The Herries Chronicles Volume 2

Hugh Walpole was born in New Zealand in 1884, the son of a clergyman. Sent to England, he was educated at Canterbury and Cambridge, becoming a schoolmaster and later a book-reviewer. His first novel, *The Wooden Horse*, was published in 1909. During the First World War he served in Russia with the Red Cross, receiving the Order of St George and being made a CBE. *The Secret City*, published in 1919, about the Russian Revolution, won the Tate Black Memorial Prize. The *Herries Chronicles*, his most ambitious work, was written in the early 1930s. He was knighted in 1937. Hugh Walpole never married. He died in 1941.

Also by Hugh Walpole
in Pan Books

The Herries Chronicles Volume 1

Hugh Walpole

The Herries Chronicles

Volume 2

Pan Books
in association with
Macmillan London

The Fortress first published in Great Britain 1932 by Macmillan & Co. Ltd
Published 1971 by Pan Books Ltd
Vanessa first published in Great Britain 1933 by Macmillan & Co. Ltd
Published 1971 by Pan Books Ltd
Both books are copyright in all countries which are signatories to the
Berne Convention
This omnibus edition first published 1985 by Pan Books Ltd,
Cavaye Place, London SW10 9PG
in association with Macmillan London Ltd
9 8 7 6 5 4 3
All rights reserved
ISBN 0 330 28853 9
Printed and bound in Great Britain by
Cox & Wyman Ltd, Reading

The Fortress

For my friends
Gertrude and Muirhead Bone

Thy gentlest dreams, thy frailest,
Even those that were
Born and lost in a heart-beat,
Shall meet thee there.
They are become immortal
In shining air.

The unattainable beauty,
The thought of which was pain,
That flickered in eyes and on lips
And vanished again;
That fugitive beauty
Thou shalt attain.

Those lights innumerable
That led thee on and on,
The masque of time ended,
Shall glow into one.
They shall be with thee for ever,
Thy travel done.

A.E.

Contents

Part One

MADAME

Part Two

ADAM AND MARGARET

Part Three

CUMBERLAND CHASE

Part Four

MOTHER AND SON

The Herries Family in the *The Fortress*

Judith **Paris**, *daughter of Rogue Herries*
Adam Paris, *her son*, m. Margaret Kraft
Vanessa, *Adam's daughter*
Sir William Herries, *son of David Herries*
Christabel, *his first wife*
Walter, *their son*, m. Agnes Bailey
Valerie, *Sir William's second wife*
Ellis, *their son*
Uhland, *Walter's son*
Elizabeth, *Walter's daughter*, m. John Herries
Francis Herries, *son of David Herries*
Jennifer, *his wife*
John, m. Elizabeth Herries ⎫
Dorothy, m. Arthur Bellairs ⎬ *their children*
Benjamin, *John's son*
Timothy Bellairs
Veronica Bellairs, m. Robert Forster ⎫
Amabel Bellairs ⎬ *Dorothy's children*
Jane Bellairs ⎭
Sir James Herries, *son of Sir Pomfret Herries*, m. Beatrice Ferry
The Ven Rodney Herries, *his brother*, m. Rebecca Fox
William ⎫
Dora ⎬ *Rodney's children*
Garth Herries, *grandson of Pelham Herries*
Sylvia, *his wife*
Amery, *his brother*
Maria, Lady Rockage
Carey Bligh, 3rd Lord Rockage, *her son*
Cecily, *his wife*
Roger, m. Janet Vane ⎫
Alice ⎬ *their children*
Phyllis, *Rockage's sister*, m. Stephen Newmark
Horace Newmark ⎫
Mary Newmark ⎪
Phyllis Newmark ⎪
Katherine Newmark ⎬ *Phyllis' children*
Stephen Newmark ⎪
Emily Newmark ⎪
Barnabas Newmark ⎭
Montague Cards, *son of Morgan Cards*
Bradley Cards, *son of Robert Cards*
Fred Ormerod, *related by marriage to Montague Cards*

Part One

Madame

'ALL IS WELL,' Judith said quietly, coming forward and stroking the red apples of the sofa. 'I shall not leave you, Jennifer. It is better I remain.'

As her hand mechanically stroked those same rosy apples, so friendly and familiar, she reflected.

Yes, this simple sentence declared the crisis of her whole existence. Nothing ever again could matter to her so deeply as this decision. With it she had cut away half her life, and perhaps the better half. She was not by nature a dramatic woman; moreover, she had but lately returned from the funeral of the best friend she had, and she was forty-seven years of age in this month of January 1822. So – for women then thought forty-seven a vast age – she should be past drama. Quietly she sat down on the sofa, leaned forward, looking into the fire. Jennifer Herries was speaking with eager excitement, but Judith did not hear her. Jennifer was fifty-two and should also be past drama but, although a lazy woman, she liked sensation when it did not put herself to discomfort.

Judith at that moment heard and saw nothing but the past, the past that she was irrevocably forsaking. Strange how the same patterns were for ever returning! Her father had been a rogue and a vagabond, a rebel against all the order and material discipline of the proper Herries. In his early years he had married Convention and of her had had a son, late in life he had married a gipsy and of her had had a daughter in his old age, when he was over seventy. David at one end of his life, Judith at the other.

In their histories again the pattern had been repeated. David of his marriage had had two sons: Will the money-maker, Francis the dreamer. Will prospered even now in the City; Francis was a failure, dead of his own hand.

And with their children again the pattern was repeated. For Will's son Walter was triumphant near by in his house at Westaways, and Francis' widow, Jennifer, and Francis' children, John and Dorothy, remained, undefended, here at Uldale.

It was here that she, Judith, came into the pattern. Daughter of two vagabonds, mother of an illegitimate boy, she should be vagrant. Half of her – the finer, truer, more happy and fortunate half – (she nodded at the fire in confirmation) was so. But the other half was proper, managing, material, straight-seeing Herries. She threw her wild half into the blaze (her hand flickered towards the fire). It was gone. She remained to fight for Jennifer, Jennifer's children, John and Dorothy, and, maybe who knows? . . . her own boy Adam.

To fight whom? Here Jennifer's voice broke through:

'. . . That will be most agreeable. I have always said that the Yellow Room needs but a trifle altering and it will make . . . but Francis would never see it. And with a new wallpaper . . . We must certainly have a new wallpaper . . .'

To fight Walter Herries, and all that were his. As 'Rogue' Herries in his tumble-down house in Borrowdale had fought all the world, as Francis his grandson had tried to fight the world and failed, so now would she fight Walter, flamboyant, triumphing Walter, made of Will and his money-bags, sworn to extinguish Jennifer and her children and all that were in Fell House, Uldale.

It had been the wish of her whole life to flee from all the Herries and live in the hills as her mother had lived before her, but Walter Herries had challenged her and she had taken up the challenge.

'. . . Not that it should be difficult,' Jennifer was saying, 'to find another girl to work with Doris. Girls will come willingly enough now that you are going to remain, Judith, dear . . .'

Walter and his two children, Uhland and Elizabeth, with all the money in the world, against Jennifer and *her* children, undefended and helpless, Judith and her Adam, fatherless and by law without a name . . .

Jennifer was going on: 'And Walter will not *dare*, now that you are remaining, Judith . . . You are the only one of us all of whom he is afraid . . . He will not *dare* . . .'

Would he not, so large and confident and powerful? Had he not said that he would snuff them out – Jennifer, John, Dorothy – raze Fell House to the ground? And what had *she*, small, elderly, alone, with no one in the world belonging to her save Adam, to oppose to that strength?

Nevertheless, she looked across to Jennifer triumphantly.

'We will give Walter something to think about,' she said.

'And you can go to Watendlath when you wish,' Jennifer said.

'Oh no. Watendlath is over for me. Watendlath is ended, a closed valley.'

'But how foolish, Judith. It is only a mile or two.'

'It is the other end of the world.'

She did not tell anyone how that night, with Adam asleep beside her, she cried. She lay awake for half the night, hearing the owl hoot, a mouse scuttle, and seeing a slow, lonely moon trace with her silver finger a question mark across the floor.

Her thoughts were wild, incoherent, most mingled. At one moment she was fiercely rebellious. She sat up, staring about her. No, she would not remain! She would tell Jennifer in the morning that she revoked her decision. She allowed her fancy then to play with the lovely sequence of events if she went. Tom Ritson should arrive in his cart. She and Adam would be packed into it, and, after tearful farewells, they would be off, down the hill with one last backward wave at the bottle-green windows of the Uldale shop and the slow friendly shoulder of the moor, along the road to Bassenthwaite, beside the Lake, Keswick, then up the hill again, above Lodore, and then— Oh, happiness! Oh, joy! The little valley closing them in, the long green field, the tumbling Punchbowl, the two farms, her own, John Green House, and the Ritsons'; below the farm the round scoop of the Tarn, black or silver or blue, the amphitheatre of the hills, the sheep nosing at the turf, the cattle moving in the byre, and best of all, Charlie Watson, straight as an arrow in spite of his years, riding towards her over the stones ... the fresh sweet air, tang of soil and bracken, glitter of stones, sweep of the changing sky ... she had to catch the sheets between her hands.

That life was for ever surrendered. Then, at once, her other practical self came running in. She was mistress of Fell House now. They would all do anything that she told them. Jennifer was her slave. She had seen, at the Ireby funeral, what the neighbours and villagers thought of her. Yes, in spite of her illegitimate son. Many things would have to be done. Had she strength enough? It was the convention that a woman over forty was an 'old thing' without savour. It was true that she had been aware, for some time past, of the troubles, melancholies, miasmas peculiar to her time of life, but she had refused to surrender to them. She felt within her a wonderful vitality and energy, as

though she were at the beginning of life rather than more than
half through the course of it. Just as in earlier days her love for
her husband Georges had filled her with fire and splendour, so
now her love for her son Adam glorified her. She was such a
woman.

Yes, many things needed to be done. Walter Herries thought
that Fell House was at an end, did he? She would show him.
Jennifer had money. They could purchase the piece of land
towards Ireby ... four more cows, two more horses. The dairy
must be enlarged. They were lucky in their servants. Bennett was
devoted, would do anything for her. Jack was a good boy. Mrs
Quinney was honest and hard-working, although she had a
tongue when she was put out. Martha Hodgson was a good God-
fearing cook, who never grumbled so long as she was not interfered with, and Doris would do well if they had a child in from
the village to help her.

They must entertain more than they had done. John and Dorothy were growing now. John was fourteen and Dorothy thirteen. It was right that they should take their proper place in the
County ... She must find a tutor for John and Adam. Someone
who would have no dealings with Walter. There was Roger
Rackstraw in Keswick, a friend of Miss Pennyfeather's. He had a
broken nose and looked altogether like a prize-fighter, but he had
been for two years tutor to the Osmaston children and had done
well there. She would see about that in the morning. She would
lose no time. And, maybe, she might, after all, shortly pay a visit
to Watendlath, stay with the Ritsons for a week, ride over to
Watson's farm ... No, no ... Better leave that alone until she
was settled here, settled deep, deep down so that she could never
pull herself up again.

Then once more desolation caught her. She lay back on her
pillow sobbing. She could not help it. She had given up all that
she loved best in the world, all save Adam. And for what? She
had been considering Walter Herries as too serious a figure?
What was he after all but a big, blundering bully? What could he
have done to Jennifer and the children? John would soon be able
to protect his mother ... But no. John was soft, sensitive, gentle.
She remembered how years ago Mrs Ponder, a servant in the
house, had thrown his pet rabbit out of the window. She had
thought then that he would have died of misery. And yet he had
courage. Only a few days before, when the rioters had set fire to
the stables, he had sat with his mother through all the noise and

confusion, reading to her, trying to comfort her ... He had courage, but he was no match for his Cousin Walter. She, and she alone ... At that she fell, at last, asleep.

It was natural that the world of Judith's son, young Adam, should be very different in shape, colour and contents from his mother's.

He was now in his seventh year and as strong as a young colt. He was, most certainly, not handsome. Even his mother could not think so. His hair was black and straight without a suspicion of a wave in it, his nose snub, his mouth large, his legs and arms too long for his body as yet. Nevertheless, he gave promise of both height and breadth. His grey eyes held both humour and caution, and he was brown with health. He was clumsy in his movements – indeed he was to move all his life short-sightedly, and this not because he was short-sighted but because he was absent-minded.

Were his interest thoroughly caught, absent-minded was the last thing that he was, but he was often thinking of the unexpected instead of the customary.

It seemed that his character would be warm and loyal, but he was sparing of words. He hated to show feeling or express it. He was independent, always venturing off on his own, busy on his own purposes. Whether he liked or disliked anyone he never said, but he had a very especial connexion with his mother and would, on a sudden, leave what he was doing and search for her because he thought that she needed him.

When he did this his intuition was always right. He was quite fearless and could be very pugnacious, but he would attack someone without warning and often when he had been smiling but a moment earlier. He was inquisitive, would ask questions and remember carefully the answers given him, although he would not always believe their truth. On the whole, his independence, his loyalty, his taciturnity and his courage were at present his strongest characteristics. He walked very much by himself.

His horizon was larger than that of many boys of his age, for his first years had been spent in France and after that he had lived like a young peasant in the Watendlath valley. His friends had been farmers like Charlie Watson and the Ritsons, farmers' wives like Alice Perry, farmers' boys like the young Perrys.

Then on coming to Fell House he had known the first attachment of his life (he was never to know very many). His mother was part of himself and he of his mother, so that did not figure as an attachment, but at the moment that he saw John Herries he adored him.

John, Jennifer's boy, who was eight years older than Adam, was fair, slender, handsome and an aristocrat. He walked with his head up, as though he were made to rule the earth. But he was too gentle and unselfish to wish to rule anyone, and it soon happened that the young black ruffian Adam did all the commanding. John was impetuous until checked, then was hurt and silent. He had a very occasional stammer that added to his shyness. He had most beautiful natural manners and was over-aware of the feelings of others. He loved to be liked, hated to be disapproved of, while Adam did not care whether anyone liked him or no. Nevertheless, Adam responded deeply to affection, although he said nothing that showed this. He forgot neither kindness nor injury, but John was always eager to heal a quarrel; John was wretched in an atmosphere of unfriendliness. Adam enjoyed a fight if he felt that the cause was a worthy one.

John's sister, Dorothy, was fair, plump and amiable. She was a type that was always recurring in the Herries families. She had some of her mother's laziness, but took a livelier interest in the outside world than her mother did.

Adam's world seemed sufficiently filled with these figures – his mother, Jennifer whom he called his aunt although she was not, John, Dorothy, Mrs Quinney the housekeeper, Mrs Hodgson the cook, Bennett the coachman, Jack the stable-boy, Doris, two dairy-maids. Until now there had also been Mr Winch the tutor, but Mr Winch was gone for ever.

Geographically his world held first the house, the garden, the stables, then the moors that fell to the very edge of the garden, Skiddaw and Blencathra under whose shadows all the life of the house passed, and beyond them Keswick, and beyond that the world of Watendlath becoming speedily to him now a dream world, a sort of fairy kingdom where all the glories and wonders of life were enclosed.

However, he had then (and he was always to have) the great gift of accepting what he was given and making the best of it. It is true that did he feel he was being given something that he ought not to be given, he would fight relentlessly to change it. He had, for instance, felt that he was *not* given Mr Winch, and he had fought Mr Winch most gallantly. It seemed only in the proper nature of things that Mr Winch should be removed.

His attitude to John changed as time passed. He did not love him less, but when he found that he could make John and Dorothy do as he wished he had his way with them. Although he was only six he knew very well on every occasion what it was that he wanted to do. The only trouble was that others did not always want to do likewise.

Like a stone flung into a pool so the fearful adventure of the rioters had broken into the settled pattern of Adam's life. That had been one of his proudest moments when his mother had told him to go into Aunt Jennifer's room and wait there until 'the men who were throwing stones at the windows' had gone away. He had known that there was more in his mother's mind than she expressed in words. She had in fact said to him: 'I shall have occupation enough. I trust *you* to guard all that I have no time for.' A strange scene that was in Aunt Jennifer's bedroom with all the familiar things, the high bed with the crimson curtains, and Aunt Jennifer's lovely black hair in a lace cap, her silver shoes and a green turban with a feather in it lying on the floor, Dorothy sitting virtuously on a chair pretending that she listened to John who was reading from Goldsmith's *History of England* (Adam did not, of course, know what the book was), John with his gentle voice reading on and on, never taking his eyes from the book – all this so quiet and ordinary, while the reflection from the flames of the burning stables played like living figures on the wallpaper, and the muffled echoes of shouts and cries came from below. He would never forget the white tenseness of John's face, the little exclamations of Aunt Jennifer: 'Oh dear! Oh dear!' 'Listen to that!' 'We shall all be murdered!' 'Children, we shall all be murdered!', the ridiculous aspect of the leather cushions that had been pushed up against the windows, the way in which everything in the room jumped and sank and jumped again in accordance with the fiery hands that stroked the walls. He himself sat on a low chair near the bed and had no doubt but that he was there on guard over them all. He was prepared that at any moment Aunt Jennifer should jump out of bed and run as she was into the passage and down the stairs. It was privately his opinion that she showed great cowardice to remain there while his mother and Bennett and Mrs Quinney were defending the house, but he had a patronizing, forgiving affection for Aunt Jennifer, as though she were a pony gone at the knees, or a dog that wouldn't fight other dogs, or a doll whose stomach oozed sawdust.

It was all that he himself could do to sit there thus quietly, but his mother had given him that piece of work and so without question there he was!

The worst moment of all was when Aunt Jennifer suddenly cried (just as John was reading about the Princes who were murdered in the Tower): 'Oh, it is me that they are after! I know it is! ... They have always hated me! They will burn the house over us! ... We mustn't remain here, children ... We must fly or we shall have the house burnt over our heads!'

Although Adam was too young to be aware of it, it was perhaps the serious regard that the three children bestowed upon her that forced her to lie back again upon her pillow, to close her eyes and await, as best she might, the outcome.

Indeed the affair was soon at an end. Quiet fell in a moment. The shadows and tremblings of the flames' reflections continued to play upon the walls of the room. John opened the door and listened. Below there were shufflings of feet, whispers, someone was weeping. They waited ... At last Judith herself came, and Adam learnt that Uncle Reuben was dead.

The news was the first real crisis in young Adam's life, the first occasion on which he had been close to a death that was real and actual to him. In France the old Curé of the village had died when paying them a call, but Adam had been too young to understand. In Watendlath a cow had died and one of Charlie Watson's horses. But Uncle Reuben had been his friend. He had spent whole days with him in the hills and, although he had been fat and puffed as he climbed a hill, he had been able to talk to hundreds of people at the same time and had known stories about Abraham, the Lord Jesus, the Giant of Poland, King Arthur's Round Table and scores of others. He had never bothered Adam with making him do things he did not want to do, as Charlie Watson sometimes did, and he carried gingerbread and lollipops in the pocket of his gown.

Now Uncle Reuben was dead, shot with a gun that had been fired by one of the wicked men who wanted to burn the house down. As the consciousness of this absolute fact, positive, not in any circumstances to be changed, sank into Adam's mind, something affected him for ever. He was, his whole life afterwards, to remember the moment when his mother, breaking off from some story that she was telling him, drew him towards her and said to him that now they were to remain at Fell House, not go to Watendlath as she had promised, and they were to remain to fight ... To fight whom? ... Was it Uncle Walter?

He suggested Uncle Walter because he himself wanted to fight him. Once in the hills when he had been bathing, Uncle Walter had ridden past on a white horse and tried to strike him with his whip. He had not forgotten that. He would never forget. So it seemed to him quite natural that he and his mother should fight Uncle Walter. And now when his mother said that they would remain here and not go to Watendlath he connected that with Uncle Reuben's death and concluded at once that it was Uncle Walter who had shot him. That being so, he, Adam, would one day shoot Uncle Walter. The sequence of ideas was quite natural and inevitable. He said nothing. He asked no questions. But he did one thing. He had a black doll, a black doll with a red coat and brass buttons. He hung the doll from a nail on the wall and threw marbles at it. Within a week he could hit the doll from a great distance. The doll's face that had been made of painted clay was no longer a face.

Then on an afternoon late in February, John and Adam had a curious adventure. Adventures were for ever happening to Adam, whether watching a carriageful of ladies tumbled into the ditch on the Carlisle Road, seeing a drunken old man fall off the top of the Kendal coach, looking at the gipsies who came and pitched with their caravans painted orange and blue on the moor above the house until they were ordered away (they had brown babies, two monkeys and a basketful of snakes; a woman in a crimson kerchief with silver coins through her ears invited Adam to join them: had it not been for his mother he would have done so). Adventures for him were perpetual, but this one had for him a new quality, terrifying had he allowed himself to be terrified.

It had been a strange day. In the forenoon there had been showers of rain that had filled the road with puddles of silver. Then Skiddaw about two of the afternoon took a step or two and came face to face with the house, dragging a stream of clouds over his shoulder with him. He had a way of doing this: a shrug of shoulders, a quiver of his sides and there he was staring in at the parlour window. The air was fresh with a sniff of spring (although spring would not be with them for a month or two). Adam walked out as far as the stream in the hollow below the Tarn; the water glided and leapt. The moss was wet on the gleaming stones above the brown water; the Fell rose straight from the hollow and was thronged with little moorland streams, for there had been heavy rains. He thought that he saw an eagle and he looked up and up into the sky that was whitish blue and empty until the clouds that clung on to Skiddaw's shoulders. All these little things belonged to the adventure. As he entered the house again Skiddaw receded and the clouds turned rose; the road beyond the garden wall was very hard and white. He could hear a young owl hooting. He climbed the stairs to find two large marbles, one crystal white, one purple, that he liked to carry in his pocket. Then slid down the banisters to the parlour. He knew that his mother and Aunt Jennifer were paying a visit. They had gone in the carriage with Bennett.

In the doorway of the parlour he found John and saw at once that he was shaking with some event. He pulled Adam by the arm into the room, which was lit only with the dusk of the falling day and the sharp jumping flames from the fire.

He spoke in a whisper.

'Adam! . . . Cousin Walter has been here!'

Adam looked to the window.

'No,' said John, 'he has gone.'

'He came into the house?'

The two boys whispered like conspirators.

'No. Not so far as the house. He was on a white horse. He got down and stood at the gate. Then he opened it and stood in the garden. He stayed looking at the house without moving, for a long while. Then he went out and rode away. I saw him through the window.'

Adam drew a deep breath and clutched the two marbles in his pocket.

'Did he look angry?' he asked at length.

'I could not see his face. Everything was so still. I thought he would knock at the door, but when he was inside the gate he never moved. He stood there looking. I thought he could see me through the window and I hid behind the curtain.'

Adam went to the window and peered out. The glow in the sky was bright and shredded now with little yellow clouds like goslings.

'He is gone,' he said, his nose pressed against the cold pane.

'Yes – but a moment back. He rode slowly up the hill. Oh, Adam, why did he come?'

'To spy on us.' Adam nodded his head. 'I shall go after him.'

'Oh, Adam, will you?'

'Yes, why not? Perhaps he has a gun and is waiting to shoot someone.'

John must go too if Adam went, but he felt an overwhelming fear, sprung from years of his mother's dread. Adam was too angry just then to be frightened. When he was angry he was possessed with rage; there was no room for any other emotion. When he had been a baby his anger had sometimes almost choked him because it boiled inside him and he could not shout nor cry. He took John by the hand, and together, as quietly as might be, they stole out of the house, closing the big heavy door gingerly behind them. The owl hooted at them as they hurried on to the road.

Outside the gate Adam halted. Something in the whiteness of the road pulled him up. But he knew what it was. A week ago he had been walking up the hill and had come upon a fat and distended frog. This frog was croaking in a despairing manner; around its neck were folded the thin spiry legs of two smaller frogs who clung thus, motionless, without sound. From the mouth of the large distended frog protruded a tip of tongue scarlet red.

Adam came the next day and found that the swollen frog was dead (the red tongue still protruding), but the two live frogs were still there, their legs interlaced, while another frog, small and green, squatted near by on guard and to see that justice had been done.

Adam was too young to feel spiritual disgust: his original instinct had been one of interest and curiosity, but now the scene around him was ghostly with evening mist, and out of the mist sprang the sharp white road; by the side of the road was a yellow-bellied frog with a tongue like blood and around him croaked a chorus of green frogs. The moor was filled with green frogs. He stood staring intently in front of him.

'What is it?' whispered John. 'He will be gone in an instant.' They stood very close together and listened. All was still. The lights of the little village were coming out; Fell House was a black mass against the mist.

It was perhaps the cold that drove them forward. They walked on the turf at the side of the road so that they should make no noise. They turned from the road and began to climb the moor, stumbling over the unevenness of the turf. Suddenly John caught Adam's arm: 'Keep down . . . He's there!'

Just in front of them a shelf of turf rose above a cutting. To the right of them, very close to them, three sheep, aware of them, held together, their sides panting. But quite clearly the boys could see the figure on the hill. He seemed gigantic in that light, his white horse colossal. The mist, into whose vapours the moon would soon pour her light, made a ghostly background to that motionless horseman, great of bulk, in a black overcoat with a high black collar. His thighs, his riding-boots, were jet against the whiteness of his horse's flanks. Neither he nor his horse moved. The sheep too seemed to be carved against the moor, and the two boys, kneeling behind the rising of turf, their hearts thumping as it seemed to them into their throats, waited to see what he would do.

He did nothing. He stayed there looking down on to Fell House. Then, as darkness fell, he turned his horse's head and rode away.

AT WESTAWAYS

WESTAWAYS was a very different place from Fell House, Uldale.

Fell House would have always, whatever were done to it, the atmosphere of the farm from which it had sprung. David Herries, John's grandfather, had in his time made certain enlargements. He was greatly proud – and so was Sarah his wife – of his dairies, the garden with its fine lawn and Gothic temple, the parlour and the best bedroom, but both David and Sarah had been simple people, nor, since their marriage, had they travelled far afield. Sarah, for a brief while, had been bitten with the London fashion, fostered by Horace Walpole, *The Castle of Otranto*, Mrs Radcliffe and the rest, for pseudo-medievalism, suits of armour, stained-glass windows and plaster gargoyles, but she was not by nature romantic and the craze had soon passed. Fell House, nestling its warm cheek against the breast of the moor, was an improved farmhouse and no more.

Utterly different from its very inception was Westaways. In the early years of the eighteenth century old Pomfret Herries, brother of 'Rogue' Herries, and so uncle to David, young John's grandfather, had had it built, not because he wanted a beautiful house but because he wished to go one better than his neighbours. However, it *was* a beautiful house because he chose for architect old John Westaway, saturnine and melancholy hermit, one of the finest architects then alive, trained in Italy, the friend of Vanbrugh and Chesterman, famous through all the north of England not only for his skill but also for his eccentricities and savage temper.

Old Pomfret had to pay for his ambitions and grumbled at the cost for years after, but he had, in the end, a lovely house. It is true that the only room in it of any value to himself was his own apartment thronged with guns and fishing-rods. He was proud, nevertheless, for people came from miles to see the house.

It was situated between Crosthwaite Church and the town of Keswick. At that time the gardens ran down to the fringe of the Lake. The virtues of the house were its beautiful tiles of rosy red, the delicate wrought-ironwork across its front, the sash windows – at that time a great rarity – the pillared hall, and especially the saloon, whose decorations were designed and executed by John Westaway himself. The subject of the design was Paris awarding the apple, and the three goddesses were painted with extreme vigour.

After old Pomfret's death the house passed out of the family for a while, but Will, David Herries' money-making son, bought it back again and thought to live in it. However, London, and especially the City, held him too strongly. He found the country both dull and fruitless. His son Walter reigned in Westaways in his stead.

Walter, who had little taste but great energy and a readiness to take the advice of others (for his own profit), enlarged and improved Westaways. For a number of years workmen were always about the place. He added a wing towards Crosthwaite, doubled the stables, extended the gardens and had a grand conservatory. He also put fine things inside the house; he had a famous piece of tapestry that showed Diana hunting, some excellent sculpture, and a Van Dyck and a small but most valuable Titian. There was also over the door of the saloon a painting of the Watteau school in deep rich colours of some French king dining with his ladies – a picture all purples, oranges and crimson that the Keswick citizens thought the finest thing they had ever seen. Only old Miss Pennyfeather laughed at it and called it 'stuff', and Mr Southey, after dining with Walter, was said never even to have noticed it.

Walter Herries himself cared for none of these things for themselves, but only in so far as they represented strength and power.

At this time he was thirty years of age and his children, Uhland and Elizabeth, who were twins, were seven; they were born in the same year as young Adam and were a few months older than he.

Walter was large in girth and limb, but could not at this period be called stout. He was in appearance a survival of the days of the Regency, now swiftly slipping into limbo. He seemed already something of an anachronism with his coats of purple and red, his high thick stock with its jewelled pin, his capacity for eating and drinking, his roaring laugh, his passion for sport. But he was not really such an anachronism as he seemed. In politics, when he bothered to speak of them, he appeared as reactionary Tory as Wellington or old Lord Eldon, but in reality he stood closer to Huskisson and Canning. The fact was that he learnt much from his father, who, one of the astutest men in the City, had his eye more firmly fixed on the past. Walter, caring for nothing but his personal power and the aggrandizement of his family, loving only in all the world his crippled little son, building his edifice in part for himself but in the main for Uhland's future, considered that future very much more deeply than anyone supposed. He suffered from the fact that no one in his immediate surroundings was of any use to him in these things. He reigned in a passionate loneliness and perhaps in that had more in common with his great-grandfather, old 'Rogue' Herries, than he would ever have dreamed possible. His wife Agnes he held to be an imbecile, and she was truly as terrified of him as all timid wives are supposed to be of tyrannous, loud-voiced husbands.

On a certain fine September morning of this year, 1822, a long-legged, supercilious individual named Posset (William Posset, son of William Posset, coachman at Levons Hall) brought into Walter Herries' dressing-room a large tin bath. The floor of this dressing-room drooped in its centre into a hollow and in the floor of this hollow was a small iron grating. Over the hollow the bath was inserted. A pinch-faced youth in a uniform of dark red and brass buttons then arrived with two vast pitchers so large as almost to conceal him. With an air of extreme relief and under the cold eye of the lengthy Posset, young Albert emptied the pitchers into the bath. Posset then with delicate tread stepped into the next room, pulled back the curtains and approached the four-poster. Walter, his mouth wide open, his chest bare, his nightshirt pulled down over one shoulder, was snoring loudly. Posset, with a gravity worthy of a tax-collector, shook the bare arm. Walter woke, gave one glance at Posset, sprang from his bed, tugged his nightshirt over his head, rushed in to the next room and plunged into the bath. Young Albert, accustomed to the fierce eruption of water, always at this point retired to the farthest corner of the room, where he stood, towels over his arm, admiring, with an amazement that custom never seemed to lessen, that great body, that splutter of exclamations, grunts and oaths, and that sudden magnificent figure of a man withdrawn from the water, suffering the lusty (but always reverent) towelling of Posset – and water dripping everywhere, running in little streams and eddies into the hollow and away safely through the iron grating. Albert always informed those less privileged that there was no sight in the world quite so fine as his master as he plunged into his bath – no lion in a show, no tiger in Indian jungle, could have the energy and vigour of his master at this moment. It was Albert's top moment of his day – a pity that it came so early; every event was a decline from it.

Walter had long ago insisted that any visitor in the house – his mother, his wife, very definitely included – must, unless a doctor forbade them, be present at the family breakfast table. It was the beginning of his patriarchal day. Only thirty years of age, he already felt himself founder of the whole of the Herries stock, and nothing pleased him better than to have Herries collected from all over the country and seated at his table.

This was not at present easy, for Keswick was tucked away in the North and travelling was difficult. Nevertheless, this was not a bad halting-place on the way to Scotland, and the number of Herries 'bagged' for Walter's dining-table in the last five years was remarkable.

Walter liked further to collect Herries who were oddities and to encourage them in their idiosyncrasies – granted, of course, that these idiosyncrasies did not inconvenience himself. Here he was instigated by the old motive of the King and his Court Jester. Walter might be said to have a great sense of fun, if no very strong sense of humour. He liked, for example, to indulge old Monty Cards in his femininities (Monty painted his cheeks and powdered his nose), in his little meannesses and his nervous terrors. He enjoyed the company of old Maria Rockage (for whom he had a real liking) that he might shock her Methodist principles. He even was childish enough to play on his wife's terrors by laying a book on a door that it should fall on her when entering a room. He was not at all above practical jokes and horseplay. They were part of his 'Regency' manner.

He had just now as his guests, Phyllis, Maria Rockage's daughter, her husband, Stephen Newmark, and three of her children – Horace aged three, Mary aged two, and Phyllis only one. She was anticipating a fourth. They were all very healthy children and Mr Newmark looked upon them as just rewards tendered to him by a grateful Deity.

For Stephen Newmark, tall, long-nosed, sanctimonious, was a perpetual joy to Walter. He took life seriously. He enjoyed Family Prayers. Walter, therefore, indulged his fancy and insisted that all of them, Agnes his wife, his mother (who was staying just then with him), his own two children, and all the household should be present on the stroke of eight and offer up, under the leadership of Mr Newmark, thanks to the Creator for the dangers of a night safely past and the glories of another day vouchsafed. It puzzled Mr Newmark a little that Walter should be so truly determined on Family Prayers. This determination did not altogether 'go' with his cock-fighting, horse racing, cardplaying, but Newmark had long ago decided (and confided to Phyllis) that his Cousin Walter was 'a strange fish'. In that conclusion he was perfectly correct.

On this morning, however, Walter had a small matter of business to discharge before breakfast. Rosy, scented, his stock starched until it glittered, his pantaloons of dark purple hiding his magnificent legs, 'rings on his fingers and bells on his toes', he descended, like Jove from Olympus, to the study where he transacted his affairs.

Here his agent, Peach, was waiting for him. Peach was a short, stocky, beetle-browed little man who had been in the service, for most of his days, of the Duke of Wrexe. He came, therefore, from the South and hated the North *and* the Northerners with a dreadful passion. He would not have stayed here a day had it not been for the odd power that Walter Herries exercised over him. He could not be said to *love* his master – he was not known to love any human being; he was not deferential, showed no servitude, disputed his master's wishes hotly and was grudging in thanks for benefits, but he seemed to have found in Walter Herries a man who had stung, reluctantly, his admiration – the only man in the world it might be. He appreciated Herries' dominating roughness, coarseness, liking for horseplay, and then something more – outside and beyond these.

In any case he made a wonderful servant and was hated cordially throughout the countryside.

He was standing now, his legs, that were slightly bowed, apart, his hand gripping the shoulder of a slim fair-haired boy who, his hands tied behind him, his eyes wide open with fear and apprehension, stayed there, his heart beating like a terrified rabbit's.

'This is the boy,' Peach said.

'Yes,' said Walter, looking at him.

The boy's eyes drooped. In his heart was the terror of death. He knew that he could be hanged for what he had done.

'I discovered him,' Peach went on, 'last evening. He had a small wheelbarrow and was placing in it some logs from the pile outside the further stables.'

'What did he say?' Walter asked.

'He said nothing. At least not then. Later when he was shut into the cellar for the night he admitted that he was hungry and had a mother who was hungry and a small brother who was hungry.' Peach gave a click in his throat, a favourite noise of his, and it resembled a key turning in a door. 'They all say they're hungry now.'

'What's your name?' asked Walter.

'Henry Burgess.'

'Well, Henry Burgess . . . You know what the Keswick Justices will say?'

The boy was understood to mutter that he didn't care.

'You don't care? Well, all the better. It's a hanging matter, you know.'

'I gave him food and drink,' Peach remarked reluctantly. 'He wouldn't have held up else.' Then he added: 'His mother's been waiting outside all night'.

There was an interruption. The door opened and Uhland came in. It was his habit to find his father here before breakfast. For a boy of seven he was tall and very spare and his face was grave and sadly lined for a child. One leg was longer than the other and he walked aided by a little ebony cane. When he saw that there was company he stopped at the door. It was characteristic of him that he stood there looking at them solemnly and said nothing.

'Well, what's your defence?' asked Walter.

The boy was understood to say they were all hungry.

'All hungry, were you? That's not much of an excuse. Couldn't you work?'

No work to be found. Hard times. Had been working for a hostler. Turned away for fighting another boy who insulted his mother.

'Young ruffian,' said Walter complacently. He stood, his chest thrust out, his thumbs in his armholes. Then he nodded to Uhland, who came limping forward. Walter put his arm round his son and held him close to him.

'Uhland, this boy has been stealing my wood. He says he did it because he was hungry. If he goes before the Justices it will be a hanging matter. Shall I send him or no?'

Uhland stared at the boy, who suddenly raised his eyes, glaring at them all.

'He doesn't *look* hungry,' he said quietly.

'No, upon my word he doesn't,' said Walter with boisterous good humour. 'That's good for a child, Peach, is it not? He does not look hungry. You are right, Uhland, my boy.' He laughed, throwing back his handsome curly head. 'Well, what shall we do with him?'

'Let him go, Papa,' said Uhland. His voice was cold, but he looked at the boy with interest. 'We have plenty of wood.'

'Yes, but we shall not have,' said Walter, 'if all the young vagabonds— Very well, let him go, Peach. He shall have the dogs on him if he comes this way again.'

Without a word Peach, pushing the boy in front of him, took him from the room.

Walter laughed, yawned, stretched his great arms.

'Well, my boy, how are you?'

'Very well, Papa, thank you.'

'Slept? No headache?'

'No, Papa, thank you.'

'Will you come with me into Keswick this morning?'

'Yes, Papa.'

There was a pause; then Uhland said:

'Elizabeth wishes to come.'

'She can go with Miss Kipe.'

'Yes, Papa.'

A roar like a wild beast's cry for his food filled the room. It was the ceremonial gong – a gong brought from India, purchased by Will and given by him to his son, a superb gong of beaten brass and carved with the figures of Indian deities.

So they went to breakfast, Uhland's small bony hand in his father's large one.

They were all assembled in the bright, high room whose wide windows looked out on to the garden with the splashing fountain, the Lake and the hills beyond. Stephen Newmark was there,

standing behind a reading-desk; Phyllis his wife; two of her
children; Elizabeth with her governess, Miss Kipe; Christabel
Herries, Walter's mother; Agnes, Walter's wife; Montague Cards
and the whole household – Posset, young Albert, the cook, the
maids and the little kitchen-help.

Walter took his place beside his wife and instantly they all
knelt. A long row of upturned boots met the interested gaze of
two robins on the window sill. After a while, with creaking of
knees, rustling of aprons, they all rose and sat down while Mr
Newmark read a selection from the New Testament. The sun
flooded the room. A large fat tortoiseshell cat came stealthily
down the garden path, its green eyes fixed on the robins. On the
bright road beyond the house the Burgess family began to trudge
in silence towards Carlisle. Walter put out his hand and laid it on
Uhland's shoulder. The cook, who was fat and had trouble with
her heart, began to breathe heavily, Posset caught the eye of the
prettiest of the maids and instantly looked away again. Little
Elizabeth, looking out, saw the cat and the birds. Her eyes
widened with apprehension.

'Let us Pray,' said Mr Newmark, and down on their knees they
all went again.

'May the blessing of the Lord rest upon us all this day,' said
Mr Newmark. There was a pause, then a rustle, a knee-cracking,
a boot-scraping, and they were all on their feet again.

The domestics were in line – Mrs Rains the cook, Posset, the
maids, Albert, the little kitchen-maid who had a round rosy face
and a neat waist – all in their proper order.

'Fresh country girls you succeed in getting, Walter,' said Newmark after they were gone, his mind meditatively on the kitchen-
maid.

'Anybody wanting the barouche this fine morning?' said
Walter genially. He was in an excellent temper, which fact the
three ladies perceived and brightened accordingly. Christabel
Herries, Walter's mother, was fifty years of age and thin to
emaciation. She wore gowns of black silk with a purple Indian
shawl thrown about her narrow shoulders. She moved
with timidity, as though she were ever expecting a rude word.
She adored her son but feared him. She had been, all through her
married life, under the domination of Herries men. Her husband
had never treated her with unkindness, but the City had swallowed him, leaving Christabel alone on shores of domesticy so
barren that she occupied half her London evenings talking to

herself in a large drawing-room all yellow silk and mirrors. Will, her husband, had hoped to make her a social success. But after a disastrous Ball that they gave in the summer of '96, a Ball that had ended with a scene between Christabel and Jennifer, then a radiant young beauty, Will, with a shrug of his shoulders, had reconciled himself to her disabilities. He very quickly saw that the thing for him to do was to make the money so that his son Walter might carry on the family glory.

Walter had always been kind to his mother, but for family rather than personal reasons. He thought her 'a poor fish', but then he had no opinion of women unless they were handsome. Christabel was, however, the mother of Walter Herries; she must therefore be honoured by the outside world. And he saw that it was so.

Agnes, as the wife of Walter Herries and the mother of his children, should also have secured honourable treatment had the thing been at all possible. But in this Walter saw that the world was not to blame, for a more miserable woebegone sickly female was not, he was assured, to be found in the civilized globe. When he married her she had been something of the type of that new rosy-cheeked kitchen-maid (whom he had noticed, and saw also that Newmark had noticed). She had been merry at first with a certain rather kittenish charm. But she was 'cold'. Marital relations had terrified her from the first. Their marriage night had been a horror, and after the birth of the twins they had occupied separate bedrooms. Then she had had one sickness after another, now did not choose to trouble to talk; 'sulky', Walter told himself. She pretended to be fond of the children but, he was happy to say, Uhland had already as much scorn of her as his father had.

He felt (and with justice surely) that Fate had dealt unfairly in giving so magnificent a man so wretched a partner. He was fair to her, he gave her everything that she needed; all that he asked of her was that she should keep out of his way and not interfere with his plans for Uhland. With Elizabeth she should do as she pleased.

Phyllis Newmark was tall, of a charming pink and white complexion, and had a laughing eye.

Her father, Lord Rockage, in his place, Grosset in Wiltshire, had given her love and kisses combined with general disorder, poverty and Methodism. On these mixed virtues she had thriven. She was kindly, cheerful, intelligent and quite uneducated. She was born to be a mother, and a mother she was most assuredly proving. She did not mind how many children she had. She adored them all. Newmark, having helped to provide her with three, must receive her grateful thanks. She gave him her obedience, laughed at his foibles and understood him better than anyone else in the world. She too had noticed his glance at the kitchen-maid although at the same time she was murmuring (with real devotion) the Lord's Prayer and observing a pimple on the neck of little Horace and wondering whether Walter would allow them the barouche that morning or force them into the post-chaise or order them to walk. She knew, however, exactly how to deal with the kitchen-maid, the pimple and the walk (if that were compulsory). Nothing could defeat her; she inherited from both her parents courage, honesty and an insatiable zest for life.

Soon they were all around the breakfast-table and set to with an eagerness that spoke well for their digestions. Rounds of beef; pies; fish, broiled and fried; eggs, baked, fried, boiled; hams, tongues, jams, marmalades, buns, scones – everything was there, and tankards of ale, tea, coffee ... Agnes Herries alone pretended to eat but did not.

'Yes, you may have the barouche,' Walter observed, 'and Phyllis shall have the barouche box if she chooses – I know that it gives her the greatest gratification both to see and be seen.' Then, having paused sufficiently to catch all their attention, he added:

'But first I have a visitor.'

'A visitor?'

'Yes. At ten o'clock precisely a lady is to come and see me.'

'A lady?'

'A friend of you all – Mrs Judith Paris.'

He allowed his words to sink in. And indeed they caused a stir. Both Christabel and Phyllis Newmark had the deepest affection for Judith. To Phyllis she had been a familiar friend since her babyhood, for Judith had once lived at Grosset, and to Christabel she was perhaps the only woman in the world who had never failed her, the one human being who did not patronize her, cared for her as she was, knew with tenderness and perception the barrenness of her life.

Yet Christabel had only seen her once in seven years. Only once since the night when Judith had dined at Westaways, the night of the news of Napoleon's escape from Elba. After that

Judith had fled to Paris, borne her illegitimate son there. Since her return to Uldale there had been war between the two houses. Whenever Christabel came up from London to stay with her son she hoped that there would be some chance meeting, in a lane, in a street. She had not dared herself to prepare a meeting.

'Oh, Judith!' Phyllis cried joyfully. 'I had been intending to ask . . .'

'She is coming,' Walter said, greatly amused at the disappointment that his womenkind would suffer, 'solely on a business matter. The visit is only to myself.'

Then Christabel showed courage.

'Walter, you should invite Judith to dinner. Bygones are bygones. You should most certainly invite her to dinner.'

'And Jennifer?' asked Walter, laughing.

Christabel's pale cheek flushed. No, she could never forgive Jennifer. That old quarrel, twenty-six years old, could never be forgotten. It had too many consequences. It had split the family; it had been the close of Christabel's social life. She had never had the courage to give a real party again. And then Jennifer had behaved scandalously. She had been another man's mistress under her husband's nose. That poor Francis had shot himself in London was all Jennifer's fault. No, Jennifer was another matter.

'Well, then,' said Walter, observing his mother's silence. 'You see, ma'am. And you cannot have Judith here without Jennifer. Judith rules that house. She has become, I hear, a perfect Turk . . . Well, well, it may not be for long.'

He added these last words in a half-murmur to himself. With a final pull at his tankard of beer, wiping his mouth, with a bow to the ladies, he got up, walked for a moment to the window and stood there, looking out, then left the room.

As soon as he was gone the children broke out into little pipings and chirrupings. The two Newmark children (who should have been in the nursery, but their father wished them to take their part, even thus early, in the morning ceremony) rolled decorously on the floor at their mother's feet. You felt that already their infant eyes were cautiously on their father. Uhland sat without moving, one leg over the other, an attitude protective of his deformity. Elizabeth, shyly crossed the room. She was a beautiful child, most delicate in colour and build. She had none of the high bones of the Herries tribe. She did not seem like a Herries until suddenly with a lift of her head you saw pride and resolve, two of the finer Herries characteristics. Her mother took her hand and they stayed quietly together, remote, in a world of their own, without speaking . . .

Judith was shown into the little parlour next the saloon. It had not been long since she had had a talk with Walter there – last Christmas-time it had been. Now, as she sat on the red morocco chair waiting for him, she thought of that, and how there had been a bowl of Christmas roses. A petal had fallen lazily, wistfully to the carpet. Their talk then had been almost friendly. She had gone with him afterwards to the nursery to see the children, and she had been touched by his protective love for his son.

But now all was changed. In the interval between that meeting and this she had had proof enough of the serious danger that this big laughing man offered to her and to hers.

She was here to defend her own, and a wave of hot fierce pride beat into her cheeks as she sat there, a small unobtrusive woman in a black bonnet, her hands in a black muff, waiting for him to come in. It was he who had written to her, a short polite note asking her whether she could give him a few moments on an important matter. She would not have come, but she also had something of her own to say. She would see that she said it.

When he came in she got up and bowed, but did not offer her hand.

'Well, Cousin Walter,' she said grimly. 'What do you wish to see me about?'

His own tone changed when he saw her attitude. He had intended to be friendly, jolly, a mood that he preferred, for he liked himself in that role. But he was like a child if anyone affronted him. It might be, too, that Judith was the only person in the world of whom he had some fear. Still, his ground was sure and he began confidently enough.

'Forgive my asking you to take this trouble, Cousin Judith. You will agree, however, that I should be deceiving myself if I fancied that my presence would be welcome at Uldale.'

'Nevertheless,' she answered, 'you have paid us already at least one visit this year.'

'Indeed?'

'Last February I believe it was. You did us the honour to ride over and even to inspect our garden.'

He was confused. He had not thought that she knew of it.

'Well – it happened that I rode that way . . . But come, Cousin

Judith. I am certain that we have neither of us time to waste . . .'
Then he added, a little awkwardly: 'I am sorry that you are
already determined that our talk shall be unfriendly.' (What was
there, he asked himself, about the little plain woman in the
homely bonnet that made him feel like a scolded schoolboy? She
had, in the last six months, acquired the devil of a manner – as
though she were already Queen of Cumberland. Well, he would
show her that she was not.)

She regarded him sternly.

'Cousin Walter, I was in this same room Christmas last. We
had a conversation that was not altogether unfriendly. Since then
facts have come to my knowledge. I know that it was through
you that Francis Herries left home and put an end to his life in
London. I know that it was because you bribed and suborned
that the riot occurred at Fell House – the riot that ended in the
undeserved death of the best friend I had in the world – Reuben
Sunwood. And since then,' – she spoke without emotion and
without removing her eyes from his face – 'since I have been in
charge of things at Fell House, your hand has been everywhere.
Those fields towards Ireby that we intended to purchase – you
paid an absurd price for them, although you could not need the
ground. You bribed the cattle-man whom we had last March
from Mungrisdale to poison our cows. Within the last month
you have attempted to bribe Mr Rackstraw, who has been with us
all this year as tutor, to spy upon us as Mr Winch did before him.
Mr Rackstraw has been gentleman enough to show us loyalty.
After these things – and I have no doubt that there are many
more with which your conscience can charge you – it is perhaps a
little without meaning to speak of friendliness between us.'

Walter did not move, did not shift his great bulk, did not turn
his eyes away. He admired her. By God, he admired her! There
was someone here worth fighting.

'Very well, then,' he said at last. 'We know at least where we
stand, you and I. I will not, however, admit responsibility either
for Francis' weakness or Sunwood's rashness. Francis would not
have shot himself had he been another sort of man. It was his
whole life condemned him, not I. As to the riot, no one regretted
more than myself its most serious consequences. And what evidence have you that I was concerned in that matter?'

'The evidence of Mr Winch,' Judith answered.

'Faugh! A wretched little time-server who cheated me quite as
steadily as he cheated yourself, Judith. As to other more recent

matters, well – do you recollect our last conversation in this room?'

'Perfectly.'

'Then you will remember the challenge I laid down. I told you – what I trust you sincerely believe – that I had no animosity whatever towards yourself. I told you also that for reasons both private and public I was resolved that Jennifer and her children should vacate Fell House, and that if I could not see to it by fair means that they went, then I would see to it by unfair. I was honest in that. I gave you warning.'

'And on what ground,' Judith cried indignantly, 'had you the right? Fell House is Jennifer's place. It is where her husband was born and his children after him.'

'My father also was born there,' said Walter quietly. 'As you may have observed, Judith, I have a great sense of family. It is perhaps the greatest quality in me. Jennifer with her rotten public history offends my sense of family. There is also an old quarrel between her and my mother that possibly you have not forgotten. In any case, I made you a fair offer then. I make you a fair offer now. Let Jennifer and her children leave Fell House and go to live in the South – and the matter is for ever ended.'

'We are only beating the old ground,' answered Judith impatiently. 'There is nothing to be said on that score. We defy you now, Cousin Walter, as we defied you then. There is only now this difference – that they have me to fight for them, and life has made me a determined woman, not easily moved.'

'No,' he answered quickly. 'I am aware that you are not. We are alike at least in that. But you know that my quarrel is neither with you nor your boy. Indeed, it has never been. That is one matter on which I wish to speak to you.'

He hesitated, then went on:

'It seems that my boy, Uhland, has met your boy Adam on several occasions.'

'Yes, I know it.'

'They are only babies, but Uhland is old for his age. He has taken an unaccountable liking for your Adam.' He paused, laughed, continued: 'Forgive me for that word "unaccountable". But for children as young as they are—' He broke off.

She felt herself, against her will, touched. When Walter mentioned his son a different character seemed to speak from his eyes, his mouth, his very hands. He was young and proud when he spoke of his son. Some better light shone through his coarse texture. But she did not want to be touched.

'You must know,' she said impatiently, 'that it was through no wish of mine that they met. It was in the woods beyond Portinscale – pure accident.'

'Oh, I know, I know ... I was not charging you with any intention. But my boy speaks of him, wishes to see him—'

'Yes,' Judith answered, 'that is a mischance that we must correct.'

'A mischance?'

'Yes. It would be good for neither of them, things being as they are, that they should be better acquainted.'

Walter choked back some reply that he was about to make. His control was remarkable.

'I had hoped,' he said steadily, 'that you would allow the children occasionally to meet. We elders may have our divisions. There is no reason—'

She broke in, jumping impetuously to her feet:

'No reason! No reason! There is *this* reason, Cousin Walter – that you are our enemy. You have killed Francis Herries, you would rob his children of the very roof over their heads. Only a moment ago you threatened me. And yet you wish that my son and your son—'

She stopped, sat down quietly, smoothing her skirt.

'I have still some of my old temper remaining although I am near fifty ... In fact, I may tell you, Cousin Walter, that I was never in better health in my life. Aye,' she nodded her bonnet, 'that is what I had come to say. You may think me an old woman, but I am young enough yet to keep my son from your influence and, pray God, I ever will be.'

He was angry; she had touched him. His hand fingered the jewelled pin in his stock. But his voice was level as he answered: 'Very well, then. You are confident, Cousin Judith. I am an impatient man by blood, but in this case I can school myself to waiting.

'Now hear my offer. It was to make it that I asked you to visit me. Last week I purchased the land at High Ireby. It was my intention, unless we come to some agreement together, to build a house there.'

High Ireby? At once she grasped the implication. The High Ireby land was on the hills above Uldale. It was at some distance, but nevertheless it overlooked Fell House. Walter there in some big place of his planning, with his fields, his cattle, his servants

, . . In spite of herself she showed some agitation.

'That would be done,' she said at length slowly, 'to spite us.'

'It would be done,' he answered, smiling (for he saw that she grasped the consequences), 'because I admire the view. It would not be perhaps altogether happy for Jennifer and her children to have me so neighbourly.' He looked at her closely. She gave him back look for look. 'But,' he went on, 'you have not heard my proposition. This house here is now too small for for me, but there are other sites that I could choose, other than High Ireby. Then it is one of two things. Either Jennifer sells me Fell House – I will give her a good price for it – and removes herself South. And in that case I would make you the offer of it. You should be my tenant at a most moderate rental. Or I build on High Ireby. There is no necessity for an immediate decision. I only wished that you should know what I had in mind.'

Judith saw then his plan; that this should hang over them night and day. If Walter built a house at High Ireby, it would kill Jennifer. And John? His nature being as it was, he could not endure it. Nor would it stop at Walter's living there. He would be able, in a thousand ways, to molest them at Fell House, to spy upon them, to break their privacy ... Yes, it was a clever notion.

'At any time, Cousin Judith,' he said, moving towards the door, 'that Jennifer is ready for me to have Fell House at a good price—'

She got up, putting her hands in her muff.

'You are clever, Walter,' she said. 'I grant you that. You are clever.'

'I am flattered,' he said, bowing. 'I must be clever to fight so brilliant an adversary.'

'Stuff!' she answered, tossing her head. 'None of your fine manners. Time's wasted by them.'

Outside the door she turned.

'You are a strange man. So much trouble to persecute two weak women.'

'One weak woman,' he corrected her.

At the top of the stairs he said: 'You understand my offer?'

'Oh yes, I understand.'

'Well, good day.'

'Good day to you, Walter.'

As she climbed into the chaise she was surprised to find herself trembling. Her desire at that moment was to hasten home and find them safe. Then to gather them all into her arms – Jennifer, John, Dorothy and Adam.

But all she said aloud for the benefit of Bennett's broad back was, once again, 'Stuff!'

ADAM'S WORLD

IT might be claimed that in spite of all that happened to him afterwards, the most important years of Adam Herries' life were from 1822 to 1826, from the age of seven to the comparative maturity of eleven.

It was true that the French years and the Watendlath years were important, but it was Mr Rackstraw who really woke him into active conscious life, and Mr Rackstraw didn't come to Uldale until after the riot at the beginning of 1822.

The five years that followed had for Adam three outstandingly influential personalities – his mother, Mr Rackstraw and John. Looking back, in later years, he sometimes fancied that everything that he did afterwards, all the things that brought him into trouble, all the things that gave him happiness, sprang in reality from those three people. At least, it is true that afterwards one person only was to influence him so deeply, and for two others only was he to care with such strong endurance as he did for his mother and for John Herries. But it was his character that was, in the main, to settle the result of events for him, as it does with all of us. What he was he was partly born, partly formed by people and events, partly fashioned by his own free will.

During those five years he lived, as all small boys do, a kind of under-water life with his own particular anemones, sea-horses, coloured weeds and stones for his absorbed attention. Of the traffic of the waters above his head he knew nothing; it mattered to him not at all, of course, that Mr Canning, staying with John Gladstone in his Liverpool home, watched a small boy called William Ewart playing on the lawn, or that there was a skirmish at Missolonghi, or that taxation grew ever higher and higher, that men and women cursed the machines that were taking the bread from their mouths, that the word 'Reform' was becoming an ever-louder battle-cry on men's lips . . .

He was always to have a great capacity for choosing at once the things that would, he thought, be useful to him and rejecting all the rest. From the very first he went his own way, and this independence was the beginning of all his trouble with his mother.

On the first occasion when he went off for a whole day without warning, indeed without word to anyone, he was on his return in the evening, tired, dirty and triumphant, beaten, and by his mother. She could not but remember, as she watched him adjusting his small trousers, the occasion so long ago when David Herries had beaten herself, hating it more than she did. The memory made her catch Adam to her breast and cover his face with kisses, an act of sentimentality that was to be, on the occasions of these punishments, her last. For she saw that he thought poorly of her for relenting, and for a day or two despised her a little.

She fought her first serious battle with him over this affair. He would neither tell her where he had been nor would he promise her not to do it again. For an awful week it seemed to her that her whole relationship with him was broken to pieces, until she discovered that she was now more intimate with him than ever before. For, when she said that she no longer wished to hear where he had been, he told her everything. He had been in the woods beyond Ireby, had had food with a farmer, had stroked a wild dog that everyone else feared, had found birds' eggs and fought a boy about tying a cat to a log and throwing stones at it. He told her everything and then tried to convey to her that he would always do so, but that he must have his freedom. He was to be always very inarticulate, and when now he found that she did not understand what he wanted, he simply fell into a complete and unyielding silence.

She explained to him that if he really loved her he could not give her anxiety and unhappiness by disappearing without telling anyone first. He wanted to say that if he told anyone he would be prevented from going and that therefore it was plain that no one must be told, but this was too deeply complicated for him, so he said nothing. Then she, the least sentimental of women, descended, in her distress, to the desperate expedient of asking him whether he loved her or no, and he, who loved her with all his being, disliked so profoundly to speak about his feelings that he said nothing at all. He, being seven, was not, of course, aware of his reasons for these things. He simply knew that he was hungry, that his posterior was sore where his mother had struck him, that

he hated to be questioned, that he had had a grand day, and that
he would go off again in a similar manner as soon as opportunity
offered itself.

Judith was a sensible woman and she had an especial talent for
understanding other people. This was not 'other people' but her
own flesh and blood, and, just as forty years ago she had climbed
out of the window and ridden away to Uncle Tom Gauntry at
Stone Ends, so now her son Adam must also be free.

She did the wisest thing – she left the whole matter to Mr
Rackstraw. This was, in fact, very remarkable on her part, for at
this time in England the great parental movement for the proper
discipline and benefit of the children was just beginning to
achieve force and power. All the children of England were learning to say 'Sir' and 'Ma'am' to their parents, never to speak
before they were spoken to, and to ask questions in the manner of
Little Henry – but Judith was never like other people, and their
ways would never be hers.

Mr Rackstraw had from the first a strong influence over
Adam. He was a man made up of very striking opposites. In
appearance he was a little, wiry fellow with a face like a slumbering coal, red, dusky and shadowed ash-colour. He had a
broken nose and sparse sandy hair. No beauty, but with clear
bright eyes and a lively mouth. He wore always rough country
clothes, his legs were a little bowed, and did he wear a straw in his
mouth would have been the perfect hostler. Nevertheless, he was
beyond mistake or question a gentleman. His rather sharp voice
that would crack in moments of excitement, his eyes, the way
that he carried his head, and the fine aristocratic shape of his
hands told you that. He was, in fact, of a very good family, the
Rackstraws of Rackstraw Manor in Rutlandshire, and his elder
brother was Sir Wilfred Rackstraw, 14 Mount Street, London,
and some minor official in the Foreign Office. He told you these
things if you asked him, said the Rackstraws were poorer than
mice, and that he had also a brother a smuggling trader on the
Whitehaven coast. Whether this last were so no one ever knew.
But he certainly had some very odd friends and some very mixed
tastes. There was not a farmer, hostler, stableman, huntsman,
poacher in the district he didn't know. But he was on social terms
too with the County families – the Osmastons, the Derricks, the
Tennants. He was an intimate friend of old Miss Pennyfeather,
and they cracked jokes continually: he often took a dish of tea
with Mr Southey and, they said, knew as much about his library

as he did himself. There was not a cock fight, a football match, a boxing match that he did not attend, and yet he gave himself nobly to the two boys, John and Adam. His passion was for Homer, and Adam owed that at least – that the *Iliad* and the *Odyssey* were to be ever friendly companions to him because of Roger Rackstraw. He had a pretty sense too of the virtues of Virgil, Horace, Thucydides and the Greek dramatists, and could make them live under his fingers. He had a poor opinion of contemporary English Letters, although he said a good word for the *Waverley* romances and told everyone that there was a young poet, John Keats, who would be remembered. For Mr Wordsworth he had more praise than was locally considered reasonable, but when alone with a friend confessed that he thought Southey's poetry 'fustian'.

However, his great and abiding passion was for this country in which he lived, and it was here that he and Adam had their great meeting-place. He was not a local bumpkin, of course, and his principal charm for Jennifer was that he seemed to have ever at his fingers' ends all the London gossip. He was always very courteous and tender to Jennifer, as though he felt that she needed protection and guarding. It might be too that she appealed to him, for, over fifty though she was, she was yet beautiful in a sort of tumbling-to-pieces, letting-herself-go fashion, and he would say, to the end of his days, that he never anywhere else saw dark hair and fair complexion to match Jennifer Herries'.

He would sit in the parlour and tell her things, how Brougham after the Queen's death, defending his not going with the body to Brunswick, had said: 'It was well known through the whole of the business he had never been much for the Queen' (and a dirty tyke Brougham was, said Mr Rackstraw); how Castlereagh's suicide was because of a pernicious blackmail that he had suffered under, how the King now is become an awful bore and talks about nothing but his old age, how Lady Holland persecuted her guests with her odious cats that were for ever scratching and clawing, how the King was seen somewhere walking with his arm round Canning's neck, how scarcely anyone went now to Lady Jersey's parties, and that the gambling saloon in St James' Street was the most splendid ever known and that young William Lennox and others were certainly being ruined there . . .

These were Jennifer's happiest hours, when lazily sitting before the fire, warming her beautiful hands, she could, without moving, transport herself into a world where indeed she did not wish herself to be, but about whose movements she was never weary of hearing.

Nevertheless, it was to Adam and Judith that Rackstraw was closest. He seemed to understand Judith exactly, submitted to her domination but treated her with a sort of quizzical honesty that she found delightful.

It was Adam, perhaps, whom he really loved, although he never showed him much liking, treated him often with roughness, lost his temper with him completely (and then he would shout and swear like a trooper) and ordered him about when he wished as though the boy were his slave. He understood, however, the child's passion for independence, and it was he who persuaded Judith to buy him his pony, Benjamin, and never, after one of the boy's disappearances, did he reproach or punish him. It was the rule, as Adam well understood, that if he went off alone he must be always back again by nightfall. He made, himself, many expeditions with the boy. These were the grandest occasions of Adam's life. Rackstraw taught him to see the country rightly. It was a country, he said, of *clouds* and *stones*. Stone walls, grey clouds, stone-coloured seagulls on dark fields like fragments of white stone, streaks of snow in winter thin cloth of stone, and above these stony crags pinnacles of stone, needles of stone, piercing a stony sky. He learnt to see a small imprisoned valley, wind-swept, as a living thing subject to growth and decay like himself. Through this vale twisted the mountain torrent, fighting with stones, letting its life be dominated by these piling stones that heaped themselves one on another, that fell in showers down the hillside, that at length perhaps choke the life of the stream and form a stony pathway that leads at last to new shapes of grass and moss and fern. The clouds feeding the streams, the streams fighting the stones, life moving ceaselessly from form to form, from pattern to pattern.

He learnt that it was impossible to live in this country, loving it, without having always in his heart the colour and shape of clouds. When, later, the drive of his life carried him to the South, he brought the clouds with him: he was never again to be rid of them. He knew all their patterns, forms and vagaries. He knew the clouds that flew in flags and pinions of flame and smoke over the brow of the hill, driven forward as though by gigantic bellows, he knew the moth-coloured clouds that with soft persistence gathered like great boneless birds around the peak of a hill, he knew the clouds of rose and silver that lay in little companies against a sky of jade in winter above sun-drenched snow, he knew the fierce arrogant clouds of jet and indigo that leapt upon a pale sky and swallowed it, he knew the gay troops of cloud that danced and quivered around the sun, he knew the shining clouds that the moon, orange-ringed, gathered round her on a frosty night when the hoar glittered on the grass and the only sound under the black trees was the chatter of the running streams. The clouds were of themselves reason enough why this country was first for him in the world.

But Rackstraw taught him also detail and reality. He learnt to know ash and oak, birch and thorn, holly and hazel. He knew about the cutting of the coppice woods for firewood and for 'spills' and how it was 'coaled', and what was a 'stander' and what a 'yarding', and from what woods houses of 'crucks' were made, and what 'dotard' oaks were. He learnt to know every variety of rain, from the stampede when it comes down like animals rushing a thicket to the murmur and whisper of a hesitating shower. He knew how sudden gusts would come as though someone threw a bucket of water at you, and again how it would be as though you walked down a staircase of rain, catching your breath for a pause, slowing up on the step's very edge while the water trickled under you.

During those five years he went on many rides with Rackstraw, and sometimes they would be away two nights, sometimes three, and once and again a whole week, he on Benjamin, and Rackstraw on his bony ugly horse Satan. He remembered all that he saw. He had in his heart and brain for evermore the Brathay, set in its circumference of meadowland, the view like a crumpled handkerchief from Pike o' Stickle, the cold, haunting loneliness of Black Sail, the glassy perfection of Small Water, the fall of screes from Melbreak, the sudden flight of birds so that the sky seemed darkened at Ravenglass, the long stretch of shore pale and lucent towards Whitehaven, the evil cleft of Simon Nick whose ghost seemed ever to be watching from the thin darkness, the great view from Yewdale to the Old Man, the Roman Fort on Hard Knott, the grand silence of Waswater where the Screes, the proudest of all the hills, plunge scornfully into unknown depths – these and hundreds more were to be his companions for ever.

He knew the dalesmen, their wives, sons, daughters, dogs, horses and cows; he knew the Herdwick sheep as though he were one of them. He knew the birds, the golden eagles, soon to be

gone for ever, the osprey, the dull heavy kite, the redshanks and
larks, the fishing cormorant. He felt like his own the flight of the
peregrine, the black-and-white wheat-ear, and the mocking little
cry of the sandpiper as it flitted in front of him along the Lake's
edge. The kingfisher and the moorhen spoke to him, one of rushing water, the other of pools so still that the reflection of a cloud
on their surface was like a whisper.

And all the singers – the willow-wren, the chiff-chaff, the
blackcap, the whitethroat, the tree-pipit – he mocked and imitated and whistled to.

From all this life there came three lives – one, the life of the
outer country; two, the life of his home, the building of Fell
House, the village and the moor; three, the personal life with the
human beings around him; and from all the events that occurred
to him during those five years three were of particular importance. One, the affair at Watendlath, was the matter of a moment
– and it was thus.

In all these five years he went over only on three occasions to
Watendlath. This abstention was proof of itself of his love for his
mother; it was because of her that he did not go more often, for
he loved Watendlath more than any other place on earth. Judith
never once told him that she did not wish him to go, but he knew
from the first that it made her unhappy. Why, he wondered,
would she herself never go? She cared for Charlie Watson and
the Ritsons and the Perrys. Once, looking out of window and he
standing at her side, after some trouble that she had had with
Mrs Quinney, she burst out: 'Why am I tied here? I am missing
my whole life!' and he knew that she was thinking of Watendlath. She never mentioned the place. Once or twice Charlie
Watson rode over to Uldale, but his visits were very brief. He
seemed constrained, and even to Adam he was sharp and curt.

It was on the third occasion – a week after Adam's ninth
birthday – that the strange thing happened. It was early autumn,
the hills were on fire with colour above the grey stone, the dead
bracken flamed, and the Tarn, rocked by a little wind, was scattered with tiny feathery waves. Adam and Mr Rackstraw had
ridden over and stayed the night with the Ritsons. Charlie
Watson never appeared, although the Ritsons said that they had
told him that Adam was coming. So it was an unsatisfactory
visit, for without Watson Watendlath was only half alive. Moreover, even the Ritsons seemed to be not quite so friendly as they
had been. Adam, who was quick for a little boy, fancied that they

were offended because his mother had not been to see them, and in arms as he always was if he thought that his mother was attacked, he attempted some sort of defence, but only made things the worse, for Alice Perry smiled and said she knew that Mrs Paris was busy, she had heard that she had much to do: they all called her 'Madame' now, she had heard, a kind of foreign way of calling a person, and, of course, were she busy they could not expect her to come all the way to Watendlath, and so on, and so on. Everyone began to speak of other things.

This made Adam angry and he went down, a rather desolate little figure, in the late afternoon to the Tarn alone. The wind had died; mists were rising. The sky that had been cloudless all day was frosty white, and the amber of the hills was fading into dun. Behind him sheep moved, like a concrete part of the dusk, up the slope. He was cold, lonely and disturbed by a sense of having betrayed his mother in coming here. He wanted to go home: he would rather not stay the night in the farm. The Perry boys, although they had known him since he was a baby, were stiff with him. And where was Charlie Watson? Why had he not ridden over? He wanted to go home.

Standing there, looking at the Tarn, he had the sense for the first time (it was to return to him very often) of being outside himself. He could see every movement that he made and he felt that, if that boy threw himself into the Tarn and disappeared, Adam Paris would still be there, nor would he feel any loss. It went so far that he pinched his arm to see whether he were real. Then he threw stones into the Tarn. The noise of the splash echoed in his ears, but even that was unreal – as though someone else, far from himself and having no relation to himself, had thrown the stones.

It was then that directly in front of him, rising from the Tarn, he saw a figure on a white horse. While he looked the figure grew clearer – a man in odd clothes, a black hat, and under the hat a wig. He wore a long, heavy, purple riding-coat, and down one spare thin cheek ran a deep scar. This man was quite clear to him in every detail to the silver buttons on his coat. He was not looking at Adam but away, gravely, up into the hills. Neither horse nor rider made any movement. They were like coloured shapes painted on the mist. Then they vanished. That was his grandfather, who had lived, years ago, below the hills at Rosthwaite. He had talked of him to his mother so often and had asked so many questions about him that he knew exactly how he would look, and in later days he might realize that it was his own imagination, at that moment of loneliness and longing for his mother, that had conjured up the figure.

But now he was only a small boy who believed in ghosts and pixies, warlocks and witches. So for once in his life he took to his heels and ran and ran until he arrived breathless in the warm and lighted kitchen.

He never told anyone of what he thought he had seen, but that night in bed, listening to the snores of Mr Rackstraw, he was comforted as though he had made a new friend.

The second affair concerned John, and this was one of the most dreadful half-hours of Adam's life, dreadful because he was not at this time old enough to meet the emotion that he encountered. When mature things break in upon childhood a picture is broken, a view destroyed; the picture and view never quite return.

Adam was nearly ten when this thing happened, and John seventeen and a half.

Their friendship had by now grown so close that they were more than brothers. They had the intimacy with that edge of strangeness and interest belonging to a friendship that has no blood relationship.

John had caught and held Adam in the only way that he could catch and hold him – by demanding his protection. He did not consciously demand it: this had grown out of Adam's fearlessness and John's sensitiveness. John was handsome beyond all ordinary standards; he was the best-looking young fellow, it was generally admitted, in the County. He was tall, slender, fair, with a straight carriage and an air of such breeding that when he moved both men and women unconsciously watched him, feeling perhaps that he was of a different strain from the rest of mankind.

When he came into a place he walked haughtily and seemed proud, his head erect, his mouth sternly set, but at once, when he was in contact with another human being, his smile shone out, lighting up his face. His proud carriage sprang from an intolerable shyness that he could never overcome. It was agony to him to meet new people or anyone of whose kindliness he was not sure. At any unfriendliness he flung on instantly an armour of reserve. With the men and women about the place he was in perfect relations; they all loved him and would do anything for him. His beauty seemed to them something rare and wonderful, and when they knew him also to be so gentle and kind they served him without further question. Nevertheless, he was no commander of men; any tale of distress touched him, however false it might be. He believed what he was told, and when he was deceived thought that it was some wrong in himself that had caused the deceit.

It was here that Adam, whom even when he was so young a child he trusted and loved as he trusted and loved none other, protected him. Adam was uncouth and rough beside him. He did not grow more handsome as he grew older. The darkness of his hair, the brown of his face and body, made him seem someone foreign and apart. He wore always the roughest country clothes. He spoke, when he did speak, with a slight Cumberland 'burr', he was often silent when he ought to speak and would look at people with a sort of frown as though he were summing them up. His worst fault was exactly the opposite of John's, namely, that he suspected everyone until he had proved his case.

It became plain to him soon that John was his charge. In spite of the difference of their ages he was already wiser about the world than John and, because he was not sensitive and because hostility only made him hostile in return and because he was afraid of no one, he was a good bodyguard.

Only one thing at this time came between the two of them. A chance meeting brought them into contact with Uhland, Walter's son. Adam had long ago decided that Walter Herries was his enemy and the enemy of all those whom he loved. He was not aware, during these years, of the developing battle between Walter Herries and his mother, but he did know that everything round Westaways was enemy country.

The queer thing was that Uhland, who was Adam's age, never missed an occasion of an encounter with Adam if one were possible. They met but seldom, in the Keswick street, once and again at the Hunt, at a sheep trial, at a running-match: once when Adam was fishing by himself beyond Crosthwaite Church, Uhland, unattended, came limping through the field. He stood looking at Adam, apparently afraid to speak. Adam would have had nothing to do with him, but the boy was lame, his face was pale, he seemed so sickly that it was a wonder he could move at all. So he spoke, and Uhland came and sat beside him. What followed was most uncomfortable, for Uhland sat there, staring out of large protruding eyes, and said nothing.

At last he felt in his jacket and offered Adam a top, a large one coloured green and crimson. Adam did not wish to take it, but Uhland clambered to his feet and went limping away across the field without another word ...

Now John had from the very first the strangest fear of Uhland. There was something about his deformity and sickliness that affected him as though the boy had a disease that he could convey to others. He saw him on the rarest occasions, but he was often conscious of him, would, in the middle of the night, think of that leg longer than the other, those protruding eyes, the little body that seemed to be bent by a head too big for it.

Once he burst out passionately to Adam and wished him to promise never to speak to Uhland again.

'But I don't speak to him,' said Adam, astonished.

'You meet him. He talked to you in Keswick a fortnight back.'

'He has a horse,' said Adam irrelevantly. 'It is called Caesar. It's coal black with a white star on its forehead.'

'I tell you,' John repeated, 'you are not to talk with him.'

'Why not?' asked Adam.

John could not say. The boy and his father hated them, would do them any harm ...

But Adam fell into one of his silences. John would not speak to him for days.

Then came this terrible distressing thing.

It came like a door banging on to a silent room. It was in the early summer. Adam had been riding, had shut Benjamin into his box, stroked his nose and talked some nonsense to him, then very happy, whistling out of tune, had wandered into the house. He had a room to himself now, one that he had chosen, an attic with a slanting roof and a fine view over the moor to the slopes of Skiddaw. He and Skiddaw were now on speaking terms, and there was nothing about Skiddaw that Adam didn't know – or so he thought.

He had but just sat down upon his bed and was thinking of the coach that had passed him with a fine tantivy and a grand cloud of dust from the horses' hoofs, thinking perhaps that he would like to see the world a bit, when the door opened and John came in. He stood without moving. He had been paying some visit and was dressed very smartly in a claret-coloured coat, the hips and chest padded, a white frill, his dark chestnut trousers strapped under his boots. Adam remembered then that, urged by Judith,

John had been to call on some people with a house on the border
of Bassenthwaite Lake. They were called Sanderson and were
new arrivals in the neighbourhood.

He stood there, his face pale, his lips quivering. He crossed to
the bed, sat down by Adam, then to Adam's horror burst out
crying, his head in his hands.

Adam put his arm around him and sat there, not knowing
what to do or say. He had never seen John cry before, and that a
man should shed tears seemed to him an awful thing.

'What is it? . . . What's the matter, John?' he said at last, his
voice a funny broken bass from his emotion. For a long while
John, crying desperately, made no answer.

Adam stared out of the window at Skiddaw and watched birds
flying slowly, dreamily, across the faint glassy sky.

'This is what it is . . .' John caught Adam's hand. 'My
mother—' He hesitated, then the words poured out of him. 'I had
visited the Sandersons. Young Robert Sanderson was there. He is
a friend of Cousin Walter's, and I could not abide him from the
first. He was affronted by something I had said in the house
about the Catholics in Ireland, that the Catholic laws were monstrous and that we should have shame for our treatment of Ireland . . . He answered hotly, and when I left came out with me to
my horse. He sneered at something I said. You know how it is – I
hate a quarrel. I answered him gently, and then he said something about the fine man Cousin Walter was, and that by what he
had heard Fell House here should be his. That was too much for
me and I called Cousin Walter what he is – a damnable blackguard. Then Sanderson told me . . . he said . . . he said it was
common knowledge that because my mother had been a man's
mistress here and because my father had found them together,
therefore my father had killed himself in London. Because my
father had been a coward and allowed that man to come to this
house, to sleep here . . . he knew of it. The whole world knew . . .
I struck Sanderson in the face – and I rode away.'

Telling his story had calmed him. He caught his breath. His
face now was as white as a peeled stick, his body trembled, but he
wept no longer.

'Everyone knows – has known for years. Only I didn't
know . . .'

They were quiet for a long time. Adam's hand tightened on
John's. He could not bear to feel John's body tremble. He longed
to do anything for him, to rush out and trample on Sanderson, to

burn Uncle Walter's house down, to ... Oh! He knew not what!
But he could neither do anything nor say anything. He was not
ignorant, young though he was. He knew – in a child's way –
about men and women, without feeling that all those things, the
making of love, the birth of children, were real in a real world.
But he understood that this was a disgraceful and terrible thing.
Nevertheless his own active feelings were those of rage against
Sanderson and a passionate instinct to defend John.

He said at last in a husky voice:

'I expect he's a liar. They are all liars, friends of Uncle
Walter's.'

'No – it's true ... I have known for a long while that mother
was afraid, afraid of everything, of Cousin Walter and people in
Keswick – and that my father had shot himself in London, but
this ...'

Then he added, still shivering as though with an intense
cold:

'I must fight Sanderson.'

'Yes, you must kill him, Adam answered eagerly. Here was
something that he could do. 'Mr Rackstraw shall help us.'

'Cousin Walter put him on to this. I know he did. Everything
we do, everywhere we go, Walter Herries is at our back. Oh, God,
if I could do him an injury for all he's done to us! And now I
know. I know why he has so much power over us, why my
mother fears him as she does ... My father was a coward, my
mother ...'

He stopped.

'Adam, you must speak of this to no one. We will settle Sanderson's affair ourselves. But that everyone should know, that
they have known for years ...'

Adam said, nodding his head:

'If it's pistols, John, you can kill him. Mr Rackstraw says
you're the best shot with a pistol for your age in Cumberland.
We'll practise in the barn. We'll go now ...'

But nothing came of it then. They learnt that young Sanderson had gone South. He never answered John's letter, and
later, joining his regiment, went abroad. The consequences were
not so easily settled. After that summer afternoon nothing was
the same again.

Adam's third affair concerned his mother.

As those years passed, Judith dominated Fell House and its
neighbourhood ever more completely.

When Adam was eleven, in 1826, Judith was nearly fifty-two. Now fifty-two was considered in those days a great age for a woman. There were old women like Mrs Tennant of Ireby who were old women, sat in a chair and had the air of prophetesses. There were old women like Mrs Summerson in Keswick who played cards night and day but were nevertheless old women. There were old women like Mrs Clare of Portinscale who rode to hounds, cursed and swore, drank and gambled, chaffed with the stable-boys, but were still old women. Judith Paris was unique. After settling in command at Fell House she seemed with every month to grow younger. Her body, taut, neat, active, appeared not to know fatigue. Her hair, once so lovely an auburn, was now grey, her face, always pale in colour (and she would use no paint as most of the older women did), knew no wrinkle. She rode a horse like a commander. She was austere and direct when about her business, but she could behave suddenly like a girl. She went to dances, card-parties, hunts, balls in Keswick. She was known everywhere as 'Madame,' famous for her kindness, her sharp and direct speech, her common sense. She had not changed in her impulsiveness, her attention to business, her loyalty, her childish pleasure in little things. Only those who knew her well were aware that something she had had was now, to all appearance, gone. It might be dead, it might be hidden. Miss Pennyfeather in Keswick knew, Jennifer unperceptively was aware ... Jennifer said that Judith was no longer romantic.

Another thing that everyone knew about her was that she was 'mad' about her boy. Of course the boy was illegitimate, although everyone could name his father, but his illegitimacy and the fact that Judith herself was the daughter of old 'Rogue' Herries (now a legend: they said that his ghost 'walked' in Borrowdale) and a gipsy, made the mother and son something apart. 'Madame' was becoming a legend like her father. Every kind of tale was told of her. When she came into a room people stared and whispered. But they invited her, they admired her; she was a 'character' and did the neighbourhood a sort of credit.

We are in part what our friends and neighbours make us and, unconsciously, Judith began at this time to respond to the demand for her to be 'queer'. Her dress was a little extravagant. Her skirts were very full in the Dutch fashion. She liked gay colours and was often seen in a shawl of red cashmere. She had hats of fine straw worn over a lace cap – far too young for another of her age, but in some way not ridiculous for her. Her turbans of figured gauze at an evening party were magnificent.

She already carried the cane of white ivory that was, later, to be so famous. People in Keswick said, 'Madame is coming,' and gathered at shop doors and windows to look.

She ruled everyone in Fell House save her son Adam. It was at the beginning of his twelfth year that she put her power over him to the test and failed. This occasion was one of the great crises that marked his boyhood.

No one knew with what passionate emotion she loved this child. E erything else that was dear to her she had surrendered — save her love of power and her love of son. As he grew her feeling for him developed into a mingling of love, admiration and exasperation. She had always wished for him to be independent and apart from other boys. His father, poor Warren, had had but too little character. Adam seemed to have no resemblance at all to his father; he was his mother and then himself as well. He reminded her continually of what she had been as a child, and it was a curious irony that she should so often feel the same bewilderment and irritation in dealing with him felt long ago by David and Sarah Herries about herself. She learnt, very soon in their relationship, that he hated any kind of demonstration. Did he love her or did he not? She knew that he did, and with all his heart, but any expression of affection silenced and removed him. But he *must* obey her. When she had surrendered her domination of his movements (no one knew what this cost her) she consoled herself with the right to order him in all other ways.

The exercise of power grows with what it feeds on. People succumbed to her so easily that she came to expect it as her right. Adam always obeyed her when he felt that her demand was just. She had one thing more to learn — that, if he thought her unjust, he was quite beyond her power.

The incident had minute beginnings. One fine morning she had driven with Adam in the chaise to Keswick. Mr Carrick the haberdasher came on to the pavement to receive her orders, and after he was gone, before she could move forward, tiresome old Major Bellenden must limp forward and, his wide-brimmed hat gallantly in hand (although the day was cold), commence one of his interminable conversations. Major Bellenden, who lived alone on the road to Threlkeld, was a purple-faced old bachelor, tyrannized over by a peevish manservant. He had served abroad, knew the East, had had an amusing adventure or two, but all these were swallowed up by the fact that he had been actually present at the famous performance on February 13th, 1820, at

the Paris Opera of *Le Carnaval de Venise* when the Duc de Berry
had been assassinated. Nay, more, he had by a lucky chance left
the Opera for a moment and returned at the very instant when
Louvel planted his dagger 'up to the hilt', had heard the Duke
cry 'What a ruffian!' and then 'I have been murdered!' Later, he
had listened to the screams of pain that came from the poor Duke
as Dupuytren probed the wound, had seen Decazes enter to
examine the murderer, and best of all had even been witness of
Louis XVIII himself as, tossed about between the banisters of the
stairs and the wall, they had tried to push his chair that he might
get to the Duke. He told over and over again how the Duke,
dying, raised himself and said: 'Forgive me, dear Uncle, forgive
me'; and Louis answered: 'There is no hurry, dear Nephew. We
will talk later about this.' And then how, at the very last,
when the Duchess was filling the room with her lamentations, the
Duke said: 'My dearest, control yourself for the sake of our
child,' and so gave France the first news that there would be an
heir to the Bourbons . . .

So often had the Major told this very long story with all the
details of it exactly repeated, that the Duc de Berry's as-
sassination seemed to many persons to have occurred in Keswick.
However, 'The Old Bore and his Murder' was the general summary of Major Bellenden.

It chanced that on this very morning the Major mentioned his
Duke. Some remark of Judith's about the weather reminded him.
'It was weather like this . . . that horrid affair of the Duc de
Berry, of which I expect I have told you . . .', and looking up
caught young Adam smiling at him in a very irritating manner.
Adam had heard his mother in her lighter moments, imitating
the Major: 'I had my foot on the stair . . . Louvel must have
brushed my arm . . .' and giving then the very half-choked, half-
important guffaw that was the Major's.

Adam smiled, and the Major saw him smiling. His mother also
saw him. The Major was deeply hurt and went limping away.

During the drive homewards Judith scolded him, speaking of
reverence to age, of impertinence and other kindred matters.

'But, Mama, you yourself laughed . . .'

'Not to his face. That is bad manners.'

'I am sorry, Mama. Look, there is Mr Southey with—'

'Now listen, Adam. You are to listen. You must apologize to
the Major.'

Adam sat grimly silent. Of all things in the world he hated

most to apologize. The matter might on an ordinary day have stopped there, but Judith had been irritated by a number of small things, by the failure of Miss Pritchett, the little dressmaker whom she patronized, to have a dress ready; by Mrs Quinney's cold; by the customary sluggishness of Jennifer.

So she pursued it.

'Promise me, then, that you will apologize.'

Adam said nothing. He sat there, his mouth pursed in an exasperating manner.

'Promise me that you will apologize.'

At last he murmured:

'It is unfair, Mama. You yourself laugh at him.'

'That is different. He was not present.'

Then again, as the chaise drew slowly up the hill to the village:

'Say that you will apologize.'

No answer.

'Well, then, I must punish you.'

Adam was enclosed in his attic for the rest of the day without food.

In the evening Judith came in to him, her head held high, her heart aching with love. She had been quite wretched all the afternoon. She had realized with a pain that was deeper than any emotion felt by her for many days that without Adam there was nothing. All this business of defying Walter, of managing the house, the servants, Jennifer, of corresponding with various Herries all over the country, of visiting and dining and being sociable – it was all nothing, nothing at all without Adam. She had loved her husband, she loved Adam. There was nothing else. And with a sudden shudder, as though a hateful wrinkled hag in a bonnet had bowed to her in the glass, she saw her old age, of which until now she had scarcely thought – her old age, empty, ugly and cruel.

She came into his room and found him standing looking out of the window, just as, centuries ago, she had stood at her window when David was to beat her. He did not turn. She put her hand on his shoulder. She was, not by much, taller than he, but when he turned her heart leapt, for he was so lovely to her, so utterly her own, so proud and so strong, just as she would have him be.

But he was relentless – and he was utterly beyond her reach. She said something. She asked him to come downstairs. No, he would not come down. Did he not see that he was wrong, that he had hurt the feelings of an old man, that it was proper to offer an apology when one had shown bad manners?

'I did not show bad manners,' Adam said, not looking at her.

She did not know it, but he himself was terrified – terrified at this resentment that he felt to her, his rebellion as though he were fighting for something very serious and important. He had never felt like this to her before. He almost hated her.

'Well, then, you will see it later on. You will see that I am right. Come down now and we will not speak of it.'

But it could not be settled in that way. His dreadful silence which he himself hated dominated him. She put her arm around his neck.

'Come, Adam.'

He dragged himself away from her and went back to the window, looking out. That infuriated her and she surrendered to one of her old tempests of passion. She stormed and stamped her feet. He was ungrateful, hard, unloving, disobedient. She had done everything for him, and thus he repaid her. Well, he should see. She was not to be insulted by a child. He should be beaten. Maybe that would teach him . . .

'Beat me,' he said, turning round upon her.

They looked at one another, each with hatred. The look was so terrible, so new, so far from anything that either of them had thought possible, that in another moment they would have been in one another's arms.

But she did nothing, said nothing, and after a moment left the room.

When she had gone he sat, swinging his legs, the unhappiest boy in the United Kingdom.

THE SUMMER FAIR

THE scarlet cloak of Oberon cast hastily on the daisied sward of the meadow, the laughter of the fairies as they fled towards the wood, the young men as they waited by the church gate, straining forward, listening for the word to go, the strange orange turban of Miss Pennyfeather, the breaking lights of violet and crimson as the fireworks burst above the Lake, the clown standing on his head in the market-place, his calves brown as berries against the sunlight, the line of chaises, barouches, waggons, the gauze and linen of the coloured dresses shining as the ladies leant forward from their carriages to watch the runners pass, the roseate haze on Skiddaw as the reflection of the setting sun threw great lines of colour across the crowded meadow, the peal of the bells from Crosthwaite Church, the gipsies with gaudy rings, crimson kerchiefs, white teeth flashing as they told fortunes in their encampment below the wood, Titania tearing her frail petticoat as she climbed the cart to ride through the town, the riot of men and women after dusk under the stars when a kind of madness seized the place, sunlight, bells, babel of voices, scents of flowers, neighing of horses, the plashing of oars upon the water, the stars and the flare of torches – for days and months and years the smoking shadow of this life was to hang about Keswick.

It was in August of 1827 that the famous Summer Fair came, blazed, vanished. For years afterwards it was remembered; for years now it has been as though it never was. And yet the town had known nothing like it before unless it were the famous Chinese Fair of nearly a century earlier. There is no record of it. Search contemporary journals and you will find nothing. For it came, it went, as many of the finest things in life come and go, by accident; it is only a background to the history of certain private lives; a handkerchief was dropped, a horse stumbled, a word was spoken. In a week the meadow was itself again, the waters of the Lake were calm, the gipsies were in Carlisle, the booths were piled boards, the bell-ringers were practising for another ceremony, the Strolling Players were drinking in a Kendal inn.

Nevertheless, there was never anything like it again. Chance, Mrs Bonaventure, sunshine, the accidental passing of the gipsies and the Players, stars and a full moon made this thing.

Mrs Bonaventure had come to Keswick six months before. She was a large stout lady with a red face, a roaring voice, and a wealthy husband almost as large as herself. They were a jolly pair, vulgar, if you like, with their loud voices and carelessness of social divisions, but it was known that she was the daughter of a Lancashire baronet, so, as Mrs Osmaston said, 'You can be sure she can speak quietly when she wishes,' and they were generous, crazy for parties and picnics and dances, and thought there was no place in the world like Keswick . . .

It was she who first had the notion of a Fête. It was in some way to be connected with the hand-loom weaving, and in some way with the birth of a baby boy to her sister who lived in Rutlandshire, and in some way with the Duke of Wellington, and in some way with a prize that Mr Bonaventure was giving for a race for young men under twenty-five, a race from Crosthwaite Church to the Druids' Circle.

In any case, there must be a Fête.

There should be booths along Main Street with gingerbread and apples and toffee. There should be dancing in the moonlight. There should be no nasty sports like bull-baiting or cock-fighting. There should be decorated boats on the Lake, and fireworks. She did not know that some Strolling Players chanced to be performing in Penrith. She did not know about the gipsies. All these delights were added unto her.

Suppose that old Herries, remembering as he must that Chinese Fair, when in an eating booth he had sold his lady for a few pieces of silver, were present, perched cross-legged on a chimney, standing upright against a tree top, what would he think of it all? A hundred years gone (but time is of course nothing to him now), and yet here was his daughter, like a little general, marshalling her family forces, and here his great-grandson Walter commanding *his* battalions, and behind them, around them, all the lively consequences, male and female, of that wild turbulent life by which *he* had once been surrounded! Yes, wild and turbulent that Chinese Fair had been, civilized and gentle *this* Fair must seem to him – but the same battle was joined now as then, and so will be, for ever and ever, change the background as you may, for ever and ever, amen!

As his long sardonic person wanders now skywards, now mingling unseen with the crowd, now peering sardonically from behind the chimneypot, he watches that same daughter with tenderness maybe, and young John and Adam and Elizabeth with concern, and great-grandson Walter with humorous sarcasm, watches and grimly smiles and vanishes into a star, wondering why they should all be so serious over a matter so brief and trivial.

For the rest, how are they, in reminiscence, to break that confusing fantastic day into some sort of shape and order: morning, afternoon, evening and the moonlight night? – or, better than that, they divide it by event – the boats on the Lake, the race through the town, the *Midsummer Night's Dream*, the dancing on the meadow – four cantos of a happy poem.

THE BOATS ON THE LAKE

By eight of the morning the booths were lining Main Street, the children were dancing like mad things down the road, the sun was blazing (for they had all the luck that day) and boats were putting out from the Islands, from Manesty, from Lodore, from Grange. By ten o'clock the carriages were rolling up, from Penrith and Ullswater and Newlands and Bassenthwaite, from Carlisle even, from Grasmere and Rydal, from Shap and Hawkshead. Very early in the morning for some of them the horses must have been led from their stables and the coaches loaded. Many came in pillion-riding as for hundreds of years they had done, while the grander farmers were proud in the 'shandy-carts'. Keswick, although Crosthwaite Church had not yet begun its peal, was ringing with bells, for teams of pack-horses, used for the carrying of pieces from the hand-loom weaving, came jingling in. Many of the women who were spreading their apples, nuts, cakes and bottles of herb beer on the trestles had been many a time to Hell Gill Bridge for the Brough Hill Fair, and with that same jingling of bells came the scents and sounds from Shaw Paddock and Aisgill and the old Thrang Bridge in Mallerstang.

But it was down by the Lake that the day was to begin. The sun lay on the water like a caressing hand, and the hills, from Walla Crag, from the Borrowdale peaks, from Cat Bells and Robinson, reflected their colour and proud forms as though they had another life beneath their glassy waters.

Mrs Bonaventure, attended by husband and friends, was soon seated like a queen on the commanding perch of Friar's Crag. She loved fine colours. She wore a hat as broad nearly as her shoulders, and from it waved four large ostrich feathers. Her dress, magnificently full, was a brilliant orange.

Very soon the borders of the Lake were thronged with figures, and the water whispered with the soft splash of oars. Across the meadows and trees suddenly broke out the bells from Crosthwaite, and from the landing-stage the blast of the Town Band. A gun was fired from the Island. The Fête was begun.

It was just before midday, when every eye was straining to see the first boat round the corner of the Island, that the party from Westaways arrived. Walter himself drove his coach from the house to the end of the Lake Road, and as his four horses galloped up Main Street everyone cheered and the little boys turned cartwheels and the pigeons flew in exulting circles above their heads.

Walter was elegant indeed as he flourished his whip decorated with coloured streamers, his many-caped riding-coat of green high above his thick neck, his chest thrust out, his head up as though to say: 'You may claim this or that for your glory today, but here is the true centre of the affair!' He had in the coach with him his wife, his children and his relations. It was a piece of fortune that these relations were present to witness his splendour, for it was only chance that the young sons of Durward Herries were passing through from Edinburgh and that James Herries (at length, after many years of weary waiting, succeeding to his old father's baronetcy) had come over from York.

But there they were: the two boys with two Oxford undergraduate friends from a house near Carlisle, and Sir James Herries, Bart., puffed out with solemn pride and complacent satisfaction. Agnes was there too, and also Uhland and Elizabeth.

After leaving the coach they walked, a cluster of splendour, to the Lake's edge.

No one could be more genial with all the world than Walter when things went as they ought to. He had left his riding-coat in Posset's care, for the day would be hot, and now at the age of thirty-five his great frame was beginning to yield at last to the stoutness that it had so long resisted. His high hat with the broad brim, rough in texture, was a dark wine-colour; his claret-coloured coat, the tails sewn on separately that it might fit his sides the better, followed the lines of his body exactly. His neck-cloth was shaped at the sides and stiffened with pig's bristles, rising to a kind of arch at the cheeks, and at its centre was the accustomed jewelled pin. He wore two waistcoats, one of dark purple, the other dark grey; his trousers, tight at the knees, widening downwards, were fawn. This must have been a warm costume for the middle of summer, but the stuff was all of a light material, and it was only at the neck as the day advanced that he was uncomfortable – which may possibly have accounted for his excitement at the end of the day: by such slender threads do human actions hang!

With his clothes, his bulk, his carriage, his merry arrogance, his vitality and *bonhomie*, he was by far the most remarkable figure on that day. Men said afterwards that to them this appeared the turning-point of his life – his last public appearance before the beginning of the Fortress!

He stationed himself with his wife, children and friends – a kind of resplendent patriarch – on a little green mound whence he could watch, above the vulgar crowd, the procession of the boats.

Scarcely, however, had the first two boats rounded the corner of the Island before the party from Fell House arrived – 'Madame', Mrs Jennifer Herries, Adam, John and Dorothy, with Mr Rackstraw in the background.

They had come almost to the water-edge before they realized that Walter Herries and his company were stationed above them. The people of Keswick could not be ignorant of the family warfare, had indeed for many years now been aware of it. The most fantastic stories were abroad: that Walter Herries had put poisoned wine in the Fell House cellar, that he had hired ruffians from Whitehaven to kidnap young John, that 'Madame' herself in the dead of night had climbed in at a Westaways window armed with a carving-knife – no tale was too absurd. Even though the procession of boats had begun, everyone watched to see what 'Madame' would do. 'But 'Madame', after a moment's glance, did nothing at all. Her Leghorn hat, trimmed with dahlias and ears of corn, her muslin dress of lilac, should have seemed ridiculous in a woman of her years. But she was not ridiculous, rather wonderfully imposing, her little figure neat and strong, her hand resting on her ivory cane, her head raised as though she ruled the world. Jennifer Herries, in a white muslin, towered above her, but was less impressive. Everyone said how handsome John Herries was, that Dorothy Herries had a fresh complexion, and that Madame's boy looked very French – the same comments were always made.

If Walter had noticed Judith, he gave no sign of it. So there they all were to watch the procession. Round the bend came the boats, the first four with twelve oars apiece. They were all decorated with flowers, and in three of the boats girls in white sang to the accompaniment of harps. The oarsmen were in white with crimson sashes at the waist. The sixth boat was a barge, and in it seated on a throne was the Guardian of the Lake. He was a stout old gentleman (Mr Barleycorn the hosier, in fact) with neck bare, garlanded, his fat legs bare to above the knees, and he carried a trident, thereby causing many of the spectators to suppose him Neptune.

In the boat that followed him was enthroned the Queen of the Lake with attendant maidens. This, as everyone knew, was Mrs

Armstrong who kept the sweet-shop just below Greta Hall. She was a commanding woman, full-breasted, and even on quite ordinary occasions, when selling a stick of liquorice to a small boy, stiff with dignity. It was because of her dignity that she had been chosen for this office.

In the boats that followed some licence of costume had been permitted: there were sailors, pirates, clowns, village maidens and Columbines. At the last there were small children carrying bouquets of flowers and watching with uneasy glances lest at any moment they should be precipitated into the water.

Oh, but it was a *grand* procession. The sun gave them his glory, the mountains wished them well, the church bells rang and the Town Band blared, the voices sang, and through it all the plash, plash of the oars gave rhythm and movement to the pattern of flowers and water and shadowed reflection.

They swept in a great circle, then drew up in line before the shore. The Guardian of the Lake rose a little unsteadily in his throne and delivered an address, not a single word of which could be heard by anyone. Then planks were thrown from boat to boat, and the goddess (Mrs Armstrong), 'every movement a symphony,' walked most majestically if uncertainly to the land, followed by her maidens, then by the little children, and last by the shouting rabble of sailors, clowns and Columbines.

Everyone now was shouting, everyone was singing; everyone rushed in unison together up to the field behind, where Mrs Bonaventure was to receive the King and Queen.

'Very pretty,' said Judith. 'Very pretty indeed.'

'Very handsome,' said Walter Herries, coming from his green mound. He took off his wine-coloured hat and bowed.

'Good day, Walter,' said Judith, looking him steadily in the face.

He smiled and seemed a boy of eighteen.

'I hope you are well,' he said.

'Never felt better,' answered Judith.

'We have a fine day.'

'An excellent day.'

Sir James bowed. Judith inclined her head.

Walter's party moved on.

Young Garth Herries asked a question.

'That, my boy,' answered Walter, 'is a relation of yours – and the most remarkable woman in England.'

THE RACE THROUGH THE TOWN

As everyone knows, the men and women of the North Country have never believed in the display of their emotions unless there is good ground for it. They prefer to wait and see what is really occurring before they venture an opinion. When they say a thing they mean it, but they mean a great many things that they never say.

The more extraordinary, then, was the outburst of singing and joy as the flowery boats circled the shore. It was a spontaneous cry as though some especial genial deity were abroad that day who, wishing for a song and laughter, saw that it was so. (In parenthesis: there had been up to this midday very little drinking. That came after.)

Adam found himself with his mother, Dorothy and John perched on a mound outside the churchyard wall, waiting with a great crowd of other spectators for the race to begin. He was, if he had cared to think of it, possibly the happiest boy in England that day. This was what he loved – the sun, the crowds, his own familiar country, every kind of sport and, as instinctively he knew, his mother as happy as he was.

In spite of the difference in their ages, mother and son were just now children together. This too was what Judith loved. She had a child's passion for small things, she adored to see other people happy. Adam's hand was in hers, and she had enjoyed her moment's challenge with Walter. There was no sign anywhere of the Westaways party, and she was quite certainly just then monarch of all she surveyed. Because she was so small of stature she stood once and again on tiptoe so that she might miss nothing. Nearly everyone around her knew who she was, and if anyone didn't he was certain to inquire; you couldn't catch a glimpse of her and not be conscious of her personality. But they were all proud of her, although they didn't quite know why. Farmers and their wives, townsmen and statesmen and better-class smiled, nodded, said it was a fine day, and she smiled and nodded back at all of them.

Adam, as was customary with him, said little but noticed everything. Dorothy stayed close beside her mother. At that time young ladies stayed as close to their mothers as though they were glued to them lest something evil should occur to them. John, very handsome in his plum-coloured coat, was apart, as he so often seemed to be. He was enjoying himself, but quietly and

with that slight nervous social tremor that never quite left him
when he went abroad. He did not know that within half an hour
the greatest event of his life was to occur.

Across the road were lined the runners, twelve of them. They
wore thin shirts open at the neck and short drawers. They were
young, strong, tanned most of them by their outdoor labour. The
two favourites were John Graham of Threlkeld, a tall, stringy
young man with a head shaped like a hammer; and Will Leathwaite of Grange, who was short, thick and simple-eyed like a
baby. Two of the men, Tom Trimble from St John's in the Vale
and Harry Pender of Keswick, were famous runners but were
older than the others. Trimble was a giant and as broad as he was
tall. His legs and arms were hairy and his chest hirsute beneath
his shirt. Good nature beamed from him and he looked round
him smiling on everyone, although his brow was wrinkled with
his serious purpose. He towered above the others. Pender was
thin and cadaverous. He was an ill-tempered man and hated to
be beaten. Mrs Pender in the hedge near at hand waited with
anxiety, for she knew that were he defeated he would be none too
pleasant a companion that evening. Trimble's mother, an old
rosy-faced woman with a basket on her arm, kept calling out to
her son to encourage him, and he would look across the road and
smile at her and shout: 'Aye, mother, I'll do my best'.

Old Major Bellenden had been appointed starter, and very
self-important he was. At the stroke of the half-hour from
Crosthwaite Church clock he would shout 'One. Two. Three,'
wave the handkerchief, and off they would go.

Adam's hopes were resting on Will Leathwaite, the thick
simple-faced young man. He knew Will a little, for Will's father
was a friend of Bennett the coachman, and Will would on occasion ride over from Grange or drive with a calf or farm produce. Will was Adam's kind of a man because he spoke little, was
good-natured and afraid of nothing.

Then, just as all eyes were staring at the clock – it wanted but
two minutes to the half-hour – up the road came Walter and his
friends. They were hastening along, laughing and talking,
making a great deal of display. Walter strode in front; his wife,
children and the two young men followed. Room was made for
them behind the Major, who began hurriedly explaining to
Walter Herries a number of things, very important things, involved in his official business.

And it was then that something happened to John. He saw, as

though for the first time, Elizabeth, Walter's young daughter.

It was not, of course, for the first time. He had seen her on several other occasions, but he had never spoken to her, and never considered her at all. Now her loveliness rose at him from the crowd, the cries, the fields and road as Venus rises (constantly, we may believe) from the sea.

Elizabeth Herries was at this time only twelve, but she was tall for her years. Her fair colouring, her air of shyness, her slim erect body, above all her quietness, enchanted John. But he could give no reasons for that sudden thundering of his heart, that queer sense of being urged by some force around him, the very air about him, to run forward, to touch her hand ... He had seen her before and she had meant nothing to him. He could not understand it. It was an enchantment, a magical turning of flowers and hedge, dusty road and churchyard wall into shining glass, feathered clouds and raining gold. To run, to touch her hand, to speak ...

Then, as though he had wheeled upwards on a rising sphere from sunlit underworlds, he caught his own state again, heard the voices, saw the lilac stuff of Aunt Judith's dress. Walter Herries' daughter! He raised his head and stared at the sun.

The clock struck, the handkerchief was waved, they were off! And Adam was off too. A moment before he had been holding his mother's hand, as docile a boy as you could find. She thought that she had him for the rest of the day. But he was gone before he knew that he was going. As the white figures flashed like birds towards the town, he, driven by an impulse entirely irresistible, was after them. His mother, his amiable placidity, were lost as though they had never been. Others were running too; there were shouts and cries, and then suddenly he was aware of a known voice and there was Farmer Leathwaite, father of Will, trotting on his black horse beside him.

'Hup! Hup!' Farmer Leathwaite cried, and a moment later had Adam in his arms, then held tightly in front of him. That was a glorious ride! Leathwaite had completely lost his Cumbrian caution. As the horse trotted on, from Leathwaite's big stomach into the very pit of Adam's back come continual cries, adjurations, shouts and cheers: 'That's it, Will, my lad! Keep goin'! Keep goin'! Not so fast through t'town ... Gently, gently, my boy. You'll beat 'em! You'll beat lot of 'em ... Keep joggin' ... That's the fancy! Go to it, my lad! Fine lad! Fine lad! Gently, gently! ...'

And Adam was caught by the same fever, crying in a cracked

voice: 'Go it, Will! Keep going, Will! Hurray! ... You're winning! ...'

But the gallant horse was also stirred by the splendour of the event and, do what the farmer would, refused to be stayed, so before they knew it they had galloped up Main Street, horses and shops, booths, women, dogs and shouting boys all left behind.

'Woh! Wey! Wey! Woh!' cried Leathwaite, trying to look back and see how his son was faring, but the mare with her ears pricked back was racing all the other mares in the world, and before they knew it they were out of the town and climbing the hill.

With shouts and curses the horse was at last pulled up. Small groups were gathered about the path. Leathwaite mopped his brow with a large yellow handkerchief.

'Do you think Will is going to win?' asked Adam breathlessly.

'Can't say . . .' Leathwaite panted. 'He's in grand condition , . . Hope so . . . Hope so . . . They'll be coming shortly . . .'

It was very quiet here. After the dust, heat, shouts and cries it was as though a heavy door had closed on the world. The trees were darkly thick above their heads, the hills like blue clouds beyond the town.

'How's he doing?' someone called from the waiting group.

'A' reet . . . a' reet,' Leathwaite shouted back.

'I think he'll win, don't you?' Adam said.

Oh, but he *had* to win! The whole of the world's happiness depended upon it. Then, after what had seemed an infinity of time, the white figures appeared, two in front neck and neck, then three, then at a considerable distance four or five. They were going more slowly now; the hill was telling on them, and they had the hardest task yet before them.

The first two were Trimble and a lad called Sawston. Trimble's big body was almost done. The sweat poured down his face, his breast was half bare, and on his face there was a set mechanical smile. But Will was in the next three and running strong . . . With him were John Graham and Pender. Leathwaite rose on his horse and waving his arms roared encouragement. Adam shouted too.

'Go on, Will ... Go on, Will ... You'll win! You'll win!'

He was one with Will then. He and Will were running together. He was inside Will, knew all his thoughts, his determination, his measuring of the hill beside him, his calculation of his strength, knew the maddening irritation of Trimble's great back in front of him, the temptation to make the spurt before it was time.

Now the horse went with them, and up the hill Adam and father and son charged together.

Trimble was giving way. Young Sawston passed him. Graham and Will drew level with him. Now Graham and Sawston were neck and neck. Here began the real steepness of the hill. The sun blazed down, the trees had drawn back as though refusing shelter.

'Now, Will, my lad! Now!' shouted his father.

'Now, Will, Now!' screamed Adam.

Sawston, Graham and Will were together. Graham, his head more than ever like a hammer, was running well. He was fresh as a skylark and breasted the hill as though he loved it. Sawston seemed on a sudden to lose heart; he looked back, missed his stride. Will passed him. At the hill-top where the path ran level to the Circle, Graham and Will were ahead.

Then, thrust on, it may be, by his father's fierce energy, Will Leathwaite made his spurt. He was ahead; Graham caught him. Graham was ahead. Will was level.

The Circle, calm, dignified, gazed indifferently out to Helvellyn and Scawfell and the Gavel. Will threw up his head; he seemed to catch all that country into his heart and, fiercely, like a swimmer fronting a terrific wave, flung himself across the string, the winner by a head.

Adam tumbled off the horse. Leathwaite, shouting his joy, caught Adam's small hand and wrung it as though he had never seen him before.

THE 'MIDSUMMER NIGHT'S DREAM'

The play was to begin at four o'clock. A platform had been erected on the rising shoulder of the fields where now St John's spire raises its finger for the friendly communion of the clustering hills. Up the slope climbed the meadows, striding to woods and sky. To the left the town, below them the Lake now richly dark under this sun with a sheen like the gloss on a blackberry; on benches raised roughly in four tiers sat the Quality. Beneath them and on either side of them crowded the citizens of England, for, although at this very moment of four o'clock of a fine afternoon in August 1827, all the Keswickians might be said to have been hovering before landing in a new world – a world of light, grime, noise, motion and confusion – yet the decencies were to be observed for a long time yet. Man still doffed his cap to Master, heads of families *were* heads of families, a mile was a mile when you had to walk it, and amusements were still simple enough and rare enough to be amusements. The little town, above whose roofs there hung a violet haze, shared in the happiness of its inhabitants as even to this day it yet does. From the days when the monks of Fountains were permitted a mill-dam on the Greta, through the stages of a weekly market in the thirteenth century over the old bridge at Portinscale, past the dark slumbering church of Crosthwaite, from the thirty citizens of Keswick in 1303, it had had its strong identity and kept it. Spirit and body were from the first lusty and self-confident. St Herbert saw to the first, the weekly market saw to the second. Through the wars of Scots and English, when Threlkeld and Millbeck must be fortified, when beacons flamed on Skiddaw, through the German invasion in Elizabeth's time until in middle seventeenth century the last smelting-house fell into ruin, comforted by the bleating of its sheep, the lowing of its cattle, resisting the constant rising of the waters that threatened to overwhelm it, Keswick stayed compact, pastoral and proud.

Then came Mr Gray riding in his post-chaise, then came the poets, and the world outside discovered it. Nevertheless, neither then nor now has that outside world even scratched the lustre of its peculiar beauty. Now it was not minerals that the invaders demanded, but scenery, so scenery Keswick would give them. Let them come and take it, for they could not diminish by a leaf, a flower or a swollen silver stream the soul of the place itself. At first wool, then shoes, then pencils, then Conventions – Keswick with an agreeable smile was generous, and could afford to be, because its soul was, and must be, intact.

But it liked best its own affairs, the fun that it had made itself for its own people, and so today it was especially happy and its chimneys purred with pleasure. There was an air of casual enjoyment about everything, and most especially about the play of Mr Shakespeare's. You would not perhaps have recognized it for Mr Shakespeare's play if you had seen it, for that was the time when actors did what they pleased to the plays that had the honour to offer them performances, and to none more than to Mr Shakespeare's.

These Players were here entirely by chance. They had been in the town from Penrith for several days, so that Mr William Greene – the chief of them – a gentleman as round as Falstaff and as jolly too, was by now almost a friend, and there was his wife, Mrs Greene, a tall lady with a deep bass voice, and his daughter Isabella, but these were known as friends always ready for a drink and none too certain about the paying for their charges.

Rain would have ruined everything, but rain for once was far, far away. It seemed, as you looked out across the purple Lake to that stainless sky, that it would never rain again.

The Quality, sitting most contently on the hard boards (for the Quality was easily pleased if there was any kind of fun toward), shared in the general cheer. Among the Keswickians there was considerable anxiety (although a happy anxiety), for a number of the Keswick children had been called in to be fairies, and no one knew how they would behave or what they would do – the children least of all – for there had been but one rehearsal, when the confusion had been so great that the final orders simply were 'to keep their eye on Titania and Oberon and follow them around'.

While they waited, the superior people held distinguished conversation together. There was not a great deal of room. Walter was pressed against James Herries, and his stout knees pushed into the thin backs of Misses Mary and Grace Pendexter, two maiden ladies who were ready to enjoy anything at any time and at any sacrifice. Evening after evening they would be out in their pattens, their old servant lighting them with a lantern, to play cards with Miss Pennyfeather or Major Bellenden, and now to have the handsome knees of the master of Westaways pressing their bones was a joy indeed. It happened, so close were they all together, that Westaways and Fell House were at last neighbours. It was as though the whole day had been working for this end, and, indeed, important consequences were to come of it. For John was near to Elizabeth Herries. When he saw how close he was to her, none of his customary shyness or caution could restrain him. In her primrose gown, sitting beside her mother, not speaking but her lips a little parted at her enjoyment of the scene, she seemed to him like a lovely bird from some Paradisal forest. It was arranged for him by some especial destiny that he should be near her. He knew that her mother, Mrs Herries, was a gentle lady who would wish him no harm. Her father, laughing and slapping his knee, was at a distance. Only one thing prevented him – Uhland, her brother, who sat staring in front of him, his brow wrinkled, his eyes like little stones, one knee – as always –

crooked over the other. As always, John was affected by a sort of cold nausea at his proximity, but today this new emotion of joy and happiness, as though like a great explorer, from the deck of his ship, over the trackless waste, he had seen the gold sands gleaming, was too strong for him to be checked.

If he moved a little from where he was sitting he would almost touch her. He rose up, stood back as though not to prevent the others' view, then raising his hat said:

'Good afternoon, Mrs Herries.'

She must have been greatly astonished that he should speak to her, but she, poor lady, bore no animosity to anyone in the world and was delighted at kindliness, so she smiled timidly and said:

'Good afternoon.' ('What a splendidly handsome boy,' she thought.)

John's eyes (he could not help himself) were fastened on Elizabeth, but he said:

'Yes, ma'am. We are fortunate in the weather.'

'It is indeed a splendid day,' Mrs Herries replied to him.

Then, boldly, he spoke to Elizabeth.

'I trust you can see well where you are sitting,' he said.

She looked up at him, and to her also he appeared as something new and wonderful. He was standing in the sunlight, very erect and tall, the sun shining on his hair. She wondered why she had never noticed before how beautiful he was. Although she was frightened of her father and had been forced all her life into the background, she was not nervous. She smiled.

'I can see most excellently, thank you.'

At her smile he could have gone on his knees and worshipped her.

'You will tell me if I am in your view,' he said, bowing. Then, just as he was moving away, he realized that two eyes were looking at him with a malignant force that seemed impossible for so small a boy. Elizabeth's brother's ... Something cold struck his heart.

The play had begun. From the first it was invalidated by the fact that Mr Greene, who was playing Bottom, wished to be in the forefront throughout, and that his wife, who was Titania, had the same desire.

So Theseus and his Court were soon bustled off the scene and the pairs of lovers were permitted to love and bicker only in brief moments while Bottom found his breath. Titania (very fine in shining ermine with a helmet – a perfect conception of Britannia) was meanwhile hovering with her attendant elves ('There's Lucy,' cried Mrs Bucket, 'her with the daisies.' 'That's our Liz — standing on one foot,' cried Mrs Ellis) near the platform and suddenly pushed forward and began, in her deep voice, to shout her lines.

'First, good Peter Quince, say what the play treats on,' shouted Mr Greene.

'What, jealous Oberon! Fairies, skip hence. I have forsworn his bed and company,' cried Mrs Greene.

For a moment it seemed that there would be trouble, but Bottom had his way, and Titania retired to sit on the grass near by and throw daisies at the children, for in spite of her size and voice she was a merry and kindly woman.

When, however, the time for the fairies was really come, they had their triumph. For one thing Oberon was a splendid young man, with a handsome red cloak and a noble pair of legs. Then the children, loving the sunshine and the freedom, exalted by the presence of parents and relations, behaved as fairies should, dancing everywhere, joining hands and singing, tumbling head over heels, running races, plucking at Oberon's cloak. The gaiety that had been in the air all day possessed the company and the audience together.

When Bottom became an ass and laid his great form on Titania's big lap everyone roared with applause, and the fairies pinched his legs, and Titania took off her helmet because it was so hot. There were fairies everywhere. When Theseus and his Court returned the sun was lower in the sky and long shadows lay across the grass. Some of the fairies, tired out, were sleeping, but behind Bottom and his companions, as they played their Play, the children danced and sang, Titania, carrying a baby in her arms, walked with half a dozen infants at her skirts (she had by now flung away most of her armour), and Bottom and Peter Quince, Theseus and Helena romped to the fiddle of an old man of the company who worked at his music in an ecstasy of enjoyment.

Puck came forward to speak his Epilogue and a sudden silence fell:

> If we shadows have offended,
> Think but this (and all is mended)
> That you have but slumber'd here
> While these visions did appear.

And this weak and idle theme,
No more yielding but a dream ...

The cheers and shouts echoed from Main Street to Cat Bells.
The gipsies under the wood heard it; an old man, driving his cart
home to Watendlath, heard it and in a piping voice began to
sing ...

THE DANCING ON THE MEADOW

The moon rose, triumphantly full, made of light and crystal,
lucent in a sky fiery with stars. The evening was so warm that
everyone brought food in baskets, in napkins and bags, and sat
about on the meadow waiting for the Town Band.

Judith, Jennifer and the children had planned to stay and see
the dancing and the fireworks, but now Jennifer wished to go
home. They had all been resting at Miss Pennyfeather's and had
started towards the Lake to see the fireworks when Jennifer
caught Judith's arm.

'I think I will go home, Judith.'

They were standing under the trees. Adam, John and Dorothy
had gone on to the margin of the Lake that they might watch the
trembling path of the moon on the water, and the boats like dark
fragments of cloud that floated into the light and out again.

'But why, Jennifer?' Judith asked. 'Are you unwell?'

'No,' said Jennifer. 'I have a foreboding.'

'A foreboding? Of what?'

'I cannot say ... Perhaps it is being so near to that wicked man
all day – the murderer of my husband.'

'Nonsense, Jennifer. You must not have these fancies, you
must not. Come. The fireworks will shortly commence.'

'No. I prefer to go home.'

'But we cannot find Bennett ... And I have no notion where
Mr Rackstraw has gone. Jennifer, dear ... Here is a seat. Rest
here for a moment.'

The two women sat down together. Judith took Jennifer's
hand, but the gaiety and happiness that had accompanied her all
day were gone. Once (what years ago it seemed!) in Paris she
had been with her friend Emma Furze, watching the dancing,
and suddenly, without warning, Warren Forster, the father of
Adam, who was shortly then to be born, appeared in front of her.
She remembered now the sharp sense that she had had of Fate
stepping up through the dark trees beside her. She had the same
sense now.

'What is it, Jennifer? ... It has been a most beautiful day. Everyone has been happy.'

'I cannot help it, Judith. I am growing an old woman now, but whenever I see that man I am afraid. He has been close to me all day – and the nearer he comes to me the greater terror I feel. And I am sure that one day he will build a house in Uldale and he will look into our windows. He will kill me; yes, he will kill me just as he murdered Francis. And then he will kill John and Dorothy.'

Judith started. Could Jennifer know of Walter's threat to build on High Ireby? She herself had never spoken of it, but someone else might have done. Walter had held his hand now for a long while; of late he had let them be except that there was a story of John's that he had looked out of window one night and seen Walter on his horse, motionless, staring at the house. But that may have been dream or fantasy. John had all the imagination of his father.

'No, no, Jennifer ... Listen – you must not think about Walter. He has forgotten us. He has not been near us for years. Really he has not. And I am looking after you. While I am there no harm can come to you.'

Judith felt as though she had a large overgrown child beside her. Jennifer was as usual untidy, her turban was a little askew. Her fine dress of white muslin that went wonderfully with her dark hair trailed at the skirt: her cashmere shawl was torn in one place. Through how many differing stages of relation she had been with Jennifer, Judith thought! From that first vision of her at Christabel's Ball in their youth when Jennifer, in her Medici dress, had been the loveliest creature in the world, through jealousy and anger, almost to hatred (she recalled vividly still that day at tea at Mrs Southey's), to this complete, kindly, but a little scornful domination!

'Come, Jennifer ... Do not go home ... It will make the children unhappy. They are having such a wonderful day. There will be the fireworks and then the dancing. It is so warm a night!'

Jennifer laid a trembling hand on Judith's.

'Judith, I know something dreadful will occur.'

'Nonsense. Nonsense ... Now this truly is nonsense. We must not spoil the children's amusement.' ('And my own amusement as well,' thought Judith. 'I have never enjoyed a day so much.')

But she had made this one appeal to Jennifer that must be successful. Selfish, apprehensive, sluggish though she was, she wished the children to be happy, and especially John, whom she adored.

So they went, arm-in-arm, to the Lakeside.

The fireworks were a great success, and when they had watched them they walked slowly up the hill to the meadow. Adam went with Judith. They were of a size now. Adam was as tall as his mother.

'Are you happy, Adam?'

'Yes, Mama.' He gave her arm a little squeeze. 'I *am* glad Will won the race.'

'Yes, so am I – but you should have told me that you were going . . . I had no notion where you were.'

'Yes, Mama . . . Can we go and see the gipsies?'

'Yes, if you stay beside me.'

When they came to the field the theatre was cleared away, and where the audience had sat the Town Band was. The great moon shone down on them all like a kindly benevolent hostess who had arranged the festivity and saw that it was good.

Young John had but one thought. His eyes roamed the scene. But poor John! He moved as we move in a nightmare seeking some person or place, but baffled at every moment by figures, mists and sudden catastrophes. The moonlight was now bright enough, the space wide enough for an army of young lovers, but fate played with him, catching him now here, now there, as though it were warning him that it would be better for him to ride home, find his bed and hide there. First he encountered one of the Miss Pendexters, who at once drew him into a babble of chatter: '. . . Well, now, that's a true saying about an ill wind, for only a moment ago I was asking your mother how you were finding it all. "John's enjoying himself, you may be sure," I said to her, "for this is just a night . . ." Oh, there's Major Bellenden. I was going to ask him . . . and a perfect little house my sister and I have moved into. We insist that you come to see us. Perfect situation, near the road so that there's always something passing, and dear Crosthwaite Church only half a mile . . . Yes, I was telling your mother – how lovely she is in the white muslin, to be sure – I was telling your mother that it will be no trouble of an evening to find our way to Miss Pennyfeather's for a game, for on a dark night Maria with a lantern is all we need, and often enough we can make up a table for ourselves. For our friends are so obliging – so very good . . .'

Escaping from this he ran into a confusion of happy life. So

dry was the night that everyone sat on the grass, watching the
dancing and exchanging all the gossip. The town, the countryside, all was represented. The music of the band came gently
through the air.

And more turbulent every moment was the evening becoming,
for there were rough fellows from Cockermouth and Whitehaven, there were the gipsies, and bottles were passing from hand
to hand. The dancing was growing wilder. Stout wives picked up
their skirts and romped. Old grandfathers with a 'tee-hee-hee'
pinched the arms of young girls, babies cried, dogs barked, but
the woods made a dark frontier, the sky a star-fretted canopy, the
mountains kept guard.

Through this whirling, noisy scene John found his way, looking into every face, thinking that maybe her mother had taken
her home, praying that that might not be.

Then, mounting the hill towards the gipsy encampment, he
saw the whole party. They had found some trestle seats – Walter,
James and the young men were exceedingly gay; Mrs Walter
Herries and Elizabeth were a little apart, quietly watching. John
waited, taking in with all his soul Elizabeth as she stood, a dark
cloak now over her shoulders; the rest of the world, the dancers,
the lighted fires, the stars that sparkled above the heavy wood,
vanished. She was alone and in her silence and quiet a saint
in a chapel secret and remote for his own single worship. He
stayed there a long while. In his twenty years he had known
no feeling like this, nothing that made him both so proud and
so humble, so resolute and so brave, but so timid also with a shy
foreboding.

She was a child, eight years younger than himself; she was the
daughter of his greatest enemy. He was conscious then of Walter,
who was being very merry and noisy, so that you could hear his
laughter above all the rest. He was aware too of Uhland, who sat
like a little ghost beside his father.

Without knowing it, he had moved nearer and then nearer
again. On any other occasion nothing could have compelled him
to approach those figures who stood to him for everything in life
that he hated and feared the most.

He had come up behind them, and then, as though she had
known, Elizabeth turned round to look at the downward slope of
the hill and the light on the water. They were all absorbed in the
dancing, and the two, as though in a trance, came together.

They had exchanged only two sentences of convention in all

their lives, but it seemed to her quite natural that he should say, looking at her but coming no closer:

'I have been searching for you everywhere.'

'Oh!' she said with a little cry of warning, looking back.

'Yes, I know ... But I must see you again. I must, I must.'

'One day – yes ... I would like it—'

'Where?' He came nearer until he almost touched her.

She shook her head.

'We must not—'

'Listen,' he said quickly. 'I will write. Our coachman will find a way to give it you—'

She stared at him as though she must see him so intensely that she would remember afterwards all his features. She nodded as though they had made a compact, then slowly she turned back.

No one can say what he would have done then, of what madness he might not have been capable, had he not seen, with a dismay that thrust him in an instant from one world into another, his mother, Judith and Dorothy approaching.

To his horror he saw that they, quite unconsciously, were walking directly into the Westaways group. He would have thought that for some mad reason they were doing this deliberately, had it not been that they were so plainly unaware. For Judith was laughing, pointing with her stick to some dancers, and Dorothy was teasing Adam as though she were trying to make him dance. He did dance a few steps, looking in the moonlight like a little animal, with his long arms and short body. They all laughed. John heard Judith say: 'Here is a fine place. We can see well from here.' He would have started forward to warn them, but it was too late.

In another moment Judith had almost stumbled on the bench where Walter was sitting.

John came forward as though to protect his mother. Walter Herries stood up. It was plain that he had been drinking heavily, for he lurched a little on his great legs as he stood.

Jennifer was transfixed with terror. In all the years since her husband's death she had never until now been face to face with him.

Walter took off his hat.

'Good evening, ladies! How agreeable a surprise! Not unexpected too. Will you not join us?'

Jennifer caught at Judith's arm.

'Oh, come, Judith. Come away!'

But Walter was delighted. Such scenes he fancied. The young Durward Herries boys, who saw something strange was abroad, stared, their laughter checked.

'Well, Jennifer,' Walter said. 'It is a long time since we met. It was my mother you knew, I think. I hope that you cherish no ill-will, though, for I assure you that I do not.'

'Thank you, Walter,' Judith broke in. 'This is too public for your wit. Jennifer, we will turn back—'

But he strode forward so that he almost touched Jennifer's arm. He made no sign that anyone existed for him but Jennifer, who shrank back against Judith.

'No, no. Why so unfriendly? We must be friends, we must indeed. For we are to be neighbours. Very near neighbours indeed. You didn't know? But, of course ... At High Ireby. I am to start building in a month or so.'

'You cannot—' Jennifer answered. 'That would be terrible. I could not—'

'Why, yes,' said Walter. He took a step nearer. Then John, seized with a wild fury, struck him in the chest. Walter tottered, for he was not at all steady, almost fell. There were cries, exclamations. Little Uhland had rushed forward, hitting at John's legs.

It was, in fact, a most ludicrous, lamentable scene, for the other young Herries men, themselves rather drunk, came forward (not very aware of what they would do). Judith lifted her stick, Agnes Herries caught Walter's arm ...

Then in a moment the publicity of it hit them all. They stood transfixed in a frozen group. Two gipsies approached and one of them, a young woman with an orange kerchief and a cage of little green birds said: 'Lady ... Pretty lady ... The birds will tell your fortune ... Happy luck, lady.'

Walter steadied himself.

'Here,' he said, 'you can tell my fortune, my girl, and give me a fine one.'

With great dignity, very slowly, Judith and Jennifer, their children following them, turned down the hill.

THE BEGINNING OF THE FORTRESS

WALTER HERRIES had told Jennifer that the building of his house on High Ireby was at once to begin. It was not, however, until the month of March 1830 that the foundations were first laid – and it happened that Jennifer was there to see.

Jennifer never recovered from that shock of the encounter with Walter on the night of the Summer Fair. It was the climax to a series of events that stretched back to that old Ball of her youth, and possibly, behind that again, to her earliest nursery escape from reality. She did not know now – she had not an analytic mind – what had happened to her or indeed why anything had ever happened to her at all. She was an old woman – this year saw her sixtieth birthday – but for all her years she felt herself to be still a young girl most unjustly treated by everyone.

In the early days – they seemed to her to be as recent as last evening – she had never had justice. Her beauty had brought her nothing: everything had been always just awry. She would have been the Duchess of Wrexe and a great woman of the world had not the Duke been so unpleasant a young man and the position of great lady so tedious and wearisome. She would have been a quiet beauty in the country had not Francis, her husband, been a weakling. She would have been a splendid Mistress had not her lover been a clod. She would have been a triumphant Mother had her children loved her. She would be now mistress of her house had not Judith taken selfishly everything out of her hands. Always injustice, everywhere injustice. No one saw what she was and no one cared.

The sluggish slackness in her that had ruined her life she did not perceive, for we never catch the causes of our fate, so clear to everyone around us. She might even now have been a fine tragic figure had she had the intelligence to look noble, the energy to tidy her hair, the wisdom to have reticence.

She had never had dignity or wisdom; she had been always the slave of trifles, small jealousies, degrading idleness, lazy avoidances of trouble.

But the terror of Walter struck into her character as a snake strikes. She was poisoned in all her being. The infection spread slowly, but from the moment that Judith consented to stay and took the house into her hands, Jennifer was lost. She had now nothing to do but brood over Walter. She cowered beneath his shadow, unable to move, waiting the awful moment.

As his shadow grew ever more terrible the figures immediately around her became themselves shadows. John had once been her darling, Judith's Adam a pleasure, the servants agreeable, her daughter Dorothy 'a good girl', Judith herself, although a tyrant, exceedingly useful and a safeguard.

After her scene with Walter all these were as unsubstantial to her as figures on a tapestry. She might have been still a fine woman; she had yet all her height, her hair (once so lovely) was white with, if she had cared, a fine lustre in its silver. But she was untidy, careless, a slattern. Any old clothes did for her, her hair escaped its pins, she would tap-tap in loose slippers, an old shawl over her shoulders, from room to room. Only her eyes were good, and the blaze in them, their intensity, belied all the rest of her, so that they were like a bright fire in a lumber-room. She would begin sentences and not finish them, eat food greedily and suddenly abandon it, pet John and Adam eagerly and then look at them as though she did not know them. The servants disregarded her; they took their orders from Madame.

Judith knew that terror was of an especial danger to anyone of even part Herries blood. She had seen, in all her active varied life, that the history of the Herries, as of so many British families, was that of a building impregnable, as its builders thought, to the attacks of all outside forces. But the outside forces are strong and immortal. Nothing tempts their malicious humour so thoroughly as the complacency of the builders. Here they twist a chimney, there a window rattles, now the wind sweeps wildly up the ordered garden, the iron-sheathed door shudders, a picture falls, the carpet rises on the floor.

Jennifer's parents had been typical Herries, good, complacent, satisfied, laughing at imagination. Jennifer, so lovely, their pride, their joy, must be safe if any Herries was. Who would dare to touch her? So, in their love for her, they took from her all her defences. Now, when a vision of another world more real than the Herries one might have saved her, she had no vision. And Judith could not help her.

From the moment of Walter's threat, for two years and a half, she waited. But life does not allow you to wait. No one knew what the matter with her was and, more tragically, no one cared.

Her children had loved her, but Dorothy was all for comfort and found her uncomfortable, while John, after he knew of the reasons for his father's suicide, shrank, against all his will and wish, from contact. Moreover, he had now something so absorbing in his life that his mother was dim to him, as he was to her.

Judith could have loved her because she pitied her and pity, with Judith, was maternal; but daily contact with Jennifer's laziness, carelessness, selfishness, turned pity into impatience, and when Judith was impatient she was at her worst.

So Jennifer was alone with her terror.

As the time advanced, that terror took strange forms. High Ireby became a place of extraordinary fascination for her. It was several miles from Uldale and uphill for most of the way, but day after day she walked through the fields, climbed the slope and then stood, under the trees, gazing at the lovely scene – the walls of a ruined cottage, a small wood of whispering trees, remnants of a garden patch, and the long slope of the melancholy fields with the village and house of Uldale tucked into the hollow.

To the right were the sprawling slopes of Blencathra and Skiddaw. They lay against the sky like the careless limbs of a giant sleeper under an enormous coverlet tossed into casual shapes. She knew here all weathers, all seasons. She would stand against the ruined wall, under the trees, a tall, motionless old woman in a tawdry hat, clutching her shawl, staring in front of her. She became a familiar figure to the inhabitants of the village near by. It was not strange that she should soon have a reputation for madness, but she was not mad in the least. She would stand there, or sit on a tumbled stone, and reflect, in a lazy way, on her misfortune – not on any very definite misfortune but on the general way in which she was ill-treated and neglected. Sometimes she would determine that on her return to Uldale that day she would tell them all what she thought of them – Judith, John, Dorothy, even Mr Rackstraw – but she never did. Partly it was too much trouble, partly when she was once again in the comfortable parlour at Uldale drinking tea before the fire or, in the summer, sitting under the tree on the lawn in the sunshine, she was cosy like a cat and smiled, lazily, on everyone.

She had too, all this time, marvellous health. Nothing ailed her.

She had perhaps the idea, as she stood in the little wood, day after day, that thus she was defying Walter. During all these two years she never saw him in the flesh. He became the more monstrous because she did not see him.

Then one day at last the thing happened. That March there was a late fall of snow. During the first week of that month a blizzard blew across the North, adding discomfort to all the hardships that the poor people were, at that time, already suffering. Waters were frozen, the sun, when it broke through, turned the snow-ridges into shining marble, the crows were spots of ink on the virgin fields.

She had had a cold for a week, and Judith had kept her in bed, but as soon as she was up she strode across the fields again, her shawl flapping behind her, climbed the hill and walked into a multitude of men.

Trees were falling. It seemed that on every side of her the trees were tumbling. The walls of the ruined cottage were no more. Men walked measuring the ground. A fire was lit on the snow and illuminated the broken whiteness of the scene that stretched back into the farther shadows of the wood.

As she stood back in the road hidden by two huge horses from whose nostrils steam struck the air, a tree fell with a great crash and a groan that seemed to come from her own heart. Men shouted joyfully, and some boys, muffled against the cold, danced round the fire.

She stepped into the middle of the road and several of them saw her. Two gentlemen on horseback, attended by little Peach, Walter's agent, were watching the proceedings: one of them was the architect, Mr Humphrey Carstairs from London, the other, young Julius Hopper, a clever lad working in old Mr Bonner's office in Keswick. Old Mr Bonner was the oldest, stupidest and laziest architect in the North of England, and no one despised him quite so deeply as did young Julius. Young Julius was slim and dark and exceedingly handsome in his high-collared dark green overcoat; Carstairs was squat, thick, his head almost hidden in the curves of his plum-coloured capes. He bent low in his saddle; he suffered severely from rheumatism.

He turned and saw the strange woman in the old-fashioned hat, drawn to her full height in the middle of the snowy road. He stared, then turned to young Julius. 'Who's the old body in the shawl?' he asked.

Young Julius stared also. He knew who she was: his first thought was that this would be amusing for Walter Herries if he rode over that afternoon. His second was of alarm. She looked crazy; he knew, of course, of the feud. She might have a pistol under that shawl of hers. He was a warm young man, fond of life, very ambitious. He had no desire to die as yet. Another tree fell; men were dragging branches across the snow that blew in little smoky spirals of silver into the air. The flames of the fire leaped, and an old man sitting by it, with a great red comforter round his neck and yellow mittens, began to play on a fiddle. The mittens made his fingers clumsy, but the men liked the music and worked with a better will.

'She's a Mrs Herries from Uldale yonder,' young Julius whispered. 'She's a sort of cousin of Walter Herries.' Then he added: 'I'll go speak to her.'

With what he felt to be exceptional bravery (for it was possible enough that she concealed a pistol) he dragged his horse's head round and rode towards her. She never moved, but stood there in the road, staring at the men, the fallen trees, the old man in the bright red comforter. Young Julius raised his hat.

'Good afternoon, Mrs Herries.' Then he said, smiling: 'Very wintry for March, ma'am.'

He wasn't sure that she saw him. He moved his horse a little to the right.

Then she said: 'What is going on here?'

He was able now to see her eyes, the pallor of her face, something dignified in her isolation. He spoke with the greatest politeness as he answered:

'Why, ma'am, Mr Walter Herries of Westaways is to build a house here.'

'Indeed?' She nodded her head. 'A house of some size?'

'Oh, yes. It is to be a very fine place indeed – gardens and a fountain, magnificent stables. A lonely spot, though, to have chosen. Mr Carstairs there from London is the architect.'

'What is your name?'

She looked at him directly and there was something in her eyes that touched him very truly.

'My name, ma'am, is Hopper – Julius Hopper. I am assistant to Mr Bonner, the architect in Keswick. I know your son, Jack Herries, well. We are very good friends.'

'Ah, yes, my son.' Her eyes went back to the fire that seemed to have a great fascination for her. The thin, reedy, uncertain squeak of the fiddle came whining through the sharp air.

'And how long will it be in the building?'

'A considerable while, ma'am. Mr Herries wishes everything to be of the best.'

'Ah ... He wishes everything to be of the best ...'

'Yes, ma'am. And these are not easy times. Although so many are without employment, it is not easy to get good workmen and wages are high. As soon as we have Reform things will be better.'

'You believe in Reform?'

'I do indeed, ma'am. We shall have Revolution else, like the French.'

'You are wrong.' She spoke with slow consideration, as though she beat every word upon the ground. 'Reform itself is Revolution. The country will be ruined. The country is in any case ruined.'

'I hope not indeed.'

'Ah, you are young . . .'

She moved away from him up the road. His horse stepped beside her. He would never forget that odd, tall, black figure with the crazy hat, moving against the snow. He thought after that it had been a kind of omen, but he was a sane practical young man who did not believe in omens, although out of habit he avoided walking under a ladder.

She came so far and then saw Peach. Mr Carstairs had come down from his horse and now he and Peach were studying a plan. Jennifer scarcely knew Peach, and yet his short bow-legged figure was in some way familiar to her. She looked up at Julius, and he, not knowing what to say, remarked:

'The snowdrops are doing bravely in spite of the snow.' There was a great patch of them under the trees. Some of them were already trodden down and, as he looked, two men, carrying a log, tramped upon the patch.

'Oh, the snowdrops!' She put her hand on his knee, leaning up to him. 'Tell Walter Herries what he is destroying.'

She turned and walked swiftly down the road, catching her shawl more closely about her. The three men turned to watch her.

Meanwhile at Uldale, as it happened on that same afternoon, Judith assisted by Dorothy Herries was entertaining four lady callers – old Miss Pennyfeather, Mrs Leyland of The Ridge, Bassenthwaite, and her two daughters Nancy and Bella.

Miss Pennyfeather had been driven over by Judith, who had been taking luncheon with her in Keswick; the Leylands had come over from Bassenthwaite in their barouche. All the ladies were very pleasantly animated: the three elders, their heads together, near the fire, and the girls laughing and chattering by the window.

For the Leyland girls this was an adventure. Dorothy Herries, blooming with health and good temper, was two years older than Nancy and Bella, who were twins and were wanting to be married, for they were already twenty years of age and soon it would be too late. They were nice simple girls who had never been to London and only visited the theatre in Newcastle and were eager for gossip and adventure. They were pale, flaxen, tall and slim, and dressed alike. They wore dresses of poplin, colour violette de Parme, with heart-shaped bodices, and the corsages long and tight at the waist. They had hats of rice straw with very wide brims, trimmed with anemones. Each thought the other looked bewitching, for they were generous and warm-hearted by nature.

They had never been to Uldale before on a visit, and this was a great adventure. 'Madame' was a 'character' through the whole countryside, and it was wonderful to be entertained in her parlour. Or was it Mrs Herries' parlour? People said that she was mad and walked about the country singing songs to herself – mad, poor thing, because her husband had discovered her with her lover and he had killed himself. Very shocking, but *how* romantic! And then her son John was so handsome, the best-looking young man in the North, a little sad and pensive as a good-looking young man ought to be. (For they adored *Thaddeus of Warsaw* and Mrs Cuthbertson's *Santo Sebastiano* and Mrs Meeke's *Midnight Weddings*.) Dorothy on the other hand – whom they loved at sight – was not melancholy at all and laughed all the while.

Then there was 'Madame's' boy whom they did hope they'd get a sight of. He was, of course, illegitimate, which made him so interesting, although everyone knew who the father had been. He *should* have been romantic and melancholy, but people said that he was ugly and silent and kept to himself. Nevertheless, it would be *adorable* to see him!

While they laughed and chattered by the window they tried to keep an ear open for the company by the fire. For Miss Pennyfeather did say such *shocking* things and their mother (Mrs Leyland was stout and jolly) had told them that on no account were they to listen to Miss Pennyfeather's wickedness, so they were naturally all ears.

But the ladies seemed to be talking of nothing but Reform, Lord John Russell, and of Brougham's attack on Lady Jersey in

The Times, and how bitter she was against Reform, and so on, and so on – dull stuff!

Then Dorothy let it out that next month 'Madame' and her son were to go to London to stay with some relations. *That* was exciting! To go to London! To see the great Simpson at Vauxhall, to visit the New Zoological Gardens in Regent's Park, to attend a Masquerade in the Argyll Rooms, to catch a glimpse of the Duke, and best of all the Theatre, the Surrey, the Royalty, or Sadler's Wells.

They knew all about it; it was as though they had been in London all their lives. They looked across to the fire and that little upright dominating woman in her crimson dress with the huge sleeves; they stared (as unobtrusively as politeness insisted) at her small pale face, her neat grey hair, her ivory cane, and watched her bright eyes, her smile, the tapping of her small foot on the carpet. People said that she was the daughter of a gipsy and that her father, although of the finest family, had been a rogue and vagabond. And here she was, with her illegitimate boy, behaving as though she were Queen of England. Ah! *What* a romantic afternoon they were having!

It was made yet more splendid by the entrance of John Herries. Both girls, at sight of him, had the same thought. What a *lover* he would make! But there was something that told them at once that he was not for them. He came over to them and made himself very charming. His voice was soft and gentle. Yes, he *was* melancholy, although he teased his sister and chaffed them about their beaux at a recent Ball in Keswick. But they felt that his mind was elsewhere.

What a *hero* of a novel he would make! He was too gentle to be truly Byronic, but he would suit *The False Step* exactly! How beautifully he went and paid his devoir to their mother, with what ease! And yet he was in no way effeminate, quite unlike that horrid William d'Arcy of Threlkeld, or, on the other hand, that oaf, young Osmaston.

Well, it was time for them to be going. Darkness would soon swallow the pale saffron twilight. Already the candles were lit in the room. Mrs Leyland rose to make her adieux when the door opened and the strangest figure stood in the doorway.

Jennifer stood there, her hat a little askew, her long thin fingers clutching her shawl. She could see but indistinctly. The candlelight blinded her, coming in as she did from the dark snow-shine road. But she saw Judith.

'Judith! Judith! He has begun to build!'

The cry, shrill, poignant, broke the comfortable cosiness of the room into fragments. Jennifer had awaked at last.

'Judith! They are trampling on the snowdrops ... The trees are falling!'

She stumbled forward, her hat ever more askew as she moved, and Judith, coming to her, caught her hand.

'Wait, Jennifer. There are guests here ...'

Mrs Leyland, good and kind woman as she was, did the right thing. She chattered:

'Well, I'm sure ... How do you do, Mrs Herries? A cold afternoon to be out in. You must be weary, and a cup of tea will be the very thing. And now we must be going. So very dark, although William is a most careful driver. We brought him from Newcastle with us. He was always careful from a boy. Might William be summoned, Mrs Herries? Thank you. Most kind. Come, girls. William will have the horses in an instant. He is always so prompt. It has been truly most delightful. I'm sure ...'

But Jennifer was not to be silenced by any chatter. She saw only one thing, one terrible thing, before her eyes – and she must declare it. Judith had seated her on the sofa, had pulled the bell-rope, was pouring a cup of hot tea. Dorothy had come round to her mother. The girls stood in the window, not knowing quite what they should do but enthralled by what they saw and heard. John had gone to hasten Mrs Leyland's horses.

'Yes, he has begun at last, Judith. All his men are there, measuring the ground, and it is to be a huge place with a fountain and fine stabling. All the trees are falling, and they have lit a fire in the snow.'

'It is Walter Herries,' Judith explained *sotto voce*. 'He has been threatening for a long while that he would build on High Ireby that he may overlook us – and now it seems that he has done it.'

'Well,' cried old Miss Pennyfeather. 'Let him, and much good may it do him! I cannot endure Walter and I don't care who hears me. Fat overgrown bully! Let him build with his limping child and puny wife! Don't you worry, Judith. 'Tis all stuff and nonsense! He can't harm you and he knows it!'

'Yes, indeed,' said Mrs Leyland, gazing anxiously at the door for news of her horses. 'I should think so indeed. So he's to be our neighbour at Ireby, is he? A pretty neighbour, and so Mr

Leyland will prove to him if he comes bothering our way. Come, girls – William must have brought the horses round.'

But Jennifer looked at them all with startled, staring eyes. 'He will not be content until he has destroyed us. I knew it from the first. All his windows will look down on us. We must leave Uldale. I always said that he would have his way!'

Judith was sitting beside her. She had one of her hands in hers.

'Jennifer, Jennifer . . . You must not be so distressed. Cousin Walter will do us no harm. How can he? What if he does build a house at Ireby? That can do us no harm. Come, come, Jennifer . . .'

How soft and gentle her voice was, thought the girls, and how crazy Mrs Herries looked, poor woman, with her hat on one side!

Mrs Leyland beamed comfortably on them. 'I am sure Ireby is no place for a house, no place at all. I cannot think why he should choose such a spot, and Westaways good enough for anyone, I should have thought. I always said he was a strange man, and Mr Leyland, who is downright if any man is, remarked to me only a week back that he was growing far too stout for his health. If he could but give some of his size to his wife, poor woman . . .'

John appeared in the doorway.

'Come, girls. Here's Mr Herries to say that William has the horses round. Has he not, Mr Herries? That's excellent. William is always so prompt. Good day to you. Good day. Good day. *Most* delightful. Never enjoyed anything more. Come, girls. *Too* kind of you, Mrs Herries. It's time we were moving on, with the snow and everything . . . You must all come over to Bassenthwaite at the nearest opportunity. Oh, I insist. I take no refusal. So very good of you, Mrs Herries—'

When the Leylands were out of the room a silence fell. Jennifer drank her tea. Then she rose.

'There is no peace for us any more here,' she said. 'You may laugh, Judith, but it is so. He will destroy us all.' Then, staring at Miss Pennyfeather as though she were seeing her for the first time, she added: 'They were trampling on the snowdrops. It is to be a tremendous place with rows of windows. I think I will go to my room.'

She walked out.

Judith sighed.

'If that isn't unfortunate! Poor Jennifer! And the Leylands will talk for weeks!' Then taking Miss Pennyfeather's arm she added: 'Janet, come up with me. You are the most sensible woman I know. Talk to her. I'm of no service when she's like this.'

So Dorothy and John were left alone. Dorothy saw at once that her brother was greatly disturbed; he stood there, fingering his high stock and looking, as she remembered her father had sometimes looked, as though he were going to be sick. At such a time she could not help him. She was good about sensible practical things like a broken leg, a bloody head, a cold in the chest, but when John was in a mood she was uncomfortable as though he were improper. Although she was the soul of good nature and almost always in a good temper, she resented the states into which her mother and brother sometimes tumbled.

John said at last:

'Nothing can help mother. Now that she has this in her head.'

'I'll see about some linden tea,' Dorothy said. 'It has soothed her many a time.' And relieved at an opportunity of escape, she bustled out.

She had been gone but a moment when Adam came in. Adam was now fourteen and a half. He had filled out in the last two years and was deep of chest, thick across the shoulders. His black hair was always untidy; a lock hung now over his forehead. He was ruddy with health, with the brown colour that made so many who didn't know him think him a foreigner, but he was English enough all the same, with the broad brow, snub nose, large mouth, square body, short sturdy legs, bright eyes like his mother's. He was English, too, in his reticence and hatred of demonstration. This affected him now, for he saw at once that John was worried and would need his help. John liked demonstrations: there were times when he wanted Adam to show him that he loved him, and although Adam did love him more than any human thing save his mother, he hated to show it. Oh! how he hated it!

He was in rough country things and his high boots were muddy, for he had been out with Rackstraw, Bennett and the dogs rabbiting and had had a glorious afternoon. When he saw that John's distress was so real he thought to himself, 'Let John do what he likes to me if it helps him.' With a backward glance he threw reluctantly behind him all the happiness of the afternoon, the crisp air, the scent of the snow, the yelping of the dogs, the sunlight breaking in silver across the slow fields.

'Adam, Mother has been to High Ireby. Walter Herries has begun to build.'

'I knew it,' Adam said quickly. 'Bennett told me.'

'Mother is very unhappy. She came in while the Leylands were here and spoke as though she were crazy. This will *send* her crazy! If I could do something! How I hate him! He comes nearer and nearer with his sneer and his crooked son and—' He broke off.

'Pooh!' said Adam, cracking his whip against his boot as grown men did. 'It's fun, John – fine fun! Why should you care? And your mother will be better now that it's happened. It has been the waiting for it . . .'

'I am afraid of nothing else,' John went on. 'Nothing but this. I'm no coward. You know that I'm not. But Cousin Walter, since the days when we were small . . . Do you remember that evening when he rode up to the house and we watched him? And now that I'm managing the estate it brings me closer to him. Oh, Adam, I wish that you and Aunt Judith were not going to London—'

'It's grand!' Adam cried, throwing out his chest. 'There'll be the coach and the lights, chimneys smoking and everyone shouting, and mother says we shall go to a theatre—'

'Adam,' John broke in. 'There's something else. I must tell you. I have been intending so for three months past, but no one knows. It makes everything so difficult—' He broke off and began to pace the room. Adam, his legs straddling, waited. 'It's this. You're to tell no one, Adam.'

'No one,' repeated Adam, and meant it.

'It's Elizabeth – Walter's daughter. We are in love. We have been so for more than two years. It began the night of the Summer Fair.'

'What!'

'Yes, yes . . . Why should it not be? There is no one so lovely, so good, so lovely—'

'But she is a child, a little girl—'

'She is your own age, Adam. In two years she will be seventeen—'

'Elizabeth! *His* daughter!'

'Yes, yes . . . I know all that you can say. I have said it all to myself again and again. But it happened at sight, and now it is for ever. Nothing can change it.'

Love – love of girls and women – as yet seemed to Adam an absurdly inexplicable business, a waste of time, a ludicrous sentimentality. And now this, for a child who was a baby, the daughter of their greatest enemy whom they had sworn always to hate, the sister of the loathsome, deformed Uhland ... An impulse to despise John rose in his heart and was at once loyally driven down again.

'Oh, John!'

'Do not pity me. Do not laugh. We love one another for ever, and so soon as she is old enough we shall marry.'

'No, no, you must not!' Adam caught his arm. 'Uncle Walter's daughter! ... I shall never speak to you again if you do!'

'Well, then, don't! I don't care!'

'But, John, how *can* you? For two years? And you've been meeting?'

'Sometimes. But not often. We write.'

Adam turned, with a gesture of disgust as though he would leave the room, but John gripped his shoulder.

'Adam, you must listen. You *must*. You are the only friend I have. The only one. I love you more than anyone in the world save Elizabeth. Again and again we have sworn that nothing should separate us—'

'Yes, but this—'

'No; you are young. You don't understand—'

'I'm not young.' Adam broke away. 'If you wish to love a girl you can, but not *his* daughter.'

'But don't you see? I could not help it. As I breathe so I love her. You will yourself one day—'

John's eyes caught Adam's and held him. There was an expression in them that struck to the very depths of Adam's loyalty and devotion. He knew then that he could never desert John, never, whatever the crisis.

He muttered something, looking away.

'Mind – it is our secret.'

Adam nodded his head, then said gruffly:

'I must go to the stables. Caesar has a sore leg. Coming?'

JUDITH AND ADAM IN LONDON

THEY – Judith and Adam – had spent the most glorious night at the George, Stamford, in the very room, so the landlord himself informed them, occupied by his Sacred Majesty, King Charles the First, when he slept there on his way from Newark to Huntingdon on the night of August 23rd, 1645. This Judith, in ordinary circumstances, would never have believed (although the room was splendid with oak beams and a huge four-poster and a small closet off it where Adam slept and snored), but the fact was that she was so greatly excited by her journey and by the expectation of London (where she had not been for so long a time) and by the temporary escape from Uldale, that she behaved like a child of ten and was ready to believe anything. One of the drawers remarked to another of the drawers that he'd never yet seen an old lady like it. They had had to wait for their adventure for it was not until the second week in October that they left Uldale.

Adam was quite as deeply excited as his mother and expressed his emotions in sudden fiery little sentences, like shots from a gun, that seemed to have little or no relation to one another.

Everything was glorious, the long ride in the coach the day before (Adam had insisted on sitting outside, although it was terribly cold and there was a place for him inside), the sound of the horn, the spanking pace of the horses, the incidental humours of the road and, most especially, the powers and personality of Mr Joe Dorset, the Coachman, with whom Adam was utterly and entirely in love.

Then had come the falling dusk, the lights of the town, the bustling courtyard of the George, the wonderful dinner when, like a gentleman, Adam had drunk his mother's health in marvellous claret, sitting up in his chair so straight that he nearly broke his back in two (he and his mother so grand at a table all to themselves, while the old gentleman with three chins and two daughters entertained the table in the middle of the room with his anecdotes of Tom Hennessey and his shooting adventures in Scotland), and then the great bedroom in which King Charles had slept, and his mother going upstairs to it in such stately fashion, the landlord himself in front with two candles, that you would have thought her Royalty.

But all this was nothing at all to the glory of the next day when they started in a pale golden dawn, frost in the air, and the roans stamping their hoofs to be off. Adam, wrapped in a hundred coats, had the glory of sitting beside the great Joe with the old three-chinned gentleman on his other side.

He could observe everything and listen to everything too. He saw the gold fade from the sky and give place to one of the loveliest mornings of the year. The fields were yet frosted, the road was hard; only once had they to travel through water, which gave Joe (who had a voice like a gurgling water-pipe) occasion to describe what had happened once to the Stamford Regent when going through St Neot's, fifty-six miles out of London – how the Ouse had overflowed its banks there, and although an extra pair of leaders were put on, ridden by a horse-keeper, yet the water was up to the axle-trees and even, for a while, the Regent was afloat, to the dreadful peril of some ladies inside it. And that led the stout gentleman to talk of Tom Hennessey's famous whip, which, as everyone knows, was a crooked one so that it could tickle the lagging wheelers in a fashion no other whip could achieve. And that led Joe to show what he could do with *his* whip, and a stout lady behind them *begged* him to be careful and not to hurt the horses, which Adam thought the funniest thing he'd ever heard. (But then women *were* peculiar, all of them, even his mother.)

There came a glorious moment, later in the morning, when Joe actually entertained Adam himself in conversation.

'And what might *your* age be, young gentleman?'

'Fifteen.'

'Fifteen! Deary me! Think of that now! . . . Learnt to fight yet?'

'A little.' (Adam was modest. Rackstraw had taught him well.)

'Going to see a Fight in London?'

'I hope so.'

'Next week, come Friday, there's the Nottingham Pet and John Willis at Islington. That'll be something.' Then, after a pause, 'Going to school in London?'

'No; just for a visit.'

'Ever been to London afore?'

'No, never.'

'Ah! That's a treat for a young lad. That's a treat, that is. All the same the country's better. Live in the North?'

'Yes, in Cumberland.'

'Ever seen the Crusher?'

'No. I'm afraid I haven't.'

'Never seen the Crusher – and live in Cumberland? Why, think of that now! I remember his fight in Newcastle when he smashed Foxy Rundle in twenty rounds – in '23 I think it was.'

But here the old gentleman broke in; he hadn't seen the fight

himself but he had heard ... and here the coach had to be
stopped for a lady with enough baggage for a journey to China,
who didn't like this, and wouldn't have that, until Joe's temper
was as purple as the capes of his riding-coat. And then – somewhere early in the afternoon – the foretaste of London began to
creep upon Adam. London! London at last! How faint suddenly
were Uldale, Skiddaw, the village shop with the green bottle
window ... Dorothy and the way she'd take the jars of preserve
out of the cupboard and examine them one by one with a seriousness ... old Bennett and the way he'd pinch his leg ... even John
standing there, looking at Adam, telling him that horrid hateful
news, that he loved Walter's daughter ... all figures as dim now
as the faded pinks and blues on the Chinese screen in his
mother's bedroom! London!

Already they were at the Peacock at Islington, and the hostler
was shouting, doors were slamming, old Joe Dorset taking up
parcels, answering silly questions from nervous ladies, drinking
out of a jug, examining the horses, reassuring a nervous old
gentleman wrapped in a vast white muffler – and then, in another
moment – Tantivy! Tantivy! Tantivy! – they were off again.

'Are you comfortable, dear?' his mother had asked him, poking
her head out of the window. 'Not too cold?'

'He's all right, ma'am,' Joe Dorset had answered, 'as right as a
'edge'og'; and Adam had been proud all down his spine. Certainly he was all right. What a pity his mother hadn't come
outside! She would have enjoyed it. Now, after Islington, lights
flared on the country road, for the dusk is creeping up and out of
it suddenly loom drovers and a herd of cattle. Then Smithfield
and Cow Lane, then up Holborn Hill. But these places were, of
course, nothing to Adam. What did he see? In detail very little,
for mist is everywhere, noise is everywhere – through the mist
lights and flares, a blazing window, a crooked chimney, a barrow
alive with flame. And the noises – hackney cabriolets, drays,
waggons, wheelbarrows, shouting boys, bawling men, screaming
women, ringing bells – and through it all, above it all, beyond it
all, his heart beating like an African drum!

He was never one to show his excitement. He sat now in absolute silence, his hands tightly clenched together under his coat,
his mouth firmly closed, but his eyes staring, staring as though
they would pierce this foggy, noisy mystery through to the other
side.

Tantivy! Tantivy! Tantivy! He felt now Joe's pride that he

was bringing his coach in on time. How they dashed over the cobbles, how the roans tossed their heads, how through the murk and gloom one could dimly feel figures sliding, horses slipping, voices shouting to be out of the way. Then, one more blast and into a courtyard of light and splendour the Stamford Regent dashes. The George and Blue Boar, Holborn: London's heart is touched at last.

He discovered then, quite to his own surprise, that he was extremely sleepy; he discovered, too, for the first time in his young life, what every traveller discovers, that once at a destination and the life that only a moment earlier had been pulsating with fire and energy is collapsed at your feet like a spent balloon.

Even Joe Dorset was fading. Not that he wouldn't be pleased to meet Joe again somewhere, but his figure was shrunk and his voice sounded miles away.

No, his mother was once again the centre of his world. She dominated the place, sending hostlers here and stable-boys there, collecting their luggage, standing over it, ordering a hackney cabriolet, and all as quietly but as imperiously as though London were at her feet and knew it.

'Now, Adam,' she commanded. 'In you get!' And in he did get, into the mustiest, smelliest, darkest interior that his enterprising life had yet known. Mice, straw, newspapers, stale beer and damp cloth all seemed to have gone to the making of that hackney cab. There was indeed straw on the floor of it and old newspaper squeezed into the hinge of one of the windows. The driver was a little man with a pinched white nose and no eyebrows. He seemed to be terrified of Judith, for when she said, 'Number Nine, Cadogan Place,' he almost bowed to the ground.

They were crushed together inside the cab, for they were piled round with parcels and small boxes. Judith put her arm around him, and so they bumped and jumped and swayed and sank as though on a tempestuous sea. Houses rose and fell beyond the misty windows, horses loomed gigantic, figures sprang up before them and vanished again, and in Adam's nostrils was that smell with which he would associate London all his life long – straw, ale, and the faint scent of violets that stole from his mother's clothes.

They had arrived. The cab had stopped with a jerk, the door creaked open, and a little boy with a large broom was there on the pavement, his hand out, begging.

When Judith had given the little boy a shilling (which astonished him very much and led the driver of the cabriolet to wet his lips in anticipation) the big solemn door (supported by black marble pillars) was slowly opened and a very thin footman with powdered hair and an ornamental waistcoat stood there staring at them. It seemed from his expression that he could not believe that anyone should be arriving in a hackney cab at that particular moment, but Judith walked straight past him as though she were the Queen of Egypt, and then, remembering that the driver had not yet been paid, hurried down again, directed the bringing-in of the luggage, smiled at the footman, said her name in a very determined manner, and entered the house a second time, on this occasion followed closely by Adam.

The hall was so extremely dark and a lamp by the staircase so exceedingly dim that a white bust of a gentleman with a lot of hair and naked shoulders, and a large picture of Moses addressing the Children of Israel, were the only things for a long while visible.

'Madame Paris,' said Judith again. 'We are expected.'

The footman disappeared and returned to say, 'This way, Madame,' disregarding Adam altogether. He, however, was determined not to be left alone in that darkness, and setting his face into its ugliest scowl (his manner when he was 'against the world') stumped along behind her. They were shown into a very large drawing room that seemed to Adam, accustomed to the bright colour of Uldale, the most funereal he had ever seen. There were two large white marble pillars at one end, dark brown curtains across the windows, a huge portrait of a gentleman with a white stock and an immense watch-chain over the white marble mantelpiece, a long bookcase buried in glass, and a marble pedestal with a simpering bust of a lady's head on it between the windows.

All this he quickly observed, and then he noticed the people present. (He had ample time for this because no one spoke to him during the first five minutes.) Mr Newmark he knew already, his high stock, his large nose, his long legs. He seemed more dignified than was possible for a flesh-and-blood human being to be. Mrs Newmark he knew too. He liked her. He noticed that she had grown very stout. There was an elderly gentleman in a brown wig, an elderly lady in a vast hat, and a very pretty young lady in a most bewitching poke-bonnet of the lightest blue. So, standing near the door, rubbing one leg against the other, he watched the greetings.

'Judith! ... Judith!' Phyllis Newmark ran forward, kissed her again and again, dragged her to the fire. There was nothing false or affected about Phyllis.

'Oh; you are here! You have arrived! After all that *dreadful* journey! You must be frozen indeed. Frozen. Simply frozen. We have been expecting you these ages, have we not, Stephen?'

Mr Newmark, unbending in a slow solemn process from the crown of his head to the middle of his extremely thin waist, greeted them with the manner of one of England's Ambassadors receiving a deputation from a foreign tribe. He hoped that the journey had not been too positively inclement. Judith, her eyes twinkling, assured him that it had not.

'And this is Mr Pomeroy.'

The gentleman in the brown wig kissed her hand.

'And Mrs Pomeroy.'

'And this is Sylvia – Sylvia Herries, Garth's wife. You know Durward's son.'

The eyes of the young lady in the poke-bonnet – eyes alive with merriment and impudence – and the eyes of Judith – also, although so much older, alive with merriment – met, and in that instant the two of them, the girl of twenty and the woman of fifty-six, were friends for life. Judith seldom made a mistake. She had not made one now.

'Is not that perfect that you are here at last? Is it not wonderful, Mrs Pomeroy? All the way from Cumberland. Oh, I must embrace you once more. I am so *very* glad to see you. Stephen, is it not excellent that they have arrived safe and sound?'

'And there is my Adam,' said Judith, turning round. She knew that it must mean some real sacrifice of his principles that Stephen should receive a little bastard into the very heart of his sanctified family. It had been Phyllis' doing, of course. Nevertheless, it was good of him. She would not forget it. Adam came forward. Although there was always something clumsy in his movements, Judith had taught him good manners. He bowed and said: 'How are you, sir?' 'How are you, ma'am?' 'Very well, I thank you, ma'am.'

What the next step might have been no one could tell, for there came, suddenly, a portentous and dramatic knocking on the door – in fact, two knocks, most solemnly delivered, with a proper interval between.

'Come in!' cried Mr Newmark.

The door slowly opened and a procession entered. First, a tall, severe woman in black silk, then in order, it seemed, of ages, all the Newmark children. When Judith had last seen them at Westaways there had been but three; now there were seven if you included (as indeed you must) an infant who, in the arms of a stout, bonneted nurse, brought up the rear. The procession assembled itself at the door and waited.

'Good evening, Miss Trindle,' said Mr Newmark in his deep bell-like tones.

'Good evening, sir. Good evening, ma'am.'

'Come, children,' said Mr Newmark. 'You may bid us good-night.'

Then they all advanced – Horace, aged eleven, first, then Mary, aged ten, Phyllis nine, Katherine seven, Stephen five, Emily four and the infant Barnabas of almost no age at all.

The Ceremony was magnificent.

Horace was a thin, pale-faced boy, large spectacles covering wide-open, anxious eyes. He advanced timidly to his father, gave an absurd little bow. 'Goodnight, Papa.'

Mr Newmark bent down and in a dignified but kindly fashion kissed his cheek. Horace then went round and bowed to the others. 'Goodnight, sir.' 'I wish you a goodnight, ma'am.' He came to Judith, who caught him up and kissed him on both cheeks, disarranging his spectacles. He looked at her quickly, then carefully straightened his glasses. He paused before Adam and gave him a comical twinkling look, as much as to say: 'This is all very absurd. Don't think I'm taken in by it.' His mother hugged him in a quite human manner.

The others followed. Mary was stout and plain. Phyllis slender and pretty. Katherine stolid. Stephen nervous of his father. Emily yawning. Barnabas from the arms of the nurse gazed at his father as though he had never seen anything so droll in his life. They were all marshalled at the door and, together, standing in a row, made a simultaneous bow.

'And now,' said Phyllis (she was blushing a little), 'let us come upstairs and I will show you and Adam your apartments. Mrs Pomeroy, pray, forgive. We shall speedily return.'

Their rooms that night were of an icy chill, but English men and women were hardened – not for them the soft and effete comforts of more degenerate nations. Nevertheless, both Judith and Adam slept like the dead, bathed next morning in round tin baths brought in elaborately by a heavily breathing, muscle-straining maidservant. They were both in time for Family Prayers, held in the long, cold dining room. Beyond the windows as Mr Newmark read (as it seemed to Judith) almost the whole of the first Epistle to the Corinthians, a yellow fog wriggled and bridled up and down the Square.

But it was afterwards, over empty eggcups, vast cold hams and two terrific coffee-pots that Judith heard a most interesting discourse from Stephen Newmark. As Judith sat there listening she decided that she liked him better, far better, than she could ever have supposed that she would. He was at his best, serious, informed and exceedingly interesting. As he propelled his long, thin body up and down the breakfast-room, speaking in his deep, measured voice, he was like some prophet of old proclaiming woe to all the world. And yet he was not unduly sensational, did not, she was convinced, go further than the facts warranted. Being an intelligent, active-minded woman, she had, even in the confines of Cumberland, realized the critical time through which England was passing – and not only England but all the civilized world. The Revolution in France that very summer had been sufficient to point a packet of morals. The riot at Uldale ending in poor Reuben Sunwood's death had driven home all the local lessons. She had felt, for years past, what every other thinking man and woman had felt, that one cry, one lifted rifle, one more revelation of the filth, degradation, misery in which half England was living, might precipitate here a Revolution worse than any France had ever known. But Newmark dealt with facts, and facts only. Huskisson's death on September 15th, at the opening of the Liverpool and Manchester Railway, seemed to him a sort of omen. He returned to it again and again: such a fine man, one of the few men of intelligence in the country, such a foolish accident! These Railways – you were at the mercy of these horrible engines. One day it would be all engines. Human beings would be crushed by them. Will Herries had been there, had been standing quite close to Mr Huskisson at the time. He would tell her all about it.

'I don't suppose that I shall be seeing Will,' said Judith grimly.

'No?' said Stephen, surprised. 'You will find him now a man of very great importance.'

'I don't doubt,' said Judith.

After that the general lawlessness, the riots at Otmoor in Oxfordshire, followed by the calling out of the military at Oxford, Captain Swing and his rick-burning, the hanging of three men by the High Sheriff in Somersetshire, an execution witnessed by

fifteen thousand people, the stirring up of the people everywhere
by Cobbett and Carlyle, outrages in Kent and Wilts, in Bucks
and Surrey, followed always by summary executions.

Then to London – dirt and starvation and wretchedness cheek
by jowl with a luxury, extravagance and heartlessness that had
never been witnessed before in any living man's memory. Materialism, immorality of the grossest, an utter scoffing disregard
of religion.

'They say,' Stephen burst out, 'that all this is still the effect of
the wars. But, good God, this is 1830 – Waterloo was in '15!'

He passed on, growing ever more agitated beneath his cold and
pedantic exterior, to the King, the Court and the burning question of Reform. The King was an old fool. They had hoped, in
the summer when George, unregretted by anyone alive, had at
last seen fit to die, that this honest, worthy old man who succeeded him would save his country. But this honest, worthy old
man was nothing but a fool, nay, a maniac. Everyone had been
pleased at first by his easy, simple manners. He was crazy from
the first, wouldn't have his own servants in mourning, but had
ordered Mrs Fitzherbert to put hers into black, put on his plain
clothes and went wandering into the streets where he was followed all the way up St James's by a mob until a woman, outside
White's, pushed her way through and kissed him; had a party at
Buckingham House and dismissed the people by saying: 'Time
you were off. Come along to bed, my Queen.'

'Well, you know, Judith, it isn't amusing. No, indeed, it is not.
In such times to have such a crazy old monarch. A bad effect on
anybody.'

And for the rest where was a man we could trust? The Duke,
Peel, Lord John Brougham – all mad about this Reform one
way or another. What's the Cabinet to do? It spends all its time
sitting to concoct proclamations offering rewards for the discovery of rioters, rick-burners. That's not the way a country
ought to be governed.

Stephen's agitation was truly genuine. You could not listen to
him and not respect him. You could not listen to him and not
think of that little procession of the night before nor see that it
was in his mind that all of them from Horace to young Barnabas
might have their throats cut by the mob any of these days. And
meanwhile, the candles guttered within, outside the yellow fog
went sliding and whispering among the tall black houses. Judith,
in spite of herself, shivered. The room was so desperately cold.

'We have forgotten God!' cried Stephen, 'and God will punish us.'

But then he cheered up a little, and, pouring himself out a cup of what must have been very chilly coffee, lifted his voice a tone and began to talk about 'Our Family'.

It amused Judith greatly to discover that he considered himself completely a Herries and his children Herries too. They were the nephews and nieces of Lord Rockage and cousins to all the Herries tribe and that was enough for him. Whoever the New-marks were or had ever been they were now altogether behind the curtain. She saw that it was his idea that the Herries were going to save the country, if not in the foreground of affairs, why, then, very active in the background.

But Will Herries *was* in the foreground; it was expected that he would be a baronet any day. And there was Carey Rockage a peer, James Herries ('stupid pompous Ass *he* is') a baronet, Sylvia Herries, Garth's wife, 'one of the loveliest, wittiest girls in town,' Walter adding field to field in the North, Jennifer's boy (as he had heard) one of the handsomest young fellows in England, and she, Judith, herself—

'And I, Stephen?' asked Judith, laughing.

'Well, anyone with half an eye—'

In short, she became aware that she had, in a very few hours, made a strong impression upon Stephen. It was idle to pretend that she was not pleased. All her old love of power came surging up within her. She began already to realize that this visit to London was going to rouse in her another crisis, a crisis not unsimilar to the one that had driven her to abandon Watendlath. She had been too long up there buried in the country. Here were the Herries going up, up, up. Here was she, even though she *was* fifty-six (and she didn't feel a day more than thirty), with all these conquests ready to her hand. A sudden violent distaste attacked her – a distaste of Jennifer with her crazy imaginings, the stout bullying form of Walter, the littleness and gossip of Keswick, the long slow curve of the Uldale hills—

'We are becoming every day more powerful as a family,' proclaimed Stephen. 'Will is intimate with Peel. He is throwing himself into these new Railways. He grows richer every hour. Carey's boy, Roger, is only nineteen but shows excellent political ambitions. My own boy Horace—' He broke off as though this were too personal. Then added: 'These are the times for people like ourselves. The best class in England, the soundest, the most solid. Money, brains, beauty – and a proper fear of God.'

He broke off and finished his cup of coffee. Strange, she thought, considering him, how although he was not a Herries he was proclaiming himself so curiously a cousin to Will, Walter, the Venerable Archdeacon Rodney, Jennifer's father and the others. All the qualities that her own father had so sadly lacked, and Francis and Reuben and now, she feared, young John. And she herself – she was a combination of the two opposites, the only one in the family who was so, which was exactly why she could, if she liked, dominate the lot of them!

'Stephen!' she cried. 'I shall enjoy my time in London!'

From the moment of that breakfast-hour she never ceased to realize that this visit was a crisis for her and for her Adam as well. Adam himself had indeed the most glorious time. It was as though Stephen relaxed his pomposity and Phyllis her house-wifely burdens under the influence of their visitors. The children – Horace, Mary, Phyllis – had never known such a time. Either with their mother or with the grim Miss Trindle they discovered all the glories of the Town for Adam's benefit. They went to Miss Linwood's Exhibition of Needlework Pictures, and saw the Malediction of Cain and Jeptha's Vow, to Barford's Panorama where were wonderful displays of foreign scenes. One of the most marvellous of all things was the Panorama of London at the Colosseum in Regent's Park, where, raised in a lift (the wonder of the Town), you saw the Conservatories, Swiss Cottage, Alpine Scenery. In St Martin's Lane was the pavilion of the gigantic whale which was found dead off the coast of Belgium on November 3rd, 1827. This skeleton was ninety-five feet long and eighteen broad, and for another shilling you might sit 'in the belly of the whale'. This both Horace and Adam were permitted to do. But better still were the Zoological Gardens in Regent's Park (only opened in 1828 and therefore still a sensation) and (best, oh, far best of all for Adam and Horace) 'Weeks' Mechanical Exhibition' in Tichborne Street, where you might see an automaton tarantula spider made of steel which moved its claws and horns, an animated white mouse formed of oriental pearls that ran about a table 'feeding at pleasure', a caterpillar of enamelled gold and brilliants feeding on the foliage of a golden tree, and an old woman who, at a call, came forth from her cottage, walked about supported by crutches 'while the joints in her arms and legs are all in apparently natural motion'.

For Judith, too, her progress about London during that first

week was one thrilling adventure. All her earlier doings there
rushed up to her as though they had occurred but yesterday, a
strange haphazard married life with Georges, money one day,
none the next, the visit to the 'Elephant' when the coach had
overturned, the famous Ball, the awful moment in the Square
when Georges told her that he must flee for his life – that other
world, a London so different from this, so ancient, gone like a
dream with its colours, its fans and powder and elegance, and
Georges, dear, dear Georges, so feckless, so venturesome, so un-
reliable, beside her now at every step, his hand through her arm
in the old persuasive way, forcing her to agree to something weak
or hopeless or mad.

Georges, Georges ... And here she was an old lady of fifty-six
with a boy of fifteen who ought to have been Georges' son but
wasn't, in this Town that Mr Nash had covered with whitewash,
where poverty of the most hideous mingled with riches of the
most extravagant, where the very pavement seemed to threaten,
at any moment, an earthquake.

At the beginning of the second week she encountered Will.

She was sitting before a small, smoky, cold fire in the marble-
pillared drawing room, her feet on the fender, plucking up her
energy to go up to her icy bedroom and dress for dinner, when
the footman opened the door, murmured something and withdrew. She looked round to see Will standing there. The same old
Will, only grander. He carried his years well. He did not look
sixty nor anything like it. Sixty! And it was only yesterday that, a
boy on a horse outside Stone Ends, he had listened to a child,
Judith, declaring firmly that she would not return to Uldale, no,
not if she died for it! He did not look sixty and he did not look as
though he could conceivably be Walter's father. He was dressed
most handsomely in black. His coat was so waisted that it gave
him an almost feminine appearance, but he was not feminine.
Oh, dear me, no!

If he was startled at seeing Judith, he gave no sign of it. Her
pale face was yet paler. She looked at him with all the distant
haughtiness that she could command, but in her heart she wished
that she did not instantly once again feel like a child in pant-
alettes.

'Why, Judith!' he said. He came forward and gravely shook
her hand. 'I thought that I should see you. I heard that you were
in Town.' Then he added, smiling a little: 'It has been unkind of
you not to pay Christabel a visit.'

She did not answer that but said:

'Phyllis has not yet returned. Won't you sit down?'

He did – with great care and dignity.

'Well – how are you, Judith?'

'In excellent health, thank you, Will.'

'I am glad to hear it. And your boy?'

'Also in excellent health.'

'Good.'

There was a pause.

'And how are all at Uldale?'

'Admirable, thank you.'

'Good. I hear that John is a fine boy. You yourself, Judith, look younger than ever.'

She said nothing to that, but wished for the millionth time that God had made her taller. Then he went on – his voice was now exceedingly measured and assured as though he were always accustomed to speaking to people of the utmost importance:

'I am glad that Phyllis has not yet returned. It gives us a moment for speaking together, Judith. You are fifty-six' (how characteristic of him to remember her age!) 'I am sixty. Is it not rather childish of us to continue this feud?'

'I am continuing no feud,' she answered. 'You had better ask Walter about feuds.'

'Ah, Walter!' he sighed. 'Walter is very headstrong. I admit that that has been in part my fault – my fault and his mother's. But he would have his own way from earliest childhood. And are you not imagining things, my dear Judith? You also, if I may say so, have always had plenty of character.'

'Imagining!' she broke out. 'Imagining!' Then, controlling herself, she went on: 'You know, perhaps, that he is building on a hill above Uldale simply that he may overlook us and interfere with us in every possible way.'

'He told me that he was to build,' Will said quietly. 'I advised him against it.'

'He murdered Francis,' she said, 'and he is frightening Jennifer into her grave.' She saw then that she touched him. At the mention of Francis a faint flush coloured his sallow cheeks.

'Francis,' he said at last. 'Poor Francis! He was his own enemy.'

'He need not have been,' she answered hotly. 'It was because of Walter's spies that Francis learnt of Jennifer's infidelity.'

But he was not to be stirred.

'Is not this all rather old history, Judith, my dear? There are two strains in our family — let us face it — and they are never at peace together. I was never at one with Francis myself. We sought different things out of the world. What he sought for was perhaps harder to obtain than what I sought for. He never found it, and in his disappointment— No, no, my dear. You cannot lay all that upon Walter. You know the world too well. You are altogether too wise.'

She considered that. There was something in what he said. Then she began in another more friendly, more impetuous tone.

'Will — cannot you persuade Walter to cease this building? Cannot you persuade him to leave Jennifer and her children in quiet? Then we will be friends. I shall be only too happy.'

He looked at her with a strange, almost human, smile.

'Persuade Walter? My dear, he has gone far beyond *my* persuading. I have no influence over him whatever. He would even rather that his mother and I did not come to Westaways.' He waited a moment and then continued: 'You know, Judith, I have all my life been pursuing money — money and power. I have got both. I do not regret it. But in that pursuit one loses other things. I have lost human relationships. I have no time for them. As I say, I do not regret it. But it is so.'

She felt herself being drawn closer to him than she had ever been before.

He went on: 'Once, years ago, when we were children — do you remember? — we were watching fireworks on the Lake, you, Francis, Reuben Sunwood and I. We all said what we would do with our lives. I have fulfilled almost exactly those early ambitions. I would not, however, say that I am a happy man. But who is happy? I have my moments. That is, I suppose, as much as one may ask.'

She heard the opening of the outer door and then the comfortable friendly tone of Phyllis's voice, so hurriedly she said:

'Will, I have no unfriendliness to yourself or Christabel — none whatever — but I will fight like a tiger to keep Jennifer and her children safe. I may be an aged tiger and not a very large one, but I can still be fierce. I am Walter's enemy so long as he is Jennifer's and John's and Dorothy's, so now you know.'

Will looked at her gravely and opened his mouth as though he would speak, but Phyllis' entry in a bustle of welcome prevented him. There was some chatter, and Will got up to depart. It was only then that he said to them with great solemnity:

'My reason for calling – I should have told you before – I thought that you would like to know. His Majesty has graciously offered me a Baronetcy which I shall accept.'

Yes, indeed, the Herries were going up, and Judith shared now in all the drama of family life to the full. It took her only a fortnight to be considered the most impressive figure among them all.

The Family Letters of this time are filled with references to her:

> Madame Paris has been the Family Sensation this week. Your father is laid up with the gout but he *permitted* me (you know what he is) to dine at Lady Rosbey's. Our cousin, Judith (*is* she a cousin?) arrived with the Newmarks and in *five minutes* had the whole room laughing. She must be *any age* and wears the most outrageous colours. Nevertheless, she was sprightly as a kitten and without losing her dignity an instant. She was as up in everything as though she'd never moved out of Belgravia and kept us all vastly amused with her Paris adventures in '15 where it appears that she . . .

And another:

> Judith Paris is the rage. I must confess that I find her charming for she is kindly as well as intelligent, enjoys everything as though she were born yesterday (she's fifty if a day!), and is no *snob* like dear William and others of our relations. She has with her an illegitimate boy (they say he is Warren Forster's son. You remember Warren – a little *peaked* man with a nervous habit of snapping his fingers) and takes him about with a great deal of pride. It is a thousand pities that she should be buried in the North for we sadly need her *esprit* and intelligence . . .

And a third:

> We dined last night at the Bulwers in Hertford Street. That amusing young man, whom you enjoyed so greatly at Barnet last year, was there, Mr Disraeli. Rosina Bulwer was a sight! Plastered with jewels and painted to the eyes, while Bulwer himself glittered all over! There were plenty of the Family as you may suppose and of all people the solemn Newmark and his fat dowdy Phyllis. However, the excuse for their coming was our cousin Judith from Cumberland. I had heard of her

often enough and was all eagerness to behold her. Well she is a
little short pale-faced thing with grey hair and had a dress of
brocaded pink gauze (of all things for a woman over fifty!).
She carried an ivory cane and should have been altogether
absurd. But she was not! Disraeli was enchanted with her and
Rosina talked to her an immense deal and even Miss Landon
admitted her 'ton'. I can tell you how she does it. By being
perfectly natural, having plenty of humour and common
sense. I never saw anyone enjoy herself so completely . . .

Indeed she did. She went everywhere, did everything, and
knew, for the moment, no weariness. Sylvia Herries was her principal companion. That girl, with her eagerness, sense of adventure and gaiety that had at its heart some undefined melancholy,
was designed for her affections. Then suddenly Judith woke.
That 'unhappiness' was everywhere, hidden by a superficial
eagerness that had no stability.

She saw that she was in a society where nothing was real, where
no one believed in anything at all, where everyone feared what
the morrow would bring. The 'Silver Fork' novels of fashionable
life, just then beginning to be so popular, were symptomatic of
the falsehood and sham, while cruel and malicious sheets like the
Age and the *John Bull* of Theodore Hook showed where the
rottenness was hidden.

Prolonged war had killed sincerity, every kind of faith, social
behaviour. The world of London that she, for a moment, invaded was dominated by a new aristocracy of wealth, an aristocracy without tradition, without breeding, an aristocracy that
in its aggressive uneasiness suffered itself to be blackmailed by the
vilest panders and the most worthless adventurers. Most of the
great houses in London were occupied by 'new men' who hurried
to learn manners that could never truly be theirs and sought
with drink, gambling, orgies and ostentation, to give a semblance
of splendour and security. The roads to prominence lay through
scandal, back-biting and jealousy. Sport, jewels, wild expenditure
covered meanness and vice. All was fake; for a woman to be
virtuous proclaimed her dowdy. Men lived by their wits and
climbed relentlessly over the backs of their dearest friends.

Such was the fashionable world of which Judith had a
glimpse. But it was in just such a world that the opportunities of
such a family as the Herries – sober, careful, traditional – lay.

The Herries in London were separated into three parts – the

business Herries, Will at their head, James the baronet following rather clumsily, and Amery Herries, Sylvia's brother-in-law, very able and sharp, a possible successor when Will was in his dotage. There were secondly the religious Herries, headed by Stephen Newmark, who, as Judith soon perceived, when he was not sensible, was *very* tiresome indeed. Stephen had his pet clergyman – Mr Aubrey Grant of St Anne's, Pimlico – a gentleman very often at Stephen's table, a stout effeminate, purring gentleman, adored by the ladies and detested by Judith. There was also in the Newmark household the Methodist tradition of the Rockage family in which Phyllis had been brought up. Maria Rockage was still alive, a kindly rheumatic old Dowager in the place in Wiltshire. She was for ever sending the Newmark family pamphlets – 'The Miner's Lament', 'The Royal Road to Hell', 'The Shopman's Vision' – interspersed with delightful, gay and very human epistles. She lamented grievously that she could not come up to London to see Judith, who had once lived with her for nearly ten years and whom she adored. Many of Mr Aubrey Grant's congregation came to Cadogan Place – old Mr and Mrs Pomeroy were very prominent – and quite awful Judith found them all. The scent on Mr Grant's handkerchief alone was enough to send her out of the room when he was there.

The third division was the social one. Into this, at times, the other two divisions penetrated, but Will and Christabel, Newmark and Phyllis, various Newmark cousins, did not truly belong.

Sylvia Herries, young though she was, was mistress here. She knew the London social, literary, Bohemian world completely. She laughingly declared that all the adventurers in London came to her tiny house in Brook Street. Indeed she did not care who came. She kept open house. Neither she nor Garth – now a very elegant, charming young man – seemed to have much money. They were for ever in desperate straits. Will – who was in these days more generous than of old – must have helped them again and again. They reminded Judith constantly of herself and Georges in those old, mad, adventurous days. That was perhaps why she came to care for them more than any other of the Herries relations, and why she made her alliance with them. Sylvia was her own kind – audacious, reckless, pleasure-loving, but also serious, practical and wise about other people.

It soon became obvious that Stephen disliked her constant

visits to the little house in Brook Street, a little house that was all light colours, jingling pianos, poodle dogs and noise. There were authors like the Bulwers, Letitia Landon, Theodore Hook, young Ainsworth, of whom he could not possibly approve. There were dancers, opera singers, racing men and ladies of extremely doubtful reputation. Judith had, alas, no more of those fine serious conversations with which on the first morning she had been honoured. It seemed to him really lamentable that a woman of her years should care for such a world. He had been right, as he constantly told Phyllis in the sacredness of their huge four-poster, in wondering whether anyone so brazen about her bastard child was a suitable guest for them, and poor Phyllis, who loved Judith with all her heart, tried to keep the peace. But what Phyllis really did not understand was that Judith should be so deeply horrified at the present state of the London world and yet enjoy the parties in Brook Street so greatly. She seemed like two different women in one.

Then the climax arrived. On an afternoon of the third week of Judith's stay, Sylvia Herries was alone with Judith in the New-mark drawing-room. Sylvia was looking most bewitching with her ringlets, rose-coloured tulle, a waist so small as to be almost invisible, and a printed satin scarf. She danced about the room like a fairy, she bowed with mock ceremony to the pedestal and the lady's head thereon, she imitated Stephen, whom she found entirely ridiculous. Judith also was seized with a devil. She valsed with Sylvia round and round the room. The 'valse' was still new enough to be divine. They danced ever more madly. They danced into a small table that held a large preposterous vase of the brightest green. It tumbled with a crash to the ground, and, of course, at that precise moment Stephen entered with old Mr Pomeroy.

There was nothing to be said, nothing to be done. There the vase was in a thousand pieces. There were the two ladies – one of them old enough to be the other's mother – hot, dishevelled, and Judith had, a moment before, lost one of her shoes. Stephen gave one of his grim sacrificial smiles, Sylvia departed with a private *moue* of amusement for Judith's benefit (seen, however, by Stephen). Judith did her best to become, quickly again, an elderly dignified lady.

'Oh, it is of no importance, no importance at all,' said Stephen, bending stiffly to pick up some pieces. 'An old family heirloom – but still – no matter, no matter.'

But he never forgave Judith that broken vase. An ivory fan, a green vase: these are the things of which family histories are made. It was quite clear – Stephen now made it plainly apparent – that it was time that the visit of Judith and Adam came to an end.

'Come and stay with us, darling,' said Sylvia. 'For as long as you please.'

'No,' said Judith. 'Cumberland is my proper place.'

And it *was*. She would not, she knew, be happy in the little house in Brook Street. *That* was not her home, any more than was Stephen's. Her holiday (and oh! how she had enjoyed it!) was at an end.

So she looked round her to collect herself and her things, and found Adam. Not that she at all had forgotten him. It had been wonderful to see him against this new background and with new people. She found that he was enterprising, reserved and extraordinarily generous. She had known all these things about him since the beginning of time, but they wore a fresh dress in this fresh world. His generosity was surely astonishing, for he had very little money unless his London relations gave him some. In any case he was always buying things for the little Newmarks, for his mother, for Phyllis. To Sylvia, whom he worshipped, he gave nothing. All the little Newmarks loved him, even the spectacled Horace, who was not lavish with his affections. Mary and her sister Phyllis would be demonstrative, but he shrank from their demonstrations with horror. He allowed no one any physical approach. He produced a toy, a doll, a horse, a rattle for the baby, flowers or whatever, and he said 'Here!' or 'That's for you, ma'am'. He looked at you sternly while he presented it, forbidding you to thank him. Then he escaped. He escaped very often, went off on his own affairs. He was, in fact, very happy during this visit.

The visit came to a close, both for Judith and Adam, with an adventure that it was not likely that they would forget. It was the recurrent adventure of Judith's life: once, in London, a boy hanging; twice, in Paris, an elephant escaping; and now, the third time.

On the evening of Monday the eighth of November, Amery Herries took Judith, Adam and his sister-in-law Sylvia to the Adelphi Theatre to witness a performance of *The Heart of London*, or *A Sharper's Progress*, by William Thomas Moncrieff. This was a glorious play, and although not intended for the young did Adam no kind of harm.

The play over, they stepped from one melodrama into another.

The Strand, lit with the flares of burning stakes carried head-high, and in the distance towards Covent Garden by an over-turned cart that had been set alight, showed a wild fantasy of faces, a mob that now was stagnant like a dead pond and then broken as though by a whipping wind, all this driven by a roar that had nothing human in it save an occasional woman's scream.

The citizens of London, excited by Mr Hunt at a meeting at the Rotunda in Blackfriars Road, were making their way to the West End that they might assist the cause of Reform. As soon as the shouts were heard the doors of the Adelphi were closed, but Amery's party had slipped out five minutes earlier, to secure a hackney coach. The doors were closed behind them; before they could consider their position they were swung forward into the street. Judith, Adam's arm through hers, saw neither Amery nor Sylvia again that night.

It was as though Judith and Adam fell into a jungle of under-growth. Above them bodies towered and whether they wished it or no they were carried forward to the cries of 'Down with the Police!' 'Reform!' 'No Peel!' 'No Wellington!'

Down there in the undergrowth they conversed:

'Never mind, Mother: I'm here,' said Adam.

'Now, don't you let go!' Judith said crossly. This was imper-tinence, to treat her and her son in this fashion. A light swung to the sky, and stars escaping, a golden net scattered among the chimney-pots. Then the sky was darkened, and a large face at-tached to a stout body in moleskins was rosy in the glare of a burning stake stinking of tar.

'No Wellington! Down with Wellington!' roared the mole-skins most good-naturedly. He stank of gin, and his hand, roughened with honest toil, stroked Judith's cheek.

At that touch fear, that she had known so seldom in her life, caught her and pressed against her. A bear tortured, a boy hanged, Adam's father clinging to her while the horses' hoofs pranced in the air, these once again encompassed her.

'Reform! Reform!' shrieked a woman, her hair about her face and a basket on her arm. Judith looked at Adam and saw that he was quite unafraid and greatly enjoying everything.

'Adam, in a moment there should be a turning to the river. Watch for it!'

But the impetuous movement ceased. Staring around her she saw that their progress had been far more rapid than she had supposed, for they were in Downing Street and had halted in front of Lord Bathurst's residence. She knew the house well, for Garth Herries had taken her to a reception there. By squirming her body through a funny jumble of legs, chests, arms and hands she found a corner for Adam and herself against some railings, and was able to observe from there how a gentleman, his face crimson with rage, came out on to the balcony. He was armed with a brace of pistols and, shouting in a voice thick with anger, told them that if they committed any illegal act he would fire. Groans, yells, shouts of 'Go it! Go it!' answered him, whereupon another gentleman arrived on the balcony and took the pistols from him. Then everyone cheered and seemed suddenly radiant with good spirits.

At that same moment Judith perceived that Adam was gone. She became at once a frenzied woman. Any self-control that she had ever learnt, any caution or reserve, was lost. She screamed like a madwoman, 'Adam! Adam!', tried to move and found that she could not, beat on some stout manly chest: 'Let me go! Let me go! Let me through! Can't you see? My boy ... Adam! Adam!'

But it happened that a strong body of the new police had just arrived from Scotland Yard that they might form themselves into a line at the end of King Street to prevent the mob from proceeding to the House of Commons. At once a great shout went up: 'The Peelers!' 'The Peelers!' 'Down with the Peelers!'. As though the ground were agitated with earthquake, the crowd rocked forward and back, seeming to rise in places like a bulging floor about to crack. A line of wavering flame ran against the walls of the houses where men with lighted wood were ranging themselves in a line of defence. But Judith saw and heard nothing. Adam was lost, Adam might be crushed underfoot, she would never see Adam again; and at that frantic thought all the world that had seemed so important, social, political, religious – yes, and all the Herries, all Uldale, all her individual life and desires, blew like scraps of burnt paper into the air. Her shawl was torn from her, her wide-puffed sleeves rent. She beat on some face with her hands, she tore some cheek with her nails. 'Let me go! Let me go! Can't you see? My boy's gone!'

But no one saw and no one cared. A general fight was toward. Inspector Lincoln of the E Division had arrived with seventy men. The tri-coloured flag that had 'Reform' painted on it – the banner of the riot – was captured by the Peelers. There was a rush to recapture it. A man, bare-breasted, his shirt hanging in ribbons from his back, black-haired, brawny, his chest tattooed with a ship in violet and green, hung above the mob like a sign. He had in his hand a hatchet. Judith, seeing him with a strange and memorable distinctness, beheld him, as it seemed to her, trample on her boy. The crowd rose and fell; she was swept off her feet and would, it may be, have ended all her adventures there and then for ever had not some man caught her to him so that she was soaked, as it were, in his sweat and ale and dripping clothes, her head against his beard, his hand upon her breast. A fine thing for an old lady of fifty-six! But it saved her. Crushed, with her face in his rough hair, seeing nothing, frantic for Adam, she heard around her the strange sough and sigh of a mob suddenly terrified, resolved to run, the wind beating from under their feet, as though it would raise them to the sky. 'Reform!' 'Reform!' 'Reform!' 'The Peelers!' 'The Peelers!'

And then sudden quiet, a child crying, a whistle sharply blown, and she herself, her cheek bleeding, was half sitting, half crumpled on the pavement. But she was up in a moment. She could run now; there was nothing to stop her. As though God had crooked His little finger, there was no one there. Some man leant against the railings moaning and nursing his head, a beaver hat lay in the roadway, a burning faggot sent up a twist of smoke, and the silence was like a miracle. A yard away there was Adam, crying 'They're on the run! They're on the run! Mother, look, look!'

He had never been more than a yard away, then. She was furious with him and, her hair about her face, did what she had never done before – slapped his face.

'You careless boy! You careless boy!'

But he was enchanted. It was the best adventure of his life so far. His mouth was bleeding, his coat and trousers torn, but he laughed and laughed as though he'd never have done.

Then she hugged and kissed him.

'I thought you were killed,' she said. She felt an old, old woman, an ache in every bone and her head like a turnip. Very characteristically, she recovered her dignity.

'Now we'll find a hackney coach,' she said.

The watchman was calling up from the street below two o'clock of the morning before Adam came in to wish her goodnight. She was sitting up, a very old lady indeed she felt, propped up with pillows and telling her different aches to mind their business and behave. There was a bruise on her forehead, one knee was lamentably swollen, but there was no real harm done ... only she was very old of a sudden. Nine hundred and ninety.

'Come here and kiss me,' she said.

Adam was in his nightdress, and, with a purple lump the size of a lemon over one eye, looked no beauty.

He laughed and sat on the bed, her arm around him. She made him put on her furred dressing-gown and furred slippers, for the room was viciously cold. There was a warming-pan inside the bed now, and she made him slide his feet inside against hers.

So he slipped into the circle of her arm, lay there with his black hair in his eyes, too eagerly excited to sleep yet. The panic of her fear that she had lost him was still with her. She had never loved him with such passionate intensity and she had never felt so old. Her brain formed odd confused pictures for her, nothing tangible, nothing consecutive. In the big stone fireplace a baby fire leapt as though it were trying its first steps in life so that it might really be a fine grown-up fire one day. An impenetrably black picture of a forest, a lonely tower, and some horsemen swayed a little on its cord, blown by all the draughts of heaven, some of whom whistled through the wallpaper like lonely spirits trying to keep their courage up. Three candles guttered on the table beside the four-poster with the green hangings; a mirror topped with heavy gilt feathers reflected the light. And under and above all this was the dreadful cold, a cold worse than Arctic, for it was damp. Soon Adam was lying inside the bed folded in his mother's arms as he had not been since he was a tiny boy at Watendlath.

Without words they reached a loving intimate security that daylight and Adam's dislike of manifestation had hindered at Uldale. It had always been there, but for long now she had not had his heart beating, as it were, inside her very body.

Idly she watched the pictures come and go: Stephen saying 'And now let us pray'; Sylvia Herries imitating some ballet-dancer at the Opera; young Mr Harrison Ainsworth (so handsome but wearing too many rings and his curls too heavy with Macassar oil) telling her about his recent Italian journey, and how he had found a rouge-pot at Pompeii; gossip about Ball Hughes and the Bulwers and Lady Blessington and Holland

House – and then, over all this nonsense, the figure of the man with the ship of violet on his chest, raising his hatchet . . .

She held Adam closely to her, kissed him, stroked his forehead. He did not resist nor move away as he would normally have done, but sleepily murmured: 'Down with the Peelers!' 'Down with Wellington!' 'Down with the Peelers!'

'Hush, dear. Don't think of the horrid thing. I wonder how Amery and Sylvia are! Dear me! how incredibly selfish! I have never thought of them until this instant!'

Then the dancing pictures vanished. She saw something else and with extraordinary clearness. She raised herself on her pillows. Adam tickled her foot with his.

'Adam, wake up! There is something that I must say!'

He took her hand in his.

'Adam – you will shortly be a grown man and I shall be an old woman. I had not thought of it until this moment. How dreadful to be old! And I shall not be a nice old woman. I shall want my way. I made the mistake of my whole life when I stayed at Uldale. We should have gone to Watendlath. I have become Herries and made you Herries and shall wish you to be more and more Herries. Adam, promise me that, however I wish it, you will keep your independence. You are not to be Herries. You are illegitimate anyway, and your father was so little Herries as not to matter. I shall want to keep you later. You will be all I shall have. But you are not to permit me. Do you hear? However much I love you . . . Dear me, dear me, what a nasty old woman I am going to be!'

Then, as there was no response, she said again:

'You are not to allow me to swallow you, do you understand? Fight me, if need be. In another ten years I shall be completely Herries, from head to toe. How horrible! Adam, do you hear me.'

'What, Mama?'

'You are to keep your independence. I love you too much for it to be good for either of us.'

'And when the Peelers were coming . . .' he murmured.

The vision passed. She saw nothing, but gathered him closer into her arms, and he slept, holding her hand tightly in his, while she gazed out into the room and watched the little fire surrender its life, and the candles blow unsteadily in the wind.

WESTAWAYS: FATHER AND SON

IT was not true to say that Walter Herries was without imagination. He could see very vividly things that were not actually in front of him, only they must, those things, if they were
going to act on him powerfully, *spring* from facts. Then, his
imagination once started, he could be obsessed, obsessed by his
own grandeur, by his sense of power, by the thought that he was
a Herries, and, above all, by the knowledge that he was Uhland's
father.

At this very time that Judith was in London breaking vases,
meeting Mr Disraeli, and scratching the cheeks of rioters, Walter
was taking his son Uhland day after day up the hill to Ireby to
watch the Fortress growing. Uhland was now fifteen years of age,
and the Fortress was half its way to heaven.

It must be remembered that it was not yet called the Fortress –
that name came to it later – but already it was beginning to be
grim of aspect. Mr Carstairs, bothered by rheumatism and this
cursed Northern climate, was not in the best of tempers. And he
was beginning to dislike Walter Herries extremely. He had never
been bullied before, being a man of some personality and temper.
Walter Herries often spoke to him as he would to his groom, and
Carstairs would have given the job up long ago were it not that he
was aware that the Herries were now important people in
London and a useful connexion, that Walter threw money about,
and (this the most important with Carstairs, who was, finally, a
man of feeling) that Walter could show, at times, an extraordinary and even pathetic charm.

He wanted the place to look like a castle. It was to have battlements and towers, towers from whose summit a flag could fly.
That was the moment of Romanticism, of the Waverley Novels,
of *Weltschmerz*, of *Pelham* and (a little late) *Childe Harold* and
Werther. There was no *Weltschmerz* in Walter, but he would
have his battlements and a flag flying. So the place was going up,
grim and grey and forbidding. Its half-grown walls could already
be seen from all the country round.

Nearly every day Walter and Uhland rode up there, Walter on
a big white horse, Uhland on a small black pony. As you watched
them together (as Carstairs watched them) you might sometimes

think their positions reversed, that Uhland was the father and
Walter the son. There *was*, Carstairs decided again and again,
something most truly pathetic in their relationship, for Walter
dearly loved his son. It was the one true, selfless, generous instinct in him. Selfless? That perhaps not, for an intense family
pride was at the root of it. But pride? Pride in that queer, misshapen, white-faced ancient child, whose sharp countenance was
always grave, whose voice was so cold and detached, whose chilly
eyes watched you so solemnly, with so deep and questioning a
gaze. Only once had Carstairs seen the boy moved by some
human emotion, and that was when, by a chance, having met
young Adam in Keswick and had a chat with him, he had said
something about him to Walter. Young Uhland had been listening; colour had crept into his cheeks, light into his eye. Walter
had made a scornful gesture, and it seemed that Uhland was
going to say something in protest. He checked himself.

It was, thought Carstairs, an interesting thing to see that stout,
red-faced man with his bright waistcoats, his pins and his rings,
his confidence and his pride, surrender to that colourless child in
his black suit, so silent, so neat and so watchful. Yes, watchful!
That was what Uhland was, watchful and waiting. Meanwhile
his sister Elizabeth, the prettiest child, Carstairs thought, that he
had ever seen, never shared her father's company. It was as
though he had no daughter.

That was a month of chills and mists, of sudden winds and
gleaming suns. One afternoon when the sun ran in and out of the
clouds like a jester, Walter and Uhland rode up to Ireby.

'Father,' said Uhland, 'why are you building this house?'

Why was he building this house? What a question! Nevertheless, this was the first occasion on which Uhland had shown
any interest in the affair. Day after day they had ridden up there,
and Walter, in a flood of talk, had shown his son how this would
be there, and that here, that the ballroom would be so long, and
the dining-room catch the sun at such a time, that he should
have a room to himself, in one of the towers if he liked, so that he
could look over the whole country, over to Keswick, over to
Scotland . . .

And Uhland had watched him gravely and plucked at his
upper lip in a way that he had, but said no word.

'Why am I building this house?' Walter explained. 'For you,
my son, and for the glory of the family, so that when you marry,
my son . . .'

'I shall never marry,' said Uhland.

'Ah, you think that now, Uhland, but the time will come when you will see a lady so beautiful . . .'

But Uhland shook his head.

'I don't care about women,' he said.

But, of course, he must marry. Did he not wish to carry on the family?

He looked at his father sardonically. There were plenty of people to do that – all the lot at Uldale, all his relations in London.

Walter felt a chill at his heart. Of course, Uhland must have sons, and they must have sons, and sons and sons!

'Look, Father – there is Mrs Herries!'

She was there again then, standing on the edge of the rough bare field, her tall black figure framed by the rough bare hills. A sensation of disgust caught him. He had not seen her for several weeks and thought that she had at last wearied of this crazy, imbecile watching. For crazy and imbecile she was! At first he had been rather pleased at the sight of her. He was having his revenge, although a revenge for what he by now would have found it rather difficult to say. Jennifer and her children had shrunk to rather poor game, although he hated the boy for his health and good looks, while his own son . . .

'Why does she come here, Father, day after day?' Uhland asked.

'She's mad,' Walter answered brusquely.

'But how mad? I thought mad people screamed and broke things.'

'She shall scream well enough before I have finished with her.' He felt vindictive today and would like to hurt someone. And yet he was not by nature cruel. If things only went well with him he could be as jolly and generous as anyone. But what was all this, what his treasures in Westaways, his position in the County, this new place of his, if Uhland were not to take pleasure in them? His big body throbbed sometimes with a savage desire to take his boy and squeeze him into some sort of life of response and activity. Here was he doing so much, striving so hard, and for what kind of return? He turned back on his horse and, seeing that dark figure against the skyline, thought for a moment of what it would be to have, indeed, John Herries for a son. He hated that young Herries. Yes, he would drive them all to perdition before he'd done.

He drew his horse closer to Uhland's pony and, speaking very gently, he asked him:

'Will you not care, Uhland, to have a son to succeed to all this when you are gone?'

'No, Father. Why should I?'

Walter sighed. 'If you cannot see that, I cannot make you.'

Uhland, after a pause, said quietly:

'I should be glad to have a brother like Adam Paris.'

'Adam Paris?' Walter, in his impatience, made his horse rear. 'That boy! Why do you think of him so much? He cares nothing for you.'

'I like him – just as I hate John Herries.' He looked about him, then asked: 'Father, when you have built this, will John Herries hate it?'

'Yes, my boy, he will.'

'Ah – then I am glad you are building it, Father.'

'Why do you hate young Herries so much? You scarcely see him.'

Uhland considered it.

'Why do people hate one another, Father?'

'Because of something they have done, some injury or harm they have done.'

'Well – that's the reason then.'

'But young Herries has never harmed you.'

'No. But I will harm *him*.'

An incomprehensible boy! But Walter had never been clever at analysing other people and, in any case, his clear view of his son would be fogged by his blinding absorbing love for him. He did not know it, but he would never have cared for a strong healthy son as he loved this weakling.

They arrived at the place. A great bustle was toward, men moving with barrows and carts, climbing ladders, shouting, hammering, cutting stone, filing and sawing. The house, half raised, lifted blind eyes to the sky. It was built of Cumberland stone, beautiful in its dim blues and greens and greys with here a soft blush of rose, there a strand of gold, but the effect of the whole was nevertheless grim and cold. It promised to be strong; nothing, it seemed, would conquer it.

Walter climbed over into the interior and Uhland stood and watched him. Within, on that misty day, everything was in a half-light. The men, accustomed to his presence, went about their work. Through a gap where a window would be, Walter

could see the sharp fall of the hill. There, in the cup of the
ground, would be Uldale. He savoured in his nostrils, for a
moment, the especial blend of rough soil, sharpened with the
grey-stone of some solitary farm blending with the bare outline
of the rising hills beyond, cold and bleak but strong and deeply
true – that meeting of strength and austerity and richness that is
Cumberland's gift to those who love her. He loved her as an
animal loves its home. But today he was restless and dissatisfied.
He climbed his way out again, and after a word or two to the
foreman, rode down the hill. He went a little ahead and Uhland,
watching, as he always did, for everything, saw something very
strange. His father had turned the corner by the little wood into
the road that ran from Uldale to Bassenthwaite. Out of the wood
came two people: Walter was already gathered into the dusk, but
they saw Uhland, and he saw them before they turned back into
the wood again.

They were his sister Elizabeth and John Herries.

He rode on after his father.

Uhland's room at Westaways was as bare as a monastic cell. The
walls held no pictures; the only furniture was a bed, two chairs, a
bookcase, a washstand and a cupboard.

There was, however, more in this room than this stiff furniture. There were the animals.

Uhland, since a very small child, had shown a strong interest
in any animal wounded, hurt or deformed. A very pretty little
picture might be elaborated of a pale-faced, limping little boy
sorry for hurt animals because he was himself hurt. But you
could not think of sentiment in connexion with Uhland – it froze
at his touch.

Nevertheless, in this lonely world through which we pass, each
of us shadowed from the other, who knows or can truly discern
the instincts of the human mind? It was enough, in the case of
Uhland, that in a cold, undemonstrative fashion he cared for any
damaged animal that came his way. The animals, on their side,
appeared to recognize him as one of themselves. They never
showed him that especial attention given by animals to
human beings who are kind to them; sometimes, we may suspect,
with a sense of conventional duty. They showed Uhland just as
much feeling as they would to another animal. They did not
trust him any more than they would trust one another. Yes, he
was one of themselves.

At this particular time, there was in his bedroom a bright parrot with pink feathers, in a gilt cage. His claw was bandaged. Uhland had bought him of a sailor in Keswick. There was a dog, mostly spaniel, in a basket. It wore, with an air of comic but patient protest, a large yellow silk handkerchief over one eye. Uhland had found it dying in a ditch near Threlkeld, minus an eye, after suffering torture at the hands of some farm-children. In another basket was a wild cat, minus a leg, that had been caught in a trap on Cat Bells. This animal, black, with fierce burning eyes, spent most of its time gathered on its haunches and spitting, but it allowed Uhland to do what he wished with it.

In vain had Walter protested that it was unwholesome to keep animals in the room where you slept. Uhland briefly stated that he would see to it that they were clean, that he would trust no one but himself to look after them. Walter submitted. If they made the boy happy there they must remain. And Uhland saw to it that they *were* clean. The room was spotless, with an odd, dried, mummified scent of the cloistered cell about it. Its only sign of life was the sudden chattering of the parrot, who would gibber unintelligibly to himself and rattle the bars of his gilt cage.

Today, coming in from his ride, Uhland squatted down on the floor and examined the dog's eye. Very skilfully, and with fingers that were strangely delicate, he undid the yellow silk handkerchief, washed the angry red eye-socket, put some ointment on a long tear above the right temple. The dog, a black spaniel with a touch of sheepdog, waited calmly while this was done. When it was over he lay down in his basket and licked his paws. Uhland gave him some water, then squatted down beside him, staring in front of him. There was a lamp on the chest of drawers near him that gave an ivory patina to his pale cheek. The black cat crouched in his basket and watched him with fiery eyes.

When he thought, he thought not like a little boy but like a man for whom all illusions are over. He had never had any illusions. He saw the things in front of him with cold clarity. He was only a small boy, but he knew an intensity of controlled feeling that was quite mature. He knew shame because he was not as other boys, haughty pride because he was the son of his father. His father was rich, powerful, had servants, horses, lands. He would have respected and cared for his father more deeply had his father cared for him less and showed less that he cared. The only two human beings who entered at all at this time into his emotions were Adam and John Herries. He loved the one and hated the other. He hated John Herries because he had been brought up from a baby to do so, because John was handsome and strong, but chiefly because he was gentle and submissive. Anyone who was submissive roused in him, child though he was, something wild and savage. To be submissive when you were strong enough to be otherwise, to bend your neck like a woman when you were hearty enough to be a proper man! It was as though someone preferred to be lame when he need not! He caught a sense perhaps also of John's dislike and fear of himself. He *knew* that John Herries was afraid of him, child though he was, and the contempt he felt for fear was closely allied to hatred.

For these same reasons he had always loved and admired Adam Paris. That stout, rough, untidy brown body with its independence, freedom, absence of all sentiment, caught and held for ever his admiration. Adam Paris did not care whether he, Uhland Herries, lived or died, and so Uhland loved him.

As he squatted there on the floor his thoughts were dark. He had guessed for a long while that his sister Elizabeth had some secret. They had nothing at all in common, he and his sister. She was afraid of him, and he thought her pretty but uninteresting. But now – she and John Herries! Uhland knew as yet nothing about the love of men and women, although the gossip of stable-boys and farm-hands had long ago told him all that there was to learn about the physical facts of conception and generation. The thing did not interest him. In any case Elizabeth was only a child as he himself was. But that John Herries should be on any kind of terms with a member of his family, roused, slowly, steadily, all his coldest anger. He looked like a little old brooding man as he sat there on the hard floor in the light of the lamp.

On the very next afternoon, as it happened, Uhland encountered John Herries.

Riding out on his pony (he was always happy when riding because his deformity was not apparent) he met John Herries walking alone on the road beyond Portinscale. John was strolling along, thinking deeply, his hands behind his back. As he walked his lips moved. He was very handsome in the dark-blue coat, fawn pantaloons, a brown beaver hat. Uhland pulled up the pony.

'Excuse me, sir,' he said in his queer grave child's voice.

John looked up and at once was seized with the chill of apprehension and discomfort that always attacked him whenever this boy was near him. He had been thinking of charming things – of

the faint pallor of the dried bracken against the hill, of the fact
that soon Aunt Judith and Adam would be back from London,
of a party that they had had at Uldale for his sister when they
had practised archery on the lawn – yes, and of Elizabeth whom
he loved with all his soul, and for whom he was waiting until she
should be old enough for marriage. And then – this hobgoblin!
To be afraid of a small boy on a fat pony! But he was afraid.

Uhland did not get down from his pony. He simply said in his
clear chill voice:

'If I see you with my sister again, you shall be beaten by my
father's servants.'

John replied contemptuously:

'How is it you are out, young Uhland, without your governess?'

But Uhland went on:

'I mean it. I saw you both at Ireby.'

John stood there looking at him. He was determined to conquer this causeless apprehension. Gentle and courteous though he
was, he had a manly spirit; it was true, perhaps, that this child
was the only creature of the world of whom he was afraid. He
might even if he looked at him long enough pity him for his pale
face, his meagre body that could not keep itself straight even on a
pony. But he looked – and dropped his eyes. He was rooted there
as one is in a nightmare.

'Now look here, young man,' he said lightly, 'you keep to your
own business, which is firing paper bullets out of pop-guns, I
should think. This is a fine day; I'm walking for my health,
you're riding for yours. We go opposite ways.'

'Then you leave my sister alone,' Uhland repeated. 'Your
family and my family hate one another, and I'm glad they do.
When I'm a man I'll do you a hurt if I can.'

'When you're a man–' John laughed. 'That's a long way.
Good afternoon.'

He passed on, but he knew in his heart that it was all he could
do to prevent himself from running.

Meanwhile Uhland rode up the hill a little way and then back
to Westaways. He would have a word or two to say to Elizabeth.
He found her in her room sewing 'or some such nonsense'. He
limped in, sat on a corner of the sofa near to her, crossed his legs
and looked at her. He recognized, of course, that she was a
beautiful girl; he had all the Herries quality of perceiving things
as they were, and he saw her fairness and delicacy, so that every

colour from the pale shadowed gold of her hair to the warm pallor of her neck and arms was in perfect harmony; he saw all this, her fragility and strength, the gentleness of her eyes, the humour of her mouth. He admired her as a valuable family possession, and the thought that young Herries should be familiar with her revolted him – but revolted him in his own quiet child's way. Nevertheless, there is no one more determined than a child when he *has* an obsession.

'I saw you and John Herries at Ireby,' he remarked.

They were twins, but to Elizabeth he had never seemed like a relation at all. They had never done anything together, never cared for the same things nor thought the same thoughts. Elizabeth had many faults but they were not Uhland's. Her worst fault just now perhaps was her almost sulky reserve. This was the result of her father's ignoring of her. That had eaten deeply into her. She would let either her father or Uhland torture her to the last point of endurance and not utter a cry. She loved John Herries, but he was a man and she was only a child. She met him secretly, wrote to him and the rest chiefly because she knew what her father and Uhland thought of him. It was therefore not probable that Uhland would get anything from her now.

'Yes?' she said, continuing her sewing.

'You are never to speak to him again,' Uhland went on.

'Who said so?'

'I say so.'

'Indeed?' She looked at him, smiling. Then she bit off her thread. 'I shall speak to exactly whom I please.'

'You shall not. If you do I shall tell your father.'

'Tell him, then.'

'He'll beat you.'

She smiled again. 'You don't think I care for that ... Uhland, what a baby you are!'

That stung him, but he showed no signs. He nursed his knee in his hands, leaning forward and looking at her.

'Those people at Uldale are our enemies,' he said. 'They will have to leave there and go somewhere else when father's house is finished.'

'Yes?' she said.

'Father will send you away to school if he knows,' he went on.

'I shall be glad to go away,' she answered. 'I am always asking him to send me to school.'

'Well,' said Uhland, getting up, 'if I see John Herries talking to you again I shall shoot him.'

'Then you'll be hung,' she said, smiling.

'Perhaps it's Herries that will be hung,' he answered. Then he limped away.

But he had no intention whatever of saying anything to his father. He liked to keep his secrets.

Walter on his side was driven, after that little talk with his son on Ireby, by a strange restlessness. What had the child meant about never marrying? He *was*, of course, a child. He knew nothing of women or marriage . . . but the thin echo of that small cold voice, like the whistle of wind through the wallpaper, frightened Walter. The boy was growing. He had now his own thoughts and plans. Walter ought to know what these were. He discovered with angry resentment that he knew almost nothing about his son. The resentment may be said to have been directed against the Deity, Who was not at that moment paying all the attention to Walter Herries' affairs that He should do.

So Walter went in to say goodnight to his son. He was sitting up in bed, propped against his pillows, reading, by the light of a candle, a book. A dark cloth was over the parrot's cage, the dog was curled up asleep, the cat sat blinking at the candle.

Uhland was reading *Ivanhoe*.

'What a silly book, Papa!' he said. 'I am certain that people never talked like that.'

Walter placed his great bulk on the bed and put his arm round his son. Under Uhland's nightdress there was a sharp rigid spine-bone that seemed to protest against the caressing warmth of Walter's hand.

'Why, not, my boy?' said Walter, who had never read *Ivanhoe*. 'Sir Walter Scott is a very great man.'

'Have you ever read a book called *Frankenstein*, Papa?'

'No, my boy.'

'That's better than this stuff. Frankenstein creates a Monster and cannot escape it. There is too much fine writing, however.'

Walter sighed. Although this room was so clean yet you were oppressively conscious of the animals in it. Their very silence was alarming. He drew Uhland closer to him and felt the hard casing of ribs on that bony little body. He kissed him. Uhland resigned himself. He knew so well, oh, so very, very well what this was, this having his face pushed into the thick hot vast territory of his father's waistcoat with its hard brass buttons. Beneath his thin cheek his father's heart pounded like an imprisoned thumping fist. If his hand slid down to the hard warm expanse of his father's thigh it was as though he touched hot steel. Moreover, he detested sentiment.

'Uhland,' said Walter, 'I was hearing this evening that they are ordering fresh troops into Carlisle. There is fear of riots over all this Reform.'

'Yes, Papa.'

'Do you understand about Reform?'

'Oh yes, Papa.' Uhland allowed his hand to be held and imprisoned in his father's. 'Parliament has chosen its members from the wrong places – little places have many representatives and big places have few. The people are not at all represented.'

('Good God!' thought Walter. 'Who *is* this son of mine?')

'Yes, Uhland,' he went on, rather heavily. 'The people want to throw us out, my boy. They want the country to belong to *them*. They're tired of seeing us have the best of everything, and I don't blame 'em. All the same it would never do if they had their way. Think what England would be like if the working-man did what he liked with it. Imagine if you had Posset in power in London instead of – well, instead of the Duke of Wellington, for example.'

Uhland agreed that it would be ridiculous. But, he added, interested:

'You see, Papa, there would be five Possets, not one Posset.'

Walter asked him to explain.

'Well, in Keswick there are hundreds of men think they're as good as Posset. But if it's you or the Duke of Wellington they *know* they're not so good, so while you or the Duke of Wellington rule there's only one of you, but if Posset were to rule all the others would want to as well.'

'Well,' said Walter after a pause, 'remember you're a Herries and belong to the finest family in England.'

'Are we the finest family in England?'

'Most certainly we are.'

'Then they are fine at Uldale too?'

'Yes,' he answered, laughing, 'so long as they go somewhere else to live.'

Then Uhland asked a strange question.

'Papa – is it part of you what your great-grandfather was?'

'What *do* you mean?'

'Well – your great-grandfather was a wicked man and married

a gipsy, who was Adam Paris' grandmother. Are you and Adam and I partly like we are because of what your great-grandfather did?'

'I can't say . . . I suppose so . . . Something.'

'But we are so different.'

'Now you go to sleep, Uhland . . . Do you love your old father?'

'Yes, Papa.'

'You are all he has, you know. All he has in the world.'

'Yes, Papa.'

'He would do anything for you.'

'Yes, Papa.'

The dog began to move restlessly in his sleep, and he snapped his teeth at the flies of his dreams.

'I am sorry that you like to keep these animals in your room, Uhland. It is not good for your health.'

Uhland threw *Ivanhoe* on to the floor; then he turned over to sleep.

'Goodnight, Papa.'

'Goodnight, my boy.'

There was a pathos in the manner of Walter's exit: the heavy man, brilliant in his claret-coloured coat and rich brown pantaloons fitting tightly to his thighs, elaborately stepping softly on his toes that he might not disturb his son. He had blown out the candle. At the door he turned back to look. He could see nothing, and the only sound in the room was the dog in his dreams snapping at flies.

ENTRY OF THE FORTRESS

HE stood on the black edge of the rock and stretched his arms. He could have shouted with joy, for today was the great day of his life.

Near him, around him, subservient to him were many of the Family. There were present his father, Sir William Herries, Bart; his son Uhland; Sir James Herries, Bart, and the Venerable Rodney Herries, his brother, Archdeacon of Polchester in Glebeshire; Carey, Lord Rockage, and his wife Cecily and their son Roger; Stephen Newmark and his wife Phyllis; Garth Herries, his wife Sylvia, and Amery his brother; and, after these, more distant cousins, cousins by marriage or anything you like, Cards and Garlands and Golds and Ildens and Titchleys – only nobody from Uldale.

It was April 2nd, 1832, and his house on Ireby was triumphantly open.

It was six in the morning of the happiest day of Walter's life. The day, which was to end with a grand dinner and a magnificent ball to which the whole County had been invited, had begun with a run with the Blencathra Pack, and now here they were on the flanks of Helvellyn, so that the sun and the hills, the whole world as God had made it, might see the mighty glories of the Herries family and Walter Herries in particular.

Walter was as happy as a child. It was not conceit that he felt; he had no small vanities because of what he had done. Everything was inevitable. Because he was English and Herries and Walter, therefore he was King of the North. No force of heaven or earth could have helped it. No especial credit to himself that it was so.

Everything was well. God had seen to it that the weather should be right. There had been early in March a very heavy fall of snow, then towards the end of the month ten days of the loveliest possible weather, when the sun had burnt through a warm rosy mist, the crocuses had flowered in the Keswick gardens, the lambs gambolled in the meadows, the waters of Derwentwater, Bassenthwaite and Thirlmere shone with a blue as deep as any Italian lake, then colder again with a further snowfall on the tops, and now, in this early-morning misty air, a blue cloudless sky spread like a field of young violets above their heads.

As his eye covered the scene he saw that all the members of his party were there. Those staying with him were of course present, save only his mother and his wife, too delicate, poor women, for such an expedition. But the others whom he had lodged in Keswick and Bassenthwaite, in Braithwaite and Portinscale, were there also, not one of them was missing. It was a grand assemblage, headed by the great John Peel himself, whose tall bony figure, clad in his grey rough garment that descended almost to his knees, could be seen on a green knoll not far away.

Yes, it was a marvellous day: weather, scent and all would be right. The morning was as still as though it held its breath for very rapture. The hills in the distance were softly coloured in every shade from the faintest mauve to that dark indigo that has the bloom of the richest plums. On the rough ground below him he could see the huntsman's scarlet coat (the huntsman alone was permitted the scarlet), and near him the hounds, little white dots, rose and fell like shining pebbles.

His heart was moved, so that there were tears in his eyes as he caught a faint note of music. Then the music swells, running like a living human voice through the still air. Somewhere hounds have struck a 'drag'. The white pebbles draw together and all move upwards towards him.

A tall gaunt shepherd at his side in his excitement catches his arm and cries: 'Sista ... Sista ... Yonder, yonder he goes!'

Then scream and scream again bursts the silence, echoing back from valley and hill. The world that had been so still is broken with movement and shouting and the stir of action. It is good. Oh yes, it is very good indeed to be alive!

Walter had with him his father, Rodney the Archdeacon, Garth Herries and Sylvia his wife, but he was at that moment conscious of none of them. The hounds, in a kind of jolly frenzy, were answering to the holloa, and he too now had to answer, for he began to pound upwards, plunging into the boggy places, knocking his stout legs against stones and boulders. The leaders have struck the line, the hounds rush past Walter as though driven by a wild windy flurry; the music of the horn, of the cries, sweet and lovely, is all about him. He is himself crying 'Holloa! Holloa! Away! Away!'

Then the hounds were hidden by a breast of the hill and he paused, puffing a bit, blowing a trifle – for he was a big man and this ground was no light stuff to cover.

Unfortunately he found that he had Rodney the Archdeacon at his side, even clinging to his arm and blowing down his neck.

'Whoof! Whoof! Walter! Deary me! Deary me! ... Most exhausting! So early in the morning too! Whoof ... Now tell me, pray, my dear Walter, in this ridiculous hunting of yours there were some quite small dogs with the huntsman ...'

'Terriers! Terriers, my dear Rodney.'

'Really! Really! Is that so? Indeed!'

'Yes, yes. We'd never get a fox out of his hole without them—'

'Indeed! ... Do you think we shall *see* a fox?'

'We did see one just now. Down below us. There they are! There they are! Out on the brow. Come on, Rodney! Stir your hams. Now we're off!'

He went pounding off and fell headlong into a lake of mist. He was quite suddenly alone. No sound. No cry. The mist eddied and whirled.

He stayed where he was and was conscious of a foreboding, as though some whispering figure had crept close to his side. Why was he, who a moment ago had been so happy and confident, now helpless? A hand had been laid on his shoulder that he should stop to hear some judgement. He looked about him, but he was blind and, it seemed, deaf as well. How unforeseen a country this was, always, when you least expected it, coming up to assert its power over you. He did not put it like that, but he was like a little boy, blundering unexpectedly into the dark. The mist clung to him like thin lawn, then moved from him and faced him in a wall of blankness, then eddied like smoke, creeping along the ground, then pressed in upon him again filling his mouth and nose. He stared, dumbfounded, as though he expected to hear a voice . . .

It broke: a gap was there no bigger than a hand; a crag leapt into air, shaped like a face, black as jet. The ground, brown and then faintly green, came sliding from space, and then, in a second of time, swimming in a wall of bright and airy colour, the whole landscape was back again; the voices were there, calling, shouting. Only a little above him was the huntsman's red coat and the hounds in a broken sequence of white and brown and grey silhouetted against the blue of the morning sky. He wiped his face. 'Dammit!' he thought. 'It don't do to be alone here,' then laughed and ran like a schoolboy again up the slope.

All the world was alive and so fresh and bright that he could shout for joy. There is the sharp call of a raven; near him to the left on the slopes of the Fell are the small bodies of the Herdwick sheep – and there, just in front of him, can it really be, is the fox himself!

He is running with a slouching, slinking movement, first straight then with a jerk upwards again, stopping for an instant by some borran where he might hide, thinking better of it, round the crag, seen for an instant, running to higher ground, then vanishing.

The sight of that fox fired Walter as though he had himself created him. He began to pound upwards again. The hills rose with him, leading him on. They were bathed now in crystalline light, purer than the purest glass, alive with their own vibrant force, stronger than any human life and far more confident of their eternity. And then another miracle! For, reaching a higher slope, he was above the mist that lay below him in a sea of white shifting cloud while he himself trod on a firm sparkling floor of brilliant snow. The snow carpeted the ground for a space, glittering with points of fire, then the rock broke from it, hard and black, only to surrender to higher fields of brightness.

He crossed the snow as though on wings, the sun and the air lifting him, rounded a boulder and had the whole pack in view. Now a dreadful fear possessed him that he would be too late for the kill. He saw Garth and Sylvia swinging along not far from him and he waved his arms crying, 'Come on! Come on! Holloa! Holloa!'

Sylvia waved back to him and, great though the excitement of the moment was, his natural instinct about women, hot and strong in him, murmured: 'That's the loveliest female . . .'

His heart hammered as he leaped a low stone wall and found himself on bracken and in the thick of the mob. They had shut the fox away from an earth near by; you could just see him tracking for the rocks. But the hounds have edged him lower and lower.

'Aye,' said a little purple-faced man to Walter. 'What he's after is that borran yonder. The terriers'll have to be after him from below. That's what he likes.'

The little purple-faced man was trembling with excitement. He smelt oddly of bracken and snuff; he was a stranger to Walter, who felt a sort of indignation that he *should* be a stranger. Everyone today was a kind of dependant of the Herries family. No one should exist who was not. The little purple-faced man began frantically to run, and Walter ran with him. The fox had gone to earth, into a borran where he was 'head on' to his adversaries.

This was a big dog-fox and worth the fighting. The excitement now was terrific: the ground seemed to quiver with it. The air shuddered with shouts and cries and the snap-snapping of the hounds. The terriers were mad to get at him; one small animal, crazy with young pride and ambition, had struggled its way far into the borran. Suddenly it emerged, looking foolish. All the terriers stopped marking, and the hounds began to rush madly round the borran, yelping, yowling, bellowing. The huntsman and the whipper-in were cursing and swearing, and John Peel himself, with his funny, ill-fitting long coat, could be heard muttering his own particular Cumberland oaths. And this was where none of the Herries were of any use at all. They hung on to the fringe of the outside world – Will and Walter, Rodney and James, Garth and Amery – all of no importance. They might just as well be dead.

For the fox had slipped away underground and bolted. He was already at a considerable distance. The fear now was that he would find a borran so deep that it would be impossible to get at him or they would lose a terrier or two there. But no! He is out again, and the hounds have steered him away from the rocks. The hounds move now as though they have absolute command of the game and are certain of the end of it. The fox is out; he is tracing a thin trod through the bracken. The hounds, running from scent to view, are hard upon him. A moment later, Mischief or Satan or Hamilton has him by the throat; he vanishes beneath a flurry of white and brown and swinging tails. Walter drew a deep sigh; he stood, his legs planted wide, his chest out, burning satisfaction in his eyes. That had been a great hour, and now he must recover his dignity and gather his family about him again.

Rodney was at his elbow, but he did not want Rodney nor that fat idiot James his brother. He despised them both, because when he was short with them (as he often was) they took it like lambs. He moved among the Herries cousins – those of them stout enough of wind and strong enough of limb to achieve the 'kill' – with an air of fine and genial patronage. He felt like a king and thought it quite natural that they should feel that he was one. But the members of the family who really attracted him were Garth, Amery, and Sylvia. Amery, slender, stern-faced, grave, was the coming 'money' man of them all, already an important figure in the City, and Garth was jolly, careless and handsome: young though he was, he could drink anyone under the table and was ready for any escapade or devilry. But Sylvia! Her eyes shining, her cheeks rosy with health and excitement, framed by the hills and the glassy blue of the morning sky, she was the loveliest thing he had ever seen. She was ready, he was sure, for any gay adventure. Harmless, of course; but tonight when the splendid house was shining with light and colour, a laugh, a smile, a pressure of the hand . . .

He moved towards them. Then he remembered Uhland. How could he have forgotten him? The whole day was to be Uhland's! This day had no meaning unless it were all for Uhland. He turned back and began to search for his son on the faint green shadows of the lower slopes . . .

*   *   *

Two Titchley cousins – old maids from Carlisle and so entirely unimportant that nobody ever learnt their names from the beginning to the end of the affair – sat on the corner of an almost concealed sofa in the ballroom and considered the sight presented to them. One was stout and one was thin; as no one ever learnt their names that is as far as the historian can go. They were dressed in the fashions of 1820, with high waists, drapery of silk netting over their busts, their ball-dresses short, with padded *rouleaux* at the bottom. One was in rose and the other in mignonette-green. Their first cousin, an eminent doctor in Carlisle, had brought them and, having brought them, completely forgot them. However, they did not care; they had rooms in Keswick but were determined not to return to them until the festivities were entirely concluded. They were in a state of ecstatic and almost drunken excitement and pleasure. A footman brought them ices and orangeade. No one else spoke to them the night long.

It was the loveliest sight they had ever beheld. They were at first inclined to be shocked by the naked goddesses displayed in the famous tapestries, they thought some of the costumes 'bare in the extreme', they discovered a young man, quite drunk, behind one of the gold curtains in a corner near to them, but soon as the air grew more heated, the noise of the band in the gallery more strident, they threw away convention and, their mouths a little open, sipping their ices, surrendered to their ecstasy.

Above their turbans of figured gauze, above the high ceiling painted with the stars of heaven and naked cherubs hanging garlands, climbed one of the two towers of the Fortress. In the highest room of the tower (which by his own choice was Uhland's room) a monkey with one eye and a face of the deepest melancholy scratched his chest; a small terrier with a broken leg whined, paused to listen, whined again; the parrot, under its green baize covering, its head on its shoulder, slept a deep, philosophic sleep. The moonlight soaked the room in a pale green light and, very faintly, the sound of the fiddles, the bassoon and the drums whispered in the air.

In the gardens everything was still and cold. Everything was new – the stone walls, the steps, the fountain whose waters flashed under the moon, the naked beds where the flowers would soon be so splendid. The trees beyond the garden walls were old; here daffodils were in bud, and the snowdrops dying. An owl cried; the music, muffled but determined, drowned its cries. Then from the heart of the trees a little wind rose and went whistling and lamenting about the garden-beds and the paths as

though looking for its familiar friends who were gone. Beyond the
high road the landscape, falling to the valley, spreading to the
smoky hills, was soaked in moonlight and lay there as still as a
pattern on glass. A man from Ireby village walking out to meet
his sweetheart stayed for a moment in the road to listen to the
music, to stare at the blaze of lighted windows, then some sudden
apprehension – as though he feared that his girl would not be
there to meet him – hurried him on.

Around and about the lighted ballroom many of the rooms
were yet empty; some of them had ladders and pots of paint and
buckets. Here a chair lay on its face, there pictures were piled
against the wall; in one room workmen had left cheese and a
hunk of bread.

The ballroom blazed with colour like the page of an illuminated missal. Agnes Herries sat with Christabel, Walter's mother,
on a little sofa, and everyone came and talked to them. Agnes was
feeling dreadfully ill; at her heart was a pain like a hand clutching and unclutching. She did not know what to say to Walter's
mother, with whom she had never been familiar. She could not
say that she liked this new house, for she hated it; nor that she
was sorry to have left Westaways, for she had hated that too; nor
that she was glad that Walter was happy, because she was not
glad. The sight of so many people whom she did not know,
whom she feared, made her sick. She knew that her little shrivelled body looked absurd in its gaudy ball-dress with the huge
sleeves like epaulettes. She knew that everyone despised her. Her
only happiness was to catch a glimpse once and again of her
lovely daughter Elizabeth, who in her dress of silver silk was, in
her mother's eyes, beautiful beyond compare. Once her son
Uhland, resting on an ebony cane that he now carried, came and
spoke to her. When he was gone Christabel said: 'What a clever
face Uhland has!'

'Yes, he is very clever.'

'I have never,' continued Christabel, who was longing for her
bed, 'seen so many of the family together in one room – never
since a Ball I once gave in London.'

She was no longer distressed by the memory of that eventful
Ball. It seemed to her now, on looking back, to have been a very
successful affair. She sought anxiously for Will, her husband.
Ah! there he was, talking to Amery Herries, a clever young man.
They would be talking about money, always Will's favourite
topic. Perhaps soon she might slip away to bed. Why, she won-

dered sleepily, had her son chosen so poor a specimen as Agnes for his wife? But her wonderings were never very active. She had long ago learnt that it was wiser not to wonder about anything very deeply.

The band broke into one of the newest valses. The floor swam with colour, green and white, purple and rose. Laughter, music, the movement of so many happy persons filled the air with a golden haze; the owl's cry could not penetrate the thick walls of Cumberland stone.

It was nearly midnight. At Uldale, John, Dorothy, Adam had all gone to bed, but Judith sat in Jennifer's room looking after Jennifer. Looking after Jennifer! An exasperating thing to do! Jennifer had been ill for weeks, but they had had to set a guard about her door to keep her in bed. She was there now, propped up with pillows, her eyes shining like fireflies. Her face was as white as dough. Even in her bed she looked dishevelled, her heavy breasts exposed, her nightdress torn above her right elbow, her lace nightcap tilted over one ear. She wanted to get up.

'You can't!' said Judith.

Judith was in a violently bad temper. All day she had ordered the maids about as though they were dirt, rapping with her stick on the floor. It had been all that she could do not to box Dorothy's ears. They had all been on edge that day. Was it because of the Ball at Ireby? Were they, in spite of themselves, conscious of it? In any case, you did not know of what the children were thinking. John had been melancholy for a while now, and Adam – Adam was silently fighting her desires. Adam wanted to get away and she knew it. She was determined to prevent it.

Meanwhile Jennifer was very ill. She had caught a chill walking in the country lanes in a thin dress with black satin shoes and silk mittens. Her heart also was bad. Her legs were swollen. She was deaf in one ear.

'You are keeping me in bed against my will. I insist on getting up.' She looked across the sheets with hatred at the neat, pale-faced woman in the red morocco chair. She listened. The house was as still as a bottomless well.

She poured out a torrent of mild, lazy abuse:

'Yes, you keep me here and think it very fine. You have grown into a bully, Judith. That's what you are. Everyone knows it. You are impossible with everyone ... impossible ... Why the maids stay in the house I don't know. I insist that I get up.'

'Don't be foolish, Jennifer. It's past midnight. You must go to sleep. I will give you your drops.'

'I don't wish for my drops. They are poisoning me. I expect that Walter has bribed the doctor to put poison in them.'

'Don't be foolish. You know that he has done nothing of the kind.'

'Oh, this woman!' thought Judith.

Jennifer slowly raised herself on her hands, climbed out of the clothes and sat on the edge of the bed, her swollen legs hanging heavily.

'So Walter has opened his house. All the countryside save ourselves is dancing there tonight. The next thing he will build a house just outside our garden.' She looked up with lazy maliciousness. 'You may say what you like; he has poisoned all our life here. John is not the same, you are not the same, Adam is not the same.'

Judith said nothing. Jennifer went on:

'You love Adam more than anyone in the world, do you not?'

'Yes, of course I do. Jennifer, get back into bed. You will catch your death—'

'Well, he is going to leave you. I can tell. I know. He will soon be seventeen and is not of such a character as to remain in a country place—'

A sharp pain, like the touch of a knife, struck Judith's heart, but she got up and, very gently, went to the bed. She patted Jennifer on the shoulder as though she were a child and urged her back into bed again. Quite placidly Jennifer obeyed.

'Oh, dear! I have such a pain in my chest! How they will be dancing now on Ireby! Everyone from Keswick will be there!' She sighed, a deep childish sigh. 'How still this house is! Only the clocks . . . Judith, what do you think life is for?'

'What is it *for*?' Judith was listening. It was, of course, only her imagination, but it seemed to her that she could hear very faintly drums and fiddles and a dim bassoon. One did fancy that one heard things in a quiet house at night.

'Yes. Why are we born? Why do we live? Why do you love Adam so intensely when it is all for nothing?'

'It is not for nothing.'

'Oh, but of course it is. He will grow up and marry and forget you just as I forgot my own mother and father. I should never have left them. I should never have come North. I should never have married Francis. My children don't care for me. No one cares for me. You are all waiting for me to die.'

'Nonsense, Jennifer.'

'No, but it is not nonsense. I cannot understand it, all the bother and the worry. People are born and they die, and other people are born and it is all for nothing.'

'It is not for nothing,' Judith repeated. 'It is that we may have some experience, that we may learn—'

'Yes, but learn what? I am sure that I have never learnt anything except to be disappointed and to be afraid of Walter.'

Judith, who was half asleep, struggled to comfort Jennifer.

'You have learnt more than you know, my dear. There is something immortal in us that must grow, and it grows with experience.'

But did it? Did she mean what she said? Her love for Adam was immortal. Her love for Georges was so – it would never die. There was something to *fight* in life, something strong and glorious . . .

She covered a yawn with her hand. 'Now, Jennifer, you must sleep.'

Jennifer lay back in the bed. 'I have such a pain near my heart. My throat is sore. I can see Walter come dancing down the hill when I am buried. And then he will finish John and Dorothy as he has finished me.'

There was something so truly pathetic in her voice; she was like a small child who is suffering she does not know why. Judith bent over the bed and smoothed her pillow. Jennifer caught her hand.

'You are good to me, Judith, although I know that you wish that I were dead.'

'Of course I don't wish that you were dead.'

'Oh yes, you do. You have never forgiven me for preventing you from living in Watendlath. Had you lived in Watendlath you would not have wanted everything your own way so.'

This was so true that Judith felt as though it were her own voice that was speaking. But she showed no signs: she stroked Jennifer's hair.

'Judith, do you not hear something?'

'Hear what?'

'Music – violins and a drum.'

'No – of course not.'

'Oh, but I do. Go to the window and pull back the curtain.'

She went. She looked out.

'What do you see?'

'I see nothing. Only the trees and the moonlight.' But that was not true. Quite clearly she could see in the far distance Walter's house on Ireby. The windows shone like little stars.

'Can you not see the house?'

'Yes; very dimly.'

'Ah ... Judith, Judith!' It was a cry. 'He will kill John as he is killing me! I can see him. I can hear him. He is coming!'

She hastened back to the bed.

Jennifer was very ill and the perspiration glistened on her forehead. Her hand was at her heart.

'Oh, I am in such pain! Such terrible pain!'

'Quiet, dear. It will soon pass. I will fetch the drops—'

'Don't leave me ... Oh! Oh! I am going to die! The room is dark ... Judith, where are you?'

'Sir Roger' was over; some of the older people were departing, Miss Pennyfeather among others. She greeted Walter with dignity and thanked him for a very enjoyable evening. Indeed, she had had one, and Mrs McCormick was to drive her back in her barouche. Mrs Walter Herries had gone to bed; Miss Elizabeth, standing beside her father, did the honours.

The old lady, who was feeling roguish, whispered in his ear:

'You have a most beautiful daughter.'

And then, to be more roguish yet, whispered:

'But I miss Judith Paris. She is a great friend of mine, you know.'

He agreed to both these propositions as perhaps he would have agreed to anything tonight in his happiness and triumph. But he was surprised at the loveliness of Elizabeth. He did not feel that he was her father any more strongly than he had ever done, but she *was* beautiful. And he would have been delighted had Judith been there. He bore her no grudge. A little later Sylvia Herries found herself beside Elizabeth and spoke to her.

'Are you enjoying yourself, Elizabeth?'

The girl smiled shyly. She thought Sylvia Herries the loveliest woman she had ever seen. She had heard that she was a beauty in London and had a Salon attended by famous men, and yet she looked little older than herself.

'Oh yes,' she said.

'Do you like the new house?'

She did not say that she hated it, that she was miserable there, that she was afraid lest her mother should die and leave her defenceless, but her colour rose in her cheeks and she answered:

'I am not perhaps accustomed . . . Later on perhaps.'

The oddest feeling rose in Sylvia's breast. This child seemed to rebuke her by her innocence and inexperience. Suddenly she hated all her London life, with Rosina Bulwer storming angrily at her overdressed husband, and young Mr Ainsworth such a coxcomb, the tables after a party scattered with cards and over-turned glasses and the grease from candles.

She looked at Elizabeth with great affection. 'Be happy while you may. You are so young and so beautiful.'

At that moment up came Walter, a little drunk. He took her away. They were dancing the valse again. He asked her to dance. He was not a bad performer for so big a man, but why had he not even looked at his daughter? His breath smelt of wine, his heavy body was pressed close to hers.

'This is a triumph for you, Cousin Walter,' she said. 'I have never seen so many of our relations before.'

His arm tightened about her slender waist.

'I'll tell you a thing,' he said. 'I have been looking forward to this day all my life.'

'The house is magnificent,' she said. But she did not think so. She found it cold and bleak. There was too much grey stone about it, and the towers and sham battlements were hideous. It was like a fortress.

But he did not pay attention. He whispered in her ear:

'I'll tell you another thing. I think that I am in love with you.'

This was no new thing to her. Men were for ever whispering it in her ear; moreover, with his physical vitality, size and strength there was something attractive . . . also tonight he was like a boy in his happiness. So she did not answer him, but said instead:

'The hunting this morning was the grandest adventure. I never enjoyed anything so much in my life.'

His hand rested on her arm; truly he danced well for so big a man.

'Yes, was it not? Glorious weather. And, do you know, this is a strange country. I took a step and was blinded by mist with sun all about me. For a moment I was lost.'

'Yes? Indeed?' She had not heard him. She saw that her

husband was watching them. She fancied that he did not care for Walter, although he had not said so.

The valse was ended, and he led her away to an alcove near the window where they were hidden by curtains, hidden from everyone save the two Titchley cousins, whose eyes were more active than ever.

She sat down, and he stood leaning over her chair, his hand very near her lovely neck. To make conversation she said:

'Is it not comic, Cousin Walter, to see so many Herries together? What do you think of us as a family?'

'What do I think? ... Well, well ... Sylvia, how lovely you are! I am sure that I have never seen anyone so lovely.'

'I hate our family when it is together in big numbers. We are all hard and material and self-seeking. When one of us is not he is gored to death by the others, like a sick animal in a herd.'

'Sylvia, would you make an objection if I kissed you? Only a cousinly kiss, you know.'

'I should certainly object most strongly. I am married, you know.'

'So am I,' he murmured laughing, and, bending forward, kissed the back of her neck.

Her husband, Garth, had seen them dancing. Sylvia was right; he did not like Walter; he wished that they had not come. He was vaguely unhappy, a rare experience for his lively, careless temperament, and, turning, found that Elizabeth, near to him at that moment, was being left with many bows by her partner, a fat, pursy little man.

'This is a grand sight,' he said. 'Who was your elderly partner, Elizabeth?'

'A doctor from Keswick.'

'Are you very happy? You should be.'

Some restraint that she had been fighting all the evening broke down. She liked Garth; he was gay and young and kind.

'No, Garth, I am not.' She held her head high, but he saw that her eyes were bright with tears. They were away by themselves, and he wanted to put his arm round her and protect her.

'Why not?' he asked her.

'Oh, this house – do you like it? It is hard and cold. And my mother is ill. And – and—'

'You are in love?' he asked her quickly.

'Yes, I am,' she said softly. 'I have been ever since I was a child.'

She was only a child now, he thought.

'Well – is there no hope of marrying?'

'None. A year ago we agreed that we would not meet any more. It is quite, quite hopeless. But I love him the same and so I always shall.'

'That is something,' he answered gravely. 'Fidelity. That is very rare, and the best way to maintain it is never to meet. Propinquity, my dear, kills love.'

'Why!' said Elizabeth, her eyes open and startled. 'Do you not love your wife?'

'I can be jealous of her. I am proud of her. I wish to be near her. Is that an answer to your question?'

'Oh!' whispered Elizabeth, staring at him and longing for John Herries with such a desperate ache that she thought that everyone must see it. 'Would you bring me some orangeade, cousin? I am thirsty.'

The band struck up a quadrille. They moved to their places. It was the climax of all the splendour and pageantry of the evening.

'Oh, did you see—?' said one of the Titchleys to the other.

Walter, his countenance shining with wine, health, exercise, success, love and triumph, led Cecily Rockage to her place in the dance.

There was a moment's pause. Then the band struck up again and all the coloured figures moved, softly, gracefully, about the shining floor.

At Uldale, Judith, her arms about Jennifer, gazed around her desperately for help. But no help could be forthcoming, for with a sigh Jennifer bent her head and, falling forward, died against Judith's breast.

Part Two

Adam and Margaret

THE BATTLE

ADAM, on the morning of his twenty-second birthday, rode
alone to Manesty Woods.

At breakfast, there had been the customary festivities. His
mother had given him a riding-whip mounted in silver, John had
given him Captain Marryat's *Mr Midshipman Easy*, Dorothy
had sent some silk handkerchiefs, and Rackstraw the *French
Revolution* of Thomas Carlyle. They had all been very kind.
Especially had the love shown him by his mother moved and
affected him. He had ridden over alone to Manesty that he might
think, that he might resolve his strong determination into unchangeable fact.

He intended, before another twenty-four hours were past, to
tell his mother that he must leave Uldale and seek his fortune in
the world. It was a fierce resolve, one towards which it seemed to
him that his whole life had been tending. It needed some girding
of the loins! The scene with his mother would be terrific!

In the quiet autumn weather he rode through Portinscale, up
the hill towards Braithwaite, then turned to the left, followed the
leaf-strewn paths until the woods closed about him and, tying
his horse to a tree, plunged down to the Lake's very edge.

There was breeze enough to run a slight murmuring ripple to
his feet: for the rest the silence was complete. Opposite him Skiddaw rose like a dividing flower in purple shadow to a shadowed
sky. Shadow veiled the Lake. Fields, hills and houses were
dim.

He sat there, his hands pressed on his broad knees, and
thought things out. Yes, there would be a devil of a row! His
mother, as she now was, was not easy to oppose – and yet, if only
because he loved her, he must oppose her. He was twenty-two
today and, as he saw it, he had wasted five years of his life. For a
young man five years seem an immense time. Ever since, at the
age of fifteen, he had visited London with his mother he had
resolved to leave Uldale, and yet here he was – seven years later,
and he was still there!

It was not that he was not resolute enough! As he sat there
with his mouth set and his thick broad shoulders squared, he was

the very image of resolution, and yet his mother had been too much for him!

He had begun, he remembered, five years back, when Walter Herries had given his first Ball at Ireby and Aunt Jennifer had died, his Grand Rebellion. He had said, his legs apart and his hands in his pockets, that he was going. And his mother had answered him: 'Well – go!'

But she had not intended for a moment that he should go. She had used Roger Rackstraw and John to assist her. Adam was greatly attached to Rackstraw in spite of his drinking, his wenching and his gambling. Rackstraw had taught him everything that he knew – how to ride, how to fight, how to read. It was from Rackstraw that he had got more than from any other the love of this country that he so deeply worshipped. Stones and clouds! Clouds and stones! He looked up at the small vaporous clouds browsing like sheep on the fields of misty sky above him. The long white stone upon which he was sitting, the boulders that lay about him, these were his intimate companions because Rackstraw had introduced him to them. Yes, he owed Rackstraw a great deal, and it was Rackstraw who had persuaded him that he must remain, for a while at least, to help John with the property, the farm at Uldale, the land towards Skiddaw, the business affairs in Keswick. Well, he had remained. He loved John Herries very dearly; there were things that he could do that John could not. He was more easily friends with the farmers and the labourers and the Keswick people. There was something in John, some reserve and shyness, that kept him apart; he inherited that from his father. But everyone liked Adam and trusted him, which was something in these days of rick-burnings in the country and starvation in the towns.

Then, two years ago, he had tried again.

'I am wasting my life here, Mother. I want to go to London.'

This time she did not say 'Go!' She had looked at him as though she would burst into a torrent of rage. She was by then over sixty; her hair was white, but her small body was as taut and erect as ever. Nevertheless, she was not quite as strong as she had been. She sat down more frequently, would take his arm when they walked in the garden. It was not so easy as it had been the first time. Nevertheless, she had not said 'No'. Dorothy had but just become engaged to a Mr Bellairs of Ryelands, near Seascale. An excellent match. Bellairs was Dorothy's age, would succeed to a fine estate, was a good, solid sound-bottomed Englishman with no nonsense about him. So Adam must wait until Dorothy was married. Dorothy *did* marry in June of 1836 and had gone to Ryelands to live. Well, then, Judith was all alone now with John. Of course, Adam must stay. Not that Judith minded in the least being the only woman in the house. She adored it. She had always had an affection for Dorothy, but of late the girl had grown into a very common-sensible house-keeping woman and had had ideas of the way that Fell House should be managed. She had married, Adam was of the private opinion, in the very nick of time.

So then it had gone on, and Adam could just see his mother nodding her little head to herself, her mouth curved in a triumphant smile. 'Now I've got him for ever! I shall marry John off, and then the two of us will be alone here together.' (Adam knew that she would never marry John off. There had ever been only one woman for him. There would never be another.)

But there was more in it than this. There was Walter Herries at Ireby.

Adam was extremely practical and saw things as they were. He was not, as John was, frightened by unsubstantial fears. But he could not deny that part of his resolve to run away to London was founded on Walter and the house at Ireby.

After Jennifer Herries' death they – Judith, Adam, John and Dorothy – had decided altogether to disregard dear Cousin Walter and his big, ugly grey house. And so in a kind of way they had. They never mentioned Walter except to joke about him, his growing corpulency, his absurd airs and the rest. When Agnes his wife died, Judith attended the funeral, and Walter spoke to her in a very friendly manner.

Nevertheless, what Jennifer had prophesied was partly true. The Fortress (as everyone in the countryside now called the place) came ever nearer to Uldale. One reason of this was that Mr Peach, Walter's agent, seemed to be on terms with all of the Uldale dependants. Even old Bennett was seen chatting with him. Mr Rackstraw drank and betted with him, and one night was deposited, dead drunk, at Fell House gates with an ironic note in Peach's handwriting.

Then Adam knew that John was always thinking of Elizabeth. He did not, Adam believed, meet her any more nor correspond with her, but John was certain that she was unhappy, in especial since her mother's death, and the thought tortured him.

Then there was the matter of Uhland Herries, his liking for

Adam, his hatred of John. For a while he was continually meeting Adam, in the roads, in Keswick, by the Lake; until at last Adam told him that he did not wish to speak to him nor have anything to do with him, that his father was the enemy of all of them at Uldale, and that, so long as it lasted, there could be no intercourse between them. Uhland just stared at him out of his strange grey eyes, nodded, and rode away. But John had the fantastic, unreal notion that Uhland was always following him, waiting for him round corners and so on, would one day do him a hurt.

Finally, Adam believed it to be true that his mother was slowly more and more conscious of Walter. When little things went wrong she attributed it to Walter, just as Jennifer used to do. Adam caught her sometimes standing in the garden, staring over at the Fortress. Of course, she was becoming an old lady now, and fancies would have more power over her than they used to do.

For Adam there was a growing atmosphere in the Uldale house that seemed to him sickly and false. He must escape from it.

There was, however, much more behind his resolve than this. He was determined to do something fine in the world.

Although his reticence hindered him from declaring his thoughts to anyone, he was filled with idealism and love for his fellow human beings. On this day, as he sat there, looking over the shadowy Lake, he felt perhaps some of the sentiment that was stirring in England just then. There was a new young Queen on the throne; all the debauchery, mismanagement, selfishness of those fat old men who had pretended to govern England had passed away. With this child who already in a few months had shown strength and honesty of purpose and purity of mind there was a new hope in the land. Adam had pictures in his mind, as all Englishmen had just then, of that girlish figure on horseback in the Park, or advancing with perfect dignity and command to meet her Ministers, so that all the old men who had known that other régime, the Duke and Peel and Melbourne, were ready to kneel down and worship her. Melbourne was already her slave. Might it not mean that a New Age of Knight-Errantry and the Brotherhood of Man was to begin?

If so, Adam meant to have his share in it. He was very young, had had little experience of the world, but it seemed to him then – as it was to seem to him all his life through – that a very little was needed to make the earth a glorious place where everyone loved his fellow-man and worked, unselfishly, for the general good of mankind.

There was nothing selfish in his desires as he sat there that morning. He never thought of himself at all. His heart swelled in him as he formed pictures of life as it ought to be, as surely it would be in time to come. It seemed to him that it would be a fine thing if himself and others of a like mind were to band together and work all with a common will for the good of the world. He was proud of his family, although he himself was illegitimate, but he was not proud of individual members of the family. Something was always taking them in the wrong direction. Even he perceived, in spite of his intense loyalty, that something had happened to his mother. It might be that she had, as she once told him, made the wrong decision when she had stayed at Uldale instead of going to live at Watendlath. Then there were Francis and Jennifer, John's father and mother, Walter and Uhland, Will and Garth and Sylvia in London. He did not feel himself better than any of them – there was never anyone with less conceit – but it seemed that in life one was for ever being tempted to take a wrong step: a quick decision and one was moving down the wrong road, never again to be in the right one.

He felt life to be good; it could not hold such beauty as he saw before him that morning and not be good. Yet so many things were wrong with it – so much poverty, suffering of women and children, dirt and shame and crime. Surely, if one worked hard enough, and if enough people in the world cared for justice and equality, everything would swing round – not to perfection, perhaps, but to something in unison with this beauty, this sense of God active and moving in men's hearts?

In any case, he meant to see what he could do; so he must go out into the world, fight his way, find others of like mind with himself. He got up, stretched his arms, felt an infinite strength and hope in him. He hated this struggle with his mother. But, if he was resolute, it would be sharp, brief, soon over, and then she would see how right he was. He smiled as he looked about him and untethered his horse. How lovely and perfect this place was! Perhaps one day he would return and have a cottage here, with the hills above him, and the Lake at his feet. Nothing the world could hold would be so good as that would be! He rode home.

But alas! How noble and ideal are we at one moment; how peevish and unkind the next! Adam stopped in Portinscale for a

bottle of stout and some cold beef. There was nothing better than
to sit in the window of the Inn, drinking the stout and eating the
beef while the grey stillness of field and Lake bound with the
hedges of the cottage gardens spread like a fan before him, to sit
there and think of the world opening, of the great deeds to be
performed therein, of the fights to be fought, the weak to be
protected, the books, maybe, to be written! He had no thought
that he was a genius, but Keats (whose *Lamia* and *St Agnes' Eve*
Rackstraw had introduced to him) had not thought himself one,
and Mr Carlyle had been a peasant, and there was the author of
Sketches by Boz . . .

So he rode slowly home through the mist and the yellow
leaves, dreaming of what was coming. What immediately came to
him was the Reverend Mr Bland, the new curate at Cockermouth, who had had a London curacy and bore a letter from
Stephen Newmark. A stout wife was with him and a stout
daughter. The visitors had been asked whether they would take
port or sherry, and the glasses, biscuits and decanters were laid
out on the table. The candles shone (gas was not yet introduced
into Fell House), a table near by was ready with the round, lacquered Pope Joan board and the mother-o'-pearl counters, for
Judith adored Pope Joan. And she sat there like a queen in a
beautiful shawl with long fringes and her snow-white hair in
long ringlets, enjoying herself tremendously.

The Reverend Mr Bland stayed an eternity. He had endless
things to say about his new church, how the Psalms were read
'too quick,' and the red cloth on the reading-desk was faded to a
dirty brown, and how at St Mary's in Islington . . . No, they
would never be gone, for Farmer Wilson had driven them over
and had gone on to some farms about some business of his own
and . . . Oh! there was Farmer Wilson at last, and soon the Bland
family was lifted into his cart, and the dusk closed down upon
their rumbling.

He followed her up to her room, watched her shake her curls,
change her shawl, do a little *pas seul* up and down her floor in
imitation of Mr Bland's mincing steps, laugh and sing a note or
two from 'Speed on, my mules, for Leila *waits* for me,' which
was one of the popular ballads of the day. It was very difficult for
him to attack her at such a moment, and yet he could not wait.
Although so thickly and sturdily built he was nervous as a young
girl when he confronted his mother. The memory of that first
awful quarrel following his laugh at old Bellenden in Keswick
never left him; there was, too, something dismaying in her swift

transition from mood to mood. Then she was sixty-three, and, let her pretend as she might, was not as strong as she had once been. And then – hardest of all – he loved her better than anyone alive.

So he burst out at once that he might get it over quickly.

'Mother – I'm going to London. I've been thinking it over. I'm going to earn my living like other men. I must, I must . . .'

Like other men! She stopped in her invocation of 'Leila', stood there in the middle of the floor and laughed at him. Like other men! To her he was still an infant, or at most a small boy who stole jam from the cupboard and bought bull's-eyes at the shop in the village. And yet he was not! She looked and saw him standing there, stolid and square, in his man's blue coat with the velvet collar and the strapped pantaloons, a lock of his black hair falling over his forehead, whiskers sprouting on his cheeks, his grave eyes confronting her without flinching. No, he was not a child any longer. This was what Jennifer had foretold. She reached out for her ivory cane that was leaning against the four-poster.

'Not on your birthday, Adam,' she said, and moved towards the door.

But he did not budge. He felt his knees shake, but now that he had begun he would go through with it.

'Yes, Mother, I must.' He cleared his throat. 'Listen, Mother, dear. I'm twenty-two today.'

'And what has that to do with it?'

'Everything. I am a man and should do a man's work.'

'You have a man's work here.'

'No, I have not. You know quite well that for all I do here I might be shut up in a cupboard. John and Rackstraw can manage everything.'

'That is not true. John is too dreamy, and Rackstraw drinks in the village.' She felt that her legs were trembling, so with great dignity she walked to the chair near the fireplace and sat down.

The devil of it was that words never came easily to him! He could think clearly enough, but when it came to words! . . . He stood nearer to her.

'Mother, pray listen. I am not being rebellious or wicked. You know how . . . how . . . devotedly I love you—'

'So devotedly that you want to break my heart,' she said.

(Something sarcastic in her said: 'Break my heart! My dear, what stuff!')

He began to be angry, which was a help to him. When he was angry his lower lip jutted out, a sign that she knew very well.

'This is a resolve,' he said. 'Nothing shall turn me from it.'

'Well – if it is a resolve – what will you live upon?'

'I have fifty pounds I've saved, thirty I got for those sheep at Threlkeld, twenty Uncle Will sent me . . .'

'Fifty! Thirty! . . . Nonsense! . . . That will last you a month or so. And then what?'

'I shall find work.'

'Yes, but what will you do? What will you do?' She stamped her cane on the floor. 'You've been trained to nothing.'

'I can find work,' he said doggedly. (He thought of saying: 'Whose fault is it that I've not been trained?' but fortunately kept it back.) 'I'm ready to do anything.'

'And starve in a gutter,' she answered contemptuously. Then her voice softened. 'Now, Adam, this is folly. You *have* work here, your proper work. John loves you. I am sure he would not know what to do without you. You are necessary to all of us here.'

As she softened so did he.

'We can soon test whether I'm necessary or no,' he said, laughing. 'I will go to London for three months, and you shall see how well you do. Why, mother, in a week you will have forgotten all about me!'

She saw then that he meant to go. She bent her head for a moment. She wanted to deal with this quietly, but she had less control of herself now than the other day. Something leapt up within her, crying, 'I want to get out!' and out it came, disclosing itself as a nasty piece of temper that took herself by surprise quite as much as anyone else. She had always had a hasty temper, but now it was as though she had her own and someone else's as well.

She was determined on two things: not to let him go and not to be angry. So she got up and walked to the door; as she passed him she laid her hand for a moment on his shoulder, smiled at him and said:

'Now you must not be naughty, Adam. Some time – later on – you shall go to London. Perhaps I shall come with you,' and left the room. There for once her tactics were altogether wrong. Those words, as it happened, were all that were needed to stiffen him. She was still treating him like a child; she *would* not see that he was a grown man. That just showed how hopeless everything would be if he stayed.

But he must go at once. He could not endure that this relationship with his mother should continue. She would beat him down

if she had time; her ruthlessness had all the old history of their
lives together to harden it.

Very soon, in fact, the battle was renewed. Next day at breakfast alone with John, drinking beer and gobbling beef pie, he told
him his decision.

'John, I've got to go.'

'Got to go?' asked John.

'Yes, to London. I'm wasting my time here. You know that as
well as I do. I've got to be of some use in the world.'

'Well, aren't you being of use here?'

'No, nothing to matter. You see, John, there's a dreadful lot of
injustice everywhere. Look at these women in the factories and
the children in the mines. Look how people are starving. Why,
they say in Whitehaven—'

'Yes, I know. But couldn't you improve things and stay here as
well? And is it your business? I mean—'

'You think I'm a bit of a prig,' said Adam. 'But I don't want to
consider myself at all. I may be a prig or not. I don't care—' He
broke off, laughing. 'Yes, I do care. I don't want to be a prig. But
I find it so difficult to say what I mean. What I *mean* is that I
think that a number of men are feeling that they want to help to
make England a grand place – without all this injustice and
division between the rich and the poor. And I want to stand with
them.'

'And you're on the side of the poor?' asked John.

'Of course I am. I haven't much myself, I'm illegitimate, I'm
nobody. Who should be on the side of the poor if I'm not? But I
don't want to preach, you know. There's none of the parson in
me. I only want that they should have more to eat and better
homes, that young children shouldn't go down the mines and be
in the dark all day—'

'I daresay they like it – being in the mines, I mean.'

'Like it! How can they like it? Would *you* like it?'

'No, but I'm not accustomed to it.'

Adam had been unusually eloquent, so now he was quiet again
although he had not, even now, said what was really in his heart.
John got up, came round to him and put his arm around him.

'I expect you're right,' he said. 'Only what it will be here
without you—'

'You need not disturb yourself,' said a sharp voice in the
doorway. 'Adam is *not* going to London.'

They both looked up, and there was 'Madame' in the doorway,

shaking on her cane with anger. 'No, I will not have it,' she said, her voice quivering. 'You get this notion out of your head, Adam, once and for all. Your duty is here. There's been enough of this nonsense.' And she went.

The two looked at one another.

'By Caesar!' said John, 'I never knew she was there.'

Adam said in a low voice: 'It's no good. She can't stop me. But it's awful fighting her.'

'Yes,' said John. 'No one likes it. That's why she always has her way.'

Meanwhile Judith went about her household duties, and the maids had a dreadful morning of it. She felt as though she were fighting for her very life. If Adam left her, what remained? Oh yes, of course she was fond of Uldale – but to be alone here with John, the stupid neighbours, Walter on the hill . . . All the morning she was closer to weeping than she had been for years. This would not have happened had she done what she should have done – gone to live in Watendlath with Adam. He would have become a farmer and she would have lived with him.

She went up to her room. She stared out at Skiddaw, veiled now by dirty, swollen clouds. What was she to do? How was she to influence him? Behind her anger and indignation was admiration of his obstinacy. She would have behaved once just as he was behaving.

But she beat these thoughts back. No weakening on her part. If she softened she was lost.

So that at dinner in the afternoon she was severe, aloof, the grand lady, the Empress. And Adam, unfortunately, because of his knowledge that he had that forenoon ridden into Keswick and drawn his money from the bank, was not at his best.

If she knew that! But she did not know it. In her heart she was quaking, but as the meal proceeded she became reassured again. She addressed most of her remarks to Mr Rackstraw, who, with his dry, red face and weatherbeaten figure, seemed to promise her that nothing here at least could change. Adam sat there, eating and drinking as though this day were like any other day. So it must be! She had been agitated by absurd alarms.

Once she said: 'The Hunt Ball in Carlisle is to be the twenty-third of October. You and John, Adam, can have a bed at the Witherings'. They will be going for sure.'

No one said anything.

'I have been hearing,' said Rackstraw, 'about this new postal scheme. All our letters to cost us but a penny wherever we send them. We live in modern times.'

She discussed the postal scheme and Lord de Ros' gambling scandal. His manner of cheating at cards had been to have a coughing fit under the table. And there had been the massacre in New Zealand – one hundred and twenty people murdered – but really so far away that one could not visualize it. She was *almost* reassured; as she moved in a manner a little more stately than usual from the room she gave Adam a quick look and thought that she had never before found him so exasperating and never loved him so dearly.

Adam told Rackstraw that same afternoon that he was going. They were in the stables and it was growing dark. A storm of rain was blowing up, and the light in the lantern that Rackstraw carried flickered.

Rackstraw nodded his head.

'I knew you would,' he said.

'I must. I can't help myself,' said Adam.

'No, of course you cannot.'

'Care for my mother, Roger. This will hit her for the moment, but she'll see it's right later.'

'Yes, she will,' said Rackstraw. 'She's a damnably sensible woman, your mother.'

He shook Adam's hand as though he were going that moment.

'Good luck to you.' He fumbled in his deep pocket, pulled out a little book and gave it to him. 'It's the *Iliad*. Grandest book in the world. I always carry it with me. Think of me sometimes.'

'But I'm not going now—' began Adam. Then stopped. He knew suddenly that he was.

By suppertime he had made his plans. He would leave the next day, drive one way or another to Manchester, then take the new railway. The very thought of this railway made his heart beat. Yes, he would certainly be seeing the world.

After supper he went out to the stables, wearing his riding-coat and hat because the storm was so fierce. As soon as he was indoors he heard his mother's voice calling him from upstairs. He went up, his spirits heavy with foreboding. She was sitting in her bedroom by the fire, wrapped in two fine cashmere shawls and looking a very amiable and kindly old lady.

'That's well, Adam,' she said, smiling. 'Come and talk to your old mother.'

No, she was not an old lady. She was as young as Eternity and vigorous. So, in order that he might be entirely honest, he stood by the door.

'I've been vexed all day by your nonsense,' she said. 'Very foolish. Now sit beside me and I'll tell you what I've arranged. You want more to do, my son. That's the trouble. Well, I've thought of that farm at Crossways. I think, with a tightening or two, it can be purchased—'

'No, Mother,' he said. 'It's no use. I'm as resolved as last night. I must go and at once. Tomorrow.'

'And why tomorrow precisely?' she asked him, her voice trembling.

'I cannot wait and have this trouble with you. I cannot endure it. Anyone else—'

She got up. 'Never mind me,' she said. 'Don't be a hypocrite, Adam.'

'I'm no hypocrite,' he answered fiercely. 'I'm your son.'

'You are not my son if you go,' she answered as fiercely as he. 'If you go I disown you.'

'Now this is nonsense,' he fought back. 'Have you no ambition for me? If I'd been another I should have gone to school and then to some business—'

She came nearer to him.

'So you reproach me?'

'No, I do not reproach you. I cannot understand that you who have so much strength of mind can never have had any ambition for me. You—'

She came close to him.

'Take care, Adam, or I'll teach you!'

She was shaking, and that touched him so deeply that his voice grew tender.

'Mother, listen. You *must* listen. You remember that once when we were in London at the Newmarks', after the riot, I was in bed with you. You told me then that if ever you threatened my liberty I was to defy you. You said that this would happen. You urged me then—'

But she had not listened to a single word. She caught hold of him and began to shake him so furiously that she drove him back against the door.

'Take off that hat and coat.'

He was now as angry as she. Anyone looking at them would have seen well enough that they were mother and son.

'No, I will not.'

'Take off that hat and coat.' Her small body had in it an extraordinary vigour.

'No.' He put out his hand to prevent her doing herself a hurt, 'You cannot use me like this. You shall not.'

'Oh, will I not?' Her words came in little passionate sobs. 'When I was a girl – we whipped our – disobedient sons—'

He tore himself away from her.

'Well, then,' she panted, 'if it is so – you shall remain here – and consider it.'

She went out, pulling the door behind her with a bang that echoed all over the house. He heard the key turn in the lock.

'By God! She's locked me in!' he heard a voice that did not seem like his own exclaim aloud. He sat down on the bed, and the room sank back into silence like a pool after a stone has splashed it. He heard the rain beating on the window. He was more angry than he had ever been in his life, and he did not care whether his mother broke her heart or whether, indeed, the whole world blew up. He looked at the window, went over to it, stared out.

Here anyhow was a way out. He could walk to Penrith, get the morning coach ... Thank heaven, he had his money.

He climbed over the sill, felt the rain sweep against his cheek, fumbling, found the water-pipe. It was the same water-pipe that his mother, escaping years ago, had used.

THE CHARTISTS

IT was while watching the return of the Procession from Westminster – the Procession on June 27th, 1838, of the Coronation of Her Gracious Majesty Queen Victoria – that the life of Adam Paris was changed. He had exactly thirty shillings in the world. After arriving in London he had found a job reading to an old blind gentleman in Bayswater, things like Pope's *Homer* and Scott's *Lady of the Lake*. The old gentleman had died, and Adam had found, after some weeks of starving, another job with Fisher and Taylor, publishers of infidel writers like Paine. For a time all was well, then Fisher took a dislike to him and dismissed him. After that he sank to starvation. He had a room in a lodging-house off the Strand, 'Wheeler's'. No one was ever to know how lonely he was and how desperately homesick he was during those months. He wrote to his mother once a month, giving an address, but had no reply. He wrote to no one else; he was too proud. He was sick and hungry for the smell of dry bracken and the tune of running water, for the small bodies of his Herdwick sheep and the little white farms ... And, by the day of the Procession, he was so hungry that he could think of nothing but food. He scarcely saw the Procession. Afterwards he had a picture of coloured fragments – horses tossing their heads, grand splashes of crimson caught and lost again, pennons waving, spurs and bridles jingling and glittering, cries and shouts: 'Here he is! ... That's the Duke! ... That's Marshal Soult! ... Who's that little man? ...' soldiers and again soldiers, backs erect, heads up behind the tossing manes of their chargers, a blare of music, a moment of deafening brass and thunder dying to a distant melody, and the air still save for the clatter of hooves; then a vague roar like a wind in the air, louder and louder, more and more personal, then 'She's here! That's her! ... Oh, how young she looks!' – and, with an odd beating of the heart and mist at the eyes, for a moment his hunger forgotten, he caught the face and figure, tiny in the great gold coach, of a girl so young and unprotected that there was something deeply appealing in the risks that she was taking. Why, she was no more than a baby! She was bowing to them. She smiled. She was gone. 'She's but a child,' Adam murmured, turning away – then thought that, for the first time in his life, he was going to faint. The street and the people were spinning up to him. He lurched sideways and was held in the arms of a tall, broad-shouldered, smiling fellow in a plain, brown beaver hat and a black coat.

'What's up, friend?'

'I'm hungry,' said Adam simply. So the tall man in the brown beaver hat took him home. This man was called Caesar Kraft and he lived with his daughter Margaret in three rooms off the Seven Dials. Kraft and Adam knew, within an hour of their first meeting, that they had that deep emotional affection for one another that men, often the manliest and strongest, sometimes experience. There was a little room on the other side of the passage from the Krafts that Adam hired. The Krafts were Chartists, and within twenty-four hours Adam was a Chartist too. By the spring of 1839, indeed, Adam was a more thorough and convinced Chartist than Caesar Kraft himself.

On the morning following his first night with them he had had

a long and critical conversation with Kraft. He knew afterwards
that this conversation was one of the turning-points of his life. It
came at a time when he was exactly ready for it – growing from
boy into man, ignorant of the world, lonely and longing for
affection. As a child he had loved John Herries, but with that
exception, and of course his devotion to his mother, which was
part of himself, he had revealed his heart to no one. Now he
opened it to Kraft, for Kraft, too, needed a friend. Adam made
no mistake here. Caesar Kraft was the noblest, purest, most
selfless human being he was ever to know.

Their alliance formed, the rest followed.

'Do you think you can write?' Kraft asked him.

'I have no idea,' Adam answered.

'Remain here for a week and study some of these.'

Kraft put in front of him a mass of documents, pamphlets,
letters, appeals, protests, from every part of the country. It was a
very remarkable collection, and Adam devoured the whole of it.

This is no place to go in detail into that documentary evidence.
It can be found in many volumes easy of access, but some things
are worth recording because of the effect that they had upon
Adam's life and outlook.

He knew that children in the mines, descending a shaft six
hundred feet deep, went along a subterranean road three miles in
length, and that at the 'workings' on either side of them the
hewers were employed in a state of complete nudity because of
the great heat. The child, sometimes not more than six years of
age, was employed there to keep the doors or 'traps' shut against
the flow of inflammable air. Here, then, the child would sit in the
dark all day opening and shutting those doors. At first he was
given a candle, but after a while when he was accustomed to the
dark the candle was taken away.

Later the child would be promoted to be a drawer or 'thrut-
cher' and then, clad only in a pair of trousers, a belt round the
waist, a chain attached to the belt at one end and the truck at the
other, the chain passing between his legs, often on all-fours because of the lowness of the gallery, he would, hour after hour, act
his part as beast of burden. The 'thrutchers' would push the
truck along with their heads and, although they were protected
with a cap, were soon bald. The women 'thrutchers' wore
nothing but a pair of short trousers.

He learnt that a hedger in the country would receive seven-
pence a day for six days of the week to find him clothes, food

and lodging. He learnt that the soldiers in barracks had for urinal
wooden tubs, and in those same tubs they must afterwards
wash.

He learnt that in the Navy the sailors lived entirely on salt
beef, salt pork and maggoty biscuit, and that they would bet with
one another as to which piece of biscuit would, unaided, crawl
across a table faster than another. He learnt that a labourer lived
almost entirely on tea (often made of crusts or twigs) and potatoes. For months together he would not taste meat. A young
man had been asked how he lived on half a crown a week. He
replied that he did not live on it. 'I poach,' he said, 'for it is better
to be hanged than to starve to death.'

Children did not go home to dinner because there was none. A
man, working in a factory, told this story: 'Up at five in the
morning to get to the factory, work till eight, half an hour for
breakfast, work till noon, dinner an hour, then work till four,
half an hour for tea, then work till nine. The master's strap, six
feet long, was kept at his right hand, two cuts at a stroke, and
every day some of it.'

The injuries of the bread-tax were beginning to be poignantly
felt. Bread was made from barley-meal. Families lived for days
on swede turnips, roasted, baked and boiled. A man had a wife
and six children to keep when flour was twelve shillings a bushel.
To have a red herring, to be shared by several, was a great treat.
If a father obtained a penny white loaf, his children would
trudge miles to meet him that they might see it the sooner. A man
would, in his hunger, eat the pig-pease and horse-beans that he
was threshing. The children would steal the cabbage-stalks and
swedes from the fields. Some families would go early out and eat
the snails. Bread was soon to be at one-and-sixpence the loaf.

So it was in factory, mine and field, in small village and large
town.

Adam's nature, the more that it was so restrained, was deeply
stirred by suffering, but hitherto the suffering that he had known
had belonged to separate incidents and individual persons. Now
it seemed to him that the whole country was spread with a cloud.
It was hard to believe that there was anyone who was aware and
yet would do nothing about it. But it was so; not only were there
thousands who did not stir a finger, but he soon came to realize
that everyone who had any power in the country was against any
change. This girl who was Queen – he heard of nothing but her
rides in the Park with Melbourne, that she danced in her Palace

until two of the morning, that at her dinner parties the plates were of gold and the cutlery of silver.

It was good for him that he fell under the influence of such people as the Krafts or he might have become a violent agitator like Henry Lunt, Kraft's friend. But Caesar and Margaret had spent their lives among these questions. Their natures were sweet and tolerant although they were as determined in the Cause as any fanatic, and it may be said that they saved Adam at this time.

One thing, however, did happen to him, and that was a suspicion of his own family. He thought of Walter and Uhland at Ireby, of Sylvia and her gay parties, of Will and his money, of James and his greedy stomach, of the Newmarks and (as it appeared to him now) their hypocrisy, of the Rockages and their snobbery, even – in his new bitterness – of Dorothy and John. Uldale with its farm, its ordered garden and orchard, its stables with the fat horses, the lawn gleaming so smoothly under the morning sun – how could they suffer it all so easily when men, their stomachs empty, bled from the master's strap, when children of six years old sat naked hour after hour, day after day, in the dark, when women and children went into the fields and grubbed for cabbage-stalks, when in the streets outside his window the stench was so terrible that you fainted under it and fever was in every house?

He began to have an obsession about the Herries. He saw them with their horse-faces bending forward with malicious pleasure to watch the sufferings of the crawling figures beneath them, Walter guzzling, Will seated on his money-bags, Sylvia with her poodle dancing across the shining floor of her boudoir. He thanked God that he was illegitimate. He was another Herries rebel – the bull that 'Rogue' Herries saw baited, Reuben's bear and the boy hanged of his mother's youth, the falling Bastille with which Francis killed his father – these were unknown to Adam, but he was forging a new link in that strong chain of protest.

And then in the middle of this he received a letter from his mother, the first that he had had since he had left Uldale.

MY DEAR ADAM – You have been very good in writing to me with such regularity. Do not think that I have not appreciated your letters but I was *determined* that I would not *weakly* submit to your self-will and *obstinacy*. Nevertheless, for a long

time now I have known that you were right to do as you did
and I was too *obstinate* myself to confess to my mistake. You
have doubtless heard from Mr Rackstraw who tells me that he
has written to you and you have all the *news* but now that I
have broken the *ice* I must further tell you that I am *longing* to
see you again and that there is no day since your departure that
I have not been of the same *mind*. I am growing an old woman
now, Adam. I am sixty-five years of age although I must say I
am extremely *vigorous* and save for a stiffness in my right arm
which only comes out in damp weather I am in excellent
health. All are well here. John has bought two more cows. We
have been very *gay* these last weeks and Dorothy with her boy
and little girl has been staying this fortnight with us. Veronica
(a most *foolish* name in my opinion) is a very *engaging* baby
and Timothy a good child when *managed*. Dorothy has much
common-sense but is anxious to have the command, even here
at Uldale, which of course, as you can suppose, I do not *allow*.
John is not so cheerful as I would wish. He had an encounter
with Peach, Walter's man, last week up at Bogshaw and they
came I fancy to some hot words. I have of course seen nothing
of the people at Ireby but I hear that Walter refuses to have
Elizabeth's name mentioned since her disappearance, of which
of course you've heard. Poor child! No one seems to *care* what
has happened to her. It would not have been so if Agnes were
still living.

I will not write more now because you are a *disobedient* son
and do not deserve a long letter but I am nevertheless (*longing*
to see you soon) – Your loving mother,

                                        JUDITH PARIS.

Adam's first impulse after reading this letter was to go at once
North, by coach, railway, or any other means that offered. This
was no new impulse. Scarcely a day of the last six months that he
had not known it, but he had always driven it back as a weakness
that he must not feel. But now with the letter in his hands his
love for his mother was for a while overwhelming. Behind the
words he saw her pride, her obstinacy, her sweetness, her
humour, her gaiety, her tenderness. It was as though she were
with him in the room. He realized, once again, that they were
part of one another, bone of bone and flesh of flesh. But for that
very reason he would not leave the work to which he had set his
hand. If he returned to her even for a day her influence over him

would be so strong that she might persuade him to remain with her. He *must* be himself, develop his own life, create his own pattern. In the end that is what she would wish him to do.

So he sat down and wrote her the most loving letter he had ever penned and then turned to his work again.

They had soon discovered that he could write. He was, in fact, just what they needed, for he was honest, indignant and accurate. His youth gave his words freshness and his sincerity prevented any fustian or melodrama.

The fanatics – one of the wildest was this man called Henry Lunt – complained that he was not strong enough. They soon discovered that he was of no use at all as a speaker. He had no power over words, and the sight of an audience was appalling to him.

He went on one occasion with a number of delegates from London to Manchester and they put him on the platform. It was one of the most horrible experiences of his life. He stood there, his brown healthy cheeks pale, fumbling his hair with his hand, moving his thick legs as though he would kick the place down. He stammered, stopped, stammered again, strung some sentences together and sat down, a lamentable failure.

When he came back to London he told Margaret about it.

'I felt as though they stripped my clothes off my back.'

'Yes,' she said, 'they say it was the worst speech ever made in Manchester.'

'They'll never ask me to do it again – that's one good thing.'

'But you can write about the bread-tax and the shilling loaf and the fever here in Seven Dials,' she answered, 'better than anyone we've had since Tom Colman.'

She was standing near to him, and he put out his hand, resting it on her shoulder. She did not move away.

'Margaret, how old are you?' he asked her.

'Let me see. I was born in February 1820. This is March 1839. I am nineteen.'

'You are not like a girl,' he said, his hand holding her arm more strongly. 'You are a woman.'

'I have been a woman ever since mother died. That night when she went and father was in my arms I thought he would die too. I never knew two people love one another as he and mother did. I grew up that night.'

'It was a happy thing for me that afternoon when Caesar spoke to me.'

'It was a happy thing for us too,' she answered.

That night in bed he knew that he loved Margaret. He had loved her, he perceived, since the first moment that he saw her. She was the first woman he had ever cared for, and this excitement and tenderness was quite new to hm. He lay there thinking of her, of her unselfishness, honesty and integrity. But he realized that he knew nothing about her feeling for himself. She was as quiet as he was; he had never seen her show any interest in men, but they were not very much together. She was out at her dressmaking all day and was often kept to very late hours. She might have a lover somewhere. There might be another side to her, a side that she never showed at home. He was extremely ignorant about women. Although he was approaching twenty-four years of age he had never kissed any woman save his mother, Jennifer and Dorothy. With the exception of his mother his deepest feelings of affection and loyalty had been roused by men – John, Rackstraw, Caesar Kraft. So this feeling for Margaret was something quite new, and that night, as he lay awake, listening to the drunken shouts in the street below, it grew and grew until he felt that he had Margaret in his arms. That seemed to him the happiest wonder, something that awed him with its mingling of worship and desire; lost in this new experience he fell asleep.

He was as cautious and careful in this as in everything else. His shyness made him shrink from any rebuff. He had nothing to offer her, no position, no prospects. And here for the first time his illegitimacy troubled him. Kraft perhaps would not want his daughter to marry a bastard. He was proud of his family, talked of his German grandfather as though he had been the grandest man in Germany. But when that seed of love is sown in a nature like Adam's nothing can hinder it.

But this new desire made life difficult for him. He was pulled in two quite opposite directions: his love for Margaret as the days went by filled itself increasingly with light and colour like a glass ball that becomes with every hour more radiant. But his discontent with the sickness and starvation all round him was something fierce and hostile, dark, jagged like lightning.

He remembered that once at home when he was on his favourite place at the bottom of Cat Bells, in Manesty, by the Lake a wind had come up, the sky had been darkened with hot saffron-edged clouds. All in a moment the breeze had lifted, and the Lake that had been placidly blue was edged with little frothy white waves. The whole expanse of water was mulberry-coloured and the islands were black-green, the tint of leaves turned backwards by the wind. Behind this angry scene Skiddaw and Blencathra and the fields below them rose drenched in light and sun – a wall of sun flashing and sparkling. As the Lake was dyed ever deeper and deeper with its mulberry stain and the little waves jumped with tongues of a dead white, the wall of light seemed to exult in its own glory: it shouted its strength aloud. Then, as a shutter closes, a hand swept wiping out all colour. Hills and lake together were dun.

He had never forgotten this scene. He had thought of it often in his first homesick days in London; now his experience seemed to be thus mixed – an exulting wall of light, a tossing discontented floor of stain. For the first time he was touching forces very much stronger and deeper than himself.

Then one of the great evenings of his life came. He went with Caesar Kraft and Margaret to a Chartist meeting in Seven Dials. Lunt and another, Philip Pider, were with them. Lunt was worked up to more than his customary indignation because a family living in the cellar of his building had been sick of the fever: two of them, an old man and a child, had died, and their bodies had been left there in the cellar two days and a night before anyone attended them. Adam noticed that behind his indignation was a kind of fierce joy because he had been given some more evidence to use in his damning account against all authority. He described with angry gusto the filthy state of that cellar, the pools of moisture, the loathsome stench, the rats.

He was this night like an animal himself, his strong dark hairy body moving like an animal's, his words, growls, mutters, little snatches of ferocity. The surroundings that evening were strange and fantastic. There had been a thick yellow fog all day, but now it had thinned, hanging in discontented wisps about the streets and buildings. The lamps in the street were damp and mildewed with moisture; the shops were for the most part closed, but some were yet open and you could see, in the candlelight, figures like shapes in the fire cross-legged over a boot or shoe, arms raised to fetch down some garment, a butcher standing with blood on his apron above slabs of red meat and dark amber-coloured entrails. Everyone moved through the wispy fog as though in secret, and there was that faint scent of sulphur in the air that a thick London fog leaves behind it.

For Adam that walk to the hall where the meeting was to be held was one of his most blissful moments. Margaret's hand was through his arm; he could feel the soft swell of her breast against his sleeve, she was so close to him. She spoke in a voice that was quiet and happy. He knew that she was happy, he could feel it in every word that she spoke. Once and again he could catch under her bonnet the gleam of her eyes, the shadow of her cheek above her dark green shawl. He was terribly anxious not to cheat himself (all this experience was so new to him), but he began to believe that his company must have something to do with her happiness – and then quite suddenly she told him that it was so.

'You know, Adam, since you came to us father and I have been happier than we used to be.'

His heart hammered with delight. He thought that she must feel its beatings against her arm. And as always when he was deeply moved, he could say nothing.

'Um—' he muttered.

'Are you not glad?'

'Of course, I am glad – if it's true, Margaret.'

'But, of course, it's true. Why should I say it if it was not? Father was often very lonely before you came. He can be passionate in his affections, and I think he loves you more than he ever loved anyone except mother.'

'And yourself?'

'Oh, myself – I am always there, you know. He has become accustomed to me.'

He plucked up his courage, although his tongue was dry in his throat.

'And some day you will marry, Margaret?'

'Yes,' she answered quietly. 'I hope so – some day.'

'Perhaps there is someone – already—'

'Oh, I don't know,' she answered, laughing. 'There is Mr Hooper – a friend of Madame's at the shop . . .'

'Oh, is there?' he said, his heart dropping to a dreadful deadness.

'I think he likes me,' she went on quietly. 'He wears two waistcoats and I am certain he has a corset. He speaks like this: "Oh, Miss Kraft . . . I'm sure . . . most exquisite . . . Pray, turn that I may see the back. I'm quite in raptures!" ' She imitated him and burst out laughing. '*I* like him, but I fear father would not. But he has a fine little villa in Islington, and he sings to his own accompaniment on the pianoforte.'

He supposed that she was teasing him, but he could not be sure. Now they had arrived at the hall, and the other world of fire and tumult drove down upon them.

The hall was a large one, and when they entered they found it packed with people. The air was thick with the warm smell of human bodies, the odour from the oil lamps; figures were indistinct – here a face, there an arm, a body flung forward – everywhere an almost ecstatic excitement and attention. Kraft, Lunt and Pider went to sit on the platform, Adam and Margaret were pressed into the wall near the door. Adam had been to many meetings by now, but thought that he had never seen such eye-strained faces, men and women and some children, one baby held aloft and waving its chubby fists in the air.

It had just begun when they entered. The Chairman, a round tubby man with thick grey side-whiskers, was speaking. The atmosphere was at present quiet and controlled. He said something about the conditions of the time, the oppression of the authorities, the iniquities of the Bread Tax, the Six Points of the new Charter. He sat down, and a long thin fellow with a straggly beard got up. He had a rather weak, piping voice and no very impressive manner: he began quietly, so there were voices from the hall; 'Speak up! We can't hear!' and a rough growl from someone: 'Sit down, damn ye, if yer can't talk.'

That last seemed to rouse him, for he raised his rather pale, watery eyes and stared down into the hall: 'If you listen you'll 'ear all right,' he said at last. 'I ain't 'ad food in my belly for the last six months, what yer can call food.' They listened. He had control over them. He had come, he said, to tell them what it was like now to work on the land. 'We're slaves to the farmer's body, slaves like they were in the old Roman times. For ten years I served Farmer Wellin in my county – aye, you don't know 'is name likely, but one name does as well as another. Then one fine day he tells me he ain't no more work for me nor my two boys – so then I goes here, I goes there. No work. Then I goes to Manchester, starves there a bit, comes 'ome again, put in the Union, turned out after a day or two, lays abed a bit, gets a day's work, then on board-day goes to them again, gets a day's work, starves a bit, lays abed a bit, goes searching for work again, eats stuff they've given the pigs because I'm that 'ungry. My boys, as good lads as ever you see, 'anging around gets into bad ways, one of 'em roots up a turnip or two and gets gaoled. 'Is mother breaks 'er 'eart and dies of weakness. That's why I'm not speaking so 'earty, begging your pardon, friends.

'I say a poor man's a slave. He can't leave his own parish – for why? – because in a foreign parish they've plenty of their own to give work to. And what are our masters doing? They're wasting

of the land, that's what I say they're doing. Give me an acre of
land and I'll live well and decent on it *and* give my boys a proper
life. I was out of work last spring from Christmas to barley-
sowing. I goes to the farmer and asks for a scrap of land to grow
potatoes on. "Oh no, you don't," says he. "Give you potatoes and
you'll want straw and a pig and I don't know what all. And one
day, maybe, I'll be wanting you to work for myself," he says. "Oh
yes," he says, "prices be so low I must lower your wages," he
says, but when prices goes up does he raise the wages again? Not
if he knows of it. What I say is, if the loaf's cheap we're ruined,
but if the loaf's dear we're starved. For myself I'm ready enough
to die, but my boys . . .'

His piping voice suddenly stopped. He wiped his eyes with the
back of his hand. Then he went on:

'The farmers say they can't live without they make four rents –
one for stock, one for rent, one for labour, one for theirselves.
Times is bad and they can't make their four rents. Well, does the
landlord as does nothing give up his rent? Of course not. Then
corn falls two pound a load and worse – farmer's forty shilling
out o' pocket on every load of wheat – eight shilling on every acre
of his land on a four-course shift. Where's that to come from? He
can't stint the landlord so he stints the labourer. Tell the landlord,
friends, what you think of him and do justice to your fellow-
men.'

He stopped, his voice ending in a funny little whistle, and he
sat down, his legs almost giving way beneath him. The majority
of the men and women in the hall had for the most part never
seen a green field in their lives – the facts and figures meant
nothing to them – but the sincerity and urgency of his starved
and feeble body stirred and moved them. You could feel it run
through the hall like a message. There was a murmur, a restlessness, voices cried out. They were all brothers together, in field
and factory, street and mine. Adam could see the faces around
him change from a vague listening absorption to a personal
human activity. A little man like a terrier leaped to his feet. He
was plainly a practised orator. He brought the personal case of
the labourer into the more general cause of them all. A woman
broke out from the centre of the hall:

'They would part me from my children!' she cried in a shrill,
agonized wail. 'How did I leave them this morning? Crying for
their breakfasts. I've had no bread to give them for the last month
and more. I've no bread. I've no fire. How can I have with one

shilling and sixpence a hundred for coals? If I snatch a bit of wood from a hedge they'll gaol me. It's the women and children you should be thinking on! Oh, if I was a man I know what I'd be doing! I know what I'd be doing!'

Another woman, on that, cried out, waving an arm hysterically: 'Ax the Queen. Go and ax the Queen to come and see for herself. She's got a heart same as us ...' And a man near her roared out: 'Why, the Queen – she's all locked up. They've got the dragoons guarding her. Do you think the Queen wants to be frightened with the like of we? She's got Melbourne, she has. What is it to him or her if poor labourers suffer and our women are stripped naked in the mines and bread's one-and-sixpence the loaf? Ax the Queen! Aye, go and ax her and see what her soldiers do to you!'

A confused babel of voices broke out. You could feel that the temperature of men's blood was rising as though with every word they moved closer together and closer and closer, so that at last they seemed to be one man, a man with eyes red and burning, a mouth hard set, cheeks hollow with hunger – a man with his hand clenched to strike.

Someone leaped up and cried shrilly: 'Let us take what is ours! Let us take what is ours! Let us take what is ours!'

Anything might have happened then. Adam, not knowing that he did it, put his arm around Margaret and drew her nearer to protect her; they were pressed back against the wall. No one thought of his or her neighbour; a stout woman in an orange shawl had her hand, without knowing it, on Adam's arm, and in a kind of strangled sob was saying over and over: 'Aye – it's the People's right – it's the People's right – it's the People's right ...'

Adam knew that in another moment there would be that strong, swaying movement beneath their feet as though the floor were stirring under them, and that then all would be swept together in some mob-hysteria beyond control.

But it did not come. Instead the rotund little Chairman in some way made himself heard. He said that Mr Kraft would speak to them and, as Caesar rose to his feet, quiet came over everyone again. How proud Adam was of him at that moment! His square shoulders were set like those of a man carrying a banner; his eyes spoke to some distance far beyond the hall and its occupants; his voice, rich, warm, sincere, had no arrogance in it and no self-seeking.

'I do not believe in disorder,' he said. 'Neither now nor at any time. I know that our cause is just, but I find it so just that it must have victory – but victory by law and not by riot. Patience—'

At the word 'Patience' someone shouted out: 'We have been patient long enough!'

Caesar went on: 'We have not been patient long enough. We can never be patient long enough so long as we are moving. And we *are* moving! We have our Six Points of our Charter, and they are so right and so just that all the world will yield to them. We are working for a prize greater and more lasting than our immediate troubles. We are working for our children and our children's children. What do we gain by fire and murder? We place ourselves in the same case as our oppressors. We must believe in justice, for there *is* justice in the world. Men may be unjust, but behind them moves something stronger, finer and wiser than man.'

He went on then to tell them what the heads of the movement were doing, showed them their plans in detail, and was so comprehensive, clear and wise that soon the hall was as quiet as a vestry, and you could hear the rumble of the carts on the cobbles outside. All then might have moved peacefully to its close, but as soon as Kraft, to a hubbub of applause and clapping of hands, had sat down, Lunt sprang to his feet. He stood swaying on his short, strong legs, his body a little forward, his dark face with its shock of black hair alive with indignation and an almost mad impetuosity.

'I am Caesar Kraft's friend!' he called out. 'I *have* been and shall be! But I say that his advice to you is the advice of a dreamer! Wait, he says! Patience, he says! Yes, we are patient, and meanwhile what happens! Our old men and children, our wives and daughters, die in cellars swimming in filth, as I have seen two dead today; our women starve naked in the fields grubbing roots that pigs would refuse. Our men are beaten by their masters until their backs drop blood. We starve. We starve. Half the men in this room are starving now! And the Government says – let them starve! The less work for us, the Government says. Let them eat one another, the Government says, if they're hungry. Let them lie closer to one another if they're cold! Why should they interfere between slave and slave?'

He began to pace the platform, his face turned to them, his body shaking with his vehemence.

'Why do we give opium to our little children? So that they may forget their hunger! We entreat the Government to have mercy on us, we send it petitions, we show it our naked backs and our fever-dying comrades. "Oh yes," they say, and send us an answer: "Sorry to say that it is altogether out of the power of Her Majesty . . ." Her Majesty! And she feeding off gold plate and riding in the Park of a morning! What does she know or care? Patience, Caesar Kraft tells you, but *I* tell you that we have had enough of patience, that they won't listen although we call, that they laugh at our tears. The Towns must win the Charter for England – men and women like yourselves – and not by patience, not by sitting down and waiting while we starve, but by rising and showing our power, by driving fear into their souls, by putting those same dragoons out of the way that we may meet the Queen face to face and say to her: "Here are your people! You haven't seen them before, but take a good look at them – see their backs how they bleed, how their stomachs are empty, their children crying for food—" '

He was interrupted by a roar of voices. 'Aye! Aye! . . . We'll go now. We'll go to the Queen . . . We've been patient enough! To the Palace! To the Palace!'

Like a wind through trees the roomful swayed, then broke. Men shouted, women called. The din was fearful, threatening, with that note in it that no individual man can recognize as his own and, after catastrophe, denies as his own.

They broke and rushed to the doors, Adam holding Margaret, who, however, was almost as strong as he.

The noisy, shouting mob tumbled into the street to be met with a fog as thick as a wall of suet. It was comic, that sudden dropping of voices, that check on the rush and impulse as though they had all found themselves on the edge of a precipice with the sea booming below them. The street was quiet and chill; the fog blew through the air in thick, yellow folds, laying its clammy touch on every mouth. Figures shot up out of the dark, some of them with flares, flamed and vanished. The crowd from the hall passed like smoke into smoke.

Adam laughed. He put his hand through her arm and they walked forward.

'Well – that is the end of *that* rioting. We must go forward, trust our luck. We will reach a clearer patch soon.' The fog was the one thing in all the world that could give him courage to speak, for they were close together, but in darkness.

So, when they had gone only a little way, he said outright:

'Margaret, I love you. Will you marry me?'

'Yes,' she said.

He stopped where he was, put his arms round her and kissed her. She did not move so he did not either. They seemed in a trance, protected by the fog, her lips on his, his arms tightly round her. At last when, very slowly, they moved on again he said:

'I must tell you, Margaret, that I have no money, no home, nothing.'

'Yes,' she said. 'Your home is with us.'

'And I have a mother whom I love more dearly than anyone but you.'

She held his hand more tightly.

'I have no father, as you know. I have no family. I am illegitimate.'

She laughed.

'You belong all the more to me for that,' she said.

Then a long while afterwards, when the fog in front of them was clearing, she said, sighing:

'Oh, I did hope, Adam, that you loved me, for I loved you from the first moment.'

HISTORY OF ELIZABETH

ADAM would have been greatly surprised had he realized that not far from where he was standing that June day in 1838 Uhland and Elizabeth had also witnessed the return of the Procession from Westminster Abbey. Will had invited them to London for the Coronation and they had accepted his invitation.

'Do you wish to go?' Walter had asked them. He also had been invited, but an affair upon which he was just then engaged (a highly exciting amorous affair with a lady who lived near Cockermouth) prevented his acceptance. Moreover, he did not wish to go; he found, if he were honest, his father a dull dog and his mother a quite unspeakable bore. Yet in his own way he loved them, wrote to his mother every month and sent his father presents of game.

When Elizabeth heard of the invitation she waited breathlessly to know whether she would be allowed to accept it. It was upon just such an invitation that she had been counting, for she was determined to escape from her father, from Ireby, from her brother, and, if possible, never return.

She was now a beautiful girl, twenty-three years of age. Her mother had died in the autumn of 1835, and since then she had not known one moment's happiness.

When, so long ago, she and John had agreed to separate and not to see one another again she had been but a child. She had forced the separation upon John because she had been certain that marriage with her would be for him a disaster. She was perhaps wrong there. Had they at that time run away and married, the whole course of their lives might have been altered to happiness, but how could he run away when he was responsible for everything at Uldale? Since then his sister had married Bellairs, but now there was something stronger than any practical reason that drove Elizabeth.

She believed – and had more reason for her belief than anyone outside the house at Ireby could know – that Uhland would kill John if she married him. Wherever they went Uhland would find them out. She had a terror of her father and brother that went far beyond actual day-by-day fact.

Uhland's hatred of John became fanatical after he learnt that Elizabeth cared for him. It became so fanatical that he did nothing about it, as though he knew that he had only to bide his time, as though he knew that there was no need for him to do anything yet because John at Uldale was well aware of it; it was as though he could see inside John's heart and feel the fear and apprehension growing there. It was as though he felt that if he did *yet* anything positive in word or deed it would hinder the full flavour of his act when the real time for it arrived.

There the two of them were, Uhland at Ireby and John at Uldale, very near together, and, like a spell in witchcraft, the power of the one over the other, although they never met, always increased.

And in the same way, on the other side of the account, Elizabeth's love for John never lessened, but increased.

She went about, saw many people in the County, made friends, led outwardly a quiet normal life; she tried with all her force (and she had much strength of character) to kill her love for John. She seldom saw him in public, for people, knowing well the old feud, took care that the two households did not meet. Sometimes

in the Keswick street, at a hunt, at a public ball, they would catch
sight of one another and turn away. John, on his side, thought
that he was only waiting until Elizabeth was old enough. He
knew that she was beautiful and rich and should make a fine
marriage. If she married him, when her father and brother hated
him so, it meant exile for her and, perhaps, disgrace. But when
she was of age she had only to make him a sign and he would act.
Nevertheless, although he was no coward in any other way, the
thought of Uhland made him sick. Often when he was busy
about the house or the farm or riding or paying a visit some
dreaminess would overtake him, it would seem to him as though
with one step, by unlocking some door he would pass into another
world infinitely more beautiful than this one. He had dreamt once
as a child of a marvellous white horse plunging through an icy
tarn and climbing, his mane flowing, the steep mountainside. He
had never forgotten the dream although it had never returned. If
he could ride that horse he would spring forward into regions of
splendour and eternal life! But again and again when such
images came to him, asleep at night, walking the fells, sitting half
awake by the fire, he seemed to hear a step behind him and would
start up, expecting to see the cold malicious face of Uhland
watching him.

So there they were, the three of them, in this summer of 1838.
Again and again afterwards Elizabeth would look back to this
time at Ireby and ask herself whether she did anything that
fostered later events. But she could not see that she was responsible. She held on during that time to the principles, first that her
father's neglect of her and his scandalous behaviour should not
touch her, secondly that Uhland's taunts should not touch her,
thirdly that her love of John should not touch her. It was the last
of the three that at length drove her to flight. She *could* not, she
could not be so near to him and not see him. Her father's behaviour she was by now accustomed to; Uhland's taunts she
could endure, but they were ingenious. He would test her suddenly, unexpectedly. He would say: 'I hear young Herries has
made a fool of himself over that farm ...' 'They are saying that
John Herries has put a girl at Jocelyn's by Troutbeck in the
family way. He can't leave farm girls alone. He has a low taste,'
or 'They say that Herries goes to Cockermouth and gambles
night after night – gambling all the estate away, poor fool ...
Hard on old Madame.' All lies of course! Walter Herries would
chuckle and shake his shoulders (he was growing immense now

although still handsome in a florid three-chin fashion). But Elizabeth would not stir. She had all the Herries pride. She would look at Uhland and smile very faintly, and he would look gravely back at her. There would be at that moment a strange subconscious alliance between them.

But by the summer of this year, 1838, she had reached the limit of all her endurance. How she hated the Fortress no words of hers could express. Even to the outside unprejudiced person it was not a happy house as Westaways had been. Westaways had been created by an artist, and it was a thousand pities that in the autumn of 1836 it was pulled down by the purchasers of the land; they had a plan for building an Almshouse there but this never came to anything. All the eighteenth-century colour and glitter, all the ambitions of Pomfret and Jannice, the childish hopes of Raiseley and Judith and Anabel, the early ambitions of Walter – all gone at the flourish of a hand, a little cloud of dust rising slowly over the tumbling brick! And the Fortress was not built by an artist! It was intended to stand for Herries independence, strength and superiority. Good English material power. Most certainly it looked strong enough with its battlements and towers, its broad high rooms, its walls and garden-paths and fountain. But it was never gay, never light-hearted, never alive! Even Walter felt this. He entertained there lavishly, had dinners and hunting-parties, dances and drinking-bouts and, after Agnes' death, made it open house for all the squires of the County. But it refused to come alive! Half the rooms 'died on him', do what he would. He complained that there was not sufficient feminine society in it. Elizabeth entertained and she was a lovely hostess, quiet, dignified, kindly. Everyone liked her, but everyone said that the place was sad. They whispered that Walter beat her when he was in a drunken temper. He did not beat her: he never ill-treated her: he gave her everything that she asked. He simply did not consider her. A Mrs Fergus, a genial stout widow, was housekeeper there during these years. She was common, voluble, gossipy, a good manager. She liked Elizabeth and tried to win her trust. But she did not. She confided to everybody that something was the matter in that house. It was as though a ghost were in every room in spite of the drinking-parties and dinners.

It may have been that Uhland was the ghost. He had certainly grown into a very severe, silent young man. Friendship with Adam might have saved Uhland at this time. He showed from a conversation that he had with Elizabeth in London that he was as lonely as she. Adam was certainly the only human being in the world to whom he would have disclosed himself. There was no doubt but that during those years from 1832 to 1838 he was as unhappy as Elizabeth was. It may be that at the end of it all he despised and hated himself quite as much as he despised and hated John Herries. No one will ever know.

Walter meanwhile, being really a foolish soul with very little understanding of other human beings, continued to persuade himself that Uhland adored him, adored the Fortress, adored the fine fortune that Walter preserved for him (already not quite so fine as it had once been: the Fortress like a heavy dull grey monster swallowed greedily all that was offered it). His love for Uhland was pathetic. He was like a big lumbering elephant cherishing a morose young wolf.

And that was how things were when Elizabeth and Uhland went to London.

When they arrived, late one evening, in Hill Street, where was Will's present town house, Uhland was in a monstrous temper because of the bad time that they had had in the coach. They had booked for the inside, of course, but there had been an asthmatic gentleman with a cough so tiresome, and an old lady with so many small packages that she was for ever undoing to see whether the contents were safe, that Uhland had sought the roof. There were not many passengers, and with extra money he had secured the box-seat, and there wrapped in the leather-covered rug might have been fairly comfortable, but then a storm had come on and the rain had driven down his neck, his overcoat was soaked, and the coachman was for ever thrusting his rein-elbow into his (Uhland's) ribs. The day following had not been much better, for the food at the inns was atrocious, and the manners of everyone appalling. Why had they not tried the new railway? It was so erratic. You never knew where it began and where it left off. Worst of all, their hackney cab, when at last they got into it, collided with a dray, and they were in perilous chance of immediate death.

So they arrived at Hill Street and discovered that a grand party was in progress. A tall gorgeously dressed footman hurried them up the stairs as though they were very criminal indeed. Everywhere were flowers; there was the distant music of a band and the crackle of many voices. Elizabeth had not been in her large cold room five minutes before a maid knocked, came in, and asked her whether she should unpack for her.

'Her ladyship is unfortunately most unwell. She has been confined to her bed for several weeks. She hopes to see you, Miss, in the morning.'

Was she supposed to come down to the party, Elizabeth wondered. Would she get anything to eat? She was inordinately hungry. The maid, who looked a nice girl, Elizabeth thought, was on her knees unpacking.

'Would you tell me your name?' Elizabeth asked.

'Ellen,' said the girl.

Elizabeth shivered. *How* hungry she was! And then, miracle of miracles, the door burst open, and in came Sylvia Herries looking radiant and lovely in pink tulle and carrying a tray!

'Oh, my dearest Elizabeth!'

'Dear Sylvia!'

'But of course I knew that you would be *starving*, and Frederick is bringing a warming-pan. You can place it under those cushions and sit on it. How are you feeling, my sweetest Elizabeth? But of course you must be *dead*! But how lovely you are looking! A little thin ... Was the journey quite, quite dreadful? Ah, here is Frederick! There, Frederick – place it beneath those cushions ... Oh, dear little Elizabeth! I am *ravished* to see you, and Cousin Will is giving the grandest party. Mr Macaulay is here and Lady Brownlow and Lady Euston and the Bishop of Oxford and *ever* so many more, and James' wife is doing the honours. You never saw anything so amazingly odd. She's wearing a turban like a pastry-cook's shop! But there's no one so lovely as you are, so you must hurry, my dearest, and eat this chicken and drink this champagne and wear your *loveliest* costume ... Now sit on the warming-pan, dearest, *quite* still for five minutes. That will warm the under part of you in any case. There's the most enravishing band and I've danced five waltzes already ...'

So Elizabeth sat on the warming-pan and then with the assistance of Ellen and Sylvia put on her dress of white organdie with a rose at her girdle, which, although it *had* been made by little Miss Trent in Keswick, suited her exactly.

When she came into the big room, blazing with lights, swimming in music, a kind of exultation seized her. How wonderful to have escaped from that cold, grey Fortress with the heavy grey clouds hanging over it, the stern dark landscape hemming it in, to this scene of splendour and magnificence! Ah! If only John were here! But one day he would be! They would be here together! She deserved some life and some fun, surely.

Will came up to her and was very kind. He was of course stiff and pompous a little, but he meant well and this was a big occasion for him. He led her up to Lady Euston who, in satin, a green turban and splendid diamonds, was the most terrifying lady she had ever seen.

'Well, my dear, and so you have come for the Coronation?'

'Yes, ma'am.'

'Let us trust that Providence will favour us with good weather. It is very cold for the summer.'

'Yes, indeed, ma'am.'

'This is your first visit to London?'

'Yes, ma'am.'

'Your cousin must bring you to Almack's, and you must visit the Opera. How do you do, Sir Henry? I hear that Mr Croker has written the most offensive article about Soult in the *Quarterly* . . .'

Soon she was dancing, once with Garth, once with Amery, once with Roger, Carey Rockage's son. Then with a gentleman whose dress-coat was so extremely waisted that she was afraid lest he should break in two at any moment. He wanted, very solemnly, to tell her about the Park: 'Until recently the Park has been most sombre and I assure you most unsafe for *anyone* after nightfall. However, lamps with gas have now been introduced and throw a noontide splendour. They combine in fact ornament with utility, and vice has been banished from her wonted haunts . . .' She supposed that he had something to do with the Parks, he seemed so very serious about it.

Then Garth introduced her to a stout rather plethoric young man, a Mr Temple, she understood. She had not waltzed with him once around the room before she realized that he was greatly charmed with her. He told her so; he led her away to a corner behind a mass of begonias and, breathing hard to recover his wind, said in a sort of wondering whisper that she was, upon his life, the most lovely girl that he had ever seen. He begged her, he implored her, not to take offence. The admission had been, to his own amazement, compelled upon him. She could not take offence. There was nothing offensive about him; he was like a baby in his tight clothes, with a large diamond in his shirt and his hair excessively pomaded. She wanted to laugh and, when he left her for a moment to bring her some champagne, she did laugh. She could not help it. She was happy. She was free. She would never go back to Ireby again, and John would come to her.

'You have made a conquest, my dear cousin,' said Garth, a little later.

'A conquest?' she asked.

'Edward Temple. He is the richest young man in London.'

In the course of the next week or so Elizabeth discovered a number of curious and amusing things. Poor Christabel was, alas, too ill to see her. She sent her loving messages and hoped that she was enjoying herself. Elizabeth was chaperoned either by Sylvia or by James' wife, Lady Herries, poor Beatrice. She was known as 'poor Beatrice' because she said such silly things, wore such hideous clothes, and tumbled into such foolish blunders, but like many who are pitied by their fellows she was a great deal happier than those who pitied her. She was good-natured, most indiscreet, and admired Elizabeth's beauty with a sincerity that was touching.

Will lived with much splendour. When they went to a ball or a theatre or Vauxhall of an evening they were carried in a fine painted 'chariot' with Frederick, the footman, in silk stockings, plush breeches and hair-powder, standing behind; the Herries family arms were on the panels. But the house in Hill Street could not be said to be comfortable. That there were often unpleasant 'whiffs' from the drains meant nothing. People even preferred that the drains should 'smell' occasionally because then they could tell which way the wind was blowing and whether 'there would likely be rain'. The furniture was fine, heavy and impressive, but the passages and rooms were dreadfully chill, and there was an air of mortality everywhere save when there was a party. Elizabeth had some very dreary days and evenings. Will was in the City all day, Uhland out and about on his own affairs, as men, lucky creatures, were able to be, but unless Sylvia or Lady Herries came for her she was sadly alone. All the Herries were good and kind to her, but she soon perceived that they were, nearly all of them, living above their means, reaching up to the new grand position that Will's money and Sylvia's social successes had brought to them. It said much for Will's dignity and tact that, having made his position by business, he and his should be admitted to Almack's and allowed the honours of Holland

House. But the Herries were a very old family, and the Rockages had most certainly not made their money in business – having exactly no money at all. Roger, Carey's boy, and his wife Janet had a house in Mayfair during the Season and ordered little dinners from the caterer (and *what* scrapes they went through in order to pay the caterer no one knew but themselves); then as soon as the Season was over they disappeared, with their only child Carey, into two very shabby rooms in Pimlico, and Janet did the cooking. The life of Sylvia and Garth, too, was one long and exciting piratical adventure – a very thrilling volume of hairbreadth peril and escape it would make. Garth spent much of his time at Crockford's, which was not on the face of it a very foolish thing to do, for the subscription was but ten guineas a year, and in the gambling-rooms there was served a splendid supper free, with excellent wine for all Mr Crockford's guests. Behind this were, of course, for many a man ruin and despair. But Garth was not a fool; he had some of his brother Amery's astuteness, and he knew his world.

Elizabeth, however, was not like Judith. She could not throw herself into whatever fun was going forward. She was quiet, reserved and shy. All she wanted of life was that she should be allowed to live quietly in a corner with John somewhere and never be disturbed by anyone again.

She sat of an evening in the great drawing room or in her bedroom, a book on her lap, and meditated her escape. For escape she must. She knew that Uhland had some plan; she felt as though with every hour he was the more closely driving her to some purpose of his own.

There came an evening at Vauxhall when she began to realize what his plan for her was. She went with Sylvia, Garth, Uhland and Phyllis Newmark. It was all very splendid. There were the 'twenty thousand lamps' shining against the soft velvety sky of a July evening, Ducrow and his horses, the famous bandstand round which, if you were an unattached gentleman out for the evening, you might swirl with the loveliest, if not the most virtuous, ladies of the town, the fireworks and the vocal concerts.

For a while she enjoyed herself, listening to Sylvia's chatter, liking the general gaiety and abandon; nevertheless, she wondered, as she always did on these occasions, why she could not throw herself into things as the others did. They must find her dreadfully stupid, she thought, and, in fact, Garth that same evening confided to Sylvia behind the bed-curtains that he thought that little cousin of theirs mighty handsome, by Jove, but she seemed to be feared of her life lest someone should kiss her or chuck her under the chin; and Sylvia was forced to confess with a sigh that she didn't come out as she'd hoped. She was more at home, she suspected, in the country.

Well, later young Mr Temple joined them and, after that, poor Elizabeth's evening was a ruin. Everyone beamed upon Mr Temple, and soon he was seated with Elizabeth as his especial charge, feeding her with chicken and ham. He had a great deal to say to her, admired her gown and told of his place in Surrey where he had horses, dogs and a piano. He said he was prodigiously fond of music and the Italian opera. Very tenderly he helped her to a 'sliced cobweb' – the famous Vauxhall ham. His favourite expression, the phrase of the moment, was, when he saw anything amusing: 'What a bit of gig!'

Soon his absorption of the famous Vauxhall punch led him to closer intimacies. He pressed her hand and wished to take her up one of the shaded walks. From this Sylvia saved her, but she observed with terror that Uhland watched these proceedings with approval.

She did not sleep that night in her huge bed. What was she to do? She felt utterly defenceless. She had not a friend in the world. Strangely, she thought of Judith and Adam. What it would have been to her just then to have seen that little old lady with her sharp nose and kind bright eyes entering at the door, or Adam with his strong, ugly, honest face standing beside her! But they seemed far away, and John farther. She had no one to whom she might turn. Beatrice Herries was too foolish and indiscreet, Sylvia too flighty, Christabel too unwell. Of Will she was afraid, Garth she did not trust. She was inexperienced in the world's ways, and London seemed now like a great web in whose sticky threads she was entangled.

Then one evening Uhland came to her room. She had but just lit the candles. Bulwer's *Last Days of Pompeii* was in her hand, but her mind was with John, running as it so often did over those earlier days when they had written and met ... He was like her, she thought, shy, not caring for the world, uneasy with others. Why could they not be together in some place where no one else could come? Uhland sat near her and was kinder to her, at first, than he had ever been. He wore black; his thin sharp features had in them a shadow of suffering. She knew that he was often in pain, and that feeling of some companionship between them, something that lay deep, deep down below all this strife and antagonism, stirred in her. They *could* be friends if only ...

He told her about some of the things that he had been doing. He seemed to be as out of everything as she.

'I hate London. I do not belong here. They laugh at us as country cousins.'

'Oh·no,' she protested. 'They are so very kind.'

'Kind! Do you know what they say of us? They find us most desperately dull, sister, and that's a fact. I hate drinking. I won't play at cards. They swagger – Lord, how they swagger! And then to be up all night and for nothing – women, drink, gambling – gambling, women, drinking. Why, Ireby were better!'

He looked at her, one of those quiet speculative looks that always made her afraid.

'I am different from everyone!' he burst out. 'They mock my lameness!'

'Oh no,' she said gently. 'They don't think of it. Why, Sylvia said—'

'Yes. Sylvia said – Sylvia said—' he answered contemptuously. 'Dear Sylvia had better take care or she'll have the bailiffs in that pretty house of hers and Garth will be in the Marshalsea ... No,' he went on more quietly. 'It is my own fault; I am no company for anyone here, not even for myself. There's a devil in me that won't let me alone. We Herries are a poor lot unless we take what's in front of our noses. We were not made to be exceptional. Not that I'm exceptional, you know, except in my temper. I despise their smugness. What do they know of what it is to have a needle stab your leg every other minute, and to be something that every woman pities? ... No matter though. I shall show them all one day ...'

She did not dare to show pity. She knew how deeply he resented it. But she said:

'We should go somewhere together, Uhland, the two of us. We could go to the Colosseum or the Panorama. I should adore to see the Panorama.'

But he did not answer her. He sat there brooding, looking down, nursing his leg. There was something, she thought, twisted, wizened about him, his thin small body bent, throwing strange humped shadows on the wall in the candlelight.

He looked up.

'You are secure at least, Elizabeth.'

'Secure?' she asked him.

'Yes. Temple is crazy about you. He will be proposing for you one of these days.'

'Oh no,' she whispered.

'Oh yes,' he answered. 'It is a fine match. There couldn't be a better. He's something of a fool, of course. But that's his age. He'll improve. I never knew a man more deeply in love.'

She said nothing. He went on:

'He is fabulously wealthy. He has his house in Belgravia and a place in Surrey. Only an old mother to care for. He doesn't play at cards and is afraid of loose women. You can do what you will with him.'

'That, Uhland, you can dismiss altogether from your mind. I should not marry him if there were no other man in the world.'

He looked at her.

'Still thinking of your friend in Cumberland?' he asked her.

'No . . . But I would never marry Mr Temple.'

He got up and walked, limping, about the room.

'Never is a long story. It would be a fine thing. Our father would think so.'

She smiled.

'There I am my own mistress.'

'Not entirely,' he said quietly. 'I think you had better consider Temple.'

'And why?'

He stood by the door, his pale eyes gravely regarding her.

'Dear sister, consider what a fine husband Temple would make. Consider it. Be wise,' and left her.

She was afraid after that and despised herself for being so. What was there about Uhland that made everyone who knew him apprehensive? Even the stable-boys at Ireby dropped their voices when he was approaching, and she knew that people in Keswick called him 'Little Mischief', although no one accused him of any actual cruelties. On the contrary, that habit of kindness to injured animals was still with him. He would be in a rage if he saw a horse ill-used or a dog tied by the tail. And yet it was not as though he cared for animals!

No, what they all felt about him was the potentiality of an outburst. Society is built up on the convention that we all *intend* to behave. That is the bargain we make the one with the other. Then, if there is one who hasn't made the bargain! . . .

In any case, Elizabeth felt some ring closing round her. She was perhaps at that time young for her age. She had been always with her mother, had known no other girls intimately. But this was a situation in which other girls than herself might have been frightened, for she knew that her father would regard this match as a heaven-sent chance. He had always wanted to be rid of her. Like so many men who are for ever making love to women he despised them heartily and wanted them for one thing only. He preferred greatly men's company, and the only chance that a woman had with him as friend was for her to have something of the downright and fearless about her as Judith had. Now Elizabeth had nothing of the downright about her whatever. She was proud and brave, but it was a pride that was too real to reveal itself and a courage that was too real for cheap display.

It was a misfortune for her that Christabel was so ill, but she did have one strange little conversation with her grandfather which was to have important after-consequences for her.

Sir William Herries was now sixty-eight years of age and as straight as a flag-pole. His hair was grizzled and he was very thin of body with a sharp nose, high Herries cheek-bones, and a severe, rather chilly eye that came from considering sums, additions, subtractions, multiplications for sixty-five years. It was at the age of three, his father David used long ago to declare, that he had added his first sum, accurately, and without assistance. He was dressed immaculately, always in black with none of those gaudy waistcoats, diamonds, pins and gold chains that ornamented the bodies of the Disraelis, the Bulwers and the Ainsworths of the day. But he was a splendid sight as you saw him step out of the carriage that had brought him up from the City, in the high hat, high stock, coat fitting perfectly at the slender waist, and tightly strapped trousers. A fine sight as, inside the cold hall with a marble statue of a goddess, handsomely robed, holding aloft a lamp, he gives his hat, gloves and cane to Frederick, passes his hand for a moment over his grey locks, pinches his side-whiskers, and walks slowly, slowly up the broad staircase.

'How is Lady Herries?' he asks Warren, the fat butler. 'Has Doctor Salter paid his visit?'

'Doctor Salter has been, Sir William. Her ladyship is much the same.'

'Ah ... Ah. Ha! ... Thank you, Warren.'

So one late afternoon, he came into the drawing room, ornamented as was the earlier drawing room in the earlier smaller house with oil-paintings of David his father and Sarah his mother, and a huge marble clock that had Virtue seated in a toga on the top of it, window hangings of a very grave mustard colour, a table or two scattered with 'Beauty Books' and 'Keepsakes', the poems of Felicia Hemans and a book of engravings of Greece and Italy – all this as chill and as damp as a mausoleum, all this bringing pride and comfort to his soul.

Today he moved about, putting a 'Keepsake' straight on a table, arranging the hanging of one of the curtains, looking out for a moment into the summer evening that was coquetting with Hill Street. Then only was it that he discovered Elizabeth seated on a sofa.

'My dear!' he exclaimed. 'I never saw you!'

'Good evening, Grandfather.'

He was weary, he was lonely, he had a pain in his side. He sat down beside her. He had never been blind to feminine beauty although he *had* married Christabel. His daughter, Alice, who had died of a chill in 1812, had been as plain as her mother. He was proud and pleased that his grand-daughter should be so beautiful. Elizabeth's beauty lay in the perfection of her delicacy, the rosy bloom of her colouring; her shoulders and arms, revealed by the low cut of her cream-coloured dress, had the soft firmness of a child's unawareness. Her hands, exquisitely shaped, were both gentle and strong. She had the fairness of a rose scarcely daring to open.

'I am afraid, my dear,' he said, 'that I have not seen so much of you during this visit as I should have wished. I am growing an old man, but I have never, all my life, learnt how to delegate business to others. If I do not see to it myself it's done wrong. I trust that you have been happy.'

'Oh yes, Grandpapa.'

'That's good. And Uhland?'

'I think he has been very happy.'

She longed to burst out: 'I am not happy at all! They want to marry me to a young man I detest. You must prevent them.' But she did not dare. She knew him so little, and he looked so very imposing with his legs spread out in front of him and his long, thin hands with the tapering fingers laid on his bony knees.

'It is a misfortune that your grandmother has been so unwell.'

'I hope she is getting better,' Elizabeth said gently.

'No, my dear, I fear not. Doctor Salter is doing all he can, but, as he constantly says, she will not make a sufficient effort. A great pity! A great pity! Your grandmother is a wonderful woman, my dear, but she has never had quite the courage needed for a life like ours. After all, she is a woman.'

'Yes, Grandpapa.'

'And what have you been doing with yourself, my dear?'

Elizabeth told him some of the things that she had been doing.

He nodded, rubbed his hands together, rose.

'Very good. Very good. I trust your grandmother will soon be sufficiently well for you to see her. It is delightful for us to have you here.'

But as he went out of the room and climbed the stairs he was vaguely uncomfortable. Was she happy? She appeared lonely. That brother of hers was a queer fish. Very queer. But then he was crippled, poor child. Odd for Walter, big and healthy as he was, to have a crippled son. What a beautiful girl! It did one good . . . But he was vaguely uneasy, and the uneasiness remained.

Two days later Mr Temple came and proposed, and after that events followed swiftly. He came with Sylvia Herries and they drank tea together in the mustard-coloured drawing room. Sylvia said that she must go and ask Mrs Arnold, the housekeeper, about some silks that she wished to match. No sooner was she out of the room than Mr Temple fell on his knees. It was a proposal in the conventional fashion!

'Dearest Miss Herries! Oh, if I may only call you Elizabeth! From the first moment I saw you I have been in a dream. You are the only woman in the whole world for me. All that I have is yours . . .' and so on and so on.

Elizabeth also behaved in the traditional manner.

'Pray, Mr Temple, rise from the floor.'

He caught her hand. He kissed it.

'I shall have to call for someone if you persist in this ridiculous—'

'Adorable Elizabeth! Most heavenly—'

He climbed on to the sofa beside her and tried to kiss her cheek.

'Please, Mr Temple.' Then she broke into sheer disgust. 'Oh, go away! No, I do not love you. I can never love you. I do not even care for you. No, not even with friendly feelings. This is absurd. This is too absurd—'

She freed herself and stood with her hand on the bell-rope.

He was amazed. He could not believe his ears. This was the first proposal of his life, for he had always believed that himself and his riches were irresistible and that when the time did come for him to honour anybody there could be but one possible result.

He was deeply chagrined. Even a tear rolled on to his fat little cheek.

'Oh, dammit!' he cried, and went indignantly from the room.

Next morning Uhland came to her in her room. His look of cold, resolved anger terrified her; she felt as though he had imprisoned her and would do what he pleased. The sense of power that he spread about him was extraordinary.

'Elizabeth – what is this I hear? Temple has proposed and you have refused him.'

'Yes.'

'You silly little fool! You are to write to him immediately and say that you have reconsidered it.'

She shook her head.

'But I say Yes. It is the very thing for you. Father will wish it. All of us.'

'No, Uhland. I don't love him. I dislike him extremely.'

'Love? What is love? It is because you have still some sentimental longing for that young prig in Cumberland.'

'You know,' she answered, 'that that was over long ago.'

'I know nothing of the kind. If you will not accept Temple I shall charge your refusal to John Herries – and I shall know what to do—'

'You can't harm him!' she answered fiercely, all her dread of him gone. 'You can't touch him and you know it. But threats can't serve you. Nor your bullying. I should never marry Mr Temple if you starved me!'

'You *shall* marry him,' he answered.

He came up to her and put his cold, damp hand on her bare shoulder. 'I know what is good for you and I will see to it.'

He looked at her and left the room.

After that she had only one thought – flight. She had already for weeks been contemplating it. She had plenty of spirit, and the thought that at last she would escape from Ireby, from this house, from her father, from all these Herries relations gave her wings. That afternoon she searched *The Times* and at last found what she wanted. A Mrs Bohun Winstanley of 21A Sloane Street had an agency for 'Governesses, Companions, Situations for Genteel Persons'. Ellen, the maid, was her next resource. She had, in these weeks, won Ellen's devoted affections, not difficult considering her beauty, charm and gentleness. It seemed too that Ellen hated her place here, hated Mrs Arnold, the housekeeper, and was only waiting an opportunity to give her notice. Elizabeth told Ellen everything, even her love for John, and Ellen's eyes grew moist with sentiment as she drank in the details of such a romance. Ellen was sworn to secrecy. On the following day, having packed Elizabeth's box, she was to take a hackney-cab and meet Elizabeth outside St Clement Danes Church at midday. To this Ellen swore: she also protested that the most horrible tortures man (Ellen's natural enemy) could devise would not tempt her to betrayal. Elizabeth kissed her.

Early the next morning, wearing her quietest bonnet, she slipped out of the house into Hill Street. It was a fine morning and she walked out of her way to Charing Cross, taking her time lest Mrs Bohun Winstanley should not yet be at work. No one interfered with her. A cheap dandy with a sham diamond pin and a double-breasted waistcoat ogled her, a policeman in a blue swallow-tailed coat and white trousers glanced at her with some curiosity, but for the most part everyone was busy about his or her own business. There was a great deal of noise with the bell of the crier, the horn of the omnibus, the Italian boy and his hurdy-gurdy, and the shops with their small-paned bow-windows were opening, somewhere church bells were ringing. Everywhere everything was entrancing, for at last, at last, she was free!

When she thought the time was come she mounted inside an omnibus and at length was put down at the top of Sloane Street. Soon Number 21A was found, a dingy door, a still dingier staircase. One flight up, in faded green letters, was Mrs Bohun Winstanley's name. Entering she found a room, grimy and disordered, with a shabby canary moulting in a shabby cage by the very dirty window, and a lady in a bonnet and mittens seated at a table strewn with papers. Standing in front of the empty grate was another lady, wearing a very gay bonnet covered with flowers, and a bright emerald-green shawl. This lady was tall, thin, and plainly in the worst of tempers. The lady at the table was small, and, at the moment, alarmed. A dewdrop trembled at the end of her nose, her mittens quivered with a life of their own, and she murmured again and again: 'Oh dear! Oh dear! But it is so *early* . . . so early, Mrs Golightly . . .'

'Early! Early!' cried the other lady, while all the flowers trembled in her bonnet in sympathy. 'Don't speak to me of "early", Mrs Winstanley. A promise is a promise!'

'But her little girl has the croup.'

'And what of *my* little girls, Mrs Winstanley? What of *my* little girls? Here have they been these three weeks, and Mr Golightly in Bath and returning tomorrow—'

It was then that both ladies together noticed Elizabeth.

'Well?' said Mrs Winstanley.

'I beg your pardon, I am sure,' said Elizabeth. 'I can wait outside—'

'But what *is* it?' said Mrs Winstanley, plainly near to tears.

'I read your advertisement in *The Times*,' said Elizabeth. 'I am looking for a place as governess or companion—'

Both ladies stared at Elizabeth. They had obviously never seen anyone so beautiful before.

'Sit down, pray,' Mrs Winstanley said at last (and it was clear that she saw, in Elizabeth, the ship of rescue). 'Now, Mrs Golightly, this is a young lady of whom I intended to have spoken yesterday—'

Mrs Golightly stared and stared.

'You are looking for a place?' she said at last.

'Yes, ma'am.'

'What is your name?'

'Mary Temple.' (Oh, how absurd! She had taken Mr Temple's name after all!)

'How old are you?'

'Twenty-three, ma'am.'

'What experience have you had?'

'I think,' broke in Mrs Winstanley, 'that you will find that she has had excellent experience.'

'Has she?' said Mrs Golightly doubtfully. 'She looks very superior, I must say.' Then she added: 'And your references?'

'I will speak for her references,' said Mrs Winstanley quickly.

'Ours is a very agreeable family,' Mrs Golightly said in a kind of dream. 'My two little girls are angelic – less than no trouble at all . . . When could you come?' she asked abruptly.

'This afternoon,' said Elizabeth.

'Very odd. Very odd, indeed. Have you French, Arithmetic, the Pianoforte, Dancing, Deportment? . . .'

'I think you will find that Miss Temple has everything that

you require,' Mrs Winstanley quickly inserted.

'Indeed!' Mrs Golightly still stared in a kind of dream. 'Very distinguished!' she murmured. 'You are familiar with the Poets?'

'I beg your pardon?' Elizabeth said.

'Shakespeare, Milton, Lord Byron, Mrs Hemans—'

'Oh yes,' said Elizabeth, 'I think so.'

'You *think* so,' said Mrs Golightly. 'Don't you *know*?'

'She is especially familiar with the Poets,' said Mrs Winstanley, speaking very gently and nodding her head.

Mrs Golightly stared and stared.

'You can come this evening?' she said at last.

'Yes, ma'am.'

'Of course,' Mrs Golightly said, turning to Mrs Winstanley, 'she may be a thief in collusion with all the thieves of the Metropolis. Pray, don't think me rude,' she went on, turning to Elizabeth again, 'but it is so very odd. I know nothing whatever about you. With whom were you last?'

'I am sure that you will find everything perfectly correct,' said Mrs Winstanley.

Mrs Golightly stared a little more.

'Well, I don't know, I'm sure. If Mr Golightly had any liking for young ladies the idea would be absurd, but as he has never given one a thought, being far too closely occupied by his beetles and butterflies . . .' She nodded her head. 'Very well, then. This evening. Mrs Winstanley will explain the terms,' and without another word she left the room, banging the little door behind her.

'And now,' said Mrs Winstanley gently, and blowing her nose, 'pray, tell me, my dear, who you are.'

THE GOVERNESS

ELIZABETH read her letter over again. In a few minutes she must go to Mrs Golightly's boudoir, where she must read for an hour while the moths buzzed about the lamp, the silly clock ticked, and the words of the novel in her hand moved in a mist of confusion before her heavy eyes. For she was very weary, as indeed she was always weary at this hour in the evening. Clarissa and Francesca were happily asleep in bed, lost in slumber, although safe neither from suffocation (for their bedroom would be hermetically sealed) nor from bugs. The little house in Islington crawled with animals, bugs and beetles and cockroaches (Alice the kitchen-maid, who slept in the kitchen, spent most of her day killing them: she was too tired at night to care), while spiders hung in every corner and dust lay on tables, sills and shelves as thick as the sand of the desert. In the meantime Mrs Golightly, surrounded with emerald-green curtains, ottomans and 'Keepsakes', sat in her evening yellow silk, her ringlets bound by her 'arcade' (a wonderful arrangement of wires twined with rosebuds, lace and ribbon), waiting for Elizabeth to continue her reading of *Agnes Serle* by Miss Ellen Pickering.

This was Elizabeth's letter:

4 PRAED STREET, ISLINGTON,
March 4th, 1839

BELOVED JOHN – I cannot, try as I may, refrain any longer from writing to you. The thought of your anxiety for me (for I do not I think flatter myself that you must be anxious) has been a motive ever more constant with me. But this I could have resisted were it not that your dear image, for so many many years now the dearest to me in all the word, refuses to leave to me the proper control of my feelings.

I know only too well, dearest John, that I am breaking all the vows that I have made and upon which I was myself formerly the most insistent. I am aware that all the reasons that kept us apart must keep us apart still: indeed their influence must be stronger with us than before since the irrevocable nature of my own desperate deed! How desperate it must seem to my own family you will realize from the fact that neither my father nor brother have made the slightest effort to find me out. I will admit to you that it is the increasing sense of my own loneliness that compels me to write to you. I had hoped that, cut off from all family ties, I might learn to forget you, but, dear John, true love is not so easily set aside and however dearly I have loved you in the past I must confess that it is only in these last weeks that I have realized to the full how deep and constant that love must be.

Perhaps it is shameful of me to make this confession to you, but shameful or not it must be made, for without some word from you I truly think that I shall die. I have not formerly been weak. I am weak now and must detest my weakness even while I yield to it.

I would not wish you to think that I am unhappy with Mrs Golightly, the lady in whose house I live and to whose little girls I am governess. She is not indeed at all unkind, only rather foolish and unable to keep her house clean or manage it with any efficiency. The two little girls are good and patient, poor little things, although entirely neglected. Mrs Golightly reads novels, recites poetry, has evening parties and attends concerts in Hanover Square, while Mr Golightly, who is fat and ab-sentminded but also kindly, collects moths and butterflies, which takes him very often into the country. Meanwhile the house is a ruin, the cooks come and go every week and only poor Alice, the kitchen-maid, is faithful and does all the work of the place.

Dear John, I think I have grown into a woman in these last months and see life more sanely than I did. I had, I do not doubt, an exaggerated picture of my father and my brother and although I know they do not love me and have never loved me, they are neither so hard nor so unkind as I at one time thought them. But do not think me cowardly, dear John, in thus writing to you. I am not thinking of changing my life but only that you should sometimes write me a letter and give me the opportunity to write to you. You understand, do you not, that NO ONE is to know of where I am nor of what I am doing. No one save yourself. It is to be a secret from everyone, but I love you so much that I think I shall be insane if I do not hear from you. Later on perhaps you will come to London and we shall meet again. Only to think of such a meeting sends me crazy with joy and happiness. But I know that you will answer this letter and that is all the happiness I wish for at this present time. Your most loving

ELIZABETH

She folded it up and sealed it.

'I am very wicked,' she thought. 'I have never done anything so really wrong as this before. But I don't care.' She further thought that she had been stupid not to have done this long ago. Her months with Mrs Golightly had made her begin to wonder whether she had not paid altogether too much attention to the decencies. She did not realize that it was the escape from the

Cumberland house that had changed her, the fact that she was emerging from the influence both of her father and brother, who until now had dominated her whole life.

She put on her bonnet and shawl, opened the door, listened, ran downstairs, down the front steps, then along the lamp-lit street to the post office. She hesitated a moment before dropping the letter in. Was it right? No, it wasn't right. Nevertheless, in it went. She stared defiantly about the street, but there was only one hackney-cab crawling along and an Italian organ-grinder with a shivering monkey in a crimson coat. She dropped a sixpence into the little monkey's cup as a sort of oblation. The monkey looked at her with eyes so old and so sad that she could not resist a little shudder. It was as though the monkey said: 'We are all cold. All lost. All doomed. There's nothing to be done about it . . .'

On the other hand, Alice, with a large smut across her nose, was looking up from the bottom of the area steps. She had a large broom in her hand which she waved in a cheerful fashion as much as to say: 'We're friends, we are. I know what you've been doing and wish you all the luck.' The thin strains of the barrel-organ echoed down the empty street as though they, too, wished her good fortune.

She ran quietly up the stairs, took off bonnet and shawl, brushed her ringlets and, with *Agnes Serle* in hand, marched down to the boudoir.

'Aren't you a little late, my love?' asked Mrs Golightly, who was reclining at ease with her velvet slippers toasting at the fire. The pug, Levilla, was on her lap, choking as usual.

'Yes, I think I am, a little,' said Elizabeth gently, and, opening her book, began to read.

She had remarked to herself again and again in these months how completely now she was separated from the Herries world. It was as though they lived, all of them, in another continent. Mrs Golightly did on occasion read out from the newspaper some social item, and once she remarked with a great deal of unction that she saw that Sir William Herries had been doing this or that. 'Let me see,' she went on. 'He is a cousin, I fancy, of Lady Rockage, and there is that lovely Mrs Garth Herries whose name you see everywhere. They are all the same family, I imagine.'

But Mrs Golightly and all her friends spoke of Gore House or Almack's as one speaks of Paradise. But with no envy. She had her world and was perfectly content with it, but the division between her world and that other one was quite complete. Mrs Golightly was a generous, unenvious person altogether. She thought her husband, children, friends and home all quite perfect. It was the fashion, moreover, for herself and her friends to be romantic about everything, and this same Romance gave them every kind of satisfaction. They liked their literature, their painting, their music, their religion to be romantic. They felt deeply and sincerely for all Oppressed Peoples. Mrs Golightly was for ever attending meetings for the poor Poles, for the Negro (whom they went so far as to call their brother), for the unhappy Greek and the neglected Hottentot. That her house was in a mess and that the slums, factories and mines quite close to home needed attention – these things were never discussed because they were *not* romantic.

Mrs Golightly enjoyed entertaining her friends in the evening (a little music on the pianoforte, a little 'dance' in the very small drawing room), she enjoyed a walk with Mr Golightly when he was at home, a visit to the theatre or a concert – but perhaps more than anything else she enjoyed sitting with her toes in front of the fire of an evening and listening to Elizabeth's reading of a novel. That original inquiry at the Agency about the Poets had been genuine enough, but when it came actually to *reading* – well, the novel was the thing! Elizabeth had a beautiful, quiet, cultivated voice, as Mrs Golightly told all her friends. It was a pleasure indeed to listen to her. So Elizabeth read, night after night, from the works of Bulwer, Ainsworth, that delightful new writer Charles Dickens, Theodore Hook, Mrs Gore, Miss Austen ('a *little* dull, my love – not enough Event') and even some of the old 'Minerva Press' romances – *Mandroni, Rinaldo Rinaldini* and *The Beggar Girl and her Benefactors*, the last in seven volumes.

Meanwhile the two little girls went on as best they might. It would not be true to say that Mrs Golightly did not love her children. She loved them very dearly. But they, too, must be romantic. She dressed them in very bright colours, showed them to her friends with pride and left Elizabeth to do the rest. They became deeply attached to Elizabeth. They never had seen anyone so lovely and, in fact, would never see anyone so lovely again. Although she dressed in the quietest way, never raised her voice and never lost her temper, they obeyed her and told her everything. Alone with her they chattered and chattered, asking her innumerable questions. She taught them what she could with the aid of Butter's *Exercises on the Globes*, Lindley Murray's

English Grammar and Goldsmith's *Poems for Young Ladies*, but she had never had very much education herself and was appalled at her own ignorance.

Although a strong offshoot of the City ran past Sadler's Wells through the High Street, Islington was nevertheless a little country town of its own, filled with trees and gardens. The Golightlys had their carriage and drove into Town on necessary occasions, but, socially, their world was their own world and they gave little thought to any other. Elizabeth's arrival here was a sensation and, during the first weeks, the bachelors, handsome young men, and gay old married ones attempted every kind of flirtation. They found her, however, so unapproachable that she achieved the reputation of an Islington mystery. It was soon asserted that she was the child of a noble lord who had attempted to marry her to a villain, that she was the child-bride of an aged marquis who violently ill-treated her, that she was heiress to a vast property and had fled from unwelcome suitors.

She was too kind and gentle to be disliked by them; she gave herself no airs; she listened to their stories and was grieved for their misfortunes. Mrs Golightly did her utmost to discover her secret, and even Mr Golightly would look up from his butterflies, smile in a mysterious manner, nod his head and say: 'We expect you to be carried off from us in a gilt chariot any day, my dear.'

Mrs Golightly's methods were more subtle. On one of the reading evenings she would break out with:

'You mentioned, did you not, my love, that your brother was in the Army?'

'Oh no,' Elizabeth would reply. 'I have no relations in the Army.'

'Indeed! Well, fancy that! It must have been the Navy you said.'

'Nor in the Navy,' Elizabeth would reply, smiling.

Or Mrs Golightly would look at her with great tenderness, remarking:

'That must have been a sweetly pretty Ball at Lady Carrington's yesterday evening. Young Lady Hermione Blossom was looking her loveliest, I understand . . . You doubtless know her, Mary, my love.'

'No,' Elizabeth would murmur. 'I have never seen her.'

'Ah, so you say!' Mrs Golightly would reply, looking very arch. 'We know what we know.'

The children were pressed into service, but they, poor dears, were so simple and innocent that they had no wiles.

'Oh, Miss Temple,' Francesca would say. 'Mama says that everyone knows that you are not Miss Temple really, and that you will be leaving us very shortly.'

'I have no intention of leaving you, Francesca.'

'Mama says that you have fled from persecuting parents.'

'Does she, Francesca? I have not fled from anyone.'

And Clarissa, who loved Elizabeth with passion, would hold her hand as though it were a pump-handle and exclaim: 'I am certain that you are a Princess in disguise, dear Miss Temple, and I *do* love you so!'

'There are no real Princesses,' Elizabeth would answer. 'Only in fairytales.'

She managed for a while well enough. They were kind to her, and it was not their fault that she knew with every week more and more unbearable loneliness and longing. Then came the egregious and appalling Mr Roberts. Mr Frederick Roberts was a stout, cheerful, noisy young man who was the practical joker of the group. He was absent during the first part of Elizabeth's sojourn, in Scotland. Everyone spoke of him with rapture.

'Wait, my love, until Mr Fred Roberts returns!' Mrs Golightly cried. 'Islington is not the same without Mr Roberts. Mr Roberts has the life of a thousand. He is the wittiest young man in London.'

Elizabeth awaited his arrival with some eagerness. He could do everything – play the pianoforte, sing a song, shoot birds, hunt the fox, dance like an angel and join anyone for any length of time at Commerce, Vingt-et-Un or Speculation. He could imitate Webster or Buckstone or Fanny Kemble as though they were in the room with you. He was the soul of good nature, and all the young ladies in Islington wanted to marry him.

When he did arrive Elizabeth found him truly terrible. He was fat, coarse, common, self-satisfied, exceedingly conceited and as noisy as the fireworks at Vauxhall. But, worst of all, he must for ever be playing practical jokes. Practical jokes were 'the thing' in Islington; everyone loved them, but no practical-joker anywhere was as inexhaustible in his energies, as fertile in his resources as Fred Roberts.

He marked down Elizabeth at once as his future bride. He proposed to her on the second evening after meeting her and, when she indignantly refused him, roared with laughter and would have slapped her on the back had she not eluded him. His 'jokes' were endless. You never knew when you were safe from him. One of his most famous was the occasion when at supper at Mrs Preedy's he poured melted butter into all the gentlemen's pockets. He loved to tie two doors together, ring both bells and watch the result round a corner. On one most laughable occasion he arrived at the Livingstone-Jones' with a tray of medicated sweets so that everyone was ill. He came to a Masquerade with mice in his pocket, let them loose and returned in another costume to enjoy the results. When Mrs Bonnington lost her husband he appeared by her bedside as the ghost of her departed (she was ill after this for weeks). Mrs Green had a stout and elderly butler into whose shoes he fastened tin-tacks so that poor James, putting them on unsuspectingly, fell down a flight of stairs and was nearly killed. How Frederick laughed when he heard of it! And the odd thing was that everyone liked him for these games! They thought him the funniest, jolliest fellow and declared that any girl who 'caught' him would be lucky indeed!

He had never, it seemed, been 'seriously inclined', although he was 'something good' in the City and could marry whenever he wished. Now he *was* 'caught', and it was Elizabeth who had 'caught' him.

Poor Elizabeth! Mr Temple had been nothing to this!

It was, however, her terror of Mr Roberts that drove her to write to John. It seemed that there was no safety for her anywhere – if not one, then another. She even discovered herself thinking of the Fortress as a place of security.

If she left the Golightlys and went elsewhere it would be the same – danger everywhere.

A few days after posting her letter a worse thing than Mr Roberts occurred – Mr Golightly fell in love with her. She had never thought of him save that he was kindly and that he passed a dazzled, bewildered existence in a maze of coloured insects. He had means of his own that he had inherited from his father, a wealthy merchant who had dealt in candles or something of the kind. He had never been known to look at a woman save Mrs Golightly, at whom, moreover, he, on the whole, looked as little as might be. His fidelity to his butterflies was absolute.

There came then an evening. Mrs Golightly went to join her two friends, Miss Sanders and Mrs Witsun, at the house of their mutual friend, Mrs Peters, for a game of Commerce. The girls had gone to bed, and Elizabeth sat in her room pretending to read and thinking of John. She thought now of John every moment of the day. How was her letter faring? How soon might there be a reply? And, surrounding John, encompassing and enveloping him, was the country of her home, the silver river through the flat Portinscale fields, Main Street in Keswick with Miss Hazlitt's bow-window and the coach standing . . .

A knock on the door. Enter Mr Golightly. She was so deeply amazed that she could not speak. There he stood with his round stomach in a flowered waistcoat, his coat-tails spreading fan-wise over his fat thighs, buckles on his shoes and spectacles on the end of his nose.

He closed the door firmly.

'This is an opportunity,' she heard him say to himself. He came forward and without another word fell immediately on his knees in front of her. His spectacles jerked to the ground and he gazed up at her with blue eyes, childlike and innocent, eyes dimmed because they had seen the world for so long behind glasses, eyes that had gazed for years upon butterflies. She tried to rise, but he put his fat hand on her knee and burst out at once:

'Miss Temple – Mary, I am well aware that this is disgraceful. I am proud that it is. I have wished for years to do something disgraceful. I doubt whether anything could be more disgraceful than this. I am old enough to be your father, but I love you passionately. I may say that I have never loved anyone passionately before. And when I say passionately I mean passionately.'

'But, Mr Golightly – this is shameful—'

'I know that it is shameful. I have been struggling against it for several weeks. At least I have been struggling against *not* struggling against it.'

She did manage to rise.

'But this is abominable. In Mrs Golightly's absence—'

'Oh, damnation take Mrs Golightly!' he burst out, clasping her skirts and holding her firmly. 'What do you think it is to sleep year after year with Mrs Golightly in a four-poster? What do you think it is to wake early in the morning and see Mrs Golightly beside you? Were it not for my butterflies I should have gone mad long ago. And you, loveliest of virgins, what do you know of four-posters? Do you realize what a four-poster *might* be? Even I, old as I am, could . . .'

But that was enough. She tore herself from his clinging hands and went, even as she had done in Hill Street, to the bell-rope.

'One word more, Mr Golightly, and I summon Alice.'

He rose to his feet. He was trembling and there were beads of perspiration on his nose. Without his spectacles he seemed oddly undressed.

'Yes,' he murmured. 'I must appear revolting to you. It is natural that I should. It is my fate that I must appear revolting to everyone save Mrs Golightly.'

He bent down and picked up his spectacles. She thought that he was near to tears.

'Forgive me,' he said. 'I could not help myself and I am glad that I could not. I am still a man, not a mummy. Oh! how beautiful you are!'

And he went, wiping his spectacles in a large orange handkerchief, from the room.

After this there was nothing for it but flight. Mr Golightly *and* Mr Roberts! And if Mrs Golightly discovered . . . But she did not want to go before she had had her letter from John. *One* letter from him and she would be better prepared to face the world again. Days went by. The beetles crawled in the kitchen. *Agnes Serle* came to her conclusion and was immediately followed by *Adelaide or the Countercharm*, the odious Mr Roberts proposed to her three times, on every occasion with peals of laughter – and still there was no letter from John.

Then came the party. This was the grandest party that Mrs Golightly had yet given in Islington – dancing, music, Commerce and Speculation, everything that the heart could desire. The whole house was 'cleared' for the event. The dining room was not far from the drawing room. In the drawing room there would be music and then dancing. Mr Fortescue would play on the violin, Mrs Porter's two daughters would sing duets, Mr Fred Roberts would give his Imitations and comic songs. It was also confidently expected that Mr Roberts had some special 'joke', a secret from everyone but himself.

The supper came from the caterer's, who also provided two long, thin men with immense side-whiskers to serve as waiters. Poor Alice was driven from one pillar to another post all day and all night, while Mrs Thackeray, the at-the-moment cook (she had given notice and was to leave directly *after* the party), for a brief while permitted herself to be amiable because, like every other servant in the world, she enjoyed a party.

When the guests were all assembled the sight was very impressive. The house was swollen with the guests. They were in the

hall, on the stairs, hanging out of window, flooding dining room
and drawing room. The gentlemen, many of them with long and
wavy hair, had high black stocks enriched with massive pins; the
white shirt-cuffs were neatly turned over the wrists, dress-coats
buttoned, trousers tight with straps and pumps. The ladies either
wore curls neatly arranged on each side, or their hair dropped in
à loop down the cheek and behind the ear, and then fastened in
some kind of band with ribbons at the back of the head. Pink was
the favourite colour, pink with plenty of lace and artificial
flowers. The older ladies were magnificent in turbans, and some
of the younger wore across the forehead a band of velvet or silk
decorated with a gold buckle, or something in pearls and diamonds. Miss Sanders, who was sixty if a day, had a black ribbon
across her brow, the ribbon containing in the middle a steel
buckle.

Every lady, of course, wore cleaned kid gloves, and the tur-
pentine that had gone to the cleaning of them gave off a pungent
and powerful odour. Quadrilles were still danced and even the
Country Dance lingered, but the Valse was the true enchantment, although in Islington it was still considered rather advanced and daring, and always everyone was afraid to be the first
to commence. Once and again the dancing was stopped for a
little music, and Miss Merryweather sang in her piercing soprano or the Misses Porter gave one of their delightful duets. At
first everyone was as polite as polite could be. The gentlemen
stood by themselves and the ladies by *themselves*, but soon the
punch-bowl had been mixed – a lovely mixture of rum, brandy,
Curaçao, lemon, hot water, sugar, grated nutmeg, cloves and
cinnamon. There was also rum-shrub. And above all, for the
gentlemen, Bishop. Bishop was a kind of punch made of port
wine instead of rum, and exceedingly potent it was. It was the
Bishop, possibly, that accounted in the end for Elizabeth's terror
and distress.

Very soon everyone became very jolly, and of course the jolliest
of them all was Fred Roberts. Before the evening had exhausted
an hour of its splendour he had fastened three girls into a cupboard, let off a squib under Miss Merryweather's skirts (and her
shriek was of a more violent soprano than any betrayed by her
singing!), piled three plates on the lintel of the door so that they
crashed on to the head of one of the long, thin waiters; but his
great feat was that he had brought a live grass-snake in his
pocket, and this he sent crawling over fair arms and necks until

ladies stood on chairs and one Miss Porter fainted (or was it, as some said, that she had enjoyed the rum-shrub?).

He was the greatest success. Everyone voted that they had never seen him in so splendid a humour, and he *was* in fine form, for he had a bet with six of his Islington cronies that before the evening was over he would be able to announce to all the world that the beautiful Miss Temple had consented to be his bride.

During the earlier hours, however, he left Elizabeth to others, although his merry eye was always upon her. At first things were not so terrible. She sat with Mrs Devizes, a lady who was vastly proud of her house, 'twice the size of this, my dear'. And must describe with perfect happiness her mahogany table and curtains of crimson rep, her gilt fleur-de-lis wallpaper and the way that she preserved her gooseberries and currants.

How Elizabeth prayed that she might be left alone with her, for she was tranquil and calm, and, as her words flowed on, it seemed that life somewhere must be secure – an enclosed world under a glass bell, mahogany, crimson rep and gooseberries.

But she was not allowed to stay where she was. For, in the first place, Mrs Golightly was so happy at the social success of her party that she was talking about Elizabeth to everyone, how she was certain that she was the daughter of a Duke, how good she was and beautiful she was, and how indebted she was to Mrs Golightly, who 'treated her just like one of her own daughters'. So naturally the young men came up and besought her to dance with them, and then, while valsing, paid her fatuous compliments and fought with one another over the honour of claiming her. Everyone began to be greatly excited, the ladies as well. Games were proposed, Forfeits, and Blind Man's Buff and Catch-in-a-Corner.

Elizabeth slipped out of the room only to find Mr Golightly, the worse for Bishop, standing in a corner near the window, staring quite desperately in front of him.

He caught her arm and drew her to the window.

'You must not tremble,' he assured her. 'You are safe with me. Indeed, indeed you are. I only wish you to be the first to know that I am leaving Mrs Golightly.'

'Oh no, no!' she cried, deeply distressed.

'I am determined, quite, quite determined. Before you came into my life I was asleep. But now I am awake and I know that my existence with Mrs Golightly is a sham!'

Oh, those poor little girls, she thought. And Mrs Golightly, who is so happy and confident. If only she could have taken him away and talked to him, for she liked him in spite of his absurdities. But she did not dare to go apart with him, and here they were besieged on all sides – people were running up and down stairs. It was quite pandemonium.

'You will feel quite differently tomorrow,' she assured him.

'Oh no, I shall not. You have changed my life. You have—'

But worse followed, for Mr Roberts appeared, carrying a glass of punch, his red face shining with happiness, his eyes fixed upon her as though she were already his bride.

Paying no attention to Mr Golightly, he caught Elizabeth's hand, dragged her with him into the room where everyone was valsing madly, and began to swing her round, dropping his glass on to the floor. She thought it better not to resist lest worse should befall.

'We are designed for one another!' he cried. 'It is Fate! I am rich, you are beautiful! Let me tell them all that you will have me! I have been waiting all my life for this moment! I am the happiest of men!. . .' Then, before them all, suddenly, ceasing to dance, he caught her in his stout arms and kissed her.

She broke from him, ran among the dancers, found her way to the door and, on the verge of tears, half tumbled down the stairs into the hall. At the moment there was no one there, but the house-door was open, Alice was on the step, and beside her some-one was standing. Alice came in.

'It is for you, miss. A gentleman asking for you—'

She went forward, trying to calm her agitation. Before her, visible enough in the pale, smoky lamp of the little hall, was John.

She was in his arms; *his* arms were round her.

'Oh, John – John – John,' was all she could hysterically cry. She was sobbing on his shoulder.

'My love . . . my adored one . . . my only, only love!'

Alice was in an ecstasy. She was practical as well.

'Oh, miss, come into the Master's room. There's no one there. Only the coats and hats.'

Into Mr Golightly's room they went, and there, among the butterflies and beetles, John told her that he had come as swiftly as he could and for one purpose only. At the first possible moment they would be married.

'Married, John?'

'Yes, married, my love. We have been too ridiculous. We have been wasting our lives.'

(Uhland? Her father? Oh, no matter. Let come what might!)

'Oh, John – I have longed for you so!'

'And I for you! When I received your letter . . .'

Mrs Golightly was in the doorway, behind her Miss Porter and others.

'Mary! Why, my love . . .'

Elizabeth, holding John's hand, and looking more beautiful than ever in her life before, said:

'Mrs Golightly – allow me to introduce you – Mr John Herries. The gentleman to whom I am to be married. He has come all the way from Cumberland—'

It was the supreme, the loveliest moment of her life.

FAMILY LETTERS

6 ACACIA ROAD, MARYLEBONE, LONDON,
April 20th, 1839

MY DEAR FATHER – Yesterday morning John and I were married at St Mary's Church, Phillamont Street, Marylebone.

I am afraid that this may make you angry and I am sorry indeed that it should do so, but as you have made no inquiry after my whereabouts I am hardened in the belief that nothing that may happen to me can give you very great concern. I am sorry indeed for this, but from my very earliest years you have shown me that you would have preferred never to have had a daughter. I find it very difficult in these unhappy circumstances to appeal to your forgiveness because indeed I do not feel that there has been anything on my part very blameworthy. I studied to love you, but you wished for the love neither of my dear mother nor myself. You are not responsible, dear father, for that. If you could not love us you could not, but neither am I responsible for wishing to make some kind of life for myself where I could be happy.

Perhaps now that I am away from you I may not cause you so much aggravation and one day you may wish to see me again. I know how greatly you have always disliked the family at Uldale but they on their part have, I am sure, felt nothing but friendliness and it is the great hope of John and myself that our marriage may heal the division between the two families. John has some means of his own and we shall be in no need of assistance from anyone. Our cousins, Garth and Sylvia, are most kind, and Carey has invited me into the country. I have written to grandfather acquainting him with our marriage. I am afraid that grandmother is no better.

With every respect, dear father. I am, Your loving daughter,

ELIZABETH

John Herries to Judith Paris

6 ACACIA ROAD, MARYLEBONE, LONDON,
April 22nd, 1839

MY DEAR AUNT JUDITH – Elizabeth and I were married on April 19th at twelve noon at St Mary's Church, Phillamont Street, Marylebone.

Dear Aunt Judith, are you very angry with me? I did wrong perhaps to leave you so suddenly with that brief letter of farewell, but I am enclosing (by her own wish) Elizabeth's letter to me that she wrote from London. Now read that and I am assured that with all your tenderness and love of others you will not be able to wish my actions other than they were. Indeed I could not help myself and arrived, as it turned out, only just in time, for my beloved Elizabeth was in the very act of escaping from an Islington ruffian when I stepped in at the door. Can you imagine it? She had been a Governess, having run away from her grandfather's, to two little girls of a lady with the astounding name of Golightly! They were kind to her, I fancy, although I cannot force very much out of her. She was never communicative about herself as you know.

But you do *not* know, dear Aunt Judith! You know one another so slightly that it will be one of my happiest pleasures to make you better acquainted! Seriously you have been so long more than a mother to me (more than my own mother ever was to me I fear) that you will, I know, rejoice in my happiness. I have not, I think, ever been truly happy before. I have been always apprehensive, fearing disasters that have never arrived. In the strangest way that house at Ireby and the inhabitants in it have hung over me like a doom. You have perceived this and thought me often faint-hearted and absurd, I know – yet these things are of the spirit and I have much of my poor father's lack of self-confidence. A Herries without conceit of himself is worse off than any other man in the world, I think! If you but knew how often I have urged myself forward to some act that I feared simply because I feared it! It seems to me now fantastic that I should have so dreaded Uhland's crooked body and the coarseness of his father – but now I have rescued Elizabeth from them, and myself as well! Do you know how, for so many years, he neglected and despised her and how patiently she bore that neglect? The end of the story is not yet. I will make myself so famous that they shall crawl on their knees to me before all is done! Now is not that an unworthy sentiment?

Elizabeth has but now entered and the kettle is on the fire and the toasting-fork ready! Our happiness is surely greater than that of any other two in the world! And yet how many lovers are there in this city at this same moment swearing the same thing. But we are such old lovers and have waited so long – longer, far longer than there was any need! How clearly I see that now!

My only unhappiness is that I have left you alone at Uldale – Dorothy, Adam, myself, all gone! And yet I am not sure that you will not be happier without us – all of us save Adam of course! I shall be seeing him tomorrow I trust. He is all Chartist now, I suppose, but he cannot think ill of me, for Elizabeth and myself are as poor as church mice and happy to be so. Sylvia came to see us last evening. She was exceedingly kind and says that Garth will soon find work for me. There will be my share of the Uldale money, but I would prefer that you send me nothing – until I ask for it.

Elizabeth is at my side. She sends her love. As she sits beside me I wonder what I have done to deserve this fortune. I have done nothing. I have been a poor feckless creature all my life but now, please God, there shall come something very different out of me. Our love for one another is beyond utterance. Dear Aunt Judith, wish us well and write to tell us that you are not angry. Your loving

JOHN

Judith Paris to Adam Paris

ULDALE,
February 8th, 1840

MY DEAREST SON – Your letter received last evening. I am *sorry* indeed that you should imagine that I am not *pleased* with your marriage. I am pleased with anything that gives you *happiness* but I am an old woman with only one passion left me and that is for my *son*. If you fancy that there is any mother in the world who gives her son willingly to *another woman* then you betray only once again that ignorance of my sex which, I fear, has been always your portion and will be so to the end.

You say that I need not fear that I shall lose you. *No, indeed, I cannot lose you*, for you are a part of myself, more perhaps than you will ever realize. You will return to me. You will bring her with you, but she can never have that part of you that is mine. You can tell her so if you wish. I am prepared to love her for as we grow old *the more one can love the better for one's health*. I have no *patience* with old women who complain of being *left*. I have always been standing on my own legs and intend to continue so. I like the name Margaret. She sounds sensible. I enclose with this my present to her. This silver box was left me by my brother who had it from a pedlar when he was a boy, and the silver chain was my grandmother's. I always intended them for your wife. Bring her soon to see me. I am quite alone here at the present although Dorothy and the children shall pay me a visit very shortly.

Bellairs is not in good health. It is his *stomach*. I am for ever telling him that he overeats but he answers that I am fanatical about food and eat like a *sparrow*. Certainly all our neighbours eat and drink far too much and I attribute my own astonishing good health to my careful feeding. Why should we behave like swine at a trough? I remember when I was a young woman in London that Georges had *incredible* stories of the amount that his friends consumed and I can remember Christabel and Jennifer in their youth guzzling like *pigs*. Well, they are all dead and here am I feeling twenty. How I run on, but I enjoy talking to my son who is now a Chartist and a husband and I don't know what! Only yesterday he was pulling cows' tails in the orchard.

John and Elizabeth were at poor Christabel's funeral. Will was a very dignified figure they say. But Sylvia writes to say that a young Mrs Morgan, widow of an Army captain, is already setting her cap at him. Is not that revolting? He is seventy this year if I am not mistaken, and she not a day over thirty! And what comedy if our fat five-chinned purple-faced Walter has a baby brother, a new uncle for our pretty Uhland! Since John left here we have had no great trouble with Ireby.

Uhland spoke to me in Keswick some days back and asked most politely after you. He has eyes like Cumberland stone and his lame leg is as lively as a spiteful old woman. I think Walter has no spite against myself but would do any hurt that he could to John and Dorothy. He and Uhland have already stories circulated in Keswick about John, and John himself seems apprehensive for in his last letter to me he says that he fancied that he saw Uhland looking at him out of a hackney coach. It may be that he was right, for Uhland has been twice to London.

All is well at Uldale. Rackstraw manages to a *marvel*. He is now at war with Peach, Walter's man. They detest one another and so carry on this ridiculous feud a stage further. We have built a new Barn in the upper field. Flossie the mare is too old for the carriage and has been put in the Paddock. I told you I think that Dorothy is coming shortly for a visit. You know me well enough to understand me when I say that I do not mind at all that I am in *sole* command here. I seem to know so very much better than anyone else the way things *ought* to be done. And I was sixty-five years of age last November! — Your most loving

MOTHER

John Herries to Adam Paris

6 ACACIA ROAD, MARYLEBONE,
October 25th, 1840

MY DEAR ADAM — The fact that you and Margaret (to whom give every loving message from Elizabeth and myself) are at Uldale encourages me to write a long letter, some of which I would wish for them all to see. Other parts of it I shall mark *Private* and they are for your ears alone.

Well, first to my great piece of personal news. The writer of this Epistle has pleasure in informing you, dear Adam, that he has been now for two days personal and private Secretary to Sir Edward Mitcham, Bart, MP for Great Cottenham. What say you to that and to whose services think you I owe it? To whom but to Grandfather Will! This is, you will all at Uldale allow, a most remarkable feat and three in the eye to my dear father-in-law and four in the nose to my beloved brother-in-law. What they will say to this villainous backsliding on old Will's part I have infinite delight in imagining. It seems that I owe this as I owe every other happiness in life to my beloved Elizabeth, for it appears that a long while back when she was staying with him he was moved by her loveliness and by her loneliness, coming in one evening and seeing her all by herself and sufficiently dejected. So he has had it in his mind for some time to do something for us and this is what he has done.

Old Mitcham is a stout claret-coloured old boy who lives in Bryanston Square with a fat wife and two plain daughters. He is amiable enough so long as he is flattered and is saved from an extravagant personal vanity by his adoration of Palmerston. Palmerston can do no wrong in his eyes and already I am myself beginning to see with a similar vision and watch the affairs in Syria as though my life depended upon it. They say that it is the Syrian business that has killed Lord Holland and that his dying word was: 'Mehemet Ali will kill me'.

I do not know that I have any Parliamentary ambitions myself. Elizabeth says that I would make a good orator, but she has a certain prejudice and I am altogether too nervous and shy to thrust myself into public notice. Meanwhile old Lady Mitcham is quite in love with Elizabeth as indeed is all the world. Sylvia says that she has come out amazingly and is another creature from when she was staying with grandfather. As well she may be, for she was at that time a lonely and deserted creature.

You have heard, I suppose, the gossip about grandfather. It is certain that this Mrs Morgan is for ever in Hill Street. She is a lively, gay, light-headed little woman, all bright colours, tinkling laughter and sharp acquisitiveness. She already touches everything in the house as though she owned it. I imagine myself that grandfather would not be averse to a child in his old age, for it is my private belief that he has suffered a long and bitter disappointment over Walter, who pays him less and less regard. I suggest that grandfather sees in Mrs Morgan a possible instrument rather than a personal pleasure.

Private. I have marked this Private because I should be ashamed were anyone but yourself to see it. But you have known me from babyhood, dear Adam, and loved me as long, I think. Listen then, brother and friend. Elizabeth and I love one another more dearly with every hour that passes. Our intimacy, our trust, our devotion is perfect. And yet there *is* one thing of which we will not speak to one another. We have both a fear, an unreasonable, foolish, crazy fear of Uhland. That she has it I know well. She speaks of him in her sleep and always in terror. By the way that she so deliberately avoids his name I know that she thinks of him. She fancies that because I married her he will do me some hurt and still more now that grandfather has volunteered this last kindness. Living with him so long has bred in her a fear of him that is beyond reason and is the stronger for its vagueness. And I must confess to you, dear Adam, that all my old terror of him persists. How often you have chided me for that! How foolish to your logical and consistent mind are such fears, but I have this from my father, who had it, perhaps, from *his* grandfather – that I live partly in a world of shadows. For a Herries that is fatal and there are times when I feel caught – held in a trap – and for no cause, no reason. How you must despise me. But no, you love me and are the most faithful and unswerving friend. Otherwise I would not have the courage to tell you. But there is more than that. The other evening at dusk coming from Bryanston Square I am certain that Uhland himself followed me.

Walking towards the Park down a narrow and ill-lit street I heard that tap of his stick and the hesitation of his step with which I have been so long dreadfully familiar. For a while, I dared myself not to turn, but at length my curiosity was too strong for me and, looking around, I saw in the light of a lamp the thin figure of Uhland, his dark beaver hat, pale face, black clothes. He stood there, without moving, leaning on his stick. I hurried on through a street now absolutely silent. He seemed to follow me now incorporeally.

Pray do not laugh at me in this. Your sturdy mind cannot imagine what such fears and terrors may be. You remain undaunted by that other world so far more real than this one. Between the Haunted and the Unhaunted there is a gulf that can only be bridged by love, and I am not one who can love more than one or two. Why does he hate me so, Adam? What have I ever done to him? What is this strange Feud in our family that is for ever forcing its way in?

But, for a moment to be practical, pray discover for me if you can, while you are at Uldale, whether Uhland has been recently in London. It would relieve my mind greatly if it had not been he. Meanwhile this is the one only subject about which Elizabeth and I do not speak. There is a shadow here, the size of a man's hand . . .

But to be cheerful and *daylighty* again, pray when you write tell me all the news of Uldale, of Aunt Judith, Roger, and in especial Margaret and yourself. When do you return to Town? You know that I do not think your *Charter* the cure for all our ills but times seem to become with every week more serious – the rick-burnings, riots and the rest – and I have little confidence in either Melbourne or Lord John. Your loving friend,

JOHN

Judith Paris to Sir William Herries, Bart

ULDALE,
January 10th, 1841

DEAR WILL – I write to congratulate you on your *Marriage* and, with that, to be as *honest* with you as I have always been. What do old people like you and me want with marriage? There is something *indecent* in it, do you not yourself think so? For you have always been the most *commonsensical* of all our Family and I cannot believe that, sitting in a corner, you do not laugh to yourself and wonder at your own action. You were lonely I must suppose. Well, so indeed are all of us. What do you say to an old woman of sixty-six sitting *all by herself* in a house under a *Mountain* miles from anywhere – or from *anyone* except your beastly Walter in his stone prison? Well, have it your own way – only I refuse to tell you that you have done a *fine* thing. If we cannot *laugh* at ourselves we are lost souls and although your sense of the *comic* has never been very strong in you, still you have a certain *dry* picture of yourself I know. I *trust* your widow will give you every *satisfaction*. Do not think me unkind nor unfriendly, dear Will. I am neither, and I have an especial *Gratitude* to you just now for what you have done for dear John and Elizabeth. That was especially noble of you seeing that your Walter hates them so (although *why* I cannot understand. Now that poor Christabel is gone he cannot *still* be thinking of that broken Fan). Moreover we were *Babies* together and that I can *never* forget although you were a dry and calculating child with a passion for *sums* (that I always detested) from the very start. Do you remember how you rode over to *Stone Ends* to fetch me back home and how I snapped my fingers at you? Yes, and would do it again if the same occasion rose. I am in marvellous health, thank God (although I doubt whether it is His doing). Dorothy comes with her babies to see me. She has now three *Girls* – one born this last November – Veronica, Amabel and Jane. Timothy is four – a fine child. Bellairs is in poor health – some disorder of the *Stomach*.

I must close. I am sending you a *Cumberland Ham* as a wedding present. You have everything in the world that you need, save only a Cumberland Ham – and there are no other Hams so good in the world anywhere. Your most affectionate

JUDITH

Margaret Paris to her father, Caesar Kraft
(This letter was never posted but was
found, many years later, by Adam Paris
among his wife's papers.)
ULDALE, CUMBERLAND,
April 6th, 1841

MY DEAR FATHER—It is very likely that this letter will never be posted. I am writing it at two of the morning, sitting under a candle in my dressing gown while Adam sleeps in the bed close behind me, sleeps so soundly as he always does, sleeps as I alas just now so seldom do!

For, Father dear, that is why in the morning I shall not post this letter, because I shall be ashamed of my mood. I am unhappy tonight, desperately unhappy, unhappy as I have never been in my life before. Now listen, father. I know that Adam loves me, I know that they all wish me well here, I know that Adam is as proud and ambitious for our work as you and I. I am well in health and so is he. We have money enough. Best of all I have you, dearest, dearest father – and yet tonight my courage is all gone. I have at the moment no resistance.

I think perhaps that my marriage has been the most dreadful mistake. I love Adam more, far, far more than when I married him and I am well assured that he loves me. I think his character noble, strong and generous. I was not mistaken in thinking it so when I married him. But, father, I think there is no woman in England so lonely as I am at this moment.

They are all so strange. This wild rough country is so strange. Adam's mother is so strange. Adam's mother! Perhaps that is where all the trouble lies! On my first visit here with Adam she was, as I told you, most friendly. She wanted to love me as a daughter, she said, and that is I know what she intended. But love does not come like that. She was resolved to feel no jealousy of me and in that very resolve felt it. You know how quiet I am, father. You have always understood that I feel more than I can say and that I cannot force myself to any feeling if it is not there. 'Madame' (as they all call her here) is the opposite of this. I have never said much about her to you. You have never seen her. You cannot imagine her. She is unlike anyone else in the world, a little tiny woman with snow-white hair, a pale brown complexion, wearing the brightest colours, her eyes sparkling, carrying an ivory cane, and alive in every inch of her! I cannot convey to you how alive she is! I do not know her exact age but it is certainly between sixty and seventy and yet she is more living than anyone else in the neighbourhood. Everyone knows it. Everyone recognizes it. She is a great figure here. She is compounded of two opposites. Her mother was I believe a gipsy and thence she has her gay colours, her restlessness, her laughter, her generosity, her tempers, her childlike pleasure in little things. She will dance to a music-box tune or pick up her skirts and run down the road, or rate a tramp like Queen Elizabeth, or play Backgammon like a baby, kiss and stroke the cheek and love you in a passion! And on the other hand she has a good business head, runs the house and property like a lawyer, disciplines the servants, has her finger in every pie.

But her passion is for Adam. Adam is everything to her. She would like to possess him, every bone and vein of him, and his soul beyond. But she is wise enough to know that she cannot and that she can only take from him what he voluntarily gives her. That is a great deal. They have the strongest bond, the two – almost without knowing it, without wishing it. It is not only a bond of mother and son but a bond of family too. All the Herries I have met, whether in London or here, have something in common although they are all so different. What it is I cannot say. It is as though, inside the family, they are all against one another, but that against the outside world they are all united. Even Adam has something of this, although he is for ever saying that he is illegitimate and does not belong to them and disapproves of their worldliness and pride and materialism. For they *are* material, grossly so *and* proud – proud with the worst kind of English pride as though they were God's people. John Herries in London is the only exception I have seen – yes, and *part* of Madame. Part of *her* is non-Herries, hates that blood and would like to escape from it.

In any case I am shut out, father, however kind they *wish* to be, I am shut out. I am shut out by them all and by this hateful hard, raining, hostile country. It is all sodden hills and grey cloud and stone walls here. When the sun shines everything is harder than ever. The stones have a hard face, the people look as though they would like to kill you, the cattle lower their heads at you. I know that it is only on visits that we are here and that Adam will never leave his work in London, but I am afraid lest one day his mother will win and bring him back here for ever. He is so silent. He cannot express his feelings at all. When I lie in his arms I know that he loves me, but he will never say so. He is so shy of expression and when others are there I sometimes think that he almost hates me. Of course he does not. He is true and loving and noble, but why cannot he say something to me once and again, only some little things to reassure me? Then he goes off – for a whole day, leaving me with his mother and without a word to any of us. He loves this country so passionately that I do not count for anything beside it. I was so happy with you, dearest father, living with you, working with you. I needed no one. And then he came and at the first sight I loved him with all my soul as I shall always love him. But here I seem to fight every stone wall, every little stream, every sulky cloud. If only he would speak to me, tell me once that he loves me, defend me against my fears ... Oh, father, why ...

Judith Paris to Adam Paris

ULDALE,
March 4th, 1842

MY DEAR SON – Dorothy and the children arrived last week. I cannot say I am sure how this *experiment* may turn out. I confess that I am not altogether easy in my mind. When Bellairs died two months back Dorothy certainly had no *idea* of it, nor had I. But she found the house more and more melancholy and longed every day more ardently for Uldale so she must have her way. We can but see and I admit that it is agreeable to have company again.

Dorothy has grown very *stout* but is kind and much *improved* I think. She was always *amiable* as you know, but had a strong conviction that she must *manage*. I have explained to her that the children are *her* business and the house *mine*. She was at first inclined somewhat to think me an *old lady*. She discovers that I am not so ancient as she supposed!

And now, Adam, I have had a great *adventure*. I have spent two nights in Watendlath! What do you say to that! I have stayed in the old house, eaten at the old table, walked the old ways. I have seen where Charlie Watson is buried and will confess to you that I shed a *tear* or two. I have seen again my Georges. Yes, standing by the Tarn, just as he used, smiling at me, because he had done something that he should not, and to-day was yesterday. I was a young girl again and all *life* was in front of me. Well, that is over, my son. As I looked across the water to the hills and down to Rosthwaite where your grandfather lived, I knew what I had *thrown away* when I remained at Uldale. I sold my *soul* perhaps that day but what does it matter? There are too many souls already in space for the loss of one little one to be of importance.

Alice Perry's son reigns and a fine fellow he is, with four fine *children*. His wife I thought a poor feckless creature and her *hodge-podge* a disgrace, but for once I kept my old tongue quiet and told her only *compliments*. For an hour I was *wild* again, old woman though I am. But the wildness passed. Here I am at my table adding accounts and the cows are going to milking beyond the window and Skiddaw is as mild and stout as Dorothy herself.

They all thought me *mad* to go. I have still a touch of madness, but·it diminishes. Rackstraw has the *gout*, Mary – the new maid (from Cockermouth – a good girl) – the toothache, her face swollen twice its size. I shall never see Watendlath again.

I *long* to have you here. It seems to be the *only thing* I live for now, but I will not force you. You will come in your own good time. I passed Walter in the road last week. We did not speak. He is *immensely* fat and is not as careful in his dress as he was. There are awful doings at Ireby from all I hear, and many people refuse to go there any longer. I hear that he vows vengeance on us all because John and dear Elizabeth are happy in London – a poor sort of reason – but he cannot harm us. Give my love to Margaret. I am sending you some of my own *Preserves*, two *Hams* and a *wool-work ottoman* that I bought at old Mr Chancey's sale in Keswick as a present to Margaret. Your loving

MOTHER

Adam Paris to Judith Paris

7 FARRIMOND STREET, LONDON,
April 3rd, 1842

MY DEAREST MOTHER – This must be only the briefest of notes as I go this afternoon to a meeting in Manchester, but I thought you would like to know how we find our new rooms.

We think them exceedingly comfortable when we have time to consider them. I was never before as busy as now. People are still talking of Peel's Income-Tax and we Chartists will most certainly not oppose it. It is a small step in our own direction but the state of the country is with every week worse and the conditions among the poor frightful.

We have seen none of our relations save John and Elizabeth. I am happy to say that Elizabeth and Margaret have become the greatest friends. I am most happy for that. Margaret has not been so well of late.

In great haste. Your loving son,

ADAM

Very many thanks for the Cheeses and Butter you so kindly sent. They are most welcome.

HOMECOMING IN WINTER

THE little town shivered under the breath of the helm-wind that, beating down from the icy caverns and hollows of Helvellyn, threw dark quivering shadows of cloud on the garden walls, set Main Street trembling with a half-worshipping, half-shuddering agitation, and caused Mrs Constantine, who had Mrs Trevelyan of Bournemouth as guest, to rub the tip of her nose with her muff a hundred times.

Fortunately at this moment of English history ladies were, by the dictates of fashion, more warmly clad than at any time before or after. So many petticoats, with solid padding, indeed did they wear that the crinoline must come in very shortly and assist them. Mrs Constantine was wearing four petticoats, and her poke-bonnet was lined with fur. Her peaked and animated face was for ever hiding itself in an enormous snowy muff. But it was right that it should be cold. Mrs Constantine, wife of one of the doctors in Keswick, told Mrs Trevelyan (whose heart, if the truth were known, was sick for Bournemouth) that it was right that it should be cold. She exulted in it, she revelled in it. It was but a week before Christmas and what was Christmas if not cold? The coach rattled down the street, old Tom Rawson blowing his horn with a fine Christmas flourish. The boys were just out of school and, wrapped up almost to the eyes in mufflers, rushed along the street screaming like sea-birds, playing 'shinny' as they went, the wooden ball lathe-turned, the 'shinny' sticks cut from the hedges. Keswick was its own quiet self in these winter months, lying peacefully beneath the purple wind-scarred hills. In the summer, as Mrs Constantine explained, it was now 'the rage', college youths from Cambridge, every house letting lodgings, the pencil-makers selling to every visitor enough black-lead pencils to last a lifetime; spar-dealers, curiosity-mongers, boat-men making a fortune; coaches tearing in and out, picnics every-where, and until lately Mr Southey to be seen at any time, taking his walk. Poor gentleman, nothing but tragedy now. So many things to see! So *many* things to see! . . . But now all is quiet. Soon sheep, their wool blown a little by the wind, move up the street, the boys with their 'shinny' sticks racing in and out among them, there is a sudden flash of sun from the wrack of cloud, piercing like a sword drawn from its scabbard the cobbles, the sheep, the boys, slashing into sudden colour the cold flanks of Blencathra.

But Mrs Constantine was historical. History was her passion. Oh, Keswick was full of history! There was Acorn Street where the Royal Oak had been (oak – acorn – did Mrs Trevelyan see the quaintness?) and the Friars Inn where Lord Derwentwater quaffed a flagon of ale before riding to the '15, and Crosthwaite Vicarage where the tithes – the wool, the pigs, the geese, the dairy produce – were brought and a grand dinner with hodge-podge followed. Here Mrs Trevelyan sneezed.

'You are not chill, my dear, I trust?'

'Oh no, not at all, not at all—'

And the old Moot Hall and the— Here she broke off to murmur :

'My dear Eliza! This is most fortunate. Here coming towards us is the most interesting person in Keswick.'

Mrs Trevelyan, blinded by the sharp wind and knowing that she had caught a cold that would endure for weeks, stared a little uncertainly.

But there was no doubt as to whom Mrs Constantine intended, for, stepping out of a barouche, standing for a moment, resting on a cane and looking about, then slowly walking up the street towards them, was a most remarkable woman. She was small of figure, but her step was astonishingly alert. She carried her head as though she commanded the town. As she approached them more nearly Mrs Trevelyan saw that her hair was snow-white under her poke-bonnet, that was of a rich blue and decorated with a feather. She wore a purple silk mantlet trimmed with a shaded ribbon. She was distinguished, most dainty, most deter-mined. Her hands were hidden in a purple muff. She tapped with her cane, she looked about her eagerly, as though she were sniffing the fragrant, frosty air. Some boys with their ball, racing up the street, slowed down as they saw her. She smiled benignly upon them. A gentleman, riding a splendid roan, touched his hat. She bowed like a queen. A bearded farmer, driving a cow, touched his hat and she bowed again. She arrived at the two ladies.

'Oh Mrs Constantine, how *do* you do?'

'Very well indeed, thank you, Madame Paris. Will you permit me to introduce to you my friend, Mrs Trevelyan, from Bournemouth.'

'With the greatest pleasure ... I hope you are well? You are paying a lengthy visit?'

Here Mrs Trevelyan unfortunately sneezed and was so deeply aggravated that instead of paying compliments, as she had intended, she could only stutter:

'The air in Bournemouth is more balmy—'

'It is indeed. But here, I fancy, it is more bracing. I am on my way to visit old Miss Pennyfeather. She has not been so well, you know. Pray, remember me to the Doctor, Mrs Constantine. If you would be so good ...'

She moved on.

'A most remarkable woman,' said Mrs Constantine eagerly. 'They say her mother was a gipsy. She has a house at Uldale and is a relation of the Herries family. Her father was a Herries – long ago here in Keswick. She has had a most remarkable history—'

They passed on to the more sheltered side of the street, but not before Mrs Trevelyan, who felt her chill gaining upon her with every cut of the wind, had remarked: 'She appears to enjoy most excellent health. I never saw such spirits!'

No, indeed. She had not and she would not, for Judith was at the height of happiness. This evening, by the Lancaster Coach, Adam her son was arriving for the Christmas festivities. Adam was coming home. She had not seen him for nearly a year; he was bringing his wife with him and that was very pleasant, but for Judith no one and nothing mattered but Adam.

She was in splendid health. This wild wind, these steel-grey hills suited her. She was exalted, lifted up. Between a break in the wall, over a dry and wind-tossed garden, she could see the distant Lake, the small waves in feathered hurry racing before the tongue of the flicking air. Were her hands not so warmly in the purple muff she could have stretched them out and embraced it all – sky, hill, water, stone and tree. The freshness, the strength, the flashing scornful sun! Snow was in the air! Snow! And Adam was coming home, Adam was coming home. She saw Dr Constantine, very thin-waisted, in his high beaver hat, riding his cob. She bowed. He bowed. It was all she could do not to give a little hop, skip and jump for sheer joy of living! Adam was coming home! Even as she rapped Miss Pennyfeather's knocker she gathered him to her heart, felt herself lost in his embrace, knew once again that neither wife nor work could take him from her. He was yet in her womb!

Little Nancy, Miss Pennyfeather's treasure, opened the door to her and she was in the parlour. It remained unchanged through all these years just as the rooms at Uldale remained unchanged, although Dorothy was for ever talking of 'new furniture'. New furniture! Judith detested the great ugly, heavy, clumsy stuff such as you saw at the Osmastons' or the Applebys'. No, this delicacy was what she loved and her eye rested with gratitude on dear Miss Pennyfeather's blue Chinese wallpaper, the nodding mandarins on the mantelpiece, the delicate harpsichord with its painting of violets on the lid, and the pretty delicate chairs with their faded gilt. But she did not look for more than a moment, for there, dancing from foot to foot in front of Miss Pennyfeather, who was sunk deep in an armchair and all wrapped up in shawls, was the strangest figure!

He was an odd little man, scarcely five feet high, his head on one side as though he had a crick in his neck, his shoulders humped; he had (Judith saw at once and recognized from olden days) the most marvellous eyes, dark, luminous, living every life in their orbs, at one moment enraged, at another amazed, at a third delighted, at a fourth swimming in fun. He had long white locks, unbrushed, dishevelled, and they seemed to have a breath of their own as they moved. He was wearing a blue-lapelled swallow-tailed coat with brass buttons, two waistcoats, a black stock and a high white collar above it. As Judith came in upon him he was dancing round like a top, his white hair waving, and nursing in his arms two white kittens, while Miss Pennyfeather's spaniel, Bonaparte, barked at his heels. Yes, Judith knew at once who he was! Back, without a moment's interval, to that afternoon at Southey's when, her heart sore and indignant at Jennifer's unkindness, that boy with the flashing eyes had broken in ... and now ... this old man ... and she ... She had never seen him between then and now ...

She bent down and kissed Miss Pennyfeather. Then she held out her hand.

'Mr Hartley Coleridge! You will not remember me ... And, indeed, of course, you cannot. It is – oh, I fear to say how many years! I was a young woman, you a boy, tea at Mr Southey's ...'

He did not remember her in the least, but he put down the kittens and held her hand and looked into her eyes with his own lambent ones and pretended that he remembered her perfectly well. They stood together, hand in hand, much of a height.

'Remember you! Why, of course, dear lady, of course, of course. Hey-diddle-diddle, but that is a long time ago – sad things, many sad things since then. So many gone, so many failing of high hopes. But we won't be sad. We refuse to be sad. I can see that you are never sad. We are like these kittens, you and I. Here – the reel of cotton – I have lost it. Here, help me!' He was down on his knees searching under the harpsichord.

He looked up pleadingly at Miss Pennyfeather.

'Claribella, Isabella, Rosamunda – may I request a glass of beer?'

She looked at him sternly, then shook her head at him.

He sat back on the floor, his hand on a kitten's back.

'Well, a glass of water then.'

She pulled the bell-rope.

Then he was on his feet again. He danced about the room, talking all the time.

'Willie and Nannie Coates; you know, Lord and Lady Bacon because they kept so many pigs ... They used to say ... And Dinah Fleming – dear, dear Dinah – and you know the Mr Briggs and the Branckens and the Hustlers – at Tail End. Oh, you know them all, Claribella, and love them, and we'll go together! We'll pay calls together! We'll go round in a gig drawn by a goat all set up with lanterns. We'll stop on Dunmail and have goat's milk and I'll write a poem ...'

He caught up the kitten, held it in front of him murmuring,

> Our birth and death alike are mysteries,
> And thou, sweet babe, art a mysterious thing

'Jeanette,' he murmured. 'That was to Jeanette.'

He almost ran to the door. 'I must be away! Off! Gone! Vanished!'

He ran back and, with the utmost tenderness and delicacy, bent down and kissed the very old lady in the chair.

'Perhaps for the last time, Claribella, Rosamunda,' he said.

'Who knows but that beer may finish me one of these warm, spidery days?'

He stood in front of Judith and smiled so enchanting, engaging a smile that there were tears in her eyes.

'You saw me last, ' he said, 'as a boy with everything in front of me. Now I can leap a brook and dance a hornpipe – not bad for an old man.'

He bent forward, kissed her hand, went to the door, bowed to both of them and was gone.

To Judith, his appearance, so unexpected, so brief, was the most extraordinary omen. He had been that to her on the only other occasion that she had met him. It had been then as though they had known one another always, sharing some secret life private to themselves. It had been so then. It was so now. All that he had lost, all that she had lost, rushed to her heart. She stared at the closed door as though it concealed a mystery. Then she recovered herself and was busy in cheering her old friend, who now was paralysed, whose doom was upon her, whose spirits were as brave and cheerful as those of the kittens that played with the ends of her shawl.

'Oh! He never had his glass of water!' Judith cried.

'Nancy will give it him. He is an old friend of Nancy's. He is with her in the kitchen now, chucking her under the chin. But she knows that she is never to give him beer – that I shall never forgive her if she does.'

Miss Pennyfeather lay back exhausted, her hands helpless, the yellow skin drawn sheath-like over the ridge of bones, only her eyes brave, defiant and amused. For an hour or more Judith made her happy.

'I enjoy seeing you so cheerful, my dear.'

'I enjoy it myself. But Adam is coming. I have not seen him this year.'

'And his wife?'

'Yes.'

'You should bring her to see me one day. I am curious. You don't care for her.'

'Oh, I do!' Judith shrugged her shoulders. 'Or I would. If she'd let me. She is a great calm, quiet woman. All the same I think she is a little afraid of me.'

Miss Pennyfeather said nothing.

'And you know that I am never my best with anyone who is afraid of me.'

'Now, Judith.' Miss Pennyfeather's eyes sought the other's very seriously. 'We have been the greatest friends for many years, have we not? Well, then, I can speak my mind. You must be good and generous to Adam's wife. Any other way lies catastrophe. Make her love you.'

'I have tried.'

'Yes – with reservations. "I will love you," you have said, "if you recognize that I come first with my son." ' Then suddenly, with an odd galvanic energy: 'Possessive love – I detest it.'

Judith bent over her friend.

'Very well, dearest . . . You are right. I will make Margaret love me.' She laid her warm white hand on the dead yellow one.

After a pause Miss Pennyfeather said:

'There is another thing, my dear. Gossip. They come in here and gossip although I tell them not to. Is it true that you are having John and Elizabeth for Christmas?'

'Yes. And Sylvia and Garth Herries also. They are coming down from Edinburgh.'

'Look out, then, for trouble from Mr Walter. I hear that he is enraged beyond all measure that you should have John and Elizabeth.'

'Why should I not have them?'

'After his casting Elizabeth off – and after John marrying Elizabeth. Oh, my dear, you are not as a rule so slow!'

'Yes . . . I see. Well, I am not afraid of him.'

'They say that young Osmaston and Fred Kelly and others are always at the Fortress – card-playing, drinking . . . Gossip. But no decent person goes to the Fortress any more.'

Judith smiled.

'I told Walter years ago that he could not do it. From the moment he laid the first stone of that building everything has gone wrong with him. Jennifer's ghost haunts him. And Uhland's ingratitude. And now his father's marriage . . . Do you know that old Will may be a father any day now?'

'Never!' cried Miss Pennyfeather.

'Yes, and he is seventy-two years old. Well, my father was the same. They are strong men, the Herries . . . Goodbye, my dear. I shall be in again very shortly and shall bring Adam's wife with me.'

When Judith was in the barouche again and turning towards home the afternoon was already gathering in. A pallid bar of shuttered light lay between heavy clouds above Skiddaw. The

wind had died, but little sobbing breaths rose and fell among the
bare trees. The hills were cold, clothed in an ashen shadow, and
over the long, thin fields a chill, hard and remorseless, laid its
hand. A few hesitating flakes of snow were already falling.

Halfway along Bassenthwaite they approached a horseman
and, in the half-light, Judith saw that it was Walter. She would
have had old Bennet drive past him, but Walter, at once
recognizing her carriage, rode his horse in front and across it.
Bennett pulled up the horses and Walter came close, laying his
gloved hand on the back of Judith's seat. She had not spoken
with him for over two years.

'Good evening, Judith,' he said.

His voice was thick and husky. Now that he was close to her
she could see the gross double-chinned face, the purple veins in
nose and cheeks, the little eyes half closed under the heavy lids.
He was very large in his riding-coat. He towered above her. He
looked rather pathetic, she thought, and she was not in the least
afraid of him.

'Good evening, Walter.'

'I shall not detain you a moment,' he went on, turning to curse
his horse that it did not keep still. 'I have only a question to ask.'

'And what is that? We shall have snow, I fancy.'

'Yes. My question is not about the weather.'

He leaned closer to her, and his breath was coarse and hot.

'Is it true, as I hear, that you are entertaining my daughter at
Uldale this Christmas?'

'Perfectly true.'

'You are aware that she disobeyed me flagrantly and that by
entertaining her you are insulting me before the whole countryside?'

His voice quivered and again she thought: 'Poor Walter!'

'Now, Walter, this is a cold, chilly moment to discuss such a
matter. I shall invite whom I please to my house.'

His big hand quivered on the board.

'Then you must take the consequences,' he said very low.

'I can look after myself – and my guests.'

'Well – I have warned you.'

She rested her hand for a moment on his.

'Come, Walter. This is foolishness. Forgive Elizabeth. Pay us a
visit. Let us slay this stupid feud that has lasted so long. Hatred
never did any good.'

He shouted: 'By God, No! ... By God, No!' – dug spurs into
his horse and charged away down the road.

Old Bennett drove on. His broad back (shoulders now bent and round) represented his proper emotions. He served Madame. If anyone did her a hurt, he would see to it. But words – words break no windows. That Herries of Ireby was crazed, and the way, so they said, that he carried on with women was shameful. Bennett, with all the virtue and fidelity of the unimaginative, scornfully flicked his horses' ears.

Judith was only for a moment perturbed. It had been strange, that dual recurrence of little Coleridge and of Walter – her past breaking in. But as she grew older she found that past, present and future began to merge. Time was becoming of less and less importance. There were these facts: her visit with Warren to Rosthwaite, the awful birth in Paris, Adam the baby teasing Walter on his white horse, Reuben as he fell mortally wounded in the lighted garden, Jennifer crying 'They've begun to build! They've begun to build!' or, long long ago, a beautiful naked woman and a young man on his knees, old Uncle Tom and Emma sitting by the fire at Stone Ends, David dropping, as though a stone had struck him, on the bright green grass, Georges throwing her out of bed at Watendlath, Georges falling, falling while the Old Man with the white beard ... She looked up through the trees to the dark sky. All these things had occurred together, at the same moment of time, and meant but this – that they had been signs to light Judith Paris the way to salvation – and she had not gone ... There was somewhere a Door ... and somewhere a Key ... and all History, whether of Nations or Families, was but this ... Have you found it? Are you in touch? Have you made the Connexion? ...

She sat back, drawing her mantlet more closely about her. No, they meant but this, all these shining moments, these figures woven into her tapestry – that she adored her son Adam, that he was coming home tonight, and her head would for a moment rest on his breast, that they would be together, together ...

Her heart began to beat so that she must lay her muff against it.

The house was alight with candles. They had not gas yet, although Dorothy was always urging it. Judith refused. Candles and lamps. This gas hurt the eyes. It was dangerous. And how pretty the candleshine against the Chinese wallpaper, or lighting you up the twisted stair.

'How modern you are!' she said, pinching Dorothy's fat cheek. Then added: 'I shall be gone soon. Then you may have gas.'

She was managing very well with Dorothy, who had grown in experience as well as in physical size. She was now a great woman with big breasts and wide beam and a face like a dairy-maid. Having children had taught her a deal; she managed them well. They obeyed her, indeed, better than they obeyed their Great-aunt Judith, as they were taught to call her. Timothy was a normal lively boy already like his father. The three little girls — Veronica, Amabel and Jane — were docile, happy-natured. Veronica was the pretty one. She had dimples and dark hair like her grandmother's. Yes, they were good children.

By eight o'clock the whole house quivered with excitement. For one thing, with the coming of Adam and Margaret the stir of the Christmas festivities might be said to commence. John and Elizabeth were arriving tomorrow, Sylvia and Garth Herries two days later. Christmas Night there was to be a dance. The children could scarcely contain themselves, and the little girls were busy, secretly, all day long, painting, sewing, cutting out, making their presents.

Adam and Margaret would take a post-chaise from Kendal, so one could not be sure when they would arrive. Judith walked all over the candlelit house, seeing that everything was right. She pushed open a window a moment and listened to the bell-ringers practising at the church a mile and a half away. She could hear the running water, and felt, with a thrill of contrasted warmth, the cold dark paths running up the mountain-sides, the gullies down whose flanks the wind was tearing. One cold flutter, then another, touched her cheeks. It was snowing.

She lingered especially in the room where Adam and Margaret would sleep. This had been Jennifer's. Here Francis had surprised Jennifer, here Jennifer had lain while John read to her and the reflection of the flames that the rioters had lighted danced on the walls. Yes, everything was well. The four-poster was ready, there were flowers (Christmas roses) on the davenport, the stamped fleur-de-lis wallpaper looked fine in the candlelight. Dorothy would like tall pier-glasses and grates of shining steel and heavy cornices. Not while Judith was in command! She came out and stood at the top of the stairs, holding a candle and listening. The house was very still, only the ticking of the clocks, a door opening and closing. Stillness, peace. A great wave of thankfulness flowed over her. She had not done so badly then. After all the turmoil of her life it had come to this — that, hale in health, honoured and trusted, in this old house that she loved, she stood there waiting for her son whom, by wise dealing, she had kept in her heart. She smiled to herself, thinking of the moment when, in that room close to her, he had defied her. He had climbed out of the window just as she had once done. Bone of her bone, flesh of her flesh . . .

The bell pealed through the house. The knocker shook the door. They were here, they were here!

She ran down the stairs, across the hall, flung open the door, was out on the paved path. Bennett and the boy had come from the stable with lanterns and all the dogs with them, barking, yelling, yelping. And there beyond the gates, like a visitant from another ghostly country, was the post-chaise. A moment later Judith was in her son's arms.

Half an hour later Margaret stood alone in the bedroom, hesitating to blow out the candles before she went down. Adam had already preceded her. She stood there beating down her fear. She saw herself in the glass, her image flickering uncertainly in the blown candlelight. Yes, she was tall, broad, plain; clear straight eyes, dark hair brushed carefully, cleanly, strong, but – dull! Oh, dull, dull, dull! And this little woman with all her oddity, liveliness, sharpness would find her with every visit more dull.

It was all she could do to keep the tears back from her eyes. The journey had been very long, the train stinking of oil from the ill-trimmed lamps, the last drive in the chaise chill and rough. She was terribly weary. Had she had her way she would have gone to bed, then and there, and slept for a night and day, but Madame would think that weak and foolish.

'What! A strong woman like Margaret! What a wife for my son!'

And Adam – why had he not *felt* her isolation, dread, loneliness? Her father would have known in an instant what she was feeling, but Adam seemed to have no intuition. Oh! he loved her, of course! But he never seemed to wish to tell her so. She scolded herself here as she had already done a thousand times. What was this need in her for reassurance? It had not been so before her marriage. She and her father had never spoken about their love. But Adam was so strange. Even now, after their years of marriage, she did not understand him. Perhaps no one understood him except his mother. He would escape from her – at any moment. At one time he was there, and then, in a second, he was gone! And it never occurred to him to suit himself to her mood, to ask what *she* was thinking! Maybe all Englishmen were like that! It was her German blood that made her ask for sentiment, sympathy, little loving words and actions. At night, in the dark, his heart beating against her heart, her arm around him as though he were her child – ah, then he was hers! But why with the first flash of daylight must he cease all demonstration as though he were afraid of the light? Oh, these Englishmen – but they were difficult as husbands!

He was downstairs now with his mother, and here was she trembling at the smell and feel of this hostile house, at the thought of the dark cold hills that closed it in, at the anticipation of that little woman with her sharp eyes, her way of suddenly looking at you as though she wondered that you *could* be such a fool!

Well, she must fight it. Adam was so happy to come home. She must make him think that she was happy too.

She came down and found them as she had expected, in the parlour seated on the sofa with the roses (Margaret *hated* that sofa), Madame's white sharp hand resting on Adam's broad knee with so proprietary an air!

Adam jumped up.

'Come here, my dear,' said Judith, patting the sofa. 'I am sure that you must be tired. Come and sit beside me.'

'Thank you,' said Margaret, feeling large and awkward and clumsy in all her limbs. 'I am not tired at all, thank you.'

She sat down beside her. There was a pause then, as though Margaret had interrupted a very intimate conversation. Then Judith continued again the excited narration of people and events that she had been pouring on to Adam before Margaret's entrance.

Then Dorothy came in, red-faced, smiling, her corsage of puckered taffeta too tight for her figure, her hair a trifle untidy. Margaret liked Dorothy. She was kind and unalarming – somehow rather German.

They went in to supper. How happy Adam was! Margaret's heart ached with love of him as she watched him across the table. He was like a small boy again, asking about everything, the dogs, the horses, the cows, the dairy, Dorothy's children, all the neighbours. He had forgotten, she saw, all his distress about the poor, the Corn Laws and the rest – the things that would make him so unhappy in London that he would walk the room, tossing his head, beating his hands against one another, crying out ...

She saw, too, Judith's happiness, how the small lady, sitting so straight at the head of the table, was almost breathless with happiness at having her son home again. How excitable she was at her age, what a child still in many ways! She would rap out an order to the parlour-maid like a general addressing a soldier, and then in a moment would forget it all and clap her hands at some joke, or throw to one of the four dogs – that sat with staring eager eyes near her chair – something from the table, or laugh at Rackstraw. And once she jumped up and walked, strutting with an affected gait to show them the absurdity of some old man in Keswick.

'Yes,' thought Margaret, 'what a poor creature I am to grudge them their happiness in being together! I will win her heart, make her love me.' But the words would not come. She could only answer in monosyllables. Some reserve stuck in her throat. 'Oh, what a fool and a spoil-sport they must think me!' she cried to herself.

After supper, the Waits came. First they could be heard behind the closed windows, faint shrill voices and the sudden plaintive squeak of a fiddle. They were summoned into the hall and stood there in a semi-circle – three boys, an old man with a white beard, a stout countryman in a smock, and a thin tall man with spectacles who was the fiddler. The servants came to listen. The dogs sat solemnly on their haunches in a group, yawning once and again.

The boys sang in piercing trebles while the old bearded man had one of the deepest voices, surely, in the world. They sang their carols without fear or hesitation, looking at no one but holding their heads up and staring into the ceiling with a kind of ecstatic frenzy. When it was over they were given money and hot drinks. They vanished into the night, and a flurry of snow blew in through the open door.

Afterwards they sat around the blazing fire in the parlour talking, listening to the wind that had sprung up and now was howling round the house.

When they all went up to bed Adam followed his mother into her room. When the door was closed she held him in her arms as though she would never let him go.

They sat down close together at the foot of the bed.

'It has been a long time, Adam.'

'Yes, Mother, I know. It is not easy. There is so much to do.'

'Are you happy?' She looked at him sharply.

'Happy? Who is happy?'

'Then you are not. Why not?'

He stared, under frowning brows, into the fire.

'The state of the country is dreadful. Never been so bad. No employment, trade fearful, no faith in Parliament, living conditions frightful – and everyone helpless. What is coming, Mother? Surely something disastrous.'

She put her arm around him, and he his around her.

'Yes,' she said. 'But I know something about life now. Nothing is so bad as you expect.'

'No. Perhaps.' He hesitated. 'I come in for a good deal of criticism, Mother. Many of them think me priggish, snobbish, out for my own hand. It was a shock the first time that I realized it. I had thought that I was so genuine, really moved by the love of my fellowmen, truly believing in them. And then when I heard myself called a self-seeker I was miserable for a while. I allowed no one to see it – not Margaret even – but I thought, "Well, perhaps I am this. I am deceived in myself." There's a little man, rather a power in London, he believes in nothing and in nobody. He says frankly that if you say that you love your fellowmen or trust your friends you are a hypocrite. He hates and despises me. I know the sort of picture he draws of me behind my back, amiable, filled with noble sentiments, but a snob because I am a Herries and making my own career under a cloak of caring for others. Yes, I was unhappy for a while – so long as I thought it might be true. But it is *not* true. There is something in me stronger and deeper than my intentions or my words or my acts. I *do* believe in my fellowmen, I *do* love them. I know that most of them intend the best. I know that Henry Cray is wrong with his bitterness and cynical mind. I have ceased to disturb myself. I am tranquil again.'

'Yes.' She drew his hand into hers.

'That is hard – the first time you really see yourself as your detractors see you. But it is grand too. At last you are seeing the whole picture. You are a spectator of yourself. That happened to me years ago in this very house, when Jennifer hated me. I could not *believe* that anyone could see me as that – mean, sly, intriguing. But only those who love you know you. There is good criticism, though, in the view of your detractors. You take yourself too seriously, Adam, I don't doubt. Pompous, sentimental! No, you are not, but you think perhaps too much of nobility and fine living. Life's a magpie's hoard – an occasional gold piece quite by accident among the broken glass and bits of coal. Take

life lightly, my son. Believe in it, but laugh at it and at yourself.'

He kissed her. 'Later on. I'm too solemn, I know. I am always
feeling it. But I live so much by myself, in my own thoughts . . .'

'And Margaret?' she asked him.

'I think I love Margaret more every day – but I don't grow
closer to her. She wants something from me. I don't know what it
is. Something I cannot give her. I have never been able to say in
words what I feel. I'm tongue-tied. It seems to threaten my freedom if I speak too much. She is very quiet, too, of course. We are
both too quiet together perhaps.'

'I am going to make Margaret love me this Christmas-time,'
Judith said. 'She is lonely, Adam, and she loves you more than
anyone else ever has – except myself.'

'You and she, Kraft, and John,' Adam said slowly, 'the four in
my life who have loved me. But for the most part men cannot
come close to me. I used to dream of helping to make a great
Brotherhood in England. Now I know that I never shall. I am
not the man.'

'No,' she answered. 'Maybe you are not. It is not for us to
choose what we shall be. We have to accept and without protest.'

She kissed him most lovingly, and he went to his wife.

THE WILD GOOSE

THE wild goose, the same bird that Orlando was afterwards
to see, flew over the house as the light was just breaking. The
whirr of its wings stirred the perfect stillness of the crystal scene.
The early sun was dim, but a pale glitter showed every tree and
blade of grass sparkling with crystal. The whiteness of the snow,
even in that thin light, dazzled the eye.

The sun rose higher – the wild goose was gone – the sheathed
snow, stretching in a translucent glory to the line where Skiddaw
cut the sky, now faintly blue, ran to the very foundations of the
house and was marked only by the tiny feet of birds.

They were all going to church – Madame, Adam, Margaret,
Elizabeth, John, Sylvia, Garth, Dorothy, Veronica, Amabel,
Timothy, Jane, Rackstraw, Bennett, old Mrs Quinney, Martha
Hodgson, Jack Turner, Alice, Clara, Wilson, Mrs Wilson.

Nearly two miles to the church. Some had walked ahead, some were driving, all the dogs had gone charging across the field, little clouds of shining iridescent powder rose up above the purple shadows that darkened the snow.

John and Elizabeth walked.

'Oh, I'm so happy!' said John. 'This is the loveliest Christmas!' But was he speaking truly, for over his head, frowning down upon him, was the Fortress? It looked sardonically threatening with its battlements and turrets; the walls met above the hill like a great hanging eyebrow; the stone was dull, heavy, squat, but snow fell in a sheet of dazzling light from its grey shoulders and it could not disown, however it might wish, the blue peerless sky that overlooked it. Light struck the walls and the preen of the two peacocks that Walter had bought. They stretched their tails on the miniature battlements.

'Is not Aunt Judith wonderful?' said John.

'I love her so much,' said Elizabeth.

She thought that it must be impossible to be happier than she was at that moment. And perhaps – who knows? – she would meet her father in the road, all would be forgiven, he would come to the Christmas party . . .

Was that, John thought, Uhland sitting his black horse under the yews? There! There! Cannot you see? His heart was chilled. No. There is no one there . . .

They were approaching the church, and the bells were ringing like mad. The quire were in a small gallery and were almost throttled with evergreens, holly and ivy and mistletoe. There was fiddler and a clarionet. The young ladies in delightful bonnets, some small boys shining with soap, the village postmaster, Mr Collins, Farmer Twistle, Farmer Donne, young Donne – they all played and sang with such a vigour that some of the holly fell with a rattle and clatter from the old beam. There was an anthem in which all the parts went wrong and nobody cared. Two of the dogs from the Hall – Satan and Mischief – strolled up the aisle and pushed with their noses at the door of Madame's high-walled pew. Then they lay down, their tongues hanging out, their eyes fixed in front of them. How everyone sang 'Oh, Come, all ye Faithful'! . . .

In the churchyard afterwards, old Mr Summers, the Vicar, stood and shook hands with everybody.

They all walked home, and it was passing through the second field that one of the important events of Adam's life occurred to him. He was to remember afterwards, with a rich sense of gratitude, that shiny expanse of snowy field, and how in the sunlight the snow turned to rills of sparkling water that glittered through the grass, and how over the hedge Sam Longford's cottage that he knew so well sent up a banner of purple smoke that fluttered against the stainless sky.

For a thick-set, broad-shouldered man, touching his cap, spoke to him.

'You won't remember me, sir?' he said. 'I've been working Penrith way the last five years – Will Leathwaite.'

Adam stopped and smiled but looked bewildered.

'You will think me very uncivil,' he said.

'Why, sir,' said the man, smiling all over his rather simple countenance. 'The Summer Fair of 'twenty-seven, when I won t'race up to Druids' Circle. Why, sir, you rode with my poor old fayther on his mare, Jessamy, and you was shouting for me fit to burst your lungs. And I won, sir, I won! Bit too heavy now, I reckon!'

Why, of course, Adam remembered! He saw the whole scene, how their horse charged the village street, and how they must pause on the road until the runners caught them up. He heard his eager cry to the old farmer: 'Do you think Will will win, Mr Leathwaite? Do you think Will will win?' And here was Will! And Adam, looking at him, liked him.

They talked a little while. Will stood there, awkwardly, kicking the snow with his boot. Then he looked up, his face red.

'Not wanting any kind of servant, sir, are you?'

'Why, no,' said Adam. 'I'm a poor man, Leathwaite, a poor man.'

'I'd come to you,' said Leathwaite, looking Adam straight in the eyes, 'just for my keep.'

'What! Aren't you married?'

'No – nor likely to be.'

Adam nodded his head and smiled.

'Well, if I ever do want one – I'll tell you.'

They shook hands and Adam moved on. The wild goose, flying in from the sea, circled over Skiddaw, then swerved towards the water of the Lake, already thinly crusted with silver, dark in the shadow under the hills.

As the afternoon lengthened excitement grew. All life was *inside* the house now. The dining room was filled with the long extended table; it was a place of mystery. Behind closed doors the preparations for the ceremony went on. On every fire all over the house the great logs blazed. Sylvia poked her head through the door of Judith's room.

'That's right, my dear. Come in.'

Sylvia came in.

'I must go and make myself grand.' She stood and looked at the old lady who sat toasting her toes at the fire. Sylvia considered her. She loved Judith, had done so from the first moment of their meeting. She would not have spent her Christmas in this outlandish place had it not been for Judith. Yes, and her curiosity. She had now, for so many years, intrigued, manipulated in her London world that she was intensely curious and inquisitive. She took it for granted that everyone intrigued, that no one was what he or she seemed, that all private lives trembled for ever on the edge of crises. And there was something – should she speak of it to Judith or no? Judith also loved her, but, considering her, now, found that she was not so lovely as she had once been. She had aged lines on her forehead, had something hard and even a little desperate about the corners of her mouth. So many Herries, she reflected, aged before their due time.

'Oh, Judith, I have never had a happier Christmas.'

'That's good. Sit down for five minutes. We have plenty of time.'

'It must make you happy to have Adam and Margaret.'

'It does,' said Judith, kicking a shoe against the fender.

'I do wish that we saw them more often in London. But with Adam's views . . .'

'Yes, I know.'

'*I* of course do not care in the least, but some of our friends think the Chartists would murder us all in our beds had they the chance—'

'Yes, dear. Absurd.'

Sylvia sighed. 'It is so restful here. I dote on the country. I hate my London life.'

'Then why do you lead it?'

'Oh, I don't know. What else should one do? Garth would be bored to death in the country.'

'I suppose he would.'

'You know that Will's wife may be brought to bed at any moment?'

'Yes, my dear.'

'Fancy – at his age! And how provoking for Walter!'

There was a pause and then Sylvia said:

'I suppose that Walter still keeps up this ridiculous feud?'

'Yes,' said Judith. 'He is furious, I believe, that I have John and Elizabeth here.'

Sylvia said:

'I saw him yesterday.'

Judith looked up sharply.

'Saw whom? Walter?'

Sylvia nodded.

'I was out walking. I had got on to the moor and was standing looking around me when he rode up behind me. You cannot imagine the start it gave me! You know – or maybe you do not know – in any case a few years back he was attracted to me. It began years ago when I stayed at Ireby for their opening Ball – the time when poor Jennifer died. I have seen him since once or twice – not for a considerable while though.'

Judith looked at her. How far had that gone? A strange shiver of repugnance – the consciousness of herself being in any close contact with Walter – for an instant held her. But Sylvia's beautiful face was quite unmoved. She was absolutely calm.

'How altered he is! Quite shocking! So gross – I must confess that I was uncomfortable. Dusk was falling and although the house was not far distant—' She broke off. 'Well, I can look after myself of course. However, he did not get down from his horse. We exchanged only a few words.'

'What did he say?' Judith asked.

'He inquired how I did, said it was long since we had met. Then he asked whether Elizabeth was staying at Uldale. I said she was.'

'Well?'

'He was very strange. Most odd. Judith, I think he may be coming here tonight.'

'Coming here?'

'Yes; he said something about it, something about a surprise visit. He said that it would make a fine bonfire if he burned this house down and everyone in it.'

Judith smiled grimly.

'We will manage him if he does come.'

Sylvia bent and kissed Judith, then went, but at the door she turned. 'The Herries men are so very peculiar,' she said. 'If they cannot have what they want they rush to destruction. Garth is just like that.'

In another room Elizabeth lay in John's arms. She murmured:

'Darling, I must dress.'

He stroked her hair, kissed her eyes, held her passionately close to him.

'Oh, Elizabeth,' he whispered, 'we must never be parted, never, never, never, never.'

'Nothing can part us,' she said.

'Nothing? No one? Never?'

'Nothing. No one. Never.'

'I could not believe that love could grow when it was from the beginning so intense. But when I look back to even a year ago it does not seem that *that* was love at all.'

They held one another in an embrace that, they thought, defied Death itself.

Before she went down to dinner Margaret looked into the nursery. Dorothy, when Margaret had asked her permission, had suddenly kissed her.

'I am fond of you, Margaret, I am indeed. We are more alike than anyone else in this house is like either of us.'

Perhaps they were. Two large, plain domestic women. Margaret had not thought that she was domestic. She had lived so long working happily with her father for a Cause. Now she was domestic. She wanted a child. It might be that all German women were so.

So she went into the nursery. When John and Dorothy had been children, there had been no nursery, but now, on the top floor, they had knocked down a wall and bludgeoned a passage. The room had sloping roofs, and wide windows stared out to Scotland. You could see the Firth stir under the sun like a slippery silver snake. When Margaret came in the four children were in bed, but of course not asleep; Timothy was five, Veronica four, Amabel three, Jane only two: Dorothy had been faithful to her duties, and then Bellairs, having planted his seed, had incontinently died.

Timothy was typical Bellairs, brave, stupid, kind and greedy. But the girls were all Herries, Veronica and Amabel of one kind and poor little Jane of the other. Veronica and Amabel were proud, sensible, determined and self-satisfied. Nice little girls, they already gave the impression that Herries little girls were much the best. But Jane, dear Jane, was the true descendant of the Rogue, of Francis, of all their cloudy ancestors before them. She dreamt dreams, she cried for no reason, brokenly she tried to explain that she saw things, a white horse, frozen water, a lady with red hair; she was a nervous, sensitive child, shy but most responsive to affection. It was to her cot that Margaret went. The children lay, their eyes staring, their cheeks hot, thinking of the marvellous day that it had been. In a heap near the window were the new toys. There was a rocking-horse, a doll's house, a 'shinny' stick and ball for Timothy.

They gave cries and shouts when they saw Margaret. They did not know who she might be, but today everyone was a friend. She talked to them, kissed them, but she knelt down beside Jane's cot. Jane, whose head was covered with yellow curls like a duckling's, smiled, stroked Margaret's cheek with a fat finger and fell asleep, and Margaret knelt there, her heart aching as though she were the loneliest woman in the world.

Down in the hall the boys from the village had arrived, Mumming, and it was a great pity that they had chosen so bad a time, for soon guests would be here and the ladies of the house were dressing.

However, Madame miraculously appeared to have time for everything, and there she was, sitting at the foot of the stairs, almost under the mistletoe, dressed in her best and beating her hands to the music. The boys, in the middle of their play, could not but look at her, she was so very fine. Her white hair gleamed, her naked shoulders shone (amazingly white for so old a lady). Her dress had three skirts – cream, silver, cream again – and was decorated with crimson roses. She wore silver shoes.

'Bravo! Bravo!' she cried, tapping with her stick. The boys were without coats and their white sleeves were tied with ribbons, their hats decorated with evergreen, and they carried thick staves.

There was a fiddle and a drum. Their dance was clever and most intricate, advancing, retreating, advancing again and striking their sticks the one against the other. They shouted Cumberland shouts and brought with them into the candlelit hall the rough tang of the mountain-stream running under grass, the windswept 'top' bare under the rushing cloud.

'Excellent! Most excellent!' Madame cried, thinking that they must go to the kitchen for beef and ale, and the kitchen in confused disorder because of the great Dinner.

One stout boy wore a fox's head and carried a fox's tail. Another boy wore a mask with a huge nose and bulbous cheeks.

'I know!' cried Madame. 'That's Willy Caine ... you can't

deceive me. How is your Aunt, Willie? She's up again, I hear.'

She drove them, hot, flushed and happy, off into the kitchen.

Then the guests began to arrive. The Reverend Mr Summers and his old, old wife, although they had the shortest way to come, were of course the first. There were the Osmastons, the Applebys, poor old Miss Keate from Keswick, a dry old maid, but she had nowhere to go for her Christmas dinner, the two Miss Blossoms all the way from Penrith (friends of Dorothy's), and Deborah's grandchildren, Fred and Anne Withering, from near Carlisle.

They would sit down twenty altogether – quite as many as the dining-room would hold – but Judith was bound to acknowledge that she was proud of her table when, seated at the head of it with stout Mr Osmaston on one side of her and old Mr Summers on the other, she looked around her. She had her dear Adam near to her and quite enough Herries to make her feel patriarchal. As you looked down the two sides of the table you could pick without any trouble the members of that family – Adam, Dorothy, John, Elizabeth, Garth, the two Witherings. Unlike though they might be, they were yet alike in these two things – in the high prominent bones, the tall erect heads and straight shoulders – and in their consciousness that they were dominating the rest of the company and came first wherever they might be.

The room is looking beautiful, she thought. The old dark green wallpaper was a fine setting to all the candlelight; the fruit, piled high between the silver candlesticks, had a hard brilliant edge of colour as though it were made of metal. Everyone smiled, laughed. There was not a care in the world.

Old Bennett, dressed up in a green coat with silver buttons, came in carrying a silver dish, and on it was a pig's head with a lemon in its mouth. Everyone stood up: there was a great clapping of hands; then, after an interval, attended by the stable-boy (also dressed in a green coat with silver buttons), who carried two lighted candles in silver candlesticks, old Bennett was back again bearing the Wassail Bowl. This was a magnificent china dish, crimson and gold, and the recipe of the drink had come all the way from old Pomfret of Westaways and he had it from the old Elizabethan Herries of the Mines. Roasted apples floated on its surface, and the aromatic scent of it was as the spices of Arabia.

Speeches were made, healths were drunk. Before the ladies left the table Madame gave the speech of the evening; proud, happy, her eye passing once and again to Adam, she was said by them all to resemble Queen Elizabeth – Queen Elizabeth in an amiable mood, be it understood.

When at last the gentlemen joined the ladies the Wassail Bowl was empty and the house was flaming with jollity. To Fred Withering it seemed there were three staircases, and old Mr Summers confided to Osmaston an affair of his in his Oxford days that was anything but clerical. Only John seemed apart from the others ('Oh, the most beautiful man I have *ever* set eyes on!' Miss Keate confided to Sylvia), his eyes resting constantly on Elizabeth with an adoration that had something poignant in its heart as though he were well aware that all was illusory, vanishing at the touch, doomed to destruction.

'Cheer up, old boy,' cried Garth, who was completely drunk but very charming.

John smiled and laughed; he was happier than he had ever been in all his life.

While the dining-room was cleared for dancing they played games – Cumberland games moreover. Instead of *Oranges and Lemons* there was the Penrith *Down the Long Lonnins:*

> Down the long lonnins we go, we go,
> To gather some lilies, heigho, heigho!
> We open the gates so wide, so wide,
> To let King George and his men go by.

And then *Sandy O.*

Here Judith, Dorothy, John and Adam, who had been all brought up on it, sang the words with all their youth in their eyes:

> My delight's in Sandy O,
> My delight's in Brandy O,
> My delight's in the red, red rose,
> Come along, my Annie O.
> Heigho for Annie O,
> Bonny Annie O.
> All the world would I give
> For my bonny Annie O.

For this game there is a girl in the middle, and she chooses one from the ring; the tune is *Hops and Peas.*

And another 'ring' game, *Hops and Peas and Barley-corn:*

> Hops and peas and barley-corn,
> Hops and peas and barley-corn,
> Hops and peas, hops and peas,
> Hops and peas and barley-corn.
>
> This is the way the farmer stands;
> This is the way he folds his arms,
> Stamps his feet, claps his hands,
> Turns around to view his land.

How they all stamped and clapped!

'Yes, well,' said Miss Keate, who was wearing, quite out of fashion, a turban, 'I never imagined for a moment—'

But best of all was *Green Gravel*.

> Round the green gravel the grass grows green,
> All the fair maidens are shame to be seen;
> Wash them in milk,
> And dry them in silk;
> Last down wedded—

At the word 'down' all slip to the ground, the last down is married. Then she stands in the middle, and they sing a song about her. Then she is asked which she likes best, butter or sugar. If she says 'sugar' it is her sweetheart she likes; if 'butter' it is some other.

After a while Margaret slipped from the room. It was very hot. She could not help it, but she felt isolated, alone. Everyone knew everyone so well. Adam had been placed some distance from her at the supper-table, and he was enjoying himself so greatly that he had thought of nothing but his enjoyment. Men were like that: children when they were happy. And she loved to see him so; that was the desire of her heart, but once she caught John's eyes as they rested on Elizabeth's young enchanting beauty and that glance stabbed her. Elizabeth was so beautiful, so young and virginal and good. Margaret seemed to herself old and soiled with all her hard life with her father, the shabby places in which she had lived, the poor desperate rebellious people who had been her companions. She had been proud of the new dress that she had been wearing, but now it seemed heavy and coarse. In the wild extravagance of her mood it appeared to her that she had lost Adam for ever . . .

She slipped upstairs and found her room. She threw herself on to her bed and burst into tears. This was, perhaps, the first time in her life that she had ever shed bitter tears; she had been always calm, controlled, and had wondered, often enough, that women should weep so readily and in front of those whom they loved. She was in years only twenty-two, but she seemed to herself to be so much older. She had felt often like a mother to Adam, to her father even, and now that she should, like a little child abandon herself to her grief! But she could not stop. Faintly she heard, coming up to her from below, the singing and laughter. Her curtains were not drawn, and she could see the snow falling in a thick tide beyond her window. How cold and desolate those hills, how bleak this North Country, how harsh the loneliness that lay like an icy hand on her heart!

The door opened and, turning on her bed, she saw that Adam had come in. He came in, happy and sweating. He was laughing, and his black hair lay damp on his forehead. His eyes shone in his brown face. His blue evening-coat with its dark velvet collar was waisted almost to effeminacy, as was the fashion of those years, and the tails of it stood out over his thick sturdy thighs. He looked always better in rather rough loosely fitting clothes. He came in laughing and humming the last notes of the *Green Gravel*; then he saw Margaret. He stopped dead, and the change in his face was almost ludicrous. Neither he nor anyone else had ever seen her cry before. No, not her father when her mother died.

'Margaret!'

It seemed to him in his astonishment that his heart turned over in his chest.

'Margaret! What is it?'

She sat up, found her handkerchief, wiped her eyes and, rather wanly, smiled.

'I suffered from a terrible headache. It was the heat.'

Clumsily, still bewildered, unable to realize what he saw, he sat down on the bed. He took her hand, which was trembling but suddenly lay quiet as it felt the tranquil reassurance and strong bones of his brown one.

'A headache? But why did you not say?'

'Why should I disturb anyone? You were all so happy.'

He looked at her more closely.

'That's not true. You would not weep for a headache.'

As he saw her, whom he loved so dearly, with her hair in disorder and her cheeks stained, his love that was so deeply secure in his heart that he never questioned it, began to be restless and uneasy.

They could neither of them lie to the other ever about anything, so she said quietly:

'No, it was not the headache.'

'Well, what then?'

'I was foolish. Nothing but foolishness.'

He put his arm around her and drew her to him, but they were not really together. He had been twenty-seven in September, so that he was not very old, and he had no experience of women at all. He began to be frightened as though something within him had whispered: 'Take care, you may lose her.'

'But what is it, Margaret?' he repeated. 'Have I done something.'

Then she said, dropping her voice, looking away from him:

'I thought you loved me no longer.'

His agitation increased. Loved her no longer, when he worshipped her? Loved her no longer when only last night? . . . But now his old trouble, that he could never find words to express himself, attacked him.

'Love you?' he stammered. 'But, Margaret, I – I . . . I could not love anyone more,' he ended, looking at her.

'No – I am sure. Of course. But perhaps it has been a great mistake. I am not handsome. I am not clever. This is your world and not mine . . .' Then she burst out with a sudden cry, a note in her voice that he had never heard before. 'Oh, Adam, I have been so lonely!'

The shock to him then was one of the worst of his life. He had taken everything for granted. He had gone quietly on, troubled about his work and his feeble achievement in it, troubled at the state of the world and the general unhappiness, but sure always of two things – his love for Margaret and his mother, and their love for him. These were so sure that he never dreamed that they needed expression. Like so many other Englishmen he lived in a man's world where expression of feeling was something too foreign to be decent.

The thought of his mother stirred, a recognized solid fact, in the middle of all his bewilderment.

'But my mother? Has she been unkind to you?'

'No. She has been very kind. It is not her fault that she cannot like me.'

'But she does like you. She said so last night.'

Ah, then they had been discussing her! The two of them together wrapped in their own intimacy! But Margaret had a noble nature, above and beyond all smallness or mean jealousy. She put her arm around Adam's neck.

'My love ... Forget this. I have had so little experience of the world, and all women are foolish sometimes. I have felt sometimes that we could speak to one another more, say more what was in our hearts – and tonight you were all together, you knew one another so well. I was foolish ... Forgive me, forgive me.'

Then, with her head against his breast, she cried again, not wishing to stop her tears that, in their flow, seemed to release and set free all her misery of the last weeks, release it so that it would never return again. He held her in his arms as though at any moment she might escape him. The shock and the surprise were to him tremendous and the effect of this would remain with him for the rest of his life. His heart was so tender, he hated so passionately to wound or hurt anything alive (unless it were an enemy, someone or something that he thought cruel and evil) that the knowledge of hurting her was terrible to him.

'Margaret! Margaret! Don't cry. You shall never cry again. What I have done, wrapped in myself, never seeing ... But I never can say what I feel. I don't deserve that you should love me. I shall make it up to you now all my life long.'

He stroked her hair. They stayed, cheek against cheek, in silence. At last he said:

'We shall understand one another now.'

She kissed him and, holding his head passionately against her breast, looking out to the falling snow beyond the window, murmured: 'Now no one can separate us. I shall never be afraid again.'

A little later, intensely happy, hand in hand they went downstairs and rejoined the company.

Now had it not been for an excellent journal known as *The Cumberland Paquet* the astonishing events that made this evening for ever memorable (so that years later they were, in a much exaggerated form, often recalled) would never have been known to the outside world. But it happened that there intervened now a short pause in the festivities – a pause between games and the dancing, and Miss Keate, hot in the head with exercise (and some of the Wassail Bowl), and young Mrs Appleby found a place on the corner of the stairs where they might cool. From their position, it must be noted, they had a perfect view of the hall and the hall door. Miss Keate had with her a copy of *The Cumberland Paquet* of December 13th which she had discovered in a corner

of the parlour. She had secretly abstracted it that she might have
'a quiet read with it at home'. She was just such a lady, a kind of
magpie, and, being of very slender fortune, picked up once and
again 'things that she was sure no one else could want'. But now
being with Mrs Appleby cooling on a corner of the stairs it was
natural that they should look over it together. Had they not done
so they would certainly have joined the company in the dining-
room and shared in the dancing.

The Cumberland Paquet was, however, of surpassing interest.
There was a leader about the Emperor of China and the vast sum
of money that he had paid to the British (most gratifying to
British pride), something about India, and something about the
very mild season so that a 'blackbird had been heard in the neighbourhood of Springfield making the neighbouring woods echo
with his melodious strains'.

'Poor blackbird,' sighed Miss Keate, whose heart was most
tender, 'he must be quite dead by now.'

There was a fascinating advertisement which both ladies, their
heads close togeher, read with absorbed interest, that 'Mrs Taylor
begs most respectively to inform the ladies of Ulverston and its
vicinity that she has just received an assortment of SIMISTER'S
PATENT WOVE STAYS, which are now ready for inspection.

'To those Ladies who have made trial of the Patent Wove Stay
comment is unnecessary, but to those Ladies who have not—'

'Have you, my dear?' asked Miss Keate.

'Well, no,' answered Mrs Appleby. 'You see ...' and then
followed five minutes of delightful intimacy.

The real news, however, that kept them glued to the stairs and
so made them witness of what followed was a thrilling account of
the doings at the Whitehaven Theatre. It was headed: THE-
ATRICAL FRACAS, and it began: 'We stated in the last number
of the *Paquet* that Mrs Paumier, the wife of the Manager of our
Theatre, would take her benefit on Friday evening, and expressed
the hope that the play-going public of this town would, as they
had done on a former occasion, give her a bumper.' Unfortunately the bumper was prevented because, just before the
rise of the curtain, the rest of the company struck for higher
wages, the audience grew restive at the delay, and 'some sharp
words passed between Mrs Paumier and the performers'. Something very like a riot followed. There was in another part of the
Paquet a public statement: 'indeed Mr and Mrs Paumier seemed
in universal trouble'.

'Why, just listen!' murmured Miss Keate, and she read to her companion:

'It being currently reported that Mr Gilfillan has signified to all persons visiting his wife for beneficial purposes, that he has received from Mr Paumier little or nothing on account of his (Mr Gilfillan's) services at the Theatre, Mr Paumier deems it his duty to publish the following receipt bearing Mr Gilfillan's signature, in order that his (Mr Paumier's) character may in some measure be redeemed until a full and printed statement of his outlay shall be given.'

'Well, did you ever?' said Miss Keate. 'Actors and actresses! What a life they lead! Quite another world from ours! Living on the edge of a volcano. I dare say if the truth were known—'

Miss Keate always afterwards said that it was at this moment (she would remember the name of the Paumiers, she said, so long as she lived) that she had the strangest premonition that something dreadful was about to happen. There was certainly no reason for any premonition, for a more perfect Christmas scene could not be imagined. Everyone now was dancing and the screech of the violin could be heard through the closed doors. Both hall and parlour were deserted; the ladies had only the mistletoe and holly for cheerful company.

But Miss Keate would for ever swear that she had her premonition. She put up her head, caught Mrs Appleby's hand, dropping the *Paquet*, and listened. Immediately after there came a terrific banging at the house-door. You would have thought that everyone within a mile would have heard it, but the door of the dining-room was closed and inside the room the music, the laughter, the tramp of feet as the country dances went their way made it a world enclosed.

Miss Keate and Mrs Appleby sprang to their feet; after a short interval the knocking was repeated and now more violently than before. Soon a maid came to the door, hesitated and then, as the knocking was renewed a third time, opened it. It was then that the two ladies knew the sensation of their lives, for with the open door the wind, carrying with it a flurry of snow, blew into the hall, set the mistletoe rocking; with the wind came a man. The ladies did not, in the first moment, see who it was, for his riding-coat blew about his face, but a second after he looked up and about, stared at the ladies, and they instantly recognized him. It was Mr Walter Herries.

The door banged behind him, and he stood there, his bulk

filling the hall, his face red and angry. The little maid did not know what to do, nor for the matter of that did the two ladies either. Then he cried out in a voice like a bull's:

'I've come for my daughter!'

Miss Keate was very good, in after years, as she pictured the scene. She had a sense of the dramatic. She described the holly and mistletoe, the sound of music and dancing, the frightened eyes of the maid, and then, about Mr Herries, she would say:

'Oh, you never saw a more enraged man! His face was crimson. You could conceive him bursting. You would have supposed that he would pull the house down. Clara Appleby trembled all over; I had to place my arm around her to steady her or she would have fainted, I am sure.'

There is something absurd, of course, in a man roaring out that he wanted his daughter, and Miss Keate, who had quite a satiric turn when she liked, saw that clearly:

'He was standing right under the mistletoe. Too absurd when you come to think of it!'

He said no more, but stood there waiting. The maidservant went to the dining-room and returned, an instant later, with Judith. *That* was a moment for the two ladies – a very great moment indeed.

'Madame,' Miss Keate would afterwards relate, 'must have known whom to expect. She came out to him like the Queen of England and she said, in a voice as clear as a bell and as though it were the most ordinary thing in the world, "Well, Walter? Good evening. And what can I do for you?"

' "Do for me! You can fetch me my daughter and be damned to the lot of you!"

' "Yes – we had better discuss it in here, I think." '

To the exquisite disappointment of the two ladies Judith and Walter vanished into the parlour. Miss Keate always afterwards said that from the very beginning Judith Paris appeared to have some power over the man. The two ladies stood there staring, and listening with all their ears. For some while there was little to hear or see. A maid knocked on the parlour door. Then the dining-room door opened, throwing into the hall a burst of music and gaiety, and out came John and Elizabeth. They had been given some message. They hesitated in the hall, then, hand in hand, went into the parlour, closing the door behind them. For a while again there was silence, and then—

But Miss Keate was never to know what exactly occurred *inside* the parlour.

And what occurred was this:

'Sit down, Walter,' said Judith, when they were both inside. He stood just by the door, glowering at her, his head thrust a little forward. Judith saw that he had been drinking, that he had a smear of mud on his chin, and that he held, in one gloved hand, a riding-whip. The room was in complete confusion, the carpet turned up, a chair on its side, holly dripping over the mantelpiece, a lady's ribbon on the ground, a lace handkerchief.

'Sit down, Walter, pray,' said Judith. 'And tell me why—'

'You know why,' he answered, his eyes shifting up and down the room. She sat on the sofa and twirled a large white feather fan in her fingers. Her ivory cane (which she was not at all sure she might not have to make use of before the end of the interview) rested near her.

'Indeed I do not, Cousin Walter.'

He came nearer to her.

'I warned you. I told you that you could go too far. Too far! By God, you've always gone too far!'

He was, she supposed, about fifty years of age and he looked sixty with the heavy black pouches under his eyes, the purple veins in cheeks and nose. Oddly, the strain of liking that, in spite of all that he had done, she had always had for him, still, she discovered, survived. Poor Walter! What a mess he had made of everything!

'I have come for my daughter.'

'Elizabeth? Certainly you shall see her.'

'She returns with me to Ireby tonight.'

Judith looked at him impatiently.

'But, Walter, that is absurd. She is no longer a child. She is a married woman.'

'We can soon stop *that* marriage. It shall be dissolved. She was married by force.'

'Indeed she was not!' answered Judith indignantly. 'If ever anyone married freely she did. The marriage has been the greatest success.'

She was listening with all her ears. At any moment dancing revellers might break from the dining-room into the hall and the parlour. She had seen Miss Keate and Mrs Appleby on the stairs. She was determined to finish this scene as quickly as possible.

'It has, has it?' said Walter, coming yet closer to her.

She saw that he was in a confused drunken rage, uncertain as to what he would do or say but determined to assert his power.

'And I know who contrived that marriage. It was you, my fine lady. It has been a long battle between us. You think I forget, but I forget nothing. Do you remember how I whipped your naked little bastard up at Hawkshead years ago? Well, I'd whip him again—'

'It is Elizabeth that we are speaking about,' Judith answered quietly.

He paused to pull himself together. Word slipped from word, sentence from sentence. There was a fog in his brain.

'I demand to see my daughter,' he muttered.

'Certainly you shall,' she answered briskly, pulling the bell at her side.

He was swaying a little on his feet.

'Why don't you sit down, Cousin Walter?' she asked him again. 'You don't look at all well.'

'I am in perfect health,' he answered furiously. 'Never better.'

'And Uhland?' she asked politely.

But this politeness bewildered him. He shook his whip at her.

'Look here, Judith!' he said. 'You're damned clever. You always were. But you don't get round me this way. Do you hear? You can't abduct my daughter from under my nose and I have nothing to say. No, I'm damned if you can. And then marry her to that young swine . . . I always swore that I'd finish him, and by God I will. The whole lot of you. Rude to my mother, was she? I told her she'd repent it.'

He was referring now apparently to Jennifer, and a picture rose before Judith of that poor bewildered lady walking in her black dress across the fields.

The maid appeared.

'Please tell Mr John and Mrs Herries to come to me here immediately.'

She turned to Walter.

'Now, Walter, pray let us have no scenes. These are old, old quarrels that should have been long ago buried. Elizabeth is a sweet girl. She and John are devoted. What else is there left to build enmity upon? I am sure that you are not angry with me. You never were. And, although you have behaved badly once and again, I forgive you everything. Now let us be friends—'

John and Elizabeth entered the room. Inside the door they

released hands and Elizabeth came forward, her head up. She held out her hand.

'She was the loveliest creature,' Judith afterwards said, 'I ever saw. There were roses all over her silk skirt, roses in her cheeks. Her curls were untidy with her dancing and she had the face of an angel. Any father would have been moved by it.'

Walter, however, was not moved. He disregarded her hand and, swaying on his heavy feet, said: 'You are to come back with me.'

She looked round at John for a moment, then smiling said:

'But I am married, Father.'

She, who had been afraid of him all her life, had no fear at all.

Then he began to storm.

'You shall obey your father, do you hear? It was no marriage. You're not married to him. You disobedient . . . disobedient . . .' He began to choke and he put his hand to his throat. He continued to look past Elizabeth to John; all his great body was increasingly agitated. Judith rose from the sofa and went up to him, putting her hand on his arm.

'Walter, this is absurd. You must see that it is. John and Elizabeth are married and have been for a long while. And why not? They love one another, and John has a fine position in London. You don't know him. You've scarcely ever seen him. All your silly hatred is built up upon nothing. Now make the best of it. Shake hands with them . . .'

But he had not been listening to her at all and, suddenly, he rushed forward catching John by the shoulder with one hand, raising the whip with the other.

'You damned puppy! I'll teach you a lesson. I'll teach you a lesson. I'll kill you for stealing my daughter. Steal my daughter, will you? I'll teach you.'

He raised his arm and, clawing John's collar, slashed at him with the whip. No one but Elizabeth saw that in that moment John turned white as the mistletoe berries above them, or that, at Walter's touch, his body seemed to collapse as though his bones had melted. She saw that and, knowing John's courage, realized even at that moment of touch that there was some additional horror here, something old and inborn, quite beyond physical terms.

But it was Judith who had the centre of the stage. Walter's touch on John seemed to swing her into one of those old rages of hers that had for long now been disciplined, for she rushed and threw herself on Walter with so much vehemence that the surprise of it tumbled him forward. She caught his arm and, small though she was, swung him right round and then slapped his face as though she were tearing paper. The whip fell; Walter put up his hand to his cheek and stood there staring.

'You dare! You dirty bully! You come into *my* house again! You blackguard! I'll show you where you are in *my* house. Go! ... There's the door! You show your face again! You dare! You ...'

She stamped her foot; she raged like a fishwife, glaring into him as though she would tear his nose out of his face.

He turned, bent half down as though he would pick up the whip, but let it lie there.

'Pick it up! Pick it up!' she stormed. 'I won't have any of your filthy things in *my* house! Christmas Day too! Where are your feelings? Where's your decency? Never you dare to set your foot ...'

He picked up the whip, stared at her still in a dazzled, confused fashion, muttered something, fumbled for the door.

As he opened it they were all suddenly aware of social conventions; they heard, with an immediate pressing clarity, the murmur of the music and the dancing feet. They all three followed him into the hall.

Judith herself opened the big door for him and stood there, with John just behind her, while the snow whirled in the wind that blew the light over the porch.

'Goodnight, Walter ... Goodnight,' Judith said.

Miss Keate saw him go out, his head down. 'As though she'd whipped him,' she always ended her story.

Elizabeth went to John, putting her arm through his; the dining-room door opened and someone ran out.

'John! Elizabeth! You must come for "Sir Roger".'

'Don't mind, John. Don't mind,' Elizabeth whispered. She was beginning a new relation with him from that moment.

But he whispered back: 'There was Uhland there – standing in the porch under the light.'

She didn't hear. She pressed his arm with her hand. 'It's nothing,' she said again. 'I have finished with my father for ever.'

But John stared at the door. It was not Walter Herries but Uhland that he was seeing.

Part Three

Cumberland Chase

UHLAND'S JOURNAL

FINISHED tonight that stuff-and-nonsense book Carlyle's *Heroes*. Wonder that I had the patience to read it on to the end, but I fancy that I was always going further to see whether all his tall words and German sentences would lead to anything. They do not any more than does this damnably silly Journal of mine. There is just this difference. Carlyle is a hypocrite and I am not. He knows he is no hero but says he is one – I know that I can be a hero as suitably as any of his Fredericks and Cromwells, but prefer not to be one. And why do I prefer? Because the world is so crammed with fools and conceited coxcombs that it is a finer thing to sit by and watch – to watch, if you like, the decline and fall of the house of Herries and myself with it. Bang – Bang – Bang – Whiskers – Whiskers – Whiskers. This is nothing but the sound a blind man makes seeing himself to bed with the light of a thick stick and the smell of the candle-end. And it is also, if you like, the noise that my beloved father and Sam Osmaston are making just under this floor of my room, both as drunk as cock-chafers in lamplight, on their knees most likely, searching for a goose's feather.

But this Journal is supposed to say what I do. Well, what do I do? Get up, you lamentable cripple, and look at yourself in the glass, examine once again your ugly wry face, your ribs, like an old mans' counting-board, and your white bit of twisted bone politely called a leg. Good, good! That's the thing, my boy! That's the way to bring your conceit down and sit on the floor to talk about Heroes. But the soul's the thing, is it not? Does not old Carlyle say so? The soul! The soul! Where may you be, soul? Stuck in that leg of mine? Hiding like a rabbit behind a rib or two? Well, come out for once! Let's have a look at you! Where are you, green, crimson or mulberry; and your shape? Are you tortoise-like with a shell like a snuff-box, or thin and spidery, catching flies for your food, or just a pincushion with pink lace and a blue silk bow?

What a week I've had too!

They've all been here. The Newmarks with all their brood,

Phyllis a female Alderman, Newmark the prize prig of the market, Horace as long in the leg as a pair of stilts and as wooden, *dear* little Emily and *dear* little Barnabas. All with the latest news of my good grandfather's new offspring. 'Oh, *what* a sweet infant! the dearest little boy!' until I thought my father would throttle the lot of them. Amery Herries too with eyes like gooseberries, the merriest drunken bachelor, and old Rodney from Polchester, sixty if he's a day, touring the Lakes and Scotland with one eye on his clerical dignity and the other on the destiny of every halfpenny! Lord, how I hate the lot of them and how they hate me! Didn't I make little Emily cry by blowing out the candle, and isn't old Rodney afraid of my humours? A family sinking to rot, my masters, cursed because, between too much money-bag on the one side and too much indecisive dreaming on the other, the way to Salvation is missed every time. Not that there *is* any Salvation, even though you search for it. Nothing but madness or death from over-eating whichever way you go.

But now when the house is silent and every stone in this building can be heard scraping its reproaches, I wonder at my indignation. Indignant? No, I have not blood enough for so bold a word. I sit here, sneezing, rubbing my knees the one against the other, healing Rob's ear in the basket, raising my perpetual theme of hatred of my dear John brother-in-law and do nothing, positively nothing. Neither lust urges me nor greed nor envy nor desire for knowledge: only if I had John's neck here I would twist it until his eyes were in his back, and even that is a fancy – nurtured lust, something bred of years of coddling. It *had* a reason once and now I've fed my brain with so many centuries of imagination that to see him tortured in my fancy is as good as the actual deed.

And yet it could have been otherwise. Only this stupid mutton-faced Journal shall know how otherwise it might have been! Another father, flat-faced Adam for a brother and a pair of legs like anyone's, and I had the power, the wish, the ambition. I could have written a book or two, I fancy, better than Bulwer at any rate, or played in a laboratory and made a discovery, or talked as wittily as any Disraeli or Palmerston of them all. I have more brains in my toenail (those on the withered foot have an especial brilliancy) than all my Herries cousins lumped together. But from the very first I was outcast. *That* at least is no imagination. I make no claim for it and I ask for no pity, but to be different from birth, to have the street children mock at you and

the dogs bark, and visitors to the house look the other way – it is a
kind of allowance for hatred. They say Carlyle has dyspepsia and
yet he thinks himself a Hero. Well, am I not a Hero that I sit here
and think, and think, and wish myself a villain? And my father
still loves me. He thinks me a miracle of brilliance and perversity.
All that is left to him, poor man, for his brain is fuddled with
drink, the ladies won't call, his fine house is a stony desert, and
they flourish at Uldale like the righteous!

Ah! there's the rub! Cousin Judith as lively as a flea, Cousin
Dorothy and her children fat as good cattle, John and Elizabeth
like sucking-doves. There! He is singing. I can hear him under
the floor. And Sam Osmaston with him – a fine out-of-tune
chorus . . .

IREBY, *November 13th, 1843*

Rob's ear has this canker again. It's his perversity, I well believe,
for he knows truly that once his ear is well, he'll go, to be
stoned by the Keswick boys again, I suppose. And the odd thing
is, I shan't care. He's been with me almost a year now. I enjoy his
face like the parson's, with its side-whiskers and a slobbery white
patch like spilt milk on his nose. He's fonder of me than any
dog's ever been, but I hate that sycophancy. I'm near shooting
him at times or hanging him from the beam with a rope – yes,
even while I wash and clean his ear with the tenderness of a
woman.

And now what do you think, O my Journal? What has our
dear father done but buy a piece of the moor just above Uldale
and build a small cottage on it and into that shove Peach and his
dirty brood. There is just one patch, it seems, that great-grandfather David neglected to buy, a measly brown bit that even the
sheep neglect. He has done it to vex Aunt Judith of course, and
vex her it must to have the filthy little Peaches at her garden gate,
and Peach at war with her drunken Rackstraw.

Since she scratched dear father's cheeks last Christmas-time
he's been all bent on vexing her, although in my view he thinks
her a damnably fine old woman. So she is! She and Adam –
another brood from the rest of them.

November 22nd

I am just back from Rosthwaite where I have been limping about
all day like an old woman looking for eggs. But something or

someone (Algebraical formula? $x + y = xy^2 =$ God?) had put it into my mind of late to be interested in my old Great-great-grand-father, the Rogue. It seems that he spent half his life longing for a gipsy girl (Aunt Judith's mother by oddity) who, when he got her at last, incontinently died. I like the smell of that old man and have picked up a pack of curiosities about him, how he sold a stout mistress at Keswick Fair, was given a scar in a duel, fought for the Pretender outside Carlisle or some such thing, married his gipsy at Rosthwaite and cuffed and kicked the guests down his stairs, how she ran away and he roamed the hills for years look-ing for her; then, catching her at last, gave her Judith whom she died of. There is something deeply sympathetic to me here, for he was outcast as I am, a rebel as I, if I had the guts, would be, a hater too, I fancy, only he would not play Hamlet by the year as I have done.

His old house is a ruin, some tumbled barns swallowed in weed and swiftly vanishing. I sat on some broken mouldy stairs this afternoon and could have sworn to seeing the old fellow watch-ing me ironically. It's his irony I like the taste of. None of the Herries have irony save Aunt Judith. I would like a picture of him, but father says there is none; however, an old cottager well over ninety years with whom I talked today – a lively cursing old man with no teeth, so that he must hiss like a snake when he talks, but his hearing is mighty sharp – he remembers him, how he came striding over the little bridge by Rosthwaite, in a plum-coloured coat with a scar down his cheek, and how he and his gipsy lay both dead in the house together and an old man rode up on a horse and carried the new-born child (Judith, by all that's comic) away on his horse with him. The only man of our family with whom I have any touch, and he dead these seventy years! Grandfather Will must remember him. Next time in London I shall harry his wits over him . . .

I am planning a long London visit. This house is the devil. It is colder than any crypt, and the stone, cover it as you may, breaks through and snarls at you. Every wind in the country whips it and the trees moan like kitchen-maids with the toothache. Also I have the ambition to touch up Cousin John a trifle. I could look in at his window and give him a queasy stomach. What is this hatred? Contempt of his mealy-mouthed propriety? Rage at his impertinent marriage with my sister? Jeal-ousy of his strength and whole limbs? Something taught to me in my cradle by my father? Yes, and more than all this. I hate him because I have always done so, because of what he is and because he is happy and I am not. These are honest reasons, but behind these there is the pleasure of the pursuit. As my old roguish ancestor pursued his gipsy so I pursue my John. We freaks in the Herries stock must have our revenge on the normal ones; there is a warfare there that has necessity in it. And I have no other emotions. I have never lusted after a woman in all my days, nor cared for a human being save Adam. Is that my own fault? I could have asked for quite another destiny, but I had no say in it. So, to my only pleasure, to see him start at the sound of my step and flinch under my hand. My leg aches in sympathy.

12 GRANGER STREET, LONDON
February 12th, 1844

Three weeks in London. What a folly! Dinner at Richmond or Blackwall, the Cave of Harmony, the Coal Hole and such; the inner sanctities of Meadows' and 'Seven's the main' of the caster, and 'Gentlemen, make your game' of the groom-porter. Cards everywhere and, even without the perils of lansquenet, with a pony on the rubber, five pound points and betting on the odd trick, you are caught before you are hooked. There is scarcely a quiet respectable house in all London where they won't rook you if you give them half a chance.

All the same there's a strange curtain of hypocritical respectability over this town since my last visit. They say it is our good little Queen and our handsome German Prince. No nonsense at Court, they say. All heading now for the Virtues.

Last night a party at my grandfather's where, if you please, we sat round in a circle and a woman with teeth like a grinning hag's read us the poems of Mr Tennyson. Poor old grandfather would have slumbered happily in his corner had not Mrs Will in a pink dress with 'volants' almost up to her waist (and there must have been at least eight rows of them) pinched him after every melancholy verse. She had time too for elegant flirtation with a fat young man whose whiskers were as long as a horse's mane! I have never disliked anyone more and her loathing of myself is badly concealed by her extreme endearments. She was frightened of me, I believe and hope. But I perceive that I throw a gloom on to every party that I encounter. All the better. This London is a meeting-place of all the snobs, hypocrites, sharps and idiots of Christendom.

But I remain, for I have my own quiet amusements. One of these is the clearing of Cousin Garth's pockets, for such a juggins at cards deserves clearing.

Another is to listen to the bombast of old James or Carey who both have the fancy that *their* England (*theirs*, mark you) is the most Christian and at the same time the most commercial miracle that this weary planet has ever beheld! To hear them talk of old Pam or of Peel you would fancy that we had no Chartists nor starving populace whatever, and to listen to their contempt of *any* foreign country is to realize to the full *one* side of the beautiful Herries shield!

I listen and then with one remark blow their soap-bubbles to air – and don't they hate me for it too! It is worth the boredom of London to see old James flush his double-chin and stutter: 'But, my dear sir – my *dear* young friend . . .'

I have a deeper pleasure than these mild amusements, though. I have discovered Cousin John's hours: he leaves Bryanston Square five of an evening and for the good of his precious health walks across the Park. Thrice a week at least I see to it that he shall encounter me. We never speak, indeed one glimpse of me is enough to destroy his peace for the rest of the day. He would take a cab were it not that he fights his cowardice, and it has happened twice that when he has taken one I have followed him in another, coming from mine as he issues from his. This game gives me a wild and sensual pleasure. There are certain streets and houses that are marked with the colour of our meetings. Best of all I learnt from Sylvia Herries last week that he and Elizabeth would be at the theatre. They had a box and I in the pit enjoyed my evening to the full. At every meeting it seems to me that we come closer together even as my father grows closer to Uldale. I am contented to bide my time, for there is no pleasure for me in life like this chase. Is this madness? It may be that it is, for it seems to me that I am now two persons and when the one is not with him the other is. I sleep but little and walk the streets at night, hearing my own step in pursuit of myself, that same halting stumble that must, I know, haunt the bowels of Cousin John. I would swear that last night, dressing for grandfather's party, I saw two figures in the mirror and neither shadowy . . .

March 13th

I have had an encounter that has moved me oddly. Yesterday afternoon in the Strand I walked straight into Adam. He was brown and ruddy and sturdy, dressed roughly, books under his arm, his eyes serious and kindly as they ever were. May the Devil forgive me, but I was pleased to see him. Our talk was thus:

'Why, Adam!'

'Why, Uhland!'

'Are you well?'

'And you?'

His hand was on my arm and I felt, for a foolish minute, that I would have followed him anywhere. He is the only one in the world not to glance at my leg, to be perfectly at ease with me, to give me some glimpse of a normal world where men are honest and mean their words. Yet I doubt not he is a prig and thinks highly of his own virtues. Yet he was kind without hypocrisy. He asked me to visit them and he meant it, I think. But I turned away. I could have struck him for moving me as he did. I could have struck him, but I looked back after him as though I were letting my best chance go. He is still on my mind today. He has given me his address and I have half an impulse to visit him. But for what? I should but despise his amiability and suspect his seriousness. There is no place where we can move side by side and I do not know that I wish that there should be.

IREBY, *April 7th, 1845*

I am so much better that I can at last get to my Journal again. Not that. I hunger for it, but it is at least a testimony to some energy. And today has been a day as warm as milk and so still that you can hear the cows munching. There was all morning a mist like thick honey with the light breathing behind it a glorious exultant spirit. The sun has been dim all day and Blencathra and Skiddaw have been like whales, unicorns, blankets of soft down, and this afternoon when the sun came fully out and the air was blue they rolled over in delight as puppies do when, deliciously expectant, they want their stomachs stroked. It is not like me to write of the weather, but I have been ill for so long and have smelt nothing but candle-ends, slops and the horsey grain of my blankets.

Last evening I had an odd talk with my father that needs recording. He came in wobbling a candle, in a bed-gown, his chest exposed, but in spite of this very sober. I have been dimly conscious of him the last months, coming in and out of my fantasies. And *what* fantasies! Myself hanging, bare save for a thin shift, from a beam, my toes turned in, and my second self

exuding like milk from an udder out of my left ear – and I was
Grandfather Will's infant, guzzling at a bottle and clutching a
money-bag, and the room was on fire and myself in the middle of
it frying like an acorn, or I hobbled on Stye Head, the mists
chasing me until I fell headlong into Eskdale, and once a white
horse, flashing up a frozen mountainside, caught me with its
teeth and flung me down into ice. In and out of this, then, has
come my good father, but only last evening did we have any
serious conversation.

He tells me that he has not had a drop of liquor for the last six
months, during my illness. And I can believe him. For once he
does not look more than his fifty odd years. His fat is dropped
from him – yes, and his spirits have gone too. He is a little
crazed, I think, as I am. This house has the seeds of craziness in
its bones. For he says that Aunt Judith has poisoned me, some
insane story about her bribing the cook to spoil my food! There's
real craziness as I told him, for whatever that old lady may be
about it will never be poisoning. He tells me, however, that Rackstraw whipped one of the Peach children within an inch of its
existence for stealing out of the Uldale kitchen window and that
one of the Uldale barns has been set on fire. He wants to have
Aunt Judith in jail, but I tell him that the countryside would
burn the jail down to get her out.

When all this loose talk of revenge and the rest had died away
he besought me not to leave him. He has a fear, it seems, that I
shall steal away just as Elizabeth did. He moved me for he loves
me with the strongest mingling of pride, fear and egotism. God
knows I don't want his love. I have no regard for him except that
it seems to me we are caught in the same trap. My illness has left
my head clear and empty. I am imprisoned and cannot be free
until some act frees me. Death, perhaps, of which I have no fear.
But death liberates only one of myself. The other remains imprisoned.

My father held my body in his arms. How lonely and isolated
an act! No one has ever held me close to their breast since I was
an infant, and my father is not a man of sentiment, but he sees
everything else going – health, reputation, wealth – save his love
for me and his hatred of the Uldale lot. I tell you we Herries are
lost men if we let our dreams go too far, be they good or bad, and
this old folly of hating one another is a dream like the rest, for
there is no satisfaction to be found in any egoistic desire. I can see
that we are intended to lose ourselves altogether in something

impersonal, and once Cousin John, the pretty, were gone I could be lost, I fancy, turning with what relief into the thick honeyed air like a child loosed from school ... But what a couple the two of us, my gross father straining my bony wasted fretfulness against his bare chest, and our eyes refusing to meet! And myself, round the corner, peering and grinning at the idiocy of the scene from behind the wardrobe.

When he kissed me I shrank into my twitching leg and he felt me shrink and for once I hated my unkindness. He is a very simple man, my father. He meant this Fortress to be a great symbol of Herries power – just as Cousin James and Rodney and Grandfather and Amery are building up their fine Victorian England – but to lay stone upon stone is not enough. That is a thing that the building Herries have never understood. I do not believe in God but I do not think that you can build anything without Him.

My father wishes me to take my proper place here when I am recovered. He is reformed, he says – no more the rake. We will attend to farms and property. Yes, but no Herries has ever wanted to accumulate property. We do not care for it enough. We think too much of ourselves and will not yield our personal conceit to anything, not even to property.

And we must get Aunt Judith out of Uldale, he says. And we must make this house warm, he says. It is always so devilish cold. He does not know that there is a rat eating away the foundations. And, when all is said, he loves me like a dog, not knowing why, and I care for nothing and nobody, not I. It is something though to see the gold light again lying evenly over the hills and to hear the stream running down the hill. I have grown, during my illness, a pale forked beard. I look, in the glass, like a green radish.

LONDON, *January 14th, 1846*

Yesterday I had a half-hour of sanity that is worth recording. I spent it with Grandfather Will. He requested me to pay him a visit. Why? Even now I do not know. Some intention perhaps of compensation because he has thrown my father and myself aside for ever and young Ellis reigns in our stead. (Why Ellis? A dreary, dry-as-dust, left-over-from-yesterday pantry kind of name, but its mother has rich cousins thusly.) Nor do I blame him for that. We are not a pair to be proud of, I suppose. And so

I went. Appalling that house in Hill Street. No rain-washed air sweeping Blencathra here, but furniture spawning everywhere, masses of it, heavy and despondent, groaning between thick rep and treading down the thick Turkey. There are pallid sightless statues and old Herries gilt-edged on every wall. I was alone in a vast room with my grandfather, and we crept together for safety. 'Keepsakes' were our only company. But I am modern for my time. I am a hundred years hence. I am sickly with the odour of 1950. He is bent now, his hair white, his clothes fitting him, black and stiff, as though they were made in a Bank. But in his old age he is kind and eager. I should judge that this baby is the only human soul for whom he has ever cared, although he spoke of Elizabeth's beauty and seeing her alone in this room one day in the past 'like a vision'. He meant, I fancy, that it could not be true that she was my sister. He thinks me misshapen and dangerous and cannot understand that I should be descended from his loins. Something has gone wrong somewhere and he is bewildered because he has always done the sensible thing. But he intended to be kind, sat close to me although I made him creep, and by not looking at my twitching leg he only looked the more intently. He asked me how I did. He had heard that I had been ill. He feared that he would never see Cumberland again although in his youth he had seen eagles sailing over Glaramara. He has a trick of fingering his coat-buttons as though they were counting-house money. He wanted me to tell him something. But what? That things have not turned out as they should do, his brother Francis a suicide, his son a drunken fool, his grandson a deformity? Well, there is little Ellis, and I see as though under glass his heart beat up again and his old eyes, weary with gazing on figures, open out at the new hope. Then he is proud of England. It is as though he had made it, put a hump on Skiddaw here, added a tomb to Westminster, straightened the Strand, bidden the sea halt in Norfolk, and run the railway to Newcastle. He is tired, he explains to me, and then with great courage lays his hot bony hand on mine.

'For I am seventy-five,' he tells me, 'and have worked hard all my days.'

He hopes that we are all now reconciled, for there was once a silly quarrel. Something about a fan. His wife, 'your grandmother,' was concerned. But that is all so old, so very very long ago, and he hopes that now all is well. Do I see Judith Paris often? A remarkable woman with much spirit and character. And

I think of the little Peach children setting a match to Aunt Judith's parlour, and Aunt Judith slapping my father's face.

But he hopes that all is well. We must be friends, all of us. Our family must stand together. They mean something to England. He talks of Palmerston and Peel and the Corn Law crisis and says the 'rotten potatoes have done it,' and how angry the Duke is and that Melbourne told the Queen 'that it was a damned dishonest act,' and that John Russell has come out of it all 'damned poorly', but they are all dim figures to him now. Ellis aged three has swallowed up the firmament. He has a little rheumatism in his legs, he tells me, but otherwise he is well enough, and so he pulls himself up and slowly, slowly, very stiff and straight, stamps from the room. And I go down into the street to meet my waiting double . . .

IREBY, *October 9th, 1846*

I have seen the 'Barguest'. I am a haunted man. I was lost yesterday afternoon in the wilds between Blencathra and Skiddaw, Skiddaw Forest way. I do not know where exactly I was. I could not find the same place again. I had plunged upward, limping and running and limping again in my own ridiculous fashion, treading down the dried bracken that in certain lights has almost a glow of fire running through it. I had looked back and seen Ireby with its stone turrets, its frowning eyebrow, squat like a discontented image staring down at Uldale. I looked forward and the rocks closed me in. They have that fashion here. They move forward of their own will; you can see them almost scratching their craggy sides. A moment before there had been the long swinging slope of bracken, fields below marked off and smelling rain, the stone wall running straight up into air, a round tufted tree holding the light, cottages and farms – and now only this pressing crowding observant rock, the ridge of the hill black against the October sky save for some little white clouds that like spies crowded to the ridge and looked over down into the amphitheatre. I am noting it down thus minutely because of what then occurred.

I seemed to be able to move neither up nor down; my leg limits me and I felt as though the slope of rock on which I was standing would slide down with me – maliciously, while the rocks round me shook with laughter. And then I saw the Barguest. An old man shaped like a whale-bone. He came along towards me on his hands and knees, and once and again he would stop, stare at me, and bite his long fingernails. But I could see through him; he swayed like water-mist, was at one time so hazily defined that there were wisps of him like clouds about the rock, then so sharp that I could count every button. It was no imagination – or I am mad perhaps with want of sleep. I stayed transfixed, and he came right up to me. I could smell his breath, an odour of mushroom and sodden leaves. He touched me with his long yellow fingernail and then dispersed into vapour. I know this is so. It is no dream and, if I am crazy, which for some months now I have suspected, what is reality? But I am sure that I shall see this place again and at some fatal time. When the Barguest had vanished I climbed a stone and all the scenery was restored again, the fields green in the October sun, and rain-clouds gathering up above the sea.

WAX FLOWERS AND THE REVOLUTION

ADAM tried, with all the self-control that belonged to his training, to forget what the day after tomorrow meant to him, but, try as he would, again and again something repeated inside himself: 'The day after tomorrow ... The day after tomorrow. Everything hangs on Monday, my whole life ... everything I've worked for.'

Margaret, in a brown bonnet, hanging on his arm, caught sight of the magnificent Beadle, whiskered, gold-laced, standing superbly at the door of the Pantheon Bazaar.

'Oh, let us go into the Pantheon ... I can find something there for poor little Daisy Bain, whose foot was crushed by that wagon last week. It won't occupy us a minute. Do you mind, Adam?'

They were both making a sublime attempt at proving that nothing was toward. Today was like any other day. And yet, with how many thousands around them, they were, it might be, on the eve of a new era, a new world, a world of light, justice and brotherhood. All London was making preparation for Monday's great Chartist rising. All clerks and officials were ordered to be sworn garrisons. Every gentleman in London was become a constable. (What a very grand carriage outside the Princess Theatre, and what a hideous befrilled Pug in the window!)

After all, what an incredible year! In the month of March

alone fearful street fighting in Berlin, flight of the Prince of Prussia, riots in Vienna and Milan, Hungary in revolt, revolution in Austria, and, above all, France tumbling either into a chaos of disaster or a triumph of a new grand order!

And on Monday – Monday, April 10th, 1848 – England too might see the turning-point of all her history. But Margaret had always a child-like desire for pleasure, and Adam was, nowadays, a great deal more easily pleased than he had once been. They had walked out into the mild spring air that they might quiet some of their almost trembling agitation. How odd it was to see the bird-stuffer's shop with the birds of paradise and parrots, crimson and gold and violent green, a statuary shop, with Canova's Graces, the staymaker's, the fitter's shop with the little cork ball bounding up and down on the perpendicular jet of water, the provision shop with the Durham mustard, the Abernethy biscuits, Iceland moss, Narbonne honey, Bologna sausages – these and many many more, and to think that in another two days all these splendours might be at the mercy of the mob, that the poor might have their wrongs righted, the just come to their own . . . It must be truth-fully added that any stranger seeing Adam and Margaret as they passed the bowing Beadle at the Pantheon door would have been astonished indeed at such revolutionary sentiments, for never did a pair look more respectable and kindly – Adam, set and solid, with his dark side-whiskers, his handsome high hat and gentle-manly cravat, and Margaret in her brown bonnet and overjacket of white embroidered muslin. Revolutionaries? Surely not this respectable pair!

In fact they did forget for ten minutes inside the Pantheon that they *were* revolutionaries. Margaret was so happy to be alone with Adam for a little that she forgot all else. Adam was changed since that Christmas at Uldale, more thoughtful, more demon-strative, but he was constantly preoccupied with his work, and their rooms were from morning to night crowded with other people. She did not often have him to herself. She was so happy that it had been *his* suggestion that they should take this walk! He did not often suggest that they should go off somewhere alone. She sometimes almost wished that there *was* no Charter, that that flamboyant boastful Feargus O'Connor had never been heard of, that she and Adam and her father need not so con-tinually be considering the wrongs of other people! And the Pan-theon, when they were inside it, was enchanting! First they went up to the gallery where they might look down on that exciting coloured maze of babbling children, beautiful ladies, attendant footmen and subservient shopmen. Behind them (and they glanced in for a moment) was that queer neglected little picture-gallery with the dusty twentieth-rate pictures and tragic Haydon's enormous spectre-like 'Lazarus' dominating with its fruitless ambition and almost emerging misconceived genius the atmosphere not only of the Pantheon but the street beyond it, the people, the carriages, the houses. Once this was a theatre; here were the Grand Staircase, the Rotunda, the green room, the con-servatories, dressing rooms. Here were *Ariadne in Naxos, Daphnis and Chloe, Bellerophon, The Cruelty of Nero*. Old Will, a stiff prosperous conceited young man of the City, must here have applauded and Christabel feebly clapped her gloved hands and old Carey have slumbered! Even the lovely radiant Jennifer, with her proud parents, must here have been the beauty of the evening. Judith's Georges must have looked in with a companion to observe the legs of the chorus; Guimard danced in a hoop that reached nearly to her ankles. Those were the pigtail days of Du-vernay and Ellsler and Taglioni! Here George III's eldest son met the lovely Perdita, and Charles Fox in a domino shouted a tipsy applause!

A church, a waxwork show, an opera, and then one night, in the middle of *Don Giovanni*, twelve demons bearing torches of resin rose to seize the guilty hero, and behold there were *thirteen* demons, one of them carrying *two* torches and disappearing in a flame of real fire while the audience fainted and the manager vanished into a madhouse!

But Margaret and Adam were not thinking of the past: the present and the future were *their* concern! They were very young – Adam young for his almost thirty-three years, Margaret only twenty-eight. Everything was in front of them.

Before they descended from the gallery Adam turned.

'Margaret, are you happy?'

'Very, Adam.'

'You know that you are everything to me now. Whatever happens on Monday, whatever way things go, nothing can alter that.'

'Yes, I know.'

He kissed her and they went down the stairs like a couple of children. To purchase something for little Daisy Bain was no easy task, for the variety of toys was extraordinary and the young ladies at the stalls so *very* polite and superior. Margaret was always easily dashed by patronage and had she been alone would have fled from those elegant young women in dismay, but Adam confronted them so calmly and with so agreeable a smile that they were ready to do anything for him. There was the monkey on a stick, the serpent made of elastic (a compound of glue and treacle), a centipede at the end of an indiarubber string, and many another; but best of all were the wax flowers. Oh! how lovely they were! Margaret clapped her hands when she saw a whole stall of them! She had no eyes then for the tortoiseshell card-cases, the pink scented invitation cards with 'on dansera' in the corner, the muslin slips, the volumes of polkas with chromo-lithographed frontispieces, the sandalwood fans, the mother-of-pearl paper-knives with coral spring handles – all these could be bought at the Pantheon, but she saw only that blazing bank of colour – crimson, orange, violet, silver – the flowers smiling from their stalks – carnations, pansies, roses, lilies-of-the-valley, peonies – their wax petals soft and iridescent, as fresh, as vernal as though but a moment ago they had opened their smiling faces to the sun!

'Oh, Adam, are they not marvellous!' she cried.

Something then touched his heart, as though he had never truly loved her before and as though he were warned that, without realizing his treasure, it might be, at a moment, lost to him. He would buy the whole store-load for her! Revolutions, tumbling thrones, the rights of the poor, these things fell down before the wax flowers like pasteboard castles!

She chose an assorted bunch – purple pansies, icily white lilies-of-the-valley, a crimson rose.

'They will live for ever!' she said, smiling into his eyes.

They were packed very carefully into a box, and lying on tissue paper looked, Margaret thought, worthy of the Queen.

'They should be kept under glass to preserve them from the dust,' she said.

The stately young woman who served her smiled with an exquisite dignity.

'That is generally considered wise, madam,' she remarked.

'Oh, Adam, how kind you are!' Margaret whispered as they walked away. 'I shall have these all my life long.' Then dropping her voice, looking at him shyly but with a deep intensity: 'I do love you so'.

They passed the refreshment counter and enjoyed, each, an arrowroot cake. Daisy Bain had been quite forgotten, so hurriedly a doll with flaxen hair was purchased for her. They enjoyed the conservatory with the fountain that contained the gold and silver fish, the exotic plants and gay flowers. But it was very hot in the conservatory, and the parrots and cockatoos made an intolerable screeching. One cockatoo, as Margaret could not help observing, strangely resembled Mr Feargus O'Connor and, for a moment, a dread caught at Margaret's heart. What would happen on Monday? Was this their last peaceful day? Would they ever be so happy again? She looked at the box that she carried in her hand and sighed. She held Adam's arm yet more closely as they passed out through the waiting-room where some grand ladies were waiting for their carriages, and so into the light and fresh air of Great Marlborough Street.

On their return home they found themselves in another world. Adam discovered suddenly, looking at the room's disorder, the bottles of beer, the smoke from pipes, books thrown on to the floor, that he wanted to be out of it all, that his enthusiasm was dead, that he did not care what happened on Monday, that there was no Cause any longer. As he saw Margaret moving quietly into the farther room, carrying the box that held her precious wax flowers as carefully as though it were glass, he discovered that with her departure all the light seemed to have gone out of his world. He had reached some new relation with her during that half-hour in the Bazaar. She was more precious to him than ever before.

So with that rather stumbling, halting movement that made him seem short-sighted, but that was only in reality because his thoughts were elsewhere, he turned and took in his company. He saw at once that Henry Lunt held the floor. He would of course in any place where he was. He was in no way different from the day when Adam had first met him, still shabby, black, fierce, denunciatory, self-confident. Adam knew that he was brave and honest, but he knew also that he was narrow-visioned, foolishly impetuous, and that his temper was so violent that it was extremely dangerous. He had been twice gaoled for his share in riots and disorders: this had not made him either wiser or more tolerant. He was more conceited than he had been, thought he knew everything and had all the gifts of leadership; tonight he seemed to Adam a noisy, tiresome demagogue. There were now too many of his sort in the movement, and, in fact, the whole impetus seemed to be slipping away from the Chartists. The Irish potato famine, the Anti-Corn Law League, above all the exciting spectacular troubles in Europe, made the Chartist movement a little old-fashioned. Louis Philippe's fall in February still possessed men's minds to the diminution of all else. After all, people said, bad though things were, they were not as bad as in France. We English are too sensible for Revolutions. We are not of that kind. Adam agreed with them. The Chartists, especially men of Lunt's type, appeared now something foreign and affected.

Undoubtedly everyone in the room this evening felt a little of this. Lunt talked the louder because of it, and, sitting on the edge of the table, swinging his stout legs, harangued Kraft, Pider, and Ben Morris and a young Jew, Solomon, as though he were, with wonderful magnanimity, screwing their courage to the striking-point.

Pider, it seemed, had said something mildly deprecatory before Adam came in, and Lunt was all on fire over it.

'Aye,' he was shouting, 'that's just what I was expecting to hear, Pider. There are too many of your sort about, and that's the truth. Here we are slaving for years back to bring this thing about and at last the moment has arrived. The great, magnificent moment, the climax of all our efforts, and what do you do but—'

'Yes, but,' Pider broke in, 'suppose the moment hasn't arrived after all? Suppose Monday's abortive and there's nothing done? Look at O'Connell!'

'Yes, look at O'Connell!' cried Lunt fiercely, jumping from the table and waving his short arms. 'He's dead, isn't he? And deserved to die. They may have given him a fine funeral in Dublin, but we know what he was, a faint-heart whose courage failed him just when it was needed. Feargus O'Connor's quite another sort of man—'

'I don't know,' said Pider doubtfully. 'I've heard men say of O'Connor—'

'And what have you heard men say of O'Connor?' Lunt shouted. 'There are always men jealous of their leaders, but I tell you that any man who says O'Connor will fail us is lying in his throat, and so I'd tell him to his face. I know O'Connor. I've eaten and slept with him, and a grander, finer leader of men the world doesn't hold! Answer me that, Pider, and tell me that you know O'Connor better than I do and I'll tell you it's a falsehood.'

Pider, who was not lacking in courage and was in no way

afraid of Lunt, started fiercely forward. Kraft came quietly in between them.

'Now, now,' he said, smiling. 'Where's the good of our arguing about what will happen on Monday? Who can say how things will turn? We've done the best we can and must leave the rest to God.'

'God! God!' Lunt shouted fiercely. 'It isn't God we're wanting, but confidence in ourselves. I tell you—'

But Kraft gave a sign to Adam and turned off into a little side-room that he used as a study. Adam followed him and closed the door behind him. He put his arm round Adam and drew him close.

'You look weary,' Adam said.

'Yes, I am weary. Their shouting makes me weary. There are times when I'm sick at heart of the whole thing, times when I wish that I'd never heard of the Cause at all, and had spent my days mending watches or keeping sheep in a field.'

'It's not like you,' Adam said, 'to be down.'

'No, maybe it's not. But tonight I have a kind of foreboding, a sinking of the heart.' He pressed Adam's shoulder. 'What is it, Adam, creeps into all Causes alike, a kind of worm that eats the heart out of them? It's a sort of egotism, I suppose. You grow to think of your own part in it all, to admire your own energy, your fine speeches, to be jealous of others who are praised, to want personal rewards. To be impersonal, to care nothing for yourself, it is the only lesson of life, and no one can learn it!'

'Yes. If there is a lesson!' Adam's dark eyes slowly clouded. 'When you watch the Churches fighting as they are, when you see Jews like Disraeli bringing off their clever fireworks, while you watch a sot like Walter Herries at home trying to frighten women ... It may be there's no lesson, no plan, no future, no God—'

Kraft shook his head.

'I feel my immortality,' he said. 'I cannot doubt it, but it is perhaps a poor kind of immortality. God *may* be a sort of flash Jew like Disraeli or a dandy like D'Orsay or a storyteller like Charles Dickens or a ranter like Lunt – it may be one long swindle – but it goes on, I *know* that it goes on.'

'Yes,' Adam continued, nodding his head, 'and emotions like my present love of Margaret. That's no present from a cheap Jew; or walking down by Sour Milk Ghyll on a summer evening when the water is whiter than snow and the hills clouds –

D'Orsay couldn't make *such* a gift to anyone. But this, Caesar, all this that we have been working for for years – I see no New Heaven and New Earth *this* way. Men don't change. Why do they not change, Caesar, that's what I want to know? Why do *I* not change with all the experience I get? I can remember when I was a tiny boy bathing one evening in a tarn above Hawkshead. My mother was there, and an old fat fellow, my uncle Reuben, a sort of itinerant preacher, who told me stories. He was a wonderful man as I remember – I daresay he was not in reality. He was killed after a riot when they tried to burn Uldale down, set on by Walter Herries. I owe Walter Herries something, you see. But what was I saying? Oh yes – that night. What was I? Four, five? I don't know. We lit a fire under the trees, there was a dog, and Uncle Reuben told me stories. All beauty, all loveliness is in that night as I look back. Not now. Not here. Not then as I knew it. I was happy, of course, but recognized nothing extraordinary. But looking back I see now that there was something divine in that wood that night. Why,' he burst out, laughing, 'there was something divine in Pantheon Bazaar this afternoon. My love for Margaret. Hers for me. Let me recognize it now and offer D'Orsay-Disraeli-Dickens-Jupiter my thanks for it.'

Kraft smiled.

'What has happened to you, Adam? You are usually so silent. Words are pouring from you.'

'I know. I'm living at an extra intensity tonight. As though there were only a thin strip of paper between myself and discovery – discovery of what? I don't know. D'Orsay's rouge-pots?'

'I know,' Kraft answered quietly. 'I am the same. It is our excitement about Monday, I suppose. A Scotsman would say I am "fey". I can see my shroud, Adam.'

Sunday night he slept so little and woke so early that while it was still dark he slipped from Margaret's side, dressed hurriedly, and went out. He walked through the quiet streets for some while without thinking of his direction, then found that he was in the City. Here it was as cool and silent as an oyster. The wall of the Custom House was a dead wall, the Coal Exchange was sleeping, but soon he was down on the wharfs where life was already active and earnest. Here were tubs smelling of oranges, shops – already opened – packed with salt fish, dried herrings, Yarmouth bloaters, mussels and periwinkles, dried sprats and cured pilchards. For he was in Billingsgate. Here the Billingsgate marketeers were

drinking from massive blue and white earthenware mugs filled to
the rough brims with coffee; here porters were busied clearing
piles of baskets away, putting forms and stools in order, in eager
preparation for the fish auction. The wharf is covered with fish,
and the great clock of Billingsgate booms forth five o'clock. The
stands are laden with salmon, shoals of fresh herring, baskets full
of turbot, while the crowds are gathering thickly, and everyone is
shouting and crying at once.

Adam watched with increasing pleasure. Close to him a fine
fellow stood, a hat tall and shiny as though he were a habitué of
Aldridge's Repository, his sporting neckcloth fastened with a
horseshoe pin, while round his giant stomach was bound the
conventional blue apron; he was wearing galligaskins and
straight tight boots of sporting cut. Here were the eight auction-
eers; here Bowler's, Bacon's and Simpson's, the noisiest taverns
(at this hour) in the whole of London. Now was the excited
selling of the 'doubles' and the 'dumbarees'. Fish, fish, fish!
Plaice, soles, haddocks, skate, cod, ling ... Suddenly he recollected. My God, this very afternoon, and the gentleman in the
galligaskins and blue apron might find all his occupation gone!
By five of the evening of this very day, all the soles and cods and
haddocks might swim peacefully in the sea for the attention paid
to them! This very street, instead of its stream of fish-scales,
bones and dirty water, might be running in blood! Instead of
gaiety, laughter, money business, there might be death, ruin, a
blaze of fire, smoking catastrophe!

There was a sick dismay at his heart. He had been working for
years with an earnestness and eagerness that had possessed every
energy he had. He had lost in these years much of the fantasy
and humour that had been part of his childhood. At this stage he
was grimly serious, taking nothing lightly. At that moment in the
Billingsgate Market he saw himself as someone fantastically
absurd, working like a labourer at piling brick upon brick, and as
he laboured the bricks turned, before his eyes, to straw.

A joke, a farce, iridescent fish-scales floating down the teeming
gutter. He hurried home.

This morning, Monday, April 10th, was a lovely day, the sun
streaming down with that soft mild radiance that brings a spring
scent of flowers into the London streets. The Chartist detach-
ment to which Kraft and Adam belonged moved off very early
to Kennington Common. There was no definite procession to the
Common; the Procession, presenting the great Petition, was to

march at least a hundred thousand strong, under the leadership of Feargus O'Connor, to the Houses of Parliament.

Here the Petition was to be presented, and what would follow after was the question on everybody's lips. Men like Lunt declared that what would follow would be the greatest Revolution in England since 1688. But how precisely that Revolution would take place, no one precisely knew. It was true that the Queen and her Consort were not supremely popular, but no one had anyone to propose in their place, and even the Lunts of the movement could not claim that the whole of England was at all ready as yet for a President or a Dictator.

The very troubles that the rest of Europe were battling with made many Englishmen proud of their own passivity.

Nevertheless, a Revolution there would be, some sort of a Revolution. What the average man, both Chartist and non-Chartist, feared was that, simply through ill-directed and undisciplined contact, there would be riot and bloodshed, meaning nothing, leading nowhere; men perceived, from the recent Paris example, that one small unexpected event could lead to vast and unexpected consequences. Let fifty thousand shouting Chartists reach Westminster ... Why, then, both sides being armed, some horrible catastrophe might take the whole civilized world by surprise. No one in London was happy on that lovely spring morning and, if the truth were known, most certainly not Mr Feargus O'Connor himself, who, in spite of his descent from Irish kings, had no wish to find himself in gaol before the evening.

Neither Adam nor Kraft was happy. They had one last word together before they set out.

'I have the oddest feeling,' Kraft said. 'I dreamt last night, of what I don't know, but I woke saying to myself, "Yes, that's the answer." Now, I know what it all means. I seemed, in that brief dream, to have passed through all experience and to have realized that envy, greed, jealousy, disappointment, lust, bodily sickness – it was not until I had known them all and tranquilly accepted them all, that I began to live. Tranquillity. I tell you, Adam, I am as tranquil this morning as a pond-weed. My anxiety is gone, but my desire too. I cannot imagine what it is that has agitated me so deeply all these years.'

Adam frowned.

'I am not tranquil. I am afraid of what a parcel of fools are likely to do before the day's out.'

It was still very early when the three of them reached the Common. On their way thither they had been impressed by the silence of the town, as of something strongly on its guard. There was little traffic in the streets, very few people about and many of the shops closed. Adam learnt afterwards that many of the important official buildings round Westminster were defended with guns and that Whitehall was in reality an armed camp.

When they arrived at the Common they saw that there was the crowd that had been confidently expected. There were many banners flaunting devices like 'The Charter, the whole Charter, and nothing but the Charter,' 'Justice for All Men and No Favour,' 'Up! Up for O'Connor!' and there were a number of brass bands.

Men, women and children sat and walked about, rather list-lessly, dressed, some of them, in their Sunday clothes, while others seemed to boast their poverty. There were many pale, thin, with angry, restless eyes and hungry faces; others appeared to have come to enjoy the sights. There were some booths with food and drinks.

Everything was very quiet, there was a murmur of voices, a sense of expectant waiting as though at any moment a miracle might break out in the sky above their heads.

Soon after their arrival Lunt joined them.

'Not so many as were expected,' Adam said.

'Pooh,' Lunt answered. 'They'll turn up. It will take many of them time to get here. And this is nothing. You wait until the Procession starts for Parliament and see how many join us. You listen to O'Connor when he makes his speech and you'll hear something.'

Soon it happened that everybody began to press together towards the centre of the Common and the crush became un-comfortable; toes were stepped on, umbrellas and sticks poked into innocent faces, women lost their children, and children were crying, pockets were freely picked.

Adam saw that it was towards O'Connor and one or two gentlemen near him that the crowd was thronging, and soon, owing to Kraft's important position in the movement and the badge that he wore, he found that they were enclosed in the magic circle. He was so close to Feargus O'Connor that he could observe him well. A wild theatrical gentleman, he seemed both over-decorated and shabby, for he had on the breast of his blue coat a number of ribbons and medals, but his pantaloons were older than they ought to be and stained with mud. His hair fell in untidy ringlets from under his high hat, and he waved with a great deal of excited gesture the cane that he was carrying. In the other hand he had a stout roll of paper that was supposed by everyone to be the famous Petition. He was, it was clear, excellently conscious of the attention that he was receiving. Once and again he would put up his hand to his rather soiled cravat, the cane would drop to the ground and be obsequiously lifted by someone. He would dart his head up rather as a suspicious hen might do, stare with proud and melancholy indignation at some small boy who, open-mouthed, was gazing at him with all his eyes.

It appeared that he had some reason for indignation, for it seemed that his pocket had been picked. Had anyone ever heard the like? The leader of the country against tyranny and oppression, and his pocket had been picked! How much had there been in his purse? He could not be sure, but a very considerable sum; also a blue silk handkerchief to which he attached sentimental value.

But Adam quickly realized that Mr O'Connor was not at all at his ease. While he talked with an excited and incoherent fervour his eyes were for ever searching the horizon and searching it with a kind of terrified preoccupation as though he expected at any moment to see a large scaly dragon, vomiting fire, issue from the Kennington trees.

He greeted Kraft absent-mindedly and shook a finger with Adam (the rest of his hand clutching the sacred roll of paper) without seeing Adam at all.

He became with every moment more deeply agitated. Beside him was a long, thin, cadaverous man who looked like a Methodist clergyman, and a stout, rubicund fellow like a butcher. There was no sign, however, of any organization or leadership. From time to time someone broke through into the magic circle, whispered mysteriously to O'Connor and vanished again. He on his part would nod his head with great self-importance or shake it or look up to the heavens or wave his cane. He alluded again and again to the fact that his pocket had been picked, and once and again would burst into a fine frenzy, invoking the Deity: 'My God, have I been chosen to lead these people at this great hour? Have they come to me hungry and shall they not be fed?' Then, dropping his voice: 'What is it, Forster? Has Cummin not arrived? Where is Whitstable? Have they got the thief that has my

purse? March to Westminster? But where are the others? This is
not the half of them! And my toes trodden on and my pocket
picked . . .'

The crowd waited with a most exemplary patience. They were,
it seemed, ready to picnic on the Common for the day if necessary. Many of them, Adam was convinced, were not Chartists at
all. Many were rogues and vagabonds who had come to gather
what they might out of so large a crowd. He saw, as he looked
about him, many incongruous figures, here a rather shabby
young dandy in pea-green gloves and a shirt embroidered with
dahlias and race-horses, then a stout serious-looking gentleman
with peg-top trousers, chin-tuft and eye-glass, and close beside
him a sturdy fellow who might have come straight from the
Billingsgate of the morning, green apron and galligaskins all
complete. It could not be said to be a very murderous crowd,
and, as Adam looked, his fears of red revolution died away. There
would be no revolution here. But for what then all these years had
he been working? Not for revolution certainly, but also not for a
contented humorous crowd like this. He drew Margaret's arm
through his and waited for what might come.

What soon came was an excited stir through the crowd. It
whispered like wind through corn. Someone had arrived. Something had occurred. Two men pushed through and spoke to
O'Connor; at once his countenance turned red and then white
again. He dropped his cane and no one picked it up. He stood,
hesitating, his head turning first this way, then that.

The crowd was dividing; it was the Constable, Mr Mayne,
followed by three of his inspectors. Mayne, a fine, resolute-look-
ing man, took his stand a little way from Adam, and sent one of
his inspectors forward to O'Connor. It was clear that O'Connor
was in a terrible fright. 'Afraid of arrest,' whispered Kraft contemptuously to Adam. O'Connor, after a second's hesitation,
clutched his cane and roll of paper and went to meet Mr Mayne.
The two men made a striking contrast, and in that moment of
seeing them together, it seemed to Adam that any alarms or hopes
on the part of anyone that Revolution would ever again break out
in England were finally dissolved.

'Mr O'Connor,' said Mayne, 'I am here to inform you that the
meeting on this Common is permitted, but no procession to
Westminster.'

O'Connor said something.

'No. No procession whatever.'

O'Connor spoke again.

'Certainly, Mr O'Connor, I am very pleased to hear it.'

O'Connor held out his hand; Mr Mayne shook it.

The Revolution was over.

Mayne, with his inspectors, disappeared, and O'Connor came forward to address the crowd. There were stands with flags and banners for him to appear on, and he did step up on to one of them, attended by some half a dozen gentlemen, but very little that he said could be heard. It appeared that he himself was going to the Home Office that he might present the famous Petition there; there would, however, be no procession; in fact, everything was over, or rather, the Meeting might continue as long as it pleased, but he, Mr O'Connor, would not appear in it.

He vanished, and there followed an extraordinary scene. Many of the more peaceful citizens, laughing and jeering, turned to leave the Common, but at the same time crowds of roughs and hooligans, urged on by the more violent Chartists, drove their way towards the stands with shouts and threats. Women were screaming, children crying, men shouting, no one seemed to be in command, someone tore down two of the banners.

'We had best be out of this,' Adam said, turning to Margaret. Then he saw Lunt. The man seemed to be in a frenzy and was orating, waving his hands, his hat off, his face congested with anger. In his hand he carried a short, thick club.

'Come,' said Kraft sadly. 'The curtain is down. The play is over.'

They turned together, but at the same moment Lunt caught sight of them. Like a madman he rushed at them, stopped in front of Kraft and shouted:

'Now where are you? You white, shaking coward! You and your friends! This is your work, with your psalm-singing, chicken-hearted caution! You have brought England to her knees, sold us like slaves!'

Kraft said quietly: 'Come, Henry. This is a farce.'

'Farce!' Lunt screamed. 'Yes! and who has turned it into a farce?'

'You and others like you,' Kraft answered sternly, his voice ringing out so that all heard him. 'I have warned you again and again, but you would not listen. With your violence you have frightened most decent men away. Aye, and lost most of our battles before they were even fought.'

Lunt's shouts had drawn a large crowd about them. Some excited men pressed forward, shouting incoherently, some laughed, some agreed with Kraft. But Lunt was beside himself; he moved in a whirlwind of passion in which he could distinguish nothing but his own disappointment, the failure of all that his egotism, yes, and his melodramatic self-sacrifice had for years been planning. He closed up to Kraft, who did not move.

'By heaven!' he shouted, 'I will show you who is a traitor! I'll teach your dirty cowardice!'

Kraft caught his arm.

'Be ashamed, man!' he cried. 'Go home to your wife and children!'

The touch infuriated Lunt, who thrust himself free, swung his club and brought it crashing on to Kraft's head. Kraft fell, his hand catching at Margaret's dress as he went down. Instantly there was silence. It was as though a hand caught the Common, the crowd, the sunlight, and, crushing it all into nothing, flung it away. There was emptiness and the sun shining on Kraft's white shirt and his twisted hand.

Adam was on his knees, his arm under Kraft's head that was crooked and veiled in blood. He looked up. 'A surgeon!' he said. 'For God's sake, someone, quickly, a surgeon.'

But he knew that Kraft was dead – the finest man in the world was gone. Tears blinded his sight as he bent again to the ground.

CHILDE ROLAND TO THE DARK TOWER

THIS was one of Judith's good days. This year, 1850, had not opened too well for her. For one thing in January she had had a splendid quarrel with Dorothy, had slapped Amabel (now a big stout girl of eleven) for riding one of the calves, had ordered Dorothy out of the house, had been told by Dorothy that she would not go, had discovered old Peach talking to one of her maids, had dismissed the maid and been of a mind to go up to the Fortress and tell Walter what she thought of him.

When this lively afternoon was over she had gone to bed, lain on her back and laughed aloud at her own bad temper. Dorothy had come in later to make the peace and discovered the old lady sitting up in bed, her lace cap a little askew on her snow-white hair, laughing and doing household accounts. They had embraced, as they always did after a quarrel, and Judith had settled down to the reading of Mr Thackeray's *Vanity Fair*. She had a passion now for novels, although she considered Thackeray too sentimental and something of a hypocrite. Becky, however, she could thoroughly enjoy and considered that there, but for the grace of God, went Judith Paris. Amelia and Dobbin she could not abide, but Rawdon had quite a deal in common with her dear Georges, who was as close to her still as he had been in 1790.

At the end of a chapter she had blown out the candle and lain down to sleep. She had slept for an hour or so and then woken suddenly to a sharp pain in the side. It was the first sharp pain she had ever known and she greeted it humorously as much as to say, 'Well, I knew you would come sometime. Now that you are here, behave as a gentleman.' The pain behaved badly at first and then, like a new acquaintance, having left his card, departed. But in the morning she felt very unwell indeed, tried to get up but could not, was finally in bed for a week. She was attended by Dr Fairchild from Keswick, a little wizened sarcastic man of middle age. They got on very well, were rude to one another, gossiped a good deal, and found that they had much in common.

He told her that she had the rheumatics and he put her on a diet. It was from this moment that she began to care about food. Food had never, all her life, been very important to her. She had always had a healthy appetite and took what came. But now that she was forbidden, she lusted. She liked to forbid herself, but hated that anyone else should forbid her anything. Moreover, Dr Fairchild, with a deliberate maliciousness, as it seemed to her, forbade her the very things for which she cared the most, and especially meat. She had encountered at odd times cranky persons who pretended to live entirely on vegetables. There was poor young Ivison, son of Mr Ivison the bookseller in Keswick, whose pale earnest countenance both amused and irritated her. It was said that he ate nothing but carrots and cabbage, and once, when she met the poor thin boy beside Mr Flintoft's Model of the Lake District, he had incontinently fainted there at her feet! So much for carrots and cabbages.

Nevertheless, she did on the whole as she was told, and now, at the beginning of March, was in fine vigour again. Her spirits were all the livelier, because just at this time John was given a holiday and came up with Elizabeth on a visit. It was a year and a half since they had been at Uldale. The house was very full and she adored it to be full. Dorothy's children were growing – Timothy was thirteen, Veronica twelve, Amabel eleven, and Jane (Judith's especial pet) was nine. Old Rackstraw taught Timothy Latin, and there was a governess, Miss Meredith. Miss Meredith Judith did not like at all, but she could not deny that she was an excellent governess. Miss Meredith, who was round and plump like a barrel, had all the present popular conventionalities. It was Judith's constant delight to shock her, for Judith could not in the least understand this great wave of propriety that had swept over the country. To allude to legs or bosoms or ardent young men or any of the processes of human creation seemed to Miss Meredith like death, and Judith perceived that not only Dorothy but the little girls themselves approved of these reticences.

'But, my dear Dorothy,' Judith would say, 'what is there shocking about being born? Why, I remember at Stone Ends when I was a girl—'

'When you were a girl, Aunt Judith,' Dorothy answered firmly, 'the world was a very different place. Not civilized at all.'

'I am sure,' Judith retorted, 'I can't say about being civilized, but babies are born in exactly the same way now as they were then. It would do Miss Meredith all the good in the world to be flung into a hedge by a tramp—'

But Dorothy was so greatly distressed that Judith desisted.

'*Please*, Aunt Judith,' Dorothy said. 'Do not offend Miss Meredith. She is the best governess in the world. Exactly right for the children. I don't know where we'd ever find such another.'

So Judith refrained, and only teased Miss Meredith when the temptation was quite irresistible.

She loved the house to be full, for she knew that she was a miracle for her age. Dorothy, with all her energy and obstinacy, had no say whatever in the running of the house. And Judith was not at all the conventional tyrannical old woman so common in works of fiction from the days of the Egyptians and maybe long before them. Everyone loved her. She was cared for now as she had never been in all her life before. How in the past she had longed to be liked! How it had hurt her when Will had disapproved and Will's mother hated her and Jennifer plotted against her! But now, when she had all the love that she could possibly desire, she did not greatly care for it. She hated sentiment and always preferred common sense.

Adam, of course, was a thing apart; she was deeply fond of John and Elizabeth, had an affection for Dorothy and the children, but, with the possible exception of little Jane, Adam was the only human being in the world whom she loved.

She certainly did not love herself, but she was proud of her age, her strength, her capability and, above all, her scorn for and successful battles over everyone at Ireby.

Of late Walter had been trying to irritate her in every way that he knew. Things were stolen, her house was spied upon, her servants were bribed, if there was any malicious story possible about anyone at Uldale it was spread in every direction. But Judith and Dorothy were exactly the women to fight a campaign like Walter's. They had much common sense and a strong feeling for the ludicrous. Dorothy was lacking in a sense of humour, but her sense of fun was so strong that to see a gentleman slip on the ice or a lady lose her bonnet in the wind made her stout sides ache with laughter.

So Walter seemed to her silly and Uhland unwholesome.

On this sunny day in March the weather was so warm that John and Elizabeth could walk comfortably up and down the lawn together. Judith, looking at them for a moment out of the parlour window, smiled with approval. John the night before had been most entertaining. If not of Parliament he was near it enough to have plenty of inside information. Both Judith and Dorothy were thrilled with interest as he told them of the hatred that the Queen and Prince Albert felt for Palmerston. Palmerston was John's hero, so he was a trifle malicious about the Queen and the Prince. Lord Clarendon, it seemed, had, a few weeks ago, dined at the Palace, and now it was all over the Town that the Queen in the drawing room after dinner had lost all control and spoken with so much vehement bitterness that Lord Clarendon had not known where to look; and when she had done the Prince had begun and, when Clarendon had visited him next day, had orated about Palmerston for two hours without stopping.

This gave the two ladies great pleasure to hear, not because they wished the Queen or Palmerston or anyone else any harm; simply that it brought the lawns and hedges of Uldale straight into the Palace.

So Judith looked out of the window at John and nodded her

approval. It was so fine a morning that she had put on a new dress for the first time, a dress made especially for her by Miss Sampson in Keswick. She wore more sombre colours now, although she still loved a touch of brightness here and there. As she was wearing long drawers trimmed with lace, a flannel petticoat, an under-petticoat, a white starched petticoat, and two muslin petticoats under the dress, she had, for an old lady, a good deal to carry. Very soon now the stiff bands of the crinoline were to relieve ladies of their outrageous burden. Judith was wearing a dress of grey taffeta with twelve flounces all of a dark shade of green. Out of this 'like a lily-stem out of a flower-tub' rose her dark-green bodice with pagoda sleeves and a very lovely white lace collar (this last a present from Sylvia Herries the preceding Christmas). Her only concession to her years was her white lace cap. Her small, alert, vigorous body carried its cumbrous clothes with grace and ease; her eyes sparkled like little fires. She had, as she had always had, an air of crystalline spotlessness. The muslins, the collar, the cap were new minted as though direct, that minute, from some most perfect laundry. And so in fact they were. Everything was laundered in the house and Mrs Kaplan the housekeeper (Judith's slave) saw that all was perfection.

They were rich now at Uldale. Dorothy had money from Bellairs and her portion of Herries money. Judith's own investments, shares in Liverpool concerns inherited from David Herries, land and property round Uldale excellently supervised for many years by Rackstraw, all mounted to an income well beyond their needs. Judith had no desire for wealth, but she liked to have everything handsome about her. Everything *was* handsome. On this lovely March morning Uldale glistened like a jewel.

She went her rounds of the house, tapping with her stick and humming a tune. She visited everything, the high-ceilinged kitchen, pantry, servants' hall, housekeeper's room complete with black cat, work-basket and flowered footstool. Then, perhaps after the dairy the place that she loved best, the still-room. Here were cakes, jams, preserves made; here was the china washed and the dessert set out. Then the lamp-room, the store-room, the meat-larder where were the weighing machine and the great pickling jars. Then the wood and coal stores, the laundry, the pump-room and the dairy. She stayed for an especial time this morning in the kitchen, for its brick-floored spaciousness bathed in sun was exceedingly pleasant. She stood there, smiling at the maids, leaning on her stick, looking at the roasting-spits, the

Dutch oven, the chopping-block, the sugar-nippers, the coffee-grinder, the pot and pan racks, everything shining, gleaming, glittering as though active and happy with conscious, individual life.

All was good; all was well; still humming her tune she went out on to the sunlit lawn to find John and Elizabeth.

For a moment she looked back at the house – dear house to whose safety and comfort she had, through all her long life, returned again and again. There had been terrible hours here. She could see David Herries fallen, stricken on this very lawn, she could catch again Sarah Herries' distracted glance, could see Jennifer waiting for her lover, Francis' mad return and frantic exit, the rioters and poor Reuben's slaughter, her own tragic surrender of Watendlath, the Christmas party and the fracas with Walter. There had been every kind of tragedy, farce, drama here; birth, death, ruin, love, humour, light easy days, pain and laughter. She had come through it all, as one always did come through if one kept on patiently enough, did not take oneself too seriously, saw the sequence of event, of change, decay and birth in proper proportion. One came through to this sunlight, to this lovely landscape, this quiet English calm; then, turning, she saw that John was walking towards her and, with that quick intuition that she always had, wondered instantly whether after all the tale was told, whether there were not a number more of chapters to be added.

For John was alone and, she saw at once, in trouble. She had never quite understood John. She had loved Francis, his father, but had never understood him either. The alarms, fears, superstitions, doubts of those two were foreign to her direct sensible nature. The part of her that had shared them she had deliberately killed.

John's slim, upright body, his pale hair, beautiful almost feminine features, had always marked him apart from other men. She thought, as she saw him approach her: 'John will never be out of trouble. He will never know what it is to rest.'

He came straight up to her and, his voice quivering a little, said:

'Aunt Judith. I have told Elizabeth I am going up to Ireby.'

She was astonished. A long grey shadow seemed to fall across the sunny lawn.

'Yes. Didn't you know? He has written her a letter: that scoundrel Peach brought it half an hour ago.'

'A letter?'

'Yes. Here it is.'

He handed her a large sheet of paper scrawled over in Walter's big clumsy hand.

DEAR ELIZABETH – As a dutiful daughter you are to pay me a visit. If you don't come of yourself I shall fetch you. Your loving father,

WALTER HERRIES

'Loving father!' said Judith, her voice shaking with anger. 'What impertinence!'

'Yes. But of course Elizabeth mustn't go. She wished it, and I forbade her even to think of it. But *I* am going – and at once.'

As she looked at him he was again the small boy when the nurse had thrown the rabbit out of the window. He stood there, his head up, his nostrils quivering (exaggerated pictures of him, she thought, but spiritually true), like a high-bred horse, defiant but afraid of the whip because of the catastrophe that a contact might bring. She, too, was afraid of some disaster. She knew, as she looked at him, that she had always been afraid of it for him.

'No. Don't you go, John. I'll pay him a visit. I've been wishing to for weeks.'

'Nonsense,' John said roughly. Then, recovering himself, added: 'Pardon me, Aunt Judith. I didn't intend to be rude, but this is *my* affair. You must see that it is—'

She did not attempt to stop him after this, but only sighed to herself as she saw him mount his bay, wave his riding-whip to her, turning with that charming, rather weak, altogether lovable smile that was so like his father's that it always made her heart ache.

Where would this thing end, she thought, as she entered the house. When had it begun? – back, back, maybe to the days when her father had been a wild young man and sold his woman at the Fair, an old eternal quarrel between beauty and ugliness, normality and abnormality, sense and nonsense – a quarrel born, as all quarrels are in this world, of jealousy and fear. But she did not care for philosophy; she took things as they came, and what immediately came now when she entered the house was a quarrel with Dorothy, who wished to buy a sofa covered with wool-work and fringed with beads that she had seen in Carlisle. To buy this monstrosity and place it in the parlour instead of the lovely old one that had the red apples.

'But it's all the mode!' cried Dorothy. 'The Osmastons have wool-work everywhere.'

'They may,' said Judith grimly, 'but so long as I'm up and about that sofa remains in the parlour. Why, I was resting my hand on it when I came to the most important decision of my life.' Then she added as she tapped away on her stick: 'It's all Prince Albert and his German taste. I detest the man.'

Meanwhile John rode down the road towards Ireby. It suited his mood that the sky became overcast as he reached the bottom of the Ireby hill. On his left a bubble of seething little white clouds rose on the Skiddaw ridge, and other clouds rushed up to the sun and, with gestures of sulky annoyance, swallowed it. He *hated* himself for this fear that had seized all his bones like water. The very thought of Uhland made him sick. But perhaps Uhland would not be there. He did not mind Walter at all; he was simply a gross, quarrelsome, bad-mannered fool. His thoughts went back to that day in his childhood when, with Adam, he had watched Walter on the moor. He had been afraid then, but he saw now that it had been Uhland's shadow behind Walter that had, like a prophecy, frightened him. He had been afraid of Uhland before he was born.

He tried now, as he rode slowly up the hill, to formulate that fear, to bring it into the open. But it would not come. That was the awful thing about it. When he forced himself to think of Uhland, or was compelled to do so, he saw him as a shapeless, boneless animal emitting some sickening odour, as one sees a creature in a dream, lurking in shadow in a dank cave or the corner of a cellar, or behind a stone. The hide-and-seek that Uhland had played with him now for so long had introduced into his own soul and body some sickly element, so that, at times, he believed that Uhland was some part of himself – that part we all have, hidden, shameful, lurking. There was nothing shameful in his life except this one cowardice. In everything else he was brave, and so all the more did he feel this one exception to be real.

He raised his head as he saw the grey stone house squatting, in its trees, on the top of the hill. Today he would force this thing into the open; it should skulk, just out of touch and feeling, no longer.

He tied his horse to the wall outside the garden and walked up the flagged path to the door. Stone frowned at him everywhere.

The gardens were trim but dead. It was late March, and the daffodils were in full golden flood under the rosy Uldale walls. Here, too, beneath the dark trees beyond the flowerbeds they flamed in little cups of fire, but the garden itself was black and gritty. As John stood there banging the knocker of the door, the whole place leered down on him.

It was not that it was so large, but that it was so dead. The windows had no faces, the stone turrets were like clenched fists, and worst of all, there was no sound at all anywhere.

At Uldale there was always sound – laughter, singing, running water and the light chatter of birds. He wondered, above the beating of his heart, that there was not a bird singing in the Ireby gardens.

At last there was a creaking of bolts and the door slowly opened. An old bent man whom John had never seen before stood there; he had bow legs and was dressed in the style of thirty years earlier, black worsted stockings, black knee-breeches, a rather soiled neckerchief, and a dull brown tye-wig that cocked a little over one eye. He had a tooth missing, and his words whistled through his lips.

'Is Mr Walter Herries at home?' John asked.

'If you'll wait I'll see,' said the old man, looking out into the garden as though he expected to see a lion rooting up the bulbs. 'What name shall I say?'

'Mr John Herries.'

His mind seemed to be on other things as he ambled away, leaving John in the hall. The hall was stony and bare. There was a fireplace with grinning fire-dogs and a large stand hung with heavy coats and stacked with whips. There was no carpet on the stone that struck the feet icily. He stood there, wondering whether the old man would not forget him, when a green baize door to his left opened and a woman came out. She was not young but not old either, and very extravagantly dressed in a Russian short jacket of gold brocade figured with bunches of flowers in coloured silks. Her skirt had so many flounces that she appeared to be robed ten times over. She wore a bonnet lined with rosebuds, and her cheeks were rosebuds too, only extremely artificial, for John had never seen a lady more brightly painted. This brilliant person brushed past him as though he were not there, and she was swearing like a trooper. She turned towards the stairs and shouted:

'Hell take your meanness, Walter!'

She was so angry that she stared at John without seeing him.

As though from nowhere a very large stout man in a night-cap and a rich flowered dressing-gown appeared on the stairs. He was grinning, his nightshirt was open at the neck and he carried a very small brown hairy dog in one hand by the scruff of its neck. Very good-humouredly he called out, leaning with his free hand on the banister: 'Au revoir, my dearest,' and threw the dog to the lady. John started forward, but the lady was quicker, caught the dog with wonderful dexterity, and rushed from the house, banging the door behind her.

Walter wiped his large hands in a handkerchief that very deliberately he took from his dressing-gown. He was about to vanish when John called out:

'Cousin Walter.'

He peered forward down into the dark hall.

'Hullo. Who's there?' he asked.

'John Herries. I wish to have a word with you.'

Walter came slowly down the stairs, drawing his dressing-gown about him, his slippers tip-tapping. He came right up to John and bent forward, peering at him.

'Oh, it's you, is it?' he said at last. 'Where's my daughter?'

He was very clean-shaved, and his cheeks, round and rosy, shone like a baby's and smelt freshly of some scent. His face was fat, but his neck and exposed chest were white and firm. His mouth, eyes, and thin hair protruding from the night-cap gave him the look of age, for he was only fifteen years older than John in reality, but looked quite of another generation. His body was of great size and had a balloon-like appearance under the dressing-gown.

'May I speak to you?' asked John.

'You may,' said Walter quite amiably. 'Come upstairs.'

John mounted after him, and Walter led the way into a room that was as untidy and uncomfortable as a room could be. There was a spitting, smoky little fire in the grate; a carpet, red with a buff pattern and a large tear, in front of the fireplace; two pier-glasses; a wool-work ottoman and a large harp leaning against the wall. The room smelt of caraway-seed and was very close.

Walter, his legs stretched, stood in front of the fireplace and motioned John to a seat.

'If you're cold,' he said, 'I can't help it. Didn't know you were coming. Have a brandy.'

'No, thank you,' said John, turning his hat round and round in his hands.

'Well, what do you want now that you are here?'

'You wrote a letter to my wife. I am here to answer it.'

Walter scratched his head under his night-cap and grinned. Then he sat down in a large faded green leather chair and stretched out his thick hairy legs, kicking off one slipper and crinkling up his toes.

'Forgive my attire, Cousin John,' he said. 'That bitch of a woman put me out this morning – and now I've put *her* out.' He threw his head back and laughed. 'Have a brandy. Pray, have a brandy,' he said again.

'No, I thank you,' said John very ceremoniously.

'Well, I will.' He pulled an old red worsted bell-rope and so still was the house that the clang of the bell could be heard echoing, echoing into eternity. 'Now then,' he said, 'why isn't my daughter here?'

'She is not here, neither is she coming.'

'Well, that's straight enough. But she *is* coming if I want her.'

'You have no sort of right to her,' John answered hotly. He was glad if he was getting angry. That made him less conscious of the silent house, less aware of his own anticipation of Uhland's entrance.

'And why have I no right? I'm her father, aren't I?'

'You ill-treated her, and then when she ran away because she was so miserable you made no kind of inquiry as to her whereabouts. She might have died for all you cared.'

Walter yawned, scratched his breast, leaned forward, shaking a fist.

'Look you here, Cousin John. Let me tell you something. You are in danger, you are. It began with your mother, who was impertinent to my mother. I gave her a warning, but she wouldn't listen, and I frightened her into her grave. When she was gone I warned you that you'd better be after her – all of you. But you wouldn't take the warning, and, more than that, you have the damned impertinence to marry my daughter – 'gainst my wishes too. I don't bear you a grudge. I don't bear anyone in this world a grudge except my old father who goes cohabiting with a woman young enough to be his daughter and gets a child by her. Disgustin' – simply disgustin'. No, I don't wish you ill, but I've been telling the lot of you these years back to move out of

Uldale, and you will not listen. You are in danger, Cousin John, and if you won't drink a brandy like a gentleman you'd better be off. I've had an irritating time already this morning, and I don't want another.'

'You needn't think,' said John, getting up, 'that we are afraid of you. We know all the dirty little games you've been playing, putting Peach on to rob and spy, bribing the servants, but it doesn't affect us, not an atom.'

'Does it not?' said Walter cheerfully. 'No, because you've that old woman in the house. She's a hard-plucked one, she is. I've been fighting her for years, and upon my soul there is no one in the world I admire more. But it won't go on for ever, you know. Dear me, no. There'll be a nasty family crisis one of these days. You can tell the old lady so.'

The old bow-legged man with the brown wig arrived with a bottle and two glasses. Walter filled one tumbler half full and drank it off.

'That's better,' he said. 'And now you'd better be going.'

He got up and shuffled his great body across the room, yawning, scratching his back, his night-cap tilted over one ear.

'Dam' bitch,' he said. 'I wish I'd broken the bones of that dog.' He kicked the harp with the toe of his slipper. 'That was her doing,' he said, jerking his head. 'Thought she could play on it. Forced me to order the thing from Carlisle . . .' He swung round at the door.

'Uhland hates you, you know,' he said, grinning like a schoolboy. 'Hates you like a poison. Don't know why. Always has.'

John said nothing.

In the passage Walter said:

'Ever been over this house? Chilly place. Draughty as hell.' He threw open a double door. This was the salon where the fine opening Ball had been given. Here were the tapestries, and the decorations, hanging garlands and the dazzling stars of heaven. But the floor was filmed with dust, there was a large patch in the gilded ceiling, a corner of the tapestry flapped drearily against the wall, a chair was overturned, and there were bird-droppings on the long windowsill.

'Fine room,' said Walter. Then, closing the doors behind him, he said: 'There are rooms and rooms in this place. Too many rooms.'

Somewhere a dog was howling and a door banged, monotonously, like a protest.

'Goodbye, then,' said Walter, nodding. 'I am sure I don't know why you came.'

'I came in answer to your letter.'

'Ah, yes. Well, it's my daughter I wish to see. No one else.'

'I came to tell you that. That she will not come.'

'Yes.' He nodded. 'She will, though – if I want her. Damn that dog. There's no peace in this house.' He shuffled off, disappearing quite suddenly. And he was replaced, for John, hearing a sound, looked to the left, and there on the stone step of a little winding stair stood Uhland.

He said nothing. He was dressed in black, with a single flashing diamond in his stock. He said nothing, he turned back up the staircase, tapping with his stick. And John followed him. The silence of the house, broken only by the distant yapping of the dog, compelled him, and the film of dust that seemed to be floating everywhere in the house compelled him. But he went because he was ashamed not to go; the fear that so maliciously squeezed his heart would mock at him all his life long if he did not go. And he went because Uhland wanted him to go.

At the top of the little stone staircase the tapping stick led him through an open door into Uhland's room. This was furnished with a four-poster, a parrot in a cage, a sheepdog lying on the floor by the window, a grand view straight down the hillside to Uldale, a bookcase, a pair of foils and a bare shabby table and two old brown chairs.

Uhland stood in the middle of the room and looked at him.

'And pray what have you come for?' he asked him.

They faced one another for the first time, as it seemed, for many years, and even now John could not bring this face and body to any definite terms. It was indistinct, floating in dust, wavering into space. The room smelt of animals, the bed was unmade, the sheets tossed about. The sheepdog paid them no attention, but slowly licked a paw that was wrapped in very fresh white linen.

John was not indistinct to Uhland. He hated, as he looked, every particle of him; the high aristocratic carriage of his head, his gentle amiable eyes, his handsome clothes and, most of all, he both hated and loved his fear of himself. He drew lines with his stick on the worn dusty carpet.

'What have you come for?' he asked again.

John's words stuck in his throat; he could not help himself. It may have been the close air and animal smell. He forced himself, as though he were beating with his foot on the floor, to speak.

'I came to see your father about a private affair,' he said at last. 'But now I am here I should wish to know what the hell you mean by following me, spying on me in London and elsewhere during these last years?'

'Ah, you've noticed that, have you?' said Uhland.

They both knew that it would need only a gesture, a careless movement, for them to be at one another's throats. If Uhland had not been lame, John must have sprung forward, and oh! the relief that that would be, the clearing away, as one sweeps off cobwebs, of years of dreams, nightmares, shame and terror. But he could not touch a cripple, and, more than that, as Uhland drew lines with his stick on the floor, he seemed to place a barrier between them.

'Well,' Uhland said, 'it has amused me to make you uncomfortable. You are such a coward, so poor a creature, that anything can frighten you. And you had the impertinence to marry my sister.'

'If you were not lame,' said John, 'I would show you whether I am a coward or no.'

'Ah, don't allow that to stop you. Lame though I am, I can look after myself. You have always been a coward. Everyone knows it.'

'If you were not Elizabeth's brother—'

'Another excuse.'

John drew a deep breath. He could not help himself, but this thick close air made the room swing about him. Uhland's stick hypnotized him.

'I'll show you—' he began. 'If I am disturbed by you any more I shall forget your weakness and make you sorry you were ever born. I've warned you. I won't warn you again.'

He turned to go. He saw the dog raise its head, heard the parrot scratch the bars, then knew that the closeness of the room gripped his windpipe, darkened his eyes. The floor swirled up like a wave and struck him. He fainted, sinking limply back against the legs of the chair.

Uhland looked at him, hesitated, then went to the washing-basin, fetched the jug and bent down, his arm under John's body, splashing his forehead with the water.

He had John's body in his arms. He put his hand beneath his shirt and felt the smooth firm warm skin above the heart. He drew the body close to his own, and his long thin fingers passed over the face, the neck, the open shirt. His own heart was beating tumultuously. With one hand he very gently bathed the forehead just as he bathed one of his wounded animals, with the other he pressed his fingers on the mouth, felt the warm lips under his touch, stroked the strong throat, looking always into the eyes.

His hand pressed more intently on the mouth; then he shuddered through all his body. He saw that John's eyes were slowly, dazedly opening, so he drew away, letting the other collapse against the chair. He got up, threw a look about the room, and, very quietly, went out.

EXHIBITION

'I AM as excited as a child,' said Judith.

'You *are* a child,' answered Dorothy severely. 'Do wrap your shawl more closely or you will catch the most dreadful chill.'

'Chill – pooh!' said Judith, leaning over the edge of Will's most handsome carriage that she might see the better an extraordinary Frenchman in beard, felt hat and full pantaloons.

They had come to London to stay with Will for the opening of the Great Exhibition.

Long before their departure from Cumberland the Exhibition had penetrated their seclusion. For weeks and weeks no one in Keswick, Bassenthwaite, Cockermouth, Buttermere Valley, Penrith or anywhere else had had any other thought but of the Exhibition and the possibilities of a visit to London. Old Bennett, for example, had received from somewhere in London a plan of a monster lodging-house that would be designed to 'put up' at least a thousand souls from the country at one and the same time 'for one and three per night', and for this small sum each and every person was to be provided 'with bedstead, good wool mattress, sheets, blankets and coverlet; with soap, towels and every accommodation for ablution, a surgeon to attend at nine o'clock every morning and instantly remove all cases of infectious disease'; there was to be 'a smoking room, detached from the main building, where a band of music was to play every evening, gratis' and 'cold roast and boiled beef and mutton, and ditto ditto sausages and bacon, and pickles, salads and fruit pies (when to be procured) were to be furnished at fixed prices', all the dormitories were to be 'well lighted with gas'; to secure the complete privacy of the occupants they were 'to be watched over by efficient wardens and police constables', and finally, 'the proprietor pledged himself that every care should be taken to ensure the comfort, convenience and *strict discipline* of so large a body.'

What could be fairer than that? Everyone was going. On a certain morning almost the whole of Uldale and Ireby villages departed in carts and carriages for the 'Travellers' Train' at Cockermouth. Others journeyed to Carlisle and met the train for London there. For hundreds of persons round and about Judith's little world this was the first real journey of their lives.

And it was, in fact, oddly enough, Dorothy's first train journey too. She was never one to allow her emotions to get the better of her, but she did cry a little as she left Timothy, Veronica, Amabel and Jane to the rotund Miss Meredith. She had never before been absent from them for a single day, but Miss Meredith was 'the safest person in the world', nothing could have appeared more secure that morning than the Uldale lawns and rosy walls happy under the soft April sun. When, at the station, she beheld the porters in their green velveteen jackets, heard the engines fizzling, and the large bells announcing the coming of a train that soon arrived, bumping and groaning as though in fearful agony; when, safely in their carriage, they were entertained by a stout gentleman with the grandest whiskers who warned them in a voice, husky and urgent, about the perils of London – the cracksmen, the rampsmen, the snorzers and thimble-screwers, all these exciting varieties of pickpockets and murderers – when at last arriving in the Metropolis and waiting outside the station for their luggage to be brought to them, there occurred, 'under their very noses, just as though they were in a theatre', a 'school of acrobats', and an 'equilibrist' spun plates high in air, balanced burning paper-bags on his chin, and caught cannon-balls in a cup on the top of his head – why, then Dorothy forgot her children entirely and surrendered completely to her adventure.

She had thought that her main occupation in London would be to take care of Judith, but she very quickly discovered that Judith took care not only of her but of everyone else in her company.

During the first evening at the house in Hill Street, Judith put the second Lady Herries in her proper place in exactly five minutes. She laughed at her, pinched her chin and exhorted her thus: 'Now you mustn't mind me, my dear. I'm seventy-seven years of age and nothing ails me. Wonderful, isn't it? I need no looking-after. I came to London as a very young girl and was not at all alarmed by it, so it's most unlikely that I shall be alarmed by it now. I knew Will long before you were born – that is the prettiest cashmere, my dear; where *did* you discover it? – yes, and Will knows me too, do you not, Will? So you are not to disturb yourself about me. I shall have *everything* I want, I am certain. And now, may I not see little Ellis? I am dying for a sight of him.'

Dorothy perceived that no one in the large cold house had anything of Judith's fire and vitality, and that that same fire burnt only quietly at Uldale. She realized for the first time how much of her personality Judith subdued in the country, and how patient Judith had often been with herself and her children.

'Judith is a marvellous woman,' said Will that evening. 'More marvellous every time I see her.'

'Yes,' said Dorothy meekly.

That was Will's opinion of Judith; Judith's opinion of Will was that he was pathetic. Will was eighty-one years of age and could only go out for an airing, sitting in his carriage, wrapped up like a mummy and with someone at his side to blow his nose, see that his feet were warm and that his hat was on straight. This 'someone' was never Lady Herries, but rather his attendant, Robins, a thin, severe, black-haired man of very religious principles. Lady Herries paid no attention to her husband whatever. She made a sort of a show on the first night of Judith's visit, gave him his pills and wrapped a shawl around his shoulders, but after that the virtuous Robins did everything, cutting his meat for him, pouring him his wine and suddenly remarking sternly: 'No, Sir William. No potatoes. They are forbidden.'

However, Will did not seem greatly to care. Judith was astonished at his subservience. Was this the stern and austere Will who had commanded so implacably poor weak-jointed Christabel? 'Shall I be like that soon?' thought Judith. 'I prefer death.'

But Will did not care, because he had one constant, eager, unceasing preoccupation – 'little Ellis'. Little Ellis was now eight years of age and as small and wizened a boy as you would be likely to find. He was accounted exceedingly sharp, had a money-box into which he was constantly putting sixpences, and inquired the price of everything. Will thought him wonderful and quite frankly now spoke of Walter and Uhland as ungrateful wretches.

He saw Judith as Walter's principal aggravator and this made him admire her more than ever. He liked to dilate on the riches that he was leaving Ellis – Walter was not to have a penny, nor Uhland, 'that surly peevish cripple', anything either. John and Elizabeth, however, were to receive a good legacy. Elizabeth he now loved. He had her to the house whenever he was able, and she, better than anyone else, seemed to understand and comfort him.

Of his wife he never spoke, but his allusions to 'poor, good Christabel' gave Judith to understand that ghosts can, once and again, have their proper revenge.

Now that it was clear that Will would not live much longer, visits of members of the Herries family to Hill Street were frequent. It was not that they were greedy: they cared neither for money nor poverty. But Will was now the most important member of their family, and the death of an important Herries was, in their eyes, a world affair. Carey Rockage, James Herries (a most tiresome and pompous old bore of seventy-two), Stephen Newmark (who considered himself a Herries and then something), Amery, Fred Ormerod (cousin by marriage of Monty Cards and a gay, drinking bachelor), Bradley Cards (a nephew of Jennifer's), Tim Trenchard (a busybody cousin of Garth's and Amery's), all these men with wives, daughters and appendages drove up to Hill Street, left cards, came and sat in the long, dreary drawing-room and asked Lady Herries to receptions.

Of them all Judith liked best to see Sylvia. She had loved Sylvia from the moment of their first meeting and she loved her still, although the beautiful, bright, impertinent girl she had first known was now a weary, over-painted, discontented middle-aged woman. Sylvia had been fighting too long the battle of living above your means. Had it been her lot to have married a man of large and assured fortune she would have been a brilliant and successful leader of Society and, at the last, a contentedly reminiscent old lady. But Garth was a cheerful, corruptible vagabond. They had neither of them morals nor honesty. They had stolen, cheated, lied all their lives long, always without any desire to hurt or damage, but hurt and damage they had – first their friends and acquaintances, last of all themselves. Moreover, the London that now surrounded them was not their own; the raffish, speculating, bouncing world of the Thirties was succeeded now by the serious, earnest, virtuous and hypocritical world of the Fifties. To be fair to Sylvia and Garth, they did not know how to be hypocritical, nor did they think it good manners to be earnest. So they were shabby and left-behind and out at heels.

Sylvia wept on Judith's bosom; the paint ran down her cheeks, and before she left she accepted ten pounds from Judith with a readiness that showed that every day of her life she was accepting small sums from someone.

Elizabeth had one talk with Judith that disturbed her greatly. Elizabeth was now thirty-six but was as remotely lovely as she had ever been. That delicate bloom and fragrance belonged to her still. On the afternoon of this talk she was wearing a costume of the new 'crystallized' gauze so that she seemed the floating cloud to which ladies at that time were so fond of comparing themselves. She was quite unaware of her loveliness: Judith, watching her with sharp, practised eyes, thought that it was as though she lived under a glass bell with John, everything and everybody shut away from them. And she was very unhappy about him.

'He cannot sleep at night,' she said. 'He thinks that I am not awake and he talks to himself. He slips out of bed very quietly and goes into the other room and walks about. I am so frightened, Aunt Judith.'

Judith kissed her, held her hand, but there was always something stiffly independent about Elizabeth. She asked for help but refused to accept it. Also she loved John, Judith thought, too deeply for it to be healthy.

'Is he worrying about your father?'

'I suppose so – or rather it is Uhland. Uhland obsesses him, and since he went up to Ireby that day last year it has been worse.'

'Well, my dear child, I've been fighting your father for years and am none the worse. John should see this sensibly.'

'But it seems like something in his blood, something inside himself. As though he were pursued by Uhland. It is a fantasy, Aunt Judith – not real at all. After all, what can Uhland do?'

'His father had the same, and his great-grandfather; something that would never let them alone. Well,' Judith sighed impatiently, 'I cannot understand it. I never could. When there's a difficulty or a danger, face it. Don't run away from it.'

'John does face it,' Elizabeth answered indignantly. 'You must not think he is a coward, Aunt Judith. He's tremendously brave in everything – but this is like a sickness.'

Judith nodded her head; there were two worlds, she knew, and unless you found the connexion between them you never found peace. Once she had herself had to make a choice. She had made it and was now the old woman she was in consequence.

Then she found that it was a very fine thing to give cheap advice to others, but that she had her own trouble to face. Her trouble – one that she had never expected nor considered – was that she was plunged, willy-nilly, into a sea of jealousy about Adam. Willy-nilly because, cry out as she might, refuse to be, at her age, so mean and small and petty, there she was in it up to the neck.

Adam had of course been the great central fact of her visit to London. To see the Great Exhibition certainly, but to see it with Adam. To lean on Adam's strong arm everywhere, to have the delicious intimate little talks with him, simply the two of them alone in her room, that had been for many years now her greatest happiness in life, to feel, above all, that no one had the close relationship with him that she herself had. It was not that she wished to shut Margaret out. She was neither so selfish nor so stupid. Moreover, she had fought that battle before and had won a victory. But her later life had been built up on the absolute intimacy of herself and her son, an intimacy that no one and nothing could break. She was, however, becoming greedy, greedy of her vitality, her uniqueness. She was 'Madame', the most marvellous old lady in Cumberland and, if she wished, the most marvellous old lady in London. This was nothing in her as cheap and petty as conceit, but the sort of amused triumph we all feel when we are clever at a game. All this was on the surface, but her very soul was possessed by her love for Adam. No one knew how deep that went. She had only loved two people in all her life, her husband and her son, but she loved them like a tigress. At the same time she had human enough wisdom and tolerance enough to keep the tigress behind bars.

Never before had her relationship with Adam been threatened as it was now. She perceived at once that the reason of it was the sudden and violent death of Margaret's father. She had not known of the scene between Margaret and Adam that Christmastime at Uldale. That would have informed her yet further had she been aware of it. But since Caesar Kraft's death she had seen very little of Adam and Margaret. They had paid only one brief visit to Uldale. She was quite unprepared for this change.

It was not that Adam was not as devoted as ever. He was there at Hill Street to meet her on the first evening. When they were alone in her room, he took her in his arms and hugged and kissed her as though he would never let her go.

'Why, how strong you are, Adam!' she cried, laughing and crying and happy as a queen. It was after this that she perceived that his thoughts were always on Margaret. *He* was of course as silent as ever, but her first sight of Margaret told her that there was here a new assurance and certainty. Margaret possessed Adam now and was quietly radiant because of it. They had three rooms in Pimlico. Adam wrote for the papers, knew Dickens and John Forster, Yates and Wilkie Collins. He was not of the writing world, stayed quietly outside it, made few friends, but made those few firmly. He wrote considerably about politics, reviewed books a little, and said cheerfully to his mother that the only things he really wanted to write were fairy stories.

'Fairy stories!' Judith cried, looking at Adam's stocky, thick-set frame and ugly unromantic countenance.

'Don't be afraid, Mother,' he said, laughing. 'I shall never write them. I must earn our bread and butter, but a good fairy story – there must be a handsome satisfaction in writing a good fairy story.'

This was nonsense of course, so she told him sharply, but it annoyed her that Margaret should think it quite a natural thing for him to do. 'Yes,' Margaret explained, 'he has found real life so very absurd.'

'Nonsense,' Judith answered. 'I never listened to such stuff. Fairy stories! A man like Adam! Why, he has a chest like a bull's!'

She soon discovered that her relations with her son and daughter-in-law were complicated by her advancing years. She was a wonderful old lady, but she could not do as she used to do. She took her breakfast in bed every morning and did not rise until midday. She was forced to confess that she returned to Hill Street exceedingly weary after her shopping expeditions. It was necessary, therefore, for Adam and Margaret to come to her rather than that she should go to them, and she thought that Margaret accompanied her husband too frequently.

Being direct and honest, she immediately said so.

'My dear boy, I am in London for a very brief visit. I have one foot in the grave. I love Margaret, of course, but I love you more.'

He said nothing (he never did say anything), but he came

alone. Then she fancied that he was thinking of Margaret and wishing that he were with her.

She would interrupt some Cumberland piece of gossip with a sharp: 'Now, Adam, you are not attending. You are thinking of Margaret.'

Jealousy began to mount in her as the tide swells a sea-pool. She slept now but badly, and before had not minded that, for she would lie and think of the old days, of Georges and Reuben and Charlie Watson and Warren, Adam's father, until the room seemed crowded with their figures; but now she could think of nothing but Adam, and, with the fantastic exaggeration that the night hours give, she would beat her thin little hands together and cry to herself that she had lost him for ever, that she was a miserable, deserted old woman, and that she might as well die. It was then that her poignant despair at the choice that so many years ago she had made for the sake of Jennifer, John and Dorothy, would strike her like a voice of doom.

'Ah! if I had but gone with Adam to Watendlath he would have been mine for ever!'

But in the daylight she was by far too sensible and blessed with too strong a sense of humour to tolerate such obvious melodrama. She laughed at herself, her fears, her selfishness. Nevertheless her jealousy mounted. She was as sweet as Tennyson's Miller's Daughter to Margaret, but Margaret was not deceived. The trouble with both Margaret and Adam was that they were so quiet. You could not tell what they were truly thinking!

Poor Judith! Jealousy is from the Devil. It was hard for her that she should have to fight her first real battle with him at so advanced an age!

The Great Day approached. The Great Day arrived!

But the whole of London was by this time an Exhibition. Foreigners were everywhere – Germans, Turks, Americans, French and even Chinamen. On every side amusements were springing up, M. Alexis Soyer opened his Restaurant of All the Nations, there was 'the Black Band of His Majesty of Tsjaddi with a hundred additional bones', the Musicians of Tongoose, the Troubadours of Far Vancouver, the Theban Brothers, and the most celebrated Band of Robbers from the Desert. Barnum provided a splendid entertainment, whereby for a rather costly ticket a guest was provided with 'a bed, a boudoir and a banquet, together with one hour's use per diem of a valet and a private chaplain, free admission to theatrical green-rooms, a seat in the House of Commons, and a cigar on the Bench of Judges'. Mr Catlin reopened his Indian Exhibition, and Mr Wyld would take you on the 'Grand Tour of Europe', or a visit to Australia or New Zealand for threepence a time.

But it was enough for Judith and Dorothy simply to view the crowds in the streets. The road to the Crystal Palace was an amazing scene. Trains of wagons lengthened far away, like an Eastern caravan, each waiting for its turn to be unloaded. Omnibuses, carriages, carts, barrows congested the road. The public houses, of which there were a great number, hung out gay and patriotic flags, and their doors were crowded with loafers, soldiers, beggars and women with shawls over their heads. Along the pavement were lined the hawkers shouting their wares, trays filled with bright silvery-seeming medals of the Exhibition, pictures of it printed in gold on 'gelatine cards', many barrows with ginger-beer, oranges and nuts.

Along Rotten Row troops of riders galloped noiselessly over the loose soft ground at the rear of the Crystal Palace, while in front of it an interminable line of carriages crawled slowly past. Close to the rails were mobs of spectators on tip-toe, their necks outstretched, seeking glimpses of progress. All along the building were ladders with painters perched high upon them and walking on the crystal covering which miraculously sustained them. At the end of the building were steam-engines puffing clouds of steam, and amid the wreckage of thousands of packing-cases were giant blocks of granite, huge lumps of coal, great anchors, the ruins of a prehistoric world. The noise, confusion, turmoil – who, asked Dorothy, could describe them? She was given to platitudes, and irritated Judith by insisting that 'such chaos is an emblem of man's energy working to a just end'. The Exhibition in fact turned her head a little spiritually, and made her so deeply proud of being a Herries that she seemed to walk like a goddess. All the Herries felt the same, that the Exhibition was their especial work and Queen Victoria the head of the family.

On the Great Day itself, the First of May, the heart of London beat with a pride and exaltation that was to affect the country for at least another fifty years.

Judith, Dorothy, Lady Herries, little Ellis, Adam, Margaret, John and Elizabeth had, all of them, thanks to old Will's power and position, splendid seats for the opening ceremony.

They started early, and that was wise, for the carriage was soon involved in a long, wearisome procession of carriages from whose windows every kind of bonnet and hat was poking and shrill feminine voices exclaiming: 'But this is monstrous! We shall miss the Queen! It is really too bad!'

John and Elizabeth were to join the others inside the building and were already there when Lady Herries, dressed in a magnificent purple bonnet and superb cashmere shawl, her head very much up, led in her little procession. Judith came last, leaning on Adam's arm.

They had excellent places, and the Sight, the Vision, the Glory – this, as Dorothy remarked, 'exceeded all Expectations and showed what Man could do when guided by the Divine Will'. (Dorothy was not, in her normal Cumberland domesticity, in the least like this. 'You are a little over-excited, my dear,' Judith had told her that morning.)

Yes, it was superb! Their seats were in one of the galleries, the galleries planted like flower-gardens with bonnets of pink, yellow and white. The Great Central Glory was the Glass Fountain. Of this Archdeacon Rodney Herries' son, Captain William Herries, RN, wrote in his *A Jolly Tar's Capers* (Weston and Mary, 1895): 'This glorious fountain in the centre of the building, shining, as the sun's rays came slanting down upon it through the crystal roof, as if it had been carved out of icicles, or as if the water streaming from the fountain had been made suddenly solid and transfixed into beautiful forms. Although but a rough, careless little Middy at the time, I can remember well that, standing beside my father, at that time Archdeacon of Polchester in Glebeshire, tears welled up into my youthful eyes and pride of my country fired my ambition.

' "It is such families as ours in such a country as ours," I remember my dear father remarking, "that, under God's Grace, can create, for the benefit of the world, such wonders." '

It must be confessed that Judith saw it all less romantically. Rodney Herries she had, incidentally, always detested. But nevertheless she was carried away, forgetting years, jealousies, aches and pains (for this morning she had a little rheumatism). For one thing the noise was terrific. The waiting multitude was quiet enough, but around them, throughout the building, all the machinery had been set in motion – the MACHINERY, key-note of the Exhibition, symbol, relentless, humourless, of the new world that this day, May 1st, 1851, was introducing. There were in the machine-room the 'self-acting mules', the Jacquard lace machines, the envelope machines, the power looms, the model locomotives, centrifugal pumps, the vertical steam-engines, all of these working like mad, while the thousands near by, in their high hats and bonnets, sat patiently waiting, passive, unwitting that the Age of Man on this Planet was doomed.

Judith and Adam, John and Elizabeth, were most certainly unwitting. Judith's little hand was thrust through Adam's thick arm, while John and Elizabeth were holding hands under Elizabeth's shawl. Margaret was thinking of her father and wishing that he were here, Dorothy's mouth was wide open, and Lady Herries was studying a coarse-grained Chambéry gauze near to her and wondering whether she could obtain one like it. Yes, a superb scene! The canopy above the royal seat, adorned with golden cornice and fringe and a small plume of blue and white feathers at each angle, the floors clean and matted, at each corner of the central square stages for illustrious visitors, from the gallery tops magnificent carpets and tapestries hanging, here the Spitalfields Trophy with its gorgeous silks, and there, the supreme triumph for many, the wonderful plaster of Paris statues, so white, so gleaming, their nudity draped so decently with red cloth. A sob rose in many throats, too, at the sight of the splendid equestrian statues of the Prince and the Queen, so large and life-like that you might imagine that at any moment the horses might start to charge down the central aisle. (This was Dorothy's fine whispered thought.) Here, to quote Captain William once again: 'Behind these was another Fountain' (it appears that he nourished a passion for fountains!) 'that made the stream as it rushed up from the centre and divided itself into a hundred drops, flashing in the sun as they fell, look like a shower of silver sparks – a kind of firework of water; and beside this rose the green plumage of the palm trees embedded in moss, while close at their feet was ranged a bed of flowers, whose tints seemed to have been dyed by the prismatic hues of the water-drops of the neighbouring fountain. Then appeared the old elm trees of the park, looking almost like the lions of the forest caught in a net of glass; and behind them again was a screen of iron tracery, so light and delicate that it seemed like a lace-work of bronze.'

A little later he continues: 'But it was when the retinue of the Court began to assemble that the scene became one – perhaps the most – gorgeous in colouring and ever beheld; for it was seen in the clear light of the transparent roof above. The gold-embroidered bosoms of the officers seemed to be almost alight with the glitter of their ornaments; there stood all the ministers of state in their glittering suits; the ambassadors of every country, some in light blues and silver, others in green and gold, others in white, with their bosoms' (incidentally a favourite word of the Captain's) 'studded with their many-coloured orders. There was the Chinese mandarin in his red cap, with peacock's feathers dangling behind, and his silken robes with quaint devices painted upon them in front and at the back. There was the turbaned Turk, and the red fez-capped Egyptian; and there were the chocolate-coloured Court suits, with their filigree steel buttons, and long, white embroidered silk waistcoats.

'There was the old DUKE too' (these are the Captain's capital letters) 'with his silver hair and crooked back showing most conspicuous amongst the whole. At the back and sides of the throne stood the gentlemen-at-arms, in their golden helmets, with the long plumes of white ribbon-like feathers drooping over them. Beside these were the portly-looking beefeaters, in their red suits and black velvet caps; and near them were the trumpeters, in their golden coats and close-fitting jockey-caps, with silver trumpets in their hands. Near these were the Aldermen, in their red gowns of office, and the Common-Councilmen in their blue silk gowns, and the Recorder in long powdered Judge's wig, the Archbishop in full lawn sleeves and close curly wig, the Musical Director in his white satin-damask robe and quaint-looking black cap, the heralds in their emblazoned robes, the Garter King-at-Arms in his gorgeous red velvet coat becrusted all over in gold – while round all these were ranged sappers and miners, in their red and yellow uniforms; and behind them were seen the dark-blue coats of the police.'

And the brave Captain complacently comments:

'It was a feast of colour and splendour to sit and gloat over – a congress of all the nations for the most hallowed and blessed of objects – one, perhaps, that made the two old soldiers, as they tottered backwards and forwards across the scene, the most noticeable, because in such a gathering for such an object, the mind could hardly help looking upon them as the last of the warriors to whom the nation would owe its future greatness. I could not but reflect,' the Captain adds, 'that my own family that has been proud to call England its mother for so many centuries had, under God's divine direction, helped sensibly by its honest devotion to duty and its consistent patriotism to bring this Great Country into its supreme world-dominating position.'

Then he continues after this little spurt of family pride: 'At a few minutes before the appointed hour the royal carriages with their bright liveries were seen to flash past the windows of the northern entrance; then darted by a troop of the Life Guards, with their steel helmets and breastplates glistening in the sunshine, and immediately after, the glass sides and roof of the Crystal Palace twanged with the flourish of trumpets that announced the arrival of the Queen. At this moment the gates were flung back, and within the crimson vestibule appeared a blaze of gold and bright colours.

'Then advanced the royal retinue, with the ushers and chamberlain in front, bowing as they moved backwards towards the throne; and after them the Prince leading the Princess Royal, and the Queen with the Prince of Wales, and followed by their Court.

'As the Queen moved onwards with her diamond tiara and little crown of brilliants scintillating in the light, the whole assembly rose and, waving their hats and fluttering their handkerchiefs, they shouted forth peal after peal of welcome.'

And here we may leave the excellent Captain in his happy state of obsequious reminiscence. His book is unquestionably of value, quite apart from its Herries interest, and is certainly worthy of a modern reprint. It attained six editions in the 'nineties.

Sad to say, Judith was not at all moved as was Rodney's son. For one thing the seat on which she was sitting was exceedingly hard, for another she was bothered by the noise of the machines, for another she was feeling odd in the head, a little as though she had been drinking. And for another she had never, in all her life, been impressed very greatly by domesticity: the Queen, the Prince, and their two children appeared to her so dreadfully domestic. That was on her father's side. On her proper Herries side she would have been undoubtedly more deeply impressed had she been quite at her ease. But she was distressed about John, about Adam, and a very little about herself. Most certainly she felt queer, as though there were a weight pressing on her heart, as though, unless she were careful, she would see double. She thought that, in all probability, this glittering and scintillating glass disturbed her. Absurd to build so large a place entirely of glass!

She could not resist, however, some beating of the heart when, as the Queen moved forward, wearing her diamond tiara and crown of brilliants, everyone rose and, waving hats, fluttering handkerchiefs, shouted their cries of welcome. Judith rose, flut-

tered her handkerchief, shouted with the rest. For a moment she
was deeply stirred. The sturdy figure of Victoria appeared to
divorce itself from all the world around it, as though it said: 'I
am lonely. I am a Queen. I represent loneliness, austerity and
power.'

She had that quality, was to have it all her life, of sudden
dignified remoteness, so that she became a symbol, a promise, a
prophecy. Judith, old enough to be that same Queen's grandmother, felt that now. The white head and light-blue coat of the
Master of the Queen's Music appeared on the rostrum, he raised
his baton, and above what Captain Herries called 'the melodious
thunder of the organ', the National Anthem – led by the choris-
ters – filled the glass dome and was caught by the light and
glitter and flung into the sunny heavens. The Archbishop asked
for a blessing (the Machinery frantically responded), the Queen
and Prince walked in procession, and then Her Majesty declared
the Exhibition open. And to end once again with Captain William: 'Immediately were heard the booming of the hundred guns
without, telling the people of the Metropolis that the Great Exhibition of the Industry of All Nations had been formally inaugur-
ated.'

Judith recovered herself and sat down. That reaction that
inevitably follows all climaxes seized her. What, after all, was all
this fuss about? It would only make the country and everyone in
it exceedingly conceited. And how tiresome the Exhibition had
already become! For months in advance of it no one had talked
of anything else, and now for months after it no one would have
any other topic. She looked down from the gallery, and the mere
thought of all the plaster statues, the great organ, the fountain,
the machinery, the furniture, the stalls covered with goods, the
endless cups of tea, the ferns and plants and blossoming shrubs,
the crying children, angry husbands and disappointed wives, all
this wearied her beyond measure.

'I think that I will return to Hill Street,' she said to Adam.

'Very well, Mother dear, but first you must see just a few of the
sights.'

She did not want to see any of the sights. She would like to be
seated safely and privately in her armchair in her room at Hill
Street.

Says Captain William Herries: 'Well might the nation be
proud of its Crystal Palace. No other people in the world could
have raised such a building...'

That is exactly what Judith thought, straining up her old eyes to the glitter and the shine. 'All this glass,' she thought, 'so ostentatious', and her dislike of Prince Albert, assuaged for a moment by the National Anthem, returned in full force.

Adam took her by the arm and she walked gaily along, with Dorothy and Lady Herries very patriotic behind her, Margaret on her other side, and John and Elizabeth not exchanging a word.

'Why don't they speak?' she thought. 'Aren't they happy?' She was wearing a soft grey bonnet and a mantilla of shaded grenadine. She walked as though she were twenty, with every once and again a step that was rebellious, originating in some quite other person. She still saw double on occasion, and there was a twinge of pain in her right shoulder.

There were of course a great many things to see, and oh dear! So many people! Bonnets and polkas, polkas and bonnets, green and brown 'wide-awakes' and fluffy beaver hats – and then the People, this time with a capital P! They will be *much* worse on the shilling days, but there seem to be a great many of them, even as it is, many with babies in their arms, many with baskets, many with fat bursting cotton umbrellas.

'There are too many people,' Judith said to Adam. The pain in her shoulder had spread to her armpit. 'Really,' she thought, 'Lady Herries is an *idiot*!'

Oh dear, there are a *great* many things to see! Here is a railwayman, family following, his japan pouch by his side, hurrying to see the locomotives; there a carpenter in a yellow fluffy flannel jacket pointing out to two small boys the beauties of a huge top formed of one section of a mahogany tree.

'Ridiculous!' Judith thought. 'No one in the world can wish for a top as big as that!'

Here is a hatless and yellow-stockinged Bluecoat boy mounting the steps of one of the huge prismatic lighthouses to see the way that it is made ... Look! There is a model of the Italian Opera House, and behold! There is a minute and most extensive model of Liverpool with a looking-glass sea and thousands of cardboard vessels. This last Adam examined with the most serious care. 'Remarkable! Very remarkable indeed!' he repeated again and again.

Judith could not explain it, she was greatly ashamed but she wanted to slap him. As with all mothers in the world there were moments when she wondered whether these very prosaic results were at all worth all the pains that she had taken.

'Did I bring him up for this?' she thought as she watched him so seriously count the cardboard ships. Then she caught Margaret's calm look of devotion and she hated Margaret. There was no doubt but that she was not at all well.

Of course they must see the machinery. For hours Judith had been dreading this moment. Pressed close against the stout limbs of a member of the National Guard— 'Really a *childish* costume,' she thought as she looked upwards to his conical hat with its little ball on top, and smelt the rough texture of his red worsted epaulettes and full-painted trousers – she was compelled to admire the power-looms, and then there was the steam brewery, then the model carriages moving along the new pneumatic railway, the hemispherical lamp-shades made out of a flat sheet of paper, the exceedingly noisy flax-crushing machine, the splashing centrifugal pump, the whirling of the cylindrical steam-press . . .

'Adam,' she whispered, drawing him a little closer to her, 'I am glad that I am an old woman. All these machines – what a very unpleasant world it is going to be!'

She whispered, because Dorothy and Lady Herries were in a state of fluttering ecstasy. 'Stupendous!' 'What an achievement!' 'Do observe those wonderful little wheels!' 'Man's triumph over Nature!' Dorothy was proving herself a true Herries. She saw Herries everywhere. If it had not been for the Herries family . . . Strange! Judith must certainly be unwell, for she wanted to slap both Dorothy and Lady Herries.

'Adam,' she whispered, 'I fear that I *must* sit down!'

There was no reply and, looking up, she saw that Adam was not there. Looking farther she discovered Adam and Margaret, a distance away, their backs turned to her, close together examining a piece of machinery. That was possibly the worst moment of her life. Absurd – so little a thing! And yet the horror of Georges' death, the tragedy of Francis' suicide, the awful evening of Adam's birth – none had touched the loneliness, the isolation of this neglect. Lady Herries was examining a miniature engine with a great assumption of technical knowledge, Elizabeth and John had disappeared.

Judith proudly, her bonnet up, walked away. As she reached the outer hall pain seized her, her heart was beating strangely. Her limbs trembled. Everyone around her seemed weary. On the steps of the red-cloth-covered pedestals weary women and children were seated, some of them munching thick slices of bread and meat. Around the fountains were gathered exhausted families drinking out of thick mugs. All over the floor were orange-skins, dirty pieces of paper; Judith sat down on one of the crimson steps, resting her head on her hands. Was she going to die in this ridiculous place with all these strangers around her? The noise of the machines rattled and quivered, piercing her very backbone. 'Am I going to die? Is this the end?'

A stout woman near to her, her legs spread, crooking a baby in one arm, was drinking out of a bottle. Strange, Judith thought, to allow such people in on the day of the Queen's first visit. But that was right. All were equal – all women together. She had read somewhere that after a certain hour the general public would be admitted. The sight of the woman strengthened and comforted her. She was herself a vagabond, born of vagabonds. No Herries, but daughter of a gipsy. Even though her son deserted her, even though all the pains in the world attacked her, even though this horrible machinery invaded the world, destroying peace and privacy, no one could touch her, she was independent.

She looked up, and there was John. He was standing quite near to her but did not see her. On his face was a look of pitiable distress. He held himself taut, his hands to his side, as if he were answering some charge. On every side of him the crowd pushed and thrust, but he was as alone as though no one else were in the world.

The sight of someone in trouble always caused her to forget herself. She rose, although her knees trembled, walked over to him and touched his arm. He started; her touch had drawn him from a dream.

'John, dear. Take me home. I am very tired.'

That charming kindly smile that she loved in him so much warmed her heart.

'Why, of course, Aunt Judith. We will find Elizabeth.'

She had her hand lightly on his arm. No one should know how ill she felt.

'Such a noise! So many people! I am realizing, my dear John, what a very old woman I am.'

'Nonsense, Aunt Judith,' he said, patting her hand. 'This would be too much for anyone.'

But as he looked at her with so kindly an expression, she realized that it was true: she was an old woman at last.

THE FUNERAL

THE last visit to London that she was ever to pay was early in 1854, and the occasion was Will's funeral.

They all said that it was defying Providence for her to go, for she was seventy-nine that Christmas, but she was determined: nothing and no one should stop her. In honest fact they all knew a fearful pride in her resolve. Seventy-nine and going to London! No one but a Herries could have done it, but the Herries always lived to a great age and died in their boots! Look at Will! Eighty-four and in the City three days before his death. It was true that he had been strapped up in his carriage like a mummy, and had held a sort of reception there in Threadneedle Street with clerks and people bowing to him on the steps of his offices: nevertheless, eighty-four and working in the City!

Judith was perfectly conscious of all the things that the different Herries, scattered about the country, would be thinking of her enterprise and, being half Herries herself, she was pleased that they should be pleased. Then of course she insisted that she must pay tribute to Will, for Will was part of her whole life, and now, when her youth was for ever present with her, intermingling with all the current events of her day so that it was often impossible to tell which was past and which was present, Will was perhaps nearer to her than he had ever been before. For as a girl she had never liked him; as a woman she had often despised him; but now, joined as they were in their old age together, she almost loved him.

She had, however, two principal motives for her departure. One was that she would see her beloved Adam, a motive sufficient to carry her *and* her coffin if necessary to the North Pole; and the other (although this she confessed to no one in the world) her desire to show Walter Herries that she was still alive and kicking.

Now, when she could not move about as she had once done, but must sit, either in the garden when it was sunny and warm, or in the parlour before the fire, or in her bed with her lace cap on her head and mittens on her fingers just like any other old lady (although she was not in the least like any other old lady!) events and persons were inclined, if you did not keep them in order, to acquire a gigantic significance.

On the one hand she was tranquil as she had never been in her life before. Old age certainly did that for you; and on the days when there was no pain to bother her (for pains of one sort and another paid her now quite constant visits), when she was neither wildly excited by some pleasure (like an unexpected dish for dinner or a sudden visit of a friend, or something entrancing that little Jane had been doing, or a piece of gossip) nor exasperated by some bit of foolishness or some alarm about Adam, why, then this tranquillity was marvellous! You just sat there, or lay there, and it lapped you round like a radiant sheet of golden light, light within you, above you, around you, while the trees burnt in gold steadily against the sky and the streams ran murmuring to your feet, and all this lovely world stood still for you. It was at such times (and they were many) that the past became the present and the present the future. Then there was no Time. She was a child again, watching them ride the horse up Tom Gauntry's staircase, and she was eating roast goose at the 'Elephant', she was walking beside dear Charlie Watson at Watendlath – all was alive again, nothing had died, she herself was immortal.

Nevertheless the things that disturbed, disturbed violently, and the thing that disturbed the worst was Walter. No climax had come as yet to their quarrel. That moment when she had turned to Jennifer and said (ah, how many years ago! Poor Jennifer!): 'Do not be distressed, my dear. I am going to remain,' that challenge had as yet reached no climax. But the climax would come. She knew it as though she were a prophetess and could see the future. Already enough unhappiness had been generated by that old, old quarrel. John's life, Elizabeth's life, Jennifer's life, Walter's life, Uhland's life – all these had been damaged by it, as hatred and jealousy and envy always damaged any lives that they touched. Her own life and Adam's had been changed by it, for she would have been in Watendlath long ago but for it, and still there was worse to come. She had stayed in Uldale and protected them all, but Walter was still there, the Fortress was still there, Peach's cottage (there was now a younger Peach in command) was just over her garden wall; Walter was a sot and Uhland a crazy misanthrope – but they were not gone, they still remained.

She had been told, only a week or two ago, that Walter had said of her: 'That old bed-ridden gipsy.' Bed-ridden, was she? She would show him! She would go to London if for no other reason!

Nevertheless, it was Will that she was thinking of as she made her departure. Her heart was soft with tenderness.

Dorothy came with her and was full of matronly care and fuss. After the day of her visit to the Great Exhibition, Judith, to everyone's surprise and offering no reason, abandoned her gay colours and adopted a kind of uniform, black with white ruffles and white lace at the throat. With her hair that had the shining softness of snow and the deep white upon white of an evening cloud, with her small pale face, her exquisite neatness and cleanliness, carrying in her hand her cane, she had the air of some austere Mistress of Ceremonies. But then her whole body and nature laughed at austerity. As she grew older her sense of fun, enjoyment of little things and active consciousness of that enjoyment, her eagerness for news, her avidity for sharing in everything, these things constantly increased in her. Her heart – she was warned that she must be careful of her heart. 'My heart?' she laughed. 'It's as sound as one of Dorothy's muffins' (for Dorothy was a good housekeeper but a heavy-handed cook). Then there was the rheumatism, and sometimes she felt faint. Once indeed she fainted in her bedroom, but no one was there with her and no one was told of it. On many days she was as well and strong as Veronica and Amabel – both very healthy girls. One afternoon she slapped Veronica very heartily indeed because that child, aged now sixteen, told her that God disapproved of reading common books on a Sunday.

'You are a prig, the most dreadful animal in Creation,' Judith cried, and when Veronica, losing her temper, shouted, 'And you're a gipsy,' Judith slapped her. Veronica, who was not a bad child, was appalled at what she had done, and Judith walked all the way upstairs and brought her down a bag of peppermints. (Judith liked peppermints and always kept a store in her bedroom.) All this in one afternoon.

Moreover, with her favourite Jane, now a wisp of a child of thirteen, she would play games by the hour and never tire. They would play backgammon and Pope Joan, and then Jane would read to her – Macaulay's *History*, Ruskin's *Seven Lamps of Architecture, Pendennis, Hypatia*. Judith thought Ruskin 'a bit of a prig' but didn't say so, because Jane thought him so beautiful. After Adam, Judith loved most in the world this dreaming romantic child who was of the tribe of Francis and Reuben and John. 'I am afraid she will be unhappy,' Judith thought, 'but she will have some of the joys none of the others will know.'

When she set off with Dorothy for London it was Jane who came into her room alone, Jane she held to her heart with all that impetuous feeling that years could not dim, Jane who gave her a parcel of three little handkerchiefs that she had worked, Jane who stood in the road staring long after the carriage had disappeared. Timothy, now a big stout fellow of seventeen, who bore a strange resemblance to the portraits of his great-grandfather David Herries, teased her:

'She's a nice old lady, but whew! what a temper!' he remarked.

Jane gave him a queer look.

'All right,' he said uneasily, pinching her ear. 'I daresay I like her as much as you do, if all the truth were known.'

She was so weary when she, at last, reached Hill Street that she felt as though her whole body had been crushed under the wheels of the train that had conveyed her.

She saw Lady Herries for a moment, and her tenderness for poor Will enveloped the stout painted lady, whom she had never liked, who, however, looked better in her full black silk than she had ever looked in gay colours. She was sitting in the vast dismal drawing room and wearing a bonnet of velvet and crêpe. Everyone was wearing velvet just then.

'That's one thing,' said Judith to Dorothy as she began to undress. 'I shall never wear velvet, my dear. Never! I shall die first!' She added: 'I am dead now, I think. The smell of gas in that train was quite awful. Give me Mr Thorpe's *Northern Mythology*. It's at the top of my bag. It will send me to sleep if anything will.'

The maid who brought her her breakfast in the morning was full of information. There was nothing that Judith liked better than to have someone with whom she might chat while she was having her breakfast.

It seemed that Will had died quite suddenly of heart failure at three o'clock in the morning. He had not felt well and had gone to his wife's room and had fallen down there dead.

The maid did not know, Judith did not know, no one would ever know of the awful little conversation that had taken place on that last morning.

It was true: he had felt very unwell and had stumbled to Lady Herries' room. He walked with great difficulty, but she had woken to see him standing there, swaying on his feet, a candle in his hand.

'I think I am going to die,' he gasped, his hand at his heart. She had jumped out of bed, found the drops that were to be given to him if there were a heart-attack. He had sunk, blue in the face, into a chair. He recovered a little, looked up into her face, and saw in those pale-blue eyes a look of eagerness.

'You are glad that I am dying,' he said.

'Will! Will!' she cried, sinking on to her knees beside the chair. 'How can you be so cruel?'

'It is very natural,' he replied. 'I don't blame you. It is perfectly right. You never even pretended to love me. No one has ever loved me. Not even Ellis—'

She protested and tried to hold his hand. He waved her away with a gesture of great dignity. Then his face became purple.

'I have wanted the wrong things—' he murmured, and died.

The funeral was to be at twelve. A great many members of the family were expected. Soon Adam came in to see her. She held out her arms and he knelt by the bed, took her small white hand in his and laughed for sheer joy at being with her again. For, when you had said everything, there was something between these two, stronger than life, stronger than death, something that no one shared with them, something that if it could be caught and held, hard and shining in one's hand like a flaming crystal, would explain, quite sufficiently, what everything is about and why we are travelling at all. But of course it can't be caught.

'Isn't this room absurd?' Judith said, laughing. She could never grow accustomed to the fashions of the time. She belonged in taste to the end of the eighteenth century. Looking back, everything of that time seemed to her to have lightness, brilliance and form. Everything in 1854 was huge, heavy and static, wrapped, too, in a sort of damp fog.

In her room there was a sofa covered with red rep, a copper scuttle and scoop (quite gigantic), a huge fender of brass, fire-irons of set steel, a hearthrug of white sheepskin, two great Minton vases with a floral design on a turquoise ground, a picture made out of seaweed in a frame of Tunbridge ware, a work-box – also of Tunbridge ware – that had a lid with a bouquet in mosaic and sides with 'Berlin wool' mosaic, and a vast dressing-table and mirror, trimmed with glazed linen and muslin. All these things and many more jostled one another in the room that was chill with the chill of the grave. In their centre, very bare, very innocent, was a tin bath.

Among these things Adam knelt and held her hand. He was a broad square man now, brown of face. She didn't like his

whiskers, although, of course, every man wore them. She loved
his eyes, which were bright, shining and most kindly. He had
great breadth of shoulders, looked as strong as an ox. He was
absentminded, but not with her. He wrote for one of Dickens'
papers, reviewed books. He was happily married. He was thirty-
eight years of age. All these things were apparently true. But the
only thing that was true for her was that he was a small child
running up the path from the Tarn at Watendlath, calling out to
her that he had seen a kingfisher.

These glorious moments came to her very seldom, but, after
that awful hour at the Exhibition, she had beaten down her jealousy. Killed it? No, perhaps not, but she was nearly eighty years
of age and must learn to accept facts. Was there anything else to
learn of life?

She stroked his brown cheek, kissed him, chattered, laughed,
then sent him away. She must get up and face the family.

It was a moment that they none of them afterwards forgot, her
entrance into the big drawing-room where they were all gathered
together. The blinds were drawn and the room was lit with gas
which giggled like a silly schoolgirl. The gas was, however, the
only jester. Everyone was immensely solemn. Lady Herries sat on
the sofa, Ellis at her side. All around her were grouped the
family. James Herries was the oldest – he was seventy-five. He
stood beside the sofa, a vast, swollen, pompous effigy in black.
There was Archdeacon Rodney, with his wife Rebecca, one of the
Foxes of Ulverston, and their son the naval officer. There was
Stephen Newmark, close to him Phyllis, now very stout, and
four of their seven offspring, Horace, Mary, Katherine and
Emily; there were, of course, Garth and Sylvia and Amery, that
gay bachelor Fred Ormerod, Bradley Cards and his little wife
who was like a pincushion in figure, Timothy Trenchard, his
wife and two daughters, Carey Rockage, only a year younger
than James and almost as stout, with his wife Cecily and their
children Roger and Alice. John and Elizabeth stood quietly by
themselves in a window. Walter, Will's eldest son, and the new
baronet, was not present, nor was his son Uhland. Everyone
thought this disgraceful.

When Judith entered, followed by Dorothy and Adam, a wave
of emotion swept the whole assembly. Even Lady Herries, who
disliked Judith and was eagerly jealous of her position as the
centre of this day's ceremony, was moved. For this was what the

Herries above all else loved. Survival. Perpetuity. To last longer than anyone else. To have life and vigour when all your contemporaries had failed to last. Even as once upon a time they had made eager bets on the centenary of Great Aunt Maria, so now their excitement and pride were kindled, for Judith Paris was seventy-nine and yet walked with a firm step, her head up, her eyes shining, the most commanding figure of them all.

But there was more than this. Judith had, in all these years, won a great reputation among them for honesty, kindliness and fair charity. They were not, on the whole, very charitable to one another. No members of any family are very charitable to one another. They know all the wrong things. But Judith, because she had lived in the North, had been outside their squabbles, rivalries and jealousies. They thought her a fine generous-hearted woman. She herself, as she saw all those Herries, so solemn and so black, felt a strange mixture of two quite opposite emotions. She thought them absurd and she felt that she would like to mother them all. They *were* absurd – old James so conscious of his baronetcy, so stout, his black legs like pillows, his grizzled whiskers like cauliflowers; Newmark, his head perched above a high stock and collar so that he resembled a dignified but anxious hen; dear Phyllis, so *fearfully* fat and her dress so voluminous that all her brood could comfortably have nestled beneath it; Sylvia, alas, no longer pretty, badly rouged, the black velvet on her dress cut to resemble pansies; Rockage, with an odd resemblance to dear old Maria, long dead, but living again in her son's untidiness and a kind of shabby good will (how well Judith remembered that occasion when she had slapped his face at the house in Wiltshire for his riding to hounds over the drawing-room chairs!); Horace Newmark, now a plump pale-faced man of thirty-five in large spectacles and resembling a little in his air of high discontent Mr Thackeray – yes, they were absurd and lovable too. How Will would be pleased did he see this great gathering! How he would approve of the black and the dignity and the solemnity! At the memory of him, to her own surprise, a tear stole down her cheek. 'Old ladies cry easily!' she thought, as she kissed the widow's plump cheek.

She walked about among them, and they were all very kind to her. It was all crêpe and black broadcloth. Robins, followed by a thin young footman with a cold, walked around offering sherry and a biscuit.

She sat down in a chair near the darkened windows, and the

low-murmured conversation went on around her like a draught creeping in through the walls and the floor. It was late February and very damp. There was a discontented, peevish fire in the huge fireplace, but as is so often the case with English fireplaces the heat went up the chimney and left the room severely alone. Nearly everyone seemed to have colds; the sneezing was prodigious. It was understood that a thin rain was falling outside.

Soon she had John and Elizabeth beside her chair. Elizabeth looked lovely but not, Judith thought, very happy. When Elizabeth moved away to talk to Margaret, Judith caught John's hand in hers and said:

'Well, dear John, how are you?'

They were away from the others. She felt his hand clutch hers, tightly, and had an impulse to put her arms around him and hold him safe.

'Very well, Aunt Judith, thank you.'

'And the Secretaryship?'

'Oh, splendid! They are so very good to me.'

'And Elizabeth?'

'We are more in love than ever.'

She nodded her head.

'That's right!'

He was the handsomest man in the room by far. But as she looked at him she caught the oddest resemblance in him to his father Francis. Just that way had his father looked at Uldale that night when he had implored her help. Her help against what? Against nightmares, ghosts, his own frustration . . .

'It's odd, isn't it,' John said, 'Walter and Uhland not coming?'

'Very wrong of them.'

'Yes, I suppose so. Have you . . . have you seen them at all?'

'No, my dear.' She smiled grimly. 'They poison our cows once and again. Walter threatened to bring an action against Bennett's boy for stealing his timber. Let him try, that's all!'

'Yes, Aunt Judith . . . You know, Elizabeth wrote a letter to Walter the other day. She thought she ought to. She heard he was ill.'

'Did she, my dear?'

'He never answered her, though.'

The time had arrived. St. Luke's Chelsea, a church that Will had attended for many years because he liked its Gothic and the length of its sermons, was their destination – a long journey at the pace that their carriages would take them. The hearse had plumes, almost as large as palm trees. The array of carriages was magnificent. Judith accompanied Lady Herries and Ellis in the first carriage.

That is always a problem, the conversation on a funeral journey, but Lady Herries made it no problem at all. First she cried, looking out of the carriage window, pleased and satisfied with the attention that the procession was securing. Then she set about the task of convincing Judith that her life was now at an end, that she had only Ellis to live for, and that she alone, of all God's mortals, had understood Will and given him what he needed. Ellis, who was now eleven years of age, less shrivelled than he had been, but bony, horse-faced like all the Herries, with sharp eyes above a large bony nose, said nothing. Did he care at all, wondered Judith? Did he know that he had been the one comfort and pride of his father's old age? At any rate, he looked like a gentleman. It was extremely difficult for any Herries *not* to look like a gentleman, which was perhaps what was the matter with them. Judith noticed that once and again Ellis stole a sharp look at her. Of what was he thinking? Of her age, in all probability. How old she must seem to him! And yet he had been accustomed to old people! A sudden sympathy for the poor child caught her. She put out her hand and held his. The little hand, in its shiny black glove, was as cold as a seashell.

'Will altered,' Lady Herries was saying. 'Altered immensely in the last years. He depended upon me for everything. I say nothing against his first wife—' ('You'd better not,' thought Judith) '—but to pretend that she understood him was absurd. Poor Will! Everyone thought – even those nearest to him' (this with a glance at Judith) 'thought that his great interest was money. Erroneous – quite erroneous. If you had heard the way that he would talk late in the night—'

Judith began to be angry. But she saw her anger coming from a long way off. She had, through many years' practice, trained herself to meet it and turn it back before it reached her heart. Bad for old ladies to be angry, and in any case waste of time. But how she did hate this woman! False and greedy and sham! Poor Will! how lonely in those last years he must have been! Old pictures began to crowd up again – that familiar one when she and Will and Francis had watched the fireworks by the Lake and had prophesied about their lives. Soon she would begin to cry. She *must* not cry. She *would* not before this woman – all scent, whale-bone and crêpe. She could not see her face for the heavy black veil that covered it, but she knew how small and mean those eyes were, how tight and hard the little mouth! Those were not the thoughts for a funeral, poor dear Will's funeral, so she looked out of window and saw a French poodle walking beside an old lady; he had a peaked nose, woolly wig, leggings and tail-band, and a horrible shaved, salmon-coloured body. The old lady was younger in years than Judith but not half so vigorous. She walked as though she were a hundred.

They were passing slowly through a mean, shabby street. Groups gathered, children ran, men took off their caps – for this moment the Herries dominated the scene. It did not make them proud. It was their right, now and always – so much their right that they gave it scarcely a thought. Here is a gin-palace, here a seedy French *pension*, children in torn pinafores gazing at the sweetshop window, here a rag shop with tobacco-pipes crossed in the window and turpentine-infected bundles of firewood. Through all this, drink, poverty, childhood, sweets and tobacco and gin, Will is grandly riding for the last time!

'Without my care and affection I shudder to think what his last years would have been—'

Judith clutched the top of her cane with her two little hands. In all her seventy-nine years, with the single exception of Mrs Ponder, she had never disliked anyone so much. She heard a sniff, a strange little strangled sniff. Ellis was crying, tears were trickling down his bony nose. She put out her arm and drew him closer to her. He stayed against her as stiff as a whalebone. But she was glad that he was crying. He *had* cared for his father then. He *had* cared! She would do something for Ellis. Ask him to Uldale, let him play with Dorothy's children ... Then she found that she too, under her veil, was crying, and suddenly she wanted to lean forward and take Lady Herries' hand. Perhaps what the woman said was true. She *had* cared for Will – in her own peculiar undemonstrative way.

They have arrived at the church. Herries wing out of carriages like crows from a nesting-tree. But silent. Immensely solemn. How broad and deep the hat-bands on the black hats, how heavy the whiskers, the stocks, the voluminous black skirts, the umbrellas, the thick black boots! A crowd has gathered about the church door. The church has all its attendant offices and officers – the stout, self-important beadle, the neatly grained high boxes, the three-decker pulpit, the wizen-faced pew-openers (two of them). The church is icily cold, and the hassock on which little Ellis kneels is hard as iron. He is miserable and feels a sense of aching loss, although loss of what he has really no idea.

Judith, sitting there, watching the big coffin draped in black, wondering about the pew-opener in the black bonnet who had already retired to a corner behind a pillar to count the pennies, thought that the Herries must have multiplied themselves three-fold since they entered the church. She thought – for her imagination was fantastic now with weariness and chill – that the ghosts of departed Herries must have joined the living. Maybe if she looked more closely she would see poor Warren there, gazing at her as he used to do with that dog-like devotion, Francis, Jennifer, even David and Sarah, and Deborah Sunwood whom she had loved so dearly in her childhood, and Jennifer's father and mother, and poor Christabel. When you reached her age the dead and the living were all equally alive – no one was dead, no one was living.

Yes, Adam was living! He sat beside her, and sometimes he would look at her to see that all was well with her. Then quietly, with that solid protection that she loved so in him, he put his strong arm round her: and then, to her shame, to her great disgrace, she fell fast asleep!

She woke hurriedly to find that the coffin was leaving the church and that she, with Lady Herries and Ellis, must immediately follow it. 'Oh, dear! How disgraceful!' she thought. 'I do hope that nobody saw me!' But she walked down the church, very firmly, all the Herries' eyes upon her. She did not care for the family now. She was thinking only of Will – Will, whose last grand ceremony was over, who would do sums on paper no longer, would be denied potatoes by Robins never again; with the exit of that body out of the church one long chapter of her life as well as his was closed.

Later they were all in the long dining-room. The table was covered with food: drink of every kind was on the vast sideboard that looked as though it had once formed part of a great mahogany mountain and was still marked with the pick-axes of ardent climbers. Judith, dizzy with an almost drunken weariness, sat in a chair near the fireplace. All that she wanted was to go to bed; meanwhile she must listen to the Family. Inhuman furniture and human bodies, high mountains of ham and beef, chickens, pies, great loaves of bread all circled round her together. There was a marble group near the window – 'Sir William Herries, Bart, and Lady Herries' – poor Christabel like an early Christian Martyr in a long icy flowing robe. The fender was of painted mahogany. There were six dessert-stands in ormolu with monkeys carrying silver nuts. On the mantelpiece were some towering vases of Copeland ware, gold on a cobalt blue ground.

'Everything is so large,' she thought, and once again had the old, old wish that her own legs were longer. Soon, however, she forgot both her weariness and the furniture in her interest in the conversation that went on around her. They had forgotten her, all save Adam and Margaret. But, more than that, they had already forgotten Will. Gone were those hushed voices, vanished that sad solemnity. As they crowded about the table, eating like wolves and drinking like the damned, their voices rose ever higher and higher, their excitement, with every moment, keener.

For now, liberated from that momentary consciousness of poor William, aware that he was safely underground and that they could therefore move freely forward with the enterprise and energy that belonged to their Herries blood, they were discussing the War.

It was, she reflected, natural that they should do so, for only yesterday, February 27th, England's ultimatum to Russia had been despatched. She herself detested war, any war, every war. She had been in Paris in 1815 and had borne Adam there, seen his father die there, suffered agonies and terrors that had affected her whole life. Why anyone should be *glad* about war she could not imagine, but not only was everyone in the room *glad*, they were *triumphant*.

She saw, too, with that detached observation that came from her mother Mirabell (who had been quite certainly not at all a Herries) that this was for them not an English war but a *Herries* war. It was the Herries who were indignant at the Massacre of Sinope, the Herries who applauded and supported every action of Lord Stratford, the Herries who had advised Lord Palmerston to resign, the Herries who thought Louis Napoleon a hero, the Herries who mocked poor Mr Cobden and silly Mr Bright for their support of the Peace Society.

As Judith listened she realized with every moment more fully what it was that separated her from the Herries clan and all the other clans in the world like them – what it was that had sep-arated her father and Francis and Reuben, what it was that gave

John his terrors and made little Jane walk apart from her healthy and energetic sisters. Here it was, this quality of the uneasy imagination, this desire for a beauty that was never to be caught, this consciousness, pursuing, relentless, unceasing, of a world *behind* the world. She could have got up from her chair and, stamping her cane on the floor, have cried: 'You fools! You fools! Will nothing teach you?' – but all she did was to smile a little, refuse a plate of ham courteously offered her by the Archdeacon, and consider pensively the silver monkeys with their silver nuts.

So, over Will's dead body, they sang their Song of Triumph.

Old James, whose chest was congested so that he wheezed like a harmonium, coughing over his plate of chicken, cried to anyone who might listen: 'I tell you, sir, these damned Russians must be put down.' He caught the ear of Cecily Rockage, a thin woman of sixty who greatly admired him (as she admired indeed everyone, for she was a humble woman). 'I can tell you for your private ear, my dear Cecily, that in the Club a day or two back Clarendon himself told me that in his opinion Newcastle had managed Palmerston exceedingly well, getting him to withdraw his resignation without any conditions, you know. Of course, the Radicals are disgusted, and so they may be. But in my opinion—'

'That's just what Carey says,' Cecily Rockage murmured, looking about her in her dim, peering way to see that her beloved son Roger was having plenty to eat and was thoroughly happy.

'They are important,' Judith thought. 'They are beginning to cover the country.'

In her Cumberland retreat she had not realized *how* important the Herries had grown. Once upon a time there were but a few of them, a gambler here, someone there riding a horse into a wilderness, an old man and an old woman drinking over the fire, but now the times had favoured them. They believed in England, they believed – almost terribly – in themselves. Oh! how they believed! What unquestioning confidence they had! Everything, everything was right with England from her Government to her furniture, and Judith realized, as she looked about her, as she heard Ormerod's gay laugh, and the Archdeacon's benevolence, and Stephen Newmark's solemn blessing, as she saw the women billowing in happy pride about their men, Sylvia a little elated with wine, Phyllis the proud mother, Rodney's Rebecca the eager listener, that there was something fine and grand in their faith, that these men and women *were* making England what she was, England the dominant Power of the world, the Queen of the Earth!

Only – was it worth the trouble: all this hard work, energy, faith? Queen of the Earth! *Was* that really important?

'I am really very tired, darling,' she whispered to Adam. 'I think I'll go up to bed if no one minds.'

No one minded. Earlier in the day, when William was still above ground, she was of importance. Now she was forgotten; England's Glory had taken her place.

Later Adam came to say goodnight to his mother. As he climbed the high stairs, leaving the boom and whisper of voices behind him, he felt a great longing to take his mother and Margaret, wrap them in shawls and whisk them off, with himself, to a desert island – a glorious island of burning sun, coral sand, heat and light and colour. The three of them alone, living for ever, always warm, always private, telling one another stories, and making necklaces of shells. He stopped on the landing opposite a dark engraving of Prince Albert and the Queen, and laughed. Two mice heard him laugh and, surprised out of their lives, whisked away.

He entered his mother's room carefully. There was a fire burning; the copper scuttle-scoop, the brass fender, the steel fire-irons shone resplendently. The old lady was lying, her pillows propped up behind her, apparently staring at a large oil painting entitled 'Little Black Sambo', which showed a small black child daintily covered with the leaf of a palm tree, sitting on the sea-shore sucking his thumb while two little white girls, clad immaculately in muslin and long pantaloons, stared at him with speculation. The firelight danced on the wall; the rain beat against the pane – it was not an uncheerful scene. She did not turn her head nor move when he entered. In spite of his heavy figure he trod very gently, sat down on a chair beside the bed and waited.

Then suddenly an awful fear seized him that she was going to die. Her face was always pale, but her small hands as they lay on the gay patchwork quilt had a marble pallor. And she lay so very still. She was, after all, of a great age. She should never have made the journey to London; this day must have been of a fearful exhaustion for her.

The thought that he might lose her at any moment now – that

she might go out like a candle carelessly blown by the wind – made him catch his breath, constricted his heart. The only three people in the world whom he loved, now that Caesar Kraft was dead, were his mother and Margaret and John. His nature was deeply modest, acutely sensitive. He could not believe that men and women liked him, and it was true that, at present, very few knew him because he was so silent about himself and thought himself a useless, cumbering failure. He had had great ambitions for the good of man and they had all failed. At that moment when Kraft had fallen and died at his feet, all his hope of helping his brother man had died. He had not the confidence nor the power nor the will. He was so shy of thrusting himself forward, so shy of display or self-advertisement, that men thought him proud and arrogant. At the newspaper office, in the little Club to which he belonged, even with a man like Charles Dickens, genial, friendly, exuberant, he could not let himself go. But these two women understood him, his mother and Margaret understood him, and to lose one of them . . .

And there was one more thing. He was only half alive in London. His soul ached for Cumberland, but Margaret did not like it. She was unhappy there. Stones and clouds, clouds and stones . . .

She turned her head and saw him. She put out her hand and caught his.

'Dear me, how nice, Adam! I have been dreaming, I suppose. But I don't know. I never know now whether I am dreaming or not . . . I was very tired, I must say, but bed is most comforting. There is no place like bed. I am sure that I never expected to feel that. I used to be so very energetic. But it's my body that's tired, not my spirit . . . How disgusting old James is, eating such a lot at his age!'

They talked quietly and happily together.

'Mother,' Adam said. 'One thing I hadn't told you. Will Leathwaite is coming to London to be my servant.'

That interested her. 'Is he indeed? What a good thing! I like Will so very much.'

'Of course it's absurd that I should have a servant with the little I make. But he wants to come. He says he doesn't care what I pay him, and it will be a little piece of home.'

'A very big piece,' Judith remarked, chuckling. 'That's nice for you, dear. Are they still guzzling and drinking down there?'

'I suppose so.'

'And what a deal they talk. Chatter, chatter, chatter. They are all delighted there's a war – why, I cannot imagine.' She closed her eyes and dreamt again. She talked as though out of a dream. 'I fancied just now that God was in the room. A God a little like Georges and a little like yourself, Adam. Perhaps that's what God will be – composed of the people we love most. He was so very kind and most reassuring. I have never been a religious woman, you know, Adam. Reuben Sunwood used to be greatly disappointed with me. He was so very certain. But I suppose an old woman may be allowed her fancies. I find that everyone is very certain about God in these days. Quite different from when I was a girl. It's as though they had made Him themselves.'

She sat up, climbing up out of her dream, full of energy again.

'I do hope you are happy, dear Adam,' she said.

'Yes,' he said. 'When I am with you and Margaret, Mother. But I'm terribly shy. It grows on me, I'm afraid.'

'Yes, your father was the same. But I shouldn't worry. We are different – you and I and poor John and little Jane. And the Herries family is an awkward family to be different in. All my life I have been fighting them. And now I am not fighting anyone any longer, even Walter. Too much trouble.'

She lay back again, closing her eyes.

'How lovely life is, all of it – having a baby, fighting Walter, pains and aches, food and riding up to Watendlath, poor Jennifer, the garden at Uldale, dear Adam, dear, dear Adam . . .'

She had fallen asleep. He sat there for some while watching her, then bent down and kissed, very gently, her forehead, then stole from the room.

CLIMAX TO A LONG SEQUENCE

I

JUDITH AND WALTER

WILL LEATHWAITE had come to say farewell. He was going at last, after six months' delay, to London to be Adam's servant. Judith was able to sit on the lawn in the September sunshine, it was so warm. The sun had the shininess of a hot sea and the lawn was like misty waters; the colours seemed gently to roll in shades of pale citron, of silver-grey, from the floor of the little Gothic temple to the walls, faintly pink, of the beloved house. Across the road, beyond the old peach-stained stones, rose the shadowed forms of the mountains, stretching themselves like great luxurious cats in the sunshine. A flight of curlews broke the pale wash of the sky, and you could feel, even though you could not see, the rough grass of the brown moorland, the icy glitter under the warm sun of the running moorland streams. Those green slopes, as yet scarcely purpled with heather, heaped up like a wave above the house answering the plaintive windy cry of the curlews.

In the middle of this peace, listening as always for her delight to the rhythm of running water, water slipping happily under the sunlight, she said goodbye to Will Leathwaite. It was as though she were sending Adam a piece of the North. Will was nearly fifty now and towered above her as he stood, his cap in his hand, staring in front of him. His colouring was very fair and there was a bald patch on the very top of his round bullet-like head. His features were stamped with simplicity, obstinacy, strength and kindliness; his cheeks were russet with good health, and there were little wrinkles at the corners of his very blue eyes that spoke of extreme good-nature. His body was large, broad, clumsy, his shoulders a little bowed. It was plain that he saw only one thing at a time and that once he had an idea in his head, nothing – no earthquake, no thunderbolt – could loosen it. He stood up in the thin Northern sunlight as though he had been created by it.

'Well, Will, you will look after Mr Adam, will you not?'

'I will, ma'am.'

'Will you like town life, do you think? It is very different from anything you've been used to.'

'So long as Mr Adam is satisfied, I'm ready,' he answered.

'It will be a great thing for Mr Adam. He hasn't many friends, you know.'

'Yes. T'nature of him is slow like my own, ma'am.' Then he smiled, a delightful slow, considering smile. 'T'best way, I think, ma'am.'

The children, Amabel and Jane, ran across the lawn, laughing and shouting, with a ball. He turned and watched them with a quiet decorous pleasure.

'Write to me, Will, and tell me how you find everything.'

'Yes, ma'am. Thank you, ma'am.'

He touched his yellow forelock and stepped slowly, steadily away, moving his great body with the ease and dignity of a gentleman in his own right. She sighed happily. It would be nice for Adam to have so trustworthy a man at his side.

She was glad that she was feeling strong and vigorous and that the air was warm, because she had much to think about. Both Margaret and John were staying in the house. Adam had written to say that Margaret was tired with the London air and needed a holiday, so she had been at Uldale a week and, so far, the visit had been a great success.

John had suddenly appeared with only a telegram's warning. No one knew why he had come. Then Elizabeth had written to say that she had sent him because he could not sleep in London. The summer had been hot: his master was in Switzerland. She herself was going to stay with the Rockages at Grosset. It was better that she and John should be apart for a while. This was sufficiently alarming, but John had said nothing until suddenly last evening, wishing Judith goodnight, he had told her that Elizabeth was going to have a baby.

'It's all wrong, Aunt Judith,' he burst out. 'I should not have a child.' He was quivering and his face was strained with distress.

'What nonsense!' she said. 'I never heard greater nonsense. Why, it's splendid for dear Elizabeth to have a baby.'

'It will be a coward – as my father was, as I am.'

He left the room without another word.

After that she slept very badly. Dream followed dream, and every dream was filled with apprehension. Every part of her past life seemed, in her dreams, to be now connected and to point to some inevitable result. She was once again with Georges at Christabel's Ball, with Charlie Watson in Watendlath, with Warren in Paris, and someone cried in her ear: 'Had it not been thus this would never have come about.'

'But what?' she cried.

But she could not see the event. She struggled, her heart full of love and fear. Adam, approaching her, tried to speak to her but was prevented. John waved to her a despairing hand before he vanished from sight. But she could do nothing. She was held, as one is in dreams, impotent, with no power in her limbs to move. Suddenly the old cruel figure of Mrs Ponder, Jennifer's servant, appeared. She was on her knees searching Judith's private papers.

'*Now* you will have to leave the house!' she cried, raising her malignant face.

'But I will not!' Judith answered.

And she had not. That was one thing upon which she could look back with pleasure, that in spite of all the odiousness and spying, in spite of Jennifer's lazy treachery, she had faced Mrs Ponder to the end, seeing the hateful woman at last out of the house. But what had Mrs Ponder to do with John? Ah, she remembered the little scene when that vile woman had thrown John's rabbit out of window. Was that, too, one link in the chain? Had every event, however slight, its inevitable result? But she must do something about John. She must not allow him to slip into tragedy as his father, Francis, had done. She must do something about John, and then she looked up to see Margaret coming across the grass towards her. She was now thirty-four years of age and a fine strongly built woman with a broad carriage, a calm open countenance and great quietness and repose in all her movements.

'She has grown,' Judith thought, 'like Adam and Adam like her, as many married people do when they have lived much together and love one another.' As she thought this a spasm of the old jealousy bit her as it might be a little animal jumping from the grass, but she brushed it away with her hand.

Margaret was wearing a simple grey muslin with panniers of white taffeta *placed* at the edges. In the bosom of her dress she had a white rose. Her dark hair was brushed back on either side, parted in the middle. She was carrying her hat in her hand. She brought peace and assurance with her.

'I like this woman,' Judith thought, as though she were seeing her for the first time. 'I am friends with her at last.'

The children had tired of their game and had run into the house. The sun was very slowly sinking, and the golden glow moved, travelling from place to place, softening the mountains with a purple flush while the sky faded slowly from bright blue into a translucent amber. Soon there will be a world of grey and silver and the hill will be dark, chill and strong. But that is not yet. The two women have half an hour to talk, the running stream the only sound in the world save their voices.

'You will not be cold, Mother?' Margaret asked, laying her broad strong hand on Judith's black dress.

'Oh no, my dear. And see that the grass is not damp for you.'

Margaret laughed. 'I have so many petticoats,' she said, 'I could sit in a stream and not be wet.'

Her voluminous grey dress spread out on the green grass and the light transmuted it.

'Have you seen John?' Judith asked.

'No; he has been away all day,' Margaret answered, sighing. 'He seems dreadfully unhappy. He has been so for months. He would talk to Adam at one time, but lately he has avoided him too, and Adam loves him so much. Elizabeth says that he will not talk to her either.'

'Yes – he is as his father was.' Judith beat her small hands impatiently on her lap. 'I can catch hold of *nothing*.'

'Adam thinks,' Margaret began, 'that it all began from the day when someone near here told him about his father and mother. He had a shock then that has weakened him like water, and it is of no use to say that he *ought* not, that I would not be like that, that *I* would not let the past touch me. We are all different, and it seems to me that the Herries who *are* weak are weaker than any others, as though someone had said once: "If you are born a Herries and refuse to have common-sense you shall suffer as no one else suffers. Have common-sense or die." Adam has just enough common-sense to save him.'

'Well, he is only half a Herries, my dear,' Judith said briskly. 'His father was only half a Herries and I am only by nature quarter a one, for my father was a wanderer and a vagabond and so was my mother. And here I am as warm and comfortable as a cat, thank goodness. It's more than I have deserved.'

Margaret hesitated. She found words no more easily than Adam, but there was something that she had been wanting for a long while to say, and now was a good time.

'Mother,' she began at last, slowly, in her deep rich voice, looking down at the grass. 'You do not hate me any longer, do you?'

'Hate you? Why, no, my child, I love you.'

'You did hate me once.'

Judith shook her head. 'No, I never hated you, of course. How could I when Adam loved you? – and besides all my life I must confess that I have found it very difficult to hate anyone. John's mother for a while once, and a horrid servant she had. Walter, perhaps, at odd moments. No. But I was jealous of you, I must confess.'

'Yes, I knew it.' Margaret stroked the grass with her hand.

'And it made me terribly unhappy. But I have never been able to express myself. I am so very shy of feeling, and women are not supposed to have any feelings. It is not thought nice.'

'In my young day,' Judith said, nodding her head vigorously, 'women had plenty of feeling and showed it. I don't know what's come over the world. Women are not supposed to have legs any more, and children are found in gooseberry bushes. Stuff!'

'And you are not jealous any more?'

'No. All my fires have died down. I sit and look on. But I love you, my dear. I do indeed. Adam has been the passion of all my life since my husband died, but a time came when I saw that someone else must do the things for him that I had done – and more things than I could ever do. How fortunate I have been that it was a woman like you, not one of these coarse painted creatures or one of these niminy-piminies all affectation, or one of those good perfect creatures like the woman in Mr Dickens' *David Copperfield*. What was her name? Agnes. But, of course, Adam would have chosen well. He would have had a whipping from me if he had not.'

'I have wanted to tell you,' Margaret said slowly, 'how grateful I am to you, how dearly I love you. I cannot say things, but I thought that once I must tell you—'

She leant up and put her arms around Judith. The two women kissed, and Judith laid her hand for a moment on Margaret's broad forehead.

'God bless you and keep you in all His ways, dear daughter. And now,' she went on quite sharply, 'I must go in. The sun will soon be down. How nice! I shall read Mrs Gaskell's *Cranford* over the fire. They say it is all about old ladies who are frightened by cows – like Mrs Potter at Threlkeld. Give me your arm, my dear. My right foot has gone fast asleep.'

A little later she was sitting in front of the parlour fire, her feet propped up on a worsted stool, a thick woollen shawl round her shoulders, and large spectacles on the end of her small nose. Her trouble was that her nose was *too* small. The spectacles *would* slip off! It was only of late that her eyes had begun to fail her. She was reading *Cranford* with many chuckles.

'How true this is! We are just the same here round Uldale. *"In the first place, Cranford is in possession of the Amazons – all the holders of houses, above a certain rent, are women. If a married couple come to settle in the town, somehow the gentleman disappears; he is either fairly frightened to death by being the only man in the Cranford evening parties, or he is accounted for by being with his regiment, his ship, or closely engaged in business all the week in the great neighbouring commercial town of Drumble, distant only twenty miles on a railroad. In short, whatever does become of the gentlemen, they are not at Cranford; ... but every man cannot be a surgeon. For keeping the trim gardens full of choice flowers without a weed to speck them; for frightening away little boys who look wistfully at the said flowers through the railings; for rushing out at the geese that occasionally venture into the gardens if the gates are left open; for deciding all questions of literature and politics without troubling themselves with unnecessary reasons or arguments; for obtaining clear and correct knowledge of everybody's affairs in the parish; for keeping their neat maidservants in admirable order; for kindness (somewhat dictatorial) to the poor, and real tender good offices to each other whenever they are in distress – the ladies of Cranford are quite sufficient." '*

Judith laid the book down on her lap and considered.

'How very excellent! That is exactly Miss Poole and Janet and Mary Darlington and Mrs Withers and Mrs Spooner. We are a world of women. Why? Why is Dorothy so important? She is not very clever nor is she at all beautiful, but she has a kind of kingdom. Now I *never* had a kingdom—'

The door opened. The little maid Eliza, her face twisted from its rosy simplicity with surprise, horror, alarm, excitement and general sense of drama, whispered something.

'What do you say, Eliza?' Judith asked, turning round and pushing her spectacles back on to her nose.

'Sir Walter Herries, ma'am.'

Walter! Her book dropped to the floor. She stayed, for a moment, listening as though she expected to hear some dreadful sound, but all that came to her was the cheerful shrill voice of someone singing in the kitchen. Then, sitting up very straight, she said:

'Ask Sir Walter to come in.'

A moment later he was standing beside the sofa, very stiffly bowing. He was dressed for riding and carried his hat in his hand. His hair was grey now (he was sixty-two) and he was clean-shaven, which was most unusual and gave him an odd babyish appearance. His red face was purple-veined, but he was not so stout as when Judith had last seen him. He was untidy, as though he had no one to look after him. Judith, against her wish, felt sorry for him.

'Well, Walter, how are you? Won't you sit down? Been poisoning any of our cows lately? How are the little Peaches? Humphrey, the stableman, found one of them in our gooseberry bushes not long ago.'

Walter sat down. He spread his legs, looked gravely at her; she noticed that his mouth was not very steady and that his hands shook.

'You are looking well, Judith,' he said.

'I am very well, thank you.' She took off her spectacles. She did not intend that he should say that her sight was going. Then sharply, as though to convey to him that she had not all day to waste:

'Why am I honoured?'

'A damned pretty place you've got,' he said, looking about him. 'Everything very fresh and charming.'

'Well – well. That's not what you've come to say.'

'No, it isn't. Sharp as ever you were!'

'Nor have you come to pay me compliments. Do you mind that window? If so, pray close it.' (For the window was open. Judith, unlike her contemporaries, loved fresh air.)

'No matter, thank you.' He hummed and hawed, then began a long rambling statement.

She could not make out what he was after. He had a lot to say about the past. Was it not foolish that they had wasted so much of their lives in quarrelling? He had been a young hot-headed fool, had done many things that he now regretted. Looking back, his ill-temper seemed to him now to have been very aimless, motiveless. But it was his father who, from the time he was a baby, had persuaded him that his mother had been insulted, and then Jennifer and Francis – well, Judith would agree that their conduct ...

'I will agree to nothing,' Judith said.

But he did not appear to hear her. He went rambling on. He was afraid that he'd taught Uhland the same doctrine. He saw now what a mistake he had made. He saw now that he had been mistaken in many things.

'Well, I'm glad of that anyway,' said Judith. 'But there is no use to go back on the past. If you are asking me to forget and forgive, Walter, frankly I cannot. Too much harm has been done – Francis, Jennifer, Reuben, and Jennifer's children. My own

life, too . . .' She coughed. She could not but be sorry for him a
little. There were spots on his waistcoat, and his stock was badly
tied. 'But what do you *want,* Walter? What have you come here
for?'

He hesitated, looked at her as though he were begging her to
help him. Then he said an extraordinary thing.

'Hatred, Judith, is a very rare quality in men. One seldom
meets it.'

She did not know what to say.

'Very rare,' she answered drily.

'I have never hated you. My mother never hated anybody.
Jennifer never hated anyone. You yourself have never hated.'

'Well?'

'What I intend to say is – I am clumsy at expressing myself –
but out of all this past quarrelling, not very real, you understand,
there has come much unhappiness.' He paused, rubbed his cheek
with his hand. 'I myself am not a happy man. All my own fault, I
admit it. I have lost my daughter quite through my own fault.
There is something bad in our blood which, if it is indulged—'

He stared at her in quite a fuddled way as though he had been
drinking, which it was likely that he had. But what was his
meaning? What was his intention? For what had he come? She
remembered the scene in this very room when she had slapped
his face. He was not the kind of man either to condone or
forget.

'Hatred, Judith, – real hatred – is a sort of madness.'

'Well?'

He went on again, finding words very difficult.

'You see . . . you know . . . you must understand . . . Upon my
word, I am extremely clumsy – you must forgive me – but my
boy – Uhland—'

'Yes – Uhland?' she said, more softly, because now, as always
when he spoke of his son, there was a new and moving note in his
voice.

'I had great hopes for Uhland. I may be a man who has made a
mess of his life. When I am sober I am ready to make such an
admission – but Uhland was to be different. He had a heavy
handicap' (his voice was gathering ardour now that Uhland was
his topic) 'his lameness – the sense that he was unlike the others.
And then his mother was not strong, and I was not the wisest
father. I was anxious to indulge him, too anxious perhaps, and he
was unusual, unlike other boys—'

He paused again, and gently, looking at him almost as though she were his friend, Judith said:

'Yes, Walter, I understand. In that at least I have always understood you.'

Encouraged, he went on:

'I am another man when I am in my cups. I will be quite honest with you. I have spoiled many things by my follies, but Uhland I have always kept apart. I saw from the beginning that he was by himself, alone. He has never cared for anyone except your Adam. He has never, I fear, cared in the least for myself, and the knowledge that he did not made me wilder, wilder than perhaps I would otherwise have been. But what I would point out is that all our quarrels, yours and mine and our parents' before us – the events in the life of your own father so many years ago – have found a kind of resting-place in poor Uhland's nature. He was born with a grudge and all his instincts have been twisted. In a fashion he is a scapegoat for the errors of the rest of us.' He stopped once more, wiped his mouth with his hand.

She was, in spite of herself, deeply touched. This was a different Walter from any that she had ever seen. She felt behind his precise, artificial, clumsy speech almost an agony of apprehension, and her own apprehension that she had been so conscious of all day rose to meet his.

She almost cried out:

'Oh, Walter, what is it? What has happened?'

Enemies though they had been all their lives, they were now almost allies.

He went on, staring at her as though that assisted him.

'Uhland has grown ever more strange. Our house is not an agreeable place. I will not pretend that it is agreeable, but of late Uhland's conduct has frightened me greatly—'

'Uhland's conduct?'

'Yes.' He found now the greatest difficulty in choosing his words. 'He is, I fear, most unhappy, but he will speak to no one. He shuts himself in his room. He walks over the house. The servants are afraid to remain where he is. And for myself, I think he hates me.'

She said nothing. He went on more swiftly.

'But it is not of myself that I wanted to speak to you. I came ... I came because—' He said urgently, leaning towards her: 'You have John staying with you?'

'Yes,' she said.

'You know, of course, that from the time of his childhood Uhland has always especially hated John.'

'Yes,' she said.

'It has been a sort of madness in him. I fear, I greatly fear that I was myself originally responsible for that. It seemed to me in those days unfair – unfair that John should be so handsome while my son—'

'Yes, I know, I know,' Judith said quickly.

'Then I implore you, Judith – I beg of you – send John back to London immediately. Immediately. Uhland knows that he is here. He has, during the last week, been very odd in his behaviour. He talks – he was talking last night – as though that old grudge had reached some kind of climax. We are, all of us, responsible for the past, I more than any, and if anything were to happen—'

'But what could happen?'

'There have been many acts of violence in our family,' he went on. 'It is as though there were an element of violence in our blood ... No. This is perhaps foolish, unreal. We are, I suppose, the most sober and sensible family in England, and just because of that when we are not sensible—'

He got up and she could see that he was greatly agitated.

'Never mind our family,' he said. 'Damn the family! This is urgent, personal to ourselves. I implore you, send John back to London tomorrow.'

She nodded. She looked up and gave him her hand for the first time for many years.

'Yes, Walter. You are right. Thank you for coming. It could not have been easy. John shall return to London. In fact this is no new thing. I have been aware of it for many years. John has been under some kind of shadow all his life, as his father was before him. I will see that he goes tomorrow.'

Walter held her hand, looked at her, bowed, then said almost defiantly:

'I have not come here to confess my sins, Judith. I shall be tomorrow as I was yesterday. I shall find myself a fool, I don't doubt, for coming to visit you. But for an hour at least I see sense. Goodbye. I can find my own way out.'

Judith sat on, her hands folded in front of her, looking into the fire, wondering as to which would be the best way to persuade John. This, had she known it, was a waste of energy, for John had heard everything, standing among some flowerpots, his hands scratched unwittingly by the nails of rose-briars fastened to the wall. He had returned from his ride and had seen Walter's horse tied to the gate. A quarter of an hour before he had seen both Walter and Uhland riding down the road from Ireby. He had come round the wing of the house towards the front door when, very clearly through the open window, he had heard the words in Walter's thick ropy voice: 'You know, of course, that from the time of his childhood Uhland has always especially hated John.'

So he stayed there, his body pressed against the wall, his eyes staring out into a sky that swam in frosty September light with one blazing diamond star. He heard everything. He heard Walter say: 'If anything were to happen—', and Judith later: 'Yes, Walter. You are right ... John has been under some kind of shadow ...'

So it had come to this! 'Under some kind of shadow! Under some kind of shadow.' And they planned to smuggle him away to London lest anything should happen ... anything should happen.

He went back to the stable and got out his horse Barnabas. A small terrier, very devoted to him, Mumps by name, little more than a puppy, came rushing across the cobbles when he saw Barnabas let out again. He had thought that the fun was over for the day, but apparently it was not. John went quickly by the gate that bordered the orchard. This brought him straight into the village street and he knew that he would be now ahead of Walter. The sun was just sinking, and hills, fields, pasture and stream lay in a mirror of light; you could fancy that if you swung, lazily, god-like in the sky, you would look down and see your Olympian features reflected in this sea of gold. Almost at once, just out of the village, at the dip in the road before it turned left to Peterfield, he found Uhland, waiting for his father, while his horse cropped the grass.

He knew that he had very little time before Walter came up, and, guiding his horse quite close to Uhland's, he said softly:

'I think that we must end this. It has gone on long enough – and by ourselves where no one can disturb us.'

It was as though because of their connexion through so many years they had grown to understand one another like the closest and dearest friends, for Uhland did not appear startled, nor did he ask 'End what?' or 'What has been long enough?' He simply drew his horse a little away from John's and nodded his head.

'Well – if you wish it. As to ending it—' Then he said sharply in his cold rather thin voice: 'What is it you want?'

'That we should have it out, the two of us, once and for all – alone.'

They both heard the tap-tap of a horse on the road. It would be, likely, Walter.

'Yes, I agree.'

They were like two schoolboys arranging a rendezvous for a fight; from the beginning there had been something childlike and something eternal too in their relationship.

Uhland went on, as though to himself: 'Yes, I have had enough of this. I must get rid of this.' He said coldly: 'Well – what do you propose?'

'Tomorrow. I will meet you somewhere.'

Uhland paused. They could see Walter coming down the hill.

'Yes. What do you say to the house opposite Calva in Skiddaw Forest? Tomorrow afternoon at four.'

'Yes. I'll be there.'

John turned his horse and a moment later passed Walter without a word or any greeting.

CLIMAX TO A LONG SEQUENCE

II

SKIDDAW FOREST

ON the following day, Uhland, waking very early in his tower, lighted his candle and began to read in a brown stubby volume. It was a translation of Vasari's *Lives of the Italian Painters*. After a while he came to this: '*Whereupon having taken this buckler with him to Florence without telling Leonardo whose it was, Ser Piero asked him to paint something upon it. Leonardo having taken one day this buckler in his hands, and seeing it twisted, ill-made and clumsy, straightened it by the fire, and having given it to a turner, from the rough and clumsy thing that it was, caused it to be made smooth and equal; and afterwards, having covered it with gesso and having prepared it after his own method, he began to think of what he might paint on it, that should be able to terrify all who should come upon it, producing the same effect as once did the head of Medusa. Leonardo therefore, to this end, carried to a room into which no one entered save himself, slow-worms, lizards, field-crickets, snakes, moths, grasshoppers, bats and other kinds of such-like animals, out of the number of which, variously put together, he evolved a most horrible and terrifying creature, which poisoned the air with its breath, and turned it into flame; and he represented it coming out of a dark and jagged rock, belching poison from its open throat, and fire from its eyes, and smoke from its nostrils, in so strange a manner that it seemed altogether a monstrous and horrible thing; and such pains did he take in executing it, that although the smell of the dead animals in the room was very noisome, it was not perceived by Leonardo, so great was the passion that he bore towards his art . . .'*

'So great was the passion that he bore towards his art,' Uhland repeated to himself and closed the book and blew out his candle to let the moth-like colour of the early morning strengthen in the room. So it was to be a great artist, such would he have done had he had the opportunity and the power. He had neither, only the longing. He had done nothing with his life, which now was over. He was certain that it was over and that this was the last time that he would see the early light spread about the room. But today he would release something from within himself that had been there since he was conceived. If he could live after that was released — ah! then perhaps he would become an artist.

He always had a headache now when he woke in the morning, a pain that pressed on his forehead like iron, and his eyes for the first hour were misted so that he had read the Vasari with great difficulty, and his lame leg hurt him sorely. But this morning when later he bathed and dressed he felt a glow, a warmth, a deep and burning excitement. That miserable coward had at last faced up to him. He would see him standing in front of him. They would be alone, removed from all the world. He would strike him in the face and see what he would do. This was the moment for which all his life he had been longing, to revenge himself upon the whole world for making him twisted and a cripple, all those people who had watched him as he walked, all the kind Herries relations who had despised and pitied him. Today he would revenge himself upon all his family — the crowd of them, so pleased with themselves and their strong bodies and the children they had begotten, so scornful of anyone unlike themselves ... and the fellow had dared – had dared – to marry his sister!

All morning he limped about the house thinking of a thousand absurd things – how his grandfather Will, now, Heaven be praised, dust and ashes, had looked at him across the dining-table in Hill Street as though he said: 'This poor misshapen creature – how can he be *my* grandson?' How Amery had invited him to ride with him, adding: 'You *can* ride, can't you?' How he had slipped on the stair at the Fortress, and Archdeacon Rodney's young son had muttered (but Uhland had heard him): 'Poor devil!' How Sylvia had looked at his leg and then blushed when he caught her – all, all, all pitying him, despising him, scorning him! Leonardo had filled his room with newts and toads and lizards and from them had constructed a figure so horrible ... There was power! Ah! there was power indeed! And today he would be revenged on them all. He would make that figure, seen all his days as the type of all that he himself despised and hated, cringe and shake and fall – a strange fire ran in his veins so that he felt almost as though his limp were gone and he as strong as any of them.

With the exception of his own place and the servants' quarters, his father's room was the only one in all the Fortress now that was cared for. The rest was tumbling to ruin. The walls were strong, but dust lay everywhere, and all the other rooms were damp-smelling and foetid. But he went everywhere as though he were saying goodbye to it all, a happy, glad goodbye. They called it the Fortress first in admiration, now in jest and mockery. So with this damned country: they thought that they were building a Fortress, eaten up with conceit they were, but one day it would be like this house, rotten and a jest to all the world. Pity he couldn't live to see that day ...

Later, with his gun over his shoulder, he went in to say farewell to his father.

Sir Walter Herries, Bart, was playing backgammon with his housekeeper, a thin painted woman called Mrs Throstle. Mrs Throstle enjoyed bright colours and was expecting friends from Keswick, so she was dressed in a worsted poplin of bright yellow and wore the most elaborate sleeves in the prevailing fashion, ruffed muslin with coloured ribbons at the wrist. She had coral bracelets. Over all this her sharp face peered anxiously at the board, for she was a mean woman, and they were playing for high stakes. Or so they seemed to her. But she always came out right in the end, because if she won she won, and if she lost she went through Herries' pockets at night after he slept and took what there was. But there was not much these days because everything was going to rack and ruin.

She was discontented, too, because Herries would not drink at present. He was sober and cross and peevish. He had struck her last night for saying that Uhland was a lame duck. She hated Uhland, as indeed did all the servants.

Walter, very soberly dressed, gave only half his attention to the game. He had been worried for weeks about Uhland, and his visit to Judith yesterday had done little to relieve him. Indeed, it had added to his discontent, for the Uldale house had looked so bright and shining. He had liked Judith too, that neat, capable, strong old woman, and all the silly enmity over which he had spent so much of his energy seemed to have blown into thin air. But enmity, hatred and all uncharitableness are never wasted, as he was to find out before many days were over.

He looked up at the door opening and hungered with love for his son. He saw that he was dressed for going out and had a gun over his shoulder; at once he was alarmed with a strange interior fear, the room seemed to fill with smoke before his eyes; his hand trembled, and he knocked the backgammon board off the table.

'There now!' said Mrs Throstle. 'And I was winning too!'

'Clear out!' said Uhland sharply. 'I want to speak to my father.'

Mrs Throstle rose, trembling. She was terrified of Uhland; one look at his contemptuous face and she shook all over. She gathered herself together, touched her coral bracelets indignantly, tossed her head and went. The round backgammon counters lay on the dirty carpet, but Walter stared at his son.

'Going out?' he asked.

'Yes, Father.'

'Shooting?'

'Maybe.'

Walter rose heavily, stretched his arms and yawned.

'I think I'll come too. Fresh air will do me good.'

'No, Father. I'm going alone today.'

Uhland looked at his father and felt, to his own surprise, a certain tenderness. He could remember – he did at this moment vividly remember – old, old days at Westaways when everything had been so rich, many people about, the house shining with colour, and his father bursting with health and self-satisfaction. But his father had wasted himself on emptiness, had let everything dribble through his hands like grain falling idly through the air. Grain falling — it lay now, in layers of dust, thick upon the floor. They had done nothing with their lives, either of them, and he saw for perhaps the first time that if he had returned some of his father's love things might have been otherwise. His father had had no return for either his love or his hate. A dry, wasted man ...

He did what of his own free will he had never done before — limped up and put his hand on his father's shoulder.

'Better I go alone,' he said. 'I'm in a sulky temper.'

Walter was so deeply moved by his son's gesture that he said angrily: 'You are always in a sulky temper.' He leaned his big heavy body towards his son's. He touched the gun.

'Going shooting?' he asked again.

'Maybe,' answered Uhland. 'Goodbye then.' He moved towards the door.

'When are you returning?'

'Oh, any time. Don't count on it,' and he went out, his backward glance from the door showing him his father bending his great stern towards the floor that he might pick up the backgammon counters.

He rode down the hill and then slowly along the ridge of the Fell towards Peter's House. He had plenty of time to be at Skiddaw House by four. It was a day in which everything seemed restrained, as though the sun were longing to break out but was held back by a strong hand. He passed an orchard where the pear trees were a bright yellow, and then in the distance he saw how the yellow hills were already autumnal, the heather resting on them in a rosy shadow from place to place. He had always been alive to beauty, although he resented it often because he felt that it, like the rest of the world, mocked at any cripple; now today the shadowed sun, the bright yellow of the leaves, the distant hills, were all part of his own purpose. They knew what would happen, and it was strange to him that they should all be able to see ahead of him, certain of the event before it had occurred.

'Everything is arranged then,' he thought. 'It is quite settled what I shall do. Every past incident contributes to this. I am what I have been made. And yet I could turn back if I wished. I would cheat God if God there be. I am greater than God, because now if I wished I could ride up Ireby Hill again and go in quietly and play backgammon with my father.' He stayed his horse for a moment, and had the fantastic thought that 'just to show them' he would ride back. But he could not; of course, he could not. Old 'Rogue' Herries; his father's words when he was very little: 'Don't you hate that conceited young cousin of yours, Uhland?'; Rodney's young son muttering 'Poor devil!' ... no, fragment after fragment had with infinite patience been brought together, all that he might ride to Skiddaw House to meet John Herries. And once again at the thought of that meeting his blood was hot.

Jane Bellairs was the only one in the house to see John go. She had two great devotions in her life – one for her great-great-aunt Judith, the other for her uncle John. She eliminated, as did her brothers and sisters, the degrees of greatness from Judith, and called her quite simply (and very proudly) 'my aunt'.

'But, dear, she cannot be your aunt,' tiresome Mrs Munberry in Keswick had years ago said to her. 'She is far too elderly. You mean great-aunt.'

But Jane had simply thought Mrs Munberry a foolish old witch, with her grey hair and sharp eyebrows. For all the children Judith was ageless. She had lived, of course, for ever, and would live for ever. She was like God, only more easily loved. But Uncle John was Jane's especial property. When he was absent in London, Jane not only prayed for him night and morning but also talked to him when she was alone, asked him whether she could fetch him anything, and thought about him before she slept, because she was certain that he was lonely. This idea that he must be lonely had come to her at a very early age when, rocking her doll by the fire in the parlour, she had looked up and seen him staring out of window.

She had given him her doll to care for, and also, although he did not perhaps know it, herself at the same time. The others laughed at her for her devotion, especially Veronica, who was a good hearty girl with no nonsense about her. But Jane did not mind when they laughed. She had long grown accustomed to having her own private life, a life that no one understood but Aunt Judith. Her mother least of all, for Dorothy would perpetually be saying: 'Dreaming again, Jane. Where's your work, child?' and Jane would pick up her piece of worsted on which she was embroidering a red rose or a ship with sails and, with a small sigh that nobody heard, pricking her forefinger and biting her lip, would set about it. She was, however, as Dorothy frequently declared, the easiest of all the children, for when she lost her temper she was quiet, not noisy like the others, and could amuse herself quite happily all the day long. Although she was nearly fourteen years of age now she was very slight and small.

'That child will never grow,' Dorothy exclaimed, and Judith replied: 'My dear, don't be foolish. I'm eighty and have never grown an inch since I was eight.'

And now she was the only one of all the family to see John go. All morning she had been painting a picture. This was her favourite pursuit, and here too the others laughed at her because she did not paint easy things like cottages and cows and the sun, very red with rays like wires, setting on a mountain, but things much too difficult for her, like the Queen in her Palace, the whale swallowing Jonah, and Noah seeing dry land. Yesterday on her walk she had seen some horses drinking from a pond, and this morning she had been drawing a great white horse swimming. Beyond the pond there were mountains, and for some reason (she did not know why) it was winter and the pond was black with ice. She covered the pond with purple paint. This painting was to be for John and, before dinner, she looked for him everywhere to give it to him. She found him coming from the stable, leading his horse Barnabas, and the small dog Mumps was with him. He smiled when he saw the little girl in her pink bonnet. Her dress, with its double skirt and fan-shaped corsage, made her quaint while on the other children it seemed quite natural. It was as though she were in fancy-dress.

'Hullo, Janey!' he said.

'Are you going to ride?'

'Yes.' He put his arm around her and kissed her.

'I've been up to Auntie's room and she's sleeping yet.'

Judith had not been well that morning and when she was not well all the house was quieter. Jane considered him. Should she show him her painting? He was busy because he was going riding.

Yes, she would. She *must* show him.

'I've done a painting and it's for you.'

'Let's see.' He bent down, while Barnabas and Mumps stood patiently waiting. All he saw was that some kind of animal was sitting on a floor of purple paint. But he guessed that the animal was a horse.

'That's a grand horse,' he said, pinching her cheek.

'Yes, and it's swimming in a pond all frozen with ice, and then it will ride up the mountain.'

'What a splendid horse! Is that for me?'

'Yes.'

He kissed her and held her for a moment close to him. Then he put the painting very carefully in his riding-coat pocket.

'Goodbye, my darling.'

'Where are you riding to?'

'Oh, only a little way.'

'Will you be back before I go to bed?'

'Yes, sweetheart.'

'Will you read *Nicholas Nickleby?*'

'Yes, if there's time enough.'

She stood in the gateway waving to him until he was out of sight. At the corner before the houses of the village hid him he turned on his horse and waved back to her. She ran into the house and wondered what there would be for dinner.

When, beyond the village, he was riding by Langlands he noticed an orchard and how yellow the leaves of the pear trees were. That made his heart beat, and the thick grass under the trees, the spikes of some of the sharper grasses, were already brown at the tips. There had been frost every morning of late. Then, as he turned towards Over Water, he realized that Mumps was running most confidently at his side, his little black eyes sparkling, his mouth open, stopping for quick snatched moments to sniff at a smell, his whole person expressing extreme content and happiness.

He must not have Mumps with him on this ride, so he pulled Barnabas up and said sharply:

'Go home, Mumps! Go home!'

Mumps stopped and looked at him as though he had just received the surprise of his life, as though he could not, in fact, believe his ears.

'Go home, Mumps! I mean it.' And he flourished his whip. Barnabas also exchanged a look with Mumps, saying: 'Yes. This is genuine.'

Mumps ran forward, pretending that he had discovered so rich a smell that John must be pleased, and being pleased, would soften his heart. Then he stood, with one paw raised, intently listening. Then when that was of no avail he sat down and

scratched his underparts. Then, that accomplished, he looked up
at John pleadingly. All of no value. The stern order was repeated,
so, after one more imploring stare, he surrendered and slunk
down the road, his tail between his legs. Round the bend, he
reconsidered the matter. He saw that his master was slowly riding
on, so, slowly, he followed, maintaining a tactful distance.

When John had Over Water on his right and was approaching
Orthwaite Hall, he heard a bell ringing, the kind of bell that rings
from the belfry of a manor-house calling the servants to a meal.
It came beautifully through the honey-misted air. 'It is as
though,' he thought, 'some giant were holding back the sun.'
Thin patches of sunlight lay on the fields, and on the hills the
heather spread in clouds of rosy shadow. All was dim, and the
little sheet of water was like a buckler on whose surface someone
had been breathing, silver under cobweb, without bounds, raised
in air above the soil.

'It's funny,' he thought. 'Aunt Judith has always said that she
could see Over Water from the windows of the house. Of course
she could not. She must have the neck of a giraffe.' And yet he
himself had often thought that he saw Over Water from those
windows – a mirage. But how friendly a little piece of water it
was! All his life he had loved it – his whole life long.

Then, with a sharp stab of anticipation, he was aware of what
he was about. Somewhere already in this misty countryside
Uhland Herries was riding. They might meet on the way. He was
somewhere near, shadow behind shadow – and the bell, still ringing, echoed in the air: 'This – Time – is – the – Last. This – Time
– is – the – Last.' He was conscious of an awful temptation to
turn back. Perspiration beaded his forehead. Why should he go
on – to his death maybe? This lovely land that all his life he
had adored; why should everything have been spoilt for him so
long by one person to whom he had never done any harm? No.
He must recognize that Uhland was only a symbol. Life would
have been for him always a place of fears and terrors even though
Uhland had never been born. What did the ordinary man – men
like Garth and Uncle Will and old James – know about such a
life, know how it was to wake in the night because you heard a
sound, to turn in the street and look back over your shoulder, to
watch a picture lest it should drop from the wall, to hear a mouse
scratch in the wainscot so that your heart thumped, to expect
with every post bad news, to fight, all your life long, shadows,
shadows, shadows? . . .

Oh, to be done with it, to throw fear out of your heart like a dirty rag, and then perhaps he would be like Adam, so quiet and sure, a little ironical about life but never afraid of it, with a heart so unalarmed that it could spend itself on love of others. He thought then that he heard a horse's hoofs knocking on the road behind him, and he turned sharply. But there was no one. The bell had ceased to ring. At last, today, it would be over. He would settle with Uhland for ever. *That* fear at least should be killed.

He rode on, past Peter's House, up on to the path across the Fell leading to the road that climbed under Dead Crag up steeply past Dash Waterfall. On his right were the Caldbeck Fells humped against the sky and stained now with every colour, the rose and purple of the heather, silver grey where the grass was thin, a bright and burning green of fields between walls, and down the side of one fell splashes of white quartz ran like spilt milk.

He looked about him to see whether anywhere there was another rider. He could see for a great distance now, to the right to the sweep of the Bassenthwaite Woods, to the left where the dark wine-stained sea of heather, grass and bare soil ran in a flood to the feet of the Caldbeck Fells, breaking, as it began to climb, into patches of field, a farm with a white wall, cows and sheep grazing. But no human being moved in all the landscape. Under Dead Crag, before he began to climb, he thought of the ravens for which the Crag was famous. He looked up to where the jagged edge cut the sky, and two birds, as though in answer to a call, floated out like black leaves, circled silently in the still air. The only sound was made by the Dash that tumbled with fierce gestures from the height above. It was full and strong, which was strange when there had been so little rain.

He was sorry that he had not been able to see Aunt Judith before he left, and yet it was perhaps as well. She had sent down word that she would like to see him in her room after her three o'clock dinner, and of course he knew what it was that she wanted – to persuade him at once to return to London. He wondered what reason she would have given: something about Elizabeth, he supposed, and at the thought of Elizabeth his heart seemed to stop its beat. If he did not return from this ride . . . if he did not return . . . Never to see her again . . . He climbed the steep road.

When Uhland reached Orthwaite Hall and looked across Over

Water the bell had ceased to ring. Then suddenly it began again, softly, steadily, persistently: 'Going – going – gone . . .'

Uhland looked at the Tarn, and then turning to the hills saw a thick tangle of mist like the ends of a woman's mantilla stray loosely over the tops. If the mists were coming down that would be serious. Many a man had been lost for hours between Calva and Skiddaw when the mist fell. The House would be hard to find, and, as though he had made a bet with some contestant, he was pledged to reach the place by four. The sun that had been shining so warmly when John half an hour before had been there, now was withdrawing. The light still lay in patches on the fields and the moor; down the Caldbeck Fells the shadow slipped, leaving the glow bare behind it as the skirts of a woman might fall.

But Uhland was aware now of a great impatience. Nothing should cheat him of this meeting. He longed to have John close to him, to see him flinch, above all to put to the final test all that those years and years of shadowing had anticipated. He urged on his horse, hearing the bell follow him as he rode up towards Dead Crag and the shining tumble of the Dash. He looked up at the steep road that ran up under the Crag and saw three birds circling like black leaves above the line of rock.

'Those must be ravens,' he thought, and remembered how, when he was a very small child, he had heard men tell of the ravens that haunted Dead Crag, and how, years ago, after the 'Forty-Five Rebellion', they had flown above the corpses of men, crying and calling in a vindictive triumph. He looked about him, down to the Bassenthwaite Woods that were now black like iron, then across to the sequence of fell-tops, but he could see no other rider.

'Is he behind me or before me?' he thought, and again that hot excitement as of wine pouring through his body exalted him. He felt a sort of grandeur that he had never known before. His lameness did not handicap him now. He was as good as anyone, and better, for he was on his way to dominate and conquer that supercilious, disdainful fool whom he would have down on his knees before the day was over.

But when he had almost reached the top of the road and the waters of the Dash were loud in his ears, he saw that the mist was beginning to pour like smoke from behind the hills. It came in eddies and whirls of movement although there was no wind. Greedily it ate up the farms, the fields, rose for a moment as though beaten by the sun, then fell again. When he was actually on the height he saw it advancing from every side. He pushed his horse forward and a moment later felt its cold fingers on his cheek. The whole world was blotted out.

The first thing that John heard when he started away from the Dash was the eager, excited breathing of a dog. He looked back and saw Mumps, his tongue out, happily racing towards him. The dog knew that now there was nothing to be done. Too late now to order him to go back. He felt a strange comfort as though this were a sign from Fell House.

He was soon lost in the spaces of Skiddaw Forest. There was no forest here; there had never perhaps been trees; the name was used in the old Scottish hunting sense of a place for game. John knew slightly General Sir Henry Wyndham whose land this was, and his keeper Donald Grant, who lived at the House, his present destination. The House was one of the loneliest dwelling-places in all the British Isles, the only building from Threlkeld to Dash. John knew also that, at this moment, Grant was in Scotland, his family with him. He had heard only the week before that the House was closed.

He could not anywhere in the whole world be more alone than he now was. A chill, in contrast with the warm valley below, was in the air, and the patches of heather, the sharp green of the grass where the bilberries had been, the grey boulders, all had lost the brilliance of their colour. He looked back once before he went on and saw the Solway lit with a shaft of sunlight that glittered and trembled under the line of Criffel and his companions. He was leaving that shining world and with every step of his horse was advancing into danger. On his right the flanks of Skiddaw began to extend and he could see the cairn that marked its peak against the sky. Calva was on his left. A moment later he saw the bounds of his journey's end, on the right Lonskill Crag, and on the left, extraordinarily black and angry, the sharp line of Foul Crag, Blencathra's edge. Between them, far away, in sunlight like the smile of another world, was the ridge of Helvellyn. Sunlight behind him, sunlight before him, but his own country dark, shadowed, without form, guarded by hostile crags. He knew that under Lonskill was the House, and at the thought that he was now so near to it a shudder that he could not control took him. Soon he would come to the Caldew river, and, crossing that, he would move into his fate, a fate that had been advancing upon nim since the day of his birth and before whose menace he had been always helpless.

It was then that he noticed the mist. It came on the right from Skiddaw, on the left from Calva. It tossed and rolled, crept almost to his feet. Was Uhland in front of him or behind? And, even as he asked himself, the whole world was blotted out.

CLIMAX TO A LONG SEQUENCE

III

IN A DARK HOUSE

WHEN Uhland felt the wet mist close in he was conscious of an almost desperate irritation. He was of so morbid and irritable a temperament that he had always been unusually susceptible to weather, to places, to trees and hills. He did not, as did John and Adam, feel that this country was in any case beloved, that, whatever it chose to do, it was to be accepted and welcomed as an ally. It had seemed to him all his life bent on his frustration, and, like others of his kind, he discounted lovely days but recorded all the disappointments and, as they seemed to him, the malignancies.

The fellow, he now contemptuously thought, would take this mist as an excuse: 'I could not find the House. When the mist came on I turned back' – and it seemed to Uhland that there would never be an opportunity again. If he missed this he missed his power over the man. He would hate him no longer but would henceforth hate himself, and, more than that, be choked till he died with this passion of which he could not rid himself.

He rode a little way and could not tell whether he were going forward or back. He had been often in such mists before, but had never been baffled and blinded as he now was, and, as always when it was damp, his lame leg began to ache, as angry as he was at this frustration.

He stopped to see whether he could hear the Caldew. It must be somewhere near, but he had never in his life known such a silence as had now fastened about him. The absence of any sound or movement closed in upon his ears like the beat of a drum. He moved on again, and as one often does in mist, thought that someone was close behind him. It would be just like that fellow to stab or shoot him in the back, an easy way once and for all to rid himself of his enemy, and, although Uhland was not afraid, it would be the last fitting irony of the injustice that he had all his life suffered under to be stabbed in the dark and dropped into space like carrion. He listened. Behind him something moved, pebbles were displaced, or there was a soft crunching of the grass.

'Herries, are you there?' he cried, and his own voice, the voice that he had always despised and hated, came back clogged with wet mist. 'Herries, are you there?'

The scene was fantastic, for at his feet and just in front of him little fragments of ground were exposed, were closed, and were exposed again. The mist immediately surrounding him was so thick that it was like fog and so wetting that he was already soaked through and through his clothes. It cleared at the top of Calva, and the round shoulder of the hill sprang out like a live thing on his left. It was so clear that he could see the patches of bright green and bare boulders lit with a chill iridescence as though in moonlight. Calva frowned at him, then raced under mist again, leaving only a fragment like a bare arm lying nonchalantly in space.

His horse struck pebbles, and then he heared the slow stealthy murmur of the Caldew. Well, he was moving forward, for not far beyond was the rising hill on which the House stood. Behind the House was a wood, and if Wyndham's keeper should be at home they could finish this affair among the trees. No one would see them on such a day.

There should be a little wooden bridge over the Caldew. He pulled in his horse, jumped off and peered around him. Now, if John Herries was really behind him, would be the time for him to come at him, and perhaps they would struggle there where they stood and end it once and for all.

He spoke again: 'Now, Herries, I'm on foot . . . Are you there?' There was no answer. If Herries *were* there he was sitting motionless on his horse, and Uhland fancied that he could *see* a horse there in the mist, and on it a gigantic figure, motionless, waiting. He stumbled and almost fell over the rocks into the stream. With an oath he pulled himself back and began to find his way along the bank. Now he had lost the horse, for the mist was around him like a wall, but the horse whinnied, and at the same moment he discovered the wooden bridge. He went back and led the horse safely across. Now he knew where he was, for at once the ground began to rise. He came to a gate, opened it, leading the horse through.

It was at this point that it was exactly as though someone stood in his path. For a moment he *could* not move, and he felt as though a great hand were pressed against his chest.

'Let me through, damn you,' he said, and stumbled and fell. His lame leg often failed him, but now it was over a rock that he had fallen. He had cut his hand, and his body pressed into the wet soil, just as though someone were on his back holding him down. The soil was filthy, soaking, deep in mire. His cheeks were muddy and the knees of his breeches heavy with water. He pushed backwards and was suddenly freed, as light as air, the mist thinning so that, as he got on to his feet again, he saw the House only a little way above him, swimming in air like a ship in the sea. He moved forward, leading the horse, unlatched the gate, passed through a small tangled garden of cabbages and currant bushes. His feet grated on a gravel path, and he saw that in one of the windows of the House a candle was shining.

Uhland's thought had not been far out. John, as the mist enfolded him, had felt stir in him that weak boneless animal, so long so hated a companion, who whimpered: 'Here is a way of escape. You can say that you were lost, had to turn back.' He stopped his horse and stayed there, listening and considering. At once an odd memory came to him, odd because he had not thought of it for years, and now it touched him as though there were suddenly a warm, strong hand on his shoulder. He remembered how once, when they were little children, Aunt Judith had told them a story of their grandfather, David Herries; how he had run away with their grandmother, years, years ago when she was a girl, and fleeing with her from Wasdale up Stye Head had been pursued by an uncle or someone of the kind – and then by the Tarn, in swirling mist, Grandfather David and the uncle had fought while Grandmother Herries watched, and Grandfather David had killed the other. It had sounded then a grand story, like a story out of a book, unrelated in any way to the warm fires and old armchairs of Uldale. Now it was real. The mist that at this moment swirled about him had swirled about David Herries then, and David Herries had won. It was almost as though someone rode beside him, smiling at him as they went. So then he rode forward, but nevertheless the memory of an old story could not kill the struggle within himself. 'Turn back! Turn back!' the boneless creature said. 'You know that you are afraid. You know that when you are face to face with him that old terror will be too strong for you, and at the first word from that voice you'll run.'

And the other companion at his side seemed to whisper: 'Go on! You have nothing to fear. All your life you have been fighting shadows, and today at last you will discover what shadows they have been.'

Yes, that was true. It had begun in his very babyhood when in his cot he had seen how the reflections from the fire had made fearful shapes on the wall. Then his nurse, old Mrs Ponder, how he had shivered as he heard her heavy step on the stair, and her voice as she said, 'Now, Mr John. I dare you to move!' and he had stood, his heart thumping, transfixed; then the day when she had thrown his rabbit out of window. The day, too, when he had first seen Uhland, Uhland limping down the Keswick street, and that pale face had turned towards him and something in him had bent down and hidden away. The evening, too, when with Adam he had seen Walter sitting his horse, silently, on the hill. But Walter Herries had never meant much to him; the dread of his whole life had been concentrated in Uhland, and it was of no use for others to say, 'But this is phantasmal. There is no reality here.' For his father, too, had found the real world a prison, and, year after year, had allowed his mother to be mistress . . .

He threw up his head. 'I am revenging my father,' he thought, 'and my son, when he is born, will be fine if I am brave now.' For he felt, as many men with imagination have done, that with the vision they are given they can see that no men are apart, that History has no Time, and that all souls struggle for victory together.

So, greatly strengthened and as though suddenly he were seeing his destiny for the first time, he pushed through the mist as someone in a cellar pushes through wet cobwebs.

He now heard the running of the Caldew, and at the same moment thought that Uhland was just behind him. He stopped Barnabas and was aware of a multitude of noises. There was the murmur of the stream, the thin breathing of the little dog, and, it seemed to him, a multitude of whispering voices. Also dimly there sounded music in the air. Since he was a boy he had known that hereabouts was the place in Cumberland for finding the Musical Stones – certain stones and boulders which, when cut, gave out musical notes when you struck them. At the Museum in Keswick there was a good set of these stones, and Mr Cunningham at Caldbeck had a set on which he and his sons played many tunes. They beat them with a leather-covered hammer. Often as children Adam and he had come up to these parts and searched for them, and he had once had a stone that gave out a great ringing sound like an organ note. He had heard that in ancient days the Romans here had used them in their houses for gongs. This memory came to him now and pleased him. There was certainly some kind of music in the air. He waited. Maybe Uhland was also there waiting, but it was hard to see in the mist. If so this would be a good place to end it.

At last he said out loud: 'Is anyone there?' and again, 'Who's there?' But there was no answer.

He dismounted from Barnabas to find the wooden bridge across the stream, and at once Mumps found it for him, going in front of him and looking back to see whether he were following. After that, it was easy to mount the rising ground, and soon, leading Barnabas, he passed through the gate, along the little garden, and up to the door of the House. The mist floated about the walls in smoking wreaths. He could see dimly the wood. He found, as he had expected, that the door was locked. There was no one there. He went to the window on the right of the door and to his surprise it was slightly open. Then he tied Barnabas to the garden wall, pushed up the lower pane and easily vaulted into the room. It was so dark that for a while he stood there accustoming his eyes to it, and the mist poured in through the open window as though all the outer world were on fire. After a time he stumbled about, knocking his knees against a chair and the edge of a table. He found the fireplace, and on the mantel his hand closed on a candle. He struck a match from a box in his inner pocket and lit it. He waited, listening. He opened the door and went into the passage.

'Is anyone in the house?' he called.

There was no answer. He heard some hens running. Then he went back into the room, and almost immediately after there were steps on the pebble path outside.

Standing back against the mantel he heard the steps go to the door, he heard the lock shaken, then back to the window, a pause, and Uhland had climbed into the room.

As they faced one another the room at once became of great importance, and when Uhland closed the window behind him the candle, that had been blowing wildly, steadied itself and seemed to watch thereafter with a piercing eye. There was very little in the room. A deal table, and on it a bright green mat and some pallid wax fruit under a dusty glass cover. On the mantelpiece were two large china dogs with bright red spots like a rash on their bodies, a clock that pointed to five minutes to four although it was not going. In the corner there was a grandfather clock that leaned forward drunkenly, on the walls a large highly-coloured print of the opening of the Great Exhibition and an engraving of the Duke of Wellington covered with yellow damp-spots. There was a wheel-back armchair with a patchwork cushion and in the corner a child's rocking-horse. In another corner there was a spinning-wheel. The floor was of brick. In the window there was a dead plant in a pot.

Uhland set his gun against the wall and sat down. His leg hurt him confoundedly. He rested his arms on the table, and stared at John. As he looked he was reassured. He had thought that perhaps now when they met at last he would find that there was nothing to be done, nothing to be said. All this chase and pursuit for so long had been a chimera. He would not be rid of the mad impatience and restlessness in his heart by any contact with this poor fool. He would just look at him contemptuously and let him go. But it was not so. The very sight of John started his rage. John had taken off his riding-coat. He wore a narrow blue tie over which his shirt collar was folded, and his shirt had an inset-breast of the finest linen. He wore a waistcoat of dark blue patterned with tiny dark red flowers. He was not a dandy, but everything about him was exquisitely clean and well-fitting. His features, pale, keen, sensitive, gave him an air of great aloofness and high breeding without, however, any conceit or arrogance, and he seemed, in some way, in spite of his years, still a boy – for his figure was slim as a boy's and his air as delicate and untouched by life as a boy's of seventeen might be.

Uhland knew that he himself was muddied, wet, and that his hand was stained with blood. There was mud on his cheek. Yes, he would spoil some of that beauty and aloofness before he left that house, and once again the blood began to beat, hot and insistent, in his veins.

He tapped with his fingers on the bare table.

'I'm here,' he said. 'What do you want to say?'

'I want to say this.' John found to his disgust that his hands were trembling. He held them tight against his sides. 'I want to ask you a question. Why for years now have you followed me – in London, here in Cumberland – everywhere? I have never done you any harm that I know.'

'I fancy,' said Uhland, 'that I may go where I please. Who says that I have been following you?'

'You know that you have, and that you have done it because it offends me. It must cease from now on.'

Uhland paused. Then he repeated softly: 'It must cease ... But why?'

'Because I say that it must.'

'You talk like a schoolboy,' Uhland replied. 'We are grown men. Of course I go where I please and do what I please. You are a coward, you know. You are the son of a coward, you were born a coward, you will be a coward until you die. Otherwise you would have faced up to me years ago.'

'No,' said John. 'I could not because you are a cripple.'

At that word Uhland's fingers ceased to beat on the table. A little shiver ran through his body.

'That makes a good excuse for you,' he said at last quietly. 'Now listen to me for a moment. It is quite true that I have always hated you. Your family is a disgrace. Your father allowed your mother to be a man's mistress for many years. I daresay the fellow paid him to keep quiet. Then your father was challenged to a duel and ran away. Then, because there was nothing else for him to do, he shot himself in London. Well, it has not been nice for the rest of us to have such relations at our very gates. It was very painful for my father. From the very first you gave yourself airs, you mocked at my lameness, you spread scandal about my father's manner of life. You were always – although you did nothing but walk about Keswick in your grand clothes – a vain fool. The very sight of you was an irritation, but an irritation that pleased me because you were, and are, so miserable a coward that a very look from me made you quake. And then you had the damned impertinence to marry my sister.'

'We will leave her out of this,' John said.

'Oh no, we will not. That is a score that I have been waiting a long while to pay ... Why, look!' he suddenly cried, with a mocking laugh. 'You are shaking now!'

'Yes,' John said, and he drew a little kitchen chair to the table and sat down. 'I will sit down. I am trembling, as you say, but that is because you always affect me so. A sort of disgust that I cannot control.'

But, as he spoke, he knew that it was more than disgust, it was fear from the disgust. Now if ever was the moment to which all his life had led. If he failed now, everything would be lost – his father, Elizabeth, their child. And he did not know that it would not be lost, for something within him – the traitor to himself that had been born with him – was urging him to run. 'Run! Run! Climb out of that window and run for your life.' His limbs were moving with a power that was not his own at all. He had to hold his feet against the brick floor. The fight within himself was so arduous that he could scarcely think of, or even see, Uhland. It was something more than Uhland, and something worse.

'If I move I'm lost,' he thought. He fixed his eyes on the pallid, deathly wax fruit. He fixed his eyes but he could not fix his heart. Ah, if only he could rise and throw himself on Uhland, that would be an escape as well as the other, but the man was a cripple, a damned cripple—

'I see,' said Uhland. 'I fill you with disgust. But it's yourself you're disgusted with. Because I found you out years ago. You've cheated the others, who think you a mighty fine fellow. I've shown you to yourself. Every time that I've been near you you've felt what you are. You have at least the grace to be ashamed . . .'

Then an odd thing occurred. Uhland stretched one of his arms out along the table, and his hand lay there, almost under John's eyes. It was a lean white hand, the knuckles red, and on the back of it thin hairs faintly yellow. The nails were long and dead. The hand seemed to John to curve and twist on the table, like a thing in a nightmare, and, when it was close to him, he was suddenly strengthened. Was it that hand that he had always been fearing? Was this the ghost? Was this all? His eyes cleared. The room was formed and plain. The spinning-wheel was real, the Duke looked at him with grave, stern eyes. His legs were no longer trembling.

'Well,' he said in a clear strong voice that had no quaver, 'whatever the past has been, I am afraid of you no longer. You should have done more with your life than to spend it over one man, in especial if he's the poor creature you think me. I am afraid of you no more, so you can follow me no more. Nor shall you insult my father and mother again. You may be lame or not lame. After those insults your lameness is of no account, and before we leave this house you are down on your knees – on your knees. When you please. Choose your time. We can be here all night if you wish.'

Would his courage last? Was this a true lasting thing that he felt? For the first time he looked Uhland straight in the face.

Uhland withdrew his hand. He now was trembling, but with anger, the choking wild anger that so constantly came to him from the sense of his own ostracism. It was as though, at John's repeated 'lameness', all the world laughed, and a little crowd of sympathizers inside himself massed together and begged him to avenge them.

'You coward!' he cried in that odd shrill voice that should have been, if fate had been fair, rich, deep and generous. 'Why, you are afraid of your own shadow! You shall stay here – do you hear? – and you shall not move! Stay there without moving until I bid you, and then it is you who shall be on your knees, and beg and pray, and beg—' He half rose, leaning forward on his arms, his thin muddied face staring into John's.

And John could not move. He would have risen and he could not. Something within him was melting, loosening ... in another moment it would be too late for ever.

It seemed that an hour passed. It was only a moment. Then, his head bent as though he were putting forth all his strength, at the instant when his power seemed gone, he pushed over the table.

It fell with a crash, the wax fruit with it, and the glass shattering on the brick floor.

His eyes shining, he stood back to the wall. He would not touch the man! He would not touch the man! But all fear was gone. He was strong with his whole strength—

'Come on, Uhland. Down!' he cried, laughing. 'I won't touch you. On your knees and then off with you. Back home—'

He saw Uhland stand. He marked every part of him, his hair thin on the top, the mud on his cheek, his damp stock, the round buttons of his coat. He saw Uhland take his gun from the wall. He thought, 'Elizabeth!' Uhland fired.

At the noise the little dog on the path outside began to bark. He barked running up and down outside the closed door. Then he began to whimper, again and again scratching at the door. The room was filled with smoke and mist. Slowly it cleared. Uhland stood for a long while with the gun in his hand, but at last he leant it carefully against the wall and went over to the empty fireplace. He bent down and looked at the body. John lay there, his face hidden in his arm. Very gently Uhland turned him over, unfastened his waistcoat, felt for his heart. John was dead.

'Well, that is the end,' he thought.

He felt no relief; only an increased grudge of injustice. He felt sick, too, with that accustomed nausea that had so often attacked him. He sat in the wheel-back chair, licking his dry lips with his tongue. The whole aim of his life was gone, and what it had been he had now no idea. He was sorry for no one but himself, and even about himself he felt now a bitter, savage irony. All those days and years for nothing. He had had a right to be in a rage, but how purposeless rage was! He was the victim of the grossest injustice, but what a poor, muddy, shabby victim! He felt an especial rage with his nausea. To be sick now would be the last indignity. But he would not be sick. At least he could prevent that. And this was all the long pursuit had come to ... nothing ... sickness ... and his hand was bleeding again. He looked about the room. He knew what he wanted. A piece of paper. He got up and limped here and there, almost stumbling once over John's body. There was no paper anywhere, and why to God was that dog outside whimpering? He blundered against the clock, and it lurched as though it tapped him on the shoulder. No paper anywhere. He knelt down, with difficulty, because his knees were stiff. Then he got up again. No, he would try first the riding-coat. In the inside pocket he found a paper and drew it out. It was once folded. What the devil was this? a crude painting, a sea of purple and some animal, a horse, a cow. But the reverse side was blank.

He sat down at the table and, taking a pencil from his pocket, wrote:

To all whom it may concern.

This is to say that John Herries of Fell House, Uldale, and I, Uhland Herries of High Ireby, met here at Skiddaw House by appointment. After a discussion we quarrelled, and I shot John Herries, he being undefended. After, I shot myself.

UHLAND HERRIES.

September 23rd, 1854

He laid the paper on the table, then unfastened his stock and laid that beside it.

He went to his gun, loaded it, placed the muzzle inside his mouth and fired.

Part Four

Mother and Son

BIRTH OF VANESSA

'EIGHTY-FIVE! Is she, by God!' said Captain O'Brien, putting up his eyeglass.

'Yes,' said Veronica, smiling. 'But you mustn't swear. You swear dreadfully, Captain O'Brien, and I don't think it's at all nice.'

'Do I, by God?' said the Captain. 'I mean to say, Miss Veronica, I'd no idea ... 'pon my soul, I must get a hold on myself. Is it our turn? Damn the game! Always getting in the way ... What I mean to say—'

'Yes, I suppose it is our turn. What do you think, Captain O'Brien? Shall we have war with France? Louis Napoleon is *very* dangerous, isn't he? But of course we've got the Volunteers.'

'Ho! the Volunteers!' shouted the Captain in derision. 'The Volunteers! That's good. Damned useful they'll be. But I tell you what, Miss Veronica.' But it *was* his turn. Amabel, who was playing (most reluctantly) with the Reverend Mr Hall, a bony, black-bearded clergyman from Penrith, had missed her hcop.

The occasion was a garden-party given by 'Madame' to her friends and neighbours on an afternoon of the summer of '59. Most fortunately it was a lovely day – fortunate because in August you never could be sure, the most treacherous month of the year in these districts. But today was lovely indeed, as Mrs O'Brien said over and over to anyone who would listen to her. 'Most lovely! Most fortunate! Who would have supposed? And such a lovely garden!'

The old house was gentle and benign under the small ivory clouds that floated in shreds and patches on the summer sky. The lawn was a smooth stainless green. The part of it that spread under the cherry-coloured wall had been laid out for croquet. Near the Gothic temple a tent had been set up for tea; the servants were coming backwards and forwards from the house.

Chairs were arranged under the wing of the house near the croquet-lawn, and in the shade of the trees by the Temple there were more chairs, two or three, placed beside Madame's. To these, people were led up in turns to talk to her – 'Not for too long, you understand,' Dorothy explained. 'So as not to tire her,

you know. But she enjoys everything. She was never better in her
life. Yes, eighty-four last Christmas. Most extraordinary! But
she has always enjoyed the best of health! She does delight in a
talk! Everything interests her!'

'A very pretty scene!' Judith thought happily. Although she
was in the shade, the sun warmed her through the trees. She was
wearing the black dress with the white lace at her throat and
wrists that had been for so many years now her costume, but
around her shoulders was the beautiful Cashmere shawl that
Adam had given to her last Christmas, a shawl light, soft and
bright, embroidered in silk with a heavy knotted silk fringe at its
edge. On her head she wore a cap of white lace and, every once
and again, she held over her head a black parasol. Against her
chair rested her famous cane. Her face now had the pallor of
ivory, but the cheeks were stouter than they used to be. Her eyes
shone with a startling brilliance. She missed nothing. On her
breast she wore a locket that contained Adam's picture. 'A very
pretty scene!' but nevertheless she thought the crinolines ridiculous. They were not, perhaps, quite so absurd for young girls
like Veronica and Jane, but Dorothy now! Yes, Dorothy was
monstrous. She was a woman of fifty-one and had grown very
stout. Her crinoline was vast and very heavy. It was of Chinese
gauze and had twelve flounces. Her sleeves also had many
flounces, and they looked as though a number of horns had been
stuck one within another. Her bertha had ruches, embroideries in
profusion, and she wore on her shoulders a Scottish plaid which
the Empress Eugénie had made the fashion after her visit to her
maternal home. A graceful woman might do something with all
this – but a woman of Dorothy's figure! And when she moved in
the house all the furniture was in constant peril!

The girls were pretty; at any rate Veronica in white, with her
bonnet far back on her head, showing her really beautiful dark
hair almost to the crown; and darling Jane, so fair, so slender,
although no one thought her pretty in comparison with Veronica, was, in Judith's eyes, bewitching.

As the figures moved across the lawn, in their wide swinging
dresses, white, rose and blue, the sun shining down so benevolently, no sounds save the click of the mallets and the balls,
the murmur of voices, the clink of the china as the servants
(Lucy and Emily – _such_ good girls) arranged the tea, Judith felt
a deep, satisfying content. The only thing was that Margaret was
not so well. Her child was due very soon now, but Doctor Bet-

tany said not for a week, he thought. But she had not been well this morning. Adam was anxious. Strange to have, after all these years of marriage, their first child! And Margaret was not so young any longer.

Ah, here was that tiresome, silly Mrs Osmaston. Mrs Osmaston was thin, withered and weary. She had had so many children that nothing remained of her but a bone or two, a nervous cough and an interest in gossip. She was neither kind nor unkind, discreet nor indiscreet. The only two facts certain about her were – one, that she had been a mother many many times, and two, that she was exceedingly stupid. She was afraid of Judith, who, she was sure, mocked at her when her back was turned. No one in the world ought to be both so old and so vigorous. There she was, a magazine on her lap, and she had been reading without glasses.

'Oh, what is it you have been reading, dear Madame Paris?' Mrs Osmaston asked, seating herself with care in the garden chair. Her crinoline was of the latest fashion, that is, its steel hoops were lowered so that they did not begin immediately below the bodice but only at the knees, and in this way the dress fitted under the hips and only began to grow wider below the knees. This scarcely suited Mrs Osmaston's thin figure, but she was very proud of it and thought herself smarter than any other woman present. And *what* she thought of Dorothy Bellairs! Oh, but she would entertain the family circle when she arrived home this evening! (She could not see, fortunately, the Shade of her great-grandmother-in-law, who, a swearing, horsy, good-natured Ghost, looked out from the Gothic Temple, remembering how she once had drunk tea on this very lawn, and wondered, in her hearty indecent fashion, at this ridiculous Ghost of a descendant-in-law.)

'Yes, what is it you have been reading, dear Madame Paris?'

'Interesting,' said Judith, picking up the *Quarterly Review*. 'There are some comments on Mr Tennyson's *Idylls of the King*.' She read: '*The chastity and moral elevation of this volume, its essential and profound though not didactic Christianity, are such as perhaps cannot be matched throughout the circle of English literature in conjunction with an equal power.*' She paused and gave Mrs Osmaston a sharp look. Then she continued, a little lower down:

'*He has had to tread upon ground which must have been slippery for any foot but his. We are far from knowing that either*

Lancelot or Guinevere would have been safe even for mature readers, were it not for the instinctive purity of his mind and the high skill of his management . . .'

Judith looked Mrs Osmaston full in the face and casting the *Quarterly* upon the grass, repeated: 'Chastity and moral elevation! Stuff! Did you ever hear such humbug and hypocritical nonsense, Mrs Osmaston?'

Mrs Osmaston, who had just been preparing to say that she thought it one of the most beautiful critical utterances she had ever listened to, sent her Adam's apple up and down in so swift a necessity for reversal of judgement. She gasped like a fish suddenly raised from the water.

'Oh yes . . . indeed, yes . . . very absurd. I have not yet read Mr Tennyson's *Idylls*.

Judith wished that she had not been so impulsive. The last thing that she wished was to make Mrs Osmaston unhappy. The older she grew the greater need she saw in the world for general kindness and charity, and the harder she found it to suffer fools gladly. That was why life was always difficult, amusing and exciting.

She knew that now, simply because of this little incident, Mrs Osmaston would go away and talk, like a hen scratching in a backyard. Judith could hear her. 'Not softened in the least by that awful tragedy of five years ago. You would have thought that such a *terrible* thing . . .'

Not softened! Judith's heart and gaze left the garden and the figures moving across the lawn, and she was caught up again, as she so constantly was, into that dreadful afternoon and evening . . . Yes, five years ago . . . when, lying in bed, she had heard first that John had ridden out, no one knew whither, and how then, with a frightened pathetic foreboding, she had lain there listening to every sound, and at last she could bear it no longer but had got up and come downstairs. And she and Dorothy had sat there, waiting, listening. Then the opening of the gate, the rap on the door, the news that his body was outside . . .

And after that, old though she was, she had held everything together. There had been a wild, mad, hysterical letter from Walter; Elizabeth had come, a lovely fragile ghost, and in February of the next year had borne a boy, here at Fell House, whom she had named Benjamin. There had been Jane, too, who for a while had seemed to be mentally unsettled. The poor child had fancied that there was something that she might have done, might have held him there, prevented him from riding ...

The excitement in the neighbourhood had gone on and on and on ... It was only, they all said, what they might have expected. There had always been a strain of madness in the Herries. Didn't old Herries in the eighteenth century sell his mistress at a Fair, kill his first wife with unkindness, and marry a gipsy for his second? Hadn't Madame always been crazy, clever though she was? And all the sorry, stale business of Francis and Jennifer came up again, over and over, and then all the drunkenness and evil living at the Fortress, and Uhland of course was mad – everyone knew – but to shoot his cousin who was defenceless, there on Skiddaw, miles from anywhere – and the little dog had been whimpering like a human being when they found the bodies.

But somehow, by sheer strength of personality, Judith had dominated it all and beaten it down. Now at last the full value and force of her character was seen. For one thing so many of them liked her. She had done so many kindnesses, she was no respecter of persons, the same to one as to another, and yet she was dignified and commanding. She was the more commanding in that she no longer went about, and only visitors to the house saw her, and not many of *them*. But when they had visited her they always returned home with wonderful stories. Everyone obeyed her as though she were a General in an army, and yet everyone loved her. She thought of everyone and everything, and yet could rap you over the knuckles with a sharp word. She didn't care who it was that she rapped. The whole County was proud of her, admired her, talked of her without end, told every sort of tale about her. She was a legend.

And here was Adam coming towards them! She knew everything that was passing through his mind. She saw his quick glance at Mrs Osmaston, his loving look at herself. She smiled back, saying at the same time: 'Well, to my mind there's far too much nowadays of making small children feel that they're born in sin. Do not you think so, Mrs Osmaston?' She liked the beard that he had grown in the last year. It suited him; he looked well, solid and muscular, not stout as she had once feared that he would be. How dearly she loved the half-humorous half-cynical brightness of his eyes. He suffered fools no more gladly than she – in fact, she thought comfortably, they grew more like one another every day. But she could not persuade him to wear his party clothes. He would wear his sack coat and round hard hat, and the checks of his trousers were so *very* pronounced. All his clothes hung about him loosely, and there was Captain O'Brien with his great moustaches and tightly fitting fawn trousers so *extremely* elegant. She did hope that Veronica would not fall in love with him nor with young Mr Eustace, the curate, who with his fluffy hair and surprised gaze resembled a chicken just out of the egg!

'How do you do, Mr Paris?' said Mrs Osmaston a little stiffly; she was no more comfortable with the son than she was with the mother. And why did he wear such very ill-fitting clothes? He also wrote for the London magazines, which made him very dangerous, for you never knew that he might not put you into something!

Adam sat very close to his mother, his big square body protecting her tiny one. He exchanged, in a whisper, one quick word with her.

'I have just been in to see Margaret, Mother. She really is not so well. Do you think that I should send James for Bettany? He is over at Greystoke, you know.'

She nodded her head.

'Yes, dear, I should. Just as well.'

Adam bowed to Mrs Osmaston (sarcastically, she felt) and strode towards the house.

Ah, now, Judith thought, they are moving to the tent for tea. She had an impulse of impatience to run across the lawn that she might see that everything was right. But of course she could run no longer. But Lucy was a *good* girl and Dorothy had sense. And one good thing – she could now rid herself of Mrs Osmaston.

'Tea, Mrs Osmaston,' she said. 'I see they are going to the tent for tea. Mr Hattick,' she cried, her voice wonderfully sweet and clear, 'will you take Mrs Osmaston to tea?'

Mr Hattick was a stout red-faced manufacturer from Birmingham who had bought a place on Bassenthwaite Lake, a very common man. The County was still undecided whether to cut him or no, but he had been kind to Judith and presented Timothy with a fine bay, and if he was kind that was enough. And now it would be good for Mrs Osmaston that she should be taken into tea by Mr Hattick.

She was watching them moving across the lawn with much amusement when an awful thing occurred. Amabel suddenly appeared, and in her voice were the notes of excited surprise and exceeding pleasure.

'Oh, Aunt Judith – what do you think? Miss Martineau has come!'

Harriet Martineau! Of all appalling things! And now, when she was already a little tired and was thinking that she would go in presently and see how Margaret was ...

Alas, Judith did not care for Miss Martineau, and had often congratulated herself that Ambleside was far distant from Uldale. She recognized that she was exceedingly wise, immensely learned, and possibly the greatest woman now alive in England, but Judith did not care for so much learning. She had never herself had much education, she was not a Positivist, she detested the thought of mesmerism, and she envied the way in which Miss Martineau milked her own cows and ploughed her own fields. Moreover, Miss Martineau never ceased to talk – about Comte, about America, about her marvellous Cure, about her weak heart, about her pigs and cows, about her novels (Judith thought *Deerbrook* a very silly book), about Mr Atkinson, about her *Guide to the Lakes*. Miss Martineau spoke always of the Lakes as though they were her own creation and would not have existed had it not been for her. She *patronized* the Lakes. In addition Harriet was all for women taking man's place; Judith did not see how they could possibly do so. They were very nice as they were: pretty Veronica twining Captain O'Brien around her little finger, and Margaret indoors about to present the world with a dear little baby. Harriet wanted women 'to rise up and take their proper place in the world'. As though, Judith thought indignantly, they had not their proper place already. And this was all very bad for Amabel, who said that she did not care for men and would like to be in Parliament. In Parliament! Women in Parliament! You might as well make doctors of them. Amabel adored Harriet Martineau, and was always hoping that she would be invited to stay at the Knoll.

But worst of all was Harriet's trumpet. Judith had, in spite of herself, a little scorn for deaf people because her own hearing was so extremely good. But a trumpet! ... And Miss Martineau was so proud of it. Moreover, in a most irritating fashion, she would remove it in the middle of one of Judith's sentences. Malicious people said that she always did that if she thought that something was coming that she did not wish to hear. However, here she was – in no time at all she was striding towards them. 'Is it a woman or a man,' an old lady once said of her to William Howitt, 'or what sort of animal is it? said I to myself; there she came – stride,

stride, stride – great heavy shoes, stout leather leggings on, and a knapsack on her back – they say she mows her own grass, and digs her own cabbages and taturs!'

She was decently enough dressed today, with no ridiculous crinoline (that is in her favour, thought Judith), large boots certainly, and a thing like a Scotsman's bonnet on her head, and one of the fashionable Scottish plaids over her shoulders. In her right hand she held her trumpet; Amabel, listening to her every word, was beside her, and Adam, coming from the house, was not far behind.

'Well, well, well, Madame Paris, and how are you? I have been for the night in Caldbeck and am to be this evening in Keswick. I am giving an address on Domestic Economy as you have doubtless seen by the papers. And I have brought you my *Letters on the Laws of Man's Nature and Development*. It was published as far back as '51, you know, but Mrs Leeds told me that she was sure that you had not read it, and I thought that I would have your opinion. And here are some peaches straight from my garden. I said to myself, "Madame Paris shall have those peaches because she is a woman I admire. She should have been a man and represented us in Parliament." '

'Indeed I should not,' Judith answered indignantly, and then discovering that she was speaking into the air when she should have spoken into the trumpet, seized that instrument and shouted down into it: 'Indeed I would not have been a man for any money!'

'Would you not?' said Miss Martineau complacently and with a look of kindness at the old lady (for she liked those bright eyes and that independence, for she was as good-hearted and free of meanness as she was egoistic and free of sensitiveness). 'Well, I had no notion that you had a party.'

'Yes,' said Judith, catching the trumpet again. 'They are in the tent having tea. You had better go and have some.'

'Indeed I will not,' said Harriet, laughing. 'I have come to see *you* and I cannot stop more than a moment. My enlargement of the heart, you know, forbids me to stay long on a visit. Old Colonel Albany in Keswick insists on a talk. He says that he has several criticisms to make on my *Suggestions for the Future Government of India*. Criticism indeed! I shall like to hear what he has to say. All these old Colonels are the same. It has needed a woman to tell them the truth about their own affairs.' She kicked one leg in front of her and thrust her trumpet almost into Judith's eye.

'Now tell me what *you* think about India.'

'I, my dear?' Judith shook her head. 'Why, I have no thoughts about anything. I live in the past and not the sort of past that interests *you*, Miss Martineau. My past is all pin-cushions, lavender-water and parasols. I assure you there was never anyone with less opinions.'

'Don't you believe her, Miss Martineau,' said Adam, laughing. 'She is a mountain of opinions. There never was anyone with so many.'

But Miss Martineau had caught only the word 'mountain'.

'Mountain! That's what I said to Coleridge once—'

'Ah, you knew Coleridge,' Adam said eagerly. She caught that and it pleased her.

'Yes. I talked to him only once. Not that I can say that his career is anything but a warning. All that transcendental conversation, you know, was all nonsense. Nothing but nonsense—'

'Yes, but,' Adam shouted down the trumpet, 'what was he like? Tell us what he was like.'

'Oh, very fine – a perfect picture of an old poet. Neatly dressed in black as I remember, with perfectly white hair. And what I especially recollect was his underlip that quivered with a very touching expression of weakness – very touching indeed. The face was neither thin nor pale as I remember it, but the eyes! No, I must declare, although in my opinion his poetry will not be remembered and as to his philosophy – I cannot express the scorn I have for his philosophy – but I never *saw* such eyes. The *glitter*! The amazing *glitter*, and shining so that one was nearly afraid to look at them! All the same, the glitter was only opium, you know, nothing but opium.'

'The father of my little Hartley,' Judith thought, smiling to herself – and in some strange way now, at this moment, while the late afternoon sun threw long purple shadows over the grass, and, behind the temple, the trees, whose leaves were tenderly touched with orange, massed like a solid cloud against the line of faint and silver hills, the thick dreaming figure of the poet seemed to wander towards them across the lawn.

The girls, moving like dancers, came smiling from the tent. In the clear still air the rich unctuous voice of the Reverend Mr Hall could be heard saying: 'Ah, but, Miss Bellairs, you misunderstand me. It is against the rule of my cloth to have a bet with you, but nevertheless . . .'

'Mr Coleridge! Mr Coleridge!' Adam could have cried. 'Come

and sit with us and we will assure you that your poetry will never die!'

But Miss Martineau must be moving on. She was pleased that that sensible-looking child (Amabel) gazed at her with such evident devotion. Maybe she would invite her to stay at the Knoll. Her heart was warm and kind, and it was not *her* fault that she knew such a terrible deal about so many very different things. But, as she wished goodbye to Judith, she thought: 'I should like to become an old lady like that.' Then she stamped away to her carriage.

She was hardly gone when Will Leathwaite appeared and, standing solidly and quietly beside Adam, said: 'The doctor is come, Mr Adam.'

'I'll be with you,' said Judith.

He gave her his arm. Veronica came running towards them.

'Aunt Judith, can I help you?'

'No, my dear, thank you. It is growing chilly for me. You must be hostess, Veronica, my dear.'

They went into the house together, she leaning on Adam's arm, Will Leathwaite following them like a bodyguard. It was splendid to have Leathwaite: he was as obstinate as he was devoted, as scornful of what he did not understand as he was faithful to all that he loved. He loved Adam and all that Adam comprehended, but only *because* Adam comprehended.

'Will tolerates me,' Judith said to Adam, laughing.

'Will loves you.'

'Only because I'm your mother.'

'And what better reason could he have, pray?'

Stopping for a moment in the hall she said: 'Ah, there are Harriet's peaches and her book. I shall eat the peaches and not read the book. She's a kind soul, but I never wish to listen to what *she* wishes to tell me. Adam, I'm weary and shall go to bed.'

It was then that, looking up, they saw the doctor coming down the stairs towards them, and in that one glance the world was changed for both of them. Gone were Miss Martineau's book and peaches, crinolines swaying in the sunshine, pleasant lawns and rose-coloured garden walls. Adam jumped to the stairs and caught the doctor's arm.

'Bettany, what is it?'

'Labour has begun,' Bettany said gravely.

'Well, well?'

'It will be difficult. You can do nothing, Paris. Best stay down here.'

But Judith at once took charge.

'Yes, Adam. Wait in the parlour. All will be perfectly well. I am sure of it. Remember Margaret is a strong woman. There, there, Adam.' She leaned up to him and kissed his cheek. 'Don't be nervous. There is nothing that you can do. Women understand these things. Come with me, Doctor. Is there anything further you require?'

Then there came to all of them a sound from above, half-moan, half-cry. It seemed to break the silence, the indifference of the house as a rough hand tears tissue paper.

'Oh, my God!' Adam whispered.

But they were gone. He was alone. He summoned all his fortitude and turned with firm step to the parlour. Will Leathwaite was standing by the hall door.

'Is the mistress bad, sir?' he asked.

'Yes – no – I don't know, Will. But the labour pains have begun. Would you go into the garden and tell Mrs Bellairs quietly? Don't draw attention to it, you know. Ask her to come in to my mother.'

Leathwaite went. In the parlour Adam sat down on the old familiar sofa with the rosy apples. Nothing was changed, for Judith had forbidden any change. There was the spinet, there was the Chinese wallpaper, the silhouettes above the fireplace of David and Sarah Herries. Only Dorothy's needlework-box spoke something alien. Without knowing what he was doing he had it in his hands, and all his life after he was to remember it – with its polished walnut wood and satin-wood edge, the painted flowers on the top and sides, and inside it a tray painted pink, the wooden bobbins wound with coloured silks, the pin-cushion, the miniature hand mirror, the folding memorandum tablet in a morocco case, the needle-cushion of red and green wool with yellow beads, and a star-shaped piece of boxwood. The red and green needle-cushion he took between his hands and turned about and about a thousand times.

He had known nothing like this since Caesar Kraft had, on the day of the Chartist meeting, fallen dead at his feet. That had been one of the great crises of his life, because at that moment when Kraft had died in his arms he had resigned for ever all his life's hopes of Men's Brotherhood, of some movement that would catch the whole world up into some heavenly universal understanding and sympathy. Resigning those hopes, he had turned to his mother and to Margaret, the two persons in the world whom he supremely loved. His nature had developed a certain cynicism about the world in general. Men were not destined to understand one another and therefore, not understanding, also would not love. Love was to be found rather in the relationship with one or two individuals and in service to them. So he had lived for his mother and Margaret, and in a lesser degree for John and Elizabeth. John's death had once again set him back, for if so fearful a thing could happen so causelessly what was God about? He understood then that there was real evil in the world, that a battle was always in progress, and that one selfish, cruel act led to many more. One bad thought even had incalculable results. He understood from watching so small an entity as his own family that a battle between good and evil was even there always in progress. His was an age that believed quite definitely in good and evil, in God and the Devil, and in so far as Adam shared that belief, Adam was a man of his period.

With Margaret, after that scene in the bedroom here at Uldale one Christmas, his relation had grown ever richer and richer. He discovered that true love between two persons means a mutual interaction of beautiful, gay and noble discoveries. Both must be fine persons if love is to be full and progressive, and unless it is progressive it is not alive. He learnt that Margaret was far nobler that he, richer in unselfishness, in uncalculating generosity, in ever-growing charity, but as she rose higher she carried him with her. Love was this and only this: a companionship that was grander in trust, in humour, in understanding with every day.

He sat there, his broad legs widely spread, fingering the furniture of the needlework-box, the little wooden bobbins, the box-wood, the needle-cushion of red and green. He was maddened by his inaction. He walked about the room, sat down again. Once Dorothy looked in.

'How is she?' he said eagerly. 'Can I not go up?'

'Oh, well enough. The doctor is doing everything possible. No, better not go up just now, Adam. Margaret is wonderful. Her courage . . .'

Yes, Margaret was wonderful. But if she were to go now . . . A hundred scenes rushed in front of him – Margaret lying in bed, her hair spread about the pillow, waiting for him; Margaret singing some German song as she went about her work; Margaret sitting opposite him, sewing; Margaret listening as he read her

some article or criticism or one of his fairy-stories that he loved
to write and was so shy of showing to anybody. All quarrels and
disputes were forgotten, or if remembered had an added colour
and glow because of their intimacy. He crushed the needle-
cushion out of shape, he jumped up and shook his fist at the
ceiling, then creeping on tiptoe to the door like a child, he opened
it and listened. There was not a sound in the house. Where were
they all? Were all the guests gone? The hall was in a half-light,
but Leathwaite stepped out of the dusk.

'It's warmer in the library,' said Will confidentially, and then
relapsed for a moment into Cumberland. 'The spumkey fire's
burning fine – and I've told Jeames to give the mare watter and a
teate o' hay for he was driving her fast to t'doctor. But t'doctor
was on t'road anyway. Lucky thing that!'

He drew near to Adam as though to protect him, and Adam
put his hand on his shoulder. They whispered in the hall like two
conspirators.

'Will – how is she, do you think? It's been a terrible long
time.'

'It's a' reet, Mr Adam. It's a' reet. Dinna fash yersel' now.'

They stood close together, shoulder to shoulder.

'I don't know what I'd do without you, Will,' Adam said. 'If I
were to lose her—'

The two men exchanged a handshake.

'It's not that she's pampered,' Will explained. 'Now some ither
lass, delicate, but t'Mistress – she's strong as a horse.'

Adam went into the parlour again and it comforted him that
Will was outside, as it were on guard. Will always fell into broad
Cumberland when he was deeply agitated, but showed his agi-
tation in no other fashion.

The minutes passed; the clock struck the half-hour. Adam's
forehead now was damp with perspiration. It was like him to do
as he was told. They would come for him when they wanted him,
but his agony gripped his stomach as though he were taking part
in *her* agony, as though he were inside her and she inside him.
The room was dark now. He did not think to light the candles.
He stood in the darkness, his hands pressed the one into the
other, the nails digging into the flesh.

In the hall Lucy had lit the gas and saw Leathwaite drawn up
stiffly outside the parlour door.

'Eh!' she cried and started. 'I didna see ye.' Then hummed,
looking at him:

The lasses lap up 'hint their lads,
Some stridin' an' some sydeways;
An' some there were that wished their lot
Had been what Ann's, the bryde was,
Ay, oft that day.

'Hist!' he whispered indignantly. 'Can't you be still?'

But she tossed her head, smiled back at him and walked slowly up the stairs, the taper in her hand.

Doctor Bettany almost knocked her over, hurrying his little fat body – all fobs and cravat – down to the hall.

As he passed Leathwaite he cried: 'It's a girl! A fine girl!'

'The Lord be praised!' said Leathwaite piously.

Bettany strode up to Adam and wrung his hand. 'A girl, Paris. A grand girl!'

'Yes – but my wife?'

'All's well. You may see her for a moment – only a moment, mind.'

As Adam tore up the staircase a slow smile lit up Leathwaite's eyes and mouth. Then, feeling in his pocket for his tobacco, he turned towards the kitchen, sharing with Adam the position of the happiest man in Cumberland.

SAYERS *VERSUS* HEENAN

ONE of the most remarkable scenes that the London Bridge terminus ever witnessed occurred in the very early morning of Tuesday, April 17th, 1860. The darkness of the early April day was illuminated only by some pallid and evil-smelling gas-lamps. The platform, the offices behind the platform, and the street outside the station were thronged with a pushing, swearing, laughing, spitting, drinking, smoking throng, all men, all happy, all strung to a key of an intense excitement. They had assembled that they might be carried by the special monster train to Farnborough to behold in the fields near by the great fight between Tom Sayers, Champion of Great Britain, and John Heenan the American. Impossible to say who were there and who not in that thick semi-darkness smelling of damp hay and train-smoke and escaping gas, unwashen bodies and morning air. At any rate there were fish-porters from Billingsgate, butchers from Newgate Market, pugilists of course, poets and journalists of course, dandies as well, celebrated statesmen, and even, so it was afterwards said, some eminent divines.

Most striking at the first showing was the amazing variety of smell – decaying vegetables, mildewed umbrellas, fumes of vile tobacco and stale corduroy suits – but nobody minded, nobody cared, everyone was happy. Clothes are of an amazing variety; there are the friends of sport, quite naturally in the majority; there may be a white neckcloth and black broadcloth, but the cut is unmistakable; hard-featured men, spare-limbed, fond of burying their hands deep in their coat-pockets and never in their trousers. Some are in fine plush galligaskins, top-boots, fur caps, and have sticks with crutches and a thong at the end. There is the 'swell', with his long surtout, double-breasted waistcoat, accurately folded scarf, peg-top trousers, eyeglasses, umbrella and drooping moustache. And there is the dandy with lofty heels to his varnished boots, great moustache and whiskers, ponderous watchchain bearing coins and trinkets, starched choking all-round collar and wonderful breezy necktie, and, lastly, there is a certain number of quiet, severe, retiring gentlemen in tremendous top-hats, dignified black with one pearl or diamond in the black necktie, sucking as likely as not the heads of their heavy canes.

The small group of Herries gentlemen going down to enjoy together the great event had members, it appeared, in all these different classes, for Garth, now purple-faced and corpulent (although he was but fifty years of age), might because of his horsy appearance be making straight for Tattersall's. His brother Amery was something of a dandy and wore an eyeglass. Barnabas Newmark (Phyllis' youngest boy, now about thirty, and known to all his friends as Barney) was altogether the 'swell', with his double-breasted waistcoat of crimson and his trousers of the loudest checks (but, as was characteristic of the Newmark strain, he was, in spite of himself, a little behind the time, coloured waistcoats having just gone out). Lord Rockage (Roger, who had succeeded his father two years earlier) was stout, very fair in colour, with light blue eyes. He was dressed gravely as became his position and sucked reflectively the marble head of his cane. (But he was not reflecting. He was thinking of nothing at all.) The remaining Herries was young Ellis, Will's son. He was now a boy of seventeen and strikingly resembled his father, thin of body with the high Herries cheek-bones and prominent nose, serious, reserved and fully conscious of his duty to the world.

Garth, Amery and young Barney were taking sips of brandy from a silver flask and were as merry as merry could be. Garth was for ever recognizing friends and acquaintances.

'Hullo, Sawyer!' he cried to a stout red-faced gentleman in tremendous checks. 'What did I tell you? Didn't I say you'd have a bid for Satan before you'd been on him half an hour? I told you what to do. Just to keep jogging on him to qualify and you'd get all you wanted.'

'We tried him, Mr Herries,' Mr Sawyer said in a deep melancholy voice, 'yesterday morning against Polly-Anne and beat her by more than a length.'

'There! What did I tell you? . . . Well, how'll the fight be?'

'I've known Tom,' said Mr Sawyer, more gloomy than ever, 'since he was a lad high as my boot. Why, I knew him when he was a bricklayer at Brighton. Why, God Almighty can't beat him!'

'Heenan is five inch taller than Sayers,' said Garth, 'and three stone heavier.'

'Why, blast my soul,' said Mr Sawyer, 'he won't bloody well get near him. There's no one on this bleeding firmament as quick as Tom is.'

It was not more than a shed under whose shelter they were all crowding, and the noise was now terrific, the back-slapping tremendous, the drinking ferocious and the oaths Rabelaisian.

' 'Pon my soul,' said Rockage vacantly, 'there's a lot of fellers crowdin' about. And there'll not be a Fight perhaps after all. Wish I was in bed, 'pon my soul I do.'

Ellis looked at him with exactly that look of cold superiority that had been his father's in *his* youth. But he was not feeling superior. He was conscious of a deep and burning excitement and of pleasure in the scene. But he would not show it. He was by temperament intensely cautious and by training suspicious, and, mingled with these two strains, there was an odd element of personless, rather noble philanthropy. He was already persuading his guardians, his mother, Stephen Newmark and Amery Herries, that he would like to assist the Institute for Necessitous Orphans in Wigmore Street, and the Home for Irish Immigrants in Penelope Place. He liked to do good with his money on condition that he need not encounter those whom he benefited.

'Odd fish!' Amery had said to his sister-in-law Sylvia. 'Damn'

generous so long as he don't have to be personal. He'd give anything to a charity and quite a bit to an Italian organ-grinder, but
he seems to me to have no heart at all — no feeling for individuals, you know.'

'Wish I were an Italian organ-grinder,' Sylvia had said with a
sigh, for although they lived now in two poky little rooms near
Victoria Station, they were always quite hopelessly in debt.'

So Ellis now felt a cold distaste for all the humanity surging
about him, but had someone on the platform begged from him he
would have plunged his hand into his pocket and given him a
handful of silver on condition that he did not speak to him after.
He had come down from Eton last Christmas, although only
seventeen, and, after the summer, was to go into the City, in his
father's firm of Herries & Herries. He had all his father's genius
for turning one penny into two, but he was more deeply concerned than Will had been with the magnificent power of his
family. He was, indeed, even at this early age, family mad. The
Herries were the greatest family in England; even at Eton, where
he had encountered heirs of all the ages and heirs with quite as
genuine a belief in their inheritances as his own, he had never
wavered. Howards, Buckinghams, Beaminsters, Warwicks, Cecils
— they had all, in his own mind, bowed before the Herries. His
closest friend at Eton had been young Beaminster, whose mother,
then a woman of thirty-eight or so, was afterwards the famous
and hideous old Duchess of Wrexe. Beaminster said to him
once:

'Someone, Ellis, told me the other day that your great-grandfather was a sort of highwayman fellow who married a gipsy.'

'Quite,' said Ellis, stretching his long thin neck, 'and now see
what we are!'

So today he felt that this fight was arranged principally for the
benefit of the Herries: it was America *versus* Herries. He looked
upon the crowd: they were all off to Farnborough to see Herries
whack America. It was high time America learnt a lesson; it was
not the last time that a Herries would be conscious of such a
need.

The bell sounded and they all crowded into the railway carriage. There was no ceremony about places, and Rockage discovered to his disgust that a great 'labouring-man' as he termed
him, in galligaskins and a fur cap, already far away in liquor,
with a black bottle in one hand and a vast ham sandwich in the
other, was spreading all over him, and even before the train had

started had planted a large red hand on his own elegant stout knee.

'Here, my good fellow,' Rockage said, trying to move his leg away. But he was wedged remorselessly and, as was his fate constantly in life, no one heard what he said.

Garth Herries and Barney Newmark had secured places together by the window. Just before the train started Garth touched Barney's hand: 'By God, young Barney, look there!'

On the platform a great scramble for places was going on. Everyone was good-natured as, in England, everyone is unless it is felt that injustice is being done. There were shouts and cries, bodies were pushed forward through crowded doors by other bodies, there was laughter and singing. A tall broad-shouldered man with a high top-hat, a rather shabby stock, white hair longer than the fashion and straggling white moustaches, waited quietly apart from the struggle. He had a body that must once have been full and strong. It seemed now to have shrunken, under the black clothes. His shoulders were bowed. At the last moment he walked forward and, without any effort, entered a carriage.

'By heaven!' said Garth. 'I thought he was coming in here.'

'Why?' said Barney. 'Who was it?'

'Walter Herries!'

'What?' whispered Barney in a voice of awed interest. 'You don't say!' He peered out of window, but the train was already moving. He looked across to Ellis who was at the opposite end of the carriage. 'Imagine if he had come in here!' he excitedly whispered. 'What a family scene!'

'Yes, poor devil.'

'What did he look like? They say he was all cut up by his son's death. A pretty little murder that was. What do you think, Garth? Was Uhland Herries mad?'

'Mad as a hatter. Young Harry Trent was up North last year and he thought he'd call on Walter – out of curiosity, you know. Besides he was some sort of relation of Jennifer Herries – John's mother. His father was her cousin or something. Well, he *did* call, and he says he never had such an hour. Gloomy house on the top of a hill. I've stayed there in the old days. They call it the Fortress. But it's all gone to ruin, and there was Walter Herries in a dirty dressing-gown drinking with an old woman. Harry says he was very courteous, walked about and tried to do the honours. And then he took him up to Uhland's room. He'd kept it just as it was when Uhland was alive – cold windy place at the top of the tower they have there. And Harry says he began a long

wandering thing about Uhland, said it was all his own fault
because it was he taught Uhland to hate John Herries or some
such nonsense. Harry says he suggested Walter should get out a
bit, do some shooting or hunting or something, but Walter just
said that he hadn't the heart ... Poor devil! Hope we don't
stumble on him at Farnborough. Wonder what he's doing down
here!'

But the train was now in the country. It was yet dark, the land
shadowy about them, but with the running into air and space the
hissing spluttering gas in its grimy glass covering seemed at once
incongruous and even itself ashamed. They had not gone far
when Garth called out: 'Why, Collins! What are you doing
here?'

A large handsome fellow with a high, broad head, plenty of
brown hair, very gay in a brown velvet coat, white waistcoat and
brown pantaloons, was sitting next to Ellis. He jumped up, re-
gardless of Herries, showing himself a man of great size and
strength, and wrung Garth's hand.

'Herries, by God! So it is.'

Garth introduced him to the other members of the family. 'Mr
Mortimer Collins, a friend of mine. One of the most promising
poets in England; one of the most important editors in England
too.'

'Now stop your codding, Herries. How are you, sir? How do
you do, sir? Fine day we're going to have. I've come all the way
from Plymouth, gentlemen, to see this fight, and by God if the
"Blues" interfere I'll know the reason why.'

'He's a friend of Adam Paris,' Garth explained, 'and editor of
the *Plymouth Mail*. Christopher North said he was the best
young poet in England – did he not, Collins? All *I* know is that
he's wiser about dogs than anyone I've ever met and he can tell a
pretty girl when he sees one – can't you, Collins?'

All the carriage looked at Collins with great interest, but
Collins was not at all abashed, laughed and ran his hand through
his brown hair and began to talk at a tremendous rate.

How was Paris? Clever fellow although lazy. Always had his
mind elsewhere, and he'd been running off when he ought to be
working. Always talking of Cumberland, but Collins could
understand that. Collins thought Cumberland a grand place.
He'd paid a visit to the poet Wordsworth once – in '48, it was –
and Wordsworth had looked like 'an old Roman Senator dressed
as an English farmer'. First-rate the Lake Country! Everyone
lived to be a hundred there. But who cared about Cumberland

this morning? He'd have walked from John o' Groats to Land's End to see this fight. Why, he'd known Tom Sayers since he was a lad. He saw his first fight with Abe Crouch in '49, and although Crouch was two stone the heavier, Sayers smashed his face to pulp. And he'd seen him fight Jack Grant of Southwark for two hours and a half and just beat him. That had been a *grand* fight!

He was so jolly in his general enthusiasm and the way in which he took the whole carriage into his confidence that they all felt very friendly even though he *was* a poet. Barney Newmark was especially taken with him because he had always had a notion that he himself might be a bit of a writer. In fact those books *Miss Rich of Manchester* and *Fox and Grapes* (which were declared at the time to be quite as good as Whyte-Melville) and, of more importance still, the *Chapters from the Life of an English Family* might never have been written had it not been for his friendship, begun at this meeting, with Collins. Nor, in all probability, would some of the best passages in *Sweet Anne Page* have been quite what they were had Collins never known Barney.

But now they were approaching Farnborough and excitement ran mountains high. Two gentlemen were so thoroughly drunk that it was little of the fight that they would see. (In fact they never got farther that day than the Farnborough pub). The train drew up and everyone swarmed out. Once outside, a frenzy seemed to seize the world. Light was in the sky, the grass was fresh to the feet, the trees in their first spring green, overhead (Collins noticed it because he was a poet) larks were soaring and singing. And he was the only one, maybe, in all those thousands who did notice it, for, from every side, multitudes were pouring (the crowd was afterwards estimated at three thousand persons), men climbing the hedges, leaping the walls, running over the grass, racing, laughing, shouting. The meadow that was to witness the great scene had been cunningly chosen, surrounded by ditches and double hedges that it might be difficult for the authorities to take anyone by surprise. Already there had appeared in *The Times* a little notice:

THE FORTHCOMING PRIZE FIGHT

HERTFORD, *Saturday*

This afternoon Colonel Archibald Robertson, Chief Constable of the Herfordshire Police Force, made application to the

justices assembled in petty session at Hertford for a warrant to
apprehend Thomas Sayers, the 'Champion of England', and
John Heenan, the American pugilist, in order that they might
be bound over to keep the peace . . .

It happened that Amery and Ellis were separated, as they approached the meadow, from the rest of their party. They could
see just in front of them the broad gesticulating figure of Collins,
Garth laughing and Rockage picking his way as carefully as a
hen in a hothouse. Amery felt his arm tapped and turned to see
Walter Herries at his side. He said afterwards it was one of the
most awful moments of his life. It was not only that he had Ellis
with him, that, so far as he knew, the two step-brothers had never
met in their lives before, but something in Walter Herries' appearance caught at his heart. He was not an emotional fellow,
Amery. He had all the caution of his kind of Herries, and then
some more, but he had not set eyes on Walter for many years.
When he had seen him last he had been stout, jolly, blustering,
self-confident, ready to shout any man down, but now he stood
beside him as though he were bewildered, lost, and as even
Amery, with all his fear of exaggeration, put it, 'he had aged a
century'.

'Why, Walter!' he said.

'How are you, Amery?' Walter said gravely. 'I trust you are
well.'

'Very, thanks. I thought you were in Cumberland!'

'Cumberland? No. Business has brought me South, and I
thought that by coming here I might recover something – might
recover something–' He looked at Ellis without any recognition,
and Ellis looked at him. There was nothing else for it.

'This is Ellis, Walter. I don't know whether–'

Walter held out his gloved hand to his brother.

'Indeed?' They shook hands. A strange emotion seized them
all. For an instant they were so isolated that they alone might
have inhabited the globe. Then Walter walked forward by himself as though he had already forgotten that the others existed. It
was from that moment of meeting, Amery said afterwards, that
young Ellis, he thought, got all his peculiar notions about the
family – his sense above all that the family must not be 'queer'.
No one knew, no one ever was to know, what Ellis had thought
about the terrible Uhland-John scandal. He must have heard
about it again and again, child though he was at the time, for all

the Herries in London were for ever discussing it. The papers
had had, of course, plenty about it, and every decent normal
Herries had felt it a dreadful slur on the family. Young Ellis had
been undoubtedly conscious of this, had, in all probability,
brooded on it. For he was simply the most normal Herries who
ever lived; all the Herries' dislike of queerness, poetry, public
immorality, all the Herries' distrust of the Arts, of anything un-
English, of odd clothes and eccentric talk, met its climax in Ellis.
The wandering ghost of the old Rogue and all his family found
at last their match in Will's younger son. If indeed there had
been for years growing in him a hatred of the unusual, of the
'sport', the 'misfit', how he must have hated the Uhland scandal!
But perhaps he did not realize this disgust of his fully until the
moment when he saw this figure of his own brother, dishevelled,
unhappy, alone, at a gathering so particularly normal, British
and Herries as this one. In any case this is certain – that after this
day he never mentioned poor John or Uhland or Walter if he
could help it. You could not offend him more than by any allusion to them.

All his later troubles and the troubles of Vanessa and Benjamin,
and of the other Herries connected with them, dated perhaps
from this meeting at Farnborough with his brother. It is not
fanciful to imagine so. And that meeting, it is also not altogether
fanciful to imagine, became inevitable when, nearly a hundred
and fifty years before, Francis Herries rode, with his children,
for the first time up Borrowdale.

Amery and Ellis soon joined Rockage, Garth, Barney and Collins
at the ringside. Garth, of course, had friends who were in the
inner circles of Pugilism, so he had seen to it that his little
company had fine places, and Mortimer Collins was with them
by the right of the Press. The arena was a twenty-four foot one.
Behind the ropes a great multitude was pressed, body against
body, and on every face was that mingled gaze of joy, expectation, anxiety and a sort of childish innocence as though no one
present were more than eight years old.

For Barney Newmark, compounded as he was of escape from
all the repressions of his early youth (his father, it may be said,
was deeply disappointed in his youngest son, who seemed to him
to have neither reverence for the things that mattered nor any
discipline of character), of imagination and sheer joy of living,
this scene with the early morning sun overhead, the turf at his

feet, the ardent eager crowd, the brilliant green of the prepared Ring, the excitement of the event, and above all his personal adoration of Tom Sayers, made up the supreme morning of his life. (And, perhaps, never again would he know anything so good.) He had never seen Sayers, but had read every scrap about him since he could remember. And he had never heard anything but good, because Sayers was a grand fellow – serious of mind, modest and unassuming, utterly fearless, generous and good-living. To do the Herries justice – men like Garth and Ormerod and Rodney – he was the kind of Englishman they *wanted* to create. They felt indeed that they had created him, and would not have been at all surprised had it been discovered that he had a drop of Herries in him somewhere. It might be that every man in that crowd felt that he had created him just as he had created this England that was beginning once again, after years of uncertainty, to dominate the whole world. Nelson, the Duke, Tom Sayers – they were all Herries men.

So Barney waited, his heart beating in his ears, his mouth a little open, and his hand resting on Collins' broad shoulder.

'That's the great Tom Oliver,' said Collins.

'Oh, where?' gasped Barney, and was pointed out an aged and grizzled gentleman superintending the last details, testing the ropes, looking up at the sky, consulting with other important gentlemen, inspecting anxiously his watch. For there was not a man in the crowd who was not aware that at any moment the authorities might arrive and the Fight be 'off'. And if that occurred this multitude of amiable citizens would be changed in one brief moment into a howling mob of savages!

It was seven-twenty by Barney's watch. A great sigh of excitement went into the air. Sayers had thrown his hat into the ring and a moment later followed it. So this was his hero! For a second of time Barney was disappointed. Sayers was no classical beauty. His face at first sight was ordinary, that of a quiet commonplace stable-man or agricultural labourer. He seemed slight in figure although he had great shoulders, but nothing, it seemed, of a chest. Nothing extraordinary, for a moment thought Barney. Heenan's hat followed, and a second later Heenan was inside. Then when he stripped a murmur of admiration followed, for this was surely the most magnificent human being God had ever made. Heenan was six feet two inches in height, Sayers but five feet eight, so that the American towered over his opponent. Moreover, Heenan was a beauty. The sun, growing ever more powerful, shone on his shoulders; his chest was superb, his face handsome and distinguished. Sayers looked an ordinary hard little middle-weight, which was what by weight he really was. Moreover, he was eight years older than Heenan.

So that when Sayers stripped Barney drew a deep breath of alarm. How could this stocky grave little fellow hope to approach that giant? The thing was absurd, and he heard comment all around him expressing the same fear. 'The match is a horse to a hen,' said a wrinkled dark man beside him. A big stout gentleman in a very high hat swore with many oaths that 'Heenan would knock Sayers into a cocked hat in ten minutes,' and someone else cried out: 'Tom may beat him, but may I be fried in hell if he can eat him.'

Collins seemed to understand Barney's alarm, for he turned to him and said: 'All right. Don't you worry. It's not that Tom's so quick – Charlie Buller was quicker and so were Langham and Ned Donally – but you wait till you see the force he uses – and his timing! There's never been such timing since the world began! It's the way he moves that saves him. You watch!'

And Barney did watch. He saw Sayers look at his man, then nod as much as to say 'I can manage that'. Then they tossed and a groan went round: 'Tom's lost the toss,' and a large crowd of Americans in Heenan's corner shouted with glee. Sayers now must take the lower ground, but Barney's hope rose again when he saw him stand in so perfect an attitude, tapping the ground with his left foot, his arms down, his head well back, and a smile on his face.

'Oh, God, make him win!' Barney whispered to himself. 'He must win! He *must* win!'

They shook hands and then, as they moved round, each man to his right in order to avoid the other's right hand, they laughed at each other, as cheery and friendly a laugh as you could see anywhere on a lovely spring morning.

They sparred, closed, and Sayers got down easily. Their seconds sponged them down, gave them water to rinse their mouths with, and they came up again. It was plain that Sayers was absolutely confident. He had beaten big men before – size was nothing to him. Heenan led and led again, but always missed; then he got one on his opponent's mouth, and Sayers reeled. Sayers returned but was banged on the forehead and went down in his own corner, whereupon the Americans whooped their delight.

And it was now that the great crowd became part of the fight. Wives, mistresses, children were forgotten. All the trades and all the labours, the small shop, the wide curve of the field as the horses ploughed it, the window at the Club, with the last private scandal, the hiss of the white wave at the boat's keel as it swept from the shore, the call on the bare windy 'top' as the sheepdog ran to his master's bidding, the gossip under lamplight at the village wall, the last climb into the dark wood before the lovers found their longed for security, all aches and pains and ills, triumph and failure, all bitterness and jealousy, all were lost and forgotten as though they had never been. Every man was drawn into that Ring and fought for a victory that seemed just then to be a whole life's aim. Garth forgot his last quarrel with Sylvia when for the thousandth time she had wept and he had sworn, Amery thought nothing of that 'pretty good thing' in Railway Shares that Ormerod had told him of, Rockage forgot his cows down in Wiltshire, Ellis forgot his dignity, and Collins thought nothing of his ambitions that he hoped would bring him from Plymouth and establish him in London as the finest writer of his time. Barney? Barney was part of Sayers' very soul. He had always *been* Sayers. Every blow that Sayers dealt was Barney's — every knock that Sayers got he felt on his own heart.

Only Walter — standing not far from his relations — remained in a world that would not set him free. He watched because something was going to happen. His loneliness would be terminated and he would return to a moving, breathing life from which, since that moment when they had told him that Uhland was dead, he had been always excluded. He bent forward, watching intently, but it was neither Sayers nor Heenan that he was seeing.

Four times Sayers was down, and every time that he fell all England fell with him. Once Heenan got in a severe right, once trying to avoid the sun he slipped, and once Heenan with a terrible left altogether floored him. Nevertheless, Tom's footwork was marvellous, in and out, in and out, avoiding that long arm and always on the retreat when a blow threatened him, so that the force of it was lessened.

Collins was in an ecstasy. 'Oh, look at his feet!' he cried. 'Look at his feet! Oh, the darling! There's beauty! There's movement!' He was beside himself with excitement, gripping Barney's arm, rolling his head to the rhythm of the fighting, stamping with his feet on the ground. Nevertheless, the sun was bothering Sayers (he tried continually to get Heenan to change his ground but always failed), he was now severely marked and had an awful cut over his eyebrow.

Would he last? Many voices, shaking with excitement, the words coming anyhow, could be heard saying that Tom was a beaten man. 'The American's too big for him.' 'He's taken a size too large for him!'

Barney caught Mortimer Collins' arm and in a piteous whisper said: 'He isn't beat, is he? Oh, he can't be! He can't be!'

'You must wait,' said Collins between his teeth. 'He hasn't begun.'

It was then that Walter Herries suddenly began to feel deep down in his loneliness that everything would be different for him henceforth if only Sayers won. Uhland could not return, but life would begin again. That strange cessation of time that for five years now he had endured would lapse. It was as though he waited for a door to open, and, even as, years before, Georges Paris had staked his future on the result of a wrestle on a hill-top in Cumberland, so now Walter Herries held his breath and waited.

'Now!' suddenly cried Collins. 'Do you see that?'

Heenan had sent out a smashing blow which Sayers had avoided, and then, jumping right back, Sayers had landed a terrific hit on the American's eye. It was one of those sliding upward hits, almost splitting Heenan's cheek.

And now Sayers was growing happy. You could see it in his quiet confident gaze, the hint of a smile that played about his bruised lips.

'I've got him now! I've got him now!' Barney whispered, his nails digging into the palms of his hands in his excitement. Indeed, it seemed that Sayers had. Stopping a hard lead with his forearm he dealt a harder one, then suddenly, as though inspired by the kindly heavens, launched out with such a thunderbolt that it seemed as though Heenan's nose must be crushed in. The tremendous fellow was all but lifted off his legs; the Americans in his corner gave a kind of 'Oh!' of wonder, and how the rest of the world shouted, Herries and all! Even Ellis cried: 'Bravo, Sayers! Bravo, my man!' just as though he had been an honest hard-working gardener in the Herries employ.

But for five foot eight to raise six foot two from the ground was no minor feat. Yes, Tom Sayers for all his quiet peace-loving friendly countenance could hit.

Again in the seventh round Sayers struck Heenan another fearful blow which sent the blood gushing from Heenan's nose; so weak and tottering was the American that he grabbed at Sayers' body and they hugged, although Sayers got in some nice body blows before they fell together.

And Barney, in his innocence, thought it all over. The American couldn't stand any more of that; another little tap and he'd be gone, put to sleep for the rest of his natural.

'Oh, he's got him! he's got him!' he cried, enchanted, dancing up and down on his two feet like a little boy, and even Walter, not far away, began to feel as though a great weight were lifting from him.

'I think Sayers is winning,' he said very gravely to a man with a broken nose, standing beside him.

'I wouldn't be so sure,' said the man with the broken nose. 'Why isn't Tom hitting more with his right?'

Barney, in fact, was increasingly aware now from the atmosphere around him that something was going wrong. What it was he couldn't tell. Everything *seemed* to be all right. To look at Sayers you wouldn't suppose that he had an anxiety in the world. His face, that would have been solemn as a churchwarden's had it not been for the twinkling crowsfeet about his eyes, was expressionless and innocent. He had the earnest and serious gaze of a student of Mr Darwin or Mr Huxley. But something was wrong.

'What is it?' Barney whispered to Collins.

'It's his arm, his right arm,' Collins whispered back. 'I think he's broken it.'

Barney always said afterwards that, of the three or four most dramatic crises in his life, that moment when Sayers broke his arm in his fight with Heenan (or a tendon as it turned out after – a happening quite as disastrous in the circumstances as a broken arm could be) was the most thrilling. Life seemed to stop: the world was held in a frozen mask, the air like ice, and no sound in the universe. Exaggerated it sounded later, but that's how it was just then.

And now it was that Barney Newmark loved Sayers, loved Sayers as he loved himself plus the love that he had just then for Miss Nellie Blossom of the Adelphi plus the love that he had for his mother, brother, and sisters, and his French bulldog Louis. All the different loves of his life were concentrated in that little stocky man when he saw him holding his right arm across his chest in the orthodox position as though nothing were the matter, relying now altogether on his feet for his defence and his left for attack, although it had always been his right that had won him his victories.

And then the beautiful thing happened, for Sayers grinned, grinned as though he were greeting an old crony, and Heenan, although his face was marked as though it had been slashed with sabre-cuts (for knuckles could cut into the flesh as gloves cannot do), grinned back. Indeed so completely was Sayers master of himself that, sending Heenan down with a horrible smasher, he used the twenty-five seconds that he might have had for resting in going over and peering into Heenan's face to see what it was like when they had wiped the blood off it. He might get some useful information that way.

Next there was a terrific round: one of the historic rounds in the history of British boxing, when they fought for a quarter of an hour and were, both of them, so badly exhausted at the end of it that they had to be carried to their corners by their respective seconds.

It was after this round that a new element entered into the fight. Heenan was now a fearful sight, for his face looked as though it were gashed with deep wounds. He was bleeding dreadfully, and one of his eyes was completely closed. The gathering of men, who felt as though they, too, had been fighting all this while, began, spiritually, to move in a new world, or rather in a very old primitive one. The tenseness was frightful. Men drew deep breaths and groaned in agony of spirit, stranger held stranger by the shoulder as though he would never let him go. Sweat was beaded thickly on Garth's forehead. Amery could not stand still but kept beating with his fist on another man's shoulder. The betting was now frantic. The Americans kept up a continual roar from their corner, and a strange rhythmical stir seemed to beat through all that multitude, the mass of human beings rising and falling with every movement of the two fighters.

They, indeed, seemed less seriously concerned than anyone else, for once Heenan picked Sayers off his legs and threw him, and then there they were both laughing at one another, and it was a strange sight to see that great American with one eye closed and his cheek in strips laughing as though this was good fun – although a trifle rough perhaps!

Indeed only once in all this time did Sayers show a sign of anger, and that was when he spat some blood and the American laughed. He was stung with that and rushed at Heenan, sent him reeling with a left, and then another and then another! When he hit him a fourth blow Heenan staggered; had Sayers had his right arm he might, indeed, have finished the whole thing with a knockout. Of one blow on Heenan's ribs *The Times* correspondent afterwards said: 'It sounded all over the meadow as if a box had been smashed in'. On the other hand, had Heenan been clever with his right the match might ere this have ended the American way!

It was now that a sort of madness seemed to swing down upon that meadow. Not an ingnoble madness either, for here were these two men, heroes if ever heroes were, laughing like boys at play, and one of them with his face a pulp, blinded, so that he struck his second in mistake for his opponent, and the other had been fighting for an hour with one arm useless, a mass of bruises and fearfully swollen. Nor was their Cause ignoble, for they were showing to all the world that their countries had strength and courage, restraint and control, fairness of mind and an honest cheerfulness, manifesting these qualities indeed a great deal more plainly than their countries often did!

And now all the Herries (save Walter only) were shouting like mad: even Ellis was crying 'Go on, sir! Well done, sir! Very fine indeed!' and with him were shouting many other Herries, the old Rogue with his saturnine humour, and stout David, his son – the best wrestler in Cumberland – and old Pomfret waving a bottle, and young Reuben in defence of the bear, young Francis rising slowly to face his invisible enemy, and poor John winning a victory in the loneliness of Skiddaw. They were fighting to be free, as every man in that crowd was fighting to be free – with every blow that Sayers struck, with every reply of the mighty blinded Heenan, three thousand men drove with them to freedom.

But the spirit of madness grew more powerful. Sayers was weakening, Heenan blinded. They had been fighting for over two hours, and in the rear of the crowd policemen – the hated 'Blues' – were trying to break their way. Once Heenan caught Sayers, closed, and hit him when on the ground. What a yell of 'Foul!' went up then, and the Americans roared back 'No foul!' and the umpire said that all was well because 'the blow was struck in the heat of fighting'. Would Sayers last? *Would* Sayers last? Barney himself now was weak at the knees, his mouth was dry, his eyes burning. He had been fighting, it seemed to him, week upon week. As for a moment he leaned forward, his head rested on Collins' shirt. It was soaked with the sweat of his body. And Walter, in his place, was shaking. He did not know it. He knew neither where he was nor how he had got there – only it seemed to him that Uhland was fighting there in the Ring, and that the moment would come when he would turn to him, crying out:

'Father, you must come and help me. I'm nearly beaten' – a cry that Walter had all his life waited for in vain.

Then, suddenly, came the climax. Heenan had Sayers' head under his left arm when in a corner. He was too weak to do anything but lean on the stake and hold on to Sayers as though trying to strangle him. He said after – and it was likely enough it was true – that he was too blind to know what he did.

Sayers did all he could to free his head, but could not; with his left he got in a blow or two. But Heenan twisted round so that Tom's neck was hard against the upper rope and then he leaned on it. Poor Tom was black in the face and it was plain that he could not breathe.

Then came pandemonium; men were fighting and yelling. 'Foul!' 'Foul!' 'Foul!' The umpire called out 'Cut the rope!' The ringside was broken and the crowd poured in, hemming the fighters round so that they could only stand up against one another. Each hit the other and they both fell down – there, prone, at the feet of their admirers.

The police stopped the fight.

They had fought for two hours and twenty minutes. The result was a draw. The last great contest of fisticuffs on English soil.

Walter moved in a dream. On a wall in front of him that seemed always to be receding, a great cock with a crimson crest was crowing. It crowed and crowed.

A little common man in a fur cap kept pace beside him.

'Well, Guv'nor, that wor' grand. I call that GR'AND!'

'Thank you,' said Walter. 'I enjoyed it greatly' – and went back to the Fortress.

SHE VISITS THE FORTRESS FOR
THE LAST TIME

ELIZABETH, forty-seven but looking oddly like a young girl in distress, confused in fact by her inexperience, stood one very wet morning beside Judith's bed and stared at the old lady with, if the truth is known, a good deal of irritation. At her side, the cause of her worry, stood her son Benjamin, now aged seven.

'It isn't,' said Elizabeth, in a clear sweet voice, 'as though he didn't know he'd done wrong, Aunt Judith. He knows perfectly well. Besides, Timothy beat him when he found out the truth. But he doesn't care in the least.'

Judith in her lace cap, mittens on her little hands, her face smiling and serene, the article in *The Times* about Mr Lincoln and the North and what the Americans had better do next open on her lap, knew two things – one, that Elizabeth wished her to be very serious in order that Benjamin should be impressed, and the other, that she thought it high time that Elizabeth gave up her widow's cap and black silk dress. Poor John had been gone nearly eight years now, and gentle colours, silver grey, dove colour, rose, suited Elizabeth so very well. Moreover, Elizabeth would be all the happier if she married. Mr Morant of Brough was eager to marry her. She was wasted as a widow, and Benjamin was altogether too much for her. Judith was smiling because she was thinking of the other children who had been too much for their relations. She had been too much for David Herries. Adam had at one time been too much for herself. Barney Newmark had been too much for Phyllis and Stephen. But Benjamin was a little different, for in this present time children, whatever they thought in secret, had outwardly to conform. All over England children were conforming, saying 'Yes, Papa' and 'No, Mama', looking up to their parents as to God, believing (apparently) all that they were told about both the creation of the world and the creation of themselves (the first in six days exactly, the second in a gooseberry bush), above all observing Sunday with the ritual and solemnity of a Sacred Order.

All this was correct, Judith supposed, although it had not been so when she was young, but she was now a very old woman and must not expect the world to stand still. (The only question was:

was it perhaps going back? But how could one ask that when
Britain was triumphant among the nations?)

It was Sunday that had been young Benjamin's trouble. He
was quite unlike Adam as a child, for although Adam had been
independent and gone his own way he had given no one any
trouble except when he had disappeared for a whole day without
warning. Moreover, he always listened to reason. But Benjamin
would never listen to anyone, and this was the stranger when you
considered that he was the son of John, who had always listened
to everyone too much. It was perhaps because of John's tragedy
that everyone had been over-indulgent to Benjamin in his babyhood. Poor little infant, born only a few months after his father
had been brutally murdered, murdered by the child's own uncle!
Could anyone have a more pitiful start in life? Had Benjamin
been a delicate, sensitive soul everyone would have approved and
everyone would have been satisfied. But, so odd are the workings
of nature, that that was the very last thing that Benjamin turned
out to be! He was plump, healthy and merry. No one had ever
known him to cry. He laughed all day. He did not of course
know as yet of his father's tragedy, but it was feared that when he
did know it would not affect him very greatly. It was not that he
was cruel, nor that he was heartless, but he had none of the right
and proper feelings. At Uldale, Veronica and Jane made much of
him. Dorothy petted him, even Tim paid him attentions. They
all thought him a sweet little child, for he was round and rosy
and had large yellow curls on the top of his head. But he yielded
to none of their blandishments. Jane was the only one who could
do anything with him, and she not very much. It was not that he
was hard or selfish. He was everybody's friend, would give everything that he possessed away to anybody (they had to stop him
giving his toys, marbles, sweets to the village children); no, the
awful thing was that he had no morals!

That seems a hard thing to say about a child who was only just
seven, but what they meant by it was that he had no idea at all of
the difference between right and wrong. The first occasion had
been when he had stolen the piece of sandalwood out of Dorothy's needlework-box. She had missed it; they had searched
everywhere for it. Benjamin had been challenged, had denied that
he had it, and then it had been found on his person. Timothy
had whipped him, Elizabeth had explained to him what a dreadful thing a lie was, but he had remained cheerful and unrepentant through it all. But unrepentant was the wrong word. He

was simply unaware that he should not tell a lie if to tell a lie was of benefit to him. He laughed like anything when Dorothy, in her vast crinoline, tried to instruct him.

Of course he was very young at the time, and Dorothy elaborately expounded to Elizabeth that very small children never knew the difference between right and wrong. They were born in sin and only later became the children of Grace. But whether Benjamin would ever be a child of Grace seemed to Elizabeth, who knew him better than the others, a sadly uncertain question.

He was for ever in hot water, and at last he committed his worst crime: he dropped a handsome silver riding-whip of Timothy's into a deep empty well at the back of the stables. On this occasion he at once confessed. He said that he wanted to see how far it would fall. He was whipped, sent to bed without supper, lectured. He minded nothing, would not say that he was sorry, and at last was brought up to Judith to see whether she could do anything with him. He looked at the old lady in the big bed and thought how small she was. His round and chubby figure smiled all over at the old lady, and the old lady smiled back at him. This, thought Elizabeth in despair, was not at all what she had wanted.

'It makes it so much worse, Aunt Judith,' she said, 'that it should be Sunday.'

'I don't know, my dear. Do you think that it does?' She drew off her mittens and then with her slender white fingers used a silver knife to peel a large rosy apple. She had always for breakfast a cup of coffee and an apple, a meal that everyone thought eccentric.

Benjamin watched the peeling of the apple with wide-eyed excitement. Would she be able to strip the whole apple without breaking the skin?

'You see, Elizabeth dear,' Judith went on in her very small voice that had a touch of tartness in it like a good preserve. 'I'm nearly ninety years of age, you know, and though I've got all my faculties, thank God, still I do live a great deal in the past. It's very hard for me to tell very often which *is* the past and which the present. You see, for one thing I've lived in this bedroom much of my life – always coming back to it. It was very much the same when I was a little girl as it is now. Of course the wallpaper's changed. It used to have blue Chinese pagodas on it. Very pretty it was. But that tallboy is the same, and this blue tester over my bed, and these charming acanthus leaves carved on the wood . . .

What was I saying? Oh yes, about Sunday. Well, you see, living
so much in the past I don't understand this not allowing children
to amuse themselves of a Sunday. Of course they get into mischief. There is nothing else for them to do.'

This was not at all what Elizabeth wanted. And the old lady
was becoming very garrulous now. Moreover, Benjamin, fascinated by the apple, had drawn ever closer and closer to the bed
and had completely forgotten that he had come there to be
scolded. He was grinning with all his might and, unconsciously,
his small chubby *and* grubby fist was stretched towards Judith.

'There! would you like a piece?' She cut off a section with the
silver knife. 'Now what do you say?'

'Thank you, Aunt Judith.'

'They all call me Aunt Judith. Isn't it charming? And I'm
ninety years old. Well, well ...' She put on her silver-rimmed
spectacles. 'That's the only thing, Elizabeth, that's beginning to
fail me. I can't see to read newspaper print as I did. Ah! there's
another poem about the poor Prince Consort, although he's been
dead six months. And as to Mr Lincoln – the *Times* man says
that if he would only—' She was aware that Elizabeth wanted
something of her. She stared at Benjamin severely over her spectacles.

'Your mother is very unhappy about you, Benjamin, because
you will not say you are sorry to Timothy. You are seven now and
quite old enough to know that you mustn't throw other people's
things down wells.'

He smiled at her.

'I'll say I'm sorry,' he said.

'But are you sorry?'

'No.'

'But are you not sorry to make others unhappy? And do you
not see that the whip belonged to Timothy? What would you say
if Timothy took your soldiers and threw them in the road?'

'He can have all my soldiers,' said Benjamin.

'You see, Aunt Judith,' Elizabeth said in despair ('it is quite
impossible to make him realize.'

A new tone came into Judith's voice, that same tone with
which once she had spoken to Will at Stone Ends, once to Mrs
Ponder, and more than once to Walter.

'Benjamin,' and he was suddenly grave, looking up into her
face. 'Will you please go at once to Timothy and make your
apologies? Without waiting another minute, please.'

'Yes, Aunt Judith,' he said, and instantly left the room.

'There, you see,' Judith said, greatly pleased. 'All that is needed is a little firmness.'

Elizabeth shook her head, smiled, shook her head again.

'I don't know. He's such a funny boy. He'll be going to school presently – that's, I suppose, what he needs. But I am so frightened for him. He seems to have no idea at all as to what is wrong. He plays with the servants just as though they were not servants at all. He is so restless. Jane tries to teach him, but he will never settle to his books.'

'There, my dear,' said Judith comfortably. 'Come and sit down for a little. Benjamin has his own idea of right and wrong just as I had when I was a little girl. He is generous and loving, is he not? And he is happy too.'

Elizabeth sat down beside the bed.

'Aunt Judith, I'm not tiring you?'

'Tiring me! Oh dear, no. Why, it is only the beginning of the day. I can do with so very little sleep now, or perhaps it is that I sleep most of the time—'

'There is another thing,' Elizabeth began.

'Yes, dear, tell me.'

'I am most unhappy about father. Oh, I know that it would be of no use to go and see him. He would not see me, I suppose, if I did go. We have talked of it before and decided that it would be of no use. But now I hear that he has a really dreadful woman there, a Mrs Pangloss – a terrible creature who bullies him and of whom he is afraid. Father afraid! Why, when I lived with him you would say that he would never be afraid ... But it is terrible to sit here and know that he is shut up in that horrible house with that woman. I don't know what I should do, but it makes me so unhappy – thinking of it – being sorry for him.'

Judith stared in front of her. Then suddenly she clapped her hands.

'I know!' she cried. 'I'll go myself and see him!'

'Oh no, Aunt Judith! No, no! Why, it's a dreadful day! It's a deluge – and you haven't been farther than the garden for months.'

'That doesn't say that I couldn't if I wanted to. I'm lazy, that's all. It's an excellent idea. I have wanted to speak to Walter – poor Walter. Yes, it is all over, our quarrel – quite finished, and it has brought misery enough on everybody. Yes, I'll go and see Walter. An excellent idea!'

There was a knock on the door. Dorothy, Margaret, Adam and the three-year-old Vanessa all entered. Every member of the family paid a visit of a few minutes every morning. This had become a ceremony as almost everything to do with Judith had now something of the ceremonial about it. Not that she wanted it to be so. All that she wanted was that she should feel that she was in touch with everybody. She loved them all, man, woman and child – and she also wished to know exactly what they were all about.

Dorothy was dressed for going out. She was in the very newest fashion – a brown 'pork-pie' but with a dark red feather, a chignon, and her crinoline raised several inches from the ground, revealing that her stout feet were encased in miniature Hessian boots. This was the first time that Judith had seen these and at once she burst out laughing.

'Oh, Dorothy, my dear. What *have* you got on?'

She sat up in bed, leaning forward, settling her spectacles exactly on her nose that she might see the better.

Dorothy blushed, but she was as phlegmatic and good-natured as she was stout.

'Very handsome *I* call it. And I am wearing an American Cage for the first time. You've always complained that my crinolines are too large.'

'I don't know, I'm sure,' said Judith, 'why with your figure you should run such risks.' Then, to Vanessa: 'Come here, my darling, and see what I've got for you. Give me that little silver box from the table, Adam.'

Vanessa promised to be a very beautiful child. She had hair as dark as Jennifer's had once been, and large dark serious eyes. She had Margaret's broad calm forehead and something of Adam's humorous, almost sarcastic twinkle. When she had been a baby sitting quietly on her mother's lap she would unexpectedly look at you inviting you to agree that the world, although pleasant, was quite absurd. She already adored her father, and he worshipped her. She had a lovely little body, slim and straight. Baby though she was, she carried herself with a beautiful easy natural gesture, bearing her head high and looking all the world in the face.

As a child she was no trouble at all. Adam had insisted that she should be called Vanessa.

'There was once a Vanessa, a lovely lady. And there was an Irish Dean – and there were some letters . . .'

'Oh, you mean Swift!' said Dorothy, who was as literal as any Herries. 'All the same it's a very odd name.'

'My grandmother,' said Adam, 'was called Mirabell, and that was a man's name out of a play by Congreve.'

'Yes,' said Dorothy. 'But I don't see why because your grandmother was odd you should be.'

'Don't you?' said Adam gravely. 'I do.'

'I do wish, Adam,' said Judith as he brought her the little silver box, 'that you wouldn't wear that hideous sack coat. You are too stout for it.'

'Yes, Mother,' he said, smiling. 'But it's comfortable.'

(And, oh, how she loved him! When he approached the bed, bent down and kissed her, her whole body thrilled and it was all she could do not to put her arms around him and hold him tight to her. But not with all those women in the room. Oh dear, no!)

'There, darling.' She took two sugared almonds out of the box. This was a daily ritual.

'Thank you, Grandmother.' Adam lifted the little girl up, and for a moment the three of them, grandmother, son and grandchild, were caught together into a loving relationship that no one else in the whole world shared.

'And now,' said Judith comfortably, 'I am going to get up. Send Lucy to me, somebody, and tell James to bring the carriage round. You can go in the barouche to Keswick, Dorothy. I am going up to Ireby to see how poor Cousin Walter is doing.'

She knew that this would be a bombshell and she enjoyed greatly the effect of it.

'What!' Dorothy cried as though she had just heard that the end of the world had come. 'Going out! On a day like this! When you haven't been out for months! To the Fortress! Why, you're crazy, Aunt Judith!'

And even Margaret, who thought now that everything that Adam's mother did was wise, said: 'Oh, but, Mother – surely that is incautious! Listen to the rain!'

'Thank you, my dear. My mind is quite made up.'

Adam, who knew that the more his mother was opposed the more determined she was, said, 'Well, then, Mother, if you go up there, I go with you.'

'Certainly not. What should I want you for? It is quite time I had a little air. Now it is settled. Go along, all of you.'

'But, Aunt Judith—' Dorothy, who was in truth deeply distressed, broke in. 'You can't—'

'Nobody says can't to me!' Judith answered. 'No one ever has, and no one ever will.'

'But Doctor Bettany—'

'Doctor Bettany doesn't know everything. It will do me a great deal of good. And there is something I must say to Walter Herries.'

'But you know what that house is. And there is some horrible woman there now. She will be rude to you and—'

'No one is ever rude to me. At any rate after the first minute. My mind is quite made up, so it's of no use your talking, Dorothy. Now I want one word alone with Adam, if you don't mind.'

Elizabeth, who had been listening in great distress, stayed behind the other two.

'Aunt Judith, *please*. If it is for my sake, I beg you not to go. I would never have said anything if I had thought you would have such an idea—'

'That is quite all right, my dear,' Judith said, smiling at her. 'Your father cannot eat me. I am too old an old lady for anyone to be rude to me. The drive will do me good. Now, go and see that Benjamin isn't getting into mischief. Jane will be teaching him his lesson.'

She was left alone with Adam.

'Mother, is it wise? Walter is very odd, they say, and the house in terrible disorder. At least let me go with you. I can remain outside in the carriage.'

He sat on the edge of the bed. She laid her hand in his large brown one.

'Is it not strange?' she said. 'Do you remember, Adam? In this very room I undressed you and bathed you and you asked all kinds of ridiculous questions. And now see what you are! You are still untidy as you were then, and you have that same brown gipsy colour. And you are not as stout as I feared you would be—'

He sighed. Then he looked at her whimsically. 'Aye, I'm brown and heavy but not fat, and I'm not a dandy – and what I am as well is a failure!'

'Oh no, Adam! Oh no!'

'Now come, Mother. You had great hopes of me, hadn't you? And I've disappointed all of them.'

'Of course not,' she said fiercely. 'All that I hoped for you when you were a baby was that you would be a farmer and live in Watendlath. That, I suppose, was the mistake of my life – that I did not go to Watendlath. But it doesn't matter now. That is the best of being old – nothing matters very much. It is very pleasant to sit outside and watch.'

He laughed '*You* watch! Why, you are in the middle of everything! No one does a thing in this house but you know it–' He paused, then added slowly: 'We are rather a multitude here. Let me see, not mentioning the servants there are – you, Dorothy, Veronica, Tim, Amabel, Jane, Elizabeth, Benjamin, Margaret, Vanessa and myself. Eleven of us.'

'And not one too many!' she said sharply. 'Now, Adam, I know what you are going to say. You are not to mention buying that land you were speaking of. We have plenty of money. The house is large. There is room for everybody.'

He looked at her with that deprecating shy glance that he had always used with her, since he was a baby, when he had something to confess.

'I have bought it, Mother. The thing was settled yesterday.'

She took her hand from his. All that old anger that rose in her when she was circumvented, all that old distress and alarm that she always felt whenever he was going away, seized her. She began to tremble all over. She glared at him through her spectacles. She pushed *The Times* away from her so violently that it fell on to the floor.

'Now listen, Mother,' he began, speaking quickly. 'I am forty-seven years of age. I have tried everything and failed at everything. Once I tried to do something for my fellow men and *that* failed. Then I tried to write, and although that did not exactly fail it has never come to anything at all. Mortimer Collins was right when he abused me one night and said that I failed at everything because I could not *stick* at anything. As soon as I was settled anywhere I wanted to run away. I have *that* from you, Mother. You know that I have. Only I haven't the character that you have, nor am I so unselfish. You would have been a wanderer all your days had you not thought so much of others. But I – except for you and Margaret, Kraft and John – I've loved no one but myself! But John's death shocked me. Kraft's death shocked me once and John's completed it. I must settle. If I do not now, I never shall – and there is only one place where I *can* settle. On my own piece of ground in this country. Then I fancy that I still can do something. They all say that I can write – Dickens said so, and Yates and Collins. I shall never write anything that matters *much*, but it will be something. It is not that I shall be far away. The piece of ground above Manesty that I have bought is no distance. I shall come here constantly. But I must have my own place, and Vanessa must have *her* home to grow up in. There are too many women in this house, nor is it fair for Margaret.'

'I am sure dear Margaret is very happy,' Judith broke in.

'Yes, she is happy, but not so happy as she would be in her own home. You *must* see it, Mother. You who are so wise and so sensible . . .'

She saw it. She had always had the capacity to see other people's point of view. But this was the end – the *End*.

She had only a few more years to live. Adam was all that she had in the world. If Adam left her . . . All that she said was:

'Pick up *The Times* for me, will you, dear? I think that it is *most* ridiculous that Germany should wish to have a Navy. I saw a very funny picture in *Punch* last week—'

He bent down and kissed her, and when he felt her body tremble, he put his arms round her. But he said no more. He knew that she would realize this was best for himself and Margaret, and that when she had realized that she would never say another word on the matter.

Nor did she. All the while that Lucy was dressing her she scarcely spoke. When the dressing was finished she sat down in a chair.

'Lucy, did I not hear that you are engaged to be married?'

'Yes, Madame.'

'I hope he is a good man.'

'Very good, Madame. He helps Mr Boulter, the butcher, in Keswick.'

'Oh yes . . . I hope he is sober.'

'He never touches a drop, Madame.'

'Well, I trust that you will be very happy. We shall be sorry to lose you.'

'Thank you, Madame.'

Veronica came in and helped her downstairs.

'Thank you, my dear. How pretty you are looking today!'

'It's terrible weather. Do you think you ought to go out, Aunt Judith?'

'I don't think – I know,' she answered. 'Now you can tell James that I am ready.'

James Bennett, son of Bennett Senior (now with God), a stout sturdy fellow and practically speechless, arrived with a very large

umbrella to shelter her over the garden-path. She was settled in
the carriage with rugs and a foot-warmer. She waved out of the
window to Veronica and Jane in the doorway, and Margaret,
Benjamin and Vanessa in an upper window.

But, so soon as the carriage had started, she fell into a fit of
melancholy – indeed saw herself, a poor little aged worn-out not-
wanted creature, lying at the very bottom of the sort of damp
dark insect-ridden well into which Benjamin had thrown Timothy's whip. Such a mood was very rare with her. Now for a
quarter of an hour she thoroughly indulged herself.

In the first place the weather helped, for it was one of the worst
days of rain and storm that the year had yet seen. From the
eastern sky the rain swung in a solid sheet – you could see it,
slanting, as though in the folds of some thin grey stuff blown by
the wind against the horses' heads. It hissed through the air and
all the ground was running with water; you could see through
the window rivulets of rain bubbling on the grass, and the rain
leaping on the roadway; the wind drove it across the land from
Solway in gusts of lines and spirals and curves.

'Dear, dear,' Judith thought. 'What a day to choose to come
out in after months indoors.' She wondered what impulse had
decided her on this visit; she was so very comfortable indoors,
and this announcement of Adam's had swallowed Walter completely as though he never had been.

It was as though her whole life through she had been trying to
catch Adam and he had always eluded her. Of course he loved
her, but not as she loved him, for she must share him with Margaret and Vanessa. Margaret was an excellent woman and Vanessa a sweet baby, but after all they were not his mother. Here to
her own surprise and disgust she felt a tear trickle down her
cheek. She took her handkerchief and wiped it indignantly away.
It was years since she had shed tears; not indeed since John's
death, and then only when she was alone. But when you were
old your body was feeble, boast as you might to others. You
could not be sure of commanding it.

This decision of Adam's was dreadful. He said that he would
see her often, but he would not. Once he was away there on the
hills above Derwentwater his visits to her would be fewer and
fewer. She cared of course for the others – for dear Jane especially – but they were not inside her heart as Adam was. And
she was not – although she would not admit it – at home in this
new world that was growing up around her, a world of material

riches and prosperity, a world in which the men seemed to be
divided from the women so that an elaborate sort of hypocrisy
sprang up between them when they met. Dorothy was shocked –
or thought it proper to be shocked – if you talked of cows calving
or sheep lambing: Jane and Amabel were quite resigned to being
old maids, it seemed. The countryside was covered with old
maids, and yet, on the other hand, all the girls in the County
thought of nothing but marriage, only they must not say so and
indeed must pretend that they had no notion of the barbarous
practices that marriage involved. It had been very different in
Judith's youth, and she had a sudden picture of herself and
Georges and Emma Furze in London and the things that they
would discuss and that other people would do!

'If it goes on much longer like this,' Judith had said to Dorothy the other day, 'there will be no more babies, for parents will
be ashamed of creating them!'

She disliked too a kind of religion that was beginning to be
prevalent, a religion that Dorothy took an interest in and that
even the beautiful Veronica pretended to admire. It came, she
believed, from Oxford, and Mr Hall and Mr Eustace were its
local prophets. It consisted, so far as Judith could discover, in
talking in a high affected voice, bowing and scraping in church
and professing the saintly life. She believed that Mr Hall *was*
perhaps a Saint – she knew that he gave everything away and
lived entirely on potatoes – but Mr Eustace with his shrill voice
and ogling eyes revolted her. She had been given to read a novel
that, so she was told, portrayed the ideal saintly character of this
religious movement – *The Heir of Redclyffe* by Miss Charlotte
Mary Yonge – but she had found it mawkish and unreal and had
wanted to throw it into the fire. In all this she was of course very
ignorant; she knew nothing at all about the Oxford Movement,
but it all helped to make her feel, when she was depressed, that
she had lived far too long and had wandered into a world that
was not hers.

However, she was not often depressed and she did not intend
to be long depressed now. She dried her eyes, blew her nose and
tried to pretend that she was as independent of Adam as she was
of everyone else in the world. If he *wished* to go and live on a
patch of ground above Derwentwater, why, let him go! How
absurd of her, when she should be thinking of her approaching
End, to be disturbed by what *anyone* wished to do! Nevertheless
the pretence was not very successful. The very thought of Adam,

smiling, untidy in his sack coat, so ludicrously absentminded, so clever (as she thought him), so well-read and wise and learned but so exceedingly modest about it ... she had only to think of him to bring him right into the carriage beside her! And so, after all, it might be when he was living on Cat Bells! He could not *really* be very far away from her!

The carriage was now driving through the storm up the hill to Ireby. She must prepare herself for the encounter with Walter. This meeting with him was in fact no new idea. She had had it in mind ever since the awful catastrophe of John's death. She must tell him, before she died, that their quarrel was ended, that she forgave him everything – yes, even the deaths of Francis and Reuben – and she must try to console him a little and try if he would not perhaps see Elizabeth and his grandson.

As Bennett, down whose cape the water was now pouring in a vicious stream, whipped the poor horses up the hill, the carriage met the full force of the storm. The wind tugged at the windows, the rain lashed them, and she rose to the vigour of it. 'This is the way I like it,' she thought. Something in her bones, that had crept into them when old Squire Tom carried her the first day of her life through the snowstorm, excited her now. She pushed her nose against the window to see whether she had arrived, but could realize nothing because the wet blur of the rain was so thick. Then the carriage stopped; Bennett got down from his seat. With difficulty he opened the carriage door and then had to push his chest right inside to avoid the wind. His rough red cheek, fresh with rain, was close against Judith.

'Well, are we there, James?'

'Yes, Madame.'

'What do we do now?'

'Well, Madame ... best for me t'pull t'bell while you stay inside t'carriage.'

'Pull it then.'

She could see dimly through the window now and thought how desolate the Fortress had become. The building was dark, naked and repellent. The stone seemed to have blackened under rain as though it had been smoked. The wood behind the house moaned and wailed. A pile of earth stood near the flagged path in the garden as though in preparation for a grave, and all the plants were beaten down with the wind. A tree somewhere rocked and screamed. She could see so dimly that she could not be sure what she saw. She could fancy that figures moved in and out through the rain, and especially her fancy, the growing faintness of the sight of her old age, made her imagine that the shape of a woman in black cloak or shawl moved out from the trees and stood motionless, staring at the carriage.

Suddenly she disliked so greatly staying in the carriage alone that she picked herself up, found her cane, adjusted her bonnet and climbed down into the rain, then walked with great assurance up the flagged path and joined Bennett.

She heard the bell pealing through the house as though the place were empty and deserted. She could smell the wet stale smell of laurels and elder bushes. Then the door opened and a slatternly girl poked her head through. Just then there was a gust of wind so violent that Judith, slight as she was, was blown into the house.

She stood in the hall and the girl gaped at her.

'You'd better close the door,' Judith said gently. 'It is terrible weather, isn't it?'

The girl's hair had been blown across her cheek, and she stared at Judith as though she were an apparition.

'I think I'll sit down,' Judith said, and so she did on a hard straight-backed oak chair with arms that she remembered well from the old Westaways house. A cat came into the hall, mewing . . .

'Who might you be wanting?' asked the girl.

'Would you tell Sir Walter Herries that Madame Paris from Uldale would like to see him for a moment?'

The cat came over to her and rubbed against her leg. She bent down and stroked it, then with her two gloved hands resting on her cane leaned forward and waited.

She did not have to wait long, for a door swung back and there stood before her a great fat woman in a mob cap. 'This,' she thought, 'must be the Mrs Pangloss of whom I have heard,' and noticed with great dislike her face red as a ham, her thick bare neck, her big uncontrolled bosom, her long peering nose and other more unagreeable features. Her personal, almost passionate, love of cleanliness made a woman such as this very unpleasing to her.

The hall was dark and the woman stared about her.

'Well?' she said, glaring at the girl. 'What are you standing there for? Haven't I told you—?'

'There's someone—' said the girl.

The woman turned to Judith.

'Yes?' she said. 'What can I do for you?'

'I was wondering,' said Judith, 'whether I might see Sir Walter Herries for a moment. Pray forgive my sitting down, but I am not so young as I once was.' She smiled.

The woman at once recognized her. She said: 'Oh yes? Indeed! Well, I fear that Sir Walter is not very well today and is unable to see anyone.'

'I am sorry to hear that. Perhaps if I were to see him for a moment only—'

'Impossible, I'm afraid.'

The woman stood staring as the maid had done. Judith was so famous a figure that this visit was astonishing. The woman's slow brain doubtless was moving through a maze of questions. What did old 'Madame' want? Did this threaten her own power here? Was there some plot hostile to herself?

'Would you at least,' said Judith patiently, 'tell Sir Walter that I am here?'

'Mustn't disturb him.'

'It is of importance that I should see him – great importance.'

'Excuse me,' said the woman more insolently, as though she had made up her mind that Judith was not to be feared. 'Another day perhaps, but today. Sir Walter is not to be disturbed. I'm in charge here. I'll tell him that you inquired.'

The door to the left of the staircase opened and Walter appeared. He was in slippers and a faded snuff-coloured dressing-gown. At first he could not see who was there. Then, almost knocking against the chair, he stumbled back.

'Why, Judith!' he cried.

She held out her hand.

'I am delighted to see you, Walter. Your housekeeper said that you were indisposed, but I shall not keep you long. Can you give me five minutes with you alone?'

He plainly did not know what to do, and she was so sorry for him and felt so strong an impulse to carry him off there and then from under the sharp nose of Mrs Pangloss that any old enmity there might ever have been fell, dead, once and for all.

The woman did not move.

'Why, certainly,' Walter said. 'I have not been well. Mrs Pangloss was correct. This is Mrs Pangloss, my housekeeper.'

Judith gave a little bow.

The woman said angrily: 'Now you know what the doctor said – that you wasn't to see anyone, no matter who it was, and you'll catch your death away from the fire, you know you will. Sorry, ma'am, it's the doctor's orders, and another day when he's more himself it won't matter, I'm sure – but I have to see to his health. If I don't, nobody does.'

Here, however, Walter plucked up courage; it must have shamed him that Judith of all people should have seen him thus.

'Very well, Mrs Pangloss. You are acting for the best, I am sure, but now that Madame Paris has come all this way on such a day . . . Pray ask Alice to light a fire in the library. That will save you the stairs, Judith. Allow me to give you an arm.'

Mrs Pangloss stood there, looking at them. She never moved and, after they had gone, stood staring at the spot where they had been.

The room into which Walter led Judith had already a fire burning in the grate and a rich brooding odour of spirits about it. A decanter and two tumblers, one half filled with something that was, Judith thought, gin and water, stood on a table. This, she realized at once, had been Mrs Pangloss' sanctum that morning. Otherwise it was desolate enough. A picture of a hunting scene hung crooked on a nail and there was a screen with pictures of boxing scenes pasted on to it. Very little else. Walter settled Judith in an armchair whose grey and disordered stuffing protruded from the seat. A window looked out on to the soaked and neglected garden. The wind whistled behind the wallpaper. Walter sat down on a hard chair near Judith. She was greatly distressed at the change in him. She had last seen him three years before, riding in Keswick, and on horseback, wrapped in a high riding-coat, he had had something of his old carriage and even, she thought, arrogance. Now he had a rugged grey beard, his cheeks had fallen, and as he sat with his old dressing-gown huddled about him he looked more than his seventy years.

'If that woman was rude to you,' he said abruptly, 'I shall dismiss her.'

'Not at all,' said Judith cheerfully. 'She said you were not well and should see nobody.'

'She's a good creature in her way,' he went on. 'She means well by me – the only one who does.'

'Now, Walter, that's nonsense. We all mean well by you if you will let us.'

'Fine words, Judith, fine words.' He drew the dressing-gown closer about him. 'I'm always cold now. This house is damp. You wouldn't think so when I built it, but the damp's come in just as everything else has gone out. What have you come for?' he asked bluntly. 'We've been meeting like this all our lives, but our meetings never come to anything.' Then as though he had said nothing: 'How old are you now?'

'I? I'm nearly eighty-eight.'

'Eighty-eight! Wonderful! And still able to get about.'

'Well, I don't get about much now, you know. There is plenty to do in the house.'

'Yes; got your fingers on everything, I suppose, just as you used to. What have you come to see *me* for?' he asked again.

'I have come for two reasons, Walter. First, I want you to know that our old feud is over. At least on my side. You must not think that I am angry or feel any enmity. The past is dead. At any rate our quarrel is dead.'

He rubbed his finger against his stubbly cheek. 'The past is never dead,' he said. 'You know that as well as I do. When you come to our age we live in the past. It is all I do live in. Back – back – to when my son was alive, when he could walk into this room just as anyone did and say "Good morning". Not that he cared for me, of course – he never did that – but he was there. He was in this house. I could hear him moving over stairs. You could tell his walk, you know, because he limped. Uhland was lame from birth, you know, Judith, and that is what made him bitter – that and my telling him when he was a baby that he had an injustice, being lame. And so he had an injustice, poor boy, and cleverer than anyone in the County. That is why he thought poorly of me. He could see I had no brains, never had any. But it's too late now. The harm's been done, done years and years ago, before we were born.'

He would have continued to talk forever. Indeed he had forgotten her, but she was so deeply touched that she rose a little in her chair, leaned over and took his hand. Even as she did so, she thought: 'Twenty years ago! If you had told me that I would ever feel so tenderly! But what does it matter now? We are both so old!'

He let her hand hold his, which was hot and dry to the touch.

'Listen, Walter!' she said. 'That is what I have come to say. You must not think that you are alone in regretting the past. That old quarrel has done us all much harm, but I feel that – that – that catastrophe eight years ago – it was terrible, tragic – but

John and Uhland by dying rid us all of an enmity, something bad in the blood, that must not come back again. John left a son, you know – a grandson whom you have never seen – and it would be wicked, *wicked*, if his life was spoilt by it. It seems to me now when I am old that we cannot do anything without affecting someone else, and one bad, selfish cruel thing can spread and spread into the lives of people we never see ... I want you now to be friends with us all, to see Elizabeth and your grandchild ... to help us all so that his life at least shall suffer no effects from all that past trouble. Let Elizabeth come ...

She had not been sure that he had heard anything that she had said, but at the repetition of Elizabeth's name his body trembled and shook, he caught his hand from hers and sprang to his feet.

'No, no!' he cried, swaying on his feet and gesticulating with his hands as though he were beating someone away from him. 'She's no daughter of mine and you shan't come round me with all your talk. She left me, and good riddance. She married my boy's murderer. Oh yes, she did! Don't you tell me now! Do you suppose that he didn't taunt him with his lameness, and she too? Uhland knew. Uhland heard what they said, the two of them. Now you can go, and pretty quick too, and don't let me catch you here again ... And put some coal on the fire before you go,' he said, his voice suddenly dropping. 'This room's as cold as hell. Hell's cold – not warm as they say. This is *my* house, and no enemy of my boy is going to sit in it.'

He stood looking at her, shaking, his legs wavering.

'Well, you are an old woman,' he said, sitting down again. 'You can stay if you like, but don't talk such nonsense. You ought to know better at your age.'

'Very well,' she said quietly. 'I'll stay, Walter, but not if you're rude and violent. We do no good by shouting at one another.'

'No, I suppose we do not,' he said, nodding his head. 'I tell you what it is, Judith. I'm not used to company. A while ago I went to London. You didn't know that, did you? And I saw a Fight – a fine Fight it was too, but the man I wanted to win didn't win, and so I came home to be by myself. I said, "Now if you win, everything will be all right. Uhland will come back." But he didn't win, and so what was the use in seeing anybody any more? So I came home, and I'm not very good company. You must forgive me.'

She saw that there was nothing more to be said just then about Elizabeth. Nevertheless something had been achieved by her visit.

They sat close together now like two old cronies.

'You see, Walter, I'm very old – very old indeed. I may die at any time. Not that I mind dying, but I wouldn't wish to leave any bad feeling behind me when I go. When you are as old as I am, bad feeling seems so very stupid – and I hope it won't continue into another generation. Your grandfather, David, used to tell me many stories about my father. Fancy! He has been dead now almost a hundred years! But David Herries used to say that he thought all the trouble in our branch of the family started when my father as a young man sold his mistress at a Fair in a temper. You've heard the old story. It's a legend, they say now, but it was all true enough, I believe. My father was a good man but he had a hot temper. That is perhaps what Uhland had too – but now those stories are all so old and so long ago and there is a new generation growing up. Dear little Vanessa, my granddaughter, such a pretty child. And Benjamin, your grandson – a very lively high-spirited boy. I don't want them to be in any family quarrel when they grow up. The world is more sensible now than when I was a girl – too sensible, I sometimes think, with people like Mr Gladstone and so much church on Sundays. Of course I think young people ought to go to church, but not as a duty. I'm rambling on, but what I really mean is that I want Vanessa and Benjamin to grow up without any hatred. Hatred is silly – waste of time and temper.'

She had talked on, but it seemed that he had listened to none of it. He only sat there staring in front of him, scratching his cheek. She was trying to reconcile him with the stout, cheerful, bullying man she had once known. How could Jennifer and the others have feared him as they did? He had never had any brains, only some instincts, and so he had collapsed under the pressure of events. You must have either intelligence or spiritual faith to stand up against life. When you had both you could be a conqueror. Jennifer had never had any brains, so she had gone the same way.

'Well, I must go now. Will you help me to my carriage?'

She rose a little unsteadily. When she stood beside him her little body was at his height, he sitting.

She kissed him.

Then, to her distress, she saw slow unmeaning tears trickle down his cheek. He did not try to stop them. He did not perhaps know that he was crying. Gently she stroked his rough unbrushed hair, speaking to him as though he were a child.

'There, there, Walter ... Things are not so bad, my dear. I will come again and see you. I am glad that we are friends at last. If you want anything, you have only to send to Uldale. There, there, Walter. Remember that we are all your friends. You are not alone any more. Uldale is no distance, you know.'

He rose slowly, looked about him in a bewildered fashion, then very courteously offered her his arm and conducted her to her carriage.

ON CAT BELLS: ESCAPE FROM ECSTASY

ADAM, turning on his side, caught the light from the window. The morning clouds, fiery with gold, were piling up above Walla Crag. *His* field – the field of all his life with its five little trees and its arch of sloping green – rolled into the glow; then, as though with a sigh of satisfaction, held the light; the little trees stood up and stretched their morning limbs. He looked at the field, thought that it was late (but they had not returned from Ambleside until one this morning), looked over his shoulder and saw that Margaret was yet deeply sleeping, then stretched out his brown hand to the bedside table and found Barney New-mark's letter.

There was light enough now to read by. Barney described Thackeray's funeral:

'... You would have been moved, Adam, although you thought the man proud and sensitive. So perhaps he was, but he had reason to be. Maybe he was the loneliest man I have ever met. One of the kindliest too. I could not but remember the first time I ever went to his house – his table covered, not with books and papers as you might think, but with compasses and pencils, bits of chalk and India ink, and little square blocks of box-wood. He was drawing, not writing. There were no signs of the author in the room, only the appliances of the draughtsman, and when we chatted he would rather talk about drawings than about books. And in what a kind, generous way, putting his hand on my arm, he said: "Well: and how can I be of any service to you?"

'And then there I was at Harlesden and a labourer going to his work said, quite casually: "You must make haste if you want to see him buried." It was a bright December day, everything shin-ing and glittering, a dense black crowd waiting by the grave, and then the hearse – quite a common one, one of those plain, dull, black-painted boxes upon wheels without feathers or any ornament, drawn by only two horses: two or three carriages following, and then the straggling mourners – Dickens looking defiant as though he would like to knock someone down, Cruikshank, Millais, Louis Blanc, and the *Punch* people – you know, Mark Lemon, Leech and Tenniel – a lot more. The eight men could scarcely carry the coffin – he was a giant, wasn't he? Then the short ceremony – thank heaven it *is* so short! – and the mourners elbowing their way through the crowd to take a last look. And wasn't this an irony? There was a heavy prosaic policeman by the grave and as we filed past he said to the man in front of me: "Now don't be in a hurry; follow each other to the right, and you will all see comfortably." Would not Thackeray himself have liked that. The younger men of course are saying that he is already old-fashioned, but I myself think . . .'

Adam did not just then discover what it was that Barney thought. He put down the letter and lay for a while looking out across the Lake to Walla Crag. Thackeray was dead and he himself was forty-eight, and his mother, amazing woman, was eighty-nine; the Americans were fighting one another, and Bismarck was bullying the Danes; he must widen the vegetable-patch beyond the trees to the right of the house, and today he would start his fairy story – the one that had been in his head for more than a year now – and young Benjamin was riding over for the day and night from Uldale. It was the last week of his holiday before he returned to school – and here he was, he, Adam Paris, who had done nothing with his life as yet at all, but was happy, happy, happy . . . here in this January of 1864, in his own cottage that he had helped to build with his own hands under the brow of the hill, and Margaret his wife lying beside him, and their child cradled in her arm (for in the night, when they had returned, she had wakened, climbed out of her cot and demanded to come to them). Well, well . . . and Thackeray was dead, dead and buried.

He stretched out his hand again, this time for a volume of a novel. The novel was called *The Ordeal of Richard Feverel*; it was written by a young man, George Meredith. Although it had been published some four years or so, he had only now heard of it. An unusual book! Fantastically written but new – new in thought, in style and in audacity. And Thackeray was old-fashioned. Thackeray was dead. He rolled over and laid his arm very lightly but protectively over Margaret. They had sailed all the perilous seas now and were in harbour, through passion (but Margaret had never been very passionate), through that strange period of isolation the one from the other, when they knew one another too well and yet not nearly well enough. (That had been ended by the scene at Uldale that Christmas-time.) Then through the wonderful stage of renewed passion and a heightened glorious intimacy. (This stage had included Caesar Kraft's death and the end of Adam's 'Brotherhood' ambitions.) Then, back in Cumberland, out of passion and into this, the real glory of every marriage that can attain it, a confidence, a trust, an intimacy so great and deep and calm that it was like Derwentwater there beyond the window.

She would never *quite* understand him. There was a vein of cynicism running through his nature that was quite foreign to her. Nor would she ever understand his restlessness. Once she had his love and the love of their child, and *knew* that she had them, nothing could ever disturb her again – except, of course, losing either himself or Vanessa. Always when he left her, even for an hour or two, a little wrinkle lined her calm brow. She was not *really* happy again until he had returned. But she was no longer possessive as she had once been. That was because she was sure of him now.

At that thought he moved a little restlessly. Did he want her to be sure of him? Did any man want his wife to be sure of him, and was not every wife unhappy unless she *was* sure? That was perhaps one of the eternal misunderstandings in marriage. And in this his mother completely understood him. In every way his mother understood him, shared his restlessness, his longings, his disappointments in himself, knew him as no one else did. He and she were wanderers constrained by the circumstances of life to be stay-at-homes. Had he not married Margaret what a useless, worthless wanderer he would have been! Like his old legendary grandfather! Yes, he had been lucky to marry a woman like Margaret, so good and loyal, faithful and true. Once he would have been wearied and irritated by too much goodness and fidelity.

He got out of bed very quietly and went down to the yard behind the house for Will to sluice him down.

Although it was early January and mortal cold, he did not shrink from the sluicing. The yard was hidden from the world save for the little wood on the rise of the ground.

No windows looked on it, and it was sheltered from the winds. Will was already there, cleaning the boots and hissing away at them like a hostler. He straightened himself when he saw Adam and stood up, grinning, his yellow forelock straggling over his forehead, his eyes as blue, direct and unflinching as those of an honest and fearless child, his body balanced easily on its strong legs.

'I'm late this morning, Will.'

'Aye. You was late last night.'

'Lovely day.'

Will looked up. The sky was blue and laced everywhere with little clouds that still had tints of amber and rose.

'Cold this morning,' Adam said.

He looked at Will with great affection. The whole day started wrongly if he did not have a brief talk alone with Will at the beginning of it, for his relation with Will was that of man to man, rid of all the uncertainties, sudden crises, sudden darknesses that haunt like ghosts the relation of the sexes. In a way Will understood him better than did either his mother or Margaret. In a way Will loved him better than did either of the women, for it was a love completely unselfish, that asked nothing in return, that was disturbed by no moods or reticences. When Adam was in a temper or caught into some creative distance far from all human agency or had a cold or a headache or felt his liver, Margaret was disturbed as though she were in danger of losing something (although she had learnt to conceal this disturbance, Adam knew that it was there and it irritated him), but Will was unchanged. Let Adam have what mood he wished, Will loved him just the same. He could be jealous, and was often confoundedly obstinate and pig-headed, but his loyalty, devotion, trustworthiness never varied a hair's breadth.

Two wooden buckets filled with cold water stood side by side. Adam threw off his shirt and breeches, then shivered as the cold air struck his bare flesh.

'Quick, Will. Quick, you devil!'

Will took up one bucket in his two arms and with a heave threw the water over Adam. Then the other. Then quickly he caught a rough towel that was hanging on the back of the kitchen door, seized Adam and rubbed him with great violence, hissing furiously.

Adam ran into the kitchen and stood naked in front of the roaring fire. Now he was glorious. He was in fine condition. Drops of water clung to his beard and his hairy chest. His flesh was firm and strong. His heart beat like a good steady hammer. He took deep breaths. Will watched the operation with high satisfaction.

'You know, Will,' Adam said, stretching out his bare arms, 'my mother has told me that her father used to have his man swill him down at Rosthwaite where he lived, in just this way. He was a queer character, he was. My mother has a heap of tales about him from his son, her stepbrother. He was years older than she was – David Herries, I mean. And now she's nearing ninety. Takes you back a long time, doesn't it?'

'Aye,' said Will. 'It does that. We're born and we're wed and we're dead before we know. 'Tis odd when you think of it, Mr Adam, that folk make the fuss they do when they're dead so quick. About little things, I mean. Now there was that man from Seathwaite last evening. Was in here with a long tale about a cow he'd lost. I told him not to fret and he was furious, as though I'd stolen the damned cow myself. Mary will be in likely. I can hear her coming.' This was the old woman from the farm halfway to Grange. She came every day as help.

Adam pulled on his shirt and breeches and went upstairs.

Later he was sitting in his room waiting to begin his fairy story. This room – not very large – was square, papered a dull rather shabby red, and the two windows looked full on to the Lake and Walla Crag. The wall opposite the windows was lined with shelves, and there were his books, not a great collection, some four or five hundred in all.

They were, moreover, a mixed lot, in no sort of order. A faded row of little blue volumes of the *Ilaid* and *Odyssey* had for companions *Pickwick* in its shilling parts (the covers of some of the numbers disgracefully torn), Rogers' *Italy* with the handsome illustrations, Arthur Young's *Travels in France* and Leigh Hunt's *Story of Rimini*. There were thirty volumes of the 'English Poets', ten of Chaucer, *Sir Charles Grandison* and *Tristram Shandy*. On the table at his side were two volumes of *Richard Feverel*, Huxley's *Man's Place in Nature*, and *The Woman in White*. By itself on the other side of him was a fresh brilliant copy in green and gold of Barney Newmark's first novel* – *Dandy Grimmett* – in three volumes.

* *Dandy Grimmett*, by Barnabas Newmark: 3 vols, Suller & Thorne 1863.

'They have bound young Barney very handsomely,' he thought. (He still looked on Barney as an infant although he was now nearly thirty-four years of age.) He felt a pang of envy, regret, sadness. There was young Barney, of whom no one had thought very much, publishing his first novel and some of it not bad either, especially the racing scenes, the fight (plainly taken from Sayers and Heenan), and the last chapter when old Dandy, dying, is brought back to his rooms in London and hears the carriages rolling to the theatres, the cries of the newsboys, and the thick heavy ticking of the clock on the marble mantelpiece. He's been influenced by Thackeray, of course – not doing anything new like this young man Meredith. But is it important to be new? Nothing is new but superficials. He can paint a scene that is real. He knows his world . . . Damned clever sketch of his father, old Stephen. He'd deny it, of course . . .'

His mind went floating away to the lake that lay in the morning sun like a snake's skin, grey and rippled, convulsed, it seemed, with little shudders. The sunlight hung above it on the flanks of the hill as though afraid to descend. He pushed open the window and looked out, heard the stream running at the back of the house, smelt the dead bracken, the gritty flakiness of the dead earth, and saw a snowdrop, solitary and beautiful, bend its stem in the breeze.

He heard Vanessa calling. His heart warmed. It was all he could do not to go out to her, but he knew that once he had left that room incident after incident would occur to prevent his return to it, as though a malicious Fate were determined for ever to hold him back from doing anything. With a sigh he closed the window and went back to the table. He picked up a number of *London Society* that had just arrived and read from the serial story:

' "*Nor need you wish to do so, Miss Fleming*," *said Jane quickly*. "*Nor, if you were thrown on the world, would you ever be what Milly and I are now. We have had unusual advantages from our cradles, and with great natural aptitude, have improved them to the uttermost*." '

He sighed again. 'Great natural aptitude . . .' 'Impoved them to the uttermost.' No, people did not talk like that. Why were novels so silly?

But this seemed to encourage him. *He* was going to write a fairy story. He sat down resolutely, drew the paper in front of him and wrote in his firm strong hand:

THE DWARF WITH THE PURPLE COMB*

He sat, looking out of window, biting the feather of his quill. Then he was off and away!

Once upon a time there was a King who had five lovely daughters. The names of the five Princesses were Hazel, Rosamond, Amaryllis, Mellicent and Mary. Mary was the youngest and she was not given so grand a name as the others because the King, her father, had wanted to have a son and was so grievously disappointed when the Doctor told him that the baby was a girl that he shut himself into his bedroom for four and a half days and refused to see anybody, even the Queen. He lived all that time on bread and water. So at least it was said. But Fortunatus, the son of the Woodcutter in the Forest near by, saw the Palace gardener climb on a ladder and hand through the King's bedroom window a gold tray that had on it a gingerbread cake, a roast goose, a Christmas pudding and a dish with oranges, plums and apricots.

Fortunatus told his father, the Woodcutter, what he had observed, and his father said that he must never mention it to anyone or he would lose his head. Mary, who was the loveliest child ever seen – she had hair as dark as the ravens and a smile so sweet that everyone at the Court loved her – was always punished when her sisters did anything wrong. For example, one fine morning Princess Rosamond was given a beautiful dress by her Fairy Godmother (it was her birthday). The dress was made of tissue and silver and it had buttons of green jade, a collar of emeralds, and the sleeves were decorated with the feathers of the Bird of Paradise. When Princess Mellicent saw this beautiful dress she was so angry because *her* Fairy Godmother had given her on *her* birthday only a needlework-case. So she took the gold scissors from her needlework-case and when Princess Rosamond was practising the piano in the Green Drawing-room she went into her sister's bedroom and cut the beautiful dress into shreds.

Now when this was discovered and Mellicent had confessed to what she had done, Mary was put to stand in the corner of the Audience Chamber with her face to the wall so that everyone who passed by could see her.

* *The Dwarf with the Purple Comb, And other Stories;* by Adam Paris, Harris & Sons, 1865.

It happened then one fine morning that Fortunatus, the Woodcutter's son, was sent by his father to the Palace with a wheelbarrow full of logs for the Royal fireplaces, and, peeping in (for he was a very inquisitive boy) at the door of the Audience Chamber, he saw the lovely little Princess standing with her face to the wall . . .

Little Vanessa ran down the path and up the road. It was time for Benjamin to be coming, and from the corner where the stream ran from the tops straight like a silver arrow into the Lake you could watch the higher bend of the road. She danced about, clapping her hands because it was cold.

She was wearing a dress of green and black checked taffeta, which was the new material. She was immensely proud of it and had begged to be allowed to wear it because Benjamin was coming. She was already tall for her age, carried herself to her full height, and now, when she was dancing, every movement was natural in its grace as the silver pattern of the stream, the dull amber of the dead bracken and the bare wood whose trees were flushed in the distance like an evening sky against the grey Lake filmed with ice. Skiddaw and Blencathra were powdered with snow, and hard round clouds like snowballs hung above their lines. Vanessa's mind was intently fixed on Benjamin. Although he was over four years older she thought that he was a perfect companion. She was even then an excellent listener; her curiosity was acute, and she could never be told enough about anything if someone wanted to tell her. Benjamin told her the most extraordinary things. Everything that happened at Uldale was of absorbing interest to her, and she spent so much of her time with grown-up people – her mother and father, Will, and Mary from the farm – that although she was entirely a child and in many things still a baby, she understood the *lives* of grown-up people, knew why they did things and could *imagine* their world. Her grandmother – the old lady who was as smart as a pin, all white and black (and the very *whitest* of white!) with her cap, her ivory cane, her shoes with the silver buckles, who was so kind, amusing, understanding, but could, all in a moment, be so sharp and commanding (very like the Queen of England) – was to Vanessa simply the most miraculous person in the world, composed of magic, fire, ice, diamonds. There she was in her room, older than anyone had ever been, but more acquainted with all that Vanessa was thinking than anyone save her mother. Then

there was Aunt Jane, the nicest of all the Aunts. Aunt Veronica
who was beautiful, Aunt Amabel who could throw a ball like a
boy, Uncle Timothy who was so big that he could take the whole
of you in his hand if he wished, Aunt Dorothy who was always
busy, James the coachman, Daniel the stableman, Martha the
cook – and so on, so on – a whole *world* was in Uldale. One could
never have enough of it.

And Benjamin was her Uldale storyteller. She would like him
to go on for hours telling her things, but he could never be still,
never stay in one place more than five minutes. And Vanessa
thought this unusual, because his mother, Aunt Elizabeth, was so
quiet. She would sit all evening in the same corner of the sofa
reading a book – only often, as Vanessa had noticed, she was not
reading, but would put down her book and sit staring in front of
her. Benjamin had no father, which, Vanessa thought, was terribly sad for him.

Ah! there Benjamin was! He came trotting round the corner
on Albert, his pony (named after the Prince Consort, who had
died the very month that Uncle Timothy gave it him). Mumps
the dog was running at the side. Mumps loved Benjamin, and
even now, when he was ten years old or more, would never leave
Benjamin's side could he help it. The boy saw Vanessa and
waved his riding-whip. When he came up to her he burst out
laughing. His round, plump face was crimson with the cold air
and the exercise, and his funny small nose needed wiping.

'You're wearing a new dress!' he shouted.

'Yes,' she said, still dancing. 'And there's ice on the Lake. It
will be frozen perhaps tomorrow – enough to skate on.'

They went up the path to the cottage, and as soon as Benjamin
was off the pony he felt in his coat-pocket and produced a large,
very sticky chunk of toffee.

'Have some!' he said, trying to break it.

'Did Uncle Timothy give it you?'

'No. I stole it from the kitchen. Mother said I wasn't to have
any because I was sick last time from eating so much, so I had to
get it from the kitchen, and Martha nearly caught me.'

Benjamin always puzzled Vanessa in this way, because he was
for ever doing things that he was told not to do. When he was
caught he never lied nor did he seem in the least to mind punishment, but it appeared that you had only to make a rule for him
to want to break it.

However, she took some of the toffee and, with their mouths

full, they went round to the back to put the pony up and see Will.
When they were in the back-yard Benjamin turned a somersault.
He had just learned to do it. 'There's a boy at school called
Turnip,' he explained. 'And he can do it and he said I couldn't,
so now I can.'

'What a funny name to have!' she remarked.

'They call him that because his *real* name is Turner – see?'
Benjamin said, turning head over heels again.

In the living-room of the cottage Adam had few books, but he
had been given two things out of the parlour at Uldale and these
he prized over all his other possessions – one was the old spinet
with roses painted on its lid, the other the music-box with the
Queen in her green dress and the King in his amber coat. When
Judith, growing too old to argue violently with Dorothy, saw
that big heavy new furniture was coming into the parlour do
what she would, she insisted that Adam should have the spinet
for his cottage. She would have given him the sofa with the red
apples also had she not felt a superstition. Her hand had rested
on that when she had made her great decision . . .

Adam's living-room had not much furniture. There were the
wax flowers that he had bought Margaret at the Pantheon. The
square carpet had eight groups of flowers on a light pink ground.
There were three carved mahogany chairs with needlework seats
and backs. There was a chiffonnier bookcase, brown and gold
with marquetry panels. These things had been presents from
various members of the family. Carey Rockage's wife had given
him two cornucopias, Will Herries the bookcase. On the walls
against some very variegated wallpaper was a watercolour called
'The Lady of the House', an engraving of Watendlath, and a
Baxter print, 'Dippers and Nest'. In one corner of the room was
Vanessa's joy, a Peepshow of the Central Hall at the Great Exhibition. Over the mantelpiece was hung a Sand Picture, 'Saddle
Horse', by James Zobel. Barney Newmark had given him this one
Christmas. So the room was an odd jumble, and he didn't care
for anything in it save the music-box and the spinet. But it was in
this room and among these things that he experienced a little
scene with young Benjamin. He had reached a point in his fairy
story where the Dwarf had tapped on the Princess Mary's
window. The Palace Garden was flooded with moonlight. She
came to the window, and, standing on top of the ladder, he
whispered to her that, if she would come with him, he would take

her to the orchard and there, hidden in the ground at the roots of
an old apple tree, he would find for her the Purple Comb . . .

At that point everything had ceased. He could see no more the
Princess, the Dwarf, young Fortunatus. All had vanished, the
Lake rippled under its silver shading of ice, and Blencathra had
the bloom of a plum. Soon it would be time for the meal. He was
hungry, so, rubbing his hands, he went into the living-room. A
moment later Benjamin came in.

'Uncle Adam,' he asked, 'can you wrestle?'

'No,' he said.

'Try,' said Benjamin, and without a moment's warning he
pushed himself on to Adam. He butted his stomach with his
round head, tried to bring his arms together around Adam's
broad thighs, twisted his small legs round Adam's thick ones. He
put a ferocious energy into this, blowing and grunting, straining
every muscle in his body. For a moment he made Adam rock.
Adam could feel the muscles of the boy's leg strung to their
utmost against his calf. The two small hands tore at his waistcoat. A button flew off. The hands groped inside his shirt,
pinched his flesh.

'Hi!' he called out. 'That's enough! You're hurting!'

'I'll do it! I'll do it!' Benjamin gasped. 'I'll bring you down!'

Adam, laughing, put out his arms, caught the boy to him with
a bear's hug, then swung him into the air and held him there.

'Now what will you do?'

Benjamin kicked. Then he was rolled on to the floor, lay there
for a moment panting.

'Things look funny from here,' he observed. He got up. 'I
haven't it right yet. There's a trick you do with your left leg. Next
time I shall manage it.' His hair was dishevelled, his cheeks crimson, his shirt open. He grinned.

'You have torn one of my buttons off,' Adam said.

'Oh, that's all right. Aunt Margaret will sew it on for you.'

He came close to Adam, leaned against him, looked up at him,
smiling, but with a strange mature glance.

Adam said: 'Are you liking school? I hear that you were in all
kinds of trouble the last term. Why was that?'

Benjamin nodded.

'I can't help it, Uncle Adam. If anyone tells me to do anything
I don't want to do it.'

'Why's that?'

'I don't know. I expect it's because my uncle killed my father.

There isn't another boy in the whole school whose uncle killed his father.'

The words came out quite easily, with no sense of self-consciousness, no unhappiness – a clear statement of simple fact. To Adam those words were like thunder in his ears. The floor seemed to rock. He didn't know that the boy had any notion of the way that his father had died. They had, all of them, for years been in a conspiracy to prevent any allusion to it before the boy, and although at first it had seemed a vain hope that he should not hear, as the years passed they all thought that they had succeeded, for when Benjamin spoke of his father it was quite naturally. He seemed to believe that he had died of some illness just like any other man.

Benjamin nodded.

'You thought I didn't know. I have known for years and years and years. First a farmer at Peter's House told me. I know just what they did. They rode through the mist to Skiddaw House. They had arranged it all, and my uncle shot my father and then shot himself. And my father hadn't a gun. So you see I'm different from all the other boys, and I'll be different all my life.'

Adam did not know what to say. He moved off and looked out of window. Then he turned round.

'Your father,' he said, 'was a very fine man and I loved him. He always did the right thing and so must you.'

Benjamin answered quickly, as though he were speaking in someone's defence.

'I love my father more than anyone, and if I had been there with him I would have taken the gun from my uncle and shot him, and all my life I'll kill men like my uncle who are beasts and cowards. I don't care. I'm not afraid of anyone, and I'll never do something just because someone tells me . . .' His voice suddenly was the voice of a small boy. 'I'll be like Robin Hood. He was an outlaw and I'll be an outlaw. I have a band of outlaws under me at school and we're not afraid of anybody.'

To Adam there came a quick picture of a wood, a pool, a man on a white horse and himself dancing in defiance of that rider's whip . . .

He came across the floor to Benjamin and put his arm around him.

'I was like that myself once and now I'm an old gentleman who writes fairy stories. The great thing,' he went on, holding the boy close to him, 'is not to be bitter against life because of what happened to your father. Don't allow things that have happened in the past, Benjamin, to spoil your life. The past is past. They are ghosts, all those dead men.'

'My father is not a ghost,' Benjamin said. 'I have his picture and a riding-whip he had and his hairbrushes. I took the hairbrushes out of Mama's room and I've hidden them. No one knows where they are but me. And one day I shall meet someone like my uncle and I will shoot him just as he shot my father, except that he shall have a gun, so that it's fair.'

Adam shook his head. 'That's no good,' he said. 'Because a wrong was done once, to do another wrong doesn't make things better.'

'Look here, Uncle,' Benjamin said. 'I can make a somersault. I *think* I can make two now. Here! Look!' and he turned two somersaults, one after the other, in the space between the chairs and the table. He tumbled straight into old Mary who was helping Margaret to bring in the meal.

Had Benjamin affected him? When they were sitting after the meal quietly watching the sunlight stain the flowers of the carpet, the gilt of the bookcase, and strike, as though maliciously, the simpering self-importance of 'The Lady of the House', he felt a curious and abnormal ecstasy of perception. It seemed to him that his senses were all tingling with an extra activity.

Margaret, opposite him, was making a basket cover in old silk patchwork. On a ground of dark green she was forming a kaleidoscope pattern of glittering scraps – flakes of crimson, sea-green, primrose, hyacinth blue, the rose of apple orchards, the gold of corn. On the grey stuff of the lap of her dress the fragments of silk lay scattered, her look so serenely safe and happy that it caught at his heart. Once and again she would glance up at him and smile. Vanessa and Benjamin were stretched on the floor, their heads together, looking at a book of Japanese drawings. From where he sat he could see the brilliant figures of birds and men in blue and crimson carrying burdens over bridges and the wide expanse of purple seas. Everything was colour and everything was peace. Tiny details seemed to wear a heightened significance, the buttons on Vanessa's dress, freckles on Benjamin's snub nose, the needlework pattern on the chairs.

He was filled with a kind of immortal ecstasy. This he had achieved. Through all the disappointments and failures of his life he had caught this and held it – love, fatherhood, security. The patch of ground upon which his feet were set was his, this hill, the silver birch gleaming in the sun beyond the window, the stream of music he could hear, this Cumberland that all his life long he had worshipped, and beyond it England, the hills running to the sea, the valleys running to the South, all this land that, now that he had his home, flowed to the North, South, East and West. Running from his door to all the seas, his for ever and ever, although his realization of it lasted only for a moment.

His happiness caught him at the throat. His eyes were blinded. He moved in his chair, and Margaret looked across at him and smiled.

Then Benjamin glanced up at them and sprang to his feet.

'I want to go out! Come along, Vanessa! I'll race you!'

They opened the doors and ran out into the garden.

It was as though he had himself spoken. He felt suddenly that his security was dangerous. He did not want it. He was bound, a prisoner. Somewhere, a small child, he was running, running, escaping, shouting, and his mother was with him. Panting, they raced up the hill to see the sun rise. The woods fell below them, the Tarn was dark, and he could hear the sheep rustling past him up the dark path. His mother was a gipsy and he was her gipsy son. He could see the lights from the painted carts – a horse neighed . . . waving his arms and shouting he breasted the hill . . .

He woke as though he had been sleeping, and saw Margaret choosing the colours from the fragments of silk, holding a scrap of rose against the light to see how it would do . . .

'I'll be back, Meg,' he said.

He went to the door and almost ran from the house. He began to climb through the dead bracken above his stone wall. As he mounted he heard the voices of the children from the garden, a cart was creaking down the road that was already a white ribbon. The Lake rose and he saw that the sun had veined it with patterns of light, here there were pools of grey and ashen pallor and there deep shadows of saffron – all confined by the hills, Skiddaw, Saddleback, Walla Crag. As he climbed, the Lake and the hills climbed with him. The air was cold like a whip, but so fresh that it struck his cheeks as the water had done when Will sluiced him that morning.

Then he began to run, he called aloud, he shouted. He

stumbled and fell over the stones and thought how old Rackstraw had told him once: 'Clouds and stones! Stones and clouds! That's what this country is!'

His breathing hurt him like a knife, for he was no child now but a stout middle-aged man with a beard and middle-aged habits of comfort and laziness. But he liked the catch at his lungs, the bruise on his knee where the stone had hit him. He climbed, stumbling, waving his arms, turning to catch the Lake and the hills with him and draw them up. He did not know that he was climbing like a madman, climbing as he had never climbed that hill before, because he was part of the hill, the wind, the sun. He hurled himself over the last boulders and flung himself on the strong, resilient turf, lying there at full length, his arms spread out, his chest heaving. Why should he ever return? Something wild and authentic in his blood beat in his brain. Margaret, Vanessa, his mother, they were nothing to him because he was not himself, Adam Paris, but something beyond himself, beyond time, the past, the present and all that was to come.

He lay on the turf, the soil was in his beard, his hands dug into the short sweet grass, the grit of the land, chilled, hardened with a frost that had outlived the midday sun. He stood up. Below him was Derwentwater to the east, Newlands to the west veiled now in the shadow of the lengthening day. He saw Catchedicam to the left of Helvellyn top, and southwards was Langdale Pike o' Stickle. Why should he ever return? He started to run again on a surface so buoyant that it seemed to run with him. Up the easy slope of Maiden Moor, Scafell and Gable coming to meet him between Eel Crag and Dale Head. Why should he ever return? Borrowdale and Grange were below and now the Pillar was in view between Dale Head and Hindscarth. He might race on for ever – Hindscarth and Robinson, then down to Buttermere across to Ennerdale, over to Waswater, to Eskdale and the sea!

He was a wandering man, a lost man, a man at last his own master!

He shouted. 'Oh, hoi! Oh, hoi!' All the hills echoed him as it seemed to him, and the waters of a thousand streams roared about his ears.

He flung out his arms and embraced the world . . .

Folly! He sat down, hugging his knees. He brushed the soil from his beard. He pulled up his trousers to see whether his knee were bleeding. It was not. He could barely see the scratch. Two sheep came wandering towards him and stood a little way off him, watching. Then, reassured, began to graze again. The sun was gone; it fell swiftly behind the hills on these January days. Helvellyn burned in a haze of rosy smoke, and all the air was frosty as though the ice had suddenly thickened on the Lake below and the hills around him. Maiden Moor, Robinson were breathing in gusts of cold thickened air. The sky paled to become the white field of one solitary star that glittered, a spark of frosted fire. Dusk and a great silence enwrapped the world.

He started home. The thought of home was comforting. Margaret sitting by the fire, and he would tell Benjamin and Vanessa a story . . .

He started down the slope, singing as he went.

A DAY IN THE LIFE OF A VERY OLD
LADY

SHE rose and then sank again, sank and rose, on a great billowy cloud of softest down. The movement was so exquisite, and she was herself so lazy, that she abandoned herself completely, although there were, she knew, a thousand things that she ought to be doing. Everything, far and near, was of a dazzling white save only Adam's nose that was purple and dripping with cold. Had she the energy she would tell him that he must blow it. There was the cloud available and it would irritate her, did she allow herself to be irritated, that he did not make use of so convenient a remedy. But she would not permit herself to be irritated. She was altogether too happy. As she rocked she sang softly to herself a song that Emma Furze had taught her, but she would not sing loudly lest she should wake Georges who was snoring on a cloud near by. How well she knew that snore – it was part of her whole life – and although she did not care for snores in general, Georges' snore was her own property and he must sleep long, here in Watendlath, for yesterday had been the clipping and he would be weary.

Moreover, just round the corner was the whole family – Dorothy, Tim, Veronica, Amabel and dear Jane. They were busy at some game. She could not quite see them, but she knew what they were about. Practising at archery, as indeed they must, for in a week's time there was the contest in Keswick and Veronica had a chance of a prize. It was winter, but in visions such as this all seasons were confused. How lovely she looked, Veronica, her body stretched, her bow held straight from her arms, her beautiful head thrown back! But Jane would be clumsy. If she were not careful they would laugh and then Jane would blush, pretending not to mind, but hurt at her clumsiness ... and she would call from her cloud, as so often she had done before, 'Jane! Jane! I want you!' simply to save her.

Things began to press in upon her consciousness. A great white bird, the sunlight glittering in silver on its sweeping wings, flew slowly above her head, and the white blossom fell, at a touch of the warm breeze, there across the lawn in the orchard, the petals hovering, wavering ... hovering, wavering! The sheep, their fleece stained with red, were pressing up the road at Watendlath, and Charlie Watson, motionless on his horse, watched them go. There was something that she must say to Charlie Watson, and so, raising herself from her cloud, she called softly 'Charlie! Charlie!'

The sky was blinded with a white radiance. The great bird, shaking showers of brilliance from its wings, beat upwards towards the sun. The radiance was so bright that she put her hand before her eyes, crying out with joy at so much loveliness, then heard – close beside here – Jane's eager laughing voice.

'Wake up, Aunt Judith! Look at the snow! It has fallen in the night! There never was such a beautiful day!'

She turned her head, rubbed her eyes, then reached for her spectacles. Putting them on she caught, in one sweep, the whole of the real world, for Jane had drawn back the blinds and, from her bed, she could see the flanks of Skiddaw glistening in crystal snow, and snow heaped on the windowsill. Above it all, there was a burning blue sky and the sun blazed over all the room. Jane stood there with the basin of water, the sponge, the soap, the towel, the silver brushes, the ivory comb, and, on a table not far away, breakfast was waiting.

'Well, my dear,' she said with a little sigh of happiness. 'I've had a very good night, thank you. I woke once and heard it strike three and that was the only time. Dear me, what a splendid sunshine! And how are you, Jane dear? I hope you slept well. I dreamt you were practising archery with Veronica.'

'I have had a very good night, thank you,' said Jane, and at once she began, with a dexterity and neatness that Judith adored (she would allow no one but Jane to perform these offices), to hold the basin, to see that the sponge was not too full, and then, when the washing was concluded, to bring the round mirror with the green wood and the gilt doves, so that Judith might see clearly to brush her silver hair.

'Mary will be in shortly to set the fire. There are plenty of logs, I told James yesterday.'

'What is there for breakfast?'

The tray was brought to the bed and carefully arranged.

'I chose those two brown eggs myself. And there is the damson preserve.'

'Dear me, how pleasant!'

'Adam is coming over today, you know.'

'As though I could forget, my dear.'

'He is bringing Vanessa.'

'Of course, of course,' Judith said, quite crossly. They would treat her – even dear Jane did this – as though she found it difficult to remember things. She remembered everything – *everything*. It was true that it seemed to her as though Georges and Charlie Watson were still in the room. Past and Present were one and the same. Jane herself would discover that one day. But because she, Judith, was ninety-five years of age (she had had her birthday a week or two ago) was no reason why they should think her helpless. It was true that she could not, any longer, walk very much, but for the rest she was as active and alive as any of them. She took off the top of one of her eggs and said:

'How is everybody? How is Timothy's cold?'

'Bad. But he doesn't mind. He has ridden off to Orpen Farm to see about the Hunt tomorrow. With the snow like this it will be difficult, but it will thaw this afternoon, I dare say. It never lies long here.'

Judith enjoyed her breakfast. Every morning as she drank her tea and ate her toast and preserve, she considered her state. She was no hypochondriac, but from a kind of outside consideration she summoned her forces. Had she a headache? Did her eyes smart? How was her throat which, a day or two ago, had been a little sore? How was that sharp pain in the right elbow? And the soreness just above the left knee? Was her stomach (which Dorothy thought it most indelicate ever to mention) preparing to upset her or was it lazy and good-natured today? (She saw her stomach as a kind of cat, sometimes full of warm milk and purring, sometimes in the worst of tempers, always selfish.)

But how was the Captain of her Ragged Army, her Heart?
Everything depended on her Heart. While she felt that her stomach was definitely hostile, didn't care a rap about her, her
Heart, she considered, was on her side, disliked extremely to
distress her, would not miss a beat and then beat twice in a hurry
if he could help it. Her Heart was a Gentleman who was making
the best of it in very difficult circumstances.

Although she held this review every morning she never spoke
to anyone about it. She could indeed carry on a perfect domestic
conversation with Jane at the very moment when she was saying
inside herself: 'Well, Knee, are you wishing to be tiresome today?
You are very quiet just now, but I dare say you've got something
up your sleeve for later on.'

And, behind all this, was her terrific pride at reaching her
present age. Every morning when she woke to find herself alive
she made another triumphant notch on the slate of her mind. It
soon might be – it might be indeed at any moment – that she
would slip into a stage of semi-consciousness when living would
be nothing but a dreaming preparation for Death. When that
came she would not be able to reckon her triumph, so now she
would make the most of it. On November 28th last, her ninety-
fifth birthday, she had had messages, letters, gifts, from Herries
all over the country – from Ellis and his mother, Janet and Roger
at Grosset, Stephen Newmark, Phyllis, Barnabas, Katherine
(who had married Colonel Winch of Forrest Hatch, Salisbury),
Emily, from Garth and Amery and Sylvia, from the Ormerods at
Harrogate and the Cards at Bournemouth, from all the Witherings near Carlisle – yes, from Herries and Herries all the
country over. They had all been kind and generous, but she
knew what it was that they had all been thinking. She must reach
her Hundredth Birthday! At all costs SHE MUST LIVE TO BE A
HUNDRED!

Not for many, many years – not in fact since old Maria
Herries who had been born on the day of the Battle of Naseby –
had any Herries come so near to a Hundred. Great-Aunt Maria
had missed it, and they were all disappointed even now, after all
this time, that she had done so.

But Judith was their pride and their hope. True that she had
not always been their pride, true that her father had been a disgrace, that she herself had married a rascal of a Frenchman who
had died shamefully in a drunken scramble, that she had lived
like a farmer's wife in the country, that she had had an illegit-

imate son, but that was all long ago. She had become a famous person, a legend. All over the country Herries said: 'Oh yes, we are a strong stock, live to a great age. There's old Madame now, ninety something, and commands a houseful of women up in Cumberland as though she were twenty. Wonderful old lady! She'll reach her Century, you may be sure. Nothing can stop her.'

Judith knew that they were saying this and she was proud of it. Of course it was foolish, but then the Herries *were* foolish — foolish and rather charming, in their childishness. When she felt well, as on a morning like this present one, she thought that she could live until two hundred. Why not? What was to stop her? There *were* days when she was infinitely weary and longed for it all to be over. But as soon as the bad days passed she forgot them.

Today her mind was as clear as a crystal. She remembered everything. Timothy's cold, the calf that had been born two nights before, the new maid Hannah from Seathwaite, the proposal that Captain Forster of Runner Hall, near Penrith, had made to Veronica a week ago (would she accept him? She was thirty-one years of age and had she not been so beautiful would have been long thought an old maid), a chair that Dorothy had bought for her in Carlisle (it was of hand-carved walnut and its seat was covered in maroon plush; Judith had thought it hideous but did not wish to hurt Dorothy's feelings), Adam's visit, a present of a miniature set in Bristol jet ware (teapot, sugar-box and cream-jug) that she had for Vanessa. Jane had found it in Keswick and it was exactly what Vanessa loved ... all these things she had in mind while Jane talked and the snow glittered, the sun flooded the room, and the damson preserve tasted most excellent ...

Afterwards she had her bath, warm and delicious, while the logs blazed and the large tortoiseshell cat purred on the rug; then Jane helped her to dress and at last she was seated in her armchair near the fire ready for the Visits.

'I think, Jane dear, I'll be able to go downstairs a little this afternoon!'

What a picture she made, Jane thought, in her black silk with her snow-white cap, the lace at her throat and wrists, the thin long gold chain that hung almost to her waist, her black shoes with the glittering buckles!

'Yes, dear, I think you can on such a lovely day.'

It was at this moment when she was not so well, just before the Visits, that she had to pull herself together, to drag herself up out of that other world, the Watendlath world where Georges and Charlie laughed and rode, where Christabel and Jennifer quarrelled before a fantasy of masked figures, where an old man with a long white beard stroked his nose ... On her bad days that past was more real than any present. But not today. She was all alert, and when Dorothy, followed by Amabel, entered with their 'Isn't it a beautiful day, Aunt Judith?' and Dorothy began at once, as was her custom, with a cheerful 'tit-tat-tat-tit' of conversation (her manner with very old people) Judith was all alive.

Dorothy was wearing a new dress, the upper skirt caught up almost to the hips and the back of the skirt descending in a straight sloping line from the waist to the ground. The upper skirt was of brown silk and the lower of bright blue taffeta. This suited her stoutness better than the old exaggerated crinoline. Judith knew at once what the new dress meant.

'You are going into Keswick, my dear?'

'Yes. Veronica is coming with me. *What* do you think? Veronica intends to accept Captain Forster!'

Here was news indeed! One less of the great virginal army! And Captain Forster was not so bad. On the stout side and not very clever, but devoted, with a charming place, money enough, a kind heart. Veronica should have been in London. She might then have married *anybody*. But she was lazy. There was something of Jennifer in her blood. She had told Judith once that the only man she had ever really loved had been a farmer from Buttermere way. That had been only her fun. Of course Veronica would never think of such a thing! But why not? Had not Charlie Watson been a farmer?

Never mind. Here was Captain Forster – plump, clean, adoring.

'Are you certain?'

'Well, she hasn't confessed it in so many words. But he is to be at the Osmastons'. I am *sure* that she means to accept him.'

Amabel, who was always dressed severely and thought men contemptible, tossed her head.

'What she can see in that fat man!'

'Well, dear,' said Dorothy complacently, 'it is she that is going to marry him, not you.'

'Yes, thank heaven.'

They talked for a little, then Dorothy said:

'We will leave you now because I think Elizabeth wants a word. She is unhappy about Benjamin.'

'What has he been doing?'

Dorothy sighed.

'What hasn't he been doing? He had a fight in the village last evening with Marston's boy, and his report from Rugby has come. It is terrible, really terrible. You must speak to him, Aunt Judith. You are the only one who can do anything with him.'

They went and Elizabeth came in.

Elizabeth was fifty-four and as beautiful now as she had been at twenty. She wore a grey dress, her fair hair flat on the top and gathered into a large bun at the back of her head, a golden glory even in that so hideous fashion. She had the air of remoteness that had been hers ever since John's death. She was not priggish nor superior in this. She joined in everything that went on, laughed, sang, played games, hunted (she was still a splendid horsewoman), but nothing could bring her into the real current of life that the others shared. She loved her son, she loved Judith, she loved Jane, but even they, even Benjamin, were shades compared with John. When he was killed she received a blow that was mortal, and Judith, seeing her, knew that the Herries battle was not yet over, and that the consequences of old long-ago histories had still their own history to make.

But because of her own story she understood Elizabeth as did none of the others. Her own Georges had suffered sudden death, as had John, and for ten years after it she, too, had been herself a dead woman. She had had the fears for Adam that Elizabeth now had for Benjamin, but she had been spared because fate had chosen John for its mark instead of Adam. All the more reason that she should help Elizabeth now.

Elizabeth, sitting close beside her, began at once.

'Aunt Judith, we have had Benjamin's report, and it is dreadful.'

'What does it say, my dear?'

'It says that we must take him away if he does not improve. They acknowledge that he is clever but he will not work, he obeys nobody. He is always fighting.'

'Well, my dear, he is a healthy boy and has to let himself go, I suppose.'

Elizabeth shook her head.

'Yes, but he will obey nobody and he does not care. When I

speak to him he only smiles. He is not cruel nor selfish. In fact, as
you know, there never was a more generous boy. It is not that he
is absent-minded. He throws himself altogether into anything
that he is doing. But there is something *wild* in him. He says he
wants to be a gipsy!'

'A gipsy!'

'Yes. He wants to go away in a caravan and eat roasted hedgehogs. Then ... there is another thing ...' She hesitated. 'Two
afternoons ago I saw him kissing Hannah; in the passage under
the backstairs. Of course it was nothing. He is only a child – he is
not yet fourteen and he is tremendously honest. He conceals
nothing. He says that he bet her a shilling that he would kiss her
... I am in despair. He is so merry, always laughing and doing
things for others – but he will listen to nobody!'

'He kissed Hannah, did he?' said Judith, thinking how
different he was from his father John. And from her own Adam
too.

'Yes,' went on Elizabeth. 'I am sure, too, that it is my fault.
Aunt Judith, I have been wrong not to *force* my way into Ireby.
But I hated it so that time I went ...'

(Two years before Elizabeth had gone to the Fortress, had
asked for her father, had suffered a fearful scene with Mrs Pangloss who had refused her entry.)

'You know that I have written again and again and he has
never answered. But if I had gone and refused to be beaten by
that horrible woman and stayed with father whatever she did, I
feel that Benjamin would respect me more. He never speaks
either of his father or his grandfather. I don't know even now
whether he knows ... whether he knows ...'

She broke down, hid her head in her hands, then suddenly
knelt at Judith's feet, burying her head in Judith's lap. The old
lady gently stroked her hair. Even on her very alert days she had
moments of slipping off into a dream. Now with her hand on
Elizabeth's hair she saw the room filled with sparkling snow:
whorls of dancing crystal filled the air, which was shot with
splinters of golden sun. The windows had faded and a great sea
of virgin snow, upon whose breast waves of iridescence quietly
formed, broke and formed again, spread from the hills' horizon
there to her very feet. She was herself as light as a snowflake, and
it seemed to her that she had to exert especial power not to float
away on the current of that white loveliness and never be seen
again ... Was this Death – and if it was so, why did men fear it?
So sweet, so friendly, so just ...

'... You see, Aunt Judith,' Elizabeth's voice came like a soft key closing a door, and the room swam back, the bed with the hangings, the ugly chair that Dorothy had given her (oh, why had she forgotten to thank her just now?), the sparkling buckles on her own shoes. 'I seem to have no will-power any longer. I do things with everyone else, but my real self is not here. It is away with John. It is as though he were always whispering to me things that I ought to do – be more firm with Benjie, live with father and make him more comfortable. I had will-power once, but John's death did something to me. Grief doesn't break your heart as the novels say, but it takes your character away. I don't *grieve* for John. I am sure that he is happier now than he ever was here. But I am not alive. When you lost your husband did you feel at all the same?'

'Yes, dear, I did. Just as you describe. For nearly ten years I lived with the Rockages in Wiltshire and I had no real life at all; but it comes back in the end. Nothing can kill you. Nothing.'

Elizabeth rose from her knees and stood before the fire, her long slim body irradiated by the leaping light, her soft grey dress like a cloud against the sparkling logs.

'Aunt Judith,' she said. 'Do you believe in God?'

'I don't know.'

'You are not certain?'

'My dear, I have been a pagan all my life long. I know now that everyone is very religious, and if you don't go to church on Sunday it's very wrong, but in my young days it wasn't so. Going to church is just a fashion, I think. At one time it's the thing and at another it's not. My husband thought it foolish to believe in anything you couldn't see, but a great friend of mine, Reuben Sunwood, was as sure of God as I am of this room. For myself, now I am so very old, there *seems* to be another world – but that may be my old age and my body failing. On some days, you know, my hearing is bad and I cannot see very well. Then I seem to be in another world. But I don't know. When one loves someone very much one seems to go beyond bodily things. When one's in a bad temper or loses one's spectacles or the servants are tiresome it's different.' She rapped her fingers impatiently on her spectacle-case.

'Dear Elizabeth, you must pull yourself together a little more. It is quite right what you say. Benjamin needs more discipline. Send him to me, my dear. This morning. In the afternoon I'm often sleepy.'

Elizabeth bent down and kissed the dry, withered cheek. How

very old Aunt Judith was! It was wrong to trouble her, but then she liked to be troubled.

'If I can find him I'll send him to you now.'

When she was alone in the room again she gave a little sigh of satisfaction. She liked to be alone, and she liked also to be in the centre of things. She was happy this morning because neither her heart nor her stomach troubled her, because it was a beautiful day and because, old though she was, they still wished to consult her. The world was whirring around her! Veronica would marry Captain Forster, Benjamin was naughty, Adam would soon be here . . . She arranged her spectacles on her nose, picked up from the table at her side a number of the *Spectator* and read its opinion of Mr Longfellow's *Hiawatha*, an old poem now but still criticized with reverence: '*Mr Longfellow's* Hiawatha *is one of the really permanent contributions to modern literature, and no other genius known to us would have been in any way equal to the work. It is not the grasp of imagination, so much as the grace and sweep of a peculiarly majestic* fancy – *a fancy like the impulsive fancy of children . . . How bright and playful is the picture of the lower animals with the little Indian prophet . . . But it is not only in the details, it is in the whole spirit of the poem – the fanciful joy and beauty, the equally fanciful weirdness and gloom – that we enjoy the touch of a master hand.*'

Well, that was very nice for Mr Longfellow. But she was not sure. The writer used the word 'fanciful' a great many times. That was perhaps a warning. In any case she could not read for very long in these days – Jane read to her every afternoon – a lengthy poem, read aloud . . . No, she thought she would not bother with *Hiawatha*.

There was a knock on the door, and Benjamin came in. He was shooting up; he was no longer the small chubby child. He would not be a handsome man, although he had fine clear eyes, a splendid colour, and a strong stocky body. As usual he seemed to be enjoying a joke of some kind. She could see that he knew that he had come to be scolded and was endeavouring to be grave.

'Is that you, Benjie? Come over here where I can see you.'

He came and stood beside the chair in the attitude of straitened attention that children must observe before their elders. His cheeks were flushed with the cold and his hair was in disorder. He tried to arrange it with his hand. He looked her in the face, giving her all his mind, not as Adam had so often done when he was small, thinking of something else.

'Now, Benjie, I have sent for you because they tell me that your report has come from Rugby and it is shocking. They say that you will be sent away if you do not behave better. Your mother is very unhappy. What have you to say?'

What had he to say? How very, *very* old Aunt Judith was! And so small and so tidy. There came from her a pleasant scent of exquisite cleanliness and the smell of some flower, a carnation perhaps. But what must it be like to be as old as that? Why, her father had been born at the very beginning of the eighteenth century! There wasn't a boy at Rugby who had a relation as old as this! Something to be proud of. He pulled himself together and tried to attend. He always attended to the thing in hand, and the thing in hand at the moment was that Aunt Judith was going to scold him about his report. He didn't mind. He liked her. He liked everybody.

'I am very sorry, Aunt Judith.'

She kicked one shoe impatiently.

'Yes, but that is not enough. You must do something about it. You are a big boy now and threaten to be a disgrace to us all.'

She looked at him and her heart melted within her. She worshipped small boys, and although Benjie was very different from her own Adam, he had Adam's independence. She adored independence.

'Why are you so naughty?'

'There are so many rules and they teach you such silly things.'

It was the tradition in England that all children obeyed absolutely their parents, did nothing that their parents didn't wish them to do, were preparing, one and all, to be the heroes and heroines of the future. But Benjie seemed unaware of the tradition.

'You know you belong to a very fine family,' she began, 'and, when you grow up, everyone will expect you to make your family proud of you.'

'I know. They are always talking about the family, but I don't see why I should think about the family. I'm myself, aren't I?'

'Yes, but—'

'When you were a little girl you ran away. Your father was always against the family. My grandfather shot himself in London and my father was killed, when he couldn't defend himself, by my uncle. I'm not like the rest of the family. I'm different and I'll always be different. Mother and Aunt Veronica and Aunt

Amabel and Ellis and Cousin Amery – *they* are the family. But I'm different. I'm by myself.'

Her heart began to beat furiously. Her eyes dimmed. She could have caught the boy to her and kissed him. And with that odd exaltation (so bad for her heart) was fear also. Would this battle *never* be ended? She seemed for an instant to behold her father, whom she had never seen, standing, erect, triumphant, against the snow . . .

She beat down her emotion and in a voice that trembled a little said: 'Yes, but, Benjie, you must understand that being different is *not* amusing – not amusing at all. It seems to you, I daresay, very splendid to stand up now and say "I'm different", but I'm a very old woman and have had great experience and I can tell you that the world does not like people to be different, and especially our family does not. You can't know yet how powerful the world is and how *right* the world is too, because if everyone was independent and refused to suit themselves to the world's rules, nothing would ever be done. My father learnt that, I have learnt it, your grandfather learnt it. You *have* to do as you are told unless you want to fight all your life long.'

'I do like to fight,' he broke in eagerly. 'You see, Aunt Judith, I think it's stupid to do things just because other people do them.'

'Yes, but do you never think of others? You must see how selfish it is always to have your own way. You can see how unhappy you make your mother—'

'But I don't *want* to make her unhappy. I don't want to make anyone sorry for what I do. They needn't be, only half the time they are glad they are sorry.'

She had nothing to say. She was on his side, so terribly on his side, and yet it would never do if he were disgraced at Rugby . . .

'Well, then,' she said as though some silent comprehending confidence had passed between them. 'You must promise me to do your best for the sake of those who love you – for your mother's sake and mine. Will you promise?'

He smiled, staring straight into her eyes. She really was a *dear* old lady and he was proud of her because she had lived to so great an age. He nodded.

'All right, Aunt Judith. I'll try.'

'And you won't fight?'

'Well, I don't know . . . I can't promise if another boy goes for me—'

'You won't be the first in any case?'

'It's so hard often to tell who *is* the first. You see—' But this was too technical.

'Kiss me then. And I shall expect a good report next term.'

He kissed her. How dry her cheek was! Towards the door he turned.

'There's one thing,' he said. 'Why do I never see my grandfather?'

'Your grandfather?'

'Yes. Up at the Fortress.'

'He is very ill and sees nobody. He was very unkind to your mother once, you know.'

'Yes, but that was years ago. You can't go on remembering things for ever, can you? I shall go one day and see him.'

Then he came back to her chair and, grinning, said: 'Aunt Judith, would you like to see my ferret?'

'A ferret? Oh, I don't like ferrets.'

'You would this one. It's grand. James gave it me.'

'Very well. You can bring it one day.'

He nodded and went humming out.

The talk had affected her deeply. She took off her spectacles, wiped her eyes, put them on again. Her heart was beating oddly. It was not good for her to be agitated, but what was she to do when all the old questions, so long answered and dismissed, came surging up again?

When Jane brought her her dinner she found her greatly excited. She had her favourite dinner – fried sole, apple-pudding – but now she did not care. The talk with Benjamin had, although it was so short, exhausted her: old terrors and alarms would surround her and hem her in, did she allow them.

'I don't think I'll come down this afternoon after all, Jane dear. I'm a trifle tired.'

'You have seen too many people, that's what it is,' Jane said firmly. She had the air a little, as she arranged the silver dish containing the apple-pudding in front of Judith, of a witch or a fairy, someone from another and slightly inhuman world. She was growing into that especial product of the British Isles, the queer old maid, someone enterprising, eccentric, kindly, and very much alone. Jane would be eccentric, she would suddenly snap her fingers, dress quaintly (she was wearing now a funny old black velvet jacket), roll her bread at a mealtime into little pellets, talk to herself, but she had a heart as rich and warm as any fairy godmother. She loved Judith with a passion that was almost unholy. Although she was religious, virtuous and indeed prudish, she would have committed any crime for Judith, married anyone, killed anyone, stolen from anyone. So now she realized that Judith was weary and had added in a moment, as old people do, twenty years to her age. An hour ago she had been seventy, now she was ninety, soon, if one were not careful, she would be a hundred and ten.

'Yes, I don't think I'll go down ... Jane, what do *you* think of Benjamin?'

'He is a fine boy. I love him!'

'Yes, yes, of course!' She knocked her silver spoon against the plate. 'We all love him, but I am afraid that he is a very naughty boy.'

'Oh, he has fights, but so do all proper boys.'

'Jane, why don't you marry someone?'

Jane blushed. She said almost in a whisper: 'I don't like men – not in that way.'

'Dear, dear!' said Judith. (She was beginning to recover.) 'It was a very nice way. Everyone is so prudish now that they are ashamed to talk of going to bed with a man. It's perfectly natural. Nothing to be ashamed of. But although they won't speak of it they think of nothing else. It's all the same whoever it is – Mrs Osmaston, Helen Withering, Mrs James Anstruther. How shall we marry our daughters? We must put our girls to bed with a man the first possible opportunity, do everything we can, dress them so as to accentuate their figures, throw them at every man we see, everything to marry them – but speak of what happens when they *are* married – oh, dear me, no!'

Jane disliked it when Judith talked like this. She did wish that she wouldn't.

'Now, there's Dorothy! In *such* a flutter this morning because Veronica is going to marry. She'd marry Amabel to *anybody* if only somebody would have her, but a pestle and mortar is the only thing Amabel will ever marry. Yes – well, that pudding was very good. I think I'll have my nap now so as to be ready for Adam.'

When Adam came she was quite ready for him. Her nap had refreshed her. The afternoon sun shone into the room like the reflection from a pale cloud of gold. The eaves were dropping with the heat of the sun and, when her spectacles were on, she could see blue shadows on Skiddaw. There was a strange mountain lightness over everything, and the logs in the fireplace were crimson with heat, and crackled like mad. As soon as Adam came in, sat beside her, took her hand, they were enclosed as though there were no one else in the world.

She wanted to talk about the Trades Unions. She had had a letter from Horace Newmark, who was in business in Manchester. 'He is as proud of all the chimneys as though they were bluebells,' she said. 'He says Manchester is nothing but smoke and dirt and it's grand. It's making England what it is, the mistress of the world. Stuff! Who wants to be mistress of the world? So like a Herries!'

Two years before, a man called Broadhead in Sheffield had, it was proved, paid for men who had rebelled against his Union to be murdered, and had paid out of the funds of the Union of which he was secretary. The tyranny of 'rattening' whereby noxious workers' tools were destroyed, women were blinded, men were shot at, was prevalent, and in Manchester, among the brick-makers, the clay which offending brick-makers were to use was sometimes stuffed with thousands of needles in order to maim the hands of those who worked on it. But the investigations into these crimes had proved, too, that many of the conditions of work were iniquitous and had remained unaltered since the days of Elizabeth.

Judith was greatly interested. 'What do you think, Adam? What about these Trades Unions?'

'I think they are necessary. The more England becomes an industrial country – and she *is* now the first industrial country in the world – the greater the power of the working-man. He will rule England one day, mark my words, and I hope he'll be wise enough to know what to do with the power when he has it. That was the trouble with the Chartists. They weren't wise enough nor clever enough. But in fifty years' time there'll be few big families left. Everything will be shared – and quite right too.'

'I don't know,' Judith said. 'England was very nice once when there were no railways and no chimneys. Isn't it strange? I've been in a sedan-chair and saw a boy hung in the streets of London. Yes, and bears were baited, and I've danced at Vauxhall. I feel sleepy. It's the fire. Where is Vanessa?'

'Vanessa is downstairs with Benjamin.'

'And how is Cat Bells?'

'Cat Bells is covered with snow.'

'And how is dear Margaret?'

'Margaret sent her love and is coming soon to see you. She is baking today and Will is helping her.'

'It all sounds very pleasant. And how are you yourself?'

'I am very well.'

'And the book?'

'Nearly finished.'

'It's not a fairy story this time.'

'No, it's about two boys at the North Pole.'

'What do you know about the North Pole? You've never been there.'

'No. That's why I know so much about it.'

'But how can you write about what you've never seen?'

'There are two sorts of writers, Mother, just as there are two sorts of Herries. One sort believes in facts, the other sort believes in things behind the facts.'

'The books I like best,' she answered, 'are those that have both sorts in them.'

'For instance?'

'Jane is reading me a very amusing story called *Under Two Flags*. It's silly, of course – not like real life at all – but most enjoyable. And then there's *Alice in Wonderland*. And then there's Mr Huxley's *Man's Place in Nature*.'

Adam laughed. 'Mother, what a ridiculous mixture!'

'They all come to the same thing in the end.'

'What thing?'

'The world is made up both of fancy and reality, I suppose. Oh dear, I don't know ... Adam, now that I cannot move from this house I can see how *nice* England is.'

He smiled.

'Yes. I know you say "Foolish old woman at her age to love anything with a passion." But I am not senile. The moment I'm senile, Adam, you shall drop a pill into my chicken-broth and finish me off. No, I am very wide awake, and I can see that all my life I've loved England. Why do you not write a book about England?'

'How would *you* do it, Mother?'

'Oh, I would put in everything – men sowing the fields, the horses ploughing, old ladies selling sweets in the village shop, Mr Disraeli with his oily hair and Mr Gladstone with his collar, Horace's Manchester chimneys, all the Herries thinking *they've* made England, my father riding up Borrowdale, the snow on Skiddaw, the apple-pudding I had at dinner, sheep on a hill, the man lighting the lamps in Hill Street – and you, Adam, running by Charlie's horse in Watendlath, at Chartist meetings in London, writing stories at Cat Bells . . .' She broke off, her finger to her lip. 'That gives me an idea – I have an idea!'

'What idea?'

'No matter. I shall tell you when it has got further on. Dear me, I've talked such a deal today. One day I talk; another day not a word. Sometimes I sleep all day. I'm ninety-five, you know.'

'Yes, I know. You're always telling me.'

She took his arm and, quickly, shyly caught his hand and kissed it.

'My whole life has been you and Georges.'

'You said it was England.'

'You *are* both England to me. We are sunk in the country, you and I, up to our necks. That's why I am so strong. Do you know, Adam, I have never had a day's illness in my life? Even when I was bearing you I was only ill for an hour or two – ugh! – that was horrid. There was an elephant . . .'

He drew his chair closer, bent over her and put his arm round her.

'Are you sure you are not tired?'

'No, indeed . . . I was a little but I had a nap. I can go to sleep whenever I wish. Oh yes, I remember! Benjamin! Adam, what do you think of Benjamin?'

'A grand boy – brave, generous. He will do fine things.'

'I am not so sure. He has had a dreadful report from Rugby.'

'All the best boys have.'

'Yes, but he was in here this morning and I scolded him, and he said that he didn't care because he was different from other boys, different because of his father and his grandfather.'

Adam nodded. 'Yes, he told me that once too. But that's all right. It's only that he feels wild sometimes. Why, I feel wild myself at times, Mother. A year or two ago I went mad and ran up Cat Bells – thought I would never come back.'

She smiled. 'I am delighted that you are wild still sometimes. I thought you were so contented that you'd never be wild again. If I had the strength I'd climb out of the window now just as I did when I was a child. Is Vanessa wild?' she asked.

He sighed. 'Vanessa is an angel. But I am sometimes troubled. She is so generous, so trusting, and believes in everyone.'

'Well, there is no harm in that as a beginning.'

'No, but she must suffer ... Oh well, we all suffer. She adores Benjie. He is her God at present.'

'Can I see her?'

'Yes. I will go and fetch her.'

He went quickly from the room. She thought – Benjamin, Vanessa, the new generation, and I shall be gone ... soon I shall be gone. How strange and how familiar that thought that this room, her old companion, would continue with Skiddaw beyond the window, the snow falling, and she not here to see it, to move the chairs, dust the china, put a log on the fire ... She looked at the table where was the parcel of the miniature teaset. She'll like that, she thought. She had always adored giving presents. Adam came in, bringing Vanessa with him. Vanessa was ten and tall for her age. She was wearing a dress of red taffeta, and her little skirt stood out stiffly. She had beautiful legs and arms, and her head with its black hair was carried with a wonderful dignity for so young a child. She came and made a curtsy, then she kissed the old lady, then waited patiently, smiling.

'I have a present for you, my dear.'

Vanessa's whole body was transformed with joy. You could see that her heart was beating with excitement; she compressed her lips so that she should not burst out into indecorous cries.

'Yes ... Bring me that parcel, darling.'

She brought it very carefully. It was unwrapped. She knelt down on the floor so that she could see the wonder. She picked up each tiny piece, the teapot, the cups, the saucers, and held them, one by one, against the light.

'Oh!' she said slowly. 'It is the loveliest ... Oh, Aunt Judith! ... I never thought ... I never expected ...' Then she reached out for her father's hand. He pulled her to her feet. Even now, with all her joy, she controlled herself. She remembered how old Aunt Judith was, she kissed her tenderly and with great care. Then she stared at the precious things as though she would never take her eyes away.

'Do you like them?'

'*Like* them!' She curtsied again, then turned to the window as though her feelings were so great that she must hide them. Once again the three of them had the sense that they were enclosed, away from all the world, rapt into a private communion of happiness.

'I must show them to Benjie,' she said.

Judith nodded. 'Yes, show them to Benjie. And come again and say goodnight before you go.'

'I will be off too,' Adam added. 'I will help her to carry the tea-things.'

'Yes,' said his mother, her sharp eyes staring with some secret excitement. 'And send Jane to me if you can find her. My idea! My idea! I must go on with my idea!'

She tapped impatiently on the silk of her dress.

'Tell Jane I want her at once. *At once* – whatever she may be at!'

Jane arrived, quite breathless. She had been washing Dorothy's bitch Maria, an old and sulky spaniel who was washed every Thursday, come what might: and today was Thursday, Dorothy was in Keswick, and there was no one else . . .

'I've left Hannah to finish her!'

'Now sit down and get your breath.'

'What is it, Aunt Judith? Adam says you have an idea.'

'Yes, I have . . . Look in that wardrobe near the window, and among those bundles of letters you will find a manuscript book in a dark-green leather cover. Yes – that fat one . . . Now you have it? There's not a word in it, is there? No, I thought not. Francis gave it to me years ago on a birthday. He thought the dark-green leather handsome. Now bring the little writing bureau closer. That's it. Near the fire so that you will be warm and will hear what I say. Excellent. Have you a pen that suits you? Now listen, my dear. I was talking to Adam about England. You know old ladies talk and talk until they are quite exhausted. I have often noticed it – the older you are the more you talk. Dear Penny-feather at Keswick was like that. Her last years you could *not* stop her . . . a constant flow. Well, now I intend to talk to some purpose. Adam and I said we love England and so we do. Then I had an idea. You know I never saw either my father or my mother, but my half-brother David – he was old enough to be my father, you know – would often, before he died, poor man, tell me stories of them. He liked to take me for a walk, or we would ride to Bassenthwaite or Caldbeck or to the Dash, and all the way there and back he would tell me about the old days and my father.

'Now I think that I should write it down – or rather that *you* should, Jane dear. I may die at any moment. Oh yes, I may – of course I may – and what a pity! All this lost for ever. No one knows it but I. And that was a very odd life my father lived in Borrowdale. David told me that he remembered exactly the night they first arrived in Keswick. No, but wait. You shall write it down. Do not you think it a good idea, Jane?'

The old lady was so eager and excited that it would have been cruelty to prevent her. But Jane did not wish to prevent her. She was herself greatly interested in that world and in that very strange man, her great-great-grandfather. How very curious that the *father* of Aunt Judith sitting there so comfortably before the fire should be her own great-great-grandfather! It was like stepping on to a magic carpet and swinging back into another fairy-world. So she took her pen and began to write in the dark-green leather book.

'Now tell me, dear, if I go too fast. Well, you'd better begin in this way. "I, Judith Paris, was born at Rosthwaite in the valley of Borrowdale, Cumberland, on November 28th, in the Year of Our Lord 1774 . . ." There! Have you got that? That's a good solid beginning, I think, rather like Macaulay's *History*. Now to continue. "I never knew my dear father and mother because they both died on the day I was born, and had I not been found and rescued from the cold by Squire Gauntry of Stone Ends, who happened to be riding past that day and heard me crying, I should undoubtedly have perished."

'Have you got that, Jane?' She peered over her spectacles on the very edge of her nose. 'Let me see, my dear. Yes, you write very nicely. Am I going too fast for you?'

'Not at all, Aunt Judith. How very interesting this will be!'

'I hope so. I certainly think it may. Well, to continue. "It is not, however, my own history about which I write, but rather about some of the early days that my father spent in the valley of Borrowdale. My father himself lived to a good age, and I myself am now a very old woman, so that I am a link with the long-ago past. I have heard very much of what happened in those long-ago times from my half-brother David Herries. David Herries was my father's son by his first wife, and he was fifty-five when I was born, so that I could have been his granddaughter. He was very famous as a young man as a boxer and wrestler and runner. He had great strength as a younger man, but when I knew him he had grown stout and was living very happily with his family at Uldale, where I also was living. He would take me for walks and rides, and it was then that he would tell me these stories.

' "He told me that he remembered exactly the night that he first arrived in Keswick. He could remember every detail, and so do I, even at this distance of time. How he was in the inn at Keswick in a big canopied bed with his sisters Mary and Deborah. The canopy that ran round the top of the bed was a faded green and had a gold thread in it. There were fire-dogs by the fire with mouths like grinning dragons. And he remembered that a woman was sitting warming herself in front of the fire, a woman he hated. Then his father came in and thought he was sleeping. He remembered that his father was wearing a beautiful coat of a claret colour and a chestnut wig, and there were red roses on his grey silk waistcoat. He remembered, too, that his father said something to the woman by the fire that made her very angry, and she began to talk in a loud, heated voice." '

Jane went on, and in that clear little voice like a bell Judith refashioned this old world to her, describing the inn and the servants running hither and thither with candles, some relations who had a meal with them, and how David's uncle wanted to make him drink wine and he would not. Then the dark mysterious night-ride to Borrowdale, and how he sat on the horse in front of his father and how proud he was, and his father asked him whether he were frightened, and he answered bravely that he was never frightened where his father was. How then they came to a house on a little hill and David ran forward and was in the house first, and there were two shining suits of armour in the hallway.

'There,' said Judith suddenly. 'I am tired. That will be enough for today. I think you shall help me to bed.'

'Oh, Aunt Judith,' said Jane. 'That *is* interesting!'

But Aunt Judith was weary. She had suddenly collapsed, her head nodded, she yawned and yawned and was almost helpless in Jane's hands as she undressed her. It was dark now beyond the window; a faint powdery blue framed the silent masses of snow; some stars, lonely in that cold sky, were like sparks blown up from a fire. Jane drew the cherry-coloured curtains. She saw that Judith was propped up with pillows and two candles lit by her side (how tiny and soft her body had been – like a child's), then she left the room to return with some tea, a small sponge-cake and some raspberry jam in a blue glass saucer. Then, most unfortunately, Aunt Judith lost her temper. It had been a tiring day, there had been something too exciting about that dropping back into the past – the past that was not only the past, but the present and future as well.

So she lost her temper over the sponge cake. It was a plum cake that she had wanted. Dorothy only yesterday had promised her a plum cake.

'But, Aunt Judith, it is not good for you. Doctor Bettany said that plum cake was too rich—'

'Doctor Bettany never said anything of the kind.'

'But indeed he did!'

'So I am a liar! Thank you, dear Jane. I am glad I know.'

'No, of course not. But you know that last time you were upset—'

'I was not upset!' She was trembling, her eyes were filled with hot tears of anger. She was in a rage, so that for tuppence she would have taken the teatray and thrown it and its contents all over the room. How dare Jane say that she was a liar! And she hated this soft soppy sponge cake! They thought they could do what they liked with her! She was so good to them all, and yet they tried to starve her! After listening all day to their troubles they could so ill-treat her!

She took the sponge cake and with a shaking hand threw it into the middle of the floor.

At the same moment Adam and Vanessa came in to say good-bye, and with them were Dorothy and Veronica back from their party. But Judith did not care. She was not ashamed. They should see whether they could bully her.

'You promised me plum cake!' she cried to Dorothy.

'Oh, I am so sorry! ... Aunt Judith, Veronica is engaged to be married! Captain Forster—'

'I don't care! You think you can do what you like with me, all of you, just because I am an old woman—'

But the sight of Veronica's beautiful happy face was too much for her.

'Oh, well ... Come here, my dear, and give me a kiss! There! That's right! Don't spill the tea-things! What did he say to you? Did he go down on his knees? Were you very gracious? ...'

A long while after as it seemed to her, the room dark save for the flicker from the fire, she lay there, very happy, on the edge of sleep. It had been a wonderful day. She had never left that room, but all the world had come into it. The elderly Dorothy, Adam, Elizabeth, with all their personal histories hot about them, and the young, Veronica engaged to be married, dear Jane so sweet and good, and the children, Vanessa and Benjamin. All the generations! They had come to her for advice and help and to tell her what they were doing. They had wanted to know what she thought. They could not get on without her.

She herself had welcomed the sun, eaten delightful food, read a little, given a present, discussed serious matters like God and the Trades Unions with Adam and Elizabeth, sunk back into the past, thought of Georges and Warren and Adam as a baby, and then gone behind that again to her own childhood and dear David, and then back beyond that to a hundred and forty years ago when her father had been a young man and worn a claret-coloured coat – all this without leaving her room, all within a day. And she was ninety-five. All the Herries all over England were waiting to see her grow to a hundred!

Well, she would. Nothing was going to stop her! How could she possibly disappoint such a great number of kind relations?

So, in that happy thought, she slipped away and once again was rocking on that billowing cloud of softest down. She rose and then sank again, sank and rose . . . Georges was sleeping near to her. He was snoring with that snore so familiar to her that it was also hers. All about them the world was of a dazzling white, shining with a million crystals.

She rose and then sank again, sank and rose . . .

AT VICTORINE'S

IN London, a boy aged fifteen stood on an October afternoon pressing his nose to the window of a house in Hill Street. This boy was young Benjamin Herries.

This was the day, the evening, the night of his life, for on this day, October 14th, 1870, he was to become a man.

It had all happened in the most surprising manner, and the cause of it had been the death, one evening while he was drinking his tea, of old Stephen Newmark. Everyone had been expecting him to die for years, but with that priggish obstinacy characteristic of him he had refused to go, degenerating into a tiresome silent old gentleman with a female nurse of whom, in the opinion of the family, he was much too fond.

Poor Phyllis had predeceased him by some years; as he was not a Herries no one had very much interest in his attaining a great age. He died in the act of pronouncing one of his almost hourly anathemas on Mr Disraeli.

Most unexpectedly it was decided that young Benjamin must be present at his funeral. It seemed that Stephen had a great regard for Elizabeth and had declared that 'he would do something for her boy one day'. So Benjamin had been sent for from Rugby (where he still survived, much to his own astonishment);

Lady Herries had invited him to stay in Hill Street for the funeral, and here he was.

The funeral, two days before, had been great fun. Everything was great fun for Benjamin, and he could not be expected to feel much grief for Stephen Newmark, whom he had rarely seen. Moreover, he noticed that Stephen's children were not greatly downcast, and his own close friend Barney made no pretence of sorrow.

'The Governor never liked me,' he confided to Benjamin on the way to the funeral. 'He disapproved of me altogether and never even looked at my novels. I don't blame him for that, but I'm not going to be a crocodile about it. I leave that to sister Emily.'

Lady Herries, who was now a rather ancient and (in Benjamin's opinion) a very silly lady, did the honours with much satisfaction, and Ellis Herries, already a man of importance in the world of affairs, was dignified and solemn. Benjamin had got considerable pleasure out of his days in town. He had never really stayed in London before.

He had had a number of projects. Why should he return to Rugby? He thought of being a stowaway in some vessel chartered for the West Indies or (his old cherished dream) joining some gipsies somewhere. He took a liking to an Italian organ-grinder, with whom he talked in Berkeley Square, and fancied that he might buy a barrel-organ. But his principal notion was that, if he could get money enough, he would escape to France and, in some way, slip into Paris and enjoy a bit of the Siege. He had followed, with eager excitement, the Franco-Prussian War from its commencement. He had cut out from the illustrated papers pictures of the Emperor, Bismarck, MacMahon, Palikao, Bazaine, Frossard, the young Prince Imperial, and many of the Empress. He was in love with the Empress; he would be delighted to die for her. He wanted nothing but to run on some mission for her, be shot in the discharge of it and fall dying at her feet. He could not understand why his companions at Rugby were on the whole so indifferent.

Then, with the catastrophe at Sedan, his whole soul was on fire. He learnt every detail of the battle by heart. He knew the exact positions of Bazeilles and Balan, of the Donchery bridge, where were the Villa Beurmann, Illy, and the fatal spot where the Prussian Guards crossed the Givonne. He was sure that, had he been in command, he would not have fallen into so complete a trap, and the moment when the Emperor, old and sick, cried out 'The firing must be stopped at all costs!' was, for him, a real agonizing piece of personal experience.

He hated and detested the Prussians; he adored the French, and Barney, listening to him, was amazed that so young and jolly a boy could feel so intensely. When he read how the Empress, escaping from Paris, hailed a cab and was recognized by a street urchin, he drew a deep breath as though he himself had only just missed a great peril.

And now that Paris was invested it was for him as though he himself shared the siege. When he heard how, on October 7th, Gambetta escaped from Paris in a balloon he shouted 'Hurray!' and gave all his pocket-money towards a dormitory feast in its celebration. However, here he was now in London, and his own immediate affairs demanded a lot of attention. Tomorrow he was to return to Rugby, and he had a sad feeling that he *would* return instead of making use of this magnificent opportunity of adventure. Indeed, had it not been for his mother and Aunt Judith, he would have certainly tried the stowaway adventure. But they would grieve, although why they should he could not understand. But women were queer and these two women he did not wish to hurt. Moreover, Aunt Judith was so *very* old. He had better wait until she was gone.

Then, this very morning, after breakfast, Barney had arrived at Hill Street and, pulling Benjamin aside, had whispered to him that he intended that evening to take Ellis and himself out to dinner. 'Not a word to a soul,' he confided. 'Emily and the others would make a terrible row if they knew. But we must do something. These last days have been too gloomy for anything.'

So Benjamin stood at the window, all ready dressed, waiting for Barney to arrive.

It was the bewitching hour when the lamp-lighter has gone his way and the lamps star the streets like nectarines. A faint wisp of fog – having in it to Benjie's excited nostrils a slight sniff of gunpowder (he was thinking possibly of Paris); from beyond the window came magical sounds of London, the clop-clop of a horse, the rattle of wheels, feet mysteriously echoing, the distant plaintive murmur of a barrel-organ. On the top of area steps belonging to the house opposite a housemaid was entertaining, for a moment, a policeman. A brougham was waiting a few doors away and down the steps came a stout, pompous, old gentleman, pilloried in starch, a red shaven face and a white waistcoat and white gloves that seemed to Benjie too big for him. The fog increased a little, the lamps spread into a hazy iridescence, some old man in a large and battered high hat came slowly down, ringing a bell and calling out something in a melancholy voice, a carriage rolled by with two footmen in cocked hats standing up at the back of it – and always that soft rumble of sound as of a fat, comfortable nurse singing lullaby to her children.

His excitement was intense; it was all that he could do not to jump about the room, turn his favourite somersault. But Lady Herries or Emily Newmark might come in at any moment. He thought them safe and secure in the great cold draughty drawing room upstairs. But you never could be sure. Grown-up people were always creeping about and opening doors unexpectedly, like that old beast 'Turker' Evans, head of his House at Rugby. His thoughts were oddly jumbled. It was a pity that Ellis was coming; it would be very much pleasanter without him. Not that he disliked Ellis, or he would not did he not patronize him. Of course Ellis was *years* older, a grown-up man who did business every day in the City. And he was very kind. He had given Benjie ten shillings only yesterday, but, for some dim obscure reason, Benjie would rather not have taken it. Ellis did not really like him – not *really*, as Barney and Adam Paris and Thornton Minor and James at Uldale liked him. And then again, looking out at the lamps and the misty street, suppose there was no God as Barney said. Barney had sprung this astonishing piece of news upon him at the funeral.

'Of course there's no God,' he had said, as though he were sure of it.

'Well, what is there then?' Benjamin asked.

'Nothing at all,' Barney had answered gaily. 'We're nothing but monkeys, old boy. You are old enough now to read Darwin. He'll tell you.'

What an astonishing idea! Then all this going to church and saying your prayers, that had been going on for hundreds of years, meant nothing at all. There was no gigantic old man with a white beard sitting on a cloud and listening! His mother and Aunt Jane and the others were all taken in! A stupendous thought! But he had only Barney's word for it, and you could never be sure whether Barney meant what he said!

Oh! there was the organ-grinder coming round the corner! He could just see him in the dim light, and there, joy of joys, from the opposite side was the muffin-man approaching! There *must* be a God, or why should there be muffin-men and organ-grinders? Would the organ-grinder have a monkey? The door opened and Lady Herries entered. She was a little, faded, old woman now, and Benjamin was certain that she painted her cheeks. He thought she looked ridiculous, her dress bunched up behind and her rather scanty hair dressed in a cascade of curls at the back of her head. She was, of course, in the deepest black and she walked with small mincing steps.

'Why, Benjamin! Dear me! Why has William not lit the gas! All alone! Emily was asking for you! Come and tell me what you have been doing. Ellis tells me that you and he are going to have dinner at some quiet place with Barnabas.'

'Yes,' said Benjamin. 'Won't it be fun?'

'I don't think this is quite the time to talk of fun, Benjamin dear. It has all been very distressing. However, you are too young yet to realize what death means.'

The front door banged. That must be Barney. They went into the hall, and there, praise be, Barney was, looking very smart in his evening dress and high black hat. He was growing stout, and looked like a very amiable clown, Benjie always thought. Chalk his face white and give him a red nose and he would be a perfect clown!

They all went upstairs to the drawing room, which was as cold as a mausoleum. They stood in a group beside the sulky peevish fire and talked in low grave voices.

Emily Newmark, a heavy stout woman in tremendous black, joined them. It is a temptation for every generation to deride any world that was fifty years its predecessor: Judith, Veronica, Elizabeth, Jane – these were, in their own kind and character, women to be proud of. They were generous, humorous, courageous and idealistic without priggishness. No period that was their background could conceivably be a period to be mocked. But Emily Newmark was frankly a pity, and was one, among others, responsible for providing our satirists with a living. She believed that Politics and the Services were the only polite careers, and the Land and the Funds the only springs of wealth that could be called decent. She was a snob and a toady. If a gentleman smoked in front of a lady he was insulting that lady's morals. She was always ready to be insulted. She looked absurd in her gathered flounces, draped skirts, and hair-plaits at the back of her head, but thought she was magnificent. She approved of the Queen in retirement and was preparing to be shocked by the Prince of Wales. (She *wanted* to be shocked.) She considered *all* foreigners (including – very much including – Americans) false, obscene, dangerous and unwashed. (Her own ablutions were neither so constant nor thorough as you would suppose.)

She approved of archery, croquet and painting in water-colours for young girls, but thought that that was enough excitement for them. She was an exceeding prude with a passionate private curiosity in sexual matters. She believed in good works, Missions to the Heathen, and patronizing visits to the slums. She was, in fact, *all* wrong, being hypocritical, snobbish, unkind to servants, a worshipper of wealth and a devout believer in a god whom she had created entirely after her own image. She was not a typical woman of her period – only typical of the section of it that was the easiest for after-generations to caricature.

She disapproved, of course, entirely of her brother Barney; she thought his novels 'horrid' with their racing, gambling, and loose women. Sometimes he brought men like Mortimer Collins to the Newmark home, and they smoked and drank together in Barney's sanctum. Now that both Phyllis and Stephen were gone, that Horace lived in Manchester, that Mary was dead, and Katherine married, Emily took charge of the Newmark remnants, Phyllis (named after her mother) who was a weak character, Barney who was not, and Stephen who was a lazy ne'er-do-well. She thought that she dominated all three, but Phyllis agreed with her in order that she might get what she wanted – new hats, novels from the library and a succession of silly young men; Stephen stole money from her, and Barney laughed at her. But Emily, in her blind self-satisfaction, arrogant patriotism and hypocritical prudery, learnt nothing. She had, however, her effect on others . . .

She had her effect on this particular and very important evening, for had she not entered the Hill Street drawing room just when she did she might not have exasperated Barney to his point of later recklessness.

'What's this I hear, Barney?' she cried. 'You are surely staying indoors this evening?'

'I am not,' said Barney.

'Well, of course,' and her voice was of a sepulchral gloom, 'it is not for me to say, but father has only been buried two days—'

'Father won't mind,' Barney said. 'He has other things to think of.'

Emily had but just sat down on the sofa. She rose.

'I will not hear such blasphemy. Nor shall this poor child, Benjamin, come with me.'

'Benjie is my guest tonight,' Barney remarked. 'He is to share my humble chop in some decent quiet place where we can think reverently of the past and pray hopefully for the future.'

Emily was aghast. She was truly and honestly aghast. This seemed to her a horrible thing. She broke into a flood of oratory in which their poor father, their poor mother, their poor sister Mary, all looked down from heaven in an agony of distress, in which childhood and vice, innocence and nasty men of the world, insults to herself and Lady Herries, all confusedly figured.

'Ellis will at least support me in this.'

'Ellis is coming with us,' said Barney.

She burst into tears.

'Oh, dammit, I can't stand this!' Barney cried. 'Come along, Benjie.' And Benjie rather sheepishly followed him out.

Down in the hall they found Ellis.

Ellis, waiting, looking up to the staircase, down which they were descending, had then the oddest hallucination. He was not an imaginative man, but, staring in the rather dim gaslight, he saw this: Barney had vanished. Benjamin, not a boy but a man of mature years, had halted on the stairs. Behind him stood a very beautiful lady in a white evening cloak with a high white collar. There was a Chinese clock at the turn of the stairs, a tall, thin clock brilliant in gilded lacquer. He noticed the time on its round face. It was twelve-thirty exactly. He was conscious of a violent, suffocating rage, and he heard his own voice, high, shrill, convulsed: 'Get out, both of you! Get out! Get out!'

As quickly as it came, it was gone.

There was no clock. Benjie jumped the last two steps.

'Hullo, Ellis!' he cried.

This only meant that Ellis was tired and had a headache. When one had a headache one did not know what one was seeing or what one was hearing. These last few days had been trying, with so many members of the family in and out of the house. But he always felt a little queer with Benjamin, never quite at his ease. He was not perhaps comfortable with small boys, and you could never be sure whether they were not laughing at you. But it was more than that. Ever since that day, ten years back, of the Heenan and Sayers fight, he had had an almost nauseating impression of Walter Herries. He could see him now, wandering,

lost, drunk, you might have said, a disgusting old man, and also
his own half-brother. He hated to think that he had any link with
him. And here was the man's grandson. They said that Walter's
life in Cumberland was a disgrace. That horrid man's son had
murdered this boy's father. Everything that was abnormal, fantastic, revolting – cruelty and illicit passion and madness – were
in the strain of that branch of the family. And he was himself
mixed in it, he who loved everything to be proper and sane and
wholesome and virtuous. He had a passion for virtue! But old
Walter and he had the same father. He would have cut all that off
as he would have cut off a diseased arm, and so he would have
been able to do were it not for this boy. The boy seemed normal
and decent enough. But he was young yet. You could not tell
what the future would be. And just as something in that branch
disgusted him, so something attracted him. He had insisted that
the boy should be invited to Hill Street. He tried to be friendly
with the boy, but he was not clever at friendliness, poor Ellis. He
wanted to be so many things that nature prevented him from
being.

'All right,' said Barney. 'Shall we go?'

They found a cab in Berkeley Square and, on the way, Barney
enlarged to Benjamin on the delights of London life.

'You shall have a night out, young 'un. We'll have dinner at
Duke's. No, be quiet, Ellis. It's my evening. What are you, Benjie?
Fifteen? Dammit, you look seventeen anyway.' He'd like to give
the boy a week. He'd take him to the Café Riche, Sally Suther-
land's, Kate Hamilton's, Rose Young's, Mott's. Cafés were open
all night. Pity he hadn't been with Barney at the fight between
King and Heenan, driving across London Bridge three in the
morning with a pork pie in your pocket. Mott's, too, where old
Freer kept guard. None of your tradesmen let in there – not that
Barney minded tradesmen. 'You're in the City, Ellis, yourself,
aren't you, my boy?' But still a gentleman was a gentleman when
it came to eating together. It was at Mott's you could have seen
'Skittles', famous for her ponies, or lovely Nelly Fowler. And
Kate Hamilton's – well, Benjie was still at school so he'd say no
more. But you should have seen a raid at Kate's – carpets turned
up, boards – under which bottles and glasses were hidden –
raised, all in the twinkling of an eye.

Or the 'Pie', where you were positively bound to have a row
before the night was up and where you tipped the Kangaroo so
that he shouldn't knock you down.

Barney wasn't a bad fellow; he was warm-hearted, generous, a famous friend, but tonight three things drove him on – the thought of his sister Emily, Ellis' air of wanting 'to be a sport' and wanting, too, to go home to his comfortable bed, and Benjie's excitement. He really loved the boy that night as he sat there, a proper little gentleman, his high hat tilted a trifle, his lips parted with his eagerness, his fresh colour, his sparkling eyes, his laugh, his readiness to trust anyone, his impulse to throw himself into whatever adventure was forward. 'I'll look after him,' he thought. 'I'll see that he comes to no harm.'

Duke's, near St Alban's Place, was half-hotel, half-hostelry. In the bedrooms the beds were cleanly enough, and most of the residents slept in them all day because they were out and about all night. A number of the residents may be said to have never been sober.

Excellent joints could be had for dinner, and the best of eggs and bacon any time of day or night, but the establishment *did* exist mainly for drinking – no one pretended other. Brandy-and-soda, rum and milk all day, sherry and bitters before breakfast, and a glass of brandy for tea.

A later generation might have thought Duke's eating room a little on the stuffy side. Everything was a trifle close, smelly, thick with tobacco and brandy fumes, linen and under-linen not quite clean, a strange air of rooms littered with feathers from an old bed, warm with the odour of unwashed bodies, cats furtively picking at fish-bones on a sanded floor, and the Chairman banging with his hammer on the table in the smoke-thickened distance. Stuffy! That was the word for the night-life of the London of the 'sixties.

But for Benjamin, Duke's room was Paradise. He gazed with eyes of wonder and admiration at old Charles, the presiding deity, who shuffled about in a tiny snuff-coloured tail suit and slippers, who – Barney told him – was never known to sleep, for at any moment of day or night he was ready to assist a drunken gentleman from a cab, or part two combatants. There were two chuckers-out, Jerry and Tom – men, it seemed, of almost legendary strength. It was nothing, Barney said, to see a long wooden coffin come down the stairs into the middle of the diners. One of the gentlemen had died upstairs, of delirium tremens. No one thought anything of it at all.

Dinner went well enough. Ellis was quiet. He seemed even to be enjoying himself and watched a young swell with an eyeglass and long moustaches drink one brandy and soda after another. 'Marvellous, isn't it?' he said in his precise careful voice. 'Can't think how he does it!'

But it was here and now that Benjamin had the first brandy and soda of his life. He had tried gin up in Cumberland, but had not liked it. Cherry-brandy had been an adventure at Rugby. But this brandy and soda was different. It may be said, in a way, to have changed his whole life. He was ready for it. In many ways he was old, very old; in others he was a baby. But the reck-lessness, the urge to do something simply because it was for-bidden, the bravado that led him again and again to challenge anybody at anything, the absence in him, not of a sense of good and bad, but altogether of a sense of right and wrong, all these were pledged by him that night in that glass of brandy and soda. As he drank it down he may be said to have whispered to his familiar spirit the words that were to be his Creed all his days: "I'll do what I want. I'll see all that I can see. I'll love and enjoy with all my heart. I'll do no one harm but nothing shall stop my adventure.'

To be fair to Barney it was true that Benjie *looked* seventeen. There was something in his hard blue eye, in his confident car-riage and his air of assurance that made him seem, even then, mature. But he was not; in one meaning of the word, he would never be. After that brandy and soda he was ready for anything and he thought that it would be amusing to tease Ellis.

Ellis was twelve years older. He was staying in Ellis' house, and Ellis had been kind to him. For all these reasons he should have been polite to Ellis. But he was happy, he was reckless, he liked old Ellis even though he *was* a bit of a woman and even though Ellis didn't like him. So, on their way to the 'Paragon', he broke out:

'I say, Ellis – what relation are you to me really? Ought I to call you Uncle?'

'No, of course not. What an idea!'

'But *what* are you? My grandfather is your brother, ain't he?'

'My half-brother,' Ellis answered stiffly.

'Oh, so you're my half-great-uncle! What a funny thing to be to anybody!'

'All right,' said Ellis, yet more stiffly. 'We'll forget it!'

'Oh, I shan't forget it! I say, Barney, isn't that funny? To be someone's half-great-uncle?'

He hadn't a notion that Ellis was minding. All life was rosy and golden. Never, never had he been so happy before. He loved Barney and would do anything in the world for him. The streets were a glory of light and splendour. Wouldn't it be fine to be going to the Opera in the Haymarket – and then, all in a moment, they are out of Piccadilly and walking down a street where the gas is flaring over coarse scraps of meat, where linen-drapers are still, at this hour, invaded by poorly dressed women wanting pennyworths of needles or farthingsworths of thread, where there are little open dens, reeking with the odour of fried fish and sausages, where a lady in a mob-cap is instructing a sailor in the mysteries of the famous dance 'Dusty Bob and Black Sal', where a huge Negro, his teeth gleaming white under the gaslight and his brown chest bare, is turning somersaults for pennies!

Then, as suddenly, they were in broad lighted streets again and passing through the wide painted doors of the 'Paragon'.

'We'll walk about,' said Barney. 'We can see just as well from here.'

Benjie had never been to a real theatre before. It was a while before he could take all the dazzling brilliance into his system. First the stage with its blaze of light held him. A group of young women in low green bodices and wide skirts were dancing while two gentlemen in evening dress, one at each corner of the stage, waved flags. A large box, protruding over the stage, contained a crowd of gentlemen, very elegant and noisy, smoking cigars and leaning over to shout encouragement to the girls. At the back of the theatre everyone was walking about, talking and laughing. There were little tables at which ladies and gentlemen were drinking. Men stood up in the pit and shouted at one another.

'Hullo, Connie!' Barney said. 'Never thought I'd see you here.'

'Oh, didn't you? Well, where were you last Friday night? I was waiting an hour and a half and wouldn't have had no supper at all if a gentleman hadn't taken pity on me. Nice treatment, I call it!'

Benjie thought that, save for his mother and Veronica, he had never seen anyone so beautiful. She was fair with bright blue eyes, ringlets and a dress the colour of primroses, gathered into great festoons at the back. She was angry, anyone could see, but Barney was not at all discomforted, only more like a clown than ever, his hat on one side of his head, grinned and stared over his shoulder to see who else might be there. Benjamin feared that she was about to do something desperate, she looked so angry, but her eyes fell on himself. She smiled, a lovely, entrancing smile.

'Hullo, baby,' she said. 'Where's your mother?'

He smiled back, and murmured something with proper bashfulness.

'Isn't he a pet? What's your name, dear?'

But Barney was, in an instant, the guardian. He put his hand on Benjie's shoulder.

'Now then, Connie, enough of that.'

Her voice was soft. She stared at Benjie as though she could eat him.

'All right,' she said quietly, 'I shan't hurt him.'

There were two chairs near to them. She sat down in one and motioned Benjie to the other.

'There! Now we are at a proper distance. Is he your guardian or something?'

'No,' said Benjie.

'What's your name then?'

'Benjamin Herries.'

'Well I never! Do you often come here?'

'It's the first time,' said Benjie.

'But not your last, I'll be sworn. Here! you want a flower in your buttonhole. Take this.'

She had two small white roses at her waist. She took out one and gave it him. Very proudly he stuck it in his buttonhole.

'You're the prettiest boy I've *ever* seen!' She drew her chair a little closer. 'Like to come and see me one day?'

'I should very much,' said Benjie. 'Only you see—' He was about to say that tomorrow he would return to school, but that seemed to him childish, so he altered it to 'I don't live in London.'

'Where do you live then?'

'In Cumberland.'

'Where's that?'

'Up in the North.'

'Oh, never mind where you live. Here, see, I'll give you my card and then—'

But it seemed that Ellis, who had been standing awkwardly by himself, was now remonstrating, in great excitement, with Barney, for Barney broke out:

'Come on, young Benjamin. We'll go and visit the Captain. Ta-ta, Connie. See you again.'

Benjamin had to go. He had just not courage enough to demand that he should stay, but as Ellis and Barney turned ahead of him, the lovely Connie, coming so close to him that his nose was suffocated in some scent that seemed to contain a whole garden of flowers, caught his neck in her fair hand and kissed him.

He ran after the others, his heart hammering, his cheeks flaming, and his mouth tasting of some sweet powder. Who had ever dreamt that life could be like this?

They went behind the stage to a large room in which ladies (performers evidently) were drinking with bearded and high-hatted gentlemen, while a funny little man in a very light waist-coat and bushy side-whiskers claimed Barney as his most intimate friend, bowed gravely to Ellis, and asked them all to have a drink.

But Benjie saw and heard nothing. He sat in a dream of happiness. Oh! what a lovely lady! How kind, how generous, how amusing! It was always his first thought when he met anyone whom he liked that he wanted to make his new friend a present. What could he give her in return for his rose? He had the ten shillings that Ellis had bestowed on him – or, at least, he had some of it. He could buy her flowers or fruit. Barney would tell him where she lived. He would go to visit her . . . Into the middle of these charming dreams Ellis gruesomely plunged.

'Benjamin, we are going home, you and I.'

'Going home?' he gasped.

'Yes. You must not be up late. You are returning to Rugby tomorrow. I myself am tired.'.

'But of course I am not going home!'

He hated Ellis, who had the sad long face of a horse pining for its stable.

'This is no proper place for you,' he said.

'Why not?'

'Well – it's plain – you are only a boy— Places like this—'

To do Ellis justice, this was one of the most difficult things that he had ever had to do. He did not wish to preach, to improve others; on the contrary, his desire was that he should be a jolly companion, a merry wit, a Prince of Good Fellows. But nature is too strong for us. Good fellows are not made, they are born. His capacity for finding life shocking was abnormally large. It was not his fault that it was so. It was simply his destiny. He did not want to spoil Benjamin's fun; he only thought it dreadful that

Benjamin should be finding this fun at all.

'You are to come with me,' he said, his voice trembling. He looked out of place, absurd, in that room.

Benjie saw it and, unhappily, Benjie laughed.

'You don't know how funny you look, Ellis!'

Then Ellis hated him. One thing he could not forgive – mockery that seemed to him unjust. It was his misfortune that all mockery of which he was the victim seemed to him unjust.

He caught Barney's arm.

'Benjamin and I are going home.'

Most regrettably Barney was by now drunk enough to find seriousness a farce and gloomy faces a pantomime. He roared with laughter.

'I say – don't be so sad, Ellis, old buck. Why, dammit – oh lor! look at your face—'

'We are going home,' Ellis, pale, tortured, terrified of a public scene, repeated.

'Well, *I'm* not,' Benjamin cried. 'I'm not, am I, Barney?'

'No, of course you're not. Here, Captain, this is my young friend, *very* young friend. Never been to a Green Room before, never seen a pretty girl.'

'Shame! Shame!' Ellis cried in the best transpontine manner. He caught Benjie's arm.

'You are coming with me!'

'I'm not,' said Benjie, struggling to be free.

Two girls laughed. A gentleman with enormous side-whiskers, holding a glass of champagne rather uncertainly, came forward.

'What's the matter?' he said.

'Let me go!' Benjie said indignantly, wrenching himself from Ellis' hold.

Ellis let him go, and in that moment hated his half-great-nephew with all the hatred that a shy, self-conscious, awkward man feels for anyone who makes him the centre of a scene. Lowering his head, picking up his hat, he slipped away.

Benjamin was invited to sit at a table. Several ladies talked to him. Somebody said: 'You can have four monkeys to one if you like.'

'Put it down,' said someone else.

'By Gad,' some voice cried, 'if you can put me on to a good thing, Gordon, I'll be eternally grateful.'

He drank some champagne. He felt a little sleepy. The ladies were kind to him, but they were nothing, nothing at all because

Connie had kissed him. Then he heard the Captain, the gentleman with the flowing whiskers and very light waistcoat, say:

'What about Victorine's, Barney, old boy?'

'I'm agreeable,' said Barney.

'What about the boy?'

'I'll look after him. We shan't be long.'

Benjamin found himself accompanying the Captain, who confided to him as they went into the street:

'I've got a boy just your age. What are you? Seventeen?'

'Yes,' said Benjie, lying proudly. 'And a half.'

He felt about forty, or what he supposed that forty would feel. Nothing excited him like something new – something he had never done before, the company of someone whom he had never seen before, a new place, a new trick, a new risk, a new danger. Now, feeling like a knight of old, he strode through the streets, trying to keep pace with his two friends so that they should not discover how short his steps were. He did a little trot, then a long step, then a little trot again. Where were they going? Would Connie be there? Victorine's! That sounded exciting. They came at length to a barren waste surrounded with railings. In the centre of the waste was an equestrian statue. Here were oyster rooms, public-houses, night-houses. Here was Jerry Fry's Coffee House and there a small theatre with a large lady in black tights painted on a crimson ground over the doorway. A four-wheeler, lonely and disconsolate, wandered from darkness into darkness.

They turned into a narrow, intensely dark street, found their way cautiously down a kind of tunnel.

'Here we are,' said Barney.

Behind the door, through a little window, two janitors were watching. They recognized both Barney and the Captain; the door swung back. As they passed in, the barren waste of Leicester Square seemed to follow them, bringing with it the 'Shades', one of the wildest eating-houses in London, where the spoons and forks were marked 'Stolen from the Shades' as a delicate hint to its patrons, and the 'Tableaux Vivants', a festive hall almost next door to Victorine's, where, for a shilling, you could listen to more filth within half an hour than in any other place in London.

'Victorine's', however, seemed as respectable as a church-service. Barney, Benjie and the Captain seated themselves in a corner and brandy and sodas were ordered from a benevolent-looking old man with a hare-lip and snow-white hair. It was not a very big room. In the far corner was a billiard-table at which several gentlemen were playing. The centre of the room was cleared for dancing and there was a shabby piano decorated with two dusty ferns in pots wrapped in green paper; at the piano a large ringleted lady in a crimson dress was playing. Two stair-cases vanished into upper regions. Several ladies were drinking at little tables with several gentlemen. But the great glory of the place was Victorine herself, a huge woman weighing over twenty stone, who sat at a raised desk near the piano. It was said that she drank champagne all day and all night. Her countenance was hideous, for her nose was flat, she had a scar across her upper lip and a number of chins. Her little eyes were wrapped in fat.

Benjie gazed at her with excited fascination. Her bodice was cut very low and her enormous bosom shook with every move-ment. He had never seen anyone so ugly and he felt that he would like to talk to her. The gentlemen at the tables embraced the ladies, and one stout female balanced herself precariously on a stout gentleman's knee. Benjie was always a great observer; he missed very little, and was capable of a detached non-moral attitude that permitted him to see life steadily and, unless his own emotions were aroused, with great fairness.

His emotions were not aroused now except that he was greatly enjoying himself – for had not Connie kissed him and given him a white rose? He was still, in the back of his mind, considering what sort of a present he should give her. He had better wait, perhaps. Christmas-time he would be in funds.

Then Victorine noticed them and beckoned Barney over to her. After a while he returned and said to Benjamin:

'Ma wants to speak to you. She won't eat you. Come along.'

Benjamin went over to her, feeling rather self-conscious as he crossed the floor, but he was ready for any adventure. He stood on the raised platform beside her, laughing. She spoke in a deep husky voice. She held out a large dirty hand.

'How are you?' she asked.

'Very well, thank you, ma'am,' said Benjie.

'How do you like my place?'

'I think it's very nice,' said Benjie.

'First time you've been here, isn't it?' she asked him, suddenly bending towards him, and he thought that he had never known anything so terrifying as that great round soiled, misshapen face with its little eyes, its flat nose, its grotesque mouth coming so close to his own.

'Yes, it's the first time.'

'You can see for yourself how quiet it is.' Her little eyes stared into his. 'There isn't a quieter house in London. It's these — — — who come with their — — — interference who make all the trouble. Take my word for it.'

It was astonishing to him, the quiet friendly manner in which she used words of a terrifying impropriety. They were not, it is sad to say, new to him, because boys at Rugby, or anywhere else, understand many words that would frighten Billingsgate. Not that they had ever done Benjie any harm, these words. They were simply counters in a normal day's play.

'You see,' Madame Victorine continued, her voice lower than ever, her manner extremely confidential, 'I am a mother to all the boys and girls who come here. You wouldn't believe all that I do for them. Saved their lives again and again. Mother I am and Mother they call me. I'm a widow, you know,' she added unexpectedly. 'My late husband was a Captain in the Army and he died in the West Indies of a yellow fever.'

'I am sorry,' Benjie said. He could think of nothing else to say.

'Yes. It was a tragedy.' There was a tear in her eye. Her vast bosom heaved. He thought that she was going to cry, but instead, to his great surprise, she banged with her fist on the desk and yelled in a voice of thunder, 'Here, you dirty —. Get out of here! Didn't I tell you last Thursday not to show your — face in my place again? Here, Cormey, put him out! Knock his — face in if there's an argument!'

Benjie turned to see a very mild-looking little man, bearded, in a dirty sack-coat and pepper-and-salt trousers talking with a big man in his shirtsleeves. The little man gave one glance round the room and vanished through the door. At the same moment Barney came and rescued Benjie, bringing him back to their table.

Barney was never so drunk that he did not know what he was doing. Now he preached Benjie a little sermon. 'You see, my boy, I've brought you here to show you life a bit. But never do anything you'd be ashamed of your mother knowing. You're young yet, but how are you to know what to avoid if you don't look round a bit?'

'I say, Barney,' said Benjamin. 'I want to give that lady a present. I'm going back to Rugby tomorrow so there isn't much time. Do you think you could give her something from me? I'll

pay you back when I get my pocket-money. I've got a bit now
that Ellis gave me, and with two weeks' pocket-money—'

'Here you are, my boy,' said Barney, diving confusedly into his
pocket.

He produced two golden sovereigns.

'I don't know what you are talking about, but if it's money
you're wanting—'

Two sovereigns!

'Oh, I say! But, Barney, I shan't have two pounds for
months!'

'Oh, never mind! Keep them.'

'No. If I give her something, you see, I want it to be with my
own money—'

He kept a sovereign. With luck he could pay that back by
Christmas. A sovereign! He could buy her something fine – a
scarf, a pin, a brooch ... And it was then that the fun began.
Over the silver image of his divine Connie he saw, rising as it
were from the floor, a thick-set squat fellow, very hairy, very
unkempt, very drunk. He wandered, as though he were describing with his feet a geometric figure, towards one of the little
tables, raised a glass of champagne stationed there in front of a
gentleman and drank from it. At the same time, grinning amiably, he knocked off the hat of the gentleman. Then, turning,
he began to orate to the room:

'In the name of our Queen, of Mr Disraeli and little Lottie
Heever, down with the French! Down, I say, with the French!
Are they eating dogs in Paris? Poodle dogs? And is elephant their
one luxury? Right and right again! To hell with the French!'

But he proceeded no further, for the two strong men, who
had been watching the billiards, were across the room, had the
man by the legs and were trundling him towards the door. At the
same time the gentleman whose drink had been abstracted –
stout, plethoric, with a beard of the colour of jet – cried something in a kind of frenzy and rushed towards one of the
staircases. Benjie, looking in that direction, saw that two young
ladies, most scantily dressed, were peering over the stair-rail. One
of them, seeing the bearded gentleman, vanished with a scream,
the gentleman after her.

Then everything happened together. The victim of the strong
men wriggled from his captors and, his trousers tumbling
towards his knees (for the strong men had burst his buttons),
lurched towards the piano; there were shouts and cries from the

upper floor which drew Madame Victorine, panting, upwards; some gentlemen ran in from the billiard table; the lady at the piano stayed with her back to it, cursing at the height of a shrill soprano; a large tortoiseshell cat crept from nowhere and began to feed eagerly upon a sandwich that had dropped; a table fell, glasses and bottles crashing with it; and the Captain, who had been dancing very solemnly with a stout lady in green, left her where she was and reeled (for he was very drunk) towards Barney.

'Here,' said Barney. 'We must be out of this.'

And then a fantastic thing occurred. At the end of the room there was a long mirror hung with yellow and green papers. Reflected in the centre of this mirror was the old waiter with the white hair and the hare-lip. He seemed to Benjie to swell and lengthen. As he grew in size, another figure, long and thin, spread out behind him, caught him from the back, in the neck, and began to twist his head round. The mirror grew ever more unusual, for now it was swinging, slowly swinging on its nail, and the two men reflected in it increased to three, to four, to five. They all struggled together, and behind them and around them the room swayed with them, tables and chairs, Madame's desk, the coloured portraits of the Queen and the Prince Consort, the piano, overturned tables, all swaying, swinging, swaying again.

Someone threw one of the flowerpots and it struck the mirror in its centre: a great crack like a spider's web struck the bodies, faces, furniture . . . Someone turned out the gas.

It was then, in that strange darkness, smelling of spirits, dust and tobacco, filled with cries and shouts, that Benjie felt a great exultation and a wild spirit of enterprise.

'Here! Benjie! Where are you?' he heard Barney crying.

But nothing could stop him. He plunged forward into the darkness, tumbled over a recumbent body, was up again, had found the piano, was enveloped by large female arms. Some woman held him to her. She was crying, sobbing.

'Oh dear, oh dear! . . . And I had a nice supper at home waiting . . .' And then, in a whisper over Benjie's head, 'Mr Archer, are you there? Are you there, Mr Archer! Oh dear, and if it hadn't been for the five shillings he promised me—'

'It's all right,' Benjie said, feeling real wet warm tears dropping on his cheek and, in sympathy, patting with his hand what was, he imagined, a huge naked arm. 'Only a moment and they'll have the lights—'

But the lady murmured, sobbing as she spoke, 'Don't you move, Charlie, my darling. You'll be killed for certain if you move a step—'

She planted a wet kiss on his cheek. She began to croon in a drunken kind of lullaby, her vast arms now tight about him, and then surprisingly, in the middle of her crooning, in a sharp businesslike voice as though she were giving an order at a shop: 'Where are you, Mr Archer? I'm here, Mr Archer, by the piano.'

He ducked his head, slipped to his knees and had escaped. Everything was wild now. Fighting was on all sides. He could hear blows struck, bodies thudding to the floor. Women were screaming, it seemed, from earth and air. Someone again embraced him. This time it was a man – someone fat, paunchy and smelling dreadfully of brandy. They were entangled, intermingled, dragging along the ground together. The man said no word but breathed desperately. He had Benjie by the slack of his breeches, and Benjie had his fist in a handful of beard. The mirror must have fallen, for there was a great crash of shattering glass. Benjie, laughing, shouting he knew not what, tore at the beard, was released like a shot from a catapult, and half flew, half fell through a door, clutched at a wall to save himself and was caught by some hand. He looked up and saw that it was Barney, Barney hatless, his neckerchief torn, but Barney quite sober.

'Thank God!' He held Benjie as though he'd never let him go. 'Here's a piece of luck. Come on, my lad. It's the lock-up for us if we are not speedy.'

A moment later they were in the deserted street, surveyed by an orange-tinted moon and two gas-lamps. Dead silence. Dead, dead silence. A little breeze rose from the pavement and fluttered on their faces. Victorine's was gone. Everything in and around Victorine's was gone. Ahead of them was the desolate waste of Leicester Square with the equestrian statue.

'Walk! Walk!' said Barney. 'Can you walk all right? Have you got your legs?'

'Oh, I'm all right,' said Benjie grandly. 'Are you all right, Barney?'

'Hush!' said Barney, who now that he had found Benjie was, all in a moment, drunk again. 'Hush! We'll wake Emily.'

Benjie's head ached, he thought that he had lost a tooth, his right leg hurt a trifle. But he felt at his buttonhole. Miraculous! The white rose was still there! How had it escaped? Was that not of itself a triumph? He was dizzy with happiness, adventure, maturity, first love, the wine of battle, the ether of recklessness, the full, complete, uncensored actuality of life.

'Barney, I've still got my rose!'

But Barney was striding on ahead. Benjie did a long step, a trot or two, a step again.

With a sudden alarm he felt in his pocket. Yes, the sovereign was there. What would he buy for her? A scarf, a chain, a pin, a brooch? . . .

He did a long step, a trot or two, a step again.

BATTLE WITH PANGLOSS

ELIZABETH, walking through the dusky afternoon up the hill to Fell House, was stopped by a little man like a ferret riding a large bay mare. She knew at once who it was – Glose, the handy-man at the Fortress, her father's handy-man – and, as always when anyone or anything connected with Ireby confronted her, she shivered with apprehension. Glose, who had sharp beady eyes and was always a trifle drunk, thought, as he looked at her: 'That's a pretty piece, although she *has* got grey hair.'

It was generally acknowledged up at the Fortress that Walter Herries' daughter, even though she was nearly sixty, was the most beautiful lady in the County. They liked to tell old Ma Pangloss so, when they dared.

'She'll be back one of these days and send you packing, Mrs Pangloss, *Madam*,' said a lively carroty-haired girl from Braithwaite who had just received her notice, 'and then we'll have a lady who *is* a lady'.

Elizabeth had a dark crimson coat with a silver-grey fur collar turned up above her slender neck, and she wore on her grey hair a feather toque with flame-coloured feathers. She was protected from the chill October wind by a thin veil. The twists and bands in which her hair was arranged at the back under the little feathered hat held lovely lights and shadows, so Glose thought. He was something of a poet where women were concerned, and afterwards in the kitchen at Ireby he declared:

'She had on a little hat all flaming feathers, and her hair was silver, you understand, and she has the figure of a girl of twenty, old as she is. Very pretty with the dusk coming on and the leaves blowing down, all the colour of her little hat.'

He was an Irishman, vagrant and worthless. He was in gaol for trying to knife a man in Keswick three months later.

But he had a letter for Mrs Herries. He was riding up to Fell House. He touched his cap, leaned down and gave her the letter.

Her hand trembled as she read it by the pale light of the saffron sky above the hill. It was written in a hand so shaky that it was difficult to decipher.

DEAR ELIZABETH – I am ill and would like to see you. – Your affectionate father,

WALTER HERRIES

That was all.

'Thank you,' she said to Glose. 'I will see to it.' She walked quickly up the hill. She was in a turmoil of emotion, but once in the house she told no one anything. She had always been quiet, reserved, by herself; her mother, who had learnt, through suffering, restraint, had taught her.

She peeped in to say goodnight to Judith, but the old lady was sleeping. Had she been awake Elizabeth might have said something, for although Judith was now ninety-eight and was being preserved as though constructed of egg-shell china, every noise, shock, sudden news kept from her, yet, inside this elegant glass case, she lived, Elizabeth fancied, an exceedingly alive and conscious existence. Judith knew more about Walter than anyone else at Uldale. It was she who had seen him last, who had known him longest. To her, Elizabeth might have spoken. But to Dorothy, who was now as fat as a tub and as contented as a pork pie, Elizabeth said not a word. Otherwise there was only Jane, for Veronica had been Mrs Forster now for two years, and Amabel had, of all mad things, gone to be a student at the Ladies' College at Hitchin. She had been there two years and was now at Cambridge, whither the College had just removed under the name of Girton. Ridiculous of Amabel, who was now between thirty and forty! She said, of all things, that she intended to study medicine!

So there were, besides Dorothy, Judith and Elizabeth, only Timothy (who showed no signs of marrying: he was fat, red-faced, cheerful – a proper Squire) and Jane. Elizabeth might have said something to Jane. She did not. Jane was such a dear old spinster, already ringleted and shawled, her face sweet and anxious and kind under her pale-gold hair, her small body *intensely* virginal. No, she would be of little use.

Of course Elizabeth must go to Ireby, and this time she would remain. From the moment that she received the note and read it in the gathering shadow of the autumn dusk she knew that there was only one thing that she must do. But oh! how she didn't want to! Her quiet, reserved, cloistered life, saturated with the memory and actual presence of John, devoted to Benjamin and Aunt Judith, was exactly right at Uldale. She was young no longer. She was nearing sixty. She shrank in every vein and pulse of her body from the roughness, violence, hateful rudeness that going to Ireby meant.

So she fortified herself with Adam and Margaret. On the morning after receiving her father's letter she told Dorothy quietly that she was going to stay at Cat Bells for a night or two.

'Are you sure that they want you, Elizabeth dear?' said Dorothy. 'Adam is just finishing his book, I believe.'

'I don't think that they will mind,' Elizabeth said. And they did not.

On that first evening, sitting by the fire after Vanessa had gone to bed, hearing Will softly singing as he occupied himself with something in the kitchen close by, Adam tranquilly smoking his pipe, they talked it all over.

The two women had a great regard for one another. Margaret had broadened into a maternal and seemingly placid woman, more German now perhaps in type than English. Her love for Adam was so strong that she could not sit with him five minutes without snatching a private glance at him to see that all was well. She knew that he loved her but she knew also, as nine out of every ten wives come to know, that she had not captured all of him; a certain wildness in him had escaped her. He was her friend and she was his, but she knew also that soon he would get up, knock his pipe against the stone of the fireplace, mutter something and slip off to Will – and that then for an hour at least those two deep voices would rumble on beyond the wall, and that they would both be happy together with a kind of happiness that neither of them could find with a woman. So she was glad to have Elizabeth then. They were two quiet, elderly women, sitting together by the fire; they were like hundreds of thousands of other elderly women sitting beside the fire that evening all over England – and the lives of those women contained sufficient courage, unselfishness and loving devotion to fill a Calendar of Saints.

Margaret, beneath her reserve, was frightened. There were many things in the Herries family that she did not understand, and what she understood least of all was that some of them were so very different from others! That you should have Garth and Amery, the Archdeacon of Polchester, Will and Ellis, Judith and Adam, poor John, crazy Uhland and his father, all of the same stock and closely related, seemed to her sober German imagination extravagantly improbable. Yet it was so, and she had long ago realized that the mad strain in the Herries family was not for her. She shrank from it with all her quiet strength because it was that element in her husband – although Adam of course was not crazy! – that prevented him from being entirely hers, and it had been that same element in his mother that had given her all her young married sorrows.

Now she was set, with all the determination of which she was capable, to keep the wildness from Vanessa! Vanessa as yet was as good and obedient and loving as a child could possibly be, but she was impulsive, fantastically generous, and – most perilous of all! – worshipped, increasingly with every year of her growth, Benjamin Herries. Now Margaret was Elizabeth's friend, but in her heart she was afraid of Elizabeth's son. Young Benjamin was wild; they said that he did wild things in London. He was eighteen years of age, and in another term he would be leaving Rugby. Then, Margaret supposed, he would come to live at Ireby and would be terribly close to Cat Bells. Margaret had to confess that when she was in the boy's company she could not but like him. He looked you straight in the face with his clear blue eye, he was merry, honest, open-handed, the friend of all the world. But he was wild. Margaret was sure that he had no principles, and although Adam sometimes laughed at principles yet he respected them as a good man should. Margaret was no narrow condemner of her fellow but she had acquired the prejudices of her time. She believed in righteousness, and for her own beloved daughter she would fight like a fish-wife if need be.

Vanessa would be beautiful – of that there was no question – and she must be guarded against Benjamin, but how she was to be guarded poor Margaret had no idea. Adam only laughed when she spoke to him of it.

And now Elizabeth was going back to that horrible place at Ireby with that drunken old wretch her father and the loose women he had with him. She was going back into all that craziness and wildness and bad living, and she intended to remain there. That quiet, frail woman, with her gentle face, shy, retiring way, so perfect and refined an English lady, thought Margaret, would live in a world that must revolt and disgust her at every turn. And, if she did remain, Benjamin would of course come to her there; he was heir, Margaret supposed, to that place, and any money the old man might have if, indeed, his dissipations had left him any. And Benjamin at Ireby meant Benjamin very near to Vanessa. At the thought of her child so peacefully sleeping in the upper room her whole protective fighting maternity was at arms. She felt inclined to cry out to Elizabeth, although she loved and admired her:

'Go away! Please, please go away and let neither your son nor yourself ever return.'

But they sat talking calmly; only once Margaret said:

'Do you think, Elizabeth dear, that it is *worth* going? Can you do anything for him? Is his life not too settled? Can it ever be your life?'

And Elizabeth answered, looking at Margaret:

'I know it's my duty, Margaret.'

Margaret shivered with some quick sense of chill and discomfort. Her German blood gave her an unusual sensitiveness to intangible influences. Many past events touched her moment's consciousness, and future events, linked to these, hung like clouds about her vision. It was as though the cheerful fire-lit room were, at that instant, fogged with smoke.

Elizabeth slept little that night and in the morning she shrank from what she was going to do as she had never shrunk from anything in her life before. After all, she was returning to the house where, it seemed to her excited fancy, Uhland's footstep must have left everywhere an imprint of blood. That was not a melodramatic exaggeration. John's death had been bloody, and, although his murderer had been her own brother, that did not make his ghost more stainless. In every room, at every turn, there would be memories, agonizing thoughts, vain, wretched recriminations. But nevertheless, she had no hesitation as to what her duty was.

Two things made the journey easier for her. One was the luxuriant splendour of the day. In October this country is often a

fantastic dream, and on this especial morning the fragment of
this world contained by the sky, the hills, the water, was a glory.
Last night there had been the first frost and the lawn glittered in
a dancing firefly extravagance under a pale autumnal mist. She
stood in the doorway of the cottage and looked out to the Lake
and Walla Crag. Near her was a mulberry tree; there were roses,
chrysanthemums, currant bushes; someone was drawing water,
and the smoke from the cottage chimney went up in a gay, fluttering pennon of thin colour. A squirrel watched her from a
branch. She could see into the living room with the bright-blue
cups on the white cloth, rough pottery with a pattern of flowers.
All this world at her hand was clear and distinct with a hard edge
to it. Then, in the space of the lawn, of a leaping jump, terrestial
existence was cut off and mirage began.

The blue cold sky ranged like a sea infinitely high and remote
from change: the tops of the larch and birch and fir suddenly, if
they were high enough, struck a hard stainless light and were
edged like cut paper, but so soon as the feathering vapours of
mist rolled curtain-like across the scene colour so rich and varied
began that the sky seemed to belong to another infinitely remote
existence, unactual and a planet away.

The mist was neither ascending nor descending in clouds; it
was not thick enough for form, it only caught the sunlight and
transmuted it, and that sunlight, joyfully enclosed, glowed within, an imprisoned fire.

It is the quality of this country that with a structure of rock,
naked fell and dark grim water, it has the power of breaking into
an opulence of light and colour. So the Lake that could be cold
as driving snow, harsh like shadowed steel, fierce with white
foam as a bird's feathers are blown angrily by storm, now was
streaked and veined with shadows of the grape that trembled, as
though a hand gently stroked its surface. This trembling was
not cold nor wind-swept, but burned with the sun-filled mist.
Above these purple shadows the hillsides were orange clouds,
orange in their brighter spaces, but like smouldering, glowing
embers where vapour enshrouded them. An isolated field, a blazing tree, a strip of bracken against the dark plum-coloured
islands, shone out like the gilt of missals, damascened, exotic,
flaming to the eye where all else was mystery, but the mist above
the gold was as dim as the white ash of burnt wood.

Because the sky was decisive with its virgin chastity of eggshell
blue, the misted land in contrast took all the colours of purple,

topaz, orange, and laid them under washes of pale gold. And yet, with all this dimness the hills were strong, striking deep into the Lake and, where they topped the mist, hard-ridged against the chill sky. And on Skiddaw there was a sudden flame-shaped crest.

Nothing but words of colour could describe this colour, but its final delight for Elizabeth was that it was friendly. The Lake, the cottage, the chrysanthemums, the sparkling lawn, wished her well. She could feel the warm quiver in the air, could think without extravagance that the sun laughed with pleasure as it struck again and again through the mist to touch with the point of its shaking lance the purple shadowy waters, the flaming autumn trees, the sharp dark ridge of Blencathra. She drew in a deep breath of the frosted air as she saw Walla Crag riding into the orange vapour like the bow of a Viking ship. The breath was as though she had leant her forehead against the pure cold of a newly riven stone . . .

And the second thing was that Will Leathwaite drove her to Ireby.

She could not have had a more perfect defence in perilous country. But before she went she had a moment with Vanessa. Vanessa came dancing on to the lawn, flinging her long arms out, running across the frosty grass, breathing in the air that stung the throat like peppermint. Her dark hair was in ringlets, her white strong neck bare. 'She will have big strong breasts,' thought Elizabeth, 'she will be very tall. I never saw a child carry her head with such majesty, and yet she is dancing about the lawn like a little pony.' She was going down with Will to Grange to fetch the carriage. They had to keep it in Grange. As she came nearer to Elizabeth the curve of her face from cheek to chin, still the face of a child innocent, open-eyed, fearless, gave promise of an almost startling beauty. You looked again to see whether that curve could be as perfect in shadowed line, in proportion and purity as you had at first supposed. And it was. Her eyes, lit now with happiness, were direct, unequivocal, so honest that they put you on your guard. What base part of myself am I going to betray here? you must ask yourself.

But Elizabeth knew that Vanessa was no perfect paragon. Her impulsiveness was always taking her into trouble; she had a temper. She was irritated often by stupid people; like her father and grandmother, she did not suffer fools gladly. Her mother was always checking her for answering back her elders (which no child was allowed to do), but, as Vanessa said, it was her father's fault because he encouraged her.

She was compassionate and generous, but not at all sentimental. At a time when both young men and young women 'gushed' and the world was on the whole more insincere than usual, Vanessa laughed. She laughed, it is to be feared, at Dorothy Bellairs, and Captain Forster who had married Veronica, and Mrs Ponsonby and a good many more. In fact Vanessa was not perfect at all. Margaret often shook her head over her.

'I am going down to Grange with Will. We'll be back in a twinkle!'

'Vanessa!' said Margaret.

'Well, but, Mama, twinkle is quite a proper word!'

'And as soon as you are back, Vanessa, you sit down to the German.'

'Oh, bother the German on this lovely day! I'm sorry, Mama; isn't it a pity that I don't like the German language better?'

She came to Elizabeth and said goodbye.

'Please, how is Benjamin?'

'Very well. He plays in the football team this term, and you know Rugby is very famous for football.'

'Yes. I am so glad.'

'Now, Vanessa, Will's waiting.'

'When you write to him will you tell him, please, that I asked?'

'Of course I will.'

'Now, Vanessa.'

Elizabeth thought it rather strange that Adam and Margaret should allow their girl when she was only fourteen to go off alone with Will – but then all the family at Uldale, except Judith, thought that Adam treated Will with far too great a familiarity. Servants were servants, and however good and valuable Will might be (certainly he was a *most* trustworthy man), still it was intended that a member of one Class should not be too intimate with a member of another Class. Emily Newmark, when she heard of it in London, tossed her head. 'Oh, well, we are none of us surprised. Adam Paris was a Chartist for years and would have burnt us all in our beds had he had the chance. Of course he *would* make friends with a common working-man.'

However, when Elizabeth was seated beside Will in the little carriage and they were driving towards Bassenthwaite she could not feel that he *was* 'a common working-man'. He was simply Will Leathwaite, and like most Cumbrian and Westmorland

men, sons of Statesmen who have owned their own land for
hundreds of years and been servants to none, he held his head
high, said nought, and feared no man. But the great thing that
Will Leathwaite was was comforting. He was a man of tremendous prejudices, prejudices often based on nothing at all, and he
disliked more people that he liked, but if he *did* take you under
his wings, then he would see that you were protected. There was
nothing he wouldn't do for you, no danger, no strife of tongues
(a thing that he greatly disliked) that he wouldn't face. His loyalty was absolute. He had long regarded Elizabeth Herries with a
tender protective affection because of John Herries' death.
Further than that, she was a member of the Herries clan. He did
not think much of several Herries whom he had met, but his
friend and master Adam was a Herries and that was enough for
him. So Elizabeth was under his wing. As he sat there, staring in
front of him, saying 'Gee-up', cracking his whip, his brow
wrinkled a little above his very clear blue eyes, his rebellious lock
of hair tumbling out across his forehead from under his old high
hat, he said very little – but she *knew* that he was protecting
her.

In actual fact he was wondering what he would do when they
reached Ireby. He did not want to leave the elderly, delicate lady
all alone there. There was every kind of bad story about the
Fortress, and that Mrs Pangloss was a holy terror. *He* could deal
with her – he would like to see any old fat whale of a woman get
the better of him – but a lady like Mrs John Herries, so quiet and
soft-spoken, what chance would *she* have?

At last when they were driving along the far end of Bassenthwaite Lake, he said: 'See here now, Mrs Herries. I don't like
leaving you all alone, by yourself as it were, at the Fortress. Please
pardon me, Mrs Herries, if I am saying what I shouldn't't.'

By now, poor lady, she was dreadfully frightened, and her
hands were trembling inside her muff, but Will must not know
that.

'No, Will. You can say anything you like, of course. But I
shan't need anyone. Sir Walter is my father, you know.'

This made it very difficult for Will, who considered that to
warn a daughter against her own father was not at all man's
work. Nevertheless, something had to be done. So he thought,
looking straight in front of him between the ears of old Bar-
tholomew the horse.

'Yes, Mrs Herries,' he said at last. 'I do hope you'll forgive me, ma'am, meaning nothing but good intentions and doing as Mr Adam would wish me to do, seeing that you are one of the family, ma'am.' He cleared his throat, gave a crack with his whip, set back his broad shoulders. 'You see, Mrs Herries, your father isn't so young as he once was, and there's a woman – Pangloss, they call her – who's no good whatever if the half they say is true. And a lady like you and a woman like her . . . I thought if I was to wait half an hour or so and you wave a handkerchief or some such article out of the window to say that she hadn't done you no kind of harm—'

'She won't harm me, thank you, Will,' Elizabeth said. 'It's very kind of you, and I've met Mrs Pangloss. I know that she isn't a very nice woman. But I'm not afraid, you know. My father himself has written to me to come and see him, so there is nothing to fear.'

'Yes, Mrs Herries, I quite understand, ma'am,' said Will. Nevertheless, he made a private resolve that he would not drive away until he was well assured that all was safe for the poor dear lady.

When they had driven slowly up Ireby Hill and the Fortress came at last into view, Elizabeth drew a deep breath of astonishment. She had seen the chimneys and the two towers, of course, every day from Uldale, but she had never, since her rebuff six years ago, been up that hill. She could not believe what she saw. How could someone as strong, as commanding, as powerful as her father had been, have allowed what had once been his pride to drop into this decay? She had seen the degradation begin in him long before her flight, but the house itself, ugly and forbidding as it was, had been proud, well cared for, the gardens kept, every kind of life and bustle about the place. And now!

She made Will stop the carriage round the bend of the trees so that they could not be seen from the house. In this part the veils of mist were thicker than above Derwentwater, and both Uldale and Skiddaw were invisible. The sun burnt strongly enough for the clouds of vapour to be faintly stained with rose, and here, as on the islands of the Lake, the upper mist was grey above the rose like the ashes of dying fires. But the top of the hill, the trees, the house, were chill and clear, crowning the shrouded valley; their detail was lined with sharpness against the cold bare sky. Elizabeth could see everything, how the trees had grown until they seemed to be throttling one another, how the garden was overgrown with weeds, grass had sprung up between the stones of the garden path, a shutter had swung off a hinge before one of the lower windows, there was an empty pane in the top window of the right-hand tower, stones had tumbled from the wall. There was something especially deserted today in the house outlined against so pale and bare a sky. As she looked it seemed to her that the house moved, its walls bulging outwards then sagging in again – an illusion of light.

She caught Will's arm.

'Is there not someone moving in the garden?'

'I don't see no one,' said Will.

'There – moving into the trees – a woman in black. No, it is my imagination. There is no one – not a soul . . .'

She put up her hand to her throat; this was so pitiful, this home of her youth where there had been so much life, now picked bare like a bone, or, to see it the other way, strangled with climbing triumphing vegetation.

'Leave the carriage here,' she said. 'I'll walk to the door. Bring my bag.'

She pulled her coat more closely about her, for it was cold up here, arranged her veil and walked quickly up the road through the gate, up the garden path.

She did not dare to hesitate for a moment lest she should lose all her courage, but it was a reassurance to hear Will's heavy certain tread behind her. Then she rang the bell and it pealed in the air as bells peal through empty houses. She looked around.

'No one has tended this garden. Look at those poor chrysanthemums. I feel as though someone were watching us.'

'Maybe it's the Pangloss woman from behind the window.'

She rang again and while the bell was still echoing the door opened. To her surprise a little girl, very ragged and tattered, wearing a woman's bonnet, was standing there. Elizabeth had thought out her plan of campaign and, taking her bag from Will, she walked into the hall and on into the small room beyond, which, in the old days, had been the gun-room. She knew it very well of course. But now it was quite different: the walls bare save for an old hunting-scene picture; there was a screen with boxing pictures pasted on it, and she remembered that this had been once an ornament of one of the spare bedrooms. There were the ashes of a fire in the grate and a stuffy stale smell of spirits in the air. She put her bag down and stood in front of the fireplace.

She saw that the child, who had large goggly eyes, was in the doorway staring at her.

'What's your will?' the child asked.

It was plain that she had not seen for a long time so grand a lady, for her gaze was rapt by the little dark green bonnet, the green coat with the velvet collar that Elizabeth was wearing.

'Will you please tell Sir Walter Herries that his daughter, Mrs John Herries, is here and would like to see him?'

The child said nothing but only gaped.

Elizabeth came over to her. She took her mottled red hand in her glove.

'Poor little thing . . . You are shivering with cold. Listen, my dear. Will you find Sir Walter for me and then say that his daughter has come to see him?'

The child vanished; the house was still. A mouse scratched behind the wainscot. She was glad that Will was waiting in the road outside. The door flung open and there stood a fat blowzy woman with a red round face, wearing a faded blue calico dress.

'I beg your pardon, madam,' she said, speaking very quickly. 'The girl shouldn't have shown you in here. This is private.'

All Elizabeth's fear had vanished at the sight of this woman, and she was so deeply filled with pity for her father that she could think of nothing else.

'It is not private to me,' she answered smiling. 'I am Mrs John Herries, Sir Walter's daughter, and I lived in this house for several years. So you see I know it well. We have met before.'

'Yes, and Sir Walter is not well enough to see anyone.'

'I know that my father is not well because he wrote to me, telling me so and asking me to come and see him.'

'Oh, did he? Excuse me for doubting your word, but he's not able to write to anyone.'

Elizabeth found the note and handed it to her. This brought them nearer to one another.

Mrs Pangloss read it very slowly, word by word.

'Silly old fool!' Elizabeth heard her mutter. Her great bosom heaved with indignation, but the letter had its effect.

'Well, I'm sorry, Mrs Herries, I'm very sorry, I'm sure. You're his daughter, as you say, and have a right – although for all the trouble his relations have taken all these years he might have been dead and buried, poor old man, for all they cared. What he *would* have done if it hadn't been for strangers taking care of him it's pitiful to think. However, perhaps you'll call another day, Mrs Herries, if it isn't a trouble. He isn't quite himself today – he's past eighty, you know, Mrs Herries – and it's the doctor's orders that he isn't to be disturbed by no one – not his nearest and dearest.'

Elizabeth walked back to the fireplace.

'I'm sorry,' she said, 'but I'm afraid, Mrs Pangloss, I can't do that. You see, I've come to stay. I have brought my bag. I intend to remain here.'

Mrs Pangloss gasped. Colour slowly mounted into her cheeks and changed them from red into a faintly streaked purple.

'Remain?' she brought out at last in a husky whisper.

'Yes. I have been far too long away. I should have come back years ago and would have done so, had I thought that my father wished for me. Now it is plain from this letter that he does. So will you take me to him, please?'

They stared at one another. This very slender elderly lady was, it seemed, nothing to be afraid of, for Mrs Pangloss changed her tone.

'No, Mrs Herries, I'm afraid I can't. Very sorry, but there it is. Doctor's orders, you see, *is* doctor's orders, and those were the doctor's very words. "I trust you to see, Mrs Pangloss, that nobody disturbs him, not on any account *whatever* – no account *whatever*. I wouldn't like to be answerable for consequences," he said. Those were the doctor's very words.'

'When was the doctor here last?' Elizabeth asked.

'Well, I'm sure, Mrs Herries, I don't see that it's any business of yours, but if you *want* to know – well, yesterday afternoon.'

'What doctor did you call in?'

'Now really and truly, Mrs Herries, you are going too far! Here you are, his only child, the only one left to him, poor old gentleman, and you living for years as you might say right at his very door and never so much as asking—'

Elizabeth's delicate face flushed and her eyes flashed – really flashed so that a light, indignant, proud, struck the thick heavy features of Mrs Pangloss. So, many, many years before, a young Buck in Islington had also been struck!

'I wrote several times,' she said, 'but received no answer. I understand now why I did not. I came once myself – perhaps you have forgotten, Mrs Pangloss? I did not wish to remind you because you were exceedingly rude and vulgar on that occasion. I admit that after seeing the kind of woman into whose hands my father had fallen I ought to have left it there, but I was anxious not to drive myself in upon him ... I was always hoping for a letter—'

'Oh yes,' Mrs Pangloss broke in. 'I can have you up for libel for
that, Mrs Herries! I can indeed – "kind of woman" indeed –
"kind of woman!" – and I the only one all these years who's been
good to him. And *that* settles it! I'm a trifle wearied of having all
his relations coming round poking their noses in, and it's got to
stop! A year or two ago it was that old French Madame who
should have been in her grave years back if she'd had any proper
decency – and her mother nothing better than a road-gipsy if all
they say is true. And now *you* coming worrying! Well, you've no
right here, Mrs Herries – no right at all – and I'll thank you to be
off!'

She had worked herself into a splendid temper and, shaking
with an anger that had been plainly fortified with both gin and
brandy, she advanced several paces into the room.

That was the very thing that Elizabeth desired. It was not very
dignified perhaps, but dignity, on such an occasion, must be forgotten. She walked swiftly to the door and then, once outside,
ran up the wide staircase, along a passage, up another stair, and
through the door into the room that had always been her father's
bedroom.

Thank God, it still was! Yes, and there was the same big four-
poster with the yellow saffron hangings that, as a tiny child at
Westaways, she had looked at with awe and terror, the picture of
a hunt with gentlemen in red coats, over the stone mantelpiece,
the two old chairs covered in green silk that she so well recollected, a walnut ring-stand, the mahogany cheval glass, the
white sheepskin hearthrug, a mahogany washstand with marble
top and two rosewood pole-screens – all articles that seemed to
be part of her very life.

And he, her father, was in the four-poster. From the door she
could see only the peaked nightcap but, at the first step forward,
he roused himself.

'Who's that!' he called out. 'Alice, you bitch, I told you to
bring me a drink. Hours back I told you.'

She came up to the bed. And this was her father whom she had
last seen, on the evening before her flight, corpulent, rosy,
covered with clothes even too strikingly elegant, master – as he
thought – of his world. Now under the nightcap there was
untidy grey hair, drawn cheeks with a week's grey stubble; his
open nightshirt showed the bones of his throat as sharp and
pointed as those of a plucked bird. For him, too, it must have
been a striking vision – this very elegant lady with her grey hair,

her little green bonnet and her long green coat fitting perfectly
her tall slender body. He did not recognize her. He raised himself
on his elbow.

'Why, what the devil—?' he said.

She stood close to the bed, smiling.

'Father, don't you know me? You wrote to me and I've come.
Elizabeth. I should have come years ago.'

'Elizabeth!' he sat up, and at the same time, with trembling
hands, pushed his nightcap straight on his head and pulled his
nightshirt about his skinny neck. 'Are you Elizabeth? Dear me!
Yes, I wrote that I was ill. But I should not receive you here. Go
into another room a moment, my dear, while I dress—'

'No, Father; I've come to stay. You must—'

But she said no more, for Mrs Pangloss, bursting in, had interrupted her.

'If this isn't *shameful*!' she cried. 'I can have the Courts on
you for this, madam. There he was just in his first sleep of the
morning and me keeping all the house quiet so that it shouldn't
be broken—'

But Walter, sitting up and grinning, said:

'Alice, you old washerwoman, this is my daughter. She has
come to pay me a visit.'

'Yes,' cried Mrs Pangloss with a ripe round oath, for she was
now too angry to care what she said (and had also, in the brief
interval between the scene downstairs and this, fortified herself
with more brandy). 'As she's come so she'll go. I'm mistress here,
and the sooner she knows it the better. Forcing herself into a
gentleman's bedroom, even if he is her own father!'

Elizabeth had crossed to the window which looked on the road
and, glancing down, saw the thick solid body of Will Leathwaite
stationed patiently by the gate. He looked up, saw her; she waved
her hand.

Turning into the room again, she said:

'Now, Mrs Pangloss, have this perfectly clear. It is not of the
slightest use for you to rant and swear. I am Sir Walter's daughter, he has asked for me – here I am and here I stay – and you
leave within the hour.'

At the audacity of this Mrs Pangloss for a moment could not
reply at all. She gasped and stuttered. Then, in jerks, the words
came.

'Me! ... within the hour! You to order me ... You!' She
strode to the door, flung it wide and called: 'Harry! Harry!

Where are you? Come here a moment! I want you!'

Walter, meanwhile, found it extremely amusing. He sat there, propped up by pillows, his eyes moving from the one to the other, grinning with his bare gums (his teeth were in a glass by the bed) and mumbling: '*That's* done it! *That's* a pretty thing! Now for a tumble!'

A moment later there arrived a heavy slouching man in corduroys, black rough hair over his eyes. He looked exceedingly sheepish, as well he might. Here was his master in bed in his nightcap, and Pangloss in one of her tantrums, and there, near the window, a beautiful lady in green. He was further embarrassed by the fact that the little girl (the child of himself and Mrs Pangloss) had crept after him (for although he beat her when drunk, she adored him as truly as she hated her mother) and, sucking her thumb, her old woman's bonnet on the back of her head, looked in.

Throughout the scene he kept muttering: 'Get away, Lucy ... 'Tisn't no place for you ... Go on or I'll larrup yer,' but the child paid no heed, and he, Harry Borden, restlessly shifted from heel to heel.

Mrs Pangloss turned to him. 'Now, Harry, you listen to me. This lady has been asked to go. Master has asked her. I've asked her. If she won't go, well – *you* shall ask her!'

Elizabeth went back to the window. She could see from there all the soft sprawling shoulders of Blencathra above the tops of the golden trees. The whole world swam in light this lovely morning. Inside the room the sun fell in coins and saucers of gold upon the faded ragged carpet. She felt the autumn sun, knew that Will was in the road below, and was conscious of a cheerfulness and high spirits that had not been here for many a day. She thought: 'Benjamin would enjoy this.'

'Well, Mrs Herries, ma'am, will you have the decency to go? You came uninvited – the sooner you go the better for all parties.'

'I did not come uninvited,' Elizabeth answered quietly. 'And I am certainly remaining.'

'You are not! You are not!' Mrs Pangloss found a glory of liquor at her heart and the fury of a righteous woman monstrously wronged in her head. 'If you won't go out you shall be put out! I'm in charge here, and so you shall know. Harry, if this lady won't go, you'll please *lead* her—'

But the ludicrous little scene was interrupted from the bed.

'Alice! Do you know to whom you are speaking? And who told

you to bring Harry Borden into my bedroom? And I want my
drink – I'm sure it's well past eleven – and *The Times* newspaper
of yesterday. You'll fetch me my drink, Alice, and give a poke to
the fire before you go.'

But Mrs Pangloss, all control lost, strode to the bed, stood over
the old man and screamed at him. Words poured from her. She
flooded the room with her life story, her virtues as a child, her
nobility as a young woman, the criminal errors of Husband One,
the positive loathsomeness of Husband Two, her patience in bearing great suffering, a struggle with Husband Two that had nearly
lost her an eye, her self-sacrifice in coming to the Fortress, her
devotion, generosity in guarding and caring for a gentleman ...
But, most unexpectedly, Walter rose to the occasion.

'Clear out, Alice. Clear out. I'm sick to death of you. I've been
sick of you for years. There's been nothing but mess and filth
here, and I'm too old to put up with you any longer. An old man
wants his comforts, and you've always thought of yourself, you
nasty old woman. And what are you thinking of, talking like that
in front of my daughter? I asked my daughter to come and I'm
glad she's here. So you be off this afternoon. Mrs Herries will pay
you what is due to you. Harry can drive you in the cart. And tell
the old hag downstairs to send up my drink. I'm parched.'

The poor woman was amazed. She was stuffed after all only
with sawdust, and perhaps, Elizabeth, watching from the
window, thought, she had a real affection for him. The look in
her face of dismay and chagrin was not only brought there by
drink and ill-temper. She stared through her stupid tear-filled
eyes. She put out her hand as though she would appeal. 'You
don't want me any more? ... After all I've done for you?'

'I'm sick to death of you, I tell you. I'm sick enough anyway,
but I'll spend my remaining days in peace. There, there! ... I
can't bear women to cry. Mrs Herries shall pay you what's due
and Harry shall drive you in the cart ...'

The catastrophe had been so sudden that she could only look
about her, turning her head now this way, now that, large fat
tears coursing down her cheeks.

She must care for him or she would not so abruptly surrender,
Elizabeth thought. She felt an impulse of pity.

But the woman turned to her, her words almost lost between
anger and tears:

'It's you that have done this, Mrs Herries, and I shan't forget it
either.'

Then, blowing her nose and wiping her eyes with a large check handkerchief, she went to the door.

'Come, Harry,' she said. 'They shall suffer for this.'

'Don't forget the drink,' Walter called after her.

When she was gone Elizabeth opened for a brief moment the window, and leaned out.

'Thank you, Will,' she called, waving her hand. 'There is no need to wait. Please tell Mr Paris that I am remaining.'

Will nodded and started down the road to the carriage.

She closed the window and came to the bed. She took off her bonnet and folded her veil.

'There are a number of things will need doing in this house,' she said.

He looked at her rather piteously.

'You'll be kind to me, won't you? I'm a very old man.'

THE HUNDREDTH BIRTHDAY

As the great day of November 28th, 1874, approached ever more nearly it may be said without very much exaggeration that all the Herries all over England held their breath. Would she do it? Could she last the course? Were they once more in their history to touch the Hundred? Or would she perhaps fail them just before reaching the post? A little chill, a window left carelessly open, a hot-water bottle neglected, the wrong food, a sudden shock . . .

Barney Newmark, who had been staying in Cumberland recently with Adam, declared: 'Pooh! She is as tough as an old hen! Not that I speak disrespectfully, for a nicer, jollier old lady you never saw. I had half an hour with her and her brain's as clear as a bell. She's got eyes like a child's. Of course, she's *old*. What do you expect at ninety-nine? She looks frail. She was always a pocket-edition but, dammit, she's sporting! *And* got a temper! But sweet-natured, you know, wants everyone to be happy. They all worship her and I don't wonder!'

In August she caught a cold and the news went right through England. Lady Herries in Hill Street (she detested Judith) gave a sniff and said the vain old woman had lived quite long enough, and for once Ellis became quite heated and said she had no right to speak so. She was an honour to all of them and it would be splendid did she live to her Hundred. Garth and Sylvia, pigging it in a little alley off Victoria Street, were genuinely concerned when they heard of the cold. 'Oh, she *must* live to a Hundred. She *must*,' Sylvia cried passionately.

'Perhaps she'll leave us something,' Garth said gloomily. Then added: 'I say, old girl, I lost on that damned horse yesterday. You'll have to pawn that ring again.'

Emily Newmark remarked virtuously that the Lord knoweth His Own Time. What He Giveth He taketh away; but Barney said:

'By gad, Emily, you'd weary a saint.'

All over the country it was the same. In Wiltshire, Carey, coming in from riding, was told by his mother and cried: 'Oh lor! I hope she isn't beat at the post! A cold, do you say? Damn' dangerous at ninety-nine.' Down at Bournemouth, where Jennifer's brother Robert had founded a little family (Robert himself was dead and his son Bradley reigned in his stead), they were greatly concerned, and Ruth, a pretty girl of twenty-two, thought of writing to Dorothy with a cure for colds that a Bournemouth doctor had given her. The Ormerods in London *did* write to Dorothy, and Horace Newmark, now extremely wealthy in Manchester, thought of running up to see the old lady.

However, all was well. Judith quickly recovered.

'Nothing the matter with her whatever,' Dorothy wrote to Sylvia. 'Of course it's very touching that everyone should be so deeply concerned, but Jane and I are *quite* capable of looking after her. And *what* do you think? Timothy is engaged at last, to a Miss Greenacre of Taunton Hall, near Grasmere. She seems a nice girl – quite a beauty but manners a little haughty. Timothy says she'll make a good mother. I trust he won't be disappointed.'

The truth was that the Herries were very ready for a public demonstration of their position. A century or so back they had been nothing at all – and now look at them! A Peerage in Wiltshire (Carey intended to stand for Parliament at the next election); Ellis, young though he was, one of the richest and most important men in the City; Barney Newmark, a famous Novelist (famous *enough* anyway); Adam Paris, a well-known writer (well known at least to all the *real* readers of literature); Horace Newmark, one of the richest men in the North of England; Rodney, Archdeacon of Polchester, and his son, a most oncoming Captain in the Navy; Lady Herries in Hill Street, a leader of fashion; the Witherings, and the Bellairs at Uldale, among the first County families of the North; and Judith Paris herself, *really* famous so that all kinds of people asked after her. Mr Disraeli had known her, Dickens and Thackeray in their day had heard of her, the Bishop of Polchester often asked Rodney about her, and as to the North itself – why, everyone knew her and everyone was proud of her!

So they were determined to make this Birthday of hers a Herries demonstration, just to show the world what a Herries could do were he or she so minded! No other family in England, so far as was known, contained so famous an old lady.

Many of them intended to be present at Uldale for the event. As the day drew near, Dorothy, Timothy and Jane, who were the managers and presenters of the Ceremony, had great difficulty in arranging for what Timothy called the 'horse-boxes'. Where were all the Herries to be put? Fell House itself would have to entertain for the night – Veronica, Captain Forster, Amabel, Lady Herries, Adam, Margaret, Ellis and Vanessa. Quite a problem! Jane and Amabel must share, Margaret and Vanessa; Forster, Ellis and Adam would have to take one of the big attic rooms. The Witherings, who would drive over, could put up Garth, Sylvia and Amery, old friends of theirs. Horace and Barney could manage in the village. Will Herries, the naval son of Rodney, his wife and sister Dora were found rooms in the Peter's House Farm. There were two distant cousins – Rose Ormerod and Sophia Fanchard – who were to stay in Bassenthwaite, and, lastly, Ruth and Richard, the grandchildren of Robert, Jennifer's brother, were young enough and lively enough not to care where they were. The two little rooms over the stables would do for them. How fortunate that Elizabeth and Benjamin were now settled at the Fortress! That left more room for everyone.

When this was all settled there arose the question of the Orders of the Day. It was decided that the procession to Judith's room with the gifts and the little speeches should take place in the morning: that would be less tiring for her. Then there should be a grand dinner at two o'clock. In the afternoon everyone should go their own sweet way, and in the evening there was to be a Ball to which everyone of any importance in the neighbourhood was to be invited.

This all settled, two great questions remained – one, the state of the weather, and two, the state of Judith's health. Were it to pour all day – to come down a regular 'posh' as so easily it might – why, then we must all put up with it, smile, and say that we liked rain rather than not. Nevertheless, it would be provoking. All the afternoon the house would be unpleasantly crowded, for these Southerners were not accustomed to Cumberland rain and had not acquired the good Cumberland habit of going out in all weathers. Tempers would be strained and it would be annoying to overhear, as one undoubtedly would: 'Of course in the Lakes it always rains.' ... 'My dear, what do you suppose you came for? Here it never *stops* raining.'

The other question – of Judith's health – was the most serious of all. Of late she had had her bad days: how at her age could you not expect it? She was often dreamy, far away, lost in some other world. Sometimes she was cross and peevish when her digestion worried her. Sometimes she was very deaf and could 'hear nothing, although Dorothy always declared that she could hear perfectly and affected this deafness simply to give herself a rest. But her heart was her real trouble: any excitement was bad for her, but how could she enjoy her Hundredth Birthday *without* excitement?

And to make everything worse, she insisted upon taking the greatest personal interest in everything. She wanted to know exactly who was coming, *where* everyone was staying, what everyone would do. Her brain was often of an astonishing clarity. 'My dear, don't be a fool,' she would say to Dorothy. 'Of course, the Herries woman must have a room to herself.' Or 'Dora? That's Rodney's girl. I remember. Her brother was at the opening of the Exhibition. In the Navy. A prig.'

It was a delight to her that Adam, Margaret and Vanessa were to sleep at Fell House. It was a long time since they had done so. It became clear, as the day approached, that almost all her anticipation was centred round Adam. It was *his* coming, that *he* should be present at her Hundredth Birthday, that gave her the keenest pleasure. Had she had the strength she would have gone herself to see the attic where they were putting Adam and Forster.

'Is the wardrobe large enough? Adam is very untidy, you know, Jane. He throws his clothes all about. Is there a nice cheval glass?'

But of course she could not move farther than to the armchair by the fire. If she had one of her bad days she must not leave her bed and they must make their speeches as quickly as possible.

But on the great morning of the Twenty-Eighth all was well. It was neither a good day nor a bad day as to weather, but at least it was not raining. Clouds shaped like ram's horns twisted above the hills, whiter than other grey clouds behind them. It might be that they held snow, for it was cold enough. The larch trees were pale gold – like gold beaten very thin – against a background of rolling hills, grey and thick like flannel, and from this vast sprawling bed a point on Blencathra, palely lit, stuck up like an old man's nose. Nevertheless it was not a bad day.

By nine o'clock of the morning they thronged the downstairs and passages. The Ceremony was to be at ten. All the women were in their loveliest dresses, and there was no question but that Veronica outshone them all. Matrimony had improved her. She knew – and dear Robert, her husband, knew – that she was to have a child; as yet there was no sign of this, but the knowledge of it (for now she loved her Robert dearly) gave her an added colour and excitement. Her dress, too, admirably suited her, with its corsage like a cavalryman's tunic, the draped back, the innumerable narrow flounces. At the back of her head her dark hair was piled in masses of curls, and she wore a little hat, very small indeed, pushed forward over her forehead. The colour of her dress was rose. She wore broad ribbons of rose on her hat. So she was the queen of the party, and Robert Forster was intensely proud of her. No one else was beautiful (Elizabeth had not yet arrived from the Fortress). Lady Herries was painted and affected, Sylvia's dress had too many flounces to suit her age, Dorothy, was too stout, Amabel too masculine, Jane was just a dear old maid, Rose Ormerod was a pretty little thing, Ruth Cards – grand-niece of Jennifer – was by far the most charming of the younger ones. She had a slight slender figure like a boy's, and the skirts of her jacket, projecting over her bustle, made her look like a boy in fancy dress. She and her brother Richard were rather new events in the life of the Herries. No one had seen them before. They won approval.

Of the men it may be said that Timothy was the most impressive, for he was host; he was large, stout and jolly, and he was but recently engaged to that stiff, haughty-looking girl in a purple dress, Violet Greenacre. He was of the type that the Herries admired, for he looked as though he would stand no nonsense and would live for ever. Barney was in splendid form, laughing with everyone. The Herries liked him because, although he *was* an author, he did not, thank God, look like one! Ellis was grave, dignified and, as usual, alone. They thought him haughty, stuck-up, and did not know that he, in his heart, was longing to be jolly, genial, generous as Timothy was, but didn't in the least know how.

And what of Judith upstairs?

She did not know, she told Jane, whether she had had a good night or no. She *thought* that she had slept well, but she could not in fact be certain because it was hard to tell when she was sleeping or when she wasn't.

She was, however, very cheerful, drank her tea and enjoyed her egg. *Of course* she would get up! She had, it soon appeared, thought out everything. The armchair was to be just here, near the fire but not too near, the small table at her side for her silver spectacle-case, her needle-case, a spare handkerchief and a silver-topped bottle of smelling-salts. She knew the Ceremony was to be at ten o'clock and she was glad that it would be early, because then 'she could have a nice time after talking to one and another'. Dressed, in her chair, she seemed, thought Jane, very small and very beautiful. Judith had never been beautiful, but it may be true to say that she approached more nearly to beauty on this her Hundredth Birthday than ever she had done before.

Her white lace cap had the brilliance of a jewel, the soft folds of her black silk dress shone in the firelight, her cane was at her hand, and on her black shoes were the diamond buckles that she wore only on very great occasions. The white lace at her wrists emphasized the fragility of her hands. Her only ring was the plain gold one that Georges had given her. Around her neck was the long thin gold chain that ended with a small gold watch in a pocket at her waist.

But it was her snow-white hair (once so brilliantly flaming) and the small face crowned by it that caught any observer's attention. That small face was wrinkled across the forehead and at the corners of the eyes and was pale ivory in colour – yet its outlines were as firm as ever they had been. The mouth had not the weak indecision of the mouths of so many old people. The lips were firm, now parting in a smile, now ironic, now commanding and sometimes bitter, for all old ladies are bitter sometimes. The eyes, though, were never bitter. Their light was astonishingly bright for so long a history, shining, penetrating, merry, questioning and, above all, loving: never weak nor sentimental unless she suffered unexpectedly some childish disappointment, when she could look like a little girl not out of the nursery.

It would be idle to pretend that she was not feeling the fullest satisfaction in this her great day. What is more, she felt that she deserved every bit of it. Very few people lived to be a Hundred and it needed a lot of doing! She was proud of herself and proud of England. She had been thinking a great deal about England during this last year, not with any weak sentiment nor any boastful patriotism. She thought, it is true, of the Queen because she was another woman like herself and had suffered a bereavement just as she once had, but she did not otherwise think of any special events or persons – neither of Mr Gladstone nor of Mr Disraeli, nor of Oxford undergraduates breaking stones in the road for Mr Ruskin, nor of Cardinal Manning advising the Irish working-man to be temperate, nor of the Monday Pops, nor of the famous new Ladies' Golf Club at Westward Ho, nor of the great bicycling race from Bath to London. Even in the mornings now when Jane read her the newspaper she did not listen very much and often fell asleep.

The England that preoccupied her now was her own personal England which seemed, when she looked at it, to spread all about her, a bright, coloured, lovely country, infinitely gentle and infinitely kind. The England of the wild life at Stone Ends, of Uncle Tom Gauntry and Emma Furze, of the fireworks at the Lake's edge, of that moment in the hall at Stone Ends when Georges had proposed to her, of mornings and evenings and nights at Watendlath with the Tarn black under the hill, the fresh smell of the new bracken, the early-morning calling of the cows, the sight of Georges coming up the path with the crimson bird in the cage, Braund Fell and Armboth, Rosthwaite and Stockley Bridge. The England of London, of the cobbles and the sedan chairs, the Ball at poor Christabel's, Mrs Ponder and the Southey's and Jennifer, the hour at Rosthwaite with Warren. The England (her happiest England of all) of Watendlath and young Adam and Charlie (dying so foolishly after of a little silly chill), of Adam above Hawkshead laughing at Walter, running up the hill with her to see the sun rise . . .

And later than that England did not seem to go. After that many things had happened to England, she supposed, and Adam had grown, married, and had a child; the hills, her beloved hills, had darkened and been lit again by the sun, had taken on every colour and been blinded by the rain – but in this later England movement had ceased. Someone called Judith had lived there, but the real Judith by then had slipped away. And yet the real Judith was still here and Adam was here. He was coming this very morning to see her have her Hundredth Birthday. She had every reason to be happy.

She smiled at Jane, who was seeing that everything in the room was right.

'I think England is very nice, dear,' Judith said.

'What, darling?' said Jane, who thought that she had not heard aright, but that Judith had been talking about her breakfast.

But Judith did not bother to repeat. However, she said something else.

'Will Walter be coming?' she asked.

Jane was startled. 'Oh no, dear. Poor Walter is much too feeble. But Elizabeth and Benjie are coming, of course.'

'Walter!' thought Jane; 'what an idea!' He was now quite a foolish, brainless old man, and although Elizabeth had done wonders so that the Fortress was now clean and alive and wholesome again, the thought of Walter coming into the middle of this happy Birthday was most distressing.

'That's a pity,' said Judith.

'What, dear?' asked Jane, who was busy all over the room, as she loved to be, dealing with trifles.

'I said "That's a pity,"' said Judith. 'You are growing a little deaf, Jane dear. I've noticed it before.'

Jane said nothing.

'It's a pity, because Walter and I once had a quarrel and I should like to tell him that it's ended.'

'He knows that,' said Jane. 'The last time you ever went out you drove up to the Fortress and made it up. Don't you remember?'

'Of course I remember. But today would be a nice day to end it all up – a very nice day. Is Adam come yet?'

She had asked that already fifty times. Jane went to the window.

'Why, yes. There he is now. Driving up.'

Judith smiled.

'Very good. I'm very glad.'

Meanwhile downstairs, Adam, Margaret and Vanessa had arrived and mingled with the family. Vanessa's beauty startled everyone. Many of them had never seen her, and for others she had been still a child. Now, although she was only fifteen, her slender height, her rich colouring, her black ringleted hair behind her little dark blue hat, her girl's dress with the white flounces, the bustle only just pronounced enough to give her waist its perfect shape, her modesty and quietness mingled with the evidence, almost impossible to control, of tremendous happiness and high spirits, created a great impression.

'That's a stunning girl!' said Captain Will to his sister Dora. 'She's Madame's grand-daughter, you know. Yes, her mother's a German. Her father married a German. That's him – that brown-faced bearded fellow over there. Writes fairy stories, books for boys – that sort of thing.'

Adam and Barney were delighted to see one another.

'I say!' cried Barney, 'that girl of yours is growing into a Beauty. 'Pon my word, she is! Regular Beauty!'

Adam laughed, pleased and proud.

'She's as good as she's beautiful, my boy.'

'Not *too* good, I hope,' said Barney. 'Don't like 'em too good, you know.'

But it was Ellis who was stricken as though by lightning. Standing by himself, near the staircase, hating it all, wishing it over, wishing that his mother would not make a fool of herself, intensely proud at the same time, saying to himself: 'You couldn't find such a set of people in the whole of England,' proud of his relations and despising them, longing to be friends with them all, hating it if any of them came up to speak to him; it was Ellis who, seeing Vanessa for the first time in his life, as she waited a little shyly behind her father, just out of the crowd, received a blow at the heart from which all his life he was never to recover. It was not that he fell in love with her at first sight; it was, more simply, that he had never known what life was before, that he moved, at the instant, into a new world of colour, light, sound. He stood there, staring. He gazed and gazed. He did not know who she might be. He turned and found Garth, already a little gay with morning brandy, at his side.

'Tell me, Garth, who is that?'

'Who is what, my boy?' said Garth, who had already borrowed a considerable amount of money from Ellis and intended to borrow a lot more.

'Why, there – over there! That young girl with the black hair – in the blue hat.'

Garth followed his directing hand.

'Oh, that! Why, she's Adam Paris' daughter, the old lady's grand-daughter ... Damn' pretty child, if you ask me.'

Ellis said no more. He stood back against the wall, gazing.

There then occurred the great sensation of the day. The clocks pointed to twenty minutes to ten, and the party from the Fortress had not yet arrived.

Dorothy was distressed, anxious. She moved about like a great green whale, saying to everyone: 'Very strange! Elizabeth is so punctual! I hope that nothing has occurred. Very strange indeed! I hope that Walter has not died, this morning of all times!'

There was a stir by the door. They *had* arrived. All was well. Dorothy hurried forward. The door opened and Elizabeth, bringing the cold November air in a gust with her, came in. Leaning on her arm, looking about him in an interested but rather aimless fashion, was her father, Walter Herries.

Walter Herries! The news went round the company in a flash. Walter Herries, who was, they all supposed, a doddering old idiot whom Elizabeth had splendidly rescued from destruction and was now nobly devoting her remaining years to succouring! Walter Herries, once the villain of the Herries piece, now a harmless old imbecile – actually he had come to Judith's Birthday!

It was a real sensation that gave way presently to a grave and general satisfaction. This was well. This was indeed most fitting! The Feud that had distressed for so long all the Herries, that had had its climax in a terrible tragedy, was now, on this splendid occasion, to be finally closed. This was Elizabeth's doing, Elizabeth who had suffered more deeply from that Feud than any other. Could anything be more proper? Soon everyone was delighted. A chair was found for Walter in the parlour and down on it he sat, looking kindly about him, smiling, seeming quite happy, yet plainly without any idea as to where he was.

'Elizabeth's smartened him up!' said Lady Herries to Amery. He looked indeed quite elegant with his snow-white beard, a handsome blue frock-coat and a dark blue neckerchief.

And that brown-faced, healthy-looking young man with the bright blue eyes was Benjamin, Elizabeth's boy. Yes, the son of poor John ... A bit of a rascal ... He had left Rugby now and was looking after his grandfather's land, or *should* be ... But they said he couldn't stick to anything, was a great anxiety to his mother. Yes, he was eighteen or nineteen, just kicking his heels ...

Benjamin himself heard none of these whispers nor would he have cared if he *had* heard. He was enjoying himself outrageously as he always did enjoy everything. Where was Vanessa? His first thought was for Vanessa. What a rum lot of old codgers these relations were! How ridiculous old Lady Herries in her paint and powder! Garth he could see had already been at the bottle. By Jove, was not Veronica a picture? *There* was a woman! Beautiful figure and what a pair of eyes! What fun bringing Grandfather into the middle of all this! It had been the old man's own idea. In a lucid interval he had grasped that Judith was having a grand birthday. He had hunted round and found a brooch that had belonged to his wife, a pretty little gold thing with three pearls and a ruby. He would give her that and he would present it himself. He explained to Elizabeth that he and Judith had not been the best of friends – but that was all over now, quite finished. Much too sensible a woman to cherish a grudge. And his excitement had been tremendous. He had got out of bed himself at about four that morning to find a box to put the pearls in. He sat in the parlour now, clutching the box in his hand, patiently waiting until he should offer it. Rum old boy, thought Benjamin, rejoicing in his own youth and strength; but he rather liked him. He was just like a child, and Benjie played draughts with him most evenings. Not that the old boy could play. He just moved the counters about, but it gave him pleasure. And there the old man sat, clutching his parcel.

However, Benjie had not come there to look at his grandfather. He moved about looking for Vanessa. And then, of course, he knocked against Ellis, the last man in the world he wanted to see.

He had encountered Ellis only briefly since that rowdy night in London four years ago. He was aware, without any question, that that evening had made a breach between himself and Ellis. Not that they were ever the kind to get on well together, Ellis so solemn and proper, and himself – well, *not* so solemn and proper! But he could not know with what profound distaste Ellis now regarded him nor the deep shudder of disapproval with which Ellis had seen Walter's entrance. What did they want to bring that old man for? He had a wild fantastic notion that it had been done in some way to insult himself. As with all egoists and men unsure of themselves, like all men sensitive to an unpopularity that they would give their lives to alter, most things in life seemed to Ellis to be directed against himself. This doddering, wandering old man was his brother! Did they not know that? Well, then . . .

It would be, he suddenly thought, just like young Benjamin to have arranged this – maliciously, simply to distress him. Ever since that night at the 'Paragon', Ellis had thought of Benjamin as wild, malicious, reckless – all the things that he hated!

'Hullo, Ellis!' said Benjamin.

They made a strange contrast, Ellis, long-nosed, pale-faced, grave, in his official dark clothes; Benjie, snub-nosed, brown-faced, in a long brown sack-coat and a dark red tie caught with a gold ring.

'How do you do, Benjamin?' said Ellis, offering his hand.

'Have a good journey up?'

'So-so. Cold, you know.'

'Yes, I suppose. Well, we'll be moving up to the old lady shortly. Quite a gathering of the clans, ain't it?'

'Quite,' said Ellis.

Benjie moved off. He had no intention of wasting his precious life over Ellis!

Where was Vanessa? He tumbled into Adam. Dear old Adam, the man he liked best in the world and Vanessa's father!

'Why, Adam! Isn't this grand? I say, where's Vanessa?'

'Somewhere,' said Adam, who was rejoicing in every minute of this great day that was to do his mother honour. 'How are you, young Benjie?'

'So-so,' said Benjie, dropping his voice and grasping Adam's arm. 'I say, this sort of thing makes a fellow restless. Ever feel restless?'

'Sometimes,' said Adam.

'Well, *I* feel restless up at the Fortress. If it weren't for mother I wouldn't stay.'

'Why, where would you go to?'

'I don't know. The sea perhaps. Or America.'

'Take my advice,' said Adam, 'and stay at home. There's no place like home.'

'You didn't always think so?'

'No.'

'Nor do I. When I'm your age, Adam, I'll settle, but as it is—'

He went off, laughing, poking Barney in the ribs, bowing ceremoniously to Lady Herries whom he detested, seeing little Ruth Cards for the first time in his life and thinking. 'That's a pretty girl. I wonder if she'd mind being kissed.' He did in fact kiss someone a moment later, for he wandered through the green-baize door at the back of the hall and there, in the passage leading to the kitchens, was Hannah, carrying a tray.

'Why, Hannah!' he cried.

'Master Benjie!' She smiled. They all adored him.

'Here, give me a kiss! No, there isn't a moment to lose! Here, I'll hold the tray!'

'No, Master Benjie, you're not to!'

But he put his arms round her, held her close to him, kissed her full on the lips. Then, laughing, ran off.

But where, oh, where was Vanessa?'

All the clocks struck ten. Everyone began to move upstairs. There had been a change in the arrangements. A very handsome volume in blue leather and gold had been provided, and in it every member of the Herries family who could be found had signed his or her name, agreeing that they from the bottom of their hearts congratulated Judith on her Hundredth Birthday and wished her health and prosperity.

It had been Barney's idea, a very pretty one. It had been intended that Adam should present this, but after Walter's unexpected arrival it had been thought that it would be excellent if Walter, the senior of them all, should make the Presentation. At first there had been some difficulty. He wanted to give his *own* present. He had come all that way to give his *own* present . . .

'But so you shall, dear,' Elizabeth whispered. 'You shall give them both. Only this is from all of us and the other is your special one . . .'

But he wanted to give his *own* present! However, at last he had consented to hold the blue leather book in one hand and his own precious little box in the other. Elizabeth guiding him, they headed the Procession up the stairs.

And up the stairs they all crowded, laughing, joking, excited, feeling that this was really a *great* Herries occasion, that, as it were, the eyes of all England were upon them.

On the way up Barney said one thing to Amery in a chuckling whisper:

'Very fitting, you know, old Walter making the Presentation. Closes the Feud. He and Judith were enemies for years. That's the end of *that*!'

At the same moment Benjie caught sight of Vanessa just ahead

of him. He brushed forward, almost, in his haste, knocking
someone over. He did not know (nor would he have cared if he
had known) that that someone was Ellis.

'I say! Vanessa! Vanessa! Where *have* you been?'

She turned. She was a stair or two higher. Her face was lit
with delight as she turned her head and saw him.

'Oh, Benjie! I've been looking for you everywhere!'

Ellis stared at her. The staircase seemed to rock beneath him.

'Hush!' Timothy said. 'We go in now, three at a time. Sir
Walter, you're first. Thank you. Elizabeth, if you wouldn't
mind!'

Judith sat looking at the door, Jane standing beside the chair.
She was quite calm, very dignified, extremely proud and
happy.

The door opened and Walter entered, led forward by
Elizabeth.

Jane gasped.

'Oh, Aunt Judith – it's Walter Herries!'

But to Judith it seemed perfectly natural.

'There, Jane, I said he would come. How extremely attentive
of him!'

Walter had no idea of anything save that it was Judith's birthday and he was giving her a present. But he realized, as he wandered, gazing about him, across the floor, that that was Judith
sitting in the chair. He knew Judith well enough. He had known
her all his life. But why was he in a bedroom? He stopped,
midway, and looked at the bed.

'Walter,' said Judith, smiling. 'How are you?'

That brought him to himself. This was, in any case, Judith,
and this was her birthday. He found himself by the chair.
Elizabeth was beside him.

'Well, Judith,' he said, his eyes still roving about the room.
'They tell me it's your birthday, so I've come and I've brought
you a present.'

He pushed the little parcel into her lap and dropped the blue
book. Elizabeth picked it up and put it into his hand again.

'Father, dear. You know what you are to say. You are to give
Aunt Judith this. It's from all of us, and you are to say that all
our names are here and that we all wish her a lovely birthday and
many more birthdays.'

'A lovely birthday and many more birthdays,' said Walter,

dropping the volume into her lap. Then, quite of his own accord, he bent forward and kissed her. Elizabeth had to steady him because his knees were very shaky.

Judith was delighted and greatly touched. She took her handkerchief from the table and wiped her eyes.

'Thank you indeed, Walter. Thank you, thank you. I am very glad you have come, because once we were not friends, were we? And now we are. I want to be friends with everyone today. And most especially with you, Walter.'

Walter began eagerly: 'And you must open *my* present, Judith.'

With very firm fingers Judith undid the parcel.

'Oh, isn't that pretty? *Isn't* that pretty? Do you see it, Jane? A lovely brooch! Walter, how *very* good of you—'

'Yes,' he said, immensely satisfied. 'It's a very pretty thing. I've had it a long time . . .' His eyes began to wander. 'Uhland would have come today, only – only – I don't know why – but—'

Elizabeth gently took his arm.

'Now, Father, you must make way for the others.' She led him to the window.

And Judith, now with her eyes bright and eager, was staring at the door. The great moment of her life had come. Adam would be next. Surely, surely Adam *must* be next!

She saw that they had all crowded to the door, and, all their faces smiling, were staring in.

A figure detached itself from the crowd. Grinning all over his face, moving his heavy body in his own rambling, comfortable way, Adam came forward.

At the sight of her son Judith's eyes and mouth broke into the loveliest smile that any member of the Herries family, here present, had ever seen.

Now her Hundredth Birthday was indeed a Triumph!

Christmas Eve, 1930
November 1, 1931

Vanessa

for Erik Palmstierna
in friendship

A Prefatory Letter

MY DEAR ERIK,

I take the greatest pleasure in dedicating this final novel in the Herries series to yourself because during those last years our friendship has been one of the best things I possess.

With that pleasure I must contrast a very real sense of loss. I am, as I write the last lines of *Vanessa*, saying goodbye to work that has been, for the last six years, my constant preoccupation. It cannot interest my readers that Judith, Benjie, Vanessa and the others have appeared to me such real and constant friends, but now, as they vanish down the wind, I feel a true and personal loneliness.

But I should like to thank those readers who have also found them friends, and to urge upon one or two critics that long novels are no new thing, and have been always in the tradition of the English novel.

Yet more boldly I would say that in this present case these four Herries novels are intended to be read as one novel, and I hope that some day there will be a reader who will both live long enough and be idle enough to read them so ? But one ambition of mine is realized. Some of those who love and know Cumberland have found in these pages a tribute to that country which has pleased them.

Affectionately,
HUGH WALPOLE

'Therefore, like as May month flowereth and flourisheth in many gardens, so in like wise let every man of worship flourish his heart in this world, first unto God, and next unto the joy of them that he promised his faith unto; for there was never worshipful man nor worshipful woman, but they loved one better than another: and worship in arms may never be foiled, but first reserve the honour to God, and secondly the quarrel must come of thy lady: and such love I call virtuous love.'

SIR THOMAS MALORY

Contents

Part One
THE RASCAL

Part Two
THE HUSBAND

Part Three
THE LOVER

Part Four
THE GHOST

The Herries Family in *Vanessa*

Judith Paris, *daughter of Rogue Herries*
Adam Paris, *her son*
Margaret, *his wife*
Vanessa, *Adam's daughter*
Sally, *Vanessa's daughter*
Sir Walter Herries, *son of Sir William Herries*
Elizabeth, *his daughter, widow of John Herries*
Benjamin, *her son, m.* Marion Halliday
Tom, *Benjamin's son*
Sir Ellis Herries, *son of Sir William, m.* Vanessa Paris
Lady Herries (Valerie), *his mother*
Dorothy Bellairs, *Jennifer's daughter*
Timothy, *her son, m.* Violet Greenacre
Timothy ⎫
Violet ⎭ *Timothy's children*
Veronica m. Robert Forster ⎫
Amabel ⎬ *Dorothy's daughters*
Jane ⎭
Captain William Herries, *son of Ven Rodney Herries*
Dorothy, *his wife*
Dora, *his sister, m.* Fred Beauchamp
Cynthia, *Dora's daughter, m.* Hon Peile Worcester
Mary Worcester ⎫
Rosalind Worcester ⎭ *Cynthia's children*
Garth Herries, *grandson of Pelham Herries*
Sylvia, *his wife*
Amery *his brother, m.* Hilda Coates
Alfred, *Amery's son, m.* Lucy Collison
Maurice ⎫
Clara ⎭ *Alfred's children*
Carey Bligh, 5th Lord Rockage
Mary, *his wife*
Maud ⎫
Helen ⎬ *their daughters*
Horace Newmark, *son of Phyllis and Stephen Newmark*
Sidney, *his son, m.* Mary Ratcliffe
Gordon ⎫
Ada ⎭ *Sidney's children*
Phyllis Newmark, *Horace's sister, m.* Clarence Rochester
Philip Rochester, *her son*
Emily Newmark, *her sister*
Barnabas Newmark, *her brother*

Part One

The Rascal

THE HUNDREDTH BIRTHDAY

AT THE SIGHT of her son Judith's eyes and mouth broke into the loveliest smile that any member of the Herries family, there present, had ever seen. It was Judith Paris' hundredth birthday. The Family was making a Presentation.

Adam bent down and kissed her. Her tiny, trembling hand rested on the velvet collar of his coat then lay against his cheek. Her triumph was complete; her exceeding happiness overflowed so that, laughing though she was, tears rolled down her cheeks.

Afterwards, at the luncheon downstairs, Adam was to make the speech, but when the time came, the one that he made was very feeble. Everyone (except of course Adam's wife, Margaret, and Adam's young daughter, Vanessa) agreed that he was no speaker; the speech of the occasion came, oddly enough, from Amery Herries, of whom no one had expected very much. There were more speeches at the dinner later in the day – Timothy, Barney Newmark, Carey Rockage, Captain Will Herries, all spoke – but it was Amery who was afterwards recalled.

'Damned good speech, d'you remember?' years later one Herries would say to another. 'At old Madame's Hundredth Birthday party up in Cumberland . . . Best speech ever I heard in my life.'

Adam was a failure. He never could say anything in public, even long ago in his Chartist days. More than that, he was thinking of his mother, the old lady upstairs, all the time. And more than that again, he couldn't sound the right Herries note. He was only *quarter* Herries anyway, and he simply wasn't able to think of them in the grand historical light that all the family, expectant round the luncheon table, desired.

But Amery could. He thought of them all (including himself) in precisely the grand manner.

All Adam said was:

'I am sure we are all very happy to be here today for my mother's hundredth birthday. You'll forgive me, I know, if I don't say very much. Not very good at expressing my feelings.

Yes – well – I know what you're all feeling. We're all very proud of my mother and we all ought to be. She's like the Queen – nothing can beat her. I don't need to tell you how good she is. Of course I know that better than the rest of you – naturally I would. There's no one like her anywhere. I ask you all to drink her health.'

And so they did – with the greatest enthusiasm. Nevertheless there was a feeling of disappointment, for he had said nothing about the Family – not a word. It was expected of him. After all, even though he *was* illegitimate, his father had been of Herries blood. They knew, they had always known, that Adam Paris failed at anything that he tried. What could you expect of a fellow who had once been a Chartist and approved of these Trades Unions, was always on the wrong side, against Disraeli, in favour of tiresome agitators like Mr Plimsoll? (They disliked any and every agitator. They disapproved of agitation.)

But Amery made everything right again with *his* speech. He didn't look his sixty-five years, so spare of figure and straight in the back; he had not run to seed like poor Garth, who led, it was feared, a most improvident and dissolute life. Amery's speech was short but entirely to the point:

'Only a word. I won't take more than a minute. But I do want to say that my friend Adam is quite right – this *is* a great occasion for all of us! There is not, I venture to say, another family in England with so remarkable a lady at the head of it as Madame whom we are gathered together to honour. It is not only that she has reached her hundredth year – although that is an achievement in itself – but that she has reached it with such vigour, such health, such courage! It is interesting to remember that nearly a hundred and fifty years ago her father, as a young man, rode pack-horse into this district, a stranger and almost you might say homeless. There were, I suppose, members of our family scattered about England at that time, but no one, I fear, had ever heard of any of them. Now, sitting round this table today we have one of England's most famous novelists – spare your blushes, Barney Newmark – the widow of one of England's most prominent financiers – I bow to you, Lady Herries – whose son is following worthily in his father's footsteps – I drink to the City, Ellis – the son of one of England's leading Divines, the gallant Captain here – one of the most active members, I'm told, of the House of Peers – never been there myself, but that's what they tell me, Carey, my son – and one of the loveliest women in the whole of England, Mrs Robert Forster – I bow towards you, Veronica!

'I promised that I would be short, so I will not point out to you how unusual a family ours is. You know it already.' (Loud and happily complacent laughter.) 'We *are* a remarkable family. Why should we not say so? We have done, we are doing something for England. England, glorious England, Mistress of the World as she deserves to be.' (He was going on to say something about foreigners but remembered just in time that Madame's husband had been a Frenchman and that Adam had married a German.) 'So here's to Madame and here's to England and here's to the Herries family! May they all three live, prosper, and help the world along the way that it should go!'

What cheers, what enthusiasm, what excitement! He had said exactly what they were all longing for someone to say – the one thing needed to make the day a perfect success!

Judith's granddaughter, Adam's daughter, little Vanessa Paris, aged fifteen, sat between her mother and father and was so happily excited that she found it difficult to keep still. Some of the ladies thought that it was not quite correct that she should be there. In 1874 the golden rule was that children should be seen (at intervals) and never heard. She was Madame's granddaughter and it was proper that she should have been present at the moving ceremony when the presentation was made to the old lady, but the right thing then was for her mother to send her back to Cat Bells where she lived. Nevertheless Lady Herries agreed with Emily Newmark that the child was tall for her age, was certainly pretty in her blue dress, and behaved with decorum. 'It's only to be hoped,' Lady Herries said with foreboding, 'that indulgence like this won't spoil her. But what can you expect? Her mother's a German. Adam Paris can have no idea of how to bring up a child. I never allowed,' Lady Herries added, 'Ellis any liberties, and no mother could wish for a more perfect son.'

Vanessa, of course, neither knew nor cared what anyone was saying. She trusted the whole world and everything and everyone in it. She loved everybody and especially her mother, her father, her grandmother, Aunt Jane Bellairs, Benjamin, Will Leathwaite (how she wished that he was here and could see all that was going on! She was storing everything up to tell him when she was home again).

From where she sat she could watch everything that Benjamin

did and said. For the rest she was sharply observant. She noticed the large and very hideous yellow brooch that Lady Herries wore on her meagre bosom, the beautiful colour of Aunt Elizabeth's hair (many of the ladies were her aunts, although not strictly so in chronology), the way that fat Garth Herries swallowed his wine and smacked his lips at intervals, the funny way that Aunt Jane (who had just come down from upstairs and reported that Madame was doing *splendidly* – not the *least* tired by all the fuss) made little pellets of her bread, Aunt Amabel's suspicious manner of eating as though she suspected poison in every mouthful, and the shy frightened air of Ellis. (She supposed that *that* was because his mother was watching him!)

Of them all there were two who especially interested her. One was Benjamin, whom she loved with all her heart, and the other was a lady whose name she did not know, whom she had never seen before, who appeared to her the perfection of grace and beauty.

First Benjamin, whom she knew so well that he was like part of herself. She had loved him from the first moment of seeing him when, himself between six and seven, and she somewhere about two, he had made her first sticky and afterward sick with toffee that he had made against orders at the kitchen fire. Her first memory of him was connected with disobedience; so she had known him ever after, always against the law, always doing things of which she shouldn't approve, but she kept sacred to the death every secret confided to her. She would never betray him; she would always love him for ever and ever. It was as simple as that. She knew with that intuitive quickness given to children that her mother did not approve of him. She knew more – that no one approved of him. He lived up at the Fortress with his mother, the lovely Elizabeth, and his grandfather, old broken-down Sir Walter, and it was supposed that Benjamin looked after the estate. In a way, as Vanessa knew, he did. In his own way. He would work like a saint and a hero for a week, really work and with good solid common sense. Then he would have a mad spell, disappear for days to the sorrow and grief of his mama. He told Vanessa that he simply couldn't help it. 'Must breathe fresh air,' he said. He never told anyone where he went. He was already, as Vanessa knew, 'suspect' by the Family. He had been a failure at Rugby: there were stories of scandalous doings in Town. 'He's going to be no good.' 'The makings of a fine Rascal,' and, as always with the Herries family when speaking of someone of whom they disapproved, their voices took on a sort of ceremonial ring, a kind of chanting sound. 'But what can you expect? His grandfather shot himself, and his uncle murdered his father. What an inheritance! And look at his other grandfather! – up at the Fortress – what a life he's led! Nothing better now than an idiot!'

No, poor Benjie has no chance at all, they decide with satisfaction. Nevertheless they could not help but like him – when they were with him. Of course it was different when their backs were turned. But in his company it was difficult not to smile. He was so merry, so gay, always laughing. So generous too. 'No one's enemy but his own,' Barney Newmark, who liked him greatly, said – and poor old Garth Herries, who had been no one's enemy but his own to such an extent that he was a complete wreck and ruin, sighed sadly in reply.

Vanessa was aware of much of this, although no one had ever told her. She was always hot in Benjie's defence, no matter what the charge might be. When someone accused him it was as though she herself were accused; she was conscious at such times of a strange pain in her heart – a feeling of tenderness, sympathy, and apprehension. Now, as she looked across the table at him, she knew that he had no need of her sympathy. He was at his very gayest. He was not large – he would be rather a small man – but his shoulders were broad, his head round, bullet-shaped, his colour red and brown like a healthy pippin, his nose snub, his blue eyes bright and sparkling. If all the Herries were like horses, as someone had said, then Benjie was like a racy little pony, ready for anything and especially mischief. 'He's wild and, I'm sure, wicked. In fact I *know* he's wicked,' Lady Herries said. 'And Ellis doesn't like him at all. But what can you expect with such a family history?' Then dropping her voice and looking into Emily Newmark's eyes with that intimate confidence felt by one upright woman for another: 'Women! Of course – I hear that already...'

Nevertheless he was happy, he loved his beautiful mother, he feared no man, he was generous, almost everything – even the tiniest things – gave him pleasure. What if he did find women enchanting, forgot to pay his debts, possessed no sense of class at all so that a tramp was exactly the same to him as a Herries, found it difficult to work at a thing for more than a week at a time, took no thought for the morrow, saw a joke in everything? – there he was, enjoying life to the uttermost, which was more than could be said for some of the other Herries seated round the table.

As to the very beautiful lady whom Vanessa so greatly admired, her name was Rose Ormerod.

After the luncheon Vanessa flung her arms round her father and kissed him.

'Happy, my darling?'

'Oh yes. Oh yes, I've never been so happy—'

'That's right. I didn't make much of a speech, did I, my pet?'

'Oh yes, Papa! It was much better than the other one because you were thinking of Grandmamma.'

'Thank you, darling. So I was. But I'm not good at speeches. That's a fact.' She laid her cheek against his. Then, remembering, straightened up.

'Papa, may I go for a walk with Benjie? He's asked me to.'

Adam hesitated. Then, taking her small white hand between his, he said:

'All right.'

He could trust her with Benjamin. And yet—

She clapped her hands and ran off, crying: 'Yes, Benjie, I can. Papa says I can.' She ran into Ellis Herries and looked up laughing. 'I beg your pardon.' She put her hand for a moment on his sleeve.

His thin anxious face looked down at her.

'My fault, I'm sure. It's – it's a nice day, isn't it?'

'Yes, it is.' She stood there, waiting, but longing to get off to Benjie. It was good manners, though, if a gentleman wished to talk to you, to wait while he did so.

Ellis Herries was tall, thin and pale. She noticed that he had a little brown mole in the middle of his left cheek.

'A very happy party we're having,' he said in his stiff anxious voice. He always spoke as though he were afraid that the words he used would betray him, laugh at him behind his back, as it were.

'Oh, it *is* nice!' She smiled, felt that she had done her duty, and ran off.

When they walked out on to the road they saw that they had but an hour before dark. Frost was sharpening the air. They mounted straight on to the moor and moved swiftly through a moth-grey world where mountains were gigantic and the turf was crisping under their feet. The house stood behind them like a lighted ship. The candles were burning in every room. Vanessa had sometimes to run to keep up with Benjamin, but in any case she ran because she was so happy, deeply excited and enchanted to be alone with him. Soon they slowed down, stood on a hillock and looked over to Scotland.

'There's Criffel,' he said, pointing.

'I can't see it,' Vanessa said.

'No, but it's there all the same.' He took her hand. 'I approve of you in that fine hat. Where did you find the feather?'

'Mama bought the hat in Keswick.'

He stood close to her.

'You are almost as tall as I am, Vanessa. You are going to be very tall.'

'Papa says I am. Will you never be taller, Benjie?'

'No, I hope not. You see, it's very useful to be short.'

'Useful?'

'Yes — if there's a row you can crawl under tables or hide behind a curtain or creep into the clock. I remember once in London—' He stopped.

Vanessa's innocence must be protected.

'Oh, do tell me about London!'

'One day, when you've been there. It wouldn't mean anything to you if you don't know the places.'

They walked on. They were both strong, sturdy, filled with health and excitement.

Benjamin flung out his arms.

'Don't you love this country? But of course you do. We belong to it. There'll never be any other country for either of us. Your father once told me that when he was a boy he had a tutor called Rackstraw who knew more about this country than anyone. He said it was all stones and clouds. One stone wall running up a hill, one sky with the clouds pouring over it, and you're happy. It's so old. There are Romans' bones under your foot. It's so strong — Border fights and Picts and Scots. It's so wide and smells so good. Don't you like the smell of dry bracken, of the trees, of the stream water when you lie flat and drink it? Which hill do you like best?'

'Cat Bells,' said Vanessa promptly.

'Oh, I mean a real hill. Skiddaw has wings, Saddleback's like a shark, Gable is a helmet . . .' He stopped suddenly, put his arms round her and kissed her. 'Oh, Vanessa, I do love you!'

'And I love you,' she said, a little breathless.

'Will you marry me when you grow up?'

'Of course I will,' she said, laughing.

They walked on, more slowly, he keeping his arm around her.

'Well, you'd better not. Everyone disapproves of me.'

'What does that matter?'

Her trust touched him most deeply.

'Would you marry me if your father and mother forbade it?'

That was an awful question. She stopped to consider it.

'Yes,' she said.

'Oh, you darling! But I won't allow you to marry me. Ask anyone. No woman ought to marry me. I couldn't be faithful.'

'You would be,' said Vanessa, 'if we had children.'

'Will you like to have children?' he asked her, wondering what she would say.

'Of course. But you can't help it. God brings you a baby. You wake up in the morning and find it lying there beside you. That must be wonderful. Mama says that God knows just when you want one.'

'So you believe in God?'

Vanessa laughed. 'Why, of course. What a silly question, Benjie! Everybody does.'

'Everybody doesn't—' He pulled up. He must not disturb her.

'Of course everyone does!' she answered indignantly. 'Why, who made everything if God didn't? God's everywhere. Will Leathwaite says that when he has been swearing too much God gives him the rheumatism just to remind him.'

Benjie thought some other topic wiser.

'Well – but if I was in disgrace with everyone, had done something shameful and no one would speak to me, would you still marry me?'

'Of course I would.'

'But if you yourself thought it shameful?'

'I shouldn't think anything *you* did shameful,' she answered.

'If I killed someone as my uncle killed my father?'

She stood, puzzled, staring into the grey cold landscape.

'Yes,' she said, nodding her head. 'I would know why you did it. There would be *some* reason that I should understand.'

He caught her hands in his.

'Will you promise me that whatever happens you will always stand by me?'

'Yes, I promise.'

'Always and for ever?'

'Yes.'

'Whatever I did?'

'Yes.'

'I'll remind you of that one day.' He turned round. 'Now we'll go back to all the cats and monkeys,' he said.

They were both quiet returning. They had to go arm in arm, very close together, because it was growing dark. For a brief while there was a faint orange glow over Skiddaw like the reflection of a distant fire; the air grew with every moment more frosty.

Once as they were nearing the house he said:

'Don't you hate Ellis? I do. *And* his old pig of a mother.'

In the hall, standing for a moment to accustom herself to the lights and splendour after the half-dark, Vanessa found her father. He had been standing there, waiting for her, hearing the voices and laughter all over the house, the distant click of billiard balls, someone singing to the piano sentimental songs like *Drink to me only* and *My hero, my Troubadour,* Elizabeth coming back from the Fortress where she had deposited poor old Walter, quite in pieces. She had put him to bed. He had fallen almost at once to sleep; all he had said, she told Adam, just before he went off to sleep, was: 'Wake me when Uhland comes in.' Very touching, but, as she said, a comfort for him to think that Uhland was still alive. Sometimes, Elizabeth confessed, she thought that he was and she could hear the tap-tap of his lame leg mounting to his tower . . . Then along the passage from the kitchen came bursting Barney Newmark and Garth and Timothy, stout, noisy, and triumphant. Why triumphant? Had they been kissing the maids? But the Herries men got like that very easily if things were going well and there were no ghosts about.

In the middle of all this Adam waited anxiously for his little daughter. His wife, Margaret, was sitting in the parlour trying to be on terms with Lady Herries and that fascinating Rose Ormerod from Harrogate (she wasn't beautiful, Adam decided – not to be compared with Elizabeth or Veronica – her nose was a little crooked, she had a faint, a very faint moustache on her upper lip. It was her colour, dark, black, crimson, like a gipsy: and then she was silent – she spoke very rarely, only smiled and used her eyes). Poor Margaret would not be happy in there; he knew how anxious *she* was about Vanessa! When he told her that the child had gone for a walk with Benjamin she gave a little cry of dismay.

'Oh, Adam! You should not have allowed her!'

'Pooh, my dear! Benjamin's safe!'

'No, he isn't! You know he isn't! And Vanessa's growing!'

'She is only fifteen.'

He had calmed her a little, but his own fears had increased. What was he to do about this? He knew that Vanessa loved Benjamin with all the fire, loyalty, ignorance of an adoring child. Benjamin's reputation was bad, very bad. And yet he liked him. He could not help it. He had always had a weakness for sinners ... But Benjamin and his own child! No, no!

As the darkness strengthened about the house his alarm grew. He was about to get his coat and go after them when in they came, Vanessa glowing with colour, her eyes shining, her body so alive that it could not keep still.

He told her that she was to come up and say goodnight to her grandmother.

'We must not stay for more than a moment. She is in bed and tired, of course, after such a fatiguing day. It's something to be a hundred, you know!'

Vanessa was at once subdued and still. She lived so entirely, at present, in her interest in other people that, in a moment, she became what they wanted her to be. That is if she loved them. She was quite otherwise, it is to be feared, with one or two – Aunt Amabel, for instance, whom she couldn't abide, and Timothy's fiancée, who had aggravated her by talking to her in baby language.

Judith's bedroom seemed now a mysterious place, quite different from the bright sunlit room of the morning, crowded with happy faces, and the old lady sitting so erect in her chair, smiling as they brought her their presents.

The curtains were drawn now, the room dark save for the fire and the dim lamplight beside the bed. That old four-poster with its dark hangings appeared like a little room in itself. Aunt Jane was moving softly about. When Adam and Vanessa appeared in the doorway she put her fingers to her lips.

She went over to the bed, leant over.

'Aunt Judith! Aunt Judith!'

'Yes, my dear,' said a very lively voice. 'What is it?'

'Adam and Vanessa are here to say goodnight.'

'Turn up the lamp.' Judith sat up, put out her hand for her

spectacles, and, her eyes as sharp behind them as a bird's, said:
'That's right. Very kind of you, Adam. Come over here, my
dears.'

They crossed the room, and Jane put the crimson armchair for
Adam. Vanessa stood close to him, her hand on his shoulder.

The old lady seemed a little breathless. She was wearing a cap
as white as snow with the sun on it, and over her shoulders Jane
laid a thick white cashmere shawl. Her little face was drawn and
lined, waxen in the lamplight. It was her eyes and hands that
were alive, and her enchanting, humorous, slightly ironical
smile.

'So I'm a hundred at last!' she said with a sigh of satisfaction.
'That's something, Adam, isn't it?'

'Indeed it is, Mother.'

'Yes, and a *very* nice day it's been.'

'You're not tired?'

'Well – a little. Yes, a little tired. My heart' – she put her hand
to her breast – 'jumps. There's nothing odd about that though.
It's been jumping for a hundred years. It was never so steady as it
ought to be.'

Vanessa smiled.

'Have you had a happy day, my darling?' She put her hand
out and took Vanessa's. How hot and dry it was, Vanessa
thought – burning bones under parchment, and at the touch of it
the child had a moment's realization of what it was to be old, to
be a hundred years old, to be burnt up with life and all the things
that you had seen and done!

'It was nice,' Judith said, 'poor old Walter coming. Very nice.
He's sadly broken up, I'm afraid. Sadly aged.' She spoke with
tenderness, satisfaction, and triumph. She had beaten Walter at
last. She was older than he and yet here she was as lively as you
like and he a poor old man who had to be led about, weak in the
head, uncertain where he was!

Yet she herself was suddenly weary. She lay back on her
pillow, her spectacles falling to the edge of her nose.

'I hope everyone is happy,' she murmured.

'Very happy, Mother dearest,' Adam answered, catching a
command from Jane's watchful eye. 'You must go to sleep now.
You will be fresh as anything tomorrow.'

'Yes, dear,' Judith murmured.

Vanessa bent forward and kissed her. Then Adam, moved by

the deepest emotion, tears rising to his eyes, kissed her, felt her hand lift for a moment and touch his cheek in the old familiar way.

Before they had stolen from the room she was, it seemed, asleep.

The first Ball of Vanessa's life!

Was Ball too grand a word to give to it? There was for orchestra Mrs Blader from Troutbeck at the piano; Mr Murdy of Keswick, violin; old Mr Bayliss of Keswick, 'cello. There was perhaps in all thirty couples, and the dining-room, cleared, within the hour following dinner, miraculously of its table and chairs, had a perfect floor. It had often been tested. The room looked lovely, Vanessa thought, with the gleaming, glittering candelabra, the candles in their silver candlesticks, the coloured paper streamers slung from corner to corner against the ceiling. It was colours everywhere, dresses – pink, white, blue, orange – billowing and surging as the dancers moved, necks and shoulders bare, jewels sparkling; almost everyone to Vanessa seemed beautiful – even old Lady Herries, although she was absurdly painted and had a neck like a writhing chicken, had diamonds in her hair that must, Vanessa thought, be worth a fortune.

Three of the women were beautiful beyond compare – Elizabeth Herries who was fifty-nine years of age but had the arms and shoulders of a girl; and Veronica, now proudly Mrs Forster, 'a queen of a woman, by Gad,' Will Herries murmured somewhat unwisely to his wife, who was a good woman but no beauty. The third was Ruth Cards, who went shortly after this to live in the wilds of Northumberland and but seldom left them.

At first Vanessa had felt a devastating shyness. At dinner she had been very quiet. She was wearing her first grand evening dress and only she and her mother knew what consultations there had been with Miss Kew of Keswick, how often they had paid visits to Miss Kew's stuffy little room near St John's, how important it had been that it should be *half* grown-up – Miss Kew had been alarmed: girls of fifteen did not go to Balls, but then of course this was a family affair, a little different . . . nevertheless, as Miss Kew confided to her brother, Mrs Paris was a German woman – 'Such things might be well in Germany' just as though she had said Shanghai!

So they had planned between them something very original,

the neck and shoulders bare – 'Miss Vanessa has such beautiful shoulders' – the skirt full, but not *too* full. A pale pink silk and round her slender neck her only piece of jewellery, a necklace of crystal beads that her father had brought her from London.

At dinner she was certain that they must *all* be saying: 'And what is *this* child doing here?' All day she had been so happy that she had not given herself a thought, but at dinner Garth Herries had been on the one side of her and Ellis on the other.

Rose Ormerod was Garth's other companion and very quickly he surrendered to her as apparently all men did. He did not speak to Vanessa once. And Ellis! Well, Ellis was very strange. He stared at her in the oddest way. He spoke to her confusedly as though he were afraid of her. He said: 'I hope you are enjoying yourself,' and then later: 'I do hope, most sincerely, that you are enjoying yourself.' He made her embarrassed. It was he perhaps who made her self-conscious. He looked at her shoulders and hands, and once he said, in a strangled fashion as though food were choking him 'I hope you will give me a dance.' Very bravely she asked him once whether he liked to live in London. 'Oh yes, indeed yes. Very pleasant. Lived there all my life, you know.'

She coloured; she felt that it had been a very silly question; she looked about her to find her father, but he was sitting on the same side of the table as herself.

Then, at first, no one asked her to dance. She sat on a little sofa with her mother, feeling that everyone must be looking at her bare shoulders, not very far, if the truth must be known, from tears. It had been a lovely day, but she had no right to be here. She thought that, in a little while, she would whisper something to her mother and slip away to bed . . .

It was Benjie who came to her rescue. The most beautiful waltz had just begun and he charged down upon them, had her on her feet before she knew, and then they were lost in Paradise.

She was a lovely dancer. She had danced all her life, danced up and down the parlour at Cat Bells while her father whistled the tunes, danced by the Lake in Manesty, danced in the kitchen with Will, had had dancing lessons in Keswick at Mr Kew's (brother to Miss Kew) dancing class. She was a dancer by all the light of her nature.

'That child dances well,' said Lady Herries to Rose Ormerod. 'Very pretty.'

'That child will be a beautiful woman,' said Miss Ormerod. The two were passing them at the moment. Miss Ormerod's intense gaze followed them round the room. In a second of time Vanessa's misery had been changed to timeless, priceless delight. They did not speak. Benjamin also loved dancing. He knew at once whether his partner was worthy of him. Already many a young woman had found herself, after a round or two, sitting to her own surprise on the sofa, and Benjie beside her, charming but static.

'You dance better than anyone else in the room, Vanessa.'

'Oh, do I?' Vanessa whispered. 'Oh, Benjie, do I really?'

He did not tell her that he had said that to many a partner in the past. He knew that he would say it to thousands in the future. But tonight he meant every word of it. When the dance was over and they were sitting on the stairs she confided to him how unhappy she had been at dinner.

'You will often be unhappy again,' he instructed her. 'Everyone is so. Dinners are the devil. You never know whom you will get. It's a game, you see, Vanessa, and the worse ninny you have beside you the better the game is. Flatter them. That's the way. Everyone likes to be flattered. You can't put it on too thick. And do it as though you meant it. Then you'll discover you *do* mean it, for the moment anyway.'

'What do you flatter them about?' she asked.

'Oh, you'll soon discover their weak point. Everyone has them. Ask them first what they like best – games or travelling or adding up sums in a stuffy office as Ellis does. After that, all you've got to do is listen. Nobody wants you to do anything but listen, no men anyway. Women are different. They like you to tell them that they are beautiful or clever. And why shouldn't they? We all get enough of the other thing. Parties are meant to cheer you up and make you feel for a moment that all the things the people who know you best think about you aren't true.'

'Well,' said Vanessa, 'whatever happens now it won't matter. I've had one lovely dance.'

But she need not have been afraid. Soon Amery came to ask her, then Will Herries, then young Richard Cards, then Carey Rockage and, at last, Ellis.

She gave them all places on her flowery programme. She swung round the room in an ecstasy. 'Isn't this lovely?' she murmured to Amery.

Amery, who was anxious about his brother Garth, now rather drunk and quarrelsome in the parlour, answered at first absent-mindedly, then realized that he was moving with a grace and charm that he hadn't known for years. 'By Gad,' he thought, 'I'm more of a dancer than I knew I was,' and wondered whether if he had been more gay in his past and his brother less gay, it wouldn't have been better for both of them! 'Poor Sylvia!' he thought, seeing Garth's wife, painted, raddled, and weary as she bumped round with Rockage, who was no dancer. 'She's had a rotten life!' He was suddenly charitable to everyone. This charming child, light as a fairy – by Jove, she was bewitching! Why had he known nothing like this? He had married late, and it hadn't lasted long. There had been others of course – Doris, whom he had had to keep so long after he was tired of her, and Alice Mason, who'd smashed all his china one night in a fit of temper, and the Frenchwoman, Marguerite Calvin, whose father's debts he had paid. Had he had much in return? No, not very much. As he felt Vanessa's hand on his arm he sighed. What was the use? He would be just the same tomorrow.

Vanessa, to her own great amusement, began at once to put Benjie's advice into practice with all these gentlemen. It worked like a miracle. Amery talked to her about money, horses, and the Family. Will Herries talked to her about the Navy, the sea, the West Indies, Glebeshire, dogs, Polchester, the sea, the Family. Young Richard (whom she liked greatly) talked about books (*Middlemarch*, Mrs Browning, Hawley Smart), gardening, riding, and the Family, and Carey talked about the place in Wiltshire, the weather, the weather, the weather, the place in Wiltshire, and the Family. She found that they soon forgot that they were talking to a child. She found that they all wanted comforting, consoling, reassuring, and so learnt one very useful never-to-be-forgotten lesson about Men. She discovered, too that all of them, except young Richard, felt that in one way or another an injustice had been done. They hadn't had fair treatment. Someone was to blame. Carey Rockage in especial was like a blinded bewildered animal whom unseen persecutors were prodding with pitchforks.

'Oh, I *am* so sorry!' she found herself saying over and over again.

And Ellis? Ellis was another matter. She had noticed that he watched her. Often, feeling that someone's eye was upon her, she saw that it was his. When their dance came it was 'Sir Roger', and he asked her whether she would mind sitting with him instead. She *did* mind because she loved 'Sir Roger' and something in her was afraid of a long talk with Ellis, but she followed him meekly out into the hall and to a top corner of the stairs.

Here the sounds of the music were very dim, the house was still, and she thought of her darling grandmother, not far away, deep in sleep. It was as though for a moment something drew her into that bedroom. She stood there, looking at the dim light by the bed.

'Are you asleep, Grandmamma?' she seemed to say.

'Yes, dear. I'm sleeping beautifully,' the answer came. She put her hand on Ellis' thin arm. 'Did you hear anything? Anyone call?'

'No,' he said.

There seemed to her a sound of light steps along the passage above them. Then she was compelled to give all her attention to Ellis. He forced her to do so. She did not know how old he was (he was in fact close on thirty-two), but he seemed to her both very old and very young.

He was unhappy, she was sure, and, like her grandmother, she could not bear that anyone should be unhappy. So, wanting to console him, she felt older than he. He was not exactly plain; he was distinguished in his thin, pale, quiet way; very serious; he scarcely ever smiled. But when he did his smile was rather beautiful. It lit up his thin face and his colourless eyes. It was as though he were pleading to be liked. He wants feeding up, she thought. His eyes were sometimes a little mad.

For a while he could do nothing but stammer out disconnected sentences. Then, following Benjie's advice, she asked him questions, about London, the City, theatres, and what he did in his spare time.

'I haven't any spare time,' he assured her. 'You see, my father had so many affairs in the City, and it all devolves upon me. I like it, you know. The City is a very agreeable place, it is indeed. Yes.' Then he said, staring at her with all his eyes: 'You must come one day, Cousin Vanessa, and stay with my mother and myself in Hill Street.'

'Thank you,' she said. 'I should love to go to London. I have never been to a theatre or a circus, and oh! how I should like to see the Queen!'

'The Queen is very much in retirement,' he said solemnly, as though he kept her in his pocket, 'but the Prince of Wales and the Princess are often to be seen driving.'

Then there was another awkward pause, until he broke out:

'I do hope you will come, Cousin Vanessa. Our house is not very gay, but if you came it would be—' He choked in his throat. 'Will you, please, not forget me? Will you think of me sometimes?'

'Of course I will think of you, Cousin Ellis,' she answered, laughing because she felt, for some strange reason, uncomfortable.

'Will you indeed? That will make me very happy ... I have not many friends,' he added. 'My own fault of course. I am shy. You may not have guessed it, but I am very shy indeed.'

She certainly *had* guessed it – not only was he shy but he made others who were with him shy too. Then the music, to her relief, began again.

'Oh, we must go!' she cried, jumping up.

'You promise to think of me?' he asked again urgently. 'I shall think of you often – very often indeed.'

When she was with them all again she sat for a while among the ladies and was aware of something that she had never thought of before (she was making so many discoveries tonight!), namely, that this family to which she belonged contained the real benefactors of the human race. Dorothy Bellairs, Veronica, Emily Newmark, even Sylvia Herries – they were all the same! If it were not for them the Poor, the Unprotected, almost everyone in fact who wasn't Herries, would perish. Vanessa had a strange picture of all the cottage women of England seeing through their window the arrival in a carriage and pair of Dorothy, Veronica, Emily, Sylvia. These ladies were armed magnificently against the cold, their hands were in muffs, the high collars of their coats reached to their bonnets. Majestically they moved down the cottage path, John, James, William following behind with basket on arm. Then the cottage woman hastens, straightens her apron, puts the children in their places, arranges grandfather by the fire, hurries to the door.

'Good afternoon, my lady.'

'Oh, good afternoon, Mrs Cottage Woman. How are you this afternoon?' The seat of the chair is dusted, even the cottage clock, the cottage cat, the cottage table are deferential. Glory has descended upon the cottage woman!

Vanessa had never thought of this before. The life that they enjoyed at Cat Bells was so very different; she had never had on every side of her so many Herries women. She had never, never realized that were it not for the Ladies of England the Poorer

Classes would fade away. She had never known that there *were* any Poorer Classes.

Even Veronica! Beautiful, lovely Aunt Veronica!

'Oh, well, I told her ... that if she didn't drink the soup ... *would* give it to her worthless old father ...'

And Rockage's wife: 'They complained about the drains, but Carey explained to them ...'

She turned it all over in her mind while she was dancing with young Richard.

Afterwards, when they were talking, she asked him:

'Are you glad you're partly a Herries?'

'Glad?' he said, turning round and smiling.

'Yes. Is it better being a Herries than being a Jones or Smith?'

(While she spoke she thought: What *is* happening to me? I've never thought of these things before.)

'Well, don'tcherknow,' said Richard slowly, 'there *is* something fine in being one of the oldest families—'

'But *are* we one of the oldest? I mean, aren't the Jones and the Smiths just as old really?'

'I suppose they are. It's being English that counts.'

'Is it better to be English than German or French?'

Richard, who had no notion that Vanessa's mother was a German, answered with no hesitation at all:

'By Gad, yes – I should jolly well think it is.' So that settled it.

As the evening went on she was aware that she had seen but little of Benjamin. She went to look for him and found him in the billiard room dancing solemnly up and down with Barney Newmark, both of them swaying a little as they moved.

Vanessa – quite suddenly a child again – stood hesitating in the doorway, and Benjamin, looking up, saw two Vanessas, both lovely, both darlings, both the beloved of his heart. But he was never so much a gentleman as when he had drunk too much, so he disengaged himself from Barney and gave a courtly bow.

'Sit down, Vanessa, and I will fetch you some lemonade.'

She stood there, bitterly disappointed. She had often seen gentlemen who drank too much, but never Benjamin. She saw that his hair was ruffled, his eyes shining, and that he swayed on his feet, but she knew also that she loved him as dearly as ever, that her impulse was to go to him, smooth his hair, straighten his tie ...

'No, thank you,' she said.

He came up to her and took her hand. He saw that she was frightened.

'Come and we'll dance, Vanessa,' he said.

'I am afraid that this one is engaged,' she answered, looking over his shoulder at Barney Newmark, who was gently singing to himself. She hurried away, leaving Benjamin staring after her.

In the dining-room again she danced once more with Amery and soon she was happy. How could she help it? Everyone was so happy around her. The musicians played like mad, the candles shone like stars, the noise filled the room so that it was like a paper bag on the point of bursting. The waltz was a lovely tune. They began to sing to it. The 'Blue Danube'. Oh! the 'Blue Danube'! How lovely! One was not on earth but swinging, swaying in an azure heaven, limitless, lit with radiance. The wide, full dresses eddied and billowed, the naked shoulders and arms were gleaming, there was that gentle undertone of music rocking, rocking . . .

Wait! What's the matter? The music had stopped! With a surge the room has reasserted itself, the candles have lost their radiance, everyone is silent, standing looking . . .

Vanessa, near to the door, saw that Aunt Jane, white-faced, shaking, Rockage's arm around her, was speaking. Amery turned to the child.

'How sad! How tragic! Madame! . . . dead!' Then realizing that it was Vanessa: 'Your grandmother . . .'

The silence that followed was so strange. Life had fled from the house.

'Yes, in her sleep . . . Jane went up five minutes ago . . . Quite quietly . . . in her sleep . . . They have sent for Doctor Bettany.'

As they stared, conscious, every one of them, of the precariousness of this moment of existence, of the folly of their pretences of safety, thinking at the same time of the figure of the morning, so upright, so grand in her pleasure and happiness, all this only a moment ago, they themselves, perhaps, before the morning . . .

But she was A Hundred! She had reached her Hundred! Nothing could deprive her of that. A great age. Best of all to go quietly in your sleep . . . A wonderful woman!

But beyond the windows the snow has begun to fall. Are there figures there on the frosty road? Old Herries, with the scar on his cheek, upright on his horse as when, so many years ago, he had

ridden up to that same gate to tell his son that his wife had run
away; stout David, young again, riding on the wind to his beloved hills; Georges, waiting now for Judith who had been in
spite of his many infidelities, his only love; Charlie Watson waiting too, after so long an uncomplaining patience; poor Warren
with that one hour of happiness to remember – and for those
silent motionless watchers was there a sudden opening of the
gates, a running out of a little figure, happy, daring, triumphant,
a moment's stare up and down the road, and then a cry?

'Georges! Georges! . . . Charlie! Warren! . . . Father!'

Vanessa felt an arm around her as Adam drew her away with
him, murmuring:

'Don't cry, my darling. It was the happiest way. Quietly –
without any fuss – while we were all dancing.'

FOUNTAIN AT THE ROADSIDE

WALTER HERRIES died in April 1880.

For the last five years of his life he was unaware of all that was
happening in the world and perfectly happy. His daughter
Elizabeth nursed him with infinite kindness and care and he was
an infant in her hands. The Fortress, during those years, was a
very quiet place. Benjamin, Elizabeth's son, managed the estate,
which was not now large in extent – two farms and a cottage or
two in Lower Ireby were the full extent of it.

He managed it, that is to say, when he was there. For much of
that period he was away; he visited the East, was said to have left
his young mark on Shanghai and to have invaded the sanctities
of Indian temples, to have assisted pirates in the South Seas and
to have been knifed within an inch of his life in Sarawak: it was
whispered even that he had five Chinese wives, numberless
Asiatic concubines. He returned, however, looking very much as
he went – brown, stubby, solid, cheerful, and without a conscience.
'I care for nobody, no, not I, and nobody cares for me' was said,
by all his friends and relations, to be his daily song.

He did, however, care for his mother, and after his third
return in '79 swore that he would settle down and become the
Cumberland squire. He loved Cumberland with passion and he

had a good head on his shoulders, so that, for a while, he was successful. Everyone liked him; for a brief time it seemed that he might be the most popular man in Cumberland. But soon stories were everywhere. He could not, it appeared, see a woman without kissing her, could not tell the truth (was it possible that his acquaintances had no humour?), had no social sense at all, so that he invited farmers' wives to meet Mrs Osmaston and took a shepherd with him to supper at Uldale. He was also, it was said, an atheist and openly defended Bradlaugh. He visited London frequently and never returned thence without a scandal hanging to his tail. It was said that the lowest ground in that city was *his* ground, that he drank, gambled, spent a fortune over horses and cheeked his relations. How many of these stories came from Hill Street, from old Lady Herries and her son Ellis, who both hated him, no one could say, but certain it was that he was himself responsible for many of them because he never denied anything and never admitted anything, cherished no grudges, accused no one and told anyone who asked him that yes, it must be true if everyone said so; he had no morals, he supposed; he would like to have some; they must be useful things, but he simply didn't know where they were to be found.

On the other hand everyone was forced to admit that, as he grew older, he did not look dissipated. His colour was of the healthiest, his body of the toughest, his eyes bright and glowing. When he bathed in the Lake or a mountain stream in the summer with young Osmaston or Timothy Bellairs or Robert Forster it could be seen that his limbs were brown and supple as though he lived for ever in the open air. He was never drunk now as many of his neighbours were; smutty stories never appealed to him in the least, and if girls were the worse for his friendliness nobody knew of it for a fact. It was said that he walked vast distances over the hills and alone. Nobody ever saw him out of spirits or out of temper. He was generous to a fault. With all this nobody really knew him and nobody trusted him. 'He's a rascal,' said the Herries in London, in Bournemouth, in Harrogate, in Manchester, in Carlisle, 'and he'll come to no good.' In fact they longed, many of them, that he *should* come to no good as quickly as possible.

His only friends among his relations were Aunt Jane at Uldale, Adam Paris and his daughter Vanessa, Barney Newmark, and Rose Ormerod at Harrogate, who always said she'd marry him tomorrow if he asked her.

His one saving grace, they all said, was that he loved his mother – loved her, they added, quite selfishly because he left her whenever he pleased and for months she had not a line from him. It was not hard, they added, for him to love his mother, for she was the sweetest and gentlest of ladies and gave him everything that he wanted.

It was also added that he possessed that strange and mysterious quality known as 'charm' – which meant that when you were with him you could not help but like him and that, as soon as his back was turned, you wondered whether he had meant a word that he said.

He happened to be at home when his grandfather died. Walter was sleeping late on a spring afternoon, and his room was bathed in sunshine. Wrapped in a padded crimson dressing-gown, his long white hair falling over his face as he slept, he seemed a bundle of clothes topped by a wig. Then he looked up, blinked at the sunlight, called for his son Uhland, saw him come slowly tap-tapping with his stick across the floor to him, grinned joyfully at the long-expected sight, and died – or, if you prefer it, went from the room, leaning on his son's arm, happy as he had not been for many a day.

That night, when the old man had been decently laid out on the four-poster in the room upstairs, Elizabeth and her son sat in the little parlour off the hall and talked. The evening was very warm and a window was open. The trees faintly rustled; there came the occasional late fluting of a bird; the scent of early spring flowers, dim and cool with the night, hung about the room.

Benjamin sat opposite his mother, his legs stretched wide, and thought how beautiful she still was, how dearly he loved her, how selfish and restless he was, how quiet and unselfish was she! Elizabeth's beauty had always been shy, delicately coloured, fragile. She was a Herries only in her strength of will and a certain opposition to new ideas. She had never cared for ideas but always for persons – and then for very few persons. As she looked across at her son she thought: 'He is all that I have left. I know that he loves me and I know that I have no power over him.' Then she raised her hand ever so slightly as though she were touching someone who bent above her chair. John Herries, her husband, had been dead for more than twenty years to everyone but herself. It was not sentiment nor vague superstition nor longing that made her aware that he was always alive at her side. It was plain fact – and as it was her own concern, her own experience, it was of no importance that others should say that this was absurd, or weak, or against facts. She worried no one else about the matter, not even her son.

Benjamin loved her so dearly that evening, thought she looked so lovely in her full black dress, felt so intensely how lonely she would be, that he was ready to do anything for her – except sacrifice anything that threatened his liberty. Everything threatened his liberty.

'So your long service is over, Mother. How wonderful you were to him! Everyone marvelled at it. I'm terribly proud of you.'

She looked at him, smiled (and with perhaps a touch of affectionate irony):

'And now, Benjie, I suppose you'll go away again?'

'Oh no, Mother. Of course not! Leave you now!'

'Well, perhaps not just now – but soon. Jane is coming to stay later. And Vanessa. Vanessa is coming tomorrow for a week.'

He looked up sharply.

'Vanessa!'

'Yes. You didn't know that she was here this evening? It was quite by chance. She had ridden over to Uldale. She had stayed the night with the Grigsbys. She came up to ask how everyone was. I told her the news, and like the darling she is she said that she would come tomorrow. Adam is away at Kendal, so it suits very well.'

'Oh, I'm glad!' He drummed his heels into the carpet.

'You know, of course, that she loves you?'

'And I love her.'

Elizabeth smiled. 'You say that very easily, Benjie.'

'Well, you know how it is.' He got up and stood in front of the fireplace. 'We've loved one another all our lives. Whatever else happens she always comes first. There's no one in the world to put beside her. But she's too fine for me to marry her. You know she is. No one knows it better than you do.'

He came and sat at her feet, his hand resting on her knee.

'How too fine?'

'You know what everyone says of me; that I'm no good, that I spoil everything I touch – a rascal, a vagabond, all the rest. And it's true, I suppose. I'm no man to marry anyone.'

She stroked his hair gently.

Is it true what they say?'

'You know me better than anyone else, Mother – or rather you and Vanessa do. I don't think about myself. I take myself as I am. But I know that I can't stick – to anyone or anything. It grows worse as I'm older. I want to do a thing – and I do it!'

'Is there any harm in that – if you don't do bad things?'

'But perhaps I do – things that you call bad. I can't tell. I don't think that I know the difference between right and wrong. Or rather my ideas of right and wrong are different from other people's. I'm too interested in everything to stop and think. I think when it's too late.'

He laughed and looked up into her face.

'I'm a bad lot – but I love you and Vanessa with all my heart.'

'Yes – but not enough to do things for us?'

'Anything you like. Tell me to fetch you something from Peking now and I'll go and get it. But I can't be tied, I can't be told what to do, I can't be preached at by anybody.'

'Perhaps,' Elizabeth said quietly, 'if you married Vanessa that would steady you.'

He shook his head vehemently.

'Vanessa is so good and so fine. She isn't strait-laced. She's wise and tolerant, but she's high-minded. She believes in God, you know, Mother.'

'And don't you?'

'You know that I don't. Not as she does. Not as she does. I may be wrong. I dare say I am. But I *must* be honest. I don't *see* things that way. I'm ignorant. I don't know any more than the next fellow and I want the next fellow to believe as he sees, but I must be allowed to see for myself. I can't *see* God anywhere. The things that people believe are fine for them but nonsense to me. To me as I am now. I've got all my life in front of me and everything to learn. God may be proved to me yet. I hope He will be.'

'Proved!' Elizabeth laid her cheek for a moment against his. 'God can't be proved, Benjie. He must be felt.'

'Yes, I suppose so. That may come to me one day. Meanwhile – a heathen and a vagabond can't marry Vanessa.'

She thought for a little and then said: 'Have you talked of these things to Vanessa?'

'No. I don't want to hurt her.'

'I don't think you would hurt her. She's very wise and very

tolerant. She doesn't want everyone's experience to be hers. Her father isn't religious in her way, but she understands him perfectly. So she may you.'

'Oh, she understands me, as much as she knows of me. But I know things about myself that I'd be ashamed for her to know. I'm not ashamed of *myself*, Mother. I'd like to be different – settled, noble, unselfish. Or would I? I can't tell. I'm not proud of myself, but I'm not *ashamed* of myself either. I'm simply what I am. All the same I don't see why I should burden someone else with the care of me. That at least I can do. Save others from troubling about me.'

'Yes,' said Elizabeth. 'But if someone loves you they want to trouble. They can't help but trouble.'

He flung his arms around her and kissed her.

'Funny I should be your son. The luck's all with me.'

Next day Vanessa came. She was now nearly twenty-one years of age. Her beauty had a quality of surprise in it. She was tall and slender. Her face was young for her age, much younger than her carriage, which was mature and controlled. She moved with such grace that you thought, as you watched her, that she was fully assured. Then when you saw her eyes and mouth, her perpetual gaiety, the sudden change of mood, the constant excitement, her stirred animation, you felt that life had not yet touched her. She was like her father in sweetness of expression but unlike him in her alertness, so that she seemed to miss nothing that went on around her. She was immensely kind, but could be sharp and irritated by slowness and stupidity and most of all by any pomposity or show of self-conceit. That is, except in the case of those whom she loved, when she simply could not criticize. For example, she loved Timothy Bellairs at Uldale and he *was* a trifle pompous.

Her hair was very dark but her colouring rather pale, unless she were excited by something. She blushed very easily, which exasperated her. When she moved she was like a queen, but often when she talked or joined with others in a game or a sport she was childish and impetuous. She was intensely loyal, obstinate, forgiving, so warm-hearted that her father often feared for her, but of late she had been learning many things about human nature. She was no fool where people were concerned.

Her mother had died in the autumn of '77 and since then she had lived with her father and Will on Cat Bells. They had been always devoted friends, she and her father, but now, after losing both his mother and his wife, Adam seemed to turn to Vanessa with an urgency that had something almost desperate about it. He remained always humorous, kindly, a little cynical, half in his fairy stories (he tried his hand at a number of things – books for boys, biographies of Nelson and Walter Raleigh, even two novels, but they were all fairy stories), half in the wild, loose, stormy Cumberland life that was in his blood and bones. Everyone liked him, nobody knew him. Many people laughed at him in an easy generous fashion. Vanessa alone understood him. She understood him because she had (although as yet she did not realize it) very much of her grandmother's character. Adam, of course, knew that. He saw his mother in his daughter again and again: her kindness, generosity, sudden flashes of temper and irritation and a constant exasperation at belonging to the Herries family.

'We don't belong, my dear,' he said one day.

'We belong enough,' she answered in a flash of prophetic perception, 'to have to fight them for the rest of our lives.'

Another thing. He knew that Vanessa loved Benjamin. It made Adam unhappy whenever he thought of it. He was himself fond of Benjie, but oh! he did not want him to marry Vanessa! Margaret's last words had been: 'Adam, you mustn't let Vanessa marry Benjamin', and he had answered: 'She must be free'.

But oh no! oh no! he did not want her to marry Benjamin! They never discussed it. That was their one silence.

Walter was buried in Ireby churchyard and, ironically, not far from the grave of Jennifer Herries, into which he once so long ago had terrified her. At the funeral, besides Elizabeth, Benjie, and Vanessa, there were Adam, Veronica and her husband, Timothy and his wife, and dear Aunt Jane. Also a few neighbours.

It was a cold windy day, one of those days when you realize how true it is that Cumberland is composed only of cloud and stone: lovely iridescent stone with green and rosy shadows but rising in pillars of smoke to meet the cloud, and the cloud coming down to settle like blocks and boulders of stone on the soil until, with the wind in your ears, you do not know which is stone and which is cloud. The little church tugged at the wind like a cloud striving to be free, and the clouds rolled in the sky as though some giant hurled rocks at his enemy.

They all stood, blown about, in the little churchyard, and poor old Walter, a capital example of the waste of energy that hatred involves, was dropped into the ground.

That same evening Vanessa and Elizabeth had a talk. Elizabeth had done all she could with the house. Her taste had never been aesthetic and she had dressed the cold bare bones of the place with heavy, very heavy, material. The big bleak rooms she had filled with large sofas, heavy carpets, big chairs, all in the manner of their period, which, if it was not a very beautiful manner, was comfortable.

She had crowds of things partly because everyone she knew did the same, partly because she hoped thus to escape the stoniness, the melancholy, the ghostliness of the place. She could not escape it. The rooms that were empty and shut up – the rooms in the two towers for instance – were heavy with ghosts. Not only she knew it. Everyone in the countryside knew it. Voices and steps were heard. Pale faces looked from behind windows, dogs barked, and parrots screeched. The Fortress, in fact, was not to surrender to a confusion of cornucopias, steel and brass fire-irons, japanned coal boxes, tables covered with beadwork, satin walnut chairs, and wax flowers under glass shades. Nevertheless in the few rooms that she herself inhabited her presence warmed and comforted. There were fires, Cumberland servants who adored her, flowers and books.

But Vanessa, in spite of the flowers, shivered. She had her father's taste, her grandmother's passion for order and arrangement. How, thought Vanessa, can Elizabeth, who is so beautiful, endure this hideous place? She did not realize that Elizabeth could endure anywhere so long as John, her husband, was with her.

Benjamin had gone that evening to see a farmer in Braithwaite. He would not be back until the following afternoon, so the two women had the house to themselves. They sat close together over a roaring fire and tried not to listen to the wind, which found the Fortress the happiest hunting ground it knew. Although Elizabeth was sixty-five and Vanessa only twenty-one they understood one another very well. They believed very much in the same things and they both loved the same man.

That evening, in fact, was a crisis for Vanessa, and in the course of it she set her feet resolutely along the path that was to lead her so very far.

'What are you going to do, Elizabeth, now?' Vanessa asked.

'Do, my dear? Why, go on as before.'

'Won't this house be very lonely for you?'

'I am used to it, you know. I'm an old woman now and like a quiet life.'

'Benjamin will be with you. That's one good thing.'

'Oh no, he won't!' Elizabeth smiled. 'He'll come and go as he's always done.'

'Oh, but he must,' Vanessa answered vigorously. 'He can't leave you all alone here. He has plenty to do, loves the country. He has wandered enough.'

'You know that he has not,' Elizabeth answered. 'He will never have wandered enough. He might settle down if you married him. Otherwise, never.'

She had spoken quietly but, as both women knew, it was a challenge of the deepest import.

There was a long silence, then Vanessa said slowly:

'Benjie has not asked me to marry him.'

'No. That is because he is afraid – afraid of himself. He loves you more than anyone in the world and does not want to make you unhappy.'

'Yes,' Vanessa said at last. 'He might make me unhappy, but I would not mind, I think.' After a pause she went on: 'You see, Elizabeth, I have Benjie in my blood. I have always had. I'm quite shameless about it – to myself, I mean. What is the use of being otherwise? I would rather be miserable with Benjie than happy with anyone else. And perhaps I should not be miserable. I understand him very well.'

She waited, but Elizabeth said nothing.

'We are very alike in some ways. I want my liberty quite as much as he does his. My great-grandmother was a gipsy, my great-grandfather a vagabond, my father illegitimate. And Benjie—' She broke off.

'Thinks he is a vagabond too,' Elizabeth went on, 'because of his father. You needn't fear, Vanessa darling, to talk about it. Here we are in the house that is filled with it. Sometimes I wake in my bed and hear the tap of Uhland's stick on the floor. I was impetuous, too, once, my dear. I ran away and married John. I had courage for anything in those days; but I know now that every impetuous step, every blow in anger, can mean tragedy for the next generation. There is no end to the consequences. They are never done.'

'Perhaps it isn't what we do,' said Vanessa, 'but something in ourselves. A strain that won't let us alone. You know, Elizabeth, that when I go over and stay with Veronica there's so much Herries stolidness and convention that I feel, I'm sure, just as Judith did when she ran away to Paris. That's where I understand Benjie. And sometimes when I'm with Timothy, although I'm very fond of him, I could whip him. I could really. He *won't* see things and is proud of not seeing them. He believes in Gladstone but has never heard of Rossetti.'

'Rossetti, dear?' asked Elizabeth.

'Yes – well, never mind. He writes poetry and paints.'

'Oh yes,' said Elizabeth. 'I'm sure I've heard the name—'

'I expect you have. But that doesn't matter. The point is that I would understand if Benjie wanted to go away by himself. I think it's silly of married people always to be together.'

'And then there's religion,' Elizabeth said. 'Benjie declares that he doesn't believe in God, foolish boy.'

'Many people say they don't believe in God,' Vanessa answered, speaking as though she were sixty and Elizabeth twenty. 'I don't think Father does, not as I do. But if you love someone those things settle themselves. I could never be as Timothy and Violet are, keeping the children in awe of them, never allowing them an idea of their own. Why, they have to come to the dining-room and bow, poor little things, after every meal! And Tim's only three, but I know he's going to be an artist. He's always drawing things. And when I spoke of it to his father the other day he was as shocked as if I'd said Tim was going to be an actor.'

'Well,' said Elizabeth, 'that wouldn't be a nice thing for little Tim to grow up into.'

'I don't know,' said Vanessa. 'There are the Bancrofts anyway. They have luncheon with the Prince of Wales.'

'Come here, dear, and give me a kiss,' Elizabeth said. 'I'd rather have you for a daughter than anyone in the world.'

Then came the last day of April, the day before Vanessa returned to Cat Bells. After dinner that night there was a large full moon. The air was warm and the moonlight filled all the garden with silver dust so that one seemed to walk on white powdery surf, now rising on a wave of quicksilver, then passing into an ebb of luminous grey. The hills were thin like silver tissue. Benjie, governed as ever by his mood, by the food that he had eaten, the wine that he had drunk, thinking Vanessa perfect in her dark dress that below the narrow waist broke out into bows and frills and trimmings, swearing that no neck and arms in all the world were so lovely as hers, seemed to see her as though this were for the first time, a new Vanessa to whom he had but just been introduced, so that under his breath he must murmur: 'This is the loveliest in all the world. All my life I have been waiting for this.'

At first she would not go out with him, as though something warned her. She stood by the fire, laughing, talking about anything, nothing. She had had a letter from Rose Ormerod, who was having a gay time in London.

'No, but you must listen to this, Benjie.'

'I don't want to listen. I don't like her. I can't think why she is your friend.'

'But she likes *you*! In this letter she says: "If you see Benjie give him my love, my *love*, mind." And she means it.'

'Oh, she gives everyone her love – far too many people.'

'She has been having a beautiful visit. Lady Herries gave a dinner party. Very sticky, she says. And she went to the Haymarket Theatre and saw *Money*. A silly old play, she says, but Marion Terry was lovely as Clara Douglas, and Mr Bancroft was Sir Frederick, and Mrs Bancroft, Lady Franklyn, and—'

'What *do* I care who they were? This is the last night of April. Tomorrow is the first of May. It is as warm as summer – silly to have a fire – and the moon is the largest—'

'Oh yes, and she went to Mr Alma-Tadema's studio to see the pictures he's sending to the Academy, and one is called "Fredegonda", and it shows an angry Queen looking out of a window at her husband—'

'Please, Vanessa.'

She looked at him and saw that he was unhappy. She nodded.

'All right. I'll come out.'

She went upstairs to fetch a shawl. Benjie, while he waited, wondered what he was going to do. This was the moment that for years he had determined to avoid. He must not marry Vanessa. He must not marry anyone. At the thought of marriage something within him warned him. But Vanessa – Vanessa ... He shivered. Outside in the garden it was warmer than in the firelit room. The house was always cold, do what you would with it. Vanessa – Vanessa ... Why had he been such a fool as to stay? He had an impulse to go round to the stable, fetch his horse, and ride off. Ride off anywhere – not seeing her again until she was safely married to someone else. But would that end it? All his life, however far away he had been, he had been tied to her, tied by her goodness, her beauty, her love for himself – and by all that was best in him. His best? A very poor thing. He had never thought so humbly of himself as at that moment when she came towards him, saying: 'I'm ready. How lovely the moonlight is!'

They walked into the garden arm in arm. Originally Walter Herries had planned a series of garden walks and a succession of little waterfalls, dropping stage after stage into a lily-covered pond. Now there were the sad ruins of these things, tangled shrubberies, little winding and melancholy paths, the doubtful splash of water and a weedy pool. Over the ruins the moon rode throwing its silver in a conceited largesse, penetrating the utter-most tangle of the trees.

'I have just finished a very amusing book,' said Vanessa, who felt as though the moon were scornfully wishing her a disastrous destiny, like the old witches her great-grandfather had known.

'What is it called?' asked Benjamin, wondering for how long he could resist to kiss Vanessa.

'*Travels with a Donkey.*'

'What a silly name!' The muscle on his arm suddenly jumped at the touch of Vanessa's hand. 'Who wrote it?'

'His name is Stevenson. I have never heard of him before, have you?'

'No. Never.'

'He writes well.' Vanessa almost whispered as they stepped into a pool of moonlight. 'Very precious, as though he'd licked every word on his tongue first before he stuck it down. Oh, look at the moon insulting Blencathra. There! Stand here! You can just see it between the trees.'

Benjie took her in his arms and kissed her with a ferocity that Ouida – a novel by whom Vanessa had recently been enjoying – describes somewhere 'as the lovely tiger's grandeur and the aban-doned wildness of the jungle'. Benjie had never kissed Vanessa before save almost as a brother. This was the first time in her life that Vanessa had ever been passionately kissed. She found it entrancing. They stayed for a long while without moving. The shawl fell from Vanessa's shoulders, but she felt no cold. The pressure of Benjie's strong hand on her shoulder was surely the thing that since the day of her birth she had longed for. Her hand touched Benjie's hair as though he were her child. He kissed her eyes, which was another thing that no one had ever done to her before. They separated. He bent down and picked up her shawl.

'This is something,' he said breathlessly, 'that I have been longing to do for years. And now we'll talk if you don't mind.'

They walked hand in hand.

'I am going away tomorrow morning and will not see you again until someone has married you.'

'I can wait,' she answered confidently. 'I will marry you any time.'

'You are not like the modern maiden, are you, Vanessa? If their young man proposes to them they faint with astonishment although they have planned nothing else all their lives.'

'No. Why should I be astonished? I always knew that we would be married one day.'

'We are not going to be married,' Benjie answered, taking his hand from hers and walking by himself. 'I ought not to have kissed you. After tonight we shall not be alone together again until you are safe. I love you as truly as any man ever loved anyone, and that is why we are not going to be married.'

Vanessa laughed and took his hand again.

'I am not a child, Benjie. I know that you are afraid of marriage – and perhaps you would be right if it were anyone else, but we are different. We know one another so well. I shall never marry anyone else.'

'Now listen.' He put his arm around her and drew her close to him. 'You must not try to shake me, Vanessa. Really you must not. You say you know me, but it isn't true. You don't know me. Everyone is right about me. I'm no good by any standards but my own. I should make you terribly unhappy, and that I won't do. No, I will not. I will not. Other women – well, that's their affair. But you – you've got to have a wonderful life, be a queen, have everyone worship you, adore you, have splendid children, a husband whom everyone looks up to . . .'

She interrupted him, laughing.

'But I don't want that kind of husband! I don't want to be a Queen! I don't want to be admired. I want to be free quite as much as you do. You talk as though it were my ambition to be head of the Herries family, live in Hill Street and give parties like old Lady Herries. Of course I *enjoy* parties and it will be fun to go to London one day, but without you I don't want *anything*!'

'Oh Lord! How can I get you to understand? Don't you see, Vanessa, that I'm no good? Really no good. One day I'm this, another day I'm that. If I see a pretty woman I want to kiss her. If I want to gamble I gamble. I'm no sooner in a place than I want to go somewhere else. My mother and yourself are the only two people I love. I have hurt my mother many times already, but you I won't hurt—'

'But, Benjie,' she broke in, 'I don't think you *could* hurt me! I should understand whatever you did.'

'You don't know.' He spoke angrily, breaking again away from her. 'You don't know *anything* about life, Vanessa. You don't know the things I've done, the company I've kept. If I could say to you, "Vanessa, I've sown my wild oats and now I'm going to settle down, go to church on Sunday, read Tennyson with you in the evening—" '

'But, Benjie, how absurd you are! I don't *want* to read Tennyson, and if you don't wish to go to church you needn't! Father never goes to church. And as to the rest, what you have done is no business of mine. I'm sure I'm no saint myself. I know that Timothy and Violet think me often disgraceful and are afraid that I shall harm the children. Look at Grandmother! *She* wasn't a saint although she was one of the finest women who ever lived *and* one of the bravest. And her father! He's a kind of legend for lawlessness and roguery. I think we should suit one another very well. And as to the relations and all they say about you – what do they matter? A stuffy lot! That's what they are!'

He shook his head. 'That's not the point, Vanessa. You may say what you like, but you are good and I'm not – that is by all that anyone means by good. You talk of Judith's father. I expect he was a fine fellow. I often think of him and wish I'd known him. I like that man. I could have been his friend, I know. But the truth is he made everyone unhappy who trusted him. And so shall I. I can't help it. It's something inside me. And I won't make you unhappy. I love you too much. It would be the one sin for me. I don't care about the rest, but *that* I'll avoid, so help me God!'

They had walked down to the weeded pool which lay now, like a foolish white face, dirtied and soiled, at their feet.

Vanessa spoke, but more gravely because she was feeling that her whole future life was to depend on the next ten minutes. What did she see? The man as he was? Perhaps ... But herself in relation to all that he might be? She did not yet know life enough for that.

'Benjie, listen. I am not asking you against your will to marry me. I don't *wan't* you to marry me. We have been friends all our lives and we can go on as we are. But if you want to marry somebody, then it had better be me. I'm sure you will never meet anyone again who knows you so well.' She put her hand again in his. 'Do you remember that time – Grandmother's hundredth birthday – the day she died?'

'Yes, of course I remember.'

'We went for a walk, and I told you that I would never marry anyone but you and that I would wait as long as you liked. I was only a child then. I'm a woman now. But it is the same. It hasn't changed. I don't see how it can. No one can ever be to either of us what we are to one another. As to risks, life's made for them. I'm not afraid.'

She felt his hand tremble as it clutched hers.

'Listen, Vanessa. You *must* listen. If I don't make you understand now you never will. You say you are not afraid of life, but that is because you don't know. How can you? You have been sheltered always. Your father worships you as he ought to. Everyone loves you. You have never been treated unkindly, never had to put up with slights, never made an enemy. You hear people say: "Oh, Benjamin Herries, he's a bad lot, he's a rascal!" But they are only words. You've never seen me *do* the things, *say* the things that they mean. I am at my best – a poor best but still my best – when I'm with you because I love you and I'm not a bad fellow if I'm in a good temper, not bored, able to get away when I want to. We've seen one another at long intervals. We've loved to be together and they have been grand times because we were free. But to *live* with me – that's another thing. I'm no man's good company for long. I've got old Rogue Herries' devil in me, I think. Sometimes I fancy I'm the old Rogue himself come again. And if that's nonsense – and I'm sure I don't know what's nonsense and what isn't in this ridiculous world – at least I'm like him in that I'm my own worst enemy, can see what's right to do and never do it, curse my best friend and all the rest. Oh, mind you, I'm not pitying myself or even condemning myself. I'm not bad as men go. I enjoy every minute of the day unless I've got the toothache or lose money at cards or some woman won't look at me. And even those things are interesting. But I'm not the man for you. You're as far above me as that moon is above this silly-faced pond and, do me justice, I've always known it.'

He had spoken swiftly, the words pouring out, his face serious, mature, almost grim, as though he were resolving that this once in his life at least the honest truth should come from him.

'All that you have said, Benjie, I know,' Vanessa answered. 'I may be a fool as you say, protected from harm and all the rest. But Father has never treated me as a child. We've been companions for years and talked freely about everything. When I stay with Veronica and Robert Forster's drunk, as he is sometimes, I can see some of the things marriage can be. You may be nasty when you're drunk, but not half as nasty as Robert is. Of course I know that marriage isn't all fun. It isn't for anybody. Only I think that you and I would be often happy together if we were married because we know one another so well. We'd be unhappy too, but I don't always want to be happy. That would be dull. When we fought we'd know that we still loved one another. If you left me I'd know that you would come back.'

'No, I might not,' he said in a low voice. 'I might never come back. Loving you as much as I do now, I might still say: "No, I can't stand this". And I'd be off – and perhaps never return.'

'Oh, Benjie, would you?'

They were standing now by the gate that led into the road. The road stretched in front of them, and beyond it the country fell to the valley like a sheet of shadowed snow.

'Oh, would you?' She was thinking. She turned, as though she had resolved a problem, and looked up at him, smiling. 'Then I'd be a grass widow. They say that they have a glorious life.'

Both laughing, they walked out into the road and at once were encompassed by a field of dazzling stars above them, sparkling and dancing as though they knew that tomorrow was the first of May and the beginning of a new summer world.

'You know, Vanessa,' Benjie said, looking over to Skiddaw, 'that I have an odd fancy. It isn't really mine. Some old shepherd told me some tale once. There's Skiddaw Forest where – where my father died. Of course it's often in my thoughts. When you stand below Skiddaw House and look over to Skiddaw you can see sometimes, just before the hill rises, a dark patch that looks like the opening of a cave. It is only a trick of light. There's no cave there, but when I was a boy I often walked there and I used to fancy that it was the opening to a great subterranean hall, a gigantic place, you know, that ran right under the mountain. I told myself tales about it. I fancied that all the men who had loved this place returned there, had great feasts there, jolly splendid affairs, with singing and drinking, everything that was fine.

All of them grand comrades, whoever they were, farmers and shepherds, huntsmen, squires and parsons – any man to whom this piece of country is the best in the world. Perhaps on a night like this there they all are singing and laughing, happy as grigs – old Rogue Herries and my grandfather, my father and my uncle, John Peel and Wordsworth and Southey, little Hartley, "auld Will" Ritson of Wasdale, James Jackson of Whitehaven, Ewan Clark, John Rooke, thousands on thousands more – I used to fancy on a still day that I could hear them laughing and singing. A great hall, you know, Vanessa, where they could wrestle and run, ride their horses, shout their songs, tell their stories ... That's where I'd like to be, Vanessa. I could do without women there. I wouldn't want to roam the world. I'd need no other company—' He broke off. 'Yes, I'd want you, I think. Wherever I was, whatever I'd be doing.'

They turned up the road and stopped at a little water trough where from a rudely carved dolphin's head water trickled into a small basin. The thin drip of the water was the only sound.

'Why don't you say,' he murmured, ' "Benjie, you're a bad lot. We'll meet no more"? It would be better for you.'

'I can't say that,' she answered, leaning close to him, 'because I love you.'

The pause that followed marked both their lives. It had a sanctity, an intimacy that went beyond all their experience. They kissed again, but quietly now, gently meeting in complete oneness.

At last he said:

'Be kind to me, Vanessa. I've tried to do the best. Maybe I'll change. Mother said that loving you might do it for me. Give me a chance.'

He waited, then went on.

'My darling – let us be engaged, here and now, for two years. This is the last day of April 1880. In April 1882, I'll come to you and ask you if you are still of the same mind. If you are – if I can trust myself – we'll be married. If, before then, you think other-wise you shall tell me. And in the two years we will tell nobody, not a word to a soul. I shall be twenty-seven then, and if I'm no good at that age I shall never be any good. Give me that chance.'

Vanessa looked in front of her, then at last turned on him, smiling.

'Yes, if that's what you'd like, Benjie.'

'Not a word to anyone.'

She waited again.

'I have always told Father everything—'

'No. Even your father. I'm on probation. If he knew he might not understand.'

'Very well. Here's my hand on it.'

They held hands, looking one another in the eyes.

'It's a poor bargain for you,' he said. 'Mind, if ever you want to be free of me you have only to tell me—'

'I shall never want to be free,' Vanessa said proudly.

'All the men under Skiddaw heard you say that,' he answered. 'And they think me a poor lot for asking you.'

'Ah, they don't know you as I do,' she answered.

As they walked up to the house she held her head high, feeling the proudest woman in England.

And Benjie, for once in his life, was humble.

HERRIES DRAWING-ROOM

VANESSA paid the first visit of her life to London in the spring of 1882.

Old Lady Herries had, during the last two years, invited her repeatedly to stay in Hill Street, but the trouble had been that her father refused to go with her and Vanessa would not leave him.

Adam was obdurate and Vanessa was obdurate.

'No, my dear, I won't go. I hope never to see London again. I am sixty-six and entitled at last to my own way. London would upset me. I know I'm nothing at all, but London would make me feel less than nothing. I'm quite contented where I am. But of course you must go. It's time that they saw you and fell down before you. It's always been the custom that the family in London should see the Cumberland branch once and again and realize how superior it is. Your grandmother took me up when I was a boy and they all fell flat before her – so they shall before you.'

Vanessa refused. She did not want to go, she did not wish to see London, they would all think her an absurd country cousin and mock at her. With her father at her side she could mock back at them, but alone she would not dare to open her mouth. (None of these were, of course, real reasons. She longed to see London and she was afraid of no one.) He wished her to go because he was afraid that they were growing, as he described it, 'inside one another'.

For the last two years Vanessa had been strange. She was, it seemed, quite content to be alone with her father and, except for visits to Elizabeth at the Fortress and to Uldale, saw nobody. She seemed happy enough, but there were times when she appeared abstracted, lost, far away. Once or twice he wondered whether Benjie Herries had anything to do with this. Benjie had been out of England for most of the two years, deserting, everyone said, his mother most shamefully. Could it be that Vanessa still cared for him. Adam put the thought violently away from him. He had an affection for Benjie, but the fellow was a wanderer, a wastrel, would come, Adam very much feared, to no kind of good. And yet some wildness that there was in Adam attracted him to the man. He might have been, had things gone otherwise, just such himself. And Vanessa had some wildness in her too. Was it that that kept the men of the county away from her? No one doubted that she was better looking than any other girl in the North of England. And she was gentle with them, gave herself no airs. But she was alone. Save for her father, Elizabeth, and little Jane Bellairs at Uldale, she had no friends. Oh yes, and the children at Uldale – she adored *them*, especially young Tim.

But there it was: she had no friends of her own age, had no gaieties, did not appear to wish for any. It was not good for her. She must go to London.

And at last she yielded. He could not tell the reason. A letter came from Lady Herries. She looked across the table at Adam and said: 'Very well, Papa; I'll go.'

Then, when it was all arranged, he did not want her to go. He realized that he would be most damnably lonely. He was sure that, after this visit, she would never be the same again. She was still, in spite of her twenty-three years, very much of a child. She could be surprisingly naïve and impetuous. She seemed at one moment to judge human nature most wisely and then she would trust someone for no reason at all. She reminded him constantly of her grandmother in her simple directness to everyone, her lack of all affectation, her complete ignoring of class differences, her generosity and warmth both of heart and temper. But she was unlike Judith in that she had many reserves and no wish to dominate anybody. In those things she resembled himself. Oh, he would be all right, he supposed. There was plenty to do – his writing, his garden, the hills of which he never wearied; he was still, in spite of his sixty-six years, strong enough to walk over Stye Head into Eskdale and so to the sea, or over Watendlath to Grasmere. He had old Will Leathwaite for company. But he would miss her – miss her damnably. There was no one else he cared for now but Will. He was growing old. He continued to write – he could not help himself – but it was poor, secondary stuff. Not at all what he had meant once to do. Why, Dickens had told him once that he would be the equal of them all. But Dickens was warm-hearted, generous, with his variegated waistcoats and passion for theatricals. A great man: no one like him now. Him and Wordsworth, that arrogant but child-hearted little man whose genius seemed now to cover all the country like a soft sunny cloud, impregnating the air, calling the scent from the flowers, echoed in the birds' call. Dickens and Wordsworth – simple men both of them – while today these Merediths and Swinburnes and Rossettis ... He picked up the *Poems and Ballads* from the table, read a line or two, turned away with a sigh. Very clever. You could not call Wordsworth clever, thank God.

And so she went. It was arranged very easily, because Mrs Osmaston was travelling to London at the same time. Mrs Osmaston was a good serious woman who would bore Vanessa considerably. That would teach her, Adam thought quite fiercely, to leave her old father!

She went: and Adam discovered, not for the first time in his history, the tactful beauties in Will Leathwaite's character. Will had all the Cumbrian gift of showing his affection without mentioning it. He scolded and grumbled and protested as he had always done. In the evening they played backgammon together, and Will invariably won.

'You have the most damnable luck,' Adam swore at him.

'Aye,' said Will, 'I have. And I play nicely too.'

Four days after her departure Adam received a letter, the first that he had ever had from his dear daughter.

'My dearest Papa,' it began.

'A letter from my daughter,' he said to Will, who was sprawling against the doorpost, his hands in his pockets. He was fat now, red in the face and grizzled in the hair. It was in his eyes that you saw his youth, for their blue was as clear, gay, and sparkling as though they were fresh from their Maker.

'Aye,' he said. 'That's grand. Hope she's enjoying herself. Not too much, you know. She's better than anything London can give her.'

Adam, after glancing through, read Will her letter. Will never stirred. His eyes, shining, luminous, and in some fashion rather sardonic, were fixed on his friend – as though he said: 'Yes. She's spreading her wings. You'll find I'm the only stay-by. We're a pair of leftovers. And who cares?'

The letter was:

MY DEAREST PAPA – I don't know how to begin I've so much to tell you. The journey was very long of course, the carriage smelt of escaping gas and oh, it was cold the last part! My feet were frozen. We couldn't see to read but it would not have been so bad had Mrs Osmaston not chattered so! She is *so* contented, *so* fortunate, has so perfect a husband, such *lovely* children (you know little Mary and James Osmaston – not lovely at all!) but the worst is that she loves all the world. Her charity is too general to be personal. We are all God's children in a kind of celestial nursery. Well, I must get on. Here I am two days in Hill Street and I *must* say that I am enjoying it. I find them very kind. Do you know that Lady Herries is seventy-eight? She is immensely proud of it and all our relations are proud of it too. If you live long enough in our family you are always looked up to whatever you may be or do. It is when you are young that you must be careful. She paints of course prodigiously and wears the brightest colours. Bustles have come in again you know, and she likes a sash and a bow at the waist! But I must not mock for she is really kind and wants me to be happy. So does Éllis. He is grave and nervous. He is dreadfully afraid of doing the wrong thing. He is exceedingly wealthy everyone tells me and ought to be married. I am very sorry for him because he does not know how to be careless and happy. Rose Ormerod says that he is always his own Governess and that no sooner does he do a thing than the Governess tells him he should not. Hill Street is a kind of Temple for the family. They come here and worship the god of the clan – a three-faced god, one face Queen Victoria, one face Commerce, and one face the Herries features, high cheek-bones, noble foreheads, and a cold eye. They are very different though. Barney Newmark, old Amery and his son Alfred, Rose and her brother Horace, Emily Newmark. These are the prin-

cipal ones who come to the house. Captain Will Herries and his
wife are in town. Also the Rockages. I think they like me. I
amuse them and perhaps shock them. I like Barney the best.
He laughs at everyone. The house is very large and very cold,
but of course you know it and I should imagine that it has not
altered at all in thirty years. Very cold, full of noise from
pipes and cisterns, masses of furniture, statues and little fires
that burn up the chimney. There is the great Charles, too.
Charles is the butler and he is so large that it is always warmer
when he is in the room with one. He is very gracious and
would be perfect if his eyes were not so glassy.

Just imagine! We have been to the theatre both nights! The
first night was *Romeo and Juliet* with Mr Irving and Miss
Ellen Terry. Shall I whisper to you, dear Papa, that I was a
little disappointed? Mr Irving is better when he is not making
love. In the balcony scene he stood behind such a ridiculous
little tree that it was difficult not to laugh. When he makes love
it is not the *real thing*. He has thought it all out beforehand.
Miss Terry is *lovely*. Oh, how beautiful and charming! But
she, too, acts better when she is *not* with Mr Irving. With the
Nurse she is perfection. I liked Mr Terriss as Mercutio but the
best of all is Mrs Stirling as the Nurse although propriety
makes them cut out all her *best* lines. The scenery is almost too
good to be true I think. You admire the moonlight when you
ought to be *lost* with the lovers. At least that is what I felt.

Will you be very ashamed of me when I tell you that I
enjoyed the second evening more? The piece was *The Manager*
at the Court Theatre. This was Barney's party and I think Ellis
was a little ashamed at *laughing* at a Farce. But he could not
help himself. There is an actress in this piece called Lottie
Venne who is *perfect* and Mr Clayton *splendid*! I laughed so
much that Rose, who was with us, said Mr Clayton played
twice as well as usual!

Of course I have not seen very much of London yet. Rose
and I are to have a morning's shopping tomorrow. There is to
be a grand party in Hill Street next week and Madame Trebelli
of the Opera is to sing. I have ridden in a hansom-cab and
found it very exciting.

And now I must go to bed. I have been writing this in my
room and I am so cold that there is an icicle on the end of my
nose! Do you miss me? I do hope so, but also I hope that you
are not lonely. Give Will my love and the children at Uldale if

you see them. If I *allow* myself I shall be homesick, but that
will never do. Last night I dreamt that you and I walked to
Robinson and met five sheep who turned into the five Miss
Clewers from Troutbeck! Have you seen Elizabeth? Is her cold
quite gone now? I am hoping there will be a letter from you
tomorrow – Your very loving daughter,

VANESSA

'That's grand,' said Will and went off to his work.

No one could guess from Vanessa's letter, nor indeed from anything that she herself said or thought, that her arrival in London
was the sensation of the year for her relations. Afterwards,
among them all, 1882 was remembered as the year 'when Vanessa
first came to town'. And this for two reasons. One was the natural astonishment at her beauty, for which they were quite unprepared, although some of them recollected that 'she had been a
damned pretty child at old Madame's Hundredth Birthday'.

By chance it happened that the fashion of the moment suited
Vanessa: the dresses looped up behind, crossed with fringed
draperies rather in the manner of the heavy window curtains of
the time, the waists very narrow (and Vanessa had, all her life, a
marvellous waist), the top portion of the costume following as
closely as possible the lines of the corset, flaring out below the
hips in frills and bows and trimmings. The violent colours just
then popular also suited her dark hair and soft skin. The dress
that she wore at her first Herries party, dark blue with an edging
of scarlet, white lace frills at the throat and wrists, was long
remembered. She arrived with only a dress or two and they of
Keswick make, but Adam had insisted that she must 'dress like a
peacock in London' and gave her money to do it with. They were
the first grand costumes of her life, and Rose Ormerod saw to it
that they were fine. Her beauty staggered them all, the more that
she seemed to be perfectly unaware of it. And they saw immediately that here was a family asset.

This raw naïve girl from Cumberland might marry anybody.
There was no limit to the possibilities. Old Amery said to his son
Alfred (Amery had married late in life a parson's infant fresh
from the schoolroom: she presented him with Alfred in '62 and
incontinently died) after his first sight of Vanessa in the Hill
Street drawing-room: 'That girl will be a Duchess – bet you a
"monkey".' These possibilities gave her at once a great import-

ance in their eyes – one more factor in the rise of Herries power!

And here that queer old Lady Herries, known familiarly as 'the witch of Hill Street', comes into the story. No one in London knew anything about that old woman save that she was useful as an entertainer and adored her son. When Will Herries had married her she had been a buxom, silly, empty-headed woman of no character and less common sense. She had given Will a son, and that was the only sensible thing she'd ever been known to do. But as Ellis grew to manhood her love for him created in her a kind of personality. People must always admire in this world any strong, undeviating, unfaltering devotion: for one thing it is rare, for another it appears unselfish although it may have all its roots in selfishness. This example was the more admired because Ellis was, most certainly, not everybody's money. Only was anybody's money, in fact, because he had himself such a profusion of that admirable commodity. They led, those two, in the Hill Street house, a life of extraordinary loneliness. In spite of the dinners, receptions, conversaziones, balls and theatre parties, they had no friends, nor did they communicate, so far as anyone could see, with one another. Old Lady Herries broke into frequent rages with her son and to these he listened with a grave and unaccommodating silence. Abroad she talked of him incessantly, his brilliance in the City, his nobility, his love for his fellow-men. At home she often told him he was stupid, ungrateful, and cold. Her extravagances grew with her age, her paint, gay colours, fantastic screams of laughter. She was a sight with her trimmings, fichus, shawls, her little hats perched high on her old head, her fingers covered with rings, bands and twists of hair, dyed, and interwoven with strands of ribbon and sprays of foliage. It remained, however, that she won respect because it was known that, selfish in everything else, clinging to life like a tigress, she would die for her son at any moment if the call came.

On the night of Vanessa's arrival, when the house was as silent as the moon, Ellis visited his mother in her bedroom. Sitting up in bed she looked the old, shrivelled, lonely, exhausted monkey that she really was. Ellis stood gravely beside her bed and said:

'Well, Mama, it is as I thought. Vanessa is the only woman whom I will ever marry.'

Lady Herries blinked her eyes. For eight years now, ever since the Hundredth Birthday in Cumberland, he had told her this. She did not care for Vanessa; she had thought Adam a country yokel, old Judith a mountebank. Moreover the girl's mother was a German. But if Ellis wanted anything he was to have it. God, she thought – she believed in a God made exactly in the image of herself – must be of the same opinion.

She could not deny that she had been struck by the girl's beauty. She had both the scorn and jealousy of beauty felt by many women who have fought life's battle without that great advantage. But this girl was exceptional. Raw, untrained, straight from the country: nevertheless with care and attention the girl could undoubtedly be turned into something. She had long made it a practice to refuse, at first, any request that Ellis might make of her, because she never lost hope that he might one day become more urgent in his prayers. She knew, in her heart, that this was one of the many hopes that would never be fulfilled.

So now she said: 'Nonsense. The girl's straight from a farm or a dairy or whatever it is. She's got no breeding.'

'She has perfect breeding,' Ellis said, and left her.

Next morning, considering the matter, she determined to make the girl devoted to her. Assuming, as do many old people, that she would live for ever, it was important that when Ellis married his wife they should continue to live in Hill Street. To lose Ellis was, of course, not to be thought of, but Vanessa might influence him. In her grinning, chattering way she did her best to be charming. It was not difficult to win Vanessa's affections if sincerity was there, and Lady Herries was, in this, sincere. Before three days were out the old woman felt that for the first time in her life someone cared for her. For the first time in her life she herself cared for someone other than her son. But truly everything was enchantment to Vanessa. She never saw London again as she saw it in those early days.

Everything about London was a miracle. The first morning she walked out she saw an old crossing-sweeper who stood at the corner of Berkeley Square and Charles Street dressed in an old faded scarlet hunting coat, given him, Barney told her, by Lord Cork, Master of the Buckhounds. That old man, with his broom, in his scarlet coat, seemed to her delighted eyes the very symbol of London, its incongruity, unexpected romance, humanity and pathos. There was an Indian crossing-sweeper, too, who stood with his broom outside the Naval and Military Club. There were the many Punch and Judy shows, the poor, dark, melancholy Italian sellers of cheap statuettes, and the old hurdy-gurdy man with his monkey.

Hyde Park was her chief delight. Lady Herries liked to drive in the afternoon, and so they paraded in a grand victoria, the old woman sitting with a back like a poker, gay as the rainbow, while Simon the coachman, in a multi-coloured livery, in figure like a sealion, drove, as though he were acting in a pageant, his magnificent horses.

But it was all like a pageant, the small phaetons with their high-stepping horses, the pony chaises conveying ladies of fashion, the victorias, the smart buggies driven by men about town, and the quiet-looking little broughams containing, it was supposed, all sorts of mysterious occupants!

This was a fine and warm April, and in the evening, between five and seven, everyone took the air in the Park. It was, it seemed, a world of infinite leisure where no one had anything to do but to see and be seen. On the other hand, there was nothing extravagant or forced in the display. No one, it appeared, wished to stagger anyone else. Everyone's position was too sure and certain. Rotten Row was, in fact, for more sophisticated eyes than Vanessa's, a superb affair.

In every way London was a magnificent show. The omnibuses alone gave it an air, for painted red, or royal blue, or green, they were always handsome and individual, with their strong horses and their swaggering, accomplished drivers who had, with the flick of their whips, the air of conjurers about to produce rabbits out of their greatcoats.

The horses indeed were wonderful, Vanessa thought, never needing the whip, the drivers' cheerful hiss all the encouragement they wanted. They were, she thought, both fiery and gentle, a glorious combination. The doors, the straw on the floor, these things were gone. The omnibuses were now the final word in the modern science of travel. But best of all were the hansom-cabs, the splendid horses driven by the most elegant cabmen who wore glossy hats and had flowers in their buttonholes. On the first day that Barney took Vanessa down Piccadilly and Westminster in a hansom-cab, she sat, her hands clasped, her eyes shining, her smart little hat perched on her dark hair, Queen, it seemed to her, of all Fairyland.

Finally London then was a town of constant surprises. You never knew what at any moment would turn up. Every building had life and character of its own, little crooked houses next to big straight ones, sudden little streets – dark, twisted, and eccentric – leading to calm dignified squares, fantastic statues, glittering fountains, shops blazing with splendour, hostelries that had not altered for hundreds of years. Everywhere colour, leisure, and, in this first superficial view, light-hearted happiness.

In that first week she spent her days with Lady Herries (Ellis was in the City all day), Rose Ormerod, and her brother Horace. The power that Rose had over Vanessa from the beginning came from her jollity, her kindness, her humour, her warm-heartedness. Rose had also other qualities which appeared later in their friendship. Horace, her brother, had a job as secretary to some big benevolent society. He was rosy-cheeked, square-shouldered, spoke well of everyone, was the friend of all the world. He was a little naïve. He talked frankly about himself. He was modest.

'I'm nothing exceptional, you know, Vanessa. I don't suppose you think I am. What I say is – why not see the best in everyone? It's easy enough if you try. People have a hard enough time. Why shouldn't we all make it pleasant for one another? I must confess that I find life a good thing.'

He was very jolly, had a hearty laugh, seemed generous and genial to everyone. There was something faintly episcopal about him as though he were in training to be a bishop. Rose was sometimes a little sarcastic about her brother, but then she was sarcastic about everyone.

Vanessa was happy, but underneath this exciting London adventure one consuming thought possessed her. Where was Benjie?

This was April 1882. The time had come when Benjie would demand the conclusion to the vow that they had made by the water dolphin of Ireby. Perhaps because she had seen him so seldom in these two years the thought of him by now completely possessed her. If she had loved him two years ago it was by this time as though he were part of her very flesh. She was neither romantic nor sentimental in her idea of him. She saw him as he was just as she saw herself as she was. Would he come? Where was he? He had written to her, on some dozen occasions, little letters, from Burma, China, India, North America. In these he had not said much, and yet she knew that he needed her, that he was thinking of her as she of him. Would he come? London brought him nearer. When the first sharp excitement of her visit paled a little she began to look for him, in the Park, the streets, the theatre. Often she thought that she saw his small stocky figure, dark face, often fancied that she recognized the quick determined step with which he walked. Would he come, and, if

April passed without him, what would she do? Was he faithless, volatile, careless, as they all said of him? Could she trust that he was faithful at least to her? Would he, oh, would he come? She spoke of him, of course, to no one, not even to Rose.

And then, in the second week of her visit, she began to be embarrassed by Ellis. She liked Ellis. She understood him better than others did. Most of all she was sorry for him. She wanted, as she so often wanted with people, to make him happy. There was something about his spare, grave figure that touched her heart. He was so *alone*. He wanted, she was sure, to be jolly with every-one but did not know how to set about it. She saw in him some-times an eagerness as though he said: 'Now this time I shall be lucky and find touch.' But always his shyness, his fear of a rebuff, checked him. As Lady Herries became more confidential the old lady poured out to Vanessa the truth about Ellis as she saw it, his goodness, kindliness of heart, diffidence. 'He can't chatter away,' Lady Herries said indignantly, 'like Barney Newmark or Horace Ormerod; but he has ten times their brains.'

Vanessa supposed that he had. He must be very clever to remain so silent for so long.

As the days passed she had an odd impression that he was approaching her ever nearer and nearer. He was not in reality; he always sat at a distance from her and when he walked with her seemed deliberately to take care that he should not by accident touch her. And yet she was ever more and more conscious of his body, his high cheekbones, the pale skin pulled tightly over them, his sharp-pointed nose, very Herries, with nostrils open, slightly raw, sensitive; his thin mouth, his high shoulder blades, his spare slim hands, his long legs that seemed always so lonely and deso-late inside his over-official London clothes. He was very tall and walked as though he had a poker down his back. He was dis-tinguished certainly with his top hat, his shining black tie, collar and cuffs almost too starched and gleaming, his pale gloves, his neatly rolled umbrella with its gold top. People looked after him and wondered who he might be, just as once they had wondered about his father. His pale thin face peered out anxiously at the world over his high collar. When he spoke you felt that his words were important although they seldom were so. He had a nervous little cough and often he blinked with his eyes.

One fine spring day he took a holiday from the City and in the company of Horace and Rose and Vanessa walked in the Park.

Very soon Vanessa found herself sitting alone with him while Rose and Horace talked to friends. She was wearing her most beautiful frock, rose and white, the pleated and flounced skirt with tucked panniers over the hips, the bodice cut high in the neck, long and pointed at the waistline. The wide skirt, the modified bustle, the little hat with roses, the different shades of rose in the dress itself, all these things were remembered by her when many times afterwards she recalled that costume as one of the loveliest of her life and the one that she was wearing when Ellis first proposed marriage.

He plunged at once like a man flinging himself with the courage of despair into icy water.

'Vanessa, I must tell you. I can avoid it no longer. I love you with all my soul. Please – please – will you marry me?'

It was then, although his seat was apart from hers, that she felt as if the moment, which for days had been approaching, had arrived. He seemed to have flung his body on to hers; she felt his thin hands at her neck, his bony cheek against hers, she could feel his heart wildly, furiously beating. She looked and saw that he had not moved. He was sitting, staring in front of him at the carriages, the riders, the colours, the sun; his gloved hands were folded on the gold knob of his umbrella.

She wanted then, as never before in her life, to be kind.

'Ellis! Marry you! But I don't want to marry anybody!'

(That was untrue. She wanted, oh, how she wanted, to marry Benjie!)

He had recovered himself a little.

'I know that it must be a shock to you, dear Vanessa. I recognize that. I must give you time. But you must not think that it is any sudden idea of mine. I have had no other thought since I first saw you, years ago, in Cumberland. That time – we were downstairs at Uldale. From that moment I knew that only you of everyone in the world could be my wife.'

She laid her hand for a moment on his knee.

'I am proud that you should think of me like that,' she said slowly, 'but I'm afraid I can't. Ellis, I like you very much, but I don't want to be married – really I don't. I couldn't leave my father. It wouldn't be kind to him now he is all alone.'

(How stupid and stiff her words were! She wanted to be good to him, to say something that would take that wistful, forlorn look from his eyes.)

'Your father could come and live with us.'

'I'm afraid he could never live in London. He is miserable now if he is away from Cumberland.'

'If you could – if you could – love me a little, Vanessa. I would wait. I would be very patient. Perhaps you could love me a little—'

She must be honest.

'No. I don't love you, Ellis. Love is very rare, isn't it? I like you so much—'

'Well, then,' he caught her up eagerly, 'that will perhaps turn into love. If you stay with us a little while. My mother likes you so much. I have never known her like anyone so much before. I can be very patient. I will give you as much time as you like—'

'I am afraid time will not alter it,' she answered gently. 'Friendship and love are so different—'

But he did not seem to hear. He went on eagerly.

'I will give you everything you can want. There's nothing you can ask for that you shan't have. I will never interfere with you. Only let me love you and serve you. I am not a man who has many friends. You have noticed that perhaps. I have been always shy in company, but with you beside me I feel that I could do anything. You are so good, so beautiful—'

Now the little scene was becoming dreadful to her. His intensity, his earnestness shamed her as though she had been caught in some misconduct.

'Ellis, dear. Listen. I don't love you. I'm afraid I never shall. We would be both of us most unhappy. Let us be friends, better and better friends, and you will find someone who *will* love you, who will make you so very happy—'

Words that every lady has used to every disconsolate lover! She knew it. She had not conceived that she could be so stupid. But, it seemed, he had not heard her. Rose and Horace gaily approached them, Horace laughing, greeting all the world as a jolly brother.

'Never mind, Vanessa,' Ellis said quietly. 'I will ask you again. It is a shock, of course. I am afraid that I was very sudden.'

'We do apologize,' cried Rose. 'That was Colonel Norton. I haven't seen him for an age. We were only gone a minute.'

It seemed to Vanessa that they had been an hour away.

When, alone in her room that night, she was dressing for dinner, she most unexpectedly had a fit of crying. She did not often cry, although young ladies thought nothing of it. But now, sitting in front of the glass, twisting her hair into ringlets, she found that the tears made ridiculous splashes on the pincushion, which was fat and round like a large white toad with a bright pink eye. She was crying, she discovered, because that Ellis should love her made her want Benjie so terribly. Oh, if it had been Benjie who had said those words in the Park! But it was not. It was Ellis. Then she found that she was crying because she felt, for the first time in her life, lonely and needed her father. She seemed to see him in the glass facing her, his brown beard, his soft rather ironical, rather sleepy eyes, his broad shoulders, rough coat ... She thought that tomorrow morning, as early as possible, she would take the train to Cumberland ...

Her tears were quickly dried because she was, she saw in the glass, so long and lanky. Now Rose might cry very prettily because she was slight and delicate in spite of her dark colour. But Vanessa was too tall for tears. She stood up in her skirt, all flounces and frills, raised her arms, threw up her head. Because Ellis had proposed to her was no reason for tears!

Then she laughed. The day before she had paid a visit with Rose to one of Rose's friends, a Mrs Pettinger. Mrs Pettinger's husband was an artist, and their little house in Pimlico had shone with the new aestheticism. The walls had Morris wallpapers, everywhere there were Japanese fans, bamboo tables, lilies in tall thin glasses, Japanese prints. Also two drawings by Mr Whistler which, privately, Vanessa had thought very beautiful. Privately, because Rose had confided to her that she found them absurd.

'Why, anyone could do that!' she said. 'I could. Just take your pencil and draw a few lines up and down. You have to stand a mile away to see what they're about.'

What made her laugh was the contrast between the room that she was in now and Mrs Pettinger's house. It seemed symbolically to be the contrast that she felt between her love for Benjie and Ellis' proposal. Her large cold bedroom had not, she supposed, been changed in detail for thirty years. Especially did she notice, as though seeing them for the first time, two armchairs of light oak carved with floral decorations and upholstered with dark-green velvet having a floral pattern. When you sat down in one of them it clung to you as though asserting its righteousness. Then the frame of Tonbridge-ware that contained a picture of a little girl outside a church made in seaweed, the Coalport toilet service, the dressing-table and mirror trimmed with glazed linen and muslin, the mahogany bedstead, the needlework bell-pulls. Yes, she thought, sitting down on the green velvet armchair, there were two worlds, as her father had always told her. Sitting there, without moving, staring before her, thinking of her mother, her father, Benjie, all those whom she loved, she moved naturally, simply into another world that had been, all her life, as real to her as the plush chair on which she was sitting. There was no effort, no conscious act of the will. An inner life flowed like a strong stream beneath all external things. This life had its own history, its own progress, its own destiny. She never spoke of it nor tried to explain it. It needed no explanation. Sometimes the two lives met, the two streams flowed together, but whereas the external life had its checks, its alarms, its vanities, and empty disappointments, this inner life flowed steadily, was always there. Yes, two worlds in everything. How to connect them? The Saints, she supposed, were those who had learnt the answer, men and women in whose lives one life always interpenetrated the other. But she, Vanessa, was no saint. She could only, at certain moments, be conscious of an awareness, an illumination, that irradiated everything so that in that brilliant light both things and people had suddenly their proper values.

Sitting on her plush chair she had now such a moment...

In the days that followed, Ellis behaved to her exactly as he had always done. It was as though their little conversation in the Park had never been. She obtained increasingly from the Herries family both instruction and amusement. Old Amery greatly amused her with his intimate stories of high places, of the adventures, for example, of King William of the Netherlands, one of whose ladies broke all the crockery in his palace during one of her tempers, of some Italian prince in Paris who disguised himself as an organ-grinder for a whole month that he might station himself outside his lady-love's door, of young Lord So-and-so who, rejected by his mistress, put a large black band on his hat, went to his rooms, and committed suicide by cutting his wrist open with a razor, remembering first to place a slop pail by the chair that there might be no mess. Young Alfred amused her because he would tolerate anyone who promised to be notable. She liked Captain Will with his breezy manner of finding the sea the only possible place, and yet now he never went there. The Rockages were redolent of the country. Carey himself, although he was tidy enough, seemed to carry good Wiltshire mud on his boots, and little Lady Rockage walked as though she were ready to spring on to a horse's back at any moment. She soon knew

them all and liked them all with the single exception of Emily,
Barney's sister, who was pious but not charitable, prudish with
an unpleasant inquisitiveness, and a mischief-maker for the best
of motives.

She found them all most strangely alike in some basic way.
They had no pose, made no attempts to assert themselves, took
everything for granted. For them all, the Herries were the backbone of England, and England was the only country in the world
that mattered at all. It was Barney Newmark, however, who best
explained the family position to her, sitting beside her on the
occasion of the splendid Herries party in Hill Street when Mme
Trebelli sang and Signor Pesto played so enthusiastically the
violin.

Vanessa liked Barney best of them all. Rose, of course, excep-
ted. Barney was now fifty-two, stout, fresh-coloured, and carelessly dressed but not untidy. He looked a little Bohemian but not
very; you would not know that he was a writer, said Vanessa.
That was a period when writers *looked* like writers. He took life
very lightly, laughed at everyone and everything, but behind that
was, she thought, a disappointed man. He had published a dozen
novels and lived comfortably on the proceeds. She had read several of them. They were not very good and not very bad. They
were like the books of other authors. But he never spoke of his
novels, laughed scornfully when they were mentioned to him.
She felt, however, that he would like it very much if someone else
praised them. At their first meeting in London she said what she
could. At once he stopped her.

'Dear Vanessa. Thank you very much. And now we need never
mention them again, need we? No friends of mine can read my
novels. That is a sign of their friendship.' Very different, had she
but known it, from the man who once at a prize-fight had
clasped Mortimer Collins by the shoulder!

They sat now in a corner of the big drawing-room and
watched the splendid affair. The room was very crowded. It
looked for the first time alive, for the heavy furniture was gone
and, save for the palms, ferns and flowers packed into the corners,
round the piano, in front of the great marble fireplace, only
human beings filled it. The ladies wore their jewels, their shoulders gleamed under the gaslight, everyone was splendid, dignified,
assured and, it appeared, happy. Vanessa would never have had
courage to penetrate the throng, but almost at once she saw
Barney, who carried her off into a corner, saying: 'Now I shall be

the proudest man here for five minutes, before you are discovered, you know. Soon there will be so many proud men that you won't be able to breathe.'

She was very happy alone with him. She would like to stay thus throughout the evening.

'Tell me who everyone is, Barney dear,' she said.

He pointed out a few. 'That dignified cleric is the Bishop of London. That fine fellow there is Mr Bancroft.'

'And oh, who is that darling old man?'

That darling old man looked like a ship's captain. He had a grey beard, grey hair erect and curly through which he often ran his hands, a florid complexion, clear eyes. He was the finest man in the room.

'That is Mr Madox Brown,' said Barney.

'And that lovely lady?'

'That lovely lady is Mrs Samuel Maguire, and her husband gives her a diamond every morning with her coffee.'

'And that very dark man?'

'That is Isaac Lowenfeld, the financier. He once blacked gentlemen's shoes in Constantinople. Jews are coming in. The Prince of Wales likes them, and why should he not? I like them myself. They have the best hearts, the best brains and the staunchest religion in London.'

She noticed two young men with high white foreheads, long pale hair and a very languishing manner.

'And those?'

'Those are the aesthetes. They look at a lily for breakfast, worship china teacups and lisp in poetry. I don't like 'em myself. They are not my kind. But they have their uses.'

'Everyone is here then? Lady Herries will be pleased.'

'Yes, it is a success because soon the room will be so crowded that no one can move, so noisy that no one will hear anyone else, and so hot that several young ladies will faint.'

She soon found members of the Herries family here and there.

'There is Emily. How nice and healthy Captain Will looks! I think Alfred is over-dressed.'

'Yes, we are all here,' said Barney. 'A great satisfaction to all of us. A fine family. And yet we are not of the first rank. Oh, I don't mean in history. We are, I suppose, as old as any family in England. But we are not, and never shall be, like the Chichesters, the Medleys. Nor like the Beaminsters, the Cecils, the Howards.

Although in fact we *are* a kind of relation of the Howards. But we're not like the new democrats either, people like the Rud-dards, the Denisons. All very poor kind of talk this, but it's important, the social history of England, partly because it's his-tory, partly because in another fifty years' time there won't be any social history. There, do you see that little woman in black with that jade pendant – with the hard mouth and the small nose? That's the Duchess of Wrexe. That's her daughter, Adela Beam-inster, with her. Well, she walks as though she owned the world, every scrap of it. Contrast her with Lady Herries. Oh, I know *she* isn't a Herries really, but she's acquired *all* the Herries charac-teristics. The wives of Herries men always do. That's what I mean. We are upper middle class. We belong in the country, small Squires, maiden ladies in places like Bournemouth and Harrogate, houses like Uldale for example. That's where *we* are. For the last hundred years we've been rising or seeming to. Will made a heap of money and Ellis is making more. Then there are the Rockages, a small pocket-nobility. But we are not first class in anything. We write – well, as I do. We are parsons and one of us becomes an Archdeacon. We make money in the City but can't *touch* Lowenfeld. We entertain, but when we bring off a party like this it's a kind of accident. Not that we see our-selves like that. We think there's nobody to touch us, but that's because we have no imagination. That's why we are of real im-portance in the country. If there's ever a revolution in England it's the Herries and others like them who will save us all. Even as we begin to die out the lower ranks take our places and become just like us. We are filled up from below, but we never *rise* any higher. We have our good points – we are not acquisitive, we are not greedy, we are kind if we are not attacked, generous even; we never lose our heads, we adore our country although we criticize it. We never have to speak foreign languages, we revel in our abominable climate, on the whole we are contented.'

'But?—' asked Vanessa.

'We have one great weakness. We are terrified of anything out of the normal. If we see it we fight and slay it. Unhappily there is a strain of the artist in our family. It breaks out again and again. Then we are shamed, disgraced, humiliated. We have never learnt how to assimilate it. That is why if we breed an artist he is always second-rate. The family is too strong for him. That is why we fight among ourselves and why some of us, if we are courageous enough not to come to terms, are so unhappy. Oh, you needn't look at me, my dear. I *have* come to terms. I couldn't fight it out. That is why I am what I am. I am always hoping that we shall breed an artist who, because he is forced to fight, becomes a *great* artist. Why have the English the finest poets in the world? Because the other members of the family have always done their best to kill them. Why was your grandmother so splendid? Because she never capitulated.'

'Father always says that she declared that she *did* capitulate,' said Vanessa.

'Capitulate? She? Think of her! Capitulate? Not she! If she were in this room tonight she'd blow out the Duchess of Wrexe like a farthing dip!'

'And have you altogether capitulated, Barney?'

'Yes, my dear. Entirely. I'm no good at all. But I tell you who *hasn't* capitulated. That's Benjie!'

At the unexpected sound of his name the lights blurred, the voices faded.

'No,' said Barney, 'but if he doesn't they'll drum him out of the field. You watch them. It will be a fight worth beholding!'

And now the room was crammed indeed. The roar of conversation, like the break of the tide on shingle with here a whisper, here a grating clatter of pebbles, here a resounding hiss, made private talk impossible, so Barney, pleased with his analysis of his relations, stood up and looked about him while Vanessa watched Mr Madox Brown roaring at the Bishop of London, and the lovely Mrs Williamson (who was reputed to bathe in milk every morning) listening kindly to one of the young aesthetes, who twisted and bent like a reed in a gale.

She caught fragments of conversation. 'I heard Trebelli at Sims Reeves' concert in February. No, he couldn't appear, so we had Trebelli and Santley instead. Oh, of course Trebelli's the best contralto in the world. But to tell you the honest truth I enjoyed better Santley's "Vicar of Bray" – irresistible. Quite irresistible . . .'

'Oh, but Bradlaugh! . . .'

'And then, my love, *what* do you think? She went to the pastrycook's round the corner and *herself* fetched a dozen cream buns in a paper bag . . .'

'Yes, but what *I* say is that they could keep Jumbo here perfectly well, doncherknow, if they wanted to – really wanted to. What I mean is, that Jumbo is important for the country, for the *Tourists*, doncherknow – something for them to go to the Zoo and look at. What I mean is, we all feel it *personally* . . .'

'Very *unkind* of *Punch*, I think. Poor Mr Irving – to print his picture and then quote "Romeo! Romeo! Wherefore are *thou* Romeo?" That's too personal in my opinion. All the same he is *not* the young, ardent lover . . .'

'Yes, but what Russell wants is to buy out the Irish landlords and present the holdings to the tenants! Simple! I should think so! If Gladstone would only say what he means . . .'

'And so, darling, Henry said to him, "That lady is intended evidently for a Chinese" – trying to be witty, poor man, and the large man with the teeth whom he'd *never* seen before said furiously, "And why, pray? That lady is my sister." And oh, wasn't Henry clever? He answered at once, "Why, because she has such exquisitely small feet." '

It was Vanessa's first London party, and, standing there, waiting before she should be drawn into the middle of it, she knew, as her grandmother had known on just such another occasion, that something in her responded to this with excitement and eagerness. It was as though, a vagabond and wanderer, peering in through a window at a splendid feast, she exclaimed to herself: 'I can do this as well as anyone. I know all the tricks.' She would never truly belong to it, but it was a part that she could play as well as anyone there. The personal drama had seized her. The drama of London, the Park with the brilliant sunlit figures, the old crossing-sweeper with the scarlet coat, Ellen Terry laughing into the wicked eyes of old Mrs Stirling, Mr Conway rebuking his errant daughter, Gladstone in his high collar thundering at the House, old Lady Herries fixing, with trembling hands, the jewels about her throat, the melancholy wail of the hurdy-gurdy two streets away, the Prince of Wales talking to Mr Lowenfeld, the 'greenery-yallery' young men yearning over a Japanese print, the carts packed with flowers arriving in the early morning at Covent Garden, Gambetta drinking his morning coffee in Paris, and that picturesque brigand Arabi ordering an execution in Egypt, an account that she had read only last week in a paper of a Professor who had invented 'little electric lamps of the Cat Bells garden, watching the thin spidery rain veil the Horace Ormerod's friendliness, and Rose's adventurousness, Barney's kindness, and, behind it all, sitting in the hut at the top of the Cat Bells garden, watching the thin spidery rain veil the Lake in webs of lawn while fragments of blue sky, as bright as speedwells, flashed and vanished and flashed again. Her mind was a jumble of this kind; at the back of the jumble was the deep unceasing preoccupation. Would Benjie come before the month was out? Would he keep his word? Was there nothing that could still this burning ceaseless preoccupation of hers? And, if he cared no longer for her, could she make her life without him? She could! She could! She was not so weak, so helpless! But her throat was dry at the thought! Her hand touched her breast to check the wild beating of her heart.

She was discovered. Rose and Horace discovered her. They led her into the throng and at once her own life was broken into little scattered fragments. She had no life. She was nothing but a laughing, smiling, murmuring adjunct to all the other laughs, smiles, murmurs.

She was introduced to Mr Madox Brown. They sat down together near the piano. At first he said nothing, pushing his strong brown hand through his curly hair, muttering a little, looking as though he wanted to escape. Then something happened. *She* did not know what it was. In actual fact it was his sudden realization of her beauty. He never saw her again, but many times after he would growl:

'One night at one of those damned musical parties I came on a girl ... you never saw anyone so lovely. Quite unconscious of it too.'

He became gentle and most friendly. He told her about his son. 'He died seven years ago. There never *was* anyone so talented. Only nineteen when he died. One day, when he was dying and I sitting at his bedside, he smiled and said I smelt of tobacco. I said, "All right. I'll not smoke again until you're better." I never *shall* smoke again. Never. Paint? Write? He could do anything. And sweet-natured. Oliver was the only genius I've known. No one else. Not *genius*. Genius is something from another world. Nothing to do with this shabby one.'

He asked her where she came from.

She told him, Cumberland.

'Oh yes, Wordsworth and all that.'

Looking at her he said:

'You have beautiful eyes. Forgive an old painter's impertinence, my dear. I always begin with the eyes, you know. Paint the eyes of the central figure first and that gives tone to the picture. I begin at the top left hand of the canvas and go straight down to the bottom. And what do *you* do?'

'I can't paint,' she answered, laughing. 'I can't do anything.'

'You don't need to,' he told her.

They could have become great friends had life arranged it.

Then she was alone with Rose, sitting behind a gigantic pessimistic palm. They were clearing the space about the piano. Trebelli was going to sing. What, she thought, was Rose's power over
her? Why was she so fond of her? Rose was like a carnation, set
deep in colour, slight, with a wine-dark air. Not beautiful, for
her eyes were too large for her small face, her nose a little snub,
and her mouth, Vanessa must confess, rather hard. Her eyes
laughed, danced, sparkled, but her mouth was always a little cold,
a little cruel. If you judged people by their eyes, then Rose was a
dear sweet girl, but if by their mouth, then Rose was nothing of
the kind. She said once to Vanessa:

'Horace and I are both completely hard and self-seeking!'

'Oh no!' protested Vanessa.

'Oh yes, we are! The only difference between us is that I look at
myself in the glass and know *exactly* what I am. Horace looks
greedily into other people's faces for his reflection and woe betide
you if it isn't a pleasant one.' She added: 'We are both adventurers. We have scarcely a penny to our name. I'm the Becky
Sharp in Thackeray's stupid novel except that I'm sometimes
sentimental. After I've been sentimental I'm so angry with everyone that I could commit murder. I dare say I shall one day.
Probably my husband. First I must get one. I'm twenty-seven,
you know.'

She talked a great deal about herself, and this Vanessa found
delightful, but Rose's real attraction for her was that she knew
life so thoroughly. Girls who were Vanessa's contemporaries knew
nothing about life at all. They were not supposed to know and,
what was more, they really did not know. Most of them married
without the slightest idea of what came next, with the simple
result that, for the rest of their days, they were a little melancholy
and looked at all men, except clergymen, with a faint distrust.
The women on the other hand, like Rose, for whom life (including men) had no secrets, were like gipsies who pitch their
caravans at their own risk. The female world looked on them with
suspicion, and the male world frequently presumed further than
slight acquaintance warranted.

Rose had by this time told Vanessa everything she knew, and
Vanessa, because she possessed certain beliefs, fidelities and a
strong sense of humour, was not at all shocked. She hoped nevertheless that Rose would be married soon. It would be wiser.

Rose, on her side, loved Vanessa. She might be herself a lost angel – and she was a great deal more lost than Vanessa realized – but she adored a good angel with a sense of humour. She admired passionately in Vanessa all the qualities that she did not herself possess. She was no fool about human nature. She knew quite well that even from her mercenary point of view the virtues pay better in the end than the vices.

So they sat together behind the pessimistic palm and talked about those present. Rose knew something about everyone. She knew just what to tell Vanessa, amusing things but not cruel ones. She kept her cruel ones for other audiences.

Then, touching Vanessa's hand, she said: 'There, I think, is the man I am going to marry.'

'Oh, where?' cried Vanessa. 'Rose, dear, do you mean it,'

'I *think* that I mean it. That man with the eyeglass, the pale whiskers, the beautiful figure.'

Vanessa looked. He was certainly very handsome.

'Oh, who is he?'

'He is Captain Fred Wycherley. He is in the Army and is very rich.'

'Oh, Rose dear, I am so glad! Has he proposed to you? Do you love him very much?'

'No, he has not proposed, but I think within the week he will. I don't love him, of course. It would never do for me to love my husband: it would give him too much power over me. But he is agreeable, amusing. I think we shall understand one another.'

Before they could say any more Trebelli began to sing. She had an extremely powerful voice and sang as though she were commanding a regiment. She was made, it appeared, of brass from head to foot.

After the singing everyone began to move about again and Vanessa was introduced to a number of people. Among them was a stout, round gentleman with fair hair and the face of a very good-natured pig, whose eyes beamed with kindliness. This, she discovered, was Lord John Beaminster, a son of the Duchess of Wrexe. He spoke in jerks, smiling upon her as though he had known her all her life.

'Very hot, these parties,' he said.

'Yes,' she said, copying Barney. 'The hotter they are the more successful they are.'

'Do you care for music?'

'Yes, sometimes.'

'That woman has deafened my eardrum. All the opera women shout. Do you like the opera?'

'I've never been in my life,' said Vanessa. 'I live in the country.'

'Oh, in the country, do you? Wouldn't want to live there. All right for a day or two. What part?'

'Up in Cumberland.'

'Doesn't it rain there?'

'Yes, when it wants to, but nobody minds the rain.'

'I do, unless I'm shooting or hunting, you know.' He smiled as though they had reached the most delightful intimacy. 'Oh, that damned feller's going to play the fiddle.'

It was then that as she looked beyond him towards the door, as though something had compelled her, the miracle of her whole life occurred. Beaminster was saying something to her. The violin began to wail. The shining shoulders of some woman at her side spread, as it appeared, into an infinite distance.

In the doorway, looking about him with a friendly grin, stood Benjie Herries.

She did not move. Beaminster, seeing a friend, said, with a bow: 'Excuse me one moment.'

Then Benjie seemed to drive, like a swimmer breasting the tide, straight towards her. She saw people greet him. She heard (for he was very near to her now) Will Herries exclaim:

'Hullo, Benjie! Where have you come from?'

She did not move until his hand was on her sleeve. She heard him say: 'Come out of this. Outside.'

She went with him down the room. In the passage above the stairs there was no one. From the room within, the violin went on and on like a voice speaking only for them.

She stood up against the wall, staring at him, feeling that at any moment she might cry, unable to speak because her heart beat so fiercely, hammering her body as though it must throw her down. But there was no need to speak, no time for it.

'You thought that I wasn't coming back. Didn't you? You thought that I had forgotten. Quick, Vanessa, tell me – do you love me? Do you love me as much as two years ago? Is there anyone else? If so, where is he? I'll kill him. Quick. Tell me. I have run all the way from Brindisi. If you knew how I've run! Tell me. Tell me. Do you love me? Are you going to marry me? Can I go in there now and tell them all? Quick. Don't waste a moment! Do you love me?'

'Benjie, wait! Of course I do. I thought you'd never come! I've been longing—'

But she did not finish her sentence. He kissed her, patting her shoulder, her arm, laying his cheek against hers. Then he caught her hand in his.

'Now come! At once! We must tell everyone! We mustn't lose a moment!'

He pulled her with him to the door. The voice of the violin came towards them, dancing over the crowd, the flowers, the palms.

Seated by the door was an old lady, blazing with diamonds, listening to the music through an ear-trumpet.

'Excuse me—' said Benjie.

'Hush! hush!' said everyone near the door. The violin rose into a thin, long, vibrating note. Then ceased.

The old lady, turning to a man beside her, said:

'And *now* it ought to be time for supper.' Then, looking up: 'Why, it's Benjamin Herries! I thought you were in China, young man.'

Benjie wrung her hand as though she were the friend of his heart.

'I was, Lady Mullion. I was – only yesterday. Let me introduce you to Miss Vanessa Paris. We are going to be married—'

'Going to be what?' she asked, her round red face ignorantly beaming.

He took the ear-trumpet, and, in a voice loud enough for all the world to hear, shouted: 'We are going to be married.'

'Oh, is that all?' said the old lady. 'I thought there'd been an accident. And now I do *hope* we are going down to supper.'

THE SEASHORE

TIMOTHY BELLAIRS took his wife and family that summer to an old house, Low Dene, in the village of Gosforth, which was situated ten miles from Wastwater and a little more than three miles from Seascale on the coast.

Young Tim, now aged five, had not lately been very well; one cold had followed the other. Sea air would do the children good, and he would have found some place *on* the sea had it not been

for Mrs Bellairs, who disliked the sea and all its works. So a
compromise was effected.

Low Dene was one of those large, rambling, untidy houses of
which at that time the country offered many examples. They
were especially suited to the large families that good English
parents thought it proper to create. The house was in a hollow
under the hill to the right of the village; fields ran to the edge of
the big scrambling garden; there was a croquet lawn, a wood,
shrubberies, a stream, everything that children desired. The place
belonged to a retired Indian colonel whose children were now
grown. He had gone with his wife and four daughters to
Brighton, where he hoped to marry the daughters and recapture
some of his own youth. It was one of those houses which here are
furnished and there are not. The drawing-room, some of the
bedrooms, were crowded with large and small impedimenta, so
crowded that you could scarcely move without disabling a china
figure, upsetting an Indian idol, or flinging a wool mat to the
floor. On the other hand most of the passages, some of the bedrooms, the bathroom, had no covering to the bare boards, the
wind whistled through the thin faded wallpapers, the piano was
altogether out of tune, every fireplace smoked, the gas hissed, the
cistern groaned, there was an odd smell of dog in every room,
and draughts played in every corner. In spite of these things
the house had an air of cosiness and comfort – why, it would be
difficult to say. It was, maybe, because a large family had grown
up in it and their games, quarrels, intimacies, pleasures had sunk
into the brick, permeated the boards of the passages, helped to
stain curtains and wallpapers into their faded homely colours.

Timothy, his wife, and children were well pleased. Fell House,
Uldale, was the joy and boast of Timothy's heart, but it was
pleasant for a while to escape its responsibilities. Timothy was
lazy although he disguised the laziness with true English aplomb.
As to the children this was the happiest summer of their young
lives. Discipline was relaxed; their father condescended to walk
with them, there was the Farm at the top of the hill, the fields
with the haymaking, the mysterious wood, the sea, and above all
Vanessa.

It was Timothy who had invited Vanessa to stay with them.
Mrs Bellairs had objected, although in her sleepy, limited fashion
she rather liked Vanessa. They had both been deeply shocked – as
had Herries up and down the country – when they heard of her
engagement to Benjamin Herries. They had thought at first that

they would never speak to Vanessa again. But Timothy had as true an affection for her as he had for anyone in the world. In his stout slow body there was little rancour, no spitefulness, temper only with his own children. He was negative in all his emotions except his family pride. He thought that he had the finest house, the finest wife, the finest children in the world, and perhaps, deep in his heart, he loved his children and had an affection for his wife. But it was not the fashion for either husbands or parents to be demonstrative. He was now forty-five years of age, laziness and corpulency made him virtuous, but he had still an eye for a pretty woman, and Vanessa's beauty, although he might not speak of it (for Mrs Bellairs could be a jealous woman), gave him the greatest pleasure to look upon. He would stare and stare at her with something of the same emotion with which he would gaze upon a fine shoulder of mutton freshly come to table. Nevertheless he cared for Vanessa. He would, at a push, do more for her than for anyone.

Discussing the tragic Vanessa–Benjie affair in the large family bed at Uldale, he declared that Vanessa should be invited to come with them to Gosforth. Mrs Bellairs groaned and lamented, but knew that if he had decided on something it was decided. They were both lazy people, but she was lazier than he. His point was that they might influence Vanessa. She had been carried off her feet by the London atmosphere. (He had the greatest contempt for London. He knew that he would not shine if he went there.) Let her spend a week or two with them in the country and they would soon show her her silly mistake.

'And her father?' murmured Mrs Bellairs.

'Let him come too,' said Timothy, who tolerated Adam but scorned him because he did nothing with his time but write books. 'The house is big enough.'

However, Adam refused. He might come over for a day or two.

Timothy, his wife, his sister Jane, now an old maid of forty-two, the children, Mrs Clopton the nurse, Agnes the young maid, Jim Wilson the coachman, Peter the dog, all moved over to Low Dene in the large family chariot.

Vanessa arrived there two days later.

The real reason of Vanessa's visit was that she wished to escape from Benjie, whom she had been seeing almost every day for the last three months.

It was not that she loved Benjie less: it was that she loved him more, and this love had plunged her into a turmoil of problems, excitements, and distresses not only about him but about herself as well.

She had never, until now, known any very close and intimate relation with anyone save her father and mother. Her life had always moved on certain fixed and stable laws. Her own faults and failings, which were many – impetuous feeling, hasty temper, neglect of obvious duties – had all, when tested by a few principles, been clearly faults and failings. There had never been any question about what she *ought* to do. Simply she had been wicked and failed.

But she was as honest as anyone alive, both with herself and everyone else, and, after a week with Benjie, she saw that neither right nor wrong conduct would ever be so clear and simple again.

That she had been carried off her feet by Benjie's return and proposal did not at all blind her to the fact that no one else had. She realized immediately at the first half-hour in the party at Hill Street that no one anywhere was going to approve of the engagement – no, not even Rose. 'She is throwing herself away,' she could hear everyone saying. Benjie's charm and light-heartedness when he was happy affected many when he was with them, and during that final week in London he was very charming indeed, but, returning to Cumberland, she found that even Elizabeth was doubtful. 'It is what I have always wanted,' Elizabeth said. 'And oh, my dear, I do hope he will make you happy!'

And her father? He kissed her and told her that her happiness was dearer to him than anything else on earth. She was a woman now. She knew where her happiness lay.

She simply said: 'I have loved him all my life.' He said no more, but she noticed in him after this a constant anxiety, an extra tenderness, and in herself, a certain reticence that had not been there before. Their relationship was for the first time in their lives a little clouded.

Benjie came up to the Fortress and lived there quietly with his mother. At first he was happy with an exuberance, a generosity to all the world, that showed him at his very best. Everyone noticed the change in him.

'I think,' Elizabeth confided to Vanessa after a week or two, 'that it will be as I hoped. You are going to change him al-together.' He told her again and again how, during those last months abroad, her image, his adoration of her, obsessed him more and more completely. On his journey home his impatience was a fever. At the sight of her at last in that silly drawing-room he nearly died! They must be married immediately. She was quite ready. She did not want to wait. Let them be married tomorrow!

Then it was he, Benjie, who postponed it. One afternoon, walking again in the garden at the Fortress, all the old doubts came forward. He was not good enough for her. Everyone was right. He would make her unhappy. When she knew him better she would hate him. She calmed him. She laughed at him. She told him once again that she had known him all her life, that she was not blind nor ignorant about men, that they must trust one another and take what came. She was so certain of her own deep, unchangeable love that they need have no fear. He asked her, in a kind of despair, why did she love him as she did. Soon against her will she was asking herself that question. What was Benjie's power over her? She loved him because he alone in all the world drew everything out of her: she loved him as a woman, as a mother, as a sister, as a friend and a companion. He was honest, generous, gay, independent, brave. He was also careless, selfish, casual, forgetful, always surrendering to the mood of the moment, hating to be tied. But that he adored her no one could doubt. He knew, his mother knew, even the men and women about the place knew that, with all his faults, this love for Vanessa was true, staunch, unyielding. Had his character been as fine as his love they would be happy for evermore!

The wildness in him was quite untamed. She knew that and reckoned with it, but to watch it working at a distance and to have it in close daily communion with herself were two quite different things.

He could conceal nothing that was in his mind, and soon he attacked what he called her 'childishness'. He attacked her religion. He told her again and again that he did not want her to change in the least and tried to change her. 'You know that there can't be a God, Vanessa. In your heart you must know it. You are a wise woman. You read and think. Well, then, ask yourself. How *can* there be a God and life be as it is? If there is one He ought to be deuced ashamed of Himself, that's all I can say.'

She disliked intensely to talk about her religion. She had never done so with anyone save her mother and Elizabeth. Her father had always respected that reticence. But quietly and with

humour she answered Benjie's indignation. 'We go by our experience, I suppose, Benjie dear. God is as real to me as you are. Of
course I don't know *why* life is as it is. I am a very ignorant
woman, and Mr Darwin's monkeys are beyond my scope. But a
hundred thousand monkeys wouldn't alter the truth that I love
you, nor would they change my love of God either. Don't worry
about it, Benjie. Let us be what we are.'

Then soon there was another thing. She had never known
before what physical love was. She had never been close to Benjie
so constantly. She had never conceived her own weakness. One
fine day they had ridden out to Borrowdale and, sitting in the
sun under some trees above Rosthwaite, they had talked. She
knew that everyone thought it very disgraceful that they went
about together without a chaperon. Even her father had shyly
spoken to her of it. She had laughed and said that he need have
no fears. But now, quite suddenly, she realized that he was right
to be afraid. It was as though she and Benjie were caught up into
a hot burning cloud of light. The world turned so that both
sound and vision were obliterated. For a fearful dumb blind
moment she was almost lost. Then by the grace of God she escaped into sight and sound again.

Next day she said

'Benjie, why should we wait? Let us marry soon.'

But there was her father. She could not endure to leave him. It
is true that she would be at the Fortress, not far away, but the
thought of his lonely days, his sitting at his table writing, looking
up out of window, thinking of her, wanting her, was intolerable.
He told her with a smile that he would be quite happy. He had
Will, he had his work and garden. She knew that he was doing
his best. He did not take her in at all. Then in June he fell ill. He
caught a cold, suffered from rheumatism, had to go to bed for a
while. When he was better Benjie, who had been wonderful
during Adam's sickness, coming constantly to visit him, laughing, cheering him up, reading to him, suffered from all his old
scruples again.

'Vanessa, give me up! I'll go away and never come back! I'm
not worth all your sacrifice. I'm not worth anyone's sacrifice.'

But he loved her more than ever and he was more charming
than ever. He was, during those weeks in July, unselfish,
thoughtful, considered her in everything. But they decided that
they would wait until the spring. 'You will know then finally,
once and for all, whether I am worth it.'

'I know it now,' she said gently. 'Nothing can change.'

But she perceived by now that, beyond any doubt, it was something he knew about himself that stirred all his self-depreciation. That, because he knew himself so well and loved her so dearly, he was determined to do this one decent honest thing – not to ruin her life.

But what was it that he knew about himself? He was not, in his attitude to anyone else, self-depreciatory. Far from it. 'Take me as I am; as I take you,' was his attitude to the world. Only he would not spoil Vanessa's life for her.

'But of course you will not spoil it.'

'You don't know me.'

'I take the risk,' she answered.

By the end of July she felt that she must, for a little while, be at a distance from him. This indecision and hesitation could not go on. It was making them both sensitive, moody, self-conscious. So she went to Gosforth.

When she had been a day there her spirit was quieted, her gaiety returned.

Gosforth itself, small quiet village that it was, contained all the past. In the churchyard there was a cross of red sandstone which represented a figure chained beneath a serpent dropping upon him poison. This was a Christian cross and yet it had on it a heathen symbol. No one could tell its age, but many Vikings, she understood, had been half Christian, half heathen. She liked to think that this had been a Viking cross. Then there was Gosforth Hall near the church, the very house where Bishop Nicolson in the seventeenth century, as a young archdeacon, courted Barbara Copley. Near the Hall was a holy well where there had been once a mediaeval chapel, and half a mile from the Hall was the Dane's Camp, and farther from that again the King's Camp, at Laconby. Many of the old houses in the neighbourhood, like Ponsonby Hall and Sella Park, were packed with history, while not far away was Calder Abbey.

In the middle of all this concentration of Time slept the perfect English countryside. There was often sunshine that August and sweeping shafts of it fell across the cornfields, warming the colours into red gold, falling at the feet of the dark shadows of the woods. It was pastoral everywhere, while on windless days the silence, made more musical by the creaking of a cart, dogs barking, the call of the farmer to his horse, seemed to carry all the summer scents of flowers and corn and trees and pile them about

you so that on the hot lawn you need not stir but gather, without
motion, everything into your heart.

Yet how strangely even in this country of cornfield, wood and
hedgerow still the mountains dominated. At every point, from
every rise, Black Combe, thrusting its head like a lazy friendly
whale into the sea, held your eye. From Black Combe's top you
could hold in your grasp the Isle of Man, the Scottish and
Welsh coasts with Snowdon greeting you, while landwards were
Lancashire and the Yorkshire Fells.

To the right from a little hill above the house you could salute
the Screes and in your mind's eye follow them as they rushed
with all their power to bury their foundations deep in the heart of
the black lake. Standing on her hill Vanessa would watch the
clouds hurrying like smoke to invade the serried tops, then to
spill themselves in storm or to break into pavilions snow-white or
crimson with fire, or to shred and scatter into strands of gold and
crimson. And she liked to sense, as she felt the motionless peace
of the cornfields below them, catching the sun and throwing it
up to her again, that above those hills the wind was raging and
that their shining, slanting surface glistened with hardness, and
the stone walls, straight as a sword, ran to the skyline over ground
that was rough and peaty and free. All history was in this small
patch of ground, and all nature too, shadowed by the triumphant
wing of the great Eagle to whose kingly progress History was but
a day.

In the house and out of it there were the children. They were
sternly disciplined. Mrs Clopton, a tall dark woman with heavy
eyebrows and a faint moustache, was a Tartar. She was not
unkind, but she thrived on her despair of human nature. She
hoped for the best but gloried in her constant disappointment.
Her God – she was a deeply religious woman – was the real God
of the Israelites, revengeful, on the watch for every blunder, cruel
in His punishments. Oddly the children liked her; they were
proud of her. She had no need to punish; a look, a word from
her was sufficient. Not that they were perfect children. They
made their own lives in their world of perpetual discipline. They
learnt their Collects on Sunday, said 'Yes, Mama' and 'No,
Mama', never spoke when with their elders unless spoken to, but
once by themselves, the official eye removed from them, they were
free, natural, and often naughty. It was as though they understood the terms under which they lived and made their plans
accordingly. Violet was delicate – fair-haired, slender, blue-eyed

and was already making her poor health her pleasant advantage.

But Tim was Vanessa's darling. He was fair and slender like Violet, but strong and wiry. She saw that he was an artist born and that nothing would stop him. He drew unconsciously without any deliberate awareness. He noticed the shapes and colours of clouds, the patterns of leaves, the path that the wind made through the corn, a snail's shiny track on the lawn, the purple shadows on the flanks of Black Combe. He was already at odds with Herries common sense.

His father would darken the doorway.

'Tim, what are you doing?'

'Making a picture, Papa.'

'Let me see.'

Then after a pause:

'Now what is this?'

'A ship with pirates, Papa.'

'Pirates! Pirates! What do you know about pirates?'

'Aunt Essie told us, Papa.'

'And you call this a ship?'

'I don't know ships very well and—'

'Well, wait until you do. Wasting your time like this! What have I often told you?'

'Not to waste my time, Papa.'

'Exactly. Now put away that rubbish.'

The children worshipped Vanessa. For half an hour before they went to bed she was allowed to tell them stories. Mrs Clopton listened in stern astonishment. There was nothing of which she disapproved so thoroughly as stories, but, while her needles clicked, she found herself attending: fairy palaces rose above her head, the Crystal Lake was at her feet and a White Horse of incomparable splendour strode the ice-bound hills.

'Time for their bed, Miss Vanessa.'

But, over her solitary supper, she wondered, against her will: 'What did the Princess find behind the secret door? Did the dwarf climb out of the cellar? Why was the Green Necklace the King's most treasured possession?'

Best of all there was the sea. On fine days they drove there in the victoria. The sand stretched in a floor of mother-of-pearl to the line of trembling white. On the horizon the Isle of Man hung between sea and sky. Timothy slept, Mrs Bellairs talked, the

children were busy with their fantasies, Mrs Clopton read her
Bible, Vanessa thought of Benjamin.

On a sunny afternoon, staring dreamily at the incoming
tide, she saw him coming towards her.

At first she was delighted, then she was angry, then delighted
again. She wanted *not* to be pleased! He was for ever breaking his
word. They had agreed that they would not meet for three weeks.
And why had he not written to her to tell her that he was
coming? Or had he perhaps ridden over and tomorrow was returning? Or did he intend? ... The children had seen him and
began to run towards him, then stopped, remembering their
elders. They loved, however, Benjie better than anyone else in the
world – far better indeed. No one, not even Aunt Vanessa nor
Aunt Jane nor any other, could create for them a world and then
live contentedly inside it as Benjie could.

'Uncle Benjie! Uncle Benjie!' Tim cried and woke up his
father. Mrs Bellairs disapproved of Benjamin completely. She
was terrified lest he should contaminate the children. She *said*
this, but in actual fact when he was in her company she always
surrendered to him. Had she been honest with herself she would
have acknowledged that to be so vicious and yet so amiable
touched the adventurous woman in her. Although stout and
forty, completely the British matron, there hid somewhere within
her a girl who longed to see what the other half of the world was
like. This girl was slowly starving to death. Once and again
she received sustenance: Benjie more than any other kept her
alive.

Nevertheless he *was* dangerous to the children with all the
horrible things he had seen and done, the dreadful women he
must know. Moreover, had they not invited Vanessa to stay for
the sole purpose of showing her how shocking, how impossible
Benjie was?

But what were you to do when in a moment he was down on
his knees in the sand helping Tim with his castle, which the
child had already decorated with a pink shell, the green stopper
of a ginger-beer bottle, and a piece of red rag tied to a stick?

And *what* were you to do when, smiling all over his face, sand
on his trousers, waving a child's spade, he came over to you
crying:

'Just think, Violet, I've come all the way from the Fortress on a
bicycle.'

'On a bicycle!' She sat up, settled her bustle, arranged the large yellow brooch neatly on her bosom and stared with what she trusted was a mixture of disapprobation and dignity.

'Now don't look like that, Violet! You know you are glad I have come. One might think I was Cetewayo by your disapproval. I'm not going to poison the children or tell them naughty stories. I *may* tell you a few later on, but to be honest with you I've come to see Vanessa, the lady to whom I'm engaged, and nobody else ... Yes, I've come on a bicycle! I bought it in Carlisle last week.'

'Where is it?' asked Mrs Bellairs, speaking as though he had brought with him the late-lamented Jumbo from the Zoo.

'It is at my lodging.'

'Your lodging? Then you are going to stay here?'

'For a day or two – as long as Vanessa will put up with me.'

'Well, we can't offer you a bed at Low Dene if that's what you want. There are rooms enough but no servants. I'm sorry, but you should have told us you were coming.'

Benjie laughed. 'But, my dear Violet, why will you not understand? I have not come to see *you*. Of course if you appear sometimes I shall be glad to talk to you and to listen to what you have to say. If you are *very* good I will tell you a story or two about Port Said. But I have not the slightest interest in either yourself or Low Dene just now. I prefer the company of Mrs Halliday and Rosemary Cottage.'

'And *who* is Mrs Halliday?'

'A retired gentlewoman with a beautiful daughter, who, an hour ago, lured me with a card in the window which said that a bedroom was to let on moderate terms. Rosemary Cottage has a sea view, the beautiful daughter was in the parlour tending the plants. Within five minutes terms were arranged, and my bicycle is now occupying all the space in the front hall.'

'Very well. If you are satisfied. But I'm sure you might leave Vanessa alone for a little. You do not mean to say that you've come thirty miles today on that bicycle?'

'No. I stayed last night in Whitehaven and transacted a little piece of business.'

'I see.' She rose with great dignity, patted her bosom, shook her dress so that the frills and ruches settled in their proper places, and said:

'Timothy, it is time we were returning. Come, children. The air is chill.'

But the victoria had to be ordered, and Benjie was able to secure a moment alone with Vanessa.

'Why have you come?' Vanessa asked him. 'Three weeks was our bargain.'

'I know. I could not help it. I had to show you the bicycle.'

'No, but I am angry. Really I am. You should not have come.'

'You haven't written, Vanessa.'

'I have only been here four days.'

'Yes, but *four days*! An intolerable time. But see how tactful I am. I am here at Rosemary Cottage. There is Mrs Halliday's beautiful daughter. I am quite happy, and we need not meet at all.'

'You know that we shall meet.'

'Let the others go in front.' He caught her hand. 'Vanessa. We must stop this nonsense. We must be married immediately. I mean it. I cannot live even four days without you.'

'Tomorrow you will say something quite different. I cannot trust you from one day to another.'

'No, I know. That is why we must be married immediately. Next month. I have told my mother. There is nothing against it.'

'There has never been anything against it,' she answered. 'Only your own indecision.' Then she laughed. 'Oh, Benjie, I am so glad to see you! I have been wanting you every minute I have been here!'

'If,' he said, 'we walk up through those sand-dunes no one can see us.'

Between the sand dunes they kissed as though they had been parted for years.

When he had seen them all drive off in the victoria he walked to his lodging, singing. Everything was settled at last. His own indecision was ended. After all, was he not changed? Did he not adore Vanessa? He knew that he did! How beautiful, how very, very beautiful she had looked in the simple blue dress with the high dark collar, the white frill at the throat, the little gold brooch that he had given her, her hair brushed from her splendid forehead, she kneeling there on the sand watching Tim's castle. No one was so lovely, no one so good and true, no one loved him so dearly! The wildness was gone from his nature. They would settle at the Fortress, soon there would be children, boys like Tim, girls better than Violet; the garden should blossom with the rose, the Fortress should burn with light and heat ...

He was approaching Rosemary Cottage. It stood by itself, its feet almost in the sand dunes, a small wind-blown desolate garden looking on to the sandy track. As he approached it he ceased to sing. The sun was setting: shadows crept over the sea and a mist veiled the little moon.

Before he entered he hesitated. Something about this place checked his high spirits. Vanessa seemed far away. A little wind, suddenly rising, blew the sand in thin spirals among the strong tufted grass.

In the sitting-room the lamp was already lit and a meal spread on the table – a ham, a dish of stewed fruit, cheese.

Mrs Halliday appeared in the doorway.

'Shall I bring the eggs and tea now?' she asked. She was a spare desolate woman in a black silk dress. He noticed that she had no eyebrows and wore mittens on her hands.

'Thank you,' he said. He pulled off his boots, changing them for slippers, found in his bag a novel by Ouida, pulled out his pipe. She reappeared with the tea and eggs.

'I trust you have no objection to smoking in here?' he asked, looking up at her with a smile.

'Oh, none at all, Mr —' She paused. 'I beg your pardon. I did not catch your name before. Pray forgive me.'

'Oh, certainly. My name is Herries.'

'Thank you. I am a little deaf in one ear.' She waited as though she expected him to speak.

'That tea looks splendid.' He moved to the table. 'I am exceedingly hungry.'

'I am very glad, I am sure.' She waited, then went on. 'I do hope we shall satisfy you. My daughter and I are not accustomed to having lodgers. We have been in this place barely a month.'

'Oh yes?' He cut the bread.

'Yes. We come from Warwickshire. My husband was a gentleman of means. He was carried off with a severe fever six months ago.'

'Oh, I *am* sorry,' said Benjie. 'What brought you, then, to this district?'

'I have a son who has taken a farm in the Buttermere direction. He always was fond of the country, but was of course in very different circumstances when my poor husband was alive.' She paused, gave a dry little cough. 'He passed away with great suddenness. His affairs were sadly involved. He was ruined by one whom he thought his friend.'

'Oh dear, I *am* sorry,' Benjie said. But he had been startled by the extreme vindictiveness of that last sentence. Up to then she had spoken so very quietly.

'Yes, and so after that my daughter and I have had to do what we can ... Thank you, Mr Herries. I hope that you have everything that you need.'

'Oh yes, thank you.'

She left the room. What an extremely quiet woman she was! It was not only that she spoke quietly, the words coming from between her thin lips reluctantly, but her movements were quiet, almost stealthy. She had been in the room before he noticed it. Had he been anyone but Benjie he would have said at once that he did not like her, but his charity was all-embracing, at any rate until he had full and sufficient reason for a stern decision. But as he ate his ham and his eggs he felt uncomfortable. He thought that perhaps tomorrow he would make a move. He had half an impulse to get up and see whether his bicycle was safe in the hall. At any rates it was stuffy in here. The room was too full of things, china dogs, pale yellow daguerreotypes, large sea-shells, little tables covered with plush fastened with bright gilt nails. There was a smell in the room as though the windows had not been opened for a very long time – a smell, was it of seaweed, of stale scent, musty and clinging? Ah well, he was an ancient mariner, he had travelled the world over and known every discomfort. He would not be disturbed by a musty smell and a china dog or two. Nevertheless he disliked intensely a large daguerreotype of a pale severe gentleman in black cloth whose cold eyes followed him wherever he moved. Possibly Mrs Halliday would not object to moving *that* picture in the morning!

There was a knock on the door; he said 'Come in!' and the daughter entered.

'Mother wished me to see whether you needed anything,' she said.

'Not at all,' he answered. 'Everything is excellent, thank you.'

The girl stood against the table looking at him.

She was certainly not beautiful, not even pretty. She was thin like her mother and very fair. Her colour was so pale as to be almost white; her large eyes were blue-grey. She looked at him and smiled faintly. No, she was not pretty but there was something striking about her. It was true that she was thin, but her very fragility seemed to claim your protection.

He smiled back at her.

'Do you like it here?' he asked her.

'No,' she said. 'I do not.' She came nearer to him and laid her hand on the cloth. He noticed at once what a beautiful hand she had, finely formed, with slender fingers. Her hand moved towards the teapot while still she looked at him.

He had a mad impulse to put out his hand towards hers.

He jumped up from the table.

'I shan't want anything else tonight, thank you,' he said, turning his back to her abruptly as he filled his pipe.

The world does not grow less mysterious as it grows older, and it is one of its more striking but less incalculable secrets that human love when it is strong enough defies physical distance. This was not the first time nor the last in their history that Vanessa, as now, riding in the victoria through the dark summer hedges to Low Dene, was quite suddenly aware that Benjie was in danger. Benjie was so often in danger, whether spiritual, mental, or physical, that there must have been many occasions when Vanessa was unaware. There is also the perfectly plausible theory that Victorian women were exceptionally sensible to chills because they wrapped up so much. In any case Vanessa, sitting in the victoria, perfectly happy, feeling that at last she was on a relationship with Benjie that was safe and secure, began to shiver. They were turning into the long straggling Gosforth street. The sky in front of them was a pale translucent green in whose bright waters some trembling silver stars were glittering.

'Why! you are shivering, my dear!' said Mrs Bellairs. 'Wrap this round you! I do trust that you haven't caught a chill!'

Young Tim was sitting beside her, and his hot damp fist was enclosed in her gloved hand. In his fist, as she knew, were several shells and a piece of golden seaweed. She had the obscure and unreasonable fancy that it was through his hot little fist that she caught the sense that Benjie was in danger. How could he be in danger? He had left her only half an hour before to walk, happy and singing, to his lodging. Rosemary Cottage! There *could* be nothing wrong about Rosemary Cottage. Nevertheless they were both of a strange ancestry, she and Benjie. Francis Herries fighting in the frosty air, Mirabell bending over her lover's body on the Carlisle stones, Francis Herries looking at a picture on the wall in a London lodging for the last time, John – his son – calling through the mist in Skiddaw Forest: 'Is anyone there?',

Judith, released at last, running into the road joyfully to greet her friends – these are only moments in a contemporary history where facts are important only as pointers, and where the significance is only externally material, and where Time has no significance at all.

'Thank you, Violet,' said Vanessa, gratefully accepting the Shetland shawl. 'It *is* cold after the sun sets.' At the same moment she had a most incongruous thought – that it was so *like* Timothy and Violet to christen their children with their own names!

She was uneasy all that evening and, next morning, a little talk that she had with Aunt Jane only increased that uneasiness.

It was a blazing summer day and they sat out on the lawn while the children, under the stern eye of Mrs Clopton, knocked the croquet balls about. Vanessa had on her knee a novel by Rhoda Broughton, and Aunt Jane had on hers a novel by Mrs Alexander. Aunt Jane had a dear little face that would soon be covered with wrinkles. Her ringlets, her shawl (even in this warm weather), the spectacles that she used when reading, her little apprehensive starts as though she expected that at any moment a bear would jump out on her from the shrubbery, a round silver biscuit tin from which she would produce suddenly sweet biscuits for the children when Mrs Clopton wasn't looking, her extreme delicacy about other people's feelings, her willing slavery to the wishes of other people, her single-hearted devotion to those whom she loved, none of these attributes concealed from Vanessa the fact that, in spite of her modesty, reserve and deep religious beliefs, she knew a great deal more about life and men and women than did either Timothy or Violet.

Vanessa had not often an opportunity of being alone with her. She was constantly busy on other people's business. Timothy especially was always providing her with occupations. She was, when others were present, very silent, and her brother and sister-in-law would have been amazed had they realized the things that she perceived and pondered. They were certain that she adored them and considered them perfect human beings. In the first of these they were correct or nearly correct (she loved people in her own way, which was not at all theirs), in the second they were altogether wrong.

The little conversation that Vanessa now had with her was punctuated with Mrs Clopton's sharp: 'Now, Master Tim, don't dirty your stockings!' and 'Let your brother have the ball now, Miss Violet', and 'What did I tell you? You must look where you are going.'

From the field above the garden came the voices of the hay-makers.

'Benjie has come to stay in Seascale, Aunt Jane,' said Vanessa.

'Yes, dear, I know. That's very nice for you.'

'And we are going to be married in the autumn.'

Aunt Jane took off her spectacles.

'I'm glad of that too. I think you have been engaged quite long enough.'

'Why do you think that?' Vanessa asked quietly.

'Oh, my dear, I know nothing about marriage of course, but Benjie, I always say, is not at all an ordinary man. I would never expect *you* to marry an ordinary man, Vanessa dear. You have too much of your grandmother in you. But when a man is *not* an ordinary man I always say that it is better that he should be married.'

'Of course Benjie's not an ordinary man. But then nobody is ordinary if you know them well enough.'

'Quite so. That's what Mrs Alexander, whose book I am finding it extremely difficult to read, does not appear to have discovered. All her characters are so *very* ordinary.'

Vanessa hesitated. Then she went on:

'Aunt Jane, I am going to ask you something. You are so very wise. You have known both Benjie and me since we were babies. Why is it, do you think, that when we are together we so often misunderstand one another?'

'That is just what I mean about marriage,' said Jane. 'People always misunderstand one another. But the point about marriage is that if you go on long enough together you arrive at an under-standing. Once you are married you are bound together. I believe all married people find the connexion very irritating for a long while, and if they were not married they would separate. But being married they cannot, and so, at last, the understanding arrives. I put it very badly of course. I am not clever as your grandmother was. But there it is. That's what marriage does.'

'We must not be engaged too long, Benjie and I,' Vanessa said, as though she were speaking to herself. 'There is something dangerous about waiting.'

'There is something dangerous, my dear, about every human relationship. That is God's intention. People would never learn anything if there were not plenty of danger about. That is what your grandmother always said.'

'Oh, how I wish she were still alive!' Vanessa cried. 'She would have helped me. I know nothing about life at all – nothing about Benjie either, I sometimes think, although I've been with him all my life. How can we know anything about men? We are never alone with them; all they do is concealed from us; when they are with us they never tell us the truth.'

'Yes, dear, you are quite right,' said Jane. 'I often think that women today are far too sheltered. Not that I like the girls that your Miss Broughton writes about. That is surely going *too* far. But when your grandmother was a girl, as she often told me, women were far more free. I dare say they will be again one day, but as it is just now they have to spend all their time guessing.'

'Aunt Jane,' Vanessa said, staring at the rising field, the sunlight that soaked the lawn, 'I'm frightened. I feel that one wrong slip and Benjie will be carried away into some place where I can't reach him. I love him so terribly, but I am only *close* to him at moments. He's here. He's gone. And when he is gone I am so helpless . . .'

Jane smiled. 'Don't be frightened, my dear. Trust God. He knows so very much more than we do. Remember always that Benjie has a tragic history behind him, his father, his grandfather . . . You know, don't you, that I was the last person to talk to his father on that dreadful day? He was leading his horse from the stable. Of course I was only a little girl then, but I have always thought that perhaps I could have stopped him if I had known what to do or say, I loved him when I was a child more than I loved anyone, and I have been haunted all my life since by the thought that I failed him. But what I say is,' she went on more cheerfully, 'that if we do right as far as we can it's all we can do. Life's a dangerous thing, my dear, and you can't escape the danger by staying in bed all day or making other people act *for* you. Don't expect things to be easy. Why should they be? God doesn't arrange the universe only for me – nor for you either. To listen to the way the people talk in this novel of Mrs Alexander's you'd think that every time they have a toothache God ought to be ashamed of Himself . . .' She nodded to herself, picked up her book. 'I'm at page one hundred and fifty-three and that's as far as I shall go. I always like to finish a book if I can; when the writer's taken so much trouble it seems only right; but *this* time I simply can't be bothered. Mrs Alexander will never know, so there's no harm done.'

For one reason or another this little talk left Vanessa – who as a
rule was sensible enough and level-headed – in a kind of panic.
That was the quality that Aunt Jane had, that when she *did* talk
she always suggested so much more than she said. Her honesty
forbade her to offer false consolations. If people did not inquire
what she thought she was too thorough a lady to tell them, but if
they *did* ask her they must accept the consequences. Vanessa now
had the conviction that Aunt Jane thought her love for Benjie a
disaster!

She endured three days of a distress and apprehension altogether new to her experience. For much of this the child that
she still was was responsible. These were perhaps the last days of
immaturity, those days when persons and events have still the
size and colours of nursery hours, moments when we are left
alone in a room where the flickering firelight throws gigantic
shadows on the wall, when the clock's tick is a menace, and the
twig snapping on the windowsill threatens the approach of some
dreadful stranger!

She had three days of nightmare – and was transported into
Paradise!

Timothy, as befitted a Bellairs, liked society if it was proper
enough, and at the houses in the neighbourhood – Muncaster
and Ponsonby and others – there was plenty. It was still the
fashion, if you went out to dinner, to take a footman with you to
assist at the meal; there were elaborate croquet parties and
magnificent picnics.

So one fine day Timothy and his wife set off to Muncaster,
and Vanessa went with the nurse and children to the sea. They
had not been settled on the shore five minutes before Benjie was
with them. He and Vanessa started to walk across the long, shining sands.

It was a day of perfect peace. Chroniclers may define that
moment as the final peaceful one in English country life – a
moment of historic tranquillity when the cornfields lay placid
beneath the sun, the hedgerows slept, woods were untrodden, and
every village sheltered under its immemorial elm while the villagers slumbered off their beer on the parochial bench. At the
final moment, then, before the trumpet of the new world
sounded, Benjamin and Vanessa crossed Seascale sands!

She knew at once that he was disturbed. There had been something, then, in her own unrest.

She said at once: 'Benjie, what is it?'

He caught her arm with his hand and pressed her against his

side so that they might walk like one man. She was taller than he. She was wearing a small, rather masculine hat ornamented with blue flowers. She held her parasol high over her head. She was smiling, she was happy. She could feel his hand within her arm against her heart. All her fears were fled.

'There is nothing the matter except that I love you. And that *is* the matter, for we must be married in a month's time. I can wait no longer. I am bad through and through. I am without a redeeming point, but I have told you all that so often that I shall never mention it again.'

'Certainly we will be married in a month's time. Tomorrow if you like! I have been dreadfully unhappy these three days. I can't tell you why, but as I was driving back the other evening I had a sudden fear that something had happened to you. That cottage – what did you call it? Where you are staying. I have been dreaming of it, crawling with spiders and earwigs. I have been thinking that if we are not married at once we never will be married. And Aunt Jane frightened me.'

'What has Aunt Jane been saying?' he asked quickly.

'Oh, nothing – dear Aunt Jane! She loves us both, I know. But she is afraid for us. I know she is. She thinks there is dangerous blood in our veins. She wants to see us *safe*.'

'She's right!' he said fiercely. 'We must be *safe* – or someone will part us, something will happen!'

They were standing at the sea edge, on a floor of mother-of-pearl. The incoming tide drew thin lines of white as with a pencil on the shore and beyond the line the sea heaved without breaking, as gently as a sigh.

'No,' she said. 'I think that *nothing* can part us. I don't mean because we love one another. I can imagine that you might come to hate me or I would be so proud that I would never see you again, but still we would not be parted. It has been like that all our lives.'

Then she added, as though to herself: 'That is my worst fault, my pride.'

He turned and looked at her as though he were seeing her newly.

'What do you mean, Vanessa – your pride?'

'I would endure anything, I think,' she answered, 'or so I feel. I would show what I was suffering to nobody, but it would remain inside me. I could not let it out. I cannot let things go – words that someone said years ago, little things that people have done.

No one knows that I remember them, but I never forget. They do something to me. I hate my pride. I would like to be free as you are, Benjie – every day a new day—'

'No, Vanessa darling,' he broke in. 'Not like me. If there were two of us, both like me, oh, what a time we would have! You are the only one in all the world who influences me! That is why you are to marry me, teach me, change me.'

'I don't think I can teach anyone.' She sighed. 'I don't know why it is, but I would rather leave people alone, leave them as they are. Father is like that too. Mother used to be constantly distressed at how bad people were. Not that she blamed them. She was too kind. But it bewildered her. Right was so right and wrong was so wrong. I have no conscience for other people, I think – not even for you, Benjie.'

He asked her again for the thousandth time: 'Why do you love me, Vanessa? Everyone tells you not to.'

'I love you,' she answered, 'as I shall always love you, because you are part of me, because you are all that I have in the world, because without you I am always lonely, because I am not alive without you. There!' she said, turning round and laughing, looking at him too with infinite tenderness, with a kind of brooding devotion as though she could not look at him enough, could not have him close enough to her. 'Now – are you satisfied?'

For a moment he was silent, then he took her hand and kissed it.

'God helping me,' he said, 'you shall not regret it.' Then, characteristically, added as they turned to walk back: 'Although I don't believe in Him, I expect Him to help me, you see.'

They discussed details. He had written to Elizabeth the night before. They would be married in Ireby church, a very quiet wedding.

'There is only Adam,' Benjie said. 'I hate to think how he will miss you. We will do everything we can. You can go and stay with him whenever you wish, and he shall stay with us.'

'He will be happy if I am,' she answered. 'And he is well now – stronger than for a long while.' But nevertheless she knew leaving him would be terrible. They must think of a plan ... some way ...

As they neared the children two women passed them. Benjie raised his hat.

'Do you know them?' she asked.

'Yes,' he said, laughing. 'That is the enchantress of Rosemary

Cottage. Two enchantresses. Mrs Halliday and her lovely daughter Marion.'

Driving home, with Violet on her lap while Mrs Clopton told her stories of the heathen in Africa and all that was being done to improve their minds, she was thinking in an ecstasy of happiness:

'We are safe! We are safe! In a month we shall be married. Nothing can touch us now.'

In the morning the old postman, bent and twisted like a gnome, brought her a letter. It was from her father.

> DEAREST VAN – I am not very well – nothing serious – but I think perhaps you had better come home – Your loving   FATHER

FALL OF THE HOUSE OF ULDALE

ADAM PARIS hovered through the whole of that autumn between life and death. His sickness began, it appeared, with some mysterious poisoning, was followed by pneumonia, and left him with a heart so weak that every excitement, every sudden movement, was a danger.

So he was told not to move, not to suffer excitement. In the early days of January he was permitted to walk a little, supported on Will Leathwaite's stout arm, in the garden. During those months Vanessa scarcely left his side; even Benjamin was almost forgotten by her.

Whatever else Adam might be, he was always a philosopher. By January 1883 he was sixty-seven years of age – sixty-seven was three years from three score and ten. To die at that age was no very terrible misfortune. He did not want to die. He did not want to leave Cumberland, nor Will, nor Vanessa. Every day held some adventure, some charm, some beauty. But he most certainly did not care to linger on an invalid, a trouble and anxiety to everyone about him. He knew that had it not been for his illness Vanessa would now be married, and although he did not wish, had never wished, that Benjamin should marry her, he wanted to see her settled before he went. Moreover, he had now perceived that it was Benjamin and Benjamin alone whom she must have, and he made the best of it.

If anybody could make anything settled and secure out of Benjamin, it was Vanessa. So great an opinion had he of her wisdom, common sense and fidelity that he thought that she might.

During those long trying days of convalescence he kept a Journal – not a very regular one, not a very original one, but he put into it his honest opinions, some of his experience. These were some pages of it:

...A long and dangerous illness is an odd enough thing, I find. It is a commonplace that it seems to you, when you are in good health, incredible that you should ever die, and that when you are very ill you do not care a hang whether you die or no. Nature has arranged that very cleverly. But now that I am growing stronger again I find that I want to live for the smallest, most insignificant reasons. I have, for example, a new dog that Benjie gave me the other day, a rough clumsy kind of terrier. I have called him Tux after Rousseau's animal – the one that the Duchess of Luxembourg gave him. I have always liked Prince de Conti and the Luxembourg for their niceness to Rousseau, who must have been, just then, as tiresome and sensitive a creature as God ever made – but the queer thing and the enduring thing about Rousseau is that he had in him something of Everyman. He would have felt, I am sure, just as I did yesterday when Timothy and Violet came up from Uldale to pay me a visit. So very well-meaning, so extremely irritating! However, in one thing I am luckier than he. I have no Thérèse for them to patronize! But I felt just as he did about presents. Timothy gave me a shawl 'to keep my knees warm' as though the whole of the Herries family were presenting me with a medal. However, it is quite natural that he should think me a fool who all his life has wasted his time over nothing! And I had my ambitions once, too, but ambitions when you get to my age are cheap affairs. Would I have been a happier man had I been Gladstone or Dizzy or Dickens? Sour grapes perhaps to say that I would not. It is natural that I should like now to clap my hand on the table and say: 'Yes, I have added *that* to the world's achievements, a law or a poem, a picture or a character.' But my illness has left me altogether indifferent. My dear mother, I suppose, went the wrong way for both of us when she stayed at Uldale instead of escaping the family and going to

Watendlath. She always said that it was the mistake of her life. Had she gone I would have been a farmer, never seen a relation, never lived in London, never married Margaret, never had Vanessa for a daughter. What I would have missed! But I might, I fancy, have been a stronger man, a more determined character, and I would certainly have had more of this country, the sight and smell and sound of it. But I would have been always a dreamer who never pursued his dreams far enough. There can be no man but is dissatisfied with his life when he looks back on it. What a confusion of shreds and patches, of starting first here and then there, of one blind move after another – walking at night along a dark road and thinking every tree a hobgoblin! But I was never much of an adventurer, too easily disheartened, too ready to be an idealist without suffering for my ideals, far too ready to shrink away into myself if I met a rebuff. A failure, I suppose, trying to conceal my failure with a certain cynicism, and yet on the whole what a happy life I have had. I have known three glorious women – my wife, my daughter, and my mother – one or two magnificent men – Dickens, Caesar Kraft, Will, and in my babyhood, Reuben Sunwood. I have been given the perception of beauty in art and in nature and, although my own writing has been less than nothing in its result, I have had, in the pursuit of it, some glorious visions. Best of all, I have never been betrayed by my own failure into thinking man a poor affair. I have never come to thinking human nature a bad blunder, although in my Chartist days I met some poor specimens. Nor, thank God, have I ever suffered a fool gladly, least of all myself.

The whole pageant of life has been, and is, of an extraordinary interest. I can see now clearly enough that Time is nothing, that each and every man is tested with the same tests and rises or falls according to what he learns. Learning is everything. But for what? I have never been sure of any kind of personal immortality. As my mother used to say: 'I don't *feel* it and so I don't *believe* it.' But Margaret was sure and Vanessa is sure and they are both wiser than I. There is a great deal of the pagan in me, as there was in my mother. We inherit that, I suppose. But even with my paganism I wonder that the world should be so beautiful and men often so fine and courageous if there is nothing more than this brief experience. I have touched some grand moments too: my first sight of Margaret in that little room off the Seven Dials, Dickens' hand on my shoulder, the day when I finished my first story, walks with Will, the day when in a kind of panic I ran away from Margaret up Cat Bells here, hours with books, sunrises and sunsets, even yesterday when looking from this window I saw the hills rosy and the Lake a misty blue. Do these mountains of perception mean nothing at all? I don't know, and up to a week or so ago in all those months of illness I certainly did not care. One night in September I was sure I would be dead before morning and everyone else was sure too. I was quite clear-headed and quite indifferent – yes, even to Will and Vanessa. But I remember that I felt intolerably wise, that I thought that I had discovered the secret. Will turned me over in bed that I might lie easier and I muttered: 'Well, *that's* it. Why didn't I discover that before?' But what I had discovered I haven't now the least idea. Nothing is certain except love, love of anything or anybody that takes you beyond yourself. This may be, for all I know, a proof of God. It's as good a one as anything the parsons can give you. 'For what we have received let us be truly thankful . . .'

January 9th, 1883

Benjie came up yesterday afternoon and we had a talk. I never saw a man look so healthy. He is a gipsy for colour and hard as iron. Nothing seems to fatigue him and nothing bores him. What is best about him is that he is an individual. He is like no one else at all: you never know where you have him, or at least I don't. If you think him happy he isn't. Behind his merriment (and I must say I like it when he throws his head back and laughs as a boy laughs) there is a strain of melancholy. That he loves Vanessa there is no mistaking, but I am certain that he has misgivings about their marriage. He is right when he says he can't stick to anything. He is always against the law, whatever the law happens to be, and in that he is, I suppose, like my romantic grandfather and the Frenchman my mother married. He is of their world and so all against the Herries world, which is altogether anti-indi-vidualist. I couldn't help thinking yesterday as I listened to him that that may be the fight the whole earth is slipping into – the type against the individual. All the troubles in our family have come from the individual refusing to conform. Do I want Van-essa to be engaged in that kind of battle? No, indeed I do not. Nor do I want her to marry a type-Herries either. The truth is, I suppose, that I love her so much that I shall never find anyone good enough for her!

Benjie yesterday was in a queer state of indecision. He came, I fancy, that I should make his mind up for him, but about what? He never said. He asked me the absurdest questions all covering something deeper that he never owned up to. Should he go to a Ball at Greystoke? Yes, I said, if he wanted to. Oh, he'd be sick of it in half an hour and do something outrageous. There's some woman and her daughter whom he met in the summer at Seascale have come to live in Keswick. Should he go and call on them? Why, yes, I said, if he liked them. But he didn't like them. Well, then, don't go. They had been friendly to him in Seascale and so on and so on. Vanessa had gone to Uldale, and I could see that he was deeply disappointed and yet was relieved. Nevertheless how charming he can be! I never knew anyone better with Will. He gets behind that man's defences in a moment. He knows by instinct what are Will's reticences. He is on a level with him completely, no patronage and no sycophancy either. His heart is good, but he is so restless and so impulsive that he is in trouble before he knows where he is. He is like a wild man who has never been tamed, and then, in a flash, a perfect courteous gentleman. Can Vanessa tame him? I believe that he fears himself that she cannot, and trembles lest he should do her a wrong. Like him I must, and fear for the future I must too. How I wish that my mother were alive! She would understand him as no other. She was the daughter of one wild man and tamed another – but my mother was unique. There will never be another like her again.

When he was gone I was tired enough and Will helped me to bed. That pain just over my heart returned like an old familiar friend. Odd how a pain, to which you are accustomed, seems in a fashion friendly. I could feel its fingers pinching my flesh, then pressing heavily, constricting the muscles, and as I laboured for breath I could almost hear its voice: 'Now we are together again, you and I. Is not our intimacy pleasant?' I could not altogether own that it was, and yet I could have almost replied: 'Yes, but don't press too hard, old fellow. Spare me what you can.'

And now this morning, this bright frosted January morning, I am well and the pain is forgotten. How quickly the past is over! How dim the pain of five minutes before! Yes, and the pleasure too! I can remember how often on a fine day, walking or sitting lazily in my boat on the Lake, the beauty has been so intense that I have longed to catch it in my fingers, hold it, wrap it up, put it away for safety. And in a moment it is gone. A rosy cloud turns grey, there is a whisper on the water, the shadow envelops the hill and *that* beauty is lost! But the intensity of the realization is caught at least. My friend Jean-Jacques, of whom for some reason I have been thinking much in these last weeks, speaks of that. I haven't the *Confessions* with me but the passage goes a little like this: 'The movement and the counter-movement of the water, the stirrings, rising, falling, gave me pleasure in mere existence. No need to think, to live at that moment was enough! Letting my boat go where it would, I would abandon myself to reverie. I was completely under Thy power, Nature! No wicked men to interpose themselves between us! Yes, all is a perpetual movement on earth. Nothing is constant. Our affections change and alter. Everything is in front or behind. We recall the past to which we are now indifferent or anticipate a future that may never come. Nothing solid for our hearts! But the soul may find a state solid enough on which it may repose with no thought of the past, no fear for the future – and so long as such a state endures he who experiences it may speak of bliss . . .

Once on a day I knew that passage by heart, I think: now it comes to me only in fragments. Poor Rousseau, demon-haunted, finding no spot where his foot might rest. How in those days when the *Confessions* were so actual to me, I hated Voltaire and the vile Grimm and the false Madame d'Epinay!

But after all I suppose that his troubles were of his own making. There would have been no genius had there been no sickness. But I think at my age I hate most in this life the jealousy and rage of men against one another. How trivial and worthless our plottings when we are here for so short a time. How easy, you would say, for Man to tolerate his brother. And yet how I myself detested old Walter, so that I would lie awake and think how I might injure him. And then at the last that poor, weak, crying old man to be fed with a spoon and have his mouth wiped! I swear that if I recover from this I will never be angry again. And yet it has been, I dare say, that I have not been angry enough in life, have not known indignation enough. I have hated injustice, but men are too often like birds in a cage. They would not be there if they could escape, and the cage is not of their own designing. This wandering along on paper has passed an hour – and now for *The Story of an African Farm* that they are all praising. New militant woman eager for her rights! If the world is to be full of them, as I suspect it will be, I shall not be sorry to have gone . . .

FELL HOUSE, ULDALE,
April 3rd, 1883

... so three days ago Vanessa and I moved to Fell House for a
week or two. I am a very great deal better, can take a walk by
myself and am not so utterly dependent on Will as I have been –
how patient, tolerant, and sensible he's been no words can say,
but I recognize sufficiently that two moments in my life have
been supremely lucky – one when as a small boy I watched Will
win a race through Keswick, the other when as Victoria returned
crowned from Westminster I tumbled up against Caesar Kraft.
The love of one man for another is an odd thing: it is bare of sex
and yet does in certain moods surpass the love of woman. Maybe
I have never been a sexual man. Looking back now I can see that
it was not virtue kept me free in my youth but a certain fastidi-
ousness that I got, as I got so much else, from my mother. I
sometimes think that had I been the child of a street-woman and,
say, a card-sharper, I could have been something of a writer. But
no matter now. Never was anything of less importance. All the
same, being what I am, I doubt whether any relationship could be
finer than mine with Will. And it has been his fineness, not mine.
Complete unselfishness, unsparing devotion, and a deep, always
by me perceptible, emotion under it all. With all that it has been
always humorous, mixed with plenty of plain speaking. I cannot
see that it has had any falseness in it anywhere. And, although I
have no belief in immortality, it is hard for me, I confess, to
imagine a state when Will and I will not be together and consciously together. Such a relationship as ours goes far beyond the
body and, maybe, survives the body. There is this at least about it
that it makes you think well of your fellow-men. It makes me
wonder sometimes whether any country but England (and sometimes I wonder any county but Cumberland) could produce such
a man as Will. He is altogether Cumbrian in his honesty, reticence, obstinacy. But this of course is nonsense. There are men
like him, I don't doubt, all the world over. My grandfather had
such a one. Quixote found one, Montaigne had one; thank God
the world is full of them.

Well, after this sentiment which no eye will ever see but my
own, here is the other side of the shield. The only other visitor
here but ourselves is Phyllis Newmark's boy, Philip Rochester.
Rochester, whom she married some thirty years ago, has something, I fancy, to do with railways and has amassed a nice fortune. Barney, I know, dislikes him and always calls him a

humbug. As for Master Philip, I have seldom disliked a young man so much. He is thin and willowy, talks in a piping voice about the 'Inevitability of Sin' and that 'Art is the only Moralist'. It happens that in this very week's *Punch* there is a little piece which I shall have great pleasure in showing him. It is apt enough to copy into this Journal:

TO BE SOLD, the whole of the Stock-in-Trade, Appliances, and Inventions of a Successful Aesthete, who is retiring from business. This will include a large stock of faded lilies, dilapidated sunflowers, and shabby peacocks' feathers, several long-haired wigs, a collection of incomprehensible poems, and a number of impossible pictures. Also, a valuable Manuscript Work, entitled *Instruction to Aesthetes*, containing a list of aesthetic catch-words, drawings of aesthetic attiudes, and many choice secrets of the craft. Also, a number of well-used dadoes, sad-coloured draperies, blue and white china, and brass fenders. To shallow-pated young men with no education, who are anxious to embark in a profitable business which requires no capital but impudence, and involves no previous knowledge of anything, this presents an unusual opportunity. No reasonable offer refused. Apply in the first instance to Messrs SUCKLEMORE and SALLOWACK, Solicitors, Chancery Lane.

A trifle sledge-hammer but it has got Mr Philip exactly. I wouldn't mind the young man's effeminacy, his ridiculous clothes, and his languor, were it not that he considers himself the Prince of the World. The scorn that he feels *and* expresses for everyone in his house is nauseating. Everyone but Vanessa, whom he condescends to admire, and talks of 'a perfect du Maurier' and how he wishes that Whistler could paint her. He would apparently make the attempt himself (for he paints the most atrocious daubs) 'had he the time'. Had he the time! When he never gets up before ten, wanders about the house like a misplanted lily, pecks at the piano and studies himself in the looking-glass. His morals would be, I have no doubt, revolting had he any blood in his poor body. He speaks of his 'soul-mates and the tyranny of the marriage laws' and such disgusting nonsense. I should shudder whenever the children approached him, but they, unlike his elders, find him a kind of clown. Amazingly, Timothy and Violet are both rather impressed, and Vanessa, in her goodness of heart, is kind to him. How my mother would have dealt with him!

April 8th

It is perhaps my illness, but whatever the reason I cling to this old house as never before. My mother's presence is everywhere, but, beyond that, the house itself for ever speaks to me as though this were the last time it would ever shelter me, as though I were the last human link it will ever have with all the life that is gone. And that is true enough. There is no one else alive but myself who knew it as it was. When I first came here Francis and Jennifer were living, David and Sarah were remembered and had seen old Rogue Herries himself ride up, looking for his wandering wife. David, Jennifer, my own mother died under its roof. Violet has done all she can to ruin it, as the house very well knows. How easy and pleasant to have left some of it as it was – at least the little parlour that my mother so dearly loved. I can yet see it as it was when I was a child – the old spinet with the roses painted on the lid, the famous music box that was played for me when I was good, with the King in his amber-coloured coat and the Queen in her green dress. Then the carpet, upon which I sprawled with John, that had the pictures of the great Battle, cannons firing and horses rising on their haunches; the Chinese wallpaper with pagodas of blue and white, temples, bridges, and flowers. Best of all the sofa, the stuff of which was decorated with apple trees and red apples. How well I remember that room and the way the clock with the gold mandarin would strike the hour, coughing a little between the strokes.

All gone now and also the things from my mother's bedroom, the red chairs, the four-poster bed. All gone, all gone, the house tonight seems to echo around me. And instead so many ugly things, mahogany wardrobes like coffins set up on end, attempts here and there to be in the fashion with imitation Morris wallpapers, sham Burne-Jones tapestry in the drawing-room – but the dining-room how awful with its circular cellarette, the vast Sheffield soup tureen, the sideboard with its malignant and obscene carved ends, the lacquered knife-tray, the needlework bellpulls that Timothy tugs at so furiously when he is impatient, the sheep-faced mahogany clock – and all these things both Violet and Timothy think so handsome! Yes, I can hear the old house groaning through all its brickwork. I am the only one who knows how deeply ashamed it feels!

April 15th

I must write tonight to banish some of this intolerable melancholy that has seized me. There is a real Cumberland wind wailing about the house, as though it had lost a thousand children. How sharp and strong it must be on the Tops! Almost impossible to keep your feet with the black heavy clouds driving furiously like chariots above you, and all the streams preparing for rain ... I have not been so well these last days and I have an assurance in my breast that my time now is short. I had my evening meal in my room and Vanessa came up to talk to me. I was allowed a fire and by the light of two candles we chatted, comfortably, easily, like the old friends we are. Why was it that I had so dreary a sense that this was to be our last talk? Nonsense, of course, and in the morning, as has happened so often before, feeling well again I shall laugh at my past terrors. But as I sat opposite over the fire I put out my hand to touch her dress as though I were frightened to lose her, and she drew her chair over to mine. She was cheerful and nonsensical as she often is, laughing at Phil Rochester who had been reading her some of his poems, one called 'The Lovers Last Cry' which was, I gathered, especially comical. Benjie is staying in Keswick. She is sure that he has some attraction there and takes it quite calmly. All she said about *that* was:

'When we marry and are together, I'll make him happy, I know.'

And to that *I* said:

'You'll have to beat him once a week. He says so himself.'

How I hate to leave her no one knows but me! She talked about herself, a thing that she very seldom does.

'I find that I'm intolerant, Papa. Intolerant and impatient.'

'Very well,' I said. 'Those are not bad things to be.'

'I was so angry with Timothy tonight that I could have smacked him. He was so extremely self-satisfied. I think all men are except yourself. Why should he talk as though he had *made* England?'

'That's a Herries habit,' I answered.

'Yes, but it's also something masculine. We were talking about Moody and Sankey and the Salvation Army and he said that such things weren't English. Englishmen never show their emotions, he said, and *that's* why England is what it is. What he meant was, "*I* never show my emotions and *that's* why England is what it is." '

'There's something in what he says,' I answered.

'Oh, well, I wanted to scream and beat that hideous Indian gong in the hall. Then he said that *The Story of an African Farm* is a disgusting book and ought to be burnt. When I asked him about it I discovered that he had only read the first chapter. And then after that he was going to say something about Benjie, but Violet stopped him.'

'Altogether a very pleasant meal,' I said.

'But why are we so different, you and I, from Timothy and Violet?'

'Two halves of the whole,' I told her. 'Life isn't complete without both of us.'

I could see that in reality she was deeply dissatisfied with herself. She is maturing, and I am sure that this long uncertain time with Benjie is affecting her seriously, although she is too proud to say anything about it.

She sat close to me, holding my hand, her splendid noble head raised high, looking into the fire.

'Well, I'm a perverse creature,' she said, nodding. 'I seem to have no control over myself at all.'

'But you *have*,' I assured her. 'You see you didn't bang the table and you didn't beat the gong.'

'No, but I can't be rational, the thing that all nice women ought to be. I laugh when I should be serious, I'm angry when there's nothing at all to be angry about. I'm not at all proper in my feelings either. Violet thinks it dreadful to mention the word adultery. She positively said the other day that the Commandments in church made her quite shy. She thinks it dreadful to be seen with a French novel. Oh! I do hope I'm not going to be a prig!'

I laughed at that.

'Why, no, I should say the very opposite.'

'No, but, Papa, virtuous about other people being *not* virtuous! ... In fact I hate myself tonight. Everything is wrong but you.'

She kissed me, laid her cheek against mine, made a fuss of me, told me again and again how she loved me, asked me to forgive her for all the trouble she had been to me. Never was she more sweet, never more my friend and companion. Before she went she turned at the door and blew me a kiss with her hand, laughing and saying: 'And now I'm going to the drawing-room to listen to Timothy telling us out of *The Times* what *he* would do if he were Gladstone.'

Tomorrow we are going for a drive.

This is the end of Adam's Journal. They were the last words that he ever wrote ...

He lay in bed for a while, rather wide-awake, watching the shadows from the fire leap on the wall, hearing the wind scream about the house, tug at the windowpanes, belabour the trees and hammer the tendrils of the vines against the glass. He thought of the cottage at Cat Bells, how cosy, warm with life and human affections. He had brought there many of his mother's things, her books, some pictures, the account she dictated to Jane of her early days, bound in a fat, green-leather volume, the presentation that they made her on that fatal Hundredth Birthday. Vanessa would have these things and would pass them on, pass them on to her children and Benjie's, and they to theirs, and so it would go on and on, until at length it might be that it would only be through Judith's green book that anyone knew that once a man sold a woman at a Fair or fought for his beloved on Stye Head ... He was growing sleepy. He laid his head on his breast inside his shirt as though to say goodnight to his heart and request it, as a favour, to keep quiet for an hour or two. He did not want to wake sharply to that grinding pain, that squeezing of the muscles between two inhuman fingers, that beating and struggling for breath ... He was falling asleep and a stout man was riding on a horse and he a little boy as bare as your hand danced to annoy him and the stout man raised his whip ...

He awoke. What had roused him he did not know. He sat up, resting on his arm. He was so deeply accustomed now to find himself woken at night by pain that that was his first thought: 'Where is the pain this time? Which part of me is misbehaving?' But there was no pain. His heart beat calmly and his back did not ache. He had no neuralgia across his forehead. The room was intensely dark. Many hours must have passed since he fell asleep, for the fire had been strong. Now there was no glimmer of dying log or fading coal. The wind was roaring like a beating lively voice in the darkness but, listening, he heard something beyond the wind – a small chattering whispering voice. Was there someone in the room? No, it sounded like several voices, human and yet not human. He raised his head, sniffing. A moment later he was out of bed. Somewhere something was on fire. He opened the door and a belly of smoke blew towards him. He cried out: 'Fire! Fire!' and ran back into the room. It was then that the strange stillness of everything struck him. The house slept like the dead, he heard clocks ticking and somewhere a snore.

He pulled on a dressing-gown, and again, calling out 'Fire! Fire!', ran into the passage. His first thought was of Vanessa. He knew that her room was on the floor above his and, covering his mouth with his arm, turned towards the stairs, but even as he did so the passage to the left leading to the servants' quarters began – as it seemed to his excited imagination – to tremble, and a moment later through the green-baize door there shot a tongue of fire exactly like a vindictive criminal struggling to be free. A second later the flame shot upwards and little tongues began to lick the green baize, and a thin line of light, clear as day, shone between the hinges and the wall. At the same time the smoke rising in the same direction began to roll in thick grey waves, and the voices that it contained grew louder and angrier. What was strange was that the rest of the house, his room, the staircase from the hall, was cold, quiet, aloof, and even as he turned to the stair leading to the other floor he heard the cuckoo-clock that was at the corner of the hall below begin to sound the ridiculous bird's voice: 'Cuckoo! Cuckoo! Cuckoo!'

Still calling out and wondering in a mad irritation why nobody had been aroused by all this commotion, he stumbled up the stairs but, halfway up them, was met by another curling strand of smoke that seemed to issue from the wall on his left. For some reason that smoke bewildered him. It increased very rapidly, seeming to come from below him and to encircle him, to beat about his head, to come even from within himself, from his heart and lungs. He should now have been outside Vanessa's door, but he did not know where he was, for his eyes were blinded and weeping with the bitter and acrid thickness that now began to fill his mouth and heart and lungs.

He knocked his knees against a box or a chair, heard something fall somewhere and, turning his head, saw below him spurts and whirls of flame and a light that had a ferocity in it and a gigantic sense of power. He called out again and thought that some voice answered him, but he spoke against a wall, almost as though some enemy held a cloth over his mouth to deaden his cries. He thought: 'But this is absurd! Where are they all? What are they doing?' Called again and again: 'Vanessa! Vanessa! Wake up! Fire! Fire!' He moved to the right where he thought that her room must be, but now was caught in a perfect fog of smoke. His feet struck some more stairs and he remembered that above this floor were the attics. If he could reach those he could fling open the windows, for even his mad anxiety for Vanessa was countered by his agony for breath. His lungs were choked, he could not see and, although his brain was clear, his limbs refused to obey him. At that same moment pain leapt on to him, pain moving in the centre of the smoke. An iron hand crushed his breast. The fingers pressed and pressed. He fell on to his knees. 'A moment,' he thought. 'This pain will pass and I shall be able to move again.' But it did not. The giant hand turned and turned, so that he could see his poor heart crushed, screwed round and then squeezed until the pain seemed to draw his very eyeballs down into his stomach.

His last conscious thought was of Vanessa. 'Vanessa,' he murmured, 'Vanessa.' He rolled over and lay there, prone, while the eddies of smoke – strong, careless, singing a song – rose, saluted the wind, filling every cranny.

Vanessa had been long in a dreamless sleep when she awoke to the sound of a loud banging on her door. Even as she opened her eyes Violet and Timothy rushed in, behind them a strange glare and everywhere in the air a crackling, murmuring, buzzing frenzy.

She did not need their cry: 'Vanessa! Get up! The whole house is on fire!'

In an instant everything was visible and clear to her. She seemed in that moment of springing out of bed to have time to notice everything – the calm undisturbed paraphernalia of the bedroom, her clothes across the chair, the yellow sofa that she always thought so ugly, the long looking-glass in which were reflected Timothy and Violet, Timothy with a riding coat over his nightshirt, Violet in a bright blue dressing-gown, and behind them that sinister glitter veiled with sudden mists. The air stank of smoke. She heard a dog bark.

Violet pulled at her arm.

'It's terrible! It's terrible!' she continued to cry. 'The whole house is on fire!'

And Timothy, running back, called:

'The children! The children! Get the children!'

But her own thought was at once for her father. She thought of nothing and nobody else. She put on her dressing-gown and slippers with a single gesture and ran out. She saw them flocking down the stairs – Philip, Timothy, Violet, the children. The stairs were still untouched. You seemed from the lower stairs to plunge into darkness while on the first floor the baize door was a sheet of flame and all around her the smoke rose like water, flooding forward, eddying back again. She ran down the first flight and crossed at once into her father's room. It was empty. At that same moment she thought that through the crackle of the fire she heard a cry from above her: 'Vanessa!' She listened, and even as she did so saw Timothy's head and shoulders above the lower banister.

'Father!' she cried. 'He is not in his room!'

Timothy shouted back. 'Come down! The whole place is falling down. It's all right – everyone's out. Yes, Adam too. He is on the lawn!'

She turned back once more into his room, saw the bed disordered, caught – without knowing what she did, obeying some blind instinct – things from the table, his Journal, a book, his gold watch; then ran out to meet in full force a towering column of smoke that rose in front of her like some genie. Gasping, her hand over her face, she ran forward, was down the stairs, through the door, and, in an instant, in a wild, chill, blowing world, the wind screaming above her, voices everywhere, shouts and cries, some child's wail, the neighing of horses, and faces white like paste in the blinding light of the fire.

She ran from figure to figure, not recognizing them at all as persons, for they also seemed to be running, moving in some kind of dance through the wind.

She called again and again:

'Father! Father! Where are you?' She pulled at some man's arm: 'My father! Is he here? Have you seen him?' and some figure that she did not know, someone holding a clock and a picture, cried, as though in an ecstasy. 'The house! The house! The roof will be in!'

Then she ran into Leathwaite. He cried before she could speak: 'Miss Vanessa! The master! He's not here!'

They turned together and ran towards the house which was now all bright with flame and alive in every part, while from its heart there came a beat like a drum and above it arms of fire strained up to the ebony sky, starred with the pigeons from the loft, flying into the light as though splashed with bright water, then vanishing into darkness.

Will dashed through the door. She would have gone after him but some man's hand held her, gripping her shoulder. 'You mustn't go, Miss Vanessa,' someone shouted in her ear as though

she were deaf. 'It's not safe—' and then called, 'Will! Will! Come
back! Everyone's out!'

She struggled. 'Let me go! What do you mean? They are not
all out. My father is there—'

A moment later Will's face, strangely unreal, appeared at a
window. He shouted to them.

'He's not here! I'm in his room!' And then, after looking into
the room again: 'I can't go back! The fire's too strong!'

'Jump!' several voices cried, and a woman screamed. He
climbed out on to the windowsill, let his legs dangle, caught his
arm in something and fell.

And, at once, as things happen in dreams, inconsequent, without reason, Vanessa saw that Benjie was beside her. She heard his
voice, as from an infinite distance, explaining that he had come
back from Keswick that evening, been roused and at once ridden
down. 'Oh, thank God you're safe, Vanessa,' he said, hurried
from her as figures do in dreams, was back again, his arm round
her, crying, 'It's all right. Will's broken a leg. No one else is
harmed. Everyone's safe.'

She tore herself away from him.

'No, no, Benjie! Don't you see? Father's in there! Father's
there!'

She ran forward. He pulled her back.

'Don't be mad. No one can live in there! The roof is falling!'

She fought him, she struck his face.

'Let me go! Let me go! We must find him!'

He held her with all his strength, pressing her against him.
The ground was covered with people; the horses that they had
taken from the stable trampled and neighed. With a great gesture, as though in a frenzy of exultation, the flames flung up their
arms, the roof crashed.

The house gave up its life.

WILD NIGHT IN THE HILLS

THERE was at that time in the hills between Derwentwater
and Cummock a very lonely farm called Hatchett's Fosse.

To this farm Benjamin Herries rode some three days after
Adam Paris' burial at Ireby.

Adam's charred and almost unrecognizable body had been found when at last the fire had died sufficiently for safe search to be made. The red brick walls of Fell House still stood, blackened and scorched but enduring. But these walls were a shell. Nothing else remained. The wind that night had been so ferocious that in any circumstances there could have been small hope of saving the house, but everything had contributed to aggravating the disaster: the ancient fire-engine at Braithwaite broke down on the road. There was nothing at the house itself, no protection of any kind. The horses and animals were saved. No life was lost but Adam's. A little furniture, some pictures, were rescued. That was all. Fell House, Uldale, was no more.

The death of Adam Paris shocked the whole countryside. He had not been widely known. He was held to be a 'shy sort of man' but he was liked. He was said to be kindly, friendly, generous. No one had anything against him. He was old Madame's son, even though he had been born on the wrong side of the blanket, and he wrote books. But more than any of these, he was the father of Vanessa, whose beauty was renowned from Silloth to Kendal. Everyone knew how she had loved him, and there was something deeply real and true in the sympathy that rose now on every side of her. Cumberland people are reputed by those who know them little to be too blunt of tongue for complacent comfort, but any man in trouble will be lucky if he has Cumbrian friends near to him. They have not been masters of their own soil for hundreds of years without learning what courtesy means, and courtesy is not in this part of England another name for heartlessness.

But Vanessa was stricken down in these first days beyond any possibility of help. With Jane Bellairs and Will she went back to Cat Bells and there she stayed, seeing nobody. On the day before the funeral she saw Benjie. He knew at once that she could not just then bear either to see him or talk to him.

She spoke in a low voice, looking beyond him at the door as though she expected someone to come in.

'I don't blame you, Benjie. You did what you thought right, but you should not have held me back.'

'Vanessa, *how* could I have let you go? The roof fell in a moment later. You would have been killed as well as Adam. What good would that have been?'

'I had rather have been killed. To think that he was alone in there! That nobody but myself and Will thought of him!'

He saw that at present there was nothing to be done. He kissed her. She made no movement, no response. She said in a low voice:

'The awful thing is that I heard him calling me. From some other part of the house. But Timothy told me he was out. I will never forgive Timothy and I will never forgive myself.'

When he went home things were no better. His mother had been unwell for some months, and the night of the fire with its tragic consequences was a shock from which it was unlikely that she would recover. The destruction of Fell House was a dreadful thing to her. She had been there so often. John, her husband, had been born there; he had walked out of there to his death. More than that, this appeared to her to be a revenge from the past. Her father had built the Fortress to triumph over Fell House. It had seemed at his death that he was defeated; but he had *not* been defeated. This was the last unexpected triumph of the Fortress, a house that she had always hated and now detested. She seemed to hear her brother Uhland tapping with his stick night and day about the passages. How satisfied he must be! These vindictive people were stronger in death than they had been in life and there was no end to their malevolence. She had loved Adam, and her heart ached now for Vanessa. She was old, alone with ghosts. No one could help her.

Benjie, her son, it seemed, least of all. She had been very patient with his selfishness, but now at last she was exasperated. He seemed to her hard and callous. For once her intuition failed her. She did not know that he was suffering more deeply than she. On the day after Adam's funeral he came into her bedroom and said:

'I can't bear this, Mother. I must go away for a day or two.'

'What can't you bear?' she asked him quietly.

'Vanessa,' he broke out in a kind of storm of indignation, 'thinks that I was responsible for Adam's death.'

She thought that he was indignant with Vanessa, but had she been well and strong she would have known that the indignation was with himself.

'She is suffering from shock,' she answered. 'You must be patient and wait.'

'Wait! Wait!' he burst out. 'For what? Everything is changed, Mother. It will never be the same again.'

The farmer at Hatchett's Fosse was Fred Halliday, the son of the woman with whom Benjie had stayed at Seascale.

Some months back Benjie, riding along Main Street, saw Mrs

Halliday and her daughter Marion looking at him from across
the street. His first impulse had been to move on, but something
had prevented him. He did not like them, he did not wish to see
them again; nevertheless he rode over and spoke to them. They
were to stay in Keswick for a while. Mrs Halliday had notions of
opening a boarding house there. Still with that strange mingling
of attraction and repulsion, he had met them a number of times.
Mrs Halliday was definitely repugnant to him: she whined, she
crept, she was genteel, she was vindictive. The girl spoke little,
had little colour in her voice or movements, but she had some
power over him. He kissed her and hated himself for doing so.
She appeared to expect his distaste; indeed she said to him
once:

'How you dislike me!'

But she did not seem at all to resent this except that, in her
still, motionless way, she resented everything. Her pale skin, thin
anaemic body, quiet, almost stealthy movements, stirred him as
though he were attracted by his own exact opposite. She did not
speak to his mind nor his heart, but his senses. When he touched
her – and always it seemed that it was by her volition and not his
– he felt no tenderness nor affection, but a sensual inquisitiveness
as though something persuaded him to explore further – as
though some sensual secret were hidden there which would,
when discovered, excite and surprise him.

He did not know – and he did not care – whether she liked him
or no. She appeared to like no one, to have no life beside that of
sudden little movements, unexpected advances and withdrawals.
One evening he met her in the dusk walking down the hill behind
St John's Church. He talked to her and then embraced her
passionately. She eagerly returned his embraces. He went home
in a mood of bitter revulsion against himself. He had met her
brother several times in Keswick. Fred Halliday was a big, broad,
red-faced hearty man, quite unlike his mother and sister, who
laughed at everything, drank a good deal, and was friend of all
the world. And yet it was true that nobody in Keswick liked him.
He was not trusted, and it was said that when drunk he was very
quarrelsome and abusive.

Not a very worthy family for Benjie to be friendly with, but
then it was always like that with him. When he was jolly, as at
most times he was, anyone would do to be jolly with. At this
period of his life almost anyone was good enough to pass the time
of day with. Who was he to be a judge? Except for his mother and

Vanessa no one alive mattered. He was proud of not caring. Life was not important and one man resembled another. He loved Vanessa, who was much too good for him, and if women liked to be kissed, why, he liked to kiss them! In spite of his escapades he had never yet got any woman into trouble. His luck in that had held. He would not hurt anyone for the world.

But as he rode out to Hatchett's Fosse he was not sure that he did not want to hurt everybody. Fred Halliday had often invited him to come and see the farm; he had never thought that he would really go. But now anywhere would do, anywhere away from his own unhappiness, his sense that he had lost Vanessa for ever and that he deserved to have lost her.

The morbid side of his character had grown stronger during this past year. Although he loved the place, this Cumberland country always increased the strain of superstition so deeply ingrained in his character. Away from his home he was as other men and could consort with them on equal terms, but at the Fortress and in the country around him he felt sometimes like a man caught in a trap. On the one hand was the small lonely house in Skiddaw Forest where his father had been murdered; on the other – and only a step away – the great cavern beneath Skiddaw where all the spirits of the true men lived and rejoiced for ever. Surely fantastic nonsense as food for a healthy man's brain! But in this Benjie was not healthy, nor are most imaginative men free of certain dreams, omens, and apprehensions. These two contrasted things were for him perhaps only symbols, but they brought with them a conviction that, whenever he returned to this country, he was not his own free master. And yet he must return! He could not keep away from it. He could not remain in it when he was there. And were his instincts altogether wrong? Had he not, in this last year, been twice prevented from marrying Vanessa, once by her father's illness and now by this cursed fire? The Men under Skiddaw would receive him in their company *if* he could reach them, but, like a man in a dream, he was held back. Who could dare to deny that the past was more powerful than the present and that you must fight like the devil or the moment you were born you were done for! That old ancestor of his, Francis Herries, might still have something to say!

All this was, of course, only a part of Benjie's mind. None of the men who knew him as he roamed the world would credit him with *this* kind of imagination! But he was compounded of stiff incongruities – proud and yet humble, faithful and yet most unfaithful, wandering but steadfast – and at this time he was still young with most of his soul-making ahead of him.

So as he rode down Bassenthwaite and on towards Braithwaite he felt only an urgent need of escape: escape from the senseless waste of Adam's death, from all the grief that that was causing (he had an eager sensitiveness to the unhappiness of others); escape from his mother, whom he knew that he should not be leaving; but above all escape from Vanessa, whom he loved now when he was sure that he had lost her, with a deeper sense of frustration than ever before.

Then he raised his head, looked up at the stormy sky and swore. 'Well, *this* has settled the business. She is better, far better, without me. She'll know that at last.'

But even while he said this he felt that they were inseparable, that however their lives went they would be bound together for ever – yes, even when he was secure and singing with the Men under Skiddaw he would be thinking of her!

As he began slowly to climb Whinlatter he felt the wind tugging at him. On the day following the fire the wind had folded its arms and stolen away as though the purpose of its coming were accomplished. Then, as is often the case in the late spring, it sprang up again and rushed about the country in flurries of excitement, blowing the daffodils silly, making the young leaves tremble and the young sheep skip, and flashing quivers of light like turning glass across the streams. The colours were all delicate – faint shadowed plum, a gold so pale that it was almost white under cloud, a wet virginal green of the young bracken. And field after field, up and up the hillsides, was silver-grey.

This afternoon, though, quite another mood was in the air, spring was forgotten. It happens sometimes here that the hills, as though an order had been given, suddenly dominate all the scene. The pastoral fields, the farms, the roads, towns, villages shrink together into nothingness and the hills step forward, spread their shoulders, swell their chests out, raise their heads and begin to march. If you listen you can almost hear the tramping. It is at such times that you can understand Benjie's fantasy of his men under the mountain, for it is no fantasy just then. Lie down on the turf and listen with your ear to the ground and you can catch the echo of the voices, a rumble of a drinking song and laughter like the cracking of a drum's skin. At such a moment when the hills take power there is a sense of menace in the air.

The sky is disturbed with a furious confusion, great sweeps of cloud smoking along with a wind behind them that is personal in its strength. The old pictures of Aeolus blowing the four winds from his mouth is true now. You can see him standing behind the hills, his strong legs spread across the sea, his broad naked shoulders stretched above his vigorous lungs. The wind and the hills act in unison. The hills, that are in actual measurement so slight, take on themselves additional properties that belong to the great mountains of the world. With white mist flanking them and black funnels of cloud eddying above their heads, they seem as powerful as Everest. Their power is menacing. They seem to crowd together in conclave: 'Now shall we step forward and crush out of existence these little fields, cowering hamlets, tiny midgets of humans?' You can watch them as they bend their heads together and twitch their shoulders with the impatience of a group of boys waiting for the word of release. The wind is enchanted with the sport promised. It goes swinging from arm to arm of the hills, crying: 'Now let us go! Now we are off!' and it sweeps whirlwinds of rain now here, now there, making it sting the earth like a hail of small shot, then raising it again in sheets of steel as though all the heavens were letting down their defensive gates. A great game that leads to no ill because the power here is friendly. They have not learnt any deep vindictiveness. This square of earth is kind to the men who settle, for a moment, upon its surface. The Genius here is benevolent.

Such a storm of wind without rain rose about Benjie as he climbed Whinlatter. The water of Bassenthwaite below him that had been a field of grey shadows as he rode beside it was now, when he looked down upon it, trembling with white waves that gleamed with an almost phosphorescent glow under the blackness of Skiddaw. The clouds were so low that when he was at the highest point of the Pass they skirted him on every side, shifting from place to place with long sweeps of spidery grey. It was bitterly cold and he had to lower his head, pulling up the collar of his riding coat.

He knew that with Lorton Fell on his right, before he turned off down to Swinside, his path branched away to the left. The farm was just here somewhere, in a hollow between Grisedale Pike and Hobcarton. He directed his horse across the rough turf, moving very slowly under the sting of the wind. To his right he looked down on to the flat plain that stretched to the Border with fields like squares of a chessboard and trees and houses like dolls' furniture. The wind raced over this flat country with a shrill whistling exultation; thin patches of white broke the grey sky above the sea. It was raining above St Bees.

It would be difficult to find this place, and if the mist came down, impossible. He might wander here for hours. He cursed himself for coming, and had an impulse to turn back. In certain moods this driving wind and cold sharp air would have exalted him, but not today, for he was sick with his own self-distrust and disapproval. Nothing grand about him today to answer the grandeur of the elements. Why should he not turn back and wait patiently for Vanessa to recover? How impulsive he had been to have taken her present mood as permanent! And how selfish he had been to ride away from her at the very moment when, in her heart, she needed him! He half turned his horse's head. He would go back. Then, as he looked round him, he saw the farm, a little to his right in the fold of the hill, a bare meagre place with a few bent trees and a stone wall. The first drops of rain stung his cheek. He rode on.

When he reached the farm two dogs ran out, wildly barking: he heard Fred's voice cursing them and then saw the big stout man filling the doorway.

He gave a shout when he saw who it was.

'Hullo, Herries! What a surprise!'

He came to meet him, his face beaming.

'You've come for the night, I hope?'

'Yes,' said Benjie. 'If you'll have me.'

'Of course I'll have you. Couldn't be better.'

They led the horse round to the stable at the back of the house, Halliday talking all the time.

'My mother and sister are staying here and some friends of ours are coming up from Lorton this evening, so you've struck the right moment. It's going to be a wild night. The wind's blowing great guns. Come along in and get warm.'

Benjie went in, hung up his hat and coat, passed into an inner room that seemed half kitchen, half living-room. Sitting beside a roaring fire were Mrs Halliday and her daughter.

At the moment when he saw them, the large smoke-stained fireplace, the window that looked out on to a little scrambling path where a cluster of primroses was hiding, two canaries in a cage, and a large sheepdog lying in front of the fire with his nose on his paws, his mood changed. This was jolly, cheerful, friendly. They were all friends of his. Other friends were coming.

They would make a night of it. He had closed a door, a heavy silent-swinging door like one that guards a cathedral, upon all that other world where his friends were burnt, those whom he loved blamed him and, worst of all, where he blamed himself. Here he loved no one and no one loved him. It was not a world of hurting, haunting intimacies. He would be happy. So, as always when he was happy, he wanted to do things for everybody, drew a chair to the fire and chattered like a boy, threw back his head and roared with laughter, his rather ugly face with friendliness and generosity in all its wrinkles. And the two women quietly answered or asked questions while Fred Halliday leaned his bulk against the kitchen dresser and, with a smile on his face, watched them.

Benjie had all the London gossip: of the success that *Iolanthe* was and the other piece that the German Reeds were running, *The Mountain Heiress*, where Corney Grain was a solicitor and sang a wonderful song called 'Our Mess', and that Goring Thomas' *Esmeralda* at the Lane, where Mr Carl Rosa had a month's opera season, contained, they say, some pretty songs but that Mme Georgina Burns couldn't act for toffee.

Mrs Halliday said that the matter with the London theatre today was that it was too expensive, not comfortable enough, and that most of the plays were silly. In fact, with a few well-chosen words, she demolished the London theatre. And Benjie said, oh, he didn't know. That was a little severe, wasn't it, and that one went to the theatre to be jolly, didn't one, and that he'd go a long way to hear Corney Grain sing 'Our Mess'. Then they discussed the Budget, which had been introduced a week or two before by Mr Childers. Certainly had forestalled the Conservatives, who had been intending to come out as Champions of Economy, but Gladstone knew two of that. Everyone talking of Economy now. Yes, said Mrs Halliday, the great thing was of course to *be* economical, but easier to say than to do. Benjie, nodding his head profoundly, agreed that that *was* the problem!

Then they discussed books, and Benjie said that he did hope that Miss Marion didn't read French novels, and Miss Marion said that she sometimes did and thought them very amusing, much nearer to real life than silly writers like Rhoda Broughton and Ouida. She liked poetry, though. Did Mr Herries read poetry? No, Mr Herries didn't. A writer like Tennyson took such a long time to say what he wanted to. No, Miss Halliday did *not* agree. Poetry could do something that nothing else could do.

Wouldn't Mr Herries agree to that? And, yes, he thought on the whole that he *did* agree to that!

So they talked in the pleasantest fashion and the time flew by while the wind roared outside and the rain that had swept up from the sea beat against the window frames. Fred Halliday had some excellent beer and Benjie drank plenty of it. The fire, the beer, the pleasant easy talk all comforted and reassured him. Yes, the door, with its heavy leather curtain, had swung to; all sounds from the outer world were deadened. Mrs Halliday, he thought, was a more agreeable woman than he supposed. She sat there knitting a stocking most domestically. Her face was grave, but after all, not repellent at all. The glow from the fire softened her rather gaunt features.

Once and again she smiled, baring her teeth with her upper lip, almost as though she were about to whistle.

And as to the girl he felt once more, and increasingly as the beer warmed him, that he would like to touch her. He must be kind to her, poor child, for she could not have much happiness in her life. He began to wonder whether she had not finer feelings, more sensitive tastes than her mother and brother could satisfy. She read French, she liked poetry. Not that she had any pride. No one could be quieter about her accomplishments. Once or twice he caught her looking at him, her pale eyes staring at him, and he felt then a little embarrassment, as though he should be ashamed of his brown face and strong body when she herself was so delicate. At the thought of her delicacy some sensuous nerve in him was touched. She was so slight, so fragile, that in his arms she would be powerless, must submit to anything that he wished. Not that he would hurt her. He would not hurt anybody in the world.

The shrill clock on the mantelpiece struck seven and, a moment later, the door was flung open and Halliday came in, bringing three men with him. These men had taken their coats off in the passage; two of them were youngish, had rough corduroy trousers with long black coats containing deep pockets. One of the two was little and wiry, with bright red hair and a small, shaggy, red beard; the other was broad, strong, very dark with bright, glancing, restless eyes and a close-clipped black moustache. He was a handsome fellow. These two men might be both between thirty and forty in age. The third, as Benjie immediately learned, was the father of these two. He was tall and thin, dressed in a long black coat with wide tails and black trousers. His hair was grey and sparse; he had little eyes and above them a very high domed forehead. He looked something like a schoolmaster.

Halliday introduced them to Benjie. Their name, he discovered, was Endicott; Thomas the elder one, George and Robert the two sons. They all sat down by the fire. Thomas Endicott had rather a shrill piercing voice, small in compass and high-pitched. He spoke with care as though, with difficulty, he had learned how to be cultured. The voices of the two younger men were rough. Robert, the little red-haired fellow, spoke with an effeminate note; he was restless and given to gestures. George's voice was deep but without any Cumbrian accent. They seemed friendly. They knew the two women and were old acquaintances, it appeared, of Halliday. Endicott the elder talked to Benjie, a little pompously and always with that slow carefulness as though he would choose the right word and never on any account drop an 'h'. Oh no, they did not live at Lorton. He himself resided in Whitehaven. Yes, oh yes, his wife and her sister lived with him. This boy George here, oh! he was a rascal, could settle to nothing, had been in the Army for a bit, hadn't he, George? Could put his hand to anything, a fine boxer; oh yes, a splendid footballer if he kept in condition – but a rascal. Wouldn't settle to anything, would he, George? They all laughed, and George smiled at Benjie in friendly fashion, as much as to say: 'I like you. I've taken to you. We shall be friends.'

Oh yes, and Robert was a wanderer too. He would go from place to place selling things, go round Fairs, you know, all over the country. What you would call a pedlar in the old days. Didn't mind what he did any more than George.

Oh, they were a wandering family. That's what his wife always complained of. Yes, an old Border family. Nothing much to boast of a hundred years ago – smugglers and worse, so he heard.

'As a matter of fact, Mr Herries,' he said, 'I have been wanting to meet you. We're almost related in a kind of way. There was a girl in our family years ago married one of your ancestors, well known in the Borrowdale district. Rogue Herries he was called.'

'What!' cried Benjie. 'Rogue Herries! Why!—'

'Aye, there were two brothers, George and Anthony Endicott, mad Tony they called him. Their sister married a man called Starr and these two had a daughter. It was her old Herries married.'

Why, that was Judith's mother! Benjie was indeed amazed;

what with the beer and the warmth of the kitchen everything seemed to him now wonderful and jolly and all that it should be. Here they were, these three nice fellows, and their ancestress was Judith's mother. Judith's mother, Vanessa's great-grandmother – but at that thought the leather-curtained door, that had for a moment swung back, was closed again. No thought of Vanessa. Vanessa was far away.

'Aye,' said Thomas Endicott. 'Funny how small the world is. I've often thought I'd like to meet one of you, although maybe those ancestors of ours are nothing to be proud of.'

'Proud of them!' cried Benjie. 'I should think I am! Francis Herries you're speaking of, was a great man, a grand fighter, and a man of his hands.'

'Aye,' said Thomas Endicott slowly. 'There are plenty of stories of him in Borrowdale. He sold his woman at a Fair once, they tell.'

'And a good thing too!' Benjie cried. 'What do you say, Mrs Halliday? If you're tired of a woman and someone else wants her? Why not sell her? Fair exchange, you know.'

But Mrs Halliday only smiled and went on knitting.

Then they had supper, a very good supper too, ham and beef and chicken, a big apple tart, rum butter and cheese and plenty of cakes. Halliday produced a wine, a good warming Burgundy, and while they ate and chattered and laughed the wind tore at the house as though it would tumble it over. But the house was strong, very old, Halliday told them.

'There was a man murdered here once,' Halliday said. 'In the 'forties it was. His wife and daughter murdered him for his money. Cut his head open with a hatchet and he bled all over this very floor.'

After supper they all helped to clear the table and then they sang songs. There was an old piano there, not strictly in tune but what did that matter? They roared out the songs and banged the piano and laughed and stood with their arms round one another's shoulders.

Soon Benjie knew that he was very merry, very merry indeed. Not drunk; oh no, not drunk at all, but as happy as a grig. He had never had a better evening. What splendid fellows they were, and especially George! His hand rested on George's shoulder. He must see George again, must see George often. This was the kind of evening he enjoyed. Yes, he would like to do something for him, put George in the way of a job if he wanted one. And

George looked at him as though he liked him. He didn't say much, but he smiled and pushed out his chest when he sang and poured beer down his throat.

The ladies said goodnight. It was time for them to retire.

'We shall see you in the morning,' said Mrs Halliday. 'What a wild night it is, to be sure!'

Some time later Benjie thought that he must go to the door for a moment to cool his head. He slipped out, opened the front door, and was almost tumbled off his feet by the wind. The world was raging outside, the rain sweeping through the air in whipping fury. With great difficulty he closed the door again and turned back to see the girl standing there quite close to him. There was a dim reflection of light from the upper floor. The voices of the men singing came raucously from the inner room.

'Why, Marion!' he said.

'I am just going up to bed.'

'It was so hot in there I came out for a breath of air.'

'Yes, I know. I was hot too.'

Her hand was touching his. He caught it, then putting his arms around her, kissed her, She kissed him passionately in return, her lips clinging to his as though they would never leave them. When he held her in his arms, so slight and slender was she that he was afraid of hurting her.

'I'm hurting you,' he whispered.

'I like you to hurt me,' she whispered back, then gently freeing herself, said 'Goodnight' and ran up the stairs.

Oh, well, he shouldn't have done that. But she was so close to him. She was in his arms before he realized it. Kissing a girl – nothing in it. It was natural to kiss a girl. There was something about her ... not that he liked her ... He stood for a moment leaning against the wall in the dark passage, and felt an odd chagrin, an almost desperate loneliness, an impulse to leave the house at once, fetch his horse from the stable and ride home ...

But he went back into the room, joining the chorus with them as he entered it.

Now that the women were gone, gaiety and friendliness rose a note higher. This was what life should be, men together with care thrown out of the window, plenty to drink, a wild night outside, all friends together. They might have known one another all their lives. Father Endicott was not such a school-master as you might suppose. He possessed, in fact, a grand fund of bawdy stories. Very funny they were. That one about the old farmer's wife of Esthwaite and the two simple young men and the lady from London. There was nothing about old Cumberland life that he didn't know, the life that was going now so fast with all the tourists in the summer and the railways everywhere. A pity, a pity! Those were the good old days when Lizzie O'Branton, the witch, jumped out of her coffin at her funeral and rode away on a broomstick, and Mrs Machell of Penrith would drive her ghostly carriage whenever a 'helm' wind was blowing, when the 'need fire' charmed the cattle, when the song was sung at the shearing. Here they broke out all together:

> *Heigh O! Heigh O! Heigh O!*
> *And he that doth this health deny,*
> *Before his face I him defy.*
> *He's fit for no good company,*
> *So let this health go round.*

Good fun, too, when they had the public whippings, or the hangings in Carlisle or the witch-drownings.

'Changed times,' said old Endicott sadly. 'All the fine spirit gone.'

But *their* spirit was not gone. It increased with every drop they drank. The table was pushed aside and George and Benjie tried a 'wrastle'. They took off their coats, waistcoats, and shoes and went to it. Solemnly they circled round and round trying for a hold. But Benjie was no very great wrestler and soon George had 'buttocked' him and, throwing him, tumbled over him. They crashed to the floor and then lay there, panting, one on the other. For they were not drunk, oh no, not drunk at all, but it was comfortable there on the floor and Benjie had his arm round George's neck, looked up at the whitewashed ceiling, pulled George's hair, said, laughing, 'I like you, George. We're friends, we are,' and George's hand rested on Benjie's back and he said nothing at all. Old Endicott played a polka on the piano and they danced heavily, clumsily, staggering about the room, and Benjie cried:

'There's a fine place under Skiddaw, George, where we'll go when we're dead and we'll dance and sing for ever and ever.'

'Aye,' said George. 'Aye. That'll be grand.'

In all the merry evening there was only one unpleasant incident, which Benjie could never after properly recall.

He said something to little red-bearded Robert, and Robert took offence. The little man was dancing with rage and screaming out:

'You're a liar, I tell you. A damned bloody liar!'

'Call me a liar?' shouted Benjie.

'Aye, and I will too. Who do you think I am?'

'Why!' cried Benjie. 'I'll tell you who you are. You're a funny little man, that's who you are!'

'I was here in this country before any of you were born. Aye, and I was too, selling laces and silver boxes, visiting the witches in Borrowdale—'

'Shut your mouth, Robert,' cried George. 'Who wants to listen to your lies? Why, man—'

'Lies, are they?' The little man was screaming, dancing up and down until to Benjie's dazzled eyes he seemed a dozen little men with peaked caps on their heads, riding through the kitchen on the wind and rain. But the little man wanted to fight, and the others, roaring with laughter, held his arms and they knocked the lamp over. The room was dark save for the firelight. Oh, but the little man's red beard shone and he was angry! And Benjie embraced him, pulled his beard, gave him a friendly kick on the pants, and he went and sat in a corner by the fireplace, waving his hands and making shadows of rabbits on the wall with his fingers.

Later, Benjie found himself with a candle wandering on his way to bed. Halliday showed him where his room was, a little whitewashed room at the top of the house. Halliday helped him into bed.

And later than that, as he lay looking at the ceiling and smiling, the door opened. The girl stood there, a candle in her hand, wearing a dressing-gown with a wool collar over her nightdress.

He sat up on his elbow and looked at her. She closed the door very softly and came over to him. She smiled and said:

'The wind's died down. Everyone's sleeping.'

He could only stare at her. She took off her dressing-gown and carefully laid it on the chair. Then she blew out the candle, climbed into bed and lay down beside him.

INSIDE THE FORTRESS

IT was early in the wet and stormy weather of that year when Vanessa came to stay with Elizabeth at the Fortress.

Elizabeth had been seriously ill ever since the fire at Fell House in April. No one could say exactly where the trouble was. It was what was known as a 'decline'. She was weak, instantly tired by any exertion; her features now had the delicacy of a thin rose-tinted shell. Her hair was snow-white, her figure still slim and erect, but ghost-like in its fragility. She walked a little from room to room: although she leaned on a stick she was still tall. She was kind and gracious to everyone, but most of her, as Mrs Harwen, the cook-housekeeper, said, was 'otherwhither'.

'It's my opinion,' John Harwen, the handyman about the place and Mrs Harwen's little hostler-like spouse, remarked, 'That the difference between her living and her dead is so slight that you'll not notice it. After she's gone she'll still be here, so to speak.'

'We've enough ghosts in this house already,' said Mrs Harwen.

Benjie had not been home since June. No one knew where he was. No one had heard from him. Elizabeth had through many years practised herself to be patient about these absences, but now it was another matter. For she knew that she had not long to live and she had only one desire in her heart – that Benjie and Vanessa should be married before she went.

She had not seen very much of Vanessa. The girl had stayed first with Timothy in Eskdale, where he had thoughts of buying a house (for he had decided not to rebuild Fell House), then had returned to Cat Bells, where Will and the old cook had looked after her.

In July she visited Elizabeth, who saw at once that here now was a woman of self-command, deep reserves and a very fine courage. Vanessa was cheerful, talked freely about her father, seemed indeed to wish to talk of him, recalling days and moments and words and phrases; saying: 'Papa always felt that' or 'Papa never troubled to be angry – he said it was waste of time.' But his death, Elizabeth saw, had made a fundamental change in Vanessa, had brought out certain qualities that were latent before, and had checked others.

She was not so impetuous: her heart was as warm but it was guarded now against shock.

Just before she went she said:

'And what about Benjie?'

Elizabeth told her that she had not heard, that she had no idea where he was.

'It's a shame!' Vanessa cried indignantly. 'You wanting him—'

'Yes,' said Elizabeth quietly. 'I am not going to live much longer, my dear, and I *must* see him. But no one knows where he is.'

'I think,' said Vanessa lowly, 'that perhaps I am partly to blame. He came to see me – after the fire. I was not myself. I didn't want Benjie or anyone. I wanted to be left alone. So he went away.'

'We'll be independent of him,' said Elizabeth gently.

Then Vanessa asked if she might come and stay. Elizabeth's pale cheek flushed.

'Oh, Vanessa dearest, do you mean it? Will you really come? How happy I shall be!'

Early in September Vanessa came. No one knew what that was to her, the first time that she looked from the long windows of the Fortress down to the valley where, very clearly, in the pale colourless moving air, the walls of Fell House were still standing. She had been dreading this moment from the instant when she made her proposal of a visit to Elizabeth. She had not seen the place since the day of the funeral. But she knew that it had to be faced, that everything had to be faced. She had learnt many things since April and one of them was that the only way to make anything of life was to fit, resolutely, with courage, into the patterns that life, in change after change, presented. To attempt to force life into *your* pattern was to challenge disaster. You must accept *everything* and turn it to good.

So she stood there that morning in her black dress, her hands clenched at her sides, the house silent about her with that dull brooding silence that seemed the Fortress' special property. In the valley the four bare walls stood, the moors climbing above them as though they already recognized that here was a spot that now they would soon reclaim, as, one day, they would reclaim everything.

Tears rolled down Vanessa's cheeks, but she made no sound. For a moment she cried within herself: 'Oh, I cannot endure this! I *cannot* endure it!' and this was followed by the strong response: 'I *can* endure it! I can endure anything!'

The hardest thing to bear was that she had not at present recovered her father for herself. When someone dearly loved passes away there is a period when everything is blurred. The personality has broken up into a thousand pieces, something here, something there, but the radiant heart is absent. Slowly the friend returns, never – if feeling has been true – to be lost again.

Elizabeth, watching her, felt at first the girl's deep loneliness. There they were alike. She, too, was lonely, had been for years, but that is a lesson that women learn and it is one of the principal bonds between them. Vanessa was only setting out on a road that Elizabeth knew by heart, of which she was even proud. At the same time they were not a gloomy pair. They laughed, drove out in the landau, had visitors, read together, played piquet and backgammon. Elizabeth's extreme weakness was what Vanessa needed. She needed, more than she had ever conceived that she would, someone to care for. It was the strongest need of her nature and would always be, as it had been her grandmother's. That was why she wanted Benjie more with every day that passed. Now that Adam was gone she had nobody else but Benjie. And, as Elizabeth needed him too, these two, although they seldom mentioned him, thought of him all the time.

But there were other things growing in Vanessa, as Elizabeth one day discovered.

A Mrs Marrable from Rosthwaite called. Now the Marrable family, its colour, personality, and circumstances, would make a very fit subject of study for anyone interested in English family life in the eighties. Mr John Marrable had interests in China. He was now retired, wore a black beard, smoked a kind of Oriental hookah, and was to be seen for the most part in green-and-red worsted carpet slippers walking up and down the glass-covered passage on the outside of his Rosthwaite house. Mrs Marrable was round, stout, full-bosomed, and her skirt so beflounced and beribboned that she was all bits and pieces. John Marrable was severe and extremely self-satisfied. Mrs Marrable very talkative, serious-minded, but gay with that nervous gaiety peculiar to wives who expect their husbands to enter at any moment in the worst of all possible tempers. The Marrables had five children, four girls and a boy; they lived entirely up to the later caricatured notion of Victorian manners in that the four Miss Marrables had been completely sacrificed to their brother Edward, for whom everything had been done. The result of doing everything for Edward was that he had turned out very badly indeed, being sent down from Cambridge for grossly insulting a Proctor and then, while supposedly following his father's Chinese interests in London, mixing in the lowest society and incurring a multitude of debts. Meanwhile the four Miss Marrables, who were not beauties, waited patiently at home for someone to marry them, were bullied by their father and grew ever more plain of feature. One of them, the third in age, Lettice, Vanessa had liked, been kind to; the result of this was that Lettice Marrable worshipped her with a passion that was made up of religion, sexual hunger, and a devastating loneliness. Lettice Marrable's adoration for Vanessa had its consequences.

In any case for the moment here Mrs Marrable was, taking tea with Elizabeth and Vanessa in the drawing-room of the Fortress. She chattered on for a long time in the eager, apprehensive, incoherent manner that was especially hers, and as she talked a large locket jumped about on her stout bosom like a thing imprisoned and mad for freedom.

'Yes, thank you, we have heard from Ned. His present enthusiasm is for Miss Mary Anderson. He goes to see her every evening in *Ingomar*, although every evening is of course the dear fellow's exaggeration. The play is a failure, he tells us, but Miss Anderson is lovelier than ever.'

'Why don't you take the girls up to London, Mrs Marrable, for a jaunt, and go and see her?'

'Take the girls up to London! My dear Miss Paris! With things in China as bad as they are! No. Mr Marrable says we must economize in every possible direction, and we are thinking of cutting down the landau. He tells the girls that we must all make sacrifices and he is quite right. Ned went with some friends to Hurlingham last weekend and seems really to have enjoyed himself, and he actually saw the Duke of Cambridge riding down a side street on a bicycle the other day! I agree with Mr Marrable that our Royal Family should keep up their position. Do not you, Mrs Herries? And Mr Marrable says that with all this odd behaviour of France in China there is no knowing where we shall all be and we look to the Royal Family to keep us all together. Although Ned writes in his letter that the Prince of Wales really *does* encourage some very light-hearted behaviour. Now is it right? What I mean, Miss Paris, is that we all look up to the

Royal Family. What kind of example is he setting our girls? And
that reminds me. They tell me that Miss Nettleship, the daughter
of Doctor Nettleship, is going up to Girton. Now I don't know
what *you* think, Miss Paris, but my opinion is – and Mr Marrable's too – that all these things that girls are wanting to do are
the *greatest* mistake. More than that, they are unwomanly – the
very word that Mr Marrable used this morning.'

'What things?' asked Vanessa, smiling.

Now it happened that that smile which Vanessa had intended
in all friendliness irritated Mrs Marrable. She had had a trying
day. John Marrable had come down to breakfast with a cold and
had been very severe with everyone. She was anxious about Ned's
doings in London, and Mrs Martin of Keswick had asked for her
bill (a thing that nobody in Keswick ever dreamt of doing unless
seized by some sudden insanity). Moreover, neither she nor Mr
Marrable really approved of Vanessa. It was true, of course, that
she was a great beauty, but was she quite nice? It was said of her
that she had some very odd opinions, and unusual she certainly
must be to engage herself to that rascal of a son of Mrs Herries,
who, poor woman, was popular with everyone, partly because she
did no harm and partly because everyone had the luxury of pitying her.

Mrs Marrable did not approve of Vanessa although she could
not deny but that black suited her, she was a very lovely girl, she
was kind to Lettice, and belonged to one of the best families in
Cumberland. This smile, however, hinted at broad views, was
patronizing, and the drive back to Rosthwaite would be very
long. She wished now that she had brought one of the girls to
bear her company . . .

'What things?' cried Mrs Marrable, a little sharply. 'Why, anything that takes a woman away from the home where she belongs.
All this gadding about, doing as men do – it isn't natural and you
know it isn't, Miss Paris.'

'Why isn't it natural?' asked Vanessa. She was suddenly weary
of Mrs Marrable. She wished that she would go. Mrs Marrable's
bright green dress was most unsuited to her figure.

'Why isn't it natural?' Mrs Marrable had a maddening habit of
repeating everything that the last speaker had said. 'Why, my
dear Miss Paris, what did Nature intend women for? Marriage
and the home. Marriage and the home.'

'But if they don't get married?' Vanessa continued, not very
wisely. 'There are more women than men in this country. Many

more. What are they to do? What do they do? Sit at home,
twiddle their thumbs, and look out of window for a husband.'

This was unwise of her because it was exactly what the Miss
Marrables spent their time in doing, as Mrs Marrable very well
knew. She bridled in every limb.

'Well, if they do sit at home it is better in my opinion than that
they should unsex themselves. Why, they are actually doctors,
some of them! It is *my* opinion, Miss Paris, that that Doctor
Garrett Anderson they are always talking about should be put in
prison!'

Elizabeth, who was watching Vanessa rather anxiously, saw
her straighten her tall body and throw back her head.

'Another cup, Mrs Marrable?'

'Oh no, thank you, Mrs Herries. I positively must be going.'

'Why should she be put in prison?' asked Vanessa.

'Well, really, Miss Paris,' Mrs Marrable said, patting her
locket and smiling rather nervously, 'I wonder you can ask such a
question! But you, of course, are of the younger generation. We
older ones wonder sometimes where the world is going to!'

'No, but, Mrs Marrable,' Vanessa persisted, 'I truly want to
know. *Why* should Doctor Garrett Anderson be put in prison?'

This was plainly intended as a challenge and Mrs Marrable
took it as such.

'I consider her a wicked woman and a dangerous influence. I
read an article about her only the other day. Do you know that
she once actually read a paper on "The Limits of Parental
Authority"? Do you happen to know, Miss Paris, that she actually supports the fantastic idea that women should have a vote? A
vote indeed! If that is not against Nature I don't know what is!
And do you know,' and here Mrs Marrable dropped her voice to
an awful trembling hush, 'that she took the part of the fallen
women in opposing an excellent Act of Parliament demanding
their supervision? – yes, and she and her friends positively succeeded in having the Act repealed.'

'If women do not protect fallen women I scarcely see who will.
Certainly not men.'

'Protect! Protect! My dear Miss Paris! And you quite a young
girl! One naturally dislikes discussing such a matter at all, but
people seem to discuss everything nowadays. All I can say is that
if you approve this condonation of gross immorality I – I – I'm
most surprised!'

'Let that be as it may, Mrs Marrable,' Vanessa said. 'I know a few things also about Doctor Anderson. She is one of the bravest and finest women alive in the world today. In fact, with the exception of Florence Nightingale, there is not a finer. I also could tell you one or two things about her that perhaps you don't know. Have you ever thought of the conditions women lived under when Doctor Anderson was a girl? A married woman was scarcely a human being. She had no rights, no property, nothing. Did you ever read Miss Leigh Smith's *Brief Summary of the Most Important Laws Concerning Women?*'

'No, indeed I have not,' said Mrs Marrable, panting with nervousness and annoyance.

'Well then, you should. It was written long ago and is still excellent reading. Do you know that when Elizabeth Garrett wanted to be a doctor she could not find a physician in England to whom she could be apprenticed? Do you know that she worked all day at the Middlesex Hospital, where there were no antiseptics and anaesthetic was scarcely used? That needed some courage, did it not? Do you know that the whole medical profession tried to stop her, that they got up a memorial against her, that London University when she tried to matriculate was closed to women? Do you know that she had to fight every step of the way and that when at last with Sophia Jex-Blake she started the School of Medicine for Women a howl went up through the whole of England? And all for why? Because, Mrs Marrable, at last women in England have grown tired of sitting still and looking out of the window for husbands! They want to have a life of their own, they want to be independent, as one day, please God, they shall be!'

Elizabeth had never seen Vanessa like this before. Her voice rang across the room as though she challenged the world. With her shoulders back and her eyes flashing she looked as though she would like to crush Mrs Marrable to powder. In fact at that moment she hated that good, kindly, and quite unoffending woman.

Unoffending but not unoffended! She was so deeply offended that she would never forget – never forget and never forgive. She was not, in her life and circumstance, a happy enough woman to forgive. Like all women who have a grievance which they refuse to admit, she made her friends take the blame. Vanessa was to be blamed for ever and ever.

The lady got up to go, smoothing her bosom and arranging her wide and voluminous skirt.

'Thank you, Mrs Herries, for a most delightful afternoon.'

'I am so glad that you came, Mrs Marrable.'

She carried it off. She shook her fingers playfully at Vanessa. 'When you are my age, Miss Paris,' she said, 'you will see the danger of these things.'

'Oh dear,' said Vanessa after her departure. 'How intolerable of me! And how unexpected! It was the very last thing I thought of doing. And in your house too.'

'You were rather vehement,' said Elizabeth. 'I have never seen you like that before.'

'No, but I am afraid you will see me like that again. I have a terrible temper and it flies up before I know that it's there. You are wise, Elizabeth. Tell me what I shall do about it.'

'No. I don't think you lost your temper, dear. You were indignant. That's all. And I agreed with every word that you said.'

Nevertheless, going to bed that night, Vanessa was very unhappy. Something was wrong, and what was wrong was that her spirit was weighed down with an intolerable loneliness. With every day that passed she realized more bitterly the agony of her father's loss. She had been wrong, perhaps, to build her life so entirely around him. It was the caring for him, the watching that he should be happy, the comfort of knowing that they loved one another – these things, gone, left in her utter desolation. Dear Elizabeth . . . but Elizabeth was now almost out of the world and did not need her. Nobody needed her, nobody anywhere.

And at that she faced the other trouble besides her father's loss. She wanted Benjie: she wanted to be married to Benjie, to care for him, understand him, comfort him, make him happy. And Benjie was away, would perhaps never return.

'That's amusing,' she thought as she lay down in bed. 'Here was I railing at Mrs Marrable about women's independence and I myself the least independent woman in the world!'

Two days later a telegram came:

'Arriving tonight. Benjie.'

Elizabeth ran to the door, flung it open, called out 'Vanessa! Vanessa!' and Vanessa came running down the stairs, thinking that Elizabeth was ill.

'Oh, what is it?'

But Elizabeth caught her hand.

'He's coming – tonight. That's all he says. It's sent from Liverpool.'

Vanessa took the telegram.

'Tonight! Oh, Elizabeth, I am so glad! He'll take the train to Carlisle, I shouldn't wonder, and then drive. He says nothing about being met.'

All day preparations were made, roses in his bedroom, Mrs Harwen roasting two ducks, the silver polished, the garden paths brushed, and everything at the end of it as dead around the house as it was at the beginning.

It was four in the afternoon. Tea had been just brought in. The hills beyond the windows lay like dark purple prehistoric animals bathing in a sea of orange mist. You could see them sprawling, burying their snouts, heaving their scaly backs, while below, all about the valley, the mist, like bales of wool, rolled from field to field.

Vanessa, holding Elizabeth close to her, stared at the hills.

'Benjie thinks there are men under Skiddaw,' she said. 'Dead men. A kind of Cumbrian Valhalla.'

But Elizabeth had not heard. She looked exceedingly frail today. Excitement was bad for her heart. She trembled a little, leaning against Vanessa's strong side.

'This house,' she said, 'whatever you do to it, it refuses to live. It was conceived in hatred, my dear. It has always hated everybody and everything just as poor Uhland did. It is this place should have been burnt, not Fell House. Look at this room. Look at the roses! I have put them here, there, everywhere. They are dropping with uneasiness. Nothing good will ever happen in this place. Benjie is bringing some bad news. I know it.'

Vanessa led her back to the sofa.

'Now lie down, Elizabeth darling. I'll bring you your tea. Don't *think* about Benjie until he's here. What bad news *could* there be?'

She was herself triumphant. She felt that she was able to deal with *any* situation that Benjie might offer. Were he in trouble through some foolishness she would stand by him. There was nothing that he could confess, as she had told him years ago, that she would not share with him. And then at last, after all these postponements, they would be married. There was nothing now to prevent it save the old obstacle of Benjie's scruples, which came, as she knew well, because he loved her so much. Now when he saw that her sorrow had only made her the more resolved, he would be as eager as she.

She went about the house, singing. She petted Mrs Harwen, who in any case adored her, went several times to Benjie's room to see that everything was right, put Elizabeth to bed.

'He will be late. He has thirty miles to drive, you know. He shall come up to you the moment he arrives.'

It was after ten when he came. She was standing at her window and saw the lights of the carriage, heard the crunch of the wheels on the road, heard the driver shout 'Whoa!' to his horses, then, with a recognition that drove her heart against her ribs, the well-known timbre of Benjie's voice.

'All right, driver. I'll get someone to help you with the box.'

He came up the path, saw the light in her window, and looked up.

'Hulloa, Vanessa. Is that you?' he called out.

'Yes. I'll come down.'

As their hands clasped she knew that he loved her as dearly as ever. She was so happy that she could have flung her arms around his neck, but all she did was to say, smiling her quiet steady smile:

'Elizabeth has gone to bed. She's longing to see you.'

Old Harwen helped the driver in with the luggage. Benjie took off his coat, nodded to her, and saying, 'I'll see Mother a moment and come down,' he ran up the stairs.

It was something in his voice and look that frightened her. *What* was it? He did not look well, but he would be tired, of course, after his journey. It was not that. As he spoke, he had avoided her eyes.

She went into the dining-room where some supper was laid out for him. She told Mrs Harwen to bring in the soup in ten minutes. Then she stood there under the gas that hissed very faintly above her head and tried to calm her fear.

Something was the matter. Had she not said that nothing that he could tell her would alarm her? Now, face to face with him, she was not sure. She felt herself quite inexperienced. She had thought that she could deal with him, but what did she *really* know about men? Perhaps he was going to tell her that he did not love her any more. No, she knew that it was not that. That first gaze into one another's eyes had told her that they still belonged to one another just as they had always done. What else could it be? Had he done anything disgraceful? She would share that with him, whatever it might be. She moved restlessly about the room, moving the things upon the table, seeing that the bowl of red and yellow roses was in the centre, arranging knives and forks.

Mrs Harwen came in with the soup tureen.

'Yes, Mrs Harwen, I think he'll be down in a minute now.'

'And you'll ring for the meat and vegetables, Miss Vanessa?'

'Yes. He must be hungry.'

'Yes, Miss. It's a couple of ducks – and an apple tart to follow.'

She walked to the window. Why did this house always fill her with apprehension? Her anxiety was needless. He was tired after his journey. After five minutes with her he would be his old self.

The door opened and he came in. He smiled at her, sat down and began to eat: she drew a chair to the table near to him.

'How well you are looking, Vanessa.'

He had not seen her since the week of the fire. They were both conscious of that, she thought. That is why he is uneasy and will not look at me; but her fear increased.

'Where have you been, Benjie, all this time? Are you hungry? Is the toast dry? I told Mrs Harwen not to make it before she heard you arriving.'

'I've come from Liverpool.' He looked at her and smiled, a pathetic smile as though he longed to be friends with her and for some reason must not be. The childishness so often apparent in him – one of his strongest appeals to women because he was quite unconscious of it – caught her heart, making her ache to take him in her arms and comfort him.

He was terribly unhappy: that was certain.

'And where have you been besides Liverpool?'

'Oh, abroad. In June I went to Germany. I thought that I'd like to see Bismarck. Not to speak to him, of course – simply to have a sight of the old man. And I did. He was driving one day in Berlin in an open carriage. It was strange, you know, Vanessa, because when I was a boy at Rugby in 1870 I hated the Prussians – I would have done anything to help the French – nearly ran away to Paris to share in the Siege. But when I saw the old boy riding through Berlin I cheered like the others.'

'What did he look like?'

'Oh, just an old man. But he sat up straight and bowed. Very striking eyes.'

Mrs Harwen came in with the ducks.

'Hulloa! Mrs Harwen! How are you?'

'Very well, thank you, sir, and I hope you're the same?'

'Oh, I'm well enough! Two ducks! I can't eat two ducks!'

'I thought if one wasn't tender you could try the other, sir.'

'Thanks. But I'm not hungry.'

'There's an apple tart to follow, sir.'

'No. Not for me tonight. I'll have it cold tomorrow.'

He carved the duck, ate a little of it, then pushed his plate aside.

'I'm not hungry, Vanessa.'

'Oh, you ought to be after that long journey.'

'No, I'm not ... Mother's not very well, I'm afraid.'

'No, she has grown much weaker lately. I'm afraid she can't live much longer, Benjie.'

His face seemed to be shadowed. The constraint between them grew deeper with every moment.

'No, I can't eat.' He got up. 'Let's go into the other room. There's something I must say to you.'

He opened the door for her and she went out, crossing the passage, down the stairs, into the little room off the hall that had been poor old Walter's sanctum.

There was a fire there and yet the room was cheerless. They sat down in the old leather armchairs opposite one another.

'Don't you hate this house?' he asked her.

'I don't like it. It is impossible to make it comfortable.'

'Old Walter sees to that,' he answered grimly. There followed an awful pause. At last she could endure it no longer.

'Benjie, what's the matter?'

'Nothing. Oh yes, there is. Of course there is.'

'Well, tell me. Don't be a coward about it.' She hesitated. 'Is it that you don't love me any longer?'

He, too, hesitated. Then he answered, looking her at last straight in the face:

'I love you more than ever.'

A wave of joy, burning with splendid warmth, swept over her. She was, for an instant, submerged by it, blind, deaf, conscious of her joy as though she were alone in space, the beautiful glass-green wave arching above her head.

'I'm glad of that,' she said at last, 'because I also love you more than ever.' She went on: 'Father's death has left me with only you. I have no one else to care for, no one else to care for *me*. When you were away so long I thought I could not endure it — not if it went on much longer. I find that I cannot live without someone to love, and as there is only you, Benjie—'

'Don't!' he broke in with a cry. 'Vanessa, don't!'

He had sprung to his feet. A panic of apprehension caught
her. Something terrible had happened. She held the arm of the
chair with her hand.

'What is it?'

'It's this. We can't be married. We can never be married.'

She waited for the next word.

'We can't be married because – because' – he turned away from
her, staring at the window – 'because I was married last week.'

He had rehearsed this moment to himself all day, and for many
days past. He had not known what he would do, nor what she
would do either. He had thought of everything – every possibility
but one.

He had not thought that, after what seemed to him an age of
silence, she would murmur:

'Oh, poor Benjie. Oh, what a dreadful thing!'

She had thought first of himself. She had guessed instantly
that he was in some bad, inescapable tangle. He could have fallen
at her feet and kissed her hands for her perception.

'We should have married last year,' she said. 'That would have
saved both of us.'

He turned and looked at her with a deep sombre gaze as
though he were fixing her for ever in his mind, just as she was,
now that he had lost her. Then he knelt down, at her feet, bowed
his head: she held his hand. Neither of them spoke for a long
time.

He got up and sat in the chair again.

'I must tell you about it,' he said. 'You must know everything.'

'Yes, tell me,' she answered.

'After the fire when I came to see you, you were upset. I
thought that you blamed me for your father's death. I'm so ready
to be blamed. I'm blamed so often. But I don't care. I don't care
perhaps enough – unless it is you who blame me. So I rode off in
a temper. You remember that in Seascale last year I stayed in
rooms with a widow and her daughter?'

Vanessa, looking at him with eyes that were so unhappy but so
resolutely determined not to flinch that he could not face them,
nodded.

'Yes, I remember. I saw them walking one day on the beach.'

'Yes. Well – a mother and daughter called Halliday – I didn't
like them – not either of them. I was thinking only of you, Van-

essa, that summer – you were obsessing me. Nevertheless I kissed the girl, disliked her more than ever, and kissed her again.'

He flashed a look at her, then dropped his glance and went on, looking at the floor.

'You and I would have been married, of course, that autumn, had it not been for Adam's illness. Fate. Call it what you like. Perhaps really the best thing. In any case the widow and her daughter came to live in Keswick.'

'Tell me,' Vanessa said, 'what she looks like. I saw her only for a moment at Seascale. Is she beautiful? *What* is she?'

'No, she is not. She is not beautiful, she is not clever. My eyes have been open from the first. She held me like one of one's pet cheap temptations – those you are always ashamed of, never resist, never confess to anyone . . . I must be fair to her, Vanessa. Whatever happens I must be fair. But you will see in a moment what she is like.'

Vanessa drew a deep, trembling breath. Her hands were folded in her lap. Benjie stared at them as though hypnotized, noticing how white they were against the black dress. He thought that he could tell the rest of the story better were he holding her hand, but he did not move.

'Yes, I must be fair to her. She knew that she had some attraction for me. She was, I think, determined from the very beginning that I should marry her, but really because, I am afraid, she loved – loves – me.'

'Yes,' said Vanessa.

'Thinking of you always, loving you more every day, yet I went to see the two of them in Keswick. I must speak of something difficult, Vanessa. It is this. The more I saw you the more I loved you – and with my body as well as the rest of me. I have always wanted my body to have power. I have liked to see it travelling about the world, getting experience, eating, drinking, strong, vigorous. I have always thought that most people do not give their bodies all the chances. Well, that spring you were occupied with Adam, of course, and I would leave you, restless and unsatisfied. Both of us were, I think. But I was doubly unsatisfied – because I wanted you so badly and because I was so unworthy of you.'

She murmured: 'That has been where the mistake was.'

'Oh, don't misunderstand me, Vanessa. I don't go about the world thinking I am unworthy of people. Of nobody else. Only you. But the one thing I must not do, I tell myself, is to spoil your life. I mustn't. I mustn't, I tell myself – and then – I do ...

'So I went to see them. Then a day or two after the fire I rode out to Halliday's farm – the brother, you know. I stayed there the night. I drank too much. The girl slept with me.'

He waited. There was a mouse scratching somewhere. They both raised their heads together, and Vanessa thought, as she had often done before, that she heard one of the dogs that Uhland used to keep in his room howling from the Tower. Somewhere a dog *was* howling, and at that moment she realized a hatred for that girl such as she had never felt before for anyone.

'Next day,' Benjie went on, 'I came back to the Fortress. I stayed for a while, then I went off with Halliday and two of his friends called Endicott shooting. I met the girl again. She was quiet, most respectable, as though now she had got what she wanted. I am sure her mother knew. I think her brother knew too. I was extremely unhappy. I wanted to come to you and ask that we might be married at once, but I was ashamed and afraid – you are the only human being I have ever been afraid of, Vanessa. I went abroad to Germany.

'When I came back the girl, her mother, and brother were in London. The girl came to see me and told me that she was going to have a child – my child, she said. I don't know whether that was the truth or no. That was a month ago. Will you believe me, Vanessa, when I tell you that I loved you during all this time more than ever?'

'Yes,' said Vanessa. 'I believe you.'

'The girl said that of course now I would marry her. The mother said the same. The brother the same. I was not frightened of them in the least. I have never been afraid of anyone or anything except your despising me or doing you harm. But also, in spite of all that I have done, I have never got a woman into trouble. I tell you that I didn't know, I don't know now, whether I was responsible in this case. I want to be fair to her in every way, but I cannot be certain of her virtue. They were all three quite friendly and quite frank. The girl said that she had always loved me, always meant to marry me. The brother said that of course it would not be pleasant for my mother if she knew of this. I agreed with that. Ill as she was it would probably kill her. But I think that my mind was entirely on you. Although I loved you so dearly I might do this again. I have never had any trust in myself. It is only myself that I blame, but from my birth, as I have always told you, there has been some strain in me that I could never trust, as there was in my father, my grandfather. And I have always been honest with you. I would have had to tell you of this, and when you knew that this was to be my child – would you marry me? Would you, Vanessa? Would you have married me knowing this?'

He waited with passionate eagerness for her answer, leaning forward, looking into her face.

At last she said:

'No. Perhaps I would not.'

He nodded his head. 'I thought not. "This ends it," I thought. All this struggle about you that I have had for years. You will be free. Perhaps you will hate me and so be clear of me, then after a while you will marry somebody splendid. One day, long after, you will acknowledge that I was right. That's what I thought. So I married her – last week in Liverpool.'

A long, long silence followed.

At last Vanessa said:

'Do you care for her? Are you fond of her in any way at all?'

'No – not in any way at all.'

Then she said:

'Thank you for telling me so honestly.' And then again, after another pause: 'This will be terrible for Elizabeth.'

'Yes,' he answered.

She got up and went over to him and laid her hand against his cheek.

'You must do all you can for her.'

He caught her hand fiercely; kissed it again and again.

'What are we to do? I can't live without seeing you.'

She shook her head.

'No. Of course we must not meet. That would be too difficult for both of us.'

She bent down and kissed him.

'How foolish we both have been, Benjie dear.' She held him close to her like a mother her son. At that moment, with his head against her breast, she realized with the utmost clarity the desolation of her loneliness. She kissed him again, then drew herself from his grasp.

'Goodnight, Benjie darling. I'll go back to Cat Bells in the morning. You won't write or anything, will you? It will be much better.'

'I'll do anything you say.'

At the door she turned back.

'I don't know whether it's right. Very wrong perhaps. But although we mustn't meet or write, if you're in trouble – real, serious trouble – you must tell me.'

'I'll tell you,' he said.

Then she went out.

THE DUCHESS OF WREXE'S BALL

ONE day in November 1884 Barney Newmark went in to drink a cup of tea with his sister, Phyllis Rochester, in her pleasant little house in Eaton Place.

He chose this afternoon because he knew that his brother-in-law, Clarence Rochester, was at Brighton. He did not like Clarence at all – he thought him a humbug. And Clarence did not like Barney – he thought him an obscene, conceited libertine. Phyllis, who cared deeply for Barney and had grown accustomed to Clarence, kept the balance between them.

Phyllis, who was now a buxom woman of sixty-three (all the Newmarks of this generation were stout), loved her comforts and adored her eccentric son Philip. So long as she had plenty of the little cakes, jams, and preserved fruits that she preferred and so long as Philip lived with her in Eaton Place she had no alarms. She had a charming complexion, and Clarence was away as often as not. Her one fear had been lest Philip should marry. But now it did not seem likely. Philip did not like women.

Barney today was in an excellent temper. He had that morning finished his novel, a novel in which Newmarket, Boulogne, and Scottish shooting parties were his principal backgrounds, where everything was very light and careless and the principal scene was a baccarat-cheating scandal. Like the majority of novelists he enjoyed, for a day or two following a novel's conclusion, an extraordinary sense of freedom and light-heartedness. Unlike most novelists these happy days were not followed by an intense gloom. He knew the thing was of no value at all. He told everybody so. He wrote to make money. He was none of your Merediths, Zolas, or Shorthouses. He couldn't write a novel like – what was its name? – that *John Inglesant* to save his life. Nor did he want to. So long as a fellow or two got his novel from a library he was perfectly satisfied – and so were his publishers.

Between the brother and sister sitting together having tea in the pleasant little drawing-room there was a strong resemblance. They were both stout, jolly, and easily amused. Barney was the best of fellows when alone with his sister. They were both glad that Clarence was at Brighton. The room was very warm, heavily curtained, and crammed with knick-knacks. There were china dogs, china shepherds and shepherdesses, china mandarins. There was even a large china copy of a Chinese temple with little bells that tinkled when there was a draught, and of this Phyllis was inordinately proud. There were photographs everywhere. Four photographs of Mary Anderson, two of Ellen Terry, three of Mr Terriss, photographs of Ellis and Garth and Emily Newmark (very forbidding) and Barney (riding a horse) and Vanessa and Carey Rockage. There were numberless little tables, all heavily loaded, a great many little chairs and a basket near the fire in which a fat pug called Charles was now wheezing. The two round tea tables were covered with cakes, pastries, muffins, piles of buttered toast.

'Good Heavens, Phil,' Barney cried, 'how many people are you expecting?'

'Nobody except you.'

'Why all the food?'

'Oh, I like to have plenty to eat. And Philip may come in.'

'Oh, may he? And what is he doing today?'

'He has gone to an Art Exhibition with Samuel Roscoe.'

'Oh, has he?'

To change the subject – which might be an unpleasant one – Phyllis asked:

'And what's the news?'

'I finished my novel this morning.'

'Oh, did you? What is it called?'

'*Neck or Nothing.*'

'What a clever title! I don't know how you think of all these things.'

'No, nor do I. I have been helping John Beaminster to choose a horse.'

'Oh, have you?' Phyllis was greatly interested. The Beaminsters were always exciting. 'Did he tell you anything about his mother?'

'No. What should he tell me?'

'Oh, I don't know, but I do think it is so extraordinary her being shut up in that Portland Place house all these years. Do you remember when she came to that party that Ellis gave a year or two ago?'

'Of course I remember.'

'Well, they say she hadn't been out of doors for years before that. Then for a week or two she was seen everywhere. Then she went back again and has shut herself up ever since.'

'That was the party,' said Barney slowly, 'when Benjie suddenly appeared. Do you remember? And that night he was engaged to Vanessa.'

Phyllis, shaking her head, choosing with great care the richest of several little cakes, answered indignantly:

'Oh, don't mention Benjie to me! I have finished with him for ever and so has everybody! I consider him a murderer!'

'Oh, come now,' said Barney, smiling.

'Well, isn't he? He killed his mother by throwing Vanessa over and marrying that horrible woman.'

'You don't know that she's horrible. You've never seen her.'

'No, but other people have. Alfred was up that way with a friend the other day and thought he'd call. They had the most dreadful visit. Benjie would do nothing but swear, and the house was a pig sty and the baby howling. Alfred said that the woman was awful! As thin as a pole and cross-eyed.'

'Oh no, not that!' said Barney, laughing.

'Well, there was something odd about her eyes, Alfred said. And she hardly spoke a word.'

'I like Benjie,' Barney said. 'I always have and I always will. There was something behind that business we don't know.'

'Nothing to Benjie's credit, you can be sure,' said Phyllis. 'Poor Vanessa. So beautiful and buried up there. She's only been to London once since it happened. She stayed with Rose for a week, you remember, and I never saw anyone more lovely. Very nice she was too. Philip was in a passion over her.'

'You needn't pity Vanessa,' said Barney sharply. 'She needs no one's pity.'

'Oh no, of course not!' Here again seemed a dangerous subject, so Phyllis, finding safety in general affairs, asked:

'And what do they say about General Gordon?'

'There is little news since Stewart's murder. Wolseley is moving up the Nile.'

'Do you think Gladstone has made a mistake?'

'Possibly. He'll hear of it if he has.'

'Some people say that Gordon is mad.'

'Mad people do most of the things in this world. That, my dear Phil, is what our family will never learn.'

'I sometimes think Emily is mad. What do you think she came in here raging about yesterday?'

'I *never* think about Emily.'

'She wants to close the Alhambra and have all the women who go there put in prison.'

'Emily will be improperly assaulted one day by a Salvation Army worker. Then she will learn something.'

The maid opened the door and said: 'Miss Ormerod and Mr Ormerod.'

Rose and Horace came in and were eagerly welcomed.

Rose looked charming indeed, in one of the Scottish plaid costumes that were then most fashionable, and her hat tilted over her hair arranged in a bun was so small as to be almost invisible. 'Where,' thought Phyllis, 'does she get the money to buy her clothes from?'

Horace, red-faced, amiable and enthusiastic, was like a successful clergyman on holiday. His vibrating enthusiasm made Barney very cynical. 'I always believe well of human nature,' Barney said, 'until Horace Ormerod comes along.'

Horace rubbed his hands together, beamed, pushed his spectacles (he had been wearing spectacles for a year or two) back on to his short nose and cried: 'Well, this is splendid indeed! Rose and I were walking in the Park and I said to her, "We'll take a hansom and see if Phil has some tea for us!" Splendid day! Fresh and bright! I never felt better in my life!'

Barney said: 'I'm glad of that, Horace. We need cheering, with so many of our fellows without employment and the City in a scare and Egypt in a muddle!'

'Nonsense! Nonsense! You *will* look on the black side of things! I have it on the best of authority that the City is doing very well indeed. And as to Egypt, you trust Gladstone. He did the right thing in sending Gordon. You can take it from me!'

'I don't take it from you!' said Barney. 'How do you know?'

'What I always say,' said Horace, 'is that you can trust Old England. She always does the right thing in the end. I hate this pessimism. It's men like you, Barney, who do all the harm. But of course you're a novelist, live in your imagination and that sort of thing.'

'Now, Horace,' Rose interrupted, 'don't be tiresome. Barney

knows more about everything than you do. But I know something that *he* doesn't know!'

They were eager for information.

'Vanessa arrived at Hill Street this morning for a long
visit!'

'No!' cried Barney. 'Vanessa! How splendid!'

'Yes. I saw Alfred in the Park, and *he* had seen Ellis in the City.
Our dear Vanessa is with us again, and it shan't be our fault if
she doesn't stay for months.'

Phyllis nodded.

'Ellis will be glad,' she said.

'And Ellis' ma will be glad,' Rose went on. 'And I have come in
only for a moment because I am going to Hill Street to see her.'

An hour later Rose was in Hill Street.

'I will tell Miss Paris,' the butler said, leaving her alone in the
big cold drawing-room.

Old Lady Herries was now eighty years of age and spent most
of her time in bed where, rumour had it, she arranged her pearls,
rubies and diamonds on the counterpane, played games with them
and counted them over and over again. But because she was in
bed and Ellis for most of the day in the City, the house was
more like a mortuary than a living-place. The drawing-room was
decorated in mustard yellow, the curtains had heavy folds of it,
the chairs and sofas were wrapped in it. On the mantelpiece was
a clock of yellow-and-white marble. The marble statues that had
been there ever since Will Herries first bought the house glim-
mered whitely under the gas. Rose shivered.

'*What* a house! But now that Vanessa has come they will entertain again. Now that Benjie is out of the way they will think
there is hope for Ellis. Is there? Vanessa is lonely enough, poor
darling, to try anything, and she has always had a kind of maternal feeling for Ellis.'

Ellis came in.

Rose did not dislike Ellis. She thought him absurd and pathetic. She was also blind neither to his baronetcy nor to his
wealth. At one time she had thought that she might herself marry
him, but her clear common sense soon showed her that she did
not attract him in the least.

'He has no eyes for anyone but Vanessa.'

Now when he came in she was compelled to admit that he
looked distinguished, and not really his forty-two years. Or

rather he might be any age. His body was slim and erect. His closely fitting black clothes and high sharp-pointed collar gave him distinction. He was Sir Ellis Herries, Bart, all right and a ridiculous physical copy of his father. A very hideous painting of his father hung on the left side of the fireplace. Yes, ludicrously alike, but the real Ellis, Rose (who was no poor judge of character) well knew, was nervous, highly strung, sensitive, unbalanced as his father had never been.

But now as she shook hands Rose liked him, for today he was radiant with happiness. When Ellis was happy you were touched because his hold on his joy seemed so precarious. He was like a man who, to his own surprise, looks to be, for once, winning a game. In the end he will in all probability lose it, but this unusual, unexpected chance gains you to his side.

'I came in only for a moment,' Rose said. 'Alfred told me that Vanessa had arrived. I couldn't wait to see her.'

'Vanessa,' said Ellis, speaking in his precise careful voice, 'is, I am happy to say, under our roof again. She will be delighted to see you.'

'But this is splendid. None of us knew that she was coming.'

'No. *We* did not know until last week. She has been staying with Carey in Wiltshire.'

'How is she looking?'

'Oh, very well. Very well indeed. But here she is. Vanessa, my dear, here is Rose to see you.'

They flung themselves into one another's arms while Ellis stood benevolently by, stroking his chin and smiling.

'But, *dear* Rose! How sweet of you to come so soon!'

'Well, of course! But why not a line to anyone that you were coming?'

'I truly did not know, did I, Ellis? You see Carey and May quite suddenly were invited to Panshanger and they thought they should go. They wanted me to stay on until they returned, but – well, I fancied a little London gaiety.'

They sat down on the sofa together.

'And now, young ladies,' said Ellis in his best paternal fashion, 'I shall leave you. I am sure you have a great deal to talk over. Dinner at seven, Vanessa.'

'Oh Lord!' Rose cried, looking at her watch. 'And it is six now.'

'No, no,' said Vanessa eagerly. 'Come up with me when I dress. It is so *lovely* to see you. And are you not engaged yet to

Captain What's-his-name and what other gentlemen are there
and have you seen dear Barney? How is Horace? How, in fact,
are all the Herries?'

They noticed at once changes in one another, as was natural
after a year's separation. The difference that Vanessa saw in Rose
was the same difference that her grandmother had once noticed
in this same room years ago in Sylvia Herries – a slight, oh, so
very slight, fading of the natural bloom, a heightening of the
artificial colour, a little hardening of the voice, the eye a trifle
more anxious. The Scottish plaid was extremely pretty, with its
red and grey, and the little hat was a beauty – very expensive
clothes. Rose looked altogether very expensive. Upon what in
reality did she and her brother live?

And Rose saw at once that Vanessa was a girl no longer. She
was even for a moment or two afraid of her. Had she lost her?
But very soon she realized the thing that she would realize
again so often – that once Vanessa was your friend it was not easy
to lose her.

Vanessa's dress was dove-grey, her dark hair brushed back
from her forehead. Her hand caught Rose's and held it.

'Rose, I want to have *fun*! I want to see people, plenty and
plenty. I want to go to the theatre. There is Mary Anderson as
Juliet, isn't there? and Mr Wilson Barrett as Hamlet, and Gilbert
and Sullivan and Mrs John Wood. I've been studying the
papers. Lady Herries has asked May and Carey to come and stay
so that May can chaperon me. They are coming from Panshanger the day after tomorrow. I want to see everybody and do
everything.'

'And everyone wants to see you. You are much the most
beautiful woman in London. Mrs Langtry is nothing at all in
comparison.'

Vanessa smiled, very happy.

'I want to be beautiful just for a week or two – after that I
don't care in the least. I want everyone to think me lovely, to say,
"Oh, who is *that* lovely girl?" In fact, Rose dear, I want some
encouragement. I've been fighting things by myself – without any
help from anyone.'

'I know, dear, I know,' Rose said, stroking her hand. There
was something feverish, she thought, in Vanessa's tone, something unlike her natural restraint.

'Yes, Timothy and Violet have been very good to me. I'stayed
there for months in the house they've bought in Eskdale. Lovely.

Not far from the sea, with the mountains behind them. But of course I couldn't *talk* to them. And there was another thing—'

She broke off, then, holding Rose's hand more tightly, went on:

'This is something I want to say and then we will never mention it again. About Benjie. I know that everyone is against him, that they think he treated me badly, that he made a wretched mess of everything, which is what they have always hoped for. Now, Rose dear, I want you to make them understand – *all* of them – that I will not hear one word against Benjie. That I will never speak again to anyone who attacks him when I'm there. Barney is the only one I'll talk to about him. Barney is his friend, I know. Will you make them all understand that?'

'Of course,' Rose hesitated. 'Vanessa, what is it? What happened? What made him do it?'

'No, Rose, I can't tell even you. It's his affair. We don't meet. We don't write. But I understand what he did. I'm his friend, and not one word shall be said against him in my presence.'

Rose felt her hand tremble, she saw that her eyes were misty. She put her arms round her and kissed her.

'And now, Rose darling,' said Vanessa cheerfully, 'tell me about yourself? How are you? When are you to be married? That hat and costume are lovely!'

'Yes, very nice,' said Rose. 'But not paid for, my dear. Never mind me. Horace and I live in a little house in Shepherd Market. Well, to tell you the truth they are four rooms over a grocer's. We got them cheap from old Lady Martindale, who lost her money at cards and had to decamp at a moment's notice. They are the very best address and are cosy even if they are small. For the rest I have debts, and gentlemen who admire me and ladies who don't, just like any other lady – and I shall marry the first decent man who proposes to me, whoever he is.'

'And Horace?'

'Oh, Horace is getting along fast on the simple plan of refusing to know anyone save those who will be useful to him. He smiles on everyone and has a genius for not seeing those he doesn't want to see. And now, dear, let us go to your room. I am longing to know what you are going to wear.'

So they went upstairs.

Vanessa dined alone with Ellis and Miss Mabel Fortescue, the

lady who now 'ran' the Hill Street house. Miss Fortescue reminded Vanessa at once of Miss Murdstone, and she herself
would have felt not unlike David Copperfield had she not
quickly seen that the situation was serious and she must rather be
Betsey Trotwood. So from the very beginning she was firm with
Miss Fortescue. Really remarkable, her resemblance to Miss
Murdstone. She had the stiff poker back, the dark complexion
and black hair, the heavy eyebrows that nearly met over a large
nose, and Vanessa was certain that in her bedroom were the 'two
uncompromising hard black boxes, with her initials on the lids in
hard brass nails'.

Ellis thought the world of her – 'Most efficient woman, Vanessa. Excellently behaved. Knows just how to treat my mother.'
Then waking in the early morning hours to hear the London
sparrows cheep beyond the window, Vanessa discovered two
other things.

'Miss Fortescue hated me at sight. And hopes to marry
Ellis.'

The dinner was a very agreeable one: Ellis was so happy and
when he was happy he was childlike. Vanessa knew, too, that he
was happy because she was there, and it was so long since she had
been cared for in this way. Timothy and Violet took her for
granted. Aunt Jane loved her but thought her still ten years old.
So also Will Leathwaite. Carey and May were fond of her, but
liked their dogs and horses still better. She was, she discovered,
hungering for affection, and placing her foot in London had as it
were set all her world alight. That afternoon, going for a walk,
the window of a florist in Piccadilly had been ablaze with chrysanthemums; down Bond Street into Piccadilly had come the
carriages, shining in the November sun, the coachmen stout and
splendid, the horses sleek, the harness glittering, and from a distance, through the walls of the houses, the echo of a barrel-organ,
heard as it always should be, a street or two away. She had
thrown up her head and sniffed the air, sharp and horsy and
honeyed with the sun. London! She adored London! She could
manage without Cumberland, clouded with unhappy memories,
for a while. Then against this background there was first Rose,
who loved her, and now Ellis, who loved her too. Ellis was improved. He was intelligent. He talked about Gladstone and
Gordon, about the 'New Radicalism' that was interesting itself in
the conditions of housing and the happiness of the poorer classes,
about the Trades Unions, about the abolishing of the Income

Tax, about the provisions of the Electric Lighting Act, about the
Redistribution Bill, about all these serious things, sensibly, with
inside knowledge. His tact with her was extraordinary, for he was
not by nature a tactful man. He studied her without appearing
to. He was affectionate, but with the affection of a brother. She
knew of course that he loved her, but he did not embarrass her
with any implied emotion.

After dinner she went upstairs to visit Lady Herries. She saw
at once a great change in her. Some of the stories they told about
her were true, for she was sitting up in bed and on a white shawl
on her lap were rings, bracelets, and necklaces. She played with
them like a child, holding them up to the light, rubbing them
with her fingers, laying one against the other.

Nevertheless she appeared quite sensible. She was enchanted to
see Vanessa.

Her great pleasure was to talk about people. Staying in her
room as she did, she brought the world around her, speculating,
gathering stories, chuckling over scandals and foibles.

'You will find London very much changed, my dear. Money is
the only thing, getting it and losing it. If you have money you
can go anywhere. That is why London is much more amusing
and not nearly so remarkable as it used to be.'

She talked about the family.

'Alfred, Amery's boy, will make a fortune. He's in with all the
Jews. His nose gets sharper every day. Dora, old Rodney's
daughter, has such a pretty child, Cynthia. Dora married
Freddie Beauchamp. Do you remember him? A thin man with a
long nose. They live in London now, and Cynthia will marry
well. Very well, I shouldn't wonder. Then Barney has made quite
a name for himself – amusing books he writes – but he has some
very odd friends. However, that doesn't matter if he's a success.
Then Phyllis' boy, Philip – you remember him? – a little affected
but very clever. He's quite a friend of Mr Oscar Wilde. I'm glad
Carey and May are coming. Their two girls, Maud and Helen,
are *very* plain, poor things, but of course they have never done
anything but ride horses, so what can you expect? They will
improve as they grow older.'

She chattered on, moving the jewels about on the white shawl,
sometimes talking to herself:

'Now *that* won't do! If Carey and May come on Friday I must
put off Miss Blades. She comes and reads to me, my dear. A very
nice woman with the funniest stories about everyone ... I will

not have that fish three days running. I must tell Miss Fort-escue.'

Then quite unexpectedly she fell asleep, letting her head, with its tousled white hair, fall on the pillow, opening her mouth and snoring.

Vanessa soon discovered that she was to be a gathering point for all the family. They had been longing for something of the kind. Hill Street sprang to life, and Ellis was rejuvenated. May Rockage was a simple creature whose heart was in the country with her horses, her dogs, and her two girls. But she had a hearty power of enjoyment and, although she dressed badly, laughed like a man and was extremely innocent of the world, she became very quickly an excellent companion for Vanessa.

Vanessa threw herself into the family interests. Soon she knew all their secrets, their fears, their ambitions, and their odd little ways.

First of all there was Rose, who, she declared to Vanessa, was going 'the primrose path'. She had two or three gentlemen friends, a Captain Rackrent, horsy and raffish, a Mr March-banks, who was some sort of a publisher and encouraged young men to write as much like the French as possible, and a Mr Easy, who was like a Jew but said he was not one, Assyrian, purple-bearded and, Rose said, very rich. He had something to do with the Theatre. Rose said that he proposed marriage to her every week – and she added, 'One day when the bailiffs are drinking beer in the parlour – the awful thing will happen – I shall marry him.'

Cynthia, Rodney's granddaughter, was the prettiest, most fairylike creature. She at once fell down at Vanessa's feet and worshipped. Her hair was spun gold, her eyes the tenderest blue, her little figure exquisite; wearing a tiny hat perched on a golden bun, her dress gathered into loops behind her, her bosom clearly defined, she was something to make men tremble. She was sweet and tender and loving but, Vanessa thought, quite ruthlessly de-termined to make the best marriage possible. All the girls were sweet, tender, and loving, and all the girls were determined to be well married. 'You would think,' said Rose, 'to listen to these infants talk that they didn't know what men were made of. But they *do* know. They know very well indeed.'

Barney's set were writers, painters, horsy men, theatrical men, and men about town. All these men – including Barney – had feminine friends who were never obtruded. Once Vanessa, going

with Rose unexpectedly to Barney's rooms, found an elegant
creature seated on his sofa, mending his stockings. She was delightful, and most maternal to Barney. Her name was Miss
Montefiore, an actress 'resting between engagements'.

Then Vanessa was forced, against her will, to see something of
Emily Newmark. Vanessa did not like Emily, but had to confess
that she did good in the world. She was for ever 'rescuing'
people, 'unfortunate women', drunkards, young pickpockets and
foreigners – Chinamen, Negroes, lost and strayed Scandinavians.
Her only interest in people was that they could be 'rescued'. She
lectured Vanessa, patronized her, and was sometimes unexpectedly human, bursting into tears and saying that she was 'mis-
judged'.

Old Amery, tottering and bewildered, thought only of his son
Alfred. That sharp young man was always adding up figures and
subtracting them again. He came to Ellis once a week with
schemes. Ellis said that many of these were clever. Alfred would
get on.

A very odd world, too, was that of young Philip, Phyllis' boy.
The young men, Philip's friends, looked and were ridiculous, but
they lived up to their gospel. They wrote little stories, painted
little pictures, and treated all the Arts as their own especial property. They arrived from Oxford in increasing numbers. They
lisped, they languished. They thought Mr Whistler, Mr Wilde,
French poets, and the art of Japan all 'too utterly beautiful'.

In short the Herries were everywhere. Into every corner of
London life they drove their strong determined wedge of
common sense. Even Philip, with his absurdities, had common
sense. England was now at the top of the world, was at a stage of
material success and triumph that exactly suited the Herries
character. No member of the family ever boasted or wondered or
explained. They simply went everywhere, into the Beaminster
house in Portland Place, into the theatres and restaurants, into
the churches and lecture halls, into the Kensington drawing-
rooms, into the City, into the slums and did their good work. No
Herries was at the *top* of anything. No Herries (with the exception of Ellis) accumulated great wealth, cared for property,
dominated politics or the Arts or the Church or the Army. They
simply were everywhere and influenced everything.

Vanessa, however, soon discerned that her arrival was for all
of them a dramatic event. At certain times in their history a
combination of circumstances produced an Event to which all

the family, gladly and joyfully, reacted. Their hatred of the eccentric, the queer, the abnormal made them respond ecstatically to anything that allowed them to display that hatred. It had been so in the old days of the Rogue, in the quarrels about the famous Fan, in the dreadful scandal of Uhland, and now it was so in the affairs of Benjamin, Vanessa, and Ellis. Benjie was their rogue, their scapegoat. Vanessa was, at this moment, their heroine. What had happened in the North about her engagement? No one knew. Would she marry Ellis and become not only the most beautiful but also one of the richest women in London? Why had she come to Hill Street if not to marry Ellis? Her presence made that winter one of the most exciting in their lives.

And Vanessa let herself go. She was there to forget all the past. She must make a world for herself in which she could be independent – never, never would she depend on anyone again. She went everywhere, to balls and theatres and Hurlingham and concerts and immensely long, elaborate dinner parties.

She and May travelled down to Brighton in the ten o'clock Pullman, lunched at Mutton's, where Barney and Alfred joined them, watched the dowagers in the carriages, the girls in the dogcarts, the invalids in the both-chairs, the babies in the goatchaises, men on bicycles. They went on the electric railways in Madeira Road, visited the Aquarium, listened to the band in the Bird-cage and had dinner at a fine hotel. A glorious day! Brighton in November, sunshine, sea air. What an enchanting world!

Vanessa went to the House and heard Mr Gladstone speak on the Maamstrasna Murders question, and when Mr O'Connor rose and called the speech 'the lamest, weakest and most halting I have ever heard', and young Mr Stanhope shouted out, 'That's what the ferret said when the lion roared', she could have clapped her hands in her delight because that was exactly what *she* thought!

She went of course to *Romeo and Juliet* at the Lyceum and thought Mary Anderson so lovely that she never troubled about the acting. She saw Mrs John Wood in *Young Mrs Winthrop* and laughed herself into tears. When Mrs Wood meets her husband, from whom she has been divorced, they do nothing but wink! Oh, *what* a wink! In fact all London went to see this not very good little play because of Mrs Wood's wink.

She was sad when Henry Fawcett died, thrilled by what Mr Ruskin had to say to his friends at Oxford, read William Black's *Judith Shakespeare*, wanted to go to a Spiritualist meeting but could find no one to accompany her, gazed at Mrs Langtry at a party, ate oysters and pheasant, drove so often in hansoms that she thought nothing at all about it, and enjoyed Mr Corney Grain in the German Reeds' entertainment. 'Nothing,' as Emily Newmark said to her severely, 'nothing but a life of idle pleasure.'

In that winter Vanessa caught a sense of London that she was never after to lose, its smells and odours, flowers and horses and fogs, its incongruities, its shabbiness, as for instance when you passed, on the way into the Underground, the faded photographs, smirking from the wall, of old burlesque actresses, Planché's ghost hovering around them, or when in some of the smaller theatres the smell of beer, the dim rose coverings of the stalls, the dirty globes of gas, the white spots of plaster between the flaking gilt, the past, mournful, pathetic, strangled the struggling present. But everywhere and in every case London was homely – homely in the clack-clack of the horses, in the scattered rumbling of the omnibuses, in the barrel-organs and the German bands, in the sudden flashing splendour of the Guard riding up St James's from the Palace, in the gentlemen's servants taking the air, in the elegant dandies of the Row, in the melancholy street-singers, the lingering notes of the church bells, in the fogs that, yellow and sulky, crept from street to street, in the comfortable laziness of afternoon tea, in the high collar of Mr Gladstone, the radiance of the Jersey Lily, the dignity and humanity of the Prince, and, above all, in that stout little regal figure, never forgotten, sitting somewhere behind the walls of plain-faced Buckingham Palace or bird-haunted Windsor, receiving an Indian prince, being sharp with Mr Gladstone or smiling at her grandchildren. All this was London and London was all this.

One further thing that winter dominated the Town: the thought of Gordon. This great victory of common sense, this triumph of plain reality – was it threatened by that figure, fanatical, heroic, and alone, fearlessly erect among his enemies? Could it be – and it was a question forced again and again upon the Herries through all their history – that common sense was not enough, that there were other things, dangerous, mysterious things of the spirit that could spring upon you and defeat you did you too long disregard them? Is there another world with which we have refused to reckon?

After the disaster of Abu Hamed there was silence. On the day that Herbert Stewart started across the desert there was a message: 'Khartoum all right. 14.12.84. C. G. Gordon.'

After that, silence again.

On the 22nd of January, the day on which London learned of
the battle of Abu Klea, Ellis proposed to Vanessa the second
time.

They were about to go up to bed. The candles with their heavy
silver snuffers stood there waiting. May Rockage had said goodnight and started up the stairs, the great drawing-room with
its yellow hangings stayed patiently for their departure. Ellis
touched Vanessa's arm.

'Vanessa – one moment.'

She turned to him, smiling, then knew at once what he was
going to say. He was very nervous, he put his hand to his throat,
looked at her with a beseeching smile.

'I have been good, have I not? You have been happy during
these weeks here?'

'Very happy, Ellis.'

'Your presence here has been a joy to all of us. My mother has
been a different being, and I – I must tell you – I have never been
so happy in all my life before.'

'I'm very glad. You have been wonderfully good to me.'

'How could one help being? But I cannot wait any longer. I
must ask you once more. It is a long time, is it not, since the last
occasion in the Park. Vanessa, will you marry me?'

Before she could answer he went on with a trembling eager
passion that touched her and made her long to be kind to him.

'Listen. I implore you not to answer before you have thought it
over. I know how much older I am. I know that you do not love
me. But you like me. You are friendly, aren't you? I can feel that
you are friendly.'

'Of course I am friendly, Ellis. And more than that. But—'

'Well, then, that's all I ask. Indeed it is. I ask nothing more. If
you will marry me everything shall be as you wish. I know that
money makes no appeal to you, but perhaps power – the power to
do good, to help others, to put wrong things right – may mean a
little. You are so good, you have so wonderful a character, that
you *should* be able to influence your generation. I will help you
to do that – under your guidance. And we are friends. We have
known one another for a long time and surely can now trust one
another completely. Think it over, Vanessa. Do not answer me
now. Please, please not now. But think of it . . . Goodnight.'

And before she could speak he was gone

In her room that night she did indeed think of it. Ellis, during
these two months, had been so kind, so unselfish and so wise –

they had been such good friends – he had talked about so many things with so much understanding – that she had come to care for him as once would have appeared impossible. She did not love him. But with the impetuous certainty both of her youth and past events she was sure that love was over for her, would never return. Or, rather, she loved as she had always done. Benjie was as truly now in her heart as he had always been. But she must never think of him, neither now nor in any possible future time. So love being over was this not perhaps the next best thing?

Men had in these London weeks gathered round her. Two had proposed to her, and in the very moments of their proposal she had realized that the very thought of any man but Benjie in *that* world of romantic passion was fantastically unreal. Well, this was not romantic passion. But Ellis was the only one save Rose who belonged to her childhood and youth. She had known him so long that he was part of all that early life. And he wanted to be cared for, and *she* wanted, now more than anything else in the world, to bestow her care on someone.

Was it also not true that she could do good in the world with the power that his money would give her? She was still very young in many things and believed that to do good to your fellows was not so very difficult. She did not want to make them better, only to make them happy. Was this not, perhaps, her duty? She knelt down and prayed, passing as she always did into a world of comfort and security. God was more real to her than Ellis, more real to her than Benjie ... But tonight she heard no reassuring voice. She rose from her knees in a struggle of bewilderment, for, coming she knew not whence, a wildness that sometimes seized her, descended on her. She did not want to be here. Her spirit was caught away into a fantastic air of wind and rain, of streams running wildly, of clouds tearing at the turf, of the sea tossing at the foot of the hill. Her blood was not tamed. Cold January night though it was, she threw up her window and, beyond the reddened haze of the gigantic town, she saw Skiddaw's dividing lines, the serried edge of Blencathra, and within the rhythm of a solitary hansom's clatter was the whisper of the running water against the shining boulder and the bark of the dog beyond the sloping hill. She thought of Judith. She thought of her father. She thought of Will Leathwaite's slow smile.

She closed the window. No. Oh no, she *could* not marry Ellis!

*　　*　　*

A few days later came the invitation to the Duchess of Wrexe's Ball, February 18th.

This Ball had been talked of all through the winter. Very very seldom was there a big function at the Portland Place house, but when they *did* have a show – well, it *was* a show! The old Duchess must have some reason for this event. Perhaps her eldest son Richard was at last to marry. Or maybe John – or Adela. But the Duchess herself of course would not appear. Somewhere hidden in the dark confines of the Portland Place house, unseen by all save a few intimates who played cards with her, her physician and the family, she plotted and planned. This Ball was to be a protest, some people said, against the new world that she detested, the Jewish financiers, the American heiresses come to search for titled husbands, the South Americans, the Theatre, and the rest. The Ball would be exceedingly exclusive. The Prince and Princess would be present.

It was very quickly an interesting question as to who among the Herries had been invited. Quite a number – Ellis, Vanessa, Carey, May, Barney, little Cynthia and her mother. It was characteristic of the family that so soon as it was known that there would be several of them there, everyone was satisfied. There was no individual jealousy. Granted that the Herries were sufficiently represented, that was all that was necessary. There was no flavour of snobbery either. It was important that members of the family should be present because it would be for the general good of English Society. Anything anywhere was better for having a mixture of Herries in it. Barney was invited because of his friendship with Johnnie Beaminster. Little Cynthia had achieved quite a friendship with Lady Adela. Moreover, the Herries were the type of English of which the Duchess approved – not Upper Ten, of course, but good sound English stock with practically no foreign mixture. The snobbery, in fact, was *English*, not *Herries*. Barney commented on this. 'The English will always be snobs because they care about caste. But it's a fine sort of snobbery as the world is at present. Keeps the right people at the top. One day when the whole world is democratic and cares more for doing things than being them, it will all seem most ridiculous. Then England will become a third-rate Power and everyone will be happier than they've been for centuries.'

They were having an artistic hour at the Winter Exhibition of the Royal Society of Painters in Water Colours, Vanessa and Barney, Horace and Rose. Very delightful, Vanessa thought the pictures. Mr Birket Foster's grand 'West Highlands' made her feel quite sick for home, and Sir John Gilbert's 'Retreat' was splendid. Mr Watson's 'Bathers' Pool' was enchanting, and Du Maurier's 'Last Look at Whitby' so very clever. But best of all Mr Goodwin's 'Strayed Sheep', so homely and English with its cawing rooks and gentle colours.

'Oh, Horace, *do* look at the pictures! What have we come here for!'

But Horace's thoughts were on England.

'Really, Barney! England a third-rate Power! What about our Empire?' Everyone was beginning to beat on the word Empire as though it were the family gong.

'Our Empire! Who says it's ours? It's ours for the moment. One day it will be off on its own.'

'Politics are *so* tiresome,' said Rose. 'Doesn't that man over there look like the Claimant? He's been appearing at a music hall. Yes, dear, I think the pictures are sweetly pretty.' She wandered off, her arm through Vanessa's. 'Vanessa darling, do you think Ellis would lend me fifty pounds if I were to ask him?'

'Oh, Rose, I shouldn't. Can't you get it in any other way?'

'Not without being under painful obligations. Oh, do look at Horace watching the door so that if anyone useful comes in he can snatch at them!'

'Rose, dear, are you in a fix?'

'Yes, I am – about ten fixes.'

'Perhaps I can help. How much do you truly need?'

'About twelve hundred pounds. But twenty would help.'

'I think I can manage that.'

'Oh, you are good to me!' Rose was charming when she was grateful. She looked so pretty, so young, so sincere. She *was* sincere. She loved to be grateful – but to the right people.

Vanessa, thinking about this and other things, discovered that the family had come to regard her as Ellis' private conscience. When anyone wanted anything of Ellis, an opinion, an invitation, a tip from the City, Vanessa was the oracle. She could do with him, they said, anything that she liked. She knew that she could.

Then a little incident occurred. One afternoon when he had just returned from the City and they were discussing the evening plans, Ellis cut his hand. He was sharpening a pencil, the knife slipped. It was a bad gash, blood flowed, he turned ashen. She rang the bell for Buller, the butler, and helped Ellis to a chair, staunching the blood with his handkerchief, which soon was soaked. Very white, he leaned back against her, her arm around him. She thought that he would faint. Smiling very wanly he kissed her cheek. She did not move. His slender body in her arm, his confident reliance on her, his touching submission, made her feel as though he were her child. As she waited for Buller to come she thought that when Ellis depended on her for comfort she could do anything for him. At that moment she loved him. He said something, and she bent forward to catch his words. Her cheek touched his.

'I think I am going to faint.'

'Buller will be here in a moment.'

Her arm tightened about him. She just heard him sigh.

'Oh, Vanessa, how I love you!'

Then Buller came in, advancing as he always did like a churchwarden to whom the morning's money offerings had proved disappointing.

'Sir Ellis has cut his hand badly. Get brandy, Buller, and something to bandage it with.'

She sat there, with Ellis in her arms. Miss Fortescue appeared in the doorway, then hurried forward.

'Oh, Sir Ellis, what *have* you done?'

'Only a slight cut, Miss Fortescue. Buller has gone for some brandy.'

Miss Fortescue looked at them darkly.

'How that woman does hate me!' Vanessa thought.

As January drew to a close and February began there were only two topics in the London world: General Gordon and the Beaminster Ball. About the first it was said on the one side that an awful mistake had been made, on the other that exactly the right thing had been done. About the Ball it was said that it would be the grandest ever given.

On the 24th of January the steamers started up the Nile on an advance on Khartoum; on February 6th it was known that Khartoum had fallen and the relief force had been too late. Meanwhile, having satisfied himself that Khartoum was wholly in the Mahdi's hands, Sir Charles Wilson had turned his steamers and gone downstream. Then for ten days England remained in suspense. On the 16th of February a telegram was published from Wolseley saying that Gordon had been killed.

Vanessa came down to breakfast on that morning to find family prayer over and Ellis standing with *The Times* shaking in his hand.

'A crime!' he cried, with an odd shrill voice that she had never heard before. 'The most monstrous crime! Gladstone will never be forgiven for this! Never! Never! Never!'

She thought for a moment that she had to do with a madman. His pale eyes were shining, his hands jerking the newspaper as though they would tear it. They were alone, for Carey and May had not yet come down and Miss Fortescue had meals in her own fierce fastnesses.

'What is it? What has happened?'

'Gordon has been murdered! We have basely deserted him. Left the bravest Saint and Hero to go to his death alone! England will be shamed before all the world!'

'Gordon murdered! Gordon killed!'

'Yes, yes; there is the telegram!'

It seemed in thousands of homes that morning as though a veil of darkness fell over the world. Nothing could be clearer, simpler than that splendid figure, selfless, a missionary thinking only of his God, fearless; it was told of him how he had gone through all the campaign in China, his only weapon a cane, of how he had thought always of everyone but himself in the Sudan. It seemed now that the blackest treachery, the meanest political chicanery had betrayed him. There were other colours in the real picture, and it says something for the accused that, through all those weeks of almost insane vituperation, they never attempted to dim the saintliness, the courage, the selflessness. But Gordon's death was, perhaps, the first warning cloud on a horizon that had been now for a whole decade stainlessly blue.

That terrible news had also its private personal repercussions.

Ellis dropped the paper to the floor, sat down by the table, then, speaking now quietly, said:

'I feel as though I had myself betrayed him. Why do we all wait and trust to a kind of luck? Why are we all so cowardly? Vanessa, I am bitterly ashamed.'

His hand trembled against the tablecloth.

'I never thought that it would happen,' he said. 'I was afraid sometimes, but Gladstone was so sure. We have come to think that Gladstone always has God in his pocket. That they have intimate talks together and Gladstone tells God what to do. Well, this time God has not listened.'

Ellis was always best when he forgot himself. He had a kind of
almost fanatical pure-mindedness at such times. Then something
robbed him of his self-consciousness, his fears, his absurd ego-
tisms. He would now have thrown his money, his physical cowardice, his fear of offending public opinion, even his Herries
blood out of the window could he, by doing so, have saved Gordon. He had a kind of grandeur.

He and Vanessa were very close at that moment. He took her
hand.

'Oh, Vanessa!' he sighed. 'You and I – if only together we
could help it to be a better world!'

Then Carey and May came in and the world was at once a
more mundane place. After breakfast Vanessa went upstairs to
find old Lady Herries in tears.

'Oh, poor General Gordon! All alone! Such a good man!
Those savages! And Gladstone worse than any of them!'

Then as though she realized that Ellis downstairs must be very
unhappy, her last word to Vanessa was:

'Be kind to Ellis, won't you, my dear?'

We quickly forget. Two days later, although Gordon's death was
the only topic, the tragedy had become impersonal. No one any
longer thought it was possible to have died at his side. Not even
perhaps quite desirable. What *was* desirable was to have Mr
Gladstone's head on a charger.

Vanessa went to the Beaminster Ball in a turmoil of varying
emotions. There was, of course, her dress, the loveliest that she
had ever had. It was a white dress, with a red rose fastened at the
narrow waist its only ornament. The bodice fitted very tightly to
the figure. She wore long white gloves and carried a beautiful
white fan of ostrich feathers, a present from Lady Herries. Her
only ornament was a diamond brooch, bequeathed her by Judith,
fastened on her right shoulder. The effect of her dark hair and all
this cloud of dazzling whiteness was very splendid, but, Ellis
thought as he glanced at her, it was the softness of her eyes, the
charm and kindliness of her eagerness, her youth, her excitement,
her happiness that made her so brilliant, so unlike anyone else.
For tonight she *was* happy. She could have taken all London into
her arms and embraced it. Her mind was set on the future, the
life that she would make for herself, the friendliness of all the
world. She was aware of her beauty and delighted that she was
beautiful. She had never *believed* that a dress could be so marvellous a fit! She would see the Prince and Princess! How good

and kind of Ellis to give her all this happiness! She let her gloved hand rest on Ellis' coat as the carriage rolled on through the lighted streets and she heard men calling as though it were for her that they were crying some message. She sat very straight, her head forward, taking all this life into her heart and intending to give it out again with all the fullness of which she was capable. Benjie was never out of her mind, but tonight he was in the back of her consciousness. One day she would be with him again, quietly, confidently, his friend. Perhaps after all it had been for the best. This was the safer way.

They halted. They were in a stream of carriages that stretched down Portland Place. Then on either side of the red carpet was a crowd of sightseers whom a large policeman kept in order. Vanessa and May passed up the steps, into the hall. Looking up for a moment before she turned to the right to the cloakroom Vanessa saw a line of footmen in red coats and velvet knee-breeches on either side of the great staircase. Dimly she heard the echoes of the band.

As she arranged her hair before the looking-glass she heard May's whisper: 'Oh, you do look lovely, Vanessa darling!'

Ellis and Carey were waiting for them and slowly they mounted the staircase. At the top Adela Beaminster, blazing in diamonds, received them.

'Lord and Lady Rockage!'

'Sir Ellis Herries!'

'Miss Vanessa Paris!'

They passed on into the ballroom. It was one of the famous rooms in London with its white walls and gold ceiling, and on the white walls were hanging the Lelys, the Van Dycks, the other famous Beaminster portraits. The far end of the great room where the band played was banked with masses of white flowers. Although so many people were standing about there was plenty of dancing space. The roar of voices rolled in waves from wall to wall.

She stood at first with May, extremely happy, quite contented to watch. Decorations were worn, the dresses of the women were superb. How ridiculous of her to have been proud of her own! She had never seen in one place so many beautiful women. The air sparkled with diamonds. A tall thin woman near her was wearing a tiara that focused all the light to itself, that made, in truth, her plain pale face shadowed like a mask. Vanessa unfolded her fan and stood, waving it slowly, smiling as though she could never have enough of this lovely scene.

She was not, however, to be left alone for long. Soon one man came up to her and then another. During these months in London she had made many friends and was in fact very much better known than she had any idea of. A Captain Verrier, who had been sending her flowers, who had taken her and May on one occasion to Hurlingham, asked her to dance. She adored to waltz – surely there was no experience in life so perfect! He talked to her, but she answered him only in monosyllables. When the music stopped and they had moved into a long narrow room beyond the ballroom and sat down, he said to her:

'I don't think you heard a word I said when we were dancing.'

'No. I love dancing so much, it seems a pity to talk.'

'I'm sorry, because I said some very amusing things.'

'You can tell them me now, Captain Verrier.'

'You know, to look at you, Miss Paris, one would imagine that you had never been to a Ball before.'

'I never have – a Ball like this. When will the Prince and Princess come?'

'Oh, later on. About midnight, I expect.'

'And is the Duchess sitting in her room upstairs all this time?'

'Yes. Like a field-marshal. And her generals deliver dispatches.'

'I saw her once. She came to a party in Hill Street.'

'Yes. She went out for a little while some years ago. But she soon went in again. She found that her importance was lessened as soon as she became visible.'

Then he began to make love to her. Laughing, she stopped him.

'Are you asking me to marry you?'

He was embarrassed.

'Well, no, not exactly. You see—'

'I should make a very bad mistress, I am afraid. I can imagine nothing more uncomfortable.'

'Oh no. You misunderstand me. I only meant—'

'I like you very much, and I am very glad we are friends.'

'You are not offended?'

'Oh dear, no. Why should I be? Only why don't you marry? There are so many nice girls who are longing to be married—'

'Well, you see, I haven't a penny. Only my pay—'

They discussed his affairs, and Vanessa was very maternal.

After that she was dancing all the time. She found everyone delightful. Some tried to make love to her, some confided their troubles to her, some laughed and behaved like schoolboys, some were extremely pompous, one asked her to go to India with him.

'India!' she cried. 'What should I do in India?'

He was not sure, except that she would make him very happy.

Then something occurred which, on looking back afterwards, affected, she found, strongly her later behaviour that night. Barney appeared and with him a charming, shy young man.

'Vanessa,' Barney said, 'here is a cousin of yours. An unknown cousin. Be kind to him.'

The boy, who looked about nineteen, was slender and tall with fair hair and bright, ingenuous blue eyes.

'I'm not a good dancer,' he said, blushing furiously. 'Shall we sit this out? I think that you will be more comfortable that way.'

She discovered that his name was Adrian Cards and that he was at New College, Oxford. He was a younger brother of the Ruth and Richard Cards who had, years ago, been present at Judith's Hundredth Birthday. He was a great-nephew of Jennifer Cards, Benjie's grandmother.

At first he was very shy, but no one could be shy for long with Vanessa. He began to pour out his heart. He had many enthusiasms. Literature. No, he did not like the Aesthetes much. They still read Swinburne, but were not he and Tennyson a little – well, pontifical? The earlier Browning, but not these 'Inn Albums' and things. Pater, yes. The *Renaissance* was wonderful. He had met Pater. A Society called 'The Passionate Pilgrims' had invited him, and there he had sat, cross-legged, looking rather like a Chinaman. He had seen Matthew Arnold and often Jowett. You could see Miss Rhoda Broughton out walking. But he was all, she discovered, for philanthropy! Toynbee Hall, W. T. Stead. They had started a Mission in Bethnal Green that he visited. Oh, Miss Paris, he did hope that she would not think him a prig. He was not that. He rowed in his College boat. He didn't like saints, he did not wish to improve people's *souls* – no, but their *bodies*! Oh, Miss Paris! Did she *know* of the distress and unemployment? Did she realize that last month four thousand men came to the Mayor in Birmingham and asked for work, that they were starving and could scarcely stand? Had she heard of the Industrial Remuneration Conference, of all the things that

the Trades Unions were doing? There was a Mr Bernard Shaw
who had read a brilliant paper, and Mr John Burns had warned
them all of what England would be in another thirty years! He
was burning with it all, words poured from him, while the splendour and almost fantastic pageantry of the evening passed backwards and forwards in front of them.

Then he checked himself with a most charming smile.

'You have been so sympathetic! I am ashamed of my
preaching. But you are staying with Cousin Ellis, are you not? I
can't help thinking of all he might do with his money if he liked!
Can't you influence him, Miss Paris?'

'Don't call me Miss Paris,' she said. 'We are cousins, you
know. My name is Vanessa.'

'Oh, thank you. And *my* name is Adrian.'

'Yes, Barney told me.'

'Cannot you influence him? The things he could do! If only
you could persuade him just once to go to Bethnal Green.'

She told him that she had very little influence with anyone.

'Someone as beautiful as you are must have influence! Oh, I
beg your pardon! Have I been impertinent?' He broke off and
then with the same eagerness he asked her about Cumberland. He
had never been there. Ruth had told him how lovely it was! She
often spoke of Madame. What a marvellous old lady she must
have been! And how sad that the house at Uldale had been burnt
down!

'Oh, your father——' He was always rushing in and then out
again!

'No, I like to talk of my father. He was the best man who ever
lived!' She began to tell him things about Adam and Cat Bells
and Uldale. She told him about Hesket and Caldbeck, of John
Peel and the Herdwick sheep and the best-cured hams in the
world. They had there the largest water-wheel and the smallest
parish in England. Of the grand old farmers and their splendid
ploughing, of an old lady she knew who had eighteen children
and was ninety today, of how if you asked an old ploughman,
strong as the horse he was leading, how old he was, he'd say 'Ah's
nobbut eighty!' of how they would sing 'Old Towler' under the
fellside, of Tom Pearson, the wrestler, who could dance a better
step-dance than any woman, of the 'Ivinson' grey tweed, the
strongest in the world – and, as she talked, all Skiddaw broke into
the London house, clouds came down over the gold ceiling, and
the bleating of the sheep was louder than the band!

She had missed a dance with someone or other. She rose and held out her hand.

'You'll come and see me, Adrian? Come tomorrow to Hill Street, tea time.'

'Yes, I will,' he said fervently.

But when she was dancing again she knew that something had happened to her. The wildness was upon her again, but now it was full of fear and warning. She must not return to Cumberland! She must make her life in another fashion. Where Benjie was, danger lay. That boy was right. It was being shown to her clearly that, at the side of Ellis she should help the world. The two of them together – what could they not do? Ellis had told her that he was waiting for her to help him. Already in these weeks in London they had grown close together. At the thought of all they could do for the world her cheeks burned, her heart beat high.

She had been living without any thought of all the unhappiness, the poverty! The things that Ellis and she might do together! ...

There was a pause. Everyone moved to the right and left. The Prince and Princess had arrived.

They walked up the room, bowing and smiling, stopping once and again to speak to a friend, while the women curtsied and the band blared. It was a glorious moment. He looked so kindly and she so beautiful. England was safe for ever and ever: the peoples of the world were bowing. A hero had died for his country in the Sudan. Here and there were a ruffian or two to be taught their place and duty! The Beaminster portraits smiled down their loyalty and patriotism, the jewels blazed, England lay like a cloak at the royal feet, and the Empire did obeisance.

'Oh! to do something splendid!' Vanessa's heart cried.

It was Ellis who took her in to supper. He was quiet, stealing glances at her once and again. She seemed to be carried high on some wave of exaltation. She looked at him so kindly that when they moved away and sat down together in a distant corner where from the hall below they could hear them summoning the carriages, he said, now for the third time:

'Vanessa, will you marry me?'

She, staring beyond him into an imagined world, nodded her head, saying:

'Yes, Ellis dear – if you want me.'

Part Two

The Husband

JUBILEE

EARLY IN JUNE of the great year 1887 Ellis and Vanessa went one evening to hear Albani in *Lucia* and, waiting in the portico of the Opera House, were caught by a breeze that, in spite of the warm evening, made Ellis its victim.

In the following days he paid no attention to his chill, sternly from morn to eve pursuing his City adventures. On the eighteenth of June there was a grand party in Hill Street, a Jubilee party, with Royalty and Colonel Cody. Next day Ellis was threatened with pneumonia. On the morning of the supreme Tuesday he was as hopelessly a prisoner as any poor wretch in Vine Street.

It was a tragedy. Ellis and Vanessa had seats in the Abbey; for months Ellis had looked forward and, in his odd way, half child, half man of importance, he had come to feel (as perhaps many other Herries were feeling) that the Jubilee was created only that he should sit with the loveliest woman in London and give his approbation to his Queen's Thanksgiving.

He lay there, his cheeks mottled, his nose sharp and white, his thin body stretched like a corpse, his eyes rheumy with cold and bitter disappointment. Vanessa refused to go to the Abbey without him. She would watch the Procession from Piccadilly with Rose and Barney and young Adrian. When she came in to say goodbye she felt so vividly his own bitterness that she cried: 'Ellis, I won't go. I'll stay here with you. Rose will tell me all about it, and besides the heat is fearful or will be soon. Ellis, I'll stay.'

He longed to agree that she should. He would not miss it so grievously if she also missed it, and the thought that she had given this up for him would be a salve to that intolerable unceasing doubt, the doubt that she loved him.

But he was not so selfish; no, no, he was not so selfish. So, in a voice thick with cold, drawing the bedclothes close to his chin, he murmured: 'Absurd! How absurd you are, my darling! You had better not kiss me. Go and enjoy yourself!'

He knew that when she was gone he would repeat to himself again and again: 'She offered to stay. One word from me and she would have stayed.'

How beautiful she was! He watched her hungrily. Her dress with its full bustle, rose-coloured, fitted her tall graceful body with exquisite symmetry. No woman in London wore clothes as Vanessa did; the little hat, perched on her dark hair, was wreathed with rosebuds. The parasol that she carried was rose. Two roses, dark and rich like the summer weather, were at her waist. She was a Queen, he thought. Had we gone to the Abbey she would have been lovelier than any other woman there. 'The beautiful Lady Herries ...' and he would have been with her, the proudest man in England.

'Give me some more of those drops, dear, before you go.'

She thought the big bare room chill and stuffy. Beyond the window the sun blazed on the street; very faintly from the far distance came the sound of a band. She could see a flag gently moving in the morning breeze from an opposite house. She was all impatience to be gone. She might be a grand lady now who must never forget her dignity, but for nothing at all she would dance down Hill Street waving her parasol. How terrible had he said: 'Yes, dear. Remain!' How terrible not to see the kings and the princes, not to hear the blare of the bands, not to see the colour and the excited happy faces of the people, not to wave to the Queen! She was so sorry for his disappointment that tears filled her eyes as she smoothed his thin hair with her hand, straightened the bedclothes, laid the books and *The Times* close to him! How old he looked when he was ill! How old and how at the same time like an ugly disappointed little boy! How near and how intimate to him she was, and how far away and separate! How kind and tender she wished to be to him! And how her very heart contracted in her breast when he made love to her! How grateful for all his kindness, how deeply irritated, against her will, by his unceasing care of her!

She sat in the chair beside his bed, holding his hot dry hand.

'You will take care not to be in the sun.'

'Oh yes, there is a large awning over our stand.'

He was moved by a sudden spasm of irritation and kicked up his knees beneath the bedclothes.

'It is too bad. It is really too bad. To happen just now! In another week I could have gone!'

'I know, I know, dear. Oh, why did we go to that silly Opera? ... Ellis, let me stay! I'll go with Rose this evening and see the illuminations ... After all it is going to be so hot, most uncomfortable, I expect, and a procession is always so quickly over ...'

He sighed. How wonderful if it had been she who was ill and he had been given the opportunity of sacrificing himself! At once he was ashamed of such a thought. His love for Vanessa prompted him to strange wicked desires. He who would give her anything in the world, to wish anything so wicked! He choked, coughed, drank a little water, smiled with wan bravery.

'What you must think me! As though I could be so selfish! Enjoy yourself, my dearest, and tell me about it . . .'

He picked up Walter Besant's novel, laid it pathetically on the bedclothes. 'I shall count the minutes until your return.'

Afterwards in the sun and splendour she felt as though she had escaped, by a miracle, from prison.

Early though it was, the streets were thronged and the stands already crowded, but she had only to slip down Berkeley Square and in at a back door, be conducted by an extremely polite young footman through a drawing-room and so out to the stand where Rose already was.

When she settled herself and looked about her she uttered a cry of childlike delight. The sky was an unbroken blue, the full green of the trees of the Green Park was soft and deep and luminous like a sunlit cloud. From her seat she could watch the hovering flutter of the flags, the massed colour of clothes, the splashes of scarlet that broke the pearl-grey of the London stone. All this colour was translated by the sunlight into something trembling and unsubstantial as though lit by some unseen fire. There was a brooding silence scored like a sheet of music with the clatter of a horse's hoofs, the echo of distant band music rising and falling on the slight morning breeze. Above the buildings flags drifted against the blue as though under the impulse of some secret rhythm. The front of the stand was banked with flowers.

She sat there, her gloved hands clasped, her lips parted, her eyes shining. At that moment, if she had been ordered, she would have died for her country, for the Queen, for any cause that needed her. For a very little thing she would have burst into tears.

Rose, who looked very exotic with her dark colour, her red dress, was as deeply excited as Vanessa.

'This is all very foolish,' she said. 'By this afternoon I shall be ashamed of myself. No matter, I like being ashamed of myself.'

Rose read from her programme:

Her Majesty will be accompanied on horseback by the

following Princes placed in the order of their relationship to Her Majesty:

Grandsons and Grandsons-in-Law of Her Majesty

HIH the Grand Duke Serge of Russia	HRH the Prince Albert Victor of Wales, KG	HRH the Prince William of Prussia, KG
HRH the Prince Henry of Prussia, GCB	HRH the Prince George of Wales, KG	HRH the Hereditary Grand Duke of Hesse
His Highness the Hereditary Prince of Saxe-Meiningen	His Highness the Prince Christian Victor of Schleswig-Holstein	His Serene Highness the Prince Louis of Battenberg, KCB

Sons-in-Law of Her Majesty

HRH the Prince Christian of Schleswig-Holstein, KG	His Imperial and Royal Highness the Crown Prince of Germany, KG	HRH the Grand Duke of Hesse, KG

Sons of Her Majesty

HRH the Duke of Connaught and Strathearn, KG	HRH The Prince of Wales, KG	HRH the Duke of Edinburgh, KG

She talked without ceasing, waving her hands, half rising from her seat, turning to look for friends. Did Vanessa know that people were paying twenty-five pounds for a good place? That nearly three hundred books of gold leaf had been used for decorating the State Coach, that there was still living a survivor of George III's Jubilee, an old lady in Gloucestershire, that the Pope is so pleased at the Jubilee that he wants England to re-establish relations with the Vatican, that so much gas was to be used in the illuminations, that? . . .

She said:

'Oh, Vanessa, I am so happy!'

She caught Vanessa's hand, then drew away again whispering:

'No, I won't spoil your fun. Don't listen to me. It isn't true. I'm too excited to know what I am saying.'

Vanessa turned to her.

'Rose, what has happened? What have you done?'

'Nothing. Nothing. I didn't mean what I said.' Then abruptly again she broke out:

'You know that Horace is engaged?'

'No. When? To whom?'

'A few nights ago – at the Ball at the Reform Club. A Miss Lindsay. A nice little girl. With money of course, And he will treat her abominably.'

'You'll be alone, Rose. You won't like that even though Horace isn't the most—'

'No. Yes. Well, perhaps.'

'Rose, you are going to do something foolish. What is it? Tell me. I insist on your telling me.'

Their lives had been bound together. Ever since that day of Judith's Hundredth Birthday when Vanessa, looking across the luncheon table, had seen her, wanted her for a friend, loved her, there had been a bond which Rose's recklessness, her risks and mistakes and gradual descent from safety into danger, had only strengthened.

'Vanessa, you will always love me, always, always, whatever I do?'

So also Benjie had claimed. She had fulfilled her promise. She laid her hand on Rose's arm.

'Rose, don't do anything without telling me. You must not. It is not fair to me. We have been friends so long and have helped one another so often. Promise me! Promise me!'

'Look! There is someone riding up the street. He is seeing that everything is clear. Doesn't he look grand with his feathers?'

'Rose, tell me. What are you doing? Not Fred Wycherley? You told me—'

'Vanessa, darling – it is all right. Really it is. I was excited. I'm always doing something silly. Look! how the stands are filling up! Why don't Barney and Adrian come? They are missing everything—'

'But it isn't Wycherley? Promise me that it isn't Wycherley – with his wife and those two children—'

'No, of course it isn't Fred. Oh, do look at that woman in that bonnet! There, to the right! Did you ever *see* such a thing?'

At that moment Barney and Adrian Cards arrived.

Adrian, who, young as he was, was now in the Foreign Office, who wrote articles for the magazines on religion, economics, French poetry, who loved Vanessa with such open devotion that everyone thought it charming, sat on one side of her, Barney, who was now very stout, on the other.

'Here we are!' said Barney. 'I have just seen Timothy and Violet and their offspring.' (Timothy had brought his family with him permanently to London.)

'I have also seen Phyllis and Rochester struggling for breath in Northumberland Avenue, Amery, son Alfred, and the new plain wife nestling under the lions in Trafalgar Square, so I have not done so badly by the family. How is poor Ellis?'

'Oh, Barney,' said Vanessa, 'he was crying with disappointment. He had been *so* looking forward—'

'Yes. It's a shame. Poor Ellis.' But he was not thinking of poor Ellis as he leant his fat body forward and drank in delightedly the scene, except perhaps, without any unkindness, to relish his own fun the more because Ellis' catastrophe made him realize that he too might have caught a cold and been prevented. He pushed out his chest, stretched his stout arms a little, wondered how little Daisy McPhail (the present lady of his apartments) was getting on somewhere along the Mall (he had loved her now for three months and still found her good company), considered (as all novelists consider) whether he would be able to describe this heat, colour, movement, expectation on paper, looked at Vanessa and marvelled yet once again at her beauty ('But this life with Ellis is telling on her, and I don't wonder'); leaned yet farther forward to gaze down Piccadilly and saw, a little to the right, only a row or two away, Benjamin Herries.

'By Heaven—'

'What is it?' Rose asked – and he could feel that she was trembling with some agitation deeper than any Jubilee warranted.

'Nothing.' He had pulled himself in. 'Only that everything is so jolly. *What* a day! Doesn't that old lady have luck with her weather?' (*Was* it Benjie? Yes, certainly. He had half turned. He had seen then.) Barney suddenly was assured that Benjie had seen Vanessa from the moment of her first entry. The little man, square-backed, brown as a berry, in some fashion independent, alone like a hill-man who had come down to study for a moment, the people of the plain, sat erect, his chin resting on the handle of his stick, the most significant thing about him his living, questing, eager eyes.

'A bandit!' Barney thought. 'For tuppence he'd hold a gun at the lot of us!'

Benjie half turned again and gave Barney a nod, slight, humorous, secret.

'His eye never leaves Vanessa. But Vanessa must not see him. Lucky that Ellis is locked away in Hill Street!'

And again, like any novelist, he considered that here was a situation, old and hackneyed though it might be, that would make a chapter or two: Benjie, Ellis, Vanessa – all of them so much more real than anything that Barney could do on paper. And he summed up for judgement the half-written efforts of his present work, *Julia Paddock* ... Poor thing, how she wilted and died before the sharp indifference of actual life!

'Look here, Adrian, change places with me, will you? I'm a bit deaf in this right ear. Creeping senility, you know.'

They changed places, Adrian seated now between Vanessa and Rose. Barney's broad body would, with decent luck, hide Benjie from Vanessa.

Young Adrian talked of the People's Palace which Besant's *All Sorts and Conditions of Men* had started as popular philanthropy. Vanessa was on a Committee. Mr Besant had come to tea in Hill Street. A nice, booming, self-confident, bustling kind of man.

'Oh, don't let's think of committees!' cried Vanessa. 'This is so much nicer. I'm not very good at committees, Adrian. My thoughts wander.'

He was only twenty-two years of age, and Vanessa was the love of his whole life. He had the imagination of the abnormal, but with it the common sense and balance of the normal. He was, in fact, closer to Will and Ellis and Timothy and old Pomfret than to Francis and John and Adam. He would never commit suicide nor dream his life away. His philanthropy, idealism, poetry, would be practical, definite things. He was the straight, normal Herries at its best. So, looking at Vanessa, he worshipped her without any thought of contact. She was the greatest lady he would ever know, the kindest, the loveliest. And how glorious to be beside her today when she was like a child in her pleasure! He had seen her of late so often as the hostess sitting at the end of her table at those endless dinner parties in Hill Street, curtsying to Royalty, talking to Ambassadors, moving down the room with all eyes upon her ... Now, for an hour, she was close to him, friend with friend. Not that she was ever affected or grand. The world in which for two years now she had moved had not touched her, but, as he had often noticed, when Ellis was not there, she was free, spontaneous, self-forgetful ...

'Oh! they are coming!' she cried. 'They are coming! I can hear the bands!'

Distant music broke across the heat and light as though some-where a door had opened. All individuality was lost; colours, blue, crimson, green, hung like painted cloths about an empty room, for here in the sunlight there was a bare space which only one figure could fill. The empty room waited for that entrance; the door would be opened and soon, for the briefest instant, a small stout old lady would be borne forward, would stay for a moment, looking about her while the colour, the music, the sun-light made a canopy over her; then, with a little bow, she would retire and all would be ended. A bell would ring, a trumpet blare, the door would close.

A kind of sanctification fell upon those people. They turned, their eyes straining down that long pathway between the banks of colour, a pathway so oddly bare. There was a fear of a last in-stant's frustration. Would a thunderbolt fall, the final trumpets for Judgement sound, and so – after the agonized anticipation – that royal carriage with the little bowing figure never appear? The sky, the trees, the flags, the splashes of crimson, all a painted prepared pattern for that instant of completion that even yet might not occur. Vanessa, looking upwards for a moment, saw three birds, dark and remote, slowly fly across the blue. At the sight of the first advancing soldier, glittering in the sun, his black horse moving with dignified austerity, she turned to Barney and whispered:

'My father met my mother for the first time on the Queen's Coronation Day.'

She wanted to evoke Adam. She wanted him there with his kind, sleepy smile and that touch of his hand on her arm ... Then she forgot everything but the Procession. Thicker and thicker they came. The pathway that had been so bare sparkled now with silver and gold. She was drawn down into a medley of colours, sounds, and, pressing close upon her, that clear clop-clop of the horses' hoofs like the ringing of little hammers on stone. Men were detached from the river of movement; a figure, the back straight as a board, the thighs stiff, one gauntleted hand raised, would become real against fantasy. You believed suddenly that it breathed, it touched its bearded cheek with its gauntlet: the rider and the horse stood out above the flood as though the trumpets had summoned it. The three Kings were in closed car-riages – very disappointing of them. The cheering increased. Now, glittering with gold, an open carriage could be seen, and then, in an instant, the air broke into cheering, the caparisoned horses, the outriders, the scarlet and the gold swung into being before the green clouded trees. The Queen, her parasol raised, in a dress of black and white, passed by. One horseman, in a silver helmet and shining cuirass, seemed her especial guardian – the Crown Prince of Germany. The door closed.

'Oh!' said Vanessa. 'How lovely that was!'

The soldiers were still marching, the drums and trumpets sounding, but the ordinary real world had assumed its place again. She heard someone behind her say: 'The twenty-sixth, remember. I'll have the carriage and we'll go straight down.'

She sat there watching for a while, happy, tranquil, remembering things to tell Ellis, suddenly thinking of Will Leathwaite in the cottage on Cat Bells. He would be going out that evening to see the bonfires and he would think of her as he always did when anything of interest happened.

'Didn't you love that, Rose? Didn't you think her splendid?'

But Rose was gone. How strange!

'Adrian, did you see Rose go?'

'Yes, she slipped away just after the Queen passed. She didn't want to disturb you.'

'Oh, I wanted to tell her—' Vanessa looked back to see whether she might yet catch her. People were rising, moving about, already many seats were empty.

Then, turning to the right, looking over Barney's head, she saw Benjie.

He was staring at her, standing up in his place. They looked at one another. He raised his hat, bowed, gave her one more long stare; then, turning his back, climbed up the wooden benches and disappeared.

She had invited Barney and Adrian to luncheon and they returned to the house with her, but, before she joined them, before she went in to see Ellis, she stood, without moving, in the middle of the floor of her bedroom, gazing in front of her. She had but a moment. Ellis, in the next room, knew that she had returned but, with the sunlight streaming about her, still wearing her hat and gloves, she stayed there, lost.

Benjie! She had not seen him for close on four years, but in that momentary glance it had been as it had always been. They had not separated. They *could* not separate. Marriage altered nothing, distance altered nothing; she must confess to herself what indeed she had never denied – that Benjie and herself could not be parted. He had looked as he always looked. His London clothes, his tall hat and dark coat could not change him, his apartness, his humorous defiance, his challenge to the world. He had been, apparently, alone. Had he been aware of her for a long while? Had he intended to speak to her? Was he staying in London? Was he here permanently, perhaps with his wife and boy? Or had he parted from his wife? Or was he on his way abroad? How strange that out of all the thousands who had watched the Procession they two should have been so close together. He could not have known where she would sit. Or had he perhaps met Barney the day before and asked him? Would he call at Hill Street or would he keep his part of their bargain? During these four years he had never written to her, nor sent a message. As she took off her hat and slowly drew off her gloves she knew that she would at that moment give everything – name, reputation, happiness – for one word with him.

Her body shivered. She knelt down for an instant beside her bed, pressing her hands against her eyes. Oh, how she wished that she had not seen him! Oh, how glad, how glad she was that she had! The sunlight fell hot upon her head like a caress. She bathed her face and hands and went through into Ellis' room.

Ellis lay there, his long hands with their prominent knuckles on the counterpane, and he looked at her steadily, following her with his eyes as she moved as a painted portrait does.

She came to the bed, sat down, took his hand and began to tell him all about everything. 'The colour, Ellis! You can't imagine it! The trees of the Park made everything so much brighter, and then the splashes of scarlet and the grey buildings and all the flowers. We had beautiful places, better than the Abbey. We could see both ways down Piccadilly and had a view of the Queen's carriage for ever so long. Rose was there. She was rather restless. I do hope she isn't getting into trouble again. And Barney and Adrian. Barney is really disgracefully fat. He said he'd seen Timothy and Violet and Amery and his son.'

'Did you see anyone else you knew?'

She realized at once that Ellis was hostile, that something had happened here in her absence. *Had* Benjie called? Had he written? Had Barney been up to see Ellis already and told him? Oh, but he would not! That was not Barney's way. Had someone else seen Benjie about London and told Ellis? Since their marriage Ellis had never uttered Benjie's name ...

She answered quickly:

'No one to speak to. We left before the Procession was over to escape the crowd. And we did. The Square was quite empty. Not a soul about. But the crush in the streets was dreadful, and what the heat must have been . . .'

He interrupted in that small cold voice always used by him when he was offended (he was very proud of it: he thought it was calculated to strike terror into any heart).

'Some letters came for you while you were away.'

So that was it! There was a letter for her in some hand that he suspected. She had noticed of late that he looked at the writing on the envelopes of her letters with an eager curiosity which he always thought that he hid.

'Miss Fortescue brought them in,' he went on. 'She thought that you were still here.'

('She *knew* that I was *not* here,' Vanessa thought indignantly.)

The letters were in a little pile on a table near the door. She went across, picked them up, then turned and smiled at Ellis. 'Well,' she said, 'what has disturbed you, Ellis? Something has made you unhappy.'

He said at once, his voice shaking:

'One of those letters is from Benjamin Herries.'

(Was it so? Then he had written to tell her that he was coming to London? He had written to make an appointment?)

She looked quickly. There was no letter from Benjie. One, in a man's hand, was from Keswick, but, as she knew at once, it was from a Doctor Harris there who had written asking if she would subscribe to some sports to be held in August at Threlkeld. She did not dare even glimpse at her own fierce disappointment. She was *not* disappointed. It was *much* better that Benjie should not write, should never write, never see her, never speak to her . . .

She came quietly to the bedside and gave Ellis the letter.

'There is nothing from Benjie. This, I suppose, is the letter you meant. Read it.'

He looked quickly at the letters, then pushed them towards her.

'No, no. Of course I will not read them. I am very ashamed. Please, please forgive me. If you knew how I have been suffering!'

'It has done your cold good anyway,' she thought, 'having something else to think about.'

Her anger and indignation, of which she was always afraid

because they were so strong when they were aroused, stirred in her eyes. She did not ask herself whether her disappointment assisted her anger.

'Please read them, Ellis, if you want to. I have no secrets from you whatever.' (Had she not?)

He looked up at her abjectly, a look that she detested, in human beings, in animals, in anyone or anything that should have pride.

'Please, please forgive me. The handwriting was like. I thought that he might be coming to London for the Jubilee. I have been lying here all these hours longing for you . . . You are so beautiful today . . . I love you so terribly. I cannot grow used to it. I used to think that in time it would become part of life, ordinary, but it does not. It is stronger every day because it is never satisfied. It is not your fault. But you don't love me. You never loved me.'

That was just. That was true. At once she felt tender towards him because of that injustice. He was like a small son who had asked for a present that she could not give him, and so she put her arms around him and comforted him. She sat down beside him and took his hand again.

'Ellis, dear, we all care for one another in different ways. That is everybody's trouble. I think perhaps I am not passionate in the way you mean. Many women are not. But we are such splendid friends. More every day. Let us be thankful for that. And don't begin to suspect things. Let's trust one another. If we do not we shall torture one another. We have been married for over two years and have trusted one another perfectly. Ask me always if anything makes you uneasy; suspicion in marriage is horrible. It's worthy of neither of us.'

He moved towards her, put his thin arms round her, laid his head on her breast.

'Love me! Love me! Love me!'

She tried to comfort him; her relief when at last he moved away made her feel ashamed. Today something new had entered their married life, something not quite new. Rather a forgotten acquaintance who unexpectedly arrives and says that now, from henceforth, he will live in the house.

She kissed him and stood up.

'I must go down to Barney and Adrian. They are waiting for luncheon. I will come up afterwards.'

He lay staring at the door long after she had left the room.

*   *   *

And even then this day was not done with her. When Adrian and
Barney were gone she went upstairs again and read Besant's
novel aloud until Ellis slept. Then she went down to the drawing-room. She had done what she could with it. There was a
portrait of her by Whistler in a white dress standing against a
dull gold wallpaper, holding a fan. She had not filled the room
with odds and ends as many of her friends liked to do. It had
now a silver-grey wallpaper, there were many flowers about,
there was a deep purple Persian carpet, but the place was not
alive. It would never live, it would never be home to her. The two
tall windows were open – a pale blue light shadowed the houses.
The sky was pale with the evening heat. There was holiday everywhere, shouts and cries, distant bands, and the flags moving
lazily in the gentle summer breeze. There was that scent of burning that a very hot day in London leaves behind it, and the odour
of flowers, roses, carnations, and the dry dusty fragrance of
geranium leaves. She turned back into the long dusky room that
was like a cool deserted cave. She walked up and down, knowing
that life, after two years of comparative quiescence, had in a
moment taken another turn. Everything from this hour was
different. Tonight there was to be a family dinner party. Ellis had
insisted that his illness should make no change. Rose and Horace,
Phyllis, Clarence Rochester and Philip, Barney, Amery and his
son and new daughter-in-law, Timothy and Violet and Aunt
Jane, Carey and May Rockage, pretty Cynthia, Rodney's granddaughter, and her husband Peile Worcester, Adrian ... they
were all coming. No one but the Family. What an odd mixed lot
they were, and yet how alike – even the wives of other stock.
They moved forward in one body, not to the outer world important and yet affecting the world by their quiet insistence on normality, confidence, the domestic virtues, patriotism, deep
suspicion of the foreigner, belief in the Church, Tennyson, the
Houses of Parliament, the Royal Family (with reservations about
the Prince of Wales, Barney's mistresses, Rose's reputation, Jews
– unless they were very rich – and one or two things more).

They had been very kindly to Vanessa. Old Lady Herries
before she died last year had said: 'My dear, never fight the
family. I know you often want to, but it isn't worth it. They
always win in the end.'

But did they? Had not Judith defeated them, and Uhland
even her own father? The battle continued. She had not, herself,
surrendered. And Benjie? Oh, *where* was he? Was he quite close

to her somewhere in London? She had the maddest impulse to go
to Barney's rooms in Duke Street. He would know, she was sure.
She went to the door, opened it, and listened. The house was as
still as the inside of a drum. Only the beating of her heart seemed
to thud down the passages. Then there was something else.
Someone was coming up the stairs.

She went back into the drawing-room with the wildest
thought that it might be Benjie. What would she do? How could
she defend both herself and him? She stood, one hand pressed to
her breast, staring at the door. But, when it opened, it was Finch,
the new butler, a man she did not like because she was sure that
he was in league with Miss Fortescue, a fat red-faced man with
sandy hair.

He had a note on the salver.

'A letter for you, my lady. A boy has just left it. He said that
he was told that there was no answer.'

She saw at once that it was in Rose's hand, and as soon as Finch
was gone, opened it, reading it there where she stood.

> DEAREST – I could not tell you this morning. I went to the
> Procession with a wild hope that something would occur, that
> I should break a leg or be strangled by the crowd. Nothing *did*
> occur, so by the time that you get this I shall be on my way to
> France with Fred. Insane. I know it. I think that we both of us
> know it. But I would not care if it were not for you. But you
> said that you would love me whatever I did. Remember – your
> love is all that I shall have in a year's time.
>
> ROSE

The note fell from her hand to the ground. She bent down and
picked it up. A foreboding, dusky and cold like the room, crept
to her side and touched her hand.

THE FLITTING

BENJIE HERRIES, a week or two after Jubilee Day, walked up
the hill on a lovely summer evening towards the Fortress. He had
been playing cricket with the young men of Ireby village. On his
shoulder he was carrying his son Tom, aged three years, and

beside him was Bob Rantwood, a famous poacher, drunkard and ne'er-do-well, one of Benjie's best friends. A sunny haze covered all the world. In the village there had been much motion, the long wagon drawn by its splendid team of horses, the chatter at the little inn with its coloured prints, its gay pictures of hunters and horses, and a grand flower-and-fruit piece that was the landlord's especial joy, left there by some travellers to pay a debt more than a hundred years ago, the flagged passage, and beyond the bottle-green windows the clear blue of the summer sky. Mrs Enderby's shop with the liquorice, bull's-eyes, bootlaces and a portrait of the Prince of Wales, the long fields rising to the grey hills, the deep oaks, the bleatings of sheep, the brilliant leaves of the copper beech, the scent of clover and bean blossom.

He was at peace and not at peace; he had enjoyed the game, the comradeship (for they liked him), the taste and sound of Cumbrian air and soil, but Rantwood unsettled him. He had poached with him many a time, knew all about salmon and trout poaching, the 'draughting' and 'poling'. Lovely nights he had had with Rantwood draughting a river, or, by himself, guiding his poles, knowing exactly where there is a spile or a crook. The thrill, in mild weather, to find a spot where the fish are spawning, or on a dark night to see the dawn steal over the fan-shaped hill, to hear the moorhen plunge! Or, draughting with Rantwood, trailing the net slowly down the river, stoning the water to frighten the salmon into the net – or best of all on a moonlight night, when an old coat had been soaked with paraffin, the thrill of the moment when this improvised torch is lit and the men with him, sticks in hand, plunge into the water . . .

Rantwood, like most poachers, was a discontented, cursing, but most amiable fellow. Nothing was ever right with him. He would swear at the game laws by the hour together, 'gloweran' aboot' like a madman, and then he would laugh, throw his thick arms around, and call Benjie, for whom he had warm friendship but no reverence, 'thoo girt daft cauf, thoo'.

He was always restless, always wanting to be somewhere where he was not – and so was Benjie. But Benjie knew what was now the matter with him. He should not have gone to London, should not have seen Vanessa . . .

Three days he had stayed there. He had not especially enjoyed his visit although he had done all the things that would, he thought, amuse him. He had visited Earl's Court and seen 'Buffalo Bill' Cody's Wild West Show, had travelled on the

Underground Railway and been stifled by the sulphur and smoke from the engine, the fumes from the oil lamp, the reeking pipes of his fellow-travellers. He had visited the Gaiety Bar and talked to the magnificent ladies who served him, had spent several hours in the Argyle Music Hall, admired the Chairman who with such militant authority banged the table with his gavel, and wondered at the amount of liquor he could consume.

He had wandered the streets and like any country yokel stared at the illuminations, had watched London Society display its elegance in Hyde Park, had been pleased with the superb procession of curricles, landaus, victorias, the powdered footmen, the silk stockings, the yellow plush; had found a beautiful lady at the Alhambra, gone with her to her room in Portland Street, but once there, after half an hour's most elegant conversation, had politely left her. He had been, in fact, the loneliest of men. That seat from which he had viewed the Procession (a pretty penny he had paid for it!) had been his ruin. He had gone to London on a sudden impulse, resolving to visit no member of the family. It had been the cruellest fate (the kind of check to his virtue that fate was for ever dealing out to him) that Vanessa should be sitting there almost at his side! For two hours he had watched her. Every detail of her dress, every movement had been absorbed by him. It was not her loveliness that had struck him to the heart, but his intimacy with her so that he knew instantly, at the first sight of her, that nothing was altered, that his four years' exile from her had hindered nothing.

He had made no attempt to speak to her. Weak, irresolute as he was, he would keep his word – at least, for a little longer. But he returned to Cumberland a haunted man.

He shifted young Tom a little, liking to feel the warmth of those small confident fingers against his neck. A funny freak of chance that Tom should have in him some kindred blood with the second wife of Vanessa's great-grandfather. After Vanessa he loved Tom – the only two in the world whom he loved.

'All the family have cleared out of the country,' he said aloud, following his thoughts. 'I'm the last here. We were all over the County a while ago.'

'Aye,' said Rantwood, who was pursuing his own thoughts. Would Herries ask him in for a drink? He had a thirst all right. But Mrs Herries – she didn't like him. Nor he her – whimsey-whumsey kind of female.

'My great-great-grandfather rode into Keswick one night from

Doncaster. That's how it all started. We were all over the place once. Oh, I've told you before. And now we're all away again.' He looked over the hedge down the valley where the summer evening breathed tranquilly under a stainless sky. Around them the insects were humming and on the other side of the hedge a brook sang beneath the willows. Voices cried through the stillness with a dying fall. As though he spoke aloud: 'I am walking up this hill and soon I will be gone. I have done my best. I have kept my vow, but soon I shall be wandering again. I can neither be free of this country nor settle in it, and when I am away I shall remember just such an evening as this, the meadow falling into dusk, and all the names that I love – Blencathra, Uldale (almost all the bricks of the house are gone now: soon there will be nothing but the turf and the sheep cropping it), Bassenthwaite, Ireby – beautiful names like the words of a vow, a vow that I have kept but can keep no longer. I hate this house I am coming to. I have always hated it. I hate this woman in the house. I have always hated her, and one day soon I shall take young Tom and we will walk away and never come back. The last Herries . . . but the place will be always in my bones. I shall never tread on such turf again nor drink such running water nor see such lithe walls running into the sky nor hear such friendly voices. But I have lived long enough away from Vanessa, and although I never speak to her again I must see her once between one day and another day.'

'That was a good catch I made to get Will Davidson,' he said aloud.

'Aye,' said Rantwood. 'Thoo can play at cricket a' reet.'

'Well, goodnight to you, Bob.' He turned in at the gate.

'I mun slacken my thirst wi' watter,' Rantwood thought discontentedly, starting down the hill.

Inside the house even on this summer evening it was damp. They had come down to live only in three rooms and the kitchen. An old woman, Mrs Cumming, was the present successor to all the in-and-out females who had done service in that place. The room at the top of the first stair-flight that had once been the drawing-room with the fine gilt chairs, the naked goddesses, the rosy cupids on the ceiling, was now the general living-room. All that remained of Walter's splendours was the long mirror with the gilded frame, and reflected in this Benjie now stood with his little son. His shirt wide open showed his brown chest, his neck firmly set, his head like a hard apple, the twinkling kindly eyes

alive and eager, his small restless body upon which clothes
seemed always an excrescence, Benjamin Herries, rogue, good
fellow, a 'deep' chap, a good-for-nothing, the kindest man in the
county, the suddenest-tempered, 'a man all by himself', a jolly
man, a man of his word, a man you couldn't trust, a gentleman, a
vagabond, a wise man, a fool – just as your personal experience
happened to be.

And his small son stood beside him, like his father because he
had the brown colour and the sparkling eyes, a child always
laughing, filled already with secret plans and plays of his own,
never wanting company, never afraid, never asking anyone to
help him.

The mirror also reflected the room, which was a scramble and
a confusion, littered with fishing rods, guns, a woman's dress, a
child's playthings, a table with the remains of a meal, and a sofa
with a hole in it.

'Vanessa,' said Benjie, looking into the mirror.

Later, to the light of a smoking lamp, Mr and Mrs Herries
enjoyed their evening meal together, old Mrs Cumming clattering in on her clogs bringing the beef and gooseberry pudding,
banging them down on the table, going out with a toss of the
head because she and Mrs Herries had but now crossed swords in
the kitchen.

Mrs Herries was the thinnest woman in all Cumberland and
her face was of a faintly green pallor. But she was the same
reserved passive woman she had ever been. In years she was still a
girl, but her features were of that ageless cast belonging to women
who have matured when very young and live on their passions.
Benjie was always kind to her; that he hated her was not her
fault. He knew that she had been many times unfaithful to him,
but she was no more personal to him than her pale reflection in
the mirror might be. It was amazing to him that they had stayed
together in this horrible house for three years, but his vow had
kept him, he supposed. He had shown Vanessa that he could be
faithful. This woman had at least done that for him; so he was
kind to her, smiled across the table at her and told her he had
made thirty runs in the cricket game. He ate his beef, seeing that
the long gilt mirror was loose on its nail and swayed ever so
slightly, so that the room rocked too a little. The two high
windows were open and the place was suffused with the summer
evening heat, with the odour of the roses that rioted about the
garden. A moon, tip-tilted on the edge of one small cloud lit

from within like cotton wool around a lantern, drunkenly grinned through the window.

'Mrs Cumming can't cook meat, that's one thing certain,' he said, smiling at his wife.

'No, she can't,' the late Miss Halliday agreed. 'But we never get a decent servant here.'

'We pay them plenty,' said Benjie, who from land, from money left him by Elizabeth, was not so badly off.

'They won't come here. They are afraid of you.'

'What! that I'll go to bed with them? You know that I've been faithful to you since our wedding day.'

(He had, marvel of marvels! Or no – to put it better, he had been faithful to Vanessa.)

'That doesn't interest me,' Mrs Herries said. 'You know you're free to do what you like. Oh, it isn't you. They would know how to deal with you if you started anything. No, it's the house.'

'Ghosts?' said Benjie.

'What you like to call them. Mrs Cumming was talking about it tonight – steps up and down the passage, a dog whining. You've heard the dog yourself up there in the Tower. Someone tapping with a stick. And that woman in black wandering about the garden.'

'Do you believe in spirits, then?' he asked her.

'Spirits!' she answered impatiently. 'These gooseberries aren't half cooked. Well, what are you to think? Those friends of my brother's, *your* friends, those Endicott men, they've seen things time and again. But there's something queer about this house.'

'Yes, from the moment the first stone was laid. My grandfather spoilt it with his obstinacy. If you see a thing isn't going to turn out well you should give it up. No good going on if the signs are against you.'

She sat leaning forward, her sharp-peaked chin resting on her hands. He noticed that she was regarding him with great attention tonight. He felt that something was in the wind.

'Ghosts!' He smiled. 'I saw one in London the other day – a beauty. She was tall like a lily, carried herself like a queen, she was dressed like a rose and a had dark, dark hair. It makes you think of a ghost like that when you see a room in the mess this is in. Why don't you tidy things a bit, Marion; keep things in order more?'

'Ah! What's the use? You're never in, and nothing would ever stay neat in this house. Three years I've had of it—'

'You're a strange woman.' They regarded one another in friendly fashion. 'You've never had any liking for the boy, and he's a fine little chap too. It has meant nothing to you, being a mother.'

'No, nothing at all,' she answered. 'Women mean nothing to me, no, nor children. But men – ah! that's another story! And you, Benjie, more than any. I want to be in your arms as badly as ever I did the first time I saw you. But what's the use? Why you've stayed with me all this time I can't imagine . . . Well, I must wash the dishes. I won't have that sneak of a woman in the house after tonight. She goes tomorrow.'

'Why, what has she been doing?'

She was standing up, her hands on her hips, staring at him as though she would never see him again.

'I like you like that with your shirt open. You're brown all over like a foreigner. Where did you get that skin from?'

'Who knows where one gets anything from? That's the mystery. Where we come from, who made us what we are, what we make ourselves into, where we are going to. And we've lived three years together, Marion, and are as far apart as ever we were.'

'Yes,' she said. 'It's all the body, what it looks like, what its clothes are. I'm not your beautiful ghost like a rose, tall as a lily. But see the rose's nose crooked and give her a black eye, and where's your love for her then?'

'I'm not so sure,' said Benjie. 'I'm not so sure.'

'But I am! It's only because you've a brown skin and are strong and haven't an ugly mark on your body that I'm in love with you. But what's the use? You don't care for me and never did. And you're the only man I've never tired of. Most men are the same after you've known them once.'

She said all this in a quiet, dispassionate voice. Was it because of her own unresting physical passion that he had once on a day been caught by her? Maybe. But that didn't matter now. It was not her fault. A pity that she didn't care about young Tom, though. That might have been something of a bond between them.

'Well, I mustn't stay talking here. That woman's stealing the spoons, I wouldn't wonder.' She went out, carrying the beef with her.

He wandered out into the garden.

Moonlight on a summer's night is a most impermanent thing. Everything is new born, but only for a moment, and when the silvery world rises it is like a dream that, even while you are enchanted, you know that you must not trust. The flowers on such a night are ghosts that at a touch will vanish away, and water, shining under the moon, belongs to no earthly stream. This garden had never yielded to any man's will. Flowers had died when you cared for them and waxed abundant when you neglected them. The moonlight poured out now from under the trees like a flood that, at the beckoning of a cloud, would be withdrawn. Only the trees stood firm, waiting the moment when they would advance, cover the ground, swallow the house and resume their kingdom. Man had never been wanted here, especially man filled with the spirit of obstinacy, revenge, and pride.

Was there some dark figure moving under the trees? He stood there watching. It was easy to imagine, with all that you had heard, that a tall woman in black, now in moonlight, now in grey shadow, moved, hesitated, moved again. He walked forward, the plants crowding about him; then he turned to the stone steps that ran to the higher ground at the side of the house. He had always disliked these steps. His mother had told him that for some reason they had always frightened her. Uhland had tap-tapped down them with his stick, Walter's drunken friends had sprawled against them and fallen from top to bottom like the helpless fools that they were. Now they were washed white in the moonlight and you could see the tufts of grass like black bunches of fingers pressing up between the broken flagstones. Here, standing half-way up, he was exactly under Uhland's stair and he could fancy that behind that dark window Uhland was standing and behind him perhaps old Rogue Herries. The two of them watching the third in that sequence. He stretched his arms. He whistled a tune. He might be of their family, but he was not of their destinies. He was fit and well and strong; he had a son and he loved a woman, he had friends and a hundred miles of country that he would not exchange, with its clouds and stones, for all the sunny kingdoms of the world. He looked down on that moonlit garden. He could hear the water falling from one pool to another. An owl hooted. *Was* not that a woman who moved from tree to tree? He whistled his tune, kicked the loose stones from under his foot and went in to see that his child was comfortably sleeping on this hot night.

Tom slept in a corner of his own bedroom, a room in Uhland's Tower, once used by Walter as a guest room. It was sparsely furnished, his bed, Tom's small one, a large tin bath, a dressing-table, his hunting prints and the faded painting of the old Elizabethan Herries that had once hung in Borrowdale. A fierce, frowning old boy with no nonsense about him! The carpet had holes, the cupboard where Benjie kept his clothes creaked with every wind, but tonight it was transformed with the moonlight and the scent of the roses. Although the window was open the room was very hot, and the child had thrown off the bedclothes and lay, his nightshirt ruffled to his chest, his little legs drawn up, one fist – clutching a small wooden horse – still clenched.

Benjie stood there, looking at him. This was his son, and not a bad son either. Pity he had that Halliday blood which was no good at all in his veins, but Benjie flattered himself that his own Herries blood could beat the Halliday mixture. Vanessa had as yet no child. That anaemic husband of hers would never give her one – and, perhaps, one day Tom would know her and love her and get his idea of women from her.

Poor Benjie sighed. He was really ashamed of himself for having a son at all. He was no sort of father for a boy to have, and he knew already what a man, who is no great hero and has done a shameful thing or two in his time, can feel when a small boy thinks him perfect. 'Well, he won't think me perfect long, and I can teach him to shoot and ride and not be afraid of anyone . . . Still, he ought to have some sort of mother to care for him.'

Then he undressed. He could not find a nightshirt so he slept naked, curling up his legs as his child had done. Father and son slept side by side and the clouds came up over the moon, drenching the room with darkness.

Tom always woke very early and came into his father's bed. He would lie, his small head against his father's chest, looking at the trees beyond the window, waiting until his father should wake. He talked to his horse, named Caesar, telling him about the things that they would do that day, bacon for breakfast, a visit to the village, and, if very lucky, a ride to Bassenthwaite. He didn't *promise* Caesar these delights. He had learnt already that it did not do to expect *anything*, that one was left alone when one least expected it, or worst of all, handed over to Mrs Cumming with her constant: 'Now don't be a worrit' or 'Keep quiet, do'. He was accustomed to being without his father for days at a time and, although his mother was never unkind to him, he knew quite well that she did not care for him. Only once had she been really angry with him, and that was when, coming into a room unexpectedly, he had seen her sitting on a fat man's knee. She had slapped him severely although he did not know what wrong he had done, and then the fat man had given him sixpence. The only fear that he had was that, when his father went away, he would never come back again. He discussed this often with Caesar, and Caesar reassured him. *Of course* his father would come back. But when he was in bed with his father he clutched him very tightly, his arm on his breast or his neck. That comforted him greatly.

At last the grand moment arrived when his father opened his eyes, grinned, yawned, stretched his arms, played a game or two. Then he watched his father splash in the tin bath, after which he was himself plunged into the same. His father helped him with his clothes, fastening his buttons, brushing his hair, and tying his boots. This was a lovely morning, as fresh as a bird's wing, and between the trees you could see Blencathra's shoulder resting against the faint early summer blue. His father whistled and sang, which showed that he was happy this morning; then, hand in hand, they went down to breakfast together.

The big untidy room was bright with sunshine, but there was no breakfast; no cloth was on the table, and, although it was by now half past eight, no sign nor sound of Mrs Herries.

Then Mrs Cumming came clopping in, carrying a plate of bacon in one hand and a dented silver coffee pot in the other.

'Where's Mrs Herries?' asked Benjie.

Mrs Herries is gone,' said Mrs Cumming, her eyes staring with a fat, half-sleepy curiosity.

'Gone?'

'Aye. Mr Ewart's trap come and fetch her seven this morning. She told me they was driving into Carlisle and she left me a letter.'

She felt in the pocket of her cotton dress and produced it; she gave him a stare and went out.

He held the letter in his hand, but, before he opened it, settled Tom in his place, cut the bread, gave him some bacon and poured out the coffee. Tom wriggled until he was comfortable, set Caesar up on the table in front of his place and set to.

The letter was as follows:

DEAR BENJAMIN – I have gone away with Charlie Ewart and shall never return. He has been pressing me for a long time. I'd have told you last night, but what's the use? There's nothing to be said. You don't want me, you never have after the first night or two. I did a wrong thing in the first place to force you to it as I did, but Mother pressed me and I was in love with you. I wonder we've stayed together as long as we have and I must say you've always been very patient, your nature being what it is. We haven't had what you could really call a cross word all these years. All the same we haven't been happy, either of us. I wish I could have felt more for the boy. I'm sure I've tried, but it isn't in my nature. I wasn't meant to have children and if I can help it shan't ever have another.

You'll be much better without me; I haven't a gift for keeping things straight and tidy. What Charlie Ewart sees in me I can't think, and I don't suppose we shall be together long although he says different. You can divorce me if you want to but I don't want any money from you and I'll never be married again. Well, goodbye, Benjie. One thing I'm glad of, that I shan't have to live in the Fortress any more. It's a place would make a cat sick – Your sincere friend,

MARION

Benjie read the letter through three times, then he gave his son some more bacon. 'Well, that settles it,' he said aloud. As though the sunshine penetrated his heart he felt a great joy and gladness. He was free again; he had been set free. He had kept his vow and now, without any act on his part, he was liberated. Charlie Ewart! That thin, shanky, lop-eared farmer! Poor Marion! He was so sorry for her that had she at that moment appeared in the doorway he would, in spite of his disappointment at her return, have been kind and considerate. But, thank Heaven, there was no need to be kind and considerate any more!

He went into the passage and called Mrs Cumming.

'Mrs Cumming, Mrs Herries has gone to London. I am going also and I want you to order Sam Bender round with the trap in an hour's time. I'll catch the train from Carlisle. I'm taking the boy with me. I don't know when I'll be back, but I'll write from London.'

So that was the end of the Fortress. He would sell the damned place and be done with it for ever. He would be in London and Vanessa would be in London. He had done what he could, and it was not his fault that now he was free to go where he would.

Poor Marion! Charlie Ewart! Well, well . . .

He went to his room and packed a few things, Tom going hand in hand with him everywhere. He dressed Tom in his best suit and his grey summer jacket.

'We are going to London,' he said. 'You, I and Caesar.'

While he was sitting waiting for the trap, he talked to his son.

'We're going away, Tom, and I don't expect we'll ever live in this house again. Years and years ago a man rode into this country with his son and went to live in a little house the other side of Keswick. He had a brother living in Keswick too. And as the years went by his son had a wife, and they went and lived in a house down in the valley there which was burnt in a fire later on. There were many of our family in the country, but, one by one, they died and went away until you and I are the only ones left. And now we're going away too. But that's not the end of it. You and I have got this country in our blood. You don't know what that means now, but you will one day. Everything you ever do will be affected by this country, and however far you travel you'll never find any other country so beautiful nor any other that's in your bones as this one is. You'll come back to it. Be sure of that. But I hope you won't come back to this house, because it was built in a bad temper and hasn't been any good to anybody.'

Tom seemed to understand. 'The funny thing is,' thought Benjie, 'that one remembers after the things that one was told although one was too young at the time. I remember things that Adam told me about birds and wrestling. Very rum that.'

'You've got to be a better man than I've been, Tom,' he added. 'And I hope you'll stay in one place sometimes. You never learn anything if you're always moving. But you'll be all right so long as you're never afraid of anyone. There's nothing to be afraid of really.'

It wasn't like him to preach, but the warm sun was comforting and he felt so happy and cheerful that he had to be talking to someone.

They took a last look at the place together, the Cumberland stone, the overgrown garden, the two cross-faced towers. A dog was whining somewhere and little flakes of plaster fell from the ceiling of the living-room.

Then Sam Bender came with his trap and took them both away.

VIOLET BELLAIRS IS PREVENTED

WHEN Timothy Bellairs and Violet his wife had been established in London a year or so they became the centre of social exchange for the London members of the Herries family.

Hill Street was of course the Temple: all the splendour and sanctification were in Hill Street. Only Vanessa of all the Herries entertained the Prince and Princess to tea (although it was said that the Prince *had* paid pretty little Cynthia a visit at her pretty little house in Charles Street); only Vanessa invited Archbishop Benson to luncheon; only Vanessa was on friendly personal terms with Mr Chamberlain.

During these years Hill Street was the Temple. But neither Ellis nor Vanessa cared for gossip. At least Vanessa enjoyed it but appeared to consider some things spiteful when they were only amusing. Now Violet Bellairs was quite different from this. A Cumberland country cousin, she had become very speedily a most entertaining London hostess. She was not, of course, very clever: you could laugh at her to her face and she seldom perceived it. She had no talent for the Arts, thought Oscar Wilde an actor, and supposed that *Robert Elsmere* was written by a clergyman, and had only just heard of young Mr Kipling. But it was not for the Arts that any Herries went to Onslow Square. They went, quite frankly, to hear about the other Herries. You could always tell when any scandal was afoot because Violet, her stout body enclosed within the brightest colours, her red face beaming, her hat elegant with a stuffed bird, her eager, friendly voice with its 'Well, how are you? Haven't seen you for an age!' was to be seen everywhere – at Charles Street, in Barney's bachelor rooms in Duke Street, in Phyllis' overcrowded drawing-room, even in the cold and gloomy place in Kensington where old Emily Newmark held her prayer meetings.

Violet was always in the best of spirits, kind and friendly to everyone, leaving a trail of scandal behind her. She *did* enjoy a gossip, she freely confessed, and liking, quite naturally, to be the centre of any company, if she had no thrilling tale to tell she invented one. Her husband, who was fat and sleepy, spent his days in the Conservative Club and his evenings at Jimmie's or the Alhambra or where you please. He was no trouble to her at all.

Violet, like so many women who married Herries men, became more Herries than the Herries. She was patriotic, strictly moral and all for the law. Nevertheless any human failing made her happy because she was never censorious, but treated a 'mishap' as a town crier treats a lost dog – rang her bell, felt kindly towards the dog but hoped that it would not be found before the whole town had had time to observe that it was lost. Her best women friends among the Herries were old Phyllis Rochester, Cynthia

Worcester, Alfred's wife (Amery's daughter-in-law) and (again oddly enough) old Emily Newmark.

She had, of course, many many friends quite outside the Herries circle, but they were not of quite the same importance to her. As she often said: 'Our family holds together. There's not another family like it in England for that.'

It happened that, early in September 1889, Violet was very busy. It had not been a dull summer, for first there had been Mrs Maybrick (dreadful woman: why was she not hung?), and then those terrible Dock Strikers who, week after week, poor abandoned creatures, went about demanding their Rights, starving and altogether behaving disgracefully. It was not, however, either Mrs Maybrick or the Strikers who gave her so agreeable a week or two at the beginning of this September. It was a real Herries sensation – *what* was happening in Hill Street?

Two years earlier, a week or two after the Jubilee, the question had been – what *will* happen in Hill Street? for Benjamin Herries had come to Town, leading his son by the hand, and one of those family crises so greatly beloved by the Herries promised to be on the way. Then, to everyone's surprise – to the surprise of old Garth, old Amery, young Alfred, heavy Emily, dear little Cynthia, even the stout Barney himself – *nothing* occurred. Benjie called on none of them. He spent an evening or two with Barney; he never went *near* Hill Street. So far as anyone could tell, he neither wrote to Vanessa nor spoke to her. Everything had been the more dramatic in that summer of 1887 because of the dreadful (but rather delightful) Rose scandal. She had escaped to Paris with Captain Fred Wycherley, leaving Mrs Wycherley, poor thing, and two young children in London. ('Did you expect him to take them with him?' Barney asked ironically.) More than that, she met Carey Rockage in the Rue de Rivoli one September day and laughed and joked with him as though nothing had occurred.

Carey was in a fine way because May, his wife, and Maud, his elder daughter, were at a hotel not two streets distant. How fearful if Rose should suggest that she should call! But Rose (who was looking both young and pretty, Carey thought) suggested nothing of the kind.

'I know you have May and Maud with you, Carey. You were at the Opéra-Comique last night. If you are making a domestic parade one day and meet Fred and myself, we shall expect to be cut, you know. So don't worry. Only, if out on a little bit of evening fun on your own, Carey, remember that Fred has his spies everywhere. He'll give you a tip or two as to the best places if you ask him! He's the kindest of creatures!' She went off, laughing, swinging her bustle. Poor Rose. She had been always a coarse woman. Horace, her brother, married last autumn and it was understood that he did not wish Rose's name to be mentioned. Simply because of the awkwardness that it caused to others. Looking more like a Bishop than ever, he let it be understood that he was devoted to Rose. 'Which of us is above reproach?' he inquired of Barney. 'What I mean, old fellow, is that charity is the finest of the virtues. For my part I look at the good qualities in my fellow-men. Who am I to judge? And Rose has loved Fred Wycherley for years.'

Nevertheless it could not be expected that Miss Ada Lindsay that was, a plain pale-faced girl, twenty-one years of age to Horace's thirty when he married her, coming as she did straight from a wealthy but Christian family in Kensington, would care to hear such things mentioned. What Ada herself thought of it nobody knew because she seldom spoke. No one knew what her thoughts were about anything – including Horace.

However, the really interesting side to Rose's disgrace was that it was well known in all Herries circles that there was a deep difference of opinion concerning it in Hill Street. Ellis was disgusted. Vanessa would not listen to a word against Rose. Cynthia Worcester was known to be devoted to Vanessa, to worship her in fact, but even she confessed that if Vanessa was going to 'bite her nose off like that all about nothing' she would think twice about visiting Hill Street again. All that she had said was that Rose had got at last what she wanted, and Vanessa had turned on her, scolded her in front of Ellis as though she were ten years old.

It was plain then that Vanessa's own views on morals were a little queer. Had they not always been queer? After all, had not Judith Paris been her grandmother, Rogue Herries her great-grandfather? Had not her own father been illegitimate and her mother a German? No one meant any of this unkindly. Vanessa was so beautiful, so generous and socially so resplendent that one could forgive her almost anything; nevertheless she belonged to the quarter from which the dangerous winds were for ever blowing, those winds that had for centuries disturbed the peace and order of the right-living, right-thinking Herries.

Benjie, however, was a disappointment. He did nothing spectacular. Nobody saw him. They said that his wife in Cumberland had run away from him after he had beaten her to jelly, that he drank like a fish and consorted with abandoned women. But these things were but rumour and Barney stoutly denied all of them. In the winter of '87 he left London for what destination no one knew.

It was in the spring of '88 that everyone began to say that things were not well in Hill Street. On the surface everything was very well indeed. Vanessa went everywhere and Ellis was often at her side, looking as proud as a peacock. Everyone *loved* Vanessa; how could you help it, so kind and generous and simple-hearted as she was? Nevertheless she made few friendships. Cynthia complained that 'there was always a barrier', but old Phyllis Rochester said that Cynthia was 'socially jealous'. Did Vanessa give herself airs? Surely not. She was the same to everyone, knew no social distinctions, and had been seen one day by Emily Newmark sitting on the top of a bus and chatting to the driver. Her only close friend was young Adrian Cards. She certainly spoilt that young man, who, because he was in the Foreign Office, looked after a Boys' Club in the East End and wrote for Mr Henley, thought himself quite out of the ordinary. *Of course* no one suggested that Vanessa was in love with him, but it was agreed that he visited Hill Street a great deal more often than Ellis cared for, and he helped Vanessa with her many charities.

Ellis was, in fact, the mystery. What went on behind that cold reserved official manner of his? He loved Vanessa madly: ever *more* madly as the time went on. He behaved to her in public with a really exaggerated courtesy and deference, but it began to be said that in private he was impossibly jealous. How do these things become known? Miss Fortescue. (who, as everyone was aware, did not like Vanessa) told a thing or two, and there was that occasion when Alfred and his wife were lunching at Hill Street. Ellis had left the table abruptly and had not appeared again. Very odd. They all shook their heads over it. Then, in the late spring of '89, Benjie Herries once more reappeared in London. He lived in two rooms in Soho Square with his little boy. Poor little boy! That was the first thing that everyone said. Benjie did not now conceal himself as he had done on the earlier occasion. He paid calls on everyone – including Vanessa – and aroused the greatest interest. They all surrendered to his charm while he was *with* them. He looked peculiar, wearing clothes of a rough tweed, sometimes the new knickerbockers, but for the most part loose baggy trousers. His tie was generally a deep red in

colour and enclosed in a gold ring, and this colour with his dark
skin gave him the nickname of 'the little gipsy'. They told one
another, however, with a rather reluctant satisfaction, that you
could never mistake him for anything but a gentleman. He was
always at his ease, laughed like a boy, was worshipped by any
Herries children who happened to be about. He made no effort to
win the affections of his relations: they could take him or leave
him, and for a while they certainly took him. After June there
was an exodus from London: Cynthia and her husband went to
Ostend; Timothy and his family to Eastbourne; Alfred and his
wife to Brighton.

Old Emily of course remained, and it was from her one must
suppose that the story spread – the story that one night at the
Alhambra, Benjie was engaged in a disgraceful scuffle, knocked a
man down and spent the night in a police station. There *had*
been a scuffle, that was certain, but Barney said that it had been
extremely creditable to Benjie. Some drunken ruffian had insulted
the lady in Benjie's company and Benjie had knocked him down.
But what was Benjie doing at the Alhambra with a lady and what
sort of a lady was she?

Then in August came the great news that Benjie had paid a
call at Hill Street and been forbidden the house for evermore by
Ellis. This was from Miss Fortescue.

Well, now, what do you think of that? Somebody said that
Ellis had slapped Benjie's face, someone else that Vanessa had
had to rush in between the two men and separate them. No one
knew what had happened because nobody was present. Ellis and
Vanessa left town to pay a series of visits. They stayed with the
Rockages in Wiltshire, and with Horace Newmark – Barney's
brother – now an old man of seventy in his grand house near
Manchester.

It was reported that Vanessa was serene and happy, but that
Ellis was 'queer'. What do you mean by queer? Well, May Rockage was bound to confess that she didn't like the look in Ellis' eye.
He seemed unhappy if Vanessa left him even for a moment.
Pathetic to see how he adored her, and Vanessa looked after him
as though he were her son, but he was restless and Carey confessed that 'he didn't seem normal', the most alarming thing that
any one Herries could say about another. All the old family scandals were revived, the misbehaviour of the ancient Rogue, the old
quarrel at Christabel's ball, the suicide of Francis, and of course
the dreadful affair of poor John and the crazy Uhland. Was the

family never to be allowed to sit down quietly by its fireside and enjoy its domesticity, serve the country and worship its Maker? What was this crazy spirit that refused to leave them alone? Benjie was as bad as the old Rogue, and the sooner he left the country for good the better.

Early in September most of the Herries were back in London again; Vanessa was at Hill Street, Amery and Alfred in Tavistock Square, Timothy and Violet in Onslow Square, and Emily remained in Tutton Street, South Kensington.

So one fine September afternoon Violet thought that she would go and see what everyone was thinking. She took her son, young Timothy, aged now twelve, with her. Timothy was a beautiful boy; she refused to cut his hair, which fell in gold ringlets to his broad white collar. For parties or calls he was dressed in a black velvet suit. He was the pride of his mother's heart. It is sad to have to record that at this period of his life he detested his mother. He was not allowed to go to school, but shared his sister's governess. He was washed and dressed and brushed morning, noon and evening. He loathed his long hair, his velvet suit, the comments of his mother's friends; he was mocked at and shouted after by little street boys; he cried himself to sleep at nights because of their insults. The only thing in the world for which he cared was to draw and paint; this he must do in secret because his father, whom he rarely saw, laughed at such nonsense and his mother showed his drawings to her friends. He had to drive in an open carriage in the Park with his mama, he had to sit on a chair in ladies' drawing-rooms and be commented on as though he were something in a circus. His settled resolve was to run away as soon as the proper moment occurred. Barney Newmark was his only friend. Barney had said to Timothy: 'What the devil do you dress the poor child up like that for? It's cruelty to children, poor little beggar,' and Violet, hearing of this, never forgave him.

On this particular afternoon in Cynthia Worcester's drawing-room, he was not altogether out of place. Two young poets were present, a lady dressed in blue velvet and peacock's feathers, and Mr Oscar Wilde. Mr Wilde was very kind to him, sat beside him in a corner and told him a story about a young Prince who ran away from his father's kingdom and became a bell ringer in a church with a wonderfully high tower. One day when the Prince was ringing the bells, a swallow flew into the tower and rested on his shoulder. The swallow had damaged its wing, so the Prince took it back with him to the cottage where he was living . . .

At this point the ladies demanded that Mr Wilde should entertain them, so the tall heavy man with the grave eyes and the
beautiful voice had reluctantly to leave young Tim, who never
afterwards forgot him.

Two more men and a girl came in. There was a great chatter.
Violet admired Cynthia's looks but she must say she couldn't
admire the way that she did her drawing-room with the pale
grey wallpaper, some flowers in a white vase, a Japanese screen,
one little table with some odd-looking thin books upon it –
nothing else. No photographs! No cosy coverings to her room,
no fans pinned to the wall, or shelves with cups and saucers and
large blue plates. However, Cynthia *loved* a good talk and was
just jealous enough of Vanessa to enjoy a story or two. You could
not find two types more exactly opposite than Cynthia – so small
and fair, with such very light-blue eyes – and Vanessa – tall,
dark, 'one of Du Maurier's women', or as Horace Ormerod liked
to say impressively, ' "A daughter of the gods divinely fair" – fair
in the sense of beautiful, you know.' So that there was just
enough difference between the two for Cynthia not to object to a
little scandal . . . no harm, only to ask where Benjie was, had
anyone seen him, did Cynthia know what Ellis, when he was
staying down in Wiltshire? . . .

So that Violet was pleased when the two young men and the
girl came in, because now it would be perfectly easy to have a
little chat with Cynthia without disturbing the others. Smiling
happily upon everyone as though she would say, 'Now I know
I'm a large woman and when I move it is a little upsetting, but I
like you all immensely and you must none of you be disturbed,'
she drew her chair closer to Cynthia's.

'Cynthia darling – what *beautiful* teacups! Where did you find
them? Everything you have is always so lovely. Listen, dear.' She
dropped her voice. '*Have* you heard what Benjie has been doing?
They tell me that Ellis . . .'

But something was wrong. For once Cynthia did not appear to
be attending.

She said: 'Yes, Violet dear, how interesting!' but her sharp
blue eyes were fastened on the heavy frock-coated man with the
pale jowl, the friendly smile, the heavily lidded eyes, who, standing in front of the fireplace, talked with a self-confidence that
awed Violet although privately she thought it a little vulgar.

One of the young men said something with a titter about the

Queen. All the patriotic Herries in Violet (acquired by marriage) was affronted. Smiling very brightly she said:

'The Queen! Surely we must be proud to *have* such a Queen. Young man, you are disloyal.' (Shaking her finger at him playfully.)

'Violet is really dreadful when she's coy,' thought Cynthia, and for the first time (because she was not interested in children) wondered whether it was not rather a shame that poor child on the sofa (to whom one of ladies was now talking) should be dressed as a doll.

Mr Wilde said: 'The Queen? Do you know, madam, what Thackeray once wrote about our Queen?'

'No,' said Violet, 'Something fine, I'm sure.'

'Very fine,' said Mr Wilde, looking at her with so kindly an expression that she wondered whether she would not invite him to luncheon. 'He wrote, as nearly as I recollect, something like this: "I salute the sovereign; the good mother; the accomplished lady; the enlightened friend of art." '

'How very fine – and how true!' said Violet.

'Not true at all, madam. The Queen has not been a good mother, she is not accomplished, and she has not been a friend to art in any fashion whatever.'

Everyone laughed. Violet felt most uncomfortable.

'We owe to her in fact the present interest in the Arts. An Englishman is only an artist when those in authority despise the Arts.'

'What about Queen Elizabeth?' said Cynthia, laughing.

'Do you imagine that Elizabeth was an artist or cared for the Arts? She wanted to be entertained and made love to, and because the Arts then were part of a man's daily life, to tempt a man to make love to you was to rouse the artist in him. The Arts today can only exist by separating themselves from daily life. That is why the real artists today are never successful lovers, live from hand to mouth and wander the streets. Very different from the life of our Queen.'

'You are forgetting Mr Kipling,' said Violet, who had been persuaded only a week or two ago to read *Soldiers Three*.

'Mr Kipling believes in the Empire,' said Mr Wilde, smiling.

'Do we not all believe in the Empire?' asked Violet, pleased that she was holding her own in this very intellectual conversation.

'Do you know what Tennyson wrote for the Jubilee?'
'A very splendid poem, I remember,' said Violet.
'He wrote:

> *'Fifty years of ever-broadening Commerce!*
> *Fifty years of ever-brightening Science!*
> *Fifty years of ever-widening Empire!'*

Everyone laughed, but Violet did not see that there was anything to laugh at. Uncomfortable without knowing why, she waited a minute or two and then attempted Cynthia again:
'Do tell me, Cynthia darling. Have you been to Hill Street since they came back from the country? How did you think Vanessa was looking?'
'No, I haven't seen Vanessa for weeks.'
'It seems that Ellis has been behaving so very strangely – not sleeping, they say, and absurdly jealous. Phyllis had a letter from May Rockage . . .'
Everyone was laughing. The young man with the flowing black tie on the sofa had been drawing a picture for Timothy, and here was Timothy actually himself drawing something!
'It's a ship! It's a ship!' he cried excitedly.
One of the other young men jumped up and began to recite dramatically:

> *'Spirit of Beauty! Tarry still awhile.*
> *They are not dead, thine ancient votaries,*
> *Some few there are to whom thy radiant smile*
> *Is better than a thousand victories,*
> *Though all the nobly slain of Waterloo*
>
> *Rise up in wrath against them! Tarry still, there are a few*
> *Who for thy sake would give their manlihood*
> *And consecrate their being. I at least*
> *Have done so, made thy lips my daily food,*
> *And in thy temples found a goodlier feast*
> *Than this starved age can give me, spite of all*
> *Its new-found creeds so sceptical and so dogmatical.'*

'A very good poem,' said Mr Wilde, 'whoever wrote it. Its fault is that it contains a philosophy. Poetry has nothing to do with philosophy, but only with feeling.'

'You had a philosophy when you wrote it, Oscar,' said one of the young men.

'Yes, and got rid of it by writing about it. Any philosophy is foolish if you look it in the face. Christ hid His face, you remember, to cover the foolishness of His disciples. And that is why He loved John, because John had no philosophy – only feeling.'

'What very bad taste,' Violet thought, 'to talk about Christ in that ordinary fashion.'

Nevertheless it was now that she was disturbed by an odd sensation. There was something in this room that deprived her of her desire for gossip. It was not that she thought the Arts important; the young men looked most unhealthy, and Mr Wilde's complexion was anything but hearty. Nor was she ashamed of wishing to talk about the family, but there was something here before which personalities seemed unimportant. She felt frustrated, prevented. Even Cynthia, whom she knew so well, was different. The things of which these men talked were not in Violet's mind beautiful, and yet beauty was in the air. Perhaps after all her drawing-room in Onslow Square was a little over-crowded. The flowers in the white vase were a pretty colour ...

It was almost as though someone had laid a hand on her mouth. She was most uncomfortable and thought at the first opportunity she would make an excuse and go.

One of the young men had, it seemed, but just returned from Paris and had seen there a performance of *Othello*.

'The absurdity about *Othello*,' Cynthia said, 'is that he should be upset so easily by so trivial a matter. A magnificent general, the strongest man in the State, and a little strawberry-spotted handkerchief—'

'You are wrong, dear lady,' said Mr Wilde. 'The tragedy of *Othello* is not Desdemona. She is only one element in his down-fall. We know, when he appears before the Senate, that he is poised above an abyss. He knows, we know, the Senate knows, that this new command is his last chance. He would have been recalled from Cyprus and Cassio given his place had there been no wife, no jealousy, no murder. Before the play begins he has reached the moment that comes to every man when the journey downhill has started. I have always seen Othello played as though he were a king of men in the majesty of purple triumph, with the trumpets sounding about him. That is wrong; he has the bitter knowledge that the glory is already in the past. It is of the past that he speaks to Desdemona, not the future. He comes to the Senate, leading Desdemona by the hand, and despair is already seated in his eyes. Great success demands great failure.' He laughed, smiling at them all. 'I am already preparing for the day when I shall know St Helena, and perhaps Calvary. I hope I shall not complain, because the only artist who can count himself fortunate is he who has learnt the value of great failure. When Othello pierced his breast with his sword and remembered Aleppo his soul cried triumphantly: "Now my experience is complete. I thank the Gods!" For Othello was undoubtedly a great artist.'

'You are making him out to be as self-conscious as yourself, Oscar,' said one of the young men.

'Not to be self-conscious is not to be conscious at all,' Mr Wilde answered.

'And not to be conscious at all – well, that is to be "Ruskin".'

Everyone laughed, although again Violet saw nothing funny in the remark. Mr Ruskin, whose name was constantly in the paper, was most certainly of a greater importance than Mr Wilde. To be important was, apparently, with these young men, to be mocked at. The Queen, Lord Tennyson, Mr Kipling, Thackeray, Mr Ruskin ... it was some comfort to her to recollect that she admired them all. She wanted to remain and she wanted to go. Something stirred in her. The house in Onslow Square, Timothy, the general trend and colour of her daily life – she was suddenly dissatisfied with them all. Family gossip, for a moment, seemed stupid and worthless.

But this was absurd. She resented her disloyalty to herself. She got up to go.

'Do tell me, Mr Wilde,' she said, 'one or two interesting new poets to read.'

He regarded her with so kindly a glance that once again she wondered whether she would not invite him to luncheon.

'I am afraid there *are* no new poets,' he answered her. 'But then there never have been. The best poets are old from the beginning. Mr Dowson there is a poet, and a very old one indeed, although he only left Oxford a year or so ago.' He indicated one of the young men on the sofa.

'I will remember.' She nodded graciously to the young man. 'Come, Timothy. Well, Cynthia, it has been most delightful. You must come to luncheon one day soon, dear, and perhaps you will bring Mr Wilde with you.'

But in the carriage she was indignant. Whatever had possessed her to be affected by two or three young men who were so irreverent and common? And how stupid of her to have determined to have a word or two with Cynthia. It was a lovely afternoon; she would drive to Kensington and see old Emily, who always loved a gossip and was certain to know the latest thing about Vanessa and Ellis.

Timothy was silent as he always was when exposed in public. But he was not unhappy. He thought longingly of the large heavy man who had begun to tell him a story and the other pale-faced man who had drawn things for him, who had not laughed at his own drawing of a ship but on the contrary had liked it so well that he had shown it to his friend.

The weather brought out the bicycles. What Timothy longed for more than any of the world's treasures was a bicycle. As a very small infant at Uldale he had seen Mr Rander, the clergyman from Ireby, ride a penny-farthing, and that glorious entrancing vehicle with its high front wheel and tiny back wheel had seemed to him the height of possible adventure. Now first Mr Stanley and then Mr Dunlop had provided safety and reasonableness. Everyone was beginning to bicycle. Timothy, sitting stiffly opposite his mama wishing that his hands were as large as umbrellas that they might cover his velvet suit, thought of the kind gentleman who had told him a story, and then with longing eyes looked out on the driver of the omnibus, yet more fervently on the driver of the hansom, but most passionately of all upon the bicyclist. It was the bicycle that must be – not, he hoped, so far distantly – his engine of escape!

'Now here we are at Miss Newmark's,' said Violet to her little son, speaking with some severity. She was still uncomfortable, still felt the touch of an unknown hand upon her mouth ...

Here at any rate there would be no hindrance to a nice heart-to-heart gossip. But, as always when she was ill at ease, she was severe with her children, and now she spoke impatiently to Timothy and told Hunter, the coachman, that she might be a long time, she might not, she did not know, she could not tell, all this in the severe irritable voice that the Herries always use when they are nervous.

She had no need to be nervous as she stood, holding Timothy's hand outside the gloomy plague-stricken door of Miss Newmark's Kensington home. She had been here so very often before and called the door 'plague-stricken' because the paint had faded and blistered until the surface represented a chart for one of the more sinister Oriental diseases. Above the door was a top hat made of iron and painted a faded green. The lower part of the house had once belonged to a hatter. Violet had often noticed how, when she called upon Emily on a sunny day, there was always a gloomy sky in Emily's street. Very odd – as though the houses in Emily's street were mountains! It was the same today. Just as Parker, Emily's viperish maid, opened the door, the first drop of rain fell. Parker had been with Emily for twenty years and hated and despised all her fellow human beings without any exception whatever, save only her mistress. She could not be said to love her mistress, because she was part of her, bone of her bone and flesh of her flesh, and both Parker and Emily were above any kind of personal vanity. But Parker was of importance at this moment in the Herries family affairs because she was on speaking terms with Miss Fortescue from Hill Street. Miss Fortescue, who as a child had lived in a family of Second Adventists, visited Emily frequently and had many a chat with Parker before she left the house. These little social contacts have made history before now.

Violet and Timothy climbed the steep dark stairs and heard the thunder roll beyond the walls.

'I said it was going to thunder,' said Violet. All the way up the staircase Timothy gazed with a terrified eye at the series of pictures from the Bible decorating the wall. He hated to come to this house for many reasons, but chiefly because of these pictures, which represented all the more dreadful scenes in Old Testament history – the murder of Abel, the destruction of the Cities of the Plain, the Flood, the Serpent in the Wilderness, the Plagues of the Egyptians. He wanted to hurry past, but his mother held him always tightly by the hand; her movements were slow and solemn. He wanted not to look, but was compelled. There was in one picture a fat snake with a flicking tongue, which writhed its coils around a shrieking woman and her child. That snake was remembered by Timothy all his life long.

'Mrs Bellairs and Master Bellairs, Miss Newmark.' So Parker always announced them in tones of the deepest dissatisfaction. She called her mistress 'Miss Newmark' on every occasion. They both preferred it.

In spite of the gloomy and uncertain light of the drawing-room, Violet saw at once that there were other visitors. Emily, now a large and heavy woman with hair of steely grey, a slight grey moustache on her upper lip, dressed always in black and having the oddest resemblance at times both in voice and features to her very different brother Barney, came forward and greeted them.

'Miss Pope. Mr Pope. Mrs Glass,' she said, introducing a pale young woman, a young man and a stout round lady wearing an old-fashioned bonnet, a very large bustle and a cashmere shawl.

On all ordinary occasions when Violet paid Emily a visit the same procedure was followed: first Timothy was put into a corner of a sofa and given a large illustrated Bible to look at and then the two ladies drew up to the fire (or the window if it were summer) and gossiped away the fortunes and happiness of every Herries in England. But today things were different. The lady in the shawl, Mrs Glass, said almost at once to Timothy: 'Oh, the pretty dear! Come and talk to me, my dear, and tell me where you got your lovely curls from.'

The room was littered with properties, sacred and reminiscent: Bibles, huge sea-shells, family albums, and volumes of poetry of a pious nature. These things gave the room the homely comfort which it needed. But today there was no homely comfort. Although the curtains were drawn and the gas lit, the thunderstorm could very distinctly be heard.

'I'll ring for some fresh tea,' said Emily.

'Oh no,' said Violet. 'I have had some tea with Cynthia' – then wished that she had not mentioned Cynthia, because Emily disapproved of her even more than she did of Vanessa. But today the mention of Cynthia roused no response. Emily seemed absent-minded. The three visitors were talking together, making a fuss of Timothy, who was struggling with a vast fragment of ancient and desiccated seed-cake.

Violet sighed, then patted Emily's knee.

'Well, how are you, my dear? I thought that I must just drive round and see how you were. For one thing Phillis has had a letter from May Rockage that would, I was certain, interest you. Vanessa and Ellis have been staying with them, you know, and it seems from what May says that Ellis's jealousy is becoming *quite* abnormal. She says that if Vanessa leaves the room for a single moment he begins—'

'There you are, Miss Pope!' Emily suddenly interrupted. 'Just what you said! A thunderstorm! Now isn't that strange after Mr Euclid's sermon last Sunday evening? Did he not foretell this very thing? God will thunder forth from His Heavens that we may be warned of the Wrath to come! Those were his very words. Violet, I've told you again and again that you should go to St Hilary's of a Sunday. Yes, and bring your husband with you. It would do him a world of good . . . Listen to that thunder! God speaking to us if ever He did and yet we will not listen . . . I beg your pardon, Violet . . . What were you saying about May Rockage?'

But here the pale young woman, Miss Pope, interrupted. She had, Violet thought, a *hysterical* face, for set like little fires in that pallor were her large burning eyes. She had a quiet, rather pleasing voice; her long, thin hands were clasped together as she spoke, and her body trembled slightly.

'Miss Newmark, you must come next time with my brother and myself. Really you must! You cannot imagine how affecting it was! The dock directors are monstrous. They could not behave as they do had they seen some of the sights that Edward and I see every day. They refuse to agree to the payment of sixpence an hour. Sixpence an hour! They would give a dog more! Dr Liddon's fund for the women and children is being wonderfully supported and that shows what the public feeling is! You should go down to the docks, Miss Newmark! They are empty. The Corn Exchange and the Coal Exchange are practically empty. You should have heard how Mr Burns and Mr Tillett were cheered last week, by big City men themselves. I cannot sleep, Miss Newmark, thinking of the women and children – the starving children—'

Violet thought that she was about to cry, and oh! how uncomfortable that would be!

Emily said: 'God is working for them. The day will come when these wicked oppressors will be punished as they deserve.' Her voice was gentle. She was touched as Violet had never seen her before. Really, with the thunder outside and this emotion inside, the atmosphere of the room was quite embarrassing, but soon the three on the sofa with Timothy began to talk eagerly together once more.

'Have you seen Vanessa since she returned, Emily?' Violet asked.

'No, my dear.'

'I do hope that everything is all right in Hill Street. You know that Benjie is in London again . . .'

'We should go through the streets,' Emily cried, 'with Christ at our head and *force* the world to listen. I suggest, Miss Pope, that you go and see Mr Euclid and suggest something of the kind to him. I know that you would find him sympathetic. We don't ask God's help enough. That's what *I* think! We try with our own feeble hands to build up His kingdom. We can do nothing of ourselves.'

'You are right, Miss Newmark,' said the young man in a voice unexpectedly deep and manly. He got up. 'Would you mind – should we not offer up a prayer now to Almighty God and ask Him to help these poor brothers and sisters of ours? Where two or three are gathered together . . .'

He went down on his knees, almost upsetting the table as he did so. The three ladies did the same and Violet was also compelled to do so, although she felt extremely awkward.

'O Lord!' said Mr Pope, 'we Thy humble servants gathered by chance together speak to Thee with one voice for our unhappy brothers and sisters. We have sinned in our selfishness. We have not asked for Thy guidance. Show us, dear Lord, in Thine own good time how these, our suffering brothers and sisters, may be rightly helped and taken out of their undeserved misery, and open the hearts of the wicked taskmasters that they may incline towards mercy and know that without Thee the temple that they build rests on sand. Show us what to do, O Lord, and give us strength so that without fear we may go forward in Thy good work to Thy glory, world without end, Amen.'

'Amen,' said everyone.

Then Emily repeated the Lord's Prayer.

When they rose from their knees they showed no shyness at all, but began eagerly to talk together.

For the second time that afternoon Violet felt that a hand had been laid on her mouth.

There was nothing to do but go.

'Come, Timothy! . . . Well, Emily,' she broke in upon their talk, 'we must be on our way. Do let me know in what way I can help. I had no idea that the poor people were suffering so. It does seem too bad indeed.'

She embraced Emily, bowed to the others and departed.

In the carriage again, as she turned towards home, she felt vexed and uneasy. There had been something very queer abroad this afternoon. Now, as they drove through the streets, the lamps seemed to blow in the breeze that had sprung up, everyone was moving swiftly as though bent on some secret mission. Her mind hung about Vanessa. Vanessa was in great trouble. She was sure

of it. It was as though the lights, the passers-by, the air of the
September evening thickening as though with a film of thin
smoke about the roofs and chimneys – all these formed a clouded
mirror in whose glass she saw pictures shaping. Real trouble. Not
something at a distant remove, about which it would be amusing
to gossip. Her heart was moved, she could not tell why. She made
Timothy sit beside her, wrapping the carriage rug round him,
then put her arm about him drawing him closer to her. She
would go and see Vanessa tomorrow . . .

Vanessa was in trouble. And then these poor people at the
Docks . . .

'How much is there in your money box, Timothy?'

'I don't know, Mama. About three shillings, I think.'

'Wouldn't it be nice to give it to those poor women who can't
give their children enough to eat?'

'Yes, Mama.'

But he thought: 'Now it will be longer than ever to buy the
bicycle.'

'We must be kind to everyone,' said his mother, kissing him.

A JOURNAL AND SOME LETTERS

BARNEY NEWMARK kept for many years a Journal. In 1896
he squeezed out of it what he felt to be some of the more interesting passages and made a volume of reminiscences which failed to
attract much attention,[1] but for the purposes of a family chron-
icle some extracts from the original diaries are of interest. It was
their misfortune, from the ordinary reader's point of view, that
they dealt with private persons rather than public, family incidents rather than general affairs. He had always kept them for his
own amusement and in that at least he had the advantage of some
of his contemporaries.

February 4th, 1890

. . . I could not conceive what he wanted me there for. I came to
the house, I'll confess, in spite of my advanced years, rather like a
naughty schoolboy ordered to the headmaster's study. He has of

[1] *Some Memories*, by Barnabus Newmark. Hatcher and Thorburn,
1896.

course never liked me. That is in fact putting it mildly. I date his positive antagonism from that evening long ago when he went with me and young Benjie on an evening out, went reluctant and returned disgusted. With the years his dislike has grown to a kind of horror. I stand for everything that he most abominates – a writer of cheap novels, irreligious, a lover of horses and women, a gambler, a drunkard. That I have been none of these things very desperately has given him only the greater displeasure. Had I gone to the dogs he could have pitied me. As it is I have kept my head just sufficiently above water to be still a danger. Vanessa's persistent loyalty to me has only aggravated the trouble. This is the first time that he has asked to see me for at least twenty years. The odd thing is that I have always rather liked him. He has an integrity that I can admire. Then I understand so well his desire to win affection and his inability to do so, his shyness, his recti-tude of conduct, his honesty. But is not his rectitude at last threatened? After yesterday I am inclined to think so.

I arrived at Hill Street punctually at four o'clock. Orders had been given that I was to be taken straight to his private Cave and I was conveyed up dark stairs and along sombre passages as though I were either a criminal or a spy – both, perhaps.

He was not there when I arrived and I had time to look about me in what is surely one of the gloomiest little rooms in London – bookcases filled with those dreary volumes of Journals and Papers marked with little white paper labels, a bald bust of some dead Roman, a large stern writing-table with silver writing things and an immaculate blotter, a grim, grizzling little fire and two leather armchairs. Poor Ellis! Many is the time, I am sure, that he has paced that little room, wondering why things are wrong when he is himself so right, shrinking from a world that he would give his soul to placate, lonely and bewildered, suspicious and uneasy.

I was not there very long. He came in, said: 'Well, Barney, how are you?' asked me to sit down, seated himself opposite me, and then, tapping his fingers together, looked all round and about him with a kind of distressed dismay on his features that was both pathetic and funny.

We hung about for a long time without coming to the point. He said that it was a long while since we had met, that it was a pity, that he understood that Allsopp's brewery was in difficulties, that the shortage of gold made separate bank reserves very difficult, that it was high time the Treasury dealt with the

Coinage question, and so on and so on. He asked me whether I
was writing anything just now in that tone in which people who
despise novels speak to novelists – as you might inquire of a
coiner whether he has been doing well lately.

I made some suitable reply and then silence fell. I had no
intention of helping him out. It was his affair, not mine.

Then suddenly it came:

Would I use my influence to persuade Benjie Herries to leave
England?

So that was it? I stared and said nothing. He was extremely
uncomfortable. He got up and began to walk the room. I must
understand that he had nothing against the fellow. He disliked
him, of course. He would be perfectly frank with me. He had
always disliked him. He dare say that he was well enough from
his own point of view, but I would have to admit that he had
never been a credit to the family – very much the opposite in fact.
His life, quite frankly, had been something of a scandal. That
was Benjie's private affair. The last thing that Ellis wanted to do
was to interfere with anyone's private life, but his continued
residence here in London was distressing to many of us, and he,
Ellis, as head of the family in London, had felt for a considerable
time that something ought to be done. He wished me to understand that he brought no kind of personal charge and he hoped
that I would regard this conversation as most strictly
confidential. I broke in there that of course he understood that I
was Benjie's friend. I also asked him did he wish me to tell Benjie
that he had spoken to me?

To which he answered in great distress, Oh no! of course not!
The last thing that he wanted was any quarrel with Benjie. It was
unfortunate, most unfortunate, that some time ago he had been
compelled to ask Benjie not to pay any more visits in Hill Street.
He regretted it, regretted it greatly, but on his last visit he had
been so outrageous in some of his views and had behaved most
insultingly to Miss Fortescue – 'My wife's lady housekeeper,' he
added, poor dear, as though he didn't know that *I* know exactly
all that Miss Fortescue is and how thoroughly Vanessa has
always detested her.

But really, he went on, the point was simply this. He did not
wish to detain me. He knew that I was an extremely busy man.
Did I think that I could persuade Benjie that a residence abroad
would be more suitable, more suitable in every way ... more
suitable in every way? ... While he was speaking my mind ran

over past family history. How odd this perpetual desire in our family for one member to rid himself of another! Old Francis the Rogue and his brother, Jennifer and Christabel, Walter and Jennifer, John and Uhland – as though it is a law with us that one half of us shall always aggravate the other to madness! Yes, to madness! As I watched Ellis, with his pale face, long restless hands, pacing up and down the room, it seemed to me that there was a kind of insanity, born of brooding unhappiness and perhaps jealousy – born anyway of a tormented unsatisfied love – not so far away!

I replied, quietly enough, that I certainly could not ask Benjie to leave the country. I could not agree with him that Benjie was a scandal. He was sometimes in London, sometimes abroad; he had his own friends, lived his own life. I could not see that he did harm to anyone.

At that Ellis became more agitated. Oh, indeed! And what had I to say to his fight at the Alhambra and a night in Vine Street? What had I to say to ... Here, with a great effort, he pulled himself up. He must repeat that he had no charges against Benjie. It was only for his own good, for his own good and the general good ... Did I think— Here he paused, seemed to be greatly agitated. Did I think that a sum of money? ... He was prepared to offer ...

At that I rose from my stiff leather chair.

'Look here Ellis,' I said. 'This goes no further of course. It ends here. But you don't know what you're saying. You send for me and suggest to me that I should bribe a friend of mine for no reason whatever to leave the country, go into exile. He has a son, you know, a fine little boy. Frankly I shall forget that we ever had this conversation. It is not worthy of you.'

I went to the door. He followed me and looked at me for a moment with such malevolence that it was a new Ellis, one I had never seen before.

'Oh, of course,' he said. 'You are his friend. I might have known ... *Good* afternoon'

And that was all. I was out of the house almost as soon as I was in it. As I walked away I thought that I had never known a queerer business. How could he have supposed for a moment that I would have listened to anything of the kind? And to what a pitch of brooding and suspicion he must have come to send for *me*, whom he has always so greatly disliked! At first I was so angry that I felt like turning back and punching his head. Then the pathos of the man himself came to me. And after that real fear and anxiety for Vanessa. I have known for some while that things are not going well with her, but she keeps up so brave a front that none of us can tell what is really happening to her. Is she meeting Benjie? Does Ellis know of something hidden from the rest of us? Of one thing I am sure – that she will be honest and straightforward in all her dealings; but all last night the thought of her enclosed behind those walls with Ellis for her companion and Fortescue in attendance – well, frankly it spoilt my evening. But I have put everything concerned with this little incident down here exactly as it occurred. The facts may be useful one day. I am Benjie's friend, Vanessa's friend, even – who knows? – Ellis' friend. A nuisance for an old, selfish, comfort-loving bachelor who hates to be disturbed. All day today I have been tempted to go and see Vanessa. But no. It is better that I avoid Hill Street for a time. The nuisance is that tonight when I should have been getting on with my novel I haven't been able to think of a thing. Quite impossible to get Vanessa and Ellis out of my head!

From Vanessa Herries to Rose Ormerod at
27 Rue Montaigne, Paris

September 6th, 1890

MY DEAREST ROSE – I have the whole evening to myself – Ellis has gone out to some meeting and I have done what I love better than anything else in the world, gone to bed, had some supper on a tray and now can write you a long letter without fear of any interruption.

After you left on Wednesday I was very unhappy. We had so short a time together and said so little although we both wanted to say so much. I was unhappy too because I knew that you were. You could not disguise it from me. All your brave talk about your loving to be alone and Fred's having been so generous in his settlement and your finding it such a relief to have done with men for ever – none of it deceived me in the least. The very fact that we had to meet as furtively as we did in Miss Mercer's rooms speaks volumes! You and I furtive! Doesn't that of itself show that there is something very wrong? Why not have come to Hill Street? Ellis would not have eaten you. You never used to be afraid of anyone. And although you pretended that it was for *my* sake. Well, I can deal with Ellis, you know. I haven't lived with him all these years for nothing! It struck me suddenly tonight with a kind of terror that for the first time in all our married life I have, in this one week, concealed two things from him – one my meeting with you, the other, well, I will tell you of the other in a moment.

But now, Rose, listen. Let me tell you here sitting alone in my room, loving you very dearly, something that I could not when we were together. The association with Fred Wycherley has been dreadfully bad for you. You know it better than I. I was shocked at the change and more shocked still at your own consciousness of it. You saw also a change in me. Yes, it is true. I know now this about life – that, far more than I had ever supposed, we affect one another. To live with another is to have to fight for your own integrity morning and night. I suppose if you love someone enough you lose your own integrity and find another much finer. But if you don't ... You know, Rose, when leaning on that hideous mantelpiece at Miss Mercer's you looked over your shoulder and said: 'Vanessa, men don't mind what they turn their women into', I knew and you knew where you have got to in these last years. Rose darling, oh darling darling Rose, let this life go. Leave Paris. Settle somewhere in England where it isn't too dull. You have some money, you have intelligence enough not to need the kind of life Fred gave you. I suppose you don't hunger for Cumberland all day and every day as I do, but why not try it for a while? Try Eskdale or Coniston or Ullswater for a month or two. They are lovely in the autumn. The Cumbrians are kindly uninquisitive folk. Why not bring that Mlle Mathieu with you whom you like? I don't know. Making plans for others is never any good, but if you were to tell me that I was to have a week on Cat Bells beginning tomorrow, I think I'd just go crazy with joy! But Ellis is frightened of Cumberland. He thinks I'll go wild there, leave him for a gipsy or something. Yes, after all these years of my good proper social behaviour he still fears it. More now than ever. Which brings me to the other thing. I nearly told you on Wednesday. I tell you now because you are the only one I can tell. I won't even say that it's a secret. If Ellis asks me tomorrow morning: 'Have you seen Benjie Herries?' I shall say yes and tell him all (or almost all) about it. But if he doesn't ask me ...

This is all it is, my grand secret. Since 1887 I have seen Benjie a few times and spoken with him, but never by arrangement. I saw him at the Jubilee Procession. I saw him once at the Theatre. On neither occasion did we exchange a word. Last week on a lovely afternoon I had been visiting Cynthia. I sent the carriage back and walked in the Park. I was wandering down one of the paths, thinking how old I was getting (I am thirty-one, you know), frightened as old married ladies will be at the way that life was passing, when I looked up and there was Benjie with his little boy walking straight into me! Well, what were we to do? We couldn't, all things considered, just pass one another with a stiff bow! I had never seen his little boy. But in any case we could not stop to reason. We have been friends since we were babies. He belongs to all my life, all of it that I love the most passionately. We – oh well, why explain anything to you? There we were and both of us so happy at meeting that we could only look at one another, without words. It was, as it always is when we are together, as though we had never parted. We sat down on a bench, the little boy beside me. We had then the happiest hour of our lives. We did not mind who saw us. People were passing all the time. If Ellis had come by, I would not have cared. What was there to be ashamed of? Even Ellis must admit that all this time we have done our duty, never tried to see one another, never written. We love one another of course. We have always loved one another. I have no doubt that if we had married as we meant to, we would have been very unhappy, but happiness and unhappiness have nothing to do with love. If Ellis asks me – as he will one day – do you love Benjie, of course I will say yes. I will never lie to him or to anyone. We thought of none of this, not of Ellis nor the family nor anyone at all but ourselves. He told me about his life, that he was lonely, that Tom his boy – who is six now – is going soon to a little day school in Bloomsbury; I told him a little about Hill Street – not everything. But we didn't talk very much as I remember. We were simply so happy to be together again. Then we walked a little way and parted. We made an arrangement to meet in Barney's rooms. He was to be there and I was to come as though by accident. But in the evening when I was home again I knew that it would not do. I wrote him a letter saying that we must not meet again and I know that I was right. Nothing stands still. At every meeting it would be harder to part and what would the end of it be? But, Rose – never forget it – Benjie has been wonderful during these years. With his character and nature to keep away as he has done, to help me by keeping away – no man has ever done anything finer.

Well, there it is. So we go on, the three of us, doing our best. The queer thing is that since that meeting, Ellis, although he can't possibly know of it, has been increasingly uneasy and suspicious. He isn't well, is working too hard and has dreadful headaches. Then there is Miss Fortescue, who hates me, of course, and would do me harm if she could. Poor Ellis – if only he would be content with what we have. All these years we have been friends. When he is happy we are *such* good friends and life goes so calmly, but lately I have been afraid. He behaved so strangely last year in Wiltshire that everyone noticed it. His love frightens me often and is becoming every week less tranquil. Can I manage all this? Of course I can. I have never been beaten by anything yet, but marriage isn't easy when it's dramatic – or perhaps it is I who hate scenes. *How* I hate them! Their childishness and extravagance ...

Rose, darling, goodnight. Come away from Paris. Come home. I saw Horace yesterday and his silent wife. He was *very* cheerful and bright and breezy – Your most loving

VANESSA

Part of a letter from Mrs Timothy Bellairs to Miss Lavinia New-mark, Constance Court, near Manchester.

June 25th, 1891

... I do hope that your father is better. Of course at his age one must expect a day in bed now and again. Timothy has been complaining of lumbago and I insisted on his staying in bed last week. As you may imagine, no one has been talking of anything but the Baccarat Case. Poor Sir William! I am quite *sure* that he did not intend cheating and I really think that some of them showed great vindictiveness. Mrs Lycett Green is quite a friend of May Rockage you know, and Timothy has often met Lord Coventry at his Club. Of course the Prince's appearance in the witness box was *the* sensation and everyone thinks that he came out of it very well and that it was most unnecessary of *The Times* to say what it did! It is all a great pity and very bad for the working classes, who are inclined in any case to be troublesome just now. Timothy says that that man Burns is a danger to the country and ought to be in gaol. I suppose you haven't heard of poor Vanessa's illness. So unlike her to be ill and nobody *quite* knows what the matter has been. They say all sorts of things, but I refuse to listen to gossip, especially of the family variety ...

Barney Newmark's Journal.

February 18th, 1892

I haven't entered anything in this Journal for weeks, but yesterday afternoon deserves a record. Stephen Bertrand, the novelist,
came in most unexpectedly to see me. And then who should enter
directly after but dear Horace Ormerod? It was really entertaining to see them together. Horace I knew had come for some
purpose. He would never waste his time on me unless he wanted
something. Bertrand had met him once or twice before and was
pleased to see him again, as well he might be, for no human alive
could better satisfy his passion for innocent copy! I could see
Bertrand's round, obese little body hurrying home that he might
not waste a moment before putting Horace's self-revelations into
his notebook! And how Horace gratified him! He was nervous a
little, I suppose, of Bertrand's cold penetrating eye and talked
therefore twice as much as ordinary! His healthy rosy face
beamed with complacency; his honest, clean, and incipiently
stout person vibrated with energy. His friendly eyes shone behind
their glasses. With jolly deprecation he told us how good he
found life to be, how easy it was to be generous, how simple to see
the best in everyone! 'Have you seen Valentine lately?' Bertrand
asked rather cruelly. Valentine at the time of the success two or
three years back had been a great friend of Horace, who liked to
be intimate with one of the most promising poets of the day. *Then*
one thought that he would be John Lane's proudest boast, that
Dowson, Lionel Johnson and the rest were not in the race compared with him! But alas, the bottle and the ladies have been too
much for poor Valentine! No one is a greater adept than Horace
at dropping a failure gracefully! There were, I swear, tears
behind his glasses as he cried:

'Poor Valentine! I wish I could do something for him. He's his
own worst enemy, I fear. I did have a word with him some six
months ago, but he has become oddly embittered, poor fellow.'

This was joy indeed to Bertrand, who most skilfully led poor
Horace on until I could not bear it any longer and had to interfere. When Bertrand was gone Horace said complacently:

'Nice fellow, Bertrand. I must invite him to lunch at the Club.
He seems to know everybody and that last novel of his had quite a
success, hadn't it?'

I told him that it had.

'What was it called?'

I told him.

'I must remember and read it before he comes to luncheon. You novelists are all so sensitive!'

Funnily enough, on reflection, I felt a strong resemblance between Bertrand and Horace, although I must confess that I like Bertrand the better of the two. Both are equally complacent, Horace because he is a fool and Bertrand because he is pleased with his gifts, with his penetration into human motives, with his cold, clear eye, with his horror of sentiment. But both are sentimentalists, Bertrand perhaps the greater of the two. Bertrand cannot understand that he is disliked (as I fear that he is) and attributes it to the fear of his fellow human beings for the naked truth. Bertrand is the kindest of men and Horace one of the unkindest, yet Bertrand is held to be cruel and Horace, although a fool, good-natured. Bertrand means no unfriendliness when he puts his acquaintances into his books. Indeed he thinks they are lucky fellows to be used for so fine a work of art! 'The artist,' he says, 'thinks only of his art', and forgets that his friends, and still more his friends' friends, think only of their reputations. And this is odd because Bertrand himself thinks a great deal of his own reputation. But I like Bertrand and give him free leave to make any use of me that he pleases!

But now to the point, Horace's point. Violet Bellairs and Horace have become great friends of late. They have many things in common. Violet, it seems, often appeals to Horace for help in her troubles. Here is the latest! Young Timothy (a very decent kid who will be an artist one day) has, it appears, been indulging a secret friendship with Tom, Benjie's boy! Where they first met, or how, I don't know. It has been a complete and most dreadful surprise to Timothy's poor mother! Tim is fourteen and Tom under eight, so you would not suppose that Tim was in great danger! But Tom is already – according to Horace (who by the way has never set eyes on the child) – a young ruffian and a moral danger to any companion. This letter was discovered by Violet Bellairs in the pocket of one of her young son's jackets. Horace left it with me and I copy it here verbatim, spelling and all:

DEAR TOM – Mother is going out tomorrow afternoon and it's a harfholiday. The old cat is in bed with inflewensa so i can meat you the same place – Your loving

TIM

I at once inquired of Horace whether 'the old cat' was Tim's

mother, but it seems not. She is apparently Violet's governess, and
I at once said that Violet deserved all she got if she wouldn't send
Tim to a decent school like any other boy. 'Oh, well,' said
Horace, who never defends his friends whole-heartedly unless
everyone around him is doing the same, 'Violet thinks Tim's
delicate.'

'She only thinks he's delicate because she's tried to make him
so,' I burst out, 'with his curls and all. The kid's a fighter and
with a will of his own. He'll be a grand artist one day. But what's
the matter anyway if Tim does make a friend of young Tom?'

Oh, then Horace broke out, forgetting all his natural caution.
Benjie was a danger to everyone. They were all coming to feel it.
I, poor fool, was the only one left to stand by him. He was
contaminating the family reputation. Ellis had done with him
long ago. Alfred hated him. Cynthia wouldn't have him in the
house, and now, through his nasty little boy, Benjie was per-
verting Violet's child. Only I and of course Vanessa ... and
everyone knew that Vanessa was in love with him even though
she *didn't* see him ...

At that I did gloriously what I haven't done for years. I lost my
temper. I lost it so that I took Horace by his fat shoulders and
shook him so that his glasses rolled on his fat nose. All my long
dislike of Horace was at last expressed. I called him every name I
could think of, obscene words that Horace's soul would shudder
at; I told him what I thought of him, that he was false, syco-
phantic, mean, treacherous. (Only one side of Horace after all,
for he is not a whit worse than the rest of us, only naïver.) I told
him that I was Benjie's friend and that Benjie was worth all the
family put together (which Benjie isn't, of course), I told him
that he was not fit to breathe in Vanessa's presence and that if I
ever heard him utter a word against Vanessa again I'd murder
him. I'm sure he thought that I would. I never saw a man look
more frightened. So I threw him out of the room, washed my
face and hands and laughed a little. But it is truly no laughing
matter. The thing grows. It is instinctive. Benjie is some wild
half-human animal to them and Vanessa *does* love him. And
Ellis' brain begins to turn. Well, God help them all, say I, and
myself no less than the rest. But how the troubles in this world
come from chatter! Fools like Horace and Violet! – and perhaps
ruin to nobler men because there are parrots on the trees. Could
we but keep silent for a little while and let men work out their
own salvation without comment. Too much ever to hope for!

A letter from Benjamin Herries to Vanessa Herries.

TOLEDO, Spain, *April 6th, 1893*

Vanessa, will you ever see this? For the first time I am breaking my vow and now I shall continue to break it, for my endurance has been tested too sharply. This goes to Barney. I have told him to let you have it. I expect no answer but I am hungering for one – only one line to tell me that you understand the sort of fate that follows me, a ridiculous fate that I cannot escape and shall no longer try to, by God! This last time was too much! As though it wasn't enough that Cynthia should be there, but Alfred and his wife as well! I had not drunk a drop that evening. You may believe it, Vanessa. I have never lied to you yet. I came into the place as sober as a church. The woman who was with me was a poor thing I used to know, hadn't seen for years, found that afternoon longing for a meal in a decent restaurant, quietly, with a friend. Well, the Café Riche is decent enough, isn't it? We were having our meal as quietly as two churchwardens all sober in our corner. I saw Cynthia come in with a man. Then a little later Alfred and his wife. We had nearly finished when Fanny Church (the girl with me) caught my arm, begged me to pay my bill and go. There was a man at the other side of the room of whom she was terrified. She had been his mistress once, it seemed, and he had treated her damnably – a heavy man with a black beard. Before I could do anything he had seen us and come to our table. He paid no attention to me, but, smiling at Fanny, said he was glad to see her again and where had she been all this time and wouldn't she tell him where she was living? She was trembling all over, poor girl, looking at me to protect her, and I, very quietly and most politely, asked him to go. He asked me who the devil I was and did I know that I was interfering with his friends, his *very* old friends. Then he put his hand on her arm. What could I do then but knock him down? Wouldn't any man have done the same? He was a big man and he fell heavily and a table went over. Of course there was a row. I waited quietly, told him that I would pay for the damage, left my card and went out with Fanny. That was all. But quite enough of course. Cynthia and Alfred had all the evidence they wanted.

But the *second* public row, Vanessa! After all these years of discipline. Was there ever anyone born more unlucky? Well, this is the end. I can do no more. I was never made for this hypocrisy

nor were *you* made for that life in Hill Street. Tom is at a good
school, that's one comfort, and I am finished for ever with
London and that farce of civilization and the damned family and
their chatter and my trying to be what I'm not. I'm finished for
ever with everything but loving you. I shall write sometimes and
tell you how I love you, for I am a boy no longer. If you do not
answer me it will make no difference. I cannot believe any longer
that you are happy, for I know that you are not. I shall always let
you hear where I am, one way or another, and one day, if it is all
too much for you, come to me. In this black town I am at peace
again. The walls go sheer down to the plain. As I look from my
window I can see the gipsies moving off along the narrow street,
and in the Cathedral it is so cool and dark that you can stay there
by the hour and hear no man's chatter. I have a room in an inn;
my room is high up. Everything is grand here, the gold in the
Cathedral, the wind against the wall, the sound of water falling
as it does in Cumberland. One thing already makes me think of
you. In a little church at the end of my street there is a picture
painted years ago, they say – *pictor ignotus* – of a Black Centaur
pawing the ground, his head up, while over the hill there goes a
Procession carrying the Host. I don't know its meaning, bringing
Christ to the Heathen or some such thing, but the Centaur is
noble. His head is up, he is ready for what may come, and he
made me think of you because of that dream you used to tell me
of – the horse that strikes the mountain with his hooves, springing from the water. I *will* not be dismayed, Vanessa! That little
London is behind me. I have only Tom and you in the world, but
you know and *I* know that as long as life lasts we will go on
finding the meaning of it, loving one another although we never
meet again, not fearing anything, not despising life until we
know that it is worthless, which it is not and never will be. I have
tried hard all these years to do as you say. *You* know how I have
tried – but I will be tied down no longer. They think, Cynthia
and Alfred and Ellis and the rest, that life is a cow to be milked –
but it is rather the Centaur on to whose back I will leap. One day
you will ride with me. When you see Barney tell him to write to
me once a week about Tom. That's a good school, they say, and I
liked the man when I saw him. There's someone playing music in
the inn room and I'm going down.

You won't despise me I know, or believe anything they say.
You are part of me and the law is we must *not* despise ourselves.
Give my love to dear Violet and Timothy and Barney's sweet

sister Emily. Oh God! but I'm glad I'm done with London! –
Your loving, loving

BENJIE

A letter from Vanessa Herries to Barney Newmark in Rome.

March 13th, 1894

MY DEAR BARNEY – The moment I received your telegram
I went down to the school. Fortunately Ellis was away on a visit
to old Horace for three days. I went down, taking Lettice Marrable with me. You don't know who she is, do you? She is a girl
from Cumberland whom I have brought to Hill Street as my
secretary – a kind of counter to Miss Fortescue. She is an odd
girl, would like to dress like a man, has all this new craze for
tennis, breeches, women's freedom – all a result of the frightful
way she has been kept down all her life at home. However, you
won't want me to waste your time with *her* except that she is the
most loyal, faithful, attached creature who ever lived and a great
comfort to me. We went by train to Salisbury and drove over to
the school. The headmaster, Mr Collins, was exceedingly kind. I
took the greatest fancy to him, his wild black beard, his black eyes
so lively behind his glasses, and his evident friendship and loyalty to Benjie. He took me to the Infirmary where Tom was. He
has been very ill, but is much better. He lay there as white as
paper, but he has Benjie's smile, hasn't he? I had only ever met
him once before – in the Park a long time ago – but he remembered me and told me about the book the nurse was reading to
him – a Talbot Baines Reed – and he was greatly amused by
Lettice's hard straw hat and the sort of golfing suit she wears! He
likes funny things, Mr Collins says. He asked me had I seen Tim,
Violet's boy? He showed me a letter Tim had written him in
secret. Awkward for me, wasn't it? He was too white-faced for
me to say it was wrong for himself and Tim to write to one
another. I said nothing. In fact, dear Barney, *all* my ideas of the
difference between right and wrong are fast vanishing! Which
brings me to this. You must send me Benjie's address, tell me
where he is. I had a letter last year from Toledo. I did not answer
it. I have not written a line to him since he left England, although
you know how I have wanted to! But I can keep it up no longer. I
must send him word about Tom, right or wrong. He worships his
father of course. He said to me over and over again: 'When is he

coming? He hasn't been here for a long time!' For the Easter holiday he is going, as you know, to the Quintires again at Longbridge Deveril. He says it is nice there, they are kind to him, pleasant girls who tell him stories. They write them themselves, he says, which seems to him marvellous. They have a magazine among themselves and oh! Tom said, wouldn't they be lucky if they could get Tim to draw pictures for it! He is a warm-hearted little boy. I wished, coming back in the train, that I had one like that of my own. Lettice slipped some money under his pillow. I saw her do it, and it's good of her because she hasn't a penny! But he's all right, Barney, and I like that master. For myself what shall I tell you? Nothing. You're in Rome and London is far away. We have been to *Charley's Aunt* and *The Second Mrs Tanqueray*. We have had a party. Cynthia has had a party. I have had a letter from Will Leathwaite, from Cat Bells. Barney, Cat Bells! Cat Bells! Cat Bells! . . . No more of that. Shall I tell you about clothes? Sleeves are very wide, waists narrower than ever. Skirts are long and trailing. My arm aches with holding mine up. Everybody is wanting to be rich. If you are rich enough you can go anywhere. Alfred gets richer every day. But this is not what you want in Rome. I have read a beautiful book by a man called Yeats, *The Celtic Twilight*. Have you heard of him? But of course you have. Ibsen is the fashion. Ellis – but I will not weary you with my silly troubles. Am I happy? No, Barney, I am not. Is anyone happy? Possibly no one. Are we all being gay and merry? Very gay and merry indeed. Send me Benjie's address – Your loving

VANESSA

Extracts from Barney Newmark's Journal.
April and May 1895

COPLEY BECK, DUDDON VALLEY.

. . . This letter. What am I to do about it? Ellis has not spoken to me for years, thinks I am altogether on Benjie's side and must know that Benjie is in England. I showed him the letter at once and asked him what I should do. It is a number of days old, forwarded with some bills and papers from Duke Street – and we have been walking from Seascale to Boot, from Boot here – that's two days. Vanessa is probably in Cumberland by now. She gives a Keswick hotel as an address. But Benjie swears that she can have no idea that he is even in England, much less that he is walking up here with me. But is Ellis likely to believe that? Can I prevent them meeting, do I even want to? I put it to Benjie on his conscience. 'My conscience says that I am to see her,' he answered, and his silly brown face lit up with such happiness at the thought that I would be a thief robbing a blind man to prevent him. Why should I stop their half-hour? She has the Marrable she-male with her, she tells me, and she is surely enough for anyone as guard! Ellis need never know – *will* never know! Benjie is even now, as I write, standing out on the sward, looking at the lambs, the water jumping the rocks of Harter Fell in a thundercloud and the sun striking like a sword on the fresh green of the larch. He is standing there kicking stones with his foot, giving little leaps. For a small man, he is a packet of vitality, but it is happiness that makes him leap! To see her, out of the blue, without arrangement on his part ... by divine accident! He will go over to the little hotel at Dungeon Ghyll for a day. Vanessa and the Marrable girl can stay the night there or drive over from Ambleside. Could anything be more discreet? And I'm tired of Ellis. He has been considerably rude to me for years and he is making Vanessa unhappy. That's enough for me ...

... Benjie and I have been talking for hours about the Wilde affair. Benjie sees her tomorrow and can think of nothing else, so I talk to divert him. But poor Oscar! What a muddle of vanity, British hypocrisy, snobbery and false judgement. As to the crime itself I say nothing. It has not, thank God, been one of my temptations, but as I have always yielded to every temptation I *have* had, if that had been one of them I might have yielded to it. How do I know? Anyway it is more mental than criminal, I suspect. But this I do know: that Oscar is always at his best with very simple childish people. He is himself a child with his vanity, heartlessness, kindness, generosities and self-confidence. I always disliked him when he was showing off, but put him with children or stupid kindly men or warm-hearted impulsive women and he is lovable indeed. Men like Whistler or Charles Brookfield or Carson really terrify him at heart, as children are frightened when, sent for by unwise parents to show off to their elders, they suddenly see the cold eye of a guest speculatively fixed upon them.

This remains at least, that never even in hypocritical England has there been such a revolting show of hypocrisy as this – and it will put Art and Letters in England back for twenty years ...

*   *   *

... Well, we are back again, and Benjie is out walking in the rain and dark by himself. I have had a happy afternoon walking for two and a half hours with the Marrable girl. We landed at last, after climbing Wrynose, back at Blea Tarn and sat there patiently. I never saw it more beautiful with the trees coming down black as thunder to the very edge, Wordsworth's 'Solitary's' cottage white in the sun and the sky pale yellow behind the Pikes. I was interested too, for she told me enough about Ellis to fill a volume. Vanessa's patience with him must be a marvellous thing, and even Lettice Marrable who hates him, pities him too. It must be a weird household now with the monstrous Fortescue, Ellis half mad with a vague torturing jealousy that has no facts at all to justify it, and this odd, masculine country girl who worships Vanessa. 'I would *die* for her!' she cries, looking into the green water of the Tarn.

'Now would you?' I ask her cynically. 'Easily said.' Then look at her and feel that she really would!

What will be the end of it?

Of what Vanessa and Benjie said to one another I know nothing. I asked nothing. I was told nothing. Vanessa is better than ever. She is surely the grand lady. To see her walk across a room is a benefit to humanity. But she is a child too. When she saw Benjie there she simply laughed, took his arm and walked off with him. I don't think I ever before realized so sharply that, behind all this present fuss and bother, there is the fact that they have been friends all their lives long. That makes a difference, of course.

I said: 'Miss Marrable, shall we take a stroll?' And so we did. *What* a plain girl! But I can't help liking her.

Part of a letter from Violet Bellairs to Cynthia Worcester.

September 9th, 1896

... We have been with the Rockages a week now. I can't say that it's a comfortable house – horses and dogs morning and night, and Carey is so far behind with *The Times* – which he intends to read every night but goes to sleep over – that he is still discussing the Jameson Raid. It has been the hottest summer ever known here and the children feel it. Timothy is being very difficult. Carey agrees with me that this painting nonsense must be knocked out of him! I never knew anyone talk so much about *Cricket* as Carey does. It's Ranjitsinhji for every meal, or whether Cambridge or Oxford bowled balls that *weren't* balls in the University Match! Men are too strange and I've simply given up trying to understand them. Timothy *will* read this nasty new paper the *Daily Mail*. I think it's the *halfpenny* that appeals to him. He always *loves* to get something for nothing. I hear that Benjie Herries is in Africa and has married a Negress. Thank heaven that friendship between his boy and Timothy was nipped in the bud. Did you ever know anything so horrible as the baby-farming murder? I hear that the Dyer woman actually ...

From Master Tom Herries to Timothy Bellairs.

LONGBRIDGE, DEVERIL

September, 9th, 1896

DEAR TIM – I will bicycle over on Tuesday and be *just inside* the farm gate by Locker Wood at half past three – Your loving

T.

ELLIS IN PRISON

ON that warm evening in July 1897 Timothy Bellairs senior left Ellis soon after dinner and went home. He was going to bed; he had a touch of lumbago and would catch it in time.

'He looks a lot more than his sixty years,' Ellis thought with some satisfaction. And he did. He had grown terribly stout. It would have been better for his health had he stayed in Cumberland.

The house was still as the tomb after Timothy's departure – and why was it never really warm even on these summer evenings? Or was it Ellis who was never warm? After seeing Timothy off, he stood in the hall listening to the silence. Vanessa was at the theatre with the Worcesters, and he had promised her to go to bed early because all day he had had one of his terrible headaches. It was she who had suggested that he should invite old Timothy to have dinner with him, because Timothy was no trouble but would chatter on and on about anything or nothing. So he had done; about the Jubilee, very different from the '87 affair – not many people in the streets and the Queen so feeble, poor old lady, that it had almost killed her; all the same, *what* a country England was! The Review at Spithead made you feel that: no other country could touch us for a Navy! Still, the country hadn't the style it used to have with cohorts of young men on bicycles and these halfpenny papers. Fine poem, Kipling's 'Recessional'. (He recited some of it as though Ellis had never heard it before!) Made you feel proud to be a Briton *and* a Herries! He could remember when he was a boy in Cumberland ... And Salisbury had said that Africa was created to be the plague of the Foreign Office. Some truth there! They had better watch President Krüger. (He spoke with scorn of Krüger as though the Herries family had decided in conclave that Krüger was a rat and ought to be stamped on.) Well, we are getting on, getting on ... Sixty last birthday, and yet it seemed only yesterday when old Madame – Judith Paris – had threatened him with the cane she always carried, for stealing gooseberries out of the Uldale garden. Pity that place was burned down! Fine place. And there was something about Cumberland which ... But Ellis did not like to hear about Cumberland, and changed the conversation. Well, he must be getting home. This damnable lumbago ... Driving with Violet yesterday in the Park. Did Ellis know that Alfred had bought one of these motor-cars, and only last year, wasn't it, they had changed the law about a man walking in front with a red flag? Pity in his opinion they *had* changed the law. How were you to protect the public with these things charging all over the place? However, they would never do away with the carriage, thank Heaven. Sensible people would always prefer the horse to those stinking, screaming engines that nobody could control. Well, well, it was a changing world and time he went home. Violet wasn't quite the woman she had been. A bit puffy in the chest and they were not quite happy about Timothy, who was at Cambridge now and not settling down as he should. Always wanting to go to Paris and paint! Ridiculous notion for a gentleman's son.

Well, well, goodnight to you, Ellis. Give my love to Vanessa. Still the handsomest woman in London ...

Why was the house so silent? When would Vanessa be back from the theatre? It was of no use to go to bed. He never slept until she came to say goodnight to him, and she knew that, and was good about returning early. Good? Was Vanessa good? As usual, so soon as he began to think of her his heart thumped in his thin bony breast, and that other man, taller than he, with the handkerchief wrapped round his head, stole out of the wall and stood beside him. *Why* was the house so silent? The servants must be moving about somewhere. Miss Fortescue must be in her room. He climbed the stairs to his study, the other figure keeping pace with him. The room was cold. The bust of Cicero watched him with its blind lidless eyes. Could you watch anyone if you were blind? Why, most certainly. His shadow with the handkerchief bound about its head was blind and yet, with ceaseless preoccupation, it watched him.

He began to pace the room as now so many, many times a day he paced it. The distance that he must cover was not of great extent *and* how well he knew it! So far to the writing-table where he would pause and arrange, rearrange, arrange again the silver writing things. Then, half turn, four paces to the wall where there hung an excellent engraving of that fine picture, 'Christ Leaving the Praetorium'. Christ, so gentle, so kindly, His hands bound in front of Him, the crowd pressing forward, the stout muscle-swelling guards restraining them. One guard Ellis had come to know well, a broad, cheerful, helmeted fellow looking over his shoulder at Ellis and, Ellis thought, in some friendly way warning him. Warning him of what? Well, and then, half turn again and down the room until you reached the door. This door, which was painted an ugly light brown, had for a handle a round cold white knob. Ellis always touched this knob, grasped it indeed with his warm fingers, for its chill indifferent hardness comforted him; it stilled his beating heart. He thought of it sometimes when he was in the City or the Park or at the Play. That cold white knob, so gloriously indifferent! What did *it* care whether he were torn with jealousy, whether Vanessa loved him? ... But of course Vanessa did not love him. That was the first fact. He stopped, as a thousand times he had stopped in the middle of that floor, and marshalled the facts that, when seen in an ordinary row, would make him a sensible clear-headed man.

It only needed that they should be properly marshalled, and he saw them like little children (cretins perhaps) with large round white heads like the doorknob, all sitting in a line, their white fleshy hands folded, waiting to be marshalled.

Bald-headed Fact One. Vanessa did not love him, had never loved him, would never love him.

Bald-headed Fact Two. He loved Vanessa with a burning, devouring fire. (It was literally that. In a cavity behind his ribs this fire was burning. He could see the flames leap and fall and leap again.)

Bald-headed Fact Three. He was jealous without reason. Jealousy. Dreadful. Like catching a disease that turned your bones to water. Intermittent. It was most devilish in this – that it left you for five, ten minutes, so that, within that space, you saw quite clearly and wondered how you ever could *be* jealous. See! See! No reason. Vanessa has never been faithless to you. She is honest, is fond of you, has been very, very good to you for more than a dozen years. And then, the more savage for its brief absence, the jealousy returns, just distorting everything so that the wallpaper is tinged with green and the cat moves to its platter of milk with private purpose in its eyes.

Bald-headed Fact Four. That he is no longer any good in the City. That his business powers have left him. That young Alfred who has come into the Firm is already taking his place. He must see to this. He is losing money.

Bald-headed Fact Five. His body. That he cannot sleep. That he has headaches. That he is suspicious of everyone. That he is drinking. That his body is hot at one moment and cold the next. That he sleeps with Vanessa when she does not wish it, which is what no gentleman should do. That the Family – Violet and Cynthia and Alfred and Emily and the effeminate Philip – are watching him just as he is watching them and everyone else. Cat and Mouse. Mouse and Cat.

Bald-headed Fact Six. That he thinks much about the past. His father who wanted him to love him, but he could not; his poor old mother; his shyness and awkwardness and longing to be liked; the first moment when, on old Madame's Hundredth Birthday, he had seen Vanessa. Shadows, shadows of the Past. That Cumberland which he hated and feared. Always trying to lure him back to it again so that it might set its fingers about his throat and hold him there while the mocking rain poured down on his upturned face and the stone walls crowded him in and the clouds came lower and lower ... All the ghosts of the Past. Old Herries, poor Francis who shot himself, John who was murdered, mad Uhland.

Bald-headed Fact Seven. That this beastly, threatening world had as its representative that brown, ragamuffin, dissolute gipsy whom Vanessa loved. Had always loved. They had been children together.

Bald-headed Fact Eight. That when all the Facts were seated quietly in the row he would see how unreal they were, would see that he was Sir Ellis Herries, third Baronet, a wealthy decent citizen of Queen Victoria, much honoured by his friends, thought well of in the City, possessing the handsomest woman in London for his wife, the kindest, the truest, most popular. There was, he would see, no reason at all for agitation. All was well. He had reason to be happy. He must go about and show people that he meant them well, that he was a likeable good man, that the hospitality for which his house was famous was practised because he wished them well, because he liked them and wished them well ...

Someone was in the room. He started as though a gun had been let off in his ear. Oh! it was Miss Fortescue.

'I beg your pardon, Sir Ellis. I thought you had gone to bed. I came to put these papers ready for you in the morning.'

Miss Fortescue was now, in appearance, completely the sinister remorseless figure of one of Mr Wilkie Collins' savage women. She was hard, black (hair, eyes, eyebrows), efficient, and humourless. Nevertheless, she was no villainess. She was sentimental, read with passion and admiration the novels of Ouida, Miss Braddon, and that comparatively new writer Mr Hall Caine. She was lonely and romantic and had, from the first moment of seeing him, decided that Ellis also was lonely and romantic. She was not in love with him; she had loved, so many times, so many heroes in fiction that no man in everyday life could satisfy her. But she had from the first considered her master as her child, to be protected, guarded, aided. Vanessa's beauty had always irritated her. She thought her kindliness a posture, for she was convinced that she had married Ellis for his money while in secret she had loved another – which was quite in agreement with her reading. She also by temperament distrusted Vanessa's general friendliness, her high spirits, her generosities. This was not a world in which women could let themselves go. There was danger, as her novels told her, on every side. She kept her romanticism and sentiment for her reading and for one or two human beings – Ellis, her ancient mother who lived at Canterbury, and an ailing brother. It had, however, taken many years for her dislike and distrust of Vanessa to grow into hatred – that true and unalterable hatred that can come to any human being who has never known passion nor independence nor compliments. In daily life she was an excellent practical woman. She gave no joy to the house in Hill Street but she managed it perfectly. Vanessa always admitted that all the burdens were taken from her shoulders. She added that she would willingly sweep the floors and make the beds were Miss Fortescue removed. She had never asked for her removal because, as the years advanced, it became more and more evident that Ellis would be a lost man without her.

She stood now, her black dress sweeping the floor in iron folds, the high puffs of her sleeves made, it seemed, of steel.

Her pale cheeks might, had she been another woman, have betrayed her excitement. The moment for which, during many long, unjust, weary years, she had been waiting, had arrived.

He had paused in his walk and seemed to be listening. Then he realized her.

'I thought you had gone to bed,' he said.

'Yes, Sir Ellis. I am just going. But there is one thing—'

'Yes?' he said, more at ease and comfortable now that the silence was broken and that the tall figure with the handkerchief on its head had slipped into the wall again. He sat down in one of the armchairs, picking up aimlessly a Society paper that was lying there. He opened it, turning over the pages, looking at the illustrations. There was a supplement illustrating the Spithead Review.

She stood near to him, her hands folded.

'You have often told me,' she said, 'that if there was anything that I thought you ought to know, I should tell you.'

'Certainly,' he answered. 'Yes, Miss Fortescue.'

'Something has come to my ears that I think you should know.' This was like a scene in one of Miss Braddon's novels. She recognized every step and movement. She was (a luxury seldom allowed her) herself a figure in one of her beloved stories. At the same time this was real life. The room was real; the persons concerned were real. She was the sort of woman who might poison an acquaintance, with no malice at all, simply that she might justify her own reading. Neverthless there was malice, true revenge for beauty, wealth, power, that she had never enjoyed.

'I learnt today from an unquestioned source that a little more than two years ago Lady Herries spent a whole day, practically alone, with Mr Benjamin Herries in Cumberland. Probably she has already told you of this; if she has not, I think it right that you should know. It is exactly information of this kind that you have said to me that you *wish* to know.'

He asked her: 'Where did you learn this, Miss Fortescue?'

'A sister of Miss Marrable's is in London. She told Miss Emily Newmark, who this afternoon told me. Both Lady Herries and Mr Herries, who are of course well known in the district, were seen in a compromising position at a hotel called the Dungeon Ghyll Hotel.'

He was shaking from head to foot, but all that Miss Fortescue saw was that his hand trembled against the paper and his foot tapped the floor.

'It is a long while ago.'

'Yes; but it can be completely substantiated by reliable witnesses if you wish it.'

Incredible that, loving Vanessa as he did, he should not have sprung from his chair and banished Miss Fortescue from the house for ever, but at her first word he had moved from the world where things are as they are, to the world, long familiar to him, where men are seen as shadows and a mist-like smoke reveals only monsters of distrust.

'Where and when do you say this occurred?'

'Just over two years ago. At a hotel called the Dungeon Ghyll Hotel in Cumberland.'

He waited a long time; then he said:

'It is of no importance. Lady Herries, I think, spoke to me about it.' He looked at her. 'You misunderstood me if you thought that I wished to hear such things. I know that you always wish to help me, but I have complete confidence in Lady Herries.'

She cleared her throat, a small, dry, mechanical sound.

'I thought it my duty; I cannot bear to see you deceived. Whatever I do, I do out of loyalty to you. You are the only interest that I have and you have taken me on many occasions into your confidence.'

'Yes, yes,' he said. 'But I do not wish you to speak of Lady Herries to me. That is not your province.'

'I understand,' she answered. 'If I have done wrong, please forgive me. I considered the matter and thought that it was better that you should hear of it from me than from someone – someone less loyal.'

He took the paper and began to read.

'Goodnight,' she said, and went.

He read very seriously with knitted brows the Society paper. He read every word.

The sight of London divested of its boards and bunting was too distressing to my aesthetic soul, so I came down to Medmenham Abbey Hotel for a few days' perfect rest, where the flags are not scarlet and blue but violet and purple, and where they rest not against crimson cotton, but on a tender background of green leaves. It is quite beautiful down here, the only drawback to its complete charm being its distance from the railway station. I have a passion for flying from my fellow-creatures, so that they can flee after me; but when it is a question of a four-mile drive after an hour's journey with a change of trains at Bourne End, their pursuing ardour seems to cool. However, Mr Playfair, whose marriage was such a blow to me last year, and who is living in the neighbourhood to write a book, offers to supply the social deficiences of my existence, and Florrie's husband has comforted me with the loan of his punt, which looks absolutely beautiful with new blue and white cushions, so I expect I shall get on very well, and by my calm acquiescence in my solitary state excite the suspicions of my unworthy family. I have seen only two dresses worthy of the name since I came here, and they were both my own; one of light drab homespun with a mauve batiste shirt, with a turn-down linen collar and a black necktie, which does duty with a white linen skirt, crowned with a pale-green mushroom-shaped hat, trimmed with a mass of shaded green wings. Now I must go out and see if I can get Mr Playfair to agree with me as to the charms of this latter.'

Of all of this he read every word; he read it all twice over, murmuring aloud some of the sentences: 'A tender background of green leaves' ... 'I have a passion for flying from my fellow-creatures' ... 'Mr Playfair, whose marriage was such a blow to me' ... 'Florrie's husband has comforted me' ... 'The suspicions of my unworthy family' ... 'A pale-green mushroom-shaped hat' ... 'A mass of shaded green wings' ... 'If I can get Mr Playfair to agree with me'.

'Mr Playfair, Mr Playfair, Mr Playfair,' he repeated, looking at the shaded eyes of Cicero. Although he read the whole of this passage with such intensity and although some of the sentences from it were to remain with him for the rest of his life, he was not, at the moment, in the least aware of anything that he had been reading. He put the paper down, got his hat, and went out.

*   *   *

It was after ten o'clock, and the streets were quiet. Berkeley Square was very still, the leaves of the trees rustling faintly in an evening breeze, the clop-clop of a hansom's horse sounding once and again from Piccadilly. At this hour London streets and houses take on themselves a listening, watching air. They resume their own proper purposeful life which has been disguised during the day by the rushing torrent of human beings; with their lighted windows they watch the traffic of the world that moves without sound, their chimneys and doorways re-establish communication one with another. Like cats they can see in the dark.

Ellis walked, his tall body bent, his head with its high black hat a little forward, his hands clasped behind his back. He passed into the light of Piccadilly, then back again into thin-shadowed streets. His companion walked with him. It is the condition of the disease of jealousy that love, self-pity and hatred move forward together. The victim can be cured, in a moment, by a word, only to be the more diseased by another. He moves always in double form, for while he sees clearly his own madness he at the same time embraces it with eager conviction. He cries out for relief from his torture and at the same time refuses to allow himself to be relieved. Every word, every sound is a significant portent, and yet he is aware how insignificant these words can, in the final truth, prove themselves.

He accepts greedily evidence that he knows to be no evidence at all.

With Ellis this was the climax to years of unsatisfied desire – a climax, the night, the trees, the houses, the lighted windows, thundered into his ears, and yet he knew also that the facts were in themselves almost nothing. Two years ago. In all the time since then Vanessa had been kind, honest, attentive. If, at any moment, he had spoken to her of the letter, he had scarcely mentioned knew that she would at once have replied: 'Yes – in Cumberland on such a day.' Thousands upon thousands of times in these twelve years he had longed to ask her this question and yet never once had he dared to do so. Since the day of the '87 Jubilee, when he had spoken to her of the letter, he had scarcely mentioned Herries, but in blind, secret, surreptitious ways he had spied upon her. That had been disgraceful. It had been disgraceful that he had permitted Miss Fortescue to speak to him tonight, but it is a symptom of jealousy that the noblest of men may commit disgraceful acts as a chaste woman will utter obscenities in delirium.

Anu Ellis was not the noblest of men. He had, all his life, been lonely, mistrustful, caught in a web that he could not break.

This remained: Vanessa had spent a day with Herries and had not told him. She had spent one day – why not others? She had deceived him in this. Then she had deceived him often. But she had not deceived him because he had not asked her. She had not lied. She had, he knew, never lied to him – but is it not a lie when a woman sees her lover in secret? Was Herries her lover? It was at that agonizing moment, a moment that had visited him often before but never with such tyranny as now, that he looked about him and saw that the starlit sky, the houses, the deserted street, were coloured a faint green. 'A tender background of green leaves.' 'A pale-green mushroom-shaped hat.' 'A mass of shaded green wings.' This faint green light trembled like the mist of a cloud of greenflies, touching the steps before dark walls, the white posters of the evening papers outside the closed and barred newspaper shop, the bent figure of an old woman in a battered straw hat picking something from the gutter, the light of a gas lamp.

A hansom clattered past. A bell from some church sounded the hour. Trembling with a terrible chilling heat, Ellis turned homewards.

He was half undressed when he heard Vanessa come in. As though he were a man with a thousand ears he had been listening ever since he entered his room for those sounds. His door was just ajar. He knew what he would hear. The closing of the hall door, the soft voice of the butler, Vanessa's softer one, a little pause. Then 'Goodnight', the butler's 'Goodnight, my lady', then the sweep of her long dress as she climbed the stairs. Then the opening of her own door, its shutting.

After that he undressed feverishly, but was extremely careful to fold his clothes, to place his studs in their silver box, to brush his scanty hair. Over his nightdress he drew on his dark grey dressing-gown, went into the passage, listened, then knocked.

She knew of course his knock. He heard her say: 'Come in.'

She was sitting in front of her mirror, a white wrap over her shoulders, brushing her long dark hair which fell to her waist. As he came in she looked at him over her shoulder, smiling.

'I thought you would be asleep. I came in as quietly as I could.'

He stood by the door staring at her; seeing her in the lamplight with that dark flood of hair, the white wrap over the loose white robe, her smile so friendly and simple, he felt so furious a storm of jealousy sweep over him that he lowered his eyes as though, in actuality, he had been overwhelmed by a tremendous arching wave of blinding deafening water.

At last he moved across the room and sat in a chair near the bed. She continued to brush her hair, talking happily. 'We went to *The Prisoner of Zenda* after all. Peile had seen it before, but as he never remembers anything *that* didn't matter. It was new to the rest of us. George Alexander and Fay Davis, you know. Miss Davis is handsome, but *what* a stick of a part, and Alexander never can forget the clothes he's wearing. The house was full, but of course it was only revived last week. I saw Johnny Beaminster and, oh yes, Alice Parlington. You remember – you danced with her at the Devonshire Ball. She was Isabella of Spain or something. Well, she asked about you and wants us to go to dinner one night . . .'

She moved into her dressing-room. For a long while he sat there, staring in front of him. She returned and got into bed, giving him a light kiss on his forehead as she passed him.

'What sort of an evening have you had? Was old Timothy a terrible bore? I thought of you when Alexander was an hour or more kissing Flavia's hand. I was most dreadfully bored, but comforted myself with thinking that you were equally bored at home. Cynthia looked so pretty, but I am sure she is harming herself with her tiny waist. It is smaller every time I see her. And the smaller her waist grows the more intellectual she becomes. Ibsen is her only wear. Elizabeth Robins and Janet Achurch her only actresses. So was so horrified when she found that I hadn't read *Esther Waters* that I thought she'd fall out of the box, and yet she puts up with Peile Worcester who can hardly spell his own name. She loves him, I really believe . . .' She stopped. She was aware that he had not spoken since he had entered the room. She sat up, resting her head on her hand.

'What is it, Ellis? Aren't you well? Is your head still bad?'

She put out her hand and touched his forehead.

'Why, you're in a fever. Let me—'

'No,' he said. 'Don't do anything. I want to speak to you.'

She saw then that he was trembling from head to foot and, as always when someone near her was suffering, she forgot everything save that distress. She got out of bed, put on the white wrap and went towards the door.

'You're ill. You're shaking all over. Wait, while I—'

He looked across the room at her.

'No, please. There's something I must say. Go back to bed.'

She did so. She knew that something had occurred while she was at the theatre. She had now for so many years been prepared for some crisis that never arrived. How many times there had been a preface like this: Ellis in misery, dumb with some hidden trouble, beginning to speak, turning away like a child afraid, and because he was always a child to her she always comforted him, not asking what his trouble was, but consoling him. Men seemed to her completely inarticulate in any real distress – her father, Benjie, Ellis, they were all the same. They could not speak when they had something important to say, and when there was nothing they chattered interminably. She had been tired, wearied with her day, the gossip, the heat of the theatre, but now she forgot herself, wondering only, as she had wondered so often before, what she could do to soothe him.

Then he said, not looking at her:

'I heard this evening that two years ago you were alone in Cumberland with Herries – alone for a whole day, seen in a compromising position.'

So *that* was it! Two years ago. Ridiculous. A compromising position. That angered her. She drew back into the bed like a child who has been hurt.

'It is quite true that I was with Benjie in Cumberland one afternoon two years ago. The "compromising position" part of it is insulting. You remember, I went to Cumberland for a week. I had no idea that Benjie was there, of course. When we found that we were so near, we met. If you had asked me I would have told you.'

'Then you admit it?'

'Admit what?'

'That you met him secretly, spent the day with him alone, and told me nothing afterwards.'

'I met him certainly. We were alone for part of the time. I would have told you had you asked me.'

She looked at him, forgetting very quickly her own anger because the fuss was about so little, was so unimportant. Once sure of that, her earlier sensation swept back – that here was something small, childlike, suffering, and that she must comfort him. She moved nearer to him. She put out her hand and let it rest very gently on his shoulder.

'Ellis dear, there is no mystery, no adultery, nothing sensational. Miss Fortescue, I suppose, told you – tonight while I was at the theatre. The "compromising position" could be only hers. Now listen, Ellis. I have seen Benjie perhaps half a dozen times since our marriage – and we have been married over twelve years – so that's not bad, is it? I have spoken to him twice alone, once in the Park, once in Cumberland. I gave no promise not to speak to him. If you had ever asked me I would have told you. You must remember that Benjie and I have been friends all our lives. I know that some of the family don't like him, that you don't like him, but when you have known someone always – you see them differently.'

She had broken off abruptly, the tone of her voice had changed, her hand had withdrawn from his shoulder, because suddenly in the middle of a sentence she saw that he, not hearing what she was saying to him, was staring at her and that his stare was crazy. Two people living together with some ill-adjustment often find that they go with slow measured steps for a long period and that then quite suddenly, and for no apparent cause, as though someone caught them in the small of their backs and jerked them forward, they are hurled into a precipitous and often catastrophic descent. It is only afterwards, on looking back, that they can see that this sudden jerk forward had the beginning of its impetus in those very first slow steps.

It was so with Vanessa now. She looked at Ellis and saw a grotesque. Under the shade of the lamp a man with a high domed forehead and a lean peaked nose was sitting. This man wore a grey dressing-gown and a nightdress that was open at the neck so that two protruding bones, pink in the lamplight, gave him a hen's neck. His bare ankles, too, were pink and sharply boned. This thin bony man with his long body looped together in the chair had two eyes that looked at Vanessa but did not see her, looked beyond her at the room but did not see that either, saw something that frightened and angered them, something that no one else saw. This separate and apart vision – which is what the sane man means when he calls his brother insane – gave the figure in the chair an aspect of loneliness, isolation. Put this man in a crowded theatre and he would be quite alone, put him in a solitary cell and he would have company.

Vanessa saw life very simply. She had some of the good sense and quiet of her father, some of the good sense and love of action of her grandmother. She was entirely sane about all things. That she was also a poet, because of the country blood in her veins, affected not at all her relations with her fellows. She had lived with Ellis for more than twelve years and had needed all her patience, sanity, humour, and common sense. Any woman, living with a man who loves her, whom she herself does not love, needs all these things, day by day and week by week. But she had learnt that you can care for a man without loving him and obtain satisfaction of your need – so she cared for Ellis. But behind her care there had grown and grown the fear that one day the situation would be too difficult for her. As she always herself said, she hated scenes, melodramas, floods of tears, self-pityings, shrieks, and beatings of the breast. She did not know how to behave in such a world. Her father and mother had been quiet people and she was a quiet person, although as with her grandmother there was a wild passionate life at the core of her nature. She had also a strong sense of the ridiculous both in herself and in others.

But now, looking at Ellis, she had no sense of the ridiculous. There was something here both real and terrible. Instinctively, as she always did in a crisis, she thought of her father. 'Help me through this,' she said, as she had done when she was a little child on Cat Bells.

She suspected that Ellis was going to scream.

'He will rouse the whole house.' She even remembered that Miss Fortescue would not yet be asleep and that her room was not far away. However, Ellis did not scream. He said very quietly:

'You are a liar. Herries has been your lover for years.'

(Even as he said it he knew that it was not true. A very quiet little animal squatting inside his head observed rather wearily: '*That* you know is not true.')

'Ellis, let us talk sense.' Vanessa held her hands tightly together under the bedclothes. 'You are fifty-four. I shall soon be thirty-eight. We have lived together for years and you know that I have never lied to you, not in the smallest, most unimportant matter. I have never been Benjie's lover nor anyone's lover. You must trust me as I trust you, otherwise we must separate.'

He leant forward towards her: her impulse was to shrink back, but courage in this dangerous moment for which, she felt now, she had for years been preparing, was of more importance than any other quality. So she sat up, put out her hand and picked up the white silk wrap from the chair on the other side of the bed;

then with it warmly around her, her hair falling darkly about her, leaning forward, her hands clasped on her raised knees, she said, very quietly:

'Ellis, listen. We are too old not to be sensible about this. We matter too much to one another to have scenes. Besides, I hate scenes. You mustn't be unhappy and there is no reason—'

'No reason!' he broke in. His thin hand shot forward and caught her upraised knee. 'No reason when you have made me unhappy for years – not loving me, pretending, taking people in, but not me. Do you hear? – never me! Do you hear? Do you hear? I've had enough of it. You drive me mad with your unkindness! You – your lover . . .'

All drama verges on the ridiculous, and especially English drama. Vanessa had once, years ago, in the Park, felt Ellis' physical contact although he had not touched her. When her protective affection was aroused Ellis' body was there for her to comfort. But when he was angry or sexually passionate she hated his touch. One hand had closed about her knee, the other was on her breast; his face was close to hers, his body stretching up to the bed. If this scene was ludicrous she was too angry to notice it.

'You are hurting me,' she said.

He threw himself on the bed, his body convulsed, trembling, thrusting against hers. He tore open her nightdress; with his knees on the bed, his arms around her body, his hands bruising her, he pushed her down into the bed. Then his hands moved to her neck: panting, murmuring unintelligible words, he twisted her head round into the pillow. His hysteria gave him great strength; she began to wonder, in a quite detached way, whether he would kill her, and she had no power at all to resist. She tried to conserve her strength, for his hands now were so tightly about her neck that she could not breathe except in little gasps of pain. A black cloud, scattered with spots of intense light, pushed against her vision.

She thought: 'This is absurd', and anger, fear of death, pain were all mingled in the dark wavering cloud.

The pressure of his hands relaxed. His body, without moving, lay heavily on hers. He was crying. She listened, as it seemed for a long time, to his sobs. At last, very wearily, she turned. He slowly raised himself, slipped off the bed. She lifted herself painfully and saw that he was kneeling on the floor, his head bowed, hidden in the bed, his body shaken with sobs.

For a long while there was no other sound in the room. At last she rose, went into the dressing-room, bathed her face and hands, stood there for a while wondering what she would do. When she came back he was still there, his body bent low, his face buried in his hands, crying.

She touched his shoulder.

'You will catch cold, Ellis.' She took her white cloak and wrapped it round him, but as her hands came into contact with his body he trembled. She went back into bed and waited for him to recover.

THE GREAT TIMOTHY SCANDAL

'YES, that is the cruel moment, when you really begin to feel old,' said Barney, nodding his head and settling his fat body more comfortably in his chair. 'I am sixty-eight, you know, Vanessa, in this year of grace eighteen hundred and ninety-eight – close on seventy – and I had no sense of age at all until last week when Nevinson took me to a Fabian Reception. There we were all walking about, already in the New Century, and every macaroon was a hard little Fact and every cup of tea an admonition not to be silly. Well, I like to be silly. In the coming century no one is going to be silly. It will be motor-cars, telephones, and all our food will be in little pills. If it weren't for things like the Klondike madness and the German Emperor and Sarah Grand I should know that the Fairy-Tale World was gone for ever. I've lived all my life in it, you know – charming world where everything had a meaning, when we believed in Faith, Hope, and Charity, assisted by Watts, when we really meant to be good even if we were not, when our children said "Sir" and "Ma'am", when we thought the Albert Memorial lovely, and were certain that it was our duty to convert every unhappy Black Man to trousers and the worship of our Sovereign. Why, in the coming century I wouldn't wonder if we don't believe in the Empire any more! I wouldn't be surprised if even adultery becomes a scientific fact rather than a moral crime. But I liked the old world. It was *my* world. My silly novels amused it (or a small fragment of it). I could lead my own life without interference so long as I didn't shock anyone in public, I could eat and drink as much as I liked. I remember, Vanessa, when I was a lad, going to the fight between Sayers and Heenan, the last great fight in England it was. It was just an adventure then, but I can see now that it was the end of an epoch. Epochs are always ending, I suppose; it doesn't matter unless you're seventy. Well, I've had a good life. I can grow as fat as I like. Nobody cares any more.'

'I care,' said Vanessa, smiling across the table at him. They were having tea alone together in Hill Street.

'While I'm getting fatter you're getting thinner.'

'Am I? I'm thirty-nine this year, you know.'

He looked at her intently. He loved her very dearly, more now than any other woman in the world.

'You haven't been very merry lately, Vanessa,' he said. 'I haven't heard you laugh as you used to do for a long time.'

'I'm not very merry,' she answered, getting up and walking about the room, her long black-and-white dress trailing behind her. She turned round, came over to him and stood beside him.

'Barney – what are the family saying?'

'The family?'

'Yes – Violet, Cynthia, Alfred – all of them.'

'Saying about what?'

'Us – Ellis. This house.'

He didn't answer at first, then he said slowly:

'Nothing much.'

'Oh! They are! In the last few months they've been closing in – nearer and nearer. For one thing Miss Fortescue's going must have been enough to start them—' She drew a chair close to him and sat down.'

'I can't keep quiet any longer. Something must be done. I've never been beaten by anything before, and I said that *this* shouldn't beat me either. Two other bad things have happened to me in my life – once when my father died, once when Benjie and I – oh, well, that's past history. Each time I held my head up and said: "I can manage this" – and manage it I did. My married life hasn't been easy, you know, but there have always been all kinds of little things to help it along. Life, I'm sure, isn't *meant* to be too tragic and I've had great consolation in feeling that I was dressing up – *pretending* to be a grand hostess, you know. Grandmother had a devil of pride inside her and so have I had, and all the time that I was longing to run away to Cumberland and be my real self I have felt as though she and father knew about this game that I was playing and wanted me to do my best

at it. Then there's been Ellis. I did him a terrible injustice in
marrying him when I didn't love him. The only thing I could do
in return was to be kind to him, protect him, be his friend ... I'm
not boasting, Barney, but I truly have played the game all these
years. Now I can play it no longer. I'm beaten.'

Barney took her hand in his.

'What's happened, my dear?'

'Last July Ellis and I had a dreadful scene. Miss Fortescue
told him one evening that I had been alone with Benjie two years
before in Cumberland. You know – that day at Dungeon Ghyll.
In itself that was nothing, but Ellis had been wretchedly jealous
long before, as you know. This was the climax. I was in bed and
he almost strangled me – a ridiculous scene, and it ended in his
crying all night, imploring me to forgive him, going to sleep at
last in my arms. For weeks after that he was abject. He dismissed
Miss Fortescue, as you know, and for a time I thought that I
could manage him. That was July. This is February. I know now
that I'll never be able to manage him again.'

She paused. Barney felt her hand tremble in his.

'What is it?' he asked.

'Ellis is mad. He has been mad for months. Oh, only at times.
We have parties here, he goes to the City. So far as I know no one
except Lettice Marrable suspects anything. The servants may. I
don't know ... You can't think, Barney, how pitiful it is! If I
could help him neither you nor anyone else should know anything, but I *can't* help him. It is I who aggravate him. I would
give him anything, anything he asks if it would help him.
Nothing can help him. I don't know whether to go or stay. But
one day it will be too much for me and I shall go. The worst of it
is that now, although I am so sorry for him, I don't feel even
kind. If I had loved him I would stay with him for ever, but the
dreadful thing now ... the dreadful thing ...' She turned her
head. 'I hate him. I fear him. I have never been afraid of anyone
or anything, but now the very sound of his step ...'

She began to cry. Barney had never seen her cry before.

'I am middle-aged. I have loved one man all my life with my
whole heart and he has loved me. Why should I lose everything?
What have I done?'

Very quickly she recovered herself. She walked to the window
and he waited. When she returned she was quite calm again.

'Listen, Barney. You are to say nothing of this to anybody.
Only ... if it gets too difficult ... I shall ask you to help me. It

may be better soon. He has been quite normal for the last month. Very quiet. Very submissive. Poor Ellis! Listen! He's coming ... I know his step now, even when I don't hear it.'

Ellis came in. But he was not alone: on either side of him walked a lady, and Barney remembered afterwards with amusement that the first sight that he had of his two relations, Miss Vera Trent and Miss Winifred Trent, was this entry, guarding and protecting Ellis.

For they were, it seemed, distant cousins. Ellis, quietly and with much courtesy, explained it. 'Henry Cards – he had a wife back in the eighteenth century, Lucilla. I can remember, dear Miss Trent, my father speaking of her. My father was born in 1770 – it seems odd, doesn't it? – and Lucilla died about 1780, I think. She painted very charming watercolours. I shouldn't wonder if there are not one or two still about somewhere. Henry and Lucilla had two sons. One of them, Prosper, was Jennifer's father, my dear Vanessa. Well, Prosper married a Miss Amelia Trent, and our two cousins descend from her younger brother. Now what does that make you to us, Miss Trent? About second cousin twice removed, does it not? Still, there's always a strong family feeling, a very strong family feeling ...'

Everyone laughed. The butler brought in fresh tea. Who were these two ladies? Vanessa had the sense that they had been in this house all their lives and had known Ellis for ever. However, it appeared not. They had never visited Hill Street. Their carriage had driven up just as Ellis had arrived from the City. They had met on the doorstep. Oh! they must apologize, but the fact is that they had lived all their lives in Bournemouth. Such a charming place, and a hundred years ago there was nothing at all but the sea waves, the sand, a tree or two! Yes, they loved Bournemouth. Vanessa interrupted. That was where Jennifer's father and mother had lived, was it not? Yes, indeed, Doctor Trent of those days had been a close friend of Mr and Mrs Cards. Mrs Cards had been *so* proud of Bournemouth, so proud that she used to speak and write of the town as a fashionable watering-place when it was really only a house or two. Doctor Trent and Mr and Mrs Cards had been among its earliest inhabitants. Oh yes, they remembered all about the beautiful Jennifer! At one time it was thought that she would become the Duchess of Wrexe. She was actually engaged to the Duke for a brief while, they believed ...

They chattered on, most happily. They were both tall and elderly women and remarkably alike. They were slim and had soft grey hair under their large black hats. They wore black feather boas, black silk dresses very long in the skirts; each lady had a big bunch of imitation Parma violets pinned to her breast and wore a very thin gold chain. Their faces resembled those of placid, extremely kindly sheep, but behind the mildness, Vanessa decided, there was a strong and possibly relentless determination. It certainly appeared that they had made complete appropriation of Ellis. They sat one on either side of him and, although they smiled at Vanessa and listened with deference to Barney, it was Ellis whom they admired. Their voices were soft with that comforting murmur that belongs to a distant mowing machine on a summer day. They took off their gloves; each wore two or three rings, thickly studded with diamonds, on the fingers. They were alike in almost every particular; the only difference perhaps being that Miss Vera was a little the more severe and determined of the two, Miss Winifred the softer and more melting. They were greatly interested in all the Herries relations – Alfred and his wife, Horace and *his* wife, Emily, Phyllis' son Philip, old Horace in Manchester, the Rockages in Wiltshire and their girls Maud and Helen, Cynthia and Peile Worcester. They seemed to have the fullest information about all of them. Vanessa noticed that they made no mention of Benjie or Rose and that they shook their heads over Timothy at Cambridge. Yesterday, it appeared, they had paid a call on Violet. With all their comments and questions they were kind and hushed. They behaved, Vanessa thought, as though they were nurses in a sickroom.

Barney watched all this in amazement. He found that he could not tear himself away. How dramatic a transition! A moment before Vanessa had been telling him the most awful things, speaking, he could not doubt, with the most absolute sincerity, and now here they were all drinking tea together, these two old maids like two cows in a field, and Ellis, calm, benign, dignified, smiling and courteous! Had Vanessa been imagining her terrors? No, he knew her too well. She was the least hysterical of women. He would not wonder but that the tears that she had just now shed were the first since her childhood. As he saw her now so quiet and so lovely in her black-and-white dress, laughing, looking after the two old women as though they were her first care in the world, smiling up at Ellis, her broad unruffled brow, her large dark eyes that had never lost the frankness, the eagerness of her earlier simplicity, her dignity as hostess, her natural friendliness as one human being with another, he thought: 'Well, I'm damned if she can't manage this. It's not so bad as she said.'

When he got up to go, Ellis most courteously went all the way downstairs with him, bending his long neck to hear what Barney had to say, rather as an Ambassador listens with the utmost attention to a diplomatic visior.

'Hullo! That's a new clock you've got!' Barney said, at the turn of the stairs. It was a long thin clock of gilded red Chinese lacquer.

'Yes,' said Ellis. 'Vanessa saw it somewhere and liked it.'

'Of course he hates me,' Barney thought. 'We both know that. Still, he's behaving very well.'

Finally, in the street, he shook his head. Ellis was not mad. He, Barney, knew a madman when he saw one!

When the ladies were gone Vanessa praised them. Ellis walked about the room and praised them too. How quiet, intelligent, and well-behaved! He had feared that the women in England were lost, with their clubs, their passion for 'this Bridge', their bicycle riding, their indecent novels, their conceit. He understood that there were in London alone thirty clubs for ladies. What did ladies want with clubs? What—

He stopped, went to a table and fidgeted with a small silver box, a paper knife, a book. He picked up the book, put it down.

'Vanessa, I did not care for that hat you were wearing yesterday.'

The room was rather dimly lit, the fire low. Her nerves had been shaken by her little talk with Barney, and as she got up and went across to him she felt an impulse, so strong that she wondered whether she would be able to conquer it, to tell him that she could endure this no longer, that she must leave the house, London, all the life that had, so ridiculously, been built up around her ... leave the house, at once, without a moment's delay ...

'What hat?' she asked.

'The one you were wearing yesterday. The one with the – green birds' wings.' He seemed to have difficulty in speaking the last words.

She was standing close to him. Her agitation fell from her because his eyes were so weary that she was suddenly filled with pity.

'Oh, Ellis, you're tired. Go and lie down until dinner. Or stay here. I'll read to you.'

'No. But you understand, Vanessa? Please don't wear that hat again.'

She laughed and was frightened. His hand was shaking against the dark stuff of his trousers.

'It's quite new. Yesterday was the first time I had worn it. I thought you would like it.'

'Then you must change its colour. You know that ... green ... I don't like it as a colour.'

She tried to speak easily. 'Certainly. You shall never see the hat again.'

He put his hand out and touched her forehead. All her strength was needed not to move away, so she came closer to him.

'How cool your forehead is! Mine is always burning.'

She put her hand through his arm and drew him to the sofa. She helped him to lie down, arranging the cushions, but he said, as though he were half asleep: 'No, sit here – close to me.'

She sat down and he laid his head on her lap. He closed his eyes. The creeping whisper of the fire, the steady determined tick of the large gold clock on the mantelpiece filled the long, shadowy room. She sat there without moving. Her childhood – the friendly figures of her father, Will Leathwaite, Elizabeth, Aunt Jane, her grandmother – the places, the Cat Bells garden with the little sturdy wood, the stream, the line of the hill above the cottage, lovely days at Uldale, the seashore at Seascale, the purple shadows of Skiddaw, sunlit brilliant clouds of snow on Blencathra, the main street of Keswick, someone riding by on a horse, the scarlet coach from Kendal, the friendliness, the small gardens of daffodils and primulas, the grey steeple of St John's above the green fields running to the Lake's edge, the hillsides flaming with bracken, the Herdwicks moving their thick sturdy bodies slowly in front of the shepherd ... her father, her father waving his hand to her from his writing-table as she passed along the garden path, her father with his soft lazy eyes, his loving ironical glance, his hand resting on Will's shoulder ...

Tears stole down her cheek. Without moving, yet she felt that she was hastening, against her will, down a dark path away from everything in life that was loving and good into a house dark and chill, with doors that would be locked behind her. How dearly she loved life! How hard she had tried to do what was right, and now she was nearly forty, frightened like a small child, and lonely! ... She had never known that it was possible for anyone to be as lonely as she was. What was she to do?

And Benjie? She had, in these hard minutes, kept him away

from her, but now, heart and mind opened, too weak any longer to resist, she threw out her arms, he came running, running to her. She clasped him to her, felt his face pressed close to hers, his heart beat against her breast.

The Chinese clock on the stairs struck. The gold clock followed it. For an hour she had not moved and Ellis, pallid as a dead man, lay with his head on her lap.

Then the Great Timothy Scandal sprang upon her. It was an excellent moment for a family excitement. There was but little in May 1898 for anyone to discuss. A small coal strike, a war between the United States and Spain, the death of poor old Mr Gladstone, the Dreyfus case, the low spirits of the Liberal Party. In none of these things did the Herries take a very extravagant interest. Cynthia redecorated her little house and gave an evening party for the Ibsen enthusiasts, Alfred introduced everywhere an astonishingly uncouth South African who was said to be worth millions, Emily discovered a Prophet from Shoreditch. The Season began and huge evening receptions rolled from house to house. The West End was populated with coachmen, footmen and men with grave diplomatic countenances hired for the evening. Every kind of carriage and every kind of horse glittered and shone. The window boxes blazed with geraniums. The Opera sparkled with diamonds. There was so much money that everyone despised it and would do anything, invite anybody, go anywhere, to obtain more. Morals were as loose as usual and manners beginning to crumble. Woman was no longer subservient to Man, and the Empire was at its apogee.

The Herries took all this for granted as every other English family was taking it for granted. The Herries concluded that everything would last for ever just as it was. Emily's Prophet said uncomfortable things, and Cynthia, Violet, Mrs Alfred, went to a meeting to hear him. They found him very sweet with his deep black eyes and flowing black hair. Melba sang at the Opera. Also at one of Vanessa's parties. A man called Conrad published a book called *Tales of Unrest*, but no member of the Herries family read it. Several ladies and gentlemen rode in electric cabs. Violet wore an evening dress with a high collar encircled with four rows of pearls. Lettice Marrable was seen bicycling in a pair of knickerbockers. For some while, however, inside this dazzling world the Herries circle had been moving quietly. There had been no family sensation. Something strange was happening in Hill Street although Vanessa appeared as usual and Ellis was stiff, courtly, and boring as usual. Rose, it was said, was drinking herself to death in Paris. Nothing had been heard of Benjie. One topic of interest was the career of the two Miss Trents, who went everywhere and were constantly at Hill Street. That, however, was not a scandal – far from it. Two quieter, gentler ladies could not be found anywhere.

The Great Timothy Scandal, then, burst brilliantly and, small though its cause, it brought in its sequence changes to many people. It struck Vanessa on a sunny May day when, coming back after a drive in the Park with Cynthia, when they had both been very gay and talked much nonsense, Lettice Marrable threw the news at the quiet tea-table. Cynthia always regarded Miss Marrable as a kind of aboriginal savage: her little hard hats, her manlike tunic, short skirt, her brusque masculine tone and quite extraordinary masculine attitudes, her public smoking of cigarettes, her abilities at tennis and golf, her passionate desire that women should sit in Parliament, all these things filled Cynthia with a wondering amaze. She was never weary of looking at her, although she did not care to be seen with her in public.

Lettice Marrable now came in and said:

'Timothy Bellairs has run away to Paris with Tom, Benjie Herries' boy. Violet has just heard. Timothy had a letter written from Paris. Violet is in a terrible way and says that Tom has perverted Timothy or some word like that. Timothy senior has left for Paris. If he sees Benjie he is going to shoot him. They are all talking at Violet's now. I've just come from there. Horace and the Miss Trents and Carey Rockage ... Benjie Herries is to be horsewhipped whenever he's found. Oh, you never saw anything so funny in your life as Horace threatening to whip Benjie – *when* he finds him! And the real joke is that Tom is only fourteen. He must have run away from school up to town and met Tim here. Anyway they are both safe in Paris.'

Cynthia said: 'I wish I was.'

Vanessa said: 'But it is ridiculous of Violet to blame anyone but herself. Tim has wanted to be a painter since he was a baby. It is nothing to do with Benjie at all.'

After that with every hour the affair grew. It seemed that Benjie *was* in Paris and that the two boys stayed with him. Then came news of a meeting between old Timothy and Benjie. Old Timothy gave it him, it was generally understood, 'hot and strong'. What really happened no one knew because no third person was present: it was difficult, however, for the Herries to believe that Timothy gave anyone anything 'hot and strong'. He was sixty-one, suffered from his heart, was as fat as a barrel. Moreover he was amiably minded.

It appeared that Benjie's attitude was that, as regarded his own boy, if he wanted to leave school and see the world, he should do so. Benjie was the same at his age. As for Timothy, he was twenty-one and ought to know his own mind. As a matter of fact he always *had* known his own mind, and it was only the stupid conventionality of his parents that held him back. It was said that at this point old Timothy called Benjie 'a damned blackguard' and that Benjie did not resent the insult as any gentleman would have done, but offered Timothy a cigarette. It was further said that the interview between Timothy and his son was extremely painful. Young Timothy declared that now that he was in Paris he was going to stay there and that Tom Herries had had nothing whatever to do with it. They had been friends all their lives, he and Tom; Tom hated his school and wanted to be with his father. By this time it was generally admitted that Benjie was the Devil. He had always been the Devil. It was time the family were rid of him.

Would Benjie come to London and face his accusers? It was understood that, with a shrug of his shoulders, he said that of course he would come to London, although he had no idea what he was to be accused of.

He came to London.

A meeting, as famous in its own small way as Christabel's Ball or Walter's historic visit to the Christmas party at Uldale, took place on the second of June at the Rockland Club between these gentlemen: Carey Rockage, Timothy Bellairs, Alfred Herries, Horace Ormerod, Barney Newmark and Benjamin Herries, Esquire.

The best evidence of what actually occurred is to be found in Barney's Journal (the Journals are all in the family archives at Centor Park, bound in faded red leather, behind glass, in the library. Judith Paris' book and the earlier eighteenth-century papers are in the same bookshelf, equally protected and equally unread).

DUKE STREET, W. *June 2nd, 1898*
I will try to put down as briefly as possible what occurred today at Rockland's, a matter purely of family interest but important

perhaps one day to young Tim and to Tom.

I met Benjie at the Criterion for lunch. I hadn't seen him for a considerable time, but there he was, just the same as ever, brown with health, cocky as a robin – very like a robin. He has just that bright, roguish, adventurous, don't-care-a-damn kind of eye and, although he's stocky, his lack of height (always a sore point with him) gives him a birdlike appearance. He looked, I'll confess, a bit odd because he wasn't wearing a hat; he had a soft nondescript collar with his usual dark red tie in its gold ring, and his clothes were a sort of wine-coloured tweed. He is always scrupulously clean, though. Benjie's careless but at the same time spruce, and his brown cheeks, bright eyes, stiff close-cropped wiry hair, hands that look as hard as iron, taut, springy body – all these, with the very kindly wrinkles about his eyes and his extremely engaging smile, prejudice you in his favour if you're an ordinary man on two legs and not a hypocrite like Horace or a prig like Ellis.

Anyway there he was, saying 'Hullo, Barney!' just as though we'd met yesterday, and walking into the big room at the Criterion as though he owned the place and at the same time found it very absurd.

As usual he ate very little. He didn't talk much either. He couldn't understand what they wanted to see him about. 'I'm not a boy, you know. I'm forty-three. I haven't harmed the family so far as I can see. They seem to think that I've lured Tim to Paris and that I may ruin his body and soul – using young Tom as a decoy. Damnable nonsense! Tim's a fine painter. I don't know much about it, but he's started away at Lucien's, which is, I believe, one of the best of those places, and old Lucien himself thinks highly of him. Tim's crazy about these men I don't understand – Gauguin, Van Gogh, Cézanne – but I'm ready to tell him he's right. How do you and I know? We may have taste but we don't care enough really to know. You can only know about Art if you happen both to love it and have a trained taste. Anyway, there he is and Tom's learning languages. He's got a passion for them and his great idea is to train for a War Correspondent. "What'll you do if there's never a war again?" I asked him. "Oh, there'll always be one somewhere," he said, and I expect he's right. He can put things down on paper pretty smartly for his age. Well, there they are, a decent pair of kids. What's the trouble? *I* had nothing to do with it. What do they want *me* to do?'

'As I understand it,' I answered, 'they want you to tell Tim to return to his parents. They think you've got some unholy influence over him.'

'Unholy be damned!' said Benjie. 'I've never had the smallest influence over anyone.'

'If you refuse they'll expel you with bell, book, and candle.'

'Expel me from what?'

'The family circle.'

'A fat lot *I* care!'

So after luncheon we went along. Rockland's is, I have always thought, the stupidest and slowest Club in London. It is just right for elderly Herries like Timothy and Carey Rockage and old Horace when he comes down from Manchester. It is small and dingy, and the room where they waited for us smelt of whisky and stale cigar-smoke. The windows looked as though they hadn't been cleaned for months. Timothy and Carey belong to grander Clubs of course, and when they want to show off they go to them, but for a real family bust-up Rockland's is the place. They were all waiting for us in an upstairs card room which we had to ourselves. When we came in it struck me at once how large physically we were compared with Benjie and how physically unfit. Carey, Timothy, Horace and myself are all stout men and Alfred is pasty. Benjie could have taken the lot of us on and thrown us all out of window! However, he was not in the least aggressive. He smiled at everyone as though he loved them and if no one smiled back that was not *his* fault! Oddly enough as I looked round the room I felt, although I'd come there of course as Benjie's friend and supporter, an acute sympathy with all of them. I understood exactly how they felt. With the exception of Horace they are all decent men, and in my opinion the decent normal Herries man is about as decent as any Englishman anywhere. He is brave, loyal, patriotic, God-fearing, good to his women and generous to all men. Simply he hasn't any imagination. A little imagination and they would understand that Benjie's type is permanent. You can't get rid of it by cursing and abusing it. You've got somehow to make terms with it. Put it in gaol, exile it, and it will always return. When men like Carey and old Timothy have learnt how to assimilate men like Benjie, the Herries family will rule the world – until then it will be always second-rate. But, of course, that assimilation will never occur. So there will be always tales to tell, poets formed out of rebellion, and wars between nations. But I understood how they felt about

Benjie. You could see, as they looked at his country clothes and his round head with its sharp little eyes and his sturdy little legs, that he was the personification of disorder to them! And they were right.

Old Timothy, as the principal sufferer, took charge, and, standing in front of the fireplace, with his legs spread, he outlined the case. Unfortunately he was both lengthy and pompous. He said the same thing over and over again. What it came to was that he wanted his son back, that Benjie had tempted him to Paris and must therefore bring him back to London again. There was nothing personal in this. He spoke as though Benjie were the kind of man with whom he could not possibly *have* any personal relations.

When Timothy had finished at last, Benjie answered quietly that he had *not* tempted young Tim to Paris, that Tim was of age, and that, although of course it was a pity that he and his father did not agree, it was nevertheless the boy's own affair. 'In fact,' said Benjie, beaming round on all of them, 'I cannot see what I have to do with it or why you have asked me to meet you here.'

At that everyone wanted to speak at once. It was interesting to me to see the strong likeness that springs up between the men of our family when we are together. Alfred with his sharp nose that is always a little shiny, his high cheekbones and short black curly hair can hardly be said to resemble short-armed, short-legged, paunchy Carey who is the perfect Country Gentleman, or Timothy who is a kind of hundred-times-cleaned-scrubbed-and-brushed pillowcase, or myself who am just fat, careless and, alas, now purple-veined about the nostrils. And yet alike we all are, alike we always have been. Is it our English beef and cabbage that has made us so? Or our politics? Or the Battle of Hastings, 1066? Or insular security?

There in any case we all were, leaning forward like one man wanting to tell Benjie what we thought of him. Carey, who always speaks as though the thick Wiltshire soil had through the years crept up and swallowed his tonsils, had his word. He spoke as an English peer who has the crops, the family, and the British reputation among foreigners all to protect at once.

'Why we have asked you here,' he said, 'is because we feel, rightly or wrongly, that you are responsible for Timothy's boy's behaviour. The lad has caused his mother and father much pain. He has carried on a clandestine correspondence with your boy, it seems, for a long time past and of that we feel that you must have been – ah – cognizant.' (Here I caricature old Carey's style a bit.) '*Therefore*, therefore we have asked you to meet us. We are representing here today the family in London. I need not emphasize to you the grief that this has caused the lad's mother, nor the necessity we all feel that her boy – her only boy – should be restored to her. The lad is a good lad – fundamentally a good lad – and we feel that he must have been under some most unfortunate influence to persuade him—'

'Rot!' Benjie broke in. 'Never was greater nonsense. Tim's been pleading since he was in that unfortunate velvet suit that his mother always made him wear, to be allowed to be a painter. There isn't one of us here who understands anything about Art, including Barney, even if he does write novels. Why the devil,' he went on, suddenly attacking Timothy, 'couldn't you have let the boy try his hand? It's none of my business or was none until I was dragged into it like this, but no one is responsible for Tim's running off to Paris except his parents – and that's the truth!'

This was from every point of view a most unfortunate speech, and after it there was no hope at all of saving anybody's bacon. I had tried to advise Benjie at luncheon that he must go slow, placate the old boys, show them that he meant them no harm. But it was of course hopeless from the start. The very sight of their London clothes, the air they had not only of owning the Rockland (to which they were thoroughly welcome) but the whole of England, annoyed him, exasperated him. However, it might not have been so bad had it not been for his allusion to Art. Now none of them – not Timothy, nor Carey, nor Alfred, nor Horace – cared a damn about pictures, but they hated to be told that they knew nothing about them. Carey said to me long afterwards: 'It was the arrogance of it, you know – telling us we don't know a picture when we see one! Why, damn it, a picture is a picture, isn't it? A feller has eyes, hasn't he?'

When Benjie had finished Carey rapped out:

'Are you going to bring young Tim back to London or not?'

'Certainly not,' said Benjie.

Horace broke in:

'Oh, but, Benjie, I'm sure that Carey misunderstands you! What you mean to say is that you will do all you can in the circumstances—'

Benjie jumped to his feet.

'I mean nothing of the sort!' (He really loathed Horace.) 'I consider it a piece of damnedest impertinence, all of you sitting round here as though you were in judgement on me. I only came to show you that I didn't care a damn for any of you! You can all go to hell for all I care!'

Both Carey and Alfred, who were hot-tempered, jumped to their feet and I thought for a moment that there would be a bit of a fight. Alfred is tall and wiry; Carey, although his arms are so short, has shoulders like a coal-heaver and is strong for his sixty-odd years. Benjie stood there, almost touching them, waiting for anything that might come. Horace was nervously pushing at his glasses in a way that he has when he is frightened (Rose used to imitate this very well), Timothy threw out his stomach as a sort of vanguard of protection.

But this was where I came in. I took Benjie by the arm and led him out of the group.

'We're not in the Klondike,' I remarked (or something equally cheap). 'Benjie doesn't see that he has any responsibility for Tim's being in Paris and I don't see that he has either. Feeling no responsibility, he doesn't see that he can do anything about it. And that's the end of it.'

I could see them looking at us and classing us together. All writers are queer to men like Carey and Timothy, and at that time, with the Wilde trial still fresh in their minds, queerer than queer. It was perhaps some feeling about the Wilde business that made them the more intolerant of Benjie although they all knew that Benjie was normal enough. The fact remains that the Wilde trial made many people in England think, for a long time, that all writers, painters, musicians, were freaks and dangerous freaks. So there we were, the 'little gipsy', the rogue of the family, and the loose-living, novel-writing eccentric. We were damned together.

'That's not the end of it,' said Carey at last. 'We don't want to be unfair, Benjie, but the fact is that we've had about enough of you. For years now you've been upsetting everyone. Even as a boy you were a family scandal. You've been mixed up in two public brawls already and now there's this business. It is the feeling of all of us that we wish to have nothing more to do with you. And if you're a gentleman we trust you'll respect our feeling.'

Then it was I who figured in the scene. I lost my temper. Never mind what I said. It's of no importance. But as I once told Horace what I thought of him, so now I told Timothy, Carey, and Alfred. I enjoyed myself for at least five minutes.

When, scant of breath (for I'm nearly seventy and my heart is not as good as it was), I had ended, it was Benjie who drew me away.

He smiled at them all. 'Goodbye, friends and relations,' he said. 'I shan't bother any of you again.' (He liked a little theatrically at times. It stirred his sense of colour.)

So, his arm through mine, we went out together.

VANESSA IN PRISON

HYSTERIA is the only word for the emotional state in which the Herries family now indulged. It is little exaggeration to say that as London once saw Jack the Ripper behind every area step, so now the Herries saw Benjie.

In 1898 and 1899, as afterwards in 1913 and 1914, London itself became hysterical. A mad craze for wealth and pleasure, an extravagance of display, a fantastic exhibitionism of non-morality raged everywhere. Diamonds and politics from Africa, an international plutocracy from the Holy Land, a pride and arrogance and self-confidence, a recklessness of materialism, the beginning of the breaking down of all barriers of caste and exclusive traditions: these things marked these years, the last defiant 'Ta-ra-ra-boom-de-ay' before the drums beat in the figures and the problems of the new world.

The Kaiser waved his theatrical arm in Potsdam, old Krüger sat in his kitchen reading his Bible, in London jumping signs for the first time illuminated the night sky and frightened the horses, *The Belle of New York* and *The Gay Lord Quex* shocked the religious, vast audiences swallowed gladly the wild tales of de Rougemont; Kipling frightened two hemispheres by threatening to die of pneumonia; the cry was everywhere, 'Let 'em all come!'

In the week of the Rockland meeting young Timothy caught pneumonia in Paris, nearly died of it and refused to see either his father or mother when they hurried over to him. But Violet saw Benjie. She could not deny that he was quiet and courteous. He was eager that she should see her son: it was Timothy who refused to allow her to enter his room. She returned to London like an insane woman. It was perhaps that she felt in her heart that she had herself been to blame in the first place. She was an old woman. She was a tiresome woman. Her passion for chatter had grown into a garrulousness that bored the world; her grievances were so many that she was herself confused by their number. She said that 'everything had begun' on an awful day when old Emily Newmark had prayed over her and Oscar Wilde had laughed at her. Violet – her daughter – married in 1897 a Colonel Caldecott. The house in Onslow Square was the stiller and emptier for old Violet's ceaseless chatter.

Bore though everyone found her, it became the accepted fact that Benjie had stolen her son from her and ruined her life. Respectable people like the Rockages and the Worcesters and the Alfred Herries were, in sober fact, terrified of what Benjie might do next. The Worcesters and the Alfreds now had young children – Cynthia had two girls, Alfred a boy and a girl; who knew but that Benjie might kidnap them and hold them for ransom?

He was seen in London and the whole Herries world shuddered. The situation was developed by the part that Adrian Cards played in it. He went everywhere – and he was now a man of importance in the London world, an Under-Secretary and a writer of witty articles ('Very malicious', Alfred and Horace thought him) – saying that Benjie Herries was the best of fellows and that his relations were ridiculous people. The Herries – the Worcesters, Alfred, Violet and old Timothy, the Rockages – felt that everywhere Adrian went they were mocked. They knew of course the reason of his championship of Benjie. It was, as they assured everyone, because of his passion for Vanessa. He went with Vanessa everywhere. She was, at last, after years of good behaviour, forgetting her position, her duty to Ellis. All that wildness that *must* be in her blood when you remember her grandmother and great-grandfather, was at last coming out. It was true that Ellis must be very trying. But could she not remember what she owed to her position? There, too, Benjie's influence could be traced. After the scene at the Rockland Club, Benjie was banished from all decent male society, and yet Vanessa was known to have said that all the Herries men, except Barney, had behaved like fools in that affair.

It was true, Vanessa was at last angry. For thirteen years she had behaved, both in public and in private, as she ought to behave. Now she was beginning not to care whether she behaved or no. For she was increasingly unhappy, frightened and indig-

nant. She was moving swiftly, with a crazy husband at her side,
no close woman friend except Lettice Marrable in the world, a
sense of deep injustice burning within her, to a climax.

The two ladies, Miss Vera and Miss Winifred Trent, helped to
precipitate it. 'What is reality? This mirror is real because I can
touch the silver tracing on the woodwork of the frame, but I
stand, looking into it, brushing my hair, and Ellis is suddenly
standing behind me. Ellis is not real. Then is the mirror not real
any longer? Ellis is listening behind the door? I open it and the
carpet on the stairs is real, the ticking from the Chinese clock is
real, but is there not the sudden sharp click of a closing door, the
very crack of the finger of unreality? And through all this I am a
woman who longs to love and be loved in return. I am nearing
forty and my life is more than half gone. I have no children, no
one – since my father died – to whom I might freely give my
whole heart. Only Benjie and Rose – both disgraced, both exiles
... Is that, then, at last *my* reality, my hunger for love, my
hunger, my *hunger* ... in a woman who is nearly forty surely
that cannot be real? ... The Miss Trents have called. As they call
now every day.'

'Dear Vanessa. We drove round to see how you and dear Ellis
are. *How* is Ellis? Is his headache better?'

'Yes,' says Vanessa. 'Tonight we are going to *The Canary*.
They say that it is a most amusing play.'

They look at her, inspect her with their large, soft and yet most
resolute gaze. Everyone is watching her just as Ellis never ceases
to watch her.

'If I don't get out of this I shall go mad, just as Ellis is ...'

Yet, with all this, she could not prevent herself from enjoying
to the full any fun that came her way. She went out and about
with Adrian, Barney, Cynthia. She had plenty of the great world,
for the Duchess of Devonshire was less formidable with her than
with any other woman in London, she watched Lady London-
derry's passion for power with all the more sympathy because she
had never herself known the passion, and she helped Lady de
Grey turn the Opera from a shabby squalling business into a
splendid tiaraed pageant. Of all the grand ladies Lady Dorothy
Nevill was to her taste the most delightful; she never tired of her
daintiness, her humour, her anecdotes, her resolute vulgarities,
and her eager curiosity about human nature. No one who came
to Hill Street thought that there was anything but peace and
plenty there. Only the Family knew and the Family didn't say. It

was the business of the Family to inform the world in general
that anything Herries was right. Vanessa was the Family public
pride and of the utmost importance to them all.

Adrian was Lady Dorothy Nevill's especial pet, and he and
Vanessa went together very often to the house in Charles
Street.

'You're not in love with the young man, are you, my dear?' she
asked.

'Not the least little bit,' said Vanessa, laughing.

'Not that it matters,' said Lady Dorothy, tossing her little head
with its marvellous auburn wig, shaking her many beads and
necklets and amulets. 'You're not like these modern girls with all
their paintin' and powderin'. How men can kiss them *I* can't
understand. What Dizzy if *he* were alive . . .'

Vanessa had friends everywhere, girls in shops, young men
from the East End in whom Adrian was interested, writers
famous like Henry James and Kipling, obscure like young Mr
Smith who brought her the tattered manuscript of his novel to
read or Mr Brown who had written an Epic on the Armada,
actresses and actors like Irving, Ellen Terry, Forbes-Robertson
and young men who walked on at the Lyceum. All were alike to
her. She had no pose, no arrogances, no prejudices. So life
whirled on the outside while within steadily the drama grew
more intolerable.

Insanity is of all things the most pathetic, the most piteous, the
most intangible. Everyone *within* the house knew that Ellis was
insane. The servants nodded their heads together and watched
him as children watch a strange and unaccountable animal. They
developed a kind of pride in him. They marvelled that towards
the outside world he was 'always all right'. Seriously, with an
almost magisterial dignity, saying very little, listening to his
guests with a sort of absorbed gravity (he was not listening; he
was watching the figures *behind* the figures), he played his part.
With Finch the butler, Mrs Martin the cook, the two men-
servants, the housemaids, Lettice Marrable, he was the master of
the house, betraying himself to them only by the twitching of his
fingers, the way in which he would look over their shoulders, the
sudden impatient 'Very well, very well' or a sharp 'Is that door
closed? I can hear someone moving upstairs.'

The servants had for both their master and mistress a new and
rather touching kindliness. They were very well treated, were
paid excellent wages. Vanessa they adored. (Even Finch, who,

after Miss Fortescue's departure, robbed right and left, drank the best wine and so had a real friendliness to his employers.) They were kind, did their duties, but they waited ... Something would happen soon ... They might all be murdered in their beds ... This made them feel privileged.

Vanessa herself wondered, often enough, whether there were not two Ellises. He was very often, when alone with her, so quiet and rational that it was almost as though the old friendly days were back again. When he slept beside her he moaned in his sleep and she drew him to her, stroked his forehead, felt as though she were protecting him against an evil demon. Yet, with this, she suffered an appalling fear of him that, do what she would, always increased. Perhaps one night he would kill her. She was always prepared for that. She would not, she thought, mind very greatly. Oddly, pity and fear went hand in hand together. She, too, waited for the next step ...

Then one day in June 1898 she received a letter saying that Will Leathwaite was dead.

She had just come in from a drive and stood in the hall, the letter in her hand. It was from Mrs Newson, who had looked after the cottage and Will for some years – a very decent woman. It simply said that Will had been ailing for some time past, hadn't cared for his food, complained of his legs. Mrs Newson had gone to Grange to see a friend and, returning about seven of the evening, found Will dying in his chair by the fire.

'I thought you'd like to know, my lady, that it was your father's name he kept saying before he died, over and over. I don't rightly think he was ever the same man after your father died. But he was tranquil up to the last, and a finer-looking man not to be found anywhere I always said. And no trouble at all, not to no one.'

She stood there, lost in the past. Will was gone: now everyone was gone. She remembered her father's description of Will winning the race at Keswick years and years ago, how he pounded up the hill to the Druids' Circle, and young Adam, himself only a boy, riding in front of Will's father on the family mare, yelled encouragement. And then how Will had come up to Adam one Christmas Day and asked if he did not want a servant. Will's love for Adam had been the best that one human being can find for another: its character was paternal, protective, selfless, and also gay, simple, unsycophantic, man to man, brother to brother. It had been perhaps the finest thing in her father's life, Vanessa thought, looking back. Was there not always antagonism in every sex relation? But in this perfect charity, honesty, and – above all, best of all – equality ...

There was no Past when you experienced a love like this, for Adam and Will would go on for ever, for ever racing up the Keswick hill, for ever meeting, the snow sun-glittering at their feet, the blue smoke rising in the silent air, for ever one waiting the other's return, for ever that exchange of glance, sure and trustful, for ever that touch of hand on hand ... In all this changing, bewildering, unstable world the one sure and certain proof that there is something eternal in man's soul; that, once in a lifetime, one touches, deep in the heart, evidence of immortality.

The letter fell to the ground: she heard the Chinese lacquered clock strike the half-hour with its sententious solemn purr. The clock's voice resembled Horace's. Will's death increased her loneliness. She had not seen him for so long a time and yet he had been behind her – they two together thinking of Adam.

She picked up the letter and saw that Ellis was standing near to her and looking at her. Why did she never hear his step these days?

'Oh, Ellis!' she cried. 'Will Leathwaite is dead!'

Ridiculously, tears stole down her cheek behind her veil.

'Will Leathwaite?' he asked.

'Yes. Father's servant. You've seen him – a big fair-haired man with blue eyes.'

She had trained herself never to mention anything in connexion with Cumberland, but at this moment she was thinking of Will, not of Ellis.

He nodded, looked at her without speaking, and walked upstairs.

A few days later a very unaccountable thing occurred. He came to her in her room where she was reading, and timidly, as though he were asking a favour, said:

'Vanessa, let us go to Cumberland for a week – to your cottage on Derwentwater.'

He stood in front of her, very tall, very pale and rigid, as though she had ordered him in front of her to be scolded.

'To Cumberland?' She was so deeply astonished that she dropped the book. 'But, Ellis, you hate Cumberland!'

'No – who told you that?'

'Nobody, of course. Only yourself.'

'When have I said that I hated Cumberland?'

'Not *hated*. But disliked it. The rain – and you don't like the North—'

'Who told you that I hated Cumberland?'

She got up and walked away. His eyes frightened her. He bent down and picked up the book. 'Why do they bind books in green? It is such an ugly colour.' Then, in rather a shrill voice: 'I don't hate Cumberland. Of course not. It will be very agreeable. I need a holiday.'

She came back to him, smiling.

'That *is* good of you, Ellis. Of course I shall love to go.'

And they went. On the evening of her arrival she could not believe that she was there. In the living-room there were all her father's things just as they had always been. His books – the little blue volumes of the *Iliad* and the *Odyssey* – the tattered shilling parts of *Pickwick*, the *English Poets, Sir Charles Grandison* and *Tristram Shandy*, Barney's novels, *Dandy Grimmett* and the rest.

And all the old beloved things, part of her very life: the two cornucopias, Zobel's sand picture, 'The Saddle Horse', the old watercolour, 'The Lady of the House', the Baxter print 'Dippers and Nest', the Peepshow of the Central Hall at the Great Exhibition, above all, the spinet from Uldale with the roses painted on the lid, and the music box with the King in his amber coat and the Queen in her green dress.

As she stood at the window, with all these beloved things around her, she held her hands tightly together lest she should show her emotion. The last evening light touched the hills: Skiddaw's twin peaks lay like islands in a clear cold silver above bars of fleecy cloud, and the ridge of Blencathra was black against the whitewashed sky. Between the trees the water of the Lake, struck by the trail of a tiny boat, fell into darker and darker shadow. The wood pigeons murmured from the wood. Some ghostly sheep wandered, just as they had so often done, slowly up the road. This was her home. How foolish she had been to be so long an exile from it! And as she watched, the years fell away from her. Twenty of those years were suddenly gone. She raised her arms above her head and, smiling, saw herself, another very different woman, moving slowly up the staircase of some grand house, hearing the names called, the distant band – Lady Herries, a middle-aged woman with a dull, stiff husband, still beautiful

but soon not to be very interesting, to be nothing more than a
London hostess who knew everyone, whom everyone knew, who
mattered to no one, to whom no one mattered. Her body seemed
to her young again; she would hear her father call her name,
Benjie would be riding over from Uldale, all life was before her
. . . All life before her? She shivered. It was behind her. She was
in prison with Ellis.

But in the following days she could not keep down her joy.
She had come home. What is it that makes in a certain square of
ground every blade of grass, every hovering uncertain cloud,
every note in a bird's song one's own? She had heard often
enough, in London, scorn of this country, its rain, its ponds, its
little hills, old Wordsworth and his daffodils, Coleridge and his
opium, reading parties from Cambridge. She had had often to
hold herself back from a ridiculous personal protest as though
the scoffers had insulted herself. She had wondered why Lettice
and Timothy and Violet, who had lived so long here, had had no
personal feeling. She had heard Timothy thank his stars that he
had done with the 'beastly climate'. She had asked Lettice
whether she did not want to go back. 'Go back? All the unhappiest part of my life was there. I never want to see the place
again.' She knew for herself that if her childhood had been one
long misery still she must return . . . and return . . .

There was something deeper here, some inheritance that was
mingled with all the truest, most importunate things in life. Her
love of this place was her key to the connexion between the two
worlds. 'Only connect . . .' 'Only connect . . .' The whole problem for man and for woman was here. They move as in a game of
blind-man's-buff from figure to figure turned, twisted, bewildered. Guess rightly and the light floods in . . .

As she stood at the window, the world beyond it sinking into
darkness, she knew with sudden certainty that to find the key of
connexion was man's only business on this earth. All else was
folly beside it. And the key for her, as it had been for her father,
her grandmother, her great-grandfather, was here – like a pot of
gold hidden in this square of ground. For Benjie too perhaps?
She had, in that instant, one of those illuminating flashes of
revelation that once and again are granted the Hoodman Blind.
God the Invisible and man exploring; she smiled as she thought
of the ironies of Barney or Benjie or Rose if she told them of her
naïveté.

'I looked out of the window as the world grew dark and knew
that there are two worlds, that they are linked together, and that

it is God's purpose that we should find the connexion. All beauty is for that. I must have courage, honesty, and I must rid myself of my Blind Man's Hood, my egotism ... I must test life by no experience but my own. For you, dear Barney, God is an exploded superstition. That is *your* experience. You are right to hold honestly by it. But for myself, standing at this window, I have another guide. Credit my honesty and I will credit yours. Let us be tolerant to one another.'

As she turned back into the lighted room she had a moment of almost blinding happiness. Her troubles faded. What matter if she were close on forty, if she loved Benjie whom she could never be with any more? What was her fear of Ellis? All the values of life were for a moment altered. She had courage for anything.

She needed that courage in the days that followed.

They were sitting quietly after supper, she reading a novel, he a newspaper. He said, still looking at his paper:

'Vanessa, when we return to London, I shall wish you to see a doctor.'

'A doctor?'

'Yes,' he said, leaning forward and laying his long bony hands on his knees. 'I have been long coming to the conclusion that you are not well. I came up here with you that I might observe you a little. In London it is so difficult. So many people to interfere. We do not see enough of one another. My suspicions – my suspicions,' he repeated the word softly, 'are quite confirmed.'

'What suspicions? I am perfectly well, Ellis dear.'

'Ah, so you think,' he went on quietly. 'That, I fear, is part of the disease.'

'Disease?' she broke in. Her heart was hammering. She looked quickly about among the old familiar things in the room to reassure herself. 'Why, I was never better in my life, and especially since I have come up here.'

'There, there. You mustn't get excited. Excitement is bad for both of us. I have said nothing until I could be certain. I did not wish to alarm you. I have myself for some while been none too well, but now I am quite recovered – quite recovered,' he repeated, nodding his head. 'But now that I have mentioned it, you can speak to me without fear. There is no one listening. At least I think not.' He got up, went very cautiously to the door and listened, then to the windows, pulling back the curtains for a moment. He walked on tiptoe.

'Listen, Vanessa. For a long time we have not been happy. Oh,

I know that it has not been altogether your fault. For a time I was accompanied everywhere by someone. Very unagreeable and difficult to account for, but now that he is gone again – and I took care not to bother you with his intrusion – I realize that your care of me during these last years, in addition to all your social duties, has been too much for your strength, your mental strength. And then it is hereditary, no doubt. Your grandmother ... You will need great quiet in the future, and an able doctor – perhaps retirement into the country to some soothing place ...'
He stopped to listen. 'You heard nothing? The city is so noisy and restless. Always something moving.'

She picked up her book. Her hands were trembling, but she answered quietly:

'There is nothing the matter with me, Ellis.' Forcing herself, she looked up at him and smiled. 'We have both been tired a little by London. That is why this week in the country was such a good idea.'

He bent down, patted her shoulder, kissed her forehead.

'There, there. You must not disturb yourself. I will see to it.' He straightened himself and tiptoed to the door. He listened, looking anxiously into the wall. 'And now I think I will go up to bed. Don't worry. Worry is bad for you. Quiet, quiet. We must all have quiet.'

She lay awake for hours that night, wondering what she should do. In the large bed that they shared he slept the peace of the insane just. He breathed like a child, never stirring. She beat herself into common sense. Panic was so near that, all the night through, she kept it off only by using her utmost strength. She could run away, leave him never to return, but that would mean defeat and cowardice. If she left him it would not be long before he would be put somewhere, in some awful, silent house, faced with dark silent windows, inhabited by poor sufferers like himself. She must not go until the last test of endurance had been reached. But this new twist of his brain was so awful that she refused to face it. If he, mad though he was, thought *her* mad, might not others also think so? Had the strain of these last years been too much for her? Had there been something hysterically unreal in her manner? In the darkness of the room she saw the Misses Trent, in their large black hats, their trailing gowns, standing close together watching her. 'Yes,' she heard one of them say to Ellis. 'You are right. Vanessa has been behaving very strangely ...' But then her common sense returned. She had

never been more sane in her life than she was now. She could deal
with this as she had dealt with everything that preceded it. She
turned on her side and slept.

Then, after one happy hour, she realized to the full the
danger that she was in. That day, the seventeenth of June 1898,
was stamped, in its tiniest detail, on her memory for ever.

In the afternoon she drove to Rosthwaite. A lady, Mrs Merriman, who lived in Borrowdale, gave a party for some of the
children from Grange, Rosthwaite, Seatoller, and invited Vanessa. They all knew her here. She was one of themselves and had
it not been for her silent, pale-faced, alarming husband they
would have asked her everywhere. They hoped, now that she had
returned to her real home, that she would often come and, although they did not say so, without her husband. They knew
that she was a grand lady in London, but Cumberland people
take things naturally. Everyone is on a level, and if anyone
behaves grandly they look foolish and are to be pitied. Vanessa
of course did not behave grandly at all. No one could be more
simple, and on this afternoon in Rosthwaite she sat on the floor
and allowed the babies to climb all over her, played musical
chairs with breathless excitement and then, to the cracked piano,
sang songs for them and afterwards played for them to dance.
Mrs Merriman, who was thin and pale, had an invalid husband
and more children than she wanted, had been inclined to be
jealous at first of this woman with her lovely clothes, her beauty,
her life in the great world. 'She has everything. How unfair it is.'
But soon she was not sure that she had everything. There was
something, she told her husband, pathetic about Vanessa. 'She
played with the children as though she could not bear to let them
go. She told me that coming back here was heaven to her. She
went to the window and looked out at the hill like a starving
woman. "Well, why don't you come here more often, Lady
Herries?" I asked her. "After all, it's your home. We are all
delighted to have you here." "Oh, how I wish I could!" she said.
I wouldn't wonder if she's not happy with her husband. I'm sure
I shouldn't be. He really frightened me, he was so stiff and
solemn. I never saw a woman carry herself so beautifully, and
such lovely dark hair as she's got and such a kind expression. But
I'm certain she's not happy. Lovely dark hair with not a grey
thread, although she can't be far off forty. No airs at all, although
the Prince and Princess often come to her house, I believe. You
know, Philip, I felt like a mother to her. There's something makes

me feel that she needs someone to love her. Oh, I know you'll call me romantic. But I can't help it. She's the most beautiful woman I've ever seen and simply sweet with the children. You could tell her anything, I'm sure.'

When the children were having tea Vanessa slipped out, crossed the road, the bridge, and looked at the solid, comfortable little Victorian house with its sloping lawn, its trim garden, the house built on the very spot where her great-grandfather had once lived. She stood there, listening to the running water, feeling the afternoon sun on her face, wondering where that old wild man now was. He, too, had stood here, looking at the hills, feeling the sun on his face, waiting for his wife to return. It had been wild then: the bare rock, the tumbling water, the valley beyond uncouth and deserted. The sun had shone on his purple coat and silver braid. She felt intimately close to him. Once again time was not. Was it fancy that a hand rested on her shoulder, comforting her? Of course it was fancy.

Here was the trim garden and on the lawn two garden chairs, a small mowing machine, a watering pot. An old bent gardener was clipping the roses. Two bicyclists passed down the road, and then a scarlet coach filled with tourists. But, after the coach was gone, silence tumbled back again, the hills, clear and defined in the sunshine, cut the cloudless sky. The gardener pushed the mowing machine, and the soft dreamy whirr filled the world with summer peace. As she turned to the bridge she whispered 'Goodbye'. Was it fancy that a figure in a purple coat watched her go?

'And now, children, we must all thank Lady Herries for helping to make our afternoon such a pleasant one.'

They all thanked her in shrill treble voices. They ran into the road to see the splendid lady in her rose-coloured coat get into the carriage, and one baby cried because it was not allowed to go with her. She kissed Mrs Merriman.

'Come back soon,' Mrs Merriman said.

'Yes, I will,' said Vanessa.

Ellis locked the door. Vanessa looked up from her book at the sound of the turning key. Why had he locked the door? She had thought that he had gone up to bed. The little clock with the painted moon and stars (as a baby she had been lifted again and again to count them) pointed to quarter to eleven.

Mrs Newson and her husband slept on the far side of the

cottage. They would hear nothing. She continued to read. This was a very clever book of short stores; it was written by a woman who must be simply too clever to do any of the ordinary things that ordinary women did. The stories were in the manner that was becoming popular; they had no beginning. One story called 'The Haystack' started with this sentence: 'Oh, but dripping is so cheap . . . and it's really not bad when you get used to it.' Nor had they any conclusion. 'The Haystack' ended: 'Yes, but half a crown – that was altogether too much for such a second-rate article.' They were depressing stories. London in the rain, hateful boarding houses, shabby men making love, the British Museum Reading Room, someone wringing a chicken's neck outside the kitchen window. They were very feminist. Men figured as poor creatures, mean, faithless, and greedy. But oh! what cleverness! What observation! Nothing escaped this lady's eye; the yellow stain on the tablecloth where mustard had been spilled at the last meal, the tear in the cheap umbrella, the shabby feather in the outworn hat . . . Vanessa knew, as she read, that one thing that was the matter with herself was that she was not clever at all. Neither clever nor witty. She could not remember that she had ever said a brilliant thing in her life. Rose, Cynthia, Lady Dorothy Nevill – what clever things they were always saying! 'I'm a bore,' thought Vanessa. 'The woman who wrote this book wouldn't endure me for five minutes.'

But why had he locked the door? He came and sat down opposite to her. The clothes that he was wearing, a dark brown cloth intended for the country, did not suit him nor did they look like country clothes. Wherever he might be, he wore always the deep sharp collar that belonged to the Gladstone caricatures, and that did not suit him either because his throat was so thin, his Adam's apple so large. She noticed tonight for the first time that the back of his pale long hand was freckled.

He sighed, then said:

'It was not kind of you, Vanessa, to have me watched all this afternoon.'

She looked at him steadily, determining that tonight at least she would not be afraid. They were returning to London tomorrow and then something must be done. For her own safety, for his, something must be done.

'What *do* you mean, Ellis? No one was watching you.'

'Ah, come, Vanessa. Why lie to me? I don't blame you, not at all. I know that you are not yourself. But it is wrong of you to embarrass me. And such an unpleasant man. I stood here for half an hour while he watched me outside the window. He never moved until I came myself to the window; then he vanished into that green bush beyond the flowerbed. Then when I returned to the fireplace, pretending not to notice him, he came to the window again. A long thin man in a green coat. I fancied that I had seen him before.'

She got up and came over to him, seeming very tall in that small room.

'Ellis dear, let's go to bed. You know that I haven't had you watched. Why should I? Now come to bed.'

'Oh, I'm not vexed, my dear. Not at all vexed. I said to myself, "If he hadn't got that green coat I really should not mind. He could watch me as long as he pleased. But I dislike green as a colour and his eyes were most unpleasant." When I went out into the garden he was gone. Then he came back again. He pressed his face to the windowpane. All the same you would dislike it if I had *you* watched, you know. You wouldn't like it at all. In fact, lately, I've had it in my mind because, being as you are, it isn't safe for you to go about alone.' He sighed, deeply, deeply as though in dreadful distress. 'The truth is that we are neither of us well. Life has been a failure for both of us. It is better for us to end it.'

She looked about the room to reassure herself with the old homely comfort of the familiar things – the spinet, the books, the music box, the pictures. She walked to the window, then from the far side of the table said: 'Ellis, give me that key. You have locked the door. Give me that key.'

'No, my dear, certainly not. Because you had me watched this afternoon is reason enough. We have not been happy for a long time; indeed I have never been happy. I cannot remember a time when I was happy. Nor are you happy. So here, very quietly, while there is no one about, is a very good opportunity to finish all this tiresome business. I feel it my duty. I have hesitated for some time, but now my duty is quite clear.'

He fumbled in his inside coat pocket and brought from it a large kitchen knife with a thick brown handle.

'You will feel nothing,' he said smiling. 'It will be no more than a cut on the finger. And then I will follow you. I can't possibly express to you how agreeable it will be to be tired no longer, to have no more headaches. For both of us it will be a relief, I am sure—'

He held the knife in one hand and stroked its edge, very gently, with the other. The little clock struck eleven.

'This is the silliest scene,' she thought, 'I have ever been in. So unreal that all the things in the room have become unreal too.' She thought also: 'But this ends everything. At last, thank Heaven, this ends everything.'

'I have thought it all out,' he said. 'Sit in that chair, Vanessa. Close your eyes. You'll feel nothing at all.' He was very close to her now, but she did not move.

'Ellis, give me the key. Put down that knife. Go to bed. You are behaving like a baby. Put that knife down on that table.'

'Perhaps I will,' he said, looking at her very cunningly. 'Perhaps I will not. But it won't matter, because nothing you can say will alter my decision. And how absurd of you not to do as I wish! But you have never done as I wish. A pale-green mushroom hat that you are always wearing. You know that I dislike it. And yet day after day you persist in wearing it.' He murmured: 'A mass of shaded green wings. A mass of shaded green wings. That's what Mr Playfair said.'

He threw out his hand and caught her arm.

'Come to the chair, Vanessa. Come to the chair. That is the easiest way.'

He looked up at her like a beseeching child. His eyes were filled with tears.

'Dear Vanessa. How I love you! How unhappy we are!'

His arm encircled her body . . . His head fell forward and rested on her breast. The knife tumbled to the floor. She led him back to the armchair, he submitting like a child.

'Please, Ellis, give me the key,' she said.

Tears pouring down his cheeks, he fumbled for the key, found it, gave it her.

'Another time,' he sobbed. 'Perhaps another time will be better. I meant it for the best . . .' Then, as she moved away, he caught her hand: 'Don't leave me. Don't leave me. I am afraid of being alone.'

She knelt down beside him, comforting him as she had done so often before. But, in her heart, she knew that this was for the last time.

ESCAPE INTO DANGER

THEY had to leave very early next morning to catch the train for London. Vanessa, who had not slept at all, stood at the lawn's edge and found that the world was rolling in rosy smoke. It would be a hot day. The smoke lifted from the Lake even as she looked, as someone lifts the covers from a bed: the Lake shivered, trembling, at the touch of the sun that itself also dared as yet only to breathe upon the water, but to breathe like God, strongly, confidently (in spite of so very many disappointments) and with the very tenderness of love. The colour flew upwards from the hills and broke into petals of rose against the sky that would soon be drenched with sun. All the hills waited – Cat Bells, Robinson, Gable, Scafell, the Langdales, Helvellyn, Blencathra – they all waited for their illumination high, high above these madmen who today are one thing and tomorrow another.

This would be a horrible journey – and so it was.

'Perhaps,' said Ellis, when they were halfway down England, 'you would like my *Times*?' He spoke to a stout fellow in a suit of loud checks who had been, ever since Penrith, staggered by Vanessa's beauty. For she wore a small toque, a spotted veil, her rose-coloured coat; behind the veil, the man in the checks was, with beating heart, assured, breathed the only woman for whom all his life he had been searching. He had money, he had rude health, a kind wife and a mistress in Carlisle, but he had not, he had never, never had, the Beauty for which he longed.

'Thank you, sir. Very kind of you. Hooley's bankruptcy means the end of the cycling boom. Mark my word.'

The fields rushed up to the window and all the houses bobbed and curtsied in the sun. Vanessa sat there, her clever book of stories on her lap, and fought down her terrors. She had not slept, and Ellis, who now looked like a Prime Minister, a director of a railway company or the real author of *Robert Elsmere*, had last night wished to cut her throat with a knife with a brown handle. He had, as usual, wept leaning against her breast. He would never weep against her breast again, for her duty there was ended. Once she had loved him as a mother her child, then she had pitied him because he was sick, now she was a weary, angry woman resolved on escape. Next week they were giving a Ball in

Hill Street, a very grand Ball indeed, and that should be the last. That should be the end, for her, of Ellis, Hill Street, London ... One need not, one must not, be stuck so deep in a quagmire of ludicrous danger ... ludicrous kitchen knives, Ellis' tears and tiptoe to the window, Ellis' man in the green bush beyond the window, Ellis' moaning in his sleep, poor Ellis ... 'To find some life that is neither false nor dangerous ...' Letting her head fall, she slept at last, dreaming that the babies in Rosthwaite pulled her with eager hands up the hill to the water falling with such cool certainty down the face of the rock. Standing waiting for her there was Benjie.

At Hill Street was a letter for her from Rose. Next day she went to see her. Rose was living in two very small dingy rooms off Baker Street. She met Vanessa defiantly, as though to say: 'I know you will find me changed and you can say, if you wish, that you never want to see me again.' Yes, Rose *was* changed. Her cheeks were painted, the puffed shoulders of her dress absurdly exaggerated, her waist too small for any comfort, her eyes unhappy. Her room was untidy, clothes thrown about, a dusty piano open with a bright green hat ornamented with a bird of paradise plume flung down on the keys.

A strange thought struck Vanessa. 'This is the world into which, very shortly, I may be moving.'

But oh! it was wonderful to be loved again! She could not believe that she had endured all these years without it! She was like a woman starved as, sitting with Rose on the shabby hole-and-corner sofa, she heard what Rose chose to tell her (a sort of fairy story in which every gentleman was kind, money sprang from the carpet, and life was one long victory).

At the end of it Vanessa said:

'I'm glad you're so happy.'

And Rose said:

'Life's hell. Don't believe a word I've said, Vanessa.'

They discovered very quickly that life just then was bad for both of them. Vanessa did not tell Rose that Ellis had wanted to cut her throat with a kitchen knife, but she *did* give her to understand that the end of Hill Street had arrived at last and that Rose must be prepared ...

There came in upon them without a word of warning the most dreadful man – Major Featherstone-Haigh. The Major was short, purple in the face, smelt of brandy, called Vanessa 'My dear' and looked at Rose as though he owned her – which, at that moment, he probably did.

Vanessa went back to Hill Street. She went back to Hill Street to find Miss Vera and Miss Winifred Trent waiting for her in the drawing-room. Standing in her room, before she went down to them, she knew a moment of fear worse than any that had preceded it. She stood, motionless, her head up as though she were listening. Then with quick nervous movements she took off her white soft-feathered toque, her veil, her long gloves. She listened again. It was a hot thundery day and her windows were wide open. A hansom clop-clopped down Hill Street; she looked out and saw a man crying his flowers which blazed in a cloud of colour on his barrow – roses, carnations, lilies. Below the windows of the houses the window boxes shone with bright blue, with scarlet, with flaunting yellows. At the end of the street was a barrel-organ that played again and again an old air from *Trovatore*. Light, colour, music: but inside the house it was cold and dark as it always was. Her dress was white and black, the shoulders very puffed, the waist very small. She looked at herself in the long silver mirror. She seemed to herself hideous, her pale face beneath the dark hair, her long white neck, her full bosom; her height was ridiculous. She hated the way that she carried her head, stiff, pompous, 'as though I were for ever at the top of the stairs, receiving. Thank Heaven, it is ended. In a week or two, in one way or another, it will be over. I will never receive anyone any more. Death, perhaps.' It did not seem impossible, for there was Ellis loose about the house, and the house so still, and those two old women in their long trailing black waiting for her in the drawing-room.

At that moment, looking at herself in the mirror with disgust as at someone for whom everything was over, someone moving in a crazy house cold as the grave, a lunatic its master, she had almost, for the first time, lost all her courage. Rose lost, Benjie somewhere wandering, no one else . . . Then also she remembered her grandmother, that small indomitable woman with the white hair and ivory cane who lived to be a hundred, who had faced everything because she knew how to be indifferent to life whilst adoring it. 'She did – so can I.' She went down to the two ladies.

'Ah, dear Vanessa, how nice to see you again. And how are you?'

'Very well indeed, thank you.'

They both kissed her, and as they did so it was as though they were graciously inviting her to stay for an hour or so in her own drawing-room. They were extremely quiet. When they moved, their long black dresses scarcely rustled. They appeared also to have a secret understanding. They had moreover the power to make you feel that you could not take a step without their permission. Finch brought in the tea, and it seemed likely for a moment that Miss Vera Trent would instruct him where the table should be placed. Their voices were what Barney once called 'boneless'.

'We have already seen dear Ellis,' said Miss Winifred.

'He says that his holiday has done him good,' said Miss Vera.

'But we advised him to be careful during these hot weeks in London,' said Miss Winifred. 'The worst thing possible for his headaches. How is he, do you think, Vanessa?'

'Oh, very well,' said Vanessa brightly. 'We had such lovely weather in Cumberland.'

'You did?' said Miss Winifred. 'Now isn't that delightful? Cumberland when it is *fine* must be indeed charming.'

'And for you – to return to your old home again – how delightful!' said Miss Vera. 'There is no place quite the same as one's childhood's home.'

'And what have you been doing?' asked Vanessa. 'What are the family scandals? Whom have you seen?'

'Oh, we lead quiet lives, you know,' said Miss Winifred. 'We had tea one day with dear Cynthia. May and her girls were in London for a week. And poor Violet – not at all well, I fear, and now that both children—' She broke off. The Misses Trent were nothing if not tactful, and, after all, Vanessa most strangely defended that horrible man who had lured poor Violet's boy—

They both looked at her together, a strange look, a look full of some knowledge that at present they would keep to themselves. Miss Vera said, smiling, raising her hand on which her diamond rings sparkled, to help herself to a little cake: 'And what is this that Ellis tells us, dear Vanessa, about your own health? Rather a sad report, I fear.'

'My health?' said Vanessa. 'Why, it was never better.'

Miss Vera shook her finger. 'Now that is not at all what dear Ellis tells us. He insists that you see a doctor. Altogether over-fatigued, he says, and I am sure that I don't wonder with all that you do. And then this great Ball next week to which Winifred and I are so greatly looking forward. But after it Ellis thinks that a quiet time in the country—'

Her anger rose. She was suddenly aware that she hated these two women as she had never hated anyone in her life before. 'I think that I am the best judge of that,' she said quietly. 'I am perfectly well.'

The door opened and she saw that Ellis had come in. The two ladies rose and moved to either side of him. He greeted them with a grave smile.

Surely, they must be aware of his strangeness, his eyes are never still nor do they see the things at which they are looking, and he walks now like a cat with padded feet . . .

All three looked at her. Then Ellis said:

'A little tea, my dear. Thundery weather.'

They all sat down.

One more move needed to complete the preparation. Next day meeting Barney at Cynthia's he put in her hand a note. It was from Benjie.

18 HALF MOON STREET.

DEAR VANESSA – I am here and shall be so for some weeks. If I may not see you I may at least be happy because I am near you.

B.

The last Ball ever given by Vanessa and Ellis in Hill Street was a brilliant success. Vanessa, in a dress of white satin and with diamonds in her hair, stood at the top of the stairs. She saw, as though it were a mechanical toy wound up for her amusement, the figures appear around the bend of the staircase – one two, one two, one two – the ladies' heads erect, bosoms thrust forward, trains draped over their arms, jewels glittering, a scent of powder and roses and the heat of the London June evening . . .

'Lord and Lady Danesborough.'

'Sir James and Lady Ford.'

'Mr Forbes-Robertson.'

'Lady Carteris.'

'Lord John Beaminster.'

'Lady Adela Beaminster.'

'Miss Rachel Beaminster.'

'Mr Timothy Herries.'

'Miss Vera Trent.'
'Miss Winifred Trent.'
'Lady Dorothy Nevill.'
'Sir Henry and Miss Nevill and Lady Wade.'
'Madame Sarah Bernhardt.'
'Mr and Mrs Peile Worcester.'
'Lord Clancarty.'
'Mr Henry James.'
'Mr Edmund Gosse.'
'Mr and Mrs Colvin.'
'Lady Sarah Meux.'
'Monsieur Felix Brun.'
'Mr Yale Ross.'
'Lady Carloes.'
'Mr Robert Hichens.'
'Sir Roderick Seddon.'
'The Honourable Lionel Talmache.'
'Mr Adrian Cards.'
'Lady Lettice Forjambe.'
'Mr and Mrs Humphrey Ward.'
'Sir Peter and Lady Thornby.'
'Miss Mary Thornby.'
'Lady Eustace.'
'Miss Pamela Eustace.'
'Mrs Clifford.'
'Mr Barnabas Newmark.'
'Lord and Lady Rockage.'
'Miss Veasey.'
'Mr and Mrs Ormerod.'
'Lady Cynthia Lamb.'
'Mr and Mrs Frederick Macmillan.'
'Mrs Grant Bingham.'
'Mr Herbert Beerbohm Tree.'
'Mr Pendle Smith.'
'Mrs Langtry.'
'General Fortescue and Mrs Fortescue.'
'Mr Max Beerbohm.'
'Miss Carlyon.'
'Mr Ross.'
'Mr Tumer.'
'Mrs Fortescue Brown.'
'Mr Brookfield.'

'Mrs Craigie.'

'Mr Charles Wyndham.'

She deflected: 'It must be midnight. The actors and acresses are arriving.' She glanced back and saw that the long room was now filled to overflowing with dancers.

'Mr Bertrand.'

'Lady Garvice.'

'Miss Garvice.'

'Mr Galleon.'

'Lady Torring.'

'Mr and Mrs Frost.'

Barney, a little later, found himself in a corner with Bertrand the novelist.

'I suppose,' Bertrand said, 'you think I'm here to pour scorn on my fellow-creatures.'

'No, not especially,' said Barney. 'Any more than anyone else.'

'As a matter of fact,' said Bertrand, 'I love my fellow-creatures. I think we are all absurd, of course. And tonight I feel something sinister in the air.'

'Sinister?' asked Barney.

'Yes. I can't explain it except that I think London *is* sinister just now. Have you read Hichens' *Londoners,* or don't you read your fellow-novelists?'

'Not very often,' said Barney.

'Neither do I. But Hichens' book is clever madness – too long, but not really exaggerated. We are all mad.' He looked around him. 'Do you see that little man over there talking to Mrs Langtry?' He pointed to a small, very dapper gentleman, with bright observant eyes, who was talking with exceeding animation and a good deal of un-English gesticulation.

'That is Felix Brun. He lives only for the social history of Europe. He knows all the moves, the undercurrents, the plots, and plotters. Whenever he appears in London, you can be sure that there is a change coming. I met him a week or two ago at the Rede Gallery where he had come to look at Ross' portrait of the old Duchess of Wrexe – a very fine painting, by the way. He was very interesting. Like myself, he has no illusions.'

'You must have been a fine gloomy pair,' Barney said, laughing.

'Oh, not gloomy at all. Why be gloomy? It has been dull, this long sleepy prosperity. Brun agrees with me that things are breaking up.'

'What things?' Barney asked. He was looking at Ellis, who,

standing near to him, alone, had in his eyes so fixed a gaze, and in his pose so odd an air of waiting for someone, that he interested Barney.

'What things?' repeated Bertrand. 'Oh, all this. The conviction that we are the finest people in the world, superior to everything and everybody. The conviction that we rule the world and it is right that we should. Brun says that England's day as ruler of the world is over.'

'That must give you great satisfaction.'

'No – why should it? We do some things very well, but we have no taste, no subtlety, no sensitiveness to what other people are feeling, and our Imperial ambitions are revolting. I am going to live in France.'

Beaminster brought up to Vanessa a very beautiful girl.

'This is my niece Rachel, Vanessa. You were at her Ball the other day. She has not been out long enough yet to be blasé. She thinks you are the most wonderful woman in London.'

Vanessa looked with great pleasure at the girl in front of her. Miss Rachel Beaminster, granddaughter of the old Duchess of Wrexe. Vanessa had gone in May to a very grand Ball in Portland Place given for this child's coming-out. The girl was tall and thin, with dark hair and beautiful eyes, a little gauche and a little foreign. Her mother had been a Russian actress, and the old Duchess had, Vanessa was told, never forgiven her son for his *mésalliance*. But the importance of this meeting for Vanessa was that this girl might be herself – herself twenty years ago.

'I do hope you're enjoying yourself.'

'Oh yes, Lady Herries. It's a lovely Ball.'

'Plenty of partners?'

The girl smiled and became at once transformed; her happiness took away that little awkwardness and you felt pleasure, excitement, anticipation beat through her body.

'Plenty. I could dance all night.'

'I have known your uncle a long time. He is one of my oldest friends.'

'Oh, Uncle John? Isn't he a dear? I should have been terrified of everything had it not been for him.'

Yes, and she might be, Vanessa thought, with that awful old grandmother and stiff, forbidding Adela for an aunt and prim, pompous Richard for an uncle!

'It's so wonderful,' Rachel said, 'seeing Sarah Bernhardt. Uncle John is taking me next week to one of her plays at the Lyric. She looks kinder, more simple—'

'Would you like to meet her?' asked Vanessa.

'Oh yes! Can I? You see, my mother was an actress—'

'Come along and I'll introduce you. Tell her about your mother.'

They went across to where the great woman was listening, with eyes half closed, to M. Brun.

Vanessa presented the girl and was pleased to see with what ease and simplicity the child behaved. She turned and, for a moment before she was caught again, watched the room, swinging under the lights to the rhythm and symmetry of the waltzes. The music softly beat into her ears: 'The last time – the last time – the last time . . .'

What if there should be a scene? What if Ellis should commit some awful indiscretion? He was looking strange tonight. Surely others had noticed it besides herself. She talked, she laughed, she walked with uplifted head. Many said afterwards that she had never seemed more splendid than at this Ball, more easily the mistress of her world. 'And for her age still such a beauty,' said little Brun. 'What is she? Nearly forty? She must be.' He remarked to Bertrand: 'An interesting family, these Herries. So typically English and yet with a strain of something—'

'*And we'll have fires out of the Grand Duke's Wood*,' quoted Bertrand.

'Fires out of the wood?'

'Yes – a quotation from one of the other Herries – the mad ones, you know.'

'Ah, there have been mad ones then?'

'Oh, plenty. There are several scandals at the moment.'

'Ah,' said Brun. 'That's what makes you English so interesting. You are madder than any other people and yet so conventional. Impossible to understand, you turn and rend your madmen while they are alive and yet are so proud of them after they are dead.'

'That,' said Bertrand, who was suddenly bored with little Brun (he tired of people very quickly – of himself also), 'is why we are so conceited. We have so much common sense that when our poets have written their poetry we kill them. Except Wordsworth and Tennyson of course. But they were mad very young and got over it.'

After that Bertrand sat by himself for a while and collected notes for his notebook. He watched Madame Bernhardt act and Henry James unravel sentences of benignity from his beard, Mrs

Langtry raise her lovely arm, bishops grow genial, politicians indiscreet and all the most beautiful girls in London manoeuvre for husbands. Then he noticed his host, who listened at first with grave intensity to a stout lady in a bright green dress, and then, when she left him, stood as though bewildered, staring about him.

'By Jove, the old boy's trembling from head to foot,' he said to himself. 'He'll have a fit or something.'

Ellis backed to the wall. He straightened himself against it. Then Bertrand saw that he felt the wall with the palm of his hand; he moved his hand up and down against the surface, and in his eyes was the most unhappy gaze that Bertrand had ever seen in a human countenance. Then Bertrand saw that two tall elderly ladies came up to him, stood on either side of him, talking to him. With his hand through the arm of one of them, Ellis moved away. Bertrand wrote in his notebook that night:

'But the strangest thing this evening was the terror of my host. A very commonplace dull man, you would say, but the dullest of us may become interesting when, lost in the bush, he hears the tom-toms of the approaching cannibals.'

The Ball reached its apogee. There was a superb and nearly riotous set of Lancers. Everyone had had supper. The summer morning was breaking beyond the windows. The carriages drove away. Finch, downstairs, entertained the footmen and the maids with his splendid imitations of the more important guests.

Vanessa, reaching her room at last, locked the door. A few minutes later there was a knock. She stood motionless, listening. The knock was several times repeated. Then silence.

As the small brown silver-faced clock that she had brought with her from Cat Bells struck eleven, she awoke. She had told them not to call her; now she rang the bell, looked at her letters, the newspaper, drank her coffee. Through and behind it all was a sense of crisis. And yet why? She had given last night one of the most successful Balls of the season; no hitch, no misadventure. And today there was no reason why anything should happen. Something *soon* must be done, but immediately, today . . .

The sun poured into the room. The paper told her that there was a new successful play at the Court – *His Excellency the Governor* – and that her friend, Irene Vanbrugh, one of the women whom for her generous spirit, unaffected good nature and cheerful courage she liked best in London, had made a great success in it. She read of a hat that sounded a miracle of loveliness:

> *A daring little toque of turquoise straw, jet pins with very big heads, white wings and a black velvet rosette in front.* She also read: *The Louis Seize bow is almost ubiquitous. We meet it on hats, it is a charming head-dress for evening wear, it occurs in almost every embroidery, every appliqué of lace, it airs itself in the lace curtains, on our walls, everywhere.*

'There shall be no Louis Seize bows on *my* walls,' she thought, half asleep, and then remembered, with the sharpness of a knife cutting through tissue paper, an unexpected little incident of the evening before. Just after she had come up from supper Ellis appeared at her elbow and with him a stout roughly bearded man. All that Ellis had said was that this was a friend of his, a Doctor Playfair. She had talked with the man for five minutes. What had they discussed? Bernhardt's season at the Lyric, the Spanish-American War, Gladstone's funeral, Cecil Rhodes – anything, nothing? He had seemed a well-informed, pleasant enough man. As soon as his back was turned she had forgotten him. She had not thought of him again until now when, suddenly, she seemed to see him in the room here with her – his untidy brown beard speckled with grey, his white waistcoat that fitted ill over his paunch, his heavy bowed shoulders, but, above all, his thick glasses behind which his large grey eyes had stared at her without blinking. How he had stared! She had not at the time thought of it, for, by now, she was accustomed that people should stare at her. But how he had stared! She fancied now that there had been some especial emphasis in Ellis' introduction . . .

She must get away! Oh! at once! at once! Somewhere, anywhere. Was she perhaps nervously overstrung? This trembling, this beating of the heart . . . Had people been thinking her ill and not cared to tell her? *Was* her mind affected by this last horrible year? She jumped out of bed, went to the mirror. Nothing ailed her. She was in the full vigorous possession of her brain, her will, her heart. She had never been more conscious of true bodily strength, of real and absolute sanity. She had been imagining the doctor . . . There had been nothing intended, nothing sinister – but with Ellis now from minute to minute you never knew . . . you never knew . . .

She had luncheon alone and afterwards drove to the Rede Art Gallery in Bond Street, where she had arranged to meet Barney. They had agreed that they must see Yale Ross' portrait of the Duchess of Wrexe. He was waiting for her inside the Gallery and she thought to herself: 'What a nice wide-awake amusing face he has for an old man of nearly seventy! How pleasant it is always to see him! What a friend he has always been to both Benjie and myself!'

They went together and looked at the portrait. It was certainly brilliant. The old woman sat, leaning a little forward, holding a black ebony cane, in a high carved chair. The most striking thing in her pose was the way in which her dry claw-like fingers clutched her cane. Her dress was black and the only colour against it was the dull green of a jade pendant. The colour of her face was almost dead white and the skin was drawn so tightly over the veins that a sigh, a breath, you felt, would snap it. She looked indomitable, remorseless, proud, nor was there a shadow of humour in her mouth (which was cruel) and her eyes (which were cold). On either side of the chair were two green and white dragons, grotesques with large flat feet and open mouths. A tapestry of dull figured gold filled the background.

'Theatrical, brilliant, and most uncomplimentary,' Vanessa said.

'She wouldn't think so,' said Barney. 'I'm told she's delighted with the picture. And she *is* theatrical – her life, I mean. She shuts herself up in Portland Place so that she may be a figure. If she went out and about she would be simply an old and tiresome woman who had outlived her time. As it is people think that she pulls all the strings.'

Vanessa thought of the young girl, Rachel, to whom she had spoken last night.

'That girl has character,' she said. 'It would be a tussle between the two of them if they fought.'

They found a quiet corner. The little room with its cool light, its gleaming pictures, its silence, was most refreshing.

'Now tell me, Barney, quite honestly, have you noticed anything strange in me lately?'

'No. Nothing. Of course not. I never saw you more beautiful, more completely mistress of yourself, than last night. Everyone said the same.'

'Thank you, my dear. And now listen.'

Vanessa told him everything; of the journey to Cumberland,

the incident of the knife, Ellis' remarks about her health, the two old women in the house, the few minutes with the doctor. Barney was horrified.

'At least that settles it. Something must be done at once – at once.'

'Yes, but what? I cannot – no, I cannot – endure another week of this. And it is not right for Ellis either. We are not safe and he is not safe.'

Barney stared in front of him. 'This is dreadful. I knew that things were bad, but not like this.'

'How much does anyone else know?'

'Well, we – the family – have realized that something was wrong with Ellis for a long time. But only vaguely. I have only known what you told me and others have guessed a little perhaps, but so long as everything was all right on the surface they have accepted it. They don't *want*, you see, that there should be anything public. There have been enough Herries scandals.'

Vanessa went on:

'And it is all my fault. The sin was my marrying Ellis in the first place when it was Benjie whom I loved. I thought of myself rather than Ellis. But there was this strain, perhaps, in him from the beginning ... I can't *deal* with it, Barney. My courage is gone, and I thought once that I had enough for anything. But how can I leave him like this, defenceless, without anybody, in that awful world of his own? If you saw how unhappy he sometimes looks, the way that he cries, the *bitterness* of his weeping! How lonely one must be!'

She trembled and put one gloved hand on Barney's knee to steady herself.

'Oh, Barney, *what* am I to do?'

'Wait,' Barney said. 'Let's be sensible about this. Under the cold eyes of the old Duchess. What would *she* do? Lock Ellis up in a Portland Place cellar and feed him on bread and water. No my dear, I'm not laughing. This is serious enough for anything, but forgive me if I'm thinking about you first. You have to be protected, you know. Let's be practical. Ellis is dangerous, poor chap. And there are the two old women. And that doctor last night.'

She asked him, dropping her voice:

'Can they do anything? I mean if they really tried to get me away into the country. Oh, I don't mean murder me. But shut me up, isolate me?'

'Oh no – not while Benjie and I are about. That is only a crazy idea of Ellis'. He honestly believes it, I shouldn't wonder. He may have persuaded the two old ladies that at least you are tired, overstrung. But you *must* leave him – for the time, anyway.'

'And precipitate everything,' she went on quickly. 'If I go and refuse to return there will be no question about Ellis – everyone will know.'

'Will they? I wonder. You will be blamed of course.' He looked at her. 'Vanessa, will you mind blame, criticism? You have had very little in your life, haven't you? Everyone has loved you. It will be different. You won't be the splendid Lady Herries any more ...'

'Oh, that! That is nothing. But there *is* something else ...'

Some people had come into the Gallery. She lowered her voice.

'I don't think, Barney, that I can go on any longer without seeing Benjie. I've had thirteen years of it, you know. I love him as deeply as ever I did – more deeply, I think. He is alone, has been for years. I know that it is wrong. I've no illusions about that at all. I'm very old-fashioned about God, my friends tell me, but of this I'm sure – that to live with Benjie would be a sin and that somewhere, sometime, I should suffer and rightly suffer. If I sinned it would be deliberately, one thing against another. But I think *now* that perhaps to sin and be punished is better than to live and die without loving anyone.'

When Vanessa talked like this she seemed to Barney so touchingly childish that he wanted to pat her hand and say: 'There! There! my dear. I'll go with you and tell them it wasn't your fault. I'll see that you're not punished.' Sin! Good Heavens! *What* a word! And the things that *he* had done, the fine times he had had, and here he was nearing seventy and as hale and hearty ...

'Well, that may be, my dear – or it may not be. Sin seems to me a vague word. If you're right and there's some old tyrant waiting to see you slip and punish you, why, then I'd defy him and tell him to do his worst. Let's be practical. Go off with Benjie, well and good. But there are two things to consider. One is the social part of it. Probably that seems unimportant to you, but it isn't so nice in practice. Men and women can be very nasty when they see someone enjoying a freedom they haven't themselves the courage for.'

'Yes,' said Vanessa, and thought of Rose.

'And there's another thing. What about Benjie? How old is he now? Forty something, isn't he? You aren't either of you very

young any longer. Benjie's a rover. He *is* a bit of the gipsy they
call him. He loves you, I know. That has been the finest, by far
the finest, thing in his life. I think if you've courage enough you
can bring it off. But you'll need all the courage you've got.'

She stood up, pulling down her veil, standing there in her pale
dress of grey and silver, for a moment, as desolate and lonely as
he'd ever seen her.

'I know,' she said. 'I'm in a muddle, aren't I? Father always
used to say that I was a careless little fool – not those words, you
know, but that's what it amounted to. And yet for so long I've
been so careful – so absurdly careful.'

As they went out she said:

'I wish we hadn't talked under the eyes of that dreadful old
woman, Barney.'

As they went down the stairs Barney caught her hand.

'Remember, Vanessa, that I'm here whenever you want me.
Always, whatever you decide.'

'Yes,' she said, smiling back at him. 'You, Benjie, Rose,
Adrian, Lettice. Five. In the whole world. Well, I suppose there
are many people would be grateful for so many.' She added, as
she got into her carriage: 'And I *am* grateful! You're a friend
worth having, Barney.'

They dined alone, very late, she and Ellis, and at once she saw
that the crisis was upon her. Ellis had some plan that was not to
wait long for its explanation. Living with him, as she had done in
these last years, she had learnt something of the strange country
in which he was now lodging. She knew that his brain always
moved along a single path, or rather the paths lay side by side like
railway tracks and he might jump at any second from one to
another, but that he was conscious *only* of the one that he was, at
that moment, treading. Tonight she was very close to him; she
could see clearly the character of the world in which he moved,
its grey uncertain darkness so that you went stumbling, hitting
your shins against sharp edges like razors, or of a sudden putting
your hand on a cold soft substance, a gelatinous mass on whose
surface spiders wove webs. And then at such contacts you
screamed. What could you do other, alone as you were, wrapped
in darkness, driving forward but with no knowledge of your
destination?

She understood, too, how bewildering were the sudden flares
of light – like the up-blazing in some works when, conducted

around by the manager, he explains the moving of some minute wheel – both of you lit by the glare of Hell. That was Ellis' world, and these flares of hot flaming light were all he had to guide him. They might be a hat with a mass of green wings, the name of Playfair, a man looking through the window, the swinging of a mirror for no cause, the whistle of a train, a book read late at night when the house is silent – these and such as these were all he had to light his path. But pursue his path he must, and would with an absorbed intensity. One track – one purpose. The burning molten substances flares to heaven, and the track and purpose are changed – changed but as intensely pursued.

She knew tonight that some intention completely absorbed him and that that intention concerned herself. Because she knew this she had a kind of prevision of what was coming. At least she was quite certain that this very evening would see the finish of all her business here. She even knew, as she smiled at Finch and said: 'No, no more asparagus, thank you, Finch', that this was the last time that she would sit at this table, the last time at least for many a day ... One might return. She speculated about that. To what did one not return? The same tests were repeated again and again. She felt that there was neither time nor space tonight but that together she, her father, grandmother, great-grandfather, Will Leathwaite, Rose, Benjie's wife, anyone you please, all in the same moment stood up to be tested while the Eagle flew across the sun ...

Just before she rose from the table to lead the way up to the drawing-room, she had the hallucination, staring at the wall-paper under the candlelight, that it would be for ever thus – she and Ellis facing one another over the broken fruit skins and half-emptied glasses, her father swinging her to and fro above the grass of the Cat Bells lawn, old David falling at the news of the Bastille, older Herries standing at his door waiting for his wife, Rose and Major Featherstone-Haigh, all the Herries, nay, all the world transfixed into immobility while God cries from His judgement seat: 'Now!' The candles blew in the wind, a picture swung very, very slightly on its cord, and it was Ellis, not God, who said 'Now!'

'Now, Vanessa, we will go upstairs. There is something I must tell you.'

So highly pitched was her sensibility that when they were alone together in the drawing-room and the door closed behind them, she felt like an animal entrapped. There was, in fact, good reasonable common sense here, for you could not one evening allow your husband to attempt to cut your throat without, after that, finding other evenings with him rather dangerous. The door was not, this time, locked. Finch and the young footman were within calling distance. She had always hated this room. She had done what she could with it, taken down the yellow hangings, allowed Whistler to paint her portrait, spread rugs, bought roses, carnations, lilies – but Whistlers, rugs, roses, carnations, lilies could not prevent that this room was still the yellow drawing-room that, even though only last night it had swung with a maze of happy figures under the crystal candelabra, was dead like a mausoleum and cold as Hell must be for those who love the warmth.

He made her sit down beside him on the sofa. He patted her hand and his hand was warm and dry.

'Are you tired, Vanessa?' He spoke to her with infinite consideration.

'Not in the least.'

'Not after last night's festivities?'

'No. I slept until eleven.'

'What have you done today?'

'Oh, nothing very much. I went to the Rede Gallery to see Ross' portrait of the old Duchess that everyone is talking of.'

'Did anyone go with you?'

'Yes. Barney.'

'Ah ... Barney ... Everyone agrees that last night's was a most successful Ball.'

'I think it was. Really Finch and the servants did excellently. Finch may have his faults, but he knows his business.'

'Did you notice last night,' Ellis asked her, 'how those who were not invited came and laughed at us? It disturbed me greatly, but I said nothing to anybody. They gathered in groups. I was afraid at one time there would be trouble.'

'No one came who was not invited.'

'Oh yes. You are quite wrong. There were many there who had no right to be present. I thought at one time that I would have them driven out of the house. But that would have made a scene. Neither of us wished for that. Everything must be done quietly.'

She moved a little away. She looked at the clock. It was five minutes to ten. The servants would go to bed early tonight.

'Well,' he went on cheerfully, patting his knee with his hand, 'we must be thankful that all went off well. It is the last Ball that we shall give for a long time, because tomorrow I am going to send you into the country.'

'And where are you sending me?' she asked, smiling.

'There is a Doctor Playfair. At least I call him that. I am not sure at the moment whether that is his right name. He has a place – in Gloucestershire, I think. But I have it all written down. I am sure that it is Gloucestershire.'

She began to speak.

'But why—'

He put up his hand. 'Now, Vanessa, please. I have one of my headaches tonight – spiders in the brain, you know. That is exactly what Doctor Playfair said when I told him about my headaches. "Like spiders in the brain?" he asked. "Exactly," I replied, "and behind the eyes." He understood as though it had been his own experience, and when I spoke to him this morning about you – he had had five minutes' conversation with you last night—'

'I remember,' said Vanessa. 'A large heavy man with spectacles and an untidy beard.'

'Exactly. Doctor Playfair. He called to see me this morning. At this house in Gloucestershire – I *think* he said Gloucestershire – you will find every comfort. It is very quiet there. There are woods. Only the other patients—'

Vanessa laughed. 'This is all nonsense, of course, about my wanting a rest. But even if it were not, do you really suppose, Ellis, that I would leave you all alone here?'

'Ah, that is what I had intended to tell you. I shall *not* be alone. Vera and Winifred will for the future live here. This will be their home.'

So *that* was it! At the same instant as she realized with a flash of discovery that her responsibility was ended – and *how* strange *that* revelation was, liberating her, she suddenly saw, from years of bondage – a horror of being caught seized her. Those two old women! Did she not act immediately she would never escape. How they would hold her she did not know, but hold her they would! So many things came to her at the same instant and with these a new view of Ellis as though he had become twice as dangerous and twice as far removed. Through all the insanity of this last year she had thought at least that he needed her; now, with that spoken sentence, she saw that he did not need her,

Those two old women had taken her place . . . But there were three against her now instead of one.

'Vera and Winifred? To make this their home? But that's preposterous. You are joking, Ellis. You—'

'It is arranged,' he answered, smiling and patting his knee. 'Very satisfactory. You will rest in the country and they will see that I am comfortable while you are away. I shall shut up part of the house. I am very tired of parties and I shall see no one – only Doctor Playfair and one or two old friends. The house will be thoroughly cleaned, swept from top to bottom. The windows need cleaning. They have grown darker every day.'

He came very close to her. He put his hand on her forehead.

'See how hot your forehead is! You have been ill for a long, long time. That is why I have myself been so very uneasy. Doctor Playfair agrees that what you need is quiet. And what *I* need is quiet. We will have shutters on the windows and someone will see to the doors. They have been far too noisy.'

He got up. 'Tomorrow afternoon,' he said, 'you shall go down to Gloucestershire.' He stood, looking down at her.

'Poor dear, poor dear!' He kissed her forehead. 'Go to bed now. Rest is what you want. I shall be in my room for a while. I have most important work – very important work indeed.'

When he was gone she sat there thinking. Her first impulse was for immediate flight. But where? Rose. Yes, Rose. Then she thought: 'No. This will be cowardice. And besides this may be all Ellis' imagination. How do I know that this absurd idea about Winifred and Vera is not invented by him? And this ridiculous notion about my going into the country. Of course he cannot *make* me go. I must talk to him again. Just now I said nothing. I must talk to Barney. Perhaps *he* will see Ellis. In any case I can't leave him like this without knowing the truth, the facts . . .'

Then she thought of Benjie. She was in a turmoil of weariness, fear, indignation. The appalling element in it was her own isolation, and she saw now that, for months, she had been becoming more isolated; everything had been closing in upon her, shutting her off.

It came to her like a cry. She would see Benjie. About her future now she was reckless. She had done her utmost, she had fought battle after battle, and now she would fight no more. The thought that half an hour from now she might be with Benjie, have, at last, after all this long waiting, his love again . . . simply to see him, to hear his voice, to escape from this fantasy of the last years so easily ... the room swam before her eyes.

She ran up to her room, found a hat and cloak, waited on the landing, listening, reached the hall in safety (no sound in all the house but the ticking of the clocks), opened the door and, at the end of Hill Street, found a hansom. She gave the man the number in Half Moon Street. Benjie would, in all probability, be out. Would she wait in his rooms for him? The old stock situation of the Society melodrama ... As the hansom turned into Half Moon Street, which was only a minute's distance from Hill Street, she tried to think what she would do, but she could not. She was ringing the bell before she came to any decision. A grave elderly manservant opened the door.

'Is Mr Herries at home?' she asked.

He did not seem in the least surprised to see her.

'If you will come in a moment, madam, I will see. What name, madam?'

'Lady Herries.'

'Very good, my lady, if you would not mind waiting.'

He disappeared around the corner of the stairs. Almost at once he appeared again, saying:

'Yes, Mr Herries is in. Will you come up, please?'

Benjie was at the door of his room. She went in and he followed her, closing the door behind him. He stared at her as though a cloud of angels had floated down to him from the ceiling.

'Vanessa!'

'Yes. This is just like a play, isn't it?' She was trembling but was determined that he should not see it. At the very sight of him she was so happy that she could only smile, stare back at him, then, with fumbling hands, take off her hat.

'Here,' he said. 'Take this chair. It is the only comfortable one. Oh, my God, Vanessa! If you knew how many times I've sat here imagining just this: saying to myself, "And now the bell will ring and Humphries will come to the door and he will say 'Lady Herries', and I ..."'

'That's in the play too.' She steadied her hands, holding them tightly together. 'But there is nothing dramatic in this, Benjie. I have come only for five minutes. But that isn't true either. It *is* dramatic, I suppose. You must give me advice. Tell me what to do.'

He sat down in the chair on the other side of the fireplace, his small body balanced forward, staring and staring and staring.

She saw that he was looking splendid, as brown and hard as a russet apple, spare, taut, not changed. Oh, not changed in the least these twenty years!

'I shouldn't have done this, I suppose,' she went on. 'At least – I don't know. There's no *shouldn't* any more. The fact is, quite simply, that Ellis is proposing to send me away to a private asylum in the country tomorrow ... It has been tonight a situation that I couldn't face by myself any longer. You know about Ellis? You have heard something?'

'My God!' Benjie shouted, springing up. 'Send *you* away? Send you to an asylum?'

'Yes. Quietly, Benjie dear. We have got to be sensible about this. The fact is that Ellis has been out of his mind for the last year or more. Twice he has tried to kill me, and still I held on. It has been miserable, tragic ... I don't want to talk about that part of it. That is past. But I must do something now, now, at once. You know Winifred and Vera Trent?'

Benjie nodded.

'They have taken charge of him. I think they intended to from the first. Oh, I don't mean that it is they who have planned to get me out of the house. I don't think they had the least idea of it. That is only Ellis' crazy notion. But it has come to this – that tonight, an hour ago, Ellis told me that they were from now on to live in the house, I was to be sent into the country, most of the house to be shut up. I don't know how much is Ellis' fantasy, how much is truth, but I *did* know, as he went on talking, that I could stand no more. I have been alone in this thing too long. And so – I came to see you.'

'Oh, Vanessa!' he sighed. 'At last!'

She nodded, smiling.

'Yes – at last. I have wasted my whole life. I can't go on without you any longer.'

He came over to her, knelt down beside her and took her hand. He sat on the floor, resting his head against her, her hand pulsing against his. They stayed for a long time quietly, without speaking, feeling as at every long-separated meeting they had always done – that there had never been any parting.

Then he became practical. He asked her every sort of question and she told him everything. For the first time in all these many years she poured everything from her heart, her unresting love for himself, her increasing loneliness, the friendship that she and Ellis had had for the first few years, the influence of Miss Fortescue, Ellis' headaches, the day of the Jubilee when he had first made her uneasy, the night when he had attacked her, and then detail after detail to the last Cumberland visit.

'But now – even now – I would not go were it not for those two old women. How I hate them! Oh, Benjie, how I hate them! But it isn't that; it is that my responsibility is over.'

He nodded.

'You have always been dreadfully conscientious, Vanessa. And now you are coming to me – for ever and ever and ever, amen.'

'Yes. I talked to Barney about it this afternoon.'

'And what did *he* say?'

'He pointed out that the world would be shocked, Violet would close her doors to me, I should no more be asked to Grosset.'

'Yes, that's true. And shall you mind?'

'I don't know – a little, perhaps. What I *do* know is that I am doing wrong. I shall suffer for it in one way or another. I suppose that, without realizing it, I have been thinking of this for a long time. I am not a fool about it. I know the delight – and I know the punishment.'

'Punishment!' he cried. 'There will be no punishment! We shall be happy for ever!'

She smiled, shaking her head.

'Of course nobody is happy for ever.' She put her hand under his chin, turning his face up towards hers. 'Benjie, are you *sure* you want me? Are you certain? I'm middle-aged, you know. You're middle-aged too, but for a man it is quite different. Are you *sure* that you want me – still – after all this time?'

'Sure? Sure? Why, Vanessa, I love you more than I did twenty years ago. Loving you has been the only good thing in me – that, and caring for Tom. Are *you* sure,' he went on, 'that *you* want me? I'm not much, you know, Vanessa. Apart from you I'm nothing at all. With you I may still do something.'

'Yes, I'm sure,' she said quietly.

'It is true, too, what Barney said. We shall be cut, you know. Wherever we live someone will be unkind. And as to the relations! Yet another scandal in the Herries history!'

'Oh yes.' She nodded her head. 'I understand just how things will be.' (Again, for a flashing instant, she thought of Rose.) 'I understand everything, I think,' she went on. 'I'm not a child now. I have seen how things go. Often and often I have been tempted to come to you. You must have known that! But I was wrong when I married Ellis, and his needing me – or my thinking that he did – kept me there. And then,' she added after a moment, 'to fly in the face of God. I know those are only words to you, but it is true reality to me. But if I can make you happy – isn't that something? You see, I've never made anyone happy since my father died. No one. Isn't that awful? If I had made *myself* happy it would have been a little, but not even that. Until tonight. Until now. Now I am so happy that there *must* be something right in it somewhere. Don't you think so?'

'I don't know about God. I think that's a tall word. But here and now we are going to do the best we can by one another. Until your God separates us we'll stay together just as years ago we meant to do.'

After a while they discussed the immediate plan.

'Tonight I'm returning to Hill Street,' Vanessa said. 'I must see Ellis once more and know what is fact and what isn't. I can't leave him until I know.'

'Then I am coming back with you,' Benjie said.

'To Hill Street?'

'Certainly. I must see that you are safe. If Ellis has gone to bed and is asleep, well and good. What time is it? Nearly twelve. He ought to be asleep. If he is not, I will talk to him. Don't be frightened. There shall be none of my famous fights. But I don't leave you until you are safe.'

She agreed. She wished now to hide nothing. If Ellis in reality intended to carry out his crazy plan it was right that she should be no longer alone. And she felt a feverish impatience that this absurd business should be settled once and for all. And she could not face Ellis alone again that night.

They walked round to Hill Street. In that clear air they heard Big Ben strike midnight as she opened the door with her key. They went up to the drawing-room. Ellis was standing there in front of the big marble fireplace.

Benjie spoke at once.

'I beg your pardon, Ellis, for coming at this impossible hour. Vanessa came round to me tonight to tell me that you intended to send her into the country tomorrow – to some doctor's. Well, Vanessa and I are very old friends, you know. We have obeyed your wishes all these years and kept apart, but when Vanessa told me this we thought it better that we should both see you. We can talk about it tomorrow if you prefer, but in that case Vanessa will go to a hotel for the night.'

Vanessa said: 'Ellis, after our talk tonight I couldn't stay here alone. For both our sakes—'

But Ellis, without moving and very quietly, waved his hand at the door.

'Would you mind,' he said to Benjie, 'coming farther into the room? They may be listening outside.'

Benjie came forward.

'Thank you.' Ellis looked at him very severely. 'I thought I told you that you were never to enter my house again?'

'Yes,' said Benjie. 'You did, and I wouldn't have come had it not been for Vanessa. Frankly, Ellis, she's frightened. You shouldn't have talked that nonsense about sending her into the country.'

'That is perfectly correct,' said Ellis. 'She is going to Doctor Playfair's.'

'Well – she is not,' said Benjie. 'Nothing of the kind. You must see, Ellis, that she can't live with you any longer after this. I didn't want her to come back here tonight at all, but she said she must know whether you *meant* what you said. It seems that you do.'

Vanessa had been standing, her hand up to the white cloak with the high white collar that she was wearing. She had been looking into Ellis' face, trying to find there some appeal to herself for help, some kindliness. If at that moment he had turned and gone to her, blindly asking her, as he used to do, that she should help him, she would, even now, have stayed . . .

But he did not seem in the least unusual. There was no sign of madness in him anywhere, and after that one sentence to Benjie about the door there was, in this scene, *no* queerness. There was no *queerness*, but there was hatred.

'You see, Ellis,' Vanessa said, 'I have realized that you don't need me any more. We haven't been happy together for a long time, have we? And as you don't need me we had better separate.'

'That is our affair,' he said. 'We can settle that tomorrow. If you were well, Vanessa, I'd have something to say to you for bringing this dirty ruffian here. As it is, Herries, get out and keep out.'

'Come on, Vanessa,' Benjie said. 'Let's go.'

She took a step forward to Ellis.

'Ellis. Don't you see how impossible it is?—'

He moved forward to her. Benjie stepped between them, then, taking her arm, he drew her away.

With quick steps Ellis followed them. He passed them as
though he did not see them and ran down the stairs. In the hall
he turned.

In a high, shrill, convulsed voice he cried:

'Get out, both of you! Get out! Get out!'

At the same moment the Chinese clock struck the half-hour.
Benjie, halfway down the stairs, put his hand on Vanessa's shoulder. They waited. He did not know what Ellis would do. But the
scene ended very quietly. Ellis did not move. Vanessa and Benjie
walked out of the house.

They found a hansom in Piccadilly.

'And now where?' Benjie asked.

'I'll go to Rose,' Vanessa answered.

She was trembling and he put his arm round her, holding her
close to him. Benjie gave the address to the cabman.

Part Three

The Lover

HAPPINESS IN RAVENGLASS

ONE FINE SEPTEMBER afternoon of that momentous year 1899, Mrs Runcing of Olive Bank, Ravenglass, came to tea with Mrs Jocelyn of Sea View Cottage. It was a most beautiful day, and the sun caressed the sea, the sea caressed the shore, and the birds rising in little flocks from the island hovered against the quivering sky like blown petals, silver-grey, and as the wing turned, of glittering metal. The cry of the gulls made the lazy sky lazier.

The two ladies sat at the window of Sea View Cottage and drank their tea.

'I'm using this room,' Mrs Jocelyn explained, 'because of my lodgers. I'm not sure that I don't like it quite as well as the other.'

A lady and gentleman rode past on a tandem bicycle. The gentleman rang his bell.

'What's that, dear?' an odd, croaking, half-strangled voice asked from within the room.

'Only a bicycle, Mother.'

On the farther side of the fireplace, almost hidden with shawls, was old Mrs Burgess, Mrs Jocelyn's mother. Mrs Burgess was ninety-two and, except that she was never warm, was a wonder for her age. She was as lively and spiteful and selfish and scandal-mongering as though she had been a young thing of twenty. There was nothing that happened from Barrow to Whitehaven in which she did not take an interest, and most especially, of course, in anything that had to do with love and – most particularly – illicit love. She was a Puritan and had all the eager questing spirit of the Puritan. Her curiosity it was that had kept her alive and would, it seemed, keep her alive for evermore.

Her daughter, Hester Jocelyn, was in every way her opposite: a little, warm-blooded, impetuous, charitable, kind-hearted woman whose husband had, ten years earlier, run away with an actress to South America. She had not loved him very much, but her loneliness was often worst at three in the morning when she could not sleep – quite terrible, yet she was cheerful, busy, charitable and infinitely patient with her horrid old mother. Something of a heroine perhaps.

Mrs Runcing, her visitor, was nothing of a heroine: a long
bony woman with three daughters whom she would sell her eyes
to marry. She threw them at the men of the district as you throw
darts at a dartboard. As with so many women of their time, they
had been trained to nothing, taught nothing. Their father
thought them too tiresome for words, their mother hated them
because no one would have them and yet loved them because they
were hers. The poor Miss Runcings!

'Things look bad in South Africa,' said Mrs Runcing. 'Henry
says we shall have war for certain. It's all the fault of that wicked
old Krüger. And so you like your lodgers, Hetty dear?' She laid
rum butter thickly on her bread. She was a greedy woman.

'Like them!' said Mrs Jocelyn. 'I should think so! No one
could help it. Mr Herries is as gay a gentleman as you'd find
anywhere, always singing and laughing. No trouble at all. But
Mrs Herries is my favourite. She's a *lovely* lady – so kind and
thoughtful, and so friendly. It's nice to see a married pair so
happy – and not young either. I've never had visitors I've taken
to so.'

There was a pause. Mrs Jocelyn looked up.

'What is it, Cecilia? You've something on your mind.'

Mrs Runcing paused yet longer, then, dropping her voice,
said: 'Hetty, there's something you ought to know.'

Mrs Jocelyn moved uneasily. She knew well this opening of
her friend's and always it meant no good.

'Know? What ought I to know?'

'It's just like you, Hetty. The last in the place to be aware of
what everyone is saying.'

'*What* is everyone saying?'

'About Mrs Herries. She isn't Mrs Herries at all. She's Lady
Herries – and she and Mr Herries are no more married than ...
than you and I are!'

'Cecilia, what *are* you saying?' Mrs Jocelyn got up from the
window. 'Now I won't have it! You've always got some story
about someone, Cecilia. It's too bad. It's a shame.'

'Oh, is it! Always got some story, have I? That's a nice thing to
say to an old friend. I'm telling you out of kindness. It's been the
talk here for days and you ought to know it.'

There was an excited movement of the shawls from the back of
the room.

'I'm sure Mr and Mrs Herries are married. I don't care what
anyone says.'

'Well, you're wrong for once. Mrs Herries is Lady Herries, wife of Sir Ellis Herries in London. She ran away from him last year, with this Mr Herries.'

'What's that you are saying, Cecilia?' the old lady from the fireplace croaked. 'Not married, you say? Not married? Well, I never! Well, I never did! Not married!'

'Of course they're not married. The affair made a sensation last year in London. And more than that, they've been lovers for years and years. Everybody knows them. The Herries are Cumberland people or, anyway, they've been in Cumberland for centuries. There was an old Mr Herries lived here in Ravenglass years ago, they say, and this Mr Herries has a house near Bassenthwaite Lake. Lady Herries was brought up on Derwentwater. She was a great lady in London for years. I call it a piece of downright impertinence for them to come back to this part of the country where everyone knows them. Disgusting, I call it. But they say there's been one scandal after another in that family. Years and years ago there was a Mr Herries who was a holy terror, and some fifty years back one of the Herries murdered another one somewhere by Keswick. It's a disgrace their coming to Ravenglass. They should be ashamed to show their faces!'

Mrs Runcing had not intended to be so violent, but, as often before, when denouncing the vices of others her own virtues grew in colour and strength. As others went down she herself went up, and the higher she went the better she felt.

Little Mrs Jocelyn had turned very pale. At last she said:

'I don't care whether they're married or not. They shall stay here as long as they like!'

'Hetty!' Here was a thing for a decent Christian woman to say!

'I don't care! I mean it!'

'Think of what people will say!'

And there was a croak from the fireplace: 'Not married ... in this house!'

Then, beyond the half-open window, they heard a step on the gravel path. Both women turned and looked. Vanessa was coming up from the sea.

'All I know,' said Mrs Jocelyn, almost sobbing with emotion, 'is that that's the finest lady I've ever met. She's welcome to this roof as long as she wishes.'

Vanessa was walking, her head back to the sea breeze, her dress blown against her legs. Her face was warm with colour. She had grown a little stouter in this last year, her bosom fuller, and, carrying herself thus strongly, she moved like a woman who was happy, free and self-confident.

This seemed to Mrs Runcing, whose own bosom, do what she would, was never what it ought to be, insulting.

'You'd think she had nothing to be ashamed of,' she said.

'Neither she has,' answered Mrs Jocelyn indignantly. 'They're happy, aren't they? And that's more than most people manage to be. I expect her husband was horrible.'

Mrs Runcing set her lips. 'You'll be sorry, Hetty,' she said. 'Encouraging immorality. You'll see how people will talk . . .'

Meanwhile Vanessa had gone into the little sitting-room on the other side of the passage, taken off her straw hat, and sat down by the window to wait for Benjie. He had gone fishing. In an hour's time he would return, they would sit reading, talking, the veils of light would fall over the sea, the stars would come out, the cries of the birds would die away; after supper they would take a last walk, then, tired and happy, return, light the lamp, play chess, go up the crooked staircase to bed.

She sat there, dreaming.

More than a year had passed and still God had not let loose His thunderbolts. She had known a period of perfect unrestrained happiness. She looked back, first to the time at Eastbourne, then to the months in France, then to the wonderful glorious experience of coming home to Cumberland. What troubles had there been? In Eastbourne she had been cut by Mrs Harbin, a friend of Violet's. Alfred and his wife had met her in the hotel lounge and that had been a little uncomfortable. On the other hand Adrian, at one time, Rose at another, Barney at another, had stayed with them. The news from London had at first been a little distressing. The talk had been, she understood, terrific. The sympathy had gone, universally, to Ellis. Winifred and Vera Trent had gone to live in Hill Street and, so far as Vanessa could discover, Ellis had been quite tranquil, had enjoyed the sympathy and had allowed it generally to be understood that he was able to bear his misfortunes like a gentleman. Often – and this was perhaps her severest trouble – she asked herself whether she had imagined all that queerness. But no: the scene in Cumberland, the frenzies and tears in Hill Street had been real enough, but how much of it had been histrionic, an attempt on Ellis' side to catch her sympathy, a passion for melodrama?

Strangely the question of Ellis' insanity was no longer the main one. She knew now, in the light of these last months, that for years she had been living in prison. It was only now that she understood how solemn, how unhumorous, how dreary that Hill Street life had been, what a *dreary* creature she herself had become! Everything in it had been false, the social fuss, the hours that she had spent with people for whom she did not care, the shamness of her interests. She thought of the balls, the receptions, the silly games, the sillier country houses and race meetings and baccarat; her weak good nature, her amiability, her own stupidity, she told herself, had kept her there long, long after she should have left it.

And Benjie? She smiled as she lay back in her chair looking at the long dune like the back of a whale over whose brown surface little waves broke in edges of white and silver. Benjie was not perfect. She had never supposed that he would be. There had been the night at Eastbourne when she had entered their bedroom to discover him kissing the chambermaid. Twice, once at Eastbourne, once in Paris, he had left her for two days without warning. Sometimes he was out of temper, sometimes (but very seldom) he was drunk. He knew some very queer people, although he was scrupulous about the company he introduced her to. Once he had declared that he must go immediately to Italy to meet a man in Siena. Tom, who, although he was only still a boy, had much wisdom, had settled that little business. Tom, by good fortune, thought Vanessa the most wonderful woman in the world.

Vanessa, on her side, was not always perfect. Far from it. She was impatient, suffered fools badly (and some of Benjie's friends were very foolish), sometimes nagged Benjie, sometimes (as she well knew) bored him with her naïveté, her religion, her obstinacy. But they had been saved, both of them, by their splendid comradeship. Because they had been friends all their lives long that business of compromise, so difficult in the first year of marriage, had been quite natural for both of them. They loved for every kind of reason, but chiefly because they knew one another so well, and admired and laughed at, for the most part, the same things. The wildness in Benjie Vanessa understood because, in her own way, she had the same wildness. They must both be free. They stayed together only because they loved one another. The troubles that they had were on the surface because the base of their relationship was firm, unshakeable. They were honest, but not so honest that they were for ever challenging weaknesses. *Of course* they were weak, mistaken, faulty in this way or that. They took these things for granted. Because Benjie kissed the chambermaid it did not mean that he did not love Vanessa. He loved *only* Vanessa. He had loved Vanessa only, all his life long.

But the best of their relationship was its gaiety. Vanessa found that she had not been gay for thirteen years but now, like a language once learnt and long unpractised, living with the natives again, back it returned.

Love, if it is to be worth anything, must be honest, trusting, humorous, protective, far-seeing. With them both it was all these things.

And under its influence Vanessa grew and developed. It had been her danger always that because of her great simplicity of nature she would become tiresome company. Her mother and father had both been very simple people and it was possible that they had bored a good many persons. Vanessa, in her London years, had learnt superficial variety – that is, she had been trained to adapt herself to a great many different characters – but her lack of subtlety sometimes revealed her. Bertrand, the novelist, whose eye was so sharp that its rather fishy, sleepy indifference often deceived the innocent, said that the only women who were interesting were the good ones who wanted to be bad, that no women were so dull as the bad women who wanted to be good. The bad ones who were content to be bad were, he said, amusing companions, but they were all the same – know one and you knew all.

Now Vanessa had, in London, been a good woman determined to be unprejudiced and open-minded. She defended Rose because she loved her, but also a little to show that she was above censorship. She had never *really* known the kind of life that a woman like Rose was leading. Her father, Barney, her husband, Lettice Marrable – from none of these did she get the real sense of it. But after a year with Benjie she knew. They talked together like two schoolboys without any reticences whatever. She was now *truly* aware of the humour, the generosity, the comradeship, the dirty untidy tragedy of the 'vicious' world. She knew that it was *not* vicious – simply a place inhabited by the uncontrolled, the needy, the weak, the greedy and, above all, the lonely. That the very last thing that it called for was superior patronage, and that those who lived in it did not wish, for the most part, for any sympathy from anybody.

So Vanessa grew wise. She learnt now to be patient, tolerant and unpriggish. This continuous love that burnt steadily from hour to hour, from day to day, warmed her heart so that it was impossible *not* to be generous. It is only the disappointed, starved, and robbed who are jealous and unfair.

Waiting now for Benjie she had on her lap and read from time to time Judith's old green-bound book. She had rescued it from her father's room at Uldale on the night of the fire. Judith, in her old age, had dictated it to Aunt Jane, and in Aunt Jane's clear spidery hand it was as fresh as though written last week. There was a piece about Ravenglass.

It seemed that, in the spring of 1737, Judith's father, Rogue Herries, had ridden over with his son David to spend a night or two with his brother Harcourt Herries, an old bachelor who had lived for many years in Ravenglass.

'David used to tell us,' Judith's book said, 'of that visit to Ravenglass as one of the striking incidents in his life because of the quarrel that he had with his father there. He would describe to us the ride over Stye Head on horseback, how gloomy his father was on that ride, suffering from one of his "demons", how they came into Ravenglass in the evening, clattering over the cobbles, smelling the sea, and hearing the gulls. Then there was Uncle Harcourt, who was a very precise old bachelor and wouldn't have a woman in his house, and he wore, David remembered, a wonderful ring on his finger with a green stone, and a rose-coloured skirted coat. After supper Uncle Harcourt talked of the London of Queen Anne, where he had been as a boy, of the Sacheverell Riots, of the Thames barge the *Folly*, and the coffee houses, and of how he had seen Mrs Rogers as Berenice.

'Uncle Harcourt was a fervent Jacobite and gave the toast of "The King over the water", breaking his wine glass after it, and he recited to them Pope's *Elegy to the Memory of an Unfortunate Lady*. Then David's father lost his temper, took David out to sea and ordered him to strip for a beating as a punishment for some fancied misdemeanour. David refused and said that he was no longer a child, and that was the beginning of a new relationship between them. This,' Judith went on, 'was one of David's favourite stories and, as a little girl, while I listened I could see it all as vividly as though I had been there – the London of Queen Anne, and the little bachelor declaiming Pope, and David and his father standing by the sea.'

'And here I am,' thought Vanessa, 'in this same place as though time never had been. Little Uncle Harcourt might walk

in at this door any moment. I knew Judith so well and she lived
in the same house with the man whose uncle saw the Sacheverell
Riots. In London now they have the telephone and there are
these new "moving pictures" and Alfred Herries has a motor-car.
Time does not separate any of us, but rather our stupidities,
selfishness, and fears. Judith, if she were here, would scold me
for moralizing. She always hated it. But, on the other hand, she
would be glad that I am happy and would altogether approve of
my running away from Ellis . . .'

She heard the hall door open and close, a quick step, and
Benjie had come in. 'They say that when you live with anyone
their features become so familiar that you can't see them any
more. Well, I can see Benjie all right, his bright eyes with the
humorous crows' feet at the corners, his brown hands, the part of
his forehead that grows white above the brown just below his
hair; I know how his arms fasten about me and how strong is his
kiss on my lips. It is all as new as though it had never happened
until now, and my heart beats at the sound of his step as though
now for the first time he was about to tell me that he loved me.'

He went up and washed. Mrs Jocelyn brought in the supper,
and after they had eaten they sat close together by the window.

'I've been reading Judith's book, Benjie,' Vanessa said. 'The
part about Ravenglass. It seemed as though time hadn't passed at
all and little Harcourt Herries might be walking in on us with his
green ring and rose-coloured coat. My great-grandfather was
born in William III's reign, and Alfred has a motor-car. So soon
as I am back in this part of the country time doesn't exist. We
none of us die here—'

'Take a step,' Benjie said lazily, 'and you are at Gosforth;
another, and it's Ennerdale. Then over the hill to Buttermere,
Honister, Borrowdale. Yes, we're back in our own country,
Vanessa. Bold of us, perhaps. The old boatman wasn't so friendly
today. He knows we're living in sin.'

She did not answer. They had been living in sin for a year and
she was not yet aware of it. Was it now, when she had returned to
her own people, that she *would* be aware?

'I've had a letter from that man Alington. He advises me to go
in for those Australian mines – at once, without losing a minute.
Shall I?'

She looked at him quietly. 'No, I don't think so.' Everyone was
speculating. The fever in London had spread everywhere, and
Gold Mines glittered on every doorstep. 'You promised me, you

know. We don't know enough about it. We have enough. We don't want to be rich, either of us.'

'Don't we?' She saw that he was restless. 'I'm not sure that I don't. I've never been rich. I wouldn't mind the sensation.'

She put out her hand and caught his.

'You're restless – what is it?'

'It's South Africa for one thing. It looks bad – or good if you like. A war would be fun. We haven't had one for ages. Tom would go as a war correspondent if he weren't so young.'

'Well, *you're* too old to go. That's one comfort.'

'Oh no, I'm not,' he answered quickly.

'You're forty-four.'

'What's that? No age at all. And I'm as fit as a fiddle.'

'Let's not talk of it.' She stilled her fear. 'I'm so happy. Don't spoil it.'

'If there *was* a war,' he said, 'it would be only for a week or two. I'd be back in no time – with a VC probably and all the Family greeting me like a hero.'

He drew his chair closer to her and leant his head on her shoulder.

'Vanessa, you're not tired of me yet?'

'No, I'm not tired of you.'

'How happy we've been and are!' He sighed. 'Why can't everyone find love like this? It seems so simple when you get it. I suppose that somewhere there's the right person for everyone – one for each – but they don't meet. Do you find there's something a little pathetic in two people of our age loving one another so? We ought to be young – we ought to be twenty – as we might have been had I not been such a fool. And I'm still a fool, Vanessa. It may break out any time.'

She laid her hand against his cheek.

'We used to say long ago that nothing could separate us. Nothing has. Nothing can now.'

'Yes – death,' he answered.

'You know that I don't think so.'

'Without our bodies? Shall we love still? You without your hair, your eyes, without the warm touch of your hand against my cheek? When I can see you smile no longer nor the way that you put your hand up to your hair, nor hear your voice. And I! I'll be a poor ghost, Vanessa—'

'What of your Valhalla under the hill, the men singing?'

'Ah, you won't be there! And I'll be such a wild ghost, flying from Top to Top, haunting old women down the chimney, stealing the butter from the dairy, pinching the young women. I love you for every conceivable reason, Vanessa, but without your body I shouldn't know you. I'd be as restless as I used to be. I'd never find you. I'd go searching from ghost to ghost ... And you'd be so good. You'd be in favour in Heaven, one of the guardian angels. They'd have no use for me, I'm afraid, and whatever job they set me to do I'd do it wrong.'

She kissed him.

'I'd find you. Wherever you went I'd go too.'

'Are you sure,' he asked her, 'that you never miss London? Not Ellis, of course, nor Hill Street – but all your friends and the good times you had with all the nobs. Don't you *mind* being a disgrace and something to make virtuous ladies shudder over?'

'I've never been so happy in all my life,' she said, her voice very low. 'I seem to have reached middle age quite emptily – as though I'd been born yesterday. There was my childhood – that was happy. And now there's this. Nothing between.'

'And now there's this,' he repeated contentedly.

They were aware that the door opened. They both turned together, thinking that it was Mrs Jocelyn who had come to say goodnight. The lamp was burning dimly and in the half-light they saw the oddest figure in the doorway. It was old Mrs Burgess, wrapped in a multitude of shawls, leaning on her stick; she stood there, her old brown wrinkled face pushed forward like the head of a tortoise. She stared at them, they could see, as though she could never satisfy her curiosity. Then she vanished.

'What did *she* want?' Benjie asked. He got up and went to the door. 'What cheek! To come in without knocking—'

'She's half crazy, poor old thing,' Vanessa said. 'Mrs Jocelyn says that she ought to be in her bed, but they can't keep her there.'

'What did she want? She looked at us as though she'd never seen us before.'

They played their game of chess and went up to bed. Long after Benjie was asleep in Vanessa's arms she lay there awake. He slept like a child, his hand on her breast. She lay there, forcing herself resolutely, quite calmly, to a new courage. Instinct, light words lightly spoken, some shadow like the finger of a cloud on a sunlit hill, told her that it would be needed.

She was right. It *was* needed. Next day Benjie had moved into his savage state. That was how she always put it to herself. It was as though he reverted into some old wild existence where the rules, objects, dangers, joys of life were all quite different from this one. He seemed physically to change. He could not stay in the same spot from one tick of the clock to another. He moved about the room as though he were unclothed, his brown finely muscled body moving naked through tall grass, his eyes shiningly alert for the enemy. As often as not he did not hear what you said to him, he snapped back replies, he suddenly started walking down the road saying that he did not know when he would return.

The happy thing was that Vanessa understood this transformed state to perfection. She was aware of it often in herself but, being a woman and therefore having all her eggs in one basket (which was Benjie), Benjie could satisfy her wildest longings. She could not satisfy Benjie's. Nor did she try. When this restlessness came on him she let him go free.

But now there was more serious trouble. His words about South Africa had clutched her heart. Was there going to be war? If so, then Benjie would be off ... Nothing could keep him ... He would revel in it. He would be killed, perhaps. People were killed in wars ...

Today was the eighteenth of September, and it seemed that, on the sixteenth, the Transvaal had replied to the British proposals of starting the argument all over again by proposing to revert to a joint Commission. There was something sinister in the tone underlying the Boer phrases.

What was it all about? For a long while she had not taken it with any seriousness. It was all due, it seemed, to Krüger's fear of Rand dominion of his country. It all went back to the old Gold Rushes into the Rand. Rather naturally, Vanessa considered, Krüger thought that to give franchise to the Rand population must entirely alter Boer rule. He was honest, perhaps, in wishing to keep the Transvaal an agricultural country. On the other hand, the British Government must protect its subjects. But ought those subjects to be in that country at all? Didn't it look as though a small, resolute, independent people were to be bullied and affronted by a big Power when all that the little people wanted was freedom to live as they wished on their own soil? On the other hand, *could* Great Britain allow her own sons to be persecuted, ill-treated, mishandled, and say nothing?

It seemed, Vanessa thought with a sigh, one of those questions that had so clearly two sides to it. And the Boers were thick-headed, obstinate, stupid, hypocritical perhaps ... On the other hand, it *was* their country! Or wasn't it? She soon, however, abandoned the wider, more public question for the private personal one. If there was a war, Benjie would go ... If Benjie went ... She pulled herself to her full height, clasping her hands behind her head, staring in front of her. The stiffest job of her whole life was approaching her.

Then a very absurd thing occurred. Coming into the house one morning she encountered old Mrs Burgess, who was shuffling along in flat slippers, trailing shawls about her and making that odd wheezy noise peculiarly her own. She saw Vanessa and, thrusting her old head forward, hissed some word. Then, with yellow convulsive hands, drawing her shawls tightly about her, she slip-slopped into her fastness.

Vanessa did not know what the word was, but it was evidently intended to express moral horror and indignation. She asked Mrs Jocelyn to come and speak to her. She told her of it. She liked Mrs Jocelyn extremely.

'Sit down, Mrs Jocelyn,' Vanessa said. 'Let's sit together by the window.' They sat down. 'Now I'm not wrong, am I, in supposing that your mother has learnt that Mr Herries and I are not married?'

Mrs Jocelyn nervously rubbed her hands together.

'No, Mrs Herries. That's correct.'

'I should have told you before. I'm not Mrs Herries. I'm Lady Herries. I left my husband last year.'

'Oh yes ...' said Mrs Jocelyn nervously.

'I should have told you. I did not mean to conceal anything. I would have told you at once if you had asked me, but I really did not feel that it was anyone's business but our own. Now I suppose you would like us to go. I quite understand and I do hope you'll forgive us for putting you into this unpleasant position. We have been so happy here and you have been so very good to us.'

Mrs Jocelyn was a sentimental and emotional little woman. Her eyes glittered with tears as she looked out of the window. Many things made her cry: the music of a band in the street, reading of a deed of heroism in the newspaper, details of a wedding, the more moving portions of almost any novel. But although she was emotional, she had the strength (and sometimes the obstinacy) of Mr Krüger himself.

'Oh no, Lady Herries,' she said. 'Please don't think of going. A friend told us, a week or so ago. It appears that you and Mr Herries are well known in Cumberland and Westmorland. You come from these parts, do you not? So of course the people here have talked about you. But please pay no attention. Mother is a very old lady and not always accountable. It doesn't matter at all. Really it doesn't.'

Vanessa smiled.

'Thank you, Mrs Jocelyn, for saying that. We'll never forget it. But of course we mustn't stay here. It would be wrong for us to make it awkward for you in any way.'

'It doesn't make it awkward,' said Mrs Jocelyn with tremendous energy. 'I hope you won't think it impertinent, but my knowing you, Lady Herries, has been the nicest thing that has ever happened to me. I don't know, of course, what reasons you had for leaving your husband, but I'm sure they were very good ones. There were times in the past when I quite easily might have left Mr Jocelyn, although now that he isn't here I wouldn't like to say anything against him. I'm sorry, of course, that you and Mr Herries can't be married, but as you can't you can't, and that's all there is to it.'

Vanessa was very much moved.

'I'm afraid that isn't all there is to it,' she said. 'I have done something that is wrong. I did it knowing that it was wrong, and the fact that we are both happy doesn't make it any more right. But I did it deliberately and I will take what comes. All the same it's not fair that anyone else should be involved, especially anyone as kind and good as you are.'

'I'm neither kind nor good,' Mrs Jocelyn replied. 'I'm often most unkind to my mother, I'm afraid. And as to being good, I'm too old now, I suppose, to be anything else very much, but when I was younger there were times when I would have run away from Mr Jocelyn most gladly if there had been anyone to run away with.'

She got up and added, smiling rather timidly:

'I've not had many friends and my life hasn't been very exciting, but when I *have* a friend – well, there it is. If you were to go away I should be very unhappy. And don't mind Mother. I'll see that she doesn't worry you.'

Vanessa went with her to the door and kissed her.

'Then we'll stay,' she said.

*　　　*　　　*

On October 9th the Boers delivered their ultimatum. For three weeks after this neither Benjie nor Vanessa spoke of the only subject in their minds.

Under the eyes of a watchful and gossiping Ravenglass they spent quiet days, bicycling to Wastwater and Black Combe, seeing the shadows turn the flanks of the Screes to purple and the bracken flame in Eskdale. Then Vanessa had a letter from Adrian.

DEAREST VANESSA – How are things going with you? Here we talk nothing but the War. General opinion is that it will be over before Christmas and everyone – except your humble servant – is turning himself into a soldier as quickly as possible that he may see something of the fun before it is finished. I am not so sure. It seems to me that we are already everywhere on the defensive. I lie low and say nothing, for the general feeling is that it is all a great lark – a sort of polo game in which even the poorest may join. I listened to Chamberlain defending the Government for three long hours and what he *did* say was all right – but how about all the things he didn't?

What is certain is that we are now beholding the end of the Victorian Era. Do you remember young Violet complaining to you and me once how, when the maid was busy elsewhere, she must sit indoors all a fine afternoon because she must not go out alone? Haven't you, at your own Balls, seen the chaperons sitting in weary rows hour after hour? I prophesy that you will never see those chaperons again and that Alfred's girl will, in another fifteen years or so, be smoking a cigarette as she enjoys her luncheon alone at the Criterion.

The Family, by the way, is amusing. They take the War of course as their own affair. Krüger is a kind of Benjie who has insulted them all personally. It is 'Our' War – Horace especially is full of club-martial ardour. Carey is going out in some capacity or another although he's sixty-three or so. Also Peile Worcester and – would you believe it? – Philip is being sent out by some paper. I am generally despised because I say that the Government must be carried on and if *I* go who will remain?

And Benjie? What is he going to do? If he goes, don't worry. Benjie will always survive things like wars. They were made for him, not he for them. Write and tell me . . .

*   *   *

Then Benjie had a letter from Paris. Tom, young though he was, had hitched himself on to some French newspaper man and was already on the sea. Tim had thrown over his painting and come home to enlist.

'You see,' Benjie said, staring at her as though he were taking her image into his very heart. 'I've got to go.'

'Yes,' said Vanessa, smiling. 'Of course you have.'

Their last night in Ravenglass they did not sleep. They lay in one another's arms while the rain lashed the windows and the wind screamed along the sea. A bird, in the early morning, beat its wings against the pane.

'You mustn't be lonely,' Benjie said over and over again. 'I shall be back almost before I've gone. I shall think of you all the time. You mustn't be lonely. You mustn't be lonely.'

As the light wove grey webs upon the wall he said, stroking her cheek:

'When I loved you a year ago, Vanessa, I didn't know what love was. This year has taught me.'

'And I love you,' she answered simply, 'more every day. I thought it couldn't grow; I didn't know . . . I didn't believe . . .'

She began to cry – a ridiculous thing, she thought, a woman of forty crying. But this once when there was no one to see . . . He kissed her tears. He had lain so often in her arms like a boy. Now he held her like a man and she was a child.

They were both very merry that morning. She would not come with him to London. She saw him drive off in the old cab; she waved her hand, laughing, while all Ravenglass watched from behind its windows.

Then she walked, her head bent to the wind, and did not return till it was dark.

THE KOPJE

SHE went back to Cat Bells.

Was not that perhaps a piece of impertinence? Everyone in the neighbourhood thought so. But she was not at all disturbed by the thoughts of her neighbours. She said to Mrs Newson on the evening of her arrival:

'You know, Mrs Newson, that I've left my husband.'

'Yes – so I've heard, my lady.'

'And since that time Mr Benjamin Herries and I have lived as man and wife. He has gone out to South Africa.'

'Yes, my lady. I hope he'll come back safe.'

'So do I,' said Vanessa, smiling. 'But I want you to tell me if you and your husband would rather get some other position. I shall be glad to help you until you are suited.'

Mrs Newson, who was a stout short woman with red cheeks and grey hair, paused. Then slowly delivered her mind.

'It's like this, my lady. It wouldn't be fair to say that me and Robert haven't talked this over. We have. We don't think it right in general for a woman to live with a man she's not married to. I wouldn't do it myself, nor would Robert. But you see, you're different. Folks can say what they like, but you're our own, so to speak. The last thing Will Leathwaite said to me while he was sensible enough to say anything was you was a grand lady and I wasn't to forget it. In Cumberland we're slow but sure, and me and Robert think you must have had good reasons for what you done, and there's no place can be to us what this cottage is after being here so long, so we'll be staying if it's all the same to you, my lady.'

After a week she could not have been more private, she thought, had she lived in a nunnery. No one came to see her; she went to see no one. She walked, read, followed with passionate interest every detail of the war. Gradually the peace of that place stole about her and enfolded her. Her father, her mother, Will, seemed to keep her company. The fell that rose above the roof of the cottage was burnished with the dying bracken; the herons sailed majestically against the sky. The little field circled with its toy-like trees on the slope above Lodore caught the morning light with such confident tranquillity that its curve, like the bowl of a cup, filled, emptied, filled again as though obeying happily its commander.

She bicycled over to the Fortress and looked down into the Uldale valley. There was a church there now and sheep were grazing where Fell House had been. The Fortress, she heard, was let to a Mr Swanwick. Children were playing in the garden, a bicycle leant against the door, two dogs ran to the gate and barked at her.

She thought day and night of Benjie. His earlier training as one of the much-bemocked Volunteers years before helped him now and he had sailed for South Africa early in November. She took a hurried journey to London, stayed there with him for two nights, seeing no one else but Barney, and returned to Cumberland. Then, some weeks later, she received her first letter.

MY DARLING – This must be only a short note. I shall soon have a chance, I hope, of a long letter. The worst part of the voyage was its monotony. From the moment we left London we were shut off from all news. To be without news for a fortnight at a time like this – you can imagine what hell it is! We thought we'd learn something at Madeira. Not a word. We were all inoculated against enteric and I to my shame took it badly. We had cinematograph men on board, but I don't myself think *that* will ever come to much! The machinery is so cumbrous that if they want to take anything that moves it is gone before their machines are ready. Then at last we sighted a sail and were so close that, when they put a board up with some news on it, we could read it easily. What they told us was: 'Three battles. Boers defeated' – and then didn't we cheer? After that no more news till we sighted Robben Island. *Then* there was news all right! . . . But you will know it all by this time and much more.

What else can I tell you but that I love you, love you, my darling? I carry you with me. You are never absent from me for a single moment, your courage, your goodness, your loyalty to a poor old devil whom no one has a good word for. But haven't they? The world has changed, Vanessa. Everyone is to me like a brother. No member of the Herries family here to tell the world what I really am – all damned good fellows – and, old though I am, I'm as lively as the youngest and will make you proud of me before I'm done. So cheer up, my sweetest, and believe in me as you have always done. Tomorrow, I believe, we are off again – whither I don't know. I'm as impatient as a flea on a hot plate. Impatient also for your first letter. Tell me *everything* – how the stream runs down through the garden, what you do every hour of the day, are the Newsons good to you? Have you had a look at the Fortress?

They are calling me. I must go – Your loving and devoted and eternally faithful

B.

A fortnight passed and there was another letter, a long one. Part of it was as follows:

... It was a bit of a battle. How can I make you see it? Looking back I can see a green hill, kopje, almost blood colour, and then grass-green veldt. The trains stopped and poured khaki into the veldt. Funny to see the confused mass, then order forming out of it, then the line of tiny dots, then a thicker line, more and more lines, then a mass of khaki. First the dots were at the base, almost lost in the brown of the hill, then altogether lost, then suddenly against the skyline. Away on the right the Imperial Light Horse. Then our guns thudded, and thud came the answer. Then the shells. Thin whirr, screaming cry. Ball after ball of white smoke struck the kopje, then little balloons of shrapnel from our guns; then the guns pealing faster and faster. Just as our own order to move came, down crashed the rain. You never saw anything like it, Vanessa. It drove through macintoshes like blotting paper. The earth underfoot melted while you looked at it into mud and the mud turned to water. Everything was blotted out in the cloud of swirling water, but the guns thundered and doggedly we pushed ahead.

Soon we were in it – my first battle, you know. What did I feel? I can't tell you – except that the ridges we must conquer seemed endless. Up one there was another! I wasn't afraid. The bugles and the pipes stirred your blood. And then I was caught into the noise. Officers shouting, swearing, cursing; all of us stumbling, falling, jumping, killing – and then, like a maniac's desired dream there at our feet the Boer camp and the Boers galloping out of it!

As I started down the hill, though, something struck me. Don't be frightened It turned out to be nothing – a slight scratch – but my face was buried in mud, all the world seemed to crash over my head and when at last I raised myself and wiped the mud from my eyes I seemed to be transfixed by a small kopje not far off. It stared at me, I at it. Brown-red in colour, it was shaped like a pig with horns. It seemed to move, to wriggle as though it wanted to scratch its back. I was dazed of course, and didn't rightly know for a moment where I was, but I thought it moved towards me, wagging its ears. Then the scene cleared. I stood up. I was all right and ran down the hill ...

Afterwards it was cold and drizzling. Some of the prisoners joined us and we were all most friendly. Decent chaps the Boers really – fine fellows with their beards and corduroys, with a grand dignity, some of them. There's been a lot of looting and you see men with the weirdest clothes. And you should watch the guns scatter at a shell. See the legs of the horses leap! You never imagined such nimbleness . . .

And who do you think has turned up? George Endicott, a friend of my wife's brother. A wild chap but I always liked him and now here he is in my own regiment. Small world, isn't it? Young Tom's shut up in Mafeking. Carey Rockage is in Ladysmith. Are you well, my darling, and keeping up your spirits? You seem to be always with me. Last night I talked to you . . .

She held on, but the strain began to tell. The loneliness of her days and nights frightened her. She became restless. She wanted to be doing something, something for the war, something, through others, for Benjie.

After the Black Week, the 10th–16th of December: Stormberg, Magersfontein, Tugela River, the feeling of the whole country changed. What was this that had happened to England? While the rest of the world looked on, jeering, hostile, longing for our humiliation – here was the most shameful time for us since the Indian Mutiny. Lord Roberts was appointed to the chief command, and Kitchener of Khartoum was to go with him. The appointment roused a storm of new energy. The gay, light-hearted jesting was over. This was a job that the country must settle. The colonies offered new contingents, a great call went out for yeomanry, and the new infantry volunteers flamed into being. The City of London would raise and equip a regiment entirely at its own expense. Everywhere there were new khaki uniforms. From all parts of the country, shipyard men, squires' sons, farmers' sons, artisans, and clerks poured into the new forces. Nothing spectacular any more. Had they but known it, that Black Week killed spectacular warfare for ever. Nothing to catch the eye was tolerated. Scarlet fled, never to return to the battlefield. A new patience, a fresh endurance, no more the reckless charge, but 'the infinitely painful crawl through the long, long day'.

For Vanessa those first months in the new year became an agony. She heard now from Benjie at the longest intervals. This country, for the first time in her life, failed her. The old beloved names – Skiddaw and Scafell, the running Derwent, the ridge of Blencathra, the slow ripple of the quiet Lake meant nothing. The valleys held no peace and the running water no music.

Her ostracism now terribly distressed her. It was a time when she wanted to have part and lot with all her fellow-beings, but on Cat Bells she was like a prisoner. Her loneliness became a horror; she could not sleep. She walked restlessly, tried to read and could not. She grew thin and pale. The Newsons heard her talking to herself, and once Mrs Newson found her crying, her head in her hands.

'Don't cry, my lady. It will be all right. 'Twill be over soon, they all say.'

Then at the beginning of April she had a brief letter from Benjie that frightened her. He had been ill in hospital; he was better, but things moved slowly. It would be all right, of course, but the Boers were obstinate fellows and Tom in Mafeking made it anxious work . . . But he was all right . . . She wasn't to worry . . . That letter was too much for her. She came to London.

She went to a little hotel called 'The Clarence', off Baker Street. A lady in the train told her of it and she thought: 'How funny! I have never stayed by myself in a hotel before!' As soon as she was in the hansom driving to the hotel she was happy. She was nearer to Benjie; she was in touch with human beings again. She had not minded at all when Mrs Hope of Portinscale cut her in the Keswick street, when Mrs Merriman, who had before been so kind to her in Rosthwaite, gave her a sharp little bow and hurried down the Borrowdale Road. No, no, she had not minded . . . She had been prepared for it. She had taken it gaily. Nevertheless, how different these things were without Benjie! Loneliness had returned, not the old spiritual loneliness of the life at Hill Street, but physical, material loneliness, hearing no voice, touching no hand, receiving no kiss. Now she was in the middle of life again. She noticed how many motors there were now; all the traffic was speedier and pedestrians were speedier too. One good thing – these new motor-cars would soon kill that London plague, the cab tout who had run at the side of your hansom pestering to serve you. She had a rich grand sense, after the silence of those Cumberland months, of plunging into a roaring new world ready to welcome her. Well, the Family would not be ready to welcome her. But she need not see them – only Barney and Adrian and Rose. And perhaps Cynthia – she had not, in the old days, been so violently shocked! It would be pleasant to have tea with Cynthia again in her pretty room, to hear the gossip, to ask about the theatres and to catch, even though from a distance, the tone and colour of that world to which she had once belonged! She sat upright in her hansom staring through the glass in front of her like a young girl free for the first time!

'The Clarence' was odd enough. A very large lady, her hair puffed out over elaborate pads, her shoulders very high, her waist almost invisible beneath her swelling bosom, her costume sweeping the floor, received Vanessa in an affected manner and directed a minute and rather shabby pageboy to show her to her room. This was dingy, with a view of chimney pots, a large portrait of Queen Victoria and a general gurgling of water pipes to give it character and life. The hotel smelt of fog and dead geraniums. At the head of the stairs was a large tank in which goldfish were swimming. The walls were everywhere very thin. As Vanessa changed her dress she heard from the next room a protesting voice:

'But, Mama, why not?'

'Because Mother thinks it better not, dear.'

'But Mama—'

'Now, Cecily. Mother knows best. He is not a young man who can possibly mean anything seriously. He has not a penny besides his Army pay.'

'But, Mama—'

The intimacy of this conversation terrified Vanessa, and when next afternoon Adrian came to visit her, and they sat in a room crowded with palms and dimmed by windows with blue and red glass, Vanessa told him that this was the most virtuous hotel in London. No indiscretion could be committed without everyone in the hotel being aware of it.

She was gay, merry, full of eagerness to enter life again.

'I must get something to do, Adrian. It was dreadful in Cumberland. I simply moped. I must work, help, tire myself to death until Benjie returns.'

She was aware of a certain awkwardness in Adrian. She remembered unexpectedly that evening, years ago, when Adrian had been led up to her at the Ball, his eagerness, his vitality, his impulsive determination to help the world. He was as kind, as affectionate as ever, but he was now a Government servant, the *Herries* Government servant. His clothes were exquisite, his manner that of one who had to carry a good many public burdens on his shoulders. Was he writing anything? No, he had little time he was afraid. H. D. Traill's death had distressed him greatly; he had given him a good deal of reviewing in *Literature*. Had she read Fleury's *Louis XV Intime*? A most interesting work with a very striking portrait of La Pompadour. And Dr Barry's *Arden Massiter*, quite good as novels go. A little over-written. And a very amusing little book, *Lambkin's Remains*. The writer signed himself H. B. He was the author of *The Bad Child's Book of Beasts*. 'You remember, Vanessa.'

But Vanessa, alas, did not remember. She had never heard of Dr Barry and was not sure whether she had met Mr Traill or no.

'Perhaps he came to one of our parties.'

Oh no, Traill never went to parties. But Vanessa was trembling for news.

'Adrian, tell me about Hill Street.'

Adrian's pale, still very youthful countenance coloured.

'Oh, no one goes there now. Winifred and Vera keep Ellis quite a prisoner. He likes it, I believe. He's queer, of course. They say he makes paper boats and has toy engines. He doesn't go to the City any more. Alfred has everything in his hands. But they say Ellis is quite happy.'

Did Vanessa imagine it or was there a new note in Adrian's voice? Was he a little, a very little, superior? Why did he seem to patronize? Vanessa's imagination. And then he must hate this hotel.

'It's a horrid hotel, isn't it?' she said.

'Yes. Beastly. But you want it quiet, don't you? I mean – you don't want to run up against any of the family.'

'Oh no – except Barney, of course.'

'Dear old Barney – he's getting pretty aged. He plays bridge all his evenings.'

'Bridge?'

'Why, of course!' Adrian expressed surprise. 'Where *have* you been? Don't they play it in Cumberland? London's crazy about it – has been for ages.'

There was a pause. Mrs Mont, the proprietress, came into the room and looked around. It was odd to see her balance her enormous bosom on two such very small feet! She patted her great head of hair and stared at the pair of them.

'Has she already heard about me?' Vanessa wondered.

'Oh yes – and do tell me about the others. Carey's shut up in Ladysmith, Benjie told me. And Cynthia's husband – he's in Natal, isn't he? Adrian! – Cynthia – how does she feel about me? Do you think I could go and see her? Would she mind? She used to be very broad-minded . . .'

There was an awkward pause. Adrian coughed, stroking the side of his nose in a manner common to many of the Herries men.

At last he spoke: 'Look here, Vanessa. There's something I ought to say. You're such a sport, you're so wise, I know you'll understand perfectly. But the whole family has taken this awfully badly. They can't get over it. You see – they admired you so much and they were so proud of Hill Street. And then – if it had been anyone but Benjie, whom they've disapproved of for years! And then there have been so many family scandals! It didn't matter so much perhaps years ago when they weren't anyone particularly, but now they are respected everywhere. Alfred's a great man in the City, and Cynthia thinks herself Queen of London. She does really. You'd be amused if you saw her. Already she's bringing her two girls up most awfully carefully. They're nice little girls too. She wants them to marry Dukes. What I mean is – there's me and there's Barney – but the others – well, I'm afraid you mustn't expect them to change. They won't. They are more respectable than you've any idea of. They can't endure Benjie and they think you – they think you were unkind to Ellis.'

'I see,' said Vanessa quietly. 'Thank you for telling me, Adrian.'

'Oh, that's all right. I say, isn't there rather a queer smell in here? It may be my fancy.'

He got up.

'Well, I must be off. Got some work to do. You tell me, Vanessa, if there's anything I can do. We'll go out one night. We'll do a play. The one at the St James's isn't bad – *The Man of Forty*. Alexander and Fay Davis.'

'Thank you, Adrian.' She stood looking at him with a wise and rather maternal smile. She could not resist saying: 'You won't be ashamed to be seen out with me, will you, Adrian?'

He blushed, looking like a boy of eighteen.

'My God, no! Why, what do you think, Vanessa? *I* haven't any prejudices. I'll be proud!'

But, a little later, sitting in her bedroom and listening to the gurgles of the water pipes, she was not so sure.

Then, next day, when old Barney came to see her, she learnt more about the Family. Barney was seventy, stout, rather untidy. There were pouches under the eyes, his cheeks were puffed out, giving him a childish pouting expression, but the eyes themselves were full of sparkle, humour, kindliness, and his grey hair, though it was untidy, was strong and wiry. He had a paunch, but he walked on his thick legs sturdily, his back straight, his head up, and always that slightly mocking boy-out-for-a-lark expression at his mouth's corners as though he found life more of a joke than ever. And yet you could, if you knew the Family, tell that he was old Emily's brother and pompous, long-buried Newmark's son. He found life a joke indeed because there had been originally enough of the solemn Herries there for him to see how ridiculous it could be.

Sitting again in the room with the palms and the coloured glass, this teatime was very different from the one of yesterday. Vanessa was one of Barney's *real* devotions. As he saw her now, seated very quietly, a middle-aged woman whose hair was turning grey, in this shabby hotel, and thought how barely two years ago he had seen her with her white satin and diamonds leading the cotillion in the Hill Street drawing-room, satin and diamonds seemed to him very vulgar things. But did she mind this shabby hotel, he wondered? Was she still satisfied with her bargain?

'Adrian came to tea yesterday,' she told him. 'I thought him a little – well, a little superior. Has he become so, or is it only with me because I'm a black sheep now, or did I imagine it?'

'Oh, Adrian's a little more Herries than he was – that's all. The Foreign Office might have been invented by our family – it's so exactly what we most approve of.'

He looked at her anxiously, rather as though he were her father.

'You're happy, Vanessa?'

'Well, I'm rather lonely, Barney, at the moment. I miss Benjie, you see – and I want work, something to do. Can you find me something? I must be busy.'

'Yes, I think I can find something. There's a Mrs Cundlip who's a friend of mine. She has a working party. They make things for the soldiers three afternoons a week. She and her friends live very quietly in Kensington. They don't gossip and they are nice kind women. I think you'd like it.'

'Oh, Barney, thank you! You *are* a dear!'

He was touched by her gratitude. Poor Vanessa, she *must* have been lonely! He told her more of the Family. Cynthia was now the star. Worcester was doing very well in South Africa. He was to join Roberts' staff. May Rockage was in London, doing war work, and desperately trying to find husbands for her girls.

Horace was rather chastened. His silent wife had developed into a grim woman who frightened him. Alfred's two children were nice little things. Richard Cards – Adrian's older brother – was now living in London. He had married rather late and had two children. Barney gave very much the same account of Hill Street as Adrian had done. No one saw Ellis and it was generally known that he was eccentric. Barney did not tell Vanessa the general opinion that her flight had turned Ellis' brain. Winifred and Vera Trent never left him. And that was that. Vanessa understood quite clearly that the Family would have nothing to do with her . . .

In another day or two she went to call on Mrs Cundlip, found her a kindly simple woman with a son at the Front and a plain energetic daughter with a passion for the clergy.

Whether Mrs Cundlip and her friend knew Vanessa's story or no, they gave no sign of interest in it. Indeed they seemed never to gossip and had, as a group, a curiously impersonal air as thought they were part of the quiet Kensington scene like the trees in the Gardens, the nurses with their perambulators, the solid policeman at the gates, the decorous shoppers in the High Street. Vanessa found them a comfort. She worked in the gentle Kensington drawing-room hung with watercolours of Switzerland and Italy and thought of Benjie and tried to be happy. As the days passed she found that increasingly she was afraid of a chance encounter with one of the Family. She remained in her unpleasant hotel because it was so safe. None of them would ever come there. When she shopped or went to the theatre her apprehension was always alive. It would hurt her, she knew now, to be cut by Cynthia or May. *Would* May cut her? – that kind, simple countrywoman in whose house she had so often stayed? But May had her girls now to think of. Old Violet Bellairs was very ill and never left her bed. The younger Violet who had married a Colonel belonged, Vanessa heard, to a very fast set (in revenge for her constricted youth) who played bridge all day and all night. And Lettice Marrable? Lettice was secretary now to a branch in Manchester of Women's Suffrage. She wrote very lovingly to Vanessa and said that she would come to see her as soon as she had time to visit London. She was very busy and talked in her letter about The Cause as though there were but one in all the world.

So there they all were.

Then one sunny afternoon early in May, Vanessa tumbled almost into Horace's arms in the Army and Navy Stores. There was no way of avoiding it! There was Horace, red-faced, stout, benignant behind his glasses, buying soap. He stepped back unexpectedly, almost trod on Vanessa, said, 'I beg your pardon' with his customary episcopal courtesy and saw who it was. His plump cheeks were scarlet.

'Vanessa!' he said.

'How are you, Horace?' she replied, holding out her hand and smiling.

They shook hands and she noticed that at once he moved with her a little out of earshot.

'I'm so glad to see you, Horace. You're looking very well.'

'Yes, I'm very well, thanks.'

'I can see you're busy. So am I.'

She smiled at him very gaily. Oh yes, it *was* pleasant to see one of the Family even though it were only Horace, with his high white forehead, large spectacles and protruding chin! For the first time in her life she *liked* Horace.

'Oh yes – indeed yes ... very busy ...' he stuttered, looking nervously about him. No one was near him, no one was looking at him. He coughed. 'Very agreeable to see you, Vanessa. Are you long in London?'

'Yes, for some time, I think.' She looked him straight between the glasses. 'Benjie is in South Africa, you know.'

'Oh yes, indeed. I had heard ...' (Why wasn't he a Bishop? Not that she had anything against Bishops. Often the noblest of men, but Horace's benevolence needed an apron.)

Now that he was assured that no one was observing them he was more at his ease. He began to talk with some of his old eager but, in some odd way, calculated friendliness. He spoke of the nobility of our men at the Front, of Britain's showing the world, of everyone doing what they could, of human nature being at its best in times of stress. He became more practical, revealing himself, as he had always liked to do, at the very centre of affairs. He had just been lunching with a most interesting man – name of Yerkes – the projector of the new electric Underground. He confidently prophesied that we should all be living at least fifty miles out of London owing to electrified trains – we should think nothing of it, nothing of it at all; said what a nuisance half-sovereigns were – he had nearly given one just now as a tip instead of a sixpence; that all the best horses had gone to South Africa, so that the omnibuses were sadly suffering. He talked as though he were delivering an address to a gathering of charity children, Vanessa thought, but he meant to be kindly. It had always been Horace's trouble that he meant so well, but had weaknesses, insincerities, tempers and absent-mindedness like the rest of us. Then he saw some ladies approaching and, raising his hat, hurried away.

'The gentleman has forgotten his soap,' the shopman said.

'He will come back for it, I'm sure,' said Vanessa.

She was very tired. It would have been nice of Horace if he had invited her to take a cup of tea. But certainly that was too much to expect. Her arm ached. She was suffering from what was known as 'skirt wrist'.

A night or two later she had a horrible dream. She dreamt that she was on a vast green plain, bounded by hills spotted with small black patches. She had lost her way and then saw coming towards her the kopje that Benjie had mentioned in one of his first letters. It was coloured red, as Benjie had said, and shaped like a pig. It came wriggling after her, flapping large naked red ears. It covered the ground with extraordinary speed. She began to run but made no advance. It came nearer and nearer; she could smell its fetid breath and see, on its back, tufts of hair. The thing rolled in its movement. It had no face, only the flapping ears. 'This is my punishment,' she thought in her despair. 'I knew that I could not escape it.' She screamed for Benjie and woke.

After that night she seemed always to be tired. The loneliness that she had felt in Cumberland returned. Both Adrian and Barney were kind, but they were busy people; the ladies in Kensington were most pleasant, but they did not invite her to their houses; she grew no nearer in intimacy to any of them, nor did she wish to. After that dream she was haunted with fear for Benjie. It was a fortnight now since she had heard from him, and his last letter had seemed to her dispirited, disappointed. With increasing unrest she looked every day at the casualties in the newspaper. She told herself that she must be calm and brave, that thousands of other women were suffering as she was, but it became soon impossible for her to be impersonal. There seemed to be no one in the world but Benjie. It was not only that he might be killed, but that his restlessness, his passion for liberty, must be fed my this adventure, that the longer he was away from her the easier it would be for him to remain away.

She suffered as all women do who love a man but are tied to him by no official bond. She had no hold on him at all but his

love for her, and he might love other women as he loved her.
When he was there she knew that he loved her, but now she was
tortured by the very indefiniteness of their relationship, although
at its heart it was anything but indefinite.

Then, on the eighteenth of May, sitting in her bedroom, reading, she heard a timid knock on the door.

'Come in!' she said.

The blowsy good-natured chambermaid, Kate by name, put
her head in through the door.

'Excuse me, mum,' she said, 'but I thought you'd like to know.
They're saying as Mafeking's been relieved!'

'Oh no!' Vanessa cried, jumping up.

'Yes, mum. Ain't it grand? Relieved yesterday, they say!'

Her first thought was for Tom. How delighted Benjie would
be! And then that it would mean that the war would be soon
ended, very soon perhaps. And, after that, that now England
could hold her head up again, the long period of doubt and
failure was over. She was so happy that, in a moment, all her
troubles seemed to be ended. Everyone would be happy! Everyone *was* happy!

At dinner in the hotel that evening even the old waiter in his
dirty dicky could scarcely carry the plates for joy. Two old ladies
who had never before spoken to her said: 'Isn't it excellent? *Such*
good news! We are so glad!' as though it had all been done for
their especial benefit.

At the table next to hers a schoolgirl with her mother was in a
state of almost frenzied excitement. She had, it seemed, been
allowed to come down to dinner in celebration of the great event.
She was a plain little girl, wearing the hideous khaki-coloured
dress then considered patriotic for schoolgirls. She was talking of
some elder girl who was allowed to wear a red, white, and blue
costume, with a regimental clasp in front. The 'thing' at school
was to pin on to yourself many penny buttons decorated with the
heads of generals, and one girl was the envy of all the others
because she had found somewhere a regular saucer with the picture of Baden-Powell and went everywhere with this pinned to
her chest.

As Vanessa listened she thought, 'I'd like to have a little girl of
my own. Would it be unfair to her that Benjie and I are not
married? Father was illegitimate and never minded. Is it worse
for a girl? Would *I* have minded? Nothing that Father had done
would have seemed to me wrong.' Soon she would be too old to

have children. She had missed that as she had missed other things. But she had not missed love ... Benjie would soon be back now, and Tom. She would love Tom with all her heart, be a splendid friend to him and, in her old age, stand by him, help his wife when he married. For Tom was unusual like all the other unusual Herries – wild at the heart, wanting often to be free of everyone; hard men for a woman to understand were these Herries!

She would go out and share in everybody's happiness. In Baker Street she boarded an omnibus, but when they reached Oxford Circus they could go no farther. She climbed down and plunged into pandemonium. She stayed for a while in a shop door and let the crowd surge past her. First, looking upwards it was as though the sky itself had gone mad. From nowhere out of nothing (for there had been little warning) the façades had created their illumination. Electric light was still rare and, at its greatest peak of grandeur, could not have rivalled the magic of those gas jets. Their wonder was that they were swayed by those little winds that came and went, running in blue-and-gold ripples like water against the grey surface, seeming for a moment to be blown out and then, with a sense of mischievous laughter, bursting into life again, as though by their own happy agency they had relighted themselves. They ran in waves of trembling light, hesitated, vanished and, with new energy, ran again. The sky was alive with beauty.

Beneath it what a world – as though a new race inhabited the earth! Men in evening dress, hats on the back of their heads, cocked sideways, evening capes flying, danced arm in arm with the ladies of the East End. These women who were to go down in history, dressed in black satin, wore great hats crowned with ostrich plumes; and so they danced, their fine bosoms swelling, the flounces of their long dresses swinging from their tiny waists, petticoats whitely revealed and vanishing. Their own gentlemen for that night at least were in 'high dress' with mother-of-pearl on their flat caps, trousers tight to the knee, flapping round the ankles. They changed hats with their Donahs, moving in the 'double-shuffle in an ecstasy of joy. The East End came West that night, and the West was glad.

And the noise! Everyone was shouting, singing, turning rattles, blowing the coiled paper springs, screaming down pink-and-white tuppenny trumpets gay with silvery angels' hair. You were 'killing Kruger with your mouth'. You were singing 'Duke's son, cook's son, son of a belted Earl'. You were shouting '*W*'ere did you get that 'at?', 'Wot price old Krüger!', 'Git yer 'air cut!' You were singing:

> *Hark! I hear the bugle calling,*
> *And I can no longer stay.*
> *Goodbye, Dolly, I must leave you.*
> *Goodbye, Dolly Gray!*

That night the British Army was worshipped. It was to be worshipped again, but in another sterner spirit, when tuppenny trumpets and mother-of-pearl could not meet a far more menacing enemy.

The soldier and the sailor were the heroes, and the 'Little Englander' was the villain of the piece. Close to Vanessa a girl, waving her arms, screamed: 'Down with Lloyd George!' and behold his image was flung deep under the dancing shoes of that multitude. And there is a god in a monocle, with an orchid in his buttonhole – 'Three cheers for Joe!' 'Not for Joseph!' 'Good old Joe!' Labour? One man named Keir Hardie has boldly walked into the House with a cloth cap on his head. So much for Labour. Squeakers and ticklers and corncrakes have, that evening, little consciousness of a new world that very soon will be demanding very different instruments . . .

Vanessa for a while was safe in her doorway, but soon the crowd was wilder. Hansoms appearing from the very bowels of the earth discharged young men in evening dress; something other than tea is the draught of the Town; here there is a fight between a cabman and a fare, there a policeman has seized some gesticulating figure, raised him above the crowd, then, as though abandoning the hopeless charge, dropped him back into the crowd again.

Vanessa has been swung from her doorstep. It is best to go with the crowd. Someone has linked arms with her and she is swayed down Regent Street, all the shouts, songs, cries seeming to catch a sudden rhythm so that it is as though the very sky itself were singing. At the edge of Piccadilly Circus the surge forward is arrested and you see a rising, falling pattern of life – not individual life now but something made up of the windy, swaying lights, tumbling bursts of sound, the very buildings swinging, it seemed, in the uncertain glare.

A woman grasped her arm: with her other hand she wielded a

toy trumpet, her straw hat at the back of her padded hair. Vanessa turned and looked. It was Rose.

'Hooray! Hooray!' she cried, waving the trumpet. 'Hooray for Joe! Hooray—' She said confidently to Vanessa: 'Come on, dear! Let's give him a cheer!'

'Rose,' Vanessa said, bending her body sideways to avoid the pressure of a stout perspiring gentleman with a tickler. 'Don't you know me?'

Rose stared. 'Vanessa!' She threw her arms around her, scratching the back of her neck with her trumpet. Her straw hat, falling, disappeared. 'Oh, Vanessa – my darling! my darling!'

Vanessa realized that Rose had been too splendidly celebrating victory. At the moment she could realize nothing further, for the impulse of the crowd swept them both off their feet. It appeared not unlikely that there and then they would find death in one another's arms, bells clanging in their ears, somewhere the trumpets of a distant band, the smell of sweating bodies, broadcloth, patchouli, against their nostrils and, against the sky, grey walls like rocks on whose surfaces flickered in the wind the jets of blue, green, red, thrown up from the tossing dark pool at their feet. It was then confusion. The fountain of the Circus stood out above the singing waters. Heads rose and fell like despairing drowning mariners. Fastened firmly in the midst was the rock of a towering hansom up whose side figures were climbing. Beyond that again an effigy with a tangled beard, a battered high hat, jerked as though in agony against the lights – Krüger moving to his bonfire.

Then the waters parted. Waves of human beings slumped like falling walls. The effigy was moving forward, followed by a great cheering procession, men waving their hats, women screaming, and under the confusion – above it, outside and within it – the steady pulse of *The Soldiers of the Queen*, into whose tune at last all the scattered sounds and voices were gathered.

Driven back at the corner of Shaftesbury Avenue, Vanessa suddenly discovered that, a wide porch of a restaurant protecting her, she was free. Miraculously, still holding to her arm was Rose.

'Oh, where is he?' Rose cried. 'The Captain! The Captain gone! He swore he wouldn't leave me. Oh, Vanessa, I'm lost – I don't know where he lives. He's got my little green bag, my little bag ...'

They stood in the shelter of the porch against the wall, shoulder to shoulder. Rose cried out as though she were demented. A lock of false hair had detached itself from the disordered pile and tickled her mouth. There was a small scratch on her cheek from which blood was trickling. Altogether a battered Rose.

She looked at Vanessa, and as she looked her wildness fell from her.

'Oh, Vanessa, I've drunk too much. Take me home. I don't care if I never see the Captain again.'

Very slowly they moved up Shaftesbury Avenue; then, turning at the first opening, found themselves in a little dark street, deserted, melancholy, shutting off like a curtain the lights, the singing, the press of the surging crowd.

'Where's your hat, dear?' Vanessa asked. She took out her handkerchief and wiped Rose's cheek. Rose began to cry.

'Oh, you must think me dreadful. Fancy your meeting me like this after all this time. But it was all the Captain's fault, and my bag had all my money in it.'

Vanessa, her hand through Rose's arm, led her from little street to little street. Near Oxford Street they found a hansom.

'Now, Rose, where are you living?'

Rose stared. 'I don't know ... Oh yes, Three Orcutt Street. That's where I was living three days ago, before I met the Captain.'

'Well – is that where you want to go?'

'Yes. You'll come with me, Vanessa? I'm not drunk really. I only had a drop in the Captain's room.'

In the hansom Rose leant her head against Vanessa's bosom and sobbed.

'Mafeking! Mafeking! I wish to God I had never heard of Mafeking or the Captain either.' In a grim little street they stopped at a grim little house.

'No. Don't come in. My room isn't very grand.' She was quite sober now, looking like a dishevelled child afraid of a scolding. 'But you'll come and see me tomorrow? Or I'll come and see *you*. May I?'

Vanessa told her the address of the hotel. Once more Rose flung her arms about her neck and passionately kissed her.

'It all feels different, meeting you. Like old times.' She wiped her eyes. 'I've lost my hat. I don't know what Mrs Blaker will think if she sees me. She doesn't think much of me anyway. Goodnight, darling.'

Later up to Vanessa's bedroom came the shouts and cries of a city madly rejoicing. Some kind of a triumph. A passionate impulse of compassion caught her heart, compassion for the world, for Rose, for all lonely and misguided creatures. The kopje could not frighten her now.

Indeed, indeed it could not. Two weeks later there was a telegram forwarded from Cumberland. Benjie had lost an arm and was being sent home at once.

She sat, with the telegram in her hand, staring in front of her. She was so happy that she could scarcely breathe lest the telegram should prove unreal. Then she knelt down by her bed and thanked God.

YOUNG TOM IN NEWLANDS

YOUNG Tom Herries, sitting one summer evening on a slope below Dale Head, the peak which closes the Newlands Valley, watched the sky. It had for some while fascinated him and distracted him from the second volume of Hardy's *The Wood-landers,* which lay on the turf beside him. He was always known as Young Tom, but even in years he was not so young any longer, for he was now seventeen years of age, but in character, in a subtle intuition of motive and feeling, in self-command, he had never been young. In looks he was something like his father, dark, short and thick with a round hard head and short wiry hair. He had also some of his father's geniality and all of his warmth of heart.

But he was different from him altogether in his self-control, in his patience, in his consideration for others. His early flight to Paris with Timothy, the free life there spent always in the company of his elders, his experiences in South Africa, his acquaintance with all the ways of humankind, bad, good, sensual, virtuous, foolish, wise, had helped him to come to terms with real life long before the common time. But, with this, there was something young in him that made folk, the country people, the townspeople, all who knew him, speak of him as Young Tom. He *was* young in this: that unlike his father he took all his responsibilities with extreme seriousness. His principal responsibilty was to his father and to Vanessa. He loved them both, but he knew his father too well to think him in any way wonderful. He felt to his father as he would to a younger brother whose faults he knew by heart but whom he loved and guarded the more for those faults, but Vanessa he worshipped.

He had been living with them now in this little house in the Vale of Newlands for six months, and the longer he lived with them the deeper did his devotion to Vanessa grow. He was thinking of her now as he lay on his back, his arms behind his head, looking at the sky. She seemed to him of another kind altogether from any women he had ever known, and he had known some very strange ones. Her love for him, which she had felt since she had visited him a little boy ill at school, made her more natural with him, perhaps, than she was with anyone else. They were very often alone together and then she talked to him as though she were a girl of his own age. She poured out all her heart to him: she told him more than she had ever told Benjie. She told him everything: of her childhood, her love for her father, her life in London with Ellis, her love for Tom's father – and they discussed, for hours together, Benjie's character, his sweetness, irresponsibility, restlessness, honesty, infidelities. When Benjie was drunk (rare occasions but unfortunate) Tom managed him to a marvel. When Benjie disappeared, Tom reassured Vanessa until he appeared again. Tom sometimes rated his father as though their positions were reversed. Benjie never resented it. He was as proud of his son as he could be. Tom himself, of course, was far from perfect. He was obstinate and sometimes sulked. He was given to fits of melancholy that he inherited from his own Herries strain, and then he would go away by himself and brood. There were many causes for these, but the chief of them was that he had always meant, since he was a tiny boy, to be a great writer and he thought now that he would never be even a good one. His early devotion to Timothy had been stirred the more by his saying to himself that Tim would be a great painter and he would be a great writer. Now Tim was, if not a great painter, a very good one. He was in Paris selling his pictures. He was known everywhere as a promising and unusual artist. But Tom, although he was a fair journalist, was no more. He talked to Vanessa again and again about this; he showed her his attempts. She was too honest and knew the value that he put on her honesty too well to encourage him.

'What is it,' he said to her in despair, 'that I can't get?'

'It is something, I suppose, that doesn't come by asking for it,

Never mind, Tom. You began so young. You're only seventeen now! There are so many writers. You will do something better in another way.'

Now, thinking of *The Woodlanders,* he felt a sort of rage against fate. Yes, he was only seventeen – there was plenty of time – and yet he did not lie to himself. *This* thing would never be his. And *what* was it? Hardy, Tom thought, was a peasant, he had scarcely moved from his countryside: he already knew far more about the wide world than Hardy could know. Hardy often made his characters talk in stilted, unnatural sentences; his books were filled with ridiculous coincidences – but here in these pages was life, the life that so many polished sophisticated writers missed altogether. Tom looked at the scene around him and his spirits fell into quiet.

For the last fortnight there had been perfect weather in Cumberland. By day the sun had shone, veiled with mist sufficient to give hill and water their rightful size. It was a late year and so the larch still stood in patterns of green flame against the smoky shadows of yew and fir, the stems of the young bracken were pellucid as are the throats of pale-green glasses. And with the sunny mist, over the green flats, up the stony sides of the fells, above the glittering chattering runnels of water, there was now thin shadow, now a breadth of light, all warm, kindly, beneficent; as a generous man's hand strokes his dog's shoulder, so God bent down from His cloud and caressed His world.

Tom, lying on his back, wondered that now the sky could be so quiet and so pure when so often he had watched clouds battling in armies for supremacy, seen one fierce cloud-captain drag another by his hair, watched the surge upward, from the hinderparts of the Tops, of whirling frenzied clouds, angrily purple, and the thick grey sullen banks of storm mount and spread until all the world was covered with them and rain fell in spears of steel upon the earth. Now the sky was pale like the inside of a pearl shell; light was translucent and softer than down. Cat Bells and Dale Head, Robinson and Maiden Moor were bathed in a peace that seemed eternal, and towards the dip where Lobstone Band hid its rocky tors, a carpet of purple shadow hung above the little fields that welcomed the evening.

Near him Herdwick sheep were browsing – the bravest little sheep in England and the most adaptable. Their wool may be harsh, but so faithful in spirit are they that all their lives they will not move far from the place where they were born, not because they are unenterprising, but because here for generations their ancestors have been and here, like proper Cumbrians, their heart is set. So, with the old forest trees, the fir, the oak, the birch, with the stones and boulders that they can, if they will, so closely resemble, with the running water and the flying clouds, they obey the law.

Soon the stars would come out, breaking the green of the evening sky, and a young crescent moon would rise, and all night long the light would last, paler than ivory, quieter than sleep. The air was scented with the newly cut hay from a field nearby, with the first honeysuckle, with the summer heat drawn from grass and fern. Birds winged slowly, making the silence vocal. The line of the hills grew with every moment sharper as the shining sky paled.

Tom's thoughts turned to his own future. This had been a fine holiday, but it could not last for ever. He loved this country as he loved none other, but soon he must go back into the world again. He had for so long now been a man – ever since he was fourteen – that he had not a boy's light indifferennce of waiting until life should begin for him. He had been kicked about in Paris, he had endured a historic siege like the other men with him, and time would not wait. For six months, too, he had been ostracized. No one came to see them at Cold Fell. His mother's cottage was only ten minutes away over the hill. It was let to a painter and his family, but that long slow slope of Cat Bells cut the three of them from the world as though they were on a separate planet. Sometimes, when he rode into Keswick, he was looked at almost as though he had a deformity. He minded in spite of himself. What did it matter that his father and Vanessa were not married? They *would* be married if only that crazy old lunatic in London would die. They loved one another more faithfully than many a married pair, and, stroking the back of *The Woodlanders* with his hand, he thought to himself that the writer of that book would understand if he were here and would come to see them and be their friend. There was something terribly wrong with the world when people as good as his father and Vanessa could be exiled simply because some old clergyman had not blessed them. He knew, though, that it all went further than this, that people thought it impertinent of his father to come back and live with his woman here in the very spot where they were so well known, and that there had been scandals before, old scandals of a hundred and fifty years ago that everyone in these valleys knew, scandals that had lost nothing in constant telling.

His young heart was passionately in sympathy with all the outlaws. It was enough for someone to be in disgrace for Tom to be on his side, so long as the outlaw was not cruel nor mean nor a coward. At his age it seemed very easy for the world to be wrong and for all the good men to be outlaws. And he was, like his father, a born champion of lost causes.

He heard voices and, sitting up, saw his father coming towards him and with him a large rough untidy-looking man. Benjie, when he saw his son, waved his one arm and, as they came up, introduced his companion.

'Tom, this is Mr George Endicott, an old friend of mine.' Then, reaching his hand up to the big man's shoulder, he said: 'George, this is my boy, Tom. I don't think you've seen him before. Tom, Endicott was with me in Africa. This boy, you know, George, was all through the Mafeking siege.'

The man, Tom thought, was one of the strongest and wildest he had ever seen. He looked like part of the countryside, belonging to the stones and bracken like the Herdwick sheep.

He wore no hat, his face was of a brick-red colour, and his shirt was wide open, showing a brown chest with a pelt of black hair. His body was solid like a stone, but he moved lightly on his feet, making no sound. He had only nodded at Tom and then passed straight up the fell, swinging his arms.

'Tom, look here. I'm glad I saw you. When you go down tell them I shan't be back tonight.'

'When will you be back?'

'Oh, tomorrow likely. Endicott has come over from White-haven. We're going for a tramp.'

Benjie looked shamefaced. He knew that Tom knew that he had gone from the house without telling Vanessa.

'All right,' Tom said shortly, and without another word, picking up his book, he started down the hill. He hated it when his father was ashamed, when Vanessa was disappointed, when rough ill-looking men from God-knows-where took his father off to drink and fool with girls and not to return for days perhaps. His father was fine, his father was the best man he knew – but why must he make Vanessa unhappy?

Cold Fell had changed not at all in the last hundred years, with its whitewashed front, its narrow passages and low-ceil-inged rooms, the rough cobbling before the door, the slope down the hill where the hens were and the broad fields that crossed the stream and the valley, the cows now clustered for the cool under a large oak, the sheep browsing on the fell slope. Great sweeping shadows of gold covered the valley, and the sun, low now above the hill, struck through the thick leafage of the oak. The river, shrunk though it was now, could be heard very clearly chattering over its stones, so still was the air.

Vanessa was standing in the doorway when Tom came up.

'Have you seen your father, Tom?'

'Yes.' Tom put his arm round her and kissed her. He did not kiss anyone easily, but he liked to kiss Vanessa – her skin was so cool and so firm. Her hair was greying but her cheek had a girl's freshness. 'Yes. He's away for the night.'

She said nothing but went in.

Later they had their supper in the porch. An old woman called Mrs Williams came every day and 'did' for them. But Benjie and Vanessa cooked, and they, all three of them, did the house, looked after the piece of garden at the back. Tom went into Keswick for the shopping. For six months Vanessa had scarcely stirred from the valley. She looked now like a woman who had always lived in the country, her hair very simply brushed back, parted in the middle, leaving her fine brow clear and broad. She wore a plain blue cotton dress, shorter by a great deal than the prevailing fashion. Her waist was not pinched nor were her shoulders puffed. She looked her age, but her body had strengthened. With her height, her broad shoulders, her firm big breasts, she was a woman who would be noticed anywhere, and all her life she had carried herself superbly.

They had cold chicken and Cumberland ham, a salad, a cold apple tart, and a cheese. A fine supper on a summer evening with the murmur of the river coming up to them and the air as sweet as honey.

Vanessa, leaning her arms on the table, looked out to the valley.

'You know, Tom, I think Benjie might have told me.'

'He was afraid to. He had a man with him.'

'A man? – what man?'

'His name was Enderby, or Enderley – something like that.'

'Endicott. George Endicott. I know him. He is an old friend of Benjie's. He met him first when he met your mother. He was a friend of your uncle's.'

'What kind of man is he?'

'Oh, all right, I dare say. Rough, wild, always on the tramp.'

'Father said he was with him in Africa.'

'I wouldn't mind,' she went on, after a pause, 'if only he'd tell me when he's going, but he slips out of the house as though he were ashamed.'

'He *is* ashamed,' said Tom.

'The trouble is that each time I say to myself: "Perhaps this time he won't come back." Judith, my grandmother, used to talk to me sometimes when I was a girl about *her* married life. She's often told me that her husband – he was a Frenchman – would go off just like that, only he would be away for months. The difference was, though, that Judith was married. I'm not. I've no hold on your father except that we love one another. That's the only hold any woman ought to want, but women are funny. I've never known a woman, Tom, who was really sure of a man. Men belong to a different world, and you can't be sure, from minute to minute, that they won't have a new idea in their head. Women are too serious about everything. They can't take things lightly. It isn't that I doubt your father. We've loved one another all our lives – but I've nothing else now. I've put all my eggs in one basket.'

'You've got me,' Tom said proudly.

'Yes. You're very faithful. You'll make a splendid husband one day.'

Tom saw that she was struggling not to be unhappy; he saw how deeply disappointed she was and, with an intuition wonderful for a boy, knew that she was dreading the long lonely summer night. He wanted terribly to help her.

'I know what it is in Father,' he said. 'It isn't anything to do with you and me. He wants to be free sometimes. He told me once that there's bad blood in us. My great-uncle killed my grandfather in Skiddaw Forest and my great-grandfather killed himself. You know all that. And I think sometimes it all comes over my father – a kind of superstition about the past. Of course the past can't do anything to you *really*, can it? But you have to fight it sometimes perhaps. So he goes away and fights and then comes back to you again. That's *how* I explain it!' he ended.

She got up and kissed him.

'The truth is, Tom dear, that I've never been a very sensible woman. I haven't enough humour. If I could only see how funny things are it would be a lot easier. When the Queen died I was unhappy for weeks. Why should I have been? I'd never known her, but I couldn't get used to her not being there. It's always been the same if I've loved anyone. You take life lightly, Tom, and people easily. It's the only way.'

'I'm rather serious-minded too, I expect,' said Tom. 'Tim's always said so. Tim used to say that I ought to have been an old nurse with families of other people's children to look after.' He laughed. 'Don't you worry. Father will be back tomorrow.' He got up and patted her on the shoulder, then moved about taking the plates and dishes into the house.

Vanessa sat there, her chin propped on her hands, staring in front of her.

Three days passed and Benjie had not returned, nor had any word come from him. This was the longest time that he had ever been away from Vanessa since her flight from Hill Street. The hours were quiet, stealthy, and packed with a secret significance. She did not know that time could be so long, and on the third day she found herself walking down the valley towards the hills, standing and looking about her, starting with an agitated excitement at the figure of a shepherd, thinking that stones were men and that every sound in the air was Benjie's voice. Tom's care of her, which he tried to make unconcerned and indifferent, irritated her. She came back to the house on the afternoon of the fourth day, driven by absurd fear. Benjie had been planning this for months past; he was weary of her and had not the courage to tell her so. Some woman somewhere had entrapped him and, as he had always been faithless, so now he proved it to her for ever. She was intensely humiliated. 'I have never been able to hold anyone to myself; there is something in me charmless, dull, wearying; everything that I touch falls away from me.' She was even haunted by the dazzling, dominating figure of her grandmother who, with her head up, stamping her ivory cane, could rule the world if she wished, but she, Vanessa, who had had beauty and all the world to charm, had been able to hold no one. Women between thirty and forty often know an especial terror and apprehension, for youth has gone; if they have had children they are being abandoned by them, men are searching for younger faces, and old age, that demands more wisdom for the subduing of its terrors from women than from men, already leers, like a cocksure arrogant old man, over the fence. Women have greater courage wherewith to meet spiritual loneliness than men have, but their capacity for spiritual experience is also greater.

She came back to the house, its floors flooded with the June sun as though to taunt her, and said passionately to Tom: 'He is never coming back. I can make my mind up to it.'

Tom said something. She turned on him furiously with one of her old tempers. 'What do you know about it? You are only a boy!'

Then she burst out of the house again and walked swiftly away from the hills. She was in a mood for anything. That old, scared, irrational Herries blood for ever mixing in the personal Herries history beat now in her brain. Why not end it? Her life had been a failure from beginning to end. Her father had died when she might have saved him, she had married a man without loving him and he had gone crazy from it, she had risked everything for another Herries who was notorious for his instability and lightness. But even now, in this passion of fear and unhappiness, she would not blame Benjie. No, it was herself – her dullness and heaviness of spirit. 'Why have I not managed life better? What is lacking, has always been lacking in me?' She came to the little church and, scarcely knowing that she did so, finding the door open, entered.

She had often, in the last six months, visited this little place and had grown to love it. Behind its wall, guarded by its trees, hills mounting to every side of it and one of the loveliest small rivers in England at its back, quiet, restrained and confident, it held something in its heart greater than change or fashion. Everything was simple, the whitewashed walls, the altar, the pews, the birds that nestled in its roof, the scents that filled it from the summer fields, and the unceasing rhythm of the river.

Very unhappy, Vanessa knelt and prayed: 'God, in this quiet place, help me to find my courage again. I knew, when I did wrong, that I would suffer, but if it be possible allow me not to suffer without anyone to help me. It is not right that I should ask You anything, for I have not yet repented of the wrong that I did. I know that You ask me to be honest, and so I say that if there was that wrong to do again I would do it again. I feel that I acted against a law and against my conscience, but I did it deliberately. God, don't take Benjie away from me. Let me care for him and watch over him and share his life later when we will need somebody. If You are my Father as, in this quiet place, I feel You to be, do as my own father would have done, and let me be good to someone I love. Don't take Benjie from me. I know him better than anyone else does. I can care for him more than anyone else can. Let me be punished in any other way, but not by losing Benjie. You have placed this church here that we should make our requests in it. This is my only prayer – let me keep Benjie . . .'

She found that she was saying aloud, her hands clenched, her eyes staring at the little altar on which was a glass bowl filled with red and white roses: 'Don't take Benjie away from me! Don't take Benjie away from me!'

The strain of her intensity snapped. She rose from her knees and sat on the hard bench. She heard a bird singing, the water swinging by, and the voice of a shepherd as he crossed the grass by the church wall, talking to another.

'Well, goodnight.'

'Goodnight.'

She knew the man by his voice and with that familiarity all the outer world swung in. She heard Barney in London saying: 'Why, no, Vanessa dear, if it makes you happy to believe in such things . . .'

She saw the Prince and Princess entering in procession into the Hill Street drawing-room . . . She was in a theatre and Bernhardt was speaking . . . Then, someone saying: 'God? Oh, God died long ago. Didn't you know?'

But the church filled with light. She heard the sheep with their gentle sleepy rustle pass beyond the wall. A fragrance of flowers and new-mown hay seemed to be carried, by the sweet, persistent note of the bird, into the church again. She knew with a sudden delighted conviction that for herself at least this presence was true. Some wise power entered into her and, falling on her knees again and hiding her face in her hands, she was pervaded, through and through, with intimate kindliness. That intimacy! To be lonely no more! 'Only connect . . .' The connexion was there, her hands were held, her bent head blessed. Time was lost. The bird continued its song as the shadows came down upon the mountains.

When she came into the house again Tom was there in the passage.

'It's all right,' he said (a little shyly, for she had been angry when she went away). 'Father's back. He's upstairs and he's awfully tired, for he's walked miles.'

She went up into the low-ceilinged bedroom and there was Benjie, lying, stripped to his trousers, on the bed, his arms behind his head. He grinned but didn't move. She saw the stump of his arm where the flesh had been joined in a sharp red line, the deep brown of his bare chest, taut and spare as a boy's, his hair tumbled over his forehead, his impudent ashamed grin, and she was drowned in a wave of triumphant happiness. But she must not show it. She must be calm, sarcastically humorous as a wise woman would be, indifferent as though whether he went or came meant little to her. So she stood where she was and looked at him.

'So you're back?'

'Yes.' Then as she still didn't move, with his bright eyes fastened on her face he said: 'Haven't you a kiss for me?'

'No, I haven't. Why did you go off without telling me?'

'Oh, I don't know. That man Endicott came over from White-haven. He wanted a walk.'

'I see. You never thought, I suppose, how anxious Tom and I would be.'

'Why should you be anxious? You knew I'd come back.'

'Four days is a long time without a word from you.' She gave him one long look, then turned to the door. 'I suppose I'd better get you something to eat. You'll be hungry.'

'Yes – famished.' He looked at her, smiling. He put out his arm. 'Here, Vanessa. Come here. Don't be so cross with me. I haven't seen you for four days.'

'I'm not cross.' She came over to the bed and stood there. He put his bare arm round her waist, then drew her down. She knelt by the bed and they embraced. Then she rested her head on his body, he stroking her hair.

'Benjie, it wasn't kind . . . four whole days . . . I was in a panic. Tom and I are all alone here. Nobody comes, and if you're away the days drag. I've been watching the hills all day.'

He turned on his side, drew her on to the bed, put his hand inside her cotton dress that it might rest on her heart. Her hand stroked his back, rejoicing in the strong muscles, the smooth skin warm and fresh like the summer evening. Through the open window she could hear the bird singing and the running water as she had done in the church. He settled himself comfortably against her.

'Now I'll tell you all about it. Quite truthfully. George End-icott turned up and as soon as I saw him I wanted to go off. He wasn't here more than a minute. You were in the back of the house. I said "Hullo, George," and he said, "Hullo." I asked him where he had come from and he said "Whitehaven". I asked him whether he wanted a walk and he said "Yes" and there we were. I *had* to go off when I saw him, Vanessa. I *had* to. I'd have told you, only I knew you'd want to know *where* I was going and how long I'd be, and I didn't know where and I didn't know how long.'

'I wouldn't,' she murmured. (But she knew that she would.)

'Then we went up the Fell and saw young Tom and I told him. It was pretty late by then, but we got on to Robinson and then at dusk on Honister. It isn't dusk, you know – there's a white light in the sky. There was a new moon, too. We found a cave on the other side of Honister. Endicott said that in the old days, years ago, his great-grandfather used the cave when they were smuggling. They were bad lots, you know – as bad as they make'em. When we came to the cave there were two others there – a man and a girl. The girl had red hair and was pretty in a way. They didn't say much, but they were cooking a hare and they let us share their meal.

'Then we all curled up and went to sleep and I was as happy, Vanessa, as I've ever been in my life. I didn't care for you or Tom or anybody or anything. It was just like that – I'm telling you honestly. I was free and the air was fine and warm. I'd drunk their whisky and eaten their meat and beyond the cave there was the misty moonlight over the hills. I was a free man and I didn't want ever to be tied again. Well, I went to sleep and, after a time, I woke to find the girl had come over and was lying close to me, right up against me she was, with her arm around me. There she lay all night. I didn't do a thing to her. I didn't even kiss her. I'm telling you honestly, mind. I'd tell you just the same if there'd been anything, I'm not being virtuous about it. I might have done a lot of things but I just didn't. In the morning we set off again, the four of us. We were together the next three days. We went down into Eskdale, then over to Coniston, on to Helvellyn, along the Saddleback. This morning we separated, and here I am. It was grand, I tell you, Vanessa – lovely days and fine nights, not saying much, any of us. George wanted me to come back to Whitehaven and stay with him a bit, but by this morning you'd all come over me again, Vanessa. I *had* to see you. I didn't feel free any longer. I didn't *want* to be free. So I kissed the red-haired girl for the first time, gave George a kick, and here I am. I know I did wrong not to tell you, but if I'd told you I wouldn't have had such a good time somehow. You've got to forgive me and believe me too. I've never told you a lie yet.'

She sat up on the bed, her arm around him. This was something of a crisis between them and she wanted to say what was best and wisest.

'Yes, Benjie, that's all right. I know you must be free. Haven't I always said so?'

'Yes, you've always *said* so,' he answered, laughing and stroking her cheek.

'Have I prevented you? Have I ever stopped you?' she asked.

'Don't be so serious, darling. Take it lightly. I've only been for a walk – and here I am.'

'That's easy to say,' she answered. 'Does no man *ever* understand these things? Every time you go off I can't be sure you'll ever come back again. Oh yes, I feel safe enough now – now that you are here and close to me – but when you are gone I say to myself, why should he come back? I've no hold on him. He may be tired of me, hiding it from me.'

'Tired of you? I love you more than I ever did. Why, Vanessa, I've loved you all my life! How could I *not* come back? I'll always return—'

'Ah yes, you think so!' she answered quickly. 'But I've seen you change your mind so often about so many things! If I were younger, gayer! But sometimes I seem to myself so dull, so heavy! Women are faithful if they're given a chance – it's the thing they like best to be! But men – when they've got what they want, they want something else. Then,' she went on, 'it's lonely when you're away. For six months here we've seen nobody. When you're with me I don't *want* to see anyone, but when you're away every minute is an hour. It wouldn't be if I knew you'd be back at such and such a time. But when you haven't said a word—'

He sat up. 'Look here, Vanessa. Let's have a child! Then you wouldn't doubt any more—'

'Oh no ,' she answered slowly. 'That would be wrong—'

'Why wrong? Your father didn't mind because he was illegitimate.'

'I think he did. It made a difference to his life.'

'If only Ellis would die!' He beat the bed with his hand. 'Now don't be hypocritical about that, Vanessa. You know it would be much better if he should die. He's old, he's crazy. Life can't be any fun for him.'

But he was afraid of alluding to Ellis. A shadow crept into her eyes. He hated that she should think of the past.

'Look, Vanessa! I have to go off sometimes. Sometimes I'm restless beyond bearing. I think of my father, my mad uncle, my grandfather. There are days when I hate myself, my ancestry, all the past and the present together. Then you can't help me – nobody can. But never doubt that you're the love of my whole life, Vanessa. If ever any man in the world loved anyone, I love you! Why, even now I couldn't be away three days from you without running back! But there's this country, every fell-side, every stream, every stone wall, is in my blood! Why, you know that as well as I! Wasn't it crazy of us to come back here where everyone knows us and all our family history? But could we help it? Of course not! No man escapes the past, nor the fields where he was as a boy if that poison is in his blood. With some of us it is, with some of us it isn't. What do Timothy or Violet or Ellis care for this country? That's why they'll never understand us nor why we do what we do! We are the gipsies, with the smell of the ground always in our nostrils. That's our history, mixed up with the country, with Cumberland, with England.'

He stretched himself and yawned.

'Lord! I'm a poet! And I'm famished too! I could eat a whole sheep!'

He held her tightly in his arm, kissing her again and again.

'Darling, don't be sad, don't be too serious. I'm yours for ever and ever. You're the one thing I'll never leave. You and this country here. And I'll be good next time – I'll tell you before I go. And I didn't make love to the red-haired girl. Remember that! Vanessa, sweetheart, darling sweetheart, don't you *know* that you've got me for ever and ever? Have you no sense? Can't you *tell* a thing like that?'

A little later, going down to prepare the food, she found Tom making, very seriously, an omelette.

'Father's frightfully hungry,' he said. Then he saw how happy she was. He sighed as though a great burden were lifted from him. She kissed him.

'I'm sorry I was angry this afternoon,' she said. Then, as she began to make the meal, she added: 'I'm afraid, Tom dear, that we both take life too seriously.'

An hour later, in front of the cottage, the moon, cherry-tinted in a white sky, rising above the hill, they had the best meal of their lives.

STORM COMING UP

'TIME, of course,' said Mr Benbow who was, during September, taking the work of the Vicar of Newlands, 'does not exist. There *is* no time.' He was, he had always been, of a mathematical mind, but he did not know, as he said this, raising his glass of beer and looking at the charming sun through its smoky depths, the strange things that his simple sentence provoked.

Here, in the September sunshine, sitting with Benjie and Vanessa outside their white house (he was a man who cared nothing for social conventions), he killed history. There was no past. Upon this square of ground, over which the Eagle was magnificently sailing, even as he spoke, across the spine of hill that rose in front of them, Francis Herries, his small son tight against his breast, rode over the wild land, not pastured now, sweeping in unchecked confusion down Borrowdale to the small house under the moon, with its shining suits of armour. 'Take me to the Fair with you,' Mrs Press cried. 'No, I will not,' he answered, while Margaret his wife lay sick in the room above.

Keswick waited basking in the sun while the coach rolled in from Kendal, and old Pomfret, a little drunken, looked out of his study window. At the same moment David, at Uldale, heard of the fall of the Bastille and cursed his son, Jennifer walked tapping with her slippers up the road to the Fortress, and Judith's boy, naked by the Tarn, mocked the big man on the white horse. In his London rooms Francis, David's son, sick of life, blew his brains out while young Tom Macaulay talked with old Rogers in Hatchard's bookshop. Judith saw the big woman count the lumps of sugar in the Paris café, and young Will raced up to the Druids' Circle while Adam cheered him on. 'It's war then,' said Judith, nodding her bonnet at Walter, and, even as she spoke, the flames leapt upon Uldale and her son fell fighting the choking fumes. The carriages moved slowly at Will's funeral, and Sayers with a broken arm faced unflinchingly the blinded Heenan.

'Thank you very much, Miss Martineau,' said Judith, shouting down the ear-trumpet, one eye on the tea tent, and John called through the mists of Skiddaw for his enemy. 'Yes, it's too late,' said Benjie, bowing his head; 'I'm married already,' and Vanessa turned, in the long drawing-room, thinking that she

heard Ellis' step on the stair. The Chinese clock strikes, and old
Emily has offered up a prayer while young Tom, his hand for a
moment on Vanessa's shoulder, says: 'He'll be back soon. He'll be
back soon, Vanessa.'

Behind these figures, mingling with them, giving them their
meaning and sharing in their destinies, fog swallows up Carlisle
to hide Prince Charlie's men, Keswick receives Mr Gray and the
young gentlemen from Cambridge who hope to have a word with
Mr Southey while on their reading party, the Reform Bill rides
in with a cheering mob behind it, trees fall, the roads are bound
with stone walls, figures from here, there, everywhere, buy lead
pencils, picnic on Skiddaw, whose green slopes young Mr Keats
and sturdy Sir Walter find adventurous. A Macclesfield paper
advertises for workers: 'Wanted, between 4,000 and 5,000
persons between the ages of 7 and 21 years.' Thick bellies of
smoke veil the Midland sky. Disraeli sees the war of the two
nations; Mr Joseph Hebergam, aged seventeen, works from five
in the morning until eight at night with a break of thirty minutes
at noon. 'Bravo! Bravo!' cry Will and Horace and the Vicar of
Little Rodney-on-the-Marsh, 'England rules the world', while a
man or two, with pens in their hands – Shelley, Carlyle, Dickens,
Ruskin, Morris – speak of 'a Golgotha of souls and bodies buried
alive'. The Herries are rising, the lights of London grow brighter,
the fields of middle England are lost in smoke, slowly, slowly
men are pushing up from under ground, are meeting, are band-
ing together, demanding their share, pulling down the Park railings, putting up bright little red houses, chasing the Squire's wife
out of the cottages, pushing into Westminster Hall, driving the
South African millionaires out of Park Lane, running here, running there, from coast to coast with their children behind them,
dancing on Primrose Hill, standing in rows of shiny black as, at
last, the old Queen passes . . .

And still on that square of ground, over which the Eagle is
hovering, nothing has changed. The coach rolls in to Keswick
square, the shepherd searches the mist under Helvellyn for his
wandering sheep, the sun falls from Seatoller on to the silent blue
of Buttermere and, under Gable, the Tarn sleeps like a rusted
shield.

'There is no time,' said Mr Benbow. 'Time is an anachronism.
At this moment Caesar falls on the steps of the Capitol and
David challenges his giant enemy.'

*   *   *

At this moment, too, Cynthia Worcester brought her two little girls on a visit to Cumberland. Strange how the Herries were drawn back, again and again, to this patch of ground. But in Cynthia's case it was perhaps Vanessa rather than Cumberland that drew her. Cynnthia had never set an eye on Vanessa since the flight from Hill Street. She had not seen her but had stepped into her place – or very nearly. Peile Worcester was not, of course, as rich as Ellis; they could not, in their house in Charles Street, entertain as Vanessa had done in Hill Street. On the other hand, they were cleverer than Vanessa. Vanessa had not been clever – kind, gentle, generous, most beautiful to look upon, but *not*, oh, most certainly not clever.

Cynthia was as pretty as a rosebud (a flower to which she had been often compared) and *also* as clever as a monkey. She had always been *inside* the Arts as Vanessa had never attempted to be. Indeed, so far was Cynthia now inside that her set embalmed her like a fly in amber. But everyone came to her afternoons, her evenings – Mr Bernard Shaw, the Sidney Webbs and Mr H. G. Wells; while on the other side there were the aesthetes, Mr Sidnney Colvin at the Museum, young Mr Binyon, a wild young man who had sailed before the mast and swept the floor in a bar, Mr Masefield, and, above all, the Homer, the Milton (who knew, perhaps the Shakespeare of our day?), honey-voiced Mr Stephen Phillips. The politicians came too – Cynthia had no Party politics: Sir Henry Campbell-Bannerman dined at her table as well as Mr Balfour. Even the new Labour candidate for Barnard Castle, Mr Arthur Henderson, came to tea ...

Cynthia had taken Vanessa's place. She was the social head of the family now, and the younger generation, Alfred's children, Maurice and Clara, Carey's girls, cousins from Manchester and cousins from Bournemouth, Philip and his odd effeminate friends, young Violet and her stupid husband – they recognized it and submitted to it.

Nevertheless (as is always the case in every family history) some things were not quite right. Cynthia was not as happy as she ought to be. She possessed just enough imagination to wish her position a little different. *Her* struggle between Prose and Poetry was, of course, all on the side of Prose. There was never any doubt as to which party she belonged to. Of the world of Judith, of Rose, of Vanessa she would never even glimpse the borders: nevertheless the world where she was was not quite good enough. Peile Worcester was not quite good enough, their income was not quite good enough, their two lovely obedient little girls were not quite good enough. In fact, in this September of 1903, Cynthia was supremely discontented, her rosebud mouth curled down at the ends; she, one afternoon, startled Mr Phillips almost out of his life by saying that today she really didn't want to listen to *Marpessa,* and she lost her temper altogether with Horace when he informed her that 'in his own small way he grew with every increasing year more and more of an optimist'. She could not *abide* Horace, she decided, with his high domed forehead, his mild eyes naked of eyebrows, his plump rosy cheeks, and his way of being able to help anyone in the world out of any trouble so long as he personally got the glory of it.

After her rudeness to Horace (for which she was sincerely sorry, for she was a kind-hearted little thing) she took herself in hand. What was the matter with her? Two things. One, her husband. The other, that she longed to see Vanessa again. She must get away from Peile for a while and she must see Vanessa, if only for a moment. With a start of surprise, staring into her mirror, she discovered that, in all probability, she cared for and admired Vanessa more than anyone else in the world. Vanessa had of course done a dreadful thing. Had she run away with anyone but Benjie Herries! Nevertheless Cynthia, feeling as she did at the moment about Peile, thought that running away from one's husband was not so extraordinary a business. Only it was a thing that a Herries must never do, because the eyes of the world were on the Herries family, they stood for domesticity, patriotism, and virtuous common sense. That was why Vanessa's affair had been so truly awful!

The matter with Peile was that he never changed. He was exactly the same as he had been when she married him, *exactly* the same, and all the things for which she had loved him then were precisely the things that exasperated her now!

He had not changed in looks; he was as good-looking as ever. He did not appear a day older (how she wished he did!) with his crinkly fair hair, his fair short moustache, his splendid figure, his immaculate clothes. He was an English Gentleman *in excelsis.* He had today precisely the same complaints against the English middle classes that he had had when he married her. *Then* they had seemed to her charming, and she had agreed with every one of them, for the Herries belonged to the Upper Middle Classes and thought therefore that almost everything that the Middle Middle Classes did was a pity. Peile's complaints and sarcasms now were just what they had always been but were more, far more, vehemently expressed, because he was older now and had all the Englishman's touching faith that the older you grew the more important your opinions were.

At this particular moment there were a number of things that made the Middle Middle Classes especially offensive to Peile. Business was bad. The country had not yet recovered from the effects of that stupid mismanaged war. How ironical to remember the cheering crowds lining the street as the CIVs marched past, or the shocking vulgar manifestations of Mafeking night! Then there was the Whitaker-Wright affair that had been dragging on for years, and only in March had the Public Prosecutor seen fit to prosecute. There was Chamberlain's absurd loan of thirty-five million pounds to South Africa. *There* was a nice burden for the Upper Middle Class (on whom now *all* the taxes were falling!) to pay! There were the unemployed walking about the streets with their collecting boxes. There was Brodrick's ridiculous 'Phantom Army Corps' of which young Winston Churchill so rightly made fun. There was this demand on the part of the Lower Middle Classes for cheap food – and they were getting it too, mostly in tins, of course, but nevertheless eating lobster and asparagus, peas and apricots, as though these things were their right instead of a luxury. There was the horrible 'Art and Craft' furniture with which the Lower Middle Classes were encumbering their homes, dreadful cheap confusions of memories of William Morris and vulgar German *Kunst*. A typist whom Alfred had engaged actually owned a mechanical piano-player, bought of course on hire-purchase. There was this new passion on the part of the Lower Middle Classes for learning things, for buying cheap books about atheism and how to put a bicycle together. There were their odd forms of entertainment and exercise – walking races to Brighton. There had been the other day a race to Brighton for waitresses! There was a sudden craze for swimming the Channel, and schools for quite inferior children were mad about hockey teams, just like the school attended by his own girls. There was this crazy ugly music by Richard Strauss that had not a tune in it, and this vulgar new halfpenny paper, the *Daily Mirror*, for women. There was the sordid excitement over the Moat Farm Murder, and there was this fearful increase in motor vehicles, so that a law was to be passed ordering them to be numbered and some 'test of efficiency' for the driver . . .

It was not that Peile was a snob. He did not think himself
better than anyone else, or only so very, very little better, but
anyone could see that this new power in the Lower Middle
Classes, their crazy desire for the best of things and intolerable
fashion of making themselves heard through the daily Press,
through Leagues and Unions and meetings and speeches was
doing old England no good, was in fact fast dragging her down
from her grand position as Mistress of the World. Something
must be done about it, and the Upper Middle Classes were the
people to do it: it was their right and their duty. Peile did not
know *what* everyone was about! The country going to wrack and
ruin and nobody cared. What was Alfred doing, and old Barney
and older Horace in Manchester? Why, simply nothing at all!

It was after Cynthia had endured months and months of this
at every meal and for an hour or so every night in the quiet of the
matrimonial chamber that she decided to take the girls for a
holiday to Cumberland.

She simply told Peile one evening and, next morning, departed.

Arrived in Keswick, she looked for rooms, preferring these to a
hotel, and found them – most charming ones – on the right side
of the road that ran down to the lake. She spent half an hour
putting the rooms' things away into a cupboard – trays from
India, china figures from Manchester, bead mats, two large
coloured portraits and three huge sea-shells. Mrs Colbourne the
landlady was a little astonished, but there was something about
Cynthia, so tiny but so charming, with such lovely hair, such
lovely eyes, and a manner that had just the right mixture of
kindliness and authority. Mrs Colbourne, who was a widow and
came from near Liverpool (had she been a Cumbrian she would
not have been so quickly melted), surrendered to Cynthia entirely, giving the governess special food (for she had a delicate
stomach), sitting up one night when Rosalind had a cough that
might become pneumonia (you never can tell), and hiring a pony
trap from her friend Mr Lewthwaite at especial terms for Cynthia's especial use. In those few days she used it in fact a great
deal. She became a familiar sight in Keswick, sitting up driving,
her little back like a ramrod, and a veil concealing her lovely
features. The citizens of Keswick are not very easily impressed –
they have too many visitors – but the Hon Mrs Peile Worcester,
driving her pony cart, her two lovely little girls sitting as stiff as

Royalty behind with their governess, Miss King, was a sight that they did not for a while forget.

Then, after four extremely happy days, there came a peremptory letter from Peile. He was not well. He had been in bed all day. He had a temperature. The doctor thought that it might be serious. He demanded her instant return.

She did not return instantly, however. She waited a day. She went with her two little girls and called on Vanessa. The pony trap arrived at the church. There they all three dismounted and walked across the meadows to the white house. Having tea by the house door were Vanessa, Benjie, and Tom. At first Cynthia thought it was the farmer and his wife. It was one of those lovely September days when, above the turning bracken, the sun lies in happy content from shoulder to shoulder of the hills and all the little streams flash with light. Perhaps one small cloud, dark as a mulberry, hangs motionless like a hawk above the glittering valley and, for a moment, the sun slips behind its shelter. Then at that instant all is sombre – the hill, the streams, the little running walls, as though a vast curving wing from the protecting Eagle shadowed the world. Then the sun is free of the cloud, and light leaps up from the heart of the soil.

It was such a day, but very warm: Benjie was in his shirt sleeves, the sleeve of his one arm rolled up; his neck was bare. He was wearing corduroy riding breeches, and Vanessa in a sun bonnet had a cotton dress – white scattered with blue flowers.

After another look Cynthia saw that it was indeed Vanessa: she ran forward with a little cry. The two women embraced.

Two days after her return to London, Cynthia wrote to May Rockage. This is part of the letter:

    ... But of course I wasn't going to miss Vanessa, the very thing I'd come up there for. So we drove over, the girls and I, to the funny little valley where they live. Peile was very annoyed when he heard that I took the girls. Very annoyed indeed, especially as he has a sore throat and thinks himself on the point of death. (He's better tonight. Nothing but a bad cold. Aren't husbands absurd?) But the girls enjoyed themselves. They went off quite alone with Benjie's boy, Tom. He's nineteen now, Vanessa told me, and *most* serious as though he was eighty. But of course he had all that time in Paris and South Africa, which makes him more grown-up. Anyway I knew the children were quite safe with him. I think both of them have fallen in love with him. They've talked of nothing else since. Benjie was nice. I should say Vanessa's calmed him down. Of course he *looks* rough. He might have been a tramp or gipsy or anything, and he's brown as a berry. But he's always a gentleman even if he hasn't always behaved like one.

But, May dear, here's the great news. Vanessa is going to have a baby. Any time. It might have come while we were there having tea! She doesn't attempt to conceal it. Really I was rather afraid what the girls would think, but they're too young, thank Heaven, to know anything about it. Miss King is *excellent* at answering awkward questions. When I went up with Vanessa to her room (*such* a small room, with whitewashed walls and smelling of hay), she told me that they hadn't meant to have one – a baby I mean – but there it is, and of course it will be illegitimate, which is a pity. Isn't it funny how we *can't* keep illegitimacy out of the family, and yet I'm sure most of us are as proper as can be? When I was with Vanessa I couldn't help feeling I'd made a mistake and it would have been much better to have run away in a caravan with a gipsy instead of all these silly London parties. Benjie and Vanessa seemed so *very* happy. But of course as soon as I was in London again I knew it would never have done. I'd *never* be happy in a caravan roasting hedgehogs and telling people's fortunes. But what *is* there about Vanessa? Of course she's still beautiful even as she is and dressed like a cottage woman with a sun bonnet. But her features are lovely, so *noble* without being a bit superior. She has the grandest eyes, the finest forehead, the kindest mouth of any woman I've ever seen. I've always adored her, even though I *was* a little jealous of her in London. She's just as quiet as she always was. She sits there, her hands on her lap, and you feel you could tell her anything. She isn't clever of course – I mean she never *says* anything that's clever – but you can trust her absolutely, which you can't do with many women. She asked about Ellis, but I couldn't tell her much except that he's quite happy looked after by those two awful old women. I asked her whether she were happy and she said she was. I think she is – part of the time. But I caught her looking at Benjie as though she expected him to go off at any moment. Not that she lets *him* see that. She's too wise. She knows that men want to *feel* they're free even though they're not really. I asked her whether she were anxious about the baby. She's forty-four you know and it's her first. But she said no. She said she didn't mind dying so long as Benjie was there. But I don't know *what* he'd do without her. He may be wild and all the rest, but if any man ever loved a woman Benjie loves Vanessa. And it was all so quiet there, with the sun on the fields and the sheep grazing and the noise of running water. If Maud and Helen are coming up next week to town do let me know. Peile says . . .

'A storm's coming up,' said Benjie, looking back towards Keskadale and Buttermere Hause. The sky was a stainless blue, but over Whiteless Pike little shreds of cloud like tags of cotton wool floated and gathered. A low whispering wind stirred the dying bracken.

'I'm coming with you,' Vanessa said. As she said it she thought: 'Now this is foolish of me. This is what I determined not to do – not to force myself on him. He doesn't want me. He will be so much happier by himself. And yet I'm determined. What is it? Is it the child? I can't bear these days to let him out of my sight.'

'Better not,' Benjie said. 'There's a storm coming. And I'm out for a long walk – Hindscarth, Robinson, over Red Pike to Ennerdale. You'll never do it, Van, as you are. It wouldn't be safe.'

How well she knew him when he thought that someone was laying a hand on him to constrain him – herself, anyone – like a hare who, with ears pricked, hears the hunter treading the long grass. But she was determined. All her cautious ways of dealing with him were gone. She could not *endure* a whole day and night just now without him. If she had asked him to stay he would have stayed – but reluctantly, behaving all day as though she had tethered him with a rope to a stone! How well she knew him! As though it were herself who was resenting it.

'I can't help it,' she said, smiling, her head up, her hands on her broad hips. 'I must come, Benjie. It will be all right. Wenlock says that it won't be yet. I never felt better in my life.'

He looked at her and she knew what he was thinking: 'This big broad woman stands over me like a gaoler. Why did I tie myself up? Can't even go off for a walk by myself!'

And yet, all these months, since they had known that there was to be a child, he had been exquisitely tender for her, taking every trouble, thinking of her, watching over her as he never would have done for anyone five years ago. Oh! he had grown. Living with her, loving her, had taught him something. Had taught *her* something too – should have taught her not to worry him, to let him go off free! But he ought not to want to go for a night and a day now, when, in spite of what the doctor had said, he knew that the child *might* be born . . . and she alone with Tom in the house. The child *might* be born . . . it was mad of her to insist that she must go with him. And yet she *did* insist.

'I'm coming,' she said obstinately.

'Look here.' He did not look at her, but slanted his eyes, bright, lively, shining in his brown face, away from her, looking at the walls of the house, the sheep cropping, the wind stirring in the bracken. 'Look here, I've told you. There's a storm coming. I must have a walk. I've been cooped up for weeks. ('Oh no, you haven't,' Vanessa thought. 'Last week you were away for two nights.') I'll be back tomorrow morning. It's madness for you to think of coming. Look here. Walk to the end of the lane with me. Then come back.'

'No, I'm coming,' she answered obstinately. She went in to get some things. As she was collecting them she thought: 'What is making me do this? And why, at moments like this, do we almost hate one another? I would give him anything, anything in the world. I would die for him. It wouldn't be hard at all. But now the more he wants me not to come with him the more I'm coming. And when it's like this it seems as though we had always been fighting one another, all our lives long. And yet soon – when we are agreed again – it will seem as though we had never had a fight in our lives worth mentioning.'

When she came down in her short skirt and with her stick and rucksack she looked in at the lower room to say goodbye to Tom. He was seated at the table, his square arm firmly planted, his honest determined eyes bent on a book. He sprang up.

'Why, where are you going?'

'I'm going with Benjie for a walk.'

The look came into his eyes that she knew so well – of fear and love and motherly anxiety.

'Oh, but you shouldn't! Not now. What's father doing to let you?—'

She smiled the old ironical mischievous smile that she had had as a child, a smile just like Adam's.

'He doesn't want me to. He's very cross about it, in fact.'

'Well, of course he is. Oh, Van, you mustn't.'

She caught him to her and kissed him.

'Dear Tom! You're going to have an awful life – always upsetting yourself about other people.'

She went outside. Benjie never said a word, but he was as sulky as a scolded schoolboy. They set off. She waved to Tom who was watching at the window, who would be, she knew, anxious and miserable all day.

'I don't care,' she thought defiantly. 'They're only men. They haven't the least idea what a woman wants. It will be good for me, this exercise. I never felt better in my life.' She walked, her head up, striding, a smile on her lips, and Benjie stepped along at her side, whistling, kicking pebbles. Only as they crossed the beck and she jumped from a stone to the bank he said:

'You're a fool, Van, you know. But on your own head be it.' Then he seemed better. He could never be sulky for long. Any little thing interrupted his mood. 'Look, Van! Look at that hawk! Like a stone on the sky! Ah! it's dropped – a fieldmouse, I expect. Here. Take my hand. This fence is a bit steep.'

Then all was well again; they were as close together as though they were one body, moving through the air, treading the turf so lightly, brushing the bracken as they began to climb. She looked back on the little stream before they left it. It played lingeringly about its gleaming stones as though loath to leave them, and the stones, too, seemed to cling to the water, stopping it, having excited murmurous chats with it, then, as though trying a last strategy, exercising in a tiny dance with flurries of silver lines and circles. All about the stream the scene was 'calm as a resting wheel' and the air so clean that trees and hill lines seemed stamped on the atmosphere like a seal on blue paper. The September day was exceptionally warm, but everywhere was the finger of decay, the leaves gold and dun and then of a sudden brightly green as though defiant of approaching death. At a cottage above the right bank of the stream a woman called to a shepherd striding uphill, two dogs at his heel: 'Well, anudder time ...' Her voice rang out in the still air like a cry.

'Oh, how happy I am!' Vanessa thought, 'and ten minutes back I was nervous, uncertain, anxious. I only want Benjie to be happy and then everything in me is tranquil.' She remembered, as they pressed past a big boulder and began to tread the turf and to feel the wind, touched with the salt of the sea, in their faces, her London life. How dead and gone that seemed! But Cynthia's visit had stirred her strangely. She had accepted her ostracism almost gladly – she had suffered so little – but she had been moved, deeply moved that Cynthia had brought her children. Yes, and had allowed Tom to take them off across the valley. Tom had thought little Mary the most beautiful creature he had

ever beheld. He had spoken of her again and again. He was to go
shortly to London. He was to be given a trial on the *Standard*
newspaper, a job that dear old Barney had found for him. How
would the Family receive him? Peile and Alfred and Horace ...
Would May and Carey invite him to Wiltshire? After all, it was
not *his* fault, poor boy, that his father had disgraced himself!
And Society was more tolerant now. Every kind of queer person
was admitted. When she had married Ellis the conventions had
been rigid, as though you belonged to a Regiment, and any social
or moral offence was as bad as desertion. She did not care for
herself – *her* case was socially hopeless and would be more so after
the birth of a child – but she *did* want Tom to have a good
time!

Benjie took her arm to help her up a steep place. At his touch
warmth poured through her body. It was always so. She had
had, in her life, so little experience, but she had always heard
that, when passion was gone, the best that a married pair could
hope for was a kind of compromising friendship. But still, after
all these years, Benjie's body was lovely to her. She would lie
awake at night, while he slept, her hand on his thigh, and know
that his vigour, his warmth, the freshness of his skin, the strength
of his bones was unique for her and always would be. Now she
understood fidelity – spiritual fidelity. Yes, that she had always
understood, but when it was aided by the body how undefeated it
must be! She understood now the tragedy of the marriage in
which physical things were disharmonized. Easy for others to
argue that it must be endured, but the touch, the kiss, the stroke
of the hand, the meeting of the cheek against cheek, the personal
flavour of the flesh, how much of spiritual contact went with
these physical things – they were the very gateway of the spirit!

So, on the brow of the hill, she said that they would sit down
for a moment and they did so. He put his arm around her and
she drew his head to her breast. She felt almost a faintness of
ecstasy here in this high air, with the smell of bracken and short
stiff grass and the sea wind. Far below them she saw a little figure
of a man leading his horse, and she thought of him, the year
going past him, rousing his horses, driving his plough through
flint and marl, the peewit wheeling above him, kestrels soaring,
his eyes always so patient, so wise about so many things, walking
as his forefathers had done in all the old ways. The child leapt in
her womb and, with that lovely sense of new life, her eyes grew
bright with comfort and she smiled.

They moved on again. She asked Benjie:

'I suppose now you think you know me better than anyone else in the world?'

'Yes, I think I do.'

'Yes, now. Father knew me; Rose – poor Rose – knew me . . . Don't you know me so well, Benjie, that it's dull?'

'Dull?'

'Yes. I never can surprise you any more. You always know what I'm going to do.'

'I know you as though you were part of myself – the better part. You *are* part of myself. You always have been.'

'A part you often want to be rid of.'

'No, not often. Sometimes. Every man is like that.' He stopped and looked at her. 'Sure you're all right? Not tired?'

'Splendid. I could walk a hundred miles.'

'You know, when you said you were coming with me I hated you for a moment. I could have run off and never come back. That's what I felt like.'

'Yes, I knew you did.'

'Aren't you wise? You resent nothing. You forgive everything.'

'Yes,' she said, laughing. 'I'm placid – like a cow.'

'No. Oh no!' He struck his stick against a stone. 'You've a fearful temper. You can be so angry that the air quivers. But you never resent. You forgive and pass on. Every day you're finer.'

'Am I? That's because I love you.'

'Yes, and I love *you*! I love you! I love you! I love you!' he called. 'Do you hear the echo? It comes from that rift of rock.' Then, looking about him, sniffing the air, he went on: 'I was right about the storm, Van. It's coming. Do you see those clouds?'

Over Newlands a fleet of small, ragged clouds were slowly gathering, as though with purpose, as though marshalled. The sun shone brightly, but the air was colder and the wind now was busy along the ground, whistling in an undertone.

She didn't care about the storm. It would be nothing. She took her last look at the valley, so small but packed with history. In the time of Elizabeth, the German company had worked the mines in Newlands: there had been the Goldscope lead mines worked at the beginning of the nineteenth century. At Stair there had been the woollen mills – all that energy and human life, lovemaking and childbearing, foreign tongues, and Elizabeth's sharp eye fixed on her profits – and now the little valley bathed in silence, the small farms, the enclosed fields, the hawks and kestrels, the shepherd calling his dogs, the farmer ploughing the stiff field . . .

'Benjie, this is the only place in the world for us! The only spot . . . and for my father, my grandmother, her father . . .'

'Yes,' he answered. 'I can't tear away from it. Try as I may I can't. Everything passes – on the surface everything passes. But underneath, Van, you land on the rock, you give a cry of delight, you defend yourself against attack, and then, in a moment, you're gone to join the others under Skiddaw perhaps. We *seem* to change but we don't.'

She stopped, leaning on her stick.

'Yes, God gives you your moment of experience – to overcome fear.'

'Oh, you and your God!' he said, laughing. 'Hasn't science taught you anything yet, Vanessa?'

'Science I don't know . . .'

He looked at her curiously. 'Then God does exist for you, Van? Just as I do?'

'Yes, if one's brave enough to believe in Him,' she said shyly. 'It needs courage like everything else. We never talk about Him, Benjie. Why? Because I'm afraid that you'll laugh, and *you're* afraid – what are you afraid of? Of looking too far. What does everyone say? That Huxley and Darwin have settled the whole question, so why argue? And they leave it like that because it's easier, because it's dangerous to look any further. I shouldn't have the courage if I were not driven to it, but I think God has tormented me all my life. Tormented isn't the right word perhaps. Moved restlessly in and around me. *You* say that that is superstition. *I* say that there's no other choice for me. I *have* to be aware that you are there; I know your step, your voice, your frown. So I'm aware that God is there. I didn't ask for it. I'm not better or worse than you or anyone else because of it. It's simply a fact.'

She had not for a very long time discussed such things with him. He knew that she prayed, that much of the tranquillity that was always increasing in her came from some inner experience, the only thing that she did not share with him. Once he had been jealous of it, angry with her because of it. Now he loved her so much that he only wanted her to be happy. Perhaps? . . . Who knows? . . .

'It's a great thing to conquer fear,' he said. 'Anyone who does that is a kind of god.'

Even as he spoke the storm broke on them. Benjie knew the dangers of this piece of country. Robinson and Hindscarth had rough faces with much scree, and the ghylls into Buttermere had loose and falling rock with water suddenly, and sodden turf on the fell-side. A nasty ground for mist. But, at the moment, he could think of nothing but the wind which, quite suddenly, leapt from the ground, rushed forward from the hillside and tore up the valley. The clouds boiled from behind the hill, and the sun was obscured. The moss, heather, bracken that had been so brightly lit lost all colour.

'Are you all right?' he shouted to Vanessa.

'Yes, yes, I'm all right,' she answered.

Could they reach the bend of the hill they would have shelter. The storm was so furious that it could not last, he thought, but how strange was this sudden roaring of waters! The rain had begun to fall in slanting whips of steel, but the becks and mountain rivulets had not had time to absorb it; yet in his ears it was as though all the thundering waters of the world had been unloosed! It was as though a spirit with inky hair strode the fell and passed, blowing a great horn summoning his army! They could see the rain sweeping from the farthest horizon in curtains of gauze, blowing, bending, but never breaking.

'Turn your back to it!' he cried to Vanessa. 'Get your breath! There'll be a rock soon that we can shelter against.'

She turned, her skirts blown against her legs, her hair in her eyes and, at that same moment, with a little gasp of pain, felt a strong hand clutch her vitals, squeeze them, let them go. She bent her head. The stab of pain passed. She hurried, pressing through the storm so swiftly that Benjie cried:

'Come on! That's the spirit! We'll find shelter beyond the brow.'

They were both soaked through their coats, but a sort of ecstasy seized Benjie. This was what he loved, all the hills bared by the wind, all the streams exulting because they would be strong and vehement again, rain and wind at their full power and the sky black with cloud. If Vanessa were not beaten by it! But there she was, her head up, striding forward, striking the earth with her stick! He ran, he jumped the stones, he sang! Then, through the rain, the mist surged forward. It rose, broke to show dark fell and shining rock, closed again with fingers on your eyes, lifted from the ground a little to reveal the short grass tugging to escape the soil . . .

Vanessa was gone . . . He shouted.

'Van! Van! Vanessa! Where are you?'

The mist broke and he saw one jet-black cloud, and towards it everything, fell and gleaming stone and line of hill, seemed to strain.

He saw Vanessa standing, her hand to her heart. He caught up with her.

'Are you all right?'

Her face was grey in that half-light, but as she answered him the mist came down again, hiding her.

But she was glad that he could not see her, for she was about to die. She knew it as certainly as though the tall figure, grey-cloaked with grave assured eyes, stood in the mist, his curving silver-gleaming scythe in his hand. Her knees bent, her head was bowed on her breast. So appalling was the pain that death held no terrors, nor her loneliness. Strange that her one thought about death for years had been that Benjie must be with her when it came. And now it was here, and she hoped that Benjie would not see her, but would pass on, striking his iron-tipped stick on the stone, and she would drop there where she was and die, alone, hidden in mist . . . She did not want anyone to see her die.

So fearful was the pain that she could not keep back a moan, and then another. But only her own heart heard. The wind screamed in her ear, and the mist, wet like a thin soaked towel, pressed on her eyes and nose and mouth. Dimly through her pain she thought how silly it had been that, only ten minutes before, she had been talking so confidently about God. God was not here. She was animal, only fighting for endurance and to die without cowardice . . .

Then the pain was so fierce that she thought of nothing, neither the storm nor any company. She knelt on the sodden turf, her head back, her teeth set, hands clenched. She fancied that, from a great distance, she heard Benjie calling, and a sudden warming thought as though it were the very last that she would have in this world came to her of his sweetness, jollity, kindliness. Nothing in this world mattered so much as kindliness . . . that men should be kind to one another because they suffered, one and all, and life was short . . .

The pain passed. It withdrew as though a figure that had been bending over her had moved away.

She looked up and saw that the mist had broken, leaving a round cup like a room suddenly revealed, a room furnished with a gleaming rock like a ship's stern. The pain was gone: she would not die yet. The child should be born. Not rain nor wind should defeat her, and she rose from her knees and breasted the wind, moving forward. The mist cleared still further and she saw Benjie moving back to her.

'It's all right,' he shouted. 'There's a farm here just on the bend. Where the trees are.'

She took his arm.

'Isn't the wind strong? It almost beat me to my knees.'

He had noticed nothing, and she now brought all her resources to the business of meeting the pain again when it returned. For return it would. She could hear it afar off as though faintly the thin warning of a distant horn.

When they came to the trees they were rocking and groaning like mad things. The mist was shredded now, blowing in crazy tears and tatters over a landscape that was all fell scattered with stone and rock. The scene was immemorial and had changed in nothing since, maybe, Roman trumpets had echoed there from distance to distance.

It was a little white farmhouse, very simple, with a small beck rushing furiously at its side, the whole world filled with wind and rain. Benjie knocked on the door, two dogs barked, then a woman opened it and looked out. The wind rushed in and they followed it, coming into a clean and bright kitchen. It was low-roofed; there were legs of cured mutton and hams hanging from the smoky rafters. On a shelf nearby there were pots and jars, little yellow cheeses, dried herbs. By the ingle there was an old white-haired man, another younger man with broad shoulders and a bull-neck standing up, the woman who had opened the door, and a pretty girl in a blue gown busy at the table.

They were very cordial and friendly, made Vanessa and Benjie come to the fire to dry themselves. Yes, they had a spare room for the night if the storm kept on. The old man was loquacious; he had light blue eyes like flowers.

'Aye,' he said. 'We're verra oot o't warld – seven mile fra a shop, eight mile fra a church – an' hard roads.'

He was proud of their isolation. The housewife asked them if they were hungry. Benjie said indeed he was. She began to be busy cooking eggs and Cumberland ham.

Vanessa sat there, her knees close together, looking into the fire, waiting for the next pain to come. She wondered how soon she might go up to bed, take her things off: Benjie had noticed nothing. He was exceedingly happy, had taken off his boots and stockings, coat and waistcoat, and sat there, smiling at them all. He told them how he had lost his arm in Africa in the war. The old man had a long story to tell about sheep – 'terrible wark' sometimes. The young man had a newspaper a week old. 'A newspaper! Aye – we mun gang a lang ways to get yan o' thame here.' Benjie laughed and chattered, loving the sound of the storm beyond the house, the smell of the frying eggs and ham. His twinkling eyes rested on the girl. *What* a pretty girl! Dark, slim, and a cheeky upturned nose such as he preferred. He smiled at her and she shyly smiled back again . . .

Later Vanessa said: 'Benjie, I am tired. I think I'll go to bed.'

'Supper's nearly ready. You must be starved. I know I am.'

'I'm not hungry,' she answered. 'I think I'll go up.'

She stood, her hand pressed to her side. He looked at her anxiously but she smiled back at him. The girl went up with her to show her the room.

The storm died down. Benjie had his supper, the woman and girl waiting on him. It was now, in a place like this with simple, friendly people, that he felt at his best. In his shirt and trousers he sat there, eating, drinking big cups of tea, laughing, telling them about South Africa and other parts of the world where he had been. Once and again he smiled at the girl and she glanced back at him, their eyes meeting, holding one another, parting quickly. The storm had died away and beyond the kitchen window a flood of primrose light laced with the tree branches spread above the bare fell.

'Hurray! The storm is over!' Benjie said.

The girl had gone. He could hear her moving on the floor above. He got up.

'I'll go and see how my wife is,' he said. But, even as he spoke, the wind came again, raging in a fury about the house, banging at the house door, rattling the windows. All the trees screamed and the colour ebbed from the sky, leaving it white.

'That was sudden,' he said, turning round. 'I thought it had died.'

He saw a scurry of leaves blow against the pane and flatten. Some stayed pressed against the window.

' 'Twill be a wild neet,' the old man said calmly.

Benjie climbed the crooked stairs that smelt of mice and white-wash. At the top was the girl just coming down. There was a ghostly light from the passage window. He caught the girl with his arm and she surrendered to him at once, pressing closely against him as though she were hungry to be loved, which indeed she was. He held her tight, kissing her eyes, her cheeks, her mouth. Then, behind the pleasure and strength and warm happiness that wrapped him in, he heard a deep breath as of someone close at his elbow. Looking past the girl he saw Vanessa at the doorway. Her hair fell about her shoulders and she had caught a patchwork quilt around her; the colours were bizarre – blue, crimson, orange, green – and above it her eyes, fixed as though fastened on some desperate resolution, stared at him. She said something, but the wind was shaking the window. All the house seemed to be quivering. The girl was as though she had never been, and as he reached Vanessa's side he said:

'Vanessa, it was nothing ... Vanessa darling ...'

She looked at him, tried to smile, but her mouth shook. He heard her murmur, 'I'm very ill ... Tell the woman to come ...'

So, as nearly ninety years ago Judith Paris, her grandmother, had borne an illegitimate child in the heart of storm and confusion, did Vanessa now.

Sally, daughter of Benjamin Herries and Vanessa Herries, was born at eleven-thirty on the night of September 21st, 1903, at Randle Farm in Cumberland.

PERFECT LOVE

VANESSA sat on the slope of the hill behind the white farm watching for Tom's coming.

Sally, now nearly three years of age, sprawled beside her. Vanessa had a book on her lap but she was not reading. It was a cold sunny May afternoon. The scene was so still that it was like a painted canvas – or a bowl with flowers, for the hills circled her in but flowers were everywhere – crab blossom, speedwell blue as a jewel, anemones. In the garden behind the farm the primroses were still in yellow clumps, violets, celandines, and pansies. Soon the blue hyacinths would be full-blown. But the bowl that held the flowers was harsh with the tang of winter. The higher hills were thinly powdered with snow and the rocks so black that they

glittered in the May sun like steel, and the little coppice beyond
the stream yet seemed to tremble as though it could not be sure
that winter was truly over.

Sally was not a pretty child but she, too, was a flower. She was
small, spare, taut. Her hair had a red shadow in its brown, and
she was always pale, but not with the pallor of ill-health. She was
the strongest child. Nothing ever ailed her. When she cried it was
from ill-temper. She had a most determined will, hated to be
frustrated, knew her own way and intention always. But she
never sulked, loved where she loved, hated where she hated, stood
no nonsense, refused to be either flattered or petted and thought
her mother the beginning and end of all things.

The love of this baby for her mother was astonishing. It had
been so from the very beginning, and Vanessa, sitting there in the
sun, felt a supreme content. Three human beings loved her –
Benjie, Tom and Sally. They would not love her for ever perhaps.
Benjie still moved towards her and then away from her again.
Tom, although he was the most faithful of men, had his own life
now and much of it she could not share. Sally would grow up and
leave her. But at this moment, in this pellucid air, happy in this
bowl of flowers, she thanked God for all that He had given her.

'Am I still frightened?' she asked herself. For, since her childhood, she had had to battle with fear. She had, all her life, given
her heart to someone of whom she could not be certain and that
was perhaps the reason that she loved him so dearly. Would the
time ever come when she would be *certain* of Benjie? He was fifty-
one now, she nearing forty-seven, but the old alarms returned,
day after day, as they had always done. When he went would he
return?

Nevertheless in the years since Sally's birth she had known
greater happiness than ever before. They had been shut off from
all the world; the friends they had made had been farmers, shepherds, wandering men. They had had almost no communication
with London. An occasional letter from old Barney, Adrian,
once from Cynthia. Benjie had been twice abroad, once to Italy,
once to Spain, but had not stayed in London on either occasion.
Anything that they knew of the outer life was from Tom. When
he came he told them all the news, journalistic, social, family. He
was happy on his newspaper; the family were kind to him, and
he was deeply, hopelessly in love with Mary, Cynthia's girl, who
was still only a child but, Tom said (he confessed only to Vanessa), the love of his life . . .

Time had passed with incredible swiftness. They were for-gotten, Vanessa said, not only by the world but by time as well. They were contented.

But for how long would this endure? Still she never woke of a morning without wondering whether before night Benjie would not leave her. He loved her – of course he loved her – but the restlessness was there in his blood as it had ever been. One day he would go, and he would be lured farther and farther, always intending to return, never returning ... What she had suffered during his two adventures out of England no one would ever know. She had, by now, trained herself to the complete hiding of her fear. She gave him no sign ...

Somewhere a dog barked and at the same moment she saw that a trap had drawn up at the gate behind the church. Someone climbed out. It was Tom.

'Sally! Sally!' she cried. 'It's Tom!' She was as excited as a child.

Sally screamed: 'Tom! Tom! Tom!'

She picked Sally up and ran down the slope to the farm.

They hurried along the green sward, she carrying the child in the crook of her arm. She waved with the other hand. Tom waved back. A moment later they were all together.

Tom was short and sturdy. He had Adam's figure before he became stout and he had Adam's quietness and certainty. You knew always exactly where you were with him. Some people would think him dull as they had thought Adam. Other people found that he was to be trusted beyond most men and that, once his loyalty and affection were engaged, nothing could cause them to waver again. A dull quality, loyalty, and an unimaginative! But valuable to some people who believe in knowing where they are.

He was not dull to Vanessa. For one thing he loved her, as he showed with every look, every movement. For another he was their herald from the outer world. As they sat that evening round the table he had a thousand things to tell them. He had taken Adrian to one of these wrestling matches, now so popular. There had been a dinner party at Cynthia's. He had met Edmund Gosse, who had told funny stories about George Eliot.

'I haven't the least notion who Edmund Gosse is, darling,' Vanessa said.

Barney had been ill with rheumatism. But the most sensational piece of news was that Maud and Helen, Carey's girls, had become desperate Suffragettes. Really desperate. They wanted to break into the Houses of Parliament. They had marched in a procession carrying banners. Their mother was dreadfully distressed.

About journalism there were many exciting things. It was rumoured that Harmsworth, now Lord Northcliffe, intended to purchase *The Times*. Everything in Fleet Street was changing. Men were dismissed from their jobs at a moment's notice. No one was safe any longer.

'Oh, it's nice here!' he said at last. 'It's so quiet. There's such a good smell.'

'How long have you got?' Benjie asked.

'A fortnight.' He wanted to walk. He wanted to go over to Haweswater and spend two days in Eskdale.

'I'll go with you,' said Benjie.

'Oh, that will be grand!' Tom said.

But Vanessa was sure that he wanted to go alone. There was something not quite intimate between himself and his father – something a little uneasy.

And that night as Benjie was undressing he said to Vanessa:

'Tom doesn't want me with him.'

He was pulling off his shirt, a little awkwardly with his one arm. His face flushed, his hair tousled, looking at her over the top of his shirt before he dragged it over his head, he seemed to her suddenly pathetic a little, and her love went out to him with an unexpected fierce rush of emotion. She was sitting before the glass brushing her hair. She turned, the brush in her hand. He, standing bare to the waist, looked back at her. They exchanged a long deep gaze. The room was lit with candles that blew in the breeze from the open window, and their shadows were gigantic on the white wall.

They stayed, transfixed, looking at one another. Then at last, with a deep breath as though he were experiencing some extraordinary new emotion, he came over to her. He put his hand on her shoulder, then moved it to her neck and so held her, her gaze still upon him. Her eyes filled with tears; her heart was hammering. It was as though he had never made love to her before, as though at last he were about to say to her the words for which she had so long been aching.

He knelt down and enfolded her with his arm, his head on her breast. With light gentle fingers she stroked his hair, staring in front of her, all the room dimmed because her eyes were dim. A ridiculous clock that had a note, Benjie always said, like an angry parrot, told the hour, but the sound was an infinite distance away. What had happened? What was then this tumultuous fiery rush of joy at her heart?

'What is it?' she said at last. 'Benjie – darling – tell me. Are you unhappy about Tom?'

He did not answer. He held her only the more tightly. At last he said:

'It's like this, Van ... It's as though I had never seen you before.'

He got up and stood there, looking at her.

'You'll catch cold with the window open.'

But he did not move; only stood there staring at her.

'Isn't it odd, Van? I'm falling in love with you all over again.'

She finished brushing her hair, although it was difficult because her hands trembled. She slipped on her nightdress and got into bed.

He always wore at night an open shirt that came no farther than the knees. For a moment he was naked and, looking at him in the candlelight, she thought how wonderfully he had preserved his body. For a man of past fifty he had an astonishing spareness and hardness. No fat. Nothing slack. And, as always, he looked as though he never wore clothes, as though his flesh were always exposed to the wind and sun. He stretched himself like an animal, raised his arm above his head, swelled out his brown chest. But he never took his bright, blue, fearless eyes from her face. She had never seen such eyes in any other man. They were so childlike, honest, dependable. But he was not a child and he was not dependable ...

She expected that her own emotion would recede. It had been but a moment, born perhaps of her maternal longing over him because he was disappointed in Tom. But the emotion did not recede. She clasped her hands under the bedclothes and tried to beat down her joy. Like many another woman she was afraid of it lest it should lead her to expect too much and bring soon some disappointment that would be almost unbearably bitter – that she would remember afterwards, when the joy was forgotten.

'I mustn't love him too much,' she told herself, as so many, many times she had told herself before. He blew out the candles and lay down beside her. She knew at once by his touch on her breast that tonight he was very gentle. He scarcely touched her and yet she was thrilled by his proximity as she had never been before. They kissed and it was a kiss far deeper than passion. They did not stir, only their two hearts beating the one against the other, but this kiss was different from any other that they had ever exchanged. It was radiant with awe and wonder and reverence at something quite beyond and outside themselves.

At last he said: 'What has happened, Van? I have never loved anyone as I do you tonight.' His hand found hers and now they lay, very quietly, side by side, hand in hand. She turned on her side, laying her cheek against his.

'How still it is! Only the running water!'

He stroked her arm with his hand, very gently, as though he were afraid lest he should hurt her.

'Van, this is heaven. I have never loved you before as I do tonight.'

'Nor I you, Benjie.'

'We'll never forget this.'

'No. Never, never.'

'I seem to understand at this moment what life ought to be.' She sighed with a deep, yearning happiness. 'I'm not afraid any more. I don't care now what happens. We have never been together like this before ...'

'No. Never. I wonder why ...'

They turned to meet one another in a passionate embrace.

And, with the morning, nothing was changed. She knew immediately that he was still moving in this new relationship. She saw that Tom was at once aware of it and that he came in an instant more closely to his father. Benjie was quiet. In ordinary he conveyed a sense of restlessness, of wanting to move from the place where he was to some other place. But this morning, after they had breakfasted, he stood in front of the farm looking at the green field, the hills, the flowers, as though he had never seen them before.

'Come for a stroll,' he said to Vanessa, and they went. But, as they walked, they scarcely spoke. They went side by side, and for Vanessa it was as though they were not walking but rather were held, in some burning cloud, alone, away from man and time and destiny. What had happened? Was it not impossible that at their age, after they had lived so long together, known one another so intimately, there could be a new relationship between them? Friendship, comradeship, yes; but a new emotion, a new passion? Surely it was impossible?

Only at the end of this walk, before they went into the house, he turned to her and said again:

'Vanessa, what has happened to us? Are we in love for the first time?'

Day followed day, week followed week; the summer passed and autumn was smoke and flame, smoke of the clouds, flame of the bracken. With November the rains fell. There was clouded light over the dales and the wind currents were as vexed and troubled as the twists and turns of a stream. A black whirlwind of cloud would rush across the tops, discharging its waters as though from a gigantic tub impatiently overset by a celestial housemaid: you would wake to a morning of universal dark; the very fire burnt dimly and the rain fell with the tramp of armies; or the wet mists would blow from Robinson, from Cat Bells, thin and airy, carrying with them all the scene, a bare hillside lit by a sudden splash of shining rock, a herd of sheep stalwart under the chill stone walls, houses of stone raised into air by the web of vapour. Or it would rain quite solemnly like a clergyman of the old school preaching into eternity, or a writer of stories for whom two hundred years are but as a day, and then nothing lovelier in the world could be seen than that quick break before dusk when a pulse of gold beats through the dark and the sun creeps from under the blanket of cloud and everything is lit with radiance for a short breathless while. In these valleys and hills rain is as beautiful as fair weather and more various, and it is rain always broken by sudden breathtaking surprises. Only in this weather and perhaps only in this country can you see what the ebon flank of a cloud may be above a misty hill, or how purple – richer than grape-bloom – can cover a fell after tempest, or the white shadow, whiter than ivory and thin like glass, that strokes the field under a pale young stormy moon.

Men who write of these things are always defeated by them, so rare and strange is their beauty, but in their hearts an eternal homesickness is created so that they are never either safe or happy again in any land where it is dry and the sun is for ever shining.

Throughout the summer, the autumn, the winter, this miracle remained for Benjie and Vanessa. Many writers for hundreds of years have written about first love, and some writers (but not so very many) have spoken of the happiness of married comradeship. But life is never settled nor arranged, nor does it behave as it ought, by the laws of the written word, to do. Many men and women would behave nobly were they given the perfect conditions and circumstances, but there is always toothache, a broken promise, a jealousy, an unreasonable desire. Only once in a lifetime perhaps a Beethoven Symphony arrives punctually and, in a lighted room, two friends forget that there is such a tyranny as Time. And, even then, sentiment may steal the prize.

Vanessa and Benjie had good fortune. Not by their own desire, and, in any case, they did not know where to look for it. It came to them and they knew what perfect love can be.

During this winter they were never parted. Their happiness was too deep and soundless for them to fear it. For Vanessa it was as though God kept them in continual company. Her ideas of God were, of course, very simple; she felt His radiance as though she moved from morning to night in sunlight. For Benjie it was simpler still. He wanted to be near Vanessa; he did not know why she irritated him no more, why he was restless no longer. He did not search for reasons. He only knew that body, soul, and spirit, he was complete.

One starlit night after Christmas they climbed the hill and sat down together. The sky was quite clear. It was as though they were wrapped in stardust. A little way above them the snow began. It was bitterly cold, but he wrapped his large shepherd's cloak around both of them and, because there was no wind, they took no hurt.

'It would not be bad, Van,' he said, 'if we were to die now, both of us together.'

Then, as she did not answer, he went on: 'That is what all lovers have always said. But *young* lovers. Lovers in their first ecstasy. We are very *old* lovers.'

'I don't feel old,' she answered at last. 'When shall we begin to feel old?'

'Oh, I suppose – with sickness, separation . . .'

'We will never be separated now,' she said quickly.

He held her to him, under the cloak, more closely.

'I don't trust life even now. I think you're the only thing in the whole world I trust. There never was anyone so trustworthy as you are.'

She laughed. 'Yes, that's why I'm dull – for everyone except you and Tom.'

'No. You're not dull. They didn't think you dull in London. But you're shy. You can't show people what you are. You're courageous enough about *things*. You'd stand up to anything.

But you're human beings. Only in these last three months have even I known what you are.'

'For the first time since my father died,' she said. 'I'm not afraid.'

Five weeks later the letter came.

It came, as catastrophic letters often come, with an almost maidenly quietness. Vanessa opened it, looking over the table to Benjie, and laughing at something that he had just said. This was the letter:

HILL STREET, LONDON, W.
February 8th, 1907

DEAR VANESSA – You will, I am sure, be extremely surprised to receive a letter from me – surprised and not altogether pleased, I fear, but Vera and I have, for some weeks now, discussed the matter and have at last decided that this letter must be written. The matter is quite simply this. For some while now – ever since last summer in fact – Ellis has been seriously ailing. He has not, of course, been strong mentally for a very long time past. That you know. But his bodily conditions have been surprisingly good: he has eaten and slept well, and, within his own mental world, has really lived with content under our care. We have done our best. It has not always been easy, but of that I wish here to say nothing. Last summer we took Ellis to Harrogate as perhaps you heard at the time. We found a small and comfortable house where we could enjoy privacy and where, at the same time, my sister (whose rheumatism has for some time been trying) and Ellis could receive medical attention.

It was during our stay in Harrogate that the change took place. He has long been given, as you must have heard, to childish pursuits. He enjoys playing with dolls, soldiers, and trains. We have always, under excellent Doctor Lancaster's advice, humoured him in this and one day in Harrogate Vera bought him a doll to give him pleasure. So soon as he saw it it reminded him of you. I must tell you that he had not, so far as my sister and I were aware, once mentioned your name during all these years. But on this occasion, on Vera's presenting him with the doll, he said at once: 'Why, this is Vanessa come back again!' At first he seemed extremely happy at his fancy, but my sister and I noticed that from this moment he began to be less well. His headaches, which you will perhaps remember, returned. His temperature was often above normal. He was restless. Many of the things that had amused him seemed to amuse him no longer. He is of course, not young any more – sixty-four years of age – and his recurrent fever made us anxious. Whatever you may feel about my sister and myself you must remember, Vanessa, that we have both for a very long time now been most deeply and sincerely attached to your husband. Throughout this last winter he has been most unwell and now for several weeks has not left his bed. Doctor Lancaster says that it is difficult to say that there is anything organically wrong, but he fears that he has not long to live. We feel, Vera and I, that if this is indeed so, we must do everything to make the last months of his life happy. We are two childless women and in these years at Hill Street we have come to feel for Ellis as though he were our son. I hope you will forgive my saying this, but the whole situation is – and has always been – so very strange!

And now to come to the point of this letter (it has not been an easy one to write). It is that, continually, during these last weeks Ellis has begged for your return. He has, it seems, a clear memory of the events that led up to your departure, but his mental decay has wiped from his recollection all bitterness and anger. He is as gentle and submissive as the child that so often he seems to be. 'I want Vanessa!' he cries and, again and again: 'When is Vanessa coming? Why does Vanessa not come?'

In these circumstances my sister and I feel it right that you should know how things stand. It is not easy for us to take this step. We cannot pretend that we approved, or now approve, of the action that you took. But it is not for us to judge and we can only assure you that if you return to Hill Street for the few remaining weeks of Ellis' life (Doctor Lancaster tells us that it cannot be much more) you will hear no single word of reproach from us and we will regard you as the mistress of this house in every way. Your place just now, Vanessa, is with your husband, whatever the past has been. You have it in your power to give him this last happiness. We feel that we would never forgive ourselves if we did not acquaint you with the facts – Yours sincerely,

WINIFRED TRENT

Vanessa read the letter. Benjie, watching her from the other side of the table, saw at once that something of the uttermost seriousness had occurred.

'What is it?' he asked, coming across to her.

She gave him the letter. He read it slowly, sometimes repeating some of the words aloud.

'But this is monstrous!' he said at last. His face was flushed with anger, and also with the beginning of a terrible fear.

She sat down, staring in front of her, then held out her hand for the letter and read it through again.

'Yes,' she said. 'I have always known that the punishment would come. It *had* to come – to make things just.'

'Now – look, Van.' He sat down beside her. 'You are not to consider this for a moment; what the old witch suggests, I mean. Go to London. I'll come with you. Go to Hill Street. Pay him a visit. We'll stay in London if you like and you shall go often and see him – anything else is preposterous.'

She shook her head.

'He wants me back. I never would have left him if he had wanted me. But he didn't. Now he does. He's dying.'

Benjie with an effort to be calm – one of the hardest things he had attempted for many a day (for this *was* preposterous; this was a plot, Hill Street all madmen and witches) – put his hand on hers, which was trembling, and summoned all his wisdom:

'Listen, Van. He doesn't want you. He can't. He doesn't know what he wants. It's some plot to get you back there again. The two old women are tired of their job, I shouldn't wonder. They think it would be a fine thing for you to take it on again. He *can't* want you with his dolls and his trains.'

'No. I don't like Vera and Winifred – but they're honest. They have no imagination and no humour, but they're honest and they've been angels to Ellis. When I wrote to Vera three years ago – you remember – to ask her to persuade Ellis to divorce me, her letter wasn't kind but it was honest and plucky. I don't like them, but there are no lies in this letter.'

She turned round and stared at him. She looked, he thought, quite suddenly an ageing woman. Her confidence and happiness had left her.

'This is awful,' she said at last. 'Terrible. The worst thing that could happen. To go back to that house, that life . . . to leave you. Oh!' she cried, her hand on her breast. 'I don't think I can! I don't think I can!'

'Of course you can't – and, I tell you, there's no need to. We'll go to London. We'll see Ellis . . .'

But she shook her head. She had recovered her courage.

'Of course I must go – and you know it, Benjie. There can be
no other way. What would I feel now if, after that letter, I didn't
go? How could I go on living with you as we have been living?
Oh, I knew it was too good to last! Something *had* to happen ...
these last six months – we've had a new life – and it was too fine,
too wonderful to be allowed much of. It's unfair, it's unfair.
That one mistake I made so long ago, to be punished for it so
many times!' Then she cried out in a kind of agony: 'That house,
Benjie! I can't *stand* that house!'

Then he was really frightened and because he was frightened
he was angry. He got up roughly, knocking his chair over.

'Look here Van – if you leave me now because two crazy old
women write a letter – if you leave me after all that has happened
to us these last months – you'll lose me. I can't keep up without
you now. I'm not young any more. I could have done without
you once, perhaps, but not now ... You owe me more than you
owe Ellis.'

'No, I don't,' she interrupted. 'I ruined Ellis' life. I've made
you happy, I made him unhappy.'

'It was his own fault. He made you marry him.' (He did not
remember that it had been *his* fault.)

'No, he did not. I need not have married him ...' Then she
turned and caught his arm. 'Benjie, there's Sally! There's
Sally!'

'You see,' he cried triumphantly. 'You see how impossible it is.
Of course you can't leave Sally. She's your child, isn't she?'

'No ... No ... Of course, I would have to have Sally with me.
I would insist on that. I would make my terms—'

Then he swore at her. 'Damn you, Vanessa, am *I* nothing?
What about me? You think of your crazy husband, you think of
your baby. But I'm to be left out of it. Anything can happen to
me—' He was not going to plead for himself. He looked at her and
saw that her mind was made up. This was the law: Vanessa's
character being what it was, this was fate.

He saw that and saw, also, for himself a future so intolerable
that he closed his eyes and bowed his head.

Then they drew together and clung together, without a word.
Both knew that in this there was no alternative.

TIMOTHY BELLAIRS PAYS SOME VISITS

OLD Barney Newmark died quite suddenly in his sleep in the autumn of 1909. The Family were sorry because they had approved of Barney's fame as a novelist. It was not, perhaps, very great and he belonged to a very different generation from the present. The obituaries were kind; he had been a genial fellow, always in London, friendly and cheerful with everyone. He was spoken of as the 'Hawley Smart of his period'. The *Referee* wrote: 'Mr Newmark could write of horses and pretty women with a grace and humour that exceeded any of his contemporaries.' But the paragraph that pleased the Family was one in *The Daily Telegraph*: 'Mr Newmark, whose loss was so widely deplored last week, was of course a member of the famous Herries family, so well known in so many directions. Lord Rockage, who owns in Wiltshire one of the finest houses in England, is a member of it; Mr Alfred Herries, the well-known financier, another; Mr Timothy Bellairs, whose picture "Mme Rochambert" created a sensation in last year's Salon, another. The Hon Mrs Peile Worcester, whose parties in Charles Street have long been famous, is a member of the family, and another member, Mr Horace Newmark, who died not so long ago, was known for many years as "the Monarch of Manchester". The Herries family is very well known in the North of England, most especially in Cumberland and the Border country. One of the most remarkable women of an earlier generation in the North was Madame Paris, also a member of the famous family. She has become almost a legend in Cumberland and Westmorland, I believe. Mr Newmark's delightful friendly, easy, and merry novels belonged to a time when the art of fiction was scarcely as seriously considered as it is today. This has been a sad year for English letters, mourning as we do both Meredith and Swinburne. Mr Newmark would have been the first to deprecate any comparison between two such giants and his own agreeable novels. Nevertheless he will be missed and for a long time to come.'

This was very pleasant. It had been for the Herries family a year of definite accomplishment. They had lived down the misadventures of the South African War and the disgrace of Vanessa's elopement (both events, in their view, of equal family importance). The Edwardian period, with its gracious (if materially minded) monarch, its common sense, its proper appreciation of money, its fostering of the upper middle class (even though the lower orders *were* behaving immodestly), its enthusiasm for Empire, its general applause for the solider English virtues, exactly suited the Herries: wildness, immorality, gambling, these things, when they appeared, became almost at once socially rationalized. The Family had no objection to immorality when it was photographed at a weekend house party during the shooting season. Private behaviour was no matter so long as it appeared publicly decent, and this was not hypocrisy on the Herries' part. It was simply that they cared for England, guarded her reputation most zealously. And this was natural, for England was Herries and Herries were England ...

At last they could sit back for a moment and see that all was well. Family feuds (ridiculous, all about nothing – a fan, a green vase, a house on a hill) were things of the past. One possible scandal, the unspeakable Rose – poor Horace Ormerod's sister – had, luckily, been hidden by the grime of mean streets. Vanessa was living once again most properly with her husband; even Barney's death was not so bad a thing, for he had outlived his reputation and had been inclined at times to say oddly sarcastic things about the Family.

England had never seemed more secure, more prosperous, more certain of the grandeur of her great destiny – and as England was, so were the Herries.

It happened that Timothy Bellairs, the painter, came over to London for Barney's funeral. The old boy had been good to him in times past. Barney and Benjie (and of course young Tom) were the only members of the Family for whom he cared. He had lived so long in Paris that he did not feel Herries any longer. Or did he? He came over to London to find out.

He was a tall thin man with very light blue eyes and hair the colour of pale corn. He wore a small pointed beard. He had a way of watching you while you talked, of agreeing with you but causing you to wonder whether he did not think you a terrible fool. His voice was gentle and he had a charming smile. He appeared detached and impersonal. He had in fact only two passions – one was for painting, the other for one or two individuals. He was capable of iron fidelity. Benjie and Tom were two of his devotions, although he had not seen either of them for a very long time. Another was a stout and extremely cynical lady who shared his bed and board in Paris.

Attending Barney's funeral he observed the Family.

Vanessa was there. He had not seen her for many years but, knowing her story and of her return to Ellis nearly three years ago, he watched her with especial interest. Her grey hair under the black hat, the pale face beneath the veil – these gave her a greater appearance of age than he had expected. But her carriage (he watched her as, attended by a little thin woman, she walked up the aisle to her seat) was very fine. She was a big woman, full-breasted, large-shouldered and, he thought, as he saw her before she turned into her seat, apart from everyone else there. 'She has learnt how to play her role.'

Tom was with him and whispered some names. That was Horace, that stout fellow in glasses, with plump cheeks, the full Herries chin and an air of self-conscious benevolence. 'Barney hated him,' Tom whispered. Cynthia swept up, Peile Worcester in atendance. Very smart, Timothy thought, with her beautifully fitting black and Parma violets – not thinking about Barney, though.

An extremely thin tall gentleman, wearing pince-nez, his black clothes rigid as though cut from wood, 'very Herries' in feature, moved to his seat as though he were taking his place as chairman of a board meeting.

'That's Alfred.'

A fat cheerful gentleman and a very fat cheerful lady hurried up the aisle, showering benevolence on all around them. 'Sidney and Mary – Horace's son from Manchester.'

Then old Carey Rockage, bent with rheumatism, May thin and short-sighted, with the two suffragette daughters who strode forward looking about them with an air of resentment.

Timothy's sister, who had married a Colonel and lived in Surbiton, was not present. Vanessa was by far the most interesting person in that church to Timothy. He thought of Barney.

'Good old boy. He had a fine life. Did what he wanted, enjoyed every moment of it.' When he remembered Barney's mistresses it amused him that the Family should come, in such numbers, to pay him the last compliments. 'They wouldn't do the same for Benjie,' he thought, feeling the touch of Tom's shoulder against his. But Barney, in some clever fashion of his own, had never openly outraged the conventions. No member of the Family had ever been brought face to face with his mistresses, while in poor Benjie's case every rebellion had been as open as it could be! And then, just as the service was about to start, Benjie walked up the aisle. He walked slowly, his brown face and bright blue eyes unconcerned, the empty sleeve of his jacket pinned to his breast. He was wearing a loose dark suit – so far he had submitted to convention – but he looked, as he always looked in public, apart, as though he were of another country, an exile and a rebellious one. 'He looks more than that,' Tim thought. 'He looks worn and strained. He's too thin.'

Had he seen Tom and Timothy he would undoubtedly have stopped and sat with them, but, his head up, seeing nobody, he walked straight ahead. 'He said he wasn't coming,' Tom whispered.

He passed the seat where Vanessa was. Some instinct seemed to tell him. He stopped for a moment, then turned and found a place on the other side of the aisle beside stout Sidney and Mary Newmark. It amused Timothy to observe the startled and frightened look that they gave him.

So old Barney Newmark, accorded by the Family full honours, joined (perhaps thankfully) the Rogue and David, Judith and young John, and was, beyond question, glad of their company.

Timothy had not as yet paid Benjie a proper visit. Tom, who shared lodgings with his father in Tite Street, told Tim that Benjie was in one of his bad moods.

'He'll tell you all about it when you go. He's very unhappy – but he'll tell you. Only you'd better wait till he chooses his day.'

Meanwhile Timothy was painting Mary Worcester's picture. He had seen, at once, that this was a thing that he had to do. She was the loveliest child he had ever beheld. She was going to be a real beauty. The modelling of her face was exquisite, her colour perfect, everything delicate, gentle, dark hair, dark eyes, already a sense of poise and movement. But, he decided very quickly, she was stupid and dull. Her voice was lovely in tone, soft and resonant, but she had nothing to say. Her eyes were large and full; she had a way of using them so that they rested on you as though they found you enchanting. But she did not find you enchanting. She was not thinking about you at all. She was only sixteen and had been kept, at home, closely guarded, but even then Timothy thought, she surely had *some* ideas about something! It seemed that she had not.

Her mother, whose little figure was still perfect but was betrayed by her too bony neck and eyes that were older than her complexion allowed for, said about her beautiful daughter that: 'You've no idea how intelligent that child is! Now Rosalind says just what's in her head and nine times out of ten it's nonsense, as I tell her – but *Mary*! No one knows what that child's thinking!'

Cynthia also unburdened herself to Timothy about Vanessa:

'Of course it's awful for her. We all realize that. She came back nearly three years ago thinking that Ellis had only a week or two to live. And now there he is quite strong and hearty! Of course he's mad as a hatter, but quite nice and gentle, I believe. He's simply Vanessa's slave, poor thing. And isn't it odd! Vera and Winifred Trent used to hate her, but since Vera died last year Winifred adores her. I must say Vanessa always had the power of making people fond of her. I always have loved her in spite of what she did. What is it about Vanessa? Perhaps you'll find out, Timothy. Because she's really dull and has no sense of humour at all. I must say she's very sporting. Right or wrong, Benjie's the love of her life and there they both are, eating their hearts out. Between you and me I wonder Benjie doesn't creep into Hill Street and poison Ellis. What's the good of his living? He's quite hopeless mentally, you know. Of course Vanessa's got Sally with her. She insisted on that. Her little girl and Benjie's. It always seems funny to me when Ellis, poor thing, has always been so proper and moral, that Vanessa's illegitimate child should be in his house under his roof. And I believe he's passionately fond of the child. Altogether very queer. Vanessa doesn't go out into society at all, but she likes people to go and see her. I go sometimes although Peile doesn't much like my doing it and I confess the place gives me the shudders.'

'Does she see Benjie?' Timothy asked.

'Oh yes, sometimes. There's nothing improper of course. The fact is, Timothy, they are the only example I know anywhere of real love. It's gone on all their lives and they're as much in love as ever they were. She's quite tamed Benjie. He used to be as wild as anything. It's a bit hard on him, isn't it? Separated from his child, too, but I believe he thinks it the right thing for Vanessa to do. They're an odd pair altogether.'

It happened that on the afternoon following the funeral Cynthia was giving a small children's party. For a brief while Timothy observed the ceremony; not for long – he detested children unless they were paintable. He was extremely sharp at catching character from face, voice, and movement. He had a number of young Herries under his eye (the coming upholders of the Herries tradition) and quickly decided that only one of them was beautiful (Mary Worcester of course) and only one charming – little Sally, Vanessa's daughter. He wondered for a moment that 'a little bastard' should be allowed in among all the true-born offspring, but decided that this was the Herries way of showing Vanessa that they had forgiven her.

The Herries children were: first Mary and Rosalind Worcester (Mary a gracious and lovely hostess; Rosalind clutching her friend little Ada Newmark – Horace's grandchild, the daughter of stout Sidney and stout Mary – and going off with her into a corner); the aforesaid Ada and her brother Gordon; Maurice and Clara, Alfred's children, plain, with good manners, but wanting the best for themselves. Mary, Rosalind, Ada, Gordon, Maurice and Clara: little ordinary Herries, all that they should be. It was amusing, he thought, as he watched, to notice the way in which these Herries children took command of the other children who were not Herries. Took command quite confidently, without arrogance or tiresome conceit, but quite as though it must be. And yet, with the notable exception of Mary, they were not very beautiful nor certainly were they brilliant. The Herries, he reflected, were never first class unless they were mad. 'I am not first class because I am not mad. Benjie, although he has never done anything with his life except love Vanessa, has something first class about him. A first-class passion for something outside oneself can make one first class. I have a passion for my Art. Why am I not first class? Because there is just enough Herries in me to prevent my escape from myself.'

Then he saw little Sally and went and talked to her. She was an odd-looking child, small with straight uncurling brown hair and a pale face. But she was all alive. She sat on a sofa and her eyes were everywhere, eager, merry, and very intelligent. She did not join in anything until she was invited, but she suffered from no self-consciousness. Little coloured balloons were handed round (they were to be blown across a tablecloth). Clara, Alfred's child, preferred the colour of Sally's balloon to her own and said so. Sally at once gave her hers, but Tim thought that she, at the same time, looked at her with a little baby irony as much as to say: 'You're like that, are you, even at your age' – a very elderly look for a child of six. 'But then,' thought Timothy, 'it will be odd if she isn't queer, born as she was and brought up in Hill Street.'

Next day he went and visited Benjie. London was very interesting to him. It was so long since he had stayed here. This was a great year for mechanical progress. The virtue of single planes advanced in a sudden leap the history of flying. In July, Blériot had crossed the Channel. In October there was a flying week at Blackpool and Mr Farman surprised everyone by flying for half an hour in wild and gusty weather.

But the great change in London was the advance of motor-cabs. Hitherto motoring had been mainly for the well-to-do. Now it was discovered that cabs could be made both cheaply and strongly. The new cabs, fitted with taximeters, were comfortable, safe, and the old uncertainty of the proper fare for the tiresome and truculent old cabby was gone. Only a little while before, motors had been the property of the rich: now, quite suddenly, they were everywhere. The whole aspect of the London streets was changed. It signified perhaps the final advent to assured power and importance of the middle classes.

Timothy felt this most emphatically during his evening ex-peditions about the town. He went everywhere: to the White City, to a first night at Wyndham's, or the Haymarket, or the St James's, to a dinner at the Savage Club, to the National Sporting Club, to the London Sketch Club, to a Sunday night at the New Lyric, and everywhere it was the same – the English Middle Class was now triumphant, subservient to nothing and nobody. The reign of the Autocrats in England was over. Sargent painted his Jew millionaires, Wells and Bennett invigorated the novel with their portraits of lower middle-class life. The word 'respect-able' had no longer any especial significance in English life. The ordinary man ruled England and he was determined to find pleasure where he could and hold to it. The ordinary man ruled England, and Herries were the ordinary man.

He found Benjie in three rooms of the upper part of a house in Tite Street, Chelsea. When he came in, Benjie was walking up and down. He was wearing an old grey jacket, grey flannel trousers, and a faded red tie. Tim was struck, more than ever, by his spareness, the fierceness of his blue eyes. He noticed that his hair was turning grey at the temples. He looked as though he had been lost in the desert and rescued in the nick of time. After half an hour's talk Tim felt that Benjie would, on the whole, have preferred that the rescue had not take place.

The room was very bare, but it had a broad bright window filled with scurrying clouds and a cold blue sky. Very shortly it would be dark. In the window was a long deal table with Vanessa's photograph (a very old one), a book which Tim picked up and found to be Hudson's *Purple Land,* some writing paper, a pen, and a long truculent-looking ruler. On the walls there was nothing save over the fireplace two grinning masks made of some dark wood. There were two shabby armchairs.

Tim knew Benjie well. In the very old days when he had gone over to Paris with Tom, Benjie had been his saviour. He had protected him against the Family. Tim, who was faithful, would stick to Benjie always because of that, were there no other reason. But there *were* other reasons, plenty of them. He liked Benjie because he was honest, generous, courageous, and his own worst enemy. Benjie had one charming quality, and a very rare one it is. He always, whatever his own personal melodramas, wanted to hear about the adventures of his friends. This was not from self-conscious duty nor from a desire to be kind. He was truly interested.

So Timothy told him – about Mlle Thérèse, his stout but charming mistress, about his new flat, about the portrait he was painting of the two little girls of the Minister of Finance, about his picking up a charming Berthe Morisot for almost nothing, of English writers whom he had met in Paris – Somerset Maugham and Arnold Bennett ('both interested in painting – very odd'), about this and that.

'And you?' he asked at last.

'Oh – I?' Benjie sat on the deal table, swinging his legs. 'I go on – as you see.'

Tim was aware, at that moment, just as a rather slatternly white-haired woman brought in the tea, that he was encountering some experience so deep and poignant that he was frightened of it. He was frightened of very little; he was certainly not frightened of Benjie. But there was something here that belonged to that rarest of all worlds – the world of absolute and positive experience. 'Because,' he thought, 'we all live one skin deep at the most. We do not, most of us, know that we can go deeper.'

So to ease things he himself talked.

'I've been observing the Family. I haven't seen it, you know, for a long time. Coming along very nicely, I should say. It ostracized me once and now it welcomes me because I'm a moderate success. I'm not exactly prejudiced in its favour. But we've

settled down. All the quarrels are over. All the same there are a
few rebels left, but they're not so grand as they used to be.' Then
he said an incautious thing. 'But I tell you what, Benjie – your
daughter's going to be a rebel. You should have seen her with the
rest of them. It persists, the divine strain. How I wish I had more
of it!'

Benjie jumped to the floor.

'You've seen Sally – where? when?'

'Oh, yesterday – at a children's party at Cynthia's.'

'Did you talk to her? She's remarkable, isn't she? Unusual?'

'Yes, I talked to her a little. I loathe children's parties, you
know. Certainly she's unusual. I was saying so.'

'I see her, you know.' Benjie came and sat down close to him,
bending eagerly forward. 'Quite often. In fact I can see her as
often as I like so long as I never go to the house. Odd situation,
isn't it?'

'Very,' said Timothy, terribly touched by his friend's emotion,
thinking, too of the old Benjie who had been a wandering kind of
rascal with no very constant attachment.

'Have you been to see Vanessa, Tim?'

'No, not yet. Do you think she would like to see me?'

'Of course she would. And you must go soon. Then come and
tell me about it.'

'Tell you about it?'

'Yes. Vanessa and I meet sometimes. Not too often or it would
be unbearable. But I never enter the house of course. And I don't
ask her about the house. When we are together in fact we don't
talk very much. Talking seems to waste the time. The only one
who told me much about what it was like inside was old Barney.
And now he's gone. Adrian goes there, but Adrian's a prig. The
rest of the family don't see much of me, you know.'

'I see,' said Timothy. 'Of course I'll go if she won't think it
impertinent.'

'Oh no, she'll love it. Especially if you tell her you've been
here. You'll have to repeat every word of our conversation, you
know.'

Tim said slowly: 'It's all damned hard on you.'

Benjie answered quickly: 'It's far worse for her. You see, the
bad part of it is that we were having such a marvellous time just
before he wanted her. And we thought it was only for a month or
two. Now it's been close on three years, and God knows how
much longer!'

'Well, if you want my opinion,' Timothy broke out, 'I think

the whole thing's preposterous! There are you, two people in the prime of life, loving one another, and on the other side Ellis who's too mad to know whether she's there or no.'

'You're wrong,' Benjie said quietly. 'Know? Why, she's his very life! He worships her. If she left him it would be like leaving a helpless child, and worse than that, because she married him. She only left him because he *didn't* want her. No, there's no other way – until Ellis dies. She would never be happy for a moment if she came away. Not that she's happy as it is, but she's got Sally.'

'And you?' Tim asked.

'Oh, I? Don't mind about me. Don't think I'm being noble either. I'm not. I curse like hell. I'd hate him if – if he were normal. As it is one can't hate anyone in the affair, more's the pity. Oh, I'm all right. I go abroad sometimes. There's Tom here for company and he's so kind that I could kill him. I'm working at a job too. I go to a travel agency every day and advise people about foreign parts. Sometimes I go wild for a day or two. I've got some awful friends, you know. But I'm never wild for long nor away for long. I come slinking back because Vanessa's here.'

'I'm glad you love her so much,' Tim said. 'Anyone's in luck to have the chance of the real thing.'

'Love her?' He threw his head back. 'Did you ever know our real story, Tim? No. Well, I'm not going to bore you with it. But we loved one another from childhood. We meant to marry. First her father died – was burnt in the fire at Uldale. That stopped it. Then – imagine it! – I married someone else! Fantastic? Not at all. My cursed imbecility that has made me do the wrong thing at the wrong time all my life. But listen. However wild I've been, however caught she's been – caught in a trap, because that's what her marriage to Ellis was – we've never ceased to love one another for a single moment. At the very instant of making love to another woman I've always known it was only Vanessa I loved. And the best time we ever had was just before we parted. And now we'll never be free of one another – I doubt if death can part us. And yet when I say that, how ridiculous, how sentimental! Hasn't every lover always said the same? But we are such *old* lovers! It goes far beyond the body – beyond – into what? Is it simply association, all that we have been through together? Vanessa isn't very clever. She isn't any longer very beautiful. But she's *lovely*, Tim. She never falters, she never lets you down, she has a childish pleasure in tiny things, she's generous, loyal, and although she thinks she's a coward, she never flinches at anything. And yet it's only a little for her character that I love her. One doesn't love people for their character, does one? Or only a little. Why? Why? Why are Vanessa and I bound together? Is she right, do you think? Is there a spiritual life that outlasts the bodily? Will Vanessa and I go on together, never apart, loving one another? ... Sometimes when I sit alone in here at night, hearing the mouse in the wall and seeing those masks grin, knowing that she's there and I here – such a little distance – I begin to believe that I can pull her spirit in here with me, her body there in Hill Street. I could swear that she comes in, sits with her head against my knee as she used to do in Cumberland – is this mad, Tim, do you think? Am I going queer a bit? Do I *look* queer?'

'No, Benjie, not in the least. Only it's bad for both of you, I should think, separated like this and yet so near to one another. Lord! I wish I loved someone like that, though! Or do I? It's a terrible strain. One can't work if one's always wanting someone ...'

He waited a while, then he said abruptly:

'Do you ever read history, Benjie?'

'History? No. Oh, I've read Macaulay and a bit of Froude—'

'You *should* read history. There's nothing so interesting. History or biography. A nation or a family or an individual – it's all the same. The point is that men's values are all wrong. The things that they *think* are happening aren't happening at all. Do you remember Tolstoi's *Anna Karénina* and the racecourse scene? Everyone *thought* that the racing was the important thing. It wasn't in the least. It was the struggle in the hearts of Anna and Karénin and Vronsky. Yes, and in thousands of other souls that day. Little temptations to meanness, lusts, sacrifices. Small tests, tests as small as a pin – but soul histories are the only histories. Write an account of a family or a county and find out where the crises of the human spirit lie. See how it meets all the tests, is beaten, is victorious, encounters its two chief enemies, greed and fear, is encouraged to extend into something wider, grander, nobler than itself. Shakespeare knew that that was the only kind of history. What are the stories of his six great kings but soul histories? What does he care for national history? It is Richard in his tent, Henry praying before the battle, the old king dying in Westminster ... I'm not religious, you know. I can't swear to heaven. I don't know whether there are pearly gates. And I'm not given to preaching. But I do know that you've got the only thing that matters, Benjie. You can feed your soul with an unselfish passion. You're not starving it. You should see old Monet painting. He's like an eagle beating his wings for joy that he's free, gross, fat old man that he is! To escape beyond oneself! To lose one's soul because one's beyond fear, and so to save it. That's the history of the endeavour of every man and woman born on this earth. The only thing that gives us grandeur, fleas on a cinder as we are!'

Benjie smiled.

'I've never heard you talk like that before.'

'No. I'm growing old. I've faced up to the fact that I shall never be the painter I hoped to be, never meet the woman I hoped to meet. We all do. I'm just of the age. I hold my tongue. I haven't talked like this for an age. The French are a cynical people, you know. All the same it's a marvel to me that men can refuse so obstinately to think of the only things that really matter. We'll suffer for it. We're bound to. Well, I must go.'

He raised his long thin body, pulled at his pale corn-coloured beard, stretched his arms and yawned.

'You're going to see Vanessa, aren't you?'

'Yes – tomorrow.'

'And you'll come and see me again?'

'I'll come and see you again.'

When he was gone Benjie sat down and wrote to Vanessa.

Next day Tim went to Hill Street. An old butler with face like a muffin, plump, boneless, without shape, received him and led him upstairs. In the long drawing-room Vanessa was entertaining Mary Newmark, wife of Sidney, old Horace's son. Mary Newmark was fat in a bright, cheerful way. She wore a dress of shining blue and she had a large hat with blue feathers. Under the hat her face, like a gigantic strawberry, beamed on the world. Beside her Vanessa, who was dressed in black, looked very quiet. But Tim was surprised. He had expected her to be grave and a little ceremonious. Not at all. She was extremely human. He could see that she was bored with Mary Newmark, who quite clearly had no idea of it. Mary was one of those women who, without any arrogance, feel that their presence is a benefit to all concerned. She was also convinced that any statement, any opinion on her part, was of the first importance.

Tim saw that Vanessa was surprised to see him and greatly

pleased. Mary Newmark was flustered a little; artists were to her strange creatures: moreover Timothy lived in Paris. She was plainly determined to be kind to him whatever he might have done.

'No, don't send for more tea,' he said. 'This is splendid. If it's stewed I like it stewed.'

'I was telling Vanessa,' Mary Newmark began, 'that Sidney and I disapprove totally of the Suffragettes.'

'Why?' asked Timothy.

'The proper place for women is the home. I don't want a vote. What would I do with one?'

As Timothy was about to speak she shook a finger at him.

'Now, Mr Bellairs, I know you're an artist and have, I'm sure, all sorts of queer ideas. But if women don't look after their homes, who will?'

'Perhaps the men will,' said Timothy.

'Men!' said Mary Newmark gaily. 'Would you like to know what I think about men?'

'Very much,' said Timothy.

'Men are children. Nothing but children. They never grow up. Once learn that about a man and you never have any more trouble.'

'Well, then, isn't it wrong if men are only children that they should have all the say in governing the country? If women are so much wiser—'

'Ah, that's just it,' said Mary Newmark with complete self-confidence. 'Women *are* much cleverer, but their proper place is behind the scenes, influencing the men. Sidney doesn't know it, but there's not a thought in his head that doesn't come from me.' She beamed on the world. 'I've no use at all for all this modern nonsense, nor has Sidney. Modern books, modern pictures, modern women – I don't mean anything personal, Mr Bellairs. I'm sure you paint very nice pictures – very pleasant, I'm sure, but what was good enough for my mother is good enough for me. What modern writers have we to compare with Charles Dickens? Answer me that now.'

'It would be a great pity, wouldn't it,' said Timothy, 'if we had Dickens over and over again? One Dickens, yes – but a hundred Dickenses!'

'Well, I don't know, I'm sure. I've certainly read *David Copperfield* over and over – my favourite bits, you know. Sidney reads aloud to me in the evenings in Manchester.'

The door opened and Sally came in. She stood for a moment, hesitating and smiling. Then she came forward.

'Say how do you do to Mrs Newmark, darling.'

'How do you do?' said Sally.

'And to Mr Bellairs. You met him the other day, you know.'

'How do you do?' said Sally, grinning.

Mary Newmark drew Sally forward and spoke to her in the voice she considered suitable to children, a voice she also used for little dogs.

'Well, darling? And what have you been doing today?'

'I've done my lessons and I've been for a walk.'

'That's a good little girl. And where did you go for a walk?'

'I went in Kensington Gardens.'

'And what did you see there?'

'Oh, nothing particular.'

Mrs Newmark pinched her cheek, a thing that she considered children adored.

'And what lessons have you done today?'

This was frightful. Vanessa intervened.

'At present she has lessons with me. I'm not a very good teacher, I'm afraid.'

There was silence. Sally was looking at Mrs Newmark with a smile that in some undefined way she felt to be sarcastic. A strange child, with her peaked face and dark brown hair. She was suddenly uncomfortable. The house was so very silent and the painter not very friendly. Moreover, there was Ellis somewhere and at any moment he might break in. How unpleasant that would be! Whenever she was uncomfortable she moved on. She moved on now.

'I'm afraid I must be going, Vanessa dear. It *has* been delightful. You must come and see us before we go back to Manchester. Goodbye, Mr Bellairs. Don't become *too* modern in your painting!' She kissed Sally and sailed away. Halfway down the stairs she stopped a moment to listen whether she could hear Ellis moving about. There was no sound anywhere.

After she had gone they all three sat on the sofa together. Timothy had at once noticed that there was a strong and deep alliance between the mother and the child. When Sally moved and spoke it was as though Vanessa moved and spoke with her. Now Sally sat beside her mother; they sat hand in hand. They made no allusion at all to Mrs Newmark. Their feelings about her were identical. They were all three very happy and confidential together.

'Now, darling, you must go to bed.'

Sally got up from the sofa. She sighed.

'Don't you wish you hadn't to go to bed?' she asked Timothy.

'I love my bed,' he answered. 'It's the best place there is.'

She looked at him sharply to see whether he were speaking the truth. She decided that he was.

'When I'm older I shall go to bed only once a week — every Friday.'

'Why Friday?'

'Because Saturday's a nice day and Thursday's a nice day, but Friday's horrid.'

She lifted her face to be kissed.

'I'll come up and see you, darling,' Vanessa said.

She walked away rather sadly. At the door she looked back and smiled.

Vanessa looked at the door for a moment after it closed. Then she turned back.

'It was extraordinarily nice of you to come and see me.'

There was something young about her, Timothy thought, and eager. She was not dull as he had half expected to find her. She had lived, he knew, for years in lonely country but she was not dowdy. Her wide clear forehead, her grey hair parted in the middle, the severity of her black dress, her breadth and height, gave her massiveness, but he had an unexpected conviction that she was younger than he, years and years younger.

'It's very strange,' Vanessa said, 'but I've never set eyes on you since you were a small boy. I can see you now sitting up in an open carriage dressed like little Lord Fauntleroy and hating it.'

'Yes, I did hate it. And I'm afraid I hated my mother too for making a show of me.'

'No — but when you were such wonderful friends with Tom and Benjie ... it's absurd that we should never have met! You were with Benjie yesterday!' she added quickly.

'Yes. How did you know?'

'I had a letter from him this morning, telling me about your visit. He writes and tells me if anything especially nice has happened. How was he? How was he looking?'

'Rather thin, I thought. No spare flesh.'

'No. I saw him last a fortnight ago. I wish he'd eat more. He doesn't look after himself.'

And then, in front of him, her face in a moment aged. She was sitting quietly, her hands folded on her lap, but he felt that behind her serenity she was enduring to the limit of everything: one burden more and she would break. He was a man who found life in general amusing and absurd rather than dramatic, but he was very sharply aware of the drama now being played in front of him – this long chill room, the house beyond it where Ellis was playing at soldiers or nursing a doll, Benjie in Tite Street, and all the Family moving like figures in a wavering tapestry as a frame to the scene. Vanessa, he thought, must be fifty or more and yet he had, at that moment, as urgent a longing to help her to escape as though she were a lovely girl of twenty!

'Benjie tells me,' she went on, 'that he talked about me – about us. Do – do you think— Do you think that it is all getting to be more than he can stand? I mean – oughtn't I perhaps to *make* him go away, to insist on it? Perhaps, away from me, he would find someone—'

'There's nothing you can do. He will never be able to go away. He will never find someone else.'

'I don't want him to go away, you know.' She smiled again. 'I think I'd die if he did. Oh, don't fancy that I'm pitying myself. I have him and Tom – and Sally of course. Don't you like Sally?'

'I do indeed. She's very unusual.'

'Yes, she is, isn't she? And – I'm telling you everything because you have been Benjie's friend so long and of course that makes you mine. Ellis . . . I have grown fond of him. No one could help it. He needs me, and he is so docile and so affectionate. So different from what he was. But of course it's not a good house for Sally to grow up in. It's not healthy here, although she's too young to understand things and behaves to Ellis as though he were her brother. I thought at first that I would keep them apart, but Sally made that impossible. She goes to him quite naturally, never seems to think it strange that an old man of sixty-six should play with dolls and soldiers. Perhaps she knows more than we think. Children may be much wiser than we suppose.'

'You are all, it seems to me,' said Timothy, 'behaving very finely.'

'Oh no, we're not! I don't see how we could behave otherwise. And I myself am not fine at all. Often I long for Ellis to die. Sometimes I feel that I *cannot* keep away from Benjie any longer. You see, we thought that it would only be for a month or two. Already it has been nearly three years . . .' She hesitated, looking down at her lap. 'The hardest part of it has been that in Cum-

berland, just before we separated, Benjie and I were happier than
ever before.'

'I know. Benjie told me.'

'Oh, did he tell you? I'm so very glad.' She went on: 'You must
think this all very sentimental, Timothy. Two old people like
Benjie and me both pouring out our hearts to you.'

'Only false things are sentimental,' Timothy said. 'And this
isn't false, Vanessa. Your grandmother, Judith Paris, wouldn't
have thought so. I gather that she was anything but sentimental.'

'No – she wouldn't have thought it false. I so often think of
her and sometimes feel as if she were here helping us both. I still
have a tiny tea-set she gave me when I was a little girl, and it
seems only yesterday that I climbed on to her bed and kissed her.'

There was a pause. He got up to go.

'I must be moving on. I'm so glad that we have met, and if
there is anything I can do, Vanessa, I always will. You can count
on me. I've got every weakness except infidelity.'

'Yes; Benjie always says that you are one of the most faithful
people in the world.'

Before he went he said, rather shyly:

'Look here! Don't let this be too much of a strain on you. One
can only stand so much, you know. Oughtn't you to go out
more?'

'Go out?'

'Yes, be gay a little – go to theatres and see the sights.'

'Oh, I do go out. And I've had so much of that in the past. But
it's all right. I'm perfectly happy.'

With that brave challenge in her ears he left the house, but for
several days he could not get her out of his mind.

When he had gone, Vanessa went up to say goodnight to Sally.
She was in bed waiting. Vanessa sat on the bed and Sally lay
within her arm, very contentedly, her eyes smiling.

'Mummy, Mrs Newmark *is* a funny lady!' (It was like Sally to
have the surname quite clearly and accurately.)

'In what way funny, darling?'

'She thinks children silly. They aren't, are they?'

'Sometimes.'

'Well, not like *that*, anyway.'

Soon she was asleep.

Then Vanessa went to Ellis. The upper part of the house had

now been made into a suite for him. He had a sitting-room, bedroom and bathroom of his own. The sitting-room was large, with high windows looking out on to chimney pots and sky. On the table was a large bowl with chrysanthemums (he loved flowers). Near the flowers was a big wooden fort with guns and soldiers. In one armchair an elaborate doll, dressed in blue silk, was lolling.

Ellis himself was sitting, when she came in, very busy with one of those puzzles the point of which is that little black balls should roll into little silver holes. He was bending over this, shaking it, holding it very still, shaking it again. He looked very old. His thin hair was white now, his shoulders very bent. He had the almost waxen cleanliness of a patient who is constantly washed and brushed by others.

'Oh, Vanessa!' he cried, when he saw her. 'I'm so glad you've come. I've been trying to do this for ever so long. As soon as one's in another rolls out.'

She sat down beside him and took the puzzle. He watched her as she manipulated it, with the eager attention of a dog who is waiting for you to throw a ball.

Soon all the little black balls were in the little silver holes. He clapped his hands.

'Oh, that's lovely! Now shake it! Now I'll see if I can do it!' She sat there quietly beside him.

He put the puzzle down.

'I'm very hungry,' he said.

'Your dinner will be coming very soon, dear.'

'What do you think it will be?'

'I don't know. Something nice.'

'Marmalade pudding?'

'Perhaps.'

'Oh, I hope so.' He sighed, laying his head against his hand. She put her arm around him.

'Did you have a nice drive?' she asked him.

'We saw some soldiers.'

'Was there a band?'

'No. There wasn't a band. I wish we could have a band – here in this room. Wouldn't it make a fine noise?' He sighed again. 'My head aches.'

'It's the weather, Ellis dear. It's been very close all day. My head's been aching all day.'

'Has it?' He put his hand up and stroked her forehead and

then her cheek. He loved to do that. At first she had shrunk from it. His hand was dry and hot and his fingernails very white, like a dead man's nails. But now it moved her strangely when he made any demonstration. And once, years and years ago, he had wanted to kill her! How queer!

With the abrupt restlessness that was characteristic of him he got up and fetched the doll from the chair.

'I've dressed and undressed her three times today,' he said. 'She doesn't seem to mind.' He gave her to Vanessa. 'Will you play for me tonight, Vanessa?'

In the corner of the room was a small piano. Vanessa did not play very well – only old and simple things, old songs, hymns tunes, waltzes. He loved her to play. He could sit for hours watching her.

'Yes, of course, dear. I'll come up when I've had my dinner.'

He was delighted.

'Oh, how nice! Play the one with mice in the can.'

'Yes, I'll play that one.'

'And the one with armies marching.'

'Yes, dear.'

She put her arm around him and he lay back against her with his eyes closed.

After a while Winifred Trent came in. She was very thin and her pale long face was covered with wrinkles.

'I think dinner is ready, Vanessa. I'll stay with Ellis while he has his.'

A gong sounded from below. Winifred Trent said every evening this same sentence.

'Thank you, Winifred.' Vanessa got up. She kissed Ellis and went downstairs.

The dining-room seemed very large and empty. Rodd, the butler with a face like a muffin, waited on her.

'Sole, my lady?'

'Thank you, Rodd.'

She sat staring in front of her. Suddenly she smiled. Benjie had enjoyed Timothy's visit. He would be happier today.

'Brussels sprouts, my lady?'

'Thank you, Rodd.'

After Ellis was in bed she would write to Benjie and tell him about Timothy's visit.

WHITE WITH SWANS

ONE night early in 1912, Vanessa woke and was assured that
she was about to die. She was conscious of no especial pain, only
a scantness of breath and a general faintness. Dimly, as though
she were many miles away, she realized that the early morning
light, very cold and thin, laid ghostly shadows on the floor. She
heard a sparrow twitter.

But so certain was she that the end had come that she felt that
she must write something to Benjie, saying goodbye, telling him
to be good to Sally ... but she found that she had no wish to
make the slightest movement. She lay there, her eyes fixed on the
ceiling upon whose dark surface some strange light, thin and
bright like a lustre bowl, seemed to hover. Her brain was quite
clear. For months past she had known that her energy was leaving her as water trickles from a cistern. Until less than three years
ago (she could fix the time exactly, for the change had come
when Timothy Bellairs, the painter, had paid her a visit and,
turning to her, had said: 'Don't let this be too much of a strain on
you') her resistance had been equal to the struggle. But after that
day (she remembered that when Timothy had gone she had been
up and said goodnight to Sally, had visited Ellis and dined
downstairs alone, and Rodd had said 'Brussels sprouts, my
lady') something had snapped. Her nobility had gone, she supposed. Lying now, about to pass away altogether from this silly
business, she could summarize the past clearly and without sentiment. Her nobility had gone. She no longer, after that day,
wanted to play her part. What she wanted was for Ellis to die and
then, for herself, that she should go to Benjie and never again, for
one single moment, night or day, leave him.

She seemed after this (it was as though she were now speaking
to God Himself, for life was over and He would understand) to
be without scruples and yet to be tied with scruples. She was now
quite shameless and, in intention, had already left Ellis and was
somewhere safe in Cumberland with Benjie, but in fact of course
she did nothing of the kind.

For three more years she did as she had already done; nursed
Ellis, played her part, ached (oh God, how her heart had ached!)
for Benjie, and there it was. But whereas in the first three years

she had acted as she did because she thought it right, in the second three she acted as she did because she had to. She could not leave Ellis because he was so helpless, but her heart became a strange confusion of disgust and misery and longing and sheer exhausted weariness.

The effort was becoming always more frightful, and not only for herself but also for Benjie. For one whole year he went abroad. They wrote and met when he was in London. They poured their very souls into their letters. But the longing became too great. He returned, thin as a stick, new lines of age and perhaps of bitterness in his face. During this last year they met more and more often, but always as though, at the very moment of meeting, they must part. As for Ellis, nothing ailed him, and Vanessa was his very life. Then Winifred Trent died. Six months ago a chill had carried her off. Before she died she said to Vanessa: 'You've been wonderful,' and Vanessa, although she had grown to be fond of Winifred Trent, had a terrible impulse to tell Winifred Trent a number of coarse truths . . .

After that strength had ebbed from her. She woke weary; she went to bed too tired to sleep. And Ellis grew stronger and stronger in the body. He liked her to play to him on the little piano by the hour. Well, now she was going to die and the whole thing would be over. She thought of Benjie and Sally and Tom, and summoned them to her side.

To Benjie she said: 'My darling, my beloved, this can't separate . . .'

To Tom: 'Thank you for looking after me, Tom dear. Mary Worcester isn't worth it . . .'

And to Sally: 'Don't forget me. Have a good life, darling . . .'

Then it seemed to her that her heart ceased to beat. She thought of God as very near to her. She clasped her hands and began the Lord's Prayer . . .

A moment later apparently Janet, the maid, came in, carrying the tea, drawing the blinds. So she had not died!

She lay there, drank her tea.

'What kind of day is it, Janet?'

'Nice and bright, my lady.'

Then Janet said:

'You don't look very well this morning, my lady. Have your breakfast in bed. Do now.'

(Janet had from the first, two years ago, been very friendly, maternal, and comforting.)

'Oh no, Janet. I must get up. I didn't sleep very well.'

'What a shame! I should stay the morning in bed, my lady.'

And she did. She was surprised at herself. Sally came in to say goodbye to her before departing to her school in Kensington. She had her luncheon with Ellis in his room.

But, after this, the obsession remained with her that she had not long to live.

One evening she was gay: that is, she went with Cynthia, Philip Rochester and Horace Ormerod to the first night of a new play. It was Tuesday, March 5th – Cynthia's birthday – and they had a very charming dinner first at Claridge's. Cynthia was very coy about her age, Horace hearty and hopeful, and Philip – who painted his face so cleverly that you wouldn't notice it unless you were a woman – was most witty at the expense of all his nearest and dearest.

'But I thought you liked Humphrey Bell!' Cynthia said, when Philip had just intimated that Humphrey cheated at cards and beat his mistresses.

'Oh, so I do! I *adore* Humphrey! He's a perfect pet! I know he wouldn't mind a *word* I've been saying!'

'Well, I'm not so sure,' observed Cynthia.

How very old, Vanessa thought, Philip was! He was all Dowsonish and Wildeish. And how long ago was that buried age with its glittering surface and tinkling music box echoes! The time when she had been a hostess and driven in the Park, had tea with Mrs Langtry in that extraordinarily cosy drawing-room, breathing that lovely lady's good-nature and kindness of heart. It had been a cosy, good-natured time – yes, and an enterprising one too! Now – what was the matter? – everyone was restless, uneasy; nothing seemed secure. She herself felt shabby, an old owl not used to the light. She sat in the back of the box with Horace, feeling a little faint, longing for Cumberland and Benjie and the Newlands farm . . .

The play seemed to answer some of her questions. It was called *Milestones* and was by Arnold Bennett and Edward Knoblock. The little Royalty Theatre contained that night many celebrated persons. The customary first-night remark was made that if a bomb were dropped on the theatre . . . In fact, all the customary first-night remarks were made. Mr Knoblock was discerned sitting in a box with his sister. Famous persons were observed, commented upon. But it was not, as it happened, a first night quite like other first nights. It was, in itself, a Milestone. This passing of time, this blindness of each generation to the significant things, the battle between the helpless imaginative and the confident unimaginative.

'Why, these are Herries!' Vanessa thought. 'These are our very selves!'

And then Haidée Wright's brilliant passionate Aunt was simply Judith Paris come to life. She seemed to Vanessa to be living there on the stage in front of her. She was eternal, immortal, as Judith was. That little figure, her voice trembling with her vitality and courage, dominated not only the theatre but the world beyond it. 'So Judith still dominates us all.' In the last Act an actress made a great success. She was extremely beautiful, and Vanessa, who had never seen her before, searched her programme. Her name was Gladys Cooper. There was something in her self-confidence and scorn of sentiment that spoke of the future. 'Will Sally be like that? Not so beautiful of course, but brave, scornful of anything that seems to her unreal?' Everyone in the theatre that night was thinking a little as Vanessa. How time passes and we don't know it! We are at the mercy of forces greater than ourselves. What if these forces grow stronger than we? What if we become their slaves? A wind of insecurity blew through the theatre that night. The actors seemed like figures in a Morality.

In the second interval, Cynthia and Philip went out to greet some friends. In the back of the box, Vanessa and Horace talked. Vanessa had never liked Horace before, but tonight he touched her sympathy. His wife had died in the preceding year. He said that he was very lonely. This big heavy man with the protruding chin, the shining forehead, the gleaming glasses, was suddenly a small and very unprotected schoolboy.

'I suppose it's my own fault,' he said. 'I'm sure I've always done my best, looked on the bright side, been cheerful very often when I really didn't feel it, but people don't want you to be cheerful and kind and jolly. They like you much better if you're sour and cynical. The fact is, I know it, people get bored with me. There was a woman once, Vanessa, whom I loved to distraction. I'd have done anything for her. For a month or so it was like heaven – it was really. I thought she loved me passionately. One weekend she went to Eastbourne and wrote me two of the most wonderful letters. Beautiful they were. And then, one night, she was to dine with me in my flat. I was all ready and waiting. I'd ordered the most beautiful little dinner. But instead of coming herself she sent a letter – a short, curt note saying that she was afraid she couldn't see me any more. She was very sorry. She had thought about it and decided that it wasn't right her seeing me and so on. But I knew that *that* wasn't the reason. It was simply that she was bored with me. And yet I'd always done my best.'

'You'd spoilt her, I expect,' said Vanessa.

'No. I'd done what any other man would have done. She found me a bore. Yes, it's very strange. People like you if you're cruel and malicious. I've never been cruel in my life to anyone.'

'Would you mind, Horace,' Vanessa said, 'getting me a glass of water? I feel rather faint.'

When he returned with one he had something he wanted to say. It was about Rose. He had seen Rose that very afternoon.

'Oh, Rose!' Vanessa exclaimed. 'Quick, Horace, tell me! I have written to her and had no answer. Once a letter from Madrid, a short one, telling me nothing.'

'I've seen her from time to time,' Horace said. 'Of course it's been very painful. But she was always determined that you shouldn't see her. It's been the one thing that she resolved. She was ashamed . . .'

'Oh no,' Vanessa cried. 'She shouldn't have been. I'm her friend. Quick, Horace, they're coming back. Where is she now? Is she in London?'

'Yes, that's why I told you. She's very ill. She's going to have a serious operation. This is her address. I've written it down.'

(Poor old Horace. Not such a bad fellow – or at any rate not so bad in old age and loneliness, much more bearable in misfortune.)

Cynthia and Philip came into the box. Vanessa had the address. She thought, as the curtain went up – 'They've forgiven me. They consider me respectable again. But Rose they have pushed down and down . . .'

On the following afternoon she found her way to the street in Bloomsbury. It was a fine March day with gay light clouds hurrying like ballerinas across the chimney pots. The pigeons fluttered on the steps of the Museum, and there was a sniff of spring in the air.

Rose's room was at the very top of the thin grey house and, halfway up, Vanessa felt once more her faintness, had to pause while the stairs slowly rose and fell and a grimy window bent anxiously towards her. At last she was there. She knocked on the door and went in. Rose was sitting, a shawl over her shoulders, before a grumbling, sulky fire. The room was stuffy and had the smell of a not very clean blanket.

'Oh! Vanessa!' Rose cried out.

Vanessa bent down and they embraced as though they would never let one another go. Rose cried a little, wiping her eyes with a rather soiled handkerchief. Then she brightened. She was fearfully thin and her complexion was a pale and dry yellow. She was wearing a shabby blue skirt and faded silver slippers. She held Vanessa's hand.

'At last I told Horace that you might come and see me. I wouldn't hear of it before. But my number's up at last and I had to have one last glimpse of you before I met St Peter.'

'I've tried to see you—'

'Yes, I know. I've been abroad. Here, let's have a look at you!'

She took Vanessa by the shoulder and held her off so that she might see her.

'This bloody gas! It isn't very gay, is it? But we don't run to electric light here yet. Well, my dear, you don't look any too grand yourself, if I may say so. You're a fine big woman, of course – always were. But you look as though you hadn't had any sleep for a month.'

'I haven't been sleeping very well, but never mind me. What about yourself? What's the matter, Rose darling?'

'Oh, the wages of sin. As a matter of fact it's cancer and that's the plain truth. Old Furry-Face the doctor says, "Only a little internal trouble. We'll have you right in no time." But *I* know. You can't cheat me. I'm starving to death and I'm sick of it. Horace has been a brick, though. He's paying for the nursing home, insists on it although I tell him any old ditch will do to die in.'

'But, Rose, you're wrong. I'm sure you are! After all, they know—'

'Wrong my foot! You can't kid me. Now look here, my dear, now you *are* here! I want to know everything. How *are* you? How's Benjie? How much longer are you going on in this ridiculous way?'

Vanessa told her something of her life, ending up: 'You see, we thought that it wouldn't be so long. It's been five years.'

'And Benjie and you eating your hearts out! Well, I think it's a bit of sentimental tosh! Giving yourself up heart, soul and body to someone who'd be just as happy with any nurse—'

'No,' Vanessa said. 'You're wrong there. I might have left him, perhaps, if he hadn't needed me. Because it hasn't been fair on Benjie. But he *does* need me. Every year it has been more impossible to leave him.'

'And now you're killing yourself! Oh, I know! It's draining all the strength out of you. I can see it. And here we are, the two of us! You've done the virtuous thing. I've done the other! Not much to choose . . .'

They talked about old times. Rose never let Vanessa's hand go. Her clutch was hot and feverish.

'You needn't be afraid, Vanessa. It's all over. There's no drunken Major coming in. Even my taste for drink has gone. I was in Madrid three years. Yes, a Professor kept me – a very nice little man he was, with a curly black beard and a wife he couldn't stand the sight of. I was fond of him. I truly was. That's a funny thing. In spite of the life I've led I haven't got tired of wanting to be fond of men – really fond of them, mend their clothes, put their buttons on, that sort of thing. Then I get tired of them. Domestic one minute, restless the next. But virtue's got nothing to do with it. I've never felt more virtuous than when I've been doing my worst . . . There was a young fellow from College once went off with me. Pretty well broke his mother's heart, too. We went on a trip to Scotland. We stopped at Keswick. I wanted to have a look at it, and there it was, same as ever – St John's spire and the square with the clock. We went down to the Lake the night we arrived and I can hear the water lapping against the jetty now. And Friar's Crag. We went on to Friar's Crag and the boy talked about Ruskin. Well, you never saw a more virtuous pair than we were that trip, reading Shelley and wondering whether there was a God and picking flowers . . . and I suppose I never did a wickeder thing than taking that young man away. Funny, isn't it? This morality! Very vexed question, if you ask me!'

After a while she asked Vanessa:

'Why do you love Benjie so, Vanessa? I've never loved anyone like that. You're the only one I've loved all my life long and you're a woman. Why do you love him so?'

'Oh, I don't know,' said Vanessa. 'He's everything I want in a man. You should ask rather why he loves me. I often tell him he should have a gay, lively woman, witty, and quick to see things. There's *one* reason I love him, I think. I can see his jokes. It used to be terrible in the old days in Hill Street when I didn't see a joke and had to pretend I did. But Benjie and I find one another amusing. We're comic to one another. That's a good reason for love.'

They fell into silence. Vanessa thought that Rose had fallen asleep. At last it was time for her to go.

'Rose darling – are you looked after here? Is there anyone to care for you?'

'Oh yes, it isn't so bad. The woman's quite decent. And I'm going to the nursing home tomorrow. You'll come and see me there, won't you?'

Vanessa promised. She looked back at the door and saw Rose's eyes – hungry, shining, feverish – fixed upon her. She went slowly away.

She visited Rose every day in the nursing home. A week later Rose had her operation and three days after that she died. She was worn out, the doctor said. Injudicious living in the past ... yes ... sad ... but, as a matter of fact, there would have been no hope. She could not have recovered.

Vanessa was happy for her sake. That was the way that she would have wished it.

Meanwhile the Family watched Vanessa with curiosity. She went round paying visits on everybody exactly as though she were going away somewhere.

Cynthia and May Rockage (who was in London just then) and stout Mary Newmark, putting their heads together, decided that she was going off with Benjie again. She was gay, light-hearted and extraordinarily kind. She said some odd things. She said to Cynthia: 'I can't get that play *Milestones* out of my head. Do you remember the girl in the last Act saying, "Please remember that we're in the year 1912"? Isn't it funny to think that for Sally, one day, 1912 will be as old-fashioned as 1812? Doesn't it make you feel queer?'

'Not in the least,' said Cynthia.

'Oh, well, then – doesn't it seem odd to you that my grandmother probably said, "Please remember that we're in the year 1812"?'

'Not in the least. Your grandmother lived to be a hundred.'

'Oh, I know. That isn't what I mean. What I mean is that people are more important than time. What I mean is that my father, who was a darling, once said in his garden on Cat Bells: "Look, Vanessa! There's the squirrel again!" That, my relationship to him, our love for one another, all of it comes back as I think of that sentence: it isn't dead, it isn't gone. He's alive because we loved one another. 1812, 1912 doesn't mean anything at all. What we think is life is nothing – the secret life has quite another history. Am I being very stupid?'

'No, dear,' said Cynthia, who was only half listening, because there were some new and extremely beautiful photographs of her daughter Mary that she was examining. 'You're being very clever – too clever for me I'm afraid.'

('One half of our family will *never* understand what the other half is after – never, never, never!' Vanessa thought.)

'Aren't these good?' said Cynthia. 'I don't want to be the fond mother, but really Mary is going to be a beauty.'

'Yes, she is,' said Vanessa eagerly, glad that Cynthia was happy and at the same time wishing, in spite of herself, that Sally was taller and had a brighter complexion.

'Do you think, Cynthia, that there is something true in what the old man said at the end of *Milestones*?'

'What did he say, dear?' asked Cynthia, holding one of the photographs at an odd angle and smiling at it.

'Don't you remember? He said women of today aren't what they used to be. They're hard. They've none of the old charm. They're unsexed. Are Sally and Mary going to be hard? They *are* different from us. I've noticed it. Sally isn't afraid of anything and she doesn't like to show her feelings. She's rather like a boy sometimes. Won't it be dreadful if all the women are like men and all the men—'

'Like Philip,' Cynthia concluded. 'Why do you think so much about the future, Vanessa? The present is so very agreeable. Peile hasn't been in a bad temper for weeks. Everything is so comfortable and settled.'

'Settled? Do you think so?' said Vanessa.

Later, the Family recalled the strangeness of Vanessa during these weeks. They had, perhaps, none of them ever really known her. She became again rather beautiful. Her pallor suited her grey hair, and her eyes were still lovely, soft, gentle, and generous. No, they had none of them really known her. There was something wild in the middle of her gentleness. You might call her timid because she disliked quarrelling, high words. Yet she had a temper, she could be most courageous. She had been, by all Herries standards, grossly immoral, living for years with a man to whom she was not married, and yet she was religious as none of them were. She had succeeded in holding a man's devotion for a whole lifetime, and a most difficult man too. And yet she was not a woman of the type, you would suppose, for Benjie. For five years she had performed a task that was, they all admitted, an exceedingly hard one. They admired her now although they had once criticized her so severely. But she was outside them all – a stranger in the end. 'There have been always odd ones in the family,' Mary Newmark said complacently. 'As Sidney says, "We're different from ordinary families." '

Vanessa meanwhile paid a visit to her doctor.

'Is there anything wrong with me? I'd like to know.'

He examined her.

'You have been under a great strain. You're very tired. Can't you go abroad for a while and have a proper rest?'

'No,' said Vanessa. 'I can't, I'm afraid.'

'Well, you aren't looking after yourself properly—'

'Is anything organically wrong?'

'No. You're nearly fifty-three, though, and should take care of yourself. A chill or an extra strain – any little thing – might be serious.'

She smiled. They were very old friends.

'Thank you. I'll try and take care.'

Then the day came (she had known that it was coming) when she could not leave Benjie. They had been having tea in his room as they did about once a fortnight. ('How old we're getting!' she said to Benjie once. 'No one thinks it immoral for us to be alone any more.') She got up to go. She could not. She stared at him helplessly.

'What is it?' he asked, getting up and coming to her.

'Oh, I don't know!' She tried to smile, but her mouth trembled. 'Suppose that this should be the last time!'

'What do you mean – the last time?'

'It's always been like that lately – harder to part.' She drew away from him. 'Oh, I was forgetting! I brought you something.'

She went to the deal table and picked something up. 'I thought I'd like you to have this.'

'What is it? You're always giving me things.'

She undid the paper wrapper.

'This is Judith's book. You know, the one we used to read out of in Cumberland.' She held it up, with its faded green cover. 'I thought I'd like *you* to have it now.'

'Why? But you are so fond of it!'

'Yes – but if anything happened ... You know, Benjie, I've always thought it such a pity that someone shouldn't publish it; it's so lively and amusing.'

'People aren't interested. We aren't a very remarkable family.'

'Aren't we?' said Vanessa. 'I think we are.'

He kissed her. 'All right. I'll look after it for you. Write your name in it – your name and mine.'

She went to the table and sat down. She wrote: 'For Benjie with love from Vanessa Herries and Judith Paris. March 29th, 1912.'

'I feel as though she were in the room with us now.'

He laughed. He was standing behind her, his hand on her shoulder.

'Ghosts! What a child you are, Van! Once we're gone we're gone!'

He felt her shiver.

'What's the matter?' he asked. 'Are you cold?'

'No.' She turned round, looked up into his face, her hands on his chest. 'Don't say that, Benjie. I can't endure to think that death – physical death – can separate us. After all – who knows? – it may be only after that that we're really together. When two people have loved one another so long and so truly as we have, isn't it absurd to think that a little thing – a cold, a stumble in the street, oh! anything – can separate us for ever?'

'Well,' he said, looking down at her with great tenderness, 'life is absurd, my darling – absurd, meaningless, cruel.'

She lowered her eyes. He felt her tremble again.

'Perhaps I'm wrong,' he said, putting his arm round her, holding her to him. 'I don't know any more than the next fellow. It's ridiculous to dogmatize. But if there's a God and He's kept us apart for five years as a cat tortures a mouse, why, then I say as many a man has said before me—'

He stopped. She was crying. He knelt down beside her.

'Oh, my darling, don't cry! After all, we've got one another. We've had years of one another. That's something. And this can't go on for ever. It mustn't. It shan't. It gets harder every day. It's killing both of us ... Darling, look up! Think of the happy times! Think of the night in Newlands when Tom arrived from London! And even now – the hours we have, the way our love grows stronger and stronger ...'

He knelt, holding her, while she sobbed against his shoulder. He caught some words.

'I'm so tired . . . I love you so much . . .'

She rose, wiping her eyes. 'There! At my age! Wait. I'll wash my face in your bedroom!'

While she was gone he stood there in perplexity. Tonight he could not endure that she should leave him and return to that house, to that dark house, that insane house . . .

This could not go on as it was. They had both endured it too long. He must think of some way.

She came back smiling, but he saw that she was dreadfully weary.

'Come with me to the King's Road until I get a cab.'

At the door they embraced, clinging to one another with an almost dreadful desperation.

'I wish I'd seen Tom,' she said. 'Say goodbye to him for me.'

'Of course. But you'll be seeing him next week.'

'Oh yes. It was so good of him to take Sally out the other day. She *did* enjoy it so!'

They went down the long stairs hand in hand. He walked beside her with the defiant boyish adventurous air that was so especially his, his hat cocked a little to the side, his empty sleeve, a flower in his coat.

In the King's Road they saw a cab, but she said:

'Let's walk a little farther. There'll be another.' The only thing that she said was: 'What do you think? Carey and May are going to America in April. Adventurous for old things like them, isn't it? They're going in this wonderful new ship, the *Titanic*.'

'We'll go to America one day!' he said.

In Sloane Square she found a cab and got in. He stood looking after it until it turned the corner.

It was a quiet, still evening with little clouds of peach blossom floating serenely across a gentle sky. The traffic moved as in a dream and she stopped the cab by the Ritz (she wanted to go to Hatchard's bookshop), got out and walked. Influenced as she always was by the world about her, all humankind seemed, in this evening hush, to be amiable and friendly. She thought of the Family, that they had all been good to her after their lights, Cynthia and Mary and May and Alfred, Horace and Adrian; two old bachelor brothers, George and Stephen Cards, who, having come to live in London, had been especially good to her, leaving flowers at Hill Street and inviting her to their funny little dinners. All the feuds were over. Into what kind of world would Sally, Mary and Rosalind and Maurice grow up? The Family had risen now above the old jealousies and causeless rivalries. She felt that she herself had done her part in the mysterious weaving of God's shuttle by her return to Ellis. Her love and Benjie's had not been wasted. Nothing was wasted, no goodness, no kindness, no little unheeded courtesy.

She lost, for a moment, under that peach-blossom sky, consciousness of her own small personal history and so was happy. But she was tired. She sat down on one of Mr Hatchard's chairs as they fastened up for her a book, *Carnival*, by some new young man. Adrian had told her that she must certainly read it. Then, as she went out into the street again, she was conscious of a small, stabbing pain in her side. As she was aware of it she knew also a sudden mysterious foreboding as though someone had whispered in her ear: 'This is what you have been waiting for. You will need now all your courage.' She put her hand to her side as though to reassure herself.

At home again she went up to Sally's room and found her sitting at her table biting her pencil over arithmetic. She sprawled over the table, the perfect schoolgirl in her dark blue dress, ink on her cheek and her hair ruffled, drumming her heels on the floor.

'I'm no good at sums, darling,' Vanessa said, sitting down beside her and loving her with a passionate desire to draw her into her arms and never let her go again. But she knew well that Sally did not care for demonstrations.

'Oh, that's all right, Mummy,' Sally said. 'I'll do the beastly things. It's in our blood, I expect, not to be good at sums.' Then she added casually: 'I'm playing for the First at Hockey on Saturday.'

Vanessa knew that this had been, during the last two months, Sally's besetting ambition, but she only said:

'Oh, are you, darling? I'm so glad.'

'Yes.' Sally pushed the book away and looked at her mother. 'You *do* look sweet! Who gave you the violets?'

'Your father.'

'Good.' She thought a moment. Then she went on: 'Mummy, ought I to mind about being illegitimate?'

'Why, dear?'

'Well, Mabel Staines said today that she wouldn't be illegitimate for anything, and that her mother wanted to ask me to tea but wouldn't when Mabel told her.'

'I shouldn't worry about it, Sally dear,' Vanessa said.

'Oh, *I* don't worry!' Sally said cheerfully. 'I told her that her mother could keep her old tea. I rather like being illegitimate. I'm different from the other girls.'

'Do most of the girls know?' asked Vanessa.

'I don't think so. They're all quite decent anyway.' Then she looked at her mother again. 'Mummy, you're tired. You want some tea. I'll get some.'

'No, dear, thank you. I've had some.'

Then Sally did what was rare with her. She threw her arms round Vanessa's neck and hugged her. She rubbed her cheek against her mother's.

'I'll look after you when you're older, and you're the only one I *will* look after.'

'Will you, darling?'

'Yes, you shall have everything you want. I'll make money for you and keep you.'

'What'll you make money with?'

'Oh, I don't know – be a secretary or a market gardener or something.'

'Perhaps you'll marry?'

'Indeed I shan't. I think boys and men are awful. All except Tom and Daddy and Ellis.' Then she dropped her voice confidentially. 'Ellis came in here crying a little while ago. He'd broken a green vase they put flowers in. I told him not to worry.'

(Extraordinary, Vanessa thought, how Sally takes everything for granted!)

'I must go up to him.'

Sally gave her a long and very wet kiss.

'Darling Mummy, I do love you so!' she murmured.

'And I love you,' Vanessa said.

She went up to Ellis and found him, quite contented, playing cards. There was a very simple Patience that Vanessa had taught him. As he played he murmured to himself. 'That's the Red Queen. Now where's the next one. What comes after nine, Vanessa?' he asked as she came in.

'Ten,' she said.

'No, the other way.'

'Eight comes before nine.

'Eight. Eight. Eight,' he said.

He had grown, in the last few weeks, to look very old. His face was wizened, very wrinkled. He looked like a pathetic old monkey.

'Play the piano,' he said, smiling at her.

She sat down at the piano, and as she played 'Annie Laurie' and 'Drink to me only' she felt the pain at her side like a knife. He came and stood beside her, humming out the tune. Then he drew a chair and sat there, all huddled up, nursing his knees.

He was like a little gnome, and with his dead white fingernails he tapped on his knee.

Soon she stopped.

'I'm tired tonight,' she said.

'Yes, I'm tired too,' he said and laid his head on her lap. She stroked his white hair as he liked her to do. Poor Ellis! Would it not be kinder? . . . Then, at the thought which sometimes came to her like a messenger falsely tempting her, she put her arms round his thin body and held him close to her.

But she was too weary to go on. She kissed him and left him, he looking after her with his pathetic wondering eyes.

She went to bed. She was brought some food, but could not eat it. When, at last, to her great relief, she was left alone, she propped her pillows up and wrote a letter to Benjie. Then she lay down to sleep. She could not sleep. Out of a cave of darkness where a dragon slumbered, she moved (carefully lest she should rouse the dragon). She thought that she would read, and she opened a book that was on the little table. It was a volume of Rossetti's poems and, to pain now stabbing her with every breath, she read some verses:

> Although the lattice had dropped loose
>   There was no wind; the heat
> Being so at rest that Amelotte
> Heard far beneath the plunge and float
> Of a hound swimming in the moat.
>
> Some minutes since, two rooks had toiled
>   Home to the nests that crowned
> Ancestral ash-trees. Through the glare
> Beating again, they seemed to tear
> With that thick caw the woof o' the air.
>
> But else, 'twas at the dead of noon
>   Absolute silence: all
> From the raised bridge and guarded sconce
> To green-clad places of pleasaunce
> Where the long lake was white with swans.

She let the book fall and lay back that she might struggle the better with her painful breathing. What was the matter with her? She was ill. She felt the heat rising, as in dry dusty wafts from the desert, through her body, and this heat seemed to be mingled with the clear, sharp picture in the poem that she had just been reading. She herself leant out from some high window on a day of fierce heat and in the general stillness she could hear the sudden cool splash of the hound, and then the caw of the rooks tearing the still air, and then, turning her weary head, she saw the lake, like a mirror in a green wall, and over its glassy green-reflected light the swans, whiter than sunny snow, floated. Ah, this heat and this coldness! This stillness behind whose surface heat beat like a drum! And the swans became horses, great white horses struggling through the lake that now was black; out of the icy water the horses struggled up on to the flank of the frozen hills and their hoofs rang against the ice! As the splendid white horses drew breath with pain, so she fought for hers. Everything moved and shifted. She was a child running across the Cat Bells lawn to greet her father, the house was burning, flames rose mountain-high, as high as Skiddaw, and she was burning too.

But Benjie came and caught her up with his one arm and they rode on the white horse over Skiddaw, Blencathra, over Helvellyn and the Pikes, sailed above Scafell and so out to sea, to the magical island on the horizon, and below them all Wastwater was a lake set in a green wall, and the white swans, with a grand remote dignity, floated on its surface . . .

At some moment, she could not tell when, she saw the crumpled face of Rodd, the butler, bending over her.

'No, Rodd,' she whispered from an infinite distance. 'I'm not very well. I don't think I'll get up today.'

Rodd went upstairs to see the nurse who tended Ellis. She was a big bony woman with a serious kindly face. She had a faint moustache and grey eyes that were both practical and gentle. Her name was Milligan.

'Nurse, her ladyship is very unwell. I don't like the look of her at all.'

The nurse went down. Vanessa recognized her and smiled at her.

'I'm not very well,' she said. 'I have a bad pain in my side. I don't think I'll get up, if you don't mind.'

'It's pneumonia,' Milligan said to Rodd. 'I'll get Doctor Lancaster at once.'

Doctor Lancaster came. Vanessa was very ill.

Later in the morning Rodd telephoned to Cynthia. Cynthia had, a moment before, been telephoning about bridge and she was annoyed because she could not, that afternoon, secure the four that she wanted. It was stupid of Anne Fellowes to bother, on that afternoon of all afternoons, about her old husband just because he had only been home from China a week. 'When he's been home another fortnight she won't bother,' she thought. She put down the receiver and wondered whom she should ask. The bell rang.

'Well,' she said, in that little voice exactly like ice knocking against a glass, a voice that was warning enough to anyone who was sensitive. 'Oh, is that you, Rodd?' she said.

'Yes, madam,' said Rodd, who was not at all sensitive. 'It's her ladyship, madam. She's very ill. Pneumonia, Doctor Lancaster said. We were wondering whether you could come to Hill Street.'

Half an hour later she was in Hill Street. As she came into the room she heard a strange sound of recurrent short breaths, something inhuman and cruel. Vanessa did not recognize her, but murmured: 'The white swans. Benjie! Benjie! Look at the swans!'

On the following morning Benjie was roused, at about half past seven, from a deep sleep by the ringing of the telephone. When he went to it he heard to his surprise Cynthia's voice:

'Benjie, is that you?'

'Yes,' he said, shivering a little in his pyjamas.

'I'm at Hill Street. I think you'd better come as soon as possible.'

'Hill Street?' he repeated, bewildered.

'Yes. It's Vanessa. She's terribly ill. Double pneumonia.'

'I'll come at once,' he answered quietly.

He was aware that Tom was in the room.

'Father's what is it?'

'It's Vanessa. She's very ill. Double pneumonia.'

'Oh no! Oh no!' Tom cried.

'Yes. I must go at once.'

He felt nothing except that he must get to Vanessa. He must get to Vanessa and save her.

He found a cab, rang in a frenzy the bell, rushed into the house and up the stairs. On the first landing he saw Cynthia.

'Oh, Benjie!' she cried and stopped. Then, the tears streaming down her face, she said: 'Vanessa's dead!'

He did not see her. He stood in the long drawing-room like a man lost, his eyes wandering from wall to wall. He was not thinking at all.

He felt a touch on his arm and, turning, saw at his side an old, wizened, bent, and wrinkle-faced man who looked up at him with questioning eyes. Moving from some infinite cold distance he came close to this strange figure. Then, with no shock of surprise, he realized that it was Ellis. From this same room Ellis had once driven him out. Now he said, in a trembling voice:

'Where is Vanessa?'

Benjie led him to the sofa and the old man sat down beside him, close to him, shivering a little.

'Vanessa's all right,' he said.

'No. But why isn't she here? Why hasn't she come upstairs? I want her to play the piano.'

He put his arm round the old man. 'We must both be patient,' he said.

'Yes, I'll be patient,' Ellis said and sat there, staring in front of him, waiting ...

Afterwards Cynthia gave him a letter.

'It is for you, Benjie. Vanessa had written on the envelope that it was to be given to you after she was gone.' Cynthia, who had loved Vanessa, looked at him as though she would like to achieve with him some new and affectionate relation, but she discovered at once that she did not know him at all, that he looked 'foreign', and that he scarcely saw her. He took the letter and walked out of the house.

He read it in his own room.

MY DARLING – I'm writing this in bed. Perhaps you will never read it, but I am writing because I feel unwell tonight and for weeks now have had a foreboding that I might die without seeing you. This is probably nothing except my being very tired, as I have been now for a long time. But in any case it is like talking to you, and is better than that in some ways because I can say some things that I might be shy to say to your face, well though I know you – or perhaps because I do know you so well.

What I want most to say is that if I were to die very
suddenly and you not see me, you are never to feel afterwards
that our love has been wasted. It has been the most wonderful
and glorious thing in both our lives, hasn't it? It has been
everything to me, not only because of our love, but because it
has shown me that there is something in life far deeper than
anything physical or material. I have sometimes thought that
the separation of these last years has been the best thing that
could have happened, because we have been separated and yet
in every important way have been closer together than ever we
were. I have wished so often that I could have been a different
kind of woman for you – I suppose every woman wishes that
for the man she loves. I would have liked to be brilliant, witty,
the kind of woman clever men describe in their books. I have
been unfortunate, I sometimes think, because I have been a
woman between two periods. Forty years ago women knew
what they were supposed to be and do. In fact there was no
choice for most of them. In times to come when Sally is grown
up, women, I expect, will be free, equal with men, afraid of
nothing. I have not, I'm sure, made a success of my life, and
yet I feel that I have, because I won and *kept* your love, and
Sally and Tom love me too. I won't say anything about religion, because I know that it bores you, but think sometimes of
me that I had no more doubt that God exists than I have of
your love for me. People nowadays seem to think that anyone
who believes in God is a hypocrite, *trying* to believe because it
is more comfortable, but it *isn't* so. There are many people who
are not stupid nor false who feel God close to them quite as
practically as they feel the people they know close to them. I
express this very badly and I don't want you to think I am
influencing you – only when I am gone remember that this was
the greatest *true* fact in my life. Perhaps you will come to feel
one day that there may be some other life that goes on side by
side with, or rather *inside*, the physical one I feel that just now
everyone is bewildered, unhappy and restless. It wasn't always
so, I am sure. People will understand God one day perhaps in
a new fashion when they have been unsatisfied and restless
long enough.

But I didn't mean this letter to be a sermon. I only meant
to thank you, again and again, for loving me so much and so
long. Don't be sad if I go. Perhaps I shall be more with you
than I have been. Who knows? Do you really think that our

love, after all it has been through, can be killed by physical death? I am sure that it cannot. Think often of all the happy times we have had, especially in Newlands. That is our country. That is where I will always be closest to you. It has been our country for nearly two hundred years and perhaps before that. Every stone and tree there is a witness that life is worth living, however hard it is, beautiful and terrible and comic and disappointing and rewarding. Go and climb Robinson or stand by the Watendlath Tarn and think of Judith and remember old Herries in Borrowdale. I *know* that nothing is lost, that everything lives, that there is no death, whatever people say.

You will care for Sally, won't you? She is very high-spirited and determined, and I sometimes think that she is the first *fearless* Herries, the first one to rise above all the jealousy and fear and greediness that there has been so long. Perhaps the world that is coming will be full of Sallies! And give Tom all the love that you can. He will miss me, I think, more than anyone. He has such a warm heart and all his happiness is bound up in other people. Forgive me for all the times that you have thought me sentimental and stupid and slow to see things. But I know you have and will. Remember that our love isn't ended, that it will never end, that nothing can destroy it now – Your most loving and devoted

VANESSA

If you have a chance, see poor Ellis sometimes.

Part Four

The Ghost

KALEIDOSCOPE

I

THE FLAME

THREE WEEKS AFTER the outbreak of war several of the
Herries family dined at Alfred's fine house in Drummond
Street.

It was a kind of farewell dinner, because Tom, Maurice –
Alfred's son – and Gordon – the son of Sidney and Mary Newmark – would be shortly departing for the Front. There were
present Alfred himself, Benjie (who, in two days' time, was leaving for Russia), Tom, Mary Worcester (now twenty-one years of
age and a frantic beauty), Rosalind (her sister), Maurice and
Clara (Alfred's children), Gordon and Ada, with Sidney and
Mary Newmark (their parents) – and Sally, who was not quite
eleven, but was allowed to stay up on this one occasion because it
might be a long time before she had dinner with Benjie and Tom
again.

There were twelve of the family in all.

Dinner was finished. Tom, Maurice and Gordon, looking very
young and innocent in uniform, were sipping Alfred's brandy
with the quiet air of practised connoisseurs.

Alfred got up to make a speech. The Herries family had always
been rather fond of making speeches. Alfred especially enjoyed it.
He was a practised hand at making speeches in the City and proving in his cold, restrained voice that everything was absolutely
for the best so long as he and his fellow-directors were in charge.

Tonight, however, his voice was not quite cold, not quite restrained. His long nose and thin horse-like face looked down at
them with a kind of anxious tenderness, and he looked especially
at Maurice, his son, whose face was round and rosy, whose tastes
were for the Arts rather than figures, who was unlike him in
everything.

And he was doing for the first time in his life, perhaps, an
artistic thing. He held in one long, bony hand a thin, beautifully
chased silver candlestick. Up its slender stem ran a pattern of
leaves and branches.

'I'm not going to make a long speech,' he said. 'But I must say something. Here we all are as a family, all together, wishing one another well. It hasn't always been so, you may remember. At one time, in the days of our grandfathers and grandmothers, there was some trouble, as I dare say you know. But now we are all united, a symbol, I like to think, of England itself – all united to fight the greatest enemy the world has ever known – Prussian militarism. Whatever else you may say about our family, no one can deny that, on the whole, we have always stood for England's best interests. One of our ancestors helped to defend Carlisle against Prince Charlie and the Scots. Benjie here lost an arm in South Africa, and in countless other ways we have backed our country. And now we are doing it again. She has never needed us as she needs us now, but because we believe she is in the right we are giving all we have, our sons, our money, our lives. Ahem! yes ... well ... It was Maurice's idea that we should do some little thing tonight that we should all remember when we are separated later on, and that when we remember it we should remember one another ... Yes ... I have, left me by my father, a pair of old candlesticks. They belonged, I believe, to an ancestor of ours, Harcourt Herries, who lived in Cumberland in the eighteenth century, and before him to an old Elizabethan Herries who had something to do with the mines in Keswick. Well, that's past history and this is present history, and it was Maurice's idea that we should link up past and present, that we should pass this candle round, each one of us standing up in his or her turn, holding the lighted candle and wishing the rest of us good luck.

'Well ... ahem ... that's all, I think. Except that Sally here, the youngest, shall be the one to light it.'

It was done as he said. Sally – standing on a chair because she was so small – lit it and round it went. The electric light was switched out and round the little flame went, very clear and bright and steady. Everyone wished everyone else good luck.

It was a frosty, sparkling morning and the guns were still. Two hours after midnight there had been a fearful bombardment. On and on went that shattering malignant thunder. Then it ended. There was a perfect cloud of silence everywhere over the desolate country. Tom was ordered to see how the land, now remorselessly altered, might look. New mounds, new pits. Four or five of the raiders lay stretched out, abandoned and desolate; one a stout officer with a snub nose and part of his face gone, another a dark squat-shaped boy who lay, his head on his arm, his wide dark eyes staring at the sky. The raid had been well planned. Tom returned. The light was strengthening, but the air was thin like stretched paper and most bitterly cold. He looked out over a land that might have been trampled by dinosaurs. The country was quite deserted save for one or two snipers at the sap-head. No sound anywhere, but he knew that all about him thousands of men were concealed. Desolation and silence . . .

He went into his dug-out and began a letter to Sally.

DARLING LITTLE SALLY – I've got half an hour to myself and everything's as quiet as the top of Cat Bells. They raided us last night and for an hour or two there was a terrible din. We lost some men, I'm afraid. It's a cold and frosty morning, which is heaps better than the mud and rain. I'm all right, feeling very well in fact. Do you remember the dinner at Alfred's when you lit the candle, and do you remember his saying that we were proud, as proper, right-minded Herries, of defending the world against Prussian Militarism? I suppose we were right at the time to feel like that, and it's still nice to think of that lighted candle going round the table, isn't it? But how long ago that all seems now, and how our point of view has altered!

I haven't had any sleep for twenty-fours hours, but last time I *did* sleep I dreamt of Vanessa. It was scarcely like a dream. She seemed to be sitting beside me holding my hand and wearing the clothes she used to wear in Newlands – just as I would wake sometimes in the morning and find her sitting on my bed. Doesn't she seem *peaceful* now in all this trouble? Do you remember how calm she used to be when something went wrong, and the way she smiled? . . .

He broke off and stared in front of him, smiling at the thought of Vanessa. Then he went on:

The thing I hate most here is being sent out to reconnoitre positions and getting lost. It's awful. Perhaps it's raining, and through the mist you see lights trembling on the horizon, or you think you do. Then, out of nowhere, someone says, as though they were fearfully angry, 'Get down!' and you find yourself in a barrage. Then you run for your life, the wet clay clinging to your legs like hands. Then you're lost again – in darkness. You go up and you go down, not knowing what is hill and what isn't. Perhaps some rifles suddenly open on you. You run and crouch, and slip and crouch and run – always lost, always alone and dirty and cold, like a nightmare after we'd eaten too much as kids.

How are you? Are you doing well at school? Remember there are the three of us – you and I and Father – or four with Vanessa. Never forget Vanessa, darling, will you? Of course I know you won't. Have you heard from Father in Russia? I haven't for ages. Have you seen Mary? Did you ask her to write to me? She promised to but she hasn't yet. *Don't forget this.* It's very important. Do you write to Father regularly? You must, even though he seems so far away. I think he's in Galicia somewhere. Isn't this funny? It's lying on the table beside me. Someone left it:

PLEASE!

Will you help your lad at the Front and all other lads, in a very simple way, and will you give your friends the chance to help as well?

Do it Thus!

Fill in THIS POSTCARD with your name and address, and post it back to us. We will then send you a number of bookmarkers . . .

Bookmarkers! You don't know how funny that sounds here. And lads! Don't you hate the word 'lads'?

Well, darling, keep up your spirits and behave just as though everything were all right. I'm fine myself and perhaps I'll get a spot of leave soon. Don't forget to write to Father and don't forget to ask Mary to write to me. Tell me what she was wearing when you saw her last. That's important – Your most loving brother,

TOM

The candle, stuck in a bottle with a collar of grease, flared up. The flame was bright, pure, steady, of gold.

'There's a flame!' cried Benjie.

The Retreat had begun and with the rest of the Otriad he had been flung into the little town of O—. It was a place of dust, whirling clouds of dust, dust in your eyes and mouth and nose. This dust was blown by the wind and behind the thin spirals of it a hot sun blazed. Everywhere there was the Russian soldier, the

Russian soldier apathetic like a cow but humorous and touching also. He was everywhere, in the streets, on the dirty staircases, crowding the tumbled untidy rooms; the Russian soldier and the dust.

'I never want to see either of them again,' thought Benjie.

But he had cried out at the sudden flame. It was evening and, after the dust storms and the hot malignant sun, the pale blue of the sky and the cool air were friendly. The members of the Otriad were lying or walking or sitting in the half-ruined building into which Molozov, their chief, had turned them. Benjie found this place intolerable. It was a long room with a naked gleaming floor and an apparently endless succession of looking-glasses. This gleaming empty reflection was broken with an infernal clatter through the open window of horses, soldiers and carts that rattled on the cobbles. There was a smell everywhere of dust and dung.

He went to see if he could be of any use with the wounded. Going out originally in August 1914 with two journalists who were friends of his, he kicked his heels in Moscow for some weary months and at last only found adventure by joining, after a week or two in a Moscow hospital, a Red Cross unit attached to the Ninth Army. They had been sent to Galicia and, after some apparent victories, had begun a retreat. He would never forget the moment of that change of fortune. He and several soldiers had gone, under the charge of a rather feckless Englishman called Trenchard, to the forest to bury the dead. This was not his own Otriad. He had come over with two of his own unit to pay this Otriad a visit. It had been pleasant to find another Englishman here, although no two men could have been found more different than Benjie with his short thick figure, his off-hand but commanding independent personality, and this untidy, seemingly foolish Englishman who would wander about singing *Early One Morning* in a cracked voice or, quite unexpectedly, looking so wretched that you thought he would burst into tears. Benjie was told that he had been engaged to a pretty, charming nurse in his Otriad who had thrown him over.

Benjie was to return that same evening to his own Otriad. But he did not. Under the trees of the forest he was looking at a dead man – a man who had been dead some three weeks perhaps. This man was all right until you came to his face. His strong blue-grey trousers were in splendid condition and he had good stout boots. Out of the top of one boot a tin spoon protruded. But he had no

face, only a grinning skull, and in and out of the mouth and eye
sockets little black creatures like ants were crawling. It was all
very peaceful there. The sanitars began to dig a grave. Some
quietly smoked cigarettes. Then a sanitar observed that the bursting of the shrapnel that had been dim and distant all day now
sounded much closer. That was the beginning of the Retreat . . .

But it was at the town of O— that he saw the sudden flame. He
had been for nearly a week now with this Otriad that was not his
own. He had begun to know them all – Molozov, the stocky
square-shouldered Chief who would say over and over again:
'There's no method . . . no system . . . nothing at all . . . By God,
there's a pretty girl!' Nikitin, a doctor who had a charming intellectual face; a surgeon, Alexei Petrovitch Semyonov, a strik-
ing-looking fellow, very thickset and muscular with a strange
square-cut beard of so fair a colour that in some lights it seemed
almost white. A man of very strong personality and great self-
confidence. There was the pretty Sister, Marie Ivanovna, and the
feckless untidy Englishman, Trenchard. He made friends with
them and liked them, but they were nevertheless all shadows on a
screen to him who had his constant, secret preoccupations.

He found work to do in the vast room at O—. This was a
strange place. It had been the theatre of the town. It was lit now
with candles stuck into bottles, and in this dim and wavering
light the doctors did their work. The busy silence was broken
with patient plaintive cries of *'Oh, Steritza! Oh, Steritza!'* or
'Borjé moi! Borjé moi!' and then the sharp official questions,
'What regiment? What division? Shrapnel or bullet?'

And across the stage at the back of the room was still hanging,
wavering in the draught, the painted backcloth of some old play.
This amused Benjie by its incongruity, for there was a picture of
a market-place in a town all very gaily painted, and down the
marble stairs flower-girls with legs like bolsters came merrily
tripping while soldiers in scarlet and blue drank with their girls
at little tables.

Meanwhile the real soldiers cried out in their agony 'Oh! Oh!
Oh! . . . *Oh! Borjé moi . . . Borjé moi!'* as Nikitin and Semyonov probed for bullets under the uncertain flame of the
candles, and a soldier in delirium sang a song about gathering the corn, in a shrill broken voice.

The dominating square-bearded man, Semyonov, had stopped
his work for a moment and stood, his arms folded, looking on,
beside Benjie.

'You seem to stand this pretty well,' he said. 'If it isn't impertinent – how old are you?'

'Just gone sixty,' said Benjie.

'Yes. You look fit. Lose your arm in this War?'

'No. In the Boer War.'

'Bad luck.'

'Oh, I'm used to it.'

'What do you think of us – the Russians, I mean?' Semyonov asked.

'Oh, you're plucky – marvellous. I never saw such courage. But you're a bit muddled high up, aren't you?'

'Yes. Hopeless. Everyone's robbing and cheating and spying and betraying. It's a mess of a war altogether. When do you think it will end?'

'Never, I should think,' said Benjie.

'I agree. Why don't you people do something on the other Front?'

'We're doing our best, I believe,' said Benjie.

'I believe you are. But they're beginning to be impatient over here.' He turned angrily, and Benjie thought he had never seen a more determined aggressive profile. 'There's that bloody fellow-countryman of yours messing things up again. Never saw a more useless fellow in my life.'

'Oh, you mean Trenchard,' Benjie said.

'Yes. I wish to God he'd get back to his own country.'

It was then that a candle, close at Benjie's elbow, flared. It was low down in its socket. In the spurt of light Benjie thought that he saw Vanessa. She stood quietly there, smiling at Trenchard, who was nervously bandaging the knee of a large patient-eyed soldier. She smiled at him, then turned her eyes to Benjie's. They drank in one another's happiness. Oh! how glad he was to see her again! But she was not there. Only the flame, bright, pure, steady.

And Sally, seeing it, said to Mary Worcester: 'Look, Mary! That light in the sky!'

Sally and Mary were looking out from behind the blinds in Cynthia's house in Eaton Place. Cynthia had taken the house six months ago. It was small, compact, could be worked with four servants. Everyone must make sacrifices now.

Ellis had died two months after Vanessa. He had been lost, bewildered; he had cried a great deal and would sit for hours, his knees hunched up, staring like an old sick monkey at the closed piano. They had found him there one morning huddled up in the chair dead. So had passed away the son of Will's old age and great hopes.

After his death Sally had gone to live with her father and Tom, and then, when war broke out, Cynthia had taken her. Although she was now, at the beginning of 1916, over twelve years of ago, she did not grow. She did not herself mind.

'I'm like my great-grandmother. She didn't grow, but nobody cared.'

She never worried in the least about her own personal appearance, as, in fact, her great-grandmother had done. How many, many times Judith Paris had wished that her legs were longer, but Sally Herries didn't care a damn!

She was, Mary thought, regrettably tomboyish. She didn't care how she looked, how she sat, what clothes she wore. She might be made to look rather striking with her brown hair and pale face. She said she simply could not bother. She was, at her present stage, direct and honest to a terrible degree. Loyal and warm-hearted, if she liked anyone. Unfortunately she did not like Mary nor did Mary like her. Mary considered that Sally was envious of her great beauty and, further, that she was jealous of her because her adored Tom thought Mary a queen and a goddess.

In the first of these there was no truth at all. Sally *did* think Mary the most beautiful woman in the world. She also thought her the coldest and most selfish, and for this reason she resented Tom's quite hopeless passion. For Mary would never dream of marrying a poor journalist like Tom. She was extremely ambitious. On the other hand, she was neither so cold nor so hard-hearted as Sally supposed her. The true basic reason for Sally's dislike of Mary, however, was that Mary had no feeling about Vanessa. Vanessa was the principal abiding fact in Sally's life. There never had been, there never would be again, anyone like Sally's mother. Sally was neither sentimental nor gushing, but deep in her nature lived intense emotion. All this, as yet, was given to the memory of her mother. She adored Tom, she liked her father, but they also were part of Vanessa.

Now, for Mary, when someone was dead someone was dead. Moreover, she had not seen Vanessa very often and remembered her only as a large rather calm lady with a broad white forehead and grey hair parted in an old-fashioned way. Also Vanessa had lived with a man not her husband and of this Sally was the result. Mary was conventional. She liked people to do the proper things. So why *should* she be passionate about Vanessa? Twice she had spoken rather slightingly to Sally about her mother – only in a joke of course, but Mary's sense of humour was not very delicate. She was neither witty nor quick-witted. Like other beautiful women, her beauty was all she needed.

But, ironically, she had, if she had known it, something of the beauty that Vanessa had had as a young woman. She was tall, dark, full-breasted. She had been told that she carried herself like a queen and never forgot it. It was her tragedy, perhaps, that she was moving into an age when carrying yourself like a queen would be no longer an asset.

Sally knelt on a chair beside Mary and stared, from behind the blind, at a dark and dead London. No light showed anywhere. Only on the horizon there had flashed a sudden finger of light.

'A flame in the sky!' Sally cried.

'It's a searchlight,' said Mary.

Rosalind, a plain-faced, good-natured girl, was seated at the table within the room, knitting. They had all been knitting, making chest-protectors. The Ladies' Committee for which they worked wanted body-belts, Warleigh leggings, gas masks, pneumonia jackets and operation shirts. Sally hated to knit and so did Mary. Rosalind enjoyed it.

'Take care you don't show any light,' she said mildly, for the penalty of failing to conform was actually One Hundred Pounds or six months' imprisonment. People were making blinds from old curtains and women's skirts.

'Oh, that's all right!' Sally came back to the table. 'I suppose I must do my beastly algebra. Oh dear, there's never any peace these days!'

At first the War had been fun, then it had been a bore, now it was rather terrible. Many girls at school had lost their fathers and brothers, and when it came to your best friend (whose name was Charlotte Greene) having to leave because her father was killed and there was no money in the family any more – why, then you positively realized it. Tom had been home on leave twice, and last time he had been pale-faced, nervous and oddly silent. But the worst was Maurice, Alfred's son, who, two nights before he went back, alone with Sally in his father's dining-room had, quite unexpectedly, burst into tears. He had been joking but a moment before.

'I don't want to go back! I don't want to go back!' he had cried.

Sally had plenty of common sense. She never lost her head, but if at that moment it had been suggested that she should return to

France instead of Maurice, she would at once have agreed to go.

She stood by the table thinking of her father (so far away in Russia, with only his one arm), of Tom who wrote such splendid letters, of poor Maurice and of Gordon Newmark, who did not seem to mind a bit and had won the DSO. Standing there, thinking, it seemed to Sally as though, across a dark stretch of water, there was a black marshy land and down its length spread a vast scaly dragon, flame issuing from its jaws.

'You funny little thing!' said Mary, who, drawn to her full height, was looking very beautiful in front of the blind. 'What are you thinking about?'

But Sally pushed past her and, on the other side of the blind, stared into the dark. Even as she looked a flame of light shot up into the sky.

'*That* was a flash!' said Maurice Herries.

This was from one of the gas-projectors from the hill behind them. They were hurling opened cylinders of gas on to the enemy position some thousand yards away. Maurice shivered. Time was short. He ordered the morning rum issue to be taken round the platoons. Then suddenly there began a procession of 'whizz-bangs'.

Maurice stood there wishing that he might 'stop one' before he had to go over the top. It was that cold, terrifying moment half an hour before the dawn when everything is clear and un-mistakable like hell. 'In another forty minutes I may be dead. In another forty minutes I may be sticking my bayonet into a Boche's belly, deep, deep, as though into butter. In forty minutes I may be mad with pain, my sight gone, my body crippled for life . . .'

Many men did not think of those things. Maurice was a poet. He thought Shakespeare, Blake and Gerard Manley Hopkins the three greatest men in the world. He loathed the mud and the filth and the smells and Berkley Cannon, his best friend, dying in his arms, and he loved the comradeship, the good humour, the courage and friendly simplicity of common men, the moments of ecstasy . . . and he hated this pause before action, hated it as he had never hated anything in his life before.

He wondered whether a Boche attack had forestalled their own. 'Perhaps they have learned our plans and will shatter our huddled groups before we leave our lines.'

Then the flame! It stabbed the sky. First the roar was one blow as on a great sheet of iron, then after a pause another, then a

pause again and another. Then one continuous throbbing thunder. The shells screamed and a pillar of fire leaned up the wall of
the dim uncertain sky. 'Our barrage,' Maurice thought. 'Zero hour.'

Maurice shouted to his little group, they jumped out of the
trench and stumbled forward. Now came the moment that he
always dreaded, when the group broke and one straggled forward
singly, one little mannikin in a world of malignant danger.
Through the noise as of cannon-balls rolling down sheets of iron,
there was the phut! phut! of rifle bullets. And there to the right
are heads of Boches in a shell hole shooting. Trotter, a giant of a
man, one of the jolliest, most carefree and kindest, staggers,
seems to leap on his feet, crashes down. 'No, there is no chance
for us tumbling through this mud with these fellows shooting at
us,' and he and Conklin, Bush and two others have slithered
down into a shell hole and are firing over the top of it. Conklin's
face is smashed in. We have got two of the Boches but more are
running up. The sky is lightening, and the roar of the guns, and
now the German guns, thunders on – but by this time it is familiar, belonging to a world that one knows, that is part of one, that
is almost friendly.

Then Maurice 'stopped one'. There was an impact on his right
shoulder as though a big stone had hit him. No pain. He slipped
down into the bottom of the shell hole and, staring upwards, was
aware now that the sky was much lighter and, to his great surprise, that he was alone there except for Conklin who, his
smashed face in the mud, huddled at his feet. His shoulder, his
arm, his hand were soaking wet, but still there was no pain. He
did not want to move. He was quite happy. A faint, a very faint
blue was stealing into the sky, and some small clouds, like rosy
petals, seemed to his eye to be dancing, gently and carefully,
against the blue.

The thundering noise withdrew, and in front of his eyes,
which he soon must close, a small and delicate flame wavered.
The flame of the candle that Sally had lit! He smiled. He would
write a poem about it, this small candleflame that neither the
wind of the great guns nor the delicate fleeciness of the morning
clouds could put out. Pity that his father hated him to write
poetry, thought all books a mistake, wanted him to add up sums
in the City. He would never add up sums, but he would write
poems to the glory of England as Rupert Brooke had done, or
about old ships like Flecker ... He would carry on the glory of
the Family, would go and live in Cumberland, near the sea, in
the valleys of which old Benjie Herries had told him. A face bent

close to his. Someone moved him and a flame of pain licked his
heart. He cried out and the flame moved up, spreading, glorious,
golden, blotting out, with its light, the whole world. There were
two flames . . .

The two flames burnt steadily, illuminating the mirror, lighting
the dressing-table, the pictures on the walls, of 'Queen Victoria
receiving the News of her Accession' and 'Dignity and Impudence', the narrow bed and the small shining table beside it.

'The electric light's fused,' said Gordon Newmark, looking in
at the door.

'I know,' said Tom. 'I've found some candles.' He sat in front
of the mirror, brushing his hair with his two old battered silver
brushes.

'Hurry up, you blighter,' Gordon said.

'All right. I won't be a minute.'

Gordon Newmark was broad and tall and the pink of self-
confidence. Tom seemed gentle, small, submissive beside him.
Tom was thirty-two and Gordon twenty-one, but Gordon had
won the D S O, loved the War – 'best time I'm ever likely to have,
old boy' – and was home now on leave as a kind of conqueror,
patronizing, in a jolly friendly way, all the family, especially his
old father and mother and his sister Ada, who all adored him.
He was, if he had known it, the recurrent Herries type, the type
of old Pomfret, of Prosper – Jennifer's father, of Rodney –
Cynthia's grandfather, and especially of Walter – Tom's great-
grandfather. But he didn't know it. He didn't care. He was the
triumphant, riding, roughshod, bullying Herries. But the type
had softened, emasculated a bit. He thought old Benjie a dissolute old rogue and Tom a 'soft 'un' and Maurice Herries 'a
decent sort of ass who writes poems'; his type was as far from the
other as ever, in the family history, it had been, but the two did
not quarrel any more. Life was beginning to move too swiftly:
you had too much to do to bother about quarrels. The Herries
didn't fight any more. But Gordon felt, all the same, a sort of
friendly scorn as he saw Tom struggling into his clothes. Under
the light of the candles Tom's face was serious, careworn, too
kindly to be aggressive. 'That's all he'll ever be,' Gordon thought,
'a sort of second-rate journalist. Thinks too much about other
people. Almost a woman – about his old father, his kid sister, his
father's mistress who died. I'd worry!' thought Gordon, who
hoped that night to pick up a pretty girl somewhere . . . you

needn't be too particular these days when you'd be returning in a week's time to be killed maybe ... But Tom didn't want a girl. He was sweet on Mary Worcester. Poor old Tom! He hadn't a dog's chance with that beautiful swollen-headed female!

Tom blew out the candles. They groped their way down the dark staircase. Tom still stuck to the rooms in Tite Street. In the dark King's Road they found a taxi, and through a town of pitch they plunged until the friendly arms of the Carlton Grill received them. Then they went to the Alhambra to see *The Bing Boys* for the twentieth time, sang *If you were the only girl in the world* with other of their slightly intoxicated fellows and roared at George Robey whenever he lifted his eyebrows.

Afterwards they found a dingy door in Soho and behind it a yet dingier nightclub known as 'The Five Pennies'. Tom had not wanted to go. 'Leave' was offering no attractions. He wanted to be back in France, although he didn't like that either. Mary tortured him. She liked him, he thought. Sometimes he fancied that she more than liked him, but he knew in his heart that he had no chance with her, and knowing it loved her only the more desperately. He had loved her always. He was chaste, having had no sexual experience whatever, and this chastity seemed, just now, to separate him from everybody. Men, all men, seemed to be caught into a passionate longing for sexual intercourse – any intercourse with anyone ... It was a hunger, the only solace for the filth, the fear, the cold, the wounds, the long drawn-out tension of this fantastic trial. And he? He thought always of Vanessa and of Mary. Of his father and Sally and his friends as well, but Vanessa and Mary were always with him, one of the kindest, gentlest, most understanding of mothers, the other the loveliest, divinest of goddesses. And he could touch neither: one was a ghost, the other a dream ...

As he sat in the small, fearfully hot and indecently smelling room of 'The Five Pennies' he screwed his courage to the sticking point. His life seemed just now to be running on hard lines, but it was worse for others. Worse for poor Maurice, for instance, who had lost his arm, worse for hundreds, for thousands of fine men. He would stick it, but he wished that he had Gordon's hardy indifference – Gordon who was, at this moment, talking to two women with a carefree gaiety that made him seem the only really happy person in the room. A girl came and sat beside Tom. He ordered her a drink; drink was being served in coffee cups. He watched Gordon a little anxiously. He knew that these places just now were haunted by 'crows', women who made their men friends drunk, took them on somewhere and robbed them of everything they had. But Gordon was no fool. He knew a thing or two.

The girl at Tom's table was tired. She complained, through the raucous jazz music, in a weary little voice, of the violence and callousness of men. Men didn't seem to care. They weren't kind any more. Generous, yes, but not kind. Life wasn't really gay although everyone pretended that it was. Food was awful. Why, fancy, eggs were a luxury food. Fancy eggs being a luxury! Butter was half a crown a pound and a chicken cost thirteen bob! Why, fancy a chicken costing ... So she went on, repeating everything twice.

Suddenly, into the middle of the jazz, the laughter, the movement of the dancers, a voice broke. A tall swaying officer had pushed into the middle of the floor, he was brushing the dancers aside. He was drunk, of course. And he cried out in a shrill scream:

'Blast this bloody war! To hell with it! Blast this bloody war! To hell with the bloody war! To hell ...'

Two waiters caught hold of him and led him away. People laughed.

'You see,' said the girl. 'That's just what I say. What I mean to say is that nobody really enjoys things much. And they aren't kind any more. If you were a woman you'd agree with me. And the women aren't kind either. What I mean to say is, it's affected everybody, and how we're ever to get back to the way we were—'

'We'll never get back,' said Tom.

He was watching a man near him who held up, with a rather unsteady hand, a lighter. He pushed at his cigarette with it. The little flame burnt bravely, with a fine uprightness. Then it went out.

KALEIDOSCOPE

II

TRIUMPHAL ARCH

IN the early days of 1917 Sally Herries had a strange experience. It was at Cynthia's house in Eaton Place.

Altogether life was strange at this time, strange and yet familiar. Sally was over thirteen years of age, went to school every day, did on the whole what she was told, was calm and quiet and collected, but suffered, at unexpected moments, extraordinary and poignant longings for her mother – also, but less poignantly, for her father and for Tom.

She had only a few friends, but in this dark uncertain world that now surrounded everyone friendships were not important. Some of the girls at school she liked, but they had all now their own especial interests – the ways in which they were helping the War, brothers, fathers at the Front, food that had become important because it was rationed, the personal experiences of air raids or the second-hand experiences of emotionalists, rumour and story and gossip; it seemed that all these things kept one apart from the ordinary relationships of ordinary life. Sally did not care. At Eaton Place she was quite alone. Mary and Rosalind were too old, Peile a silly (but kindly) old man, Cynthia infinitely distant.

But *how* fantastic a world it was! That moment after dusk when all the world was dark, the first experience of an air raid with the alarm, the silence, the distant firing, the expectancy (not at all frightening – pleasurable, like being at the theatre just before the curtain went up), the rumours, the stories that people told, the anxieties about Tom, about Gordon, the many women wearing black, the tales that reached even her ears of the funny ways that soldiers and their girlfriends had in places like Trafalgar Square after dark . . .

She was aware that her family were behaving very finely. She herself caught some of the family pride. It was really true, she felt, that but for her family England and the War would be lost. When she went to other people's houses – the houses of the parents of her friends – she heard many very despairing remarks. It would make no difference, they said, that America had severed diplomatic relations with Germany. America would not be able to be in time, we would all be defeated before America could do anything. Someone told a story about going into a tear-shell factory and weeping tears enough to fill a jug. People recounted horrible details of wounds and suffering and lonely agonies. Sally tried not to listen but she *had* to . . . Her imagination was vivid. She saw these dreadful things as though they were happening in front of her. She grew older very quickly. People said that we were bound to be beaten. All the glory was gone. We were led by idiotic Generals, our politicians were impossible fools. People

said that it would be better if we made terms with the Germans.
Let *them* have the glory!

'Oh no!' Sally cried out in the house of kind Mrs Mickleham,
the mother of Connie Mickleham who was so clever at algebra.
'That would be wicked!' And for once she burst into tears and
ran from the room.

But *inside* the family it was *all* quite different. No one dreamt
of anything but complete victory. We would go on for ever and
ever but victory must certainly be ours.

It was now that the Herries were seen at their very best. Their
normality, their common sense, the absence of *grab* in their
natures, their non-property qualities, so to speak, their courage,
their indifference to facts that they refused to realize, enabled
them to become completely patriotic. They loved their country
because their country depended on them and while *they* were
there all must be well.

Maurice came home without an arm and sat, with a white face,
staring into distance. They were sorry for him but disregarded
him. Gordon came home, filled with the War. It was glorious.
When the Americans came in we would soon sweep the dirty
Boche back to Berlin. He had extraordinary stories about the
dirtiness of the Boche, his meanness, cruelty, cowardice and sav-
agery. The Herries on one side, the Germans on the other. Who
could doubt of the result?

It was on one March evening that Sally had her funny little
adventure.

She had been doing her schoolwork in her cold little room at
the top of the house and remembered that her geography book
was in the dining-room. She came downstairs for it. The house
was still and plunged into that eerie dusk that seemed now to be
always the atmosphere of rooms and passages. She reached the
hall that had only a light at the farthest end, near the kitchen
stairs. She walked forward to the dining-room door and saw that
a man was hiding, close up against the wall, behind the umbrella
stand. He was a little man with spectacles, a rather dirty face, and
he was in uniform. As she saw him he whispered, but without
moving from the wall to which he seemed to be fastened, 'If yer
say a word I'll throttle yer.'

It was all part of the general strangeness, the half-light, the
silent streets, the sense of the War, prowling like a large cat
almost at one's very door, of Benjie somewhere in Russia, of Tom
underground in France eating plum and apple jam to the light of

a single candle, of that man weeping a bucket of tears in the factory, of Maurice without an arm, that this little man should be pinned against the wall of the house in Eaton Place.

She saw that he was very frightened and she wanted to give him something. She gave him half a crown that she was saving to buy something for Tom with.

He said 'Gawd bless yer, miss', and in another moment had opened the hall door and slipped away, letting into the house a blast of cold biting air before the door closed. She stood there wondering. What had he wanted? Had he come to steal? He looked very unhappy. He was a piece of the War. She had encountered the War. She continued quickly to grow up.

Her father, crossing a small snow-covered square in Petrograd, heard a strange sound. He was walking with a little black-bearded Jew, Konrad Mathias. Mathias had just said: 'It is between personality and non-personality. Everything comes down to that. Am I, Konrad Mathias, an individual with a history, an important history like no one else's, or am I a little gas, a little acid, a little water, dissipated at the prick of a pin? ... Do you see? Am I Konrad Mathias? Am I? Am I?'

'I should think you probably are,' Benjie had said, looking at a church dome, a brilliant green against the burning blue of the sky. The snow sparkled at his feet. 'I like this,' he said. 'The green, the blue, the sparkling snow. It stirs me – not the acid and water in me, I think. Or is it?'

'No, no!' Little Mathias, in his black woolly fur cap, jumped on the snow.

'Well, I don't know,' Benjie said. 'The individual can't be very important. If the world goes topsy-turvy the individual starves and is very quickly gas and water again. There's a revolution in South America and Mr Smith in London loses his job. His child dies because it hasn't enough nourishment. It's the revolution that matters. Certainly not Mr Smith.'

'Oh, you're wrong,' Mathias cried. 'What if he does lose his job? He's losing it or gaining it all the time. Everyone in a lifetime meets his personal crisis whether there's a revolution or not. Birth, love, death, economic struggle, falling out of love with one's wife, seeing a pretty girl round the corner, having a suspicion there's a God, then deciding there isn't. Always the same crisis turning up for everybody. The hoops of the circus – you must jump through them. That's fate. The way you jump. That's free will and is the only thing that matters. It's the individual who is always different. How will you meet this? A toothache, syphilis, cancer, a sudden bit of success. That's history.'

'Then you believe in God?'

'Of course I do. Only He doesn't interfere. He sets the scene. You play your part. I've been about the world a lot. It's everywhere the same. Are you a realist or a romantic? If you're the first it will be the dates, the scientific facts, the large movements, the cold truth that will seem to you to be important. If you're the second it will be the things behind the facts – what each man does with his soul.'

'You think man has a soul?'

'A spiritual life? Of course. It's the only thing that squares the facts.'

'Is there a life after death, do you think?' Benjie asked more eagerly than he had intended.

'Life? Death? There's always death. Every man is living and dying all the time. But *physical* death – that's not important. Men are so thoughtless. And they worry about the wrong things.'

'So you think the old world is finished?'

'Of course it is. And the new one will take a long while settling itself. But that doesn't matter. Men will have their personal histories just the same. Why, take myself! I'm fifty-five – a Jew of no importance whatever. But I was afraid for years, afraid of everything and everyone. Thought people despised me. And I was greedy too. Now I'm not often afraid and not greedy. That's more important than a revolution. Not because I am important, mind you – no more and no less than the next man – but it's important to God that I should get a move on. More important than that Napoleon should win Austerlitz or Rasputin be murdered.'

'But Rasputin's death has affected millions.'

'No. Only provided situations for men to meet. They'd meet them in one fashion or another in any case.'

It was then that Benjie heard the noise. It was like the sharp cracking of twigs. The scene was very peaceful. At the end of the square was the canal and along the side of it a cab was slowly crawling, the *isvostchik*, in his fat clothes, bunched up on the seat. Some birds flew slowly across the blue. Some church bells were ringing. It was about three in the afternoon.

A moment later it was as though the blue sky had burst and

poured confusion on to the earth. Down the path by the canal a mob of people, shouting, crying, came pouring, and on to the square from the other end rolled a lorry, piled high with soldiers, bristling with rifles. The lorry stayed still. A man came running from the canal. He ran a little way into the square, outlined very sharply against the snow. He stopped and looked back at the people. Then from the lorry there came a noise like the clearing of a throat, and the man ran a step, stood, crumpled at the knees, fell, raised himself, fell flat, wriggled like a worm and lay still.

Benjie had known many bad moments in his life but none so bad as this one – for there he was, isolated, alone in all that gleaming, glittering colour. He must run for miles, it seemed, before he could reach security. But Mathias was already running. An absurd notion came to Benjie that it would be undignified to run. He walked slowly, his hand in his pocket. But now many people were running into the square, and as they did so a red light rose like a fan above the houses and spread into the blue.

He walked slowly and as he went repeated to himself like a man in a dream, aloud: 'This is Revolution. This is Revolution.' Then he saw the square flooded with people. They were shouting: 'To the Nevski!' 'No, no, to the Duma!'

He was carried with the crowd . . .

And it was now September. Tom on leave, walking down Piccadilly, heard the air-raid warning. Instinctively he hurried his step and then slowed down again. For what did it matter?

He had come from half an hour with the lovely Mary. On his way there he had thought: 'Well, now, tonight I'll ask her. She will be sorry for me, perhaps, moved because next week I return to France. She will think "Oh, poor boy". And she will be kind.' As he had walked towards Eaton Place his love – that had been part of him for so long now, that had gained so terribly in intensity out there where every homeward vision shone with a mystical light – his love had dried and constricted his heart so that it was a shrivelling little ball in his body. Away, beyond the houses, not far distant, somewhere hanging in the pale September sky was his hope. He would say:

'Mary, I have loved you so long. Let me go back with just this to remember! I may not return. Be kind to me.' A weak, cowardly sort of prayer, but he was beyond all pride now. He wanted her so. His thoughts were lascivious and pure, of the body and the soul, all things together. Oh! if she would only be kind!

And she had been kind – kind and abstracted. Her eyes had rested on him without seeing him, and then she had been suddenly aware that she must do something about this poor man who had loved her since she was a child and was so good and patient and so tiresome. And next week he would return to France and would suffer horrors, perhaps, would be frightened and tired and lonely.

Comprehension came into her eyes. She saw Tom. She wanted to be good to him. She asked him questions about the Front.

But he knew that it was only kindness. He refused a second cup of tea and went.

So he did not mind now if there were an air raid. The omnibuses seemed to hasten, and soon, as he neared the Circus, the streets were quite empty. This was the week when there were almost daily air raids. They said that people's nerves were beginning to go, and Tom remembered how a friend had told him that, two nights ago, he had walked down a street in Pimlico during a raid and that it had been naked, empty, shining, but that behind every window people were playing pianos.

No pianos here. Nothing but the Circus, bare as though set for a scene in a theatre. The firing came nearer and flashes lit the sky. Light hit the Circus and sprang away. But nothing happened. The all-clear sounded. He went on a bus back to Chelsea.

During the remaining days of his leave he found that he could endure no one but Sally. For the first time he was afraid that his nerve was breaking. He was so *tired* of it – sick to death of it all, he was. And worst was the chatter. He lunched with Alfred and listened to Gordon. He lunched with Cynthia and listened to poor old Peile. He heard that Sir Henry Wilson was sold to the French, that £100,000,000 had been spent on gas, that German cruisers were lying off Harwich, that . . . Oh, what did it matter? Everything was unreal now. Life itself was unreal, the physical processes of the body, the putting on of a collar, brushing one's teeth . . .

He went to entertainments, heard Beecham conduct *Figaro*, saw a farce, was made miserable by a musical comedy. All these were unreal.

But Sally was real. He had always loved her with that patient, unchanging, unfaltering devotion that was so especially his. He delighted in the growth that he saw in her. Although she was so young she had great common sense, courage and much humour. And, in one way or another, she constantly reminded him of Vanessa. She had Vanessa's integrity.

On the last evening before his return they talked.

'I wish I was going with you, Tom,' Sally said.

'Do you?' he laughed. 'You wouldn't like it.'

'No, of course I shouldn't. The girls at school all wanted to go once, were dying for the time when they'd be grown up enough to be nurses or something, but now they're not so keen. I don't want to go for any adventurous reason. Only to help.'

'You do help,' he said, 'by staying quietly here and being good-humoured and patient.'

'How long do you think it will last, Tom?'

'Oh, I don't know.' He was holding her small but strong hand in his. 'I've given up prophesying.'

'Do you think that after all we may be beaten?' Her voice sank into an awed whisper.

'No. The Germans won't last as long as we will – not now the Americans have come in.'

'Yes – but the Russians won't fight any more now, will they?' She seemed to be looking into great distances. 'I wonder how Daddy is?'

'Oh, he'll be all right wherever he is,' said Tom.

'When I grow up I hope I shan't forget all I feel now. Don't you, Tom? It would be awful if when we're older we all forgot how horrid it all is and let there be another war.'

She sat on the edge of his chair and put her arms round his neck.

She produced a present, a scarf that she had knitted.

'It isn't very good. I'm not clever with my fingers and, to tell you the truth, I'd have hated the bother if it had been for anyone else.'

So he went back again, trying not to think of Mary. But he didn't think of anyone much. He was terribly tired, not in the body but in the head. And he dreaded the noise. It would be almost better to be dead, because then at least there would be quiet.

And Maurice, the son of Alfred, the son of Amery (thin-legged, dyspeptic, high-stocked, over-large Adam's apple), the son of Durward (of Rocklington Hall; stout, plethoric, fine calves), the son of Pelham (stubborn, hot-tempered), the son of Grandison (exceedingly stout, dewlapped like a bull, intimate with St John), son of Robert (stout, good-natured sot, gambler and humorist, a friend of Charles II), son of Robert who first brought distinction on the family by breeding bullocks in Wiltshire and marrying a Scottish heiress – (he was son of the Herries who came to watch

German miners in Borrowdale in his Queen's service. that cross-grained bitter fellow whose portrait hung in the Herries house in Rosthwaite and later at the Fortress) – well, what of Maurice?

Not very much. 'A poor reward for all the trouble I've taken,' his father would think, looking at him. 'What if he *has* lost an arm? So have lots of other fellows, and worse, blinded, tubes in their stomach, mice in the brain – and there he sits, doing nothing but stare or read or listen to high-class music on the gramophone. Can hardly believe he's my son. Rotten pessimist too. No patriotism. I believe he likes the Germans better than the English.'

So Alfred told him one day at lunch:

'My God, Maurice, I believe you'd rather be a German than an Englishman.'

Maurice gave him a queer look.

'I'd rather be anything than a Herries,' he said.

For by this time in the spring of 1918 he was very, very tired of his family. It was May and the Billing-Maud Allan case was amusing everyone at the Courts. That the case was poisonously hysterical startled nobody. The Family – Alfred, Gordon, Cynthia – alluded darkly to perversion. 'We must sweep these abnormalities from our national life,' wheezed old Horace. 'It's a splendid thing for England that this cancer should be revealed.' But he confided privately to Maurice: 'I know what you're feeling, my boy. To tell you the truth, I'm not as optimistic as I used to be. But one has to put a brave face on things.'

'Why?' asked Maurice.

Horace didn't exactly know. He supposed that he had always been determined to see the bright side of things. All his life it had been the same. After all it wasn't life that was important but the way that you dealt with it. Some writer had said that somewhere, and he thought that it was very true. He wheezed in his chair (his heart was bad) and looked bravely, through rheumy eyes, into Maurice's face.

'I've been laughed at all my life,' he said. 'I've wanted people to like me and they've only laughed at me. I've thought I've done my best, but I can see now that I've failed. My sister went on the streets and died there, and everyone's found me a bore.' He sat there; a thick heavy tear trickled on to his fat cheek and stayed there. He brushed it away.

'All the same,' he said, 'even if I've made a mess of things, what I say is true all the same. It's better to be cheerful and it needs a lot of obstinacy. Cheer up, Maurice. You might have lost both your legs, you know.'

But Maurice couldn't cheer up. His father, his sister, all the Herries save little Sally, drove him mad. He thought perhaps that he was going mad. There were times when the guns sounded so loudly in his ears that he could hear nothing else. He would sit in his bedroom and try to read Joyce or T. S. Eliot or D. H. Lawrence. Beautiful, wonderful things their books had in them. They told the truth at last. For centuries writers had been lying about life, but now no honest writer need ever deceive again. Lawrence seemed to him a kind of young god, fighting all the hypocrisies, the prejudices, the falsities of mankind, and fighting all alone, his back to the wall. He had been persecuted by the damned interfering authorities simply because he protested against this bloody war. And then, when Maurice thought of the authorities (he saw them as a fat, red-tabbed crimson-faced officer screaming at some trembling private ...), he would get up and walk about his room, and the stump of his arm would ache and the guns would sound in his ears and strange fierce lights would flash over the dressing-table and crimson the eiderdown on his bed.

There came a night when he thought that he would end it. He woke at an early hour of grey dawn and a voice said, quite clearly, in his ear: 'Come on. Put an end to this. You've had enough of it. You're never going to be any good at anything. Never. Life is endless.'

So, as though obedient to a command, he got out of bed and wondered what he would do. Should he go down to the kitchen and turn on the gas? That seemed a long business and would need a lot of arranging. He had a penknife. Should he cut an artery? A messy affair. Should he throw himself from his bedroom window? That might not finish him. He walked up and down, followed, it seemed to him, by this persuasive voice.

'Go on, you're no good. You're spoilt and finished. Better get out of it ...'

At last he sat down in the chair by the ash-strewn fire and burst into tears. He cried and cried as though he never would stop. Then he fell asleep in the chair where he was.

A poor affair. Nothing fine about it anywhere. He had a job those last months in the Ministry of Information and so he walked, alone and unattended save by his private demon, from one place to another ...

* * *

About half past ten on Monday morning, November 11th, Benjie went into Hatchard's bookshop. While waiting there he was accosted by a stout pale-faced gentleman who said to him: 'I say – the Armistice is signed.'

'Oh, is it?' said Benjie, bought his book and walked into Piccadilly. There was no sign anywhere of excitement – the buses rolled along, people passed on their business, a young man stood with his eyes seriously fixed on Mr Jackson's appetizing window.

Benjie had moved from Chelsea after his return from Russia and had rooms now in Ryder Street. As he was about to turn into Jermyn Street he spoke to an old man with newspapers.

'Is it true,' he asked, 'that the Armistice is signed?'

'Can't say, sir, I'm sure,' the old man answered, rubbing his nose with the back of his hand.

'Very strange,' Benjie thought. 'This is the moment for which we have all been passionately waiting and no one cares, no one cares at all.'

Entering his flat he saw Sally and Tom sitting together on the sofa.

'Hullo!' he said. 'What are you two doing here?'

'Tom found me in Piccadilly,' Sally explained.

'Why aren't you at school?'

'There's mumps. We were all sent off this morning.' Then she added: 'Tom says the Armistice is signed.'

The valet of the flats came out of Benjie's bedroom with a suit over his arm.

'Bailey,' Benjie said, 'the Armistice is signed.'

'Indeed, sir,' said Bailey. 'I'm very glad, I'm sure. A great relief to everyone. Will you be in to luncheon?'

'Yes – no. Look here, we'll go and celebrate somewhere.'

He looked at both of them.

'Are you sure it's true?' he asked Tom.

'Oh yes – quite sure. The paper had it in an hour ago.'

'This is all wrong,' Benjie thought. He went to the window and glanced down into Ryder Street. No one was stirring.

He looked back at them. 'One day in Russia,' he said, 'about a week after the March Revolution, I got caught in the crowd. We all marched singing through the streets. Everybody was singing. It was the most marvellous thing ... Well, why aren't we singing? The greatest and most horrible war in history is over.'

'I suppose we can't realize it,' said Tom. 'And we're all rather tired.'

'Yes, we're all rather tired,' Benjie thought, 'and we're going to be tired for years and years. Perhaps nobody will have the energy to sing again.'

'All the same,' he added aloud, 'it's something that men aren't going to be killed any more. That's something.'

At that moment they heard the maroons going off and the silver clock on the mantelpiece struck in its thin surprised tone eleven o'clock. They all went to the window and saw people pouring into the street. From every door they seemed to be coming. Men, without hats, rushed out, waving their arms. Flinging the window open, Benjie could hear distant shouting.

'Come on,' he said. 'Let's go out and see the sights.'

After that they were part of a vast, wild, cheering and yet oddly unexcited crowd. That at least was what Benjie felt, as though all these people said to him with one voice (not a loud voice – almost a whisper): 'It is right for us to be excited. We've won a great war, but life is changed. We can never be quite so light-hearted and careless again. Once, not so very long ago, on Mafeking night, we all went mad. But we shan't go mad now. We have to behave as though we were gloriously happy. But we are not. By tonight we may be drunk a little and make a noise, but it doesn't mean anything.'

Nevertheless, with Sally close at his side, he could not but feel that something was accomplished. Another phase of history, another phase of his own life, was closed. His adventurous days were over and so too, maybe, were the adventurous days of the world. It would be all cold mechanism now – mechanism, science, a remorseless progress.

He had a sudden longing for Vanessa and at that same moment Sally said: 'How I wish that Mother was here!' He pressed her arm close to him. So long as Sally was alive things would not be mechanical. She was too individual for that.

They had pushed their way to Trafalgar Square, but here they were brought to a standstill. A thick unbroken mass of humanity. Men were shouting and singing, girls waving. But Benjie felt that everyone was waiting for something. That moment of singing in Petrograd would not be recovered here. It would never be recovered. It had been a moment of extravagant idealistic hope.

'There should be a Triumphal Arch,' he thought. 'Here in front of the lions. And everyone should march away under it, swearing as they passed beneath it that never again would men hate, plunder, be greedy ... Never again!' He smiled. Not bad nonsense for an old cynic like himself. That was the sort of thing that old Horace would say. Alfred and Gordon and the others would have a fine time tonight. They at least would be happy, for they had won the War and were Lords of the Earth.

But not perhaps for long. The battle was not over yet between the Maurices and the Gordons, the Cynthias and the Vanessas.

'Come on,' he said. 'We'll go to the Berkeley and have a feed.'

A thin rain had begun to fall. There was no Triumphal Arch. As they pushed their way slowly Benjie saw a soldier, motionless, staring, unshifted by the crowd. 'Perhaps he's thinking that now he won't be killed. He won't have to go back to that hell. That's something anyway.'

He thought constantly of Vanessa. If she were here how happy she would be that he was safe now, and that Tom was safe. She would be happy for all the women all over the world.

All the women! Yes, that was something.

But there was no Triumphal Arch.

SALLY AND TOM

CYNTHIA gave Gordon Newmark a theatre party on his thirtieth birthday (he was thirty on February 4th, 1925) and Sally and old Horace Ormerod and Rosalind and Adrian came too. Cynthia (who was now over sixty, although you would never think it unless you looked at her neck), had a weakness for Gordon and hoped that, with judicious management, he might be induced to marry her daughter Rosalind. Rosalind was a good girl, had the best character in the world, and, although she was on the plain side and was now over thirty, would make a good wife for Gordon. Gordon once might have married her, for he was just the kind of man to appreciate good solid wearing qualities in a wife, but after the deaths of old Sidney and Mary Newmark (they died within a week or two of one another) it was discovered that their children, Gordon and Ada, would have large fortunes. Gordon was, of course, in his grandfather's business but made his headquarters in London. He was of another generation from old Horace Newmark, who thought that there was no city in the world to equal Manchester. Gordon was good-looking, with clear-cut features (a little too clear-cut perhaps) and that fashion that cropped up again and again in Herries businessmen of wearing clothes that looked too immaculate to be human. He was an agreeable well-mannered fellow, proud of his own looks, his DSO, his business ability, his family and his 'I like a man with no nonsense about him' – one of his favourite sayings. He intended a little later to go into politics and he would have a peerage before he finished. But first he must marry, and Cynthia hoped that in spite of his money, his profile and his self-confidence he might marry Rosalind.

For alas, neither Mary nor Rosalind was yet married. It was too extraordinary! Mary was still lovely, but for some reason young men didn't propose to her. They came up to her, looked at her with wonder in their eyes and went away again. The fact was that, thirty years earlier, when Vanessa ruled Hill Street, Mary would have been exactly what everyone wanted – beautiful, dignified, graceful, and not too clever. Now the young men (who after all had served their country) wanted something more lively.

So Cynthia had her troubles. Peile was aged and, although his figure was still good, this new post-War world appeared to have struck him dumb with amazement. It had been, at one time, the middle classes that had seemed to him astonishing. He had appealed to his Herries relations to save the country. But the job had been, it seemed, altogether too much for his relatives. So now, standing on his thin aristocratic legs, looking at the Income Tax and the closing of the great houses of England and the young women who looked like boys and the young men who looked like girls, he could only stare and stutter and gasp.

So he was not of very much use to Cynthia, who, from the house in Eaton Place, did what she could, looking now like a rather pretty little pig, with her hair a little too yellow, her cheeks a little too pink, her skirts a little too short, and her neck (in spite of all she could do) a little too wrinkled.

She had invited Sally to the theatre party because she had invited old Horace. She had had no intention of asking Horace, but one afternoon when he had called on her and had sat there looking so old and pathetic, her heart (which was still kindly when she gave it an opportunity) was moved to say: 'Well, Horace, you must come to the theatre with us. Come next week. We are going to that play that everyone is talking about – by a new young man whose name I forget. They say he's extraordinarily clever and only left school last year.' Horace, who was now nearing seventy, had purple streaks on either side of his nose, an unwieldy stomach, and a cheery smile that was habit rather than intention (and so seemed to Cynthia terribly pathetic), said eagerly that he'd love to come. He was free practically any night next week.

('What a bore!' thought Cynthia. 'Whatever did I ask him for?')

Having done so she must also invite Sally, for the strange thing was (one of the many strange things about Sally) that she was attached to Horace; she was kind to him and never showed him that sharp tongue and penetrating criticism only too apparent with others. Sally would look after Horace. It was a pity that Gordon did not like Sally. That, however, would throw Gordon all the more into Rosalind's company, and she, Cynthia, could be amused by Adrian, who was elegant, witty, drily cynical, and knew the private behaviour of everyone.

So they went to *The Vortex*. They met at the theatre because the play began early, and instead of dinner before they would have supper at the Savoy Grill afterwards. Sally was the first to arrive and Gordon the second. Each was annoyed at seeing the other.

'Who else is coming?' asked Gordon.

'Horace.'

'Horace? Oh Lord, what a bore!'

'Why?' said Sally.

'Oh, well, he's a bit comic,' said Gordon.

'Comic?' said Sally. 'So's everyone. I am – you are.'

Gordon said nothing but he was greatly annoyed. *He* comic? You might call him anything you like – everyone with personality has detractors – but comic? He looked at Sally with great distaste. Her hair, which had now lost its carroty shade and was a plain dark brown, was bobbed in the new fashion. With a few more inches and a little more colour she would not have been so bad. She was slim, her eyes and mouth were bright, alive – too alive, perhaps, for he hated young girls to look sarcastic. She was unlike other girls and that he also disliked. The height of good form, he thought, was that you should not attract attention in a crowd. Of course if you were a *beautiful* woman, that was another matter. No one could call Sally Herries beautiful, and there she was, thinking no end of herself, secretary to some old Jew (she worked because she liked it, not because she had to), living in the most independent manner with another girl, illegitimate (although of course in these days no one minded that) and, worst of all, Benjie Herries' daughter. Now that Gordon considered himself the head of the Herries family and responsible for its good behaviour, he greatly regretted Benjie, who, in spite of his being seventy and having only one arm, often behaved outrageously and had some dreadful friends.

So Gordon ('Who *is* that handsome man?' someone, standing near him in the foyer, asked her companion. 'What splendid features! He looks like an actor.') and Sally stood there disliking one another exceedingly. The others arrived and they all went in. Soon the curtain went up, and the young author of the play, himself playing the lead, began to tell the other characters exactly what he thought of them.

Cynthia, as she listened, became more and more uncomfortable. What a *very* queer collection of people! The mother, with her cropped hair, her painted face, her passion for cigarettes and cocktails, was of course nothing like Cynthia, and it made it all the queerer that the part should be acted by nice Miss Lilian Braithwaite, whom Cynthia knew well, a charming woman with nothing very modern about her. No, the mother on the stage was nothing like Cynthia, who was received everywhere, and by the young people especially, with the greatest warmth. She so often said: 'I don't feel a day more than thirty', and it was true, she did not, unless her neuritis bothered, or chance had forced upon her a succession of late nights. No, she did not resemble this woman in any way nor did any of the friends of Mary or Rosalind resemble the girl with the Eton crop, played by Miss Molly Kerr, or the dreadful young man whom Noel Coward presented so vigorously. When the curtain went down she turned to Adrian.

'Well I never – what an extraordinary lot of people!'

Adrian, whose eyelids were always a little weary like Mr Pater's Monna Lisa's, said: 'Oh, do you think so? There are lots like them nowadays!'

'Surely not!'

He waited a little. Then he said:

'When I see this sort of thing, I think of Vanessa. I never forget her as I saw her first at a ball. She was dressed in white, with her dark hair piled on the top of her head. I have never seen anything so beautiful before or since.'

'Poor Vanessa!' said Cynthia. 'How terrible she would think all of this!'

'Not at all,' Adrian said sharply. 'She was too simple to be frightened off by external differences. She would be shy, of course, and think that she was being stupid, but she would make friends with that boy and girl in no time. There's been nobody like her since she died.'

'Oh, do you think so? Well, if you come to that, nobody's like anybody, are they? But I can't agree with you, Adrian. Vanessa would be miserable in a world like this. She wouldn't know how to adapt herself.'

'She wouldn't try to,' said Adrian rather crossly. 'She'd just be natural. Of course some people would find her dull. Some people always did. But others – she'd be just what they are always looking for now and can't find.'

('Adrian's getting a bore,' Cynthia thought. 'And old – a fussy old Foreign Office bachelor.')

Sally took Horace for a stroll.

'Are you enjoying yourself, Horace dear?' she asked him.

'Oh, I should just think I am!' he answered her in his full philanthropic voice. 'I enjoy everything. When you get to my age, my dear, you'll realize how true it is what Stevenson once said: "We all ought to be as happy as kings." '

'Your tie's up at the back of your collar,' Sally said critically. 'What a whacking lie if Stevenson ever did say that. And you know you don't mean it, Horace. Even though you've been pretending to be jolly all your life you needn't pretend it now with me.'

'But I *am* enjoying the play,' he said a little sheepishly. 'I don't go so often to the theatre nowadays, you know. I like a jaunt. I'm a lonely old widower and a bit of fun does me good.'

Behind his red cheeks and large round glasses and protruding chin there was fear: fear of illness, fear of being laughed at, fear of solitude at the last and, above all, fear of being left behind. Sally knew that it was true, that the world found Horace a dreadful bore, that men at the Club slipped away as he approached, that young men laughed at him and that all his relations despised him. She was fond of him because she knew all these things.

'Lonely! Of course you're not!' she said cheerfully. 'Look here, come and have tea with Margaret and me tomorrow afternoon. I've got an afternoon off. My old Jew's going down to Brighton.'

'Oh, thank you, my dear.' Horace's glasses beamed. 'I should enjoy it immensely. I like your friend Margaret.'

'Margaret's a pet,' said Sally.

'And when is your father returning from South Africa?'

'Oh, any day now.'

'And Tom – how's Tom getting on?'

'Very well indeed. He writes some of the leaders now.'

'That's fine,' said Horace, looking proudly about him. Here he was with a splendid girl – a true representative of the young generation – and she had asked him to tea, and Cynthia, one of the smartest women in London, had invited him to the theatre, and he belonged to one of the most prominent families in England. He forgot, in his sudden exuberance, the faded gloom of his rooms in Jermyn Street, the surly indifference of his man-servant, and the rude manner with which Alfred had turned his back on him a few days ago.

He had always said: 'I don't know what it is, but there's a sort of inner happiness in me which nothing can destroy.' It wasn't quite true any longer and he had never realized that his consciousness of it had been, in the past, one of the principal reasons for his unpopularity, but it was true enough at the moment for him to look at all the men near him with a certain kindly condescension as though they had all just fallen into the water and he was there, with a strong manly hand, ready to pull them out again.

Cynthia and Adrian joined them.

('Why is it,' Sally had once asked Tom, 'that all the members of our family move about as though they had just opened public buildings?')

'I think the play's absurd,' said Cynthia. 'I never saw such people!'

'Oh, do you?' said Sally. 'There are lots of them about. I'm rather like it myself.'

She wasn't and she knew that she wasn't, but it pleased her to irritate Cynthia.

At that moment Adrian brought up a man. 'Cynthia, this is a friend of mine at the Foreign Office – Arnold Young.'

The man was perhaps about five-and-twenty, slim, tall, fair-haired. He had a weak chin, a mouth with humour and bright blue eyes. He looked weak and amiable, as though he needed caring for and would be charming if you cared for him.

Sally looked at him and her heart was moved. He instantly smiled. 'You were rather like a choir boy,' he told her afterwards, 'who was bored to death with the sermon.'

The bell rang and they turned into the passage.

'Do you like this play?' the young man asked Sally.

'Oh, frightfully!'

'Isn't Noel Coward marvellous?'

'Simply marvellous.'

And just as they reached the stalls he said to her:

'I say – I hope we meet again somewhere.'

They must have met somewhere again very shortly after this, because, about a week later, Sally had this conversation with Tom.

Tom, who was a concrete Conservative, still inhabited the rooms in Tite Street.

Tom was now forty-one years of age. He was heavily built but not stout, short and square-shouldered, with a pale, anxious, extremely kindly face. Many years of journalism had not changed him. He was dressed in a black coat, black tie, striped dark trousers always. He played golf a little, and in the summer tennis a little. He liked his work but was not enthusiastic about it. He had only two passions – Cumberland and the few people he loved – Vanessa, his father, Mary and Sally. Over these four (Vanessa's ghost was certainly one of them) he watched and worried until they would sometimes scream with annoyance. He knew this and now did all he could to hide his care for them. He pretended to be quite indifferent as to whether they came or went. He was even a little afraid of letting Vanessa's ghost know how often he thought of her! Because he cared for his father less than for the others he irritated him the least. Besides, in these days, Benjie was often abroad. But Mary and Sally were simply his whole world. When they snapped at him, as they frequently did, he would slowly flush and blame himself for being so tiresome. Curiously, in relation to the rest of the world he was rather indifferent. Men in Fleet Street both respected and liked him. He was not clever enough to rouse their jealousy and he was always ready to do someone a turn, not from sentiment but simply because he was good-natured.

But that world hardly existed for him. He would have been a better journalist if it had. When he could snatch a night or two he would hurry up to Cumberland. There was a farm between Grange and Cat Bells where he always had a bedroom. Then he would walk, generally alone. He knew the Tops like his London bedroom wallpaper.

Sally loved him and bullied him. It exasperated her that year after year he should long for Mary Worcester who would never marry him. With glee she told him one day that people said that she was going to marry the young Duke of Wrexe.

'Funny, isn't it? History repeats itself. Our great-grandmother was engaged for a while to the Duke of Wrexe of her day. The lovely Jennifer – lovely and stupid like Mary.'

However, the young Duke of Wrexe married an American girl.

'Why do you tease me about Mary, Sally?' Tom asked her once. 'I never mention her.'

'Why do you go on year after year when it's hopeless! I want you to marry a nice good girl and make me an aunt.'

'You wouldn't like it if I did,' he said truthfully.

On this particular day when Sally had tea with him in Tite Street she did not tease him. She was very affectionate. He loved her dearly when she was kind. All the best in her came out. Her eternal qualities of courage and honesty were transmuted when she was kind into a true nobility. When she was not kind she seemed sometimes hard and selfish.

But today she looked at him with eyes of love. She sat on the edge of his armchair, swinging her legs, his arm round her.

'When's Father coming home?'

'Any time now.'

'I wonder what he's been doing in South Africa. I hope he's been behaving himself. Every year I think he's getting too old to misbehave any more, but he doesn't. Vanessa managed him, but no one else ever has.' She waved her arms. 'I love him! He's such a pet with his little ruddy face and his sharp eyes and his one arm and his eagerness to fall into any scrap that's coming! He'll startle us all yet and shock the family once again before he's done.'

She looked at Tom meditatively.

'Tom, I'm going to tell you something. You'll probably hate it. I'm in love – for the first time in my life.'

His arm clutched her a little more tightly. His heart began to hammer and he told himself: 'Now be careful. Don't show her that you mind. Don't show her that you're anxious. She's a modern girl. She won't stand being warned or advised.' He was able to say very quietly:

'Who with, Sally darling?'

She stroked his head.

'That's right, my pet. You're taking it well. He's a man in the Foreign Office. He's a friend of Adrian's and his name is Arnold Young.'

'Oh yes? I don't think I've met him.'

(Inside he was saying to himself: 'Now I shall have to protect Sally without her knowing it and see that he treats her right. She thinks she knows everything about life, like all girls now, but she doesn't.')

'No, you wouldn't have. Well, he's tall and got a lovely figure and he's very fair with blue eyes. On the other hand, he has no chin and wants looking after. He has a mother who plays bridge, morning, noon and night.'

'Does he know you're in love with him? Where did you meet him?'

'I met him when I went to *The Vortex* with Cynthia. I don't think he knows I'm in love with him. We've only met twice. I'm very rude to him. I've never been in love before and it's a funny feeling.'

'Would you like to marry him?'

'Yes, I think so – if he asked me. Of course all Margaret's friends think marriage is rot nowadays. As long as you don't have a baby there's no point about marriage, they say. But I don't quite agree. It's all very well going away with a man for a week-end, but I think it would be nice to *look after* Arnold, run his home for him and everything. I expect I'm old-fashioned. Margaret says I am.'

'Is he a decent fellow?' Tom asked. 'I mean has he got a mistress somewhere or anything like that?'

'Oh no,' said Sally. 'He doesn't seem to care for girls. He's terribly under his mother's influence. That's the worst thing about him. But he isn't one of those, you know, or anything like that. Not a bit nancy. I don't say he's very fine or grand or wonderful. I'm just in love with him, that's all – here in the pit of the stomach!'

Then to Tom's astonishment she put her arms round his neck, kissed him and laid her cheek against his. She hardly ever kissed him.

'Do you know,' she said, 'we're all by ourselves – Vanessa, Father, you and I. Misfits. Still, we don't have a bad time.'

She began to roam round the room. Looking up, on a shelf above her head she saw an old green book. She stood on her toes and brought it down. She looked into it. It was a large fat book filled with rather faded writing in an old-fashioned female hand.

'What's this?' she asked.

'Oh, don't you know? That's some recollections Judith Paris

wrote when she was an old lady – or rather she dictated them.'

'How marvellous! May I read them?'

'You'd better not take them away. Father asked me to take care of them for him.'

'Why – are they shocking?'

'Not in the least. But Judith gave them to Adam, Vanessa's father, and Vanessa gave them to Father.'

'Oh, but listen, Tom! They go back ever so far – almost to the beginning of the eighteenth century.'

'Yes; Judith lived to be a hundred, you know.'

'Oh, let me take them! I'll be frightfully careful.'

He hesitated. 'Well, if you're *fearfully* careful—'

'Of course I will. I must go now.' She came to him and kissed him. 'Dear old Tom. I don't want to be sloppy, but you *are* a darling.'

He held her with his hand on her arm.

'Sally. Look here. I know you hate my being serious, but – well, what I mean is you haven't got anyone but me, in a way. Father isn't here and he wouldn't be much use. Vanessa told me to look after you.'

She smiled.

'Well – what is it?'

'You will be careful, won't you? I know girls know everything these days. Since the War they don't care *what* they do. But – you'll be careful, won't you? Tell me if you want any help about anything. Are you sure he's a decent fellow?'

'Of course he is. I can look after myself.'

After she was gone Tom walked about the room sighing. She looked such a baby. She was such a good sort. He loved her so dearly. But there you were. It wasn't the thing now to show your feelings. He had such a lot. Had he only been able to write! He sat down and soon was lost in a book of Santayana's. Now *there* was a writer!

On a day in April Adrian gave a luncheon party at his rooms in Lincoln's Inn. He invited Sally, Maurice, Maurice's young woman, Arnold Young, Miss Culloden, the well-known novelist, and her friend Miss James.

Sally hadn't known that Arnold was to be there. She had not seen him for three weeks. Adrian had asked her very casually and she had thought that very possibly she would be the only guest besides Maurice and Emily Tempest, to whom he was engaged.

When she saw Miss Culloden she was afflicted with the shyness
that she inherited from her mother. She was always sorry when
she was shy, because shyness made her rude and abrupt in self-
defence. Sally had read none of Miss Culloden's books. She read
very little and for the most part the authors whom her friend
Margaret admired – Lawrence and Aldous Huxley. She had attempted *Women in Love* and *Ulysses* and found them very tiresome. Then one evening she had found an old faded copy of
Rider Haggard's *She* tucked away on a shelf. Scornfully she had
begun it, and Margaret, coming in at one in the morning, had
found her, curled up in a corner of the sofa, entranced.

'Whatever are you reading?' said Margaret. And then, when
she saw, all she said was: 'My God!'

So Sally did not know what her real taste in books was. But she
did know that she had read nothing by Miss Culloden.

Miss Culloden was a large cheerful friendly woman who reminded Sally of one of those broad-backed white horses at the
circus, who go patiently round and round while ladies spring on
to them and off them again. Miss James was her little friend who
went with her everywhere and 'brought her out' on the subject of
her works. Sally could not conceive why Adrian had invited her,
for Adrian's taste in the Arts was severe, but it afterwards appeared that Miss Culloden had met him somewhere and had
insisted on being invited. That was why the party today was
mainly 'Family'. No celebrated persons. Miss Culloden was the
life and soul. She was one of those fortunate writers (very rare)
who are completely satisfied with everything – their own works,
their publishers, their public and everything concerning them.

'You remember, Molly,' said Miss James, 'there was that chapter about Venice in *Grapes and Thistles* – one of your best bits, I
always thought.'

Adrian changed the conversation to Sargent, who was recently
dead.

'Everyone said at the time,' said Miss James 'that the artist in
Models for Sale was intended for Sargent.'

'Well, he wasn't,' said Miss Culloden very firmly. 'He was a
composite portrait.'

'I remember you were very anxious at the time,' said Miss
James.

'Well, I'd have hated Sargent's feelings to be hurt. People are
terribly sensitive. They're hurt if they think they're *in* a book and
they're hurt if they're not.'

After a while Miss Culloden surveyed the table. 'You're quite a family party, aren't you? Netta and I feel honoured at being made one of you like this. Oh yes, I know what I wanted to say. I was hearing about a marvellous member of your family the other day, an old lady who lived to be a hundred. And she'd actually seen Napoleon just before Waterloo, and knew Disraeli and all sorts of famous people. Wouldn't she be wonderful for a novel? I wonder if you'd all mind if I wrote a book about her one day?'

'I don't think she actually *saw* Napoleon,' Adrian said. 'She was Sally's great-grandmother—'

'Was she *really?*' Miss Culloden beamed upon Sally. 'Oh, how splendid! Now do tell me!'

'If you ever *dare* to put her in a book,' Sally said, her voice trembling, 'I'll bring an action.'

Everyone was uncomfortable. That was just like the girl, Adrian thought, to take the old fool seriously. You never knew what she *would* be serious over! But of course with Benjie for a father . . .

However, Miss Culloden didn't mind in the least, but thought: 'What a strange, unusual little girl! I'll see more of her.'

Adrian changed the conversation yet once again and asked Miss Culloden whether she had been to the theatre. Had she seen *No, No, Nanette?*

'Yes, indeed – and it's simply splendid—' she began.

But Sally was miserable. There she was, making a fool of herself before Arnold. She could remember when she was seven or six or some absurd age that Vanessa had warned her about her tempers. She could see Vanessa standing by the window in the room at Hill Street, the room with the two yellow globes and the picture with 'Miss Muffet and the Spider'. Yes, Vanessa was there, wanting not to laugh, wanting to be stern and severe, but Sally had made a face and Vanessa had laughed . . .

'—and if Miss Herries *ever* forgives me,' Miss Culloden was saying, 'I shall ask her one day—'

Everyone was looking at Sally as though they expected her to do something, so she smiled at Miss Culloden, hating herself, one of those horrible smiles that you fastened on to your mouth as a dentist fastens on a gag.

And not only was Vanessa standing there, but now also Judith Paris, for, in the last few weeks, Sally had absorbed that old green book into her very blood and bones. She knew it almost by heart and it was agony to her when it stopped, stopped at one of its most thrilling moments when Judith was remembering the terrible quarrel about the fan at Christabel's Ball. Why, conceive it! Here was Sally and there at her very elbow was Judith who, going on a jaunt with her French husband to the 'Elephant and Castle', had worn a dress – 'a jaquette of pale silver-coloured silk and the bodice and underdress were of dark wine colour: I wore a hat of light straw and my shoes had silver buckles'. There was Judith in her old age dictating to her great-great-niece Jane Bellairs, who, a sweet old maiden lady with ringlets, had died as recently as 1905, and here was she, Sally, in 1925, feeling that Judith was in the very room with her, the hat of light straw perched on her red hair ...

'I'm sure you are wrong, dear,' Miss James was saying in her firm even voice that was like a ruler drawing lines on a piece of white paper. 'It wasn't until *Love in a Garret* that America really took you to its heart. I remember so well your telling me that the Americans were fickle and that you were not going to allow yourself to be persuaded by the success of one book into thinking that it would last. You told me, I remember, that Sir Philip Gibbs said—'

'Oh, God! this is awful!' Adrian thought. He looked at Maurice, who was one of the discontented members of the family. 'A legacy of the War' Cynthia called Maurice, and it was certainly true that he had lost an arm and written a little book about Blake and got himself engaged, when he had no money at all, to a young woman who painted ladies with green hair and the oddest legs, all things – in the opinion of Cynthia and Alfred and Gordon – that might be classed together as a 'pity'.

'Oh, these awful women!' thought Adrian. 'What *can* Maurice be thinking of them?'

He had a high opinion of Maurice, who had bought a Matisse in Paris very cheap, and had had tea with James Joyce. But he was wrong about Maurice, who liked Miss Culloden very much. She reassured him. Obviously to her the world was not a bloody, menacing place in which everything and everybody was going to hell. He liked her, whereas he loathed Gordon, who also believed in life. But then Gordon believed in life because Gordon was such a wonderful fellow, and Miss Culloden believed in life because she was naturally happy, like a lark in the sky ...

When the party was breaking up, Arnold said to Sally: 'Can I take you anywhere? I've got a car.'

Sally's heart leapt for joy.

'Yes, you can,' she said. 'Anywhere you like. I haven't got to be at the office till four.' She was so happy that, on bidding farewell, she looked up at Miss Culloden and said, smiling (this time with real if rather childlike sincerity):

'Please forgive me if I was rude.'

'Rude, my dear!' cried Miss Culloden. 'Why, you're too sweet for anything! Now you must come and have lunch with me, you really must – and I promise not to say a word about your great-aunt or whatever she was. Now what day can you come?' She produced a small silver-edged notebook. 'I'm talking to the Soroptimists on Tuesday and there's Marie Lowndes on Wednesday. Thursday I'm going out to Surbiton. Now what about Friday? Friday's quite all right. There's only the Tallboys Club Committee in the afternoon . . . Now *what* about Friday?'

So Sally was engaged for Friday.

In the little car (which was bright red in colour and *very* smart) Sally said: 'Where are we going?'

'Anywhere you like.'

'Haven't you any work or anything?'

'Oh yes, but I *must* talk to you.'

'Well, let's go to the National Gallery and look at the Sargents.'

Side by side on a settee alone in the room, looking at one lovely woman after another, Sally said:

'I like Mrs Charles Hunter's hat.' Then she added: 'They're all quite unreal, aren't they?'

'Yes,' said Arnold. 'He despised women. The only thing he admired about them was their clothes. You can see how he hated his sitters. His hatred is real in the pictures even if nothing else is.'

'Yes,' said Sally, who, sitting there very meekly, wishing that her legs were a little longer and that altogether she was built on a larger scale, was nevertheless a great deal happier than any girl of her generation thought it fitting to be.

'Will you marry me?' Arnold said suddenly.

'Yes,' Sally said. 'I'd love to.'

'I'm terribly glad,' Arnold said. 'I loved you from the first moment I saw you.'

As he said this Sally thought that he'd never wanted looking after so badly as now. She longed to put her arm round him. All she said was:

'You know I'm illegitimate.'

'What on earth does that matter?'

'Have you any money, Arnold darling?'

'Well, not a lot. There's what I get in the Foreign Office and my mother makes me an allowance.'

'Your mother doesn't like me,' Sally said quickly.

'She will when she knows you, darling.'

'No, she never will. She thinks I'm Bohemian and she's heard things about Father. She knows Father and Mother weren't married. These things matter to *her* and always will.'

A shadow seemed to pass very swiftly over Arnold's face. (Poor dear! he certainly *did* need looking after!)

'She wants you to marry a fine girl of a noble family. Her generation are *like* that.'

'Well, your family's all right. It's one of the best in England.'

'I know, dear – but don't let's be snobbish. The point about our family is that there are the right ones and the wrong ones. There always have been. Cynthia Worcester and Alfred and Gordon are the right ones – but my father and I are the wrong ones, I'm afraid.'

'What nonsense you're talking, Sally darling. You're splendid! You're wonderful! And my mother isn't going to say whom I'm going to marry! It's my life, not hers!' It was the bravest thing Arnold had ever said.

'Well, you go and talk to her,' Sally said, laying her hand for a moment on his. 'I won't be engaged until you've talked to her, but I do love you frightfully and I think I always will.'

There, in that public room, in front of all the Sargent ladies, they kissed, and as he felt Sally's small body tremble against his he swore to himself that he would defy a thousand mothers ...

'Oh, of course,' young Mr Elton was saying, 'if you prefer to read people like Galsworthy and Barrie—'

'Why shouldn't I?' said Mary Worcester. 'I don't, if you want to know. But why shouldn't I?'

'Because they're false as hell,' said young Mr Elton. Then he saw that his audience was despicable, made his adieus and departed.

'I suppose I'd better be going too,' said Tom.

'I don't think Mother will be in now. She's playing bridge and *said* she'd be back, but with bridge you never know ...'

Tom stood in the middle of the charming little drawing-room,

which in the fashion of the moment had only one French picture
on its walls – a late and not-at-all-good Utrillo – a bronze by
Dobson on the mantelpiece, and very little else.

Then, hiding his fear, he spoke the words that, for almost all
his life, had been trembling on his lips. Why now? Was it less
hopeless than ever? Certainly not. Mary, who in these days was
often depressed, was very depressed indeed at the moment. An
extremely agreeable handsome young man, who would have been
an excellent escort to all kinds of places, had found her, like all
the other agreeable young men, most appallingly dull. She didn't
want to be dull. She was ready to admire their painters, their
poets, their morals, their cynicism, their atheism, although in her
heart she found all these things unpleasant, but it was of no use.
They found her a bore and practically said so. She was thirty-
two. Life was ghastly.

Nevertheless the words came pouring from Tom's lips.

'Mary, I can't help it. I've wanted to say this so often. You
know I have. Won't you marry me? I've loved you all my life. It
mightn't turn out so badly. I've got a rise. I'm doing leaders on
the paper now, and there are articles too I write for the weeklies.
It isn't such a bad income and, if you married me, I believe I
could do ever so much better still. I would look after you – I
would care for you—'

He stopped because the words choked him. He looked away
from her at the Dobson bronze, a figure with thighs so enormous
and a head so small that it filled him, at this moment, with terror.

Mary looked at him with great kindness. She patted the grey
sofa with her hand.

'Tom, come and sit down.' He came and sat down. 'You know
I can't.'

'Why not? No one has loved you so long nor so faithfully—'

'Yes, I know. But there are other things beside fidelity. One
thing is that I don't love you. You know that I don't. That isn't
my fault or yours. Another is that I'm frightfully stupid. If I
lived with you I'd bore you terribly. Another is that I must marry
someone with money. And another – perhaps the most important
– is that I never would marry any member of our family.'

He came closer to her and she allowed him to take her hand.

'Then there's another. You're *too* good, you're *too* faithful. I
couldn't bear anyone who loved me as you do. I know I'm not
worth it, but it isn't that. No one's worth it. But I like people who
are independent of me, who don't give a damn whether I'm nice

to them or no. If I snap at you it's as though I struck you. You
wince. But I *do* like you. I don't mean that. Only to live with you
– never, dear Tom.'

She hesitated, then went on:

'You see, you're old-fashioned. You believe in God and kindness and charity and all the old things. How you can, I can't
think! It's a rotten world run by stupid people. It may come right
again one day, although not in our time, I expect. You're like old
Horace in that, except that you really *do* believe in the things you
say. You're like Vanessa, who was, I'm sure, the finest woman
who ever lived, but she simply doesn't *belong* to our time.'

'You're not to say a word—' began Tom.

'There you are, you see? You won't face the facts. You never
do. I didn't know Vanessa very well, but I *do* think she was
splendid – much finer than any of us are! But she seems old-
fashioned now – she was Victorian – and you're a bit Victorian
too.'

There was a long pause. Then he said:

'What do you mean – you wouldn't marry one of the
family?'

'Just what I say! I hate and loathe our family! Either we're
prigs or we're mad. We are so damnably English whatever we are.
Mother's all right, I suppose, but look at Father and Rosalind
and Alfred and Gordon – and poor Maurice who's as cracked as
can be; and there was Ellis who was mad for years; and Rose,
Horace's sister, who died in the gutter. And if you go back it's just
the same. Your grandfather was murdered by your great-uncle,
and before that there was a Herries shot himself in London, and
there was the crazy Herries in the eighteenth century. And in
between the others have all been dull and self-satisfied and self-
righteous. I shall marry someone or other just to get away. But I
won't marry to stay.'

Tom answered slowly: 'You're wrong, Mary. Whether we've
been mad or sane we've been alive. You may laugh at England,
but it's the finest— Oh, don't let's talk about the family! What
does it matter? I'm only half Herries! The family can't make any
difference! And I won't fuss over you, Mary, really I won't. You
shall have your own life. You shan't see more of me than you
want to! We get on together. We have for years. You like being
with me. If you married me—'

She sighed. 'It's a shame,' she said at last. 'I'm glad you've told
me, though, because – now that you see that it's hopeless perhaps
you'll find someone else. I've wanted for years to tell you how

hopeless it is. Of course I like you and like being with you – sometimes. But I'm not worth it – not worth your kind of devotion, Tom. And you'd regret it like anything. I shall get fat and plain and peevish. I haven't an idea in my head, only scraps of other people's ideas. And I want money. It's the only thing that can save me. With money I can make things do, perhaps. Without it—'

'If you loved me,' he said at last, 'would any of these other things have mattered?'

'Once they wouldn't. But now – it isn't love I want but money and comfort and safety.'

He got up. She liked him at that moment very much. She got up and held out her hand.

'Goodbye, Tom dear,' she said.

'Goodbye,' he answered and left her.

He went back to Tite Street, sat in his room, his head between his hands, thinking. This was awful. Mary's refusal had made no difference to his love for her. How could it when it was part of his vrey being? But now he had got to make terms with it, he thought. He must manage his life henceforth so that this dead hope did not spread like a cancer into all his energies. For, until today, there had always been a hope – for years and years that hope had been a light in his room. Now he must manage without it.

He was so desperately tired that he slept in his chair, his head forward on his breast.

He woke to find that the light had been switched on and his father was standing there. He rubbed his eyes, for he was only half awake, and Benjie was like a figure in a dream, standing in a rough heather-coloured overcoat and holding on a chain a very alert, eye-shining, panting rough-haired terrier.

'Good God!' Tom cried, jumping up.

'Yes,' said Benjie smiling. 'Here I am.'

'Why didn't you send a wire?'

'Well, you see, Tom, I didn't know when I'd arrive. As it is I've been in the New Forest a whole week wandering about. That's where I bought this.'

The dog, its tongue out and its brilliant deep brown eyes almost jumping from its head, strained at the hold. The colour of its coat was black and tan, with a fine rough white patch across the neck.

'Why didn't you write from the New Forest?' asked Tom.

'Oh Lord, I don't know! Don't badger me. My bags are in the

other room. Isn't this a nice overcoat? I won it in a bet on the boat. Luckily the other fellow was just my size. Heavens! but I'm tired!'

He took his coat off. He was thinner and browner than ever, thought Tom, and his eyes had the same desperate brightness as the dog's. He went and poured himself out a whisky and soda. He sat on the edge of the deal table, swinging his thin legs, his little animal-like face cocked a bit over his glass. Tom had noticed that the very first thing he had looked at across the room was a large photograph of Vanessa.

'Any news?'

'Sally's engaged.'

'What!' Benjie sprang off the table. 'Sally! My little Sally! Heavens! Who to?'

'A fellow called Young – Arnold Young. He's in the Foreign Office.'

Benjie was excited. He came over to Tom, holding up his glass with his one hand.

'What's he like?'

'Oh, he's all right, I suppose. Sally thinks so. But he's just the sort of chap Sally would pick up – a bit weak, I should think, and wants looking after.'

'Any money?'

'Got a rich mother, and I should think she's bloody from what Sally says. Nor does she like Sally. She goes about everywhere, I believe, saying that there's no engagement and it's preposterous and so on.'

'Why, what has she got against my Sally?'

'Oh, I don't know.'

'Born out of wedlock, scamp of a father – that sort of thing?'

'I don't know. I haven't seen her.'

Then, very like Benjie, he drove the thing right out of his mind. He had released the dog, who now bounded all over the room, sometimes prancing on four legs at once like a young lamb, and examining everything.

'What's it's name?'

'Sam.'

'It's a shame to keep a dog like that in London.'

'I shan't keep it in London. I'm going up to Cumberland.'

'Oh, I say, are you really!' Tom's eyes shone.

Benjie put his glass down and rested his hand on Tom's shoulder.

'Like to come too?'

'Wouldn't I, though!'

'Could you get off?'

'Yes, for a bit, I think.'

Benjie looked at him critically, then drew him closer until shoulder touched shoulder.

'You're not looking any too fine.'

'Oh, I'm all right.'

Father and son gave one another a glance and each smiled.

'What's the matter? Mary turned you down?'

'Yes. How did you know?'

'Oh, I guessed. I'm a bit lonely too. South Africa was all right – interesting seeing it again after all these years. But it would have been better if Vanessa had been there.' Then he added cheerfully: 'I say – Mary's damned dull, you know.'

Tom shook his head.

'You don't understand how it is.'

'Oh, don't I?' He laughed. 'You bet I do! I've been in love with the same woman fifty years. How about that?' For a brief moment he held Tom closely to him.

'Come on and eat.'

'What about the dog?' asked Tom.

'Oh, he'll come too. I know a place where they don't mind dogs.'

Meanwhile on that same evening another member of the family was carrying on the Herries history a further stage. Arnold had taken Sally out to the theatre – to Mr Lonsdale's play *Spring Cleaning*. Sally enjoyed the play, although she thought it old-fashioned. They were having supper at 'The Gargoyle', they were dancing a little, talking a little. They were, both of them, terribly in love.

'Yes,' said Sally. 'I think all these plays about how wicked we are seem very Victorian – *East Lynne*, you know. There's *The Vortex* and *Fallen Angels* and the one tonight. All the young men are – well, you know, and the young women have monocles and Eton crops. Everyone drinks and they go to bed with one another in the bathroom. Just as they did in Mrs Henry Wood's day—'

'Well, aren't we all like that just now? Look round you, my pet, and observe.'

'There are just about forty million people,' said Sally, 'who've

never heard of "The Gargoyle" or Noel Coward. They don't
sleep together in the bathroom nor do their young men powder
their faces.'

'What do they do then?' asked Arnold.

'They go to football matches, read the *News of the World* and
sleep cosily with their wives and husbands.'

He drove her to her door. Then he asked her whether he might
come in for a moment. She hesitated, for Margaret was away. But
then she nodded. The sitting-room that she shared with Margaret
had a very comfortable sofa, a long well-filled bookcase, a gas
stove, and posters by Mr McKnight Kauffer pinned to the walls.
Over the mantelpiece there was a watercolour by Charles Holmes
of a black hill with a shaft of sunlight breaking on it and illuminating a field that shone with the brilliance of a missal.

'That's nice,' said Arnold. 'Where is it?'

'It's Stonethwaite Valley in Cumberland.'

There was also an old photograph of Vanessa. She was standing, her hand on a chair; her dress had the puffed sleeves and the
small waist of the period. But she did not look absurd. She
looked very charming indeed.

'Who's that?' Arnold asked.

'That's my mother.'

'By Jove, she was a beauty.'

'Yes, wasn't she?'

On the sofa she gathered him into her thin childish arms.

'Oh, Arnold,' she said. 'I want you to be happy!'

(She was not aware that more than a hundred years before in a
ragged deserted house in Borrowdale, Judith Paris had said the
same words. But Judith had not loved Vanessa's grandfather.)

He strained up to her, putting his arm up to hold her round
boyish head as in a cup.

'And so do I you.' He kissed her, holding her so closely to him
that their two hearts seemed to beat as one.

'Well, you can make me happy – frightfully happy—'

'Yes, darling?' Sally said, stroking his hair.

'Let me stay here tonight.'

She drew away from him, placing her hand firmly on his arm.
She sat back against the corner of the sofa and looked at him.

'Well, really, Arnold!' She was suddenly frightened, frightened in a way that a modern girl with all her knowledge of life
should never be.

He began to speak eagerly.

'See here, Sally. There's nothing so very dreadful. I know how to look after you. Why shouldn't we have a good time? Everyone else does. You don't believe in God or hell-fire or any of that old junk, do you?' He laughed rather nervously. He was not a practised seducer. He had never seduced anyone before. He did not feel that he was trying to seduce Sally. He simply, he thought, loved her so madly that he wanted to be as close to her as possible.

'I don't believe in hell-fire,' she said slowly. 'But I'm not sure about God. My mother believed in God.'

'Of course. So does mine. All their generation did, but ours doesn't. We're simply some sort of chemical mixture. There's no future or past or anything, so why shouldn't we enjoy ourselves? We'll only be young once, and perhaps before we're much older there'll be another war like the last and we'll all be blown to bits.'

'I think it would be nicer,' Sally said slowly, 'to wait till we're married. If we have everything now there won't be anything new to experience later on.'

'Yes, but don't you see, Sally? As we are going to be married it doesn't matter anticipating it a bit, does it?'

She knelt on the sofa, turning her little body towards him, holding his head between her hands, looking at him very seriously.

'Arnold – we *are* going to be married, aren't we?'

'But of course we are!' He moved his soft cheek against her hand.

'Yes, but what if your mother goes on hating me?'

'She doesn't hate you. She doesn't know you.'

'No, she *won't* know me! Now tell me – it's true, isn't it? – she told you that our engagement is absurd, that I'm no good and my father's no good and that she won't have her darling wee pet of an Arnold marrying a little bastard.'

'No, of course not, darling. How absurd you are!'

She jumped back from him, sprang to her feet. She stood there, small, pale-faced, but dominating.

'Now listen, Arnold! She *does* say that. You know it and I know it! And I'll tell you something – I'm as good as anyone in England, as proud, as independent. I had the grandest mother anyone ever had. There never has been, and there never will be again, anyone as fine as Vanessa. And I don't want your damned charity. And your mother can be as superior as she likes, I'm not going on to my knees and imploring, but her—'

He was in a dreadful state. He had never loved her so much as at that moment. He had in fact (and this was true) never loved anyone before.

'Sally, my sweet, my pet. We'll be married when you like. Tomorrow if you wish. Anything you say—' He caught her with his arms, carried her back to the sofa, and they lay there, close together, saying nothing, he kissing her mouth, her eyes, her hair.

And she thought: 'How terribly I love him. I'd give him anything. Why not be kind while one may?' As his body trembled in her arms she was infinitely touched. Oh, darling Arnold, darling, darling Arnold! Judith had loved a man outside marriage, and her own mother . . . She was herself illegitimate . . . and in these days, when everyone was free . . . He was right . . . Who knew how long their happiness might last?

Why should she not be kind? Why should she not give anything she could that would make him happy? She sighed, touched his cheek.

'All right, Arnold darling,' she said. 'You can stay.'

MEN AT WAR

ON this evening of May 3rd, 1926, Benjie took the dog Sam out for a little exercise. He had, only the day before, returned from Morocco and found that he was plunged into a world of turmoil. Tom, who was pale and tired and plainly overworked, said that by next morning we might find ourselves plunged into Revolution. 'Revolution,' said Benjie; 'how absurd!' But to himself, perhaps, more than to anyone else in London it did not seem absurd, for he carried, always present with him, that picture of a ragged mob crossing a bridge, of the skaters vanishing, of a sudden rifle shot, of a square frozen and bare under a shining sun but quivering with danger, and, most tremendous of all, a multitude of people singing as though Paradise had come. And had Paradise come? Not at all. Murder, destruction, and the slow agonizing beginning of a new world . . . So here it might be also.

But what, he inquired, had been happening? Tom entered into a slow and tortuous explanation. The Secretary of the Miners' Federation, Arthur Cook, had made the trouble. After the

Samuel Commission had recommended reduction in pay, Arthur Cook had replied: 'Not a cent off the pay, not a minute on the day', and all the miners of England had repeated his words with emphasis. The Government had announced the withdrawal of the subsidy, and on April 23rd the owners had delivered an ultimatum. Cook had not liked the terms of the ultimatum, his men had appealed for help to the Trades Union Congress, and that body, in its turn, had put the question of a General Strike to a ballot of its unions.

No one supposed that the Trades Union Congress really *wanted* a General Strike – of course they didn't – but they thought that mild Mr Baldwin would capitulate. However, mild Mr Baldwin gave a puff or two at his pipe and *didn't* capitulate. (It happened that the Government had been making their preparations ever since 1925.) Well, then, on this very Monday, members of the Association of Printers' Assistants working for the *Daily Mail* had demanded the withdrawal of a leading article entitled 'For King and Country', and the men on the *Daily Mirror* had objected to a news article directing anti-strike volunteers to recruiting stations in the London area. The General Council Committee thought that they would go and have a talk with Mr Baldwin, but when they went to see him he was not there. They were greatly surprised.

At midnight the General Strike was to begin. On the evening of the Monday, Benjie took Sam for a little walk. It was a fine night, and he went to Hyde Park, thinking that it would be a good occasion for himself and Sam (who was in excellent spirits) to listen to the Marble Arch orators. They would surely be at their best at such a crisis and most amusingly violent. But the gates at Hyde Park Corner were closed. A cordon of police was stationed there, and the policemen said, quietly and coldly as though they were thinking of something else: 'Move on there, please!'

He joined the crowd pressed against the railings, and in this crowd no one spoke – only they gazed. Very odd, thought Benjie, on this fine May evening, and the strike not yet declared, to see Hyde Park a camp. Inside the railings there were fleets of lorries and huts and tents rising. No one spoke: only Sam barked at a chow tethered by a blue cord to the arm of a lady. Benjie looked at the lady and saw that she was fair. Her figure was as slim as fashion dictated figures should be (to Benjie's constant chagrin, for he liked figures to be plump). She was wearing a little blue hat, her hair was pale gold, and she had the face of an innocent, rather bewildered child. Her chow was aloof and dignified. Sam, at the end of his lead, strained towards it. Benjie raised his hat.

'The Government seems to have got in first,' he said.

'Oh yes,' she answered in a voice that was all music. 'Isn't it splendid of them?'

It had been difficult, with his one arm, to raise his hat and control Sam at the same time. His movement had for a moment jerked Sam on to his hind feet. She smiled at that. After all he was seventy-one, but no one would know it. He was spare and tough as he had been at forty.

'What is going to happen, do you think?' she asked him.

They walked away together. Half an hour later she had given him her address. She had rooms, it appeared, on the Chelsea Embankment. Her name, it seemed, was Miss Grace Mortimer.

He took her, that same evening, out to supper.

When he reached his own place at three or four o'clock the following morning he was aware of a deep and bitter unhappiness. He sat on his bed in his shirt, staring at his own abasement. He was not abased because he had been friendly to Miss Mortimer. He had done no harm to the pretty lady, to whom sudden meetings with strange gentlemen were no novel affair. She had been charming, had talked of her father, a General, now deceased, had shrugged her bare shoulders at the way the world was going, had thanked him for his generous gift, had begged him to come and have tea with her on the following afternoon. He had not told her that he was over seventy, and he was certain that she had not supposed him a day more than fifty. He had been ashamed of nothing that he had done, and yet he was most utterly ashamed.

At that hour of the morning with the chilly room hostile and the town preparing in a ghastly silence for the coming day's warfare, he was as lonely an old man as the world contained. Sam was sleeping in his basket near the window, comfortable and indifferent.

'Vanessa! Vanessa! I want you, I want you! Where are you? Why aren't you here to keep me company in this damnable world?'

Then he got off to bed, pulled his shirt over his head, did his exercises. Afterwards he lay sleepless, seeing the lorry, projecting rifles like a hedgehog, hearing the wild shouts beneath the window, starting at that sudden flame on the horizon of a burning building ... He had never loved London so dearly as in those hours.

When daylight came he was still ashamed and abashed. He was saying to himself, as he had said so often before, that he was finished with women, but that statement did not lessen his abasement. He lay in bed, his head resting on his arm, wondering what was happening to the world and hating and despising himself. Here was the country tumbling into ruin and he doing nothing about it, but worse than that, here was he himself a hale and hearty old man who did nothing but wander about the world, sigh for a woman long dead, and appease his appetites in any selfish easy way that appeared to him. He was not convicted of sin. He did not feel a sinner who must hurry to repentance; but he *was* convicted of waste, of sterility.

He had achieved some kind of relation with his son, it was true, but in spite of their greater friendliness Tom still bored him. Tom wanted to mother him, and oh, God! he hated to be mothered!

And then there was Sally. Before he had left for Morocco he had taken Sally to the theatre. He could see that she was unhappy, but she wouldn't tell him anything. Just like these modern children; got no confidence in their parents. There was a gulf fixed between his generation and theirs. She was unhappy This young man of hers was no good. Benjie didn't like him, a weak backboneless kind of fellow, the sort of man women wanted to help. He was making Sally miserable, and Benjie's heart ached for her. He wanted, in fact, to be allowed to love someone – yes, although he was past seventy. He was damnably lonely and no use to anyone. Perhaps after all there was something in what Vanessa said. There was somewhere another, a secret life, and if you didn't find it you were 'left' when you were old. Oh, but he was not going to whine! He didn't care if he *was* alone. Everyone was alone if it came to that. He had better be up and doing, see what was happening to this crazy world.

While he was dressing Tom came in.

'Look here,' said Benjie. 'How can I make myself useful?'

'Oh, easily. They want volunteers for every kind of thing. You can take that car of yours and drive people to their offices. Everyone's walking. It's a sight, I can tell you. Outside the Foreign Office it's packed with people waiting to enrol. They've enlisted a hundred thousand in the Volunteer Service Corps already.

They're going to supply two million gallons of milk a day from Hyde Park. It's marvellous! England's middle class counts for something in a crisis.'

'Yes, that's what Russia hadn't got,' said Benjie. He added, smiling: 'Our family will be pleased. I bet they're all busy serving the country. Any fighting yet?' Benjie asked.

'No, I don't think so. But I dare say there will be. I've got to go down to Limehouse.'

Benjie looked out of the window. Not a soul was to be seen. He went out. Everyone was walking. He came to Birdcage Walk and found it packed with cars, crawling along four abreast. He discovered that the gates of Charing Cross railway station were locked. No one seemed to know quite what to do. It was a new world, a new life, but beneath the uncertainty he was aware of a strong united determination. He seemed to feel it in the very stones of the street. 'The Strike hasn't got a chance,' he thought. He decided that he would get his car from the garage and be of some use. He climbed on to a pirate omnibus driven by a very bright but determined young man in knickerbockers. Two young men standing beside him were going down to Dover to assist in the unloading of ships. He thought that he would offer to go with them, but an unwonted shyness stopped him. He saw an omnibus that had been in the wars, standing derelict surrounded by a large, gazing, meditative crowd. He noticed a big advertisement on its boards: 'Maurice Moscovitch: The Great Lover.'

The great lover! Well, he was done with women and all the silly, sterile, messy things in his life, and then he saw a girl near to him, swaying uncomfortably as the bus moved. A pretty girl looking defenceless and a little frightened. He wondered whether she would not like his assistance. A fat, rather breathless man near him said: 'This bloody Strike's being helped by the bloody Germans. Give you my word! Syndicate of German financiers. I happen to know. They're landing bullion on the East Coast from a small ship.'

Instantly Benjie's temper, which was easily moved, was up. Silly damned liar! He'd like to tell him so. He nearly did, but got off at the top of Knightsbridge instead. Yes, he got off and walked straight into Gordon Newmark.

'Hullo!' said Gordon. 'Why, it's Benjie!'

'Yes,' said Benjie. 'It is!'

'Isn't this splendid!' said Gordon. 'We'll show them, the dirty tykes. No one knew what England was capable of until now.'

He was swelled with elation, triumph, pride and satisfaction. His handsome face (Benjie always thought that he looked like a horse that was one of the best and smartest performers in the most famous of circuses) was carved into a proper model of all that the English ruling classes should be.

'Here!' cried Gordon. 'What are you doing to help?'

'What ought I to do?' Benjie asked modestly.

'Go down to the Mansion House. They'll soon enrol you there and tell you what to do.'

'I will,' said Benjie. 'Thanks very much.'

At the same moment his daughter Sally was saying to her employer, Mr Bimberg:

'No, thank you, Mr Bimberg. I can get home quite all right this afternoon.'

Mr Bimberg was plump, bald and very neatly dressed. She had been quite comfortable with him for a long time now, but of late – within the last few months – he had taken, it seemed, a new interest in her. He put his soft round hand on her arm, he patted her shoulder. A pity, because the job suited her.

But this morning she was too deeply involved in her own private history to consider the outside world very deeply. She was fighting with all the strength that she had to keep dreadful terror at bay. As she sat taking down Mr Bimberg's letters her thoughts were wild. Arnold had not kept his appointment last night. She had waited and waited. He had arranged to take her to *The Best People* that they might together admire the fine art of Miss Olga Lindo. She had sat in her evening frock (she had worn it only twice before) for a whole hour. How horrible that hour had been! Sally was tutored to conceal her emotions, but after that agony of suspense she had burst into tears, torn off her frock and lain on her bed. He might come. Something had kept him. Ten. Eleven. Midnight. But why had he not telephoned? In the morning there would be a letter. But there was no letter. Choking her independence, she had telephoned. He had left the house half an hour before. So, her head up, looking gravely at Mr Bimberg, she had taken down his letters.

At lunchtime, alone in the room, she had telephoned again. Arnold answered her. Her heart hammering, her voice a little breathless in spite of herself, she said:

'Arnold, whatever happened last night?' (She would forgive him whatever his excuse might be.)

'Oh, my dear, I'm too frightfully sorry.'

'No – but whatever was it? I waited and waited.'

She knew that he hesitated.

'Darling, I'll explain everything. It wasn't my fault. Really it wasn't.'

'But what *was* it?' Her knees were trembling. She steadied herself with her hand on a chair.

'I can't explain here.'

'But why didn't you telephone?'

'I couldn't. It was impossible where I was.'

'But where were you?'

'Don't be so difficult, sweet. You know how difficult it is on a telephone.'

'But we can't leave it like this. I waited and waited. It was awful. How soon can I see you?'

Again he hesitated. Then he said:

'All right. I'll come along to your place about six.'

'You *will* come?'

'Of course I will.'

A little reassured she sat there, thinking. She did not go out to lunch, but stayed there without moving. She ought not to have told him that she cared. It was the doctrine of her friends that a girl never showed that she cared for a man. She could hear Margaret saying: 'So of course I told him that if he wanted to go he could. *I* didn't mind. So off he went, and I rang up Archie and we had a grand time at Ciro's. *Of course* he came round the next day ...'

But she wasn't quite like that. She had been Arnold's mistress for nearly a year and that did make a difference, didn't it? It made a difference in every kind of way, because Arnold now had everything he wanted while she ... she wanted more and more. Not physical things, but for him to *want* her and to need her, to depend on her ... The physical thing was nothing, and yet it was everything because, after it happened, Sally was his mother, his sister, his friend, his companion, while Arnold was still only Sally's lover and that not so warmly as once he had been. He should have married her. It was not perhaps very fine of him to fear so abjectly his mother, and yet Sally understood that too. *She* was not afraid of his mother, but it was natural that Arnold should be. For he was afraid of a great many things, which was partly the reason of Sally's love for him because she wanted to shelter and protect him.

As the afternoon went on her fears grew again. *Why* had he not come?

'Yes,' said Mr Bimberg. 'You had really better let me drive you home.'

'Oh no, thank you, Mr Bimberg.'

'You'll have to walk all the way, you know.'

'I'm not going very far.' (Which was untrue.)

He looked at her with his round eyes like rather damp marbles. She thought that he was going to touch her. She stood her ground. But he did not. He sighed and ambled away.

The streets were very strange. Crowds of people were walking, all rather quickly and rather silently. Was this Revolution, the kind of thing that had happened in Russia? She did not care in the least if it were. She only cared about Arnold. They all walked together like an army obeying orders. She began to be conscious of something corporate in this movement. She saw an omnibus, ran for it, stood packed in a confusion of legs and bodies, had her penny collected by a very pleasant red-faced man in a brown suit, jumped off again, stood in a side street listening to the sudden silence as though she expected to hear a gun fired or to see a flare of light against the sky. *Was* this Revolution? Would there be fighting and barricades? Perhaps Arnold would need her more if there was fighting – and she had a curious quick picture of herself as a small child, looking up from her book in the Hill Street house, seeing Ellis in the doorway and hearing him say: 'Sally, do come and play soldiers ...' She looked at her wristwatch and hurried on.

'I mustn't show him that I care,' she thought. 'I must be quite indifferent. I *know* that he wants me. He *can't* do without me.'

When she reached the flat Arnold was already there, standing in front of the fireplace. When she saw him she loved him so dreadfully that it was all she could do not to hurry into his arms. But she did not. She went into her room, took off her small brown hat, gave her cropped hair a shake, waited for a moment staring at, but not seeing, the photograph of her mother on the mantelpiece. Then she came in, sat down, lit a cigarette and said:

'Well, you're a beauty, Arnold. Whatever did you let me down for like that last night?'

He did not move towards her, and there was a constricted movement at her heart as though a cold finger had touched it. But she looked at him quietly, noticed his tie of blue and red stripes, his pale long hands, his eager, easily startled eyes. Yes, she knew him so very well.

'Look here, darling,' he began. 'I'm most awfully sorry about last night.'

'No – but what *was* it? Of course I'd have understood if something had kept you, but even then you should have phoned, shouldn't you?'

She knew that her voice slipped into a sharper pitch, not from anger but from fear.

'Oh yes, I should. I meant to. But you see I was at home—'

'Well, you've *got* a telephone in your house, haven't you?'

'Yes. Of course. Don't be facetious, Sally ...' He came forward a few steps, hesitated, then plunged.

('Why,' thought Sally to herself, 'he's just like a piece of seaweed, yellow, and if you pressed any part of him with your finger it would go "pop".' At the same time she wanted to take him and smooth his hair, calm his fears, give him a present, offer him a drink, lie down on the outside of the bed with him, draw his head to her breast and listen to a catalogue of his troubles. At the same time she also wanted to throw the book on the table – she even saw the title, *Jacob's Room* – at his head and stamp on his toes. She always said that he wore shoes with too shiny a toe.)

These things passed through her mind and like odds and ends caught up with a shower were drowned in the one and only insistent drumming consciousness:

'He's come to tell me something. He's not going to see me any more.'

'The fact is, Sally, I had an awful row with my mother last night.'

'Oh, did you? What about?' (But she knew quite well what about.)

'About you. She says that I have to choose.'

'Choose?'

'Yes. Between you and her.'

Sally stared at him and saw the seaweed, gold with dark brown fronds swaying in a sea pool, swaying indeterminately while the breeze ruffled the water of the pool into little angry protests.

'Oh, I see. She's told you that before.'

He went back to the fireplace, hanging his head at the gritty little fire and kicking the fender with his shoe.

'Yes, I know.' He turned round and faced her. 'Look here, Sally. I'm no good. You've got to give me up. I can't stand it. I've had more than a year of it, facing Mother. It's more than my being afraid of her. It's like being afraid of oneself. Oh! I can't explain these things, but I'm sort of inside her. Part of me thinks just as she does – I've loved you frightfully, I do love you frightfully now, but all the time I'm wanting to be right with Mother again. I thought, perhaps, she'd get over it. I thought she'd get used to the idea. But she doesn't. She hates it more and more.'

'*Why* does she hate me?' Sally asked in a small sharp voice.

'Oh, it isn't *you* that she hates! I think she'd make a fuss about my marrying anyone. She doesn't want to lose me. Of course that's all wrong and very selfish, but in a way I understand it. I don't really want to lose her either. All the same she'd get over that – because she's really an awfully good sort – if you ... if you–' He hesitated. 'You see, Sally, she's heard a lot about your father and she says that there's one side of your family that's mad and it always has been. Of course that's all rot–'

'It isn't all rot at all,' Sally interrupted. 'If you look at it from one point of view it's true, I suppose.'

'Mother isn't conventional exactly, but–'

'Does she know,' Sally interrupted, 'that I'm your mistress?'

'No, she doesn't.' He squared his shoulders. His face was so white and miserable that something in Sally cried: 'I hate both these women who are making you so unhappy. Pay no attention to either of them.' And something else in her cried: 'You're a wretched weak creature and I'm a fool to have bothered over you for a single moment.'

'To tell you the truth, Sally, I'd be afraid for her to know. She's old-fashioned about those things. And it wouldn't make it better if she did know.'

'She'd see me as the designing siren, I suppose,' Sally said. 'Well, perhaps I have been.' Then, after a pause, she asked: 'What exactly did happen last night?'

'I was dressed and just going out to you when she came into my room. She asked me where I was going and I told her. She made a most awful scene. Oh, it went on for hours! She cried. She wouldn't let me telephone or anything.'

'I see,' said Sally. 'And then?'

'Oh, then – at last–'

'You promised to give me up?'

He nodded his head.

He began a torrent of explanation. She cut him short.

'All right, Arnold. I understand perfectly.'

She went up to him, kissed him gently on the forehead, held out her hand.

'Goodbye, my dear.'

'No, but Sally–' He tried to catch her in his arms. Quietly she moved away from him, stood looking at him for a moment, then said:

'Now cut along. We've had a lovely time and I don't blame you a little bit.'

He was going to speak again but, looking at her, decided not to. He picked up his hat and coat and went out.

Into his small room at the Mansion House, Benjie was aware just as the clock struck seven of the intrusion of panic. A stout General with very bright red tabs on his shoulders was shouting down the telephone: 'Oh, but, look here, the thing's absurd! Give the feller a kick in the pants and tell him to clear out. What do you say? I can't hear . . . very bad at Camden Town? Well, tell Ritchie to cut along . . . Hullo! hullo! are you there, Ward? Well, why couldn't you say so? Can you hear me? Hullo! hullo!'

Benjie, his gaze idly fixed on the General's large posterior, wondered for the first time whether after all the Herries would manage to hold the fort. Everyone seemed to him to be Herries down here, and he himself, in these few days, had become civilized Herries too. He had enrolled countless men and women, urging them to do their utmost for King and Country, and as, with serious and patient faces, they had promised him to do so, he had thought: 'By God, this country is all right. The heart of this old country is sound', almost as though he had been Cynthia or Alfred or Gordon or Adrian or even old Horace, who, the night before at Cynthia's, had beamed sentimentally through his glasses and, like a bishop pronouncing the blessing, had said: 'This will go down in history. England has proved herself.' It *would* go down in history, but he was not sure whether it would be quite in the fashion that his family had desired. What was happening beyond this quiet and dignified room?

The Government in its *British Gazette* proclaimed that it was maintaining with complete success all the vital services of supply – light, food and power. Communications were improving every day. On the other hand, fifty London General omnibuses had not returned to their depot last night; at Middlesbrough some women and boys had held up a train; a motor-bus had been set on fire in East London; shops were being looted in Edinburgh; and Mr Saklatvala had been sentenced to two months' imprisonment. On this very morning the *British Gazette* announced that they had discovered that the General Council had issued a new order to 'paralyse and break down the supply of food and the necessaries of life'. How far would this spread? Every day increased the danger. He did not know that at any moment returning through Piccadilly he might not see the appearance of the lorry bristling like a hedgehog, the pieces of red cloth tied to the rifles, the windows of the Ritz smashed with machine-gun fire. 'They don't know. They haven't had the experience, any of them. They are blind to everything. Their whole social order has crumbled to pieces under their very eyes and they are not aware of it. This machinery – the machinery they've been used to so long – may vanish in a moment's temper ... They don't know it. They haven't seen it ...'

'By God!' the General was shouting into the telephone, 'tell them they've *got* to or it will be worse for them. This isn't Russia, you know.'

No, it wasn't Russia. The Herries were here. There had been no Herries in Russia. All the same ...

'Coming along, Herries?' the General said, his face beaming. 'I told the bastards where *they* got off. Coming my way? I'll drive you.'

So he sat in the back of the car with the General and discovered as, with throngs of pedestrians on every side of them, they pushed their way towards Trafalgar Square, that this fine stout kindly officer was happier than ever he had been in his life before.

'This is what I've been wanting, Herries. Teach the blighters a lesson. I'll be damned glad myself if it does come to real trouble. Give us an excuse to be rid of a few of them. That feller Saklatvala – I'd string him up on a lamp-post if I had *my* way. By God, I've never been so proud of my country as I am tonight.'

So the Herries were saying. They'd all like to string Saklatvala up on a lamp-post. Old Judith Paris, he remembered, had written in her book somewhere of seeing a boy hanged outside a butcher's shop. She hadn't liked it. But then she'd always been a queer one. And the Herries were right. Civilization had got to be kept on its feet. But suppose the old world was gone. Gone for ever and ever? Suppose on that evening when the whole world had burst out singing (he had sung like the others) they had sung the old world out of existence? Why, then *where* would the Herries be?

The town seemed to him sinister tonight. It had started to rain and soon it was a downpour. Through the rain the town was walking home. In the heart of the crowd the motor-cars, loaded with people – shopgirls, secretaries, elderly women, old men like himself – ploughed the way. The lights flared and the darkness stifled the lights. The whole town seemed on the move as though the order had been given to abandon it, and everyone was fleeing for safety. And yet they were not fleeing. That was the very last thing that they were doing. These people were defending the town, nobly, gallantly, without a thought for themselves. But what about the enemy? *He* knew how silent a thin street could be, and behind every window a concealed rifle. *He* knew how men could gather, in secret, in silence, and then, at a spoken word, the familiar places – so old, so safe, so complacent – would be filled with death. This was no melodrama. Efficient, historical fact. One machine gun at the Oxford Circus end of Regent Street, where they now were, and that crowd would turn in upon itself, would scream, cry aloud, bodies crushed into the mud, and the rain pouring down ... Oh, he was an old man! What had happened to his nerve?

'And that, my dear feller,' the General was saying, 'is the way *I'd* deal with them!'

At the top of Portland Place, where several roads meet, there was a complete confusion. Under torrential rain a mass of cars, coming from different directions, faced one another like angry herds of cattle. Horns hooted, men shouted, nothing could move. A policeman, his black cape shining in the rain, appeared as it seemed from the bowels of the earth, waving his hand. He came right up to the General's car, placing his hand on the bonnet, and Benjie saw his face, his blue eyes, his cheeks wet with the rain, and a clear, unflinching, unhesitating power of direction and order in his every movement. He seemed a giant from some other planet, impersonal and inhuman. He called out, waved his hand, and at once the disorder was composed into order: the cars separated and divided. Benjie was reassured. 'That man wasn't in Russia,' he thought. But just before his own car moved on he saw a girl, almost slipping, recovering, placing her hand for an instant against the window. It was Sally.

'Here. Let me out. Goodnight, General. See you tomorrow.'

A moment later he had caught his girl's arm.

'Hi! Sally! What are you doing here?'

The rain was driving in their faces, and the collar of her waterproof was drawn up. He held on to her arm, but he could feel that she was resisting him. They had moved away from the roar and confusion and stopped under a lamp. She looked up at him.

'Hullo, Father!' she said. 'What a coincidence!'

'The lamplight,' he thought, 'is making her look like this, and the rain. By God! something has happened to her, though. She's as though she were walking in her sleep.' Then she woke up. He felt her arm tremble under his hand, and her small pale face under the light little hat from which the rain was dripping hardened into that look of angry determination that was often exactly his own.

'I must get on,' she said. 'I'm late.'

'Where are you going?'

'Oh – I've got an engagement with a friend.'

Then her lower lip began to tremble. He saw that she was on the edge of tears. He put his arm round her.

'You haven't any engagement, my dear,' he said. 'Nor have I. I'll take you home.'

She had ceased to resist.

'All right,' she said. 'I don't care.'

They walked back to Oxford Street and not a word was spoken. Then they found an omnibus that was driven by quite an elderly party with a white moustache and was crowded with rowdy young men who were going off on some job.

'They say there's been terrible fighting in Camberwell tonight,' an elderly lady said.

'We'll protect you, ma'am,' the young men shouted. 'Lenin shan't get you.'

When they were in Sally's room and had taken off their wet things they sat opposite one another on either side of the fire.

'Margaret coming in?' Benjie asked.

'No, I don't think so,' Sally said. Then she added: 'I've nothing to give you to eat, Father. There isn't a scrap in the place.'

'That doesn't matter.' He pulled out his pipe, crossed his thin legs, leaned back. He was weary. This was a life, when all was said and done, for an old man of seventy-one, and, fit though he was, his back ached and his legs told him that they had done enough for one day.

'Look here, Sally – that was all my eye about your going anywhere. You didn't know where you were going.'

She didn't answer him.

'What's the matter?'

Still she didn't answer him, but sat up straight in her chair, her hands crossed over her knees.

'Why don't you let me take you out and give you a meal?'

'Oh, it's all right, thanks.'

He said at last: 'I wish to God Vanessa was here.' He went on to cover the silence:

'You know, Sally, we ought to see more of one another. I've been a bit shy, I dare say, but it's been my fault that I've never, in all my life, been able to get on any very sound terms with anyone except your mother. Light come and light go. And now I'm paying for it. All the same,' he said, 'you and I and Tom – we've only got one another now. You've got your young man, I suppose.'

'He's gone,' she said.

'What do you mean – he's gone?'

'Oh, he left me three or four days ago. His mother didn't like me.'

'Oh, so that's it,' said Benjie softly.

There was a long silence.

'Well, my dear,' Benjie said at last, 'I shouldn't worry about him too much. You'll find someone much better.'

'Oh, I dare say,' said Sally.

'He was frightened of his mother, wasn't he?'

'He was very fond of her. He hoped for a long time that she would get used to me. But she didn't.'

'Was it partly,' Benjie asked, 'because you had a bad lot for a father?'

'It was all of us. You and I and Vanessa and Judith Paris and your father being shot. Right away back. She seemed to know all about us. Now if I had been Rosalind or Mary it would have been all right.'

'I see,' said Benjie. 'Sins of the fathers. Very unfair, I always think.'

'She didn't know I was sleeping with Arnold,' said Sally in a dull toneless voice. 'That would only have made it worse.'

'He was a bit of a cad, I should say,' Benjie remarked. 'All the same I'm glad he didn't marry you.'

'No, he wasn't a cad at all. I understand him perfectly.'

'You'll get over it, my dear. One gets over everything. (All the same, he thought, I've never got over being without Vanessa.) I've come to the conclusion there's a lot to be said for marriage. Oh, I know, your generation don't think so, and I know that Vanessa had the hell of a time with Ellis. All the same I can see now that it would have been very pleasant if your mother and I had been married. It's the best arrangement society's discovered yet.'

'I didn't care,' Sally said, 'whether I was married to Arnold or not. I wanted to look after him. I wanted – I wanted—'

Her voice broke. She tried to recover herself, beating her hand against her knee. Her mouth moved and quivered and shook. Then she began to cry.

Benjie went over to her.

'Here, Sally – don't cry. It's all right. You've got your life in front of you. Darling – Sally darling.'

He knelt down beside her, putting his arm round her.

'These days – I didn't know anything could be so bad ... I didn't know I could miss anyone so much. I thought I knew enough not to be hurt by anything. He was so sweet ... He loved me ... he did really ...'

'There, Sally, it will be all right. Really it will. It's been my fault. I haven't been with you as I ought to be. We'll stick together now. You can tell me anything. I've been very lonely too ... Hellish ...'

He drew her with him to the other chair, a big roomy one. He sat back and, with his arm around her, wrapped her into his embrace. She was folded up in his arm like a child. She was so small that he could hold her easily. Her hand was clenched inside his. She dried her eyes and with little convulsive sobs told him everything: how Arnold had not taken her to the theatre, of their last meeting, of how, next day, she had not known what she was doing, had wandered about in the crowds, had worked for Bimberg mechanically, had not slept at all for three nights – and tonight she had not known, she had thought that perhaps now that everything was over it would be better ...

He held her more tightly, feeling her quiver against his heart.

'I know. We all go through it. It doesn't matter what generation we belong to, how much we think we know. It doesn't make any difference ...'

He thought of that last talk with Vanessa in his room, the agony and distress of letting her go. He was ashamed of his casual life, his neglect of his promise – 'I swear, Vanessa, I'll never let her go again.'

A long time after, Sally got up from her chair, went into her room and washed her face and hands.

She stood looking at him, and smiled.

'You're rather a pet,' she said. 'You've been awfully nice to me.'

'What shall we do?' he asked. 'Go out and have a meal?'

'Oh no. I don't think I could eat anything.'

'Let's see how the Strike's going.' He went to the wireless and turned it on. Someone was speaking. 'Why, it's old Baldwin!' Benjie said.

Mr Baldwin was saying:

'The Government is not fighting to lower the standard of living of the miners. That suggestion is being spread abroad. It is not true. No honest person can doubf that my whole desire is to maintain the standard of living of every worker.'

Then after a while there were the sonorous tones of Lord Oxford:

'The real victims of a general strike are what is called the common people. We should have lost all self-respect if we were to allow any section of the community, at its own will and for whatever motives, to bring to a standstill the industrial and social life of the nation. That would be to acquiesce in the substitution for Free Government of a Dictatorship. This the British People will never do.'

The voice died away. Sally's eyes were closing.

'Go on. Go to bed,' said Benjie.

He went with her into her bedroom and, with a little sigh, without taking off even her slippers, she lay down on the bed. He lay down beside her, taking her in his arm again. In a moment, her head against his waistcoat, she was asleep, and he lay there, looking with his sharp, ironical eyes at the ceiling, happier than he had been for many a year.

BELOVED MOUNTAIN

'AND now,' said Tom, 'as we cross the bridge you'll see how beautiful it is!'

'And I hope to God she will,' he thought, for he was convinced now that the visit, the visit to which he had looked forward with such eagerness, would prove a terrible failure. Sally had invited herself: he would never have dared, of himself, to ask her. He had taken his three weeks' holiday late this year – it was now early in November 1928 – and, as always, had come up to Cumberland. He wanted to be nowhere else. It was lovelier with every visit. He had taken rooms in a house, Bella Vista, on the road from Grange to Manesty, and settled in there, very happy with Mrs Zanazzi, his hostess, and Miss Zanazzi her daughter, and his books, walking every day, sometimes a long tramp, when he would be away in Eskdale, or by Esthwaite, or Patterdale for the night. He was forty-four now and used to being alone. His father was in Spain. He had friends in London, but no one whom he wished to have with him.

And then Sally had written, saying that she would come and stay with him for a week, Sally who had been so strange and hard for so long, who had scarcely seen him, who had had nothing to say to him when they were together.

He had been terribly excited. Mrs Zanazzi had arranged that Sally should have the best bedroom in the house, the room with the view out over the shelving fields to Skiddaw and the Lake.

They would have a glorious week. He and Sally would recover one another again. He knew how unhappy she was and, if he were very careful and did not show her in any way that he wanted to help her, he might give her something that she needed. Oh yes! how *very* careful he would be!

So he had gone to the station full of eager expectation. She wouldn't think much of his small Austin, but he would explain to her that it was better to have a small car in this country; so often the bridges were narrow and the roads little more than lanes . . .

When he saw her come from the train he had gone eagerly forward.

'Hullo, Tom!' she had said, and, at once (so sensitive he was) he had known that there was no change, that she was hundreds of miles away from him, that she didn't care for him, that she didn't know why she had come.

And the drive in the Austin had been terrible. She had shown no interest in anything. When he had asked her about London and had she been to parties and how was old Bimberg and Cynthia and Maurice and Margaret, she had assured him, 'Oh yes' and 'Oh no' and 'Everything's just the same'.

'And now,' he said, 'as we cross the bridge you'll see how beautiful it is!'

To himself it was exquisite. The brilliant autumn colouring was gone. Everything was silver-grey. There had been much rain and the Lake had flooded; the stream ran under the bridge in tumbling curves and circles, watched gravely by the dark hills while the last pale leaves clung to the trees; the fields were faintly green, floating in the last light of the autumn day towards the Lake like green smoke gently stirred by the wind.

He did not know that as Sally looked out she was caught by a quick apprehension. 'Something awful is going to happen. Why did I come? Whatever made me write and ask to come?' Tom's kind and serious face, his short heavy body bent a little forward at the wheel, his eagerness to make her happy ... Oh, why was Tom always the same, why was he not some heavenly messenger who had swung down in a silver aeroplane and whispered to her: 'You have had enough of this. You have had more than two years of it. I will catch you up and we will fly, like the golden Eagle, into coloured clouds and a foaming brilliant sea'? But Tom was no heavenly messenger, and like green smoke those sleepy fields rolled into the Lake.

A pale ivory twilight lay over the landscape when Sally looked from her window. She could distinguish no detail, only over-head, above the dark shadows of clustering trees, the sky broke into spaces of dim ghostly light as though a moon were some-where hiding. When she heard running water something caught at her heart. Since her babyhood she had never been in this country, but now it was as though something familiar were re-turning to her; the smell of wet leaves, the sky that revealed nothing and yet seemed a world of motion and movement, the queer windy whisper in the air, dark shapes on the horizon that were, she knew, the mountains, these things were all familiar to her and unique. No country of hill and field where she had been was like this one, and yet she could see nothing but shadow and, when a dog barked, it was a voice welcoming her, reproach-ing her for being so long away.

After supper when she sat opposite Tom in the sitting-room she smiled.

'I like being here, Tom,' she said. 'It's as though I'd been here before.'

'Well you have. You were born not far away from here.'

'I know. In a farm, in a storm. Mother nearly died getting to the farm. She often told me.'

'The funny thing is,' Tom said, 'that we came into this country two hundred years ago – old Rogue Herries riding a horse with his small son in front of him. Then we grew and multiplied like the Israelites. We covered the country. And now we've died away again. There are none of us here any more. But it's caught one after another of us, set its seal on us, made us influence others. Perhaps, although we haven't any of us been important, we've altered England's history by coming here.

That's what a small piece of country can do.'

'You ought to write about it, Tom,' she said, laughing and thinking that he was nicer here, sitting back, smoking his pipe, than he was anywhere else.

'I can't. That's what's so damnable.' He picked up an orange-covered book on a table near him. 'Listen to this, Sally.'

He read:

> 'So she let her book lie unburied and dishevelled on the ground, and watched the vast view, varied like an ocean floor this evening with the sun lightening it and the shadows darkening it. There was a village with a church tower among elm trees; a grey domed manor house in a park; a spark of light burning on some glasshouse; a farmyard with yellow corn stacks. The fields were marked with black tree clumps and beyond the fields stretched long woodlands, and there was the gleam of a river, and then hills again. In the far distance Snowdon's crags broke white among the clouds; she saw the far Scottish hills and the wild tides that swirl about the Hebrides. She listened for the sound of gun-firing out at sea. No — only the wind blew. There was no war today. Drake had gone; Nelson had gone. "And there," she thought, letting her eyes, which had been looking at these far distances, drop once more to the land beneath her, "was my land once; that Castle between the downs was mine; and all that moor running to the sea was mine". Here the landscape (it must have been some trick of the fading light) shook itself, heaped itself, let all this encumbrance of houses, castles, and woods slide off its tent-shaped sides. The bare mountains of Turkey were before her. It was blazing noon. She looked straight at the baked hillside. Goats cropped the sandy tufts at her feet. An eagle soared above her. The raucous voice of old Rustum, the gipsy, croaked in her ears, "What is your antiquity and your race, and your possessions compared with this? What do you need with four hundred bedrooms and silver lids on your dishes, and housemaids dusting?"'

'Whatever's that?' asked Sally.

'It's *Orlando,* by Virginia Woolf. Just out.'

'I don't understand a word of it. What's it mean?'

'It means what it says. You must forget things like space and time.'

'How can you?'

'You can if you like to go far enough. Do you remember in Judith's book, little Harcourt Herries reciting Pope to Francis and David at Ravenglass? Well, he's still reciting it. He's still moved by the beauty of it as I'm moved now by the beauty of this.'

'That's nonsense,' said Sally.

'Yes, if you like to think so.'

They sat in silence, quite happy, coming closer to one another with every tick of the clock.

'I'm beginning,' said Tom, 'to see why we are all so restless and unhappy. It's an awful time really. No one seems to be sure of anything any more – religion, economics, politics. So many people out of jobs. Why, look at you and me and Father. I lost Mary, you lost Arnold, Father lost Vanessa. And so in a way everyone we know seems to have lost something. But then, as the gipsy says in *Orlando*, "What do you need with four hundred bedrooms and silver lids on your dishes?" You don't need them if you discover the other world. Do you think I'm talking rot?'

'I don't understand a word that you're saying.'

'Well, I'm a failure, a complete and absolute failure. I wanted to be a good writer. I wanted to marry Mary. I adored Vanessa and she died. I wanted you and Father to need me – and you don't. Nobody needs me. So I'm a good example of times like these. I've been unhappy and restless for years. But lately I've been finding out that there's a world that has nothing to do with my needs, nothing to do with space and time, a world that has been showing me points of light for years like the sun flashing on a window, but I haven't seen ... If I could *live* in that world, Sally, it wouldn't matter how much a failure I myself was because it's so beautiful, so timeless and so alive that personal failure is of no importance at all.'

'It all sounds very vague to me,' said Sally, but looking at him with curiosity. It was so odd to see Tom with his heavy body, thick shoulders, quiet ways, bursting like this into fantasy.

'But I too can be fantastic,' she thought, realizing suddenly why it was that, through all these years, she had never been really intimate with Margaret. 'I too can be fantastic,' and, looking into the fire, she let her mind wander back over the past year, which had, in truth, been as nasty and spiteful a year as she had ever known. Later, lying in bed, unable to sleep, she reviewed it and discovered that it had already altered its colours under the influence of this place. Like the families in Genesis, Margaret led to Olive Stane and Olive Stane to Miss Bourchier and Miss Bourchier to Freddie Tallent and Freddie to Freda and Freda to William Blake and William Blake (so *very* unlike the poet!) to Mrs Carslake-King and Mrs Carslake-King to stout, solid and feminist Mrs Brent. At the stopping place of Mrs Brent, Sally considered herself as a feminist. She had not been a very good one. Why? It had seemed, after the tragedy of Arnold, the natural thing to consider men feeble and conceited and exasperating creatures. There was, if you were to believe them, a regular war of the sexes. All the men stood up for one another and were most unfair about it, and all the women stood up for one another and were not unfair about it. Some of the women were grand – Olive Stane and Miss Bourchier for instance. They had wit, humour, generosity, courage. What did they lack? They lacked nothing perhaps, but spent their time altogether too much in London literary sets, never really meeting anyone but one another, although they thought they did.

And so, not one of them reached the first class. As writers they were clever and no more, as politicians they were not effective, as women they left men cold and frightened.

So Sally, who had never really been at home with them because she was not clever enough, admired them and left them. She went for a while to parties, but this life she soon abandoned. She disliked to be made love to in an absent-minded way, which was what the young men did; she disliked to be drunk; she disliked not to know the name of the hostess who was entertaining her. She disliked to drink gin dressed (for it was, that night, an Infant Party) as a babe-in-arms. She disliked people to take it for granted that unless she was Lesbian she was uninteresting. Nevertheless she did not make the mistake of supposing that the whole of her generation were worthless. On the contrary, she found among them enough courage, honesty and common sense to save Europe were someone really worthwhile to get hold of it. Only there was not, it appeared, anyone worthwhile. Lenin was dead and Mussolini was in Italy.

So, unable to be intellectual, and weary of parties, she fell back on the Family. There were not many just now, of her own generation. There were two distant cousins, Phyllis and Anstey Veasey. Their great-grandfather had been the younger brother of Anna Veasey, who had married Warren, Adam Paris' father. Their own father was a Judge and they lived, in considerable

splendour, in Connaught Place. They were amusing, full of vitality and very sure of themselves. Then there were two girls,
Mabel and Jessie Rossiter, relations of Adrian's, who lived with a
widowed mother in Chelsea. They were nice girls but extremely
serious, believing in Bertrand Russell and determining, as soon as
they had children, to encourage them in complete freedom of
expression.

No, so far as Sally was concerned, her only friends in the
Family were poor old Horace and Maurice.

Maurice's marriage was unhappy, but just now everything
about him was unhappy. He could not forget the War. He could
not translate his experience of it into indifference and a kind of
shoulder-shrugging tolerance as did so many of his contemporaries. Sally did what she could for him and he loved
her.

No, she decided, turning over restlessly on her bed (which was
comfortable because Mrs Zanazzi knew how to please her guests),
everything for ages had been awful except her father. There the
relationship begun on the week of the Strike had bloomed. They
were friends now and always would be. They enjoyed their times
together, they understood one another, they cared for one
another. And it was Benjie who, just before he had gone away to
Spain, had suggested that she should go up to Cumberland and
stay with Tom.

'You'll find it's like going home,' he had said.

Two things still troubled her, though. One was that she could
not forget Arnold. He had married a Miss Thurston. Their pictures had been in the papers. That was all that Sally knew. But
surely by now she, a sensible modern girl who would stand no
nonsense, would have rid herself of his presence. But she could
not. He still haunted her at every turn. Little things that he had
said, done, looked, been . . .

And the other ghost was Vanessa. It was, she supposed, because she had been so unhappy that she had thought of her
mother so constantly. But it had been more than thought. In
London she had been constantly expecting that her mother
would appear. She had even at times run up the long dark staircase to her rooms, thinking – in spite of all common sense and
practical wisdom – that Vanessa would be there, waiting for her.
This was a ghost that had no sense in it at all.

So, lying restlessly on her comfortable bed, she decided that
things in general had been altogether rotten. Was there something

in what Tom had said that evening about finding another world? Was that what everyone was wanting? Was this other world ... and, so wondering, she fell asleep.

In the days that followed, the country opened up on every side of her. Miss Zanazzi was a great walker and climber. What she said was: 'There's no end to all of this, Miss Herries. You can go to the same spot every day for a year and it's always different. The changing clouds and the light, I suppose.' She explained to her that every part of the country had its own personality: Wastwater and Wasdale were savage, Windermere polite, Ullswater a fortress, Buttermere a fairytale, and every hill a separate character. Of course Scotland was bigger and finer, but the charm of this country was that it was so close together. With every step the view changed and the colours altered. 'It's mysterious, Miss Herries. You'll never come to the end of it.'

She went with Tom to Rosthwaite and saw the little hill where old Rogue Herries' house had been. There was a sturdy little stone house there now. They went to Uldale and saw the green field, on the edge of the moor, next to the church (that had not been there in the old days) where David's house had been, where Judith had grown up, where Adam had died. They climbed Ireby hill and looked over the wall at the Fortress and saw an old lady come to the dining-room window and stare at them.

'Uhland still walks there. I'm sure he does,' said Tom.

They walked up the road from Bella Vista and looked at the cottage on Cat Bells.

'Who lives there now?' Sally asked, and Tom told her that it was a novelist, none of whose books Sally had ever read.

'What a shame!' said Sally.

'Oh, I don't know,' said Tom. 'If he's happy – only I wish he hadn't painted his garage door blue.'

So everything was gone and yet everything remained. They went up from Rosthwaite to Watendlath and visited John Green's House where Judith had lived with her French husband. The sun was shining on a birch tree, and they noticed, as Dorothy Wordsworth once had noticed before them, how *'it glanced in the wind like a flying sunshiny shower'*. Tom found the place in the *Journal* that evening and read from it:

> *'It was yielding to the gusty wind with all its tender twigs. The sun shone upon it, and it glanced in the wind like a flying sunshiny shower. It was a tree in shape, with stem and*

*branches, but it was like a Spirit of water. The sun went in,
and it resumed its purplish appearance, the twigs still yielding
to the wind. The other birch trees that were near it looked
bright and cheerful, but it was a creature by its own self among
them ... We went through the wood. It became fair. There
was a rainbow which spanned the lake from the island-house
to the foot of Bainriggs. The village looked populous and
beautiful. Catkins are coming out; palm trees budding; the
alder, with its plum-coloured buds.*

'Now isn't that lovely?' said Tom. 'As fine as any poem by her
brother. But how does she do it? There's hardly a word of more
than two syllables. I suppose it's partly that she was so honest –
no humbug – and partly that she found everything beautiful
from the village to the smallest twig of the birch.'

But Sally was thinking of Judith in Watendlath:

'Do you remember how she saw her husband coming down the
path, after he had been away so long, with the bright bird in the
cage? It's as though it happened while we were there.'

'Do you see?' said Tom triumphantly. 'I told you that Time's a
fallacy. Live here long enough and you'll see that that's true.'

She felt that the process going on within her was mysterious. It
was, as Benjie had told her, that she felt as though she had come
home. 'I belong here. All my friends are here – and Tom is really
a darling.' For the first time she began to forget Arnold.

But the days were passing and soon she must return to Mr
Bimberg. They decided that they would do one grand expedition
before she returned to London. But it was late in the year for
grand expeditions, and Miss Zanazzi warned them: 'The weather
can be funny this time of year. Mists, you know, and there might
even be some snow. It's turning colder.'

It was. One night there was a furious gale and the wind tore up
the valley, whipping the trees on the right of the house, lashing
the windows with rain, screaming with an exultation that Sally
found splendid as it galloped up the mountainside.

The streams began to beat like drums and, behind the uproar,
it seemed to Sally that men were shouting, calling, crying aloud.
Yet, next morning, a shining and placid peace lay over the
country. A frost glittered on the chrysanthemums and a long
stretch of purple lay above the faint browns and greens, staining
the bare trees and spreading on the hillsides in a thin grape-
coloured cloud.

'How lovely!' Sally thought. 'It is as still as a dream.'

So they decided to make their expedition next day. Tom would drive the Austin to Seathwaite, leave it there, and then they would go up Stye Head, climb Scafell and be back for supper.

Next morning the sky was flurried with little white clouds and the air was sharply cold. Miss Zanazzi told them that the glass was going down, but she thought that they would be safe for the day. They started out in splendid spirits.

As they began to walk from Seathwaite, Tom said:

'You know, Sally, I think this has been the happiest week of my life.'

Sally, who disliked very much to express her feelings, said:

'Well, that's all right.' But she added, because she could not help herself: 'We'll come up here together again, won't we? – just the two of us. And perhaps Father.'

'Oh, Father knows every inch of it. He loves it more than I do.'

Tom chattered away. He wasn't tiresome any more and Sally realized that people who need affection are natural and easy once they have got it. They are embarrassing only because they are starved. 'I don't believe I'll ever be annoyed by him again,' she thought.

They crossed the little Stockley Bridge. They had been hemmed in by Glaramara on the left and Base Brown on the right, and now the sharp precipices of Great End filled up the valley in front. It was here that Sally had the first perception that she was moving into an uncertain world.

'You'd think,' Tom said, 'that you're looking at the same hill all the time, Great End. Well, you're not – halfway between Seathwaite and Seatoller it's Lingmell you've been looking at.'

The tops did indeed appear to be different with every step, and soon after leaving Seathwaite all the civilized state of man dropped out of existence. Sour Milk Gill was a raging torrent, and the wind that blew in between crevices of rock and boulder frothed it to a spume. They were shut in by a barricade of hills, Glaramara on the left and Base Brown on the right.

'Base Brown,' Sally said. 'What a horrid name!' She was conscious of a return of the apprehension that she had felt on her drive from the station the first day. It was as though a wall of grey menacing stone rose in front of her and on the other side of it was Margaret throwing a book on to the sofa and crying: 'Well, of all the tosh!' and Humphrey Bell, the novelist, who could not forget that the War had personally insulted him and was therefore most blameworthy (as though the War were an absconding solicitor!) ... and the wooden barricades in Piccadilly Circus, and Olive Stane saying: 'Oh, I'll make it a Gin and It', and poor old Horace leading her so proudly in to dinner at the Piccadilly Grill, and the shimmering rug with purple trees and dark green birds on Cynthia's dining-room floor, and Adrian giving her tea in his lovely flat with the Duncan Grant landscape that had a barn in it of so deep an amber-red, and the green Elk of Carl Milles, and Unamuno's *Quixote* open on the table, and the old blind man in Piccadilly with the cup and his fat body and patient, patient face.

'And now we climb,' said Tom. 'Not much of one. That's Taylor Gill on the right. I've never seen it so fierce.'

She was both frightened and exhilarated. Everything seemed fierce and angry. The wind rose as they rose. In an incredibly short time the Borrowdale valley was far below, and at the far end of it over Skiddaw and Blencathra a grim wall of grey cloud was mounting but, miraculously, from some unseen place, a tongue of sunlight struck the valley, quivering across it like a searchlight.

At the top they were on a long boggy flat through which a stream ran. Lingmell was in front of them and Scafell Pike to the left of it.

Now they were truly in no-man's-land. A bird flew slowly, mournfully over their heads, but otherwise there was no sign of life at all. Sally saw that Tom was now completely happy, and in his happiness he had a strong family likeness to Benjie and Vanessa when *they* were happy. The true Tom appeared as he never appeared in London. His body did not seem thick and clumsy now. Sally was surprised at the easy agility with which he moved. In London, when he was in a room, you always watched with anxiety lest he should knock something over. Every teacup was in peril from him, but now you felt that he could shoulder a mountain with safety. He began to sing slightly out of tune, and soon Sally began to sing too. Really this was a splendid day.

They reached Stye Head Tarn and, as they did so, a pale sun, dim and veiled, burst the grey paper tissue of the clouds and shivered with a queer iridescent shimmer on the black surface of the little Tarn.

It was very cold, but they found shelter behind a rock on the slope of Green Gable, looked down to the Tarn across the flat, and ate their luncheon. This was the very wildest scenery that Sally had ever beheld. There were of course many places of far greater splendour and terror in the world, but the intimacy and closeness of this place made it personal, as though it had a quality of fairy tale – one of the old stories when the hero reaches at last his perilous destiny, and from the dark rock, the shaggy tree, the awful enemy emerges. And yet, with this peril there was also friendliness. Gable with its great rounded top is the least hostile of all mountains, and the whole plateau with its stream and tarn is kind because it has been there for so long and is so sure of its passive power.

'It was just above here,' Tom said, 'by the other tarn that David fought his duel.' As he spoke a ripple of light ran across the Tarn. Everything sprang to life as though it answered him, then fell into a waiting silence again.

It was too cold to remain long where they were and, after they had eaten, they walked slowly up the slope to Esk House. Here, when Sally looked down into Eskdale, she gave a cry. The valley was sombre today and for many an observer would have seemed little more than a tumble of rock and rough grass falling away to the sea, but at that moment, more than any other, Sally felt that she had come home. On every side of her the hills rose darkly to a dark sky and there was a strength in all those uncouth forms, a strength and patience, a wildness controlled, that seemed to her lovelier than anything that she had ever known. She caught Tom's arm and held it. 'I feel as though I could never be unhappy again,' she said.

Then they started slowly to climb the Scafell Pike track. The wind was rising, murmuring from top to top, and the faint illumination of the pale sun vanished suddenly as though at a word of command. The heavy sky seemed to move down in a lower band above their heads.

'I thought I felt a flake of snow on my cheek,' Sally said.

'Oh, that's all right. It won't come to anything. Not at this time of year,' Tom answered. 'We'll soon be at the top.'

They turned slightly to the right up a green slope which was not difficult, although beyond them the eastern buttress of the Pike had a grim look.

Tom glanced at his wristwatch. It was later than he had supposed; you grew, through the summer, accustomed to Summer Time and fancied that the light would last for ever. There should, for a long while yet, be enough, but it was a dark day and, in the last half-hour, had grown very swiftly darker.

Instinctively he hurried his steps and Sally called out: 'It's all right, isn't it? We've got plenty of time, haven't we?' She had to shout, for the wind whistled in the air.

'Quite all right,' Tom called cheerfully.

She wondered whether she should suggest that they should turn back. Something would have frightened her had she not been determined against any sort of fright. Where Tom could go she could, and she knew that these were little hills and that, in summer, the slopes of Scafell were like a picnic party. Nevertheless she had spent her life in the town; this was the first day she had ever had on the Tops and her feet ached: if she stopped for a moment the wind cut her with its cold, and again she felt some lingering flakes of snow against her cheek. But more than these things it was the changed aspect of the scene that alarmed her. The hills appeared to have doubled their size, and instead of that entire intimacy they had drawn apart, lifting black shoulders and ragged edges against a sky that seemed now to be alive with dark motion, piles of cloud with the dead whiteness of dried bones running before grey unsubstantial vapour. Still, where Tom could go she could.

He stopped for her and held out his hand.

'We'll go back if you like,' he said.

'Oh no – we're near the top, aren't we?'

'Very near – and then we can run down in five minutes.'

When the Pillar and Steeple came into view Tom, who had often climbed this before, although always in fine weather, knew that the rest of the way would be rough.

'Look here, Sally. Perhaps we'd better go back.'

'Oh no. Let's do it now we're here.'

The path now was a confusion of rough stones and the wind seemed to meet them from every quarter. A scurry came up from the valley and with it a whirl of light wet snow.

Then, a moment later, from no quarter at all as it seemed, a blinding storm came upon them. There was snow in it and a wet mist, and it appeared to Tom that from below them, on either side, a boiling vapour of mist rushed, edging up.

They were near the top, he supposed, but he could see nothing. He caught Sally close to him. It was as though they both of them stood on air. If there was ground it rocked under their feet, and the gale lashed their faces like the sharp whip of stinging twigs.

With his arm round her he shouted: 'I say, this is awful. We must find shelter somewhere. This will soon be over.'

The trouble was that it had become suddenly unknown country. He knew that on the one side of the Pike it was easy descent but on the other it was rock and precipice. They moved forward together, step by step, stumbling over the stones. The wind was ferocious, and the sleet came in waves as though it were timed and obeyed a certain rhythm.

Sally stumbled, she caught his arm, then put her hand up to his wet cheek.

'I wanted to be sure you were there. It's the cold – it takes your breath.'

He must shelter her somewhere until this gust was over, but he feared the whirling dusk that was now so thick and clinging that he was like a blind man who, sightless, yet knows his room is turning about him. He felt that all round them was a world of rock; stones that would seem minute enough in daylight now were gigantic. It was as though one single rock moved with them, maliciously keeping them company.

'Look here, Sally,' he said. 'What do you think we had best do? I don't know where we're going. If I could tell which way the wind's blowing, but it seems to be coming in every direction at once. If we could touch grass we'd be all right, but the fact is I'm afraid of striking the rocks on the other side.'

She scarcely heard him. She was ready for anything, but this icy wind was beyond any experience that she had ever had. The cold seemed to grip and shake her; she had never known before what it was to lose faith in her own power of resistance, but her knees were cut with the cold, her head was buffeted and her hands were gone.

She realized that they were beginning to descend, and the wind now leapt up from below, tugging at their feet.

They turned the edge of a rock and the gale fell. Bending down Tom saw that the rock was arched. He groped round it and found that within the curve there was shelter.

He manoeuvred her into its hollow. 'Look here. Rest your back against the rock here. Now bend your knees up. You can't feel the wind now.'

The relief was blessed, for the roar had died, her face was no longer torn with the cold, and she could feel her hands again. He knelt in front of her.

'Thank God. You'll be all right there till the storm's over. I don't suppose it will last long. It doesn't as a rule when it gets up as suddenly as that.'

She pulled at his arm.

'Come in too.'

'No. There isn't room. I'll stay here for a moment. Any second the mist can blow away and I'll see where we are.'

She held on to his arm.

'Tom, you're grand – as though you'd been in storms all your life. You are a brick to look after me.'

She'd never before praised him for looking after her. Well, that was something. He had his back to the gale and it was as though a thudding door of ice beat upon it. He turned sideways, lying up partly against her. So they waited, her hand on his knee.

He thought: 'Now I can do something. I'll see that she's all right. We'll be laughing at this in half an hour.'

Then the sleet changed to snow. There was a thin bright whiteness in the air; in spite of its thinness the general scene was no clearer. Nothing was more visible, but now the touch of the storm was soft and clinging while the wind moaned through the web with a singing, whining cry.

They waited. Time passed.

A long time later Tom put his hand on Sally's. It was icily cold. He bent forward and touched her cheek. She whispered, in a voice strangely unlike hers: 'It's fearfully cold, Tom.'

He took off his waterproof and his coat, then his thick woollen jersey.

'Look here. You've got to put this on.'

She acquiesced, and he knew at once that she was already sleepy with the cold, for, in her own self, she would have eagerly resisted.

But, as he held her against himself, he felt her whole body slacken. He pulled the jersey over her head, then laid his coat over her, thrusting her hands into its pockets. Lastly he took the waterproof and wrapped it round her legs. He saw that she was curled up well within the shelter of the rock. Her head fell forward and he knew that she was asleep . . .

He waited. His eyes stared into the dancing thickness that now had, it seemed, a rosy light at its heart. Then the cold bit him; he felt its teeth at his breast and a warm breath against his nostrils as though out of the storm an animal had crept to him for shelter . . .

Circles, crimson at the edge with centres of dazzling white, floated, hung, fell slowly and rose like telephone wires seen from a train. With a terrific effort he rose to his feet, tottered, balanced himself against the rock.

'Sally!' he whispered. 'Are you all right, Sally?' But of course she was all right. He smiled. Then he moved. He must move or he would sleep.

He stumbled into the light. For now the world broke into a dazzling brightness. He stepped forward to greet it. Soft hands caressed his cheeks and someone stroked his eyes.

Oh! Beloved Mountain! This place of light and splendour for which all his life long he had been waiting. Beloved Mountain that took him now with the warm strong caressing grasp of a friend.

Everywhere about him, from the height and the depth, voices greeted him. A light, more splendid than any that he had ever known, dazzled his closing eyes. He ran forward and fell.

Later a shepherd, looking for his sheep, found Sally sleeping under the rock.

FAMILY DINNER

Two events of the first importance occurred during the spring of 1930 in the Herries family: one was the marriage on April 3rd at St Margaret's, Westminster, of Miss Mary Worcester to the Marquis of Paignton, the other was Alfred's removal to a very fine and spacious house in Hampstead. The two events were celebrated by the dinner that Alfred gave in the second week of May.

Lord Paignton was thirty-eight years of age when he invited Mary to be his Machioness, and Mary was thirty-seven, so there was, as Adrian said, 'nothing of the virginal about it'. All the same Paignton was a very 'virginal' man. He had proposed to other ladies on other occasions and had twice been engaged, but none of these young women had been serious enough for him. He was himself intensely serious-minded as was right and proper in the future Duke of Wendover. He was famous for his conversational opening gambit: 'If you are at all interested in my opinion of the matter ...' He had excellent views on Tariffs, Russia, Unemployment, the Pound Sterling, Agriculture, and Why Our Churches are Empty Today. But the interesting thing about him, Adrian thought, was that he was marrying Mary for her brains rather than her looks.

She still *had* looks of a statuary, marble kind and he would, Adrian thought, be just the man to admire her poise, her immobility and air of watching repose. But no, her brain was the lure. 'I'm marrying the most intelligent woman in England,' he told his friends at the Bendish, a little club in St James's Street where gatherings were held of so solemn a character that it was said that a waiter there hung himself because he hadn't seen anyone smile for five years.

'Does he think her clever because she never says anything?' Adrian wondered. But it did not matter. The Herries were pleased, although by this time they were so firmly the backbone of England that nothing either here or there could make any difference. Cynthia was now entirely swallowed up in the waters of bridge, and was so weary with her long, long efforts to find a husband for Mary that, when at last Mary found a husband for herself, she had very little to say about it.

Rosalind had married a Major Brigstock, a good fellow who luckily believed the Herries the finest family in the world, and Peile had died two years ago from influenza, so Cynthia thought now of nothing at all but Contract, her two Pekinese – Tang and Ming – and her figure, which was by this time as thin and sharp as a needle.

Alfred bought the house in Hampstead because money was very uncertain and he thought it not a bad thing to have it in property. He also saw quite clearly that very soon now the West End would be nothing but shops, and anyone who had to live in London would be ashamed to be seen south of St John's Wood. He had also a very charming house near Sunningdale and, although he was sixty-eight this year, played a good game of golf every weekend. He was a dry self-satisfied old man with supreme confidence in himself and a contempt for anyone who was not practical. But he could be generous and, when his liver was in good order, could tell a funny story. He was now deeply disappointed with his son, Maurice, who settled down to nothing, thought that he could write poetry, and led a cat-and-dog life with his wife. On the other hand his girl, Clara, had married a rich American, Borden Wadsworth, and entertained regally in Chicago.

His only trouble, had been that he liked women around him. Men as companions were only useful for golf and an exchange of opinions about the money market. Quite recently this lack in his life had been strangely supplied. A woman called Abigail Hill, a single lady of forty or so, occupied the position of his best friend. The true story of Abigail Hill was a most interesting one and her influence on the whole Herries family already promised to be remarkable. She was a tall, gaunt, extremely fashionable woman who had lived, it appeared, for many years at Eastbourne with an old invalid father. He, dying, had left her a large sum of money. She had come to London and had taken a large flat at the Marble Arch end of Park Lane. Here she entertained, and with excellent taste. She was, apparently, cynical and plain-spoken. She won a reputation for her caustic remarks. But, cynical or no, she became attached to old Alfred and he to her.

No one suggested for a moment that there was anything lyrical in their association. They were quite simply good friends and, whenever he gave a dinner party, it became natural to find her there as hostess. She furnished the Hampstead house for him and did it magnificently. She was modern and not too modern. This was a good time, because of the growing distress in Europe and America, for 'picking up' things cheaply, and Alfred's pictures and furniture were worth seeing. He, like the other Herries before him, cared little or nothing for property as such. It was beneath a Herries' dignity to think that he or she was valuable because of possessions. All Alfred wanted was that he should be suitably surrounded. Abigail Hill saw that it was so.

In a short time she had made her mark on every member of the family. She played bridge with Cynthia, talking cynically with Adrian, flattered Gordon, soothed Maurice and even bothered to have tea with poor old Horace. The only members of the family with whom she could do nothing at all were Benjie and Sally. She complained of them to Alfred.

'They're too sentimental for anything. They don't seem like your relations.'

'Benjie's always been a bad lot,' Alfred said, 'and his daughter takes after him.'

Nevertheless they were invited to the dinner party because Abigail said that what was needed was a little variety. 'You're all a little monotonous in the lump,' she said, 'and as a matter of fact I rather like Benjie even though he detests me.'

Adrian was engaged and therefore a young Frenchman and his sister, children of a French financier of importance to Alfred, were invited. They were the only two present who were not of the family circle, and only at the last moment was it discovered that the Frenchman, Raymond Herriot, was blind – blinded in the War.

'That's uncomfortable,' Alfred said. 'I wish we hadn't asked them.'

'I believe he's no trouble at all,' Abigail answered. 'He goes about quite a lot.'

The dinner party consisted of Alfred, Miss Hill, Gordon, Maurice and his wife, Tim Bellairs the painter, now living in London, Phyllis and Anstey Veasey, Mary and Lord Paignton, Cynthia, Rosalind (her husband the Major was away in Ireland), Raymond and Mlle Herriot, Sally and Benjie.

Yes, quite a party.

Sally had given up her rooms and lived with her father ever since Tom's death. They got on splendidly. Now as she drove him up to Hampstead in her small bright-red Midget he thought of her with most loving affection. Tom's death had wrought a deep change in her. It was strange, when you thought of it, that Tom had longed all his life to do something for those he loved, and in his death, which had seemed accidental, gratuitous, he had at last won his desire. Well, perhaps nothing was gratuitous, accidental ...

But with Sally it was the three great unhappinesses of her life – her mother's death, her misadventure with Arnold, and Tom's death – that made her what she now was, and Benjie, looking at her, knowing her courage, common sense, humour and kindness, wondered whether ever in England before there had been created a generation so fine and intelligent as this one of Sally's. 'Only we can't tell yet. We can't tell for another twenty years.'

Assembled in Alfred's grand drawing-room, panelled, the splendid possessor of three lovely Canalettos, they found that they were the last of the party.

'Yes, this *is* the Family!' Benjie thought, sarcastically, for whenever he encountered them *en masse* he disliked them, felt that they disliked him and would be relieved if he left them for ever. He could never be with the Family without, at the same time, feeling rather ashamed of himself, and that made him both shy and angry. For they had succeeded. As a family (for they had only the slenderest connexion with the Scottish Herries) in 1730 they had been nothing, in 1780 a little something, in 1820 people were aware of them, in 1850 they counted, in 1900 they were prominent, and now in 1930 they were everywhere ... And yet for him now as he looked at them, the romantic period of their history was closing. They no longer fought, struggled, were

jealous, cruel ... Cynthia, Alfred, Mary, Gordon, Rosalind ...
They had become part of England, and future history would be
made of struggles elsewhere and of another kind.

'We've been interesting for just two hundred years,' he
thought. 'Sally and Maurice and the Veasey children may make
history, but it will be a new chapter.'

For he was old enough now to be a philosopher and have a
perspective. And, physically, he was in splendid condition for an
old boy who had led a life, had only one arm and was seventy-five
years of age.

They marched into the dining-room. The long shining table
was lit by tall candles in high silver candlesticks. Over the mantelpiece was a fine picture by John of a peasant in a blue cloak
standing against a background of dark hills.

Benjie threw his eye around him. He was himself sitting between Phyllis Veasey and a grave dark girl with charming intelligent eyes whose name he did not know.

'Who is it on the other side of me?' he asked Phyllis under
cover of the opening babble of conversation.

'French,' said Phyllis. 'A Mademoiselle Herriot. That's her
brother over there next to Sally. He's blind.'

He looked across and saw, next to Abigail Hill, a young man
with black hair and a strong watchful face. He was watchful
because he was blind. His brown eyes gazed with a steady absorbed look in front of him and, instead of appearing sightless,
had a penetration that seemed to go beyond all things physical, to
rest calmly on a world where everything was quiet, profound and
real ...

'Vanessa's world,' Benjie thought.

Phyllis Veasey began at once to talk. She found it difficult to
keep still. She was gay, bright, like a coloured bird who had just
risen from the water and must shake the sparkling drops from its
wings.

She had been reading a very long book called *Kristin Lavransdatter*.

'I'm afraid you don't read much, Cousin Benjie.'

'No, not very much. I never have. I'm an old man and want to
see everything I can before my time's up. I like a man called
Hudson who writes about birds.'

'Well, *Kirstin Lavransdatter*'s miles long. I like long books,
don't you? You go on and on and on. I got this one from the
Book Society.

'What's the Book Society?'

'Oh, five writers tell you what to read.'

'Why five?'

'Oh, I don't know. Five's better than one. Not so prejudiced.'

'I should have thought five times as prejudiced. Anyway, what do you want anyone to tell you what to read for? Why don't you decide for yourself?'

'Oh, there isn't any time and one wants to read what other people are reading.'

'The girl's an idiot,' thought Benjie crossly. He found that his temper rose just as quickly as ever it had done in spite of his seventy-five years. So he turned to Mlle Herriot and found, to his relief, that she talked perfect English. For his own French was nothing to be proud of.

'Don't we seem odd to you,' he asked her; 'an English family all dining together inside the security of one's own fortress?'

'In what way – odd?' She had a most charming smile, gay and gentle. And, at that same moment, he realized that young Herriot, turning to Sally, had the same smile.

'Well, the French and English never really understand one another, do they? And never will. You are so realistic. We so sentimental. Now we don't look sentimental, all of us in this room. But I assure that we are. We believe devoutly in our fairy stories – the splendour of England, that hearts are more than coronets, although we are the most snobbish people on earth, and that the Herries family is unique in the world for its qualities of good sense, patriotism and fine breeding.'

'But I think England *is* splendid – and France too. You see, I also am romantic. I think, too, that England has her faults, her stupidities, and France too. Now is not that a safe answer?'

'Very safe,' he said, smiling. 'That is your brother – on the other side to the left, sitting next to my daughter?'

'Yes. Oh, is that your daughter? What an amusing face she has! And how intelligent! She is more alive than anyone else here.' Then she hurried on lest he should think that she was paying obvious compliments. 'My brother, Raymond, was blinded in the War. He is the most splendid man I know. His blindness hardly handicaps him at all. He lives in Berlin. He is working with a group of other young men for international understanding.'

'Not an easy job,' said Benjie.

'No,' Mlle Herriot said eagerly. 'But most interesting. He gets on with the Germans splendidly. His blindness seems to help him. He says that people accept from him, because he is blind, more than they would from others.'

'Perhaps it would be better if some more of us were blind. We might see farther.'

Just then he caught Sally's eyes and they smiled at one another. He could see that she was very happy. She was. She had not looked forward with great pleasure to this party. Big dinners were out of fashion now, family groups were out of fashion, and old Alfred and Abigail were not, in Sally's view, an interesting pair.

She had left Bimberg long ago, and now (because work she must) was helping the famous Lady Connington in an effort to rouse the people of England to an interest in the League of Nations. Benjie was not rich, nor had she inherited anything from Ellis who, in a will written shortly after Vanessa's flight, had left his wealth first to the Miss Trents, and at their death to charities. Lady Connington was a fool, and the League was not, at times, very encouraging. It attracted so many half-baked nitwits. Nevertheless, Sally was staunch to it. It was, Mr Rack-Bunden told her, 'the only thing there is. Without it our civilization is ruined. We go tottering into the abyss.' So Sally held on to the League, went about the country in her MG speaking for it, and explained to Sheffield and Newark and Doncaster what Gandhi's theory was and what was happening in China . . .

She had felt, in fact, after Tom's death that she must try and do some good somewhere. Do something for him in return, as it were. She had long ago understood that among her friends the worst thing that anyone could say about anyone else was that he or she was trying to do good. It was simply too 'shy-making', in the phrase of the moment. At the same time she realized that many of them did a great deal of good in a humorous, cynical, and 'Don't you dare to remind me of it' manner. She hid her motives; she tried to pretend that Lady Connington and the League satisfied her. She was exceedingly lonely. Here she was, twenty-six years of age, and she had achieved nothing whatever except to be considered, by a stupid, ignorant woman, not good enough for a weak, helpless young man. She had lost her mother, her lover and her brother. She was beginning to wonder, in spite of her twentieth-century materialism, whether there was not a curse on her father and herself. They were, both of them, so plainly isolated, by themselves, not wanted.

So she had not looked forward to the dinner. Abigail Hill did not like her; Alfred thought that she encouraged Maurice in his discontents; Gordon disliked her; the Veaseys were afraid of her.

And then, when, after five minutes, a few words with Gordon, her neighbour on her left, had convinced her that their hatred of one another was entirely mutual, she turned to her other companion. He turned also with eyes that seemed to stare with a gentle, almost indecent obstinacy into her heart. They did, indeed, make her heart suddenly beat with a confusing rapidity. She did not know him. She had never seen him before. Why did he stare at her so? And then she saw that his hands moved round his plate, touched, very quickly, the knives and forks. Then that his duck had been cut into small pieces before it was brought to him. She knew now why his eyes so unwinkingly stared.

'You must forgive me,' she heard him say (his English was good, but it had a pleasing accent). 'I am blind, and so am unable to be sure whether you want to talk with me or not. I don't even know whether you are looking my way.'

She touched his sleeve with her hand.

'I am looking your way and I want to talk.'

'*Bien*. Thank you very much. I don't often go to dinner parties because I'm afraid of being tiresome. Or, rather, I did not. But now my life in Berlin includes a good deal of – what do you say? – sociability, so I am getting over my shyness.'

'Oh, do you live in Berlin?' asked Sally.

'Yes. I was blinded in the War. At Verdun. I was in hospital for two years and did not know what to do with myself. And then in '25 a very brilliant man, a Swiss, a Monsieur Holthois, formed an International Group with members in all the principal cities in Europe – also in America. His purpose was no more than for internationally-minded people of every country to be in constant communication – see each other often, you know. We are all patriots, but internationalists as well – not so difficult as you suppose. Our only rules are that we deliberately discuss everything – are not afraid to – and that we see one another's point of view and that we allow no difference of opinion to separate us. We are growing very fast, and I am the principal French representative in Berlin. But, dear me, I talk only of myself. Tell me about *you*. What are you called? Who are you? Married or single? What do you look like? You see, you must help me.'

'Yes,' said Sally, rather breathlessly. 'I want to. My name is Sally Herries. I'm twenty-six years of age and not married. I help

Lady Connington about the League of Nations, or try to, but I'm not much use, I'm afraid. My father is sitting on the other side of the table. He and I live together. My mother died when I was only nine, but I've never forgotten her. She was the finest person I've ever known. Then my only brother was killed in Cumberland in 1928 – we were caught in a storm on a mountain, and he kept me warm by wrapping his clothes round me, and he fell over a rock and was stunned and died of the cold.'

'I'm very sorry,' said Raymond Herriot.

'Yes, so you see there's nothing very special about *me*.'

'Would you please tell me,' he asked, dropping his voice a little, 'if you do not think it impertinent, what you look like?'

'Of course.' She laughed. 'Shall I be honest? I'd better be, because other people would tell you the truth if I didn't. I'm short and small. I've got dark-brown hair – short, you know – a sallow complexion which I try to brighten up a bit, a snub nose and not a very pretty mouth. On the other hand, my eyes are nice. I've quite good hands and very small feet – only my legs are too short.'

'Thank you,' he said.

She did not know whether she had been impertinent and too familiar or too hasty. She had never had an experience like this before. She felt that she would tell him anything.

'One thing you have not said. You have a beautiful voice.'

'My voice isn't bad,' she answered recklessly, 'when I'm in a good mood. I have an awful temper. I get that from Father, and then, when I lose it, my temper I mean, my voice has a nasty edge to it.' She added, thinking that it was time to get away from the personal: 'What a wonderful thing to do! To work like that in Berlin! I do envy you.'

'Come and work there too,' he said earnestly.

'Oh, do you think I could?'

'Why not?' Then he added: 'I feel as though we were meant to meet tonight. Please let this not be our last meeting.'

'Oh no!' Sally said. 'Oh no! We'll meet as often as you like!'

It was after that that her eyes met Benjie's and they smiled.

By this time everyone was very gay. Alfred's wines were excellent, and that spirit of self-confidence that always developed when members of the family were for a time together was now most happily universal.

Dessert came and Alfred made a little speech (he liked to make speeches).

'I welcome you all to my new house and I hope you will be

very often here. It may seem ostentatious for an old man like me to have a new house, but it is intended for the Family as much as for myself. I don't know whether some of you remember,' he went on. 'It is a long time ago but it is very vivid to myself. At the beginning of the War, before Gordon and Maurice went to the Front, some of you had dinner with me, and Sally here, who was only a child then, lit a candle which we passed from one to another. I must say that I think there has been something that has held us all together through all the hard times, and will, I am convinced, hold us together still.

'I would like to say how pleased I am that on this occasion we should have with us two friends from that splendid country so grandly our ally then and now. I drink to the health of glorious France.'

Everyone stood up and drank.

Then young Herriot replied. He said only a few words:

'I must thank you very much on behalf of my country and my sister and myself. We are all proud of the countries to which we belong: it is, I think, that pride, one of the finest things in human nature – but with it there must go something as fine – pride in the whole world, a desire to see the whole world one, so that so dreadful a thing as war can never return to the world again.'

Then there was a very regrettable episode – one of those episodes for ever recurring in the Herries history. Young Anstey Veasey had been drinking. He was a nice young fellow. Everyone agreed about that afterwards. What he did any one of his generation might have done. Luckily the little affair was very soon over. Fifty years ago there would have been more lasting consequences; a hundred years ago perhaps a family feud as in the famous ancient story of poor Christabel and the fan. But now – well, now in the twentieth century the Herries temper had mellowed, the hysterical element in it had been taught discipline.

What occurred was that young Veasey cried out:

'It's all very well for you fellows who had all the fun to say that there's to be no war – but what about us? Are we never to have any adventure again? Oh, I know what all you older people say – that the last war was horrible and the next one will be worse. But how do we know? You had some pretty good times in the War. I've heard lots of fellows say it was the best time in their lives. Of course men were killed and wounded, but we've all got to die some time, and after all it's the greatest adventure can happen to anybody. I don't think another war would be such a bad thing when all's said and done. It would clear up some of the mess the world's in anyway. After all, you can't stop men fighting. It's their nature to fight, and I think a jolly old scrap with the Russians or someone would do a lot of good.'

He was, of course, only a boy who had had too much to drink, and his silly nonsense should have passed unnoticed.

But what happened was that before anyone else could speak Maurice had sprung to his feet.

'It's a damnable lie!' he cried out. He stood there, white-faced, his thin nervous body trembling, his voice pitched high. 'I say it's a lie! My God, is this what we went through all that hell for? Only a few years and already there are fools daring to talk that blasphemy. We suffered – we suffered, millions of us, men, women and children suffered. We went through hell day after day, month after month, year after year. Our lives have been wrecked. We've lost everything, friends, faith, belief in God ... We've been ruined, been damned ... The only hope we've ever had is that at least what we suffered has made it impossible for anyone to suffer that way again. And now, now – already – it's coming back, and men dare to say they want it back – and all we've been through has been no good. Anyone, anyone – who helps another war is damned. They're enemies of their fellow-men – the cruellest—'

He stopped short and, to everyone's horror, burst into tears. He stood there, his hand in front of his face, sobbing. Then, with a gesture of his hand, his head down, he turned and hurried from the room.

There was a moment's silence then. Rosalind got up and went after him.

'I say,' said young Anstey, 'I'm most awfully sorry—'

Paignton broke in: 'If anyone cares to hear what I think—'

Conversation became general. It was very unpleasant, of course, and especially because there were those present who were not English and because Maurice was Alfred's son.

But all the concentrated common sense of the Family rose like a calming breeze. They knew nowadays – Alfred and Cynthia and Gordon and Mary – how to deal with that sort of hysteria. Poor Maurice! It was natural enough that he should feel as he did, but at his age he should really have learnt to control his emotions – one of the first and most important lessons.

Soon everyone was easy again. Rosalind returned and said that Maurice had gone.

'He's been having his headaches,' she explained.

'Poor boy!' Alfred said. 'You'd think that after all these years his nerves would be in better control. I think of sending him to Vienna. There's a doctor there . . .'

Later, in a corner of the drawing-room under the enchanting Canaletto that showed the gondolas like butterflies, the figures of rose and silver in their masks crossing the bridge, Sally had some last words with Raymond Herriot. His sister was saying her farewells to Alfred.

They were partly concealed from the others by the folds of a curtain of dark shadowed gold. He put out his hand and touched her sleeve. Then his hand rested firmly on her arm.

'It is,' he said, 'how do you say? – up to you, our next meeting.'

'I will meet you whenever and wherever you like,' she answered.

'Well, then – why not tomorrow? Would you come and have tea, perhaps, with my sister and me? We are at Brown's Hotel.'

'Yes. Of course I will.'

'*Bien*. And then one day perhaps you will come to Berlin?'

'Yes, if you would like me to.'

'Yes, I would like you to.' His face broke into a beautiful smile. 'I have a perfect picture of you in my mind – already.'

'You must ask your sister,' Sally answered.

'I don't need to ask anyone.' Then very abruptly he said: 'Now, how old do you suppose I am?'

'Oh—' She moved a little closer to him. 'I should say – thirty-five.'

'Yes – thirty-six. And still a bachelor. Strange, is it not?'

'I don't know. I'm not married either.'

'Yes, that is very strange. But you are ten years younger.'

She said nothing.

With that quiet gentle voice that she found extremely charming he asked her: 'That is not too great a difference in years – between us?'

'No. Of course not.'

She could not help herself. She put out her hand and caught his. He held hers and then, raising it, kissed it.

She sat beside her father, driving the car, staring in front of her.

'Did you enjoy it?' he asked her.

'Yes, Father – most awfully.'

'Pity Maurice had that outburst. I hate to see a man cry. Poor chap. If I had my way, I'd give young Anstey a good leathering. Rotten manners with Herriot there!'

'Lots of his generation think like that.'

'Do they? More fools they.' He looked at her. 'You seemed to get on well with that young Frenchman.'

'Yes. I'm going to tea with him and his sister tomorrow.' Then she added:

'He thinks I might help him in their work in Berlin.'

'Oh, does he? Would you like to?'

'Yes, I think I would.'

He sighed, but so gently that Sally did not hear him. So that was Sally's destiny. Just what she wanted, someone with her own notions, someone for her to look after. But blind? And a Frenchman?

Sally would manage it. She'd found what she wanted. And so the last link was broken. He would be alone now – the last of the bad Herries. They were all good now ...

Cumberland.

It was as though the Derwent suddenly broke in a torrent across Piccadilly and Glaramara rose towering above the Ritz.

He put his hand on Sally's knee.

'He looks a fine fellow,' he said, 'if you want to know what I think about it. And when you're married I shall take the next train for Keswick.'

Sally laughed.

'Father, how ridiculous! I don't know that he even likes me.'

'No, but I do. Look out! You nearly had that taxi.'

When later she kissed him goodnight she was quite especially affectionate, and, after she had gone to bed, he sat for a long while looking at Vanessa's photograph.

'Sentimental,' he said, knocking his pipe out on the fender. 'That's what I've become! All the same – Vanessa would have approved of that man. He's her sort.'

COUNTRY FAIR

SALLY HERRIES was engaged to Raymond Herriot just before Christmas 1930. They were married in London at a register office on the 14th of November, 1931.

In February 1932 Benjie paid them a visit in Berlin. He stayed with them for a fortnight and had a grand time. The more he saw of young Herriot the better he liked him, and Sally's happiness was founded on excellent reason. The only thing that distressed him was that she might become *too* international. She had, in a few weeks, the troubles of Germany at her fingertips. She knew what Schleicher wanted, what Hitler said, and what the German Princes were doing. She also knew why the middle-class German was starving. At the same time she understood to a marvel what were the difficulties of M. Herriot (no relation at all of her husband's). She understood the ambitions of Mussolini, the restlessness of the Japanese, the confusion of the Chinese, why America would be Democratic before the end of the year and just how far the Five Year Plan had collapsed.

'You know,' said Benjie when he had listened to a great deal of discussion, 'I'm so old now that none of these things seem to me of the least importance.' He patted Sally on the shoulder. 'When you are busy making the new world don't forget there's such a place as Cumberland.'

'There you are, you see,' Sally said. 'How can you say that the state of the world isn't important? How can Cumberland be happy if there isn't enough to eat?'

'Temporary questions, temporary questions,' Benjie murmured. 'There's something more important.'

'What is?' She put her arm around his neck. He was such a fine old man, so sturdy on his legs, so irascible and jolly and indignant and easily placated, so strong and healthy for his years.

'I don't know – and I don't care, as long as I know that *something* is—'

He kissed her. They were saying farewell. It was in the Kurfürstendamm on a Sunday evening. They had been seeing Jannings' new film *Tempest* with the new actress Anna Sten. She had excited Benjie and he would have given anything to be able to kiss her adorable and most mysterious almond eyes. 'But I don't kiss women any more,' he told Sally. 'Or hardly ever. Old men of my age should look and not touch.'

He was catching the night train to the Hook, and in the train he felt for a while very melancholy. The last link was gone. Not only was he alone now, but the romantic history of the Herries family was closed and finished. He would go back to Cumberland and never leave it till he died. He hated to feel lonely, so he thought of Vanessa. He opened a novel that he had been told was good – *The Fountain*, by Charles Morgan. He was very quickly interested in it although he seldom read novels. 'Sort of book Vanessa would like,' he thought.

In the summer he did a ridiculous thing. He bought a caravan. He had been staying for some days near Canterbury and he saw this thing. It looked very handsome, for it was painted a deep crimson and the curtains of the little windows were pink and white. It contained, he discovered, every possible requirement and was remarkably cheap because its owner had just been declared bankrupt. He found that his motor-car could be attached to it very comfortably. He bought it there and then. Afterwards he had the difficult task of explaining its advantages to John Holly. Holly was his man, chauffeur, cook, bottle-washer, general factotum, friend and perpetual grumbler, who had been with him now for several years. He was a small spindle-shanked man whose appearance was never as smart as Benjie wished. He had a passion for engines, dogs and women. He was sober and industrious, but an abominable gossip and a Bolshevik in politics. He was no respecter of persons.

'Gor blimey! What do you want a bloody caravan for?'

'To live in.'

'To live in? You can't live in a caravan in London.'

'We aren't going to live in London any more, John. We shall probably never see it again. We are going up to Cumberland to stay.'

'Oh, well, you can take my notice. I'm not going to live in the country.'

'All right. You can go as soon as you like.'

'I damned well would go it if weren't for the dog.'

'There you are, you see. It's much better for Sam to live in the country. You're always saying he doesn't get enough exercise.'

Sam, although he was no longer young, behaved like a puppy still. Holly adored him.

'A caravan! My God! We *will* look a couple of pretties!'

Before his departure for Cumberland, Benjie went round and said goodbye to the Family. They were none of them sorry to see him go, as he very well knew. Only Horace perhaps regretted him, which was ironic, because Benjie had for so long detested Horace. However, Sally had cared for him, and now at the age of seventy-four he put up, on the whole, a very brave show.

He was as optimistic as ever and even quoted 'God's in His heaven: All's right with the world'.

'Everything possible is wrong with it,' said Benjie, 'and we're two old derelicts who ought to have been dead long ago.'

'I'm remarkably well,' Horace said, 'except for a twinge of rheumatism. I'll come up and visit you in Cumberland one day.'

'I'm damned if you will,' thought Benjie. However, he shook him warmly by the hand.

Cynthia's Pekinese barked at him until he was deafened (he detested toy dogs), Alfred showed him round the Hampstead garden, Gordon slapped him on the back, Adrian, who was now a weary dyspeptic pessimist, said to him:

'I'll be sorry not to see you about, Benjie. I've always admired you, you know.'

'Admired me? Good God – why?'

'You've always gone your way. I might have done once. And then you make me think of Vanessa, the only woman I ever really loved.'

They weren't so bad, he thought, when he'd said goodbye to all of them. He had fought them all his life and was glad to be rid of them, but he saw quite clearly their integrity, their wholesome common sense, their loyalty to their own beliefs.

'There have to be the imaginative and the unimaginative, but they'll never understand one another. And that's that.'

August this year was luckily a dry fine month. Everyone was astonished – as everyone in England always is when holidays are fine – astonished and a little indignant, as though England were posing slightly. The caravan was most amusing. Benjie, Holly, and Sam all slept in the little cupboard behind the general living-room unless the nights were dry, when Holly and Sam slept out of doors. But they got on very well. They were all quiet and unemotional sleepers.

There was a great deal of traffic and general holiday rejoicing. Holly, as was the way of his kind, was extremely proud of the caravan in the presence of strangers and very indignant about it to Benjie.

'Blasted old inculus' (he meant 'incubus'). 'It wobbles like an old fat woman.' But he talked to everyone – farmers, hotel girls, motor-cyclists and the AA officials.

'Ought to have one,' Benjie heard him say. 'Everyone will be having them soon. They say we all got to economize. Well, what about it? Most economic thing going.'

When they were north of Doncaster, Benjie's spirits rose higher and higher. For one thing, he'd never felt better in his life.

'What do you think of me for seventy-seven?' he would ask John. He would be doing his exercises, half stripped on a sunny morning outside the caravan, while Sam sniffed for rabbits under the hedge.

'Take care you don't catch no cold,' John would say. 'And another thing. Don't let no women see you. They'll think we're nudists.' Then, with a reluctant and cynical smile he would add: 'You've got a fine brown skin – like the gipsies. I'm a gipsy now myself, I reckon, but I can't get that brown colour. Lived too much in towns.'

On the whole they found that farmers, proprietors of fields, publicans and sinners were all very agreeable to them. A very good thing, for Benjie's temper was up in a minute.

'I give what I get – always have. Give me sauce and you'll know it.'

Then, when they came to Kendal, it was just like going home. There's a brow of the hill between Kendal and Windermere when the waters of the Lake are suddenly revealed. It is as though a door were unlocked. Benjie caught Holly's shoulder. 'Look at that, John, and thank your Maker.'

'Here, look out – I'll be driving into the hedge.'

'Well, stop the damned thing.'

All three of them got out and looked at the Promised Land.

'The only woman I ever loved lived with me there. I was born there. My children were born there.'

'What!' said Holly, astonished, 'Only loved one woman in your life? A gay old man like you? Glad I can't say the same.'

But Benjie didn't answer.

They came into Keswick on a fine summer's afternoon and attracted a good deal of attention, but they didn't stop there. They found that on the following day, September 3rd, were the Braithwaite Games, so Benjie said that they should pitch their caravan in a field nearby. They found a nice green one under the beneficent shadow of Grisedale and Grasmoor. They found a farmer too, a little bouncing man with a red face.

At first he was very angry and then he was very friendly. He told them to clear out and Benjie spoke his mind. Holly, watching them, found it amusing to see two little men so furious.

'What I want to know,' Benjie remarked, 'is why you can't keep a civil tongue in your head. We aren't doing any harm to your blasted field. I'll pay you properly, if that's your trouble.'

'Aye,' said the farmer, 'but I don't want your money or your company either.'

Then he smiled. Benjie was standing, with his hat off, his blue eyes fiery as though he wanted nothing better than a hand-to-hand encounter.

'It's a nice day,' the farmer said. 'You can stay if you like – and I don't want your money either.'

They shook hands and finally sat down on the steps of the caravan and had a chat.

And next morning it came down a regular posh. Not only did it pour, but the wind blew, and not only did the wind blow, but it blew from every possible direction. The whole world was a turmoil of wind and water. But Braithwaite people are not easily discouraged. Have they not the finest village hall for entertainments in the County? No, they are not the people to be defeated. Benjie in a mackintosh and Sam with his stiff short hair blown sideways and one ear over one eye (all the work of the wind) went along to see how things were progressing. They discovered that the tea tent had just been blown down for the third time. Everyone was in a state of mind. As the *Mid-Cumberland Herald* afterwards neatly put it: '*All morning wind and rain conspired to make conditions as unpleasant as possible. While the caterers were manfully struggling to erect a marquee in which to feed the spectators, and had to give up after the third attempt, the would-be spectators were debating in their own minds whether to attend or not. The secretary and committee were wondering what the patrons would do.*'

Benjie and Sam assisted for a while and then, feeling that they were wet enough for anything, went back to the caravan. Here, for the rest of the morning, while the rain beat and the wind blew, Benjie wrote to Sally and entertained Sam.

Sam had never grown up. He had not changed in the slightest since Benjie first had him; the white and brown curls of his coat were as charming as ever, his brown eyes as alive and his body as packed with quivering and alert eagerness. A small rubber ball was everything that he needed to turn life from a dull sombre business into a matter of quicksilver daring and adventure.

The caravan apartment was small and loaded with cooking things, clothes, a rifle, a broken-down armchair, a radio and a number of books. In and out of this confusion Benjie and Sam enjoyed an entertainment that had surprise for motive and confusion for its atmosphere. As the ball bounced man and dog rushed for it together. Benjie was, after many years of practice, up to every kind of guile, but Sam knew all the tricks. He stood, the stump of his tail erect and quivering, his eyes on fire, his nose twitching, his right foreleg trembling! Had you shouted in his ear that the Last Trumpet was at hand it would have been no matter. Benjie, his arm raised, held the ball: he feinted towards the cooking stove and Sam's body swung in that direction but his eyes did not shift. He knew, too, of that. When the ball bounced his teeth snapped, he sprang and Benjie grabbed. Books fell, tins rattled, clothes swung in mid-air. Benjie was on his belly groping under the chair while Sam, in no way deceived in this manoeuvre, knowing well that Benjie had the ball set in his hand, stayed, his legs parted, his eyes burning, his complete soul (for he had one) concentrated ...

Meanwhile the rain lashed the caravan, sweeping across the field in sheeted splendour.

'Not bad for seventy-seven!' Benjie cried to Holly, who, standing disdainful in his yellow ulster, saw his master with his shirt open, on his knees, and dust on his cheeks.

'Gawd, what weather!' Holly said.

Nevertheless in the afternoon they ventured and had their reward. Cumberland people are not to be shaken by the weather and there was a good crowd. The weather in fact shook its head and decided to improve. The rain when it did come was a deluge, but in between the sun shone and the colours came out like a picture show. The clouds rushed like mad things across the sky. The sun fell, as though the light had been spilled from a bucket, on to Skiddaw and at once the purple glow of the heather on its flanks spread like a living shadow from shoulder to shoulder while above and below it the green turf almost hurt the eye with its brightness. Then, on the other side of the valley you might see (if you had time to notice) the dark clouds piling up over the tops and swinging through Coledale Pass like an army. On the clouds came and a minute later the rain poured down. The army marched on to invade Keswick and out the sun came again. If you cared to watch you could time the showers and run for shelter.

In the heavens it was all life and movement and on the ground the same stir and constant change.

Benjie drew a deep breath of satisfaction. When he saw Mr Bowe, the secretary, who for weeks past had been saying to all and sundry, 'Now, whatever you do you mustn't miss Braithwaite', hastening hither and thither to see that everything was up to time, his own excitement was intense. He was home again; he was among friends again; he was breathing the air that was, by right of birth, his own. He knew exactly what they were all feeling and wanting and hoping, and he felt and wanted and hoped with them. The clouds were his and the grass was his and the surrounding watching hills.

In a noisy crowd the bookies shouted their odds. In spite of the rain the booths with sweets and apples and ginger-beer drove their trade. Dogs were everywhere, and children and anxious parents, farmers and Keswick citizens and men from Cockermouth and Bassenthwaite, from Under Skiddaw and Threlkeld and Grange and Portinscale.

Soon everything was in motion. In the centre of the field were the wrestlers, the twelve-stoners and the ten-stoners, moving slowly round and round one another with a heavy foot-treading solemnity. Round and round they would go, arms out, broad backs straining; they would seem thus like nothing so much as dreamers who find that meditation on the Deity, the character of the soil they tread, the end of their mysterious destinies, can be obtained best by this slow motion and steady contemplation. Western mystics with their proper sacred ceremonies – and then suddenly there is a start, a jerk, they are locked in one another's arms like lovers, a face stares to the sky, a vast leg stiffens, there is a fall.

'Aye, it will be Blakeney's for sartain,' a farmer beside Benjie prophesied to him gravely.

'Why Blakeney?'

'Didn't ye know? Three times nine and a half stone world champion – aye. He's a lad . . .'

Round the circle of the field the flat-racers were already arranging themselves.

But it was the Puppy Trail that made Benjie's heart beat. In his excitement he dragged Holly by the arm, for that man of a mechanical world was gazing about him with an urban civilized scorn for these poor countrymen who knew nothing better than, on a wet day, to strip almost to the buff and circle slowly round and round on a sodden field.

Benjie might be seventy-seven, but he ran as well as anyone, climbed the low wall and hurried into the next field to see the start of the Trail. At the sight of the men holding the hounds in leash, at the sight of those same hounds straining, yelping, pulling, he sniffed the air as though he were an old hound himself. The last hound trail he had seen he had been with Vanessa over Loweswater way. It had been a glorious day, he remembered, so hot that they had sheltered together under a thick tree for the cool. Afterwards they had had their tea there, and the shadows, moving to the sound of the running beck at their side, had slowly covered the slope of the hill. Then the first stars had come out and, as they had walked together to the road, they had heard from the tent the softened buzzing of the band . . .

Now, as he waited, the sun flashed between the showers, the two trail runners with their 'pads' of old stockings and their aniseed bottles came running in, someone dashed down the flag and the hounds were off. Up the hill, over the wall, across the field and they were lost to view.

After they were gone there was a strange silence, a vacuum, a sense of 'How shall we fill in the time until they're back again?' Some with field glasses climbed the slope, others stood in clusters discussing results – was it to be Starlight or Saturn or Meg?

They turned back for a brief while to watch the wrestling. As Benjie stopped before the wall he felt his shoulder gripped. Against him, at his shoulder, was a strong old man roughly dressed in corduroys, black-haired, bent a little in the back. It was George Endicott.

Benjie stared, feeling that now at this very moment he was wrestling with George on that parlour floor while on the staircase above the woman stood with the candle, waiting, listening . . . that moment that had twisted wrongly his whole life. He had not seen Endicott for ten years.

'George!'

'Funny to see you here. Thought you were dead.'

'And you.'

'Come and have a drink.' It was as though they had never parted. It was his last struggle. He was old and Endicott was old, but there was time yet, old though they were, for the ancient shabbiness, wildness, waste, to return. George had still his black

eyes, his loose mouth, that animal lurch of his shoulders. Benjie
had never gone away with George yet but that one thing had led
to another and so, step by step, into a craziness that ended in
darkness. Odd how, at the sight of George, that other world
crowded in, all the women he had kissed, the silly toasts he had
drunk, the fights he had fought, yes, and further back through
that, striking back to some old scene when a woman had been
sold in a tent and on a starlit night swords had flashed, and on
the Carlisle wall, befogged, he had seen the Devil ... Had he or
had he not? Was this the last touch of that wild hand on his
shoulder?

It seemed that it was, for, smiling he said:

'No, George, thank you.'

'What?' said George. 'Too old for drinking?'

'Oh, I'll drink with you some time, but I'm waiting for the
hounds to come back.'

George's dark eyes covered him. They studied him from head
to toe.

'You look fit.'

'Yes, very fit, thanks. Only a stiffness in my right leg once and
again. Are you staying round here?'

'No. I'm moving on to Carlisle tonight. Like to come?'

'What are you doing there?'

'Eh, I don't know. Meeting a man about a dog, you know.'

There flamed up in him one final tempting impulse. He was
lonely. He had thought, this morning, that it was happiness
enough wandering the country with John and Sam. But he
didn't know ... It would be good to be with George again, to
move, ancient though he was, into that old world without law,
without order, without discipline.

Then he shook his head.

'Afraid I can't.'

'Sure?'

'Yes. Can't get away.'

'So long then. See you some time.'

George vanished and Benjie turned back to see where Holly
was, almost as though he needed protection.

He felt an intense relief as though a weight that had hampered
him for years past were gone. A relief – and a loneliness – for he
was old and, in the final stage of life, with every added year our
fellows recede from us further.

He waited on the edge of the hill, watching for the first sight of the hounds. To John at his side he explained the mysteries. 'You must be careful laying your trail. You've got to watch out that it isn't too dangerous for the hounds, loose scree or falling boulders, and your curve mustn't have too small a radius because a clever hound will pick up the scent on the far side and cut off a troublesome corner. There are hounds who'll be half a mile ahead of the others again and again simply by cutting off corners. And you've got to watch out for men stopping them on the course, giving them meat or something. Once you have betting, men will do anything. All the same it's the prettiest thing in the world, this and sheepdog trials. You've come to the right country, John.'

'Well – so you say –'

Then, suddenly, there was a shout. Over the top of Barrow the hounds had been sighted. Against the dark green slopes you could see the light-coloured bodies moving now in spots of colour, hidden by trees and then, in a moment, all in a line along the fell path.

'There they are!' 'I can see Starlight!' 'Meg's in front.' 'Nay, that's Saturn!'

Now they had all vanished behind a knoll. There was a breathless pause and then a great shout as two hounds appeared abreast.

' 'Tis Starlight!'

'Nay – Saturn! Saturn! Saturn!'

'Yes, 'tis Starlight all right!'

Then down, down the hill they came all together over the hedge on to the roadway. At the last fence Saturn was over first, Starlight just behind him.

'By God! a grand finish!' someone shouted.

But the hullabaloo was now fearful, for all the trainers, with signals perfectly understood by their hounds, let them know, with plenty of time to spare, where the finishing point may be. The shrieks, yells, howls, whistles can be heard a mile away, and some farmer driving his cart up a country lane catches the din on the breeze and will say:

'Yes. Yon's t'hound trail at Braithwaite.'

Starlight and Saturn were up the field together, and had either slackened victory would have been to the other. Did they slacken? Not they. It was one of the best finishes for years – and Saturn has it, two lengths ahead of Starlight, and Granite close behind him.

The rain came, the rain cleared. A lovely mellow light covered the earth. It was the final of the twelve-stone wrestling – Bob Greatouse of Arradfoot had been beaten in the final of the twelve-stone by Blakeney the champion, but the other Greatouse of Arradfoot was in the final of the ten-stone. He was wrestling Pickthall of Cleator Moor. All men held their breath. The two figures went round and round. There was a clinch. Everyone said 'Ah!' Pickthall was thrown with a back-heel ... Round and round again. Another 'Ah!' Pickthall was thrown again, this time with a twist off the breast and a back-heel. Arradfoot could be proud that night.

Benjie was talking, he did not know to whom. Everyone was friendly. Someone asked him whence he had come.

'Oh, from the South.'

And where would he be going to?

'I'm going nowhere. I'm staying here.'

'Aye. Nowt t'matter wi' Coomberland.'

He turned back and looked up to Barrow.

Yes, he was staying. He'd come home.

THE EAGLE

DURING the following weeks Benjie made a number of friends. He was of course quickly recognized, the wild young Herries who had grown up with his mother at Ireby, married beneath him, disappeared and then returned with a woman not his wife, shut himself up for years in Newlands.

In the old days you might have disapproved or not disapproved according to your own uprightness of character. But now he was no longer a danger. They called him 'an old rascal' but his teeth were drawn now. He was a character with his one arm, his short-cropped grey curly hair, face like a russet apple, bright blue eyes. And he liked to wear blue shirts and dark-red ties. So he went about the district with his caravan and his man and his dog.

'Yes, he's a rascal,' they'd say, but he never did any harm to anyone. He had a fiery temper and knocked a man down in Cockermouth in spite of his seventy-seven years, but for the most part he was ready to be friendly.

Moreover he was a Herries, and the Herries, although they'd been queer, had been fond of the district for two hundred years.

And Judith Paris was still remembered everywhere – Madame with her white hair and grand manner and walking stick.

'Glad you've come back,' they said to Benjie, and they were.

There came a day in October at last when he thought he would pitch his caravan in a field by Rosthwaite. He had avoided this for weeks: some superstitious feeling had kept him away, as though that ride from Keswick to Rosthwaite and his sitting down there at the spot where the Herries house had once been under the shadow of Watendlath, had some kind of deep spiritual significance for him. He didn't believe much in deep spiritual significances, but there came times when a man stopped, like Balaam's ass, at a shadow on the path. He had been everywhere else – Uldale and Ireby and Cat Bells and Newlands and Seascale and Gosforth and Ravensglass – all the places that kept anything of Vanessa in their atmosphere – but he had held back from Rosthwaite.

'When I get there I'm closing the chapter.' He didn't know, but he thought it likely that he would end his days in Borrowdale. 'And then that's the finish. No Herries here any more.'

But at last, on a lovely October day, he decided to move on to Rosthwaite. First he had luncheon at the Keswick Hotel, by invitation, with two Keswick residents – Mr Glossop and Mr Blane. Mr Glossop was a bachelor, a large stout cheery man in very baggy knickerbockers. He lived in St John's in the Vale and was reputed to be wealthy. Mr Blane was married, had three children and a small income. He had been a Civil Servant in India, had retired, and suffered from a very uncertain digestion. It was natural that Glossop should be an optimist and Blane a pessimist, but Benjie was interested to realize, as luncheon continued, how very much less certain he was of his opinions than were these two much younger men. He neither knew so certainly nor cared so deeply.

As they walked into the hotel Glossop was waving his arms and crying out cheerily: 'What a day! What a grand day! How are you, Mrs Wivell? Pretty good? That's right ... No, Herries, as I was saying, this Government seems to be doing wonderfully well. Of course we know that people complain about the Means Test, but what I say is this ...'

Later at luncheon Mr Blane looked at Mr Glossop with his rather dim yellow-shadowed eyes and remarked, nervously crumbling his bread:

'Really, Glossop, how you dare! Why, we're on the edge of the pit, the whole lot of us. Hasn't sterling gone down eight points this very week? Isn't France at her wits' end to balance her budget? Haven't those poor fellows from all parts of the country been marching through the rain all this week on London? Isn't Germany making ready to fight Poland and shan't we be compelled because of Locarno to join in? Really, Glossop, I'd be surprised if I didn't know you. Don't be taken in by him, Mr Herries. His spirits go down to zero the minute he has the toothache—'

'Ha! Bah!' said Glossop. 'You're a defeatist, Blane, that's what you are! One would think that a little bit of discomfort means the ruin of the universe! Why, after the Napoleonic Wars they had thirty years of distress and a much worse distress than anything we're experiencing. You just wait until after the American election. You'll be surprised how quickly things settle themselves and trade's booming again! Why, Davis from America is over here consulting with MacDonald this very week, and I see that today's *Express* says . . .'

So it went on and Benjie's mind wandered. He pulled himself together to say once:

'I've got a girl in Berlin working on international affairs.'

'And what does she tell you?' said Glossop, beaming.

'Well, she doesn't tell me anything.'

And then a little later he remarked:

'Of course if they can teach Doyle to defend himself he'll make some of those Americans look silly. He's a natural fighter.'

But he couldn't really attend. Mr Blane cried:

'Well, I simply can't understand you, Glossop. There you are, fiddling while Rome is burning.' He added, 'We're bewildered, that's what we all are. Don't feel safe any more.'

And Benjie thought: 'That's his generation – afraid. Sally's isn't.'

He remarked: 'Sam had a great fight yesterday in Penrith. One of those nasty Aberdeens some fat woman was carrying round with her. He just about bit its ear off.'

And after luncheon he could not fix his mind on serious matters. It was as though this going out to Rosthwaite were all-absorbing. They went with him through the town to where his caravan was pitched between the Art School and Crosthwaite Church. All the way along Mr Glossop was heartily greeting his friends.

'How are you, Mrs Fox?' and then in parenthesis, 'Mrs Fox of

Fawe Park – American – charming woman', or 'Fine day, Mrs
Johnson. How's the boy getting on at Cambridge?' or 'How do,
Todd', or 'How are you, Lewin?' as a clergyman passed them on
a bicycle. While on the other hand Mr Blane recognized no one,
nor did he see the charm of the old tower nor the break between
the houses which showed the sunlit hills rolling through the
mortar and brick, nor the white cloud like a gigantic bird's nest
perched between the breasts of Skiddaw. He saw nothing, for,
defeated once again by the malignant obstinacy of his greed, he
had eaten Cumberland ham at luncheon, the richest ham in the
world and for him the most destructive. Already he saw pain and
discomfort approaching him down the road . . .

Before Benjie sat with Holly in the front of the motor that
pulled the caravan (and Sam on his knee) he shouted to Mr Blane:

'Try five-minute exercises with your colon like that fellow I
read about in a book the other day. Nothing like it for the digestion.' But Mr Blane didn't think that funny. He assumed a
rather sinister air.

As they sputtered off along Main Street, Benjie was cross.

'Having a joke with some men about their digestion is as
serious as joking about their religion.'

'That's all right,' said Holly, 'if your stomach's behaving
proper. You've got a stomach like an ostrich. I've always said
so.'

As usual, they were a sensation in the town, and today, under
the blue sky, the red caravan with all the handles to the doors
highly polished was a fine sight. Benjie, his hat cocked on one
side, a late rosebud in his buttonhole, was a throw-back, as he
himself had observed, to Britannia seated on her throne in the old
circus processions.

'You know, Holly,' he said, 'two hundred years ago on a dark
night a very wicked ancestor of mine rode out into Borrowdale
just as we're doing.'

He was thinking a lot about Francis Herries just then, for a
fortnight ago he had read Judith's book once again right
through. Times weren't so good, with investments down as they
were. It was true that now that Sally was settled his needs were
small, but he had wondered whether, after all, Judith's book
mightn't be worth publishing. After reading it he decided that it
would be sacrilege. But the whole world of that book was very
present to him. When you were as old as he was time vanished
and had no meaning.

Holly had no interest whatever in the Herries family, but he *was* interested in scandal.

'What way was he wicked?' he asked.

'Oh, the usual way.'

'Wine, women and song! Oh, boy!' said Holly.

'There's no need to be American, John,' Benjie remarked. 'They're fine people and their own language suits them, but you're English.'

'You bet,' Holly said. 'No damned foreigners for me.'

When they reached the Ashness gate Benjie made him pull up. He got out and looked across the Lake. There was not a ripple on the water, which was coloured so faintly blue that it was almost white, to the Manesty bank. Here the trees, the chesnuts, the maples, the larches flamed on the water's edge. They seemed in actual fact to be burning. You might fancy that, across the still water, you heard the branches crackle in the blaze. From the darkest crimson, through amber, orange, the rich yellow of a canary's wing, to the faint gold pallor of Chinese lacquer, they were massed against the red cloud of bracken that covered the fell. To the right the cloud that had been a bird's nest on Skiddaw had grown until it enveloped the peaks in a tumbled mass that glittered like frozen snow. There was no sound nor breath of stirring.

'It's a fine day,' he said, climbing back beside Holly.

'And it'll rain tomorrow, I bet you,' said Holly.

With every yard of ground – past the Lodore Hotel, the Borrowdale, Grange Bridge, the Bowder Stone, down the hill into the valley – Benjie's spirits rose. The outer world slipped behind them. The old valley was still shut in even as in ancient days, when its citizens had, as the legend went, tried to build a wall to enclose the cuckoo. Glaramara and Grey Knotts and Brandreth were the advance guard; Gable, Scafell, Great End, Bowfell were still guardians at the close, as for so many hundreds of years they had been. The valley was as still as the Lake had been, and above the green fields, to the right at the side of the streams, the leaves in orange and crimson lifted their glory to the blue.

'Where are we going?' asked Holly. 'Does this valley lead to anywhere?'

'No. It does not. We're stopping for the night near the place where that same ancestor of mine built a house.'

'Kind of lost sort of place, this valley,' said Holly.

Where the path leads off the high road up to Watendlath they halted. Here there was a little stone bridge that crossed a stream flecked now with the blue of the sky, and just above it was a solid little stone house.

'Is that the place your ancestor built?'

'No. That's not the house, but it's the spot. Two ladies lived there, but now it's sold. There's nobody in it, I fancy, just now.'

After some trouble they found a spot on the level below the house where the caravan could remain.

When they were settled Benjie lit a pipe, and taking with him that day's *Times* which he had procured in Keswick, Judith's book at which he thought he would have another look, and Casson's *Wise Kings of Borrowdale* (an old friend of his that he had not seen for many a year but had found today in Chaplin's shop), he seated himself comfortably on the step of the caravan while Sam pursued idyllic scents on the border of the stream.

He had only to raise his eyes, he reflected, and there was old Rogue Herries riding up the path with the little boy in his arms ... The boy runs forward and flings open the door ...

He opened Judith's book at the beginning and read:

'I, Judith Paris, was born at Rosthwaite in the valley of Borrowdale, Cumberland, on the 28th of November in the Year of Our Lord 1774 ...' He skipped a little, but old Aunt Jane's feminine mid-Victorian hand was wonderfully clear. 'I have heard very much of what happened in those long-ago times from my half-brother David Herries. David Herries was my father's son by his first wife, and he was fifty-five when I was born, so that I could have been his granddaughter ... He told me that he remembered exactly the night that he first arrived in Keswick. He could remember every detail, and so do I, even at this distance of time. How he was in the inn at Keswick in a big canopied bed with his sisters Mary and Deborah. The canopy that ran round the top of the bed was a faded green and had a gold thread in it. There were fire-dogs by the fire with mouths like grinning dragons. And he remembered that a woman was sitting warming herself in front of the fire, a woman he hated. Then his father came in and thought he was sleeping. He remembered that his father was wearing a beautiful coat of claret colour and a chestnut wig, and there were red roses on his grey silk waistcoat ...'

Benjie skipped a page or two. He came to the ride through Borrowdale. 'David was wide awake now and knew that his father was happily drunk. He sang a song that was popular with children then. David had played it as a game:

'Lady Queen Anne who sits in her stand,
And a pair of green gloves upon her hand.
As white as a lily, as fair as a swan,
The fairest lady in a' the land.

'They rode on and suddenly the clouds broke and a moon sailed out and the sky was covered with stars. Then they moved up the little hill and it was all very quiet. It all seemed very wonderful to David, who had never seen mountains before, and of course they were very large in the moonlight.

'Then they stopped and someone said:

' "That is the house on the left of us."

'They went on through a thick group of trees and now they were outside a rough stone wall guarding a courtyard where grass was growing. David remembered that he was sadly disappointed in his first view of the house, for it looked so small under the hill. Then some dogs ran out, barking, and his father put him to the ground and he ran forward and was first into the house. In the hall, which through the open door was moonlit, he saw two shining suits of armour . . .'

'It's all very vivid,' thought Benjie; 'if I try hard enough I can see it just as it was and the boy running across the courtyard.' The air was so still that it was not difficult to fancy that there were figures standing listening, and that the old house was still there with the moon shining in on the suits of armour.

The fresh air made him feel sleepy. The past was so much more real to him than the present, as it is perhaps to all old people. The things that the two men had discussed at luncheon were dim and shadowy.

'It may be,' he thought, 'that it is only when you are old that you see things in their true perspective. The world seems to be crumbling but it has crumbled so often before, changing into a new shape that will appear as solid to another generation as its earlier form seemed to the older people. But I'm no philosopher. I've been better at doing things than thinking them.' And his life crowded up into his consciousness, all of it moving at the same time. He was with Barney and Ellis at the music hall and a lady gave him a white rose, he asked Vanessa to marry him in the moonlight in the Fortress garden, he wrestled with Endicott; once again, misery at his heart, he told Vanessa that he was married, and once again he stood by the Chinese clock while Ellis shouted at them from below; he was in Newlands and there came the most wonderful moment of his life when Vanessa, brushing her hair, turned and looked at him ...

He would go no further. But how strange that all these things should be still so alive and other things that had nothing to do with his heart – Africa and Spain and (the greatest moment in his life apart from Vanessa) the sunlit day in Petrograd when they had marched, singing, into the new world. Why, he thought, were the only things that counted in a man's life, when you looked back, the things that touched his spirit – if he had one?

Was it true, as Vanessa believed, that there was a secret life, progressive, unceasing, all-important?

Holly had come to the caravan door, a frying-pan in his hand. 'John, do you think there's a secret life?'

'Will you have your eggs scrambled or fried?' John asked, disregarding, as he so often did, Benjie's mad way of asking questions that meant nothing.

Benjie turned back to the scene. It was growing cold. As fire dies into ash so the sky was fading into grey. He was very happy. His memories and this country made him so.

He opened Casson's thin green book, but could scarcely see to read.

> *I bid ye mourn not for the death of beauty.*
> *For, though the Springtide fades from Cumberland,*
> *Her streams and tarns, there is eternal spring*
> *In heaven. And, on my island where I live,*
> *I dream that heaven is very like this land,*
> *Mountains and lakes and rivers undecaying,*
> *And simple woodlands and wild cherry flowers.*
> *At least I know no better. But weep not.*
> *For, though this land is but the shadow of heaven,*
> *It yet is heaven's shadow.*

He was almost asleep. His pipe fell from his hand. It was so small a country – this green valley, up the Pass into the hollow guarded by Gable, and the Scafells with dark Wastwater to one side, lonely Ennerdale to another, Eskdale, and, to the south the Pikes and Langdale, Esthwaite and Windermere and Coniston. One turn of the hand to the north, and in close company Grasmere and Rydal, Ullswater, and so, towards the Border, Derwentwater, Buttermere, Crummock ... a land that the sweep of a bird might in a flash of the sun cover with its shadow. England itself, from these little hills and lakes, through the dark space of the Midlands, in a moment of time, over field and stream and sloping hill to the sea . . .

The Eagle's wing embraced it. The White Horse, striking upward from the dark water, climbed the icy hill. The Eagle free, the White Horse triumphant, the same Eagle, the same Horse as in captivity, now lost themselves in a larger liberty, in a purpose far grander than their individual struggle . . .

Was he asleep? He thought he heard Holly's voice:

'You'll get cold out there. Supper's nearly ready.'

But he rested his head against the upper step. He sighed with happiness because all the struggle was over. No one was afraid any longer. Vanessa was all right. Tom was all right. Sally, who knew no fear, was building the new world. And he himself was at home where he had always wanted to be.

He turned his head, smiling, and sleepily murmured, as in the past he had so often done:

'Goodnight, Vanessa.'

Over this country, when the giant Eagle flings the shadow of his wing, the land is darkened. So compact is it that the wing covers all its extent in one pause of the flight. The sea breaks on the pale line of the shore; to the Eagle's proud glance waves run in to the foot of the hills that are like rocks planted in green water.

From Whinlatter to Black Combe the clouds are never still. The Tarns like black unwinking eyes watch their chase, and the colours are laid out in patterns on the rocks and are continually changed. The Eagle can see the shadows rise from their knees at the base of Scafell and Gable, he can see the black precipitous flanks of the Screes washed with rain and the dark purple hummocks of Borrowdale crags flash suddenly with gold.

So small is the extent of this country that the sweep of the Eagle's wing caresses all of it, but there is no ground in the world more mysterious, no land at once so bare in its nakedness and so rich in its luxury, so warm with sun and so cold in pitiless rain, so gentle and pastoral, so wild and lonely; with sea and lake and river there is always the sound of moving water, and its strong people have their feet in the soil and are independent of all men.

During the flight of the Eagle two hundred years are but as a day – and the life of a man, as against all odds he pushes towards immortality, is eternal . . .